RHINEGOLD

RHINEGOLD

Stephan Grundy

BANTAM BOOKS

NEW YORK   TORONTO   LONDON
SYDNEY   AUCKLAND

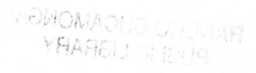

RHINEGOLD
A Bantam Book / April 1994

BOOK DESIGN BY SIGNET M DESIGN, INC.

Library of Congress Cataloging-in-Publication Data
Grundy, Stephan.
    Rhinegold / Stephan Grundy.
        p.   cm.
    ISBN 0-553-09545-5
    1. Mythology, Norse—Fiction.   2. Northmen—Fiction.   I. Title.
PS3557.R8365R45   1994   93-39747
813'.54—dc20   CIP

Published simultaneously in the United States and Canada

Bantam Books are published by Bantam Books, a division of Bantam Doubleday Dell Publishing
Group, Inc. Its trademark, consisting of the words "Bantam Books" and the portrayal of a rooster,
is Registered in U.S. Patent and Trademark Office and in other countries. Marca Registrada.
Bantam Books, 1540 Broadway, New York, New York 10036.

PRINTED IN THE UNITED STATES OF AMERICA

RRH   0 9 8 7 6 5 4 3 2 1

CONTENTS

BOOK 1: THE DRAUGHT OF MEMORY

I sing of the gold   that glitters in darkness,
treasure long bound   in mound of white bone.
There gleams fire silent   where gold is long hidden,
where years weigh like stones   the way long forgotten . . .
Now standing on green earth   see in the sunrise
the web that weaves onward   wyrd writhing around . . .
Forth comes the dragon   fire in the blood-paths,
glitters the rune-hoard   gleams fairer than gold.
From dark mind-shadows   mysteries of forebears,
bright gems and swords   brought forth for the sib.
Hail, those who claim   the clan's hidden treasures!
from skull-darkness, bring   wisdom out to the day!

—Kveldúlfr Gundarsson, from *The Hoard*

The first book of this tripartite novel, "The Draught of Memory," is given to J.R.R. Tolkien and Richard Wagner, who first in our time brought the gold forth from the dragon's mound and the dark waters of the Rhine to awaken our memories of our northern forebears.

The second book, "Sigifrith the Walsing," is given to Freya Aswynn, Bill Bainbridge, Sveinbjorn Beinteinsson, James Chisholm, Will von Dauster, Thorfinn Einarsson, Gamlinginn, Hulda Hauser, Ingvar, Alice Karlsdottir, Garman Lord, Tadhg MacCrossan, Steve McNallen, Gert McQueen, Valgard Murray, Diana Paxson, Prudence Priest, Dianne Ross, Stubba, Edred Thorsson and all the many other good folk and true who have taken up the shards of their heritage and worked to reforge the sword of the northern soul.

The third book, "The Death of Athelings," is given to the memory of Anne Harrington, brutally murdered on the night of February 17, 1991 by her husband, Rob Meek. No woman was ever truer to a less worthy man.

I owe many thanks to the people without whom this book could not have been written: my teachers W. H. Jackson, Bonnie Wheeler, Jeremy Adams, Donald Bullough and C. W. Smith, to whom very special thanks are due for his good redes and help. I am indebted to Stephen E. Flowers for his work *Siguror: Rebirth and Initiation* and to D. H. Green for *The Carolingian Lord*. Above all, I thank Paul Bibire for his matchless friendship, inspiration and philological assistance.

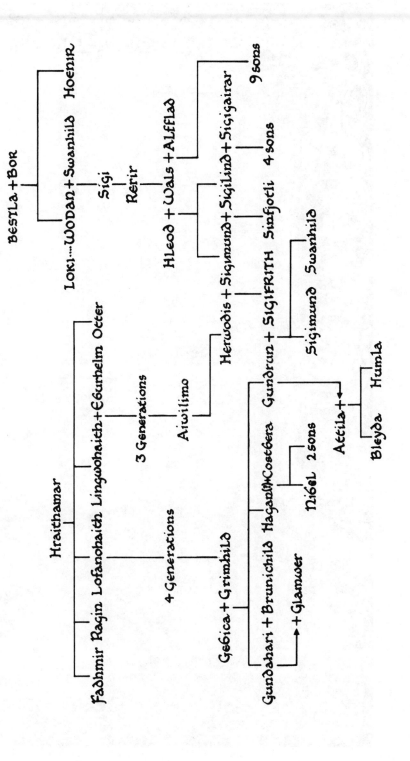

Huns

Alan

Saxons

Walsings

Elbe

Baltic
Sea

Inglings

Rhine

Burgundians

• Worms

uin

Franks

The
Dragon's Crag
(Drachenfels)

Rhine

Frisians

Danes

ings

Under

Roman

Rule

North

Sea

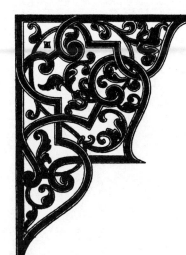

RHINEGOLD

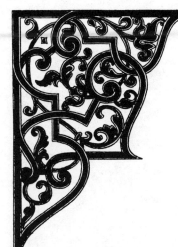

BOOK I

THE DRAUGHT OF  MEMORY

(Gold) causes strife among kinsmen,
the wolf grows up in the wood.

—OLD NORWEGIAN RUNE POEM

PRELUDE: SIGIFRITH'S GIFT

Golden sunlight glittered from the Rhine's depths like a fire in the flood, brightening the dark waters into the torchlit grandeur of a river-king's hall. With a shout, Sigifrith, the weariness and sore muscles of his day at the forge forgotten, stripped off his filthy tunic, ran out on the edge of a rocky jetty and dived into the water laughing.

"Hai!" he shouted, head and shoulders bursting up into the air, arms upraised and a shower of icy droplets flying around him. The thong holding one of his long braids had come loose, so that his water-darkened hair floated around his right shoulder and flopped in a wet rope over his left. "Hai, old dwarf, what's taking you so long? Are you going to hunt fish with that axe?"

"If I were a wolf," Ragin's grumbling bass answered, "I'd hide behind a tree till my dinner came out of the water, fresh-washed, defenseless and ready to eat."

"If you were a wolf," Sigifrith replied lightly, "I'd kick your snout in so that your teeth scattered all over the wood and you had to live on soup and grass, if I didn't skin you right there for a wolf's-hide coat."

"Your heart is too high, Sigifrith," Ragin mumbled, shaking his heavy head. "It will get you killed someday."

"So? Everyone dies, that's what the skops at my father's court sing about. Why should I make things worse by being afraid of it?" He screwed up his face in an exaggerated mask of misery and dripped water over his cheeks like a flood of tears. "Oooh, oooh, oooh," he moaned in falsetto. "Oooh, Sigifrith is dead, the hero is dead."

Finally an unwilling chuckle forced its way from the grim old dwarf. "All right, Sigifrith. But King Alapercht didn't send you to me to learn bravery, he sent you to learn wisdom—if you can." He stumped to the end of the jetty, laying his axe down carefully on a dry rock. "There, no one can get it without us seeing them, unless they swim underwater for a very long way. Remember,

'Always be wary and watchful be;
for man's wits know never when may be need
to meet hidden foe in hall.'"

Ragin took off his tunic. His short, muscular torso was covered with the scars of old burns gleaming pink-white against the dark soot that had soaked into his sweaty pores over five man-lives of smithing. Slowly, grimacing, Ragin lowered himself into the cold water. The current did not swing him about as it swung Sigifrith, but neither did it bear him up as it bore the youth, so that he had to cling to the rocks with one hand as he scrubbed at his thick body with the other.

Sigifrith swam nearer; then his mouth opened in a horrible gasp and he went under, clawing at the water as if something were dragging him down.

Ragin clung to the rock, head underwater and eyes open, trying to see through the darkening river to find out where Sigifrith, or else his attacker, was. He came up for a breath, beginning to pull himself out of the water, when a cold slimy hand like a piece of river weed grabbed his ankle and silenced his bubbling scream in the Rhine.

The smith grabbed at the rocks of the jetty's side, his powerful arms pulling him desperately upward, bulging belly scraping against the stones till he could breathe again. The cold hand let go; behind him he heard a splash and the loud pant of breath bursting free.

Sigifrith, laughing, loose hair plastered to his slim shoulders, held up a dripping leaf of slimy waterweed.

"Out of the damn water!" Ragin shouted, scrambling out himself and grabbing up his axe and tunic before the boy could get any ideas. Sigifrith followed, a little chastened but still grinning, picking bits of green stuff from his long mat of wet hair. "You're not touching hammer or anvil for a week, boy! How in the gods' names do you expect to learn anything if you treat your teacher—your foster-father—like this? I was going to tell you to-night—look, boy, how dare you act this way? I spoke with the gods before your father was born, when the Rhine's gold was first brought forth from the water. Look!"

In the setting sunlight, Sigifrith thought he saw a pale ghost of flame burning upon the rushing river.

"Do you see the fire?"

Sigifrith nodded, half-entranced.

"When I was young here, before your father's father's birth, it was a true blaze, a flood of fire flaming over the gold below. Such gold . . ." Ragin's eyes stared blindly into the water, through the swelling of two salt-crusted tears. "I was young then, young and fair and almost as tall as you," he told Sigifrith. Crawling into his grimy tunic again, he fixed the boy with a red-rimmed gaze for a moment. Sigifrith looked back; in a moment the dwarf turned away from his ward's keen glance, sighing. "But you—you don't want to listen to anything from a miserable old dwarf, no matter that he is your foster-father and you were sent to learn from him. You'd rather eat my food, take what you want from what I can teach and then run away laughing, no matter what a shame you are to the laws of guest and host. Go back to Alapercht's hall; I've no more time for your bad manners."

"I'm sorry," Sigifrith said softly. "I really am. I only meant to tease you a little, truly, because you always seem so grim."

Ragin turned and started to walk up the path. The sun had sunk behind one of the black peaks, and the sky was darkening swiftly now. A cold wind blew soft as snow down from the mountaintops, chilling Sigifrith's wet skin so that he was glad to pull his sooty tunic over his goosepimpled back, wringing out his hair so it wouldn't drip cold water down his spine.

"Please tell me about the Rhine's gold," he coaxed, climbing swiftly up beside Ragin. The dwarf hefted his axe over his shoulder and grunted. "I'll carry that for you, if you like."

"Back from my weapon!" Ragin snarled, raising his axe as if to strike Sigifrith. Dodge in and out, grab it between fore and backstroke, the boy thought, his breath coming faster as excitement warmed in his blood. "Back, I won't let you touch it, I saw you kill—" Then the strange glitter faded from Ragin's eyes, as it always did after a few moments of his mad fits. His axe dropped to dangle loosely from his hand. "Ach, it's only you, Sigifrith. Pick a few mushrooms and we'll have enough for a stew for supper." He hefted his axe again over his wide shoulder and stumped on upward, leaving Sigifrith alone in the darkening wood.

When Sigifrith returned to Ragin's small hut, he could see a gray plume wafting the smell of seething meat out of the smokehole, a scent pleasantly blended with burning pine wood and toasting bread. Sigifrith knocked cautiously at the carven door, into which Ragin's craft had wrought the image of a man thrusting a sword into a huge-footed wyrm, a ribbon of runes running along the dragon's twisted shape. Sigifrith could not read runes, but Ragin had told him that it said, "SIGIFRITH DRAGON'S-SLAYER SHALL RULE THE HOARD."

ᛋᛁᚷᛁᚠᚱᛁᚦ᛬ᛞᚱᚨᚷᛟᛏᛋ᛬ᛋᛚᚨᛖᚱ᛬
ᛋᚺᚨᛚ᛬ᚦᛟᚱᚲ᛬ᛗᛞ᛬ᚹᛁᚱ᛬᛬

The door opened and Ragin's strong hand closed on Sigifrith's wrist, dragging him into the hut and pushing him down into a chair. In the dim flickering of the firelight, it seemed much bigger than in the daytime, vaulting away into darkness. From the corner of his eye, Sigifrith thought he could see the red shadow-shapes of runes burning invisibly around him like images seared on his eye by the sun, but they vanished when he tried to look straight at them. The herb- and smoke-scented air of the hut felt charged with a strange tingling, as though lightning were about to strike.

"Do you know what night this is, Sigifrith?" Ragin's deep, husky voice asked him. Its eerie tone sent a shiver up Sigifrith's spine, as for the first time he felt Ragin's strangeness: dwarf, men called the old smith, but Sigifrith had never felt before how far from human his foster-father was. The sudden realization made him feel electrically alive, standing on the border of a great adventure.

"No," Sigifrith answered honestly, breathing deeply and trying to hold down his excitement. "Please tell me."

"This is the first eve of Thrimilci, the night of the goddess Haith—of Frowe Holda as the Witch. Now I tell you the first hidden thing: though you were begotten at Ostara's feast and born at Yule, a seed of your birth was planted on a Thrimilci Eve these years ago. Do you understand?"

"No."

"You may—you will, if you truly have the wisdom of your ancestors in your blood. Sigifrith, descended of Sigimund and Sigilind the Walsings, son of Herwodis, the daughter of the line of Hraithamar, I have a birthing gift for you."

Ragin put a horn of dark ale into Sigifrith's hand. The drink was black in the firelight, its depths unfathomable; the horn was graven with a twisting tracery of brown-stained runes.

"An old woman gave me this for you when you were born. Are you afraid to drink? What bale do you think she might have brewed into it? Do I see your hand shaking, Sigifrith?"

"I'm not afraid of any witch living," Sigifrith answered. His own boldness felt like a fire within him, kindled by the sparking air and the mystery of the ale. "And it would be rude of me to refuse a naming gift or a drink given me by a woman."

Sigifrith raised the frothing horn to his lips and drank deeply. The cool, foaming ale was strong and good, tasting of grain and rich soil, of quickening yeast and running burn water and the dark secrets of the unknown roots from which trees rise and waters spring. Its warmth spread through his body, strengthening him and clearing everything about him till the embers of the fireplace were red-glowing gold, till the whisper of the Rhine far below was a roaring cataract and the polished wooden chair he sat in was carved from the very bones of the earth, the bones of the first great giant Ymir from whose body Wodan, Wili and Wih had shaped the Middle-Garth, bones like his own, which the gods had once shaped from ash, as they had shaped woman's from elm.

"Are you ready to hear the story now, Sigifrith?" whispered Ragin, his voice like rock grating on ancient rock, but with a hint of dark venom and the scratching of scales over a dry boulder. "Are you ready to hear the tale of your mother's line, of her great-great grandmother Lingwohaith, daughter of Hraithamar, and of the Rhine's gold, which doomed all of Hraithamar's kin? Are you ready to learn of the deeds of your father and his twin sister, the Walsings whom Wodan begot and raised to victory and death? From these two strands was twisted at last the rope of all you are: high-hearted, foolish boy, are you ready to look into the depths of your wyrd?"

"I am," Sigifrith said, hearing his own pure high voice as if from very far away, like the hail of a golden horn.

THE FIRST BEGINNING

The great rush of a stormwind howled through the pines like a wolf, sending raven-black clouds scudding along as swiftly as the galloping of an eight-legged shadowsteed. With the wind came the rain, a gray waterfall from the sky that tasted a little of wine or mead, mysterious, magical, and the flickering, fiery laughter of the lightning. Thus Wodan, Hoenir and Loki came to the Middle-Garth, men's earth, swift as the storm raging between the worlds.

Men make images of their gods, trying to set their might forth into earth; but the true power lies in names and songs. Ygg the Terrifying, All-Father, Father of the Slain, Father of Magic, One-Eyed, Grim, Graybeard, Lord of the Ravens, God of the Hanged, Lord of Ghosts: all these are Wodan, the god of wod-fury and song, whom men of the Middle-Garth, lacking soul-sight, sense in the night wind rushing through the trees. Hoenir is his watery, mysterious mirror; Loki leaps from place to place, sputtering and sparking fire, a dangerous servant, a deadly master, but an indispensable companion. So the soul feels their mights; what the spirit could see became clearer and clearer now, as the gods chose to walk in the Middle-Garth in the shapes of those trees they had once made human with the breath of life, the mead of thought and dreams and the quickening fires.

Taking shape in earth, Wodan was tall and gaunt, wrapped in a deep blue cloak whose hood darkened his gray-bearded face. The pool of darkness in his shadowed right eyesocket was a well of mystery; the left eye gleamed like starlight from the keen tip of a spear, matching the sharp glint of the rune-carved weapon whose ashen shaft he leaned upon. His boots were worn by much wandering, scuffed but still sturdy; the fire of the runes on Gungnir's shaft was hidden within the wood, only a tinge of red in the graven staves showing the power that burned within. His great mead horn was slung about his body, curling round his narrow hip like a wide-bodied wyrm. Raven wings beat shadowy behind his head, dark Hugin and Munin, Thought and Memory, that only spirit-sight could see clearly. Where Wodan's shadow passed there sprang up crimson-capped mushrooms, fly-flecked with tiny white bumps. Behind him, Hoenir was almost a shadow himself, his pale cloak wrapped about his lanky, long-legged body, eyes and hair colorless. The grass sprang green with new life where his feet trod, as if sprinkled by a cool rain. Loki was short and slim, with wild red hair tossed about by the wind, dressed in a bright red tunic, yellow hose and a cloak of leafy birch-green. His glittering amber eyes darted here and there, his feet skipping to one side of the path or the other, and his nimble fingers were constantly, nervously, plucking leaves and sprigs from the trees and bushes along the way, searing and shredding at the same time.

The descent from pure spirit to the earthly body always felt like a slowing and a cooling to Wodan, the blurred edges of his windlike rushing resolving into the limited, yet amazingly clear, sight of a mortal man. Still, he could see the dark green lines of earth-strength thrumming up from the roots of gnarled trees and bushes, the cruel white face of the Birch-Maiden whose touch drives men mad, the cold dark glitter of the dreaming adder under a boulder, and the faint fiery flashes of will-o'-the-wisps drawing nearer, gathering to the hidden glimmer of flame sparkling around Loki. Barely human ears heard the shrill death cry of a mouse—a true mouse, no witch's fetch—and, a few moments later, the triumphant *Hoo-ooo!* of the owl; he heard the echoing songs of bats, clear as a chorus of small birds for those with the ears to hear.

As a man, Wodan hungered and thirsted; and his hunger was always strongest just after coming forth into earth, when the body, craving solidity, made its most urgent demands. The sating of any hunger would do, whether with crusty bread and soft cheese or with the warmest places of a woman's love; indeed, Wodan often came to the Middle-Garth through a maiden's bedchamber. There was no woman here; but Loki, knowing what his brother and master needed, flickered and shrank till the sharp and knowing mask of a red fox laughed up at Wodan and Hoenir. He shimmered away and was gone, a four-footed flame running too swiftly to set the heaps of fallen leaves afire. As if in a dream, Wodan and Hoenir pulled down dead branches, clearing a space between two great roots and laying the wood for their quick brother to spark.

Only a short time later, the fox darted back into the clearing. Two rabbits dangled from his slim muzzle by their ears; dried blood and charred fur rimmed his chops. In mockery of a hunting dog, he dropped the small corpses into Wodan's outstretched hands, then flared, laughing, into man-shape with a burst of flame so bright that Wodan's human eyes had to blink.

The fire was already roaring merrily, devouring the wood. Loki sat cross-legged before it, licking singed blood from the corner of his mouth. Wodan skinned the rabbits with a few flickers of his keen knife and gave them back to Loki to cook, flinging the bloody hides aside.

The three gods ate swiftly, their shapes flickering in the shadows of Loki's fire but becoming more solid as they took the earthly flesh in. They tossed the bones over their shoulders to be splintered by the teeth of the two shadow-wolves that stalked, almost invisible, behind Wodan. This was their way: to walk as men, to bear the burden of what they had shaped at the threshold of time.

The grease on Loki's fingers flared with a crackle. He dusted the ashes from his hands.

"Well, well, my brothers," he said lightly. "I haven't lost any of my skill, have I? No matter how long it's been between farings, you can always count on crafty Loki to find what you need."

Wodan nodded, unslinging his mead horn. He held it out, murmuring a few words and tracing a single rune: *ansuz*, ᚠ, the god-rune of inflowing wod. The sweet fiery scent of the poet's honey brew rose from its depths, from the magical mead that flowed in from an unseen cauldron to fill the horn with its golden galdor-might. The one-eyed god drank deeply, its rush of wild inspiration mounting to his head at once, then passed it to Hoenir and Loki.

"Good mead," Loki commented. "And made all the sweeter by the way you got it, hmm?" He nudged Wodan knowingly. "So tell me, why are we eating rabbit in the Middle-Garth instead of feasting in the Ases' Garth? Is there a great battle tomorrow? More dead heroes for your collection? What brings Frija's husband so far from her loving clasp and nagging advice?"

Wodan turned to his companion, looking down at him as from a great height. A small, grim smile curved his lips; a glint shone in his left eye, though the shadowed socket remained deep and unfathomable. "You'll have to wait a while to find out," he said.

The three gods rested there a while longer; then, as the first light of dawn began to show pale through the trees, they stood and began walking towards the river.

The Rhine flowed slowly, its dark waters following a curving path around the feet of the crags that loomed above it. The gods travelled upstream in the brightening morning light, as Sunna rose high above them. When she was almost at her height, Wodan stopped, looking at the shore.

A large otter was basking on a rock beside the river, the sun drying its sleek, glossy brown fur. It rolled over, scratching its back on the boulder like a cat and stretching luxuriously, then crept on its belly to the edge of its rock, staring into the Rhine. Something silver flashed below; the otter poured into the river like a stream of dark fur, without so much as a splash. Wodan, Hoenir and Loki stood watching the place where it had vanished for a few moments, seemingly enchanted by the little creature's playful grace. As they looked, the otter, its fur plastered dark and wet against its body, crept out of the river with a huge salmon in its mouth. It held the fish up triumphantly as it shook a shower of glinting droplets from its water-spiked fur, then lay down on its belly, half-closing its eyes in pleasure as it slowly began to gnaw on the salmon, savoring its meal.

Casually, Loki stooped for a stone and flung it straight and true at the otter's head. It had no time to dodge; its brown eyes opened in humanlike shock just as the rock crashed into its skull and it slumped down, the salmon falling from its open mouth.

Loki scampered forward to examine his trophy. The rock had caved the side of the otter's head in, its blood and brains matting the wet fur. An unnerving look of horror glazed its wide eyes, still staring sightlessly at the death that had suddenly struck it down. Laughing, Loki held the salmon in one hand, the otter in the other, its long body dangling limply from his grasp.

"Look!" he called to the other gods. "I only wanted the fish, but now we have fish and otter both. Trust crafty Loki to do more than anyone guessed."

Wodan and Hoenir watched him as he skinned the otter, neatly peeling its pelt from its body. He shook his head in disgust at the damage his rock had done to the head. "Pity there, really. I probably won't be able to do anything with that part. Oh, well, these things happen."

The skinned carcass of the otter lay pink and bloody by his feet, its lithe, graceful muscles naked, its bare face already drawing into a rictus of death. Loki kicked its stiffening body to splash heavily into the waters of the Rhine and went back to Wodan and Hoenir, rolling the pelt up and stuffing it into his belt pouch.

"Where to now, High One?" he asked Wodan breezily.

The one-eyed god pointed upriver with his spear. "Hraithamar's home is that way. We should be able to get there by nightfall, and he'll offer us hospitality for the evening. I think he'll be particularly impressed by your catch. One of his sons is a great fisherman who would have been proud of that salmon, but never caught an otter at the same time as a fish."

Loki preened, pulling the pelt out again and unrolling it for display. "Trust cunning Loki to beat a man at his own game," he laughed. His slim fingers stroked the sleek fur as a man might caress a cat, drying and smoothing it till it was as glossy as it had been while the otter lay in the sun. The gods walked onward along the shore of the Rhine.

As the Sun began to set, the river's depths gleamed with fiery gold, a phantom blaze dancing through the dark waters as if in answer to the red of evening that burned between the mountains. Loki glanced lustfully into the depths, his greedy amber eyes alight.

Wodan fixed him with a single sharp gaze. "No," he said quietly, "it's not for you."

Still Loki stole closer to the edge of the river, staring at the half-visible bale-fire above that showed the ruddy glow beneath to be true treasure. Once he had stolen the fire-gemmed Brisingamen from Frowe Holda's neck, coveting its burning splendor; once he had filched a torch from Agwijar's hall, the sea-lord's dwelling that was lit by the light of gold alone. Wodan had commanded him not to try for this; yet he yearned for it, fire calling to fire. He hung back a little; but though the Allfather's back was turned, he could feel the keen spirit-gazes of Hugin and Munin still upon him and hurried to catch up with the other two gods before he roused the Raven-Lord's wrath.

Hraithamar's hall was built on top of a stony crag overlooking the river: a squat, square, timbered fortress. The gods could see his banner clearly through the darkening twilight: two red swords crossed on a deep blue field, warning men of the well-known warchief whose band waited within.

"Looks like rather a gloomy place," Loki said as they began to climb upward. "Does this Hraithamar have a beautiful wife? Pretty daughters? Anything to liven the night?"

"Hraithamar's wife is dead, and I believe his daughters are rather plain," Wodan answered. "However, he has strong sons, which should delight you just as much, and there are stallions in the stable—mother of Sleipnir."

Loki flushed angrily; no one in the Ases' Garth did not know how he had changed into a mare to lure away the stallion that had helped the giant mason to build the walls of the gods' dwelling—and how he had returned nine months later with the eight-legged colt behind him.

"You're hardly the man to say that to me," he started hotly. "I remember when you . . ." But they were near the walls of the keep, and two armed sentries stood before the door, so there was no more time for the old flyting between them. Wodan straightened his dark blue cloak and strode ahead of the other two.

"Halt!" one of the sentries, a big, burly fellow wearing a tunic of heavy leather, called. "What are your names and what do you wish here?" In spite of his challenging words, his voice was open and friendly, his broad face cheerful between the two reddish brown plaits dangling from his leather cap. Wodan knew him already from earlier battles: this was Hraithamar's eldest son, a good warrior, if rather too easy-going. Though he lacked the bloodlust of a berserk or a true champion, he enjoyed fighting and did it well.

"We are three wanderers," Wodan answered. "I am called Eagle, my brother here"—he pointed to Hoenir—"is called Stork, and this one"—he indicated Loki with a wave of his hand—"is Fox."

"Eagle, Stork and Fox. A strange group of animals to be wandering together," the big man remarked. "What is your business here, then? Have you come to see the drighten Hraithamar, or have you kin in his warband?"

"We are traveling to the mouth of the Rhine. There is a man named Sigimund there whom I shall meet in a while if all goes as it should. In the meantime, we ask guest-right for the night, for we have wandered over the fells a long way and are hungry and tired."

"Then be welcome, you three wanderers," the sentry said, stepping forward to clasp Wodan's wrist with rough enthusiasm. His eyes widened a little at the strength of the wiry old man's grip on his own huge forearm, but he bore it well. When he had greeted Hoenir, he turned to clasp Loki's arm, but the grip only lasted a moment before he jerked back, singed.

"Do you carry a fire in your cloak, Fox?" he asked. His voice was jesting, but Wodan could hear the edge of fear in it as the man began to guess at the uncanny nature of those he had asked into his father's hall. The god traced the shape of a rune, ᚹ , with one hidden finger, whispering its name, *wunjo*, joy, as he sent forth its might to calm and cheer this man.

"I'm Fadhmir, Hraithamar's son," the sentry said. He raised his head, sniffing at the scent of cooking meat that crept through the cracks of the hall. "I think they're about ready to start serving dinner in there, and my watch is just about up. Harimann, would you hold things down till our reliefs arrive, make sure the hall doesn't grow legs and run away or something?"

The other sentry tugged at his scraggly blond moustache. "Lazy, aren't you? I guess I can do that."

Fadhmir pulled the heavy oaken doors open and led his guests in. Two long, narrow tables ran down the center of the hall. Warriors lined the benches on either side of the tables, talking so loudly that the din rang off the sooty rafters. A huge fire burned at the far end of the hall and torches flamed up and down its sides, filling the great room with flickering warmth beneath the cold starlight that shone through the smokehole at the end of the room.

A plump girl with curly dark brown hair, dressed in a neat linen skirt and tunic under a short hide cape, hurried up to the travellers, smiling breathlessly. Fadhmir nodded to her, and she spoke in a rush, saying, "Lofanohaith, Hraithamar's daughter, bids you welcome to his hall." She looked flirtatiously up into Wodan's eye, then to Hoenir and Loki; it took no magic for Wodan to feel her dreams of powerful chieftains in disguise and a marriage of love and adventure. What he did sense beneath her fuzzy little mind, to his surprise, was the low glow of a slumbering power: this girl was one of Frowe Holda-Haith's own, though she would never know it unless some need awakened the hidden might within her.

Fadhmir gestured for his sister to bring food. Quickly she scampered off to get four wooden platters of bread and meat and four horns of ale, glancing swiftly under lowered eyelashes at the strange guests her brother had brought in. Loki grinned at her as he took his ale and food from her hands, his slim fingers giving her plump ones a hidden squeeze, and she giggled and flushed. Wodan cast a warning glance at his brother, who smiled innocently up at him as Fadhmir shooed Lofanohaith away and led them down the hall to the fire, where a carved wooden chair sat at the end of one of the tables. He seated them on the bench to the right of the large chair, himself settling down on the bench to the left.

"My father's often late," he shouted across the table to them. "Don't stand on ceremony. I've welcomed you in his name." He raised his horn. "Hail the gods and goddesses!"

"Hail the gods and goddesses!" the three gods answered, drinking with him. The golden ale was yeast-muddied, as it often was when first brewed, but strong and good.

A tall, burly man was making his way toward them; he bore no outward sign of rank except for one gold ring spiralling about his right arm, but his men raised their horns as he passed and he greeted each with a few words.

"Ha, Eburhelm, how's your son doing? I knew that chill couldn't keep him down long. Harimann, I heard you've been letting my lazy son get off watch early. You're supposed to set an example, not fill in for the idiot. Aiwimund, did you get the herbwife to look at that ankle? Good man, you know I need you fit and sound."

Hraithamar stopped when he came to where Fadhmir and his guests sat, his quick eyes passing over them, lingering suspiciously on Wodan's spear before he spoke. "Hraithamar welcomes you to his hall, wanderers. I can see that my son has already done his duty by you—one of his duties, anyway," he added. Fadhmir glanced away for a moment, a smile of embarrassment glancing across his wide face. "So, where have Ragin and Otter gone to? I was expecting to see them this evening."

"I'm here, Father," a quiet voice came from behind Hraithamar. He glanced around as the slim, broad-shouldered figure of his second son came from the shadows beside the table to take his place beside his tall brother. Ragin's light brown hair was neat and his hide tunic clean, but the wide pores of his face were stippled with the black of the forge that would never wash off. He was no better than most as a warrior, but, Wodan knew, he was a fine craftsman who had already taken the first steps on the path of runic wisdom as well; even now, men knew that the weapons he made cut keener than others and moved more lightly in the hand. "I don't know where Otter is. He said he wanted to come by my forge this afternoon, but he never did. He's probably off fishing again."

"Otter's the famous fisherman?" Loki broke in, his high tenor voice cutting easily through the din of the hall. "I'm called Fox, and I'll wager you a gold ring that this day the Fox made a better catch than the Otter ever did."

"That's an easy wager to take, guest," Fadhmir boomed. "Either you don't know much about my little brother or you're not too fond of your gold, but I won't quibble either way. You can't be carrying much in that wee bag of yours; tell me what you've caught."

"This very afternoon," Loki began, "I came on an otter that had just caught a salmon. With one simple toss of a stone I made both of them my catch; what do you think of that? The salmon was big enough for the three of us to have more than our fill, and here in this wee bag you see I have the prettiest otter pelt you ever saw." Loki scrabbled with the knot on his bag, pulling it open without noticing, as Wodan noticed, the frozen silence that had fallen on Hraithamar, Fadhmir and Ragin and was spreading outward to the men around them as they saw the face of their lord. Opening the bag, Loki pulled the otter's skin out—and pulled, and pulled, and kept on pulling as more and more of the glossy dark fur unfolded beneath his hands till he held an otter's pelt big enough to cover a middle-sized man. Open-mouthed, he stared at it in the sudden stillness.

"Murder!" Ragin shouted, grabbing for the eating knife at his belt.

"Murder!" Fadhmir answered, steel ringing softly as he drew his sword. Then every man in the hall was on his feet, reaching for whatever weapon he could grasp; the oaken doors burst open and the sentries pounded in, sword and spear at the ready.

"Hold!" Hraithamar's deep voice boomed. He held his hands out. Wodan felt him pushing back the anger and fury of his men, though tears of rage and sorrow stood in his eyes. "These are guests here; we must hear them out."

The shouting fell to a dull murmur, but the firelight glinted off knives and sword-sharp glares of hatred all through the hall. Hraithamar gestured, and his men moved slowly into a ring around Wodan, Hoenir and Loki.

"Know, strangers," Hraithamar said, his voice full of grief, "that you have murdered my son Otter, called Otter the Fisherman and Otter the Skin-changer. In that pelt that proves your guilt, he went to the river to catch fish, and there, by his own admission, Fox slew him. What defense do you have for your lives?"

Loki looked at Wodan. "How should I have known it was anything but an otter?" he said, loudly enough for everyone to hear. Wodan's gray gaze met his in a moment of silent speaking, and he fell still.

"First, you have given us guest-right," Wodan said calmly, "and even though one of us has slain your son, you can take no revenge on us this night while we are your guests."

"Men have broken guest-right before," muttered one of the warriors, a tall, dark-haired man with a scar on his cheek that drew half his face down into a permanent scowl. Hraithamar's glance silenced him.

"Secondly, as Fox says, there was no way for us to know that his stone was striking more than an ordinary otter. By right, you must admit that by taking on the shape and skill of a beast, Otter also took the risk that every beast suffers in the lands of men. Had he thought of the dangers of his own talent, he would be living now. Fox did what any man might have been expected to do; consider that, as you judge a right geld for his deed."

Hraithamar stepped forward and took the man-sized otter's skin from Loki's hands, sweeping the wooden platters of food from the table and spreading the skin out. Otter's empty legs dangled almost to the floor, the rent in the head of the pelt clearly visible.

"A geld," he said slowly. "Yes, a geld must be paid, gold to fill the place of grief. Will you accept my deeming peacefully, or will you choose to fight instead?"

"We will accept it peacefully," Wodan answered. "Name your price for weregild and we will meet it with our gold or our heads."

"Hear me, you men of Hraithamar, you gods and goddesses," Hraithamar cried, his voice cracking, raising his hands up toward the heavens. "My son Otter has been slain; now I name judgment. Let his pelt be filled with gold to match the worth of his body to me; let each hair on it be covered with gold to match the worth of his life to me, or else, by their own word, be the heads of his slayer and those who let him be slain forfeit to match the price of his life. By Tiw's judgement, by Thonar's might, so shall it be!"

"So shall it be!" the men of his warband roared, their voices full of fury. There was not one of them, Wodan knew, who had not loved Otter's bright cheer, his grace and his laughter; not one of them who would not want to see revenge taken for Otter's death. Loki glanced swiftly at Wodan who stood, grim and still, waiting; as Hoenir stood still beside him, whatever thoughts stirring through the dark waters in his mind hidden beneath the surface of his plain human face.

"Show us your gold, murderer," Fadhmir growled, moving forward, his broad face like a slab of stone lit by the twin fires that burned from the depths of his eyes, more hard and purposeful than Wodan had ever seen it from his high seat during battles. "Do you have my brother's worth in those small bags?"

Wodan, Hoenir and Loki silently turned their belt pouches inside out to disclose a few coppers and scraps of meat.

Ragin grinned, stepping up beside Fadhmir. "You'll need more than that, murderers."

"As you say," Wodan answered. "Hraithamar, we can and will meet your price, but our wealth is all at home. Will you let one of us go to fetch it, and the other two stay as hostage?"

"Fetch it, you say," said Hraithamar. He looked at the huge pelt spread over the table, then back at the three wanderers, glaring suspiciously. "What manner of men are you to promise that so lightly? Why should I trust you?"

"We are men who have enough gold to meet your price. As for trust— we will be two, helpless in your hands. Would one of your men leave you to the blood eagle, or whatever tortures a father could devise to avenge his son's death? Nor need you fear that our folk will come with an army; if Fox has not returned within three days you may slay us then and, as you know, there are no hosts near enough to reach your hall in that time."

"Why should I let the slayer himself go? If I have my revenge on any of you, I will have it on him." The firelight carved deep furrows of grief into Hraithamar's face, as though he had borne his sorrow for a century; he stood unmoving as a mountain, but Wodan could see the faint spark of greed already beginning to kindle in the depths of his soul and drew in breath to fan it.

"Because only Fox can reach our home and return with the gold within three days. He is my messenger, with the key to my hoard; only he can safely bear so much gold back alone. Surely you have noticed"—Wodan lowered his voice, murmuring softly to Hraithamar alone—"he is not as other men. When I command him, he will go and return, and the glow-red gold will be yours alone."

Hraithamar looked at the pelt of his son again, thinking of how much gold it would take to fill the man-sized hide, how much gold it would take to cover each hair of it. If Otter had fallen in battle, he thought . . . and did not finish the thought, but Wodan knew that he had won. If Otter had fallen in battle, he could never have won his father enough gold to fill his skin and cover it without, more gold than any man had seen or heard of except in tales whispered by grandmothers or spun by drunken, lying merchants from the southern lands beyond Rome; and Hraithamar had two other sons.

"You swear it?" he asked.

"I swear by the point of my spear," Wodan replied, handing the hilt of the weapon to Hraithamar and laying his right hand on the gleaming tip. A droplet of blood rolled down from the keen edge to soak into Gungnir's wood, leaving no trail of its passing on the shining metal.

"That would be a worthy weregild," Fadhmir mused. He shook his head, glancing at the pelt of his brother. He opened his mouth as if about to speak, but something choked in his throat and he turned his head away.

"Honor to our brother, for whose worth it was given," murmured Ragin. Misted by tears, his dark eyes, too, passed quickly over the hide. Enough gold to fill it and cover each hair—for Otter, the bright sleek otter, whose graceful movements had been stilled forever, whose sharp eyes would never watch him at his forging, who would never laugh across the feast table at him again. Otter was dead, but a brother's portion of such a weregild would be enough gold—enough for Otter's life? Otter, his gold; his gold, Otter; and what when Hraithamar died and left half another portion as well? Otter was dead, fared to Walhall or Hellajo, and nothing would bring him back now, and for those who lived . . . ? But no king or hero would ever boast of such a weregild again; well might songs remember Otter the Fisherman, Otter the Shape-changer, Otter whose worth had been set at enough gold to buy a kingdom and willingly paid. So much gold . . .

"Send your Fox, then," Hraithamar commanded. "I'll keep this spear and your knives as surety for your pledge." Wodan took his hand from Gungnir's point. He drew his eating knife and, holding it by the blade, handed it to Hraithamar, the smooth wooden hilt fitting snugly into the big man's hand. Hoenir did the same.

"You don't expect me to give up my weapons, do you?" Loki asked. "After all, I'm the one who has to do the dangerous work."

Wodan looked at Loki. "Go," he said softly. Loki's golden eyes met his, thoughts sparking into his mind. Where shall I get the gold? Loki asked. What do you have in mind?

You killed the otter, Sly One, Wodan answered. You keep boasting of your cleverness; now go and prove it. Find an earthly hoard and bring it back, and make sure there's enough there to fill the hide and pile around it till every hair is covered.

Loki's fiery glance would have set a burst of agony flaring through the head of any mortal man, but Wodan merely gazed coldly at him till he bowed mockingly to the High One and to Hraithamar.

"You set a high price on hunting in your land," he commented. "I hope I don't get hungry along the way and kill another of your sons in a rabbit hide."

Fadhmir raised his sword threateningly, a snarl of rage distorting his face, but Loki was already gone. Fadhmir turned to face Wodan and Hoenir, looming darkly in front of the firelight.

"You should thank the gods I was fool enough to give you guest-right here before you showed my brother's skin, murderers. I hope your Fox gets back late . . . I'll be glad to take his pelt and your heads to go with it. I—"

Ragin put a restraining hand on his brother's arm, holding him firmly. "Enough, Fadhmir." The two of them looked at each other for a moment, shadows flickering harshly over their faces. "One way or another, they'll pay."

Fadhmir looked at the pelt again. The flames of the torches shone from Otter's glossy coat, golden highlights gleaming from the brown fur. He thought of his brother's lithe body sprawling naked in the river, slim legs and arms dangling limply below the water's surface and sharp face half-crushed by the rock that had broken his otter's hide. How much gold would fill his place . . . and how much would a brother's share be?

He lowered his sword. "Yes," he said. "They'll pay."

A circle of warriors moved forward, closing around Wodan and Hoenir.

"Take them to one of the storage huts," Hraithamar ordered. "There'll be enough room in there."

"What if they spoil the grain?" a heavyset blond man asked, rubbing his thumb along the wide oaken hilt of his sax.

"Then they'll pay for it."

"Is this how you keep the laws of guest-right?" Wodan asked mildly, looking around at the circle of knives.

Hraithamar met his eyes without flinching. "You'll have food and blankets, and I haven't killed you yet, but I won't sit at table with you and I won't let you run around loose, especially with that Fox creature gone. If you think you have a fair complaint, there are plenty of men here to listen."

"We'll go peacefully, as I said," Wodan replied. The warriors then took Wodan and Hoenir roughly by the arms and marched them out of the hall. In the darkness, the shadow-smile of satisfaction on Wodan's face was hidden from all but himself.

THE GOLD

Once out of the hall, Loki's shape blurred into a flash of fire, a will-o'-the-wisp floating swiftly through the forest. Tiny flames of balefire burned here and there over pinpricks of gold in the soil; he could feel the thin veins of hot ore beneath the earth, like veins carrying a dragon's burning blood through its stony body. He laughed, floating free in the wind, flickering here and there between the dark trees as his fancy drove him, but drawing ever nearer to the glow that shone from the river's bed, the hoard hidden deep in the Rhine.

The dark waters flowed swiftly; the err-light hovered in the rising mist for a moment, then sank down, fading to pass into the hidden world beneath the waters. The Rhine moved around Loki like a cool breeze, bearing its fish and other things, dark and hungry things that lurked at the bottom by day but came out to hunt when the Sun no longer lit the waters and the shores around. Slimy shapes moved past Loki, curving sinuously to avoid his burning touch. A mortal man might have seen fair maidens swimming and weaving about beneath the river's ripples, but out beyond the borders of earthly being nothing that was foul could hide itself from Loki of the dark etin-kin; and he, treacherous fire, knew well how little water could be trusted. He might have stayed to play with them, but the glow lured him downward to where the treasure lay in the water's depths.

Reaching down, Loki touched only sand and waterweed again and again, though he could feel the gold burning there. At last he cried out in fury and frustration, his anger shivering through water and earth and reverberating between the towering cliffs on either side of the river, and children clutched at their parents and adults reached hastily for weapons or drew sticks from the fire to scratch fresh hex symbols and runes on the hard earthen floors of their mud-daubed wicker huts. Loki damped down his fury, rising up through the river again and out, a plan already kindling in his mind.

He followed the course of the river till he came to a sandy shoal at the foot of a mountain. The glowing ball of his might shrank to a spark, hidden behind a rock; he gathered himself to wait for dawn.

The first blue streaks of light were beginning to glow through the clouds when Loki saw what he was waiting for. Three swans, their great white wings beating slowly, circled above the Rhine and settled down through the faint morning mist, floating slowly toward shore. Loki's excitement flared; a flash of light showed from the rocks where he was hiding, and the swans turned their narrow heads toward him, snaky white necks drawing back as their black beaks opened to hiss at him in mockery. Serenely, they let the current bear them away toward the north and they faded into the silvered mist of sunrise. Loki flashed after them, but they were gone already.

"Stupid geese," he murmured to himself. "I'll see how they hiss when I've caught them."

He moved along the river, searching for a place that would draw the three swans to it; a place where he could weave himself, hidden, into rock and sand where their wise eyes could not see him. At last, upstream some miles near the path to Hraithamar's hall, he found a jetty of stone that jutted out into the water; neither river nor shore, not water nor earth, its own magic would hide his traces and bring the swans to his hand. He waited for them at sunset, as the red glow of evening shone through the craggy peaks and lit up the depths of the Rhine; but only a woodbird called bright clear nonsense at him. In his own banked coals among the river-lapped stones, he hatched a thousand plans and cast them away, weaving an intricate web of guile in his mind.

The next dawn came dark and stormy, the wind whipping a veil of heavy rain across the waves of the river. Above, Loki saw the white wings beating, flashes of silver-white light through the clouds, but he knew that the three swans would fly till the storm ended. It rained all that day, as gray light faded into darkness; but after midnight a strong, sharp wind began to rip the clouds to tatters and let the cold starlight shine through.

Light outlined the mountain peaks to the east when the three white shapes came floating down the dark water like clouds. Craning their necks about and peering with keen dark eyes, they came to rest by the jetty, clambering up on webbed black feet. Voiceless whispers hissed from their beaks, whispers that Loki heard and understood.

"There are no men about."

"No men on the shore, no men on the wood, no boats on the rushing river."

"Still my heart trembles."

"What of the fire-thing who waited before?"

"He must be far; this place holds its own might."

"Not water nor earth nor height of air."

"Here are we safe? May lay feathers aside?"

"Here on this border of river and shore?"

"We may wash us in peace, sisters all."

Loki held himself utterly still as the swans cast off their cloaks of white feathers, rising from their snowy hides as tall maidens, white-skinned with gleaming pale hair and the dark eyes and powerful grace of the great birds. Silently they slipped into the waters, letting the current of the river wash around them as they stared joyously upward to the pink and gold of new sunlight warming the faint silver-blue of early dawn.

In a sudden flash, Loki appeared in his man-shape, gathering up the soft cloaks of swan feathers with one sweep of his slim arm, his light laughter ringing out across the Rhine.

"Ha, ha, my maidens!" he crowed. "You may be safe from men, but not from crafty Loki."

The swan-maidens threw back their heads, long hair streaming into the dark water and white breasts swelling up from it as they cried out, a harsh, high wordless scream of betrayal.

"Stop wailing," Loki commanded irritably. He pinched a feather from one hide; it curled into smoke in his hand. Silent tears streamed down the faces of the three maidens like a flood of river water, but they did not cry out again. "That's better. Do you want your hides back?"

"Please give them back," one of the swan-maidens whispered. "You can't use them. Only a woman can wear a swan's cloak. Give us our hides again and we'll teach you our magic. We'll show you all the secrets you want to know."

Loki smiled, tossing the three feather cloaks lightly over his arm. The maidens swam to the edge of the jetty, pulling themselves half out of the water so that their bare shoulders and breasts gleamed in Frowe Sunna's new golden light.

"That's better," Loki said, his gaze running appraisingly over their bodies. He could . . . but how to keep hold of the three cloaks then? He would have to wait till he knew what he needed to do. "And you're wrong; your feathered hides are very useful to me, because you'll do what I want to get them back, won't you?"

The three maidens nodded, staring at the white swan skins he held, their dark eyes sharp with longing and rage.

"Right. Well, the first thing I want is for you to tell me how I can get the gold from the river's bed."

The swan-maidens looked at each other warily.

"We can't tell," one whispered voicelessly. "If we do—"

"If we don't? We'll be bound to earthly life for ever, serving dull husbands, our wisdom forgotten, never to fly through the air or watch our heroes in their battles again. What is Andward to us? A dull clod of earth and stone, a miser, a cold and scaly fish."

"Would you let this one take the Rhine's gold? This betrayer, this sly one, who murdered the otter in an idle moment? Better for him to suffer."

"But not us with him, sister."

"Not us, no. Once we have our hides back, the Nine Worlds may go as Wyrd shall turn them. Let her turn, as long as we are free."

They looked up at Loki again. "The dwarf Andward keeps the keys to the hoard," the one who had argued for telling him said. Her sister raised a hand to slap her, but the words were spoken and the blow never fell. "He is a coward, his heart cold with fear. You can easily find him and force him to give up the hoard with that Wounding-Twig that hangs so sharp at your belt."

"Good girl," Loki said approvingly. He tossed her one of the cloaks; it fell over her like a mist, shaping her into a swan again. She floated out on the river, circling anxiously and hissing, careful to keep her distance from Loki. "Now, what can you two do to convince me that I should give your hides back? I know all I need to, but I think you might have something else to offer." He bent down and pinched the breast of the nearest maiden, the one who had spoken against him. She flinched back, making an ugly sound in her throat, but could not stop his hand from moving on her.

"You don't know all you need to," the other swan-maiden broke in. "You'll never find Andward unless you leave her alone and listen to what I have to say, and I'll never tell you unless you give me back my cloak."

Loki laughed, straightening up. "And why should I expect you to tell me when you have it, my girl? You'll fly away as soon as you can. No, tell me now, and if I think your wisdom is worth it, I'll give you your feathers. Your sister got hers, didn't she?"

The maiden glanced at the swan. Eyes downcast, she whispered, "Andward takes the form of a fish from sunup to sundown. Look for the huge pike which bears a golden ring fixed to his fin. Catch him and hold him by the ring; then you can force him to give up his hoard."

Loki held her cloak high above the water. "Come and get it, then."

Swiftly the swan-maiden climbed out of the river, water dripping from her white body in a shower of sunlit drops as Loki watched her lustfully. She grabbed her feather hide from Loki's outstretched hand and leapt quickly back, but not quickly enough to avoid his burning caress of her firm buttocks. Splashing into the water and swimming away, she pulled the cloak over herself as if its cool touch would soothe away the feeling of Loki's hand on her.

"Silly girl," Loki called. "Your sister will be able to tell you what you're missing, since I know all I need to." He stretched his foot out, catching the third swan-maiden beneath the chin and turning her head up toward him. "Do you want your cloak back?"

"Yes," she replied.

"Well, you'll have to earn it. A trinket as pretty as this is a high price for a woman's favor, but I'm in a generous mood this morning. Don't look so furious; half the goddesses in the Ases' Garth would give more than a feather cloak to be in your place now. Come on . . ."

In a mockery of respect, he helped her out of the water, pulling her up to stand naked before him. The new sunlight gleamed off the drops that jewelled her body, the fine tangle of hair between her thighs glimmering like a dew-hung spiderweb. Loki walked around her, pinching her breasts and buttocks as if appraising a cow for sale. "Not bad, not bad at all," he commented. "White as ice—but Loki has melted snowy maidens before this. So, let's see if there's blood in your pale veins."

He stroked her here and there, caressing her with his fiery skill; but she stood still without responding or resisting, and Loki began to grow angry. "Down, girl!" he commanded. "If you don't show a little more enthusiasm,

I'll start wondering if you're worth your price." He pushed her down roughly, the harsh rocks scraping her skin so that beads of crimson began to ooze through the whiteness; his touch was burning now instead of warm, teeth instead of tongue.

When Loki was done, the swan-maiden's pale breasts were an angry, sore pink; blood stained her white thighs and the marks of burning bites glowed red on her shoulders and throat.

"Clumsy," he said dismissively as she sat up, bringing her legs together and clutching her arms about her. "I don't think you've quite earned your cloak yet; I rather think, in fact, that I may have a use for it. Watch closely."

Loki flared and flashed; instead of the slight man, a red-haired, amber-eyed woman in a leaf-green gown stood before the trembling swan-maiden, her pure, high laugh pealing out across the Rhine. "No barriers hold crafty Loki back. I do as I please and become what pleases me. I wonder how my new cloak will fit me."

"You said you'd give it back," the maiden whispered miserably, staring at the gleaming white feathers draped over Loki's slim, shapely arm. "If I . . . you said . . . "

Loki wagged a finger at the woman who shivered at his feet. "You should have listened more carefully. I said, if you earned it, and instead you lay there like a lump of porridge. No, I can make plenty of use of this. How are swans at catching pike? Better than men, I suspect. Perhaps when I've done what I need and you've had some practice earning your bread with your body I'll give you another chance to win it back."

The swan-maiden raised her head as though suddenly awakened, her dark eyes glimmering with hatred. She scrambled to her feet with a hiss of pain, the burns on her body glowing redder. "Take it if you will, but you'll never get the Rhine's gold till you've learned what I know about it, not if you fly up and down the river in a stolen hide for ever."

"What could you know that your sisters didn't? They wanted to tell me what I needed to know. Why should I expect the truth from you?"

"Because I am older and wiser than they are; because only I have sunk down into the water's depths and talked with the ancient salmon who dwells in the river's bed. You are a wight of power; you can see yourself that I am the keeper of secrets about which my sisters know nothing."

Loki considered her carefully; the glinting darkness, the shifting shadows and radiance within her soul enthralled the fire god for a moment. Loki shook long, glowing red hair back from softly rounded shoulders; then, in a spray of sparks, became his male self again.

"Tell me what you know, then," he said. "If it's worth it, I'll give your coat back."

"You lie," the swan-maiden spat at him. "You are an ancient liar, false as the shadows of your flame, and seeing you fail in your goal might be worth losing my feathers for ever. But if you give me my hide I'll tell you the last secret of the Rhine's gold, even though you don't deserve to know it."

Loki paused a moment, running his fingers over the cloudy feathers. Her soul shone diamond, unmoving; he knew he could not sway her will now.

"So be it," he said, flinging her cloak at her. She drew it halfway on, great swan's wings arching pure and white from her ravaged shoulders. A mighty gust of wind fanned Loki's hair and cloak back as she beat her wings, rising into the air and hovering above his head.

"Take the Rhine's gold from its depths, and it will be a cruel orlog to all who hold it till it returns to the waters. The secret is death, if you follow through with your thoughts, death for athelings and the children of athelings. But take the dwarf's ring of power, and hold it for yourself if you can; and remember his fish shape when your greatest need is upon you, for no beast is harder to find or fasten upon. And take my nith with it: as you bound me with my dearest cloak, may you be bound with the guts of your son one day; as your fires burned me, so may the bale of the wyrm fall ever to burn you, till you break forth to lead the host before Muspell's flames at the world's end. For all your pride, Loki, your wyrd is writ already, and may your downfall come soon!"

She stretched out her hand, fingers splayed toward him and hate flowing forth in a tingling, painful stream like the bite of a hundred nettles. For a moment Loki was too shaken to reply; then the maiden pulled her hide completely over her and flew up as a swan, her sisters rising from the Rhine to follow her away.

Loki spat contemptuously after them. "A goose's cackling," he said to himself. "What made her think her nithing could touch me?" He looked down into the depths of the Rhine. "A pike with a gold ring in his fin, hmm? Well, fiery Loki may be many things, but he's not a water-wight by choice. I'll do better if I fare to someone who knows about catching what lies in the waters."

Regretfully turning from the glow that still mocked him from the Rhine's bottom, he flickered away, a faint streak of lightning flashing through the hidden paths to the shore of the North Sea where Agwijar rose in his first winter fury to batter the land with great fists of frothing gray water, where the seagulls blew about like leaves in the stormwind, their screaming lost in the crashing of the waves. The wild shapes of etin-women—the daughters of Agwijar and Ran—crested and leapt on the sea, reaching up hungrily in search of ships to drag down, their long white hair streaming to the wind in torrents of spray. Loki stood on the stony beach for a few moments, staring into the icy waves eating at the land, the fringe of froth rising ever higher. He sighed, shivering a little.

"Pity the poor wights who have to live in that," he said to himself. "It's well that crafty Loki is wiser, dwelling in the fire's warm heart." But Ran held the silver-twisted net that caught the souls of the drowned—the net that would do to catch the pike Andward. Loki stretched out, lying along the beach, his clothes melting into the warm brown pelt of a seal as his body rose and swelled.

When Loki took man shape by the shore of the Rhine again, Ran's net was in his hand. He twirled it lightly, its cold silver web hissing through the air like an arrow of ice, then glanced up to see how much daylight was left. His haggling with the sea queen had been long: the Sun had already started down from the heavens' height, and Loki had only a few hours left before the threads of Wodan's plan, whatever they might be, were broken and he was set to pay yet another price.

"Bitch," he hissed, spitting toward the North Sea. His spittle seared the grass with a crackle of fiery venom, leaving a small circle of scorched black earth.

"Grow," Loki whispered to the net. "Grow to the width of the Rhine, so that no crack nor cranny escapes you. Catch me the dwarf that swims in a fish's hide; catch me the gold-ringed pike, for I want no other fish."

As though unrolled from an invisible coil, the net grew longer and longer, its silver strands spilling down the shore and into the water till the threads glimmered on the other side. Swiftly it swept along the river, Loki flashing beside it, along meadows tinged with winter's first brown, up from the plains and around the craggy feet of the hills that rose higher as he whisked southward, until suddenly it began to tug and jerk like a live thing.

"Ha!" whispered Loki in a fury of triumph and relief. He reeled the net in swiftly, hand over hand. The heavy body of the pike that thrashed and jumped within made it a difficult load, almost pulling Loki's slight man form into the water; but a few sharp words to the net drew it up tightly enough to bind the struggling pike into stillness.

Loki heaved the fish on to the rock where it lay, gills opening and shutting, glaring balefully at him through the bright strands. The pike Andward was half as long as Loki was tall, a glittering golden ring fixed on one of the small fins on his right side. Loki looked down at him for a moment, then shook the net sharply so that it cut into the fish's green scales.

"Well, Andward," he said lightly. "You look uncomfortable. Why don't you get back into your natural shape so that we can talk about things more easily? I have an offer for you, and it begins by giving you a chance to get out of this net and stay alive instead of being roasted for my supper."

Loki loosened the net just a little. The scaly mail of the pike cracked down its belly and the dwarf crawled out of his fish hide. Andward was no taller than the fish's length, bandy-legged and pot-bellied with a scraggly black beard and a face as craggy and grooved as water-eaten sandstone, set in an ugly, sour grimace. The fish's gold ring now gleamed on his finger: a dragon carved down to the tiniest scale, coiled about a huge star ruby. Its intricate beauty was all the more surprising against the gnarled, hairy finger around which the dragon's tail twisted.

"What do you want?" Andward growled in a deep, harsh bass. "I don't have any time for your games, and I don't have anything you want anyway. Go away and leave me be."

"You're wrong, old dwarf," Loki answered. "You have something I want very much: you have the key to the treasure of the Rhine. I want the gold—

exactly as much as you want your life, or perhaps a little more. We can haggle over it if you like, but that's what it's going to come down to." He drew his slim sword, Wounding-Twig, and put the tip to Andward's throat through a hole in the net's loose weave.

"Do I have a choice?" Andward rumbled.

"No. Admit it, dwarf: Loki's got you in a net from which there're only two ways out. One is through the Rhine's gold, and the other is through this sword here. Choose quickly, I haven't got any time to waste."

Andward breathed, as though about to speak. The point of Wounding-Twig pushed harder against his throat.

"One swift question before we start. Andward, do you know what weird befalls those who speak false words, when they have fared to Hella's home?"

"They wade, waist-high, in the knife-filled stream of Wathgelmir, which flows from Hwergelmir to the depths of Hella's realm, long do they linger in that stream of sorrows," the dwarf answered. "And ill-luck to you, who know every turn a lie can take."

"You're a wise dwarf, not to set your wits against cunning Loki," Loki said, highly pleased with himself. "Down to the Rhine's gold, my trusty guide; but one wrong move, and we'll see whether Ran's net can strangle you faster than my sword can slit your throat."

Andward pulled the pike's skin over his wretched body, muttering and grumbling under his breath. Loki lifted the net and plunged into the water with it, loosening it further so the pike could swim ahead to guide him.

The two of them sank to the bottom of the river and swam upstream for a few moments; then Andward turned, pulling Loki toward a great river-smoothed boulder. As they sank into the stone, the glittering scales of the pike fell back from the dwarf's body, leaving him dark and twisted within the darkness of the river-rocks where he dwelt. Here in the stone, Andward must take his own shape as the stone that had shaped him.

Gold blazed around and through the craggy rocks: Roman gold pieces, rune-graven fibulas from the North, neck-rings and arm-rings of twisted gold, wound about itself in a braid or spiraling upward. Lumpy ropes of amber twisted through the heaps like red-glowing serpents' backbones; gems gleamed ruddy or dark from the intertwinings of chip-carved brooches, discs and squares of gold wrought with spiraling weaves too complex for the eyes to follow. Jewel-eyed beasts' heads gleamed golden from the tips of rotting horns and the ends of gold-wound torcs; serpentine finger-rings coiled brightly in little piles like golden adders' nests. And woven through the gold everywhere was the brighter flame of magic, glittering red through graven runes, hovering over spearheads inlaid with golden signs, burning almost blue white over a small coif of gold ring-mail. Loki laughed, melting into fire himself and spreading through the hoard so he could feel the gold touching him at once, its tingling might flowing through him. He wanted to lie there for ever in the Rhine's bed of pure gold and magic, but Wodan's will bound him too tightly yet so that he must rise from his fires and pull himself into human shape again.

Still laughing, Loki stooped, gathering the gold into his belt pouch in great, greedy armfuls as Andward watched bitterly from the net's grasp. Soon the cave was dark and grim, lit only by the faint fox-fire of rotting moss on its walls and the hoar-cold glimmer of Ran's silver net.

When he had shut his pouch on the last piece of gold, Loki stood and dusted his hands off briskly. "Well, that's that," he said, then stopped, staring at the faint gleam struggling between the finger cracks of Andward's fist. "You'll excuse my forgetfulness," he said politely to the dwarf. "It's been a long day, and I'm really such a scatterbrain sometimes. I'm supposed to take that wretched ring off your hand as well."

Andward clutched the ring more tightly to him, stifling its light against his crooked chest and cringing back against the net. "What good will it do you? You have the hoard of the Rhine; now go. Surely you can afford to leave me my one tiny treasure? No wight in the worlds is richer than you; be generous, as befits such a fro, and the weal you do will come back to you."

"Save flattery for those who care about it," Loki advised. "Loki's wits are all he needs, in the Nine Worlds or elsewhere. Andward, I know your name and I have you caught; now give me the ring, or my sword will send you to Hella and my magic will bind you in the darkest part of her realm, among wyrms and ice and knives."

The dwarf clung to his ring, shivering, but did not fight when Loki reached through the net and prised his thick, gnarled fingers away from it one by one. Loki tossed the glowing dragon ring in the air; it landed in his palm with a heavy, solid thunk. As he slipped it on to his slim finger, it seemed to writhe about itself and draw in to fit him more closely.

"Nice work," he commented. "Did you make it yourself, dwarf?"

Andward did not answer. His dark, knobby face twisted into a grimace of hatred and fear as he stared fixedly at the ring on Loki's finger. Loki laughed and released the net.

S
T
E
P
H
A
N

G
R
U
N
D
Y

⌘
2
6

The dwarf scuttled away between the rocks, slithering into them until Loki could no longer see where dwarf ended and stone began. Only the red sparks of his eyes glowed out of the darkness as his voice hissed, "My curse on the ring I made, on all who wear it! Gold fired in blood, ruby blood-red, be you bathed in your holder's blood again and again, the death of athelings and the sorrow of women. Death to every man who takes you, make each woman who keeps you the bringer of death to her kind. Be strife of kinsmen, be breaker of bonds, let no gift and no oath hold where the river's fire burns, let no love bear lasting fruit, but cut all kin of your keepers down. My curse on the hoard I kept, held by the ring! Let no craft work its might to weal, let no need turn round nithing's might, but smith-craft's torch and need-fire's glow burn but to funeral pyres. Brothers' bane and drighten's doom: thus Andward names the hoard! Norns, lay this orlog from the Rhine's depths. Write this wyrd—so shall it be!" The ruddy light of Andward's eyes winked out and he was gone into the rock.

Loki clapped his hands together delightedly. "A well-wrought curse, dwarf!" he applauded. "Lucky for me I'm not planning to keep the hoard—though I'm not too worried about the ring either; few have accused Loki of being a calmer of strife, even among his kin. In fact, you've taken a great load of work off my shoulders. Hraithamar really went a little too far, and I would have had to even the scales anyway, but now you've done it for me. My thanks, dwarf."

Loki waved merrily at the dark rock where Andward had vanished, then started up again, back to Hraithamar's hall.

OTTER'S WEREGILD

The western sky was just turning gold around the slowly reddening Sun when Fadhmir and Ragin came to take Wodan and Hoenir out of the hut where they had sat among the bales of grain for three days. As Hraithamar had promised, the two prisoners had been fed and treated well, though the men who brought them food often cursed under their breath and spat at the floor near their feet. They had heard the far-off sounds of the funeral feast's wailing, the memory toasts shouted over the noise of the hall as the men drank to the dead and the occasional scuffles and grunts of a fight. They knew that Hraithamar had sent men out to search the Rhine for the body of his son and not found either the skinned otter or the corpse of the man. Had Wodan wished, he might have told Hraithamar what fish or water-wight had stripped Otter's flesh from the bones that lay at the bottom of the river, but he did not.

Hraithamar's surviving sons were both fully armed, wearing leather tunics with iron plates across chest and back and iron-bound leather caps. Their trousers were grubby from three days of mourning, stained with spilled ale and dirt. The bright keen gleam of the naked sword in Fadhmir's hand shone in stark contrast to his filthy clothing and the spots of rust that had already dappled his armor. Ragin held a length of rope, his blade sheathed at his side.

When Fadhmir spoke, his voice was strained and hoarse, hardly louder than a whisper. "Your Fox hasn't come. Come out, murderers, come out and pay my brother's weregild."

Wodan and Hoenir walked out slowly, keeping a careful distance from Fadhmir as his sword rose to point at Wodan's throat. Silently Ragin moved before them and they put out their hands to be tied. Hraithamar's younger son did not speak, but Wodan could feel the murderous hate in the tension that cramped Ragin's smith's muscles rock-tight, curling his calloused hands into claws that could barely tie the rope and roughly jerking his clumsy knots tight till the fibers bit into flesh.

Ragin yanked on the rope, trying to make the two gods stumble behind him, but to no effect. Wodan stared at him calmly, meeting his bloodshot dark eyes with an impassive, icy glance. "Come along," the smith husked, starting toward the hall. He did not, however, jerk the rope again. The two gods followed him quietly, watching Fadhmir: if the big warrior gave in to the madness lurking near the strained borders of his mind and attacked, Wodan knew that his plan would be warped beyond recovery. But Fadhmir held himself back as his brother led the prisoners to the front of Hraithamar's hall, where a roughly hewn gallows already dangled its line into the air, rope swaying with the current of the wind. Sunna was sinking rapidly, her red light staining the sky behind the wind-borne banners of black cloud streaming from the north.

Hraithamar, his huge body muffled in a black cloak, stood before the gallows with a circle of men behind him. In his hand, he held Wodan's spear, though his face twisted now and then with his effort to keep a grasp on the weapon, which was never meant for the touch of such mortal men as he. His blue eyes were wide and wild, lit with hate—and fired, Wodan sensed, with the bitter edge of disappointment, like a faint, sharp hint of poison at the border of his mind.

"The judgment has been made and the oath has been kept," he intoned. "Eagle and Stork, you have had your three days and your messenger has not returned. Therefore, the weregild which you cannot pay in gold, you must pay with your lives."

"The Sun has not set yet," Wodan answered.

"Nevertheless, she is setting, and no one has come within the borders of my land since noon. Whatever your Fox is, he has not passed here. Up, Eagle, we'll see how you fly." He laughed harshly, a sound matched by the grating echo of the laugh that rang from the dark cave of Fadhmir's open mouth. The big warrior's sword flashed as he cut the rope binding Wodan and Hoenir in two, just missing Ragin's hands.

"Crazy fool," Ragin hissed under his breath, scrabbling for the loose ropes. He shoved the end dangling from Hoenir's bound wrists roughly at Fadhmir and pulled, more cautiously, on Wodan's rope, leading him to the edge of the gallows.

Wodan walked up the stacked logs to the top of the pile. His sword held menacingly in his free hand now, Ragin clambered up beside him, reaching for the noose. Wodan knew Loki was already there, waiting for his moment and, no doubt, laughing quietly at the sight of the Lord of the Hanged about to have the noose put around his neck by simple men.

Enough, Wodan said silently to the hidden fire-wight. Out. Now.

Loki stepped from the shadow of the gallows and out into the last dim red rays of the sun. "Your scouts have been feasting too hard, Hraithamar.

You really ought to keep them under better control, you know." He looked up at Wodan. "Happy there, old gallows-bird? You might as well come down. I believe we have something to discuss with Hraithamar and his family."

Slowly, uncertainly, the circle of men broke up, staring at Loki with eyes shadowed by mistrust and terror. Wodan saw many of them make the sign of Thonar's hammer surreptitiously or thrust thumb through fist to avert the evil of his amber glance.

"You aren't carrying any gold with you," Fadhmir's voice rumbled from deep in his chest. "Only that same little bag. We should kill you now and have done with it."

"Ach, but you're wrong, Fadhmir," Loki answered cheerfully. "Wrong and half-mad, by the looks of you. What makes you think you can trust eyes as bloodshot as yours?"

Wodan glanced at Loki warningly. "Come inside, Hraithamar, and you two, Fadhmir and Ragin. And summon your daughters as well, Hraithamar, for a share of the weregild goes to them too, according to the laws you've called on."

"They'll be inside," Hraithamar muttered. He shambled forward, staring keenly at Wodan, Hoenir and Loki a moment before he turned to his sons. "Come on, what are you waiting for? We'll have the weregild, one way or another, in a few minutes."

Fadhmir and Ragin ushered the three gods into the hall with their swords. Hraithamar's two daughters, Lingwohaith and Lofanohaith, stood by the fire, tending it. Their dark gowns were cleaner than the clothing of their brothers, but their faces were swollen and red from crying. Lingwohaith's golden brown hair hung down lankly; Lofanohaith's darker curls tangled dirty and dull about her plump, ravaged features. Otter's empty hide was still on the table where Hraithamar had spread it out. A musty odor of rot tainted the cold air of the hall.

Hraithamar beckoned to his daughters. "Bring Otter's hide here and help me hold it out. We'll see if you can really pay what you've promised or not."

Silently Lingwohaith and Lofanohaith picked up their brother's pelt, one at each end. Lofanohaith held it gingerly, as far away from herself as she could; her face twisted as she struggled to avoid breathing too deeply. Lingwohaith's grip was firmer, her narrow jaw tightly clenched against the new tears rising in her red-rimmed blue eyes.

"Stretch it out as far as you can," Hraithamar commanded them. He stood in a firm stance a little way from the hide and leaned over to spread the sides of the pelt as far as he could. The otter's dangling feet barely touched the floor. "Now, Fox, show us your gold."

Loki opened his bag with a flourish and reached in to pull out handful after handful of gold. He began by pouring Roman coins down the otter's legs till they hung straight and heavy; by the time all four of them were filled, the arms of Hraithamar's daughters were trembling. Lofanohaith cast a piteous look at her father, her soft brown eyes full of pain, but Hraithamar could not or would not see that the girls were already at the end of their strength.

"Enough to cover it, inside and out," Hraithamar said, the corner of his mouth twitching. As Loki began to load the armrings and torcs, the carefully crafted brooches and rings into a heap around the gold-weighted feet, Ragin sheathed his sword, fascinated both by the intricate craft of the work before him and the sheer mass of the gold; coin rang on gemmed buckle, on spiral ring with a pure high thin note that seemed to sing on and on inside his brain till he could no longer tell the clinking of the piled hoard from the ringing within his skull. Beside him, Fadhmir gasped, dropping his weapon; light gleamed from the fire on to the hoard, into his eyes, a ruddy myriad of glittering lights that grew and grew as Loki piled the gold ever higher to hide the legs of the huge otter pelt, up to fill the empty space where Otter's heart and entrails had been and stuff the head full with a skull and brain of pure precious metal. Rings for a child or small woman's finger rounded out even the thin hollow tip of Otter's tail. Loki's slim hands bent a few of the thin spiral bracelets straight and slipped them in to fill the rings completely before Hraithamar could open his mouth to cry cheat. Lingwohaith, Lofa-nohaith and their father stepped back, no longer needed; the hoard alone supported the pelt now. The gold rose waist high around the giant otterskin, over the gold-filled curve of its slim shoulders and arched back, over the uptilted head, till the last piece, a thin, palm-broad disc from the far north, had been placed over the tip of Otter's brown nose.

Lingwohaith and Lofanohaith, rubbing their sore arms, stared in wonder along with their father and brothers. It was Fadhmir who moved forward first, his big shoulders shaking a little as he bent close, drawn by the firelight flickering off the gold, to see if maybe, if possibly . . .

When he reached the raised part of the pile over Otter's head, he jerked back with a sharp cry of triumph. "Here!" he shouted, pointing a thick, scarred finger at a tiny crack in the pile. "You haven't covered him. I can still see the tip of one whisker. The weregild isn't paid yet."

Wodan looked at Loki, who made a great show of turning out his bag to show that it was empty. Only a few crumbs of dust tumbled from the rough leather seams.

"If you can't pay the weregild in full, your lives are forfeit," Ragin said. His voice was gleeful, but his dark eyes were blank except for the reflected glitter of the fire, a thousand points of light dancing, infinitely small, in the depths of his pupils.

Loki shrugged expressively, spreading his hands, and the fire caught a circle of golden sparks from the dragon ring on his finger.

Hraithamar turned his head quickly. "That ring will cover the whisker," he said. "I'll have it, with or without your blood on it."

Loki drew off the ring and placed it over the tip of hair that protruded from the gold like the tiniest of loose black threads. "Have it if you will, but a wise pike told me you won't get much joy of it."

Hraithamar smiled. "We'll see." He put the ring on his finger, then gestured to Wodan's spear standing by the door. "Go now," he said. "My men are outside; get through them or not as you can, but go and leave my family in peace. The weregild is paid in full and I want nothing more to do with you."

Without looking back, Wodan walked over to take his spear. The gods went silently from Hraithamar's hall. The ring of men that stood waiting by the door with ready spears and knives felt only the passing of a sudden gust of wind with a few spatters of rain; one or two thought he might have seen a flash of light as he blinked, but no more. Then they stood wordless, for the touch of Wodan's wind on their faces had bound their eyes to blindness, fettering their thoughts and movements as though their muscles had turned to chains of iron binding their bones, and his whispered word had deafened their ears. So they would stand like day-struck trolls until the dawn's light loosed them, and by then the web Wodan had left to weave itself in the hall could not be undone.

The longer Hraithamar gazed at the gold, the hotter its light seemed to burn in his body, shaking him with a sudden fever of desire. Hardly aware of what he was doing, he fell to his knees before the pile, running his hands through it again and again. A brooch clanged to the ground; a ring dropped with a sharp clear note and rolled away. Hraithamar clutched for them, pushing them back on to the pile to start a small clinking avalanche of coins.

Lofanohaith brought her fist to her mouth, chewing on her knuckles in terror as she stared at her father. She, too, could hear the high, sharp ringing of the gold, but it filled her with fear; she could almost sense a deep bass rumbling beneath it, the sound of a huge glacier grinding forward or a great mass of snow and rock slowly beginning to slither down a mountain, unturnable and deadly.

Lingwohaith glanced at the enthralled faces of her father and brothers in alarm. She had tried her best to keep some calmness in the hall since the terrible strangers had brought Otter's empty hide home, as Fadhmir drank and wept and swore himself hoarse till she could almost feel his reason stretching like the seam of an overloaded bag, as her father gritted his teeth and stared from the depth of his horn into the flames and back again, as Ragin sat, saying nothing at all, the muscles of his shoulder and back raised into ridges of fury beneath his dirty feast tunic. Her sister was no help, turning and twisting in the bed they shared at night and screaming about blood on the sheets and slain children and the hall burning down till Lingwohaith was ready to kill her herself for the sake of a little sleep. Now it seemed as though everything she knew had been pulled on too hard and torn into tatters, but still she tried to force her panic down. Breathing deeply, she dug her nails into the palms of her hands and shoved her grubby hair out of her face with her fists.

But it was Lofanohaith who spoke first. "Stop that!" she screamed shrilly at Hraithamar. The noise seemed to jerk him away from his furious scrabbling after the fallen pieces of gold; still on his knees, he turned his head toward her, a look of wrath on his face. "Father, you're frightening me," she pleaded. "They're gone now, and the weregild is paid. Let's do what we need to for Otter's . . . p-pelt. . . . There's enough gold there to give him a real atheling's pyre and still be richer than anyone on the Rhine. Please?"

For a moment Hraithamar's expression shifted, and he wore the broad, open face Lofanohaith knew, marked only by a furrow of concern between the brows. "Burn the gold? What are you talking about, child? Weregild is for the living, and this is only a coat your brother wore. It would be ridiculous to make a full funeral pyre for it."

"But it's all we have of him. We ought to . . . " Her voice trailed off as Hraithamar turned back to the gold.

"We ought to divide out the shares of the weregild," Ragin said, his voice as raspy as dry rock. He stumbled forward to where Hraithamar stood, drawn, like his father, to the glittering pile. "Each of us gets one share, isn't that the way things are always done?"

"One share?" Hraithamar asked, not looking up as he caressed the gold over his dead son's pelt. "But we don't want to split this hoard up, do we? Where would you go? What kind of warband could each of you gather alone, even with a share of this gold? No; it's better that we should stay together. Follow your father, as you always have, and let me administer our hoard to everyone's good."

Fadhmir stooped to pick something up. The firelight that glittered so hotly on the gold shone cold and red as a winter sunset from the steel blade of his sword.

Ragin felt the hilt of his own weapon in his hand, the smooth oak he had carved with such care for the strongest and keenest sword he had ever wrought, engraved with ↑, Tiw's rune, on blade and hilt for victory. He could not look away from the glowing dragon ring on his father's finger, scaly gold and smooth ruby vanishing into the pile and reappearing again as his own hand moved with Fadhmir's, plunging their swords deep between Hraithamar's ribs. Metal scraped across bone and against metal within Hraithamar's chest and he screamed horribly, falling back from the gold as his sons released their weapons. Lingwohaith and Lofanohaith's high screams echoed his, the two girls backing away in horror from their brothers who stood staring into the bloodied heap of glistening treasure.

Then there was only the sound of Hraithamar's hoarse, rattling breathing and the ringing of the gold as Fadhmir and Ragin swept the hoard into their cloaks, armful by armful, roughly shaking out Otter's pelt and tossing it away. When the gold overflowed the edges of their makeshift bags, they ran to the two great chests against the wall where Hraithamar's household goods were kept, flinging the fine linens and smooth bowls of Roman clay on to the earthen floor with tearing sweeps of their arms. They did not see what they were doing; they never turned their gazes from the gold, though

Hraithamar's fine drinking cup of Roman glass shattered into glittering splinters against the wall where Ragin tossed it.

The delicate weaves of cloth had been their mother's pride; her sight blurred with tears, Lingwohaith ran after her brothers, thinking only to save her mother's work from their rending and trampling. Perhaps she was clumsy, or did not look where she was going; Fadhmir's backhanded swing burst against her face in a shower of bright lights, throwing her against the wall where she sat stunned as they tumbled the gold into the empty chests until no more was left. Like ravenous hounds, Fadhmir and Ragin swung their heads back and forth to see if they had missed any tiny piece.

Fadhmir just beat his younger brother to the ring on his father's finger by the edge of a moment. Hraithamar's hand curled weakly, but his son yanked the finger straight and the ring off, pushing it on to his own hand. Ragin stood glaring at him for a moment, but turned swiftly back to his cloakful of gold.

"Together!" Fadhmir said. "We won't get far alone. One to watch while the other sleeps . . . we have to watch . . . Go and get the horses."

Ragin half turned from habit, then whirled back. "Both of us. Together."

"What about them? What if we leave it with them?"

Lingwohaith bit her lip as her brothers' eyes met in perfect, mad understanding. Fadhmir nodded; they said nothing more. She did not dare to move as she watched them tie up the corners of their gold-filled cloaks and heave the huge makeshift bags—more weight, she knew, than even Fadhmir's might should be able to lift—on to their backs, hurrying out of the hall. Father's men are out there, she thought. They will do something. But no sound of challenge or weapon came on the cold draft that blew through the open door; only the sound of heavy-laden hooves, then her brothers' footsteps hurrying back. Their measuring gazes scanned over their sisters. Lingwohaith's breath choked in her throat, but silently she thanked the gods that she had not moved, hoping that Fadhmir and Ragin had mind enough left to know it.

Fadhmir and Ragin turned their dreadful eyes away from the women, and Lingwohaith's breath began to flow again. Together the brothers lifted the first chest and bore it out of the door, then came back for the second.

Lingwohaith heard the slow hoofbeats moving away, and pushed herself up. Weak-legged with a terrible relief, she tottered over to her father's side and sank to the ground beside him. The pool of hot blood around him soaked quickly through her thick woolen skirt, warm against her knees. She could hear Lofanohaith sobbing noisily.

"Lofanohaith," Hraithamar said in a hoarse whisper. "Is that you? I can't see, my eyes are burnt."

"It's Lingwohaith, Father." Lingwohaith choked. "I'm here." She bent to put her arms around his shoulder, careful not to jostle the swords that crossed inside him. His racking, agonized cough brought up a gout of blood: the swords had gone through his lungs. High enough, praise the gods, to kill him soon. It was not a gut wound; he would not linger in agony for days.

"Revenge me. That's all I need, all you have left. Promise!"

"Father." She felt eerily clear-headed and light. The fire's flickering lit the hall in sharp-edged shadows around her sister and Hraithamar's fallen body; she could feel the rough texture of his tunic under her hands as though she had never touched linen before, but her legs were so numb that the blood soaking them might have been from a wound of her own. "Father, I can't kill my brothers. No matter what they've"—become, she was about to say— "done. They're my brothers. Not after Otter, I can't."

"Your son, then. Or if you have a daughter, her son. My kin must avenge me for what has been done."

"Father," Lingwohaith said pleadingly. Hraithamar coughed up another huge spurt of blood, black in the firelight; then his throat filled with a gurgling rattle and his head drooped to one side. More blood drooled in a steady stream out of his mouth, and Lingwohaith knew he was dead.

She was not sure how long she sat there, but her father's blood was cold on her dress and legs when she stood up. Lofanohaith had stopped crying, her teeth clenched tight and her plump face tautened into a mask, flesh seeming to fall away from high cheekbones and stern jawline.

"They'll have to be outlawed, you know," Lofanohaith said to her sister. "There's no way we can hide everything."

Lingwohaith could see the resolution stark and startling on her sister's face, and suddenly she remembered how Lofanohaith, when she was younger, had sometimes dreamed things before they happened, soberly telling her sister in a voice that sounded like a very old woman speaking through a child's throat. Lingwohaith had been secretly relieved when the frightening visions had ceased, hoping that whatever had caused them had been out-grown or died away; but now she knew with terrible certainty that Lofa-nohaith's hidden power had only been slumbering for a while, like an adder sleeping through winter's cold. She could feel that weird hot strength beating up and through her sister's body again, pushing against her like a mighty current. Yet the old habit of sensible assertion and control was still strong in Lingwohaith. "If we can say the strangers did it?"

Lofanohaith's glance went to the rune-carved hilt of Ragin's sword and the handspan of Fadhmir's broad blade protruding from their father's body. "I don't think we can. Only that . . . Fox . . . had a sword, and it was a little thin thing. And, besides, they killed our father for that cursed"—she shud-dered, the memory of its brightness still flickering behind her eyes—"that cursed gold. Do you want them to come back? To be able to sit in his hall?"

"But they're our brothers," Lingwohaith protested, knowing how feeble it was. She thought of the mad, blank looks that had twisted the faces of Fadhmir and Ragin as their swords met in their father's body, and knew she could never look upon them again without screaming in terror.

"They're gone," Lofanohaith said. "They're gone, as if they were dead. And another thing." She clenched her fists, moving closer to stare straight into her taller sister's eyes. Lingwohaith stared at the frozen mask of Lofa-nohaith's face in shock, amazed at this grim, resolute thing that wore her sister's soft flesh now. "There was no gold. There was never any gold. It was a spell those wanderers wove that drove our brothers mad. No more."

"But I saw," Lingwohaith insisted, then stopped as Lofanohaith's hands closed on her slim shoulders.

"It doesn't matter what you saw. Do you want men to think Fadhmir and Ragin killed our father from greed? Do you want our brothers to be hunted down like wolves? It was a spell, and that's all. They may have . . . If we never see them again, that's good enough, but I won't have my own kin disgraced any further."

Lingwohaith breathed in several times, letting the roaring in her ears fade away. "Of course," she said. "Of course. They must have gone for horses, so we'll give them a while to get away before we call our father's men . . . our men," she added fiercely, "in. Then we'll hold the funeral feast for our father and burn everything that's left, and we'll have to see about marriages straight-away. Who would you say is the best man in the band?"

"Eburhelm," her sister said without hesitation. Despite his stinking teeth and big belly, the older warrior was still the most skilled and wisest of the lot; except for Hraithamar, only Fadhmir had been able to offer him challenge. The others would follow him without question, which was all Lingwohaith cared about at the moment.

"Right. I'll ask him tonight. We have to think about holding things together first, then we'll see about getting you well settled. I know our father was looking at a couple of possible alliances; he wanted to hold off till he could get someone he thought you might be happy with, but now . . ."

"Absolutely." Lofanohaith's face was still locked up, its stark intensity almost frightening to Lingwohaith, if anything could be frightening to her any more. She wondered—dear Frija, it seemed impossible—if her merry little sister would ever giggle and blush again, or if this strange, steely resolution that had overcome her would fasten her in its grip to the end of her life.

It seemed to Lingwohaith suddenly, in an odd flight of dizziness, that the firelight's flickerings over the other girl's face showed her Lofanohaith as an old woman, flesh sunken off sharp bones, still staring out with burning, furious intentness. The light seemed to circle inward, leaving the hall blank except for Lofanohaith's aged features. As Lingwohaith stared, caught in the web of her own sight, her sister's face was overlaid with the sharp features of a bird-boned younger woman, whose brittle, polite smile cracked into a snarl of cruel triumph. The woman's face shifted again, into the dark mask of a young man whose grimness had never been lightened by any laughter, whose high-boned, icy-pale face was hardly human at all. The shadow of a spear-tip darkened one of his eyes, cutting a shadow scar down his cheek; then Lingwohaith's seeing blurred, and it was her younger sister she saw. She shut her eyes hard and opened them again, trying to drive the image from her memory as it had fled her sight.

Lingwohaith and Lofanohaith bent down, Lofanohaith holding her father's body while Lingwohaith, bracing her feet hard against the floor, tugged out first Fadhmir's sword, then Ragin's. She was panting when the job was done, but together they managed to heave the huge, stone-heavy body of Hraithamar up onto one of the wooden tables. Lofanohaith pulled his tunic straight, breaking off some of the crusted blood, and Lingwohaith gently tried to straighten his twisted features and close his wide, staring eyes, wiping the blood from his mouth and beard with the long sleeve of her dress.

Without looking at her sister, Lofanohaith laid the bloody swords on the table beside Hraithamar. They sat down together, one on either side of the bench, waiting for their brothers to be long enough fled. Lingwohaith stared into the fire, Lofanohaith into the darkness of the hall. Neither of them spoke to the other about what they saw in the light or the shadows.

DRAGON AND DWARF

Wodan and Hoenir walked through the dark night until the cold gray light of first dawn showed their shapes clearly against the rushing water of the Rhine and the cliffs beyond. Hoenir said nothing: it was his way to wait and to hold his thoughts. Of their kin, he was closest to their mother's brother Mimir, who kept the Well of Memory and doled out draughts from its water sparingly. So, though he had little love for Wodan's oath-brother Loki, he would wait and watch what came to pass without speech or judgment until the waters of Mimir's Well had closed over the last of Wodan's works.

They walked on until the faraway hill on which Hraithamar's burg stood was only a dark blur through the thin morning mist, now tinted palely with gold and pink in the light of the rising sun. As the dawn grew more fiery, the faint gray blue of Hoenir's garb faded farther into the brightening fog until he could be seen no longer. The light drew together near where he had been, coalescing into the slight, gaudy figure of Loki, breathless from his long night's faring to Ran's hall and back.

The tall man in the dark cloak stopped and turned, leaning on the shaft of the spear that served him as a staff.

"Well, Loki?" he said mildly.

The red-haired man cocked his head swiftly to one side, orange-gold eyes flickering like heat lightning as he looked up at his companion. "'Well, Loki?'" he mimicked, cruelly exaggerating the hint of age in the other's voice. "Well, what, Wodan? You want me to go away again, I suppose. You always do, when I've done all the work you want. 'Brother,' you call me when you need my help; but when Loki has saved your neck and taken the blame for what you willed, it's always, 'Go away, All-Father is busy remaking the worlds.'"

He stopped, staring at what Wodan held out to him. The silver-bound aurochs horn brimmed over with golden mead, the ruby eyes of the eagle's head at its tip glinting mockingly at him. As Loki watched, a few drops spilled over the silvered rim, tracing their way down the deep-etched tracks of the runes that covered the length of the horn in a carven tracery of mystery and pattering on to the grass like sunlit dew.

Wodan smiled grimly, his one gray eye glimmering. "I am mindful, Loki, of how in earlier days we blended our blood together. I swore that I would never drink ale unless it were borne to us both. Drink well, my brother, for we have a long way ahead of us."

Loki took the horn and drank noisily, dribbles of mead hissing into steam as they ran to the sharp point of his beardless chin. He emptied it halfway and handed it back to Wodan, grinning. "It's still good mead," he said flippantly. "And all you had to do for it was diddle an etin's daughter? I want your job someday." He was gone in a flash of flame before Wodan could reply.

The one-eyed god stood with the half-full horn in his hand, staring at the bright after-image of the momentary fire on the flood. Sighing, he raised the horn to his lips and drank well of the mead, now pleasantly warmed by Loki's touch.

Freshly inspired by the bright stream of wod, Wodan breathed in deeply and breathed a cloud of steam out into the cold air. When the frozen puff drifted away, an empty raft was bumping gently against the rocks at the Rhine's edge. Steadying himself with his spear, the Father of the Slain stepped onto the rocking raft, drawing his dark blue cloak up and wide-brimmed hat down. With his long gray hair and beard flowing loose and Gungnir's point hidden in the depths of the Rhine, Wodan looked like a mere aged ferryman whose hire might be had for two eggs or a mug of ale. He pushed off from the shore, floating against the strong grip of the current, his own wind-might bearing him to his next goal.

Ragin and Fadhmir rode till after daybreak, leading the two horses that bore the chests of gold on their backs. The light of the gold still filled their eyes, its pure power thrumming through the heavy sacks they carried and ringing through their bodies, driving them onward. Swords and blood and fire leapt in Ragin's mind, swirled and swept away by the gold that burned like a ring of fire around his sight, till the twisting light ate the edges of the night forest and left him riding blind, trusting to the dumb wisdom of the horse that labored under him and his burden. He did not hear how its breath came harsher and harsher, nor feel its sweat soaking through the sides of his breeches as the bright morning mist faded into daylight.

It was Fadhmir's steed that foundered first, dark eyes rolling desperately as its slim legs broke down and heart burst beneath the great weight it bore. Fadhmir clung to his gold, cursing; the horse fell into a splayed dark heap beneath him.

If he's dead, Ragin thought, I'll have all the gold; but to his disappointment, his brother rose from the wreckage of his horse's body, snarling under his breath.

Slowly Ragin dismounted. "Where do we go now?" he asked.

Fadhmir gestured up the river, at one peak that rose higher above the wood than the rest. "There," he said. "Where the Romans sometimes quarry stone. There's a large cave in there, with a small entrance, easy to guard. I used to meet . . . anyway, we can go there and keep watch over our gold; one of us can hold the entrance well enough while the other sleeps."

"How will we get there, then?"

The big warrior pointed upstream. A raft was floating toward them, the aged ferryman poling it toward the shore.

"Can we trust him?" Ragin asked suspiciously. "Suppose he figures out what we have and tries to betray us? Or tells someone where we've gone?"

A horrible smile lit Fadhmir's wide features. "We'll kill him when we are across, of course. Sometimes I think you're a little simple, my brother."

Ragin reached to the sword at his belt, but his searching fingers found only the tooled leather of its scabbard.

Fadhmir's grin spread wider, showing teeth like jagged yellow pebbles. "With our hands, if we have to." His big fingers tightened on the knot tying the corners of his cloak together, as Ragin's steely fist closed involuntarily. The ferryman's gray hair and beard blew behind him in the wind; Ragin knew that the old man could never stand against his own blacksmith's grip.

The raft swung to shore, the ferryman pushing his pole between the rocks to hold it against the strong current. "Are you two going down the river?" he asked in a cracked voice. "Have you the money for a ferryman's fee?"

Without answering, Fadhmir stepped onto the raft, which sank a few inches beneath his weight, teetering precariously till he moved to its center. I can't trust him; I could ride away with my share now, Ragin thought. But he knew his horses were too tired to move faster than a man could walk— and half the gold was on the raft with his brother; he could not leave it behind. Slowly he followed his brother on, carefully picking his way between the rocks to the raft as he guided his horses along behind him. The river's ripples splashed onto the log planking as the raft tilted under him, wetting his boots to the ankle.

When Ragin and Fadhmir had settled themselves, one man and his gold on each side with the third horse in the middle, the ferryman turned his back to them. Without speaking, he began to pole the raft straight toward the mountain Fadhmir had pointed out.

He knows, he knows, Ragin thought in a sudden panic. He looked at his brother, whose eyes darted about in a wild fury. Although Fadhmir, too, had set his burden down for a moment, he stood bent over, holding to the cloak's knotted hem with a death grip. The Sun's light set the white six-pointed star blazing from the ruby on his finger, white as the clenched knuckles of the fist that bore it.

The raft's movement down the river was slow, the ferryman struggling to keep the heavy load in an even line against the flow of the water that swung it from side to side. But bit by bit they moved forward, and finally the wood bumped against rock.

"What do you have to pay me with, then?" the aged man cackled. The gleam beneath his hood fixed Fadhmir first, and the big warrior stood dumb for a moment. As he turned his sharp gaze to Ragin, Fadhmir leapt forward, one hand held back by the weight of his gold and one hand stretched out toward the ferryman's neck, reaching through the tattered gray shroud of beard for a withered throat that was no longer there, melting into mist under his hand.

Ragin and Fadhmir stared at one another for a moment, eyes wild. Ragin's limbs were trembling with terror; he felt as though his body was only a hollow shell like the shed skin of a snake, too weak to hold his own weight up. Leading the horses off again was a tricky business; twice the raft nearly went over, and as it slanted under the weight of the third horse coming to the edge the chest of gold began to tilt toward the river. Ragin threw himself under it desperately, pushing it straight again with a wrench of his body that tore through his back. Panting with pain, he followed the horse off. He knew what lay in the dark hollows of Fadhmir's gaze, and so he forced himself to take his hand from his back and show his teeth.

"I'm not hurt," he said roughly.

"Good, then you can help me carry this."

Ragin took two corners of Fadhmir's cloak bag, and the two men began to bear their burden along the path that led up to the mountain, their horses following behind them. Ragin plodded head down, doggedly setting one foot in front of another, chanting the lines of a song he had heard . . . two nights ago? . . . to himself, his feet clumping down in a steady drumbeat:

Onward, for we march to war
on to death and Walhall
Warriors win the highest seat
within the barriers' hold.

Forget the ferryman, he said to himself, forget the strangers' strange words; you have the gold, nothing else in the world, nothing else matters.

Swords bite bitter, steel burning
walkurjas' gray steeds howl
Flow red rivers from our blade-teeth
run to thirsty earth.

The path was partially overgrown with brownish grass; Ragin's boots trod the dry blades down, carrying him upward, upward, to the cave where he could sit and loose his load. His sight was focusing inward, away from the Rhine far below, away from the sky spread out like a clear cloud-stained blanket around him, away from the dark peak towering above him where his goal waited, to the narrow path before his feet, avoiding the rocks that made the going more treacherous as he climbed upward, stepping over the tendrils of weed that stretched across the track. His body felt entirely numb except for the sharp, piercing vibration of the gold through it, stilling the rapid amazement of his mind and dulling his senses till only his vision of boot toes moving onward and the shifting pattern of stones and grass told him that he was still walking. Only when he followed his brother into the darkness of the iron-shored quarry cave and, knees sagging, let the terrible weight of the gold down at last, did feeling return to him.

Too tired to stand, Ragin dropped to the ground, looking up at Fadhmir's exhausted face. Tiny lines creased the edges of his brother's eyes and mouth, as though he had aged twenty years in the course of the night.

"I'll watch," Fadhmir said shortly, moving to the narrow cave's mouth with a wary blue eye turned toward his brother. "You sleep now. You look like you need it."

The darkness was already overcoming Ragin's vision, but he struggled to stand as Fadhmir walked toward him. He thought he saw a gray rock in his brother's hand, but everything was gray, gray around him as his eyes closed and he slumped back.

Fadhmir brought the rock down hard on his brother's head, then picked his body up and slung it powerfully out of the cave. It rolled down the mountain, finally stopping against a small, crooked tree halfway to the river. For a moment he thought about getting up and throwing it the rest of the way. . . . Ragin might be a threat, might be . . . but the gold sang ever louder in his head. What if he left it for the time it would take to make sure of Ragin? Might not someone else come along and try to take it from him? No, there was only one way to be sure.

He crept back into the dark cave a little way. Untying the tight knots with fingernails and teeth, he let the gold spill out, the two loads merging into one huge heap, glimmering softly in the faint light from the cave's narrow mouth. Its pure high note called painfully to him till every bit of his body resonated with the music of the gold. Feverishly, he pulled his dirty tunic and breeches off, lying down and rolling over and over in the hoard, giving himself to the precious edges of sharp metal cutting into him and its cold fire shivering through him. He twisted the spiral armbands wider to fit his heavy-muscled arms and legs, and pushed rings onto his strong fingers. Then his hands touched something that sent a tingling shock up through his arms: a coif of close-knit rings, heavy with the weight of pure gold. The gold plate over the middle of the forehead had a symbol carved into it: eight crossed tridents radiating, forks outward, from a central point. Ecstatically Fadhmir pulled the gold chainmail over his long itchy hair, feeling its intensity burning away his own dirty, pitiful humanity. It seemed to him that he could feel his soul curling around the gold like a great serpent, like the dragon of his ring around its ruby, free of the weakness of his human body, eyes always watchful. So Fadhmir gave himself over to his own dream, willingly trapped by the might of his hoard and the magic of the Helm of Awe, which he now wore on his head.

Ragin awoke with the red of the late afternoon Sun throbbing painfully through his eyes and in his head. His mouth was as dry and musty as old hay, and he ached terribly in every limb, but most of all at the back of his skull. Carefully he reached up to touch the point from which the spiderweb of pain radiated and cried out when his fingers made contact with the swollen lump. Below the Rhine flowed, cool and inviting; above he could still feel the pure fiery singing of the gold, calling him up. For a moment he paused, torn, then began to crawl up the side of the mountain. Sweat poured down his forehead and stung deep and sickening as an adder's bite where Fadhmir's rock had struck him, but he kept on, drawn by the might that had touched him, pulling himself over the rocks and weeds to the mouth of the cave against the heavy weight of black fear and oppression that seemed to press down from its narrow dark opening.

Looking within, Ragin saw his brother spread out in the gold, his body half-hidden and face covered by the gleaming metal. A shimmering shadow seemed to rise above him: the ghost of a wyrm coiling around the hoard, its scales glittering faintly like a great river of transparent gold coins and Fadhmir's mad eyes lidlessly open in its huge head. A trembling terror seized Ragin as the half-seen dragon opened its mouth, darting an insubstantial tongue toward him. Even his desire for the gold could not stand against the mad panic that had him halfway down the mountain before he could think again. The inner parts of his breeches clung hot and wet to his legs, the smell of piss sharp in his nostrils. He leaned over and vomited, a streak of agony stabbing through his head with every convulsion. Sobbing, he crawled toward the cool waters of the Rhine to wash the stink from his body and the foulness from his mouth.

When Ragin had taken his bath, shivering, he put his grubby clothes on. Dizziness rushed over him as he tried to stand, and he quickly sat down. A cold wind was blowing down the river, its edge sharpening as the Sun sank lower. He pulled himself in between a few large rocks, huddling to the ground to keep warm.

The night passed for him in feverish fits of shivering against the cold and painful, haunted interludes of semiconscious sleep where he thrashed and cried out, with the vision of the gold burning behind his eyes, flames leaping through it and the bright wyrm twining around it, its scales shifting and glimmering through his skull. Once he called out for Lofanohaith, and once for his father, only to remember in despair that he was far from his sister and something had happened to his father, though he wasn't quite sure what. He thought the strangers who brought the gold might have done it, or else Fadhmir; but when he pictured his father's fall it was as though he could feel the Tiw rune on his sword's hilt in his hand, and that disturbed him deeply. It was the blow to my head, he told himself; but further down, beneath the range of thought, something wondered if it hadn't been the sheer blast of power from the gold that had burnt out his brains and left him stranded by the edge of the Rhine while Fadhmir lay, half-buried, guarding his hoard— and, if so, if the scattered pieces of his mind would ever come together again. Only when the Sun had risen again, drying the heavy dew from Ragin's cold, damp clothes and warming his shivering body, did he fall fully asleep, free of the night's mad half-dreams.

When Ragin woke the second time, the sky was clouded over and a few drops of rain were beginning to spatter down. The lump on his head still hurt when he touched it, but the pain no longer turned his empty stomach. When, supporting himself slowly on the boulders around him, he eased himself to his feet, his sight remained clear and his legs steady; and now he was aware that he was terribly hungry and rather cold as well.

But I can go home, Ragin thought. Though the ride had seemed to last forever, he realized now that their heavy-burdened horses had moved slowly. The Roman quarry was not so far from Hraithamar's hall: if Ragin could find the good path through the wood he might possibly get home by nightfall, or just a little after. Carefully he started walking, trying not to jostle his sore skull.

Ragin heard the men before he saw them, their voices—voices he knew, that had been raised with the other warriors' in Hraithamar's hall at every feast since he could remember—carrying straight through the tree-shadowed windings of the path.

"We'll make those bastards pay if we catch them," one grated. Ragin recognized Wolfger's surly tones.

Ragin heard the sound of a muffled blow. "You shut up," someone else— Harimann, from his slight eastern accent—shouted. "It was a spell, didn't the frowe Lingwohaith tell us so? It's those strange wanderers we should be looking for, not Fadhmir and Ragin. They never would have done something like that if they hadn't been enchanted. And we . . . " He was quiet a moment, then went on. "You weren't there. We never saw nor heard anything. Not till dawn. Didn't hear fighting, didn't see the strangers come out, didn't see Fadhmir or Ragin go. Nothing. We were struck, like someone laid war-fetter on us. Could have been something like it happened to them."

While Harimann was talking, Ragin wriggled around the roots of a clump of blueberry bushes and crouched behind the trunk of a huge oak tree that rose from the nest of shrubbery, hoping that the sound of the warrior's voice would hide his own rustlings. His heart thudded painfully in his chest and his hands shook with the fear of hearing the words spoken that would bring his horrible dreams into being; but all his fear could not drown out the remembered sound of steel grating against bone, or the gold-blurred vision of Hraithamar falling back from the hoard.

Harimann, Frithirik, Wolfger and Hlothowig came around the corner. The scarred side of Wolfger's scowling face was bright red from Harimann's blow, his black sideways look vicious.

"They did it anyway. He was our drighten and their father, and they killed him together. Even if they was enchanted, they ought to come back for judgment and tell us what happened. They would if they was innocent, wouldn't they?"

Harimann cast his blue glance down to the side of the path, heavy brow creased. "Might have," he muttered. "But we don't know what those wargs did to them. It could be they're still running out of their wits somewhere—could be, till they die. We ought to find them and see what we can do."

"You hear something in there?" Hlothowig asked, thick knuckles rubbing at the itchy corner of one pale eye as he pointed into the bushes with his other hand. He sneezed, then wiped his nose with the sleeve of his tunic.

"Nothing but you sniffling," Wolfger muttered. "You're so jumpy that, if a rabbit jumped out at you you'd run away swearing you'd been attacked by a wild boar." They kept walking, turning out of sight.

"That's enough, Wolf," Frithirik's deep, slow voice came through the brush. "If there was anyone here, I'm sure all this talking has scared them back across the river."

Wolfger said something else, but it was too indistinct for Ragin to make it out. He hugged his arms around himself, shivering and crying silently for everything he had lost, waiting for the night.

In full darkness, Ragin crept out of the bushes and walked along the path, ready to run at the sound of any human noise. Small furry things rustled in the dead leaves; far away, an owl called. Ragin stifled a startled cry of fright as something dark burst from the bushes in front of him and whisked across the path, but it was only a fox with something wriggling in its mouth.

Near the hall, he had to move more slowly, keeping his head down as he crept between trees and through the cover of bushes. The light of the Moon's sharp crescent silvered the spear points and leather byrnies of the sentries before the door, and a few more armed men were walking around, talking in low voices. Ragin could not hear the words, but the tones of shock and venom were clear enough to his keen ears. He waited as the Moon followed his road up the sky, not sure what he was waiting for until he saw Lofanohaith come out of the hall.

One of the sentries tried to stop her for a moment, talking to her. Ragin guessed that he was trying to get her to let him come along. Lofanohaith said something that caused a brief burst of laughter, then patted the knife at her belt in a way that sent a shudder through Ragin's cold body. Proudly, the Moon bright on her light gray shift, Lofanohaith walked around the hall and into the trees where her brother stood waiting. The Moon's light cast shadowed hollows into her cheeks and frosted her dark hair with a tint of silver. Ragin stared at her, almost unable to believe that this grim vision with her hand on her knife hilt was the sister he knew.

"What do you want?" Lofanohaith hissed.

Ragin sagged back against a tree trunk, too tired to stand anymore. "Help me," he whispered. "Tell me what happened. Fadhmir hit me on the head and . . . I'm tired, I'm hungry and I'm confused. Only the gold . . ." His voice trailed off into the fire that leapt up to blind him for a moment, clearing away in dizzy spots of light before his eyes.

Lofanohaith's face did not soften, but her voice was a bit quieter when she spoke again. "You and Fadhmir killed our father. He wouldn't share it out, so the two of you stabbed him and took—it—away. Lingwohaith's married Eburhelm already and the two of you have been declared outlaws, 'like wargs in the wood, that any man may slay.' They've been out looking for you—and for the strangers, but no one's found so much as a footprint of them." Lofanohaith leaned closer, the Moon reflecting silver from the pools of her eyes. "Go away, Ragin," she whispered harshly. "Change your name and find another drighten to follow. Set up as a smith somewhere, but find a way to get back inside a hall or hearth. Otherwise . . . you remember the dreams I had when I was small, the dreams that always told us when guests would arrive or when battles were coming?"

Ragin nodded.

"I was right every time, wasn't I?"

"Yes," he admitted. He wanted to look away, but the icy light spilling out of Lofanohaith's eyes held him in fast fetters.

"Last night I dreamed again. I knew you were coming, and I know what's happening to Fadhmir. Ragin, forget . . . it. Forget it and go away as far and fast as you can, but don't leave the human kind behind you, otherwise you'll lose everything you have left of your humanity. The hoard will kill you as surely as Fadhmir is dying already, and the hand that fells you will be the hand of the only person who has reason to love you. Do you believe me?"

"Fadhmir is dying?" he asked. "Then the gold . . ."

"Fadhmir's body is fading into his spirit. The first thing I saw in my dream was you looking into a cave at a dragon curled round the hoard. You saw it then: everything that used to be our brother is becoming the guardian of our gold. He will lie there, his spirit feeding on the strength of his earthly body until it starves to death and crumbles to dust, and between that power and the might of the gold that sustains him, the shape of his soul will slowly come forth until a true dragon guards Fadhmir's cave. You yourself will never be able to overcome him; I saw you running from the Helm of Awe when you might still have been able to slay his body and soul together. Look: you're a warg, an outcast now, but it's not too late. You can still turn back and turn away the wyrd I dreamed. Let it go, Ragin. What you do in the next few days is going to lay your orlog and decide your doom forever, and right now your own brains are no more use to you than a scrambled heap of ashes, so you need to listen to me."

"I'm listening," he whispered, cowering back from his sister's terrible piercing eyes. "Tell me what to do. Please." A violent fit of shivering came over him; he wrapped his arms about himself, hugging his chest tight as his teeth chattered till it was over.

"Go to your forge and gather as many of your tools as you can carry. I'll bring you your horse—he came home by himself yesterday evening, he knew the way, just as you always said he did—some food and something to protect yourself with. They burned your sword and Fadhmir's, but I can probably steal a spear without being noticed. Go on, it's safe."

Obediently Ragin scuttled away, following the narrow path to his forge. The fire was cold, tools scattered—had he left them like that? It was odd, he had always been so careful before. He hefted hammers and tested the edges of chisels, judging weight against need till Lofanohaith came, laden with bags, through the door.

She wrapped a thick wool cloak around his heavy-muscled, trembling shoulders and handed him a belt with a good long knife dangling from it. Ragin fumbled with the clasp of his empty-scabbarded swordbelt until, impatient, Lofanohaith unhooked it for him and locked the other around his waist, tossing the finely tooled sheath and belt into the dead coals.

"Here's food for a few days, and a little silver. I couldn't get more. Some ale, and there's more food and some clean clothes in Irminafaxen's saddlebag. I've got him tied outside for you. You might try crossing the river and going to one of the Roman camps. I've heard they don't care about outlawry as long as a man has some sort of useful skills, and you're the best smith north of the Danube, as far as I've ever heard. Go on, now, and don't come back."

Ragin wanted to reach out and embrace her, to say . . . he didn't know what, but something to loose the hard knot in his throat and the hot flood behind his gritty eyes. But Lofanohaith had already turned on her heel and was striding out of the forge, too upright and remote to touch.

As Lofanohaith had promised, Irminafaxen was outside, his reins looped over a low branch on a nearby oak; a short thrusting spear leaned against the tree's gnarled trunk. The piebald horse rolled his eyeballs suspiciously, sniffing and dancing about as Ragin came nearer, but he allowed his master to grab his reins and quiet him. Ragin loaded his tools and food onto the horse. Using the spear as a prop, he pulled himself into the saddle then slapped the horse softly on the neck. "Go on," he whispered.

Irminafaxen turned around three times, as if trying to locate a sound in the distance, then began to trot swiftly toward the southeast. Ragin slumped back, too tired to keep a watch for Eburhelm's men or to do anything but let his horse go where he would, as the painful glimmering rose up inside his skull again.

Ragin rode for several days, huddling inside makeshift lean-tos of branches at night, eating the food his sister had given him and drinking out of streams along the way. Under the thickening coarseness of his winter coat, Irminafaxen grew thinner, nosing through the fallen leaves for the sparse grass of summer's end or chewing at bushes as he carried Ragin along. The sky had clouded over, a light rain drizzling steadily since the young blacksmith had left his sisters' hall. He thought he was going south to the Roman territories as Lofanohaith had counseled him, but he was out of the lands and away from the paths he knew; he had not dared to ride along the Rhine, so he had borne far to the west before turning southward. His fits of shivering and burning blindness had gradually eased, but the gold sang soft and distant in the back of his mind all the time, like the faintest of ringings in his ears.

Ragin thought that he had been riding for five days when his food gave out. He wasn't sure quite where he was, only that he had to keep going in the hope of finding some other human beings, and if that didn't happen soon he'd have to start looking for food in the wood. He knew how to set snares for rabbits; he had a vague idea of how to tell poisonous toadstools from good ones most of the time, and at least he could recognize the thick-stemmed, brown-capped rock mushrooms that made the best eating.

With a new clearness of sight, Ragin pulled Irminafaxen to a stop and looked around the dripping wood. He could hear the swift running of a stream nearby, full from the days of rain and splashing loudly over its rocks; deep in the trees, a small bird called and was answered by another. The sharp hoofprints of a deer were stamped deep into the leaf mold on the path, half-full of water. Orange platters grew from the wet mossy bark of trees and the white-capped, orange-gilled witches' mushrooms leaned about their roots along with a few pinkish brown toadstools.

Ragin slid from Irminafaxen's back, boots squelching into the fermenting leaves and mud, and took the horse's reins to lead it along. "Well, Irmina-faxen, you won't have to envy my food any longer. I'm living off the road, same as you." His voice was shockingly cracked, dusty and dry; when he laughed, it came out as a brief, barking cackle. The horse swung its white-splotched head away, rolling its eyes and pawing the ground with one fore-hoof at the unexpected noise. Ragin patted its neck and led it onward, carefully scanning the drifts of rotting leaves at the forest's roots and stopping, every now and then, to examine a decaying tree trunk or piece of wood.

Intent on the ground, he did not know how long the hart had been standing like a deer's dark shadow in the trees before him, its antlers raised into their branches. It was a magnificent beast, heavily muscled with a strangely deep-hued coat, as though it had been dusted with coal.

Ragin grasped for his spear and hurled it at once, but the stag stepped gracefully to the side, avoiding the weapon with casual swiftness. Slowly it turned and started walking away, speeding up as the young man ran for his spear but not breaking into a run.

Snatching up his weapon, Ragin pulled himself on to Irminafaxen's back and urged the horse after the swarthy hart. Now it began to run, leaping rocks and streams with careless grace, as horse and man pounded after it, Irminafaxen panting and Ragin clinging to saddle and mane with desperate intensity as his steed soared over water and fallen tree trunk, bush and boulder in pursuit of the dark stag, which never faltered, yet never passed out of their sight. It slowed when they did, glancing back every so often as if to be sure that they were still following.

It's only a deer, Ragin told himself. Meat for weeks. I can build a shelter and smoke it—sinews for a bow, warm hide for a blanket—I can't let it go. His shrunken stomach rumbled loudly at the thought of roast venison and his mouth filled with water. Again he urged his tired horse on, trying to get close enough to trust his spear cast. If only I had a bow now, he thought.

The gray sky was darkening when the stag finally rounded the rocky side of a hill and vanished from Ragin's sight. He rode after it, but it was gone, no track or trace marring the cracked gray rock that clacked under Irmina-faxen's hooves and rose high before him. In rage and frustration, he slid from the horse's back and beat his fists upon the mossy stone hillside.

Suddenly Ragin's hands were still. He felt, beyond doubt or wonder, that something was watching him from within the crags, something mighty and old as the bones of the earth. Awe rose over him like a great wave; his hands shook as he carefully uncurled his fists and laid his palms flat against the damp rock. Enter, said a deep voice in his mind. Its tone resonated eerily through his skull, as though it rang through several realms at once. Unquestioning, Ragin stepped forward into the stone, which seemed to turn inside out as he moved from his earthly body, becoming the doorway to a dark, sloping tunnel through the hill. He had to crouch down and creep with bent knees and hunched shoulders along its twists to the red firelight glowing at the end.

The tunnel widened into a craggy rock cave, lit by the brightness of a forge's fire. Before the flames stood a wight shaped like a man, but a man no taller than Ragin's chest with shoulders as wide and muscular as those of the biggest man Ragin had ever seen. He wore only a sleeveless brown tunic, plain brown breeches and heavy boots. The dwarf's skin was almost black with ingrained charcoal, his huge bare arms scarred with the same pink-white burns of the forge that Ragin bore. His fringe of dark hair and waist-long beard were frosted like the pelt of a silver fox, the beard's end tucked under his belt. Ragin crouched under the low roof, staring at him as he threw back his round head in a deep, eerie laugh.

"What brings you to Wind-Alf's door, man?" he asked. "Did you hope to find your stag within my hill?"

Ragin's gaze turned to the forge, where a half-made sword lay glinting, light running and coiling along the serpent patterns of metal, then to the dwarf's keenly crafted buckle in the shape of a leaping stag, perfect to the last bronze hair and tiny black jewel of its eye. Only in the hoard had he seen . . . only in the hoard . . . dwarves' work that no man could match, treasures to break the heart and swords to slay . . . to slay . . .

"I've come to learn craft, to forge a sword that will slay a dragon," Ragin said, his voice sounding thin and weak after the dwarf's booming laughter. "Will you teach me, Wind-Alf?"

"Teach a child of Ash and Elm the crafts of the dwarves? What have you to offer? You have no gold, and you can't give Frowe Holda's price."

"I'll work for you as an apprentice, as it's done among men," Ragin offered desperately. "I'll carry wood and make charcoal, turn the grindstone and fetch water. I'll do whatever you like, but I have to learn from you."

The dwarf's grin disappeared. He moved closer to Ragin, staring into his face for a long time, then reached out and squeezed his shoulders and arms in a grip like iron pincers. Ragin winced, but did not cry out.

"Sound enough, I'll grant," Wind-Alf allowed. "You've swung a hammer for a little while. You might even have started learning a bit of wisdom, am I right?"

Ragin nodded. "I know the names of the runes, and some of their uses. I know which to sing when I'm hammering and what to say when I quench the metal. I know some of the herbs that go into the water and all the trees that go to make charcoal."

"Fair enough, for a child of men, though you've a long way to go to match even the rawest of new-made dwarves. Ha, I'll call my brothers and see what they think of you." Wind-Alf stepped back, breathing deeply. The light of the forge dimmed down to a soft red glow beneath the ashes and left a green after-image before Ragin's eyes. "Northren and Suthren, Austren and Westren, Dwalan's kin, I, your brother Wind-Alf, call. Nar and Nawan; Nibel, Dawan; Wegg and Thekk, Thrawan and Thror; Gand-Alf, Nali and Glowen, Aikinaskildhijen, come to judge this son of Ash and Elm."

Ragin felt the darkness grow crowded with heavy shapes, sparks of gold and red shining like foxfire from the eyes of the unseen dwarves who jostled and poked at him, running what felt like hammer-calloused hands over his bent body and murmuring to each other in voices like rock sliding over rock.

"No fear here; he's left men far behind. He won't betray our craft."

"He'll steal your gold if you look away a moment. See here where Andward's nith has burned him."

"He's not the first and he won't be the only. He wants to forge the sword to kill his brother who keeps it, but it wasn't he who stole it. It was Loki. Ha, our kin will be revenged on Loki someday before he stands on his ship of dead men's nails, when the Muspilli come to burn the world."

"Revenge, that's in his soul right enough. Revenge and greed, sure as we all know them. No better tool to use than that forged for the task, and no better metal than that smelted for the work. Here he is, with the curse's gold alloyed into his heart; who better to craft the cursed dragon's death?"

"Loki thinks Fadhmir's death will free the gold's fire to burn through the worlds again, but if we work well, Ragin's hands will grasp and hold it. And if he should gain the gold, won't it come back to the stone?"

"When the dragon is dead, we'll rule the Rhine again. Loki will find no friendship there, no hole to hide in when he needs it, though he take the shape of a fish and seek out Andward's cave again."

"Finely crafted; well be it wrought."

"This one loves the craft. You can see the smith's torch burning in his head when he looks at fine work. Teaching won't be wasted on him, even if he is a son of Ash and Elm."

"He's not Weland."

"There was only one Weland. But he'll do."

"He'll do."

Slowly the thronging presences faded away until only Ragin and Wind-Alf were left in the low-roofed cave.

"It looks like I've got an apprentice, then," Wind-Alf said gruffly. "The first thing you'll learn is how to stoke the crafter's fire—no, you'll learn what it is. Do you know the story of how Frowe Holda got her necklace Brisin-gamen from us? How she paid for the four rings of gold with four nights of her love? Well then, you have the first secret. Her burning love-might was what gave my brothers the strength and the vision to forge the necklace, the fire that melted and purified the gold for their shaping. The same power lurks in everyone, but only awakens in a few, sometimes through need and sometimes through the touch of another fire. Now you've been burnt by both and you have to shape it before it destroys you, bring the wildfire together into the clear light of a torch and shape it to your work. Do you feel it? Do you feel your flame?"

And as the dwarf spoke Ragin could feel the fire running through his spirit in burning veins, flushing him with its heat.

"Yes," Wind-Alf hissed. "Yes. Not so much there yet, but it will grow as your strength grows. Now come over to the forge and let it flow in."

Ragin followed him to the coals. The dwarf grabbed his hands, pushing the fingers together and thumbs out at an angle, then turned them palms downward. Ragin breathed deeply, bringing the flame through his palms and wrists till it flowed, red-gold and clear, to leap up from the coals underneath his hands. He moved back slowly without changing the position of his fingers, feeding and controlling the fire till it had grown again to what it had been when he came in.

"Keep it like that," Wind-Alf commanded. "Pay attention to what you're doing; don't worry about what I'm doing, or your mind will slip and you'll spoil my work." He picked the half-done sword blade up in a set of iron tongs and plunged it into the fire as Ragin struggled to maintain his strength and his control over the flames. "The heat must be straight and firm; don't let it flicker."

By the time Wind-Alf had pulled the sword out of the flames and beaten it on the anvil thrice, Ragin's arms were trembling and the fire was starting to jump about a little bit.

"All right, let it go," the dwarf told him. "Get back to your body before it freezes and go to sleep. You may as well set up your own forge for the daytime by the side of my hill; you'll need to practice. Come back at sunset tomorrow."

Ragin started to thank him, but Wind-Alf cut him off with a sharp gesture. "You think it's going to stay this easy? You won't be thanking me tomorrow, boy; you'll be lucky if you haven't fled by the time the Moon's full. Go away now."

Ragin turned and scuttled down the passage, out of the hill and into his body. His back and legs were sore and cramped, as though his spirit's crouching had strained them as well, and he felt as exhausted as if he had just run for twenty miles. Amazingly, Irminafaxen was still there, nudging his master's body anxiously with a warm, soft nose.

Ragin levered himself up from the rock and patted the horse, then began to build another of his makeshift shelters. He knew it wouldn't be very good, but at least it would keep the worst of the wind and rain off for the night, and tomorrow he could start building a real hut for himself.

As he gathered brush and wood, Ragin thought of Lofanohaith's warning about leaving humankind behind him. Had it been a last stab at revenge on her part, trying to keep him from his rightful craft? It must have been; he could not imagine anything finer than dwelling here by Wind-Alf's stone and learning from him . . . for when he could forge a keen enough sword, one better than any man could make, he could slay the Fadhmir-dragon and take the hoard for his own. It was his sister's pitiful trickery, telling him to keep to humankind and to forget the hoard, that the hoard would kill him; no more. She might be a spae-woman, whose visions showed her the earth and the realms beyond—she was, she had to be to know about Fadhmir and what he was becoming—but there was no law of magic or man that said Holda's handmaidens had to tell the truth about what they saw.

Ragin slept well in his damp brush shelter that night, dreaming of a forge of his own in the center of the dragon's hoard, of enough gold to craft for a thousand years, of swords such as no man or dwarf had made before, and of a low-roofed cave in the rock where he could work till the end of time. And in his dreams, he could already stand upright in Wind-Alf's hill without having to hunch his shoulders or bend his knees and neck.

PLANTING THE SEED

The raft floated south, the boatman poling it against the current with a leisurely hand. He did not stop for fares, but continued with the curses of those who needed to cross at his back—those who did not mark how easily his raft moved against the flowing of the river and make the sign of Thonar's hammer over themselves or clutch the amber amulets at their throats.

When Wodan left the river at last, he moved swiftly along the road, faring eastward with the steady wind at his back billowing out his dark cloak like a raven's wings as it bore him along. Sometimes he passed through villages where a little smoke still rose from the ashes of thatch and woven wicker walls; sometimes he passed through towns where dogs barked cautiously at him or whined and crept away and plump children, sucking their thumbs, stared at the strange wizard-man from behind their nervous mothers' skirts. In such hamlets he stopped where he could sense a sick goat or a child with a broken leg, where the tracing of a few runes and singing of a healing chant would get him a night's lodging and a bag of food. Once, as he walked away, a skinny boy of six or seven shook off the hand of the mousy blond girl holding him and darted forward to touch the staff of Wodan's spear. His mother gasped and swiftly grabbed him back, smacking him till he howled. Wodan turned his head to fix the boy in his glittering gaze, and the child went quiet at once, trembling with excitement.

"Later, Ansuger," Wodan murmured, and moved on, stalking at a steady pace along the muddy road past the fields and into another thick wood where a wolf could travel more swiftly than a man, guided by the rich scents of stag droppings and rabbit trails and the markings his brothers and sisters made to warn others away from the lands ruled by their packs.

Out of human sight, gray fur sprouted as cloak and clothing vanished, long man's hands fused to paws and grim face lengthened to a snout till a great grizzled wolf gazed at gray tangles of bush, gray trees and clouding heavens through a single eye. The wind still blew toward the west, bringing a steady drizzle to dew the wolf's thick fur and drip from wet black branches around him.

Three days had passed by the time Wodan rose to two feet again at the other side of the wood. He raised his hooded head, his eye straining through the shadows of the rapidly darkening sky and the thickening veil of rain. Above the clouds, a raven's harsh voice called and another croaked an answer, calling Wodan on to the stead he had seen from his high seat, the next step on his long faring.

The god tightened his grip on his spear, pulling his boots loose from the mud with a wet sucking sound. Wrapping his damp cloak more closely against the edge of ice in the wind, Wodan strode along, following the unseen shapes of Hugin and Munin as they flew blackly through night and the gathering storm. A far-off flash of lightning showed the shadow-ravens a little ahead, wheeling like the ghosts of bats in the sudden blinding whiteness before the dark beat down in an icy torrent.

The faint glimmer ahead might have seemed only a wishful dream, a trick of lightning and mind, to anyone but a fore-sighted god; but the Wanderer quickened his step, moving eagerly onward. Another flash of Thonar's hammer showed the shape of a small keep towering over the little wicker huts around it. Light showed through the smokeholes, spilled through the door as a man stumbled out.

Wodan heard his muffled cursing through the downpour drowning his small trickle. "Wodan and Thonar! The gods've been drinking too much tonight!" He hurried back in, shutting the heavy oaken door hard behind himself.

The echoes of Nothger's hasty slamming had barely died away when another banging sounded through the hall. The knocking was not so loud, but every man in the hall—and the frowe Swanachild—looked up, startled and wary, like hounds catching the first whiff of wolf on the wind. The knock sounded three times and stopped; those within the garth glanced at each other.

"Hard to imagine an honest man out tonight," Dagabercht, the lord of the hall, mused slowly. "Nothger, did you see anything out there?"

"See anything?" the warrior said, shaking rain from his matted hair and beard. "I couldn't see my . . . excuse me, Frowe Swanachild . . . it was too dark to see anything out there."

Swanachild blushed, and Dagabercht laughed, leaning over to kiss her on the cheek.

The hollow triple knock sounded again, cutting Dagabercht's mirth off to a soft choking noise. Swanachild felt the resonance of the sound thrilling through her large-boned body, tingling through her flesh and ringing inside her skull as if the whole hall had become a great bell. She breathed in, a sudden rush of air filling her and lifting her to her feet with a giddy wod such as she had never felt in her sixteen years, not even in the drunken excitement of her wedding night. Dagabercht put a big restraining hand on her arm, holding her back gently.

"I don't think you should, Swan," he said. As always, his speech was slow but firm. "You don't know who—or what—that was. Let me go."

Swanachild looked down at the broad, muscular form of her husband sitting up straight in his high seat, a flower-wrought goblet of precious Roman glass in one hand and her arm in the other. He held both with the same careful, gentle firmness, as if equally afraid of crushing or losing the fragile glass and the sturdy young woman. His weatherbeaten face was flushed with drink and the heat of the fire that roared in the middle of the hall. The worry lines on his wide forehead now creased a little deeper. At any other time, she would never have thought of gainsaying him, but the strange ringing of that knock still blew through her soul like the wild call of a hunting horn through a misty morning at winter's edge.

"Man or troll, it's no night for anyone to be left standing outside our hall," Swanachild said, her high, soft voice definite as the sound of a stone dropping to earth. She took the empty goblet from Dagabercht's hands and refilled it from the ale pitcher of Roman bronze before them, then walked between the tables down the length of the hall, wishing suddenly that the brown hair plaited about her head were thicker and not so mousy, feeling the generous curves of her breasts move against her fine white woolen dress in a way that Dagabercht's touch had never made her move.

Thrice more the knock sounded, stilling Swanachild's heart and breath in a transport of awe. Her hand trembling, she tossed the heavy bar of the door aside as if it were a twig and pushed it open hastily, suddenly terrified lest the mysterious knocker turn away and leave her waiting forever.

At first she saw only a tall dark shadow standing in the light that poured from the hall's open door. She caught her breath sharply as it glided toward her, stretching out its hand, a single bright glint from beneath its lowered hood catching her like the blow of a spear.

Belatedly she remembered the goblet of ale in her hand. Shaking in every limb, she stepped forward, unable to withstand the great force that had seized upon her and now seemed to be bearing her onward.

The strange shape moved into the hall, taking the glass and draining the dark beer in a single draught then handing it back to her. As Swanachild's eyes cleared, she saw a tall man—at least a head taller than herself, and she was the height of a good warrior—graybearded, but powerful, wrapped in a sodden dark cloak with a wide hood that fell over one eye. The shaft of his spear was worn and ancient; for a moment she thought she could see a fiery tracery of markings on it, but when she looked straight at it, it was plain and dark.

Behind Swanachild, the tense bubble of silence in the hall burst into shards of laughter.

"This must be an atheling's hall, ruled by the highest born of men!" someone shouted. "Even an old beggar gets a drighten's greeting here!"

Dagabercht's deep guffaw growled out in answer, "Yes, an atheling's hall! Swanachild, bring our guest up! No visitor goes hungry or unhonored where Dagabercht is drighten!"

The men banged their horns on the long tables, ale slopping on to the knotted, stained wood. Swanachild glanced up at the wanderer, her fair cheeks reddening with embarrassment for her husband and his warband as she thought, A beggar? How could they miss seeing . . . ? But the wanderer's one eye gleamed with grim laughter at the blindness of men, and Swanachild understood in a breath of inspiration that what they saw was what he wanted them to see. So she smiled sheepishly, as if she had given a drighten's greeting to a wandering beggar, and led her guest to the seat beside her husband at the high table, refilling the glass goblet with her own hands and fetching Dagabercht the sculpted goblet of Roman bronze, which matched the pitcher.

"Tell us your name, guest, if you will, and say where you're going," Dagabercht bellowed over the noise of the hall.

"My name is Herobart," the wanderer answered, "and I travel north and west to the mouth of the Rhine to meet a man called Sigimund, with whom I have a meeting arranged."

Dagabercht stroked his curly brown beard, his half-drunken merriment quieting. "The road can be hard, especially with winter coming on. Are you hoping to find a band to travel with?"

The wanderer—Herobart—shook his hooded head. "I fare swiftly enough by myself. I don't carry gold or jewels, and my spear is enough for me to trust in. Not every drighten is as generous and hospitable as yourself, but a singer can always find a place to stay for a night or two."

Swanachild saw her husband relax, the lines of his forehead smoothing as he sat back in his heavy oaken chair.

"A singer, hmm?" Dagabercht said, his deep voice lightening. "And would more beer loosen your throat enough to sing for us?"

The corner of Herobart's mouth quirked into a silent grin as Swanachild poured the dark ale into the blue-green horn. Only she saw, and smiled back at him, her face bright with understanding.

"Dagabercht's hall is always glad to honor a singer," she said, as graciously as she remembered her mother saying in her father's hall. She struggled to hold back a mad laugh of ecstasy as the wanderer's long, powerful hand touched hers on the cool glass of the horn, sending a bolt of tingling warmth through her body.

Herobart drank deeply, wiping a few brown drops from his hoary beard, then stood and thumped the butt of his spear on the floor. A few nervous eyes went to the weapon, and twitchy hands to eating knives, but the hall grew quiet. The skop leaned his spear against the wall again.

"At your will, drighten Dagabercht, and yours, frowe Swanachild," he began, bowing to them, "I shall sing the tale of how Mannaz fathered the three races of men."

Dagabercht nodded, waving the bronze goblet whose sculpted stem he clutched clumsily in a hand more used to horn or clay pot. Herobart drew in a deep breath and raised the glass horn once more before he began to chant in a powerful voice that stilled every whisper, thrumming through the hall like the wind through a great harp.

> *Twisto himself   first tore from the earth,*
> *forth, he was mother   and father both*
> *to Mannaz the shining   mighty and wise,*
> *Hail to Mannaz   men's father bright!*
> *Over earth haring   to a hut came he . . .*

Swanachild refilled the common pitcher with ale and walked about the hall, pouring drink for the men of Dagabercht's warband. Bearded faces turned toward the shadowed figure of the singer, eyes misted as they stared into the depths of time for the vision his story brought forth. Only horn moved to mouth to prove them living and feed the power of his song on good strong ale as Herobart told of how Mannaz lay between man and wife for three nights to father the son Thrall, who then wedded a wife fitting to him.

> *From these two came   the kin of the thralls,*
> *the daughters and sons   of serf-clans all.*
> *Mannaz walked on   mighty and wise,*

Hail to Mannaz   men's father bright!
Over earth haring   to a house came he . . .

Over and over Swanachild glided, soft as in a dream, to refill her husband's cup. She was a little alarmed at how much Dagabercht was drinking, his heavy, scarred hand plunking the Roman goblet down more and more clumsily. He would sleep like the dead, as surely as if she had given him poppy gum or the black, sweet, dangerous berries of dwale, the enchanter's nightshade. Again she refilled his cup, though he had stopped raising it to her. His sense seemed stolen away already, a tattered leaf on the stormwind-wod of drink and song.

Swanachild drank her matching cup dry, then downed another, letting herself be borne up by the sound of Herobart's voice, strong above the howling gale outside, as he told of Mannaz's second son, Carl—the free farmer, the first of yeomen.

He wedded a wife   worthy of free kin,
from them came kind   of the carles all:
Mannaz walked on   mighty and wise,
Hail to Mannaz   men's father bright!
Over earth haring   to high hall he came . . .

Swanachild hardly heard the singer's words, she was so caught up in the sweeping chant of his voice; but he told of how Mannaz stayed with the fair atheling couple, who drank wine from glass and wore the whitest linen.

A length of three nights   lay he between them,
high-minded Mannaz   mighty and wise.
Got him atheling-son there   Earl the shining,
the keen blade's wielder   of king-kin the first.

Herobart told of Earl's deeds, of how he learned rune-lore and did battle, and at last,

Won he atheling-maid   a wife swan-white shining,
fathered on her   the highest of lines.
Shine Earl's sons mightiest   of Mannaz's kin,
Hail to Mannaz   men's father bright!

There were a few moments of silence as Herobart finished. To Swanachild, it seemed as though a mist of light was slowly clearing from the hall, leaving it in the dull shadows of the fire's burning down. Then the men banged horns and mugs on the table, shouting acclaim as they broke from their spellbound enthrallment. A few called, "More! More!," but Dagabercht banged the side of his empty goblet down, denting a carefully sculpted cluster of bronze grapes and spilling a few dark drops onto the table. He stood, swaying.

"Thass . . . great song. Great singer. Keep horn, you've earned it." Swanachild heard a few gasps: gold was given often enough, but the glass horn was a gift more fit for a drighten, a gift such as drightens seldom gave away. Dagabercht nodded his head, almost falling over. "Yes. Keep it."

"A true atheling's gift, well worthy of Earl's kin," Herobart answered. "You shall be remembered in my songs, even to Walhall."

"Good. Good." Dagabercht turned to Swanachild. "Come, my dear . . . dearest frowe. On to bed."

He took Swanachild's arm, leaning heavily on her as they made their way through the small and smoky kitchen to the chamber they shared. Strong as she was, Swanachild found it hard to support her husband's thick, muscular body as he staggered and swayed from one side to the other. She was careful to keep between him and the banked cooking fire, whose glow shifted mockingly through the ashes with the wind of their passing. She had once seen a warrior in her father's hall fall into coals that looked dead: the memory of his hair and beard flaring up, flesh bubbling beneath them, made her cringe whenever she caught the first whiff of roasting meat.

The ale she had drunk had left her dizzy and exhilarated, breathing hard. She was glad when she could help Dagabercht through their dark room to lower himself to the clean, feather-stuffed mattress and thick furs of their bed. He was asleep almost at once. Swanachild could hear his low snuffling snores before she had even taken his boots off him. She unwrapped her own shoes, then unlaced her key-jangling belt, crossed her arms behind her and pulled her dress over her head, finding her way to the chest near the far wall by touch and laying her garments over it.

Swanachild did not hear the door open or see any glow of firelight or flickering shadow in the darkness of the chamber, but she felt the rush of air on her naked body, stiffening her nipples and sending a shiver up from the base of her spine, and she knew that Herobart was there. He did not speak; she heard only the howling of the wind outside, but his touch as he stroked her hair, letting it down in a silky wave as all the pins and thongs and bindings dropped from it, was as cool as a rushing river, warm as a fire whose heat tingled without burning, bringing her to him as he seized her and bore her up and forth to the bed where her drunken husband snuffled in his sleep, whirling her away and open in a sweet wod of mad desire, filling her as gently as a breath of air and as furiously as a wild wolf, a stallion covering her, an eagle whose wings wrapped around her and bore her up, a serpent seeking her depths, creeping ever inward to her roots, driving with a fury that she could only let herself be gripped and flung about by as she tossed her head back and cried out in the storm again and again, her voice lost in the gale till it rose to a high harsh falcon's scream, till the lightning flashed within the room and she stared up in her gripping wod to see the one-eyed and storm-swept face of the god whose might filled her, eagle wings beating and claws gripping as her sense was lost in one great eagle's cry.

Swanachild's moan rose to the eagle's scream again as the pain ripped her apart in a burst of brilliant lightning, her child-swollen belly clamping down.

"Push," the old midwife Berchta commanded her, looking down a long nanny-goat nose and tightening her grip on Swanachild's white-knuckled hand. "Push harder. Now!"

Thunder rumbled; she could hear the rain of the unseasonable summer thunderstorm beating down outside, feel the hot wetness of waters and blood between her legs as she pushed, crying out once more.

"The head's coming. Go on, push!"

The old woman's swollen, lumpy fingers pushed down on Swanachild's belly, forcing out the thing that was stretching her till she tore, howling in her agony. Her body, wiser than her pain-racked mind, tightened again and again, hips tilting. She could feel it coming through, struggling out of the bloody passageway of her body, kicking against her.

"Push!" the midwife shouted, and she pushed, every muscle in her back and her distended abdomen cramping with the effort. Great beads of sweat matted her thin mousy hair and rolled down her face. "Push!" and then suddenly the pressure eased and, with a last rending effort, the small struggling body slid out of her.

Through clouded, dizzy eyes, Swanachild saw Berchta biting through the dark slimy cord that ran from her child's navel back into her womb and tying it off, the old woman's arthritic fingers handling its slippery length with practiced swiftness. Berchta handed the baby to one of the two younger women, Swanachild's attendants Audhrid and Sigiruna, who stood by the bed with cloths and hot water like a fair and a dark shadow. She bent over Swanachild again.

Another sudden contraction racked the new mother's body, and she screamed in surprise as well as pain, thinking, Twins?

"The afterbirth," the midwife hissed to her. "Bear down, now; push it out so I don't have to go in after it."

Swanachild bore down and pushed, but the ravaged muscles of her pelvis were too weak to bring the afterbirth out.

Berchta sighed gustily. "Brace yourself, girl. This is going to hurt." She slid her calloused hand into Swanachild's torn body, its roughness scraping along the ripped flesh within while Swanachild screamed, flinging her head from side to side and trying to move away; but the attendant women held her shoulders until the midwife had finished her job, bringing out the floppy meat of the afterbirth dripping with blood. Little blond Audhrid quickly held out a large bowl of birchwood, its paleness stained with the old blood of numberless births, and the midwife plopped the afterbirth into it. "There, girl. That's all."

The baby howled, a high piercing cry, and the old woman's wrinkled face creased more deeply in satisfaction. "Sound of a good healthy . . . Fro Ingwe be praised, it is a boy! A strong heir for Dagabercht!" She took the birch bowl from Audhrid's shaking hands. "You clean her up now. Let the boy nurse a while, then put three drops of what's in that clay bottle there into a large pot of beer and have her drink it."

Swanachild looked anxiously at the midwife, who gave her a toothless smile. "Don't worry, I'm taking this to bury under an elder tree, as is right for Frowe Holda's blessing."

Berchta dipped her right index finger into the blood of the afterbirth and traced the rune, B, *berkano*, on the newborn baby's forehead. "Frowe Berkano, Birch-Mother, and idises all! Bless this man, be his shield in battle, give him bright rede in peace. Holda, hold him hale; Frowe, keep him free from ill; idises of his line, ancient kin-women all, bring him joy and ward him well. These be the birthing-gifts I give, and great his line shall grow." The midwife put the child in Swanachild's arms and waited until he had fastened his small mouth on her nipple and begun to suck lustily before she bore the bowl and its bloody contents out into the storm.

Audhrid and Sigiruna dipped their cloths into the warm water and sponged off Swanachild's bloody thighs and pelvis, their gentle hands soothing her cramped and torn muscles. She lay very still, letting the worst of the pain drain away like a great wave sinking slowly down the beach of her body as her son's tiny lips on her milk-swollen breast sent little twinges through her.

When the baby would drink no more, Sigiruna lifted him carefully from her and Audhrid held a pot of steaming, honey-sweetened beer to her lips. Swanachild drank gratefully, the warmth of the draught spreading quickly out from her empty stomach, and slid into a deep, peaceful drowsiness. The last thing she heard was Dagabercht's joyous bellow, "A son! The gods have given me a son for Midsummer's!"

By the ninth night after her son's birth, Swanachild was still weak and sore, but she could stand and even walk a little way without having to lean on her husband or one of her maidens. Wrapped in a light blue cloak against the cool breezes of the clear summer night, she slowly bore the fair swaddled babe outside to the harrow stone in the middle of the hallowed grove by the hall. Audhrid stood on her right side and Sigiruna on her left, ready to hold her up if she should need it; old Berchta walked behind her, unseen but comforting.

Dagabercht and the thanes of his warband stood in a half-circle around the great boulder. A soft wind rustled through the leaves of ash and oak and birch above them; the stars shone clear and unclouded and the new Moon silvered the holy stone and the leek that lay upon it. Swanachild looked down at the adorable face of her son, very fair in the light of the Moon, and smiled happily at him, tickling him through the woolen swaddling cloths that wrapped his sturdy little limbs.

"Ga," he said comfortably, and her heart swelled with love. She hugged him tightly to her, standing straighter and walking to her husband's side beside the harrow stone.

"Hear me, you high ones, in this holy grove," Dagabercht called. "Hear me, Tiw, Wodan, Thonar; hear me, Fro Ingwe and Frowe Holda, Nerthuz and all you of the giving earth. I, Dagabercht the son of Wigabercht, take this child as my son, fathered by me and born into my own blood and line, and so do I give him the name Sigibercht, for the bright victories he shall win."

Dagabercht dipped his fingers into the ancient ritual aurochs horn that his thane Arnuwolf held out to him, sprinkling the baby's head with the hallowed water that had been drawn from a running burn at dawn. He curled Sigibercht's small fingers around the thick pale stem of the leek, its dark green fountain of flat leaves springing above the baby's wool-nested head, and held him up to the sky. "Sigibercht, Dagabercht's son!" he shouted.

But Swanachild remembered the night of storm and wod when the wanderer Herobart had planted the seed as her dear husband lay deathlike in the fetters of drink beside them, and smiled to herself, whispering, "Sigibercht, son of Wodan," so that only she and the unseen powers around the harrow stone could hear.

THE SWORD

The white gleam of stars and Moon from the harrow stone reddened to glimmering fire, its shifting patterns glowing like molten gold in Sigifrith's blurred sight. He struggled to open his eyes—was it Wind-Alf's shadow he saw dark and hunched against the ruddy light of the forge? Forging a sword to kill a dragon . . . no, it was the shadow of Fadhmir's head rising above the howe fires of his stolen gold, the wyrm coiling and gleaming over the dead man's body and the treasures heaped around it. It seemed to him that he could see Ragin's craggy face near his own, the firelight gilding the old dwarf's gray hair and beard. But no, Ragin was young, dark-haired and shaven, and a man who stood straight in the sunlight; Wind-Alf was the ancient stone-dweller . . .

A low muttering sound rasped against Sigifrith's ears: scales on stone? A file on metal? He thought that he could hear words in it, but the darkness was already roaring around him, echoing Swanachild's voice.

"Sigibercht, son of Wodan . . . Sigibercht . . . Sigibercht . . ." The woman's words rose and cracked, sinking from his hearing even as they trembled through his very blood and bones, their twisting rope pulling him onward. He let himself follow, seeking sight to go with the shifting muddle of sound, till the wind caught him again, bearing him along its low howling to a hillside of cracked gray rock standing high against the light of the new Moon. A gleam of fire showed through one of the cracks, and the ringing of a hammer on metal echoed through the stone. A body lay against the stone, darker shadow on the shadowed rock. It did not move as the tall shape of a cloaked man came nearer, although the starlight glinted from the tip of his spear.

The god smiled grimly as his eye took in the one who lay there. "So, Ragin," he whispered, although his hidden eye, the eye which lay in the depths of Mimir's Well, had already turned to another sight—to the harrow where Swanachild murmured the name of his son Sigibercht. A fair night for beginning the forging, he thought: his kin would be well-wrought. Wodan stepped into the stone, stooping low to move along the narrow way.

Ragin and the dwarf, both stripped to the waist, strove at the forge, beads of sweat dripping down their faces from hair to beard. Wodan marked how the young man's shoulders had grown broader, and how he hardly had to stoop in Wind-Alf's low hall, though Ragin still seemed tall and slim next to the dwarf. The young man did not look up from his work at the bellows until Wind-Alf drew the half-formed helm from the flame and laid it upon the anvil.

"What are you doing here?" the dwarf asked Wodan roughly.

Ragin was already speaking before his master had finished. "Send him away! He was with Fox, he'll betray you if you let him speak." The youth's voice rose on his last words; his face was flushed and Wodan saw the sparks of the Rhine-fire glittering behind Ragin's widened eyes again. This time the god had no wish to fan the sparks to flame. His finger hidden so that the dwarf would not see his magic, Wodan traced *wunjo*, ᚹ, the rune of peace. The fierceness of Ragin's face eased as the rune's warmth settled around his mind.

"Be still, boy," Wind-Alf said to his apprentice. "Wodan's always dealt fairly enough with the dwarves; he'll ween our friendship needful for a long while yet. Now, what have you come for this time?"

The words were there in Mimir's Well, as Ragin had spoken them; Wodan, whose hidden eye had been the pledge for his draught of those waters, had only to look. "I want you to forge a sword that will slay a dragon."

Ragin's breath hissed like red-hot metal plunging into the quenching bucket, but he said nothing. Wind-Alf nodded slowly. "We work together this time. What have you brought?"

Wodan drew what he carried from the depths of his dark cloak. First the metal: star iron that he had claimed as it fell through the sky. Harder lumps and softer lumps, scarred black from the heat of their falling; the dwarf could forge these into a sword that would cut through stone. Secondly, three staves of ash-wood, written with runes to fill the blade with the might it needed to wreak the works Wodan meant that it should do. The first: ᚹᛟᛞᚨᚾᚨᚨᚨ, his own name and the rune *ansuz* written thrice—the rune of his winds blowing through the worlds, blowing the soul of his line to life. The second bore "Sig," "Victory," ᛋᛁᚷᛋᛋᛋ, for the victories his kin would be sure to win with the blade, and the rune *sowilo* written thrice for the wills that would win the victories. Third was written ᚹᚨᛚᛋᛁᚾᚷᛋᚾ , "Walsing," the name the children of Sigibercht's line would bear when the sword was full-forged. This stave was carved with *othala*, the rune of inheritance; *eihwaz*, the yew tree, which would hold the soul and memories of the line through death and rebirth; and *nauthiz*, the rune of the need and pain which would shape Wodan's kin into the heroes he needed them to be. Lastly, Wodan brought forth the stone which would bind the sword to the soul of his children—an ice stone which he had wrought from his own seed, hex-cut, smooth and milky white.

Wind-Alf took the bag of star iron from Wodan's hand. He reached in, stirring the lumps of metal with his fingers, then brought the bag to his face and sniffed at it. "Our fire's not hot enough to melt that yet. Give my boy here time enough and he might be stoked up to the job, though it'll take more than a human's short life."

"The forging will take longer than that, and I have no doubt he'll be here for its end," Wodan murmured. "Still, you must start now. Will you let Loki guest within your stones?"

"I've had more welcome guests," the dwarf answered grudgingly. "I suppose I'll have to. Don't tremble so, Ragin; you'll need your anger for feeding the fire, and without craft your feelings are no better than raw ore. All right, Wodan, call up Loki if you must. And call the other one too, the quiet one; he gave his gift to these tree-shaped creatures at the beginning, and he must give it again now."

Hoenir was already at Wodan's back, silent and soft as a cloud crossing the moon; but Loki, contrary as was his way, or bent on seeming unmastered, would not come to his blood-brother's silent calling.

Wodan had no space to raise his spear in the low-roofed room: he stretched it forward instead, crashing the tip against the stone anvil. "Loki! I hail you forth by the blood we shared! Flickering flame, you fled from me, but could not come away. I made you my brother, now I call you forth. Loki! Loki! Arise!"

The forge fires flared suddenly, and Loki stood there, dusting his hands as if he had just finished a piece of work. He reached out a finger and pushed the point of Wodan's spear to the side. "You didn't have to shout," he said casually. "I was thinking about dropping by anyway. Hai, Ragin, I heard your sister Lingwohaith just got married to a man named Eburhelm. He's a fat old fart with bad teeth, but I guess a woman with a dead father and runaway brothers can't hope for much better. Did you send her a wedding gift?"

Wind-Alf looked at his apprentice, who held quite still without saying a word, and nodded. "Good, Ragin. Get to the fire again, and watch him. You'll never find a better teacher in its ways."

Loki's shape melted again, brightening within the forge. Wodan set the first rune-carved stave into the flames, and the five of them began their work.

Many things drew Wodan's eye in that time, as the folk who called on him in battle fought with the Romans on their southern borders; as the seething cauldron of the northernmost lands spawned warbands seeking gold and tribes seeking lands away from their most warlike neighbors; and he often wandered to the Middle-Garth or sent his walkurjas to turn the tide of fighting as he chose; but always he kept a watch on the line he had fathered, the line that began with Swanachild's son Sigibercht.

The forging of the sword went on, the twisting and beating and folding of the star-iron rods, as Wodan's son Sigibercht won his battles and his fierceness made more foes on every side. Wodan came often to Wind-Alf's hill to blow up the bellows, strengthening Loki's fires to the forging as the fires of hate grew in the hearts of Sigibercht's allies as well as his foemen. Wodan was not at his son's last battle; he sent his walkurja Hleod in his stead, to choose Sigibercht's death while he himself held the white stone in his hand, watching it clear until he could see the gleam of the firelight through its milky depths, and knew that Sigibercht had fallen.

The sword was a rough bar of wave-marked iron now; but the sword that Sigibercht's son Rerir bore against his mother's brothers was sharp enough for its work. Now the pattern was well forged into the sword with the wyrm twistings of light and dark metal, and Wodan was well-pleased with the fires of the second rune stave that had forged it there, and with the way his son's son was turning out.

The blade was closer and closer to being finished, its wyrm mottlings shining forth along its finely shaped length, but its final tempering and sharpening were yet to come. Rerir died, but his frowe bore a son; and when, nine days after the birth, her brother lifted him up and gave him the name Wals, Wodan saw that the stone in the sword's hilt was clear in and without flaw.

When Wals and the walkurja Hleod lay in their wedding bed together, Wodan, Hoenir and Loki came to Wind-Alf's hill again. Ragin's long beard had turned gray; his skin was not as dark with ingrained charcoal as his master's, but his pores were deeply stippled with the stains of his smithing, and if Wodan had seen with a human's eyes and not known them well, he would have found it hard to tell which of the two had been born a child of Ash and Elm.

"Now," said Wodan, and Loki melted into flame, coiling into the forge fires as the third rune stave flared to light. His own breath fanned the flames higher and higher as Ragin and Wind-Alf put the sword into the forge together and Hoenir stood by quietly, filling the quenching bucket. Hleod did not cry out in her birthing pain; the scream Wodan heard was that of her maidservant as the walkurja's agonized grip broke the bones of her hand.

Wals' axe blow smashed the door in and he brushed the women aside, taking his wife's hand in his so that she could grip him as hard as she needed to. The sword glowed red hot now, the steel deep apple-red. As Hleod's next pang came, Wals dug his feet into the earth he had piled around his grandfather's mound when he built the great hill on which the hall stood above the fury of the North Sea in winter. Wodan knew that Wals could not see the wolf that stood by Hleod's bedside, but the warrior shuddered as the echo of its howl scraped down his spine and the blade brightened to orange in Loki's fires, wyrm mottling running white down its blade. Hleod sucked at the blood from her bitten lip; her eyes closed again, and the young midwife moved forward between her legs to draw the child forth.

"A girl," Wals said. "If she lives, I shall name her Sigilind," and Ragin drew the blade from the fire and struck the last blows upon the star iron. Ragin raised the sword above the bucket to quench it, and Hleod's body convulsed once more. The midwife hastily laid the first child down; she was just in time to catch the second before it could squirm free to the floor, and Ragin plunged the flame-bright sword into the water in a great hiss of steam.

"A boy!" Wals cried out, taking the second child from the midwife's arms and holding it high. "He shall be named Sigimund."

Wind-Alf took the sword from the water, weighing it with his hand. It rang clearly when he flicked it with a thick nail, the echo resonating through the stone. "A bit of sharpening and polishing, and then it's done. You three go on; you can pick it up when you're ready. Good work, Ragin. I think there's hardly anything more for me to teach you."

7

SIGILIND'S WEDDING

... a flying arrow, a crashing wave,
night old ice, a coiled snake,
a bride's bed talk, a broken sword,
the play of bears, a king's son.

—HAVAMAL 86

"There was a man called Sigi, who was said to be the son of Wodan. There was also a man called Skadhi. Skadhi had a thrall called Bredi: he was well-taught in the things he had to do, as great in skill and strength as those who were of better standing. Now Sigi went hunting once, and that thrall with him, and they chased game all day. And when they gathered their booty together, Bredi had more than Sigi. And Sigi took it ill that a thrall should have hunted better than he; so he fell upon him and killed him.

"It became known that Sigi had murdered the thrall. Therefore they named him a warg and an out-dweller, cast from all holy places, and he might no longer stay in the home of his father. Wodan followed him out of the land a great way, and he did not leave him till he had found him some warships. Now Sigi went harrying with the host that his father had led him to, and it was his orlog at last to win a land for his own, after which he made an atheling-marriage. He had a son by his wife, called Rerir.

"Sigi began to grow old. He had many foes, so that at the last those men that he trusted most, his wife's brothers, fell upon him when he was least on his guard and had only a few thanes about him; they overpowered him with greater numbers. Rerir his son was not there at that slaying; but he gathered so great a band of thanes and chieftains of the country that he got him both land and lordship after Sigi his father. And when he was sure of his rule he gathered a great host and attacked his mother's brothers who had slain his sire; they were the first to misdo, though he likewise put little worth on their friendship; and so before they parted he slew all those who were his father's bane, though it was unfitting for him to raise hand against his kin. And then he was fro over land and men and wealth, and made himself yet mightier than his father.

"Rerir won himself great booty, and likewise a wife who seemed well matched with him; but they were together a long time and yet they had no child or heir. This was a soreness to them, and they prayed often and earnestly to the gods that they might have a child. Now it is said that Frija heard their prayer and told it to Wodan, and well he could give rede in this. He called a wish-maiden of his, the daughter of Hrimnir the giant, and put an apple into her hand, bidding her to take it to the fro. She put on her mantle of feathers and flew till she found the fro, who was sitting on his father's howe. She let the apple fall on to his knee; he took it up, and it seemed to him that he knew what end it would serve. He went home from the mound to his men, and there he met the frowe, and he and she both ate some of that apple.

"The frowe soon found that she might be with child, but she was a very long time in bearing it. Then Rerir went to war, as kings must do; and news came that he had died of illness on his faring. But the frowe's sickness went on, with the child kept within her past its time. Now she knew that she could not thole much longer and so she bade her maidens to cut out the child, and so it was done. The child was a boy, and he was very large when he was brought forth. A name was given to him and he was called Wals; he was fro in these lands after his father. Very early, he was strong and large and bold in all things calling for manhood and bravery; he became the greatest warrior, always victorious in the battles he fought when he went harrying.

"Now when he had become a grown man, Hrimnir the giant sent him his daughter Hleod, who had come to Wals' father Rerir with the apple. Thus he wedded her, and they dwelt long together in good fellowship. She grew heavy with twins; but the birth was difficult, and afterward she fared back to Wodan as his walkurja again.

"That is the story of your line, my hero-children," the old woman said to the boy and the girl who sat before her with the warm sun of summer's beginning gilding their pale heads. "Remember it, Sigilind, when you go to the land of the Gauts with your husband; let it strengthen you, Sigimund, when you fight beside your father."

Sigimund raised his head, ice-blue eyes shining from his clean-featured face. "I won't disgrace my line," he said proudly. His high baritone voice was as strong as a battle horn, with just a hint of roughness marring its clarity, as though something had scarred his throat long ago. "I shall be the best of my father Wals' thanes this summer when we go to war."

"I am ready for my husband," Sigilind said, her voice echoing her brother's an octave above. "My children will be true Walsings, or they will not be my children."

The old woman, Hulde, smiled toothlessly, her wrinkled eyelids lowering. She had nursed these twins since the death of their mother; though Wals' second wife Alfflad had tried to raise them, they would only listen to old Hulde. Now they were ready to go forth from her, Sigilind to her wedding and Sigimund to battle. It seemed to her as she looked at them that she could see their spirits shining silver-white, pure and hard as starlight through their skin, clear fires that would burn without flickering or dimming. Indeed, they are worthy of Wals, she thought; worthy of their father and of the true father of their line, may he always bless them with wisdom and the victory of their names.

Sigilind and Sigimund stood up gracefully together, uncurling their long limbs from where they sat on the damp spring earth. Both of them were slender, but well-formed, Sigimund's muscles sharply defined against his sky-blue tunic, Sigilind's firm body gently curving her white dress. Their faces were finely molded with high, strong cheekbones; a thin pelt of gold was just beginning to blur Sigimund's sharp jawline. Their eyes were keen and clear beneath arched, pale brows and wide foreheads; fourteen years old, they were almost the same height, although Sigimund was beginning to grow more swiftly than his twin sister as his shoulders broadened with muscle and her hips and breasts became rounder. Sigilind's long blond hair fell straight down her back; Sigimund's was bound into two tight warrior's plaits that could be tucked up to cushion a steel helm.

Together they rushed forward to enfold Hulde in a double embrace. She hugged them with an arm around each, tears blurring her rheumy eyes. "My dear little wolf cubs," she murmured, stroking their silky heads. "I know you'll make me proud of you."

They stayed in the embrace a moment, then broke, Sigimund and Sigilind raising their heads and staring at the river's mouth.

"Sails!" Sigilind said, pointing into the distance. "It must be Sigigairar!" She darted off towards the edge of the flat mound which raised their village above the winter and spring floodings, dodging around two black-splotched cows who stood stolidly chewing their cuds. Unhampered by skirts, Sigimund caught up with his twin quickly. He could see the white sails in the distance, moving slowly up the river.

"There's not much wind, so it's a good hard row for them," he commented. "Your husband will be all sweaty when he gets here."

Sigilind darted a quick mock punch at his face which he slapped away, hitting him solidly on the shoulder with her other fist. "My husband is a drighten, you idiot. Drightens don't have to row, at least not when they want to make a good impression on their brides."

"Why should he bother? The wedding's already been set, and I don't recall him asking you anything anyway."

"He will because it's the proper thing to do," Sigilind replied smugly. "I can tell you, it's going to be a long time before any fro lets his daughter marry a wild man like you."

Sigimund aimed a blow at his sister and the two of them sparred for a moment before Sigilind leapt lightly back, smugly brushing her hair behind her delicate ears. "That's quite enough of that," she said with great dignity. "I want to look nice when my husband gets here."

"Your brooch is on crooked," Sigimund told her. "Here, let me, I can see it better." He unpinned the small four-armed brooch of gold on her shoulder and repinned it straight. So close, he could feel the quickness of her soft breaths and the nervous excitement trembling through her. He knew, as if it were his own, the thrill of curious anticipation quickening her heartbeat and flushing her cheeks; he felt it every time his hand closed on the smooth wood of a sword's hilt and he thought of the summer fighting that neared with every moment of the lengthening days.

Sigimund brought his sister's horn comb out of his belt pouch, running his fingers over the grooves of the runes engraved into it. "Do you want me to comb your hair? You've made it untidy."

"Please," Sigilind said, crouching down to feel the grass for a dry spot between the cow pats before she carefully arranged her dress around her and sat. Sigimund began to work the comb gently through her fine, glittering hair, but she leapt up within a few moments. "You're too slow," she complained. "Give that to me, I'll do it myself." She grabbed the comb from his hand, her swift, strong touch smoothing and arranging the offending pale tangles in a couple of hard strokes. Handing the comb back to her brother, she whisked her palms down her skirts. "My dress isn't spotted, is it?" she asked. "Look at the back, I can't see it."

"Your dress is fine," Sigimund assured her.

Sigilind craned her neck, pulling her skirt around to look at it more closely. "You're as blind as a toad," she said crossly. "There is a spot there. What'll I do, Sigimund? This is my wedding dress."

"No one will notice. I promise you, no one will ever see it," Sigimund began, but his sister had already whirled and dashed off for the hall, flashes of ankles showing through the criss-crossed leather thongs of her shoes. The wind from the North Sea was freshening, blowing the ships more swiftly upriver and tossing the new green leaves and white flowers of the huge apple tree, the Barnstock, which stood in the center of Wals' hall, its branches rising high above the thatched roof. Sigimund could see the yellow glitter of the sunlight from the golden adornments of Sigigairar's men as they strove at the oars, struggling up the river, which, still swollen from the storms of winter's end, rushed against them in a greenish brown flood.

Wals' thanes were already coming out of the hall, drawn up in a fine array to greet Sigilind's betrothed and his warband. Cloaks of dark madder-red, clear yellow and deep or pale blue fluttered in the sharp breeze; to show Wals' wealth and open-handedness, gold rings gleamed from the arms of his warriors and costly swords, their leather scabbards finely worked with gold and silver wires, swung from the sides of a few. Sigimund glanced along the line: there two of his cousins, Adalwald and Alfwald, stood side by side, their wide chests and shoulders braced like a shield wall; there the sun shone off the balding head of Wals' foster brother Berhtnoth. The row dipped sharply where the little black-haired Dane Hrothwulfar stretched to his full height, chin jutting out and fists clenched as if he were already answering a challenge; and again where Sigimund's next brother, Berhtwini, stood on tiptoes and craned his skinny neck to catch a first glimpse of the man who had come for his sister. Many of the thanes were Sigimund's kinsmen; the rest had come from the lands around, men rich or strong enough to leave their farms for the life of a full-time warrior, or else landless men drawn by Wals' fame and the promise of winning gold in the name of such a mighty drighten.

Sigimund hurried up the gentle rise of the meadow to the line of warriors standing before the carven oak doors of the hall, standing straight and slim as a young sapling in his own place beside Berhtwini. The great doors opened and Wals came out into the sunshine, blinking clear blue eyes against the sudden light. Dressed only in his sky-hued feast tunic and white cloak embroidered with intertwining red dragons, he was broader and heavier than other men in full battle armor, overtopping most of his thanes by a good handspan. Fifty winters had silvered his straw-pale hair and thick beard with a light coat of hoar frost; a few wrinkles straggled like unraveling threads across his weather-darkened face, but his step was swift and graceful as he came out to greet his daughter's wooer. Sigimund stretched himself as tall as he could, throwing back his shoulders and filling his chest with air as he prayed earnestly to Wodan that someday he, too, would be as mighty and noble as his father.

Wals led the procession of his thanes down to the waterside as the white-winged ships of Sigigairar the Ingling made themselves fast by the land and lowered their gangplanks. To Sigimund's disappointment, they did not bear the dragon heads that all the war stories of Gauts and Danes spoke of; but they were every bit as large as those of his own father's fleet, their curved sides finely wrought and covered with fine and intricate carving along their arching prows.

"Ho, Wals!" the tall man coming down the gangplank, the Gauts' drighten Sigigairar, shouted. "I've come for my bride." Sigigairar's voice, pleasant except for a sharp nasal edge, carried easily across the meadow. His red-gold hair was braided into a fuzzy, wavy plait; his features were storklike, with thin eyebrows and a long, crooked nose over a sparse, pointed beard. Sigimund noticed that, though tall, Sigigairar did not come near to his father's height, and his arms and shoulders were stringy and wiry rather than full like Wals'. Gold and gemmed brooches hung richly on his tunic; his sword hilt gleamed with bright inlay.

"Bring your men down, then, and we'll see if you can take her," Wals called back in a rough, powerful bellow.

Sigigairar leapt lightly to the land, landing in a fighting stance like a man who was used to raiding from the sea. He straightened and moved to clasp arms with Wals, looking the bigger man in the eye.

"You can be sure that Sigilind won't be able to ask for more than I can offer her," the Gaut said. His thanes came up behind him, the host of tall, powerful men in their fur cloaks ranging themselves around him as if prepared for battle. Sigimund nodded to himself in approval. His twin's husband knew how a drighten should show himself to his allies; if his display showed the worth of his fighting truly, he would never bring shame to Wals' daughter. "Well, where is she? I want to see my bride."

"My daughter Sigilind is waiting in her father's hall, as befits a maiden," Wals answered. "Be welcome, Sigigairar, as guest and kinsman."

Wals and Sigigairar walked up the meadow to the hall together, followed by their warriors. Sigimund covertly studied the Gauts around him. They were sweating profusely in the warm sun of summer's beginning, one by one throwing off their furs and tugging at the necks of their thick wool tunics. Most of them were a little taller than the Saxons, some with the wiry build and fair hair of their king and some darker and more heavily set, like Danes. They were talking quickly in their own hard, clipped tongue. Sigimund felt that if he could listen long enough, or if they would speak more slowly, he might be able to understand their speech; it annoyed him to be almost able to tell what they were saying.

The inside of Wals' hall was cool and dark after the bright day, lit only through the open door and by the shadow-dappled sunlight pouring in through the new leaves and white flowers of the Barnstock. Fresh straw was strewn on the hard-packed dirt floor, and the sweet scent of rosemary and thyme rose beneath the boots of the warriors as they thronged in. Sigilind and Alfflad, Wals' second wife, came around the side of the benches, Sigilind bearing a gold-bound horn of mead to her father and Alfflad carrying its mate to Sigigairar.

Sigilind cast a sideways glance at her husband-to-be, who was watching her with a penetrating, appraising glance, as though she was a fine colt or falcon that he was considering buying. Well, he's only got himself to blame if he doesn't like what he's got, Sigilind thought; it wasn't I that arranged to marry him.

Sigigairar's thin face split into a wide smile, showing broken yellow teeth. "Greetings to you, my lady Sigilind," he said. He fumbled in his belt pouch for a moment, bringing out a thick chain of gold. "Take this gift from your husband, as a sign that all I own is yours."

Sigilind lifted the cold, heavy chain from his hands and put it around her neck, looking Sigigairar straight in his pale eyes. "As I am to be yours, my drighten," she replied clearly and calmly.

Sigigairar made the sign of Thonar's hammer over the horn before lifting it to her and drinking deeply. He stifled his belch, dashing a few golden drops of mead from his sparse moustache and ruddy beard with the back of his ringed hand. Turning to Wals, he asked, "Well, what are the marriage ways of the Saxons? When shall the wedding be, and when the feast? Do we wait for Freyja's night to speak our oaths, or do it now under Sunna's brightness?"

"Of course you're eager to get on with wedding my Sigilind," Wals replied, "but my frowe Alfflad says that you have to wait till sunset. Women will have their ways in these things."

"Tonight is Thrimilci Eve, the Frowe's night," Alfflad's low, alto voice broke in. "The wedding shall be held under her blessing, so that it may be holy and fruitful."

Sigigairar nodded, taking another long swig from the horn in his hand. "Thrimilci Eve's a witch-night, but I think Sigilind's already cast a spell over me. Hai, Sigilind, you're beautiful enough to be one of Wodan's walkurja daughters."

Sigilind tossed her long straight fall of blond hair back over her slender shoulders. "It takes a brave man to wed a walkurja," she said lightly, glancing up at him through her fair eyelashes. "Are you such a high hero, then?"

To Sigilind's shock, Sigigairar began to chant in a high, penetrating tone, his voice rising and falling:

> I've won meat for witch-steeds
> —walkurjas' thorn I've hurled—
> and Gauts' speech-friend gladdened
> giving athelings to spear.
> Bright my war-snake's bitten
> byrnies' rings of iron,
> now the necklace-goddess
> knows what man comes to woo.

Something of Sigilind's surprise must have shown on her face, because Wals explained quickly, "In the Northlands, a great man should be a maker of songs as well as a warrior. You are honored to have a husband of such skill. You made that verse straight from your head, didn't you, Sigigairar?"

Sigigairar inclined his head slightly, his light eyes glittering with satisfaction. "It is a gift of mine," he said. "I hope it pleases you, Sigilind."

"Oh, yes," she said quickly. "Perhaps you can teach me the art one day?"

"It's a difficult skill to teach. The true skald's wod comes from Wodan alone, and men's wits can only aid in the crafting—but if you like, I can try."

"I would, very much," Sigilind said at once.

Wals smiled proudly at her, his strong white teeth gleaming in the daylight from the hall's roof. His huge hand tousled her fine hair lightly. "You'll have plenty of time later to learn the shaping skill, Sigilind. Now why don't you and Alfflad go and get your women to bring these men some food and drink? They've fared a long way for you, my girl, and it's only fair for you to get them a good meal."

"So it is," Sigilind answered. She looked at Alfflad, who nodded her dark, braid-crowned head. The woman and the girl went out of the hall together, to the little cool hut where tall barrels of mead and beer stood stacked upon each other.

Caithlin, an Irish thrall whom Wals had captured in a raid ten years back, was already filling tall clay pitchers, her fat hands moving deftly to the task. She glanced cheerfully at her mistress, brushing a loose tangle of red hair off her freckled forehead. "That's a fine lot of men after coming for the frowe Sigilind," she said. "I'm glad they've got the peace strings tied on their swords. Those Gauts were a wild lot when the fro was fighting them, and they don't look too much tamer now, all muscles and fur they are." She let out a coy giggle. "Why, I remember back in Eriu . . . " She hushed at Alfflad's sharp look.

"That's all you know," Sigilind said. "The drighten Sigigairar can make verses up out of his head like a trained skop. He made one to honor me, and he promised to teach me how."

Caithlin clicked her tongue, whether in admiration or disapproval it was hard for Sigilind to tell. She heaved herself to her feet and handed a pitcher to each of her mistresses, straightening her brown skirts around her hefty bulk. "Well, well. I'll be going and seeing to the food then, and having some of the girls to bring it in, shall I?"

"Do that," Alfflad said. "And try to keep your tongue still while you're doing it, hmm?"

The thrall woman ducked her head in a sort of curtsy and bustled out. Alfflad sighed, gazing after her. "Don't pay any attention to her, Sigilind. You know Wals wouldn't have chosen Sigigairar as your husband if he didn't think he was as worthy of you as any man could be."

"I know," Sigilind said, closing the door of the hut behind her as they stepped out into the sunlight. "Why is everyone so worried? I know Sigigairar and my father used to be fighting, but that was years ago. They seem friendly enough now."

"Well. They are, as friendly as two great drightens can be, but two of Sigigairar's cousins died in one of their last skirmishes." Sigilind's stepmother looked her directly in the face, creamy forehead creasing over her soft brown eyes. "Now it may be that he looks on getting you as a prize to make up for that, even though there was no judgment of weregild ever asked; but you can see why there might be reason to worry, even with peace strings on everyone's swords."

"Umm. Yes." A prize to make up for slain kin, Sigilind thought. She didn't like the idea very much. Nor did she like the thought that followed hard on its heels: what if he wants to take his vengeance out on me? She dismissed it angrily; only a coward would hurt his wife for revenge, and no story she had ever heard of Sigigairar, whether as her father's foe or his friend, had named him a coward. And besides, whatever lay in her wedding, she reminded herself, it was her duty as a Walsing to endure it like a warrior, just as it was Sigimund's duty to bear his sword into battle and endure his wounds and hardships.

Alfflad noticed the grim look that hardened Sigilind's fine, strong features, and set her pitcher down so that she could hug her stepdaughter for a moment. Sigilind felt her own body thrumming as tense and hard as a steel harpstring against her stepmother's, her excitement now underlaid with the dark hum of fear that would not go away.

"Don't be frightened, darling," Alfflad's low, clear voice murmured.

"Wals' children are never frightened," Sigilind lied, straightening her back and stepping away from the woman's soft embrace. Then, seeing the faint twinge of pain that rippled across her stepmother's still face, she added, "I love you, Alfflad. Don't worry about me. I'll be all right, truly."

"Of course you will," Alfflad said. "It's just hard for a mother to let her children go." She paused and shook her head in annoyance. "And I'm getting as bad as . . . as Caithlin, standing here gabbling when the hall is full of thirsty Gauts." She picked up her pitcher and the two of them walked back to the hall.

When the Barnstock was only a rustling shadow against the darkening sky and the light through the hall's door had faded to a faint gray glow, the thralls came in to light the fire and the torches. Sigigairar's men put on the furs they had taken off in the afternoon heat, and the thanes of Wals wrapped their cloaks around them. Sigimund sat up and craned his neck to watch as Wals, Sigigairar, Alfflad and Sigilind got to their feet.

Berhtwini's sharp elbow poked him in the side, the younger boy's pointed nose aimed straight up at his brother's face like a dagger. "Are they going to go out to the harrow, or do it in here at the Barnstock?" Berhtwini whispered.

Sigimund elbowed his brother back. "They've got a private house ready for them to do it in, you fool."

"That's not what I mean," Berhtwini hissed, screwing up his narrow features in annoyance and impatience. "I mean the wedding, stupid."

"I don't know where they're going to have the wedding. If you'd be quiet, we might be able to hear what's going on."

Two of Alfflad's attendant maidens, the sisters Fridha and Wynfridh, came forth from the shadows, the light green of their gowns and dark green of their cloaks turned to eerie-hued fire by the flickering light. They took torches from the sockets in the wall; Alfflad stepped between them and they began to walk between the tables. Behind them followed Sigigairar and Sigilind, then Wals. The thanes rose by rank, Saxon pairing off with Gaut. The fur-clad bulks of the Northerners loomed huge and frightening in the shadows, as though they were half-beasts. Sigimund could smell the badly cured hide of the Gaut who walked beside him, his heavy body swaying with the faint limp of an old leg wound. Admiration for his sister's bravery rose in him as he thought of her living ringed around by these wild Northmen for the rest of her life.

Sigilind's white shape gleamed ahead of him as they wove over the hill, across the meadow and through the trees. In the gathering purple dusk, Sigimund could see need-fires beginning to glow on the distant hilltops, blurred black shadows dancing around the flames and leaping through them for Frowe Haith's blessing and for warding against the power of the witches who rode abroad on that night. The plaintive lowing of cattle floated across from mound to mound as their owners drove them through the smoke and over the fires to smoke out any sickness or ill-wishing wights that might trouble them. The darkening twilight felt charged with magic, sparkling at the corner of Sigimund's eyes; he was breathless with excitement, feeling that he stood on a threshold between what he knew and something that drew him on into a misty world whose shapes were just beginning to turn into reality around him. A tiny moth, as gray-white as lichen, fluttered past his face, its wings brushing feathery against his cheek and sending a shiver down his spine.

The need-fire was already kindled on the heaped rocks of the harrow, glinting sparks from the quartz in the stones and casting deep shadows into their cracks and crevasses, glowing like bale-flames above the gold oath ring before it. The warriors stood silent except for the rustle of fur and wool as they moved uneasily from one foot to another. Here, in the holy place, Sigimund could feel the Frowe's rising summertide might curling from the earth and around the clearing like a great serpent. Alfflad stood behind the harrow, Fridha and Wynfridh holding their torches on either side. Behind them loomed the shadowy figure of a large dark mare, whose reins the frowe held in one hand.

"Hail, Haith, goddess holy!" Alfflad cried, her voice ringing deep through the clearing. Sigimund could feel the sound resonating through the earth, thrumming up through his boots in a tingle of power. "Hail, thou all-giving earth. Hear the words that are spoken this night; hold them true, whatever betide. Frowe Holda, Nerthuz, Fro Ingwe, bless this wedding; be it fruitful, full of frith and joy. Hold Sigigairar and Sigilind together till the day of their deaths; and may that day be far. We give you this gift for the wedding, this mare, that you may bless them with many strong children." The knife glittered red in her hand as she turned to cut the mare's throat with one powerful sweep of her arm, dark blood flowing out over the sleeve of her dress and hissing in the fire on the harrow. Fridha was ready with the wooden blessing bowl to catch the steaming flow as the mare collapsed to her knees, then to the earth before the heaped stones. Wynfridh handed her mistress a sharp-needled pine twig; Alfflad dipped it to trace a sign in the blood. Bringing the thickly dripping twig out, she splashed a few drops to sizzle on the harrow stones. At her gesture, Sigigairar and Sigilind clasped crossed hands on the gold oath ring before the fire.

"By Holda-Freyja, Ingwar-Freyjar, and all the gods and goddesses, I swear to keep you as my wife, in trust and honor; to stand by your side while I shall live and never to do harm to you," Sigigairar said, his voice low and trembling.

"By Frowe Holda, Fro Ingwe, and all the gods and goddesses," Sigilind said, "I swear to follow you as my husband"—her voice caught for a mo- ment—"in trust and honor; to stand by your side while I shall live and never to do harm to you."

"So shall it be." Alfflad's deep voice cut through the night in a keen- edged, eerie half-chant. She sprinkled Sigilind and Sigigairar on their heads and clasped hands with the blood from the blessing bowl. "Now the oaths are spoke and sealed, here in the holy place. May they never be broken! Now wend your way in blessing's weal, frowe and fro; hale in frith, fare well to your hall."

All was silent for a moment, the only rustling that of the breeze stirring the moon-silvered spring leaves. Sigimund felt a sudden chill; glancing up, it seemed for a second that he could see a pair of winged black shadows circling overhead. Wodan, father of our line, he prayed, bless my sister's wedding. In the far distance of his mind, he thought he could hear two faint wolf howls, sending a shiver like the stroke of a cold whetstone up his spine.

The wind was strengthening, blowing the flames toward Sigilind and Sigigairar until Sigilind had to let go of the ring with one hand to wipe tears of smoke from her eyes. Her gesture broke the spell holding the gathered warriors still. Wals and Sigigairar came forward to heave the mare's body up on their shoulders, and the rest of the thanes followed them as they bore it back to the hall, where a great cauldron already bubbled over the fire by the Barnstock's roots. With a soft grunt, the two drightens let the heavy corpse down in front of the flowering apple tree.

Sigigairar stretched creakily and rubbed his shoulders. Trickles of sweat mixed with the mare's blood on his face, tracing red trails down his forehead. The dark spatters on Sigilind's pale skin and dress were dried already, bride-markings that all the Nine Worlds could read as surely as runes. The Gautish drighten whirled his bride off her feet, lifting her up and kissing her soundly as the warriors cheered and slammed hard fists on the oaken tables in applause. "Feast!" he shouted. "Feast to the honor of my bride and the goddesses who give good weddings, and hail to my new father Wals!"

"Hail to my new son Sigigairar and his bride!" Wals answered, raising his horn as Alfflad's serving women and the wives and daughters of his thanes came forth with pitchers of ale and mead for the warriors.

Alfflad, Fridha, and Wynfridh swiftly cut the horse to pieces and cast the flesh into the cauldron to seethe; the two green-clad maidens stirred the pot while Alfflad left the hall and returned with a handful of leaves and roots, which she cast into the frothing waters, a pleasant herbal smell rising to fill the room almost at once. Sigimund watched her curiously as she murmured over the pot, but the words were too soft for him to hear. In any case, it was the goddesses of women she was calling on and the work of a woman she was doing; unlike the galdor magic of Wodan's runes, it was a wisdom unfit for a warrior.

There was already bread on the tables, platters of cheese and bowls of little wild strawberries into which the thanes plunged their hands, bringing the fruit out in dripping fistfuls of red sweetness. Sigimund and his brother took two wooden plates from the stack at the end of the table and helped themselves to generous portions of food. One of the Gauts, a big, balding man whose fur cloak made him even bigger, had grabbed Caithlin as she filled his horn and her shrill protests mingled with giggles as he lifted her hefty body onto his lap. Sigimund saw the Gautish drighten's quick glare at his man, who paid him no attention; it was Haith's night, and only the most highly born maidens would be barred from her play. But he'll want his thanes to behave themselves, Sigimund thought. The last thing anyone wants is a fight at this feast.

A sudden gust of wind banged the hall's open doors off the walls, blowing the smoke from the cooking fire and the steam of the cauldron around the Barnstock to shroud its branches in a misty cloud. On the heels of the blast came a tall, barefooted figure in a cloak of deep mottled blue, its hood flung back beneath the wide-brimmed hat that he wore tilted over one eye; below a pale tunic, he wore dark linen breeks tied at the knee. In his hand was a great, naked sword, its keen edges shining as silvery as his hoary beard and hair even in the firelight and a clear ice stone, smooth and pure as water, gleaming in its hilt. Silently, as the drightens and their bands stared, he strode up to the huge apple tree and stabbed the blade in to the hilt. A shiver ran through the Barnstock from its deep roots to its crown, trembling through the earthen floor and thatched roof of Wals' hall.

The stranger turned, a star gleam of light from his one eye raking over the assembled men who gawped at him. Sigimund saw Gautish and Saxon hands reaching nervously for the hilts of swords bound down with peace strings, saw others grasping at amulets, bearded lips whispering the names of gods as a deep bell of awe rang through the hall.

"I give this sword as a gift to the man who can draw it," the stranger said. His powerful voice hummed with a weird roughness, resonating as scratchy as hemp through the rope scar on his throat. "Truly, he shall never bear a better in his hand; nor shall any here have more need of it in the time to come."

Turning, the old man glided swiftly out of the hall. By the time anyone arose to go after him, he had vanished into the faint moonlit mist rising from the river.

The warriors began to clamor, each pushing toward the tree with all thought of guest manners forgotten. They crowded alarmingly close to the fire and the bubbling cauldron, staring at the gleam of the hex-shaped crystal in the sword's hilt and shouting at each other in Saxon and Gautish.

"Wait!" Wals bellowed, forcing his way through the throng and shoving a couple of men back from the tree with his powerful shoulders. "Quiet!" Slowly the babble stilled, the men looking up at his great figure. Lit by the low-burning fire and wreathed with steam from the seething meat before him, he seemed inhumanly huge, towering over the smaller men before him like a kingly clad bear. He stretched his gigantic arms out, pushing the men back before him as with a mighty invisible shield. "This is my hall, and by the gods I'll have order in it if I have to kill everyone to do it. Each of us shall try in turn, or none shall; do you doubt that our guest knew whom he was giving it to, or think that the wrong man may get it?"

Heavy heads shook. Uncertain and frightened, the warriors glanced at each other. Sigigairar, standing just before Wals, glared at him narrow-eyed; but before he had time to speak, the Saxon drighten had turned and wrapped both big hands around the hilt of the sword, bracing his feet on one of the Barnstock's wide, ridged roots and pulling with all the strength in his mighty frame, twisting back and forth in a series of hard jerks. A few of the apple tree's leaves and flowers trembled; but the sword stayed unmoved, sunken as firmly as the old man had left it.

Sigigairar stepped up beside him, his narrow features drawn with anger. "Back, Wals, and let me try," he said sharply. Wals met his eyes for a moment, and Sigimund held his breath, waiting for his father to strike the other lord.

Wals shrugged his massive shoulders. "We'll see," he said calmly.

Sigimund could see the jaw muscles working under Sigigairar's patchy beard as the leader of the Gautish band grasped the hilt and pulled furiously, every muscle on his lean, sinewy arms standing out under a sudden gloss of light sweat. His thin face was red with fury, little rivulets dripping down his forehead and pale eyes bulging as he strove to move the sword. Finally, panting, he let go and beckoned to one of his thanes. "You're next, Bernu. Let's see if your bear's-sarker strength helps against the charm on this blade."

Caithlin's ample charms forgotten, the big man in the bear's cloak came through the crowd to the tree, leaving the Irish thrall muttering to herself in annoyance. The men around the Barnstock backed off as Bernu drew the bear's-head hood of his furry cloak over his head. He crouched down and growled before he flung himself at the sword hilt with a horrible snarling noise, froth running out of his bear mouth. The branches of the huge tree wavered a little beneath his furied attack; the sword did not, though blood from Bernu's hands dulled the brightness of its clear jewel.

As suddenly as it had begun, his storm was over; he stepped back from the tree, swinging his bear's head from side to side. "It's not mine," he muttered softly, taking off his hood. The thin fringe of hair around his bald crown was dark and wet, his big beard sodden with froth. "He didn't give it to me." He shambled back to the bench and collapsed heavily beside Caithlin.

One by one, Gaut and Saxon strained, heaved and cursed at the hilt of the sword, held fast by the Barnstock's gnarled trunk, till at last only Sigimund and Berhtwini, standing at the outskirts of the crowd, had not tried to pull it out. Sigimund looked questioningly at his younger brother.

"No, you go," Berhtwini whispered. "You're the elder."

Sigimund walked forward. Too dignified to try to force his way through the bigger bodies of the men around him, he moved slowly till Wals' gesture cleared a path for him.

"Come on, Sigimund!" his father called. "It's your turn now."

Sigimund could see Sigilind standing up on the bench to watch him, her narrow hands clutched before her blood-flecked bosom. Something like a spark coursed between them as their eyes met, flowing through Sigimund as he reached out to take the tingling hilt of the sword. It thrummed in his hand as though it had been struck a great blow, numbing his arm to the elbow. He struggled to hold on to it as it slipped out of the trembling apple tree. Then it was loosed and he held it aloft, the painful shock of its might easing as the power coursed through his arm, running through his body like the glow of strong mead. A mist of light blurred Sigimund's eyes, glowing from the brilliant edges of the sword; a great wind roared about his head as he heard his own voice crying out an unknown word from a great distance, a strange word that howled through his soul and through all the hidden worlds around him, its echo resonating in Sigilind's higher octave.

Slowly the light faded back into the blade of the sword and Sigimund's body, leaving them dark. The sword tingled only a little in his hand now, as though eager for battle. It felt amazingly light and keen as he swung it to cleave the steam of the cauldron in a hissing steel stroke.

"Just a boy," Sigigairar said in harsh, angry wonder. He turned on Sigimund, his light eyes flicking from the youth to Sigilind and back. Quickly he twisted his shocked face into a conciliatory smile. "You're my Sigilind's twin, aren't you? Sigimund?"

Sigimund nodded, trying to focus his eyes on the lean figure of the drighten before him. To his wonder-dazed sight, Sigigairar was only a blurred ghost, his voice muted as the buzzing of a fly trapped under an overturned clay pot. Only the sword in his hand and the echoes ringing through his skull seemed real to him; but the vision was ended and his eyes were already adjusting to the firelit dark of the hall again.

"What price would you name for that sword?" Sigigairar asked him. "Whatever it is, Sigimund, I can meet it. Gold? Men for your own band? A fine Gautish ship to go harrying in? Whatever you want, I can pay it."

Sigimund did not, could not, tell Sigigairar that all he wanted was to go back to the moment of drawing his sword from the tree, to the feeling of endless might and wisdom at his hand and the light that at once dazzled and cleared his eyes till he knew all the Nine Worlds interwoven around him. Instead he whipped his sword around in a whistling practice stroke. "I have what I want," he said simply. He waited for Sigigairar to challenge him, but no challenge came.

"So you have spoken," the Gautish leader said mildly. He turned and walked to his seat as Sigilind, remembering her new dignity, climbed down from the table. Her eyes were still fixed on her brother, breath coming quick and soft in the joyous echo of their cry as his hand (their hand) had drawn the sword forth from the Barnstock. Sigigairar put his arm around her, drawing her bright, half-seeing gaze to himself. He kissed her gently, but deeply, though his own eyes flickered over her shoulder to watch Sigimund and Wals.

Wals clapped his eldest son on the back, nearly bowling him over. "A good sword's all you want, is it?" he said, not bothering to lower his voice. "By the gods, Sigimund, you're a true Walsing. You'll win wealth and ships for yourself with it, as I did, won't you?"

Sigimund grinned at his father. The quieter hearth fire of love and pride was already glowing beneath his rib cage, lighting the darkness left by the sinking of the furious might that had burned so brightly before him. "I will," he said. He hefted his sword, looking to his sister to see her joy in him.

The fair river of her hair rippled beneath Sigigairar's hand as he caressed her, her back turned to her brother. Sigimund clenched his hand tight on the clear crystal in the sword's hilt. She was a bride, he reminded himself, her oath sworn to her husband now; but he longed to have her beside him as she had always been, trying his new weapon's weight and balance as she did with all his practice swords—feeling, as he did, how its smooth hexagonal crystal cleaved to his hand as though it had always gleamed from his palm, how the echo of its might still tingled in his arm as its serpent-mottled blade swept, swift and weightless, to cut keen-edged through the air. In this sword, he knew, she would find no flaw to warn him about, as she had with every other weapon they had touched.

The men crowded around Sigimund, staring at the blade and discussing it with admiration.

"Good as Weland's work," a short, heavyset Gaut with a cast in his left eye said approvingly, nodding his head in a decisive manner.

"Yah," the Saxon thane Alfhari, Alfflad's brother, agreed, scratching the shiny pink scar that cut crosswise through one side of his bristly brown beard. "I knew a man who had a sword with that snake pattern on the blade—he always said it'd been made for his father by the dwarves, but he said a lot of things."

"They say some of the little dark men down south past Rome, at the edge of Muspell, make blades like that," the Saxon Oswald cut in.

"Muspell, shit. I heard there's a dwarf-sized smith on the Rhine who's forging 'em," the short Gaut replied. "My brother talked to a man who'd got a dagger from him. He looked at the blade, and he said it was the prettiest thing he'd ever seen. He wanted to buy it, but the man wouldn't sell—just like the boy here. Thonar, if I had a weapon like that I wouldn't sell either, but saying no to our drighten's a good way to end up with your head on a pole and your body in a shitheap."

"Wals' son can say what he likes to whoever he likes," Alfhari said, looming over the Gaut with his fists clenched, ready to strike.

Wals' deep cough cut through the steamy air. Gritting broken teeth, Alfhari moved back a pace, opening his fists and forcing a grin. "Sigimund can say what he likes," he repeated. "I wouldn't argue with the boy while he's got a sword like that in his hand—would you?"

The Gaut scowled at him a moment, his left eye sliding in Sigigairar's direction. He cleared his throat noisily and spat on the floor, heavy boot scraping the spittle into mud. "Suppose not," he said reluctantly. He turned away; Sigimund thought he could hear him muttering under his breath, ". . . told us not to get into fights."

Softly, her lips moving in a whisper, Alfflad began to ladle the steaming broth and chunks of horsemeat into the clay bowls her maidens and thralls held out to her. The warriors began to drift back to the benches, Saxon sitting with Saxon and Gaut with Gaut as they murmured together and cast sideways glances at Sigimund, who still stood in the middle of the hall with the naked sword in his hand, beginning to feel rather uncomfortable.

"Take it to my chamber," Wals told him, bending close and speaking low. "It'll be safe there; in the morning we can get you a proper scabbard for it."

Sigimund nodded. He took a torch from the wall and went out of the little door near Wals' high seat that led to the room the drighten and Alfflad shared. Alone with his sword, the torchlight rippling down its blade, Sigimund felt an almost unbearable, piercing joy. He stood for a long time, torch in one hand and sword in the other, staring at the waves of light and shadow that flowed along its length as he turned it over and over. At last, hating to let go of its hilt, he wrapped it in one of the blankets from his father's bed and stretched up to lay it on the cross-beam above the fireplace. He could hear the feasting noises becoming louder and louder outside as the men ate and drank, shouting their boasts to each other, till the sound swelled to the huge roar of seventy-odd throats shouting, "Frowe bless!" and he knew that Sigilind and Sigigairar had left the hall for the private hut of woven branches that he had helped to adorn with elder and birch for Holda and Nerthuz, with white-flowering rowan and red ribbons to ward away evil witchcraft and with the pale star blossoms of houseleek, Thonar's Beard, to break through Sigilind's maidenhead and ripen the fruit within her as Thonar's summer lightning ripened the growing wheat. Then Sigimund stood on tiptoe again and dragged his blanketed sword down from the rafter, and he curled up on Wals' bed with the blade clutched close to him (for he knew, deep within where thought could not sink, that its keen edges might slice wool and linen easy as thought, but they would never cut his own flesh).

Sigimund went to sleep like that, and he dreamed of his sister, frightened and eager as Sigigairar's sword-calloused hands fondled her swelling breasts and touched her gently so that she moved like a young filly under his guidance. He dreamed of her shock—for she had seen men swimming naked in summer, seen hound and cat and horse rutting a hundred times, but never a man in his full pride—and the pain at first, as she clenched her fists and bit her lip to keep from trying to throw her husband from her or striking out at him in answer to his battering at the walls of her body. But Sigigairar must have known virgins before, for he stopped, stroking her till her breathing calmed and soothing her tightened muscles, till, still aching but eager again, she reached for him; and this time his weight was easier for her to bear and she caught her breath with the beginnings of pleasure—and love, for this stranger?—who was neither the foe nor the beast she had feared, but a man who was kind enough and wise enough to keep the oath he had made on the holy ring to her, even though . . . and she gasped as the joy of his touch rose within her body, sparking up to light her mind . . . even though he hated her father and would bring his death to being in time.

Sigigairar kissed Sigilind as the waves of warmth sank down her body; but beneath the flow of feeling between them, Holda's gift, she could already hear the distant, low sound of her father's doom, like surf crashing on a shore far away, and in the darkness of the bridal hut she thought for a fleeting moment how near and unguarded her husband's throat might be. But she had sworn as he on the ring before the Frowe's fire, and eaten of the holy mare's seethed flesh with him; and so she let herself soften to his caresses, and at last sank to sleep in his arms.

Sigimund awoke to the sound of men running through the hall, talking furiously. He got up quickly, thrusting his sword through his belt, and went to the door. Sigigairar's men were gathering their rolls of bedding together, carrying all they had out of the hall. Wals and Sigigairar stood near the Barnstock, whose leaves were dripping with light morning rain, talking in quiet voices as Sigilind waited by her husband's side. On one shoulder, she wore a new golden brooch as big as her palm, set with clear green gems like little glowing cats' eyes—Sigigairar's morning gift to his bride. Seeing Sigimund, she slipped quietly away and darted over to him.

"Why is everyone leaving?" Sigimund whispered to his sister. "I thought Sigigairar was going to stay for a proper length of time."

"He was supposed to, but he claims we have to go back to Gautland now. He's invited Father to a feast in three months to make up for being so rude, but . . ." Sigilind hugged her brother to her tightly, the thick links of her gold chain pressing painfully into his chest. "He wants to kill you," she hissed. "I told Father—I wanted to break off the wedding—and he said that he meant to hold by his oath to Sigigairar and that, if I were a true Walsing, I would have to keep to mine."

"Sigigairar didn't hurt you, did he?" Sigimund murmured fiercely, putting his arms around his sister's shoulders.

She shook her head, long disheveled hair falling silky over his hands. "Oh, no. No, he was kind to me. He'll be a good husband to me. It's you and Father I'm afraid for."

Sigimund laughed. "Is that all? There's not a warrior from Rome to Finland who could stand up to Wals in a fight, and you know that as well as I do. You don't need to worry about us. Just take care of yourself and be sure to make him treat you properly, because if he doesn't I'll give him a good reason for worry."

Sigilind's sky-bright eyes looked up into her twin's, glistening with tears that mirrored the crystal blurring of Sigimund's own sight. "I'm going to miss you, Sigimund. I don't know how I'll be able to wait three months for you to come north—but if you can avoid it, don't do it, and if you do come, be wary and don't trust my husband in anything. And keep Father warned as well. I think he's trusted his own strength for so long that he forgets men can be slain in all sorts of ways."

Sigimund clung to his twin as he had in childhood, forgetting for a moment that he was a grown warrior with a sword of his own and she was a new bride whose womb might already have been quickened with the growing seed of a child of her own. "I'm going to miss you too, 'Linde. But it's only going to be for a while, you wait and see." They held each other quietly.

"Sigilind!" Sigigairar's nasal call cut through their embrace. "Will you be ready soon?"

Slowly Sigilind unwrapped her arms from her brother and turned to her husband. "Just a moment," she answered. "Let me get my baggage. I'll need a couple of men to help carry it."

With a sharp gesture, Sigigairar intercepted two sturdy Gauts and waved them over to Sigilind. Obediently they followed her out of the hall, to the storage hut where the chests full of embroidered linen sheets and pillows stuffed with goose-down and sweet-smelling herbs for sleep, of cups and needles and all the other things a new bride might need had been stored. She pointed out what they were to take; they heaved the wooden boxes onto their shoulders, carrying her bridal portion down the gentle slope of the meadow and wading out to one of the ships.

Wals, Alfflad and Sigilind's brothers, from Sigimund with his glistening new sword stuck through his belt down to three-year-old Alfwald who stood sucking his chubby little thumb gravely, were waiting by the water's edge for her. Crying openly now, she embraced them all: her father's bulk, solid and wide as the Barnstock; Alfflad's tender warmth; Sigimund's body—her own body—made hard with a young warrior's muscles, but trembling, as was she, with expectation, with sorrow for the wyrd that had to rend them so far apart, and with, perhaps, the hidden echo of fear like waves heard at the faraway mouth of a sea cave; Berhtwini's elbowy boniness, and so on down to Alfwald, whom she kissed on the upturned tip of his nose.

"Siggy-lindy going away," he piped firmly. "Siggy-lindy coming back soon?"

"I hope so, little one," she answered. She brushed away her tears and turned to Wals, who looked down at her solemnly.

Out of his belt pouch he drew a small, slim dagger, the pommel of its hilt carved into the keen head of a falcon. "This belonged to your mother Hleod," he said, his rough voice cracking. "Bear it well, my Sigilind, in memory of her."

"I swear I shall never give Wodan's wish-maiden cause to be ashamed of me, but only to be proud as befits a daughter of Wals," Sigilind answered as she accepted the dagger from her father and thrust it under the silken cord girdling her waist.

She looked again at Wals, at Alfflad's slight figure beside him, at her own face mirrored in Sigimund's and at the line of her half-brothers: Berhtwini, Wulfger, Alfger, Oddwig, Orngrim, Wynbercht, Wihtric, Alfarik and Alfwald. "I love you," she said to all of them, and turned away before she could begin to weep in earnest. Burly Bernu lowered a plank from the ship to the bank of the river; Sigilind walked up it with her back straight, slow and dignified as befitted a married woman who was still the daughter of Wals and the walkyrige Hleod.

Sigimund stood watching as the plank was withdrawn and the wooden oar legs began to move up and down, carrying the fleet swiftly along with the current. He watched till the white wings of the sails shrank from huge billows to tiny clouds in the distance and vanished into the gray spread of the North Sea. Only then did he realize that he was standing alone; Wals,

Alfflad, Berhtwini and the rest had gone to go about the work that Sigigairar's unexpected departure had made. Sigimund touched the smooth crystal in the hilt of his sword, feeling the echo of its might thrumming softly through him like the blood through his veins and, a more distant echo, the soul of his twin given heart by his touch, reaching out to renew his own brave mood as he thought of her.

THE FROWE

Sigilind stood in the sun before her husband's long hall, stretching her arms upward and letting her thick braid of fair hair fall, heavy as gold, down her back. A light breeze rippled through the pale sea of ripe grain that covered the swells of hill and valley up to the dark edges of the wood where the pines rustled softly together and down to the glittering blue of the still sea. She smoothed down the woolen folds of her sky-colored dress and her hands lingered a little over the slight swelling of her belly, trying to feel some movement of the tiny life within her.

"You won't see them first from here, darling," an old woman's voice crackled behind her. Sigilind jumped, whirling about to stare at the tall figure of Sigigairar's aged mother.

Kara overtopped her daughter-in-law by a couple of inches. Her hair was ash-dusted gray and the flesh of her face had pulled back somewhat from her strong cheekbones and square jawline, but she was still remarkably young and powerful-looking. Only her voice, like the rotten hollow in the middle of a strong-limbed old tree, showed her true age. A musty scent of dried herbs clung to her madder-red linen skirt and tunic and the deep green shawl about her broad shoulders.

A snakelike shudder writhed up Sigilind's spine as she met Kara's flat, pale eyes. "Whatever do you mean?" she said, as casually as she could.

"Your family, of course. My dear, the Moon is dark tonight and you've been cleaning the hall and staring at the water since it was full. What else could you be waiting for?" Kara reached out to pat her on the shoulder with a heavy-ringed hand. Sigilind kept herself from drawing back, but she twitched at the prickling touch of her husband's mother. "There, there, it's all right," Kara crooned. "I remember how lonely I was when I left my father's hall—I'm not so old yet, darling." Her pupils seemed to be widening as though she had stepped into a shadowy keep, drawing Sigilind in. "But you've got a fine husband and a strong babe growing in you, and it won't be long before you've forgotten about your brothers. What you'll really love is what you have here."

A sudden warning thrill ran through Sigilind, clenching her fists and driving her nails tight into her palm. With an effort she pulled her gaze away from Kara's darkening eyes, lowering her head and nodding so as not to seem rude. "I suppose so," she murmured.

"Of course, darling," whispered Kara softly. The gold coiled around her fingers touched the underside of Sigilind's chin coldly as she lifted the young woman's gaze to meet hers.

Sigilind felt suddenly dizzy, but she straightened her back, calling on all her strength to look Kara in the eyes without falling wholly into her. "I love Sigigairar and my baby," she said firmly, "but I'll never forget what my brothers and my father are to me."

Kara showed her strong, wolfish-white teeth. "You're a faithful girl, Sigilind," she rasped. "You'll never forget your duty to your husband, either, will you?"

"I will not," Sigilind said.

Kara nodded, tiny snakes of annoyance still wrinkling her wide brow. It seemed as if she were about to say something more, but the sound of bare feet slapping against the hard dirt path through the wheat field and a young boy's high panting broke through the edge of the moment.

"Ship! Ship!" the boy called. "Down around the point! Looks like a Saxon!"

Her dignity forgotten, Sigilind scooped up her skirts and broke into a run, her wooden-soled sandals kicking up a cloudy trail of dust behind her and her long braid trailing in the wind of her flight as she pelted in excitement and terror down through the field and over the hump of the point. She could almost hear the soft keening of Sigigairar's whetstone on his blade as he had sharpened it the night before; for the past two weeks, she had seen his men oiling their axes as if to slaughter cattle for the feast.

Looking down from the raised rocks, she could see that the ship coming in beside the others at Sigigairar's dock, though it bore Wals' apple banner, was too small to be his flagship. She slowed to a walk, panting in great gasps like sobs. They're safe, she thought, they're not going to come after all. Then a tendril of icy fear reached into her bowels as she thought of why a messenger might have come in Wals' place, and she began to hurry again.

Wals' messenger, Osfridh, was dressed in a rusty tunic and bright yellow cloak fastened with a big silver brooch; Sigilind relaxed somewhat when she could see no sign of mourning about him. He lifted his cloak to wade ashore, his boots splashing loudly through the clear water of the Baltic Sea. Politely he waited on the beach until Sigilind had made her way down the rocky path to him, as the other men looped the ship's ropes around one of the posts between two of Sigigairar's boats.

"Greetings, frowe Sigilind," Osfridh said, his tenor voice slicing through the air between them and the noise of the sailors making the ship fast. "I hope you are well this day?"

"Er . . ." Sigilind said. Flustered, she brushed back a few wisps of glittering hair that had escaped from her braid, cleared her throat and tried again. "Greetings, Osfridh. What message do you bring from the drighten Wals' hall?"

Osfridh smiled at her, his open brown eyes meeting her gaze with affection. Only a few broken teeth marred the handsomeness of the messenger who spoke for Wals in all the lesser affairs of state, when the drighten could not or would not be there himself. "No great ill, though battles will delay Wals' visit for a while. But surely the gracious frowe Sigilind will ask these poor seafarers to come to the hall of her husband and sit while she hears the news of her home."

"Oh!" Sigilind gasped, remembering proper manners at last. "I am sorry. It seems that my eagerness to hear of my kin has driven everything else from my mind. Good messenger Osfridh, would you and your men care to come to the hall of the drighten Sigigairar for refreshment and rest after your long faring?"

"We would be honored, gracious frowe," Osfridh answered. For a moment, he held his long face in a perfectly sober and proper expression, except for a certain crinkling about the eyes; then he gave it up and laughed. "Don't worry, Sigilind. You'll get used to being the frowe of the hall soon enough."

Sigilind led Osfridh and the eight men who had come with him up the pathway to Sigigairar's hall. She showed them in through the room in front where the beer casks were kept—in winter it would have been small joy for the women to walk to the storage huts and back each time they needed to fill their pitchers. Sigilind saw the thanes glancing curiously at the stalled aisles that ran along half the length of the hall, and thought a few noses might tighten against the barn smell. Although the thralls, both men and maids, had striven for days to clean the hall after the cattle were taken out to the fields at winter's end, season after season of bringing the animals in for warmth had worked their smell deep into the wooden walls. Instead of a large fire in the middle of the hall, as was usual in more southerly lands, long firepits ran the building's length from the stalls down to the other end where a small door behind the high seat led into the room Sigigairar and Sigilind shared. Sigilind wondered if her father's thanes, used to the rustling leaves of the Barnstock and the light from the sky above it, would find Sigigairar's hall as dark and musty as she had when her husband carried her proudly in.

Sigigairar and twelve of his thanes stood at the door in byrnies and helms, bows leaning on the wooden wall behind them and swords at their sides. Sigilind could feel the tightening of her husband's long muscles, his body clenching in anger as the eyes behind the helmet's grating flicked over the small band of Saxons. She shut her eyes for a second, but the knowledge only grew clearer to her hidden sight: Sigigairar's men had seen the small ship long before it came to the point. He had known how many men he had to face, but not whom; if Wals and his sons had come by themselves as he had bidden, he would have had them in a neat ambush. Yet, he wanted no more men there than must be: perhaps because a messenger such as

Osfridh would bear the news of a waiting host back to Wals, perhaps because he knew the deed was ill—Sigilind could not tell. Thank you, Wodan Warfather, she thought, for the battles that keep my father among enemies of whom he knows he must be wary.

"Greetings, Saxon," Sigigairar called. "Do you bring tidings of my kinsman Wals?"

"I do indeed," Osfridh answered.

"Come and be welcome, then," Sigigairar said, pushing the door open. He and his thanes filed in, followed by Sigilind, Osfridh and the Saxon band.

Sigilind led Osfridh to the seat of honor beside Sigigairar's and seated his men along the bench before him, then went to the outer chamber to fetch ale for them. When she returned bearing her husband's horn and one for Osfridh, Sigigairar and the messenger were already talking. Sigilind desperately wanted to sit and listen, but she had her duty to the other guests.

At last each man had his ale, though one or two of the Saxons, used to the richer drink of Wals' hall, scowled balefully down into the sour dark Northern brew. Sigilind took her seat next to her husband, waiting a few moments for him to stop the conversation and let her find out what Osfridh was saying.

Not until she coughed gently did Sigigairar at last turn toward her, his mouth twisted into a crooked grin. "It seems your brother is doing well with that sword," he said, bitterness as sharp as poison on his tongue.

"Tell me," she said eagerly to Osfridh. Once or twice she had dreamed—sunlight gleaming off snake-patterned metal, blood running hot over smooth crystal, cold steel slicing through spear shaft and sword blade, byrnie and flesh alike—but she clenched her hands tightly and leaned toward the messenger to hear him tell her the dreams were true.

Memory lit Osfridh's even features with a fierce grin. "Ah, I've never seen anyone but Wals fight like Sigimund. He was good enough before, but with that sword in his hand, there was nothing and nobody that could stand against him. He went right through that wild tribe from the north like fire through dried grass. Nothing could touch him, except that once one of them got behind him and knocked him on the head. That put him down for a little while, but your father got there before the bastard could finish his job, and Sigimund was up again before the fight was over. No damage done," he added hastily, seeing Sigilind's face twist with worry. "He was just sore enough to make him mad. He won his share of treasure, too, though there wasn't as much of it as there might have been. I've heard that some of the folk we were fighting were coming over our way because some other clans had shoved them out of their homelands—Northerners coming south and Easterners coming west. I don't know how things are turning, but it doesn't look as though we'll have much peace for a while."

"So I should not expect Wals and his sons to honor my hall with their presence this year?" Sigigairar asked, tapping his long fingers irritably on the rough oaken tabletop.

"The drighten Wals regrets that he will not be able to feast with his daughter's husband until peace has been completely restored to his realm," Osfridh replied.

"And next year? How do things look? Surely a drighten of Wals' fame has established his hold well enough to trust his land to those loyal to him for a few weeks?"

"Wals says that he will come as soon as he is able, although only the Norns know when that may be," Osfridh stated firmly, inclining his brown head a little in a gesture of respect to Sigigairar.

Sigigairar sighed. "Indeed. I had heard . . . well, no matter. Sigilind, dearest, would you fill our guest's horn again and have the girls bring in some food? As I know full well, it is a long faring from Wals' hall."

The whisper of fear that had nagged at Sigilind for the last three months was eased now; she smiled at her husband in relief, thinking, Father heeded my warning and now I can love Sigigairar with my heart, without fearing that I may betray my kin.

"Of course, my love," she answered sweetly, already on her way to the outer chamber.

As Sigilind, arching her shoulders back for balance, rose to her feet with two full, heavy pitchers of beer, the tall shape of Kara came suddenly from the shadows of the ale casks. The Walsing started, spilling a thin waterfall of foam over the earthen rims of the jugs. "Kara," Sigilind said quickly before the old woman could speak, "have you seen Helche and the Welsh girl anywhere? I need them to bring in some bread and cheese, and perhaps also some fish, if there is any fresh."

"We have fresh fish," Kara croaked, "but it won't keep as long as you wish."

"What are you talking about? Wals' messenger and his men have to be fed now."

Kara hunched down to look Sigilind in the eye. "But not Wals or your brothers. The Walsings push west and south even as they try to hold their lands against the folk crammed against their borders, and I know—I have a little wisdom—it will be years before Wals is satisfied again with what he has. Trust the words of an old woman: when you see them again, they must be strangers to you and this must be your only home."

"How do you know?" Sigilind asked, bewildered. "Why do you say this?"

"Because I do know, and because I love my son's pretty wife who bears the life of my kin within her. Because, Sigilind, I want you to be joyful with Sigigairar, untroubled by the strife men make with each other."

Sigilind clutched her hand on the hilt of the dagger Wals had given her on the day of her departure: the walkurja's knife. "Before my mother was married, she rode through the air above battling warriors," she said proudly. "Wals' clan have never sought peace above all else, and Wodan, from whom we are sprung, is often a stirrer of strife."

"You have a strong spirit," Kara said, shaking her head, "but time and love will still your fierceness, and you will grow to be glad of that when your

STEPHAN GRUNDY

☩ 8 6

brothers are gone and your husband alone remains with you. Go on, go back in there, and I'll see to our thrall-maidens. They're probably sleeping in the sun somewhere. Do you trust me to arrange things for our clan?"

"No one better," Sigilind answered truthfully. And for nothing else, she thought.

"Go on, then, and tend to our guests. I know you'll make our Sigigairar proud."

Kara patted Sigilind on the shoulder, her palm as leathery as the footpads of an old hound even through the light woolen dress. The young woman hurried away from her husband's mother, eager to hear more news of her kin.

A VICTORY

Wals' messenger came to the hall of Sigigairar at each summer's end, bringing news of more wars, more strife from the invaders to the north and east or the conquered folk in the west and south that kept Wals and his sons away from their kinswoman's hall. When Sigilind's first son, Theudorikijar, was five and her second son, Harigastir, four, a heavyset young man named Odward with black hair and a broken nose came in Osfridh's place to tell her that the other messenger had died in a fever that had swept through Wals' land but, thank the gods, not slain any of his line, though Alfwald and Berhtwini had fallen ill of it and would always bear pockmarks on their faces. The name of Sigimund was always first in the songs Odward chanted; and Sigigairar watched, his pale eyes narrow and big-jointed fingers tapping on his knee as the Saxon spoke of Sigimund's sword carving roasts for wolves and eagles, winning him a name that would soon grow as mighty as his father's. And Sigilind stroked the fair heads of her sons, her heart filled with gladness for her twin and a greater gladness for the ocean that kept her husband's brooding heart from him, because though Sigigairar was unfailingly kind and loving to her, there was something in his sideways glance that never ceased to remind her that he had not forgotten his shame at Wals' hall.

Sigilind stood watching her sons at play under the shadow of the wood's edge. Three days of storm had kept them in the hall, and they were busy

screaming and fighting off the last of their captivity. Nine-year-old Theudorikijar had his younger brother Harigastir in a headlock and was trying to
wrestle him toward a patch of brambles; Harigastir writhed his shoulders
and shook his brother around; stubbornly refusing to be wrestled. They were
both large for their age, tall and well-knit; only a little tinge of their father's
red stained their golden hair, though his crooked nose jutted out from both
narrow faces. Sigilind gazed tolerantly at them, remembering how she had
fought with her brothers, snapping and biting like wolf cubs as well as wrestling and punching—almost ten years ago? She was twenty-three years old
now, her heavy coiled braids bedecked, as befitted a frowe and mother, with
a circlet of wrought Irish silver that Sigigairar had won on a raid two years
ago; she wondered if she would remember which end of a practice sword to
take up now. Carefully she felt the grass under her to be sure it was dry and
sank down, arranging her skirts about herself.

Harigastir had broken out of his brother's hold and was chasing him
farther into the wood. They had just gone out of sight in the undergrowth
when Sigilind jerked her head up. "Theudorikijar! Harigastir! Get back here!"

The bushes rustled and two small fair heads poked out. "We weren't going
far," Theudorikijar said in a tone of wounded dignity.

"We could still see you," Harigastir chimed in.

"When you have your swords," Sigilind told them severely, "you will be
men and then you may go where you please and fight with whatever you
like. Until then, there are wolves in the wood. Do you remember how many
children were lost last winter?"

"Three," said Harigastir sulkily. "But it's summer now, and the wolves don't
come near the hold in summer."

"Still," Sigilind stated. "And nevertheless. You must stay within my sight,
or you'll find that your mother can be worse than a wolf when she's angry."

"Aw," Theudorikijar complained.

Harigastir glanced sharply at him. "Whiner."

"Am not. Who cried this morning because he stepped on a thorn?"

"I shouted a battle shout. That's not crying."

"You cried, I heard you. Whiner, whiner, whiner."

"Whiner yourself. You start wailing whenever you stub your toe, and you
know it."

"Why don't you shut your mouth before I shut it for you, you little
nithling?" Theudorikijar threatened, moving toward his brother with murderous intent. Sigilind settled herself more comfortably to watch, ready to
step in if things went too far.

The sound of a far-off steerhorn shivered through the air, shattering the
taunts of the two boys to silence. Sigilind and her sons looked up at Sigigairar's hall, then down to the point where a watchman suddenly stood,
raising a horn to his lips. Its rough note, deep and close, answered the far-
off call.

Sigilind's heart fluttered and leapt, her throat choking in a spasm of fear.
She picked up one boy under each arm and ran up the hill through the

wheat. Theudorikijar and Harigastir stared silently at their mother, more terrified by her sudden flight than by the warning horns.

Reaching the door of the hall, Sigilind pushed her sons inside and turned to look for signs of the foe. The men were gathering slowly: Sigigairar's thanes in chain-mail byrnies were the first to the hall, the free carls, armored in boiled leather, came after, roused from their summertime weeding and tending of beasts. As yet she could see no invader; but the horns had blown news of an enemy in their lands.

Sigigairar came out of the hall, fully armed and armored. He took Sigilind by the shoulder, the metal plates of his leather gloves icy through her summer dress. "Go on in, darling," he said, his voice muffled and distorted as though his winter wrappings were still around his face. "There's going to be fighting, and I don't want you to be in danger. Are the boys? . . . Yes, you sent them in, didn't you? Come and watch over them."

"Who is it?" Sigilind asked, her voice rising almost to a shriek. "Is it safe for our sons here?"

Sigigairar's breath caught. Behind the interlaced metal that shielded his face, his eyes turned away from Sigilind's for a moment, and she knew the answer—after nine years, she had almost stopped fearing. "It's safe," he said heavily. "Go on in. You don't want to see this. Let us get it over with."

Sigilind tightened her hand on the dagger at her belt, thinking, for a moment, to throw herself on her husband. But she was a Walsing and she had sworn an oath; an oath that Sigigairar, too, had sworn and never broken. Silently she turned and walked back into the darkness of the hall, not looking out over the water to see Wals' great ship riding off-shore—and anchoring just out of reach.

Trembling with a cold sickness, clammy sweat sticking her linen dress to her body, Sigilind went to the two boys who crouched at the end of the hall by their father's high seat. She embraced their shaking bodies fiercely, as though their warmth could somehow ease the ice that seemed to lay all her strength in fetters. Outside, she could hear the sound of men's low voices, though she could not make out what they were saying. When Harigastir and Theudorikijar began to wriggle, she whispered nonsense to them, stroking their heads as if they were restless puppies; and after a while they were asleep, Harigastir in her lap and Theudorikijar leaning against her shoulder.

Sigilind did not know how long she had waited before Sigigairar came into the hall, pulling his helmet off and throwing his gloves on the table.

"Tell me, my wife," he said, voice thick and nose twisted as if in disgust, "is it the way of your folk to feast on board after weathering a storm at sea?"

Sigilind breathed in deeply, squirming to ease her numb feet without waking her sons. "It is, in thanks to Nerthuz, who gives good winds and wards us from the Robber's greedy net."

"It is, is it?" Sigigairar murmured, running his thumbnail along the edge of his sparse beard. "And do you know how many ships are in Wals' fleet?"

"I did once, but no more," Sigilind said. "You have been south many times since I have. Now leave me alone about this, because I cannot bear any more." Her voice cracked with tears. Sigigairar crouched down swiftly beside her, wiping the droplets from the corners of her eyes with a gentle fingertip.

"My wife, my love, I will let it be, if you give me your word on one single thing. Only swear to me that you will not try to fare away with them, but will hold to the oath of our wedding, and then you will stay in our house with our sons and this will not touch you at all."

His eyes met Sigilind's; they were wide open, shining with water. Does he believe this? she wondered. How can he . . . ? But his knuckles were white where he clutched her arms, mouth tight as a seaman's knot and freckled skin stretched over his long bones like rawhide drying on a rack. She could feel how badly Sigigairar wanted to believe that she would still love him; and because she was Wals' daughter and her father had told her to be true, she reached out and embraced him. "I promise that I will stay with you," she said.

Sigilind's words dropped heavily, rocks splashing into the waters of a well. Sigigairar kissed her desperately, his arms tightening on her until she ached from his touch before he let her go.

Awakened and dislodged from his comfortable resting place on his mother's shoulder, Theudorikijar set up a wailing. In a moment his brother's disgusted howl matched his.

Sigigairar twisted his face into a grin. "I love you, Sigilind. Please remember that." He picked up his gloves and helmet and walked back to his men.

Sigilind shook herself, brushing off the dusty marks his chain mail had left on her white dress, and stood, stamping prickly life back into her numb limbs. Stretching, she was suddenly aware of how much she needed to empty her bladder. "Come on, boys," she said, pulling her sons to their feet. "We're going to be safe for a little while, and Mother needs to go behind a tree."

"Are we going to fight someone?" Theudorikijar asked eagerly, his thoughts drawn away from his complaint.

"Not today." Sigilind's voice was grim, the faint rough undertone rasping harshly through its usual high clearness. Subdued, her sons followed her through the back door of the hall and down the other side of the hill, where they could no longer see the sea.

Sigilind crouched behind a clump of bushes to relieve herself, dizzy and confused. Without thinking, she had lied to Sigigairar about the Walsings' ways to back up what Wals himself must have said—but why had he said it? And Sigigairar's question about the ships . . . ? Of course, she thought, some of Wals' fleet must have been blown off-course in the storm. If he comes with a great enough host, Sigigairar will let him come in peace; angry as he is, he's not mad enough to destroy himself for revenge—or for Sigimund's sword.

Nerthuz, she prayed, blow Wals' ships to us soon, before his pride drives him ashore to his death. Begetter of Fro Ingwe, the Frith-King Ingwar-Freyjar, giver of fruitful peace—Nerthuz, give them the winds they need so that this can end without the killing of kin.

She looked toward the southern sky above the sea, hoping for a sign that Nerthuz had heard her—even a breath of breeze—but the sky was as clear and calm as an empty bowl.

After a little while, Sigilind called her sons together and went back into the hall. Kara was waiting for her in the fore-chamber, a frothing aurochs horn in her hand. Sigilind waved the boys on to the feasting room; the hall door shut behind them, leaving the two women alone.

As she had grown in height and strength and learned to ward herself against Kara's glance, the years had dimmed Sigilind's fear of Sigigairar's mother to a wariness like the faint throbbing of a long-healed wound; now, looking down at her, Sigilind wondered why she had ever been worried about what Kara might do to her. In the light from the smokehole, the aged woman seemed suddenly withered, her old strength drained from her like ale from a cask. The dark horn she held gleamed dully, almost too heavy for her shaking grip.

"Take this, Sigilind," Sigigairar's mother croaked. "The gods know you need something to soothe you."

Gratefully Sigilind took the horn from Kara's hand and raised it to her lips, breathing in the rich malty scent. Only a slight sweet undertone caught at the back of her throat, just enough so that she lowered the drink warily. "What did you put in it?"

"A herb to soothe you and another to give you good dreams and easy sleep—the same that I gave Harigastir when he had the fever. No others, I swear it."

Sigilind sniffed more carefully at the drink. "Dwale to make me sleep, and sleep a long time. What else?"

The Walsing's voice dropped to a rough hiss as she closed with the old woman, her anguish bursting forth through her veins. "You want me to sleep and to forget my kin—you've wanted that since I came here. I've had to fight off your witch-gaze for nine years and now, since you can't beat me with your strength alone, you want to drug me!" A wave of ale slopped over the rim of the horn, its cold stilling her shaking hand. "Hella take you, you old witch! Get out of here! I'm oathbound to Sigigairar, but I never swore anything to you. Go, go, I never want to see you again and if you try to bewitch me one more time I swear I'll kill you. Get out!" Her voice had risen to a harsh raven's scream, her mother's dagger gripped before her in her trembling, white-knuckled fist. Kara stared at her son's wife for a moment, then turned and fled, followed by Sigilind's wordless howl of rage and frustration.

Sigilind reined her body back tightly, bending to set the horn carefully upright against the wall with its end stuck into the earthen floor. Then she curled upon herself, pressing her fists against her thighs, shaking so hard that she could barely stand.

After a while, Sigilind picked up the horn. She knew that she ought to throw the drugged drink out, somewhere far from the settlement where neither farm beasts nor children might stumble across its bale, but a thought was already twisting to her mind. Here was a weapon that would not harm nor slay: its magic of forgetfulness was set against her alone, but the dwale in the draught would bring a night of deep unbroken sleep to anyone—even if the hall should burn down around the drinker.

Sigilind carried the horn through into the chamber she shared with Sigigairar. She moved one of their chests a few inches away from the wall, setting the horn down behind it and pushing the chest back to hold the vessel upright. Unless someone looked very closely, the shadows would hide it from all sight.

Sigigairar's men sat at feast that night, the thanes at the upper benches and the carls below, farmers enjoying that night of the best food at their drighten's expense. Dice clattered on the benches; the men drank and laughed, wagering weapons or silver against their luck for the next day's battle. The Welsh thrall-girl came in and out of the hall, fetching platters of food for the men who stood at the shore watching Wals' ship; Sigilind, sitting silent and pale by her husband's side, wondered darkly if Kara had chosen the mute for that task because she could bear no messages from Sigilind to the ship. Kara herself was nowhere to be seen: whether she was helping the thrall Helche to tend to Theudorikijar and Harigastir or had crawled off into the woods to die, Sigilind neither knew nor cared.

The summer sky was almost wholly dark when Sigilind, filling her pitcher of ale, heard a knock on the outer door of the hall. She twisted the barrel's tap shut so fast it cracked, a thin chain of droplets dripping from it to muddy the earthen floor below. Holding tightly to her dagger, she crept into the shadows and crouched down behind the ale casks, looking through a crack between two of them. She saw Sigigairar's long legs and the helmet dangling from his hand as he strode through the chamber to open the door himself.

Outside stood a panting youth dressed only in a pair of breeches, the light from Sigigairar's torch casting a red sheen over his sweaty chest and face.

"Hlewagastir sent me," he gasped. "I'm to tell you . . ." He bent over, rubbing his stomach as if cramped.

"Yes?" Sigigairar snapped impatiently. "Tell me!"

The boy drew a few deep breaths, coughed and tried again. "Five ships . . . wrecked in the storm. No living men cast up. Found a banner with the Walsings' apple on it."

Sigilind gasped silently through locked jaws, frozen for a moment as she stared out of the door at the darkened sky. Sigigairar's back was to her; she could not hear his next words, but he led the youth in. Sigilind came out of her hiding place and finished filling her pitcher from the cracked tap. She must make sure the other women knew to draw from that barrel first—the northern fields were not so free with grain that ale could easily be wasted.

When Sigilind finally came into the great hall again, Hlewagastir's youth was tearing at a hunk of cheese; the cheese rinds and breadcrumbs scattered around his wooden plate showed that he had already devoured a fair part. Sigilind refilled his empty mug, fresh ale foaming up from the dark droplets within, and sat down next to Sigigairar. Her husband said nothing to her, and she tried to keep from looking at him.

At last the men started to wander out to their own homes or roll themselves in blankets or straw. The first set of guards came in and the second group went out, swearing half-drunkenly at the ill-minded idises ruling the lots that had drawn them a lack of sleep that night. Sigilind rose quickly from her seat and went to get Kara's horn from their room, topping it off with the last ale from a pitcher on the table and swirling the horn about so that the herbs within would be well mixed with the ale and the draught froth freshly.

"Let this renew the frith between us, my husband," she said. She drew in a deep breath, chanting in the skaldic way he had taught her,

> Fierce beast's ear-forest branch,
> froths with Agwijar's craft,
> Bright, necklace-goddess brings
> brew for the war-Thing's oak.
> Herobart's wife heard once
> how we swore our love-runes,
> word-fetters will not break,
> will I keep troth with you.

To Sigilind's surprise, her voice was cracking and her eyes hot with tears by the time she was done, as she thought of the winter nights she had spent in the crook of Sigigairar's arm learning the way of word-weavings and riddle-kennings, the two of them wrapped in one great bearskin cloak before the fire.

Sigigairar coughed, his voice husky as he spoke. "Let our wedding never be broken, my beloved." He raised the horn, draining it in one mighty draught. Rather unsteadily, he rose to his feet and put his arm around her, leading her back to their bedchamber.

The Ingling fell asleep before they had finished taking their clothes off. His head drooped back, a snore resonating through his open mouth.

Sigilind waited a few moments, then drew her dress back on, wrapped her shoes about her feet and carefully stole out of the back door. Thanking the gods for the dark moon, she realized belatedly that her pale dress would make her stand out in the night like a raven on snow. Quickly she crept back in and found a cloak to hide herself with before beginning the careful, roundabout way to the shore.

Sigilind had walked, she thought, close to a mile before she came to a good-sized fisher's hut with a boat drawn up on the beach before it. She stared at the multitude of ropes running from the slack sail and the six oars made fast in their locks. Not until she had rounded the smooth hull did she see the small rowing boat in the darkness behind the ship's other side. Without further thought, she sliced the ropes that bound the tiny craft and pushed it out into the water as quickly as she could, straining, slipping and cursing under her breath in the Saxon speech that she had grown away from in the past nine years. When the waves were lapping around her thighs and the boat tugging hard at her grip, she gritted her teeth, crouched down in the water and leapt, scrabbling to keep the boat upright as she flung herself over its side. It tilted alarmingly under her weight, but she managed to get aboard without capsizing it, and, grabbing the oars, began to shove herself determinedly toward Wals' ship. She was panting like a dog after a summertime hunt by the time she had rowed a few minutes, and had to keep shifting her grip and wrapping more of her cloak around her hands against the rough rasp of the oar on her palms, but she kept going, praying grimly to all the gods to bring her safe and unseen to Wals' ship.

At last she could see the black shape looming against the darkness. She did not know how to guide the boat in better than the most general direction, but her luck favored her: no arrows came arching out from the watchmen on shore, and soon the current had carried her to bump gently against the side of Wals' ship.

"Who is there?" a deep, rough voice asked. Sigilind bit her tongue; after nine years, she could still recognize her father's call. His shape loomed over the side of the ship; he had thickened a little, but even his silhouette in the darkness could show her that he had lost none of his drighten's awe.

"It's Sigilind," she hissed back. "Please take me in."

Wals bent down, his huge hands grasping his daughter under the armpits and lifting her up as easily as if she were a child—though she was only a few inches shorter than he now, as tall as most warriors. "What are you doing here, Sigilind?" he asked gently, his face set as if in pain. The faint starlight showed her the claws of age gripping around his eyes and the shadows sunken in his flesh.

Sigilind embraced her father's wide shoulders tightly. "How many ships did you have when you left?"

"There were six others," Wals answered slowly. "One sprang a leak and had to put ashore shortly after we left; the others were parted from us in the storm."

Sigilind lowered her head. "And you were waiting for them to catch up before coming ashore."

Wals nodded. "I'm not such a fool as to walk into the dragon's mound with less strength than I can bring. What's wrong? Have they . . . ?"

"A messenger came this night. They were found wrecked. None of the men lived."

Wals clenched his hands on his daughter's shoulders for a moment, then relaxed, letting her go. "The Norns write wyrd as they will," he murmured. "Go back to your husband, Sigilind. There is nothing else for you here."

"Are you going to give yourself to your enemy like this, when you know

S
T
E
P
H
A
N

G
R
U
N
D
y

☩
9
4

he's set a trap for you? Father, if you must come to Sigigairar's hall, gather your host again and come for victory."

But Wals' age-ravaged face at once seemed younger and stronger, his eyes wide as if he already saw the brightness of the shields shingling Walhall's roof. "As an unborn babe," he murmured softly, "I swore an oath that I would never flee from fire nor iron for the sake of fear, and so I have not; why therefore should I not fulfill it in my old age? Nor will maidens mock my sons for fearing death, for every man must die once, and no man may avoid death when his time is come. No, we shall not turn back, but use our hands as boldly as we may. I have gone into a hundred battles, and at some times I have had greater numbers, at others less, but always the victory was mine, and it shall not be said that I now flee or beg for peace."

Sigilind stood breathless before her father. Then suddenly she was whirled off her feet, grasped and swung in a gasping arch through the air.

"Sigilind!" Sigimund's voice cried joyfully; an octave above, she echoed, "Sigimund!"

The twins embraced, staring into each other's mirror faces in the darkness, still so well-known that only a faint glimmer of starlight was enough to show each every shadow of the other's expression. Sigimund had grown as tall as Wals, an unwashed tangle of fair hair falling down over his broad, powerful shoulders. Except for a large chip out of one front tooth, Sigilind could see no hurt on him from all the battles of which she had heard tell. A pang went through her as she held her twin's body against her, as though her longing for him were a wire harpstring which had sagged for nine years and was now twisted tight, twanging its painful vibration through her whole body. Too close to speak, they hugged for a few moments.

Looking closely at his sister, Sigimund's fierce grin of joy muted as he traced under her eyes with a gentle, calloused fingertip. "You've been crying," he said softly. "Did he hurt you?"

Sigilind shook her head. "Sigigairar has been a good husband to me. But I hoped . . . Oh, Sigimund, I'm so glad to see you, but I hoped you'd never come here." Too exhausted for tears, she laid her head on her brother's muscular chest. She felt Sigimund smoothing her hair, then heard his easy laugh.

"You worry about me too much, 'Linde. With this sword in my hand"—he touched the smooth hex of the ice stone in its hilt—"what does Wals' son have to fear from a Gaut?"

The deep voice thrummed through Sigilind's mind like a rope drawn tight and plucked, as she had heard it nine years ago when the speaker had thrust Sigimund's sword into the Barnstock: "Nor shall any here have more need of it in the time to come." Sigilind straightened her back and forced a smile to her face; need Sigimund might have, but he had been given the sword to meet it.

"If it comes to it," she said softly, but clearly enough so that her father could hear as well, "if the battle goes ill and you—any of you—get away, about two miles into the woods, well to the north of Sigigairar's holding, is a great howe of white stones. Men stay away from it because it was raised over one of the old Herulians before they went south. They were a tribe of rune-masters and shape-shifters, berserk warriors who wore the skins of beasts to fight, or raised the dead to battle beside them when they came on their foes by night—but it's safe enough in the daytime, if you don't stay too long. I'll leave food by it, and whatever else you need that I can get. In the mountains farther along to the north are a lot of caves and such. Sigigairar has trouble with outlaws and trolls every year, but he's never been able to do more than keep the roads clear; there are too many caves and they're too well hidden. A band of men could stay there easily if they had to."

Listening, Wals nodded soberly. "That's good to know, though I think that I myself shall never go there. Go back to your husband now, Sigilind. You've done what you can. Your mother must be proud of you."

Sigilind embraced her father again, then Sigimund lifted her over the side into the rowboat. "Can you get back alone?" he whispered down to her.

"I can," she answered softly, biting off a hiss of pain as she closed her raw palms on the oar shafts. She pushed off from the side of Wals' ship and pulled her cloak's hood up to cover her fair hair again, then let the current carry her silently downshore till she was out of sight of the guards. The waves caught her craft, bearing her in to the beach; when the boat's hull grated against sand, she climbed out and waded ashore, water squishing out through the sides of her shoes as she took the long, roundabout path through the woods to the back of Sigigairar's hall.

Sigilind woke to a dark and empty room, the sounds of battle outside reaching her ears only faintly. Men's shouting, the crashing of metal, were dulled by stone and wood to the roaring of the sea. Quickly she pulled on a woolen shift and ran outside, the dew cold on her feet and fog damp on her bare arms and face. Through the mists, she could make out the shapes of men fighting below in the wheat field, but she could not tell who was who, nor, though she strained her eyes, could she find either her twin or Sigigairar in the mob of struggling warriors.

Clutching her walkurja mother's dagger, Sigilind closed her eyes, willing herself to Sigimund's side. For just a moment it seemed to her that she hovered above the field where rivulets of red blood ran, mixed with dripping fog, down the blade of Sigimund's sword; that his helm tilted on his head, leaving part of his nape bare; that Sigigairar's rangy figure came up behind Sigimund as his blade cut through the mail shirt of the thane in front of him; that she reached down to block Sigigairar's blow rising from behind, but could only turn it upward so that it struck against helm instead of flesh, the ringing steel shock flinging her back to herself with a horrible pain throbbing in the back of her head. She sat down hard on the wet grass, dizzy and shivering; after a few minutes, sick at heart, she crawled back into her chamber, waiting dully for the shouting to die down.

After a while Sigilind heard a horde of footsteps rushing into the hall. She raised her throbbing head as Sigigairar, bearing a torch, came through the door. His byrnie was streaked with blood, but whole; he walked too easily to have taken a body wound, she thought. A wide strip of dirty cloth bound up his sword arm. The clear crystal of Sigimund's sword hilt gleamed above his belt.

"My brother?" she asked. "All my brothers . . . ?"

"They live, for now," Sigigairar replied. "Sigimund was struck on the head; we forced the rest to surrender. Wals fell fighting. I swear to you that he shall have a fit pyre. I would not dishonor the lich of my wife's father—or such a noble hero."

"What will you do with my brothers?"

Sigigairar only looked away, staring at the flame of the torch in his shield hand.

"Please," Sigilind said softly, and he glanced down at her in startlement. "Please don't kill them straightaway. If you will not free them, then bind them in a stocks in the woods and let the gods do as they will, but let no more kin-slaughter curse our house." She paused, gritting her teeth, before she forced the words past the acorn-hard knot in her throat. "I beg of you, do not shed their blood."

"And should I tie them up so that you can free them?" Sigigairar asked sadly. "Or do you want them to suffer more before they die?" He looked at Sigilind, who lay miserably at his feet, then, wincing, touched the wide bandage on his sword arm. "One of them may have crippled me, you know," he murmured, his voice reflective. Sigilind could hear his next words as plainly as if he had spoken them aloud, although his thin lips whitened with holding them back: And you asked after them before thinking of me, although you could see I was wounded.

"Because you ask it," Sigigairar said finally, "I shall; but you must swear not to try to see them or free them. And I shall tell them it was your wish. If, after sitting in the stocks for a few days, they begin to curse you, it is not my fault. Is that really what you want?"

"It is," said Sigilind more firmly, pushing herself to her feet. Deep in her heart, a faint coal of hope began to glow, although she had no idea what she could do.

"Then swear."

"I swear that I shall not try to see my brothers while they sit bound, or free them. Let Wodan hear that I"—and her voice caught, but she finished strongly—"I, Wals' daughter, swear it."

"Good enough," Sigigairar said. "Do you want to ready your father's body for the flames yourself, or shall I have someone else do it? I will not ask you to arrange or sit at tonight's feast, if you do not wish to."

"I will ready both my father's body and the feast. It shall be an arvel-drinking as well, for all those who fell today, and it would hardly be fitting honor for the dead if the frowe of the hall sat sulking in a corner."

"True enough. Get the men to help you with whatever you need. I'm going to my mother's house so she can see to my arm. I bear you no mistrust, but no herbwife in my lands is her match." Sigigairar turned to stalk out, stopped and came back. "Would you help me take my byrnie off?"

Sigilind thrust the butt of his torch into the earthen floor. Sigigairar bent over, his sword arm held out at a stiff angle. Carefully she eased the chain mail over his shoulders, holding its weight up so that he could pull his wounded limb out. He bit his lip and his face went pale as the links caught against the bandage, but he made no sound. "Thank you," he said, draping the link-shirt over his good arm and going out.

Sigilind waited a few heartbeats before she pulled a warm dress over her shift and laced on her shoes. The fog had lifted when she stepped outside again, but the day was still gray and cold. Bodies lay strewn through the wheat field, its green-gold now crushed down in great dark patches as though a giant's hailstones had beaten down the grain. A few of Sigigairar's men were pulling the bodies into a heap, stripping each of their weapons and jewelry, which they separated into two piles: those who had fallen for Si-gigairar's sake would have their goods given back to their families or burned with them as the living chose; what Wals' men had owned would be divided among the victors.

Sigilind stepped gingerly over the corpses, glancing quickly at each. She knew many of Sigigairar's dead: there was fair little Hlewagairar, who had married last year, with a spear half through him; there in his drying blood lay Arnuwulfar, stern and craggy-faced, who had fled a blood feud in Throndheim; there was the stout farmer with a wen over one eyebrow whose name she had never heard, but who always had a bit of honey or one of his wife's cakes for Theudorikijar and Harigastir, with a seax knife buried deeply in his skull between his glazed blue eyes. Among them, bodies twisted together or flung apart, were Wals' thanes. Some were the kinsmen and friends she had grown up with—Hrothwulfar's head, half-severed, dangled over his shoulder; broken stalks of wheat were tangled in Berhtnoth's trampled guts. Others were strange to her.

Wals' corpse was almost hidden by the pile of bodies around him. His broken sword had fallen beside him and over him lay the huge furry body of the old berserk Bernu, his swollen purple head choked almost off by Wals' death grip and his teeth fixed in Wals' throat. Wals' blue eyes were wide open, staring brightly into the clouds.

Looking down at her father's body, walled in by a barrow built of his fallen foes, Sigilind felt some of her grief and anger drain out of her into the bloody ground. Her father would feast in Walhall that night, and her mother would bear him drink; he had died as such a hero ought, and she had no need to dampen his feasting tunic with tears. Drawing herself up to her full height, she gestured to the men who were gathering the dead.

"Hai! Over here!" she shouted, her voice carrying clear over the silent field. "I want your help, now!"

Three of the men—Agilar, Ingwanthewar and Aiwimundur—hurried through the wheat to her. Even in victory, the exhaustion of battling still hung heavy on them.

"This was my father Wals," Sigilind said firmly to them. "My husband has given me leave to ready his body for the pyre as befits the greatest drighten and hero who has yet walked in the Middle-Garth. You, Ingwanthewar and Agilar, free him from his slain; Aiwimundur, fetch me as much water as you can so that I may wash him properly . . . no, go to the ship before someone else empties it and find the best tunic of his size that you can. There is no sark big enough for him in this land."

Ingwanthewar and Agilar bent at once to the task of unlocking Bernu's jaws and prying Wals' hands from the berserk's throat. Aiwimundur lingered a moment, his rain-gray eyes gazing straight across at Sigilind. A look of sorrow shadowed the middle-aged thane's plain, wide-boned face like a stirring of sand through clear water. "Frowe, do you know what our drighten has ordered for your brothers?"

"I know."

"I will not flout the drighten's will," he said softly, "but if I can do anything else to ease your sorrow, I shall." Aiwimundur paused. "My brother was killed by his wife's family. I avenged him—but I have never forgotten. I would not have the beer of our hall brewed with that bitterness."

Aiwimundur's eyes searched Sigilind's for a moment. When she did not answer, he coughed deep in his throat and started down to the shore where men were already unloading bundles of goods from Wals' ship to the dock.

THE WARG

Sigimund woke up to the stink of vomit rising from his own clothes, his head aching abominably. He was sitting up, dizziness blurring his eyes. How did I get so drunk? he thought as he retched emptily. Then his memory drifted back on heavy wings: fighting through Sigigairar's wheat field, a blow crashing down on the back of his helmet. Carefully Sigimund moved his head to look down, feeling as though his brains were sloshing about inside his skull. An empty scabbard hung at his side, and his hands were bound behind him. His feet were locked into a low stocks that ran the length of the clearing: a split log with leg holes bored in it, the two halves bound together by wrist-thick rivets of iron and the whole anchored in the earth by thicker bonds yet. Sigimund and his nine brothers sat on another log behind it, roughly ranged from eldest to youngest. Sigimund knew that he must have been unconscious for at least a day, for the stocks could not have been swiftly built, but they looked as though they could have been made for no purpose but to bind the sons of Wals: sticky sap bled from the split log that gripped his lower legs and the file marks were bright on the iron rivets, no rust marring the metal yet. Sigimund groaned softly. Nasal laughter sounded behind him.

"Are you awake, Sigimund?" Sigigairar asked, walking around in front of the row of stocks. "Good. We have a saying here in the Northlands: a thrall takes his revenge at once; a coward never. I've had to wait—but do I have a fit revenge now for the insults you and your father gave me at my marriage?" He touched the hilt of Sigimund's sword, which hung at his belt. Sigimund felt some satisfaction at seeing the heavy bandage and stiff movement of Sigigairar's sword arm.

"There are still Walsings living," Sigimund answered. Though the words choked in his swollen throat, they were clear enough.

"You may thank your sister for that; she begged me not to shed your blood myself. She asked that you be tied here in the forest, and it is her wish that will keep you here in the rain and the cold and your own dung, helpless before whatever walks in the wild. Do you thank her for making your death a hard one in captivity, rather than a quick one at the end of a sword?" Sigigairar smiled viciously, the lines of his grin slashing through his thin cheeks like merry sword cuts.

"You're lying!" Alfwald shouted from the other end of the stocks. "Sigilind would never do that!"

Sigigairar's sharp, twisted face suddenly uncreased into soberness. "I swear before all the gods that I would have slain you had she not begged me otherwise. If you feel betrayed by this, know that it was Sigilind who chose it for you." He grinned at them again in mockery, then turned on his heel and strode away. The Walsings watched him go, glancing sideways at each other.

"Sigilind wouldn't have," Alfwald said, more softly. "Would she?"

"She's been gone a long time," said Wihtric, shifting uncomfortably on the log. "She may have meant it as a kindness."

"Or she's planning to come and set us free," Wulfger suggested. "Surely a Walsing wouldn't stand by while her brothers died."

Sigimund only leaned forward as far as he could, resting his pounding forehead on his knees. For some reason that he could not put words to, he felt less sure than his brothers, who discussed how Sigilind would surely come for them and how they would burn down Sigigairar's hall and avenge Wals in tones of excited fury. He told himself it was only the blow to his head and the loss of his sword; he could not be faulted for losing a little of his brave mood. Sigilind must have planned—but Sigigairar was no fool and must be keeping a close guard on her. What could she do, if she were also held prisoner? Had an impulsive hope of freeing her brothers turned awry in her hands? Waves of dizziness were beginning to wash over Sigimund again. He breathed deeply, closing his eyes, and sank into a sick and fitful sleep, half-wakened every now and then by shooting cramps in his back and neck as the light of the sky slowly darkened.

It was full dark when he jerked upright, fully awake at once. At first he could see no danger; then, from the far end of the stocks, he heard a low, eerie snarling that raised the hairs along his spine and head. Sitting up to his full height and stretching to see over his brothers, he saw a gray shape creeping—almost floating—between the trees. The huge gaunt wolf growled again, an unnaturally resonant sound that seemed to vibrate through Sigimund's whole body. He tensed his muscles, pushing against the stocks and twisting his bonds with all his might; his brothers realized what he was doing and added their strength to his own, but the two planks of oak were set too deep and solid, hammered somehow into the rock beneath, so that the strength of all Wals' sons together could do no more than shake it.

The warg glided closer to the stocks, its feet hidden in the low, eddying mist that veiled the ground. It turned its head to Sigimund, tongue lolling and teeth showing. For a moment, it almost seemed to Sigimund—dizzy and sick again from his struggles—that he could see through it as if it were only a ghost shaped of cloud. Then it crouched down into the mist and sprang up again, straight at Alfwald's throat.

His last word, "Sig—," choked on blood as the wolf snarled and began to feed. Sigimund howled in anger, thrashing against the stocks that held him; Berhtwini struggled and cursed, and the rest of them shouted and shook as if they could frighten the wolf away; but it only growled softly in its throat as, fearfully solid now to Sigimund's blurred sight, it gnawed at the body of his youngest brother.

When the warg had had enough it stood and loped away into the thickening mist, leaving the Walsings cursing and weeping behind it. Alfwald's chewed bones and rags of bloody flesh had, mercifully, toppled from the log; in the faint light of the new moon, Sigimund could only see the shadows of his feet in the stocks, whole as if he still sat there.

"It ate . . ." Alfarik's voice muttered, soft and sickened. "I can't . . . " He turned his head away from what lay next to him.

"He called out for Sigilind," Orngrim said, his words ringing bitterly hard through the darkness. "If she was planning to save us, she ran off course."

"All we heard was 'Sig,'" Wynberht pointed out in an unnaturally calm tone, his voice thick as though his tongue had gone numb. " 'Victory.' We don't know what he meant. We can't know. He never finished. Don't say things like that."

The Walsings sat without speaking for a long while. As the sky started to pale, a cold wind curled around them from the north, wafting the smell of blood to gag in Sigimund's throat. His back, neck and shoulders hurt miserably; his feet had gone numb with cold and wriggling his toes hardly helped. His bladder felt horribly swollen as well. Sigimund could smell the sharp spoor of piss and the heavier foulness of shit through the reeking blood. It did not matter which of his brothers had soiled himself; they would all have to, sooner or later. He concentrated on clearing his mind of the humiliation of fouling his breeches like a swaddled child. I am Wals' son, he thought to himself. Only cowardice or my own failure can shame me. Though I piss in my trousers now, I will live to take my sword back and piss on Sigigairar's grave. I piss on Sigigairar's land and his wretched head. Let this be his shame, not mine. For all his thoughts, Sigimund could feel his face heating as the warmth puddled down his leg and under his buttocks; but he was grateful for the acrid smell that rose around him, masking the scent of blood and meat in the clearing.

Oddwig laughed harshly, a short sharp bark. "My breeches're done for too. Shit, and I left my other pair back on the ship. I knew I should have packed more clothes for coming to be a Gaut's guest."

"It's all right," Berhtwini said. "No one up here will notice a few stains on your breeches. They'll just think you're a Gaut coming back from battle."

"Hai! Get away from there!" Orngrim shouted suddenly, half-rising from the stocks. Sigimund saw the snakelike wiggle of a weasel's back disappearing through the grass, the little beast dragging a piece of meat in its mouth. Sigimund wanted to rise and shout outrage with his brother, but he knew it would do no good. Most animals would not be frightened off from their feasting so easily; the Walsings would be lucky if nothing larger than a weasel followed the scent of blood to the shreds of Alfwald's body.

The flies were already buzzing around, clustering on the torn flesh like black clots of blood and hastening to the scent of the waste in the Walsings' breeches. Sigimund tried to keep his bound hands moving, to chase the swarm away from his back and buttocks. The movement chafed the rope against his skin, scraping forth blood to draw more and more flies, and sent terrible pains shooting up his arms and through his shoulders, so that he had to give it up at last. He could blink and shake his head to keep them away from his eyes and out of his nose; now and again he twitched as a bull would to shake the flies away, but he could do no more.

The sun was high when a man came into the clearing, bearing a large wooden bowl and two pitchers. He held his plain wide face blank and vague, his eyes averted. Crouching down, he began carefully to feed the Walsings, one after another, and give them water. The bowl held oatmeal mixed with dried fish, cold and salty, but filling; the man got up to refill the pitchers from a nearby stream several times. He would not speak to them until they were all fed; then he said only, "Sigilind sent me," and walked away.

"She hasn't forgotten us," said Sigimund, grateful for the break in thought that took his mind away from the flies buzzing about his bloodied wrists and the line of ants filing up his leg.

"Why didn't he free us, then?" Wynberht wondered, his freckled brow wrinkling. He shook back his dirty thatch of fair hair and looked up the row to Sigimund, then down to Alfarik who sat, pale and silent, as far from the end of the log as he could.

"Sigigairar may have guards around," suggested Alfger. "He may—"

"Then what hope is there for us?" asked Alfarik quietly.

"To die like Walsings," Wynberht answered, then started to chant softly:

If our wyrd is crueler, let our courage be keener
harder be hearts   and higher be souls
unweakened by fear   though with horror fraught
then shall Wals' sons   all worthy be named.

He stopped, brown eyes darting back and forth and plump cheeks reddening with sudden embarrassment.

"I never knew you had any word-craft, Wynberht," Berhtwini said.

"I never had any songs worth speaking aloud," Wynberht replied. "I believe being bound has loosed my wits." He smiled ruefully.

"When we get back home, we'll tie you up every night if that's what it takes to make you sing," Alfger threatened, smiling broken-toothedly across Oddwig and Orngrim at the newly revealed skop. "How did that go again? 'If our wyrd is crueler . . . '?"

" 'Let our courage be keener,' " Wynberht supplied. By the third time round, the Walsings chanted it together, the ragged chorus of their voices rising above the flies buzzing at the end of the log.

The man came to them again at sunset with more food and water. To all their questions—"Where is our sister?" "Are we guarded?" "Is Sigilind able to come herself?"—he turned only a blank expression, till Sigimund began to wonder if he was actually simple-minded or if indeed there were guards hidden within earshot. He did not wrinkle his nose at the rank aroma that hung around the stocks or turn his face away from their smell as he bent down to feed each of the Walsings; even when he came to Alfarik, he showed no disgust at what lay beside Wals' youngest living son, less than Alfarik himself who could only choke down a couple of mouthfuls before biting his gorge down and shaking his head violently.

One by one, the Walsings began to drop into the cramped half-sleep that was all their bonds would allow, shifting restlessly to ease the chafing of the ropes at their raw wrists and shivering in the growing cold as the wind began to blow feathers of cloud across the darkening sky. Sigimund awoke in darkness to spatters of rain—awoke anxious, aware of an eerie stillness under the rustling of the wind and pattering of the raindrops. He peered around, but could see nothing . . . nothing, till a patch of blackness faded to ghostly gray and the wolf's snarl froze his breath in his throat.

Alfarik, suddenly roused, leapt forward. The stocks on his ankles stopped him hard; Sigimund heard the cracking of bone a second before the wolf was upon the youngest living Walsing. Wals' sons sat shocked still until Wynberht's cracked voice rose above the wolf's low snufflings in their brother's body to break the horror that bound them. Once again, he chanted his song,

If our wyrd is crueler   let our courage be keener . . .

and the rest of them joined in gladly to drown out the sounds of the beast,

harder be hearts   and higher be souls,
unweakened by fear   though with horror fraught,
then shall Wals' sons   all worthy be named.

As the Walsings called out their father's name, the wolf whirled, leaping into the air in a long arc that ended in Wynberht's throat. The stocks rocked as it struck; Wynberht's head bounced back from a bloody torrent, hanging from his neck by a thin tatter of flesh and broken bone. The wolf turned on the log, eating its way through Wihtric's guts back to Alfarik's corpse, taking a few bites before it whirled and leapt over the dead to Orngrim, its mighty jaws cracking through his skull.

Those Walsings who were still living shouted Wynberht's song louder and more defiantly as the wolf's wod grew. Sigimund felt no fear as he stared at the blood and froth dripping from its mouth; only a fierce hot gladness that they had been able to mark its heart, if not its body, before they died. It was upon Oddwig now, chewing through his belly to tear out his living lungs: a painful death, but a swift end to the dull agony that racked the Walsings' bound bodies and the festering of the sores on their limbs and buttocks. Together, as we lived, Sigimund thought as the wolf turned on Alfger and the warriors began the verse again; but the beast paused with the strings of Alfger's rent throat dangling bloody from its muzzle. It shook its shaggy coat, spattering a fine warm spray over Wulfger, Berhtwini and Sigimund, and trotted back into the woods, wet grass swishing against its legs. The rain was coming down hard now, a chill, clean shower washing down the hot coppery scent of fresh blood and sluicing away the worst of the stench that hung about the log.

The rain fell until late the next day; neither able to sleep nor wake, Wals' sons sat in their bonds, rousing only when Sigilind's man—if such he was— came to feed them. Wulfger muttered darkly in his half-doze, his pale cheeks flushed with fever. Looking behind their backs, Sigimund could see the wide pink streaks beginning to darken up his brothers' arms from the pus-rotten flesh swelling around their bonds. Although the fever was beginning to blur his own sight, he thought he could see the first twitchings of maggots beneath the shiny black meat flies gathered about the oozing wounds, and he turned his face away swiftly. The burning sickness in his body might yet cheat the wolf, he thought.

Toward evening the wind began to grow stronger, sweeping the breaking clouds into long trails across the reddening sky. Painfully Sigimund leaned his head back, watching two ravens tilt their wings against the wind, one spiraling downward and one circling ahead. The raven landed on Alfger's body, digging its talons into his gaping throat and twisting its head downward to get at his eyes. It lifted its beak up, gulping.

Wulfger's fever-glazed gaze was fixed on something he seemed to see across the clearing; he did not appear to mark the raven beside him, but Berhtwini grunted harshly, twisting his body against the stocks as if he could move the logs to shake the bird off. Sigimund added his own strength, but the log bit deep into the festering sores on his buttocks as he scraped against it, and the two of them soon had to stop.

The raven cocked its head, looking Sigimund in the eye, and uttered a single resonant croak before going back to its meal.

"If my hands were free, bird, I'd send you to Wodan faster than you can wing by yourself, and you could bear my greetings to my kin in Walhall then," Sigimund told it. The raven lifted its beak from Alfger's empty eye-socket and gulped again, then raised its feet and walked slowly across Wulfger's body. He hardly twitched beneath its claws. Berhtwini began to thrash about as soon as it neared him, but he could not shake the raven off. Fresh blood welled from beneath its talons as it made its way from him to Sigimund.

Sigimund let his head slump down for a moment, then flung it up and, as loudly as he could, shouted "Go away!" in the raven's face. It stumbled, digging its claws more deeply into Berhtwini's shoulder. Sigimund leaned over, closing his eyes as he swung his head, and tried to butt it away. He felt the beating of strong wings about his head, then the raven's grip biting deep into his own shoulder where his shakings and twistings could not dislodge it.

At last the raven's beak moved toward Sigimund's eyes. He closed them as tightly as he could, turning his head away from the bird. Its feathers were cool and smooth against his face as it reached over; he felt the hard horn tip of its beak against his right eyelid for a moment. Then the wings beat against his head again; the claws unclenched from his flesh and the bird's weight lifted from his shoulder.

Sigimund looked up. The raven was winging to join its mate who circled above. He looked down again. It had been no dream: the blood was still flowing from his shoulder and darkening Berhtwini's tunic along the raven's path.

Although Sigimund and Berhtwini shouted Wynberht's song till their voices failed them, the wolf took only Wulfger that night, and he was so ill that he hardly twitched beneath its teeth. Then only the two of them were left on the log, the remains of their brothers spread out beside them under a crawling black carpet of flies.

Night blurred into day, the swirling of time marked only by the water Sigilind's man poured down Sigimund's throat and, when his croaking voice asked for it, over his head to ease the burning inside him. Then a woman's strong, slender hand was stroking Sigimund's brow, coolness stilling the heat of his fever—or was her touch warming him as he shivered in the cold wind?

His foggy eyes tried to focus on her, but could see only the gleam of wheat gold hair, pale skin and the bright sky-light of her eyes like a blue lantern through the mist of his sight. "Sigilind?" he asked, and then, "Mother?"

"Be true," a high ringing voice murmured in his ears. "Keep your heart high and have no fear; there are still Walsings living."

"But what can I do?" he cried out desperately.

The sound of his own shout jerked Sigimund awake with a start; he stared around wildly, but saw nothing except his brother Berhtwini beside him, the rustling oak leaves stained with the first tinge of brown above and the stained grass below.

Berhtwini raised his head wearily to stare at his brother. The flesh had fallen away from his sharp cheekbones and his skin had gone as white as death beneath the old purple scars of the fever, so that his eyes seemed to stare from a pock-marked skull already. "I don't know," he said, his voice a grating whisper; then, "Sigimund, how did we end up here? Everything was going so well at home when we left. We had all those ships, we could never have lost a fight with Sigigairar if he had dared to start one . . . how could three nights of bad wind have destroyed everything Wals built? They say Wodan was the father of our line and he's always stood by us, but where is he now?"

"They also say Wodan betrays his chosen at the last," Sigimund answered slowly. "He gave Wals enough victories; it was only fair that he took him in battle, rather than letting him become a useless old man."

"But what about us? What about our brothers? This is no way for a man to die, tied up and be . . . betrayed by our . . . "

"Betrayed by our sister's husband," Sigimund rasped as firmly as he could, trying desperately to believe it. He coughed several times and spat out a gobbet of green phlegm. "If this is our wyrd, then so it is, but we're not dead yet. I don't mean to give up while there are Walsings living." Shifting his weight, he bit back a moan as the fouled wood scraped against the sores festering on his buttocks.

Berhtwini looked at him for a moment, half-accusing, half-questioning; then his head drooped down again and his eyes shut. Sigimund stared sadly at his last brother, wishing that he, like Wynberht, had some gift of words that he could use to strengthen Berhtwini's heart in his last hours.

"I love you, my brother," he said finally. "If we are not freed while we live, we shall feast together in Walhall before two nights have passed; nor, I think, will men soon forget what befell the sons of Wals."

"But who is there to remember?" Berhtwini asked, a faint tinge of hope brightening his voice.

"Sigilind will remember, and tell her sons that no men ever met a crueler fate with greater courage than her brothers; and they may in time grow to avenge us."

"On their own father?"

"If they have any of Sigilind's soul in them, they will turn away from the traitor and reclaim the line of Wals from death. And who should be closer to us than our sister's sons?"

A ghost of a smile came to Berhtwini's lips. "Then, if there is hope that we may be avenged, Wodan has not wholly betrayed us after all." He shivered, his body racked with a coughing spasm. "I think I shall find the warg more welcome than a slow death by fever, anyway. Now let me sleep so that I can meet it with all my strength."

Sigimund nodded, exhausted, and sank back into his own daze.

That night, both Sigimund and Berhtwini sat for a long time peering into the darkness before the warg appeared. For a second it seemed to be only a whirl of smoke or mist; to Sigimund, it looked for a second as if it were actually shaping itself out of a nebulous patch of darkness. It was the size of a small horse now, glowing faintly through the darkness with a power that pressed him backward on the log as it neared.

"There are still Walsings living!" Berhtwini shouted out. Then the warg's cold swept over Sigimund as it attacked his brother; it had no animal's scent, but only a faint musty odor of dried herbs and smoke. Drops of hot blood, already cooling, spattered Sigimund's fevered face. He could not look at what it was doing to his brother, but he could not turn his glance from the beast—the she-beast, whose eight wrinkled dugs drooped from her flesh-swollen belly, shaking as she snuffled and dug with muzzle and claws in Berhtwini's limp body.

When the warg was done, she turned her bloodied muzzle to Sigimund, laughing silently. Through her cruel, narrow grin, it seemed to him that he could almost see the vicious face of an old woman mocking him. Then she turned and loped away, melting, in his blurred vision, to a patch of fog before fading into the night. Alone, with no one to see him, two fever-hot tears burned their way down from Sigimund's eyes, drying quickly to crusted salt on his warm-flushed cheeks.

The man came to feed him early in the morning. Sigimund's throat was swollen and it was hard for him to speak, but between one mouthful and the next, he managed to choke out, "It wasn't a wolf."

The man stopped, his gray eyes meeting Sigimund's glance squarely for the first time. "What did you say?" he demanded. Not simple, Sigimund thought vaguely.

"It was . . . I don't know. A thing. A shapechanger. Female. No real wolf would . . . "

The man looked down the fly-covered, crawling length of the log, from Berhtwini's freshly torn remains to Alfwald's yellowing bones. Thoughtfulness drew his thick brown brows together, a keen gaze lightening his eyes.

"Old, or young?" he asked.

"It was old. It . . . it laughed at me."

"I will tell Sigilind. As yet she knows nothing," he added. "I had thought I might spare her your pain." He walked away quickly before Sigimund could say anything more.

It was full dark when Sigilind's man came back, not long before midnight. He walked quickly and lightly, glancing about himself. Though he carried a stabbing spear in one hand, the sword at his belt proved him to be not the thrall Sigimund had thought but a thane of high rank, and his cloak was fastened with a brooch of smoothly Roman-worked silver. In his shield hand he held a small pot.

"Sit still," Sigilind's man ordered sharply. "I am going to cover your face with this honey, and fill your mouth with it. You must be careful not to swallow, but to hold it till the warg is done with you—or you with her. This is the rede which your sister gave me to give to you."

He pulled Sigimund's filthy hair back and tied it with a leather thong, then reached into the pot and brought out a dripping handful of honey, which he smeared over Sigimund's face, drops trickling down to stick the Walsing's eyes together and gum up his beard. Obediently Sigimund opened his mouth for the next glob; its sweetness sent an aching pang through his teeth and his throat convulsed in an involuntary swallow. Sigilind's man poured honey into him until it flowed over his lips and into his beard.

"Farewell," he said. "My name is Aiwimundur. If you get out of this remember that, though I am true to Sigigairar, I would not aid in this foul trollcraft."

Sigimund nodded his sticky head uncomfortably, concentrating on blocking his throat with his tongue and ignoring the sweet drool on his chin, snuffling through his nose.

His eyes clogged by honey, Sigimund could not see the she-warg when she strode into the clearing, but the sudden eerie stillness and the cold prickling over his body warned him that she was there. Sigimund tensed, waiting for her teeth. Her leathery pads whispered through the grass to him; he felt the dizzying tingle of her weird might around him, then the soft rasp of her tongue caressed his face warmly as she began to lick the honey from him.

Sigimund waited patiently, though his heart was beating wild with sudden hope. He did not dare to open his eyes for fear that she would see his thoughts.

The gigantic she-wolf cleaned his forehead and worked down one cheek, then the other, giving his beard a few licks up to his mouth. Eagerly she thrust her muzzle into his face and her tongue all the way into his mouth to eat the honey within.

All Sigimund's fury and frustration, compounded by this final humiliation, burst forth in him at once. He pushed his head forward and, before the she-warg could pull away, clamped his teeth into the root of her tongue. Her hot, salty blood welled up, mixing with the honey still in his mouth; fiercely he swallowed again and again, feeling the fire of her unnatural strength burning through his veins. She whined horribly, trying to tear herself from the grip of his jaws, but he held on, fighting against her as she flung him back and forth on the log, shaking the stocks about till the wood began to creak and crack around the shredded flesh of Sigimund's ankles.

As the huge wolf's struggles grew more furious, Sigimund bit more deeply. Then a river of blood gushed forth into his mouth; involuntarily he swallowed something thick and slippery. The she-warg, freed, fled, her howl of agony bubbling with dark blood.

Sigimund's head was light and dizzy, but he felt eerily strong. He realized that he was standing; that the stock was turned on its side, the nails that had anchored it shut against the struggles of Wals' sons bent and half-broken from the wood. Though he could see blood running freely from his ankles, he felt no pain; kicking and stamping, he was free in a few moments. He bent and twisted, forcing the arc of his bound arms over his numb hips and buttocks. Sitting with his back to the log, he doubled up his legs and brought his wrists over his heels, then lowered his head and began to chew at the ropes, spitting every so often from the foul taste of the pus that had soaked into them. When the last strands had parted, Sigimund began to limp north, away from the clearing where the bones and flesh of his brothers lay so scattered that no one could have told which of them was which. The unnatural strength that had filled him was beginning to drain out again, the deepest aches in his wrists and ankles chafing once more as if he still wore his bonds. Every one of his muscles moaned with low voices of pain which rose steadily as he staggered from tree to tree; fever fogged his sight till he could not tell whether the dawn had begun to lighten or not and strange voices seemed to call to him from the side of the path. Only a faint vision of a white mound before him kept him going, until at last he stumbled against its stones and fell to his knees.

Crawling around, fumbling at its walls, Sigimund saw that some of the stones had tumbled from the mound, leaving a narrow passageway. Forcing his wide shoulders through—moaning as a new series of vicious cramps stabbed through his abused back—he pulled himself inside the howe, into the open chamber of quiet darkness.

REVENGE'S BEGINNING

Curled against the warmth of Sigigairar's bony back, Sigilind lay awake most of the night, staring into the darkness. *What have I done to my brothers?* she asked herself over and over. Aiwimundur had told her only that they fared well—until that morn. Now—even now—she thought, Sigimund might be waiting for the warg to come, or fighting with it, or have already died, or slain his foe.

When she finally fell asleep, she jerked awake almost at once, the taste of blood hot and sweet in her mouth, trembling with a fierce fury. She thought she heard something howling in the distance; then, only a minute later, a soft moan sounded nearby, but she did not go to the door. No matter how wounded, Sigimund would not come back to Sigigairar's hall.

Suddenly Sigilind heard a horrible scratching at the door, a raucous noise that scraped shudderingly against her eardrums. She put her hands to her ears, looking in disbelief at the dark shape of her husband whose soft breathing was undisturbed by the noise. She lifted the blanket and rolled away without disturbing Sigigairar, getting her dagger from the belt that hung over her chest of clothes and creeping softly to the door, ready to meet whatever might be trying to come in. She waited a long time after the scratching had stopped before she resheathed the knife and went back to bed.

The first light was beginning to creep through the door from the great hall where it shone through the smokehole when Sigilind pushed the woolen blankets away and wrapped her shoes on. Rubbing her eyes blearily, she stepped out of the back door.

She tripped over something cold and hard; only a vague memory of practicing fights with her brothers turned her sprawling fall into an agile roll. Sitting up and rubbing her shoulder, Sigilind drew in her breath to scream as she saw what lay before the door of her chamber, then let it out in a long slow gust of quiet triumph.

Kara's withered corpse lay on the grass, dried blood caked down from the black hole of her tongueless mouth and gray hair frizzed in a wild mane around her skull. One hand was raised in a claw; deep, ragged gouges, pale against the dark wood, showed where, with her last strength, she had tried to scratch through the door. A strange shift, woven of coarse gray-white hairs, had fallen down about her waist, leaving her shoulders and wrinkled dugs bare. Her body seemed oddly shrunken within her loose skin, as though she had grown grossly and then starved to death.

Sigilind heard footsteps through the grass behind her. Standing and turning, she found herself face to face with Aiwimundur. The middle-aged thane's eyes were veined with a fine tracery of blood, the wrinkles around them as clear as etchings on silver in the growing morning light.

"Sigimund is gone," he whispered to her. "Nor, I think, between . . . the warg and the struggle last night will the drighten be able to tell that one of the Walsings escaped by piecing bones together."

"What shall we do with this?" she asked him, gesturing at Kara's body.

Aiwimundur shook his round head. "We will take her to her house and lay her out as befits the mother of our drighten. Her trollcraft was enough of a shame; let no one but ourselves know that she died of it." He bent to pick Kara's corpse up, but she was too heavy for him to move her from the ground. Sigilind crouched down beside him. Together they heaved and pushed, moving her a couple of inches before their strength failed them.

"This is an ill sign," Aiwimundur said heavily. "If she's not laid properly, she'll be sure to walk again. Do you know any ways of dealing with such things?" Sigilind shook her head. "I didn't think so. You rouse Sigigairar and get him out to watch her. I don't think there's danger in daylight, but I've heard it's not good to leave them alone, and kin may quiet her ghost. I'm going to Hlewagastir's lands to fetch his spae-woman Freyjadis. We should be back around midday."

Sigilind stepped back into the hall, leaving the door open. Sigigairar had turned in his sleep, his long arm sprawled out over the hollow in the blankets where Sigilind had nestled. She took him by the shoulder and shook him, not gently.

"Sigigairar," she called. "Wake up, Sigigairar."

His eyes opened slowly, blinking as he searched for her. "What is it?" he said in a voice softened by sleep.

"You have to get up, Sigigairar. Your mother . . . "

Sigigairar was out of bed in an instant, bony knees catching in his night garment as he strode to the door. Sigilind heard his sickened gasp of breath, then his awful cry, "Mother! Who has done this to you?"

Sigilind hurried up beside him, fright cold in her veins. A fresh drop of blood welled from Kara's crusted mouth as she neared, plopping silently onto the earth; but though the old woman's ghost might still lurk within the rigid lich, her tongue was gone: she would accuse no one, nor would she betray Sigimund's life.

"See how her shift is torn and stained, and the mud on her feet," Sigilind said. "She must have been walking in the woods last night."

Sigigairar bent, as Aiwimundur had, to lift the corpse; and, like Aiwimundur, was unable to move her, though he strained till the hard edges of his muscles seemed ready to break through his freckled skin. He lifted his eyes, shadowed with wild horror, to stare at his wife. "What sort of trollcraft did this?" he asked.

"Aiwimundur has gone to fetch a spae-woman, so we can lay her to rest," answered Sigilind.

"Rest. Yes." He jerked his narrow head about like a frightened bird. "You cover her up and sit with her. There's something I have to . . . "

Sigigairar ran back into their chamber; Sigilind could hear the sounds of him dressing hastily. She pulled the old woman's coarse shift up over her withered breasts and the loose white skin of her shoulders, trying to move her to a more seemly position. The corpse would not be budged; Sigilind might as well have been trying to arrange the limbs of a stone carving. When she finally rocked back on her heels, her hands were as cold as if she had been dabbling in icy water.

Sigigairar, his red tunic on askew and Sigimund's sword dangling from his belt, ran from the hall and out into the woods, hardly glancing at his wife. Sigilind waited, her face down to hide her faint smile. When Sigigairar returned, his mouth was set in a grimace of grim satisfaction. "They're all dead. They must have been for a few days," he said to Sigilind.

"How?" she asked, her voice trembling. She hoped he would think the quaver was one of shock and grief.

"A bear, I think. The stocks was broken. I didn't stay to look more closely." Sigilind flinched, breathing an inward sigh of relief. "I'll have someone gather the bodies for burning," Sigigairar went on. "You don't want to see them. You'll have enough to do as it is."

"Mama, Mama," Harigastir's clear voice rang out. The short, square-built thrall-woman Helche had Sigigairar's elder son firmly by the hand, but Harigastir had managed to squirm away from her and came running ahead of his brother. "Mama, guess what I did this morning. You'll never—" He stopped short, looking up at his parents then down to the ground, taking in the situation at a glance. "Grandmama!" he wailed piercingly, throwing himself on the grass beside Kara's corpse. He hugged her as if trying to shake her awake. In a second Theudorikijar, too, had broken Helche's grip and came running to Kara's side, streams of tears flooding down his face.

"What happened to Grandmama?" Theudorikijar asked piteously, turning his gaze to Sigigairar, who in turn looked helplessly at Sigilind.

"Your grandmother is dead," said Sigilind calmly. "It may have been a troll or an outlaw who killed her."

"We loved her more than anybody," Harigastir snuffled.

Helche came panting up, shaking her head, her short-cropped blond hair fraying out around her jowly face. "Lady, I tried to hold them, but they're getting too strong for me. Dear gods, shall I take them away from this? They're too young . . ."

"They've seen dead bodies before," stated Sigilind. She looked at her sons, coldly judging them for the first time. Strong and healthy, yes; but were these sniveling children truly of Wals' heroic line? Still, time and testing might prove them to be of better metal than they seemed now, as they would have to be to avenge Wals and his sons on their father.

"But this is different," Sigigairar protested, reaching down as if he would shield his sons from the sight of their dead grandmother—or from her glazed, baleful glare.

"How?"

Sigigairar looked at Kara's corpse, opened his mouth as if to speak, then shut it again.

"Good lady, he's right," Helche insisted. "There's some trollcraft here, and it's not good for children to be touched by such things."

"They can't hide behind my skirts forever," said Sigilind. "Let them see what they can. And bear it like men," she added loudly, trying to catch her sons' attention. Their howls sank to soft murmurs as they stared at their grandmother's ravaged mouth and stiffly upraised claw. Harigastir wiped a bubble from his nose with the embroidered sleeve of his blue tunic.

"Don't do that," Helche said by habit, slapping the boy lightly on his wet cheek. Harigastir spared her a quick glare before he grasped Kara's crooked hand in his own small fingers and gingerly tried to straighten it out.

"That will be enough!" Sigigairar snapped. "Helche, get these children away from here and make sure they don't have a chance to talk to anyone about this. Sigilind, send Gunthormar here; he'll have to muster some men to set a watch around the hall until this has been dealt with. Then you'll start making the hall ready for my mother's arvel. I mean to hold the funeral drinking tonight, so that she'll have no cause to doubt that she has the honor she deserves from my folk. Now, one of you bring a blanket to cover her with. I won't have her seen like this."

"You won't keep the Sun's light from her, will you?" Helche quavered. "Surely the full light of day is best in such matters."

Sigilind could see the water swelling in her husband's eyes, but Sigigairar's voice was quite firm as he said, "I shall sit with my mother as long as is needful, then. All that she did when she lived was for my sake, and now that she is dead I have no fear of her hate, nor have my folk any reason to fear her while I am here. Get the blanket and take my children away; they should not see this."

Helche would come no closer to Kara's body. Sigilind had to disentangle Harigastir's hand from his grandmother's and lift both boys to their feet so that Helche could lead them into the hall, then she hurried down the hill to Gunthormar's house.

The blue woolen blanket from their bed lay over Kara's body when Sigilind came up to the hall again. She could not help shuddering at the thought that she might lie under it again, but said nothing; it would be simple enough to put it with the grave goods for burning. Sigilind went into the hall, where Helche was trying vainly to quiet the boys.

"Go to the storehouses and start readying linen and goods for her," Sigilind ordered the thrall. "I'll take care of them for the moment."

As Helche went away, Sigilind took each of her children by the hand. There was good strength in their grips; it heartened her to feel it. She squatted down, looking first into Theudorikijar's eyes, then into Harigastir's. She could not feel the answering spark that had met her from Sigimund's eyes or her father's. It seemed to her that the Walsing blood must be slumbering in them like a snake in winter, waiting for the need that would kindle the fire out of their still souls, and it was her task to awaken it so they would be strong enough for the vengeance that must be done—even vengeance against their own father: that would call for stern souls and hard hearts indeed, and a courage that feared no curse. Harsh as it must be, her frost would not wither young Walsings, but ripen them.

And if the true metal is not in them? Sigilind thought. But it must be: they are my sons, and if they are not, they are only the strength of Sigigairar's line, and shall become foe in their hearts to us in time. But that cannot be! she added fiercely to herself.

"You see," Sigilind said softly to her children, as she led them toward the woods, "the Nine Worlds are full of dangerous and horrible things, and you have to be strong enough to fight them—as you will be. Your great-great-grandfather, Sigibercht, was the son of the god Wodan, and because he killed another man's thrall he had to live like a wolf in the woods, among the wild beasts and ghosts and trolls that dwell in the forest, but he won all his fights and gathered men together so he could win himself a realm to rule . . . " She went on, telling them the story of Sigibercht's death and Rerir's revenge, of Wals' birth and the things that had happened when she married Sigigairar. The children walked quietly on the forest path beside her, listening, she hoped, though their gazes flickered over tree and stone and bush, drawn by every fluttering moth or mouse's rustle. "And so Sigigairar invited your grandfather to a feast; and when he finally came—when all the fighting was—Sigigairar gathered his men together and treacherously killed Wals and all his thanes, except for his ten sons—my brothers."

"Mama, what smells so bad?" Harigastir asked.

"There's something dead nearby," Theudorikijar answered him. "Something big, I bet, like a bear."

"There's not any bears in this part of the woods, is there?" Harigastir questioned Sigilind, clinging a little closer.

"Whether there are or not, you will not be frightened, because you are of the line of Sigibercht and Rerir and Wals, and you will grow up to kill bears if you please," Sigilind told him sternly, levering him away from her skirts. She sniffed the air, wrinkling her nose at the stench and steeling herself for what she knew she would soon see. "Now, my sons, you must be very strong, because I am going to show you something horrible. You must face this because, when you are grown to be warriors, you will not only see but make your share of dead, and you will risk your own deaths whenever you go into battle, so you must learn to know it and not to fear it."

Pale, her sons stared up at her, one clinging to each hand as she led them along the path. A streak of red-orange flashed ahead of them as a fox scampered from the clearing with a small bone in its mouth. Sigilind did not let her sons turn away as the stench struck them, nor did she turn her own eyes from the wreckage of bones and rotting flesh that lay scattered around the log and the broken stocks before it. Harigastir tried to twist out of her grip and run away, but her slim fingers held his wrist so tightly that he began to wail. Theudorikijar gulped, his mouth twitching as if he were fighting down his gorge.

"These were my brothers," Sigilind said to her sons. "They died because of Sigigairar's treachery. For your honor and the honor of your line, you must avenge them, or you must die trying."

"Avenge them on our father?" Theudorikijar asked, his high voice trembling. He glanced around the clearing wildly, staring up at the cloud-swept sky as if to find some release from the scattered bones and fly-blown meat that covered the earth around him like broken tree limbs cast down by a great storm.

"Swear it to me." Sigilind's voice sounded strange and hard in her own ears, like icicles shattering on stone. An icy, cruel wind blew through her, lifting her up to a dizzying height from which she seemed to look down at her two children, their little faces now set by an excess of horror into twin masks of resignation in which only a light glimmer of tears showed life. "Swear that you will avenge Wals and his sons Alfwald, Alfarik, Wihtric, Wynberht, Orngrim, Oddwig, Alfger, Wulfger, and Berhtwini, or die trying."

"I swear," Theudorikijar said numbly.

Harigastir nodded his head, too choked to speak. Sigilind stared piercingly at him until, finally, he too forced out the words, "I swear."

"So Wodan, first father of our line, takes your oath."

Sigilind turned and led her sons from the clearing. They said nothing, though after a few minutes silent tears began to stream down Theudorikijar's face.

Sigilind took the boys to the cluster of storehouses below the hall, looking through the doors of each until they found the one where Helche was sorting through linen. Her wide-shouldered, thick body bent over the chest where it was kept; Helche did not look up as Sigilind and her sons walked in.

"You can leave that, I'll do it," she told the thrall. Helche jumped, brown eyes wild and white-rimmed as the eyes of a frightened cow as she turned to stare at her lady. "Take the boys out—see if you can find one of the thanes to give them a workout with practice swords."

Helche bobbed her cropped head. "Yes, my lady," she murmured, and crouched to wipe the tears from the boys' eyes with her heavy, calloused hands. "Don't cry, darlings," she crooned. "Come on . . . there, now."

Sigilind had a fair pile of linen, combs, cups, and such things as a woman would want with her in Holda's halls picked out by the time she heard the sound of Aiwimundur's voice outside the storage hut.

"Aye, we found her around the back door of the hall, where the drighten Sigigairar and his lady Sigilind sleep. She'll still be there; she was too heavy to move."

The voice that answered him was a sweet, light alto, though husky as if from years of breathing the smoke of burning herbs. "That's good. You really shouldn't have touched her at all, but I'll know in a minute whether any harm's been done. No one's tried to go into her house, have they?"

"Not as far as I know. Not when I left, anyway."

Sigilind came out of the storage hut. Aiwimundur was leading a dark brown horse by the reins. Beside him walked a woman in a loose tunic of light green and dark green skirt, her strong, well-formed calves and bare feet moving swiftly beneath its swishing folds. A black bag dangled from her right hand like a dead goose, its loose neck flopping over her plump arm. When the swiftly passing clouds above fled from the sun, its light caught fiery glints from the warm golden-brown glow of her thick, wavy hair and from the rope of amber around her neck. Although her stride was firm and determined, her round hips moved freely, with a joyful womanliness that made Sigilind feel stiff and cold within her own womb. She was only an inch or two shorter than the Walsing, but much heavier of build, hills and valleys of flesh swelling and curving richly beneath her green garments.

Suddenly the spae-woman stopped, turning to fix Sigilind directly in her gaze. Her eyes were blue with a burning ring of yellow-white around the pupil; transfixed in her glance, Sigilind found it hard to breathe, but felt none of the cloudy oppression that had always borne her down under Kara's gaze. Rather, it seemed to her that Freyjadis was staring straight through her, weighing her soul on a balance keen enough to sway with less than a fingernail's length of thin gold wire in the difference.

"Sigilind," she said. "You were the one who found the body. What did you do to it?" Suddenly the piercing intensity of her gaze eased so that Sigilind was able to look at her face. She guessed the spae-woman was about thirty, though no wrinkles marred her lightly tanned skin. Her cheekbones and jaw were strong but delicately pointed beneath her plumpness, giving her a look of girlishness despite her age; her nose was long and rather heavy for her face, as though it had been broken once or twice.

"Aiwimundur and I tried to lift her, and I pulled her shift up to cover her," Sigilind answered.

"I'll want to talk to you later, in private." Freyjadis glanced at the sun. "We need to get this done before sunset. You're lucky it didn't happen in winter."

A ring of armed thanes stood around the hall. Their muttering stopped as Sigilind, Aiwimundur and the spae-woman came closer, though now and again one of the men would look anxiously at the blanket-draped heap lying beside their drighten.

"Let us through," Sigilind said, and Gunthormar and Ingwanthewar moved aside so the three of them could pass.

Freyjadis went to the corpse of Kara and stripped her coverlet away. "What fool hid her from the light of the Sun?" she asked as she crouched down beside it. "You've only strengthened her, and you'll have to burn the blanket now." The spae-wife stared into Kara's glazed dark eyes, murmuring under her breath. Once her head rocked back as though a strong arm had slapped her; she snapped it straight, stretching her splayed hand out toward the body. Sigigairar, still sitting with his back to the door, watched her without speaking. His light eyes were not red with weeping, but his sorrow had ploughed deep furrows down the narrow length of his face.

From her bag, the spae-wife took a few handfuls of something that looked like brown gravel at first. Looking closer, Sigilind could see that it was some sort of root, finely chopped and dried. Freyjadis sprinkled the herb around Kara's body in a rough oblong, then forced the rest under her with the point of her bone-handled knife. Her chant grew louder, though to Sigilind it sounded like nothing but strange, melodious gibberish.

She stood, dusting her hands off. "That will take a little while to do its job. Take me to her house."

"What did you do?" Sigilind asked nervously.

"I've broken part of her tie to Hella's realm. Now that she no longer touches the Death-Frowe so closely, nor draws so much strength from the Dark One's land, we can lift her from the earth and take her where she needs to go. Come, Sigilind. Aiwimundur, you fetch me a torch."

Sigigairar uncurled his length from the ground, stamping life back into his feet. "Can you tell who did it?" he asked the spae-woman.

She hardly glanced at him as she answered, "No. Not without calling her ghost forth. That would be a very stupid and dangerous thing to do, and I am not going to do it."

Sigigairar did not sit down again, but he slumped against the door of his hall, his long bones loose as sticks in a sack. Freyjadis pulled a small brown packet out of her bag and held it out to him. "Take this and have one of your women brew it with hot water when you go to bed tonight. It will give you a peaceful sleep and help in healing. You ought to take it now . . . but you won't, will you? Very well; stay with her until we get back. Don't let anyone take your place, and don't even think of covering her up again. Then you can go and see to your men before the tale becomes three times its size in the telling."

Sigigairar said nothing, only stared at Freyjadis until she turned back to Sigilind. "Take me to her house."

Sigilind led the spae-wife to the sunken hut where Kara had dwelt since Sigigairar had brought his bride home. The hut was set a little way from the main settlement. Its turf-chinked stones rose to waist height, roof timbers slanting up to just above Sigilind's head at the central peak. The four corners of the roof were crudely carved into the heads of horses, their eyes huge and staring.

Freyjadis walked around the house three times. Once she turned her head over her shoulder, seeming to speak silently to something unseen behind her. Coming to the door at the northern side of the hut, she bent and twisted her body, going down the earthen steps backward with her head looking up from between her legs as her chanting rose to a soft eerie wail. Startlingly swift, like a birch-limb bent into a loop and suddenly released, she sprang straight and whirled in midair, her powerful forearm striking the door so that the latch burst and it flew in before her. A breath of something cold and foul blew out of the open door, brushing against Sigilind and chilling her to the marrow, and was gone. Eyes wary, Freyjadis stalked in like a great cat, her head low as if she were sniffing about for something, swinging from side to side. In the shadows within, Sigilind could see her striking with blinding speed at a furry bundle of something that hung from the ceiling and it fell to the earthen floor with a clatter of bone against bone. Suddenly she was kicking and whirling in a wild, furious dance all around the hut, her blows shaking its bare stone walls. A sound of shattering rose and echoed deafeningly around her, as though she were bursting links of frozen iron asunder; as Sigilind watched, it seemed that she could see each strike breaking another line in an angular pattern of red light that wove and traced in an intricate basketwork pattern around Kara's house. The spae-woman finished by kicking the half-charred sticks of the hearth up in an arc of charcoal and powdery gray ash with one foot and, with the other, coming down squarely through the center of a wide, thin, oblong drum with dark brown figures painted over its hide surface. It crashed resoundingly; then silence dropped at once, as though a hand had clapped itself over the vibrating hut to still it as a man would still a drum's echo.

Freyjadis shook her bare foot free of the tattered hide and limped out into the open air, panting. She took the torch from Aiwimundur and set it to each of the horse's heads in turn, murmuring under her breath. They caught at once, four pillars of fire leaping up, and soon a black cloud of musty smoke was rising from Kara's roof above the bright clear glow of the orange flames that gnawed greedily at the thatch and flickered down to the turf of the walls. Freyjadis cast the torch in through the open door, straight at the ruined drum. It flared with a sudden silent boom; then all was fire within.

Freyjadis smiled. "Well, that wasn't as bad as some I've seen. Have you got anything for me to eat?"

The sudden question took Sigilind by surprise. "W-well," she stuttered, then, "yes, of course. What do you want?"

"I need something strengthening—bread and cheese, with butter and honey if you have any. Meat would also be good, and ale or mead, if there's anything that old seith-witch didn't have a chance to brew her mind-twisting magics into, otherwise milk will do."

Sigilind hurried off to fetch the spae-woman her food. When she returned with a large wooden platter heaped high with food and a clay pot of creamy milk, Freyjadis was already giving Aiwimundur her next orders.

"I need a large, thick stake with a sharp point, of either oak or alder; four strong forked branches of alder or willow, large enough to pin her arms and legs with; six smaller forked branches, and three thick bands of willow. Also, you should start someone to digging a hole in the peat bog, large enough for her stretched full-length and deeper than a tall man's height."

Aiwimundur nodded and walked away. Freyjadis sat down cross-legged on the ground and took the food from Sigilind's hands. She threw back her head and drained the pot of milk in one long draught, wiping creamy froth from her upper lip with the back of her hand, then began to devour the bread, meat and cheese as if she were half-starved, cramming handfuls into her mouth and letting the crumbs shower onto her dark green skirt and the earth around her. After a few moments, Sigilind realized that she was staring rudely at the other woman and quickly glanced away before the spae-wife could take offense.

The wooden platter was empty in a frighteningly swift time. Freyjadis rose to her feet, brushing crumbs from her skirts, and smiled graciously at Sigilind. Though her teeth were brown and some of them broken, none were missing.

"Would you like any more?" Sigilind asked.

"That'll do me fine for the moment, thanks. How did you do it?"

"How did I—?"

"Kill Kara."

Sigilind clapped a hand to her breasts, stumbling a step backward from the spae-wife whose hot gold-white gaze bored into her own again.

The shorter woman moved closer, not allowing Sigilind to back away any farther. "I'm not going to hurt you, Sigilind, and I'm not going to tell anyone, but it's very important that I know what happened."

Sigilind glanced around swiftly. She could see a few of the carls and their wives going about their business among the little houses of the village; a young girl, blond braids swaying like loose ropes in the wind, led her sheep around the bottom of the hill; and farther up at the hall's door, Aiwimundur was talking to a group of men, but no one was close enough to them to hear. Lowering her eyes, she swiftly told Freyjadis of Wals, of her brothers, and of the honey that she had sent to Sigimund. "I don't know what I expected would happen," she confessed softly. "I thought—maybe I thought that if he could catch hold of her somehow, he could force her to free him. I had been waiting for Wodan to do something for them, but when Aiwimundur told me that all my brothers were dead, I realized I had to do something, and I had vowed to not go to them or try to free them."

The spae-wife sighed deeply. "So your twin brother bit her tongue out, and I suppose he couldn't help swallowing some of her blood. You know that the taint is on your soul as well? That you stand in danger of becoming something like the warg your brother slew, or some other outdwelling wight? By the words of judgment, an outlaw is a warg; an out-lying man, a forest-goer, is a troll as well as an outlaw, and your brother drank of Kara's trollcraft together with her blood."

"Sigimund and I . . . " Sigilind started, and could not finish. "What should I do, then?"

"Try to hold to the bounds of men—your wedding, the kin you have left within the hall and the vows you have made before the gods."

"But I must see Wals avenged!" Sigilind cried out. "And my brothers— how can I not work for the vengeance that will honor their deaths?"

Freyjadis shrugged. "Clearly you've made up your mind and nothing I can say will make any difference. Come and help me with the body, then. I can't get her onto my mare alone."

Sigilind followed the spae-wife back to the hall, where the dark brown mare stood patiently by Kara's body as if keeping guard over it. Freyjadis nodded to her, and together the two women bent and heaved. Though Kara was still unnaturally heavy, and touching her even through her shift froze Sigilind's fingers to useless numbness, they were able to lift the corpse from the ground and wrestle it onto the back of the horse, who rolled her white-rimmed eyes wildly at them, flaring her nostrils and whickering, but standing staunch as a stone under her weird burden.

In a little while Aiwimundur came back, bearing a bundle of thick sticks. "I've got the men down at the bog," he said. "I expect we can take her there whenever you think we should."

Freyjadis took the stakes from his arm one at a time, looking carefully at each, running her hands up and down them as if searching for hidden flaws. "These are very good," she said. "I'll need a few minutes by myself."

Aiwimundur and Sigilind walked down the hill together. The black pillar of smoke from Kara's hall had faded to a cleaner gray, scented only by turf and wood, the wind whipping it sideways into a huge feather. They stood and gazed at it for a few moments.

"What are you going to do now?" he asked her.

"Do?"

"About your brother."

Sigilind looked down at the ground. A bumblebee hummed heavily above a clover blossom like a little white snowball near her feet; beside the patch of clover was a small hole and a lump of mud childishly sculpted into something that might, from the right angle, bear a very faint resemblance to a loaf of bread. "He knows where to go," she said at last. "I'm not going with him, if that's what you mean."

"No. Is he going to stay here in Gautland, or will he go back to reclaim Wals' country?"

Sigilind didn't say anything, only stared at the fading plume of smoke and the trees beyond it. The oak leaves hung limply, their dark green already dulled by a touch of brown, as though a fine layer of dust had sifted unevenly over the wood. Aiwimundur waited for her a long time, his eyes never wavering from her face. Finally he said, "If your brother needs help getting a passage home, I'll help him. If you, or he, are planning anything else— anything to Sigigairar's harm—don't let me know about it. I've done all I can for you."

"You've done all we needed," Sigilind said, her voice suddenly rushing out warmly. She took Aiwimundur's square jaw in her hands and kissed him firmly on the lips. He stood stolidly, neither pulling away nor returning the kiss, as though he were unsure of what to do. "Thank you."

"I've done all I can," Aiwimundur repeated. "No more. If you want to thank me, let things go as they were before."

They stood, neither looking at the other, till Freyjadis led her mare slowly down the hill. A white bandage, splotched with dusty brown fingerprints and the bright red of fresh blood, wound her left wrist; a twisted ribbon of brown-stained runes cut through the naked white wood of the freshly stripped oaken stake. Aiwimundur and Sigilind followed the corpse-laden horse and her mistress past the village, over the road through the rustling fields and along the narrow, winding track through the sparse alder and birch trees that fringed the edges of the bog like an old woman's beard. A stark cloak of cloud had blown across the sky to shield the sun; a few spatters of rain were beginning to fall.

Three men—two thralls and a farmer from the village—stood beside a deep hole, the bottom of which was already beginning to fill with black, peaty water. Freyjadis gestured to Sigilind, and the two women rolled Kara's corpse from the horse, dumping it to splash facedown into the grave pit. The spae-woman lowered herself in after, heedless of the mud staining her clothing with great black smears. Standing knee deep in water and sucking bog above the body of Sigigairar's mother, she drew a square-headed hammer from her bag, set the point of the oaken stake on Kara's back over her heart, breathed in deeply and brought the hammer down with an explosive shout. The body jerked and splashed as the stake sank in. Freyjadis struck it twice more till only a foot of rune-carved oak stood out from Kara's back.

Taking the four large forked sticks from her bundle, she used them to pin the corpse to the bog by knees and elbows, then bent three sturdy willow bands over Kara's neck, the middle of her body and her buttocks, securing the bonds by a forked stick at each end.

"So lie, Hella-runester, borne to earth by your ill," Freyjadis commanded in a loud, ringing voice. "Thurse-sister, troll-wife, thrice cursed, bound thrice to the bog. Lie as long as you may, you shall never break free, nor unravel the runes that the Ginn-Reginn wrought when first were the worlds made. Your hide is held here, your fetch held unfree with your lich fettered while worlds may last. So I have spoken, Freyjadis the wise, at the ancient well, at the Ases' seat. So shall it be!" She brought her hand down, striking the oaken stake with her fist nine times.

Those watching above waited, breathless, till she stretched her arms out to them. The two thralls each grasped a limb and helped her out to the accompaniment of her muffled grunts. When the spae-woman was finally out of the pit, the front of her tunic was slimy with black mud and her wet skirt stuck to her muddy legs. "Thank you," she gasped to them. She spread her legs out, breathing deeply as though she were drinking strength in directly from the air. "Fill it in," she directed. The thralls began to shovel mud in at once, great gloppy spadefuls splashing into the dark water, which had almost risen to cover the corpse already.

Freyjadis pulled herself onto the back of her horse. "I'm going home. You know where you can find me if you need me—and where you can send my payment."

She nudged the mare into a trot, chunks of wet turf flying up from the horse's trim hooves as the spae-woman rode to the path that led around the edge of the bog.

"What do we pay her?" Sigilind asked Aiwimundur.

He shrugged. "She generally lets people decide for themselves what her help is worth. If someone puts too low a value on her, she lets them fend for themselves next time they have trouble."

"How shall I find her?"

"She lives on Hlewagastir's lands at the other side of the bog. If you follow the path around and turn right when you get to the stone Hlewagastir raised for his son Holtigastir, then follow the creek to the north, you'll come to her hut at the bottom of a hill. When the way isn't too muddy, you can start at breakfast time and be there by mid-morning. But I'll go for you if you like."

"Yes," Sigilind said. She was not eager to look into the spae-wife's burning eyes again or to hear another of her warnings. She and Aiwimundur followed the track to Sigigairar's hall. "If you'll be here tomorrow morning, I'll have something ready for her then."

"Good enough," Aiwimundur acknowledged, starting along the road that led through the hamlet to his own home. Sigilind went to the storehouses, taking a bit here and a bit there until she had a good load of dried fish and meal, a worn knife and a well-oiled spearhead. Luck was with her; she found two tunics and a pair of breeches big enough to have been Wals' or Sigimund's, which must have been taken from the ship and not yet given away or cut down to fit a lesser man. She tied all of it inside an old woolen blanket and carried the bundle outside.

She had meant to take it straight to the Herulian's howe, but as she stepped out of the storehouse, a sudden fit of yawning overtook her. She felt her eyelids drooping, her limbs becoming heavy and sight dim with sleep as though a leaden cloak had fallen over her head. She wondered vaguely if Freyjadis had somehow managed to enchant her, but she was too tired to worry about it.

Putting the bundle back inside, Sigilind went to the great hall. A few folk were still drinking, muffling their toasts as soon as Sigilind came in—she guessed they were thanking the gods that Kara was dead at last.

Sigigairar, drugged by the ale of his mother's arvel, was already asleep. He lay snoring on his back, fully clothed with Sigimund's sword still at his belt. Sigilind lay down beside him, pulling a blanket over herself as her eyes closed. With her last thought, she reached out to curl her fingers around the smooth crystal of the sword's hilt, then plummeted into the depths of her dream.

Sigimund awoke in complete darkness, a chill shivering out from within his bones. Before falling asleep, he had stripped his fouled clothes from his body to keep them from caking into his sores and lain naked on the cold clay. Now he wanted them again, but he felt too tired and ached too deeply to stretch his hand out. He stared into the blackness, phantom lights spreading their illusionary tracery before his eyeballs, fading and reforming. Only one ball of foxfire at the corner of his eye glowed steady, slowly brightening as the cold within the mound grew deeper and deeper as though it were stealing the heat from his very body.

Sigimund turned his head toward the ghostly fire burning beside him. It cast no light over the howe, which was still locked in midnight blackness, but it showed the dry body of a man lying on a wolfskin, the darkness of his shape lit by the flame above the round gold medallion on his chest and the twin sparks flaring in his hollow eyes. His long hair and beard twined through the red-glowing chain; the medallion itself burned with twenty-four tiny runes scratched around its golden rim, red light glittering from the lines that formed the stylized figures of man, horse and eagle at its centre.

As the Herulian's corpse began to sit up, Sigimund threw himself back to where he thought the passage had been, but found only cold, mossy stone behind him. The dead man's skeletal hands, criss-crossed with ragged sinews and tipped with long black nails like a raven's claws, reached out for Sigimund. He scrabbled away; the corpse rose to its feet and walked after him, its movements slow but filled with a dreadful strength and purpose. In a second, Sigimund realized that he was trapped; that he was in the world of death and was going to die; and that he refused to die like a rabbit trapped in a burrow. Curling his legs under him, he waited until the Herulian was almost on top of him, its nails reaching to fix in his shoulders, then sprang at it with all his strength, bringing both of them down to the earthen floor of the howe. It was fearfully strong, but its dry body had only the weight of its bones; to Sigimund, even exhausted as he was, it felt as light as down. Whenever he tried to pin it, it twisted away, its claws coming again and again for his eyes; he fared worse when it gripped him, for its nails dug in and the strength of its dry grasp was almost impossible to break. Sigimund's breath rang harsh against the stones of the howe as he and the Herulian wrestled each other around the death-chamber. Blood from a near-miss stung blindingly in his right eye; he could feel its trickles running hot from his wrists and ankles again, and springing out in droplets in all the places on his arms and legs where the corpse had grabbed him.

His foot caught in the wolfskin on the floor. A sickening fear shot through him as he fell with the Herulian on top, the dead man's eye-sparks flaring before him. He felt its dry grip on his neck, its nails beginning to dig in; then it seemed to him that he could feel the smooth crystal of his sword's hilt in his palm, a warm might flowing from it through his limbs to melt the icy fetters that seemed to have bound his body under the dead man's gaze. Straining with all his desperate might, he pressed the writhing, twisting corpse upward to the limits of his arms' length—far enough away that it could claw at his arms and kick viciously at his doubled-up legs, but no more. Sigimund rolled and sprang to his feet, holding the Herulian away from him; he bore it to the wall of the mound and held it there, pressing the dry dead body to the stones with all his weight and strength.

Slowly its struggles lessened, till it hung unmoving in his hands. The faint foxfire about it glowed more brightly; in its phantom light, Sigimund could see the corpse's jaw drop open. A cold breath blew steadily out of its mouth, a wind tainted with the faraway scent of rot. In the silence broken only by his own raspy panting and coughs, he heard the faint hoarseness of a man's breathy voice as if it rang not through the stones of the howe, but through the darkness of his own skull.

"Who has woken Widuhundaz from his sleep?" it said. Sigimund had learned to understand the Northern speech, but the Herulian's words sounded archaic and distorted to him, so that he could only barely tell what it was saying. Yet as he stared into the red sparks of its eyes, he felt the sense underlying the strange words becoming clearer and clearer. "Who has called me from the hallowed hall where I sat, in the wet pathways and the far roads through the worlds to wander?"

"I am Sigimund, the son of Wals," Sigimund said, his own speech half a whisper and half a hiss. "Who are you, dead man?"

"I am called Widuhundaz and Wodila, Hrabanaz and Widugastaz, Wiwaz and Ansula of the Heruli, Rune-Master and Mannaz-Wodhanas. Sigimund Wargaz-Bane, what wouldst thou of me know? Why hast thou come, the silence of my howe to break? Three questions I will answer; no more."

"When shall I avenge my father?" Sigimund whispered to the Herulian.

"One of thy sister's sons will be a true Walsing. When thou hast made that one a worthy hero and beside thee he stands, tested in might, thy sword shall be won back again and Wals shall be avenged by the fire thou and he set, Sigigairar's hall to burn."

"How shall I know which of Sigilind's sons to trust?"

"This thou hast won by thy might: that thee thyself shall be able to bear poison both within and upon thy hide, and the men of thy true line shall be able to bear it without, though not within. Now once more ask, ere back to the land from which thou calledst me I fare."

"How may I learn the wisdom of the Herulians?" Sigimund asked, his heart beating hard and the breath suddenly chokingly thick in his throat. The wind from Widuhundaz's mouth grew colder, the stench of rot heavier upon it, as though Sigimund had drawn closer to the land of the dead from which it blew.

"Take the knife which lies beneath my wolfskin and cut my head from my shoulders. Wrap it in my tunic and the wolf's hide—wrap it well, so that no ray of sun can touch it—and find a place in the darkness to hide it. Take also the bracteate around my neck, that was a sign of my lore. When thou wishest to learn aught from me, at midnight bring out my head, around thy own neck place the bracteate, and call upon Widuhundaz of the Heruli in the name of Wodhanaz, Wilijaz and Wihaz. And when thou my wolf's hide upon thy body settest, then shall the wolf's wod upon thee come with the wolf's shape; and of that hast thou great need in the times that are to come. Now upon my hide place me, that I may ride along the wet wilderness ways and from thence back to the hallowed hall from which thou hast called me, Sigimund Wargaz-bane, last son of Wals."

The wind from the corpse's mouth faded to a last faint sigh from the dead man's leathery lungs as the ghostly crimson sparks in his eyes went out. Sigimund carried him to the wolfskin, fumbling under it for the knife before he stretched it out and laid Widuhundaz's dry body upon it. After a few moments the cold of the howe lightened and Sigimund knew that the Herulian's ghost had left that place. With one quick stroke of the knife, he severed the brittle skin and tendons of the neck, snapping the dry spine like a twig. The hollow head dropped into his other hand, fine hair slipping silkily through his fingers; the gold bracteate fell to the floor with a soft tinkle. When Sigimund reached down for the tunic, everything within had already crumbled to dust. He wrapped the head as he had been told, feeling around on the floor till his touch met the thin, cold metal of the golden medallion. Its etchings were rough against his fingertips as he picked it up and set it carefully on top of the head, sitting down beside it to think for a moment.

Something was nagging at the back of Sigimund's mind, a worry that he couldn't quite place. In spite of his nakedness, he felt quite warm now. The blood from the fight had dried, and there was no pain . . . there was no pain! He tested his wrists and ankles gingerly, but could feel only the raised lumps of healed scars; the open sores on his buttocks were gone, and the deep aching that nine nights in the stocks had left in his muscles had faded to a vague tiredness. He breathed deeply: no phlegm rattled in his lungs. Indeed, he felt quite well and strong.

The darkness of the howe no longer seemed so black; looking around, Sigimund saw a faint light beginning to shine through the breach in its wall. He put the fur-wrapped head of the Herulian through the hole, then crawled out into the dawn, the morning breeze cold on his naked body. Sigilind stood there waiting for him, pale as a birch tree in her white shift, holding a large bundle in her arms. As Sigimund strode forward, she ran toward him to embrace him, careless of the stains his filthy touch would leave on her. Corners of sharp metal poked painfully into them from her bundle, squashed between them, but they hugged each other with a furious gratefulness that they yet lived.

Still wrapped in her brother's arms, Sigilind looked down at what lay on the ground beside the hole and gasped. "My dream," she murmured. "I saw . . ."

"My fight with the Herulian?"

She nodded.

"And did you also hear his rede to me?"

"That one of my sons would be a true Walsing, and that only when he stood beside you would you gain your sword back and avenge Wals and our brothers?"

"Yes."

The rising light of the day glowed in Sigilind's blue gaze as she gazed upward into her brother's eyes. "I had thought—for a while I had thought that I would have to break my oath and end our line in shame. But while you live, and while one of my sons has such a fair doom, the Walsings shall still be worthy of our father."

"As we swore when we were children. Sigilind, do you remember how old Hulde kept telling us and telling us about our ancestry from Sigibercht, the son of Wodan, onward and insisting that we would have to live up to every one of the heroes who had gone before us?"

"She hardly talked about anything else."

"If she could have lived to see us now—if she could know what had happened here—what would she have told us?"

"To be strong and never to yield; to gather our strength and take vengeance as our grandfather Rerir did," Sigilind answered at once. The dawn light cast the silvery sheen of good steel over the tears on her cheeks; her face was as white as a swan's feather, its finely wrought strength tempered and set in her resolution.

Tears prickled hot behind Sigimund's own eyes as he looked at his sister. Tenderly he reached out to stroke the softness of her fair hair with one hand, drawing her in closer to him with the other.

"I love you," Sigimund murmured to her. "Give me a few days to make a dwelling place, then send your son to the caves where you told me to go and I will get on with what I need to do. It may be that the worst of your work is over now."

"Far from over," Sigilind said, her high voice as bleak as a snowy crag, rough beneath the clear ice. "But you shouldn't fear for me; I am Wals' daughter and I can do what I must."

Sigimund stared questioningly at her, but the clear pools of his sister's eyes reflected only the sky; he could not see through that blue gleaming. Sigilind ducked her head and pulled a tunic and breeches out of her bundle. Sigimund recognized the trousers as Wals', the yellow tunic as his own. He put them on quickly, turning his glance away from his sister as a flush warmed his cheeks. Taking the bundle from her arms, he retied it and tucked it under one arm, picking up the fur-wrapped head of the Herulian under the other.

"Fare well, my brother," Sigilind said, her voice soft with a whisper of tears.

"Stay well, my sister." Sigimund bent to kiss her, her mouth melting into his as the unspoken warmth flowed between them to strengthen them both, then stepped lithely over a fallen branch and made his way between the trees, starting northward to the mountain.

12

THE TESTING

The brisk wind of Heilagmonth, winter's edge, carried clouds like great gray boulders swiftly across the cold sky, blowing the rustling leaves to their first glow of orange and gold and whipping Sigilind's hair across her face as she stood behind Sigigairar's hall staring out over the wood. One gust caught her dark red cloak, unwrapping it to flap behind her, the brooch that fastened it tugging against her neck. Irritably she grabbed it and pulled it back again, turning so the wind would blow it against her rather than away from her. Below her, Theudorikijar and Hari-gastir were playing at birds, running a little way up the hill and leaping into the air with their arms out and their capes spread behind them like wings for the wind to lift.

Straining her eyes, Sigilind looked past the hamlet, trying to see through the trees beyond to the white mound of the Herulian's howe, but the dry leaves hid it from her view. Only when the wood was bare with winter would she be able to see the cairn through the branches of the trees. Past that—far past—the dark swell of the mountain rose against the wind-stirred sky, where somewhere Sigimund lived among the trolls and outlaws, troubling her sleep at nights with the skull of the Herulian Widuhundaz and the fiery burning of runes before her eyes, the galdor magic of their names and power singing through her dreams as Sigimund learned their secrets from the Herulian's head.

A shrill wail rose from the bottom of the hill. Harigastir had tripped and scraped his knee on a rock, and now sat howling while Theudorikijar looked at him scornfully.

"Mama, says heroes don't cry when they're hurt," he told his brother. "I don't cry. Our father doesn't."

Harigastir shut his mouth firmly and wiped his tears away, rubbing the back of one grubby hand over his bloodied knee. "See what you know," he said at last. "I heard him, the day after Grandmama died."

"That's different. I bet you could hit me with a sword and I wouldn't cry from it."

Harigastir brightened, standing up. "Can I? Let's see."

"You know what I mean, you little stupid. In battle, like a warrior."

Did Theudorikijar stand a bit straighter than Sigilind had thought, his pale eyes shine keener, as though he, too, had been touched by the gifts of the Herulian? Watching him in the shifting light, as the shadows of clouds chased each other across the sun, she thought he did. And how much longer can I wait? she said to herself. The sooner he's away from Sigigairar, the less he thinks of Sigigairar and Kara and the closer he can grow to Sigimund and his duty, the more likely he is to grow into the hero Sigimund needs to stand beside him as he takes our revenge. She glanced again at the mountain. It was a long day's journey for a boy alone—a grueling journey, and what if he had not found Sigimund by the time night fell? The days were getting swiftly shorter; even if Theudorikijar left at dawn, he might well not be at the mountain by sunset. But if he were the one the Herulian meant, he and Sigimund would find each other; if not . . .

I made them swear to avenge Wals and my brothers or die trying, Sigilind thought. But now? Is it fair? They're only children.

But one of them is a child of Wals' line. The other? "My children will be true Walsings, or they will not be my children," Sigilind reminded herself, her whisper ringing with the high note of her youthful steel. Theudorikijar and Harigastir were leaping before the wind again, trying to make it bear them upward higher and higher before they came crashing down into the brown-rustling grass.

It was not yet dawn the next morning when Sigilind came creeping through the drizzling darkness to the sunken hut where Theudorikijar and Harigastir slept with Helche. A child's belt hung over her arm, threaded through the scabbard of a large dagger. The hefty thrall-woman snorted resonantly in her sleep; the two boys' breathing was soft and high, gentle as the snores of two slumbering puppies. In the darkness, Sigilind could not tell which of the boys was which; after a few moments, she bent down and shook one shoulder at random.

"Lemme sleep," Harigastir's muffled voice mumbled. Sigilind shook her other son more vigorously.

"What?" Theudorikijar muttered. "Stoppit. Goway."

"You must get up, Theudorikijar," Sigilind whispered harshly into her son's ear. "It is time for you to prove your line."

"Urmph," he said, sitting up. "Mama? What?"

Sigilind lifted him bodily to his feet. "Get your clothes without waking your brother or Helche and come outside. If they should wake up, don't say anything," she murmured softly. She glided back out, closing the door behind her. Struck by a sudden thought, she went to the storage house and fumbled around for a few moments. She found the bronze needle she was looking for when it stuck in her finger; the thread took a little longer.

When she got back, Theudorikijar was standing outside the hut, his clothes draped over his arms. His light hair peaked over his head like waves on a stormy day, though the steady drizzle was already beginning to damp it down. Without speaking, Sigilind took his nightshirt off. He shivered in the morning damp, rubbing at the goosebumps on his bare chest and arms. "It's cold out here," he complained. "Let me have my clothes."

Quickly Sigilind helped him put his trousers on and laced his shoes on to his feet for the journey, then tossed his tunic over his head and guided his arms through. "Turn around," she whispered. "It's got a hole in it." She licked the end of the thread, twisting it down till she could pull it through the hole in the needle. Can I do this? she asked herself. She set one hand on Theudorikijar's shoulder to hold him still, trying to feel the glow of the Walsing soul within his small body. Kara's death had not been the means to bring it forth, nor had the oath the child had sworn in the clearing among the dead. Now she must try a straighter means in hopes of awakening his spirit so that he might live through Sigimund's testing.

Holding her hands as steady as she could, Sigilind began to sew the sark to Theudorikijar's shoulders. At the first stab of the needle into his hide, he yelped.

"Be still," Sigilind hissed, pushing the needle into his skin and pulling it out through the sark again. Awake, awake, she murmured silently to him, trying to send the brightness of her own might out through her fingers to kindle the might within her son. Let this thorn prick you awake: be a Walsing, and live!

"You're sticking me, Mama," Theudorikijar complained, whimpering as she stuck the point into him again. "Ow, that hurts. Stop it, please, that hurts."

"If you are hurt, you must bear it like a Walsing," Sigilind said sternly to him. "Far worse than this lies ahead of you."

With the third stitch, Theudorikijar began to whine and cry loudly. Sigilind's heart quailed within her at the sound. He's only a child, she reminded herself, even if he is a Walsing; and between Kara and Helche, he's never had a chance to learn to bear pain like a warrior. Sigimund will be able to test him better than I.

"Hush," she said. "Remember that you are of a heroic line, and ready yourself." With one quick jerk she yanked the tunic, seam and all, from Theudorikijar's body. He let out a yowl as the thread tore through his skin, three trickles of blood running down his white back. Sigilind wiped the blood away with the hem of her shift, then put the tunic back on Theudorikijar and pinned his blue cloak around his shoulders. The glare of bale in his eyes heartened her somewhat; his anger made his gaze more like the piercing glance of the hero he would need to be if he was to avenge Wals against his own father.

"Why are you doing this to me?" Theudorikijar muttered furiously. "What have I done?"

"You haven't done anything wrong, except that you must learn to bear your wounds like a man and not like a child. You are to go to the mountain where the trolls live and seek out Sigimund my brother, who is dwelling in a cave there. He will teach you to be a true hero."

She walked beside her son to the beginning of the path into the woods. Every so often he snuffled, glancing sideways at her. "You always told me not to go into the woods alone," Theudorikijar said when they stopped beneath the dripping leaves. "What will I do if I get attacked by a troll or something?"

Sigilind unslung the belt from her arm and buckled it around Theudorikijar's waist. The big dagger at his left side, which she had taken from the storehouse where Sigigairar kept those weapons he meant to give as gifts, was almost long enough to be a short sword for him. His tear-damp face brightened as he drew the knife from its scabbard and held it before him. Sigilind turned his hand, correcting his grip. "Like that," she said. "Now there is nothing in the woods or the caves you need to fear. Go on, Theudorikijar, and prove yourself to be a son of Wals' line."

"How will I know where to find Sigimund?" Theudorikijar asked. She could hear the excitement of adventure beginning to froth in his voice, like beer foaming up from the bottom of a horn.

"Trust to your own wits and strong heart, and to Wodan who fathered our line," Sigilind answered, sounding more certain than she felt. She put a bag into his hand, a bag with just enough bread and dried fish for two meals. Bending down, she brushed a wet lock of Theudorikijar's hair away and kissed him lightly on his narrow forehead. "Go on, now."

Theudorikijar hefted the dagger, glancing around as if he expected a wolf to come out of the trees at any minute. Slowly at first, gingerly picking his way among the twigs and stones, he started down the path; as Sigilind watched, he began to walk faster and was almost skipping as he went out of sight.

Sigimund left when he saw that the sun was beginning to sink, the shadows of the rocks at his cave's mouth creeping long and dark within. Carefully, quietly, he followed the track that he had made his own to the edge of a stream that ran from the mountain's softly rounded top down through the woods, his calloused footpads gliding through the first fallen leaves without crack or rustle. He drew in a breath of quiet satisfaction when he saw the snared body of a rabbit lying, brown and stiff, between two trees. He untangled the sinew from its neck and reset the trap, scattering leaves and dirt around to hide the rabbit's struggles and the wood of the snare. The second trap was empty.

As he went on he heard a rustling and scrabbling. The third snare's victim still lived, its eyes rolling and teeth bared as its strong back legs tried to kick it free of the trap. Sigimund crouched down and broke the rabbit's neck with a swift twist, its body flopping loose and warm over the other's as he put them aside and repaired his snare. Picking up his dinner, he had begun to walk back to his cave when the sound of ragged whistling pierced through his ears, interspersed with the occasional snuffle. Silent as a fair shadow, Sigimund ghosted through the trees, crouching down behind a clump of bushes as he came nearer to the source of the sounds. A small boy, his blue cloak covered with blackberry stains, stumbled along the pathway. His reddish-fair hair was tangled with burrs and twigs; the hems of his trousers were muddy and dripping. The grim set of his narrow face crumpled occasionally as his whistles grew shorter and shorter. One fist was clenched on the hilt of the huge dagger that hung from his belt; the other wiped drips from his long, crooked nose.

As Sigimund stepped from the bushes, the boy jumped back, drawing his dagger. "You look like my mother. Are you Sigimund?" he said, his high, slightly nasal voice shaking. "If you're not, either get out of my way or lead me to him."

"I am Sigimund. Are you the son of Sigilind the Walsing?"

"I am Theudorikijar, son of Sigilind and her husband the drighten Sigigairar," the boy answered proudly, drawing himself up straighter. "My mother sent me to find you and prove myself a true hero."

Sigimund looked at the boy, trying to weigh his worth. Theudorikijar looked like a strong child; for a ten-year-old, he was quite large, as large as some of Wals' sons had been at his age. And he must have had some of his mother's soul to have come so far alone; his challenge certainly showed he had some courage.

"Then be welcome, Theudorikijar, son of Sigilind the Walsing," Sigimund said. "My home is no hall, but it has done well enough for me. Are you hungry?"

"I'm starving," Theudorikijar said eagerly. "My mother got me up before breakfast and hardly gave me anything to eat on the way. What do you have?"

"Roast rabbit," Sigimund said, lifting the two stiffening bodies that dangled from his fist by their ears. "And I have kept some meal for bread. I was waiting for you to get here."

"How did you know I was coming?"

"It's a long story, and we have dinner to cook. If you still want to know tomorrow, I'll tell you then."

Theudorikijar hurried along beside his mother's brother. Although Sigimund had slowed his walk, the boy had to stretch his legs to keep up with his uncle's long stride. "Have you seen any trolls yet?" he asked breathlessly.

Sigimund smiled down at the boy, thinking of his brothers, from Berhtwini to Alfwald, asking him about his battles and his journeys in the same wondering, anticipating tone of voice, stretching toward a world that they could see glittering just beyond their reach, brighter for its year or two of distance from them. "Not yet," he answered.

"They'll come out when the nights get long," Theudorikijar asserted. "Daylights turn them to stone. Do you have trolls in Saxony?"

"Not like the mountain trolls I've heard about here," Sigimund said. "Saxony is a very flat land with no mountains, and what hills we have we or our fathers or grandfathers built to live on because the sea sometimes floods in."

Theudorikijar's eyes went wide, as though he were trying to see through the miles separating Gautland from Saxony. Gazing up at Sigimund, he stumbled on a stone and only his uncle's swift hand kept him from falling down. His face crumpled.

"We're almost at my home now," Sigimund said. "Just a short way up the mountain . . . come on, you've walked a long way today, but the last mile of the journey is where heroes part from the rest of the world." He slowed even more for the sake of the boy, who plodded grimly on, only letting out little whimpers when his feet turned on the loose stones that strewed the path.

A sharp wind cut around the side of the mountain, its cold raising Sigimund's hairs in a shiver. He led Theudorikijar through the boulders that hid his cave from the outside.

"It's cold in here," Theudorikijar complained. "How do you sleep?"

"Let me blow up the fire, and you'll be warmer in a bit."

Sigimund sat down, blowing on the coals and feeding them with twigs, then sticks, until a bright blaze cast its flickering shadows over the rough, dripping rock of the cave's walls, sending the shadow of the bundle at the back up to loom, huge and thin, over his dwelling. His blankets lay rolled beside the firepit; his spear stood straight against the rear wall, like a sentry warding the Herulian's wrapped head. There was a large flat stone that he used for cooking sometimes by the firepit; on it were two black, flame-hardened stakes of a length to lie between the forked sticks that stuck up on either side of his fire. Beside the stone stood a rack made of sticks lashed together by sinew, on which several rabbit hides hung drying. He prodded at the lumpy bag of meal that sat near the coals and was rewarded by a muscular squirming under his fingers. For a moment he gazed into the glow of the fire, settling himself for what he knew must follow.

He handed the bag of meal to Theudorikijar. "Take this and knead it well on that stone there," he told the child. "I must go out and get some firewood so that we can roast our rabbits properly."

Theudorikijar accepted the bag from his hand, looking at it dubiously. "I've never kneaded bread before," he said. "Helche the thrall says that's women's work."

"But there are no women here, so we men must do for ourselves or do without," Sigimund told him. "Get to it, now, and we'll have a nice dinner when I come back with the firewood."

Sigimund walked down to the wood; once there, he picked slowly through the fallen sticks, tossing one away as too small, another too big, a third (although it was growing dark and he could hardly see) as too green. At last he realized that he could no longer stay away; he would know his answer when he got back to the cave. He felt along the ground till he had a good armful of thick wood, then went back to the mountain and up to his cave, forcing his pace to stay even and swift.

Theudorikijar sat on the flat rock by the fire, pointed chin cupped in his hands. A little way from his feet the bag of meal lay, a squirming bulge pushing its woolen sides out here and there.

"Have you done anything with the bread?" Sigimund asked.

"I didn't dare open the bag of meal, because there was something living in it," Theudorikijar answered him, staring into his face with wide eyes.

"Well, we shall have rabbit anyway," Sigimund said. Not looking at the boy, he sat down cross-legged beside the flames, quickly skinned and gutted the two rabbits and hung their hides and sinews on the rack by the fire. He stuck the pointed stakes through their bodies and laid them across the forked sticks to roast, turning them every so often. Theudorikijar plied him with questions about Saxony and about battles he had fought in, moving closer to him. Sigimund answered as well as he could, though his thoughts were already cold and distant.

When Theudorikijar, wrapped in all Sigimund's blankets, had gone to sleep, Sigimund left his cave and began to run through the darkness, his steady pace carrying him swiftly down the mountain and along the path through the woods. While he ran he chanted (as Widuhundaz had taught him) the rune *ansuz*, calling on its thought-wind to bear his words to Sigilind across the shimmering bond stretching between them, awakening her and bringing her out to meet him.

Her face shone white in the darkness beside the glimmering howe; she huddled into a thick black cloak against the wind. "What happened?" she asked as soon as she saw her brother.

Sigimund shook his head. "I am no nearer to having a man's help with Theudorikijar than without him."

"Take him and slay him, then; there is no need for him to live any longer," Sigilind said. In the thin moonlight, her eyes were as cold and keen as those of the adder Sigimund had hidden in the bag of meal. "I tricked myself into believing that he was the one because he was the older and seemed braver than his brother." She clenched her fist on the falcon-head hilt of her dagger. When she opened her hand again a dribble of blood showed where the falcon's beak had pierced her palm. "He is his father's son, not mine. Let this be the first payment on our weregild—but since he is a child, whose only fault is cowardice, slay him quickly, without causing him fear or pain."

"He sleeps soundly in my cave," Sigimund assured her. "I can get back before dawn; he will never awaken."

Sigilind nodded. "So it shall be, then. Give me the winter to raise my son in the ways of bravery, and I will send him to you at the first thaw. Is there anything you need?" she asked, her voice suddenly lighter, as though a heavy beam had been pulled aside from it.

"If you can, leave out a cooking pot or two. What is Sigigairar doing with my sword?"

"He has it always with him. I dare not take it from him while he sleeps, because if I do he will know that you still live."

"So he will," said Sigimund grimly. A thrill of anger shot through him as he thought of his sword at his foe's belt, its hilt sullied by the touch of a hand not his own and its keen blade cleaving at Sigigairar's will—his sword, drawn from the Barnstock, the heart and root of Wals' line, ravished from him by the man who had sought to bring that line to an end. "I must go now, if I am to get back before Theudorikijar wakes up. Tomorrow or the next day, if men come out searching for him in the woods, they will find his body by a tree with his neck snapped, a freshly broken branch beside him as though he had climbed out too far. I think no one will ask further."

"I think not," Sigilind agreed. "Go, then."

The cloudy eastern sky had grown pale by the time Sigimund, breathing hard, ran up the rocky slope of the mountain. He rested outside the cave for a few minutes, then crept within. Theudorikijar still slept, curled beside the firepit. The flames had died down and only a faint warmth glowed from beneath the ash. Sigimund squatted, positioned one hand above the boy's chin and the other above the back of his narrow head, and with a single, quick jerk snapped his neck. Theudorikijar kicked once, settling down in a series of small shudders; a dark patch soaked slowly through the blanket. Sigimund stared down at the body for a moment. He picked up the bag of meal which now lay quiet on the floor of the cave and walked outside, untying it and reaching in. The cold, jewel-smooth body of the snake slipped under his fingers like water. Its black forked tongue flickered out of its blunt snout as he brought it from the bag, testing the lingering scent of rabbits on his skin before it struck. The adder's fangs sank into the muscle between Sigimund's thumb and forefinger with a sharp pain. He let it hang on, working its poison into him for a few moments, its brown and black-patterned body writhing in his hands. Then he pried it loose, holding it behind its head and looking into its keen, thoughtless eyes. The wyrm's lidless stare was as cold as crystal, unlit within. Gently Sigimund set it down to slither away into the rocks. His hand was bleeding where the snake had bitten him, but its fangs' bale did not swell or blacken the wound.

Sigimund unwrapped the blankets from Theudorikijar's body and carried the child out. Tired as he was, he would need to hurry if he wanted to do his work before Sigigairar's men came upon him.

13

SIGILIND AND SIGIMUND

The winter after Theudorikijar's death bit deep and cold, snows howling down from the north before the Winternights' full moon. One of Sigigairar's best milch cows was frozen before the beasts could be herded into the long stalls that ran along the sides of the hall, and a young ox went missing in a blizzard and was never found. Sigigairar sat more often by the fire in his chamber than in the great hall with his men, staring into the flames moodily, and when Sigilind went among the thanes she heard them whispering that he had lost his luck, that his kinslaying had turned the gods against them and come spring they might seek another drighten to follow. Men quarreled and sulked in the cold hall; now and again knives would flash over dice or a careless word. Sigilind kept Harigastir with her as much as she could, making him walk through the blowing snow with her to fetch cheese or grain from the storeroom, then swing his little wooden practice sword till his arms could no longer lift it. When the wind was still, Sigilind went out alone in the darkness, walking through the black trees that writhed and twisted around her to the clearing where a waist-high drift of snow hid the rotting log and the broken stocks where her brothers had died. Beneath the whiteness, she could feel, turning in uneasy sleep, the pain of their bondage and deaths festering in the icy earth, waiting for the vengeance that would unbind the ill that had soaked into that place and loose the horror that wound the clearing about like the coils of a huge frozen snake—the accusation that cried silently and piercingly through her head. When she came back from her walks, those few men who still came from their homes to the hall turned away from her haunted gaze and she heard them whispering below their breaths.

The Yule feast was scanty; most of their ale had gone for the funeral feasts of the autumn, and the fighting through the wheat field had left less grain than they needed. The voices of carls and thanes rang loud and hollow through the low rafters of the hall, the men shouting out their vows as Sigigairar led a black-splotched boar—the best boar of the herd, hallowed to Ingwar-Freyjar—around the hall. The Ingling drighten's voice penetrated through the sharp-edged laughter as he spoke his own oath with his hands on the bristles of the boar.

"By the bristles of the boar, I swear that Ingwar-Freyjar has not forsaken me! Though I have lost my mother, I shall win more of my mother Earth for my inheritance; though I have lost my elder son, I shall sire another, and stronger, to make good his loss. So I swear it—I, Sigigairar the Ingling!"

The cheer that went up was ragged, but full of heart for the first time since snow had begun to fall, drowning out Sigilind's whisper as her fingers touched the rough bristles of the boar's back. Still, as the noise sank down, she could hear the soft murmuring among the men, and knew what they whispered. Now her husband had dared the gods: if he had lost his luck, if her womb did not fill before next Yule, if his battles went ill or the seeds failed to sprout from the field in their time, his folk would spill his life to feed the land and win their luck again, for that was the geld the Ingling kings paid for their rule.

The month of Thonri was cold and bitter, the snow and hail fists of the rime-thurses hammering at the walls of hall and hut as they howled in the wind. Only Angantiwar, Gunthormar, Aiwimundur and Hailgi forced their way through the storm to keep the feast of Thonar with their drighten, drinking to the Middle-Garth's red-bearded Warder in thin ale mixed with melted snow and calling upon him to drive back the frost giants again. A month and a half had passed between Yule and the time that the icicles began to drip from the eaves of the hall and the frozen earth no longer rang hard and sharp underfoot, but sucked muddily at the soles of Sigilind's boots. She could see the axe edges of hipbones and the bands of ribs pressing against the clothing of thanes and thralls alike, the farmers' faces pinched and gray with hunger as they mixed their meal with more water each day. Some of the cattle and horses, too weak to stand, had gone down to their knees, staring huge-eyed and mournful over the wooden planks that blocked their aisles from the rest of the hall; a mare and a bull had already died, their meatless bones and hides boiled for soup till no more could be cooked out of them. But near the middle of Solmonth the ewes began to drop their lambs; the waters came roaring down from the mountains, their wild white froth stained brown with mud and clumps of dead leaves; a crust of dirty ice crystals refroze every night over the snow on the fields, but dripped away in the sun; and Sigilind knew that she could hold back no longer from sending Harigastir to her brother.

Sigigairar and Sigilind were sitting in the hall together three days later when the searchers came back bearing the dripping body of Sigigairar's second son. His body was broken and battered, the back of his skull bashed in, though the water had washed the stains of brain and blood from his fair hair. Sigilind closed her eyes for a moment: she had known, she thought, from Harigastir's first howl when she stuck the needle through his sark and skin that he would fare no better under her twin's testing than his brother had; but the sight of his small corpse, dressed in the brown tunic she had tried to sew on to him, wrenched through her hunger-shrunken entrails as though a hand had swept through her belly to gather their cords and yank.

Sigigairar did not move as he listened to the tall, black-haired farmer Arnuwaldar tell him, "We found him in the river. Maybe he hit his head on the rock first, or maybe he drowned and the rest happened as it carried him along. The flood's running cruel this year, and you know the nicor-kind are hungry at winter's end."

The drighten turned to look at his wife. "Now both our sons are gone, but we have the hammer and anvil to forge more," he said to Sigilind. He stroked a chapped finger gently down the hollow side of her cheek. "Let Harigastir be set in the earth with such as he will need—let our seed sprout again." The skin of his face was drawn into harsh, deep folds, flesh eaten down to bedrock by old hunger and new sorrow. It did not change as he stood, pulled his wife to her feet and led her into the back chamber, leaving Arnuwaldar to stand with Harigastir's drenched corpse in his arms, nor did it change as their hipbones and ribs grated against each other, thin lips flat over hard teeth as Sigigairar kissed his wife, trying to caress her shrunken womb back to life with his rough, cold hands and awaken the hoard of seed that lay within the bony cradle of her pelvis. Slowly Sigilind felt herself thawing a little at his familiar touch; but the fetters of winter still locked her up within, unfreed by his returning warmth. She could feel how her husband eased when he was done, wiry muscles uncoiling and the deep straight lines of his brow fading like the furrows of a ploughed field blurring under a heavy rain. "You see," he breathed softly, holding her bone-sharp body close to him, "we haven't lost everything, my love."

"No," Sigilind murmured, "we haven't." Already a thought was beginning to rise from the darkness in her mind—a thought that made her tremble with both excitement and fear as she saw her own face mirrored within her mind, felt her own touch strong upon her body in place of Sigigairar's. She could not, would not put a name to what she wanted, thinking only, No son of Sigigairar's will take my revenge for me.

The days lengthened swiftly through the end of Solmonath and beginning of Hrethmonth, each one easing the cold a little and bringing a little more brightness to the evenings till Freyjar's wain came rolling down from the great hof at Uppsala where the gudhes and gydhjas kept the holy images of the gods and sacrificed to them on the great feast days. The gydhja who rode in the wain with Freyjar this year was a young woman of no more than fifteen or sixteen. Long white birch twigs, just budding pale green, wove through her long blond curls; she wore nothing else under the heavy green cloak that kept her warm. All the folk gathered as the wain passed, their thin cheers rising through the cold air to hail the might that brought life back to the earth and all who lived on her. They feasted the gydhja as best they could, everyone who had lived through the winter gathering in the hall to honor Freyjar and his priestess. The rough-cut wooden image of the god towered in the drighten's seat, his great phallus jutting out before him to show the blessing of life that he brought. Its head, big as a man's fist, was worn to a soft brown gleam by years of hands touching it for his fruitfulness. They poured out the last of the ale for Freyjar and his priestess and ate the last food they could spare at that feast to show their trust that Freyjar would not betray them by sending another snow.

Laughing, the half-starved men and women gathered before him to touch his stock of life, making ribald jokes and verses in voices feeble from hunger. The gydhja sat sipping her ale, smiling quietly as she watched them like a mother watching her children.

"You never grabbed mine like that!" the carl Hathulaikar shouted at his wife Guthrid when she wrapped her swollen-jointed fingers around the god's maleness as if she were grabbing the hilt of an axe. She shook a winter-dulled brown braid, tilting her pointed nose as she answered, "Could you get it to stand up like that, I might!"

Hathulaikar's one front tooth gleamed as he cupped his palm over the rounded end. "Freyjar'll see that this stallion has more than enough for you, you old mare," he said, tugging at her braid with rough affection.

One of the village boys, Thalir, guffawed hoarsely as he pushed Angantiwar's daughter Hildgunnar toward the image.

"Lively you'll be, you won't lie still, nor will that be boring between your thighs," he chanted at her, grabbing her bottom. A winter of hunger had made her too weak to leap away, but she squeaked and shuffled out of reach, pulling her skirts straight as Thalir chased her up to the god. He was reaching out for her again when he bumped into a bench; too hunger-slowed to catch himself, he toppled like a tall scraggly pine, stretching his length on the floor amid the laughter of the others. Hildgunnar tousled his mat of hair quickly with her foot before she went to brush her fingers over Freyjar's phallus. "Let me marry a better man than Thalir," she said slyly.

Old Tati the Woodcarver, Thalir's grandfather, sucked at his gums and cackled, "That won't be hard! Ask for something else!"

When all the folk had touched the god, Sigilind and Sigigairar rose from the bench and came up together in a sudden hush of stillness, the hall more silent in the wake of the raucous laughter than it had been in its winter emptiness. Sigilind laid her hand on the apple-smooth knob, Sigigairar's long fingers wrapping over and around hers. Freyjar's deep-rooted might and warmth flowed in through her hand to soothe and strengthen her heart with the gentleness and power that she remembered in her father's embrace, making her feel more unshakably safe and loved than she had since leaving Wals' hall. Freyjar, she prayed, Fro Ingwe, give me the strength to bear a true Walsing. Bless my son with the might of the earth, and your warrior-might too, that he be as strong as the atheling-beast, the stag, and brave as a wild boar in battle. Let him be a true fro who can win lands and keep them safe and fruitful in victory and frith. For a moment it seemed to her that an answering tingle glinted in her womb, like a golden grain shining for a moment from the darkness of earth.

The men carried the weak cattle out to pasture through the muddy tracks of Freyjar's wain as it rolled away; two died on their first day out, but the rest gorged greedily on the springing carpet of rich thick grass, their dull winter coats coming away in patches to show glossy hides beneath and their mooing sounding stronger and stronger through the evenings. Everyone labored from sunrise to sunset in the fields, dragging the plows through the early summer mud and planting the rows of seeds along the brown furrows; even Sigigairar strode through the mud, watching his people and bending, now and again, to toss aside a new-turned rock or press a seed more deeply into the wet earth. Despite his nightly strainings, a trickle of blood ran from Sigilind's womb at the full moons of Hrethmonth and Eostre; the runes that came to her from Sigimund in her dreams kept the gates of her body barred so that, push as Sigigairar might, he could never break through the frozen wall that blocked him from the fruitfulness sleeping within her. The thanes and carls began to come to the hall in the evenings again, sharpening their weapons while Sigigairar spoke to them of what they had won harrying down the coast of Gaul in years past, of how the weather seemed good for ships, and how there was land nearby that might be won either by Roman gold or Gautish steel. The hard edges of hackles that had been raised all winter lowered as hands clenched on sword hilts and voices that had whispered and muttered now cheered and shouted their drighten on.

The cut of ice in the Eostre wind had softened to a cool rushing like a stream in summer by the morning of Thrimilci Eve when Sigilind went out to the pasture and saddled up a strong bay horse. She wore a white dress and a dark green cloak; around her neck was the thick gold chain that Sigigairar had given her at their wedding, and her hair, unbound and combed till it shone, flowed heavy and pale behind her. Though still thin from the winter's hunger, she had gained some of her strength back, and as she urged her horse along the muddy path to the edge of the bog, she could feel the muscles of her cheeks twitching from the unaccustomed strain of a smile. The light green leaves of birch and alder trees rustled softly in the breeze; a mist of green veiled the mud, bog daisies shining white and yellow near the edges of the dark pools that lay open under the bright sky. Sigilind's veins tingled almost painfully within her, as though her whole body had lain numb and unmoving and only now was the blood beginning to flow again.

The gelding trotted cheerfully around the edge of the bog, and Sigilind patted its neck affectionately. "Hai, you're glad to be out again, aren't you?" she said to it. "Even if you do have to bear an old crone like me on your back." She stopped suddenly: she had not spoken so lightly since chatting with her children last summer. Not my children, she told herself. Sigigairar's alone. She clenched her hands on the horse's reins, overcome by a sudden trembling as she tried to think of what she could possibly say to the spae-wife to explain her need. And if she doesn't . . . ?

"I am a Walsing and I will do what I must," Sigilind whispered. But if Sigimund didn't . . . ? It was not he who bore the guilt of his brothers' fettered deaths, or an oath of love and troth to their slayer; he had not borne Theudorikijar and Harigastir within his body and watched them grow with love and pride, nor had he chosen their deaths. And a man was not made like a woman; steel his heart as he might, his body could betray him as hers could not.

Sigilind stopped at the tall, flat stone beside the path at the other side of the bog. A lightly carved wheel with four spiral arms whirled red above the thin curve of a ship; between them ran a crude row of runes:

ᚺᛁᛗᛈᚠᚷᚨᛊᛏᛁᛁ:ᚱᛁᛊᛏᛗᛗᛥ:ᚱᛁ ᚠᛟᚱ:

ᚺᛟᛚᛏᛁᚷᚨᛊᛏᛁᛁ:ᛊᛟᛁᛁ::. Leaning closer, Sigilind made out the words, "I Hlewagastir risted r . . ." That must be "runes," she thought . . . "for Holtagastir son." A small burn tinkled and splashed down past it. She pulled on her horse's reins, and its hooves squashing through the mossy bank of the stream. She followed the water upstream for a while, till the land began to rise and she came out of the sparse trees. A hill rose ahead of her and at the bottom was a small house. Freyjadis' brown mare stood by the fence, now and then rubbing against the rough wooden posts to scrape off hunks of her matted winter coat. Two large cats sunned themselves between the herbs growing around the house, one slim, long-legged and black, the other husky, white with black splotches. The house bore no outer adornments, but it seemed to Sigilind, looking at it as her dreams had taught her, that a creature, unseen and winged, sat watching her from the roof; that the turf-chinked stone walls were interwoven with a golden-red basketwork of power; and that something more than beasts stared at her from the yellow eyes of the cats. She stopped at the fence that ringed Freyjadis' yard, unwilling to go farther without announcing herself and yet (as she had dreamed Sigimund's deep trances, his mind and soul bent on the silent whispering of the Herulian's head) afraid to disturb the spae-woman at whatever work busied her on the day of Thrimilci Eve.

The black cat eyed Sigilind with a scornful, narrow glance. Stretching and rising to her feet, her sharp-toothed yawn showing the startling pink of her inner mouth, she let out a loud miaow, stalked to the door of the hut and raised a paw to scratch on it. When no answer came forth from within, she sat down and cocked her leg at Sigilind, licking her own bottom in a most insulting way. Sigilind had to laugh as she watched the black cat industriously grooming her private parts; and with her high, clear giggle came the creak of the door's hinges. The cat scurried away as her mistress came out of the door, raising a hand to shield her eyes against the bright light.

"Sigilind!" she said. "Come in. You can tie your horse to the fence. It's not as flimsy as it looks."

Sigilind tied the horse up near Freyjadis', leaving the two of them to nose each other over the fence, and opened the gate, stepping gingerly past the boundary of the spae-wife's yard. A warm feeling of well-being washed over her as she did, and the sense of being watched that had made her feel uneasy when she stood outside now made her feel safe and cozy.

The inside of Freyjadis' house was comfortably messy with scattered clothes and clay dishes. Bunches of dried herbs hung from the central beam of the ceiling, their sweet scent filling the house. A big-bellied clay cauldron, its sides deeply cut with dark-stained lines, squatted over the ash-furred coals of the hearth in the center of the floor, and to the south of the firepit was a three-footed stool, its legs carved into trailing roots and its seat covered with hide. A flat round drum with dark brown stick figures shattering its pale flatness hung on the smoke-blackened wall beside a rack of wooden bowls and spoons. A pile of thick down quilts and pillows, disarranged as though a giant cat had made her nest amid them, lay on the floor near the south wall. At the east and west sides of the fire sat two large chairs, their wooden sides and backs carved with intertwining spirals and their seats padded with heavy cushions of down-stuffed wool. Freyjadis eased her generous body into one chair and gestured Sigilind to the other.

"What brings you to my house today?" she asked. "Are you coming just to greet the summertime with me? Or do you want Freyja's help to melt the ice so that seed can grow in your womb again?"

To Sigilind's horror, she found that she was weeping, a hot flood of tears rushing down her face. The spae-woman came over to her, holding her head to her soft side and stroking her hair as she cried out all the winter's burdens. After a little while, she gave Sigilind a square of yellowed linen to blow her nose on and wipe her eyes with.

"Now are you ready to tell me what you need?" Freyjadis said gently, her arms still around the younger woman's bony shoulders.

Sigilind raised her head, looking straight into the spae-wife's blue eyes. "I need for you to change shapes with me and lie beside my husband tonight," she said in a rush of breath. "And I need . . . I need to conceive a son."

Like metal set on the smith's fire, Freyjadis' eyes began to glow, the rings around her pupils heating first to gold, then to the piercing gold-white Sigilind remembered. The Walsing met her gaze firmly, strengthened by the heat of her own need-fire glowing from the darkness of her soul.

"By whom? Is making Sigigairar a cuckold part of your revenge?"

"By my brother Sigimund," Sigilind answered. "I must bear a true Walsing, and I can see no other way to do it."

Freyjadis stood gazing at her for a few moments, then padded gracefully around the room, reaching to pull handfuls of dried leaves off the bundles of herbs that hung from the ceiling. She cast them into the cauldron, crouching to blow on the coals and poking, first twigs, then larger sticks, under the pot until the fire burned strongly. A sudden gust of fresh summer wind blew the door open and the two cats stalked in, sitting tall on either side of their mistress with their tails coiled about them. At Freyjadis' gesture, Sigilind closed the door. A heavy, sweet-scented steam was already coiling up from the cauldron, its smell making Sigilind feel dizzy and light-headed. Half-seen waves of green and gold and red flowed to darken the Walsing's sight, tinging the turf-chinked stone walls with their shifting hues. Freyjadis rocked back and forth on her heels, breathing in the steam, her sweet husky voice rising to a keening chant, as strange and pleasant as the scent of herbs filling the house. It seemed to Sigilind that she could almost see the steam twisting into ghosts as the spae-wife chanted, hot gray mist turning and seething before her eyes, never still long enough for her to do more than half-guess at its shape before it changed. Strands of Freyjadis' hair rose as though drawn by fur-rubbed amber, the firelight glinting red-gold from its darkness. Her searing gaze stared into the steam, blind to all around her. Sigilind felt her own hairs prickling; though she could not see the spirits above the cauldron clearly, her spine tingled with their presence and the power around her. Suddenly it seemed to her that she could hear the high voices in her head above the spae-wife's voice, singing, "It must be so, a Walsing must be born. So Wyrd has written already, deep in the roots of the Well, so is the orlog laid. Do not hinder, do not harm, the time to turn it is long gone, nor will it come soon again. Let Freyja and Freyjar bless Wodan's work. Sigilind shall bear the weight of its woe."

A whorl of sparks spun and whirled Sigilind's eyes to darkness; she was breathing hard when her sight cleared and the dizziness faded, as though she had swum a long way underwater. The cats scattered away, scampering out in two wide arcs around the hut as Freyjadis stood up, rubbing at the backs of her legs. A tinge of sadness hung over her face like the shadow of a snow-weighted branch as she looked at the young woman before her. Sigilind straightened her back; she knew nothing she had not known before.

"Take off your clothes and sit down," Freyjadis said. "Wait: if you have to piss, go out and do it now, because once I've begun to work, you won't be able to break the ring."

When Sigilind came back in, the floor was covered by signs and runes painted in a red ochre circle about the firepit, with only one gate left through which she might pass. She knew the runes and some of the signs; others were strange to her, their interweaving angles and curves drawing her sight into a twisting maze. Gingerly she stepped through the opening in the ring, walking carefully around the piles of herbs, bones, rocks and scraps of hide that the spae-woman had arranged neatly within. Freyjadis watched her, nodding slightly as Sigilind traced her path inward.

The older woman stood, stretching, then pulled her pale green tunic over her head and reached behind to unhook her red skirt, which floated down into a bright puddle around her bare feet. Her full breasts sagged only a little, her widely curved body firmer and stronger than her loose garments had made it look. Flushing, Sigilind loosed her key-jangling girdle, then unhooked the buttons down the back of her white dress and stepped out of it. She was acutely aware of how her hipbones and ribs stuck out, the round-ness of motherhood starved from her by the long winter, of how thin her legs and arms were beside the strong limbs of the spae-woman. It's as well we're changing shapes, she thought bitterly. What could Sigimund see in me now?

But Freyjadis, too, sighed as she looked at the other woman's body. "Are you sure you want to change shapes with a fat old bag like me?" she asked Sigilind. "I think you're getting the worst of the bargain."

"Oh, no," Sigilind protested. Unaccountably she giggled. The spae-wife smiled back at her, showing her yellowed, broken teeth.

"You see?" she said. "You have nice white teeth and your nose doesn't look like a snowshoe. What makes you think a pretty girl like you won't have a better chance to get what you want than an old crone?" She made an awful face at Sigilind, crossing her eyes and letting her tongue flop limply out of her mouth. Sigilind laughed harder, feeling suddenly lightheaded. Freyjadis rearranged her features. "Well, if you're sure, then."

"I'm sure," Sigilind said, her laughter calming to the odd spurt of a giggle.

"All right. The first thing . . . " Freyjadis came over to Sigilind and put her hand on the younger woman's belly, just below the navel. Her touch was very warm, as warm as the body of a cat or a hound. "You set this block up yourself, didn't you?" she asked.

"Yes. I didn't want any more children of Sigigairar's."

"Three ice-runes—simple, I suppose, but powerful enough against some-one who doesn't know how to break them. You know the runes, then? Did Kara teach you?"

"No. I learned from Sigimund, who learned them from the Herulian in the howe."

Freyjadis muttered something that Sigilind couldn't quite hear, then said, "All right, I want you to think hard on *uruz*—that's a rune of water which will melt this ice without harming you and ready your womb for new growth. Then, when I tell you, think of *fehu*, the rune of Freyja's fire that will quicken your fruitfulness for tonight so that you can win your brother's love and the son you want."

Sigilind nodded. The spae-woman traced ᚢ, the rising and falling stream of *uruz*, above her womb; together their voices rose to chant the rune name as Sigilind felt the flood of power roaring into her pelvic cradle. The frozen knot within melted like ice floating in the river at winter's end, easing the tightness that had bound her; warmth trickled down from her womb. Frey-jadis' hand traced the straight stave and two upright branches of *fehu*, ᚠ ; they changed their chant. It seemed to Sigilind that she could see within herself; see the emptiness of her womb now filling with a ruddy glow like molten gold as the warmth spread out from it through her pelvis with the familiar, urgent pleasure that she had never hoped to feel again. Her breasts were beginning to flush, her nipples swollen as if with milk by the time the spae-woman stepped back. Freyjadis' face was pink and beaded with drops of sweat; her breath, like Sigilind's, was coming fast.

"That should do it for you," she said. "Stay there." Dipping her finger in her pot of red ochre, she went over to the gap in the circle and painted it closed. "Now, when you put my clothes on, remember that you're not only changing your dress. You will not be Sigilind any more; you will have no revenge to seek, no sorrow burdening your heart and no cold iron bracing your spine. You are becoming Freyjadis the spae-woman, fire below and green earth above; you go about at night, as Freyja does, like a nanny goat among the bucks or a cat in heat, sharing your love with whom you will— and enjoying every minute of it."

Sigilind could feel the heat rising to her face, but she did not turn her gaze away modestly; instead she grinned with excitement as she pulled the spae-woman's green tunic over her head and stepped into her red skirt. Both garments were far too big for her; she felt silly, but also free enough to slouch a little and shake her thin hips in their vasty envelopment. The spae-wife's amber necklace felt light and warm as she lifted it on. Freyjadis grunted as she tugged Sigilind's white dress over her body, its tightness straining over her hips and squashing her breasts down into huge flat ovals. Sigilind was wider-shouldered than she; she could just fasten the top two buttons, but the rest of the back gaped widely down past her buttocks. She could barely tie the two dangling ends of Sigilind's girdle together. The falcon-headed dagger pressed cruelly into the fat of her side, and Sigilind's gold chain, which fell loosely between the Walsing's breasts, only came a little below Freyjadis' collar. In the tight dress, the spae-woman stood ramrod straight, her movements stiff and slow as though she were laced into leather and weighted by a byrnie's metal. She walked around the circle thrice, turn-ing as if pierced by an unseen axis, then bent her knees slowly and sank down to throw some of her little piles into the kettle, others onto the fire. The black cat beside her gave a loud, anxious miaow as the acrid scent of burning hide rose from the flames together with a pungent smoke.

Freyjadis reached out her arms across the fire to Sigilind, who raised her own to join hands with the spae-woman, staring into her eyes and trying to feel the delicate points of bone beneath the plumpness of her cheeks, her slightly tilted nose lengthening and thickening to lumpy straightness, heavy fullness weighting her breasts and belly as it had when she was pregnant, rounding and widening her buttocks and thighs, filling out the drooping folds of the vastly oversized skirt which was nearly falling off her hips. She could almost feel her arms swelling with softly padded strength, her eyes

R
H
I
N
E
G
O
L
D

ᚻ
1
4
3

burning gold-white with the reflection of the bright eyes glowing into her own through the thickening smoke as Freyjadis and she began to chant together:

> I wear thy hide,   thy hair to hood,
> thy shape my own   in seeming be,
> Freyja's smoke   this fire-night
> turning round   the thoughts of all
> Haith in falcon   hood flies forth
> mazing all   the minds of men
> Gullveig's glittering,   gleaming glow
> blaze and all   but seeming blind
> I wear thy hide,   thy hair to hood,
> thy shape my own   in seeming be!

Once they chanted it, Sigilind could hear her voice rising high above the spae-woman's. The second time they sang on one pitch, both voices slightly rough and blurred; by the third, Sigilind could hear the other woman's clear voice with its faint resonant undertone ringing above her own low, smoky chanting. With the last words, "Thy shape my own in seeming be!" they leaped up together over the fire, changing places. Sigilind looked through the fading steam, staring in wonder at her own plump, tanned hands grasping the slender white fingers of Freyjadis. Wavy strands of dark hair straggled around her face; she tossed her head, flinging her heavy mane back and gazing at the long straight fall of pale hair around Freyjadis' high, remote features. She laughed the spae-woman's deep, husky laugh, twirling around and reveling in the way her wide hips swayed under her flowing red skirt, the freedom of her heavy breasts shifting within her loose green tunic beneath the rope of amber.

Freyjadis spread out her arms, slowly spinning. She walked thrice about the circle again, almost too proud and stiff to release the power she had bound up in its ring. With a sharp kick she scattered the red ochre and broke the line, and Sigilind sagged a bit as the pent-up might sprang free. The cats rubbed about Freyjadis' thin ankles, mewing and glaring yellowly at Sigilind.

"It is done," Sigilind's own voice said to her. "Go on, and Freyja be with you. I'll meet you here in three nights."

"Thank you," Sigilind said breathily, swaying out of the hut. The grass was soft under her thickly calloused feet. She stretched like a cat in the sunshine, enjoying the warmth through her light clothing. Freyjadis' dark mare looked down a long brown nose at her, then snorted and picked her way surefootedly through the herb garden to the other side of the house; but the bay tied at the gate rolled its eyes at her, whickering and stamping one foot as she drew near. "You don't recognize me now, do you?" she said, light-hearted as a girl. She took a bag from its back, despite its restless

shifting, then walked down to the snowmelt-swollen stream, following its
rushing path up along the way to the mountain.

Sigimund sat on one of the boulders outside his cave, staring bitterly at the
flaming crimson and pink of the Sun as she sank down to the dark ocean.
Since he had thrown Harigastir's body into the river, he had not called on
Widuhundaz, nor had he had any mood to do more than he needed to for
survival. At times, he thought that perhaps he should travel south, take
passage on some ship and fight his way back to his father's realm. What
good could there be in skulking here in his cave for ten or twelve years
more, waiting for Sigilind to bear more sons—for him to slaughter till he
found the one the Herulian had promised? For all he knew, the ghost might
have lied to him out of vengefulness, bent on punishing his howe-breaking
in this subtler way since it could not slay him outright. Sunken deep in his
dark thoughts, he did not notice the sound of the woman's footsteps till she
stood, breathing heavily, before him.

Jerking his head up, Sigimund grasped for the spear that leaned on the
rock beside him. The woman laughed softly, huskily, tossing back a thick
mane of amber-glinting dark hair.

"I promise I won't hurt you," she said, her voice rich as the scent of musk.
She moved closer, casting a sideways glance up at him. "But I've lost my
way and I need a place to stay for the night." Sigimund felt a wave of warmth
spreading out from her, sending a tingle up his spine as he looked down at
the gentle sway of her full, free breasts beneath the loose green linen. She
wore a fine amber necklace, but her feet were bare, her arms strong and her
skin browned like that of a farmer's wife. Was she expecting to be raped?
he wondered darkly. If she would come to a mountain where outlaws were
known to live and ask strange men for shelter, she certainly had no right to
complain of whatever happened. Not that he would . . . but some might . . .
He glanced at the hands that had slain his sister's two children. How, stained
by kinslaying, could he think of begetting a child himself? Surely Fro Ingwe
and Frowe Holda would raise their curses to freeze his ballocks to cold
stones, to wither all his strength in the act?

Sigimund leapt down from the rock, landing lightly in front of her. "I will
be glad to share my dinner with you, and give you shelter for the night,"
he said. "But I will warn you now, you may find my food meagre and myself
ill company."

She smiled, showing him teeth that were stained and broken, but sound
at the roots. "I brought some food for my journey, so I have enough to share
with you. It's true, you do look grim, but I think I may not find you the
worst of companions. Now tell me your name, if you will, forest-goer?"

"I am called Grim, the son of Nawan," Sigimund answered slowly. "I have
no other kin, save a sister who is parted farther from me than Sunna from

her brother Moon. And who are you, woman who wanders through the haunt of trolls and wolves?"

"I am called Freyjadis," the woman answered. "Which are you, Grim? A troll or a wolf? Answer quickly now, you can't be both."

Her ready wit surprised Sigimund into laughter. No woman had spoken to him like that since Sigilind sailed away with Sigigairar.

"A wolf, I suppose," he said. "Will you come into my den?"

Freyjadis giggled, brushing back a few wisps of hair and lowering her blue eyes, then glancing up at him. "I don't know," she said slowly, teasingly. "I understand it's dangerous in the dens of wolves. Horrible things can happen to a woman alone." She laughed again, a strangely light and girlish sound; her plump hands fluttered. Sigimund could tell that she was older than he, thirty or so, yet—he thought suddenly—she seemed like a maiden on the brink of her bridal, excited in her new womanhood but still unsure in it. Ridiculous, he said to himself; you've been away from women too long. Maybe . . .

Only the red rim of Frowe Sunna showed above the horizon when the two of them went in, but the early summer evening was still bright with a blue light and a few small flames writhed up from the sticks to light Sigimund's cave. The cloak of ill-tanned rabbit skins that had kept him warm all winter was now spread over the blankets of his bed; the head of the Herulian was hidden within a rough wooden box with a circle of blood-stained runes cut deeply into its lid; and two chairs made of elkhide stretched over sinew-tied branches, one large and one smaller, stood to either side of the firepit. From the roof of the cave hung a haunch of smoked meat, and a stew of elk and wild spear leeks simmered in the clay pot that sat on a raised platform of sticks and bones above the fire.

Freyjadis flopped down into the smaller chair, wriggling her ample bottom until she was comfortable. She pulled a large round of cheese and a long-necked, stoppered pot out of her bag. "No bread, I'm afraid. It's been a bad winter."

Sigimund looked at the cheese, his mouth starting to water as he smelled its rich scent. Freyjadis unstopped the pot and offered it to him. His breath caught as the thick, creamy milk flowed down his throat and he had to clamp his teeth together to keep from spewing it over the woman as he coughed. She went over to him and patted him on the back with a strong hand until he could breathe again. "I expect you haven't had any of that in a while, have you?" she said. Her breasts swung as she broke the cheese in two and handed the larger piece to him. Belatedly he thanked her, dipping his bone-handled ladle into the pot and filling two wooden bowls with elk stew.

The taste of the cheese wrenched something inside Sigimund. He had not eaten cheese since he left home, and it reminded him painfully of Wals' hall with the Barnstock rustling above, of the pride he had felt when he stood at his father's side and looked over the warband gathered before them, over the lands they had won and held from the Northern pirates and Eastern invaders.

"Why so sad?" Freyjadis asked him. "Does it taste ill?" She sniffed carefully at her own piece before taking a bite.

"When I last ate like this, I was first among my father's thanes, sitting in a great wooden hall with nine brave brothers and a band of the best warriors around me," Sigimund answered slowly. "Gold rings wound my arms. I dressed in the finest of linens and my father's wife brought me ale in a cup of Roman glass. Now, if that lady still lives, she is a captive; if that hall is not yet burnt, a drighten who is no kin of mine rules within it. My sword was the best of swords, truly Weland's work; now it sleeps on the thigh of my foe, and his hand brings its serpent-wrought blade to bite for his glory, while I live like a wild beast, outlaw—and kinslayer. Why then should I not be sad?"

Freyjadis' eyes were bright with tears in the firelight. "But surely you only wait for your time to strike? You seem to be too strong to let your ill-luck fell you; you are—from what you tell me, you must be—of an atheling's line. Do you not hope to win back what you held, and more? If the gods should forsake you, it seems to me that your own might and main are enough for you to gain as many victories as any man."

"If the gods should forsake me," Sigimund said softly. And had not Wodan left him to face the wolf alone; and had not he himself, with Sigilind's help, won his way out of the stocks and overcome the dweller in the howe? "True, I have more strength than most, but I have also heard it said that I shall win back the sword Wodan gave me in my hour of need and avenge my father."

"What more could you ask, then?"

"Not to have slain my sister's sons!" The cry tore its way out of Sigimund before he could stop it. "They were not . . . truly of our line, and lacked courage. And she told me herself that I should do it."

"Then let hers be the doom for it." Freyjadis' low voice rang grimly. "If you bear fear or regret in your heart, it will weaken your arm when the time comes to strike. For the sake of your slain, put these away till your foe lies dead before you." Her voice softened as she tilted her head to look up into his eyes, her lips curving into a smile. "But you're not going out to take your revenge tonight, are you?"

"No," Sigimund admitted.

"Then let it be till the time has come." She stared directly at him. "Believe me: you have no need for shame." The fire cast a strange whitish glow around her pupils; it seemed to Sigimund as though a fetter had sprung free within him. Witchcraft? he thought, wary for a moment as a tingle ran through his body. But the relief he felt was so great that he could not find it in himself to question her or to search within his soul for the charms Widuhundaz had taught him against witches' work on the mind.

Freyjadis smiled again. "Stop your brooding and eat your stew before it gets cold," she ordered. "You'll curdle it if you keep frowning at it."

To please her, Sigimund began to force a smile, and found that it came easily as he looked at her sprawling comfortably—almost wantonly—over his chair. They ate quickly, passing the milk back and forth between them. Sigimund noticed that she kept looking at him and then glancing quickly away when he looked back, as if she were embarrassed.

"This is very good stew," Freyjadis said. "You've learned to cook . . . I mean, being all alone, I suppose?" She flavored the comment with another of her teasing sideways glances.

"I suppose so," Sigimund muttered. "I've been eating it long enough not to notice."

The woman delicately licked her bowl clean and finished off her cheese, leaving the last drink of milk for him. A warm breeze, scented with new leaves, was blowing around the boulders that hid the cave's opening; the sunset had dimmed to a purple twilight. Hidden fire seemed to glimmer at the edges of Sigimund's sight, sparking up his back and filling him with a vibrant, swelling might. He rose to his feet and took Freyjadis by her plump hands, helping her to stand. His cave seemed too cramped to him, smelling of badly tanned rabbit, old elk bones and unwashed blankets. Following the urges that pulsed more and more strongly through his heart and body, he put his arm around the woman's shoulders, leading her outside. Her hips swayed against his thigh; she nestled more firmly into the crook of his arm as they rounded the boulders and came out into the light of the new Moon.

Freyjadis tilted her head back, her eyes closed and lips parted a little. Sigimund bent to kiss her, breathing in her sweet herbal smell and pressing her rounded body to him. Her breath was coming quick and soft when the kiss ended; she opened her eyes, their bright-ringed blue glow drawing him inward as if into a watery cavern lit by white-burning gold. Together they walked down the rocky slope of the mountain and into the rustling wood where the wild flowers starring the grass breathed sweetness around them and the Moon's silvery light flooded cool through the new leaves to wash away the wintry storms that had raged in Sigimund's heart and open him to the fire that seemed to thrum up through his feet from the damp earth. He embraced Freyjadis again, reaching around to unhook her skirt and caress her buttocks as it dropped. She was already pulling off her tunic, her thick waves of hair cascading around her bare shoulders as she cast it aside, then untied his breeches and lifted them carefully off. Her hands trembled on his body; together they sank down to the cool tangle of wet grass. Sigimund could feel the power flowing between their bodies as he thrust into her, between their eyes as their gazes met and locked in a single burning spark. For a wishful moment it almost seemed to him that he was looking down into Sigilind's face, that pale hair, rather than dark, flowed over the grass and that he pressed against the slender, steely litheness of the woman's body that was twin to his own; but Freyjadis' strong arms embraced him, her wide thighs locked about his body as her sweet low voice whispered, "Sigimund, Sigimund," breathlessly, and there was nothing but her and the ecstasy flaring through him. Sigimund gasped and cried out wordlessly, flashes of darkness and light searing his eyes and roaring through his ears like a great wind as he spilled and she tightened about him, knotting his seed deep within her as he, slain, unwillingly began to draw out of her.

Sigimund and Freyjadis lay against one another, caressing each other lazily for a while, till the swiftly cooling breeze raised a stippled filigree of goosebumps across their naked bodies. They helped each other to dress and walked quietly up to Sigimund's cave, where Freyjadis curled against Sigimund under his smelly rabbit-skin cloak and itchy winter blankets. He was almost asleep when a single thought surfaced from the darkness.

"How did you know my name was Sigimund?" he asked. He felt the muscles under her softness jerk stiffly, then relax.

"I'm a witch," Freyjadis murmured softly. "Don't worry. It's our secret. No one but Sigilind and I will know."

Sigimund felt vaguely that he ought to ask her something else, but he was already falling asleep in her comforting warmness, one arm over her and the other turned out behind him. Tomorrow, he thought, and then the thought sank into a golden glimmer that dazzled all but Freyjadis's nearness from his dreams and his thoughts, till he awoke wrapped in the scent of her thick rich hair, remembering nothing except their love, and reached for her again.

Sigilind stayed in the cave with her brother for three nights—three nights and two days of making love, of wrestling playfully in the grass, of laughing and singing and walking through the woods in summer's beginning together. But the wind came up before the third dawn, waking Sigilind with a sharp drum roll of rain spattering on rocks, and she knew that she would have to go back to Freyjadis' house. She slid out of the blankets silently, bending down to kiss her sleeping brother one last time before she pulled on Freyjadis' clothes again and steeled herself for the cold, dark walk back to the spae-woman's hut.

The dawn was just beginning to glimmer gray behind the clouds when Sigilind came to the fence where her horse was tied. Freyjadis stood at the gate, her slim white figure shining through the morning darkness, her high-boned face fair and grave.

"Have you done what you had to do?" she asked. Sigilind's smug grin answered her question. "Come in, then. I'm sorry," she added irrelevantly.

The fire was burning under the cauldron within, its pungent smoke filling the air. "This will be easier, since we're returning to our own shapes. All you have to do is change clothes with me again and say, 'I, Sigilind, the daughter of Wals, take back my own hide,' as you dress."

The two women took off their clothes, exchanging them silently. Her voice wavering upward as she spoke, Sigilind said, "I, Sigilind, daughter of Wals," (as Freyjadis' voice cracked downward on "I, Freyjadis, daughter of Anulaibhar") "take back my own hide." She laced her white dress easily up her back with fingers that felt thin and hard as a bird's claws, pulling her hair out to fall straight and pale over her shoulders and hooked her loose girdle around her slender waist. But she was still a little sore between the legs, as she had been; she could still feel the faint stickiness of Sigimund's seed when she moved, and she knew that what he had planted in her would stay and grow.

With a sigh of relief, Freyjadis relaxed lumpily into her own clothing, settling her skirt over her wide hips and shaking her amber necklace out over her heavy breasts. "Well, that's that," she said. She stood looking at Sigilind for a moment, then set one pudgy palm on her hip and extended the other teasingly, raising her eyebrows. "Come on, girl. Give. Your husband's awfully nice, but three nights of fun isn't quite enough for a working like that."

"I . . ." Sigilind started.

The spae-woman laughed. "Oh, go on. I'm just teasing you. I didn't expect you to have brought anything with you. You can send whatever you think it was worth. If you like, you can wait to make sure you caught."

Sigilind took the gold chain from her neck, its glittering smoothness running through her fingers like heavy river water. "Here," she said. "Will you take this?"

Freyjadis drew her eyebrows together, whistling softly. "Are you sure, Sigilind? You were raised as a drighten's daughter—do you know what this is worth?"

"I know. Sigigairar's given me more gold than I want, and you . . . you've given me something I . . . " She couldn't finish her words. Freyjadis embraced her, the pillowy softness of her body feeling strange to Sigilind after her three nights of lying against Sigimund.

"There, go on, girl," she said. "Your husband will be getting up now, and he'll want to see you before he leaves. For the last two days he's been getting his men and ships ready to go raiding again. You told him you were going to the spae-woman to make sure he left you with something before he went out fighting; he'll be ready for that, and the gods know he won't be surprised when your tummy starts to swell."

"Thank you," Sigilind said as Freyjadis turned her around and pointed her out of the door.

"Don't thank me yet," she said. "Go on. Scat!"

Sigilind's horse, ridden here by Freyjadis, was still saddled; she untied the reins, got on and started riding back. Halfway there it began to rain again, and by the time she had put the horse in the barn and walked to Sigigairar's hall she was soaked to the skin.

Sigigairar met her at the door, his hair disheveled and red tunic skewed on his shoulders. His long face was more alive than she had seen it since Harigastir's death, his eyes fully open as if he liked what he saw and his mouth quirked up in a grin. He grabbed her and kissed her soundly, their lips making a little boglike sucking noise as they broke.

"Did the spae-wife do what you went for?" he asked breathlessly. She reached up to straighten the neck of his tunic and brush his hair back into place.

"She did," Sigilind answered. She slipped her arm around her husband's waist, her elbow resting on the pommel of Sigimund's sword, and thought: if only I dared to grab it! One yank, one thrust; but that would shame Wals' line as surely as if he were never avenged. She could afford to be generous, with Sigimund's child in her womb. So she moved her hands to caress Sigigairar as they walked into their chambers, murmuring love words as they undressed. Once his touch was too rough; he slowed to a gentler movement as she murmured a complaint of soreness, his grin showing that he took the signs of Sigimund's ardor for his own.

"No, stay there," he said when he was done, standing up and girding on his sword belt. "I've heard if you rest all day, you won't risk shaking the seed loose. One last kiss for luck, and then I've got to go—you know we would have sailed at dawn if I didn't love you too much to miss this one last chance. But I'll bring you back a silk dress, see if I don't, and maybe some Roman work from the Gaulish coast."

He bent to kiss her lingeringly, the warmth of his lips stiflingly close. Outside rose the rough bass of his steersman Gunthaharir: "Hai! Sigigairar, the damn tide's about to turn. Are we going now, or do we wait till night?"

"We leave now!" Sigigairar roared back. He caressed the sunken hollow between Sigilind's hipbones as though he could already feel the seed beginning to grow in it, his thin lips trembling as though he were trying to say—or not to say—something else.

"Fare well," Sigilind said.

"Stay well, my wife," Sigigairar answered.

She pulled the blankets up to cover herself as he banged the door open and hurried out, one hand flying out behind him as an afterthought to fling it closed.

Sigilind wiped the wetness of Sigigairar's kiss off with the corner of a blanket. She lay back dreamily, her husband's spent seed running out of her. As she drifted back to sleep again, she crossed her hands over her womb to shield the Walsing child within.

14

SIGILIND'S SON

The snows were piled in drifts higher than a man's head when Sigilind lay in her birthing bed, heavy white flakes whirling through the darkness of a winter morning and thunder rumbling softly over the windswept sea. By late in the afternoon, she still lay straining and white, biting her lip to keep from moaning; Helche and the Welsh girl looked and shook their heads.

"It's too big," the squat thrall said gloomily. "We'll have to send for the spae-wife. Poor Sigigairar, and after it seemed his luck had turned well again." She went out, leaving the other to tend to Sigilind.

The edge of Sigigairar's voice cut shrilly through the door. "I don't care how hard it's snowing. You nithling, Sigilind and my son are lying on the edge of death in there—are you afraid of a little weather? All right, the gods curse you, I'll go myself." There was a slight pause, the mumbling of a deeper voice, then, "She'll come if I have to pick her up and carry her every step of the way! Get my horse ready, since you don't have the spirit to go out yourself."

As another contraction seized her, Sigilind grasped the Welsh girl's hand so hard that the thrall cried out in pain. She slackened off, gritting her teeth.

"Get me the sword," she rasped. "Get the sword from Sigigairar and bring it to me. Hurry, before he leaves."

The girl scurried away, leaving Sigilind alone in the shadowy room. From the corner of her eye, she could see the dark figures of ghost-women around her: the idises, the dead women of her kindred, come to bring her child to birth or carry them both away to Holda's quiet kingdom. She had not seen them so clearly in her easy birthing of Sigigairar's children, but now they bent over her, shadows wavering with the firelight. Their faces were veiled in the darkness that wrapped them. She knew that her mother could not be among them; if Wodan's wish-maiden was nearby she rode above in the storm, warding her daughter from all the ill things that howled in the wind and scratched at the door of the hall with icy claws. Sigilind's womb cramped again and she bore down hard, gripping at the shadowy hands of the women by her bedside, their ghostly strength steadying her till the Welsh girl bore Sigimund's sword back in.

Sigilind grasped the sword firmly by the hilt; the sheath slid from it. The firelight gleaming down the wyrmlike twinings of light steel and dark on its blade drew her mind, easing her pain as her body pushed again at the huge burden of the child within her, trying to force it out of her belly's mound through a passageway that was too narrow. A dizzying wave of darkness rose over her mind; as if from a great height, she thought she saw Sigimund huddled within his cave, wrapped in deerskins and rabbit fur before the Herulian's head that rested on top of its chest within the circle of runes. His face was pink and sweaty; his lips paled and he gripped his knife's hilt tightly as each contraction rippled through Sigilind's body, as though he, too, strained to give their child birth. He was carving runes on a white piece of birchwood: ᛒ, *berkano*, the birch rune for the birthing, ᛗ, *dagaz*, day, to bring the child to life; ᚠ, *ansuz* the third, rune of Wodan, to loose her womb and open the way to bring the soul of their line from the hidden worlds. Drawing the edge of his knife across the palm of his hand so that a line of bright blood sprang out, he dipped the point in the blood and dyed the runes, chanting their names in a deep voice. His magical song's scratchy resonance rang through Sigilind, who echoed the galdor-chant in a whisper; but it was not enough. She could feel the child tearing at her—claws of a wolf, teeth of a wolf, as if Kara had come again in its new-formed body—and clutched more tightly the sword hilt to strengthen her against the whimper beating at the barred gate of her mouth. Then the Herulian was speaking, his hoarse murmur breathing through her skull. "Now Sigilind the wod of the wolf bears; thou must to thee draw it, or else she shall to Walhall fare upon it. Take the hide, Sigimund Wargaz-Bane; the wolf-shape upon thee thou must take, before it her steed becomes."

Sigilind saw the shadow of the wolf's head rise above her brother's own as he lifted the Herulian's hide up, lowering it onto himself. As Sigimund fell to all fours, howling and slavering with the wolf's hide tightening his body into its own shape, Sigilind felt a wave of wind bearing her up and the rending pain in her womb easing. She breathed deeply, pushing the air out in a long slow stream; she could feel her body opening to the might thrumming through her, and with one huge, tearing heave, she forced her child out.

The Welsh girl carefully peeled the milky caul back from its big head. As soon as its mouth was free, it let out a lusty howl that rang through the room, drowning the screaming of the blizzard outside. She held it up to Sigilind, her empty mouth stretched into a dark grin. Sigilind laughed through her pain when she saw the little penis hanging between his legs, hearing, like a faint roaring in her ears, Sigimund's cry of joy.

Her son wriggled and kicked so that the thrall could barely hang on to him. Sigilind laid the sword beside her and reached out for the baby, hissing as her last contraction forced the slippery sack of the afterbirth out into the Welsh girl's hands. Putting him to her breast, oblivious to the thrall cleaning her lower body, she whispered in his ear, "Now you are born of Wals' true line, and you shall grow to avenge him."

Sigilind had slept and woken again, and was chewing on a piece of dried fish when she heard Sigigairar's shivering whoop of joy and his shout for hot ale. Her husband and the spae-wife came into the chamber together, their cloaks dripping with melting snow and droplets running from Sigigair-ar's icy beard.

"Is it true?" Sigigairar said. "Have I a son?"

"He is strong and healthy," Sigilind answered, lifting the baby up for Sigigairar to see him more closely.

The drighten nodded in satisfaction. "He's bigger than the other ones were." Sigigairar reached out to tickle the child under the chin with one cold finger. Sigilind's son howled at the touch and snapped his tiny pink gums as if he were trying to bite Sigigairar, unfocused blue eyes glittering almost frighteningly. "Ha, he's a warrior already," the drighten said proudly. He turned to Freyjadis, embracing her thick figure so hard that the air whuffed out of her lungs like a horse whose rider had suddenly tightened the saddle girth. "Nine months since my wife came to you," he said. "What can I give you that will pay for this rightly?"

"You owe me nothing, Drighten Sigigairar," Freyjadis answered. The cloak and scarves that had muffled her face from the blizzard's fury hid her ex-pression, but her voice sounded resigned and rather sad. "Let your joy in Sigilind's son be enough."

"I must give you some payment," Sigigairar argued. "Land? Gold? Cattle? Tell me what you want, and I will give it to you gladly."

It seemed to Sigilind for a moment that she could feel the brief spark of Freyjadis' glance passing over the naked sword by her side, too swift for thought or eyes to follow. Then the spae-woman shook her hooded head. "Truly, I have done only what I needed to—only what the gods would have me do. I will take no payment from you for it."

"Tell me if you change your mind," Sigigairar said. "Will you at least stay till my son's naming feast?"

Freyjadis looked up at the covered smokehole, then removed her wet hood and began to unwrap the scarves from around her face. "I don't think I have much choice, do I? I will stay gladly."

And so in nine days Sigilind broke the ice on the river and drew out the water that ran beneath its cold bridge. She had healed quickly; she was able to bear her son along the twisting path that led from the hall through the wood to the holy grove where the harrow stone dwelt. The snowy road was well trodden before her; nearly all of Sigigairar's folk had wrapped them-selves in thick wool and hides with the fur turned inward, braving the winter to come to the name-giving of their drighten's son. Sigilind knew they would be watching the boy closely to see how he grew, for the Ingling king's fruitfulness was the luck of his land. She was sorry that—even for a few years—the might of Sigimund's seed would help to strengthen Sigigairar's name, but it could not be helped.

Sigilind's son yelled loudly as the icy water touched his forehead, bellowing bright rage as Sigigairar lifted him up. "So I give you the name Sinfjotli, Sigigairar's son, and take you into the Ingling line," the drighten cried out. But even as he spoke, Sigilind saw the wolf's pelt peeling back from her brother's face, leaving him pale and naked against the mountain top's snow with the grayish white fur in a heap at his feet. She made a sign of warding—hand formed into the *thurse* rune ▷, with thumb thrust through fist—to break the Ingling's words as he called her child "Sigigairar's son." Sigigairar did not seem to hear the lightning crackle that leapt from her; of all the folk there, only Freyjadis started, and she did not look at Sigilind, but pulled her fur-lined hood more tightly about her ears.

Sinfjotli grew quickly under his mother's unsparing care. At four he was as large as many children of seven and able to recite the tale of the Walsings' lineage in a high voice like the echo of his mother's; he delighted in catching bees within his cupped palm and laughing at the stings that hurt him no more than the pricking of thorns. By the Eostre after his eighth birthday, Sinfjotli was bigger and stronger than Theudorikijar had been at ten years, and Sigilind decided that she would delay no longer.

As she had with Harigastir and Theudorikijar, Sigilind woke Sinfjotli up before dawn. A cold wind sliced through her woolen dress and cloak, and she was pleased to see that, although her son wore only his breeches, he did not rub at his goosepimpled arms, but stood facing the wind as firmly as if he expected to fight a holmgang with it. Sigilind tossed his red tunic over his head and, without a word, stuck her needle and thread through fabric and skin alike. Sinfjotli bore it without a word, only baring his teeth in a fierce grin. When she had sewn across his back she whipped the tunic off, gritting her own teeth as she tore his skin away with the seam. Rivulets of blood ran down Sinfjotli's back, but he laughed, the rough undertone of his voice ringing out grimly.

Sigilind's palms were wet, a fine sweat of nervousness sticking strands of hair to her forehead. "Doesn't that hurt?" she asked her son, her heart beating swiftly with hope.

"Such pain is little to a Walsing," Sinfjotli answered, as she had taught him from his earliest days. He turned to hug his mother around her waist, his ice-bright blue eyes looking up into hers. His face was as like hers as Sigimund's was: pale, high ridges of bone rising like the snowy arches of mountain cliffs above his sharply planed cheeks. Like theirs, his brow was wide, his jawline strong and clear.

Sigilind hugged her son tightly, his trickling blood warm on her hands. She put his tunic back on and wrapped him in a deep blue cloak. For a moment she stood thinking; then, before she could change her mind, she unloosed her girdle and tied it around him, setting his hand to the falcon-head hilt of her mother's dagger.

"Bear this knife well," she said, her voice raspy, like a bronze horn un-blown for years. "It was my mother's; my father gave it to me when I left my home. Bear it well and bring pride to the Walsing line."

"Wals shall never have cause to be ashamed of me," Sinfjotli replied, drawing the dagger and twirling it, its edge slicing through the cold wind with a clean whistle. He slid it back into the sheath at his waist, then stood on tiptoes to kiss his mother. "I love you, Mother," he said. "I promise I won't fail you."

"I love you too, my son," Sigilind said. She looked toward the eastern sky. "Go on, then. I've given you what a mother can give; now it's time for you to go to my brother and learn the ways of a man. Go to the mountain and find his cave: you will know him when you see him, I promise you."

Sinfjotli nodded. He stood poised on one foot a moment, staring at her, then, his eagerness for adventure overcoming him, he dashed down the hill and into the dark rustling forest. Sigilind heard the faint echo of his joyous laughter and smiled grimly to herself, looking northward to the mountain whose snowy top was beginning to glow more palely with the light of day.

Sigimund sat on a flat cracked rock in the wood, his eyes open, but blind to the white sunlight slanting down through the thin green leaves of early summer as he stared into the swirling patterns of might that curled like snakes through the earth around him, spurting up in great fountains through the roots of the trees and spraying in droplets through the grass and the small flowers that carpeted the forest floor. He breathed deeply, stretching his own roots down through the rock to draw in the power of the earth. He had been listening to the singing for a little while before his mind took it as anything more than another part of the wood-sound, but the song was one he had last heard in Wals' hall, sung in the Saxon tongue by a high voice with only a vague sense of tune or key.

> Dark is the day   in the dawn before battle,
> wild the wind as it   howls through the wood,
> grim are the warriors   grinding their spear points,
> gray is the horse whose   hooves ride the wind.
> Ravens are gathered   to watch the grim reaving,
> wolves wait in wood for   the feast that will fall.
> Up, Harimann's warriors!   weapons shall give them
> meat for their merriment   mead running red.

Sigimund knew that high voice with the hint of rough-scarred strangeness at once. It was too pure for a woman's; there was only one in the world who could sound like that. Grinning, he raised his own voice on the next verse.

> Hosts of these harsh men   have harried our homeland
> Rome's growing might   ruthless foe to the free.
> Fire and horn call   our folk to the forest,
> this day shall be dawn for   our folk, or else doom.

With the last words, the singer came into sight. The shifting sunlight through the new leaves dappled his shoulder-length blond hair with gleaming and shadows. He carried a pair of shoes carelessly in his hand, his bare feet, caked with mud and dead leaves, stepped lightly over the first blossoming of summer's edge.

"Hai!" Sigilind's son called. "Sigimund! Your sister sent me here. Are you ready for me?"

Sigimund glanced at the boy, weighing his worth swiftly. He was much taller and stronger of build than Sigilind's other sons had been; no tears stained his fairness as he looked up fearlessly into the eyes of his mother's twin, nor did any hint of Sigigairar's looks catch an aftertaste of bitterness in the back of Sigimund's mind. Sigimund knew that he must seem strange and frightening to a child raised in an atheling's hall, even one in Gautland; but Sigilind's son looked straight back at him, showing no sign of fear or surprise at the sight of this big man whose long hair and beard glittered in a wild blond mane around his weather-worn face, and who wore only the wolf's hide tied around his middle.

"How old are you?" Sigimund asked in surprise. "Surely . . ." Surely my count of winters isn't so far off, he thought. But this boy must be ten or eleven, at least.

"I have eight winters," the boy answered, "but I can wrestle anyone of fourteen to his knees, and Sigigairar's thanes have not found me so weak. And I would have killed any wolf that attacked me; did you kill that one yourself?"

"Let's see how you wrestle," Sigimund said, and sprang at the boy. Sigimund was surprised at the strength with which the sturdy little figure met his playful assault; they wrestled for several minutes before Sigimund finally scooped Sigilind's son off the ground and plunked him gently down on his back, tickling him till he squirmed away. Sigimund nodded approvingly as the boy dusted himself off and crouched down again. "If you go on as you've begun," he said, "I can see that you'll be a man worthy of your mother's line."

The boy didn't speak, but his grin of delight told Sigimund what he needed to know.

"All right, then. What's your name?"

"Mother says it's not always wise to tell people your true name, but I know yours and I'm not afraid of you so it's all right. I'm Sinfjotli."

"Well, Sinfjotli, are you as good at running as you are at wrestling? Can you follow me up the mountain?"

"Try me and see," Sinfjotli boasted, flexing his knees and poising himself for a race. Sigimund whirled and was off, dashing through the trees as swiftly as he could and casting his mind ahead for the cold coiling on the warming stone that would prove in all fairness what he wanted to believe already. His long legs carrying him far ahead of Sigilind's son, he turned aside and scooped up the adder that writhed furiously through his fingers, hissing and striking at him without effect.

The knot was already tied in the wriggling bag of meal and Sigimund seated in his chair beside the embers by the time he heard the sound of Sinfjotli's houndlike panting outside. He waited a few moments, until the boy called out, "Sigimund! Here I am! Where are you?"

Nine years of living through the ferocious Gautish winters and hiding from the sight of men had given Sigimund time to conceal the opening of his cave so cunningly that no one but himself could find it, so that light came in but wind and snow were barred from his door. Now he came out to Sinfjotli and led the boy in through the twisting maze of boulders. Sinfjotli looked around, bright eyes wide as he took in the carved chairs with their cushions of fox fur, the bearskin lying over the bed of deerhides stuffed with feathers, grass and sweet-scented herbs, the large wooden rack on which hung haunches of smoked elk and deer, strips of dried fish and a large round cheese. The sweet musty scent of brewing mead rose from a tall clay crock at the back of the cave; beside Sigimund's spear now leaned a bow with a quiver of arrows by it and a sword in a well-wrought leather sheath. Angular, red-stained patterns of runes were chipped into the rocky walls—runes to ward Sigimund and runes to strengthen him, hallowing his dwelling place and all within.

"Did you do this yourself?" Sinfjotli asked. "Mother said you were living like a wolf in the woods, with only a few scrawny rabbit hides to cover you and nothing to eat except what you could catch or she could leave for you."

"And so I was in the first year," Sigimund said. "Now I have been here nine years, time enough to make most of what I need and to find a place far enough away to sell my furs where no one asks too many questions of a man who comes out of the mountains, if his prices are low and his silver is pure. That keeps me in food well enough; and whatever I can't make or catch, I take from those travelers whose might is less than mine. Did your mother tell you she was sending you to a wild warg, who cares nothing for the laws or the men of these lands where his father was slain? If you stay with me, you will learn to fight by falling upon those who pass through the lands in which we roam and there will be no going back to the world of men for you till we are done with our vengeance."

"Whatever you do, I will do it as well," answered Sinfjotli. "I will fight with you and win myself weapons and armor so that I can aid you in avenging Wals on the drighten Sigigairar."

His eagerness pricked at Sigimund like a thorn. He gazed down at the boy, whose fair hair streamed as ragged and soft as wind-swept clouds, flopping half over one ice-blue eye. Sinfjotli's face was lit by a fierce grin as he stared up at his mother's brother. *If the thought of slaying his own father bothers him,* Sigimund thought, *he hides it remarkably well. He has a Walsing's strength and courage; but does he also have Sigigairar's ill nature, if he cares so little for his own kin?* He shook the thought away. Sinfjotli was young yet; he would have years to test his soul before the two of them stood together against Sigigairar.

"The first task you have to do is a simple one," Sigimund said. He handed the bag of meal to the boy. "Take this meal, knead it well and make bread from it. There is water in that pot by the hearth."

"I don't know much about bread-making. The only grains my mother would have me touch were the Welsh-grains, that is gold in the skald-talk, and she herself played at swords with me more often than she worked with the women at baking. But I will do my best, and if it doesn't taste very good you will know why."

"I believe I will risk it," Sigmund said. "My bread was not worthy of much fame in my first winter here, either. I'll go to gather some firewood. I expect the meal to be well-kneaded when I get back."

As before, Sigmund delayed over gathering the firewood, although the sky was still light. He walked over the wet earth, breathing in the fresh scents of summer's beginning as he wondered what he would do if Sinfjotli's heart failed to match his bold words or if, for all the boy's courage, the bite of the worm were to swell with black poison. The woman Freyjadis had lightened the weight he bore from the deaths of Harigastir and Theudori-kijar; nevertheless, he thought that he could not bring himself to slay another of Sigilind's sons. And if, though he kneaded the worm and took no hurt, Sinfjotli had gotten his father's treachery with his blood, what would Sigmund do then? Could he trust a tainted son of Sigigairar beside him for the work of avenging his father's death and freeing the soul of his line? The question coiled coldly at the bottom of his heart; he knew it would lie there waiting for each careless or malicious word of Sinfjotli's to disturb it till an end was reached. Slowly he turned his steps back up to the mountain.

As he neared the mouth of the cave, he could hear Sinfjotli's clear tuneless voice raised in song again, words that he remembered Sigilind singing long ago.

> Bright above   my battles baleful,
> White are swan-wings'   shining snow.
> Shield-maiden's   sword is swinging,
> bright, sings burning   battle runes.
> Fair hair streams   from steel helmet . . .

Sigmund breathed in deeply, then sighed in a long slow hiss of relief as the scent of baking bread curled around the boulders at the door of the cave.

Two flat lumpy loaves like discolored mudpies lay on the rack above the embers; the bag lay empty by the dangling feet of Sinfjotli, who sat in the larger of the two chairs.

"I have made bread," the boy said proudly. He folded his arms and sat back, looking up at Sigmund as though daring him to find fault with his baking.

"And did you find anything in the meal?" Sigmund asked.

Sinfjotli cocked his head to one side, tugging at his smooth chin as though a beard already grew there. "I rather think there might have been something living in it when I started to knead, but whatever it was, I kneaded it in and it will not disturb our dinner, I think."

Sigimund laughed aloud, impulsively bending down to hug the boy around his solid shoulders. "It will not disturb my dinner," he said. "I don't mean for you to eat it, for you have kneaded a most venomous snake into this bread, and I think it would not sit well in your stomach. But there is plenty of other food for you, and you'll want to become used to it because you'll be eating it for a long time. Wolves like us don't get bread too often!"

He crouched to build up the fire, Sinfjotli watching him intently. "What's in that chest at the back of the cave?" the boy asked. "I tried to open it and have a look, but it wouldn't come open and when I kept pushing at it I started to feel very ill. Is it magic? Mother told me that you learned runes and galdor-songs from a Herulian."

"It is magic," Sigimund said. "I think that you are still too young to learn from what I have in there, but I will teach you in time. Till then, it is best that you leave it be."

Sinfjotli nodded, his arched brows drawing together into a frown. "When will you teach me?"

"When you are a grown warrior—in two or three years, perhaps. Are you hungry?"

"I could eat a bear!" Sinfjotli declared, glancing longingly at his loaves, then at the rack of meats and cheese.

"Help yourself, then. This is your home as much as mine now, and I expect that you'll be helping to refill my larder soon."

"So I will," Sinfjotli agreed. He got out of Sigimund's chair, drew his dagger and cut off portions of dried meat and cheese that would have done credit to a grown man, sitting down to devour them with remarkable speed and then getting up for more. Sigimund broke off a piece of lumpy bread and sat chewing meditatively on it, his strong teeth occasionally crunching through a piece of bone. He felt a growing warmth beneath his breastbone as he watched his sister's son gobble down his food. The Herulian's rede had been good after all; now he need only wait and work as he had planned till he held his sword again and his father's blood had been avenged, and then he, Sigilind and Sinfjotli could fare far away from this cold Northern land and win a kingdom as rich and fair as Wals' had been. With his sister and such a man as this boy promised to be at his side, might he not even raise a host to claim lands from Rome and rule beside the empire that spanned the world? Useless dreaming, he thought; I have a long road to fare before ever I can turn south again. But the last light of the sun glittered from Sinfjotli's tangled golden hair like a distant promise, and Sigimund felt that his long waiting had earned him the right to a useless dream or two before he began to teach his sister's son how to fight and, as he himself had learned here in Gautland, to bear hardship as he must for what lay ahead.

SINFJOTLI

Although Sigigairar sent his men far and wide through the wood, seeking for Sinfjotli, they did not find him. When Sigilind went among the folk, she began to mark their sideways glances and the way they would stop talking when she approached. Now she walked as warily as a fox through the village, on her way to buy two skeins of blue embroidery wool from Thonardis the Dyer. She did not quite creep, but moved softly through the long shadows of summer morning. As her path bent around the house of Stanagrimar, the sound of her own name in a man's mouth stopped her and she drew back from where the three men stood talking with their backs to her.

"It's Sigilind's fault," Stanagrimar was saying. "The weather's been good and the barley's growing fine, but Sigigairar's seed isn't meant to be mixed with that line. Not after . . ."

"It was no betrayal. They came armed for war, didn't they?" Angantiwar answered him. "Still, I take your meaning. She's brought us no luck since she came here, and more ill than good."

"What about . . . her?" Hrabanahelm asked. "The old seith-witch is dead, isn't she? And Sigilind helped lay her. I'd call that good."

"One traded for another," Angantiwar replied. "I don't know how the drighten bears to spend his nights with her when she comes in from the wood."

"Ah," said Stanagrimar, tugging at the woven braid of his beard. "He's a true Ingling, isn't he? They know how to make magic work their way, if it's got to be worked. I've never seen the Winternights blessings made as richly by anyone else, and short of that one bad winter before Sinfjotli came we haven't gone hungry a year since he took the land. Sigigairar hasn't lost his luck yet. He knows how to deal with her, never fear—though it would be best if there were a second wife beside her to bear his seed; he can easily afford two women."

"He's lost his sons, hasn't he?" said Angantiwar. "Three out of three—and that woman's been a long time barren since Sinfjotli was born. I say he ought to drown her in the bog beside Kara before he takes another wife."

"Shut your mouth," Stanagrimar told him. "The gods will show us soon enough; there's no need to talk of those gifts while the land is fruitful. If a ninth year passes before she quickens, it's like as not that things will turn and then we'll see."

Sigilind had heard enough and walked on. The three men fell silent when she passed them. She could feel their guilty glances prickling down her back, but held her head high, refusing to answer them with her look. The full moon would bring her courses on her that day or the next, as it had every month since Sinfjotli's birth. Perhaps her struggles then had broken something within her. Sigigairar's seed would not take root in her womb, and she was glad of it.

Sigilind's courses did not come on her that night, nor the next either. I am old enough to have stopped bleeding, she thought. But by the time the Moon had waned to a thin sliver of sharp-edged light, her nipples had grown tender and her stomach churned uneasily in the morning, and she knew that there was a child in her body again.

When she could not deny it any longer to herself, she left the day's bread-baking to Helche and the Welsh girl and walked out of the hall. The grain was already growing tall, the wind rippling silver patterns across the green field. It seemed to her that the old bloodshed should have blighted the ground or at least left some scar, even as Sigigairar's right arm would never quite heal from the wound he had taken in the fight; but there was none to be seen. Although it was early in the morning, the day was already growing warm, Sunna's light hot on her hair, and she was glad to come into the shadows of the wood.

Sigilind did not think about where she was going, but her feet followed the path to the clearing where her brothers had died. Rust had eaten the nails of the broken stocks; the log where they had been slain had collapsed into itself, the rotting heap overgrown with mushrooms and a few shoots of wild spear leek: ten years, and they were yet unavenged. She whispered their names softly: Alfwald, Alfarik, Wihtric, Wynberht, Orngrim, Oddwig, Alfger, Wulfger, Berhtwini. A sudden pang took her; she bent over, crushing her fist into her belly as though she could push the child out of her. It is none of mine, I will not be forced to bear it! she muttered fiercely to herself. She thought of swelling for nine months, the weight on her bladder making her piss more and more often; of waddling about clumsily as Sigigairar's brood mare while men like Stanagrimar spoke proudly of their drighten's strength in filling her and how his luck had sprung high again.

Sigilind knew, as most women did, the herbs that could unroot a child from the womb before the man who had put it there ever knew that his seed had begun to sprout. The thought had hardly shaped itself in her mind before her gaze turned to the earth, running through the fronds of the leaves and flowers springing up among the grasses.

It took her a while to find the herbs she wanted—the herbs that made the womb cramp and cast out its fruit before its time; she would try those first. At the last, when her hands were full, she came to a shady place where deep purple flowers bloomed—the dwale, whose dark sweet berries might bring sleep or madness or death, according to the dose. It was too early in the year for the berries to be out; instead, Sigilind crouched down, taking each dwale shoot by the stem and pulling it carefully out. Its bale was strongest in the roots, but she had no fear of it. If the other plants, that worked by poisoning the mother a little, did her no good, then a heavy dose of dwale might slay the child within her while leaving the Walsing unscathed.

Sigigairar had gone down to see to his ships that morning, readying for another raid southward. Sigilind knew that she would have her chamber to herself for most of the day, and so she did not hurry as she heated water in a small iron pot to steep the brew that would free her of her unwanted load. The harsh bitterness lingered in the back of her throat when she had downed it; she coughed and spat into the fire. After making sure the chamber pot was close at hand, she lay down to wait for her brew to work.

Night and dawn came again, and nothing had happened. Sigilind waited until Sigigairar had gone out to his work again, then took the three dwale roots from the chest where she had hidden them. They were plump, pale brown with crumbs of earth caught in their rough skin, and the three of them together could have poisoned half a host. Holding her breath, Sigilind chewed them swiftly, washing them down with clear water from her horn. Her mouth felt numb when she was done, and she began to wonder if she had been wise—if the Herulian's gift had been only to her twin. But she, too, was a Walsing; she would not dare less than her son had.

Before long, the walls began to shimmer in Sigilind's sight, showers of rainbow sparks spraying over the rough wood. She felt drowsy, as though she had drunk several horns of mead and then crept beneath a thick blanket of soft wool, and after a while she lay down. It seemed to her that she was not sleeping, but she could see Sigimund and Sinfjotli sitting together beneath a roof of leaves where a spear leaned against a tree trunk, their fair heads bent close together. Sigimund was speaking, drawing something in the dirt with a stick . . . a little closer, and she could hear him . . .

Sinfjotli leaned closer to his mother's brother, staring at the rune Sigimund had scratched into the earth. "What is it? What does it do?" he asked eagerly.

Sigimund laughed and tousled Sinfjotli's hair. "You'll learn as I did. First the shape, then the name and the heart, and lastly the use." He began to scratch others in the order of their aett, the family of eight that bound the twenty-four runes to their three rows, then chanted, pointing to each rune with his stick:

ᚠ Fehu, "gold": the kinsmen's strife,
serpent-path and flood-tide flame,
the wolf grows up in the woods.

ᚢ Uruz, "aurochs": the fearless beast,
drizzle shrinks the glacier's rim,
often the reindeer runs on hard snow.

ᚦ Thurisaz, *"giant"*: the torment of women,
the rock's dweller, old hag's mate,
sharp is the thorn to each thane.
ᚨ Ansuz, *"god"*: the oldest father,
Ase-Garth's chieftain, words' wise lord,
the wind is bound by no chains.

Sigimund would have gone on, but he heard the sound of horses' hooves, a wain's wheels squeaking behind them. He hefted his spear in his right hand, putting the forefinger of his left to his lips, and led Sinfjotli closer to the road.

One of the men looked like a well-off carl, his belly swelling beneath his yellow tunic and his balding head bare to the sun; the other, taller and thinner, wore a byrnie and carried a sword. No helm covered his dark hair: they were clearly awaiting no attack this close to Sigigairar's hall. The wain they rode in carried a load of thin planks, finely shaped for ship-building.

Sigimund's flying spear pierced through the links of the warrior's byrnie and burst out through his back. The other man dropped down in the wain, scrabbling for something as he shouted his horses onward. Sinfjotli burst out of the wood in front of them, waving his arms and screaming shrilly, and the beasts shied aside. The wagon tipped precariously; then Sigimund had leapt up onto it with his knife out. His victim was not quite fast enough to get his own spear up in time, and in the next moment Sigimund had yanked his head back and cut his throat. The horses, able neither to go forward nor backward, had stopped in their tracks.

"What shall we do now?" Sinfjotli asked. "I know these horses, they belong to Sigigairar. Can we keep them? I should like to learn to ride."

"We have no place for horses," Sigimund answered gravely. "Now I mean that none of Sigigairar's works shall do well, for no one shall pass safely along this road or into the woods unless he comes with a host—and such things swiftly become known to men. I know what an Ingling king's luck means to him too . . . and these horses must fare as their drivers did."

"I'll see to it, then," Sigilind's son boasted. "I'm not afraid of them. Just show me where to cut."

When the horses had been slain and laid before the wagon, Sigimund struck a spark with flint and iron and soon had the wood blazing; but he did not put the men on the pyre. He and Sinfjotli took the broken byrnie—it would not be hard to mend—and the dead men's weapons. While they walked back to the cave, Sigimund watched the boy carefully. Sinfjotli was a little pale, but otherwise seemed untouched by the killings he had seen.

As they sat cleaning the blood from the metal, the young Walsing turned to look at Sigimund. "I'm not going to be sick," he said. "My mother raised me for this, and had me watch whenever men were fighting."

"Have you ever seen a man killed before?"

"When Hildigairar and Red Wulfar fought at holmgang, and Red Wulfar stuck his sword through Hildigairar's guts," Sinfjotli answered promptly. "He was a long time dying, too. That was when I was five."

Sigimund thought back, but he could not remember when he had seen his first man slain. "Well enough." There was no more good in thinking on it; he had done what he needed, and it was good that Sinfjotli had the stomach for the work. He put his scoured spear aside and began to murmur the rune song softly, tracing the staves in the firepit's ashes. His sister's son chanted the first four runes with him, then Sigimund went on alone.

ᚱ Raidho, "riding": for horses worst,
The Ginn-Reginn wrought in elder times,
The steed does not run nor rest.
ᚲ Kenaz, "torch": the crafter's light,
clear it burns at the atheling's bier,
sore is the house of rot.
ᚷ Gebo, "gift": the praise of each man,
alike to gods go their friends oft,
the good drighten freely gives rings.
ᚹ Wunjo, "joy": the hero's high soul,
with kinsmen about, sorrows but few,
blithe is he whose burg is strong.

The Sun was shining straight down through the smokehole when Sigilind's sight cleared again. Her womb was still whole, with no pangs of loosing, and it seemed to her that she could feel the unscathed growth within her—soulless yet, without brain or breath or name, but alive with the unshaped life of the blindly seeking seed that had quickened it. Either her own body had warded it from the dwale, or some other charm kept it within her. Whichever might be the case, there was only one from whom she could seek rede in the matter. She did not look forward to seeing the spae-woman again, and less to telling her what she wanted, but she saw no other way open before her.

Freyjadis was out in the sunshine, brushing her mare and talking softly to it. She did not look round as Sigilind rode up to her gate, but said only, "Come in."

Sigilind dismounted and tied her horse's reins to the fence. The soles of her feet prickled as she stepped within Freyjadis' garth, a prickling that rose to set the hairs on edge along her spine. She felt as if something were pressing against her, trying to push her into flight, but she made her way forward as though she were walking against a strong wind.

Freyjadis took Sigilind's hand in her own hot grip and led the Walsing into her house as if she were leading a child along. When the door had swung shut behind them, the spae-wife turned to face Sigilind. Freyjadis' eyes glowed hot gold in the dimness of the hut, and the musty scent of old smoke and herbs choked Sigilind's throat.

"Tell me," Freyjadis ordered.

"I want to get rid of the child I carry," Sigilind said, all in a rush. Despite the bitter taste in her mouth, she felt cleaner at once, as if she had vomited up the dwale roots and her stomach lay light and empty.

"You know how to do that well enough."

"I don't. I tried and it didn't work." Her face burning beneath the spae-woman's steady gaze, Sigilind told Freyjadis what she had done.

Freyjadis swung her head slowly back and forth, as if listening to some music that Sigilind could not hear. "It takes little spae-sight to see what is amiss. Were you the wife of a simple carl or thane, you might empty your womb easily, for no woman should be made to bear when her heart is against it. But you are wedded to Sigigairar the Ingling, and though your brother lurks in the woods, Sigigairar has not lost his luck yet, nor has Ingwar-Freyjar turned his face from him. If I should lend my might to yours, we might be able to cast this child out. Then the land would wither and rot, and Sigigairar would be leader here no longer—and that is not my choice to make while the gods give him leave to rule. It may be that Sigimund shall overcome Sigigairar at the last and slay him or break his might, and then things will be different. Then it may be that Sigigairar shall slay Sigimund and your son, and then he shall live long and rule with better luck than any before him: the gods wait to see who shall prove worthiest."

"What can I do?"

"If you would hold to your oaths, bear Sigigairar's children and wait."

Freyjadis' voice was as stark as bedrock with the earth scraped from it, and Sigilind could not answer her. Finally, the Walsing gathered the strings of her courage together and said, "What do I owe you for this rede?"

"Nothing. I take pay only where I can help. Hasten back now: the dead have been found and Sigigairar is greatly afraid for you."

The light was beginning to dim when Sigilind dismounted and led her mare into the stable. She heard footsteps behind her, and the next moment her breath was almost crushed out of her as Sigigairar grasped her in a tight embrace and whirled her off her feet.

"Where have you been?" he asked, holding her close to him.

"I went to see the spae-woman," Sigilind answered. She was unwilling to tell him the tidings that would bring him joy, but he would find out soon enough. "I'm pregnant again."

"Hail to Ingwar-Freyjar!" Sigigairar let her down carefully, a grin of relief lightening his thin face. "Fair news on a dark day—you must not go on the roads alone."

"Why not?" Sigilind asked, doing her best to sound startled.

"Someone slew Haribaldur and Hildiormar, and burned their wagon with the planking they were bringing. Outlaws down from where they hide in the mountains, I'd guess. They took the weapons, but left the horses dead. It was one thing when they were stealing a sheep or two, but . . ."

Sigilind could guess the shape of the shadow behind her husband's eyes: he had loved Harigastir and Theudorikijar, but Sinfjotli had been the very flower of his pride. If he finds them he will not slay the boy, she murmured silently to her heart, and felt the cold coal in her breast warming as if a breath of wind had fanned it to fire.

"Are you going out after them?" she asked.

"Tomorrow at first light, and we won't come home without a warg's corpse to hang before the gates of the garth."

Sigilind hoped that Sigigairar would see only womanly softness in the trembling of her smile. She leaned her head against his shoulder to hide her face. "You'll take care, my husband?" she said. "How many men are you taking with you?"

"All the thanes of the warband, though I won't call any carls away for this. We'll be as safe as any hunters who go after wolves, anyway."

Sigilind lay awake after Sigigairar had gone to sleep, staring at the dim summer light glimmering through the smokehole. She wished she could get out Sigimund's sword, to hold it while she sent her thoughts of warning to him, but Sigigairar had not slept easily since Sinfjotli had left the hall and she knew it would disturb him if she got up.

Sigimund, Sigimund! she thought. She could see their shadows against the twilit summer sky, as if they were sitting on a high rock; see the lightless glimmering of the rune staves Sigimund traced in the air, the angular shapes shining like red after-images behind closed lids.

H Hagalaz, "hail": the whitest of grains,
Wodan the worlds in elder time wrought,
Ice-stone is sickness of snakes.

ᚾ Nauthiz, "need": the bondmaiden's grief,
hard to bear, to heroes help,
the naked freeze in the frost.

I Isa, "ice": the broadest bridge,
glistens like glass, fair is the frost,
the river's rind is fey men's foe.

ᛃ Jera, "year": the harvest men's hope,
Fro Ing the Fruitful gives well,
from good summer comes a ripe field.

Sigimund, Sigimund! Sigilind whispered silently. Beware, my brother, beware! But the shadow sight was fading from her already, and no matter how she tried she could not bring it back.

Sigigairar and his men were gone four days. When they came back, as Sigigairar had promised, they bore two corpses with them; but even from the top of the hill, Sigilind could see that the bodies were both grown men, one ruddy-haired and one dark. Sigigairar had the corpses hung up just outside the village on the broad-limbed oak tree where the men sometimes hung the bodies of sheep-stealing wolves. Still, it was not the last of the matter. Half a month later the smith's apprentice went into the forest to gather wood for charcoal and did not come back; three days afterward, Hroarar and Gunthormar found what the foxes had left of him. In other years, the traders had come over the roads in summertime with furs from the far north and fine goods from the south, but this year only those who came by boat visited Sigigairar's halls. As the child grew within her, Sigilind turned her thoughts more and more to Sigimund and Sinfjotli wandering free in the woods, fighting whenever they came across men. Sometimes she knew they were hunting, stalking after deer or loosing their arrows at birds; sometimes she could feel them at rest, sprawled in the sun among the blueberry bushes that grew thickly on the mountainside, and often the Herulian's rune-song rang through her head.

Eihwaz, "yew": the winter-green wood,
rough-barked flame-keeper, estate's joy,
his own words knows Wodan alone.
Perthro, "fruit": the great tree's treasure,
rising from roots; women keep seed within,
the lot-box is bold men's mirth.
Elhaz, "elk": the antlers ward sharply,
all but the bold are burned by the fire-ring,
mighty is the talon-span of the hawk.
Sowilo, "sun": the shield of the clouds,
light of the lands and ice's woe,
the seamen fare far over waves.

A few days before Winternights, when the first flakes of snow had fallen, Sigigairar led his host to the mountains a second time, scouring the woods. The path from Sigigairar's hall to the holy grove was a long and twisted road to tread in the darkness, and a few foemen could wreak great havoc at the holy time: Sigilind knew her husband was thinking this when he called his men to make a second search after the outlaws who walked in the wood. Sigigairar's host passed so close to the hidden way into Sigimund's cave that the two Walsings could hear their voices and the pebbles grating beneath their feet, but the warriors walked on without marking that a path might lie between the sides of the great stones. As he heard them moving by, Sinfjotli raised his head, his hand tight on the falcon hilt of his dagger and a smile glowing through his face.

"We could come through the boulders alongside them and slay Sigigairar now," he whispered. "Why don't we?"

"It's not yet time. You must come to a man's strength and be fully tested in might before we can win our vengeance," Sigimund murmured back. The boy's eagerness to slay his own father lay oddly cold against Sigimund's heart; it seemed to him that no good could come from the greed for kin-slaying, although Sigilind and he had brought Sinfjotli up for the sake of revenge.

It was not long after Winternights that the harsh winds from the sea began to whirl snowflakes around the mountains in earnest, cloaking the cave's hidden entrance with another concealment of icy whiteness. Then, as they crouched around the fireplace in their robes of fox fur and the woolen blankets they had taken from traders they had slain, Sigimund taught more and more of the Herulian's wisdom to his sister's son. Together they drew the runes in the ash with a pointed stake, chanting their names and verses in a two-toned chord that reverberated till the cave rang like a great hollow bell with the echoes of their galdor.

↑ Tiwaz, *"Tiw": the one-handed god,*
the temple's ruler, the wolf's leavings,
often the smith has to blow.

ᛒ Berkano, *"birch": the greenest with leaves,*
Loki brought the luck of deceit,
deep the bog at winter's end.

ᛗ Ehwaz, *"horse": the highborn's joy,*
heroes speak from the war steed's back,
Sleipnir is fleetest of beasts.

ᛗ Mannaz, *"man": the growth of dust,*
the joy of kin, the ship's adornment,
of etins is Mimir most wise.

Half a year pregnant now, Sigilind sat often with a horn of ale in her hand, staring into the fire. She had not felt so lonely since she had first left her father's hall; but then the bairn in her womb had been a blessing, something to love and hold tenderly within her, and now the kicks against belly or bladder were the blows of a small foe.

Last winter, she and Sinfjotli had run through the snow, shouting and throwing snowballs at each other. Heedless of her skirts, she had even wrestled with her son as she had with her brothers when she was young, until they rolled laughing in the snow together with ice crystals melting on their eyebrows and hair. But now she lay fettered by Freyjadis' wisdom while her son learned the Herulian's galdor-magic, listening to Sigimund and tracing the runes in the ash on the hearth as Sigimund chanted them.

Sigilind knew how Sinfjotli's sky-blue sight was swept by the wind of the galdor-songs that called, though he hardly understood them, to something within him that coiled and wove through the depths of his soul and burned in his head like the whirling wheel of the Sun. She saw, as Sigimund did, the fire awakening in Sinfjotli, glowing red-gold around him in a hidden shadow of brightness, and rejoiced at each new sign of the blood of the Walsings, the blood stemming from Wodan, as Sinfjotli spoke the rune-songs more and more surely.

ᛚ Laguz, "water": the might falls from mountain,
fearsome the waves when men fare from land,
the leek is brightest of herbs.

◇ Ingwaz, "Ing": the hero of gods,
faring from east, his wain comes behind,
the swordless fights with a stag horn.

ᛞ Dagaz, "day": Delling's bright door,
dawn weds the night with shining,
the thorn pricks the sleeper awake.

ᛟ Othala, "estate": the father's realm,
a joy to each man who bears it,
the garth bars the warg from within.

By the time the shifting banners of shining color had faded before the true light beginning to glow in the winter sky as the Sun's horses drew her upward again, Sinfjotli could chant the rune-song and knew at least three uses for each stave; he was beginning to learn how to weave them together into patterns of might and he could carve and color the runes with red ochre or his own blood at need. And so, when the days were just beginning to lengthen past the nights and the Moon had come to his first summertide fullness for Eostre's holy day, Sigimund took Sinfjotli up to the mountain's peak at sunset, bearing with him the last of their mead, a rune-carved wand of yew wood, the Herulian's chest and a pot of water that had been drawn forth at dawn from the wellspring of the clear burn that ran down the mountain. Though he seemed a Walsing in every way, Sinfjotli had still been born of Sigigairar's line, and named as an Ingling. Sigimund meant to cut Sigilind's son free from the Gautish clan's soul and hallow him as a Walsing before all the gods and ghosts—to let him die from the holy garth ring, and bring him to its life again at dawn.

The wind was cold and bitter, the Sun sinking in a glow of red wrath as the two Walsings stood on top of the mountain and together traced a circle of flame around themselves, chanting the names of the runes as Sigimund shaped the staves to glow invisibly in the darkening air. Stretching his arms upward, Sigimund called,

Ase-Garth's might above me awe,
Wodan, your wisdom hail your sons,
Here to this holy place flow shining might.

A whirlwind of bright power, unseen rainbow fire, seemed to spin deosil from above into his open arms, filling him with tingling warmth. He spread his legs, planting his feet firmly on the earth, and sang,

Holda's might below me held,
Rising from deepest hidden roots,
Here to this holy place flow mirky might.

He could feel a whirlpool swirling up widdershins through the mountain, flowing up through his feet, rooting him to the earth. For a moment he stood, poised between heavens and depths, gazing out into the vastness of the Nine Worlds spread before him.

"Wodan, father of Wals' line!" Sigimund chanted, his voice ringing through the endless depths around the mountain-top.

> With my sister's son I have warred,
> here to mountain's height we have fared
> that shall now his soul be seen.
> Cast out he from Sigigairar's clan,
> warg shall he in night world wander
> till I call him my own kin,
> within the ring of Wals' realm,
> or else the trolls shall take him.

With his last words, he lifted Sinfjotli by the neck of his cloak and the seat of his breeches and heaved him out of the circle. The boy rolled with his fall, coming swiftly to his feet. His mouth was open in shock; Sigimund had told him only that they would watch till sunrise. But he recovered quickly, letting out an ear-splitting shriek and running around the edge of the circle, leaping up against the hidden wall of fire that barred his way and making fierce faces at the one who watched within.

Sigimund settled himself for the night's watch, breathing slowly as he sank into a deep trance, shutting out Sinfjotli's shouting and taunts, aware of the boy's angry excitement only as a blot at the edge of his senses. Slowly the stars turned above him; slowly the Moon's rime-maned horses drew his cold crescent across his faint-glittering black road. He could feel the wyrms below him coiling and uncoiling restlessly, gnawing at the roots of the World-Tree. A cold wind was blowing from the wings of the great eagle, Hraiwiswelg the Corpse-Gulper, who sat on the easternmost branch, stirring the leaves of the Tree ever more strongly, its whispered breath rising slowly toward a great gale that was stirring all the tides of the Middle-Garth up to seething, shifting war and endless struggle. As from far away, he heard the sharp, high battle shrieks, weird as the voices of trolls, of a strange foe who rode on the wind from the east and swept all the tribes of Mannaz's kin before them. The streams flowing from the well of Wyrd, the well at the World-Tree's roots, wove and twisted through the worlds. Sigimund saw his own, shining white, twining with burning gold to sink down and rise again in a hero's red brilliance, twisting through the path of one of the wind-blown tribes till the two were so meshed that he could not unravel them, then shining forth once more in a blackness so bright that it hurt his eyes. The three streams knotted into the three interwoven triangles of Wodan's sign, the walknot, the knot of the slain by which the god bound his own from birth; and blazing forth from its center was the image of a tiny golden dragon coiled about a ruby that burned with a white star.

Sigimund blinked away the after-image as the vision faded into darkness. He was breathing hard, as if he had just come up from deep water. Outside the edge of the circle, he could see Sinfjotli sitting with his chin in his hands. The boy's winter-thin face was shadowed, but Sigimund could feel his baleful glare.

By the stars, Sigimund knew that it was almost midnight. He allowed himself a quick hidden smile as he settled himself more comfortably on the ground, rubbing prickling life into his sleeping feet. He had half-expected Sinfjotli to go back down to the cave; but now the boy's patience would be rewarded and the question he had been pestering Sigimund with for a year would be answered. He opened the Herulian's chest, taking the gold bracteate out to hang it around his neck and spreading the wolfskin on the ground before he lifted out the head of Widuhundaz.

The eerie cold pierced through his fingers and ran up his arms like a little bolt of icy lightning as soon as he touched the Herulian's head. He did not need to call the ancient wizard's names, as he had so often; only to look into the deep pits of his eyesockets where a cold red spark was beginning to glow and to listen as Widuhundaz's jaw fell open and the wintry rot-tinged wind began to blow out of his mouth in its steady stream.

"Sigimund Wargaz-Bane, Wals' son," the Herulian's hoarse rasp breathed through his skull. "Why on this night hailest thou me forth? What sight has stirred the Walsing's soul, after rune-master's rede to ask?"

"I have found the true Walsing of my sister's line, but I am not yet sure of him. What of his father's soul does he hold?"

"He is wholly like his father, and wholly like thy sister as well, nor shalt thou find aught else in him. What more wouldst thou wish to know?"

"What is the meaning of that which I have seen this night?"

"Thou hast seen the wandering of the folks, which is bound already to the wyrd of thy line. This wind that blows them blows up the fire of thy fame; thy strength and thy sons' shall be great in these struggles, and songs of your might fade not while Midhgardhaz shall stand. This the Norns have writ first for thee thyself and Sinfjotli; secondly comes your son Sigifrith, by a woman yet unborn; thirdly the orlog for his slayer is laid, his kin by oath and his mother's line. This is the knot of heroes, by which you shall all be bound. Wouldst thou know further, or how?"

"What more must I do to test my sister's son's soul, to ready him for our revenge?"

"When he is a man of thirteen, together through the wood you shall fare; there the wood hounds' hides shall you take, and the last way of Wodhanaz learn. Wargs in truth, you shall cross the garth's bounds and the fires free within you, for only thus can thou and he gain the might to turn wyrd as you must and claim thy sword from the foe. With Wodhanaz's berserk-blessing, no sword shall scathe you; your fierceness from all bonds will free you, as need you shall have before this work to its end is turned."

The Herulian's cold breath faded away; the ice melted from Sigimund's hands and the sparks of Widuhundaz's eyes blinked out. Sigimund wrapped the head in its wolfskin and put it back into the chest, laying the bracteate carefully on top of it before he closed the lid and retraced the runes that warded it. He sat back to think on the strange rede that had been given to him; and so he thought till the stars turned around him again and the cooling wind warned him that dawn was drawing near.

For a time he stood, doubting, looking at the drowsing figure of Sinfjotli outside his circle's garth. Wholly like his father, the Herulian had said. Could he take such a one into his line? What doom would come to Wals' kin if the son of his slayer were brought within it? Yet by the ancient rune-master's rede, his revenge could not be wreaked without this youth. So it should be, then: he could not turn from his wyrd.

Sigimund gazed eastward as the red glow of dawn spread up into the lightening sky, brightening to pink-flushed gold. On the mountain's peak, between day and night, he reached out across the unseen flames to Sinfjotli, who leaped from his rocky seat and, grasping Sigimund's hands, strode boldly into the holy ring. As Sigimund embraced the youth—new-born in the Walsing clan—a spring of joy welled up within him, breaking forth into words:

> Hail, Day! Hail, ye Day's sons!
> Hail to Night and the daughters of Night!
> Here at Delling's door I stand,
> in the holy garth of kin-home.
> With waters bright I wet the youth,
> Sinfjotli, take thy name from me,
> thou son of Wals' line!

Sigimund sprinkled the spring water on Sinfjotli's pale head, droplets scattering like dew in the rising light, then heaved the boy up in his arms, lifting him toward each of the eight winds. Unbinding the sword from his side, he girded it about the waist of his sister's son, drawing the leather belt in till its end flopped halfway down the youth's thigh. "This sword is your naming gift," he said. "Carry it well. I shall not bear another till I have my own in my hand."

Sinfjotli drew the sword; new sunlight flashed from it as he twirled it about his head.

"Hail the gods and goddesses!" he cried, his voice ringing high and shrill through the cold dawn air. "Sinfjotli am I, son of Wals' line; hail the day of our kin!"

Sigimund poured the last of their mead into the rune-carved horn and held it toward the golden edge of the Sun.

> Hail the spring of Eostre's day,
> white-clad sig-wife rising bright,
> Sun her shining sword and shield,
> Eostre takes her swan-white siege!

Hail to Wodan, drighten old,
wedding now the woman fair.
High upon the mountain peak,
We welcome the new day!

He traced the three interwoven triangles of the walknot above the mead and drained a third of it, the sweet fiery liquid flowing down his throat like sunlight as its rush of holy wod mounted to his head, then passed the horn to Sinfjotli. The boy drank deeply; his face flushed red for a moment as he held back a cough. He was gasping when he gave the horn back to Sigimund.

This mead we give ye mighty ones,
that we shall wax to the heroes' wyrd
and win what is our will!

He poured the mead out in a glittering golden stream onto the earth. For a moment he and Sinfjotli stood silent; then, impulsively, Sigimund embraced his sister's son. Sinfjotli hugged him back tightly, tears of joy gleaming like melting ice in his sky-bright eyes. Sigimund could feel the little tremble of relief in the youth's strong body and suddenly he knew that Sigilind had, through some magic or godwork, kept Sinfjotli's soul fatherless and without kinsmen save his mother until he himself had accepted the boy as his own—yet still the Herulian had said, "He is wholly like his father," and the Walsing could not quite still the adder-writhing of that thought.

Sigimund's nose was beginning to drip in the cold morning wind. He blew it roughly on the sleeve of his tunic and raised his wand again to break the circle so he and Sinfjotli could go back to their cave for breakfast.

As Sinfjotli grew, he and Sigimund fared more widely together in their search for new adventures and new deeds to test the boy's might. By the end of Sinfjotli's thirteenth summer, he was as tall as most grown men, the top of his head almost reaching to Sigimund's nose. He was as skillful with a bow as Sigimund himself, though he could not yet match his mother's brother with other weapons. When Heilagmonth's first ice dried the birch leaves' soft green rustling to musty gold and brown whispers, oak and maple flaring to red embers in the wind of summer's death and the white-flecked crimson caps of the maddening fly-mushrooms spreading in clusters above the rotting leaf mold, Sigimund knew that he could hold back no longer. He had half-feared the last test the Herulian had set upon him for Sigilind's son, but half-awaited it in eagerness as well; and now the Moon was turning toward his first winter fullness and the spoor of hunt blood was on the wind.

Last winter, the two of them had struggled bare-handed with hungry wolves, and Sinfjotli had slain the pack leader. The great wolf's gray hide now lay over the chest that held the Herulian's head; Sinfjotli had wanted to make a cape of it, but Sigmund had forbidden him to. Now the older Walsing draped the hide over his arm, then opened the chest and took out the Herulian's wolfskin as well.

Sinfjotli watched his mother's brother keenly. The youth said nothing, but even in the firelight Sigmund could see how Sinfjotli's hairs prickled with excitement. Sigilind's son clenched his fists in a sudden twinging spasm, his shining teeth bared in a sharp grin.

"Come," said Sigmund, and the two of them walked out of the cave and down the mountainside. The Moon glared whitely down at Sigmund and Sinfjotli as they moved silently through the shadowy woods. Their huge shapes twisted and slid like water among the branches that clawed down at them, swept and tossed by the wind that leapt through the trees with a rattling like the hooves of a faraway host pounding to battle.

They were halfway to Sigigairar's hall when Sigmund signed a halt and handed Sinfjotli his hide, lifting up his own. It leapt in the wind, clawed feet and plumelike tail flying out behind it as though the wolf were running through the air. Though he could hardly see it, he knew a slit opened the thick pelt of the underbelly—the slit where he could creep in. The hot tingle of the wolf-hide's furry touch ran through his veins, calling the thing that lay just below his skin to awake and turn outward.

"Are we going to put them on?" Sinfjotli asked. "I wondered how long it would be."

"How long have you known?"

"Since I met you. I saw the wolf's eyes in your gaze, when I first knew you for my mother's kinsman."

They stripped off their deerskin tunics and breeches, unwrapping their leather shoes and kicking them away. Sinfjotli's body gleamed white as stone in the Moon's light, muscles raised like slabs of steel to armor him against the cold river of wind roaring around them.

The youth stood with the wolf's hide swinging from his hand, watching Sigmund. "Is there anything we need to do? Should we make a circle to ward ourselves?"

"It will not be we who need warding," answered Sigmund. "And who in these lands should we ward from ourselves? No. Wodan and the turnings of wyrd have led us here, and we must take the moment as we have come to it."

Sigmund took a deep breath and spread the wolfskin out, sliding his head up through the slit in its neck and his hands into its narrow paws. It seemed to him as though he tasted the she-warg's blood at the back of his tongue again, feeling the fierce troll-strength raging through him. A great howl ripped its way up through his throat; unable to control himself, he fell to all fours, snarling and slavering as he stared at the whirling wheel of the Moon that dazzled a burning white wind through his shadowed eyes and howled through his brain till there was no thought left to him but running wild through the night wood with the other wolf at his side, drunk on the

Moon and the mead-strong wind in his mouth and the delicious scent of an elk growing closer as he followed its spoor with burning wod rising through him. For a moment he saw the antlered shadow looming between two trees; then, with a great bound, he and Sinfjotli had fallen upon it, too swift for hooves or horns to ward them off, ripping with teeth and claws, strong hot blood spurting into their mouths with each bite of the musky dark flesh. Sigimund threw back his head, blood trickling down his throat from his muzzle, and howled in fierce triumph; dimly, as the meat of his kill sated the wolf-soul that had whelmed him, he knew that he had never felt such wholeness of self and act.

Across the elk's shredded body, Sinfjotli raised his dark-stained head and answered Sigimund's howl; in his wordless cry, Sigimund heard the same joyous wod that burned through his own veins. Together they turned to run again, the wind in their faces flattening the fur along their backs and whipping the air from their mouths so that they had to bite each breath from it. They ran like that till past dawn, when the wind had faded to stillness and they stood, panting, at the edge of a forest whose red and gold and brown had faded to shades of twilight gray in their wolfish eyes. Before them lay a field of dry dead stalks; the grain was harvested for the winter, the Yule ale brewing within the huts that lay below the hall on the hill's top. Sigimund's nose caught the scent of Sigilind's passing, the smell so like his own but tinged with the salty femaleness of a woman-mother and underlaid with the heaviness of sorrow; he smelled the dung-caked boots of farmers and the musky sweat of men who played and fought at swords, and the acrid spoor of Sigigairar, piercing sharp as a thorn to bleed a tear of bitterness into his eyes. The blurred shapes of the farmers and their wives were already moving in the hamlet; he and Sinfjotli turned back into the forest before anyone could see the two wolves standing there.

Sinfjotli growled questioningly. Sigimund heard, as clearly as if his sister's son had spoken with human words, "What shall we do now? Shall we wait for Sigigairar to come out and fall upon him? Surely he and his men could not withstand us, if we took them by surprise; he cannot have so many with him that we two cannot overcome them."

"No," Sigimund answered in the same wolf-speech, half-growled, half-spoken through scent and the lay of his ears and his eyes meeting the gray-white human gaze of Sinfjotli. "It is not written that I shall slay him with tooth and claw. I must regain my sword first. No, what we shall do is to go our ways through the forest and seek men to fight. Each of us shall battle alone with seven men, but no more, and if one of us should chance upon more he shall call out and the other will come to his aid."

"I am worth more than seven," said Sinfjotli, his ruff bristling and his tongue lolling from his muzzle. "Why should I need aid for so few?"

"Because you are young and bold, and men will think it good to hunt you," Sigimund answered, bristling out his own fur and looming menacingly over the smaller warg. Sinfjotli sprang at his throat and they rolled over and over, snapping at each other, till finally the younger wolf, pinned beneath the weight of Sigimund's body, stretched out his neck in a sign of submission. Sigimund closed his jaws carefully, till his teeth just touched Sinfjotli's hide, then let him go. The two of them shook their fur out and trotted off their separate ways into the wood.

It was not long before Sigimund heard the sound of men's boots crashing through the fallen branches and deep voices ringing through the crisp air of winter's edge like the low barking of the hounds who padded along beside them. He crept through the undergrowth till he could see them clearly with his short wolf-sight. There were a number of them carrying boar spears and bows; a couple were armed with swords as well as spears and knives. One of the dogs, a big brute with a scarred muzzle and a cast in one eye, sprang against his leash snarling when he caught Sigimund's scent. The dark-haired man who held him yanked him back roughly. "Hai, Faralik, we're not even close to the old one's den," he said. "I won't spend the day chasing foxes with you." The other men laughed as though they were about to start chaffing him over his wild hound.

Sigimund raised his wolf-voice in a horrible howl, stilling their laughter as they grasped at spears and looked about.

"Foxes, eh?" said an older man, one of the sword-bearing thanes, whose hair was thickly overlaid with silver-white strands. "Agilar, that was a wolf and close by us. Your hound's wiser than you are. Let him go, see what he can chase out to whet our appetite for boar." Beneath the creased wrinkles that traced over his broad, plain face like spiderweb-thin runes, he seemed vaguely familiar to Sigimund—something to do with the cool touch of water, the sweetness of honey in his mouth—but the warg's soul howled through him, knowing no man.

"All right, then, Aiwimundur, we'll see what kind of wisdom comes out of the mouth of the aged," Agilar answered, snapping Faralik's leash from his collar. The hound needed no further urging; in one leap he was through the bushes and spilling his guts on the damp leaves. Sigimund spat out the foul taste of the dog's blood. He could hear Sinfjotli running through the wood toward him, and he thought that he had no need to wait any longer.

Sigimund sprang over the body of the hound who curled whimpering around his own entrails and was among the men, snapping and tearing at their flesh as he danced and wove through the points of their spears in a mad and joyous wod of blood, hot and furious as the taste of the she-warg's tongue in his mouth. A sword sliced down his shoulder, cutting off a hank of fur but not biting on his hide; the point of a spear pushed against his chest, but could not pierce. The hounds jumped at him and fell away like waves leaping against the side of a boat and splashing harmlessly back. Sinfjotli was there with him, pale mask covered in black blood and bones cracking beneath his jaws. The last one living was the old man who had known the wolf's howl; he stood with his back to an oak's trunk, beating them back with a sword in one hand and a broken branch in the other.

The man's eyes met Sigimund's for a moment as they struggled. He gasped, then cried out, "Kara! Thonar ward me! I helped Freyjadis and Sigilind lay you. Back to the bog with you, ill ghost!" The branch fell from his hand as he grasped for the Hammer-amulet at his neck; and Sinfjotli's jaws snapped through hand and neck together.

Now nothing stood living on the path save the two wargs, trembling with tiredness and hunger from the wod that had whelmed them. Afterward, Sigimund was not sure which of them first lowered his jaws to the dead men whose blood ran salty-sweet from their muzzles and down their throats; but he and Sinfjotli ate till they were full, snuffling out rich bits of liver and tearing mouthfuls of flesh away from the broken bodies here and there. Sated at last, feeling their strength beginning to return, the two wargs walked away from the tatters of bone and meat that strewed the pathway like hay cast about by a strong wind.

When they had gone a little way, they settled down to clean themselves and rest. The burning white wheel of the Sun was low when they awoke, the shifting dappled light grays of the forest beginning to darken to deep gray and shadowed black around them. They parted as before, Sigimund reminding his sister's son to call out to him if he came upon a band of more than seven.

Sigimund had wandered a long way through the shifting twilight, snapping at mice and following the twisting trails of rabbits through the fallen leaves as his wolf-soul would, when he heard the far-off sounds of shouting and struggling. Lithe as a snake, he turned his narrow body around on itself, leaping swiftly over bushes and dashing through the shadows to follow the sounds and the rising smell of fresh blood on the breeze.

He was still a way from the battle when the last of the screaming stopped. Panting, he walked the rest of the way to find Sinfjotli slumping against a tree by the slain bodies of—more than seven men, ten or eleven, with their hounds scattered about them. Even in the deep twilight, Sigimund could see that Sinfjotli was half-dead from the aftermath of the fit, and that blood ran from a lump on the side of his head. Yes, there was a spear with a broken shaft. One of the dead must have had the wit to strike at Sinfjotli with the wood that would wound a berserk where iron would glance unfelt off the wod-maddened warrior's hide.

"Why didn't you call me?" Sigimund snarled furiously. "Has the wolfskin so addled your wits that you can't count past seven?"

Sinfjotli looked up, his long tongue lolling out between his sharp teeth. Tired and wounded as he was, his warg-grin had, to Sigimund's angry eyes, something of a sneer in it, and it roused Sigimund's blood near to fighting heat.

"You had help in the killing of eight men. I am but a child in years beside you, yet I asked no help in the killing of eleven. I told you—"

He got no further. Sigimund, enraged past bearing, let the wolf's hide bear him up in a leap that ended with his jaws in the front of his sister's son's windpipe. Sinfjotli staggered and fell beneath him; he lay, gurgling a little blood in his breath, and did not raise himself when Sigimund got off him.

Sigimund drew his breath through his teeth in a sharp hiss as he looked at Sinfjotli lying before him. The vessels of the youth's throat had not been pierced: only a trickle of fresh darkness stained his fight-clotted fur, but the bubbling of his breath spoke clearly of how sore his wound might be. The eyes of the warg could not weep, and so Sigimund raised his muzzle to the half-eye of the twilight Moon and howled long and bitterly, his piercing voice wavering high through the cold wind. He rubbed his chin against the ground, trying to loose the hold of the wolfskin on his head so that he might peel it back and become a man again, but it was as tight as if it had grown to him, shake and scrape as he might. Finally he bent down and gently tugged Sinfjotli up on to his back, pulling the other wolf's forelegs down over his shoulders with his jaws and heaving him on to the ridge of his spine.

Sigimund carried Sinfjotli step by painful, unbalanced step to their cave in the mountain. When he got there, he laid his sister's son on one blanket of furs and tugged the other over him to keep him as warm as he could be, since there was no way for Sigimund to start a fire with his paws. Bitterly he scratched at the dead ashes, sneezing as a fine powdery cloud flew up to sting his sensitive nose.

"May the trolls take these wolf-shapes," he growled to himself. He sniffed about, looking up at the rack above his head. It was too dark to see what was there, but he could smell the strips of smoked meat where he himself had hung them out of the reach of any wild beast that might find his cave by chance. Finally he turned about thrice and lay down beside Sinfjotli, nose between his paws, listening to the other's bubbling breath till, assured that his sister's son's death was no nearer than it had been, he went to sleep.

Sigimund was awake at dawn, rolling over and trying to stand upright before the shock of falling down on to all fours and the gentle gurgle beside him brought everything that had happened in the wolfskins to him, as clear and painful as morning sunlight in his short-sighted eyes. He nudged anxiously at Sinfjotli; but the other wolf would not move, though his blood was warm and his breath steady. Gently he nosed the youth's left eyelid upward. The eye beneath was a well of darkness; whatever Sinfjotli saw, it was not lit by the Middle-Garth's day.

Sigimund padded over to the row of clay pots where he kept the dried herbs and other things Widuhundaz had taught him to use. He pushed one over and a few yew berries rolled out, deep red and wrinkled as tiny withered apples. Careful of the poison within, he delicately lifted one between the points of two fangs and carried it over to Sinfjotli, laying it on his body. It would shield the fire of his soul wherever he wandered, and none would now stir Sinfjotli's sleep in the Middle-Garth. He would find his body as whole as it might be when—if—he came back.

The warg hunted through the wood in the morning, and what he caught he bore back to the cave, looking anxiously to see if Sinfjotli had woken or died; but he lay unchanged. Sigimund slept through the afternoon, waking to howl restlessly at the swelling white Moon. He wondered if his sister's son could hear his voice; again and again he howled his name, but he heard no answer.

The next day went the same way, except that Sigimund woke well before sunset. Going out into the woods, the Walsing wandered restlessly here and there, casting after tracks and turning aside before he found the small beasts that had made them, till he came upon a pair of weasels dashing about, writhing between and over each other like furry snakes, darting sharp beady glances up as if to tell Sigimund that his first move would see them away and gone faster than the flicker of lightning. He stood there staring at them. He was not hungry or overcome by the wod of his hide, and felt no need to slay them amid their dancing, snapping play.

As he watched, one of them sprang at the other with a fierce little cry. They rolled, slim bodies knotted together, and when they came apart, one did not get up again. Sigimund saw that it was bleeding little bubbles on to the pale fur of its throat. The other made a slithering dash beneath the bushes, leaving its comrade on the ground.

Cautiously Sigimund moved closer. He lowered his nose, sniffing at the fallen weasel. He had just opened his jaws when he heard a muffled hiss from the underbrush and saw the tiny dark jewels of the other weasel's eyes glaring at him above a wide leaf.

Sigimund stepped back and watched the weasels from behind a tree. The one scampered out of the bushes and laid the leaf across the throat of the other. To Sigimund's amazement, the wounded weasel at once sprang up and leapt at its comrade, and, tumbling and playing as before, the two of them writhed off into the grass and were gone.

At once Sigimund nosed frantically through the grass, trying to find the leaf which had fallen from the weasel's wound. After some time, when he had no luck at it, he followed the path he thought he had seen the first weasel take; but a wolf, lithe and narrow-shouldered though he might be, could not go where a beast made for slithering down rabbit holes could, and a tangle of thorn bushes finally stopped him. Though he closed his eyes and the thickness of his fur protected him from the worst spines, he could not break through the branches, nor could his highest leap carry him over the woven wall. Bleeding and sick at heart, he sat down on his tail and raised his howl to the clouds sweeping across the silvery sky.

A raven wheeled above Sigimund, its harsh cry scraping down his spine. No; it was not that raven that had called, for it carried something in its mouth, a mouse or . . .

Not daring to breathe, Sigimund waited, stock-still, as the raven glided down to him. In its beak it held a wide pale leaf exactly like the one the weasel had borne to its fallen comrade. The wind of its black wings ruffled through Sigimund's fur as it hovered just above his head. It opened its beak; a gust of air whipped the leaf out, and Sigimund jerked his head sideways to catch it in his jaws. The raven turned, wheeling upward again. Its rough croak echoed raspily through Sigimund's skull as he ran for the cave, strings of silvery drool whipping from the edges of his muzzle around the leaf that he held so carefully.

Sigimund leapt over the rocks and into the cave. He nudged the younger wolf's sleeping body from his side to his back, stretching out his throat so that the wound was uppermost, then laid the leaf down on the bubbling sore as he had seen the weasel do. At once Sinfjotli stretched and sprang up. Though the darkness that had drowned his eyes drew in only slowly, he was as whole as he had ever been and Sigimund raised his head and howled for joy.

"What I have seen . . . " Sinfjotli growled, his voice soft and unsure. He shook his head from side to side as though to encompass a vision too wide for his wolf's skull. Once he opened his mouth and closed it again; wolf-speech failed, and indeed, Sigimund thought, the tongues of men might fare no better at showing what one lying at Hella's door might find beyond the Middle-Garth's walls. Sinfjotli turned to the pile of game that Sigimund had left and gobbled it up greedily until only clean-licked splinters of bone were left. Still hungry, he made a high jump at the rack where the smoked meat hung and brought it crashing down around him. He cocked his head and rolled his eyes up at the older wolf apologetically.

Sigimund gave him a brief lick on the muzzle. "Eat all you want. We won't need it this winter. Indeed, as soon as we are free of these hides, we are going to feed other wolves on a feast cooked in Sigigairar's hall!"

The two of them devoured the last of the winter's provisions, growling happily as they broke apart the rack and scattered its sticks around like puppies at play.

It was two more days before Sigimund awoke and found that he was a man with a wolfskin blanket laid over him. He pulled his head out of the wolf's neck and woke Sinfjotli, who dragged the skin off and stared at the faint brown stains around the muzzle with wonder, even as Sigimund stared at the blue of the sky, the gold of Sinfjotli's hair and the deep red of the runes carved into the cave's stone walls. Joyfully he crouched with bow-drill and dried leaves, twirling and twirling the wood until a wisp of smoke began to curl from its glow and he could feed it into a fire.

When the flames were burning well in the middle of the cave, Sigimund and Sinfjotli held up their wolfskins, looking at one another for a moment.

"Ought we to burn them?" Sigimund wondered. "Might they not be useful later?"

"I think we will not need the hides now," Sinfjotli answered. "Indeed, I do not think that even when they are burned to ash we shall be without them; and I would not have another take them up." It seemed to Sigimund that Sinfjotli's pupils had widened to wells of darkness again for a second as he spoke.

Sigimund nodded. "So it shall be, then," he said.

They cast their hides into the fire. The fur blazed quickly. Sigimund doubled over with a sudden rush of burning might as though the full wod of the warg had come upon him at once. Gradually he forced the spasm down and saw Sinfjotli, too, writhing with clenched fists and bared teeth till he could grip the might that had whelmed his soul and wrestle it back to stillness.

"Dress and weapon yourself," Sigimund said when his sister's son stood clear-eyed as a man again. "We shall travel lightly when we go from here."

"What about the Herulian?" Sinfjotli asked. "Will we not take him with us?"

Sigimund pondered the question for a few moments, staring at the chest against the back wall. "I think not," he said. "I mean for us to bear him, and all the goods we have gained in our years of harrying, back to his howe, and leave him there with the honor he deserves."

Sinfjotli nodded, his high-boned face grave with thought. So much like Sigilind; how could there be anything of Sigigairar in him? wondered Sigimund. Yet the Herulian had said it. . . . He sent the prickle of foreboding away from his spine—unworthy of a Walsing!—and straightened his back.

"But there's no way into the howe," the young Walsing pointed out. "Will we have to break its walls?"

"There was a way in and a way out when I first found the Herulian," Sigimund said. "I doubt if we shall have trouble finding it again."

Laden with five years of booty and the Herulian's chest, clad in helmets and chain-mail byrnies that they had won in their fighting, Sigimund and Sinfjotli strode through the wood laughing at the gold, brown and red of the leaves around them, the deep green of the pines and the yellow-fringed orange of the layered shelf-mushrooms growing from wet bark. It was strange to scent no longer the trails twisting along the ground, to see the sharp edges of brown branches and sunset-flaming leaves in treetops that had been gray blurs, and to speak with the voices of men, half-deaf again to the speech of scent and eye. The cold wind bore them easily along their path; careless as they were, Sigimund knew they were lucky not to be spied by other men. But they had made the forest a terror themselves, so others now traveled there only in large bands, and the Walsings could hear them from far away and avoid them easily.

Two large stones had fallen from the northern edge of the Herulian's howe, but the passage was too small for either Sigimund or Sinfjotli to force their shoulders through it. So they crouched to lay their riches of gold and silver and furs in as carefully as they might, and last of all to pass the chest where the Herulian's head lay through the hole and set it on his new grave-goods. Each of them moved one stone to block the pathway again and stood, unburdened save by Sigimund's spear and Sinfjotli's sword.

"Ready?" Sigimund asked his sister's son.

"I've been ready for five years," Sinfjotli answered with the taunting grin that Sigimund had grown used to—was it not his own, the one he had once worn as he boasted that he would be the best of his father's thanes? "Are you ready?"

"We'll see, won't we?" Sigimund said, swinging his spear in a whistling arc through the wind.

16

REVENGE

As Sigimund and Sinfjotli drew nearer to Sigigairar's hall, they became more cautious, falling silent and moving shadowlike through the branches far from the pathways through the wood. They could see bands of men traveling up the hill, with women and children walking or riding within the rings of warriors. Sigigairar must have invited every human being for several days' ride to his hall, perhaps to stave off the whispers of ill-luck that must have followed the day of terror in the woods. There would be no taking him in the hall that night. Even as wolves, Sigimund and Sinfjotli could not have hoped to overcome the gathered host.

"What shall we do?" Sinfjotli whispered to Sigimund.

"Wait."

The two of them squatted down behind a stone. Sigimund breathed deeply, spinning his thoughts out into a long thread, casting them toward Sigigairar's hall where Sigilind, her face flushed from the heat of the cooking fires and strands of golden hair straggling out of the coils on her head, stood directing a thronging horde of thrall-women, carls' wives and children as they cleaned and cooked and brought in fresh straw to strew the floor. Sigimund remembered Alfflad readying great feasts in his father's hall just so, and his pang of homesickness twanged down the thin cord that bound the twins.

Sigimund opened his eyes and settled himself to wait with his back against the rock. It was not long before they heard light footsteps through the dried leaves.

Sigilind had not changed into her feast clothing yet. The dress she wore for cooking was plain and stained. She was as slim and graceful as ever, but Sunna's gleam off her coiled plaits of hair was more silver ice than golden warmth, and Sigimund could see the wrinkles beginning to crimp the corners of her eyes. He could not help glancing from Sigilind to Sinfjotli and back again: only the first glitter of hair along the youth's jaw was not mirrored in his mother's face. Warning pricked down his spine as he gazed at them; he put it aside and rose to his feet.

The joy that lit Sigilind's face washed away the creases about her eyes as she embraced her brother, then her son. She held Sinfjotli longer—clutching him as tightly as though she were wrestling with the walking dead, staring breathlessly into the face that mirrored hers so closely—and Sigimund understood that it must seem to her as though she were looking at her twin, as if he had stepped unchanged through the twenty-one years and the horrors that had drawn her face closer to the bone and worn the gilt from her hair.

"My son," she murmured, her voice blurring with tears. Sigimund saw Sinfjotli's throat move as if the youth were gulping back a sob; his mouth opened, but no sound came out. Sigilind let go of him, stepping back. "You have grown well, Sinfjotli. I could not have hoped better for you."

"I . . . I wish I could have come to you before," Sinfjotli said. "But now you will have only a little longer to wait, and then we shall not be parted again."

Sigilind's gaze flickered from her son to her brother, then back again. "Has the time come at last?"

"The time has come," Sigimund said. "Your son is a man grown, than whom I could ask for no better at my side. Then be glad, my sister, for soon we shall be far from here."

"We shall, indeed," Sigilind agreed. "When do you mean to do it?"

"We had not looked for such a host to be there tonight," Sigimund admitted.

"This is the feast at which Freyjar and Freyja are most worshiped, together with the alfs and idises. To keep their favor and his place, Sigigairar must show himself worthy both to them and to all the folk around—and now there is much doubt, since he cannot keep the woods safe. And because of that, you shall have your chance at him. Follow me."

Sigilind led them along a twisty way through the trees until they came to the grove of ash and birch trees where the harrow stone stood. The grove lay at the foot of a small hill, with a wide path—almost a road—winding around it.

"Here, where the way turns to round the hill. Sigigairar and I shall leave the grove last, while the rest of the folk wait for us just beyond sight: the fro and frowe must always stay alone with the gods for a little time after the blessing is made. If you catch him here, as we step out of the grove, you will have a few moments before the others can reach you—time enough to slay him and be away. I think they will not follow after you, for his death now will prove that he was no longer worthy of rule. But you must be swift and sure, for he will just have come from the gods who shall not turn from him until you have proven your might greater, and he bears the sword by his side. Strike high; his sword arm has not wholly healed from the hurt he took in the fight with our father, and he does not raise it with ease."

Sinfjotli flung his arms around Sigilind again, swinging her off her feet and around in a circle. "Well thought, Mother! And so we'll do it."

Sigilind tucked a loose trail of hair back under her crown of braids, then leaned forward to kiss her son. "I'm proud of you, Sinfjotli. You are a true Walsing, my dear son." She turned to embrace Sigimund again. "I must hurry back, or they'll start wondering where I am."

"Fare well till later, then."

The setting Sun glowed through the sparse-leaved trees; the sky was darkening rapidly overhead when the wind first brought Sigimund and Sinfjotli
the sound of voices raised in song and the rich pine-sap scent of torch
smoke.

> Now die the days   and dark comes night,
> sleep the seeds   set in earth's womb.
> cows come in   when chill blows wind,
> soon shall fall   the snow all white.

Sigimund and Sinfjotli moved away from the path, crouching down behind
the bushes where they could watch the folk pass by without being seen
themselves.

Sigigairar and Sigilind led the folk to the holy grove. Sigigairar's head
was crowned with oak leaves flaming red-gold over his gray hair. His cloak
and tunic were dark green and his breeches yellow. Spirals of gold wound
around his arm, covering the scar of the wound Sigilind had told them of.
Sigimund's sword hung at Sigigairar's side, and as the Walsing saw the sunset
glowing from the ice stone in its hilt, all his strength was hardly enough to
stem the growl growing in his throat. Sigilind wore a gold-leaved crown of
birch twigs and carried a gold-bound aurochs horn. Beneath her green cloak,
her dark gown of southern silk was richly adorned with fine embroidery.
Soon we shall be together again, Sigimund told himself, trying to ease the
cold grasp of longing beneath his breastbone.

Even in the fading light, Sigimund could see how much the two small
children who walked behind the rulers looked like Harigastir and Theudorikijar with their mother's fairness and father's red, her fine features and his
crooked nose, and his breath caught in his throat. They must have no part
in this, he said to himself. Though they might seek vengeance in their turn
when grown, Sigimund had no fear of Sigigairar's sons, and he thought he
could not bear to kill more of Sigilind's children. But they will go out with
the others, he thought; our meeting shall be with Sigigairar alone.

Four cattle followed the children: two bulls and two cows, well-fed beasts
with glossy hides. Most often, here as in the Saxon lands, it was the weakest
beasts with the least hope of living out the winter who were slaughtered for
the Winternights' blessing, but Sigigairar sought holy favor more strongly
now than ever before and had chosen among the best of his herd.

As the folk neared, singing, Sigimund marked how they glanced through
the trees, peering into the shadows. There was no iron in their voices beneath the gilded shell of their song. Though the words were joyful, their
loud brightness glittered only to defy their fear as the feasters walked
through the woods where the wargs had fed nine days before.

Shorn the fields' shining hair,
growing's ended grain is reaped.
Froths harvest beer and horn runs full,
hail we Freyjar fruitful god!

Then it was well for Sigimund that they sang: their voices covered his gasp
as he saw the woman Freyjadis stalking ahead of a knot of warriors, breasts
swinging beneath her light green tunic and dark green skirts swishing about
her legs. Although Sigimund knew she could not have heard him, she
glanced sharply upward. For a moment their eyes met, the fire of her amber
and gold necklaces swirling up and flaring in her gaze till it seemed to
Sigimund that he stared dazzled into the setting Sun. Cold chilling down
his back, he blinked the brightness away as she turned her head and walked
on. Although Freyjadis had not changed since those days in his cave he
could not have mistaken her—he felt a sudden, unreasonable sureness that
this was not the woman with whom he had lain. Shaken, Sigimund closed
his eyes, breathing deeply until he was calmer. There will be time to unweave
mysteries later, he reminded himself. Now we have only one task; when it
is done, we shall see what comes next.

Not only the clearing, but the whole holy grove, was full of folk standing
close enough to breathe one another's breath when the last warriors had
come down the path and the singing stopped. Sigimund and Sinfjotli crept
to the top of the hill and looked down through the trees into the torchlit
clearing. Sigigairar and Sigilind stood closest to the harrow stone, with the
cattle before them and a keg of ale on the ground beside them. Sigimund
could not see their children, but Freyjadis stood at Sigigairar's back. Her
shadow hunched oddly behind her, like a lynx about to spring, and again
Sigimund felt sure that he had never touched this woman. He slithered back
as she looked up again, gesturing to Sinfjotli that they should take their
places beside the path.

Sigigairar's voice came clearly to them over the rising autumn wind that
rattled the branches again. "Now the summer is ending; the time of harvest
is done. We stand at winter's door, at the sunset of the year; at the holy
stone we give worship to the gods and ghosts of our folk, as our kin before
us have always done. Ingwar-Freyjar, we hail thee with harvest thanks! Freyja
holy, we hail thee! Idises and alfs of our kin, wend your way here: hear our
call to this blessing!"

Sigimund stroked the shaft of his spear as Sigigairar went on speaking.
Smooth and well-shaped, it would fly easily from his hand. Sigigairar had
taken Sigimund's gift from Wodan: Sigimund meant to make him a gift to
the god in turn.

Wrapped in his thoughts, he did not mark the movement on the path
until a little golden ring flew over the bushes to land somewhere near his
feet and a child's voice murmured, "There, you've lost it! I think it went over
there." Then he saw that the two children—bored by the length of time it
had taken the folk to gather and having scant care for their father's call to

the gods and wights—had wandered out of the grove and were pushing their way to where Sigimund and Sinfjotli lurked.

The full Moon shone white off the children's upturned faces, freezing Sigimund's hand on his spear. Then one mouth opened darkly to scream. Sinfjotli's sword was already out, opening a leaping spring of blood from the child's throat, but the other one got out a single piercing howl before the backstroke sliced through its body. Sigigairar's voice broke off as his children dropped, as though Sinfjotli's stroke had slain him too; then a wave of men broke out of the clearing, swarming around the hill and up it as the women below reached for their knives and shouted their men on.

"Take them!" Sigigairar cried, his cracking voice slicing through the din. Gray-haired as he was, he leapt lithely toward the fight, the sword in his hand whirling with a speed that Sigimund had forgotten. Sigimund snarled and howled, froth running into his beard as the madness of the wolf's hide came upon him. He beat his way down the hill toward Sigigairar, fighting into the holy grove, but there were too many bodies in the way for him to hack through. Though the edges of their weapons did not bite on his hide— *did a wolf's fur blur through the rings of his byrnie?*—the force of the blows slowed him. Slipping in the blood-mixed mud around his feet, Sigimund howled and howled again at the man who was trying to press through the mob to him. He struggled through a sea of corpses that rose around his knees, then his thighs; the blurred shapes around him had stopped using weapons, pressing against him with shields instead and bearing him down thus. Again and again he threw them off; yet in the end there were too many, too much weight on him, and the moment he stopped moving his berserk might faded away, leaving him too weak to lift his own limbs.

Vaguely he heard Sigigairar's sharp command, "Take them and fetter them firmly; take them back to the hall and keep them till morning. I shall think on their fate. They have fouled the holy grove with men's blood, and Freyjar shall have his geld for it." The roaring in Sigimund's ears drowned Sigigairar's next words to sea-loud silence, but a few aching breaths later he heard the Gautish drighten's cry: "My sons!"

Then Sigigairar's voice was cold and still, so that it hardly seemed like the voice of a living man. "I know this man, though I had thought him dead. The Walsing must have won his way free somehow, and got this cub on a wolf in the woods. You, Gunthormar and Hroarar, take Sigilind to a hut and watch her, though remember that she is my wife and treat her with due honor. I wish only that she be watched until these wargs are dead."

Sigimund came to himself to find that he and Sinfjotli were fettered like cattle on shipboard, their ankles and wrists bound by iron chains. They lay face down in two heaps under a hail of freezing rain; before them, several thralls were building a mound around a slab of stone that lay on its side, its edge higher than a man's head. One of Sigigairar's sons rested on a wooden

bier at either side of the stone, their wounds covered by their fine clothes
and the gold at their throats. Sigigairar himself stood beyond the mound,
his iron-gray hair and black cloak blowing in the wind, staring fiercely down
at his foes with his hand on the hilt of Sigimund's sword.

Sigimund's feet and hands were numb, his ears aching with cold. He could
see ripples of shivering running through Sinfjotli's body. The young Walsing
turned his head to look at him, bearding his downy chin with icy mud. To
Sigimund's pride, he spoke no word that Sigigairar might take as a sign of
pain or fear. It had not, after all, been Sinfjotli's weakness or cruelty that
betrayed him; once wyrd had sent the child's golden ring arching over the
bushes to his feet, nothing except flight might have changed what happened.
Though he could see little hope, his heart was not dimmed within him: if
he could not come out of the howe living, he resolved, he would use the
last of his life to bind his soul to his corpse. Then the undead might do
what the living could not, and if he gained his sword back only for it to lie
in his barrow, he would be content enough. Who knew what wyrd might
shape the strangeness of his vision and the Herulian's words, or what might
befall him after death? For the Herulian had said that Sigifrith's mother was
yet unborn, and it was often said that men were born again into the Middle-
Garth when they had fallen.

When the stone walls had risen almost to the height of the great slab's
edge, Sigigairar gestured to the thralls to stop their work and stalked over
to the Walsings. Sigimund steeled himself for a kick that he could do nothing
to stop, but the Gautish drighten only stood there looking at them. The
years and his sorrows had cut wrinkles sharp as scars across his high brow,
carved deep gorges like empty riverbeds into the stone of his thin face, dry
channels running down to crease his sparse beard. His look did not change
as he gazed down at the men who had slain his sons.

"Are you Sigimund, in truth?" Sigigairar asked. "Or some troll who has
taken his shape to mock me?" His voice shook, but less that Sigimund might
have thought; it seemed to him that the Gaut's sorrow had drowned all
surprise or fear. Sigimund could not tell whether Sigigairar was speaking to
himself or Sinfjotli, but he swallowed hard to wet his throat, then answered
as boldly as he could.

"I am Sigimund: you could not slay me, nor could the warg who came
by night. I was her death, and the line of the Walsings lives yet—it will
take a mightier one than you to bring it to an end!"

"You speak bravely, but I think your luck is at an end. You shall pay
Freyjar's geld for defiling his holy grove with man-slaughter, and be thralls
of my sons in their lives to come, whether they be born to the Middle-
Garth's ring again or fare to the holy halls," Sigigairar said. "Now you may
curse the god who armed you against fire and iron: for you shall starve
together within the burial mound of my children, where you can neither
touch nor see each other. Some ill magic must have freed you from the
stocks, Sigimund, but you and this wolf cub you got in the woods will have

no such way out this time. And when you are dead my ill-luck shall die with you."

Sigimund waited to see if Sinfjotli would speak out—would say that he was the son of Sigigairar and Sigilind, not of Sigimund—but the youth was silent. A true Walsing, Sigimund thought again, and the thought brought a small prick of joy through his numb shock.

Sigigairar beckoned to one of the thralls, a short, burly man with black hair and olive skin like a Roman's. Together the two of them bent down to pick up Sinfjotli and heave him roughly over the wall. He landed heavily with a clatter of iron, and Sigigairar and the thrall turned toward Sigimund.

The Gautish drighten's grasp was hard and as clawlike as a bird's talon, his sinews wiry strings over his long bones as though he were dead already; but his breath had the morning stink of a living man's, and the wet wind blew a clear drop from the end of his cold-reddened nose. He and the thrall carried Sigimund to the side of the mound and swung him up. For a sickening moment, Sigimund spun through the air, unable to do more than twist around to break his fall, and then he crashed into the cold mud, the ground knocking his breath out of him. He could hear Sinfjotli gasping and choking on the other side of the stone slab.

"Seal them up," Sigigairar ordered. Sigimund heard the sound of his boots sloshing through the mud. At least the walls kept the worst of the wind off, though small gusts whined through cracks in the stones: they would not freeze to death at once. The Walsing clenched his fists and feet rhythmically to keep the blood flowing through them, stilling himself in readiness for what might befall him.

Sigilind paced up and down the narrow ring of the storage hut, her head bent beneath its low roof. She heard the sounds of stone on stone outside; when the clinking stopped, she clearly heard her husband's voice speaking the doom he had chosen for Sigimund and Sinfjotli. To this? she thought. Is all I worked for come to this? She thought of her sons, Ingwar and Ingwawulfar. She had not borne them willingly, nor let them suck from her breasts, but they had grown into fair children—and like enough to Theudorikijar and Harigastir that she had sometimes hoped the two had been born again to a better wyrd.

Sigilind wiped the tears from her eyes with a corner of her shawl. Mourning would do no good. She had chosen revenge herself, nor would she have haggled over the price even if she had known it. She sat down cross-legged, wrapping her shawl about her shoulders, and began to breathe deeply as Sigimund (and in her dreams, she) had learned to do from the Herulian. The men outside were talking softly, Gunthormar's deep rumble answered by the breathy whisper of Hroarar. Sigilind touched the golden brooch on her left shoulder, wondering if she might bribe them to let her loose. She doubted it. She must try what she had heard her brother learning in her dreams; she must see if she, too, could work magics to bind her foes' minds and loose fetters from her chosen heroes as her walkurja mother must have done before her.

Her deep breaths became a slow hiss of ice, solidifying into black chains that sank, in the sight behind her closed eyes, through the reddish-fringed bald crown of Hroarar, through the curly chestnut hair of Gunthormar, the cold dark glitter fettering them to silence of thought, silence of motion, as their voices muttered and faded. Softly she hummed, lulling them to sleep—easy, yes, had they not watched all night? The heaviness of ice weighted their lids down, sealing their eyelashes with a thick glitter of numbing frost; their hands fell limply to their sides, their backs slumped against the wall of the hut, nothing moved except their slow, deep, sleeping breath.

When Sigilind opened her eyes again, she heard nothing from outside. She picked up two large pieces of smoked meat and hid them under her cloak, then crept to the door and pushed it open with a sweaty palm, ready to tell Hroarar and Gunthormar that she needed to piss again. She drew in a deep gasp as she saw them, not quite asleep, but slumped against the hut, their eyes moving very slowly toward her.

"Where are you going, Sigilind?" Hroarar asked, his voice slowed and thickened so that she could hardly understand it.

"I'm just going out to the wood to piss," she murmured in a soft, half-chanting monotone. "You stay here and rest, stay here, stay still, don't worry. I'll come straight back." She looked directly into his eyes, feeling the flow of might through her gaze settling the bonds more firmly within the ring of his skull. "Rest, Hroarar. Rest, Gunthormar," she commanded, turning her eyes to the dull brown gaze of the other guard. They eased back a little more, their lids settling over their foggy eyes. Sigilind moved away slowly, careful not to startle or disturb them.

Once around the hut, she ran light-footedly up to the back of the hall. Now she would have to risk everything; if the gods were not kind to her, she would have no second chance.

Sigilind pulled the door to their chamber open and stepped in. She sighed in relief as she heard Sigigairar's grating snore. He lay on top of the bed-clothes wrapped in his black cloak, his knuckly hands clutching each other above his breastbone. Sigimund's sword still hung at his belt. Sigilind did not mark the cloaked shadow behind the sleeping man until the dark head raised to meet her gaze.

Freyjadis' eyes were as huge as a cat's in the dimness, drawing Sigilind's own sight into their molten white core. Sigilind did not break their gaze, but moved very slowly to the chest where Sigigairar's old sword had been kept and lifted the lid, fumbling through the neatly folded linen and scented herbs till her hand touched the cold roughness of leather. She shoved the clothes aside and pulled the weapon out of its sheath. It was not as long as Sigimund's, nor so wide in the blade; it would fit easily into the other's place. Quickly, her fingers light as a flicker of flame, she drew Sigimund's sword and replaced it with the other, her hands moving to weave a web of invisible light around its grip, a silvery sphere to turn attention from it so that no one—not even Sigigairar himself, unless something brought him to look closely at it—would notice that no ice stone gleamed from its hilt. Freyjadis did not move nor speak, only stared at Sigilind as she thrust the weapon through the meat and hid it all under her cloak.

Sigilind left the hall and closed the door behind her, glad to be free of the spae-woman's gaze. She ran down the field to the growing mound, stopping only to pull up an armful of wet dead stalks and wrap them around the hilt of Sigimund's weapon.

The thralls looked suspiciously at her as she approached.

"What do you want here?" Frank Chlodowig, who had been directing their work, asked her.

"Only to throw in some meat and straw, that my brother and his son not die too quickly—and for you to hide it from the king, for he blames me unfairly." Before the thrall could move to stop her, she whirled on to her toes and tossed the bundle through the gap in the top of the mound. "Now you must hide it from him, for he will be angry with you for letting me do it if he finds out, and I can promise you that thralls will suffer worse from Sigigairar's wrath than a queen will."

Chlodowig stared balefully at her for a moment, dark eyes set like an angry bull's. "I think you have plotted ill against your husband. If I were one of his men instead of a thrall, I'd tell him, too." He spat on the ground. "But you're right. I'd get a worse reward than you would if I did. Be glad of your place, lady." He turned back to the others who stood watching him, rubbing their heavy arms against the cold wind. "Get going, you lazy slugs! Nothing happened, and you'd better remember that if you don't want your hides hanging from your backs."

Sigilind hurried back to the hut and past her sleeping guards, slipping in without waking them. For a second she grinned in triumph, clenching her fists: through Wodan's gifts and her own strength she had won Sigimund and Sinfjotli their chance. Reluctantly she sank down to the ground again, turning herself to melting the bonds she had set on her guards before their sleep became endless.

In a few minutes, she heard a drowsy mutter of, "Shit! Gunthormar, did you go to sleep?" answered by, "Huh? What?"

Sigilind lay down on her side, half-curled with her head pillowed on a sack of grain. She closed her eyes and dropped her mouth open just before the door of the hut creaked.

"It's all right," Gunthormar mumbled. "She's sleeping like the dead. Why doesn't Sigigairar send out someone else to watch? I want to go home, I want some food and I want to go to bed."

"Probably forgotten us," Hroarar said. "Between you and me, I think he might be getting a little fey. Anyway, we'll be able to let her out as soon as those thralls finish building the mound. Even berserks won't be able to get out of that, and she sure as shit can't get anything in to them through rock."

"Urhm. They're all going crazy, if you ask me. Did you ever think about packing up and going north to Hlewagastir?"

"Another old fart with dead sons? No, thank you. When I go, I'm going south. They say a man with a strong arm can win as much land as he wants, either through war or as a gift from the Romans."

"You've been listening to sailors, my friend. The Romans don't give anything away."

"No, really. My cousin went to Britain two years ago and he said he met a whole bunch of Alamanns that the Romans had settled there, land and houses and all, to watch their coast for them and keep raiders like us out."

"Your cousin . . ."

Sigilind let their voices fade from her mind as she sat up and began to concentrate on sending all her might to her brother and their son.

Sigimund saw the bundle of straw flying through the gap in the mound to land on Sinfjotli's side, then heard chains clinking as the youth hitched himself over to look at it.

"We won't be hungry for a while, anyway." Sinfjotli's voice came through the thin gaps around the edge of the stone slab between them. "My mother has given us plenty of meat." Breath hissed between his teeth. Sigimund listened anxiously, but heard nothing else.

The thralls were heaving stones above them, filling in the top of the mound and turfing it over till only a little light came through the cracks between the stones. Sigimund and Sinfjotli did not speak again until the sounds of work stopped at nightfall, though a thrill of expectation was tingling through Sigimund's body as he thought of what else Sigilind, if she was free, might have given them. He could almost see the ice stone glittering like frost in the straw . . . almost . . .

"Sigimund?" Sinfjotli's voice called quietly. "There's a sword here. I think—it's got a stone in the hilt, a hex-cut stone."

Sigimund shouted softly with joy. "Can you reach it over the top of the slab?" he asked. "If we can hold it for each other it will cut our chains, and then we can see about getting out of here." He wriggled over to the slab and used it to shove himself up—thank the gods, his hands were bound in front—bending his knees to keep from hitting his head on the top of the mound.

"Just a second," Sinfjotli's muffled voice muttered. Sigimund heard a clink of metal and a sharp hiss of triumph. "Got it! Holy gods, this sword is sharp! It sliced right through the iron. Are you ready?"

"I'm ready," Sigimund answered. He followed the slight scrape of metal on stone till the touch of his sword's cold sharpness thrummed through his numb hands, leaving him breathless with reawakening memory. In a sudden violent motion, he forced his fettered hands around the side of his head and brought them across onto the sword's edge. The chains shattered upon its sharpness.

Sigimund stretched out his arms, shaking cramps from his shoulders before he grasped the point of the blade and pulled it to him. The blade came easily, but the hilt was too wide to fit through the gap. They turned it this way and that, trying to ease it through. Sigimund heard it scratching on the rock, and for the first time he feared that the blade's edge might be dulled or harmed. He put his hand to the weapon. It was as sharp as ever, but it had dug a long groove deep into the stone.

"Pull it back, turn it on edge and thrust it straight through," Sigimund told Sinfjotli.

The young Walsing did as he was told and with only a slight moan of protest the blade cut through the rock. Sigimund took hold of the point again—it did not bite him, as it never would—and he and Sinfjotli began to saw through the slab of stone with all their strength till they had room enough to bring Sigimund's sword down in a great blow that cracked right through the rock. It fell apart in two pieces between them, and they were loose in the mound.

Sinfjotli felt about Sigimund's feet for the chains and cut him free. The two of them embraced fiercely, exultantly, in the darkness for a moment, then Sigimund put his hand on the sword's hilt over Sinfjotli's and together they pried and heaved their way out of the mound. The wind was blowing harder than ever, whipping back their long hair and Sigimund's beard, but the stars glittered starkly in the clear black sky and the cataract-white Moon, just past his full, stared blindly down at them.

"Now our luck has overcome Sigigairar's!" Sigimund said. "We have won the right to meet him face to face. His folk cannot stand against us."

The two of them ran joyfully to the hall. A slim young man stood guarding. At the sight of them, he gripped his spear in shaking hands and moved in front of the door.

"How did you come out of the mound?" he asked. "Are you living men, or dead?" Though his voice shook and broke on the last word, Sigimund deemed him a brave man to stand instead of fleeing.

"We are living. We broke our chains and came alive out of the hall of the slain," Sinfjotli answered. "Now stand aside: it is Sigigairar the Ingling we want, and you have no right to keep us from him. We mean for him to know that not all the Walsings are dead!"

The door warder stepped aside, letting them in. They passed through the beer room and flung open the door to the great hall.

No one spoke as Sigimund and Sinfjotli stepped between the door posts: the hall was as still as if no one breathed within. Sigigairar stared at them, tongueless with shock. Beside him, Sigilind sat calmly waiting.

Then Freyjadis, who sat at Sigigairar's other side, rose slowly to her feet and flung back her cloak, turning to point at the drighten. "Now, Sigigairar of the line of Ingwar-Freyjar, your idises have turned against you and your luck is at an end. You could not hold the hallowed grove free from blood-shed, nor keep your children alive; and the Walsings have won free out of their mound. See: Sigimund has his sword back, that is the luck of his line, and you have lost your seed and your lands. So, Sigigairar Ingling, you must pay the geld of your troth at last."

Sigigairar half-drew his sword as he began to rise from his seat, then he looked down at its stoneless hilt. His mouth opened, but he said nothing. He sagged back into his chair, his head drooping.

Freyjadis looked at the gathered folk. One by one they rose from their benches and began to file toward the door. Some of the carls opened the stalls, leading cows and horses out into the night.

Sigimund and Sinfjotli waited by the door until only Sigigairar and Sigilind still sat there. "Sigigairar, let my sister go," Sigimund said.

"She shall go if she wills," Sigigairar said, and his voice was that of an old man. "It is I alone who must pay this geld."

Slowly Sigilind rose to her feet and walked the length of the hall, not looking back. Sigimund's heart leapt like a salmon in his breast as she came to him, but her face was very grave.

Freyjadis stood outside with a torch in her hand. Two byrnie-clad thanes were piling wood by the side of the hall, heaping up a pile for the kindling. When the three Walsings were out and the door closed behind them, Freyjadis bent down and thrust her brand into the branches.

The damp leaves sputtered and sparked, twigs flaring up and dying down. Only slowly did the flames begin to creep onto the larger pieces of wood, reaching up to the scarred door. The brand had burned almost down to Freyjadis' knuckles by the time the door of Sigigairar's keep began to char and crackle under the flames that rose swiftly to catch in the thatch.

The fire leapt up to the roof, swept higher and higher by the wind that flung the black smoke over the stars in a long thin veil. It took two men to hold each of the horses; the beasts tossed their heads, stamping and neighing in fear of the fire burning so close to them.

"Sigilind," Sigimund said softly. A gust of wind whipped smoke around to choke his throat and burn his eyes with tears; he coughed it away. "Come away with us, and I shall make good to you all you have suffered. Together we and your son shall take back our father's land and more, and no frowe will have greater honor than you who have borne so many woes for our father's sake."

He embraced her tenderly and kissed her. Though tears ran from Sigimund's eyes, Sigilind's face was dry and hot, her back straight. When she finally answered him, her voice was raspy with smoke.

"Now all shall know," Sigilind said, "whether I cherished against Sigigairar the memory of the slaying of the fro Wals: I had you kill his children and mine who seemed over-slow in the avenging of our father; and I came out to you in the shape of the witch-woman Freyjadis, and now Sinfjotli is the son of us two. He is so mighty a hero because he is the child of both the son and the daughter of Wals. I have wrought at all times for the slaying of Sigigairar. So mightily have I worked to bring about this revenge that I may no longer stay in the ring of the Middle-Garth, but I am still a Walsing and I will not break my oath to my husband, although he has cast me out. Therefore I shall gladly die with the drighten Sigigairar, though I went with him against my will."

Sigilind reached up to Sigimund again, drawing his face down to hers for a last kiss. Only now, after the many years, Freyja's spell faded from his mind and he remembered how the witch-woman had cried, "Sigimund!" when they had first loved; he remembered how he had thought himself mad or dreaming when he saw Sigilind's face behind hers, like his own in a clouded mirror; and he wept with thirteen years of loss for what he had not known and what had always been before him in Sinfjotli—who, if he had only trusted his mortal eyes, he could have seen was wholly like his father, and wholly like Sigimund's sister also, with nothing else in him.

Sigilind pulled away from her twin. The flames were roaring in the thatch above; the crashing of roof beams within the hall drowned out the whinnying of the horses and the murmuring of the folk around them. Sigilind kissed her son quickly, touching the falcon head of the dagger at his belt.

"Sigilind!" cried Sigimund in anguish, leaping forward to grasp her; but with the hero's strength that he had forgotten must flow through her as through him, she threw her brother aside and opened the door of the hall.

The rush of fire knocked Sigimund back a step, dazzling his eyes. He blinked, blinked again: Sigilind was already a black shadow within the flames, walking slowly into the fiery hall for a few steps before she went down and the brightness flared around her. The roof caved in, fire and smoke collapsing toward the center and then shooting up, brighter than ever, to cast terrible twisting shadows around the hill and over the fields and huts below.

Sigimund and Sinfjotli watched till dawn, till only charred posts and heaps of smoking ash stood where Sigigairar's hall had been. Sigimund rubbed his thumb over and over the smoothness of the ice stone in his sword hilt, wondering: did I give Sigilind's life for this? But she had spoken of doom in his cave thirteen years ago; he realized that she must have known even then, when she came to him, and borne the weight of her knowledge and their guilt so that he might be free to avenge Wals. He looked down at his big scarred hands, the hands that had held the Herulian's head, that had cut runes so skillfully and drawn circles of flame to ward him in his search for the wisdom he had needed. For all his pride and craft, all his deeds, he had not been able to compass the one thing that Sigilind had known almost from the start, that, knowing, he might have saved her as she, with her wits and the wardings of her soul-might, had (he understood suddenly) saved him so often before.

"She never told me," Sinfjotli said. "She only said that Sigigairar was not my true father, but that she had gotten me through magic." His man's voice wavered and cracked upward on the last word. The youth dashed water from his red-rimmed eyes with the back of a sooty hand, leaving a black smudge on one cheek.

"My son," Sigimund murmured, the tears coming to his own eyes again as he struggled for the betraying words that would not, no matter how he tried, loose the mingled flood of sorrow and awe in his soul. "Your mother was a true Walsing—and a stronger hero than either of us, she who bore her wyrd in stillness within the hall of our foe while we ran free through the woods. Now she has fallen as befits one of Wodan's walkurjas, keeping her oath with her enemies dead around her. May she fare to Walhall in joy and be born forth in the Middle-Garth's ring again as befits her. The gods grant that we be not parted for ever!"

Heedless of the thanes and carls who stood around them, the two Walsings wept unashamedly until Sinfjotli finally sneezed and wiped his eyes. Then they saw that they stood in the middle of a ring of armed men. Most of the women were farther away, tending to the beasts or to their children, but Freyjadis stood within the warriors' circle, facing the Walsings. The spae-wife's golden-brown hair flowed out behind her in the wind, and she stood with the rising sun at her back so that Sigimund could not look straight at her. Still, the sight of her shape against the sunrise wrenched at him, and the more so now that he knew who had worn her hide for those three nights in the cave: he ached uselessly for what might have been.

"You cannot stay here," Freyjadis told them. "You have brought too much ill to these lands; the wights here will never look well on you, and there are others of the Ingling line who may come to rule in Sigigairar's stead. Go where you will, but leave our land behind you. We will give you a ship and goods enough to take you back to Saxony. If you leave now, the winds shall hold good long enough for you to reach your home before the worst of the winter storms blow up."

"It is a fair offer," Sigimund said slowly. He looked around at Sigigairar's men. Some scowled and turned their faces from him and others glanced nervously away, but a few young men met his gaze, their eyes opening to him with a touch of awe. The luck of the Walsings had overcome Sigigairar: and here, as in Saxony, some youths would always long for battle and gold, good fame and a high seat in the band of a mighty drighten. "We go to reclaim the land of the drighten Wals. Who among you will come with us? We can offer you fame and gold and a fair seat in a greater mead hall than you have yet known, or else a warrior's death in battle and a place in Wal-hall—and as you have seen, we fare with Wodan's blessing. Who will come with us?"

The first to step forward was the slim youth who had stood guard the night before. The sleepless circles under his eyes were very dark, red hair and scanty beard very bright against his pale face, but his voice was strong as he answered, "Thonarstanar the son of Wulfastanar." One by one, five others broke the ring, speaking their names as they came to stand with the Walsings.

Freyjadis led Sigimund and Sinfjotli to the storehouses as their new thanes went to gather their belongings for the faring and say their good-byes to their families. As she turned to go, Sigimund reached out and put a hand on her arm.

"Yes?"

"Thank you," he said quietly.

17

SIGIMUND'S WOOING

Sigimund sat alone on the deck of his flagship, a horn of strong mead in his hand, staring at the Moon's glimmering in the rippling of the Rhine. His ships were tied upstream of the river's mouth for the night, and most of his men had gone on shore, setting up their tents and lighting campfires. The sound of singing carried easily over the water, a song he had heard many times in his hall which told of how he and Sinfjotli had overcome one of the great drightens of the Saxon folk to take back Wals' lands and more.

> Stark was the strife in storm of white hail,
> awful flew arrows with ice storm all mixed,
> when Wals' bairn at Wodan's game played,
> Sigimund's spear was Saxon lord's doom.

Sigimund's hand clenched on the horn; he raised it, drinking deeply, as if to drown out the memories the song raised in him. He had heard it last while sitting in the huge carved chair at the end of his great hall, one hand holding a horn of mead and the other resting on the delicate fingers of the woman who sat beside him, his Danish wife Borghild, as he listened to the singing of a skop who had asked guest-right in their hall for the evening. He had looked along the fire-lined hall to the mound in the center where the Barnstock had stood more than twenty years ago before Wals' dwelling had fallen to flames. Once the hall had been rebuilt by a Saxon drighten named Adalrad, who had taken the Walsings' lands for his own. Sigimund had slain Adalrad when he returned, and had parts of the new hall torn down and remade as he remembered it, but the Barnstock was gone and could not be planted again: it had been only five years since he and Sinfjotli had won their revenge in Gautland, and an apple tree would not grow as high as the

Barnstock in ten times as long—if a sapling could grow at all with no more light than came through the smokehole.

"High above hero's   head rode the sig-wife . . . "

The skop sang of a walkurja who shielded Sigimund in battle, a shining maid whose whiteness his blurred berserk's eyes had seen flashing above him in the winter storm as he fought. Had he truly seen a sword twin to his own in her hand, had he really seen the flowing pale hair and high-boned face of his fallen sister riding over his head, or was it only the dream of his battle-madness and the wish of his heart that Widuhundaz had warned him might twist his soul's sight?

In Sigimund's ten years as a drighten in the Saxon lands, the Herulian's lessons had sunk deeper and deeper beneath the daily worries of men. Now, though he tried to still his mind as he had learned to do in Gautland, it came harder to him than it had the first time; and when he tried to reach out, to see if he could feel some spoor of Sigilind close to him, his need for her choked his mind and blinded him to all but his fear that he would not find her. Only the Moon's light on the river answered him, the whiteness betraying his eyes into hope when he did not look straight at the ripples. Even when Sinfjotli had still been beside him, Sigimund could not think of his twin without wishing to cast aside everything he had won, though he could never bring himself to silence songs that spoke of her.

So it had been, he thought, turning his gaze from the light on the river to the shadowed mead in the depths of his horn; just so it had been on the night that had first turned him toward this need-faring. Sigimund drank deeply, letting the mead's warmth numb the aching within him as he thought back to what had passed between himself and Borghild, in that time before Winternights when Sinfjotli had just come back from a summer of fighting in the warband of Hailgi Hunding's-Bane. It lived within him: it would not pass away.

S
T
E
P
H
A
N

G
R
U
N
D
Y

ᚼ
1
9
8

Borghild's delicate fingers curled around Sigimund's hand as she looked up into her husband's face, tilting her plait-crowned head so that one gold earring dangled teasingly free, the other lying against her neck like a curl of hair brighter than her own ash-blond. "Why do you look like that?" she murmured softly to him. "Have you grown tired of hearing songs about your victories? You've kept every skop in the north busy enough for these past eight years."

"No," Sigimund answered. "I was thinking of past times, that's all." He took a deep drink of the strong mead, then another. There was no fear that it would run out; even at the end of the worst winters, the household of the fro Sigimund had food and drink enough to consume as they would, and now the harvest-tide was nearing its end.

Sinfjotli's sword   sang on linden-shields,
hewing down hardiest   heroes before him,

> *so well he warred   withstand him could no one,*
> *— stark foe to his foes   feasts for ravens he made.*

Sinfjotli's teeth flashed through his beard as he unwound a ring of gold from his arm. He hefted it lightly in one hand. Mead and the warmth of the fire beside him tinged his fairness with a pinkish flush, but his eyes were clear as he watched the skop who sang of his deeds. When the song was over, Sinfjotli leaned forward and tossed the gold arm-ring in a glittering arc. It thunked neatly into the hand of the skop, whose freckled face cracked into a wide grin as he raised it up, calling, "Hail the Walsings!" He twisted it around his wiry arm; the gold that wound Sinfjotli's thews twice coiled four and a half times around his.

"Where have you come from?" Sinfjotli shouted to him.

"I'm Paltwini, of the Alamanns by birth, but I've just come down from the Danish lands. I was last in the host of Hailgi Hunding's-Bane, over this summer. I saw you there, though maybe you didn't see me, and I heard your flyting with Gunthamundur and saw how you fought at Hailgi's side against the sons of Granamarar."

"Do you know any songs of that yet? I think my father's heart would be gladdened to hear the full tale of my harrying to the glory of the Walsings this year."

The skop struck a chord on his harp and began to sing again, his high voice carrying easily through the smoky hall above the murmuring of the men gathered there.

> *There shone a light   from Loga Fells*
> *and from that light   a lightning flashed . . .*

Sigimund finished his mead and leaned back in his chair, resting his hands on the heads of the two dragons coiling about its carven arms as Borghild went to refill his horn and her empty pitcher. Sinfjotli stamped his right boot on the hard-packed floor in time with the chant, tossing his long fair hair back from his eyes and grinning at the thanes who raised their drinking vessels to him as the skop told of how he and Hailgi had weathered the great storm at sea with their ships and men, bidding the sailors not to be afraid nor to reef the sails, but to hoist them higher and let the fury of wind and wave bear them to land the more swiftly.

> *. . . and Sigrun on high   hovered in cloud,*
> *shielded them starkly   ships warded all,*
> *till out of Ran's clutching   claws came the brine-steeds*
> *safely to Gnipa Grove   glided they then.*

Smiling, Sigimund took his refilled horn from his wife's hands, passing it through the arch of his son's elbow. The two of them drank with arms linked together. Sinfjotli had truly grown into a man to be proud of, thought Sigimund. He remembered how he himself had stood at Wals' side before battles, shouting similar insults at his foemen, and after asking Wals' speaker Osfridh—no, Odward; Osfridh had died in the great fever—to chant the songs of his own deeds. Looking at the fairness of the face he remembered from his youth before the tiny wrinkles had snaked into the corners of his eyes and the hoarfrost had settled its first silver glitter on his hair, Sigimund knew that he lived again in his son's young boldness, even as Wals still lived in his own drighten's adornments of victory wound on victory and fame on fame.

> Ever with Hailgi   the Hunding's slayer,
> first in the fray   at fighting of heroes,
> fiercest in fight   to flee aye unready,
> stouthearted hero   Sinfjotli ever.

Sigimund joined heartily in the shouts of applause, and this time it was he who slipped the twisted gold from his arm and flung it to the skop. Beside him, Borghild tapped the glass foot of her goblet gently on the arm of her chair, its soft ring almost silent under the shouting.

"Will you give us another song?" Sigimund asked. "Do you know tales of the gods and of how they walked in the Middle-Garth in elder times?"

"A song of Loki!" shouted merry-hearted Ehumari from his place near the head of one bench.

"Of Thonar!" Cunthwulf boomed across the hall, heaving his great bulk upright in his seat.

"Do you know the tale of how Mannaz fathered the three kinds of men?" another voice shouted from the benches near the door.

"I know a great many, good thanes, gracious drighten," Paltwini answered. "But my voice is growing tired now. If you would have me stay in your hall, I will sing for you tomorrow and as many nights as you please. Truly, I have not yet been among a more noble band or sung for such far-famed rulers."

"Stay as long as you choose; you are welcome here!" Sigimund called out, his men stamping and whistling in approval. The wiry skop tucked his harp into the bag that hung at his side and bowed. Two of the thanes, Theodibald and Adalstein, made a place for him on a nearby bench. Without being asked, Borghild glided to refill his clay mug herself, her slim body slipping as gracefully as a small fish through the rippling shadows of the firelight. Sigimund could not help glancing at her from the corner of his eye: in the betraying torchlight, he could half-imagine her crown of hair fairer than it was; his eyes blurred with smoke and mead, and he might see her features stronger and more like his own. But then she would come closer, and she did not look so much like Sigilind—and in the dark of the bedchamber, when he could not see Borghild's face, every touch told him that she did not have his sister's height or strength.

When Borghild came back, Sigimund noticed a fine straight line of thought between her light brows, one corner of her mouth twisted downward as though she were trying to chew a stubborn piece of gristle without showing it. Her hazel eyes flickered over Sinfjotli and back to her husband as she seated herself at Sigimund's left side again.

"So Hailgi has won himself a wife at last, has he?" Borghild said, looking at both Sigimund and Sinfjotli. "My father thought once of wedding me to him, though that was before he slew Hunding and gained his fame. He was certainly no match for you, Sigimund."

Sigimund caressed the back of his wife's hand, his sword-calloused palm passing lightly over silky skin and the warm smoothness of her gold rings. "It was well for him that we never came to fighting," he allowed. "Still, Sinfjotli has won a fair portion of fame at his side this summer while I held my lands in peace, haven't you, my son?"

"A fair portion," Sinfjotli agreed, rubbing his beard. He shook his horn gently, sloshing the last inch of mead around before he raised it and drained the drink.

"Would you care for more?" Borghild asked. "You certainly learned to drink like a hero in Hailgi's hall." She smiled at her stepson to take out any sting that might lie in her words. Her teeth were white and sound, but a little uneven.

"I would," Sinfjotli said. She poured out the drink for him and refilled her own vessel, the wavering golden stream splashing from the conical bottom to stain the blue glass green.

"Indeed, Sigimund, I think you would say," she said, settling herself back into her chair and glancing up at Sigimund through her pale lashes, "that Sinfjotli has become as much of a hero and as well-famed as any young man in the Northlands, would you not?"

"I think I would say that," Sigimund said, glancing from his wife to his son. "And I would be right, too."

"No one has any doubt of it," Sinfjotli said. "It is no little thing to have fought beside drightens such as my father and Hailgi, and not to be forgotten when the skops sing of their deeds. Indeed, the thought has come to me that if I were not so glad to stay in my father's hall and to fight for the fame of the Walsings that it would not be hard for me to gather men together under my name and go south to win lands of my own."

"It would not be," Borghild said. "But if you will not leave Sigimund's realm for more than a summer, why haven't you at least thought of going to win a bride for yourself? It seems rather shameful to me that you, as famed and strong as you are, sit here and drink and watch my serving maids' bottoms as though you were not mighty enough to find a bride worthy of Sigimund's line. Even my younger brother Hlothwer is betrothed now, and he is not half so famed as you."

"Do you want him to leave our hall so soon, then?" Sigimund asked Borghild. Looking at Sinfjotli's flushed face and glittering eyes as his son leaned forward in his chair, a sharp pang struck through Sigimund's entrails; wedded,

Sinfjotli would have his own hall and keep his own feasts, whether he dwelt within his father's lands or not.

"You can't keep your son with you forever, Sigimund," Borghild said more softly. "Sinfjotli is a man and must go a man's ways—and if the gods are kind, we will have sons of our own to fill his empty chambers."

"Yes, we will," Sigimund murmured, feeling in his heart that his words were only empty wind. "So, Sinfjotli, are you ready to go out wooing? Have you heard of any maidens who might be worthy of Wals' line? If you have anyone in mind, Borghild and I will gladly send to arrange things for you."

Sinfjotli leapt to his feet, facing Sigimund. "Except for one thing, I hardly need even a father's help in winning a woman," he said. "But will you give me leave to ask twelve of your thanes to follow me when the winter's storms are done?"

"I will give it gladly," Sigimund answered.

Sinfjotli tossed his blond hair back in two cresting waves about his face. The smooth gems of his wide belt buckle gleamed deep red and green; firelight shone cold from the torc of twisted silver about his neck and from his golden arm-rings as he raised his drinking horn. A little mead slopped over the edge to stain the earthen floor in dark droplets.

"Then I will be back by Midsummer's with an atheling-wife at my side. This I swear, and drink upon it thus!" In one long draught, his high cheeks reddening above the edge of his beard, Sinfjotli drank the horn dry. He lowered it with a gasping laugh and sat down quickly. "Your brewing gets stronger every year, Borghild!" he said. "The Danes were fools to let you leave their land. I never had such mead in Hailgi's hall."

Borghild's lips curved upward in satisfaction, but she said only, "You'll be lucky if you don't have a headache tomorrow."

"Do you have a woman in mind?" Sigimund asked.

Sinfjotli stared into the depths of his empty horn for a moment, then met his father's gaze. "I might," he admitted, grinning. "You'll see."

"To your bride, whoever she may be!" Sigimund shouted. He drained his own horn, the mead rushing to his head in a dizzy wave of exhilaration. Leaping to his feet as lightly as his son had, he swept Borghild off her chair, her glass of mead spilling down the front of his tunic. She made a squeaking noise, then giggled, leaning her head against his broad shoulder. "Sleep well, my son," he said to Sinfjotli. "We have a night's work ahead of us." He lifted Borghild up farther and kissed her, his lower lip snagging, as it often did, on her uneven teeth. Something white flashed in the corner of his eye; Sigimund turned his head sharply, his heart thudding hard, but it was only one of the serving women in a pale tunic.

"What's wrong?" asked Borghild.

"I thought I saw . . . someone it wasn't. Don't worry about it." He kissed her again and began to carry her toward their chambers, thinking: if I went out alone tonight, if I did as the Herulian taught me . . .

But Borghild would want to know where he went and why at such a strange hour, and he could not tell her: she would have little patience if she knew that his heart was wedded to a dead woman, and he had to bear his duty to himself and his men above his own joy.

Looking away from his memory, Sigimund stood up and walked over the ship's deck to the keg of mead that stood beside the mast. He refilled his horn, swirling the drink around inside. It had been this ship he gave to Sinfjotli to sail forth from his hall with his small band of thanes at the beginning of Hrethmonth, as soon as the winter storms had blown out the worst of their fury and the green spears of leek leaves were starting to thrust upward from the thawing earth. His son had needed a stark ship: the tides were higher that year than Sigimund ever remembered them being, waves frothing up almost over the great flat-topped mounds on which the farms and villages of his land had been built, the hills that the folk of his father's and grandfather's time had raised to escape the flooding at winter's end. So while the thralls had spread manure on the fields at the foaming edge of the North Sea and the carls had gone about their planting, Sigimund and his thanes had readied themselves for battle. It had seemed to Sigimund then— as it was more and more in his mind now, on this southward faring up the Rhine—that if the floods grew any worse, he might soon have to widen his rule and move his folk farther away from Agwijar's hungry grip. But the thwarted waters had drawn back after the feast of Eostre on the first full moon of summer, and soon the cattle had slipped down the muddy clay sides of the mounds, lowing plaintively as they searched the devastated earth for grass and found only ropes of reddish brown seaweed; and Sigimund had stayed in his lands after all, waiting for word of Sinfjotli's wooing to come back to him.

Sigimund sat down, gazing into his horn again. Enough mead would make him drunk, in time, but it would do him no harm. He thought of the Walsing might against poison as he drank, and the mead's strength curdled bitter in the back of his throat. And he had been drunk then, first with joy, then with Borghild's strong ale. So he remembered: so he lived it again, on these nights when he drank alone.

It was a bright warm day half a month before Midsummer's when the sound of a horn broke through Sigimund's concentration on his sparring. He put up his practice sword, stepping back from Ehumari a pace and wiping the dripping sweat from his eyes before he looked toward the river to see the snarling wolf's head of Sinfjotli's banner waving proudly over the ship whose oars drove it against the current. He recognized the ship he had given his son when Sinfjotli left. Behind it rowed two more, richly fitted; the young

Walsing had done well for himself in his years of raiding the coasts of Britain and Gaul with his father's band and fighting in Denmark with Hailgi.

"Is it him?" Ehumari asked, leaning on his wooden weapon and shading his eyes with one hand. His hair had frizzed out around the band tying it back, and he was breathing hard—harder than Sigimund, though he was fifteen years younger. "Holy gods, it is! And do I see a woman there on the deck with him?"

Sigimund blinked a couple of times, straining to see more closely. His eyes were less keen than they had been, he thought. He could just see Sinfjotli's light hair above the white of his tunic, and so close to him that they almost blended into a single blur, a smaller figure in . . . yes, a long dress of pale blue, head wound with heavy dark plaits like a great helmet. "I believe so," he said, grinning. "Run and tell Borghild to ready a welcome for my son and his bride. I'm going down to meet them."

Ehumari turned and sped off to the hall, his lanky legs pounding furiously. Sigimund watched the ship for a moment more, then, his heart lifting within him, raced through the hamlet and down the side of the hill. The children weeding in the fields looked up in giggling astonishment to see the fro Sigimund running like a boy, skidding every now and again in the mud as he hurried joyfully to meet his son.

"Don't bust a gut!" called the old blacksmith, Eggberht, looking up from where he sat filing an axehead in the sunlight and wiping sweat from his bald head. Laughing, Sigimund raised a hand in greeting to him as he sped past.

The ship had reached the edge of the hill by the time Sigimund got down to it, and a crewman was throwing a rope around the posts sunk into the earth. Sinfjotli picked up his wife and moved to the edge of the ship, teetering for a moment before he sprang to land with her. When he put her down, Sigimund saw that she was of middle height and slightly plump, though hardly a burden for a man of his son's size. A few light freckles sprinkled her face like dust flecks on cream; the shining coils of dark brown hair wound about her head were adorned with ornaments of gold. She straightened her sky-blue dress with great dignity as the thanes lowered a plank from the edge of the ship and began to carry chests to shore under the sharp-tongued direction of a fat little brown woman.

"Greetings, Fro Sigimund," Sinfjotli's bride said, looking up to meet his eyes with a clear blue gaze. Her quiet voice was high and pure, almost a birdlike chirp. "I am Sigrid, the daughter of the fro Frodrik of the Frisians and now the wife of Sinfjotli, who has won me by the strength of his sword."

"Welcome to our home!" Sigimund said, stepping forward to enfold her in a carefully gentle embrace.

"What do you think of your new daughter, Father?" Sinfjotli asked. "Have I done well? She is the most noble frowe in the northern lands, and I had a hard fight to win her. You will hear the song of it soon." He put his arm around Sigrid's shoulders, drawing her closer to him. Her head hardly came past his chest, but she showed no sign of being daunted by the two Walsings who loomed over her. She cocked her head to smile brightly at Sigimund and his son.

"I am very glad to be here," she said. "I have heard the tales of the Walsings for most of my life, and never hoped that I should have the joy of such a hero as Sinfjotli for my husband."

Sigimund looked warmly at the young pair standing before him in the sunlight. "Come up to our hall, then. Borghild my wife is making things ready for you. You must be hungry after your long faring."

"Even the women of the Frisians are used to going by ship," Sigrid answered him. "But I thank you for your care, and I have been looking forward to seeing the hall of which so many songs have been sung."

Sinfjotli held his bride close while the three of them walked up the hill together, as though he could not get enough of cuddling her to him or gazing on her sweet face. Sigimund felt a sort of mellow sadness, like the mists of summer's end, stealing over him as he watched his son and Sigrid; he loved Borghild well enough, but he had never felt the need for her that drew Sinfjotli and the Frisian woman together even as they walked.

Borghild's serving women were sweeping the hall, sending clouds of dust and flecks of straw billowing around the hem of the frowe's dress as she strode here and there, shooing out chickens and trying to bring the hall into some kind of order. Her ash-blond hair was down, falling in smooth waves around her slender shoulders; her hazel eyes darted here and there, pointed fingers snapping nervously. Distracted as she seemed, a large plate of cheese and fresh berries lay ready on the table beside a tall gilded pitcher and four matching goblets, and another fine chair had been set on the raised mound next to Sinfjotli's seat.

Borghild was turning toward the door when Sinfjotli, Sigrid and Sigimund came in. She looked up with a nervous smile waving the thrall-women away. "Welcome to our hall," she said breathlessly. "And may you always be welcome here, frowe."

"This is Sigrid, daughter of the fro Frodrik of Frisia," Sinfjotli said, ushering his wife before him as if to display her.

Borghild stopped still, her face stark white.

"What did you say?" she asked him in a queer little voice, as though she were about to be ill.

"Borghild?" Sigimund asked, two steps of his long legs bringing him to his wife's side. "Are you well?" She hunched her shoulders away from the touch of his arm.

"How did you get this woman as your wife?" Borghild demanded of Sinfjotli, her voice very low, but trembling with intensity.

"I won her by my own strength," Sinfjotli answered. He stretched his arms around Sigrid in an unthinking gesture of protection. "How else should I have done it, when your brother courted her? She wished to come with me, but he would not let that happen without battle between us. He fought bravely and well—you may be proud of him—but I slew him. It was a fair fight."

Sigimund froze in shock, the blood draining from his face. Only then did he see Sinfjotli's ice-blue eyes open in sudden awareness and hear the inward hissing of his son's breath; and for a moment, though he had never wished to strike Sinfjotli before, Sigimund wanted to clout the young man on the head. How could you have been so stupid? he thought.

Sigrid stepped back against her husband, her hand coming to her mouth as she stared at Borghild. For a moment the only sound was the whispering of the thrall-women and the clucking of the chickens wandering through the open door.

Borghild's scream pierced the air like the whistling of an arrow in flight, "My brother!" She drew the dagger at her belt and sprang at Sinfjotli, but Sigimund was quicker, plucking her up as her feet left the ground and holding her tight to him with one arm, wrenching the knife away with the other. She glared up wildly into his face. "Get him out of here!" she screamed. "Get him out of my sight. Warg, accursed, never let me see him again!" Borghild collapsed, sobbing against his shoulder.

"The bridal hut is almost ready," Sigimund said softly to Sinfjotli. "Take your wife there and see to her things. If you leave us alone, I think I can make amends here."

Sinfjotli nodded gravely. He led Sigrid out, stopping only to take two platters of food from the end of the table. At Sigimund's gesture, the serving women followed the young couple, leaving the king and his wife alone.

Sigimund sat down with Borghild on one of the benches, his arm still around her. A shaft of dusty sunlight slanted through the open door, gilding Borghild's tarnished hair and making her blink as she looked tearfully at him.

"My parents had been working for years to get Hlothwer wedded to her," she said. "When the last messenger from them came before Winternights, he told me that the betrothal was set. The wedding would have been next spring. And your son came . . . like a robber on the road, and killed him for her. Oh, Hlothwer had no fame like Sinfjotli's, but he had no ill name either. He had done his share of fighting and not fled; it would have been no shame for that woman to be married to him, and Sinfjotli could have won any other he pleased." She fastened her fingers into the ridged muscles of Sigimund's shoulders, bringing her wet face close to his. "Why did he do it?" she demanded of him. "Why didn't he honor the vows Frodrik had already made, and leave my brother to what was rightfully his?"

Sigimund looked uncomfortably away from her glance. "Men get their gains by strife," he answered at last. "Hailgi also won his bride so, and was he not honored for it? And would you have been so sorrowful if I had fought for your hand and won you by my sword instead of by treaties and oaths?"

"I was not yet promised, and you didn't steal me away by murder," Borghild answered bitterly.

"It was no murder!" Sigimund protested. "Sinfjotli must have fought with your brother like a man. Surely he didn't need any secret craft to best him . . ." He choked off his words, but they were already said and true. He had met Hlothwer while wooing Borghild. He vaguely remembered sandy hair and hazel eyes, a square frame and a quiet manner; nothing except his family had particularly distinguished Hlothwer beyond other thanes, and Borghild knew that as well as he.

"It was done for a lawless purpose, and there was nothing fair about it," replied Borghild, turning her head to stare at the motes of dust that dimmed the sunlight. She ignored Sigimund's touch as he smoothed her disheveled hair. "Either send that warg you fathered and his ill-won bride from our realm now, or I swear I will bring you more sorrow than ever a woman has brought a man." Her voice choked and her slim shoulders began to shake with weeping again.

"Borghild, Borghild," Sigimund murmured, holding her close till her tears had flowed their course. "I know there was no dishonor in your brother's fate, and all men must die in time; he, at least, will not be forgotten in the songs made of this. And if that will not comfort you, then let me pay a fitting weregild to honor him. You know I have never paid weregild to anyone in my life, but I will pay it to you now, if it will quiet your wrath and soothe you enough to let my son dwell in our lands. I have lost brothers too. I have lost all my kin but Sinfjotli, and I would not lose him as well."

Borghild drew the hem of her sleeve across her face and met his gaze again, blinking against the sun that caught green glints from the pooled depths of her hazel eyes. "No matter what I say, you will not let Sinfjotli go from you. It seems to me that you are as much of a mother as a father to him." She spoke the insult in a low monotone, as though she were too tired to taunt him as befitted the bitter flyting of her words.

Strangely enough, Sigimund felt no anger. "Perhaps I am," he said softly. "But I do not want to send my son away. Will you take the weregild?"

"You are the king here. You must decide what is fitting. Only let me hold a funeral feast for Hlothwer, and name his death a murder."

"Weregilds are not often paid for a man felled in fair battle. Let that be enough. I will not quarrel with you. Hold your funeral feast when you will, if this can make peace in our hall and our family again."

"Peace enough," Borghild said. She stood up. "But promise me that I will not see Sinfjotli or his woman again till the ale is done brewing, because I don't think I could bear the sight of them. I will send my women to finish readying the bridal house and to do what they need."

Sigimund enfolded his wife in his arms and kissed the saltiness from her lips, shutting his eyes for a moment as he embraced her stiff body. She did not warm to him, but she did not pull away either, waiting till he was done before she went about her business.

The Walsing walked out into the sunlight, feeling troubled and sick within. He went toward the bridal hut, which was finished except for the greenery that the women and children would deck it with before nightfall. Borghild's serving maids were already bearing branches of birch and pine up the hill together with flowers and herbs.

Sigimund stopped at the door of the hut, hearing Sigrid's clear giggle and Sinfjotli's laughter as cloth rustled within. There would be time to speak to his son later, he decided.

The Moon hung low and large in the misty sky of late summer on the night of Hlothwer's funeral feast. All the leaders of the tribes within Sigimund's realm sat at the benches of his hall, together with their thanes and his; Hlothwer's weregild, an atheling's price in gold and goods, lay heaped about the feet of Borghild's chair where all could see it, ropes of amber twining through rich fox pelts and fine linen. The precious metals and stones glinted from the furs, half-hidden by ruddy brown and silvered black as though the rocks from which they had been brought forth still held them. Sinfjotli sat where he always had, at his father's right hand, Sigimund looming like a wall between his son and his wife. A place had been set for Sigrid beside her husband, but she was not there; she had sent her fat little serving woman to the hall with the message of her illness.

Borghild was pale and quiet, simply dressed in a long gray overshift, her ash-blond plaits held about her head by pins of plain horn. Though rich jewels lay at her feet, her only adornments were the amber beads dangling from her belt. She carried the ale about as though she were dreaming, often splashing drops onto the stained wood of the tables or the earthen floor. Her silence did not dampen the shouting that rang through the hall's rafters or mute the sound of Sinfjotli's laughter for long as he called greetings to the men he had fought with.

The feasting had started early; when it came time to drink the toasts to the gods and the dead, Sigimund was already well mellowed by Borghild's strong ale, and so he hardly marked when she took Sinfjotli's empty horn from his hand and carried it away instead of filling it from the half-full pitcher by her chair.

The drightens, thanes and carls stood for the first toast. Sigimund, his voice hoarsened from years of shouting on the battlefield, called it out loudly.

"Hail to Wodan, who gives the gift of victory in battle!" Some echoed him before they drank; others, who trusted more in their own might than Wodan's troth, made the sign of Thonar's hammer and drank to the trusty Warder of the Middle-Garth. Sigimund drained his drink in one swallow; lowering it, he saw that Sinfjotli was staring into the full horn in his hand.

"Will you not drink to Wodan or Thonar?" Borghild asked him. For the first time that night she smiled, showing her uneven row of white teeth.

Sinfjotli looked at his father, his face strangely grave and stark. "The drink is bespelled, Father," he said with an unsureness that Sigimund had not heard since they left their cave in Gautland.

"Give it to me!" Sigimund said. He took the horn from Sinfjotli and emptied it, returning it quickly before too many men began to stare at them. His head was beginning to swim; he knew that the two horns of ale left for the toasting would have him as drunk as he had ever been, but there was no way to get out of it without showing weakness to the great men of his lands.

Borghild went around with her serving women, filling cups and horns. She took one man's drinking vessel back with her whenever she went to refill her pitcher. Sigimund rose halfway out of his chair when she carried Sinfjotli's horn away, almost ready to go with her, but she had done nothing more than she had done for each third man whom she served.

Sigimund stood again. "Hail to Nerthuz and Fro Ingwe, who give us good winds and good harvest!" he shouted, and this time all his men answered his hail alike. He drank his horn dry, belching out the bloat that was beginning to swell him. Again, Sinfjotli had not drunk.

"The drink is full of deceit," Sigimund's son said sadly. "I think I should not drink ale brewed with hate."

Sigimund looked at Borghild. The tears were beginning to pool in her eyes again. "Hasn't your son done enough to me? Why should he shame me before the great men of your land at this feast of all feasts?" she asked softly.

Sigimund glanced back and forth between them for a moment. Sinfjotli's eyes were dark in the smoky firelight, only a thin rim showing pale around the swollen pupils. Drunk as he was getting, Sigimund felt a thrill of worry run through him.

"Give it to me," he said again, grasping Sinfjotli's horn and draining it. "Now there will be no talk of shame."

More than full, he rose from his seat and stumbled outside to piss in a stream that seemed to flow forever. With a sigh of relief, he retied his breeches, looking up at the hazy face of the Moon, whose silver-gilt roundness swam mockingly in front of his drunken eyes, hovering low and fuzzy-edged through the mists.

When Sigimund went back in, Borghild stood by his chair. Her pitcher was full; she poured a dark stream of ale into his horn first, then into that of his son.

"Now, Sinfjotli, you have no reason for fear. Drink this toast, if you have the courage of the Walsings, or else show these thanes that you are a nithling in spite of your strength." She raised her glass, the ale a solid darkness beneath its blue rim, and cried out, "Drink to my slain brother Hlothwer, for whom we hold this feast!"

"To Hlothwer!" the men roared back at her. Sigimund drank again. Even fuddled as he was, he could feel the thickness of yeast in his mouth when he reached the bottom.

Sinfjotli stared into his horn. "The ale is muddied," he said. Sigimund had never seen him so cast down. He remembered how his son had kneaded the adder into the meal and laughed, and a drunken fury began to grow in him as he saw how Sinfjotli's hand trembled on the silver rim of the horn. He could not imagine how this strange fear of Borghild's nith had come over his son to steal his mood of bravery from him—from Sinfjotli, who had never turned away from fights of soul or body in the Northlands.

"You are no Walsing!" Borghild said loudly. "You flinch from a little yeast in your ale."

"Let your beard filter it, my son!" Sigimund cried, shaken and angry, trying to drown her out. But Sinfjotli was already raising his horn and tilting his head back. Sigimund saw the knot of his son's throat leap thrice beneath the glittering edge of his beard; then Sinfjotli plunged down, face forward, the horn spinning out a shower of dark drops as it fell from his hand.

The crash of his fall shattered through the talking of the men. "Treachery!" cried a sharp thin voice from among them, then they were still, all staring at Sigimund, who rose from his seat with a howl of despair. His heart swelled and clenched around a tight stone of agony, shooting an arrow of pain down his left arm. For a moment he staggered and gasped through suddenly numb lips, holding himself up against one of the wooden dragons of his seat. He could not bear to look at Borghild or at the thanes whose faces showed pale through firelight and darkness. Bending his knees carefully, he cradled Sinfjotli's body and stood, the young man's long legs dangling down over one arm and his head flopping over the other.

Sigimund carried his son's body down the side of the mound and into the thick mists that shifted and eddied below like a moonlit flood. Drunk and mad with grief, he staggered along, his chest throbbing with a pulsing ache. Now he wept; now he almost laughed; he stumbled from tree to tree, his feet turning on stones as though he had never walked through a wood; he could not think about where he was going or what he would do.

Sinfjotli's eyes were open, wholly swallowed up by the darkness of his pupils. His body was cooling and beginning to stiffen. As Sigimund walked, a dribble of ale drained from his son's mouth. Only now, with the soulsight he had almost forgotten in his years of simple war and rulership, did Sigimund look at it to see the faint green gleam of the bale Borghild had brewed into the draught. That bale must have been in all three; Sinfjotli must have seen it, but Sigimund's strength to bear poison, within or without, had betrayed them both.

Stinging tears mingled with the fog in Sigimund's eyes. Might he not have laughed at his wife's taunts; might he not have drained the third horn and bid Sinfjotli make do with mead? The fame of the Walsings, or else their swords, could have held up such a joke.

Sigimund did not turn till he splashed knee-deep through the waters of a salt marsh. Faint err-lights gleamed through the mists that rose from it like cold steam from a murky cauldron, shining ghostly on the weed-rippled waters. The Walsing walked along the edge of the marsh, his boots sloshing through the sucking mud. He could not see any pathway through it; it seemed to stretch forever into the light of the Moon, who glowed as fuzzy as a will-o'-the-wisp in the fog above him.

Sigimund became aware of the sound of splashing behind him. He sank up to his ankles in the mud as he stood looking over the water to where a small boat floated slowly out of the mist. Only the faint plashing of the oars as they rose and fell, dripping dark waterweed, proved that it was more than a ghost or a dream in Sigimund's drunken eyes.

The man rowing the boat was wrapped in a dark cloak that shadowed his face. He thrust an oar down to the bottom of the marsh, halting his vessel some way from Sigimund.

"Do you want me to ferry you across?" the man called, his rough raven-croak carrying easily over the water.

"I do," Sigimund answered.

"The boat is too small for all of us. Let me take your burden first, and you will pay me when I come back for you."

He rowed in closer and Sigimund waded out, the cold water soaking through his breeches and the lower part of his tunic as he dragged his feet through the deep muck. He uncurled his numb arms and laid Sinfjotli's body into the bottom of the boat. The ferryman began to row away at once, leaving Sigimund to stumble back to land.

The vessel was only a dark shadow against the flitting marshlights when Sigimund saw that the boatman was turning out toward the sea. He hurried along the edge of the water, shouting after him, "Wait! Where are you going?" But no answer came back. The boat vanished into the mists and darkness, and Sigimund could no longer see it. Though he stood waiting until the Moon had sunk into darkness, the ferryman did not come back for him.

Sigimund had lost his path walking along the marsh, so his journey back to the hall was long and twisting. The pain in his chest had dulled to a faint throbbing, but his head ached and his gut roiled with sickness. When he finally got home, the fires had burned down and the guests had gone else-where for the night. Sigimund could just make out Borghild's shadow in her chair, her brother's weregild heaped untouched about her feet.

"What are you doing here?" he asked roughly. He drew his sword and stumbled forward, looming over her where she sat without flinching.

"Where else should I go?" Her upturned face was a pale blur in the dark-ness below him. "I avenged my brother as best I could. Do you blame me? You?"

Sigimund thrust his sword back into its sheath. "No," he said, his voice falling heavy against his own ears. "Go in and go to sleep. You have a journey ahead tomorrow."

"What do you mean to do?"

"You will go back to your parents with all that is yours and a fair payment. You can find another husband. I will not have you stay with me any longer."

"Do you want to shame me?"

"No. You will go as befits a frowe of your station. I do not think you can ask for more."

"No," said Borghild. She stood, stepping over the pile at her feet, and went into the chambers behind the feasting hall without another word. Sigimund sat down in his chair and strained his sight against the darkness until his head sagged down onto his chest.

Now, on the Rhine, Sigimund wondered: if Sigilind had been there, why had she not warned him? Was it her fault as well as his? But that seemed unlikely. Another thought was worse: had she called to him, and had he, dulled by the years of his half-marriage to Borghild and his life within the world of men, not been able to hear her voice? That seemed ill to him, but worst was the thought that she was not there at all. He would not think of that: he would finish tracing the steps that had brought him here, and see if he could gain more from them—if he could unravel the web of wyrd in his mind.

After Borghild had been sent back to the Danes' land and Sigrid, grieving, had gone home to Frisia, Sigimund had begun to send out his messengers to the edges of the Roman marches in search of another woman who would be a fitting bride for him, readying his warriors and gathering his ships meanwhile to move southward in search of better lands to win. But harvest time had come soon, and then no one could be taken from the land. It had not been until well into the winter, when the gales from the North Sea swept the waves around the mound villages to froth and hiss under the driving showers of hail, that the skop Paltwini had stumbled dripping and shivering into Sigimund's hall, grinning at the drighten through bluish lips. Sigimund seated him next to the fire, throwing his own fur cloak around the skop's narrow shoulders, and ordered hot ale to be brought for him.

"What news do you have from the south?" Sigimund had asked when Paltwini's teeth had stopped chattering and the ice had melted out of the water-dark ringlets of hair across his forehead.

"No news from the Alamanns, but Aiwilimo, the ruler of the Salian Franks on the Roman side of the Rhine, has a daughter named Herwodis, fourteen years old and already as fair and wise as a woman may hope to be. I have seen her and spoken to her myself, and I think you could not do better."

"Tell me about her," Sigimund had said, settling himself more comfortably on the bench and stretching his feet out to the fire.

"She is quite tall and strong of build, with brown hair and gray eyes. She is afraid of little. She does not speak too much, but her mind is very deep, and she is well skilled in all the things a woman should know. If you ask me, I should say that she will bear you fine and strong children."

Sigimund had thought about it for a moment, tugging at his beard and staring into the flames. "Since you have spoken to Herwodis, you must have spoken to her father as well. What did he say?"

"He answered with fair words, saying that he was honored by the interest of a drighten such as yourself, but that he would have till the beginning of summer to think about it. There was another messenger there, sent by Lingwe, the son of that Hunding whom Hailgi slew, and Aiwilimo gave the same answer to him."

"Hmm," Sigimund had mused. He had known then that there might come more fighting, but he had dwelt in peace for a long time—too long, it had seemed to him then as he had gazed down at the red-gold firelight shining from the ice stone in his sword's hilt, and the sleeping wolf within his soul had begun to stir.

"We will go as soon as the Solmonth planting is done," he had said, touching the sword's stone, which thrummed softly under his fingers.

And so, as soon as the summertide seeds had been safely tucked into the wet ground, Sigimund's fleet of ships had sailed around the Frisian coast and began the long faring up the Rhine to the land of the Franks; and so he sat here now, the last of his line—a man growing old with the weight of forty-seven winters—setting out to woo a maid of fourteen. Now, more than ever, he wished for Sigilind's rede; but she was silent, if she was there at all.

The next day was fair, but colder. A stiffening wind blew from the North Sea behind them. Sigimund, standing behind the prow of the first ship, felt it like a strong hand at his back pushing him onward. His thanes, dressed in bright-dyed new tunics and cloaks with their gold arm-rings and brooches freshly polished, feet bare for shipboard, stood about or lounged on the deck behind him. Some were casting dice and arguing good-naturedly over whose throw it was, others were stretched out to enjoy the sunshine. One of them, Odger, wandered up to Sigimund, standing beside him for a while before he spoke.

"It's a fine day to go wooing on, isn't it?" the thane said, looking up at the clear blue sky as he spat a wind-blown lock of red moustache out of his mouth. "The gods must favor this wedding."

"You mean as they didn't favor the last one?" Sigimund asked with a rueful half-grin.

Odger tilted his head downward, looking at Sigimund's bare feet. "Wouldn't have said that myself," he muttered, his tough square face set in an uncomfortable frown. He was silent for a moment, then a brown-toothed smile cracked through his ruddy beard. "Do you think there's going to be fighting? I've heard Hunding's sons are a quarrelsome bunch. I wouldn't mind trying them. And the Frankish lands might be worth a look, too. I'll bet they don't have to wade through half the North Sea every winter."

"While Hailgi Hunding's-Bane lives, I don't think there's much to fear from the bravery of the sons of Hunding," Sigimund answered lightly. "As for Frankish land, we've been talking about going south for a couple of years." He paused, gazing down at the dark green depths of the Rhine. "This wedding might be just the thing to give us our foothold."

"To tell you the truth," Odger said softly, "I haven't felt quite comfortable in the old hall since . . . well, since what happened last summer. It gives me a funny kind of feeling." He coughed deep in his throat, the thin scar across his left cheekbone flushing red. "I wouldn't be surprised if a lot of the men felt the same," he added.

In a sudden gesture of relief, Sigimund clapped the thane on his shoulder. To his surprise, he realized that he had been thinking the same thing all winter as he sat in his lonely chair at the head of the hall, though he had never managed to bring the idea of leaving Wals' home far enough up in his mind to have a look at it. "There we go, then," he said. He looked around at his men. There, lanky Ehumari cast a makeshift fishing line over the side of the boat: he had made no secret of his wish to fare southward in search of fame and gold. Hairy Oshelm crouched over his dice like a bear over a salmon, his big paw flashing out to flip them into the air. He complained often enough of the winds and the flooding, as did the fair-headed brothers who diced with him, Alfrad the Short and Cunithruth. Paltwini sat with his back to the mast, curly brown hair hiding his eyes as he restretched the seven wires of his little harp; surely he would hardly mind moving closer to the lands from which he first hailed. And the rest of them, who talked and laughed so loudly in the fresh air: Oldhun, Harthberht, Wilfrid, Cunthwulf, Hrodger; did they not seem happier now than they had since before Sinfjot-li's death, now that their drighten led them out again to new lands and perhaps a new battle? So, in one swift blow, the doubts that had brewed in Sigimund's mind for months were decided.

They traveled up the Rhine for several days, rowing when the wind stilled. Flatlands rose to soft hills, then to low mountains; the line of ships wound around their jagged feet like a many-jointed wyrm crawling on the long white legs of the oars.

It was Harthberht whose keen eyes first pierced through the morning mists to spot the small boat floating swiftly down the current. The banner that drifted above it in the light wind showed a Frankish throwing-axe embossed in gold on a red field. Sigimund called Paltwini to the prow; the skop put down his ale cup and hurried to see.

"That's Aiwilimo's banner, all right," he confirmed.

Sigimund unslung his father's blowing horn and put it to his lips, sounding a deep blast that echoed back and forth between the low mountains on either side of the Rhine.

"Put up the white shield of peace," commanded Sigimund, steadying its rim himself as Alfrad the Short heaved it up beside the prow with a grunt. "Ho!" he shouted across the water to the man in the craft. "The fro Sigimund has come to wed Herwodis. What welcome does King Aiwilimo give him?"

"A welcome feast is set, if you come in peace," the man's thin voice answered him. "If you come for war, Aiwilimo's sword and the swords of his Franks are sharp and ready."

"We come in peace!" Sigimund called back.

"Then be welcome!" The messenger rowed about, his powerful arms pulling him against the current and up the river before them. Sigimund's thanes put on their newly burnished chain-mail, brushing the last dust off their shields and sleeking down their hair and beards.

Several other ships already bumped against the dock on the west bank of the Rhine, the current tugging them against their ropes. Three were heavy-bottomed river craft, and the other four were the long, slim seafaring vessels of the north. The messenger stood on the dock, the cool breeze blowing his thin cloak tight against his powerful frame and stirring the waist-length mane of dark hair curling down his back. Brown eyes surveyed them keenly from a heavy-boned, skeptical face as Sigimund's thanes lowered the planks and marched off the boat in a glittering throng behind their drighten. Sigimund strode up to the messenger, inclining his head to meet the other's eyes.

"You will be King Sigimund the Walsing," Aiwilimo's man said. Even speaking normally, his voice was strained and thin; a purple scar puckered beneath his deep brown beard. This was a man of some luck to have lived through such a wound; it spoke well for Aiwilimo himself. "I am Hathubarth, the brother of Aiwilimo. King Lingwe, the son of Hunding, has been here for three days, but neither King Aiwilimo nor his daughter Herwodis has wished to make a betrothal till they have seen and spoken with you as well. Will you keep peace in Aiwilimo's hall, even if they choose against you?"

"I will," Sigimund said.

"Then come with me and I will lead you to them. You will want to bring what you can. It is most of a day's march to Aiwilimo's hall."

Sigimund and his men unloaded the ships. Quickly Sigimund marked the number of guards on Lingwe's boats, then called to Wilfrid, Cunithruth, Oshelm, Hrodger, Swafrad and Eormengild. "You stay here and watch things," he said softly to them. "I don't think I trust Lingwe any more than I think he trusts us."

"Yah," Swafrad mumbled through the gap where his front teeth had been, spitting over the side of the boat in the general direction of Lingwe's ships. A low burst of laughter came from three of the men who sat on one of Lingwe's decks playing dice. One, hairy and blond, stuck his thick finger up his nose and then flicked it casually over his shoulder toward Sigimund's boats.

Hathubarth led Sigimund and his thanes down the stone-marked path that led along the edge of the hill. In spite of their burdens, they set a swift pace, sighting Aiwilimo's hall before the Sun's wain had rolled far down from her noontide stead. The hall and the houses around it lay in the middle of a wide plain, its greenness sectioned off by farms and enclosures of cattle and long-limbed horses. The hall itself was made of stone, stretching both longer and wider than Sigimund's own, like the buildings he had heard of in tales of the Romans. Head up, Sigimund led his warband proudly down the road to stand before the great oaken door of Aiwilimo's keep.

Hathubarth flung the door open. The hall was hung with woven rugs and brightly lit by torches within; the platters of food lining the benches were half-empty, and the few men who slept beneath bore snoring witness to the ampleness of Aiwilimo's hospitality. Two women moved about, the taller of them strewing fresh herbs among the stained straw with a slow, quiet grace and the smaller one tidying up the tables. Seeing Sigimund and his band outside, the larger maiden set down her herbs with an unhurried movement and walked out to greet them. She was as tall as Sigilind had been, though heavier of bone and without his sister's spearlike slimness. Sigimund glanced sideways at Paltwini, who nodded slightly.

"Well met, frowe Herwodis," Sigimund said to her. He drew out the gift he had brought for her: a golden comb ornamented with intertwining lines and spirals of dots punched so fine and close together that they seemed to draw clean, deep grooves through the precious metal. "Please take this as a sign of my honor for you and your noble line."

"I am honored by your regard, King Sigimund," Herwodis said. Her voice was deep and pleasant with a faintly muffled softness, as though she were deliberately muting the full strength of the sound rising from her heavy chest. She took the comb from his hand, turning it over and looking at its whorling ornamentation with keen interest. "It is beautiful work," she stated. "The craftsmen of the north deserve their fame." She stepped back into the hold, one white arm sweeping in a gesture of invitation. "Please come into our hall. I am sorry it is not better prepared for you, but my father and King Lingwe are off hunting, so there will be finer fare tonight."

Sigimund and his thanes came into the hall and Herwodis seated them at the bench laid lengthwise at its head where the honored guests would sit together with the drighten. She called to the other maiden, "Hilde, go and fetch wine for our noble visitors." Hilde let out a piercing giggle, then clapped her delicate hands over her mouth, ducking her red-kerchiefed head, and scampered from the hall. When she returned, Herwodis took the tall silver pitcher and a blue glass goblet from her hands. The drink that flowed into the glass was as pale as greenish straw, with a few tiny golden bubbles rising from its depths. Sigimund had tasted wine, captured on raids against Britain and Gaul, three times before, but it had always been the deep red wine of the Roman lands. He bowed slightly from the waist as he received the draught from Herwodis, breathing deeply to catch its sharp scent without actually sniffing at it.

He waited until Herwodis and Hilde had served all of his men and Herwodis had poured out half a cupful for herself before he raised his goblet and said, "Hail to our noble hostess, whom I hope shall soon adorn our hall."

An uneven row of grins, most of them broken-toothed and pocked with gaps, answered him along the faces of his thanes as they echoed his hail. Herwodis' maid giggled again, shaking a couple of wavy blond strands free from the restraining kerchief. Herwodis, her lips curved into a calm smile, glanced along the line of men. Her eyes met the eyes of each for a moment as though silently thanking him for his accolade and Sigimund noticed a few of them actually smirking where her glance had passed, as though her look had blessed them with some high honor. He emptied his glass. The wine was sweeter than the wine he had had before. It was not so sweet as mead, but a faint bitter undercurrent of wormwood sharpened its delicate fruitiness. Cuthwulf choked back a cough, his round face going red; Ehumari wrinkled his long nose, but the others bore the unfamiliar draught well enough.

"Tell me about your journey here and the land you rule," Herwodis said to Sigimund when the cups had been filled again. "I have heard many of the songs about you—even before your skop came to speak to my father," she added with a little smile toward Paltwini, "but I would like to know more."

So Sigimund talked to her, drinking sparingly from the glass goblet that she refilled whenever he emptied it. As Paltwini had said, Herwodis did not speak much, but she listened very attentively, watching each change in his expression with the same keenness that he had marked when she looked at the workmanship of the comb he had brought her. He could not tell whether she was weighing him well or ill. Her strong-boned face stayed calmly smooth and pleasant at all that he said, her only response being, every now and again, to ask him another question. Still he found something reassuring in her calmness, as he had in his youth when, troubled, he had sat with his back to the great apple tree that stood silent and enduring in the middle of Wals' hall.

It was growing late in the day when Sigimund heard the sound of hounds barking and men shouting outside the hall. The oaken door banged open and two men came in, carrying a stag slung over their shoulders. Sigimund recognized the elder of them at once. Though he was clean-shaven, with gray staining the dark brown braids that hung to his waist and a scar splitting the tufts of his right eyebrow to fix his expression in a continuous question, his heavy-boned, sardonic features were almost twin to those of Hathubarth and not so far from the solid dignity of Herwodis's face. The younger man was of middle height, muscular, though slim-waisted. A mass of blond hair curled around his broad shoulders; a long fair moustache straggled down the edges of his clean-shaven chin like pale grass drooping at winter's edge. A noisy horde of warriors and woofing, gamboling dogs pressed through the door behind them, the echoing of their din through the stone walls only somewhat muffled by the hanging rugs and straw on the floor. The leaders were not the only ones with game: two half-grown wild swine and a doe, easily enough to feed the gathered company, were carried in behind the hart.

Aiwilimo and his companion dumped the body of the stag before the large fire burning in the middle of the hall. Other men in the rough brown tunics of thralls came in to spit their game and begin the work of roasting it. Herwodis got up to bring the two of them wine while Hilde and more servant girls who had eddied into the hall in the wake of the men began to carry refreshment to the other hunters and refill the cups of Sigimund's thanes.

Sigimund stood as Aiwilimo and the other man neared him, stretching out his arm to clasp the Frankish king's. Aiwilimo's grip was firm, and he did not flinch from Sigimund's strength. The other man dug his callused fingers deeply into Sigimund's muscles till Sigimund tightened his own grip enough to make his rival's lips go white for a moment. "Lingwe, Hunding's son," Sigimund said. "Your family is very famed in the north."

Lingwe's thin, flaring nostrils tightened as though scenting something unpleasant; his blue-green eyes flicked up and down Sigimund's body. "As is yours, Sigimund," he replied. "And here in the Frankish lands as well, I should hope."

"Herwodis tells me that the songs of my deeds and those of my son Sinfjotli, who fought in the band of Hailgi, are often sung here." Sigimund smiled blandly down at his rival. One corner of Aiwilimo's mouth was twisted up in what might have been a faint grin as he observed the two rivals.

"It's a pity that you arrived so late," Lingwe went on. "There was good hunting today, and I have heard it said that in your youth you were well known as a hunter in the forests of the northlands."

"Indeed, I did many mighty deeds in my youth, but I have done more as a man full-grown and now I have almost reached the age at which my father stood in his fullest might. The Walsings are a long-lived kind, though few of us have ever died in the straw. We have that gift from Wodan, who was the father of my grandfather Sigi."

Lingwe coughed dryly, as though a bone had caught in his throat. He glanced at Aiwilimo and Herwodis, who stood by her father's side watching them quietly. In the moment of silence, she stepped forward to refill their cups.

"It is a great honor to me to be courted by two athelings of such fame," Herwodis said, meeting the gaze of each of them in turn. "But surely, King Lingwe, you are weary from your hunting. Will you both not come and sit beside me?" She led them to Aiwilimo's high table, seating Lingwe at her right and Sigimund to her left, while Aiwilimo took his place next to Sigimund.

The questions that the Frankish king asked the Walsing through the course of the feast were, Sigimund was amused to note, not unlike those his daughter had been asking in the afternoon; and his manner was like hers as well as he leaned forward to hear Sigimund through the noise, eyes observing his guest sharply, heavy face as calm as the blocks of Roman stone from which his hall was built. Sigimund made no secret of his readiness to come and settle in a land south of his own. "The North Sea is flooding in on us," he said, gnawing the last bite of deer's meat off a bone, "and it seems to me that a flood of peoples will soon be streaming before it. You could do worse than to have the strongest of those at your northern march as your son and ally."

"And I expect that you would like as much help as you can get in bringing your folk south," Aiwilimo replied, his mouth quirking up into his sardonic half-grin. The thralls were beginning to carry the tables out one by one, as Sigimund had heard was the Frankish custom after a feast. "Now tell me, how did you come to put Borghild aside? I have heard many things from many people."

"My son Sinfjotli went wooing. He would not tell us where or whom till he returned with Sigrid the daughter of Frodrik of the Frisians. He had slain the brother of Borghild, who had also sought her hand. Borghild would not be comforted, though I let her hold a funeral feast and even paid a weregild, although my son had killed her brother in a fair fight. She brought him a drinking horn full of poison, and he had his death from it. I sent her back to her home in full honor, with two ships and full payment for the breaking of our wedding agreements. I could no longer bear to have her with me."

Aiwilimo nodded. "You did more fairly by her than most would have," he commented. "Indeed, you have a name for generosity and fair dealings to those against whom you are not warring."

"I can well afford it," Sigimund stated plainly. "I have won enough to give freely, and I do not need to hoard my goods because if I should give them all away today I can win as much or more tomorrow. I think you know the tale of how I came to Wals' kingdom again, so I shall not bore you with that."

"I do know it," Aiwilimo agreed. The tufts of his scarred eyebrow twitched. "There is one story of note about my line, one which goes back to my great-grandmother Lingwohaith and her brothers Fadhmir and Ragin. It is a strange tale, but one I think might interest you—you especially, for you have somewhat of a name for strange dealings yourself, as well as for no little bravery."

"I should like to hear it," Sigimund said.

Aiwilimo sat up straight, shouting over the noise in the hall. The full strength of his deep voice drowned out the laughter and arguments of the other men. "Ho! Arnhelm! Where is my skop? Quiet for him, now!"

A fattish, ginger-haired man got up from one of the benches, wiping greasy fingers on his blue tunic before he picked up the small triangular harp that had lain beside him and came forward to stand in front of the high table.

"What do you want to hear, my king?" Arnhelm asked. "Songs of your atheling guests? There are many that I know."

"Sing them the story of the gold from the Rhine," Aiwilimo commanded.

The skop scratched at the short fringe of beard that rimmed his jowls a moment, as though thinking of how to begin, then struck a chord on his harp and started to sing in a high, powerful voice:

Wodan and Hoenir   wandered with Loki,
to Middle-Garth   as men by the Rhine
there an otter   eating saw they,
a goodly fish   the flood beside . . .

Sigimund sipped his wine absently as he listened to the skop tell of how Otter's weregild had been paid with cursed gold; how Fadhmir and Ragin had slain their father, and how Fadhmir had taken the gold from his siblings.

> . . . then grim on gold   grew he to wyrm,
> the Helm of Awe   his eyes between,
> but Ragin fled   into the rock,
> dwelt with dwarves   all Dwalan's kin.

"Men say that Fadhmir still guards the hoard north of us, in the mountain above Gnita Heath, which we call the Dragon's Crag," Aiwilimo told Sigimund when the song was done and the skop had caught a flashing Roman coin to carry back to his bench. "Lingwohaith was married to the warrior Eburhelm and they held the lands that had been Hraithamar's. In the time of their daughter's son, my father, there was a famine and he and all his men took service with Rome. The Empire was glad to have us settled here, if we would help in keeping the other tribes across the Rhine and out of Roman lands. I do not know what became of Lofanohaith and her line. Ragin the dwarf keeps a forge not far from the Dragon's Crag, but he often wanders south to us. He makes swords so fine that no human could equal them. From looking at the hilt of your own, I should almost think that it is one of his workings."

"I am not sure who forged it," Sigimund confessed. "It was given to me for my greatest need, when, as the songs may have told you, it served me very well." He touched the smooth ice stone of the hilt. "It seems to me," he went on, "that it might serve for slaying a dragon as well. If all your skop sang is true, there would be some good to be gained by such a deed."

"Indeed," Aiwilimo murmured, drawing the word out like thread from a spindle. "So I have heard. But he would need to be a fearless man who goes against Fadhmir. A few even in my lifetime have climbed up from Gnita Heath and, brave men though they were, found themselves seized by a madness of terror before they ever saw Fadhmir. This, I have been told, is due to the Helm of Awe by the craft of which he became a dragon and which he is said to wear still."

"I have dealt with the secret crafts before by my own might," Sigimund said. "And she who wards my soul is no stranger to magic. I believe I would put my trust in her in front of any fear I might feel about the workings of another."

Aiwilimo tapped his thick fingers on the table. The only adornment on his hand was a heavy gold ring set with a black stone on which a helmeted head was embossed in the Roman style.

"It may be that you will have a chance to show me," he said at last. "I won't speak for my daughter's choice, though. She is wise enough that I have promised to let her make her own decision between you and King Lingwe. Although I may counsel her, I won't force her into anything. On the other hand, I would like to have you as a friend and ally, whichever way Herwodis may turn."

Sigimund glanced at Herwodis, who sat with her head tilted to hear Lingwe. She looked as calm and polite as she had when listening to Sigimund talk that afternoon; Lingwe's eyes glittered like blue-green glass and he swept his arms around in wide gestures of enthusiasm for whatever he was saying, the ridged muscles of his shoulders moving snakily beneath the intertwining embroidery of his red tunic. Deep-minded as Herwodis might be, Sigimund thought, she was only fourteen. Surely the handsome young son of Hunding would be more attractive to her than an old man, mighty and famed though he was? And her quiet gray gaze had rested on Lingwe all evening, while Sigimund had spoken to Aiwilimo. The thought of Herwodis marrying Lingwe sent a sudden flash of heat lightning through Sigimund as he looked at the dark head bent toward the fair, but he knew that he was old enough to put that sort of thought by and get what he could out of the journey. He had not come here to marry for love so much as gain for his line and his folk, he reminded himself.

"That would please me as well," he said.

It was beginning to grow late when Herwodis took her leave of Sigimund and Lingwe. Not long after, Aiwilimo picked up his goblet and stood.

"You will excuse me," he said to the two drightens who sat with an empty space between them. "I don't stay up this late very often, and I have things to talk over with my daughter. When you are ready to sleep, please ask any of the men or maids of my hall and they will show you to the rooms set for you. I hope that Herwodis will have made up her mind by tomorrow, and I trust you to keep your men at peace in the meantime."

"Of course," Lingwe murmured smoothly. Sigimund merely nodded.

"Well, then. Good night, King Lingwe. Good night, King Sigimund."

They each bade him goodnight, and it seemed to Sigimund that a touch of a smile lightened Aiwilimo's square-cut cheeks and stubble-shadowed jaw as the Frankish king looked upon him.

"You don't think you can win Herwodis the way your son won his wife, do you?" Lingwe challenged Sigimund as soon as Aiwilimo had left them. His clipped speech was beginning to grow thick from the strong Frankish wine.

Sigimund stared coldly down at his younger rival. "I certainly know that you can't," he answered.

"A spae-woman told me that you would end up with reason to regret this wooing if you kept on with it," Lingwe hissed. "I've heard men say that you trust in such things. If you do, take her advice and go from here before Herwodis brings you either to shame by her judgment or to death." He twisted the drooping end of his moustache around his ringed finger like a second thick coil of tarnished gold above the first.

"I have more trust in my sword and my own might and main than in the words of seith-women and such folk," said Sigimund. "I have learned how deceiving they can be, even when they speak truest. Do you really think whispers in the dark frighten me any more than the threat of your sword? Avenge your father first, son of Hunding; then you may think about attacking stronger men."

Lingwe's eyes narrowed. His hand dropped from his moustache to caress the axe-shaped amber bead that hung from the hilt of his sword. "If we were not bound by peace, I would say that your deeds are more shameful than my father's death. Have you told Herwodis how you got a son on your own sister and ate corpses of men with him in the wood?"

"I expect that you have told her that, and more," Sigimund answered. "And if we were not bound by peace, I would say that it was the part of a woman to try and meet a foe with whisperings rather than deeds. I would say, indeed, that I would be wary of drink taken from your hands, since a womanish coward is likely to be a brewer of seith-craft and bale as well."

Lingwe grasped his sword, springing to his feet. Sigimund caught him by the wrist and forced him down to the bench again, smiling broadly. "But we are bound by peace, and it wouldn't be fitting for us to either fight or flyte in the atheling-hall of our host. I will be glad to finish this conversation with you when the matter for which we came is done."

"I shall look forward to that," Lingwe answered. "Now may the gods keep me from the shame of sitting at table with you again!"

Sigimund loosened his grip so that Lingwe could pull free and stalk away. After a few moments he began to laugh softly. He knew he had gone too far; but why shouldn't he have? The son of Hunding would have been his enemy in any case, and now each of them knew where the other stood. Although he had been sparing with the Frankish wine, it had done its work: he felt eerily lightheaded when he stood, still laughing, and looked around for someone to show him where he would sleep that night.

Sigimund awoke early, lying between the soft sheets of his bed for a little while in a dreamy doze. There were fewer fleas than in his bed at home, he had to admit; but the stone floor was very cold on his bare feet when he stood to push his splayed palms against the ceiling as he stretched to his full height. Fuzzy gray light came through the flat plane of translucent glass over the window, warped by bubbles and ripples. Sigimund thought it was very fine, though he wondered how such a thing would do in his own land against the winds and hail from the North Sea. Perhaps when he built his hall in the south, he could get Roman craftsmen to make him windows like that.

The door opened and Sigimund modestly turned away as the maid Hilde came in lugging a big clay pot of steaming water in both arms. She let out a shriek and jumped, splashing hot water on the floor. Sigimund slid back between the sheets. "It's all right now," he called. "You can come in."

Giggling and blushing, Hilde set the pot down beside his bed. She unfolded the linen towels that were draped over her arm and laid them over the middle part of his body. On top of the towels she put a fine horn comb with a silver-inlaid shaft. She glanced at him to see how he would answer her familiarity. Sigimund smiled tolerantly, waiting for her to withdraw.

"Would you like me to bring you something to eat? I'm setting food out in the great hall, but there's someone sleeping wherever you might want to sit and they snore like a host of pigs in the mud, really they do."

"That's all right," Sigimund said. "Tell me, is Herwodis or King Aiwilimo up yet? Or Lingwe?"

"The king and his daughter are already up. Herwodis rises quite early, and she always has something to do. I tell you, you won't find a better frowe than she is. I've been with her for three years, ever since my father's farm was burned in a Burgundian raid, and I haven't regretted it for a moment." She put her hand over her mouth, then another secretive giggle fluttered out. "She says I might expect to find a husband in her husband's warband. I couldn't have asked for anything like that when I was mucking out the cows, now could I?"

"I suppose not." Sigimund thought of the stolid farmwomen who herded their cows and sheep up and down the sides of the mounds, and had to smile himself; not many carl's daughters kept such a light heart for long. "Go on, then. Let me wash before the water gets cold."

"Oh . . . I'm sorry. I didn't mean to keep you. You're not angry with me, are you?" she asked, flicking her hair back with a mouse-swift gesture.

"Don't be silly. Run along." Sigimund waved his hand in a vague shooing gesture. Hilde tripped out of his room with another of her bubbling giggles.

Sigimund washed and dressed himself quickly. He wondered whether hot water in the morning was a Roman custom or a Frankish one, and if Herwodis would expect it every day. There was something to be said for it, he decided. He combed his hair and beard till they were dry, hoping that Herwodis had not marked the light silvering through their gilt. Going to the hall, he ate the crusty cheese and drank the new warm milk without tasting them, watching the doors at every moment to see if Herwodis or Aiwilimo would come through as the men around him snored or groaned and heaved themselves upward, rubbing at bleary eyes and stumbling outside to piss. When Lingwe came in, he took his food and ate standing, his back pointedly turned to Sigimund who ignored him with equal aplomb.

It was well past midmorning by the time Herwodis, Aiwilimo and Hathubarth finally came into their feasting hall. They were dressed richly: the men's tunics and Herwodis' long white dress gleamed with the sheen of silk, and Herwodis folded her ringed hands modestly above a large square golden buckle. Lingwe turned around as they entered, striding confidently up to stand a little before Sigimund, though not crowding him enough for Sigimund to take offense.

"We wish it to be known," Aiwilimo said, letting his voice ring out with its full power, "that my daughter Herwodis has chosen to be married to King Sigimund the son of Wals, and if all are willing, the wedding shall take place this night. Let King Lingwe son of Hunding know that he and his men are welcome here at our feast, should he choose to stay, and that there is no ill will borne toward him here."

Most of the bleary-eyed men, Sigimund's and Aiwilimo's both, rose to their feet to cheer; but those who had come with Lingwe stayed seated or prone upon the floor, muttering darkly. Lingwe himself narrowed his eyes, dark red staining his fair cheeks like spilt wine, but he spoke courteously enough. "I thank you for your invitation, King Aiwilimo, but there are many affairs pressing me from my homelands, and I think I should leave as soon as I may to attend to them. I trust this will not offend you."

"Not at all," Aiwilimo said. "Stay or go as you wish, you are welcome."

Lingwe backed away from Sigimund a good pace before turning around and beginning to gather his men together. Sigimund stepped forward and clasped Herwodis in his arms, her silken dress slippery under his calloused palms as he bent to kiss her. She met him warmly, though a little clumsily. He held her in his clasp until her faint shaking had eased.

For the first time since they had met, Aiwilimo was grinning openly at him. "It seems strange to have a son older than I am," he said. "But you are more than welcome to our family, Sigimund."

Hathubarth looked gloomily at Lingwe, who had bent over to shake one of his men who had drunk too deeply the night before. Then he, too, showed his teeth to Sigimund. "I hope you won't regret this," he rasped thinly. "Now, what are the marriage ways of the Saxons? Is there anything you will not be wedded without?"

"I'll be happy to follow whatever rite you want, as long as I can keep my sword by me."

Hathubarth drew his brows together, speaking to Herwodis. "That's not usual. What do you think?"

Herwodis closed her eyes for a moment. "I think," she said, her muted voice slow, "that while Sigimund has his sword and his luck, the favor of his drighten Wodan will be with him. I think it will give Fro Ing and Frowe Holda no insult at our wedding."

And so Sigimund and Herwodis were married before the hall that night, Aiwilimo himself calling upon Fro Ing and Frowe Holda to hallow the wedding and to bless it with strong sons and daughters, and to Tiw to hold the wedding oaths in troth and victory. The men of both warbands stood mixed together, holding clear-burning torches to cast their light over the two as they swore on the oath ring and drank ale from a horn of Frankish glass. Sigimund stood with an arm around his bride's sturdy shoulders as Hathubarth cut the throat of the great white bull that had been brought as a gift for the gods and flesh for the wedding feast, sprinkling its blood over the gathered folk with an oaken twig. Lighthearted joy flowed through the Walsing as the dark drops touched him; embracing Herwodis, he felt dizzily young and free from all that had bound him.

Wormwood-tinged Frankish wine and flickering torchlight and the warm solidness of Herwodis beside him blurred the evening in Sigimund's mind till he lay stroking the trembling from his new wife's virgin body with the river ripples of the moon shining through the bridal chamber's glass window washing over them.

"I've watched my father's men breeding horses before," she said softly. "I know what to expect. Go on."

"It's not quite like horses," Sigimund murmured to her. "There's more than that . . . I'll show you." He kissed her again and again, touching her with a gentleness he had almost forgotten, until her breathing and murmurs told him that she was ready for him. Sigimund held himself back as much as he could, moving on her slowly; she bore the pain of his first thrusts well, only clenching her teeth and hissing a little till her body eased and opened to him. A sharp pang, like the sweetness of honey on a bad tooth, went through Sigimund as her glimmering whiteness against the dark sheets brought the memory of Sigilind through his unwilling mind again to brighten the fire hidden in their mingled loins. Sigilind; Sinfjotli; Sigimund cried out word-lessly in a pain like pleasure as the streams of memory swept through him, spilling in his seed with a pang that flared red-gold in his sight, sinking into Herwodis' dark eyes below him.

As he withdrew from Herwodis, she reached up with a finger to wipe a tear from his face. "You're crying," she said wonderingly. "Why? You didn't hurt me so badly, really. I was expecting it to be much worse."

Sigimund only kissed her again, letting the strange flood from the depths of his soul sink back with the throbbing of his body. He stroked her head, clinging to her solid warmth as a man might cling to a deeply rooted tree against the fury of a torrential flood. "You're so young," he whispered, his voice choking in on him. He coughed, clearing the thickness away as he held tight to his new wife. "And beautiful, and wise . . . why did you choose an old man like me?"

"Because you are mightier now than Lingwe, handsome and young as he is, can ever hope to be. You will be a strong shield to my father . . . and I mistrust Lingwe. I don't think I could ever love him."

"Fair enough," Sigimund said. He brushed the thick dark hair back from her forehead, gently straightening its tangles with fingers calloused as hard as horn from his sword's hilt.

They lay there together for a little while, till Herwodis said, "Do you think we could . . . ? I've heard the second time . . . ?"

"Again?"

"Could we try?"

"I think so."

FARING HOME

Sigimund stayed in Aiwilimo's hall for a month, feasting and hunting and sitting to talk with Herwodis, her father and her uncle. Together they planned that he and Aiwilimo should fare back to the north to gather Sigimund's folk and goods and bring them back to the lands they had chosen, along the German bank of the Rhine south of the Dragon's Crag. Aiwilimo also sent to the Roman Sebastianus with whom he had made his own arrangements. He had no doubt, he confided to Sigimund, that there would be any difficulty in gaining Rome's blessing; the Imperial servants who had given Aiwilimo his lands were terrified by the hordes of wild Eastern tribes that had streamed through Germania in their flight from the Huns, and Rome itself lived in fear of the day when the tribes might band together and cross the Rhine against them.

The Saxons kept the holy day of Eostre, whom the Franks called Ostara, in Aiwilimo's hall. Everyone was up before dawn, shivering in the first cold light as Sigimund and Aiwilimo together kindled the need-fire and thrust their brand to light the bonfire of nine woods that had been laid the night before. Franks and Saxons gave each other eggs that the Frankish women and children had painted for luck and fruitfulness and ate cakes flavored with fresh tansy, as their ancestors had always done to welcome Frowe Eostre and the beginning of summer. Hilde said that she had seen a white-gowned woman, a light alf, standing on one of the faraway wooded hills for a moment in the sunrise; when Sigimund asked Herwodis if she, too, had seen the alf-frowe, his wife only smiled teasingly at him. "I wouldn't tell," she said.

It was not long after the feast of Eostre that the Roman envoy Sebastianus came alone to Aiwilimo's hall. He was a small man, whose head barely reached the middle of Sigimund's chest, but he carried himself with great dignity beneath the odd draped garment he wore over his tunic. The sword at his belt was very short, its handle plain, but well polished by use. Although Sigimund had heard that the Romans were swarthy, Sebastianus' curly hair was a light brown and his skin fair beneath his tan. He was clean-shaven except for a little tuft of beard in the deep cleft of his jutting chin. The Roman's glance flicked up the great length of Sigimund's body with a sort of tolerant admiration as he accepted a goblet of wine from Herwodis, addressing Aiwilimo and his daughter in a speech so heavily accented that Sigimund couldn't tell what he was saying, although the accent sounded rather like that of the Gautish tongue. In a few minutes, he turned to speak to the Saxon, who shrugged.

"I'm afraid I don't understand you," Sigimund admitted. Sebastianus regarded him for a moment, then nodded and started talking to the Frankish king again.

Aiwilimo waited until the Roman had finished what he had to say, then said to Sigimund, "You'll have to excuse his speech. He learned it among the Goths in the east, and we all sound the same to Roman ears. Anyway, he does well enough here, because the Burgundians speak a Gothic tongue and most of us have come to understand them. He is saying that Rome will be glad to offer you the treaty they call *foedus:* they will give you the lands to the north of mine, on the Rhine's west bank, to hold for them if you will fight against their foes for them. Although you will be responsible to the Emperor, you will rule your own folk and keep your own ways, as I do. Everything is just as we'd talked about already, but he insists that I say it again for you so that it will be right according to their laws."

"I will be glad to accept your *foedus,* Roman," Sigimund said to Sebastianus, speaking very slowly and repeating himself in Gautish. The Roman's wide brow crinkled, then he smiled, showing an even row of white teeth. He pulled a scroll of parchment, a cake of ink and a thin stylus from a small bag, unfolding the scroll to show Sigimund that it was written about with runes that were largely strange to Sigimund. Spitting on the ink stick, he handed it and the stylus to Sigimund and pointed to an empty place at the bottom of the parchment.

"Romans insist on having all things written down," Aiwilimo explained. "They sign their names to these things. He wants you to make a mark of some sort to show that you agree to Rome's terms."

Sigimund thought for a few moments. He had not heard that Roman law included magic to bind those who followed it; but he meant to keep troth with the treaty, as long as Rome behaved fairly toward him. He dipped the point of the stylus in the ink and scratched the runes of his name onto the scroll.

Sebastianus blew on the ink to dry it and rolled the parchment up again. He reached out to clasp wrists with Sigimund. Though his fingers hardly spanned half the Saxon's arm, his grip was firm and his eyes steady as he looked up at his new ally.

"Welcome to the Empire, Sigimund, King of the Saxons," he said, slowly and clearly enough for Sigimund to make some sense of his Gothic speech.

The treaty with Rome concluded, Sigimund and his new kin decided that it was time for them to begin their journey north. The ships were loaded with their goods, both those that Sigimund had brought for Herwodis and those that Aiwilimo was providing for the expenses of bringing the Saxon folk south.

They moved swiftly down the Rhine; it was only a day's sail before they came to the mountain that Aiwilimo pointed out to Sigimund as the Dragon's Crag.

"You see that wide pathway through the rocks there? That, men say, is where Fadhmir comes down to drink from the river."

The broad trail that wound from halfway up the mount was like the track of a snake, blackened as though by fire. Cold shivered up Sigimund's spine as he looked at it, but he forced himself to stare boldly at the dark crevice from which it issued, his hand on the hilt of his sword. Aiwilimo himself had turned his head away; Sigimund saw Ehumari making the sign of the Hammer and Theodibald moved to the other side of the boat. Herwodis did not turn away, but she clutched so tightly to the edge of the ship that her nails dug little crescents into the wood, nor did she look past the beginning of the charred track.

"Are you still eager to meet with Fadhmir?" Aiwilimo asked ironically. The square edges of his cheekbones reddened as though he were ashamed of his own fear.

"I shall," said Sigimund. "When my realm is fastened down here, I shall." He raised his eyes again, looking deliberately at the cave as they sailed past it. Deep within its darkness, he thought he saw a spark of red gold glowing.

It was nearing evening and, if Sigimund's memory was right, they were half a day from the mouth of the river, at a point where a thick wood ended and open plains began, when they heard the sound of a horn blowing and saw a fleet of fifteen or twenty ships on the river before them. Sigimund raised Wals' horn to his mouth and blew it in answer. When the lead ship rowed forward, he saw sunlight glinting from the curly blond head of Lingwe and anger arched his ribcage like a bent bow.

"What treacherous ambush is this?" Sigimund roared across the river.

"Only the treacherous see treachery in an honest challenge!" Lingwe's answer came back. "Put ashore and fight now, or we will wait till tomorrow if you need so long to prepare yourselves. Call your kin to aid, if you wish, as I have called mine; but I will have satisfaction for the insults you gave me in Aiwilimo's hall."

Sigimund was ready to shout out his challenge for that moment, but Herwodis had appeared beside him and put her arms around his waist. "Wait till tomorrow," she whispered. "That will give you and my father time to plan. I don't know much about battle, but even I can see that no matter how mighty you are, only wisdom can win this one for you."

The Walsing breathed deeply, calming the wolf-rush of anger. She was right, of course; only his fury at being blocked when he had been so close to achieving all he had hoped for would have goaded him on.

"We will meet you tomorrow at dawn!" Sigimund shouted. He took hold of the rudder and turned his ship to shore himself, landing at the edge of the wood. The other five in his fleet followed him, shouts and cursing running from ship to ship. Lingwe's fleet, likewise, came to land a good distance away from them. Sigimund and Aiwilimo helped their men to unload and to set up tents; Herwodis and, to Sigimund's surprise, Hilde also worked till the camp was fully set, carrying bundles and driving in tent stakes along with the men.

Sigimund, Aiwilimo and Herwodis came together in their tent to plan the battle as best they could, though there was little they could do. Their strength was known; it would do them no good to hold part of it back, nor, in these flatlands, was there anywhere they could hide or mount an ambush. Sigimund almost frothed with fury, cursing and stamping; and once, as his wolf-wod whelmed him, he threw back his head and howled to the skies. He could barely understand the quietness with which Aiwilimo and Herwodis faced the situation before them.

"I think," said Aiwilimo finally, "that we must ready ourselves to fight or die as well as we can. My brother may be able to avenge us, but short of running away there is nothing else we can do."

Herwodis looked from her father to her husband and back again. "You know, there may be something in that. I would never suggest it for you," she added, "but if Hilde and I were to go into the woods tonight, and we were to hide as much as we can of what we have with us, then nothing would be lost if you win the battle, and if Lingwe wins at least he will have only half a victory."

Her calmness calmed Sigimund; spontaneously he put his arms around her and kissed her. Herwodis' deep wisdom and still dignity made her seem unutterably precious to him now, the more so as he remembered how she clung to him and whispered in the night, half a young girl and half a woman with full-grown love. It would be cruel for him to leave her, he thought; surely Wodan would not betray his last happiness, after all his struggles?

"I have never except once lost a battle while I had my sword in my hand, and that once it was only because I was struck from behind," Sigimund said. "With our father to guard my back and myself to guard his, I believe it will go harder with Lingwe than he expects, no matter how great his numbers may be. But I agree that nothing can be hurt if you go to the woods. Truly, I think it would be best, because many things can happen in the course of a battle, and you are too dear to me for me to want to risk you in any way. Let me stay with you one last time till Sunna has gone down, and then we will have time to see to your safety."

Aiwilimo coughed tactfully, his mouth quirking into his ironic grin as he looked at his daughter and her husband. "There are things I must do outside. I'll come back to you after sunset." He went out of the tent, fastening the flap carefully behind himself.

Sigimund and Herwodis undressed quickly, clinging to each other with all the might in their bodies. Sigimund knew that he would have bruises; her arms and legs clutched him as though she wished to hold him to her forever by her earthly strength. He himself was not afraid to hold her as tightly as he could, pounding at her in his haste and yet trying to hold himself back, to make it last as long as he could so that he would not have to break away from her again.

"Do you really believe you can win?" Herwodis whispered when they were holding each other after, unshed tears making her eyes as bright and clear as gray glass filled with water.

"I've won my way out of worse than this," Sigimund answered. "I had less hope when I was bound in Sigigairar's stocks. I was in a worse case than this fettered within his mound, and I had fewer men beside me than I have now when I came to win my father's kingdom back. Now my hands and feet are free: what do I have to fear from Lingwe's men?"

"That was why I married you, you know," she murmured back. "One of the reasons, anyway. You're like a yew tree: you can stay green through every winter. I think the first frost will wither Lingwe."

"I hope so," said Sigimund, helping Herwodis put her dress back on as she pulled his breeches up and tied them.

"Sigimund? Herwodis?" Aiwilimo called softly outside. "It's time."

Sigimund, Aiwilimo, Alfrad and one of Aiwilimo's men whose name Sigimund had never caught carried the three great chests of fine goods into the forest as far as they could, till they came to a clump of thornbushes whose sharp spines gleamed silver in the light of the waning Moon. Sigimund pushed prickly branches aside, bending the thin trunks of the bushes back, and lifted the heavy chests in far enough (he hoped) that they would be hidden even in full daylight. Herwodis stood watching; beside her Hilde was—the gods be thanked—silent, her fair face as pale as a bare skull in the moonlight.

Herwodis embraced Aiwilimo. Sigimund saw no tears on her face, but the harshness of her breath and of her voice as she whispered, "I love you," to her father told him all he needed to know.

Aiwilimo held his daughter gently for a moment. "I love you too, Herwodis. Don't be afraid, whatever happens. I know your wisdom will bring you safely through, and I trust you to make me proud of you." He released her and she turned toward her husband.

"I love you, Sigimund. Promise me that I'll see you alive after tomorrow."

"I promise," Sigimund said. He hugged her to him, her breasts pressing against him and her warm breath on his neck. Reluctantly he let go of her. "Go on now, my love. Hide as well as you can till you know what's happened."

Herwodis stood on tiptoes to kiss him one last time. Poised, she trembled for a moment, then walked slowly off into the woods, Hilde fluttering behind her like a frightened moth.

"Your daughter's worth every bit of this," Sigimund said to Aiwilimo. "No matter what happens, I will not regret having won her."

"I know."

Sigimund lay awake late that night, listening to the soft noises of the wood and the river. Alone in the darkness with only faint cracks of moonlight seeping in, the tent seemed much bigger to him: he might have been lying on the floor of a hall, if a hall's fires were as silver and thin as swords.

Sigimund rolled out of his blankets and got to his feet. The roof was well above his head, and he did not have to crouch nor duck through the flap when he made his way outside.

The Moon shone brilliantly, his silver bright as Sunna's gold. Thonarstanar was standing watch, but the Gaut's eyes were closed as he leaned against his spear. Sigimund walked past him, down to the river where his ships were anchored.

Sigilind stood waiting for him, her long unbound hair flowing white beneath her helm and her byrnie glittering in the Moon's light. The sword belted to her side was twin to his own, its ice stone glowing whitely. Sigimund rushed toward her, but she held up a hand to stop him.

"Sigimund," she called, and her voice thrilled sweet ice through his veins. "Come no farther. You must turn away from this battle, or tomorrow you shall surely die."

"What rede are you giving me?" Sigimund asked her, shaken. "Should I flee from a foeman, and shame our father's memory?"

"This is the rede Wodan has given me to bring you. It is he who has chosen you for death, if you go on in this battle: he does not mean for you to win victory. Because he has often favored you, he has sent you this warning—and I mean that you shall live, for you have reason past your pride. You have planted a Walsing son in Herwodis' womb, a son who is our son born again. Should Lingwe slay you and find where she has hidden in the woods, that child's wyrd shall be ill indeed. If you die tomorrow, he shall bear your soul bound with the soul of our son; and if Lingwe captures your wife, then the last of the Walsings, who should have been the greatest and most famed of our line, shall thole a far worse shame at his hands than you could think of elsewise."

"I cannot flee," Sigimund replied. "If Wodan withdraws his favor from me, well enough; it is his to give or withdraw as he pleases. Is it truly written that Lingwe shall capture Herwodis, if I am slain?"

"It is a thing that may be, and more like than not. Wodan told me to warn you of it."

"But it is not set fast. If I am slain, then you must ward Herwodis and the son in her womb. But it will take more than Lingwe's sword to cut me down: the wolf's wod is still within me, to ward me from iron, and should some ill magic fetter it, I am yet as mighty as I ever was."

"I do not wish you to die," Sigilind said, and the tear rolling down her white face was as black as blood. "For then we shall be parted a long time, and I fear that the ill you might suffer at Lingwe's hands would break our bond forever."

"My sister," Sigimund murmured. "I would not leave you—but you died for the sake of an oath to a man you hated, and I can do no less for those to whom I have sworn my help. Aid me in the fight if you can; if Wodan wills that you choose my death instead, then go to Herwodis and hold her safe from my foes."

"That I shall do," Sigilind answered.

It seemed to Sigimund that his sister's shape was growing fainter as the Moon's light brightened. He stepped forward to embrace her, but her body was cold and insubstantial against his, and the touch of her lips on his face was no more than a breath of cool mist as he closed his eyes. When he opened them again, he was back in his tent, and he knew from the chill and dampness in the air that it was near to dawn, and time for him to arise.

Aiwilimo was already up when Sigimund came out of the tent, and the other warriors were just starting to emerge. The two leaders walked among their men in the wind and early damp, talking to them as they laced on their leather or pulled ringed byrnies over their heads, till the first light of day began to show faint blue through the swift dark clouds. Across the field, Sigimund could see the huddled shadows of Lingwe's army. His sword rang softly from its sheath; he held it up, its thrumming might tingling down his arm. He knew that while he had his sword in his hand, the wod of the wolf within him and Sigilind above (he believed; he had to believe) to ward him from ill magics and harm, he could not be beaten. He grinned with the battle-joy rising within him, then threw back his head and howled, the high eerie sound echoing over the field. His wolf-cry would be no comfort to his foes, he knew; but Oshelm and Hrodger, who were closest to him, clashed their swords against their shields in applause. A few spatters of rain fell in Sigimund's face; the new light was growing grayer through the army of tattered clouds that streamed across the sky.

Aiwilimo, fully weaponed and helmed, came to stand beside Sigimund. "We can't wait much longer," he said.

Sigimund, rising higher into his battle-wod, saw a red-gold light around the other king that blurred the outlines of his body into a man-shaped will-o'-the-wisp. His answer was a deep growl in his own ears, slowed almost past bearing.

"No. Call them."

Aiwilimo shouted. Paltwini brought Wals' horn to Sigimund, who blew it with a mighty blast that rent the tattered sky like lightning. The thanes gathered behind them and they began to move toward the other army. A spear blurred up from the host before them, its point a silver thorn tip in the rain, arching over their heads. Bows were drawn, arrows hissing through the air like long, deadly hailstones. Above, Sigimund saw a glimmering lightning of white through the clouds, like the flash of a swan's wing. He howled again, running ahead of the warband that pounded slowly behind him. None of the arrows that screamed past his head could touch him. Lingwe's host parted before him like waves before the prow of a ship, and no byrnie or shield could stand up to the touch of his sword, splitting open to free the spurts and rivers of blood that fed his wolf-wod, clotting on his flame-ringed arms up to the shoulders, staining his face and beard and tunic. He struck again and again through the shifting halos of light that, brighter or dimmer, ringed the men before him, cleaving through the webs of luck and strength that warded them in a dance of joyful madness as he snarled and frothed, the wolf's fur shimmering through his fiery skin, hand on the sword blurring in his sight to a paw, to a hand, as Sigilind's white shield flashed before him to knock aside every weapon that might have touched him.

A flash of sunlight shone on to Sigimund's blood-running sword through the shifting clouds; his sight began to clear, till before him he saw a huge man in a deep blue cloak whose wide hat tilted down to hide one eye. The man lifted his spear against Sigimund, runes shimmering red down its great dark shaft. For a single moment he saw Sigilind's white shape above him clearly, fair hair flying back as she stretched down her shield to push the weapon aside.

"No!" Sigimund cried, for he saw at once what she meant to do. "Sigilind, no!" But she did not heed him; she stretched down her shield to push the weapon aside. The cloaked man's mouth opened in a booming cry of wordless wrath that shivered through Sigimund's bones. He raised his spear again, pointing it at Sigilind.

Sigimund leapt forward, striking with all his might. His sword rang clearly, the shock running down his arm as it broke in two pieces on the spear. The one-eyed warrior swung his weapon around; its shaft knocked Sigilind aside, and Sigimund could see her no more. Then the man was gone, and with him the last of Sigimund's battle-wod, leaving him unarmed and unarmored to face his foe.

"Wals!" he shouted hoarsely, wresting the axe from the hand of the man in front of him and sinking it through leather cap and skull. His eyes no longer blurred by berserkergang, Sigimund could see the remnants of his band and Aiwilimo's fighting fiercely and cut his way through to them, shouting them on.

Something struck his eye, stinging and blinding. Sigimund thought an arrow had hit him, but then he saw the torrent of white hailstones streaming down from the blackened sky, ringing on helmets like hammer blows. A flash of lightning scarred the sky, its thunder half-stunning the men below.

"Odger, Oshelm, to me!" Sigimund called. "Onward, on, we still can win!" But Lingwe's host was pressing in on them from all sides. Ehumari's iron-bound leather cap had fallen off; the shaft of a spear caught him across the temple and he dropped without getting up again. One of Aiwilimo's Franks hurled his axe at the man before him; it stuck in his foe's shield, and before he could draw his own sword a slash of the other's had opened his throat. And so one by one they fell, till Sigimund stumbled through the corpses of friends and enemies alike. Tired from the unaccustomed work of axe-fighting, his arm could not come across in time to strike aside the spear that came hurtling through his body, its massive blow knocking him to the ground. He curled around the shaft, sucking his agonized breath in as the boots trampled around him.

For a long time there was nothing but the huge pulsing pain throbbing out from the center of his body and the white wheel of the Sun burning now and again through the dark mists fogging his eyes, growing redder and redder as she sank into blackness. The boots had gone away, the dim grumbling of men's voices fading to silence till only the harsh croaking of the ravens and crows feeding on the fallen sounded over the battlefield, its quiet disturbed by the rustling of their wings and the chewing of foxes and other small beasts.

"Sigimund? Aiwilimo? Father, are you here? Sigimund?" a woman's voice called.

"Sigilind?" he whispered, moaning as he raised his head and strained his eyes open. The half-waned Moon cast a pale light over the field; he could see the dark shadows of two women making their slow way through the heaped corpses.

"Sigimund?" she called again. Her voice was too low for his twin's; he thought of Alfflad first, then remembered Herwodis. So she had escaped, then. It was enough.

"Herwodis," Sigimund answered, honey-thick blood bubbling with his breath to clog his words. His ribs scraped against the spear's shaft as he called out. He coughed out more blood. It would not be long now. "I'm over here." Feebly he stretched up one hand, then let it drop.

Herwodis lifted her skirts and stepped over and through the stiffening bodies, nearly tripping several times in her haste as she hurried to her husband's side. She crouched down beside him, bending to kiss his bloody lips. Sigimund closed his eyes, sighing in pain. It was getting harder and harder for him to breathe through the blood filling his lungs.

"Can you be healed?" she asked anxiously. "Do you think . . . ?"

"I've seen many men live again when there was little hope of it, but now my luck has left me, so that I will not be healed," he said. It seemed to him that his agony was fading; he could no longer feel his hands or his feet, and his speech came haltingly through numb lips. "It is not Wodan's will that I draw sword again, since mine is broken. I have had my battles as long as it pleased him."

"But what of my father? I saw his body—surely you must be healed to avenge him?" Her tears were as silver as snail-tracks in the moonlight.

"That is the orlog of another," Sigimund replied. The pain was almost gone; he felt quite calm and peaceful, as though warm waters lapped around and over him. "I know that you are carrying a child. Rear him carefully and well, and the boy will grow to be the greatest and most famed of our kind. Also find the shatters of my sword and keep them. A goodly one shall be forged anew from them, and it shall be called Gram and our son shall bear it and do with it great deeds, which shall never grow old, for his name shall live on while the worlds last. Be content with that. But I am weary with my wounds, and I must go to seek our kinsmen who have gone before."

He raised a shaking hand and laid its palm flat against Herwodis' belly as the darkness rose around him. Within he could see a white spark brightening to burning red, twisting into the intertwining triangles of the walknot as he had seen it so many years ago; and he was content to sink down into the darkness again.

Herwodis crouched by Sigimund, her ankles aching and her feet growing numb. She stayed there until she felt his hand becoming cold over her womb; then she rose to her feet and called softly to Hilde, "He is dead. We must find his sword."

Together the two women heaved and tugged at the dead, shooing away the carrion birds and kicking at weasels and rats as they felt their way along the battlefield. Staunch as she was, Herwodis shuddered at the cold slippery entrails beneath her hands and the glazed eyes of the dead gleaming light-lessly beneath the Moon—from faces she knew, her father's men who had lifted her on their shoulders when she was small and the thanes of Sigimund's warband whose names she had just started to learn. It seemed to her that they looked at her accusingly; that it was her fault they lay there dead, with no one to give them a proper funeral pyre or mound, and she shivered as she pushed their heavy bodies aside and felt beneath them for Sigimund's broken sword, now and again wiping slime and stench from her hands.

"Help me!" Hilde screamed suddenly. Herwodis, startled, let out a shriek as she turned to see her maid held fast by her cloak. The girl struggled wildly, striking out at Herwodis as she stepped quickly over the bodies. "Help, he's got me!" She burst into a torrent of hysterical screaming and sobbing.

Herwodis ignored her, crouching down. One of the bodies—she could not tell whom, an axe blow had caved his face in—had rolled to trap Hilde's cloak under him. She shoved the corpse up and pulled the cloak free while her maid screamed and twisted as though mad. Herwodis, sick and terrified, grabbed her by the arm and slapped her across the cheek till she quieted. Her own hands were trembling uncontrollably when she let go. "Go on," she said roughly. "Go and wait in the wood. You don't need to do this any more."

"B-but you'll be alone here with all these dead men," Hilde sniffed. "What if . . . ?"

"Go," Herwodis said firmly, her unmuted voice so loud that she started again. "Go on."

Hilde fled stumbling from the battlefield, leaving Herwodis to search till. . . at last, thank the gods . . . her hand touched the smooth hex-cut stone in the hilt of Sigimund's sword. It was broken jaggedly halfway down its length. She crawled about through the bloody mud until she cut her hand on the broken edge of the other half. Her breath hissing through her teeth, she wiped the wound on her sleeve and held the two twisted halves of the weapon together. Yes; that was it. She cleaned the sword with her dress, trying to keep her hand from dripping fresh blood on to it, and picked her way off the field of slaughter to where Hilde waited in the woods, trembling and staring around as though every rustling tree branch were a wolf or a ghost.

"Did you find it?" the maid whispered, standing as close to her mistress as she could.

"Yes."

"What are we going to do now?"

"First we're going to find a place that's not too wet and has some bushes to shelter us from the wind, and then we're going to go to sleep. I don't think there's anything else we can do tonight."

"Oh, I couldn't sleep," Hilde whimpered. "All those dead men. When that one grabbed my cloak, I thought I was going to die . . . I thought he was going to pull me down with him." She started to sob again, clinging tightly to Herwodis, who stroked her hair with a trembling hand as she tried to gather her own thoughts. Sigimund was dead: it seemed impossible. He had towered over the men around him like an age-old tree, hard-wooded and enduring; she had thought he had the strength to live forever, that no lesser man would ever fell him. But now his sword was shattered and his lich lay cooling in the mud with her father's, their plans for a kingdom together fallen with the two of them, and it was left to her alone to go on as best she might.

"Hsh, hsh," Herwodis said to her maid, as she would calm a child. "Hsh, hsh, we need to rest. Who knows what may happen in the morning? We need to get back to my father's lands. Hathubarth will keep us as we were before. Hsh, hsh, little Hilde, be quiet so nothing can hear us."

Hilde's sobs subsided to noisy snuffles. The two of them wandered around for a while, finally curling up in each other's warmth at the roots of a big ash tree whose wide trunk shielded them from the wind as its leaves would from the drizzle beginning to mist down. Despite her protests, Hilde fell asleep almost at once, her breath soft and measured against Herwodis' cheek; but the cold hard root pressing into her back, the aching of the wound that throbbed up her arm, and the waves of grief and guilt surging through her body kept Herwodis awake and terribly alone till dawn, thinking (she could not help it) of her father's body growing chill among the dead.

Herwodis awoke, hungry, tired and sore, a couple of hours into the day. Hilde was already starting to stretch, moaning about how cold she was and how badly her back hurt from sleeping on the ground.

"Let's go and see if there is anything left of the tents of our camp," Herwodis said. "There may be some food there."

But the sons of Hunding and their men, in a fury at not finding either treasure or women, had destroyed what they could not take, smashing and shredding everything that the bands of Aiwilimo and Sigimund had left. Herwodis and Hilde had to crawl through the wreckage, heaving aside the splintered wood and pulling the heavy cloth and leather away to see what was left to them. The chest that held Herwodis' clothes was broken and her jewelry gone, but many of the dresses were still whole or only somewhat torn. All the wine casks had been taken; the bread had spilled out of its bags and gone sour and moldy in the night.

Herwodis emerged from the ruins of the last tent, blinking and rubbing her eyes as she saw the sails of a fleet coming up the Rhine from the North Sea.

"Is that Lingwe?" Hilde asked anxiously. "Has he come back for us?"

"I don't know. Let's hide till we can see better."

The two of them went a little way into the woods. A gust of wind fluttered out the standard, showing a golden horse stitched on to a white field.

"It's not the sons of Hunding," Herwodis stated. "I don't know who it might be."

"What will we do? What if they . . . ? I'm sure they won't harm you when you tell them who you are, but I'm only a maid. What if those men . . . ?" She crouched in upon herself, crossing her arms across her breasts in a gesture that showed clearly what she feared.

Herwodis stripped off her embroidered cloak and her gilt-buckled belt, fastening them around Hilde's body and taking her maid's plainer adornments. The only things she kept for her own were the comb from Sigimund, tucked into the small bag at her waist, a small gold ring that her father had given her and Sigimund's broken sword, which she hid under Hilde's cloak.

"Now, till we get home, you are the atheling and I am the maid," she said. "I think I can defend myself rather better than you. Also, I have lost my maidenhead honorably and a babe grows in my womb already, so I can suffer no more than a little if things turn out badly. Now for the gods' sakes, pull yourself together and try to act like a king's daughter. If you see that these are atheling-men, tell them what happened here and we will show them to the treasure."

Hilde nodded, biting her lower lip. They could hear deep voices calling through the wood, "Hai! You maids, come out! Have no fear! The drighten Alapercht would speak with you! Come out!" By their accents, Herwodis could tell they were Alamanns and the first kindling of hope began to cast a flickering shadow of fear over her heart.

With the last words, three men came through the bushes. They were armed only with spears and not armored, but their tunics were of fine cloth. They stopped before Herwodis and Hilde, not reaching out to take them, and Herwodis breathed a bit more freely.

"Come with us, if you will," said the shortest of them, a square-built man with a houndlike face beneath a thatch of shaggy brown hair. "The drighten Alapercht saw you going from the battlefield and wishes to ask you about what has happened and who has fallen there."

For a moment Herwodis and Hilde stood silently, each waiting for the other to speak. Then Herwodis nudged her maid's ankle sharply and Hilde stepped forward. "We will come with you," she said.

The two women followed the thanes to the ships. A well-dressed man stood on the shore, waiting for them. He was about the same height as Herwodis, a slight plumpness layering his heavy muscles. His features were strong and pleasant, aquiline nose jutting over a close-cropped, thick sandy moustache. As he stepped forward to meet them, Herwodis saw that he carried himself with the bearing of a king, though his curly brown hair was chopped off just above his shoulders.

"Greetings, gracious frowes," he said. "I am Alapercht, son of King Chilpirich of the Alamanns. Will you tell me who you are and what you know of the battle here?"

Hilde tugged at her dirty hair self-consciously, turning her glance away from his hazel eyes. "I'm Herwodis the daughter of Aiwilimo, and this is my maid Hilde here," she said. "The kings who fought here were Aiwilimo of the Salian Franks and Sigimund the Walsing . . . my husband." She let out a brief giggle like a yelp of pain. "They fought against Lingwe and the sons of Hunding, who had brought a great host against them as they sailed back toward Sigimund's lands from wooing the king's daughter Herwodis . . . myself. Lingwe wanted to get both me and my bridal treasures, but although he won the fight he found neither of us, for me and my maid had hidden and the treasure is buried."

"I see," murmured Alapercht thoughtfully. He scratched along the side of his prominent nose, hand slipping down to tug at his moustache. "And would you be willing to tell me where the treasure is hidden?"

Hilde looked fleetingly at Herwodis, who smiled in encouragement. "I think, Frowe, there would be no harm in leading these athelings to it. This drighten seems like a man who will honor both you and that which is yours as is fitting."

"Your maidservant has keen eyes," Alapercht said. "Now I will tell you what I mean to do, and you can decide for yourselves how you like it. I will take the two of you home to my father's realm, for I have been away too long and it is not good in these times for a great part of a warband to be gone from its home in the summertime, lest they come back and find that another folk has fallen upon those they left behind. Also, I don't know the lands of the Franks very well and I am not willing to turn aside to march through a stranger's country. But I will promise you safety, both from whomever we might meet on the way and from my own men. Then when there is a chance I will have you taken wherever you wish to go. What do you think?"

"Surely that is fair enough, Frowe?" Herwodis told Hilde. "I myself would rather ride in ships with a strong guard than walk back to Aiwilimo's . . . to Hathubarth's realm. And this drighten's promise of safety is very comforting, the more so since I have a child in my womb to think of." She put her hands protectively over her stomach where Sigimund had touched her last, holding back her tears.

"We'll take it," said Hilde. "Noble drighten, we'll be glad to go with you. If you'll follow us, we'll show you where the treasure is buried. It took four men to take it there, but one of them was King Sigimund, so you might want a few extra hands to help get it out."

When Alapercht and ten of his thanes had lugged the chests back to the ships and the sails had been raised, the drighten seated himself by the stern and had stools set for the two women.

"You spoke of your child," he said to Herwodis. "Is your husband living?"

"He fell in the battle," she answered, her eyes cast down.

"And you?" he asked Hilde. "Do you carry a child of King Sigimund's?"

Hilde's delicate hand fluttered to her mouth; she gasped and looked at him wide-eyed for a moment before remembering herself. "No," she answered. "I . . . no."

"It is a pity that such a mighty king should have died as the last of his line," Alapercht commented. "Surely King Sigimund was the most well known of heroes, and King Aiwilimo was also not without his share of fame. I am sorry that I was never able to meet either of them."

The settlement from which Chilpirich ruled was fenced from the mountainous forest around it with a ring of stout posts. His hall was fine enough, Herwodis thought, though it was made of woven wattle chinked by clay on a wooden framework rather than stone like her father's. The cattle grazing within the hamlet were fat, with glossy coats; the grain seemed to be growing well, a sign that Chilpirich was a good fro to the land. She was glad to be out of the ship and away from Hilde's chatter, though from the smoke she had seen rising along the banks of the Rhine and the ruins of settlements she feared it might be some time before Alapercht deemed the lands peaceful enough for Hilde and herself to fare home.

A small silver-haired woman stood by the door of Chilpirich's hall. Her eyes were half-closed against the lowering sun when she stepped forward to meet Alapercht and his band. The drighten embraced her warmly, then took her by the hand and drew her over to where Herwodis and Hilde stood. "Mother, I have here the wife of the slain King Sigimund the Walsing and her maid. Would you see to making them comfortable? They will stay with us till things are settled enough for them to be sent back to the lands that King Aiwilimo held from Rome."

"I will be glad to," Alapercht's mother answered. To Herwodis and Hilde, she said, "I am Perchte, the wife of King Chilpirich. Poor dears, I wish some occasion of more joy could have brought you to our home." Her clear blue eyes scrutinized the two of them, taking a careful measure. "If you'll come with me, I will have a place made ready for the two of you. I expect you'll want to wash and rest before dinner."

"We would be grateful for that," Herwodis answered, before she remembered that she was supposed to be Hilde's maid.

Perchte blinked, looking closely at both of them again. Herwodis felt a flush of embarrassment warming her cheeks, but the woman before her said only, "I hope you won't be disappointed by our home. I fear that Roman builders are harder to come by on this side of the Rhine than on your own."

She led Herwodis and Hilde through the central aisle of the hall and into her own torchlit chambers. Without windows, they were darker and dirtier than Herwodis was used to, a musty smell underlying the scent of the herbs and straw strewn upon the dirt floor. "I'll send in a girl with water for washing and see to having your clothes brought up from the ship, and a house will be ready for you by the time the feast is over," Perchte promised. She went out, leaving the two Frankish women alone.

"Do you really think I can do this? At a proper feast?" Hilde whispered. "Why don't you tell Alapercht? I'm not afraid of anything happening anymore."

"I don't know why," Herwodis whispered back. "I suppose . . . well, it would be insulting, after we've gone on this long. He'd have a perfect right to take offense, and then we might never get home." The wound on her hand still ached; though it was beginning to heal, drops of blood wept from it when she clenched her fist around the pain. "No; let's go on as we have. I don't want to risk anything now. Besides, it won't be for too much longer, and you're doing very well as a frowe. Really."

"You think?"

"I do," Herwodis answered firmly. She patted the other girl's round shoulder. "But don't giggle whenever someone asks you about Sigimund. You're supposed to be grieving for him."

"I know. It's just the thought of me married to a man like him . . ."

Hard as she was biting the inside of her cheek, Herwodis held her expression quite still. She breathed deeply several times, trying to loosen the tight knot within her.

"Hush," she said severely. "Someone's coming."

A blond maid came in with two bowls of steaming water and towels, withdrawing quickly. Herwodis and Hilde washed themselves and set to looking through their things for clothes that would fit their changed stations and themselves alike. The shortest of Herwodis' dresses trailed a full handspan's length on the floor behind Hilde, sagging over her belt of woven silk like an empty sack; the longest of Hilde's left Herwodis' calves half-bare and pulled so tight across her breasts and back that she was sure the seam would burst if she breathed too deeply or lifted her arms. However, they could do no better than change clothes, for Herwodis had adorned her own dresses with rich embroidery along the seams, and the plainest of them was of fine linen dyed a rich deep blue, such as a serving maid could not be expected to wear; while none of Hilde's clothing was too good to be dirtied by cooking and cleaning.

"Our cloaks shall cover a great deal," Herwodis said hopefully. She did not dare to bend down; she bent her knees instead, squatting carefully. Tucking the extra length of dress beneath the belt whose knotted ends dangled almost to Hilde's knees, she pinned one on each side. "There; that will keep you from dragging on the floor."

As she had while they were on shipboard, Hilde wore Herwodis' cloak folded down to her own size, but Hilde's cloak hardly fell lower down Herwodis' legs than the maid's dress. Still, Herwodis thought, the athelings were not likely to mark or care about a serving maid's ankles, and much could go unseen in a torchlit hall. She pinned the golden brooch of her cloak above Hilde's left breast, tightening her gilded belt buckle a notch around the other girl's waist, then shook Hilde's cloak on her own shoulders so it would fall a little farther down her legs.

Standing back and looking at what she had done, Herwodis thought Hilde looked quite like a well-born frowe—indeed, with the maid's delicate features cleaned and her blond hair coiled neatly around her dainty head, Hilde seemed more of an atheling than Herwodis herself must have even at her best, as much as she had always tried to mute her loud voice and move slowly enough to hide her size and clumsiness. As for herself, though she felt like a carl's ox in a tight harness, a plain serving maid needed far less grace than a king's daughter.

The sounds of feasting were beginning to rise outside as Perchte rapped on the door. "Are you ready?" she called. Herwodis opened the door and held it for Hilde to scamper out before following her companion.

Hilde was seated next to Alapercht at the feast; as a serving maid, even one who was a guest, Herwodis stood behind her frowe, seeing to her needs as Hilde had done for her in her father's hall. On Hilde's other side sat Perchte and a dignified man whose black hair and beard were mixed with gray; Herwodis guessed that this must be King Chilpirich.

Alapercht chatted amiably with the maid. Herwodis, no longer responsible for giving rede in council, hardly paid any attention to what they were saying until the young drighten addressed a question over Hilde's shoulder to her. "And tell me, Hilde," he said. "I noticed on shipboard that you wake up just before dawn as well. Is there any sign that lets you know the time, when you can't see the moon or stars?"

Caught off guard, she answered, "My father gave me a small gold ring, which grows chill on my finger toward dawn."

"The ways of the Franks are strange, if the daughters of kings take drinks of milk from the cows every morning and the serving maids are given gold!" Alapercht said. A shock of fright thrilled through Herwodis, but he was laughing up at her, his hazel eyes friendly. "I think the two of you have played your game long enough, Herwodis. You should know by now that you have nothing to fear from me. I would have treated you properly, as we are both the children of kings, if you had told me, but I shall deal even better with you. If you will, you shall be my wife and I shall give you dowry when your child is born."

Perchte and Chilpirich were also smiling up at her, the queen's eyes bright with excitement and amusement mellowing the king's dignified face like sunlight warming a craggy cliff.

"Please do," Perchte urged her. "We'll send to your father's brother and have everything done properly as soon as we can, but we want you to stay with us. And you don't need to be afraid that your child won't get a proper raising here. We've heard the songs about the Walsings, and we couldn't think of any greater honor than to have Sigimund's bairn among us."

"Nor," Chilpirich added, his voice slow and deliberate, "could you ask, I think, for any better protectors from the man who has wronged you till your child has grown old enough to take revenge. Although Wyrd has taken your husband and your father from you, Alapercht and I will be glad to fulfill their duties toward you and toward your child if you wish it."

Herwodis stared at the three of them looking up at her as she stood in a serving maid's place, dressed in a cloak too small for her over a stained shift. But there was no mockery in the friendly smiles of king and queen, nor was there any in Alapercht's handsome face as he stood to pull his own chair out for her. She wavered between turning to flee and sitting down. Lingwe's narrow-eyed face flashed through her memory, and the stone floors and glass vessels of her father's hall. But she had left as a bride; and now, with the pretense that had protected her from the duties of a king's daughter shattered, she knew that eventually she would have to marry again. If she did not wed Alapercht, then Lingwe would return or another king would come across the Rhine to claim her—perhaps even a wild Burgundian with a Hunnishly warped skull.

Herwodis seated herself in Alapercht's chair with as much dignity as she could, smoothing Hilde's cloak around her. "I had not hoped for such kindness," she said, softening her voice to hide its trembling. "I will be glad indeed to marry you, Alapercht, and to stay in the home of our kin."

Impulsively, Perchte stood and came to embrace her, the queen's kiss on her cheek as soft and fleeting as the touch of a butterfly. "I'm so glad," she murmured. "Poor girl, you've had such a time, but it's over now and you're safe."

Alapercht gave Herwodis his own drinking horn, clasping his hands over hers on its polished surface for a moment. She took a good-sized swallow of the strong ale before she gave it back to him. He tilted his head back, the knob of his throat working as he drained the horn. "So we shall do all that we do between us," he said, taking her hands in his again and looking into her eyes. He was not Sigimund, but he was sturdy and gentle, his warm protective touch as comforting as the shaggy body of the guard hound that had been her companion as a child.

"So we shall," Herwodis answered, closing her eyes as he bent to kiss her.

"When do you think you may be ready for the wedding feast?" Chilpirich questioned after a little while.

"Let me wait till after my babe is born," Herwodis said at once. "That way no one will be able to question my trueness."

"No one would anyway, darling," Perchte assured her, but her mind was already made up.

"Still I will wait." Unseen tears flooded over her cheeks as the knot of fear loosed in her breast and an old song rang through her thoughts:

Better to have a son   though late-born the heir,
*   bairn, after his father's death.*
Few stones are set   to stand by road,
*   save by kinfolk for kin.*

He spun through a dizzy whirl of darkness lit with fiery gleams, floating like a feather in the wind till he could no longer remember who or where he was. Then the winds were all coming together, knotting into a great fist that pressed against him. Gasping, he tried to breathe, but only warm saltiness filled his mouth and nose as the darkness around him tightened again and again, pushing him unstoppably onward into a close passageway. His sight blurred faster and faster from firelight to blindness. Once he caught the glimpse of a bearded, black-pored face leaning over him, gray-fringed lips forming words he couldn't hear; then ahead flashed milk-clouded light as the way opened wider and the might at his back bore him on and outward. He cried out, but his mouth was clogged by a thick film that stilled his howl till something tore the wet shroud from his face and freed his breath. Then he shouted a great shout, staring up at the fuzzy dark shapes that loomed over him as his sight split into two parts. He seemed to hover in the middle of a torchlit room, looking down at the silver-haired woman who held a wrinkled newborn to her slim body with one hand, stroking the sweaty forehead of the young mother who lay, splayed and naked, in the birthing blood with the other; and yet he looked through unformed eyes at a world of mingling shadow and fire where no shapes were clear to his sight and only the warmth of the bony hip he rested upon seemed real.

"It's a son," the silver-haired woman said, her voice echoing distantly into nonsense through his ears: a son . . . ssson . . . onnn . . . nnn . . .

The brightness hurt his eyes; he lifted his heavy head, his voice rising in a wavering howl as he glared into the light and the icy wind that numbed his face. He saw the man with the silver-black hair and beard take the babe from his mother's arms, the warrior's muscular clasp strange and rough after the milk-soft embraces of the women who had tended him.

"Fro Ingwe, Frowe Holda," the man's voice said, a deep slow growl in his ears. "Ziw, Wodan, Donar, Nerthus, all ye gods and goddesses, hear! I name this child Sigifrith: may he be born to victory and may all his victories lead to frith, to fruitfulness and to joy."

Freezing water splattered onto his face; he glared up at the vague pale blur above him as it growled more unknown words. The droplets splashing onto the babe shone bright as ice in the cold winter sunlight, but his blue eyes glimmered more brightly, and the man who held him said joyfully, "Look how keen his eyes are! No one will ever be his like."

Then he could not hold any longer, both sights fading as he spun into the darkness. Once he opened his eyes to look up at the shadowed rafters of a sunken hut and the short wide shape looming above him; though, sick and dizzy, he struggled to hold the vision, then his lids fell again and he saw no more.

Ragin waited worrying, not daring to touch his foster-son until the harsh hissing of Sigifrith's breath faded to high, measured snoring. The wind had risen outside, whining coldly through a chink in the sunken hut's roof; it would soon be morning. He squatted down to gather the youth's slim body from the floor where he had fallen.

Sigifrith was a light burden to Ragin's thick arms as the smith bore his foster-son to the straw pallet where the boy usually slept, carefully drawing the blanket up to cover him. The dwarf waited another moment to see that his ward was sleeping naturally before he went to the keg in one corner and drew off a mug of his own heavy, bitter ale.

The polished wood of his chair curved about Ragin's body to hold up his back, easing the aches of his long night's watch. He put his feet on the furry cushion of an intricately carved stool, sipping at his drink and looking into the last flames of his fireplace. Ragin was tired, very tired, but not yet willing to give himself up to sleep, though he knew it would be a long time before Sigifrith woke to begin the next turning of the wyrd that the smith had written with the runes carved in the shape of the wyrm that twined about the door, which Sigifrith had not the craft to read:

ᛋᛁᚷᛁᚠᚱᛁᚦ᛬ᛞᚱᚨᚷᛟᚾᛋ᛬ᛋᛚᚨᛖᚱ᛬
ᛋᚺᚨᛖ᛬ᚦᛟᚱᚲᛁᛗᚤ᛬ᚹᛁᛚ᛬᛬

SIGIFRITH DRAGON'S-SLAYER SHALL WORK MY WILL.

BOOK II

SIGIFRITH THE

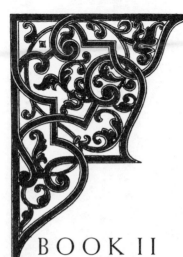

WALSING

Nothung! Nothung! Neidliches Schwert!
Jetzt haftest du wieder im Heft . . .
Dem sterbenden Vater zersprang der Stahl,
der lebende Sohn schuf ihn neu.
Nun lacht ihm sein heller Schein,
seine Schärfe schneidet ihm hart.
Nothung! Nothung! Neidliches Schwert!
Zum Leben weckt' ich dich wieder . . .

—RICHARD WAGNER, *Siegfried*
(Act I, Scene iii)

(Nothung! Nothung! Sword of need!
Now you are fixed in the haft again . . .
The steel shattered for the dying father,
the living son shaped it anew.
Now its bright shine smiles on him,
its sharpness cuts hard for him.
Nothung! Nothung! Sword of need!
I waked you to life again . . .)

1

THE SMITH'S APPRENTICE

The smell of seething meat and wild leeks began to seep into Sigifrith's awareness, the darkness behind his closed eyelids lightening to a pulsing dull red in the ray of warmth falling across his face. The youth opened his eyes a crack, squinting against the brightness of the afternoon sunlight that streamed through the open door of the hut. The crowlike rasp of Ragin's cough sounded behind him, and Sigifrith turned his head away from the Sun to look half-blindly into the shadows cast by the old dwarf's cooking fire.

"Awake at last," Ragin grunted. "Well, what do you remember?"

Sigifrith shut his eyes with a silent gasp as the weight of his night's vision pounded through him again, racking his body with a long shudder. It was too much for him: try as he might, he could not grasp it or hold anything beyond a fleeting impression of burning gold; a woman's face, fair and stark as an icy winter's dawn; and the sharp metal ring of a sword breaking in two. Slowly, though he could not say why, a sense came to him that he knew what he must do. "I must avenge my father," he said. He cast back through his mind, trying to remember—the five man-ages since the gold first came from the Rhine—but no more than thirteen winters of memory filled his hoard, thirteen winters of childhood and growth since his naming . . .

Feeling horribly robbed, cheated of his most precious inheritance, Sigifrith clenched his fists, striking them wildly against the cot and crying out in frustrated fury, "I can't remember, I can't remember! The gods curse you, I had it, I saw it all and now it's gone!" Tears flooded hotly down his face as he struggled to grasp the fading shape of his dream again.

The wooden frame of the cot broke under Sigifrith's fists with a crack, toppling him to the floor in a mess of blankets and sticks. He drew a deep, shuddering breath and climbed out of the wreckage. As he stood looking down at Ragin, the dwarf moved away uneasily, red-rimmed eyes flicking toward the axe resting against the wall.

"It's gone," Sigifrith said again, more softly. "Did you know that would happen? Was it your revenge on me for teasing you?"

Ragin shook his heavy head. "It's still there, Sigifrith—in your bones, in your blood, where it always was. The drink let you see everything hidden in the depths of your memory for a moment, but you have to rewin that inheritance for yourself. When you have slain Fadhmir and taken the part of Otter's weregild which is yours through your mother, then you will know more than you do now."

"Otter's weregild," Sigifrith murmured. An empty pelt dangling, gold clinking on gold . . . the ghostly head of a dragon rising over a man's body. There was more, he knew, far more, but it was too deeply hidden for him to see. He grated his teeth in frustration. "Tell me about it. Please," he added, smoothing the angry edge from his voice.

"You'll be very hungry," Ragin said calmly, turning to the fire and ladling out two generous helpings of stew. The dwarf sat down in his chair, leaving the plain three-legged stool for Sigifrith. When the youth had taken his first bite, he realized that he was ravenous. He swallowed without chewing, slurping his stew straight out of the bowl, which he refilled over and over till the cooking pot was empty. Only then did he fold his hands over his stomach and burp with satisfaction.

Ragin eyed him dourly. "Sigifrith," he said.

Sigifrith knew the lecture that was coming. "I won't do it at feasts. I promise. Even though most of the thanes do," he added under his breath. "Now will you please tell me about Otter's weregild? Or about my father?" A pang of longing twisted his guts as he spoke the last words. He felt as if he could see his father's lost world glittering just beyond his reach, all the brighter for its distance.

"Not yet," Ragin answered, his eyes glinting darkly from the shadowed caves under his thick gray brows. "If we get to work again, though, you might be able to finish that dagger by dark."

"What good is a silly knife to me?" Sigifrith asked in despair. "I need to forge a sword, a sword to avenge my father with—"

"A sword that will slay a dragon . . ." Ragin murmured. A faint mist seemed to cloud his craggy face, blurring the harsh lines age had carved into its stone. "Patience, Sigifrith. All in its time. I've waited five generations, and I haven't forged that sword yet. I've been waiting for the right metal, you might say. But you have to learn what you're doing and why before you can start on something like the sword you want, so you need to get to work and finish that knife. Come on, now."

Ragin picked up his tongs and began to tend the fire, shuffling about the ashes to make sure that no drips from the cooking pot had contaminated his flames. Piece by piece he added more charcoal till he had a strong blaze going, the clean scent of burning ashwood curling up in tendrils of light smoke. Sigifrith walked over to the granite anvil and picked up the half-forged blade he had been working on. It was a large, heavy knife, the length of his forearm from tang end to blade tip; it would be good to take hunting when he got back to Alapercht's hall. The cutting edge was just beginning to take shape as a tapering curve, arching up to the straight thick back edge. This would be a knife that could chop bone as easily as it parted hide from flesh, if Sigifrith could bring out its raw promise.

Sigifrith grasped the knife in his tongs and brought it over to the fire.

Vigorously he pumped the bellows, the blast of wind feeding the blaze around the dark steel in its core.

"Slowly," Ragin reminded him. "Slowly. If you heat it too fast, or try to do too much too soon, it will crack and you'll have to start again. There," he said as Sigifrith slowed to a more measured pace. "Better. Count it with your breaths . . . you're breathing life into the blade."

The metal heated slowly, its dull glow brightening to cherry red. As it began to shade into orange, Sigifrith pulled it from the fire and laid it on the anvil's smooth stone top, hammering along the edge to work in the curve he wanted.

"Turn it," Ragin cautioned. "Keep it even—don't hit it too hard, you don't need your full strength for this. Careful. . . . Strike the flat as well, you want to keep the thickness more constant." Finally he nodded his satisfaction. "All right. Put it back in the fire."

It was well past midday the next day when Sigifrith sat at the grindstone, putting the edge on to his knife. Because the day was warm and sunny, he and Ragin had brought the stone outside; now he pumped it with tiring legs as rock whined and rasped against steel. His right hand was bleeding from an earlier slip, and he stopped every so often to wipe it on his breeches, staining the wool with smears of rusty brown. Intent on his work, he didn't notice the sound of hooves on the path below till he heard the rider cursing at a fallen tree blocking his path, his voice as sharp as the crack of breaking wood.

"Rotten piece of shit! Around this way, Whitetail . . . no, here! Stupid horse!"

Sigifrith sprang up laughing as he recognized the voice of Alapercht's thane Hildkar. He hurried down the path to meet the man, shafts of sunlight through the new summer leaves flashing against his eyes as he ran.

"Hildkar!" he shouted. "Up here!" Leaping on a rock beside the path, he waited for Hildkar to ride to him.

"Sigifrith?" the young thane called, then, as he came around a bend in the path, "Damn, you've grown. Is it much farther? Get on and I'll take you the rest of the way."

Hildkar's long, narrow face was pale, eyes bloodshot and dark hair rumpled on one side. Sigifrith could see his thin hands trembling on Whitetail's reins. The horse's dun head was lowered; it plodded along the path with the slow unenthusiasm of a mule. Hildkar pulled it to a stop before Sigifrith's rock.

"What's happened?" Sigifrith asked. "Is something wrong at home? Nobody's dead, are they?" He climbed from the boulder to Whitetail's back, breathing in the rich smell of horse's sweat that almost masked the musty traveler's staleness hanging about Hildkar.

"No. Wait till we get to wherever it is you're supposed to be and I've had a chance to sit down and maybe even eat and drink something, if the old dwarf isn't too stingy to feed his guests. I've been riding myself to the bone to get here in time. I got lost along the way, and if an old man hadn't told

me where Ragin usually kept his forge, I'd be halfway to Hunland by now."
He nudged his horse with the tip of a dust-dulled boot. With a shuddering
sigh, Whitetail heaved himself to a walk again, hauling his doubled burden
up the path to Ragin's forge.

When they came to the clearing before the hut, Ragin was nowhere to
be seen. Sigifrith knew that the dwarf was either waiting in the woods or
inside the hut, ready to attack or flee.

"Hai! Ragin!" he shouted. "It's all right! It's one of King Alapercht's thanes!"

Ragin came around the hut, his axe in one hand and a bundle of firewood
under the other arm. Slowly, as though appraising a piece of metal for pur-
chase, he considered Hildkar, weighing Sigifrith's words and the young man's
clear exhaustion against the spear in his hand. Finally he nodded.

"Come in, then," he said. "But I don't have a place for the horse. You'll
have to find something to do with him for yourself."

Sigifrith sprang down to the ground and helped Hildkar slide from his
horse's back. He was pleased to notice that the thane, who had been several
fingers' width taller than he when he left Alapercht's hall, now met his eyes
on a level. "Go on in," he said. "I'll take care of him."

"Thanks," Hildkar said. "Everything's in the bag to the right of the saddle."
He followed Ragin. Whitetail stood with his head down, puffing through
wide nostrils and rolling the whites of his eyes at Sigifrith every so often.
The youth took the saddle from the horse, rubbed dust and sweat from his
dull coat, then lifted each hoof to check for stones. When he had finished
those chores, Sigifrith ran breathlessly into the hut.

Ragin frowned at his foster son. "You always forget something when
you're in a hurry, Sigifrith. What was it this time?" Sigifrith thought for a
moment, then reluctantly went out again. Not only had he forgotten to water
the horse, he had forgotten to tie him.

Fortunately, Whitetail had not moved far. He stood at the edge of the
clearing, grazing placidly on the new shoots of summer grass. Sigifrith took
him by the reins and led him around to the clear stream that ran down
behind the hut.

When Whitetail had drunk enough, Sigifrith tied him to the black-
budding branch of a sturdy ash tree and ran into the hut. Hildkar sat on the
hard clay floor, leaning back against the wall as Ragin watched him from his
chair. Sigifrith offered his stool to the thane, but Hildkar gestured him away.
Sigifrith noticed that, much as the dwarf had always stressed the need for
him to show proper hospitality when he should rule a hall of his own, Ragin
had offered the guest neither food nor drink. He took the last of the week's
bread and some cheese and dried cherries from the small chest where Ragin
kept food, and filled his own cup with ale for Hildkar.

"So you've decided to be the host in my hut, have you?" Ragin grumbled
at Sigifrith, tugging at his beard. "Without asking me first. A king's son needs
better manners."

"I'm sorry," Sigifrith said. "May I make Hildkar welcome in your home?"

"I suppose it's too late to say no now," Ragin growled. "Go on, then."

Sigifrith gave the food and drink to Hildkar, who nodded his thanks and began to devour it eagerly. The youth stood moving from foot to foot as he waited for Hildkar to finish. As the thane licked the last bits of cheese from his fingers and drained the last swallow of ale, Sigifrith finally burst out, "Can you tell me now? Why are you here? What's happened?"

Hildkar sighed as he looked up at Herwodis' son. "All right. The Burgundian king Gebica has signed a treaty of *foederatus* with Rome which gives him the lands on the western side of the Rhine directly to the north of ours. He and his band are coming to make a treaty with King Alapercht, and the king wants you to be there for it. They're due to arrive at the Thrimilci full moon, so you have enough time to make it back if you leave tomorrow morning."

As Sigifrith glanced at Ragin, he thought he could see the twisting of heavy jaw muscles under the dwarf's thick beard. Ragin stared into the fires of his forge as though searching for something among the writhing patterns glowing through the coals. For a moment, it seemed as though he had not heard the thane's words. Then the smith swung his hoary head about to face Hildkar again.

"Does Gebica bring his wife and children with him?" he demanded.

Hildkar blinked eyes wrinkled by exhaustion, seemingly scrabbling to collect scattered thoughts. "His wife and children?"

"Grimhild, Gundahari, Gundrun and Hagan," Ragin growled impatiently. "Do they come with him, or is it the king and his warband alone?"

"I don't know," the young thane said. "No one told me. Alapercht just said that I should be sure to fetch Sigifrith back before the next full moon."

Ragin snorted. "And you never thought to ask, I suppose. It can't be helped now, anyway. Is the frowe Herwodis well?"

"Yes. And . . . she sent a message for you." Hildkar drew his sparse dark brows together, running a hand through his rumpled hair as he dredged the words from his memory. " 'Herwodis greets her great-grand-uncle and bids him to dress his nephew in his best when he brings him to Alapercht's hall.' "

The dwarf made a rough noise of satisfaction. "So," he whispered, the wind of the word hissing through his jagged teeth. He stood, clumping over to the anvil where a twisted bundle of metal rods, half-welded into a rippling bar of steel, lay on the smooth stone. "Go on outside and get back to work, Sigifrith. If you hurry, you'll have a new knife to take with you. I want you to get this piece done, because I don't think you'll be forging steel again for a while."

"Why?" Sigifrith asked. Ragin only waved his hand irritably, as though swatting at a fly, and turned back to his work. Bewildered, Sigifrith looked at Hildkar. "Is there something else I don't know about?"

"You know all I do," the tired thane answered, letting his long body sag down closer to the floor.

Sigifrith had opened his mouth to offer Hildkar his own cot when his glance fell on the wreckage of boards piled neatly in the corner. Instead he gestured to the folded blankets on the floor beside the broken wood. "Help yourself," he invited. "You look as though you need a rest."

"I do. You know," he murmured softly to Sigifrith, "if Ragin would take one of those horses Chilpirich and Alaperlcht keep offering him, it would make things easier for everyone. I had to ride like a madman so that you two could have time to walk back."

Sigifrith shrugged helplessly. "Who knows why Ragin does anything?" he whispered, glancing over his shoulder at the squat dark shape silhouetted against the firelight of the forge. "Look, I've got to get back to work, or I'll hear nothing but nagging for a week. Make yourself comfortable."

Hildkar pulled himself the short distance to the piled blankets and began to arrange them around himself. Sigifrith went out into the sunlight, sat down at the grindstone and began to turn it. He winced at the grating whine as steel met stone, and pumped a little harder so that he could get the job done more quickly.

Sigifrith and Ragin traveled no more swiftly than the old dwarf could walk. Ragin stumped along at a slow pace that soon began to get on Sigifrith's nerves, and the boy would run off into the forest for hours before returning to the pathway along the Rhine. "Are you a dwarf or a snail?" he would shout in exasperation at Ragin, who merely raised his shaggy gray head to fix Sigifrith with a baleful glare, muttering under his breath as his foster son tossed his new knife up in a high glittering arc and snatched it from the air again. "Pick up your feet, old clumper! The moon's getting fuller every day."

As they came from the Frankish territories into the lands ruled by Gebica, Ragin grew ever more cautious, avoiding the main road and keeping to the small paths through the woods.

"Why should we hide?" Sigifrith argued. "You come through here often enough for them to know you, and none of the Burgundians has any reason to recognize me. Besides, I thought they were about to negotiate a peace treaty with us or something."

"Peace treaties have a way of failing unexpectedly when something more advantageous comes up," Ragin said darkly. "And no time is less safe than the time between war and peace. Till the treaty is sealed, you're living in a border march—and therefore vulnerable."

Sigifrith chose another angle of attack. "There's a better road on the other side. I bet if we crossed at the next ferry or ford we could get home almost a day earlier and I could have more time to get ready. And if we were on the main road instead of skulking in the underbrush like wargs, we probably wouldn't look as suspicious, either. Besides, if any Burgundians try to give me trouble, I'll chop them up for stew." He drew his knife and flourished it, the blade blurring into a wheel of polished metal flinging out dazzling flashes of sunlight.

"Don't draw if you're not going to use it," Ragin said with the weariness of long habit. The dwarf stopped, letting his bag of tools and new-made weapons down carefully and rubbing his thick shoulders. He squinted across the river, to the territories that the Burgundians had taken in the great break-through seven years ago—when Alapercht had taken his own lands across the Rhine from his father Chilpirich's—and now held by law and treaty with Rome.

"We came through on that side before without any trouble, didn't we?" Sigifrith persisted. "And we could stop at that inn we passed up last time. I'm getting sick of rabbit stew, and you make so much noise you scare the deer away before I can reach them. I bet if you didn't I could kill one with my knife. Ansbrand said he knew someone whose mother's brother killed a full-grown stag with nothing but a dagger. Or if you'd let me fix a shaft on one of those spearheads you've got, it wouldn't matter how far off I was. Anyone can kill a stag with a spear."

"You must not be recognized while you're in these lands," Ragin croaked. "Do you think, if we stop at that inn, that you can be a simple smith's apprentice for the night? Quiet and obedient—not just to me, but to every man who calls you 'boy' and sends you to fetch him ale or tie his horse? Do you think you can keep your eyes down and your mouth closed? I don't think so."

"But I can!" Sigifrith said, laughing. The thought of a masked adventure pleased him enormously. "I'll be the meekest little thrall you ever saw. I will! No one will ever guess that I'm . . . " He trailed off. Not Sigifrith the son of King Alapercht, as he was often called by courtesy. Heir to the Alamannic kingdoms? What had become of his father's lands?

"We'll see," Ragin muttered dubiously. "It might be worth the risk just to keep you quiet." He eyed the straight length of Sigifrith's body as though measuring the shaft for a spearhead. "Slump down a bit. Act tired, even if you're not. And don't look anyone in the eye."

Sigifrith slouched, lowering his lids and bending his shoulders as though he were used to bearing burdens. "Better?" he said. Sigifrith thought Ragin was about to nod. Then, in spite of his attempt to look downcast, a giggle escaped Sigifrith's mouth.

The old dwarf sighed. "None of this is a game, Sigifrith. If you can't disguise yourself better than that . . . " He heaved up his burden and began to walk again.

The Rhine was running high with the floods of winter's end: here in the south, he rushed wild and muddy from the mountains of the Mirkwood, his torrents sweeping much harder and faster than at Ragin's forge near the Dragon's Crag. Sigifrith and Ragin had to wait for the ferryman to come out of the inn on the other side, patting his wide belly in contentment. He puttered about on the shore for a while before Sigifrith, impatient, finally shouted to him, "Hai! Ferryman! We want to cross!"

Ragin's hard elbow hit the edge of Sigifrith's hipbone. The youth slouched from his proud height and tried to settle himself into a more patient pose.

The raft began to move across the turbulent river, its steersman's heavy muscles bulging beneath a thick layer of fat as he wrestled his craft across the swift-running current that tried to sweep it downstream.

The ferryman thrust his pole down to stop a little way from the river's bank, leaning on the stick as he got his breath back. "You want to cross, do you? And who are you supposed to be?" His voice was pleasant and smooth; he smiled as he spoke, showing crooked buck teeth with a wide gap between them. Around his neck was a plain wooden cross with a long stem.

Ragin trod heavily on Sigifrith's foot as he pushed in front of the youth. "You know me, Anshelm—Ragin the Smith, you've carried me before. This is my apprentice, Wulfi."

"Bit old to be an apprentice, ain't he?" Anshelm asked.

"Thirteen winters," Ragin replied shortly.

The fat ferryman looked Sigifrith up and down, then whistled. "If he grows any more, he's going to be a damn big one. The two of you aren't going to be an easy haul in these waters, you can bet on it."

"How much?"

"Well, your boy's a man's size, and you'll pay me a man's full price for him—two mugs of ale, same as for you. And I get another cup for the season."

"Ostara's feast was close to a moon ago," the dwarf reminded Anshelm.

"All right, but look at that water. Have you ever seen storms like the ones we had this year?"

"Three years ago they were worse. And the Rhine was high enough to overflow his banks and wash out half the road ten years back. Old as I am, Anshelm, I haven't lost my mind yet. I'll buy you three mugs for all of us, and Wulfi will help you pole."

Anshelm snorted. "Help me? You want me to trust my raft to a smith's raw apprentice? Besides, he may be tall, but he's too skinny to do me any damn good—a man needs some meat on him to do my job." He slapped his ample gut, laughing. Ragin waited. "All right. Three cups and a loaf of bread, and your boy helps pole."

"Half a loaf."

"Half a loaf," the ferryman sighed. "If I didn't know you . . ."

"You'd think you could squeeze more out of me."

"No one else complains about paying an honest worker a decent wage." He pulled the raft in to shore, moving to balance it as it tilted under the weight of Ragin and his tools. Sigifrith crouched and sprang, landing lightly in the middle of the raft as Anshelm gaped and Ragin shook his head. Sigifrith laughed, shaking his long tangle of wavy hair away from his face.

"Crazy idiot!" the ferryman said, his pleasant voice going as sharp as rancid cheese. "You'll have us all overboard. If you want to help on my boat, you'll do what I tell you, understand?"

Sigifrith smiled sweetly at him, looking down before Anshelm could turn away from his glance. "All right," he said. "I'm sorry."

Somewhat mollified, the ferryman adjusted Sigifrith's hands on the pole. "Now shove on the bottom—shove hard."

Sigifrith pushed down with a mighty heave, sending the raft spinning wildly out into the current. He laughed again with excitement as Anshelm shouted and Ragin dropped down to cling tightly to the planks of the raft. Sigifrith pushed again, but the water was too deep for him to touch bottom. As he swung the pole with all his strength, trying to row up the current, it cracked with the force of his first stroke against the water.

"What the . . . ? Stop that, you fool! Stop and let me row!" Anshelm shouted. The Rhine was carrying them swiftly downstream toward a treacherous stretch of river where black rocks whipped the water into a white froth. The ferryman grabbed the oars from the bottom of the raft and madly strove to turn it to a straight course across the river again, streams of sweat rolling down his deeply creased forehead. His face was bright red, breath coming in great shuddering gasps, when the raft finally bumped shore again.

"How are you . . . at . . . carrying things, boy?" Anshelm panted. "I hope . . . damn good . . .'cause you've got to . . . haul this raft . . . back up . . . you wretch." He dropped the oars and bent over in a sudden cramp, grabbing his stomach as if to hold his entrails in.

Sigifrith looked at the raft, then at the river. It hadn't felt so strong . . . Suddenly he grabbed the oars and pushed off again, rowing straight into the current. The raft swung one way, then the other, as he tried to straighten it out and get the oars to swing in the same rhythm; but it moved slowly upstream.

The raft floated more easily as Sigifrith found his balance between right and left, rowing them upriver. The youth's arms were aching painfully and he, too, was panting by the time the raft came to shore in front of the inn, but he grinned triumphantly at ferryman and dwarf.

"Jesu . . . Christus," gasped the ferryman. "What in . . . Hella's halls are you?"

"He's a young fool with more strength than he knows how to use," Ragin answered dryly, picking himself up from the bottom of the raft. "In other words, he's a clumsy idiot. And he'll be a tired one tomorrow, because while you and I are sleeping, he'll be making a new pole for you—won't you, Wulfi?"

"I suppose so," Sigifrith answered, light-headed. He pushed the oars back into Anshelm's shaking hands and jumped to the shore, leaving the raft to rock behind him. "There was enough meat on me after all, wasn't there?" he added.

The ferryman and Ragin both ignored him as they climbed off and pulled the raft up the bank. Sigifrith shrugged and raced ahead to the inn, where the light summer wind swung a wooden sign from side to side above the open door. The peeling paint showed a crude black wolf's head with a long red tongue dangling from its jaws into a frothing cup of ale.

Sigifrith stepped into the cool shadows of the inn's common room. A black-splotched goat eyed him for a moment, then swung its head away to munch a mouthful of straw off the floor. A couple of men and a fat little woman sat at one end of the long table, tossing dice. The woman looked up at Sigifrith, snorting disdainfully.

"What do you want?" she demanded. Sigifrith stared at her in bewilderment. No one except Ragin had ever spoken to him like that before . . . and Ragin was different, he could be rude to everybody.

The innkeeper waved her hand, shooing him away. "Go on, boy, get out," she said. "I'm very busy."

Sigifrith glanced around at the empty room, then at the dice cup in her other hand. "But there's hardly anyone here," he said.

"I'm very busy," the woman repeated.

Sigifrith drew himself up to his full height and started toward her. The men eyed him with a rising suspicion beginning to crest into anger, the elder of the two starting to heave his bulk from the bench.

"Hai! Wulfi! Your master wants you down at the raft," Anshelm's voice said from behind him. The plump ferryman stood in the doorway, mopping his brow. "He's got something for you to carry. I must say, I don't envy him having to teach anything to a wild creature like you." Anshelm turned to the innkeeper. "You'd better get a room ready, Guthrid, you've got guests coming. But make sure all the breakables are out of it." He laughed, moving away from the door to give Sigifrith a wide berth as the youth went out. "Let me tell you, though," Sigifrith heard him say, "I've never seen anything like it . . . "

Ragin stood by his bag, boots planted firmly as he glared at his foster son from beneath lowered brows. "What kind of apprentice do you think you are?" he hissed. "What kind of apprentice leaves his master to do the heavy work?"

"But you've never let me touch your things before," Sigifrith protested. "How can I know what to do when I've never been told?"

"Urmph. Try paying attention. Haven't you ever seen an apprentice with his master before?"

"I suppose I never thought about them much," Sigifrith admitted.

"No. Well, go on, then, if your arms aren't too sore to move. They will be tomorrow," Ragin warned, a hint of malicious glee sparkling in his raspy voice.

Sigifrith swung the sack up and carried it into the inn. The innkeeper's face eased when she saw Ragin.

"Ragin the Smith." Guthrid spoke the name firmly, as though she found it to be something, if not wholly welcome, at least trustworthy. "You'll have your usual place."

"Yes. And a blanket for my boy Wulfi."

"That's extra for him, you know. Anshelm told me . . . "

Ragin's foot caught the side of Sigifrith's calf as the youth was about to drop the sack. Under the smith's sharp glare, Sigifrith let his load down carefully and went out again as Ragin and Guthrid bickered. He stretched his sore shoulders with a soft grunt, standing in the comforting warmth of Sunna's light for a few moments and letting her melt his frustrations away. His cheerful mood coming back to him as his tiredness faded, Sigifrith looked about him for a few moments, then wandered into the wood by the roadside in search of a sapling to replace the ferryman's broken pole.

As Sigifrith, pole in hand, walked back toward the inn, he heard the sound of horses' tack jingling and men's voices speaking the heavily accented Gothic speech of the Burgundians. He hurried out in front of the inn to get a better look at the travelers. It was a largish band—he guessed twenty-five or thirty warriors in byrnies, arrayed around a finely clad drighten and frowe behind whom rode two boys and one girl of about Sigifrith's age and a pair of maidservants. A tall, thin man in strange robes with a long topknot of streaming gray hair rode before the pair in the middle. Dark eyes hazed by a thin milky film stared at Sigifrith for a moment before the old man looked away.

The horses were smaller than Alapercht's, puny and graceless-looking to Sigifrith's eyes until he noticed how they moved in perfect step and perfect formation. He had heard that the Burgundians could ride and shoot like Huns, the little steeds under them ruled by magic and obedient to the softest thought. At first it looked to Sigifrith as though a number of the Burgundian warriors were wearing strange hats or helms; it wasn't until the second glance that he realized that their skulls were actually deformed, sloping up to near-conical points. *Maybe they really do mate with trolls!* Sigifrith thought, his breath coming faster with excitement. He waited, clutching the roughly cut staff tightly in one hand, to see if they would stop at the inn.

To Sigifrith's great pleasure, the drighten called out, "Halt! We sleep here tonight."

The warriors wheeled their horses around the middle group in a swift flourish of skill, hooves flying in unison. "Hai! Gebica!" they shouted, horses stamping the ground in a single final thunderclap before they stopped dead. The black-haired boy's steed jerked uncomfortably under him, as though trying belatedly to join the display; he pulled at its reins, biting his lip unhappily.

Sigifrith felt the laughter bubbling in him as he watched the Burgundians dismount. The man in the middle there, the drighten—that must be King Gebica, and the bird-boned frowe he was lifting from her horse must be his wife Grimhild. Then the white-gowned girl with the long thick mass of golden-brown hair curling down her back was Gundrun, and the boys Gundahari and Hagan, though he had no way of knowing which was which. Gebica was a man of middle height, just a little shorter than Sigifrith. He was broad-shouldered and hefty, with chestnut hair and sturdy, plumpish features; the sword at his side was unornamented, but sunlight gleamed off its hand-polished hilt and its scabbard was well worn. One of his sons was heavily built with the rich brown hair, wide cheeks and small, indented chin of his father; the other—the one who had had trouble with his horse—was wiry-slim, though heavily muscled in the shoulders and chest. The steely links of a chain-mail byrnie gleamed dully beneath the sleeves and hem of his black tunic, although his brother was unarmored. The two youths were almost of a height, so Sigifrith couldn't tell which was the elder. Grimhild's blue linen dress was embroidered all over with golden and red threads in intricate, turning knotwork; a huge saucer-shaped brooch of gold set with deep red garnets pinned her dark green cloak at the shoulder. She moved as quickly as a shrike, long fingernails tapping restlessly at the sharp beak curling down from her falcon-shaped belt buckle. About to hand the reins of her horse to one of her boys, she jerked her head to the side as she noticed Sigifrith.

"You!" she called. "You there, boy!" Sigifrith could hear a Frankish over-tone ringing through her Burgundian speech. "Can you tend horses?"

"I can," Sigifrith answered, leaning his pole against the wall of the inn before going through the throng and taking the reins from Grimhild's bony hands. He kept his glance down, trying to look as meek as he could.

The brown-haired boy stood by Gundrun's side as she dismounted, but it was clear that he was only there for courtesy; Sigifrith saw her kick at him when he tried to lift her down. She handed her reins to Sigifrith as her mother had done. The slimmer boy, his high-boned, icy-pale face set in a stern and oddly adult frown, took his brother's horse.

"Let the inn boy do it," the other said. "That's what he's here for, isn't it?"

"I'll do it myself," the black-haired boy answered. His voice was startlingly deep, grating and monotonous with an eerie overtone that raised the hairs on the back of Sigifrith's neck. Surprised, Sigifrith forgot Ragin's orders and looked him straight in the eyes. He did not turn away, but returned the gaze as though expecting a challenge—or giving one. As the other youth's dark gray eyes stared at him, a strange tingle rang through Sigifrith's blood like the roughly resounding note of a steer's horn calling out battle's begin-ning. He noticed that the Burgundian's high, upswept cheekbones made his eyes look slanted beneath their sharply arched black brows; that his fine, narrow features bore only a little resemblance to Grimhild's and none at all to Gebica's.

The two youths stared at each other for what felt like several minutes before the Burgundian had to turn his gaze away from Sigifrith's eyes. They followed Gebica and his steed through to the watering trough. Sigifrith's companion did not speak again, but Sigifrith could feel his harsh scrutiny as the two of them watered their charges, then rubbed them down and looked at their hooves. Sigifrith noticed that the other seemed ill at ease with the horses, which, sensing his nervousness, shifted restlessly around him and eyed him suspiciously.

"You sure you don't want me to help you?" Sigifrith offered lightly. He recalled scraps of words that had been used to him by servants, inn boys. "Surely a king's son shouldn't have to be his brother's groom."

The Burgundian's angular face did not move, nor did the painful monotone of his voice change as he rasped again, "I'll do it myself." His brother's chestnut shifted, stamped and came down on his foot; he bore the pain without any sign as he nudged the horse and pulled at its reins till it moved. He looked at Sigifrith again, as if defying him to say something, and again Sigifrith felt that strange tingling along his spine. He kept silent, however, finishing his work and tying the horses to one of the posts before the inn.

"Your master's gone out back, boy," Anshelm said when Sigifrith went in. "He's doing some ironwork to pay for your food and lodging, but you'll be sleeping in here with everyone else tonight, because King Gebica and his family want the private rooms. It's always like that, hey? Is that my new pole in your hand?" He looked at the sapling trunk Sigifrith carried, sap oozing from its ends and the broken stumps of branches along its length. "It'll take you a bit of work to clean that up," he said, satisfied.

Guthrid bustled into the common room, wiping a few strands of loose hair from her sweaty forehead with the back of one hand and waving the broom she held in the other at the placid goat, which ambled out as the Burgundians began to crowd in. Sigifrith found a spot on the bench and sat down to watch as the fat little woman dithered and flustered back and forth with cups of beer and wine for her atheling guests. A thin maiden with straggly blond hair, her face red from the heat of the kitchen, carried plates of steaming lamb stew and fresh bread out into the gathered throng.

Sigifrith noticed that the black-haired youth was careful to sit with his back to the wall, grimly eyeing the room and everyone in it as though he expected an attack at any moment, and that he sniffed the cup Guthrid brought him suspiciously before he sipped. Holy gods, thought Sigifrith, he's a strange one.

Gundrun wrinkled her nose at the first taste of her wine; the other boy blew foam from the top of his beer and drank it straight down. To Sigifrith's amusement, he stifled his belch as his mother's sharp eyes lit on him. Gebica, sinking into his place at the head of the bench beside Grimhild and quaffing his beer, burped without bothering to muffle it and held out his cup for more.

Hungry and thirsty as Sigifrith was, he—remembering his role—waited until the warriors had been served before claiming his portion of garlicky stew, bread and beer. He gobbled it greedily, looking around for Ragin; but the old dwarf was nowhere to be seen.

Sigifrith went back for more food, but Guthrid, a cup of beer in each hand, forestalled him with a shake of her head. "You'll wait till the athelings have had their fill, boy," she snapped. "And your master's eaten already, so don't think you can trick more out of me by claiming it's for him." She snorted disdainfully and hurried back to her other guests. Annoyed as he was, Sigifrith had to smile to himself, thinking: if she only knew. He sat down beside the low fire, peeling his sapling and trimming the broken stubs of branches from it, tossing the green chips and long curls of bark into the flames.

In time Guthrid closed the door against the night cold and lit the smoky torches on the walls. It was not too long after that the Burgundian royal family went off to their private rooms and the warriors began unrolling blankets on the floor, pushing and jostling for the places nearest to the fire. In the shadowy torchlight, Sigifrith mingled easily with them, unlacing his boots and wriggling around till he found a place where his face wasn't too close to anyone else's feet. It felt strange for him, used as he was to sleeping alone or with only Ragin in the room, to be crowded together with these people, but he was tired and in no mood to complain. When Sigifrith wasn't listening carefully and trying to understand it, the Burgundian speech became a soft and garbled growling in his ears; now the arguments and the night talk of men, punctuated every so often by a belch or sneeze, faded to a dull mumble around him as he eased into sleep.

Sigifrith tossed and turned his way up from uneasy sleep, sweating in the warmth and smell of the crowded room. The fire had burned down to a dull glow; the warriors snored or shifted in their sleep. The reek of the garlic the Burgundians had eaten and the butter with which some of them had greased their hair days ago mixed with the stink of road sweat and farts to fill the room with an overpowering fug. Sigifrith felt stifled in the close atmosphere, overheated and restless. Silently he got to his feet, pulling his boots on, and crept out, easing the door on its leather hinges closed behind him.

The waxing Moon cast an eerie silvery light over the road and the woods beyond it, shadows harsh and black on the moonlit ground. A soft breeze ruffled Sigifrith's mane of hair, prickling cold up his back as he crept toward the Rhine. As he came nearer to the slope of the riverbank, he could see a slim black figure sitting on a rock, seemingly looking into the silver-rippling water or across at the darkness of the other side. Sigifrith's breath came soft and quick with excitement as he neared the silent watcher—a night-alf? A river-ghost? What human being would be out here this late at night when everyone was sleeping? Sigifrith glided over stones and grass as quietly as he could, hoping to get close enough to see its face before it vanished into rock or water again.

He was a few steps away when a twig cracked loudly beneath the thick leather sole of his boot. At once the dark shape whirled with a muted jingling of mail, one hand going up as if to block a blow and the other drawing the long dagger at its side.

The moonlight shone cold off the white face of the black-haired Burgundian boy from the inn. His lips were drawn back from his teeth, his dark eyes wide and blank.

Sigifrith stepped back quickly, spreading out his hands to show that he held no weapon. He gave the Burgundian his friendliest smile. "Easy," he said. "It's only me—the boy from the inn, remember? I didn't mean to startle you."

The Burgundian's face relaxed into a frown as he sheathed his dagger. He straightened from his fighting crouch, his eyes focusing on Sigifrith at last. "What are you doing here?" he asked. Now Sigifrith knew what to expect, the other boy's grating bass was less of a shock, but Sigifrith still found its strained single tone painful to listen to.

"I woke up. It was too hot in there for me to sleep," he answered. "What about you?"

"I couldn't go to sleep. I often . . . Anyway, I thought I should come out and keep watch. This close to the Alamannic lands, one never knows what might happen. No insult meant."

"How did you know I am Alamannish?"

"By your speech, although you don't chew your words as badly as an Alamann. Are you part Frankish?"

"My mother is Frankish," Sigifrith said. "What's your name, then? Are you Gundahari or Hagan?"

The Burgundian boy stared at him for a moment, his grim face unchanging. "We'll trade questions," he offered. "Like a riddle game, and the first one who can't—or won't—answer loses . . . not his head . . . he has to tell his true name and lineage, as well as he knows how to."

"All right," said Sigifrith. The other youth sat down on the rock again and Sigifrith settled himself beside him, looking at the silvery eddies of froth over the black water. A faint mist was beginning to rise from the river, glowing softly in the moonlit distance.

The Burgundian's byrnie clinked as he turned to look at his new companion. "You go first," he grated.

"Why do some of your warriors have such oddly shaped skulls? Is it really because your folk mate with trolls?"

"That's two questions. Which are you asking?"

"The first."

"It's a custom we learned from the Huns after our folk traveled from Gautland and Burgundarholm, back when we lived on the eastern steppes at the march between the Gothic lands and the wild folks beyond. They're shaped for helmets. It makes the men better warriors. What are you doing here at this inn?"

"I'm not really a servant here. I'm just staying for the night with my foster-father Ragin the Smith." Quickly, afraid that he might have given too much away, Sigifrith asked, "Who was that strange man with the long gray hair who rode in with you?"

"He's our Sinwist—our head gudhija. He will hold his place as long as he lives, speaking to the gods of our folk and the ghosts who came west with us. How old are you?"

"Thirteen winters, counting the Midwinter of my birth. You?"

"Twelve winters. I was born at Midsummer—six months after you, I suppose. Where did you learn to tend horses as well as you do?"

"My . . . the Alamanns have always had the best horses. Even Chilpirich and Alapercht see to the breeding and tending of their own stock. Why are your horses so small?"

"We brought them with us from the steppes. They may be small, but they can trot for hours under the full weight of a warrior in armor and never be tired, and they can go longer without food or water than any other breed. They can be trained better than any others, as well. Which gods do you follow?"

"The Alamanns hold Ziw highest. We also honor Wodan, Frija, Donar, Fro Ingwe and Frowe Holda, Voll and Volla, Nerth and the other dwellers in the Ases' Garth and Wans' Home." Sigifrith paused, letting the words he scarcely understood well up from the darkness of his mind into the moonlight. "I myself call on Wodan as my father did before me, for Wodan was the first father of my line, and he has gathered all my kin who have gone before me into Walhall: it is he who gives us the gifts of victory and binds us with the knot of the slain." Sigifrith breathed deeply, coughing to hide his confusion and wonder as he stared down at the river's flowing serpent-patterns of silver and black, shiny as polished steel beneath the Moon's cold light. "What about you, then?" he asked, for lack of a better question.

"The Burgundians believe in all the gods and goddesses, together with the ghosts of the steppes, to whom our Sinwist sets poles and pours out mares' milk. Some of our folk also follow the Roman Christus, even a few of the athelings. Have you ever seen any of the gods or goddesses, or any ghosts?"

"A statue to Ziw stands in our holy grove. Otherwise, no . . . Not since my birth," Sigifrith added slowly. "Have you?"

The Burgundian youth paused, his slightly slanted eyes gazing into the river's shadows. "I saw the Wild Hunt once," he said, his deep voice little more than a distant rumble. "Last Yule-time . . . I couldn't sleep, so I went out. First I heard the wargs howling through the wind and snow, then the sound of a horn." His gravelly voice slipped into a chanting rhythm, as compelling as it was painful to hear. "Like clouds the ghosts rode through the tree tops behind the eight-legged shadow-steed. Their faces shone lightning-white through the storm; to hunt the living the mirk-wights rose, the sleepless dead rode from the dark earth halls. Ygg, the Terrible, rode before them, grim and one-eyed, grasping his spear; Sleipnir bore the draugs' drighten to the Middle-Garth from the grave-holds. I saw the wild wod in his glance, as he led the ghosts through the sky; his ravens' wings beat black on the wind and his gray wolves ran beside. And I . . . " He stopped suddenly, as though afraid of what more he might say. "What were you making with that stick in there?"

"A new pole for the ferryman. I broke his other one." Sigifrith met the Burgundian's dark-pooled eyes again, trying to pierce through their blackness and see whatever it was that stirred his own awareness so—to find the root of the eeriness that troubled his senses, coupled with the nagging feeling that he had glimpsed that grim, high-boned paleness before. The gentle breeze was rising to a sharp cold wind, shivering through his body. "What did you see in the river before I came out?"

The Burgundian turned away from Sigifrith's stare. "My name is Hagan, of the family of the Hending—you would say King—Gebica of the Burgundians. My mother is Grimhild, daughter of Hildelind, the daughter of Sigrid, the daughter of Audhrid, the daughter of Wulfrun, the daughter of Lofanohaith, the daughter of Hraithamar. And you are Sigifrith, the son of Herwodis, Aiwilimo's daughter, and Sigimund the Walsing, now of the house of the kings Chilpirich and Alapercht to whose lands we are traveling."

"How did you know?" Sigifrith asked in amazement, staring at Hagan, whose set face showed no sign of his triumph.

"I knew from the keenness of your eyes when I first saw you," Hagan answered. "I didn't say anything then, because I thought that if you were hiding your name and place, you must have a reason—and then I wanted to be absolutely sure. Why are you pretending to be a common apprentice?"

"Because Ragin said I had to if we were to stay in this inn, and because I thought it would be fun. No one else has guessed, have they? Did I do it that badly?"

"No." Hagan rose from the rock and stretched, rubbing the light coating of misty dew from the edges of his byrnie with the sleeves and hems of his tunic. He put his hand up to his mouth to cover a yawn. "I don't believe anyone else has any idea of whom you might be. And I'll keep your secret, as long as it doesn't mean any threat to my family or my folk—and if you swear not to tell anyone else about how you passed yourself off as a servant boy to spy on the Burgundians. Do you understand?"

"I won't tell anyone. But what difference could it possibly make?" Sigifrith asked, also standing to his full height and tugging his tunic straight.

Hagan stood where he was, looking up into Sigifrith's face. "It's a risk. Do you swear not to tell anyone?"

"I swear," Sigifrith said.

The Burgundian nodded. "All right. We have to rise at dawn, and I expect you will too. If you and Ragin make good time you should be there before we are—the Hending Gebica is stopping along the way to visit Hariulf, one of the Burgundian drightens along the new march between our lands and yours. You're sleeping in the common room?"

"Yes."

"You'll wake up early enough, then." Hagan gazed at the Moon, whose silver light was taking on a gilded tinge as he sank toward the low, mist-shrouded hills on the other side of the Rhine. "And you won't have much more time to sleep," he added as the two of them started back toward the inn.

"What about you, then? Have you been up all night? You're the one that's going to be tired in the morning."

"I'm used to it," Hagan answered.

Quietly the two of them crept back into the inn, stepping over—and sometimes on—the sleeping bodies of men who mumbled curses under their feet. Even the stuffy warmth of the common room felt good after the cold outside, though its smells seemed to reek more strongly than before. The Burgundian made his way through the inner door without a sound. Sigifrith, knowing that he would never find his place again, stretched his full length on one of the narrow benches. He yawned deeply, letting himself fall asleep without another thought.

THE GEBICUNGS

Sigifrith and Ragin crossed into Alapercht's territory without more happening, though Ragin grumbled at the laxness of the sentries who failed to meet them along the march-lands. Although Sigifrith pestered him, the smith refused to say why he had hidden himself during their night at the inn; and finally Sigifrith put it down to simple cowardice.

The lands Alapercht had won when the Alamanns crossed the Rhine were pleasant, green fields and softly rolling hills covered with the skeleton fences over which, in another moon or two, the green tendrils and leaves of grape-vines would curl. As they neared his home, Sigifrith often ran a mile or two ahead of Ragin, only to turn aside from the road and stop to look at the horses in which the Alamanns took such pride, the tall stallions tossing their noble manes and the long-legged mares with their new foals tottering at their sides.

Alapercht's hall stood near the edge of a forest, where the king and his adopted son had often gone hunting with the thanes. When Sigifrith saw the dark edge of the trees far ahead, he broke into a run again, sprinting down the road and leaping up the hill on which Alapercht's keep stood with great strides as he saw the tall, heavily rounded figure of his mother standing at the door. He caught Herwodis by her waist, exuberantly lifting her up and swinging her round in a circle before setting her on her feet again. When he put her down, she rubbed her well-padded ribs gingerly.

"I don't think you've broken anything," she commented ironically. She eyed him in that careful way she had, then smiled. She had lost a side tooth since he'd been away, but otherwise Sigifrith couldn't see any change in her. "You've certainly grown and become stronger. It looks as though Ragin's been taking good care of you." She embraced him again; he hugged her back, being careful not to squeeze too tightly this time. "And you're looking more and more like your father," Herwodis added, her muted voice tinged by a faint mist of wistfulness. She coughed. "It's good to have you back, Sigifrith," she went on, more briskly. "You've come just in time, too. King Gebica and his family will be coming tomorrow morning, and you need a bath and—" She stood back, her keen gray eyes measuring her son again. Sigifrith drew himself up to his full height, breathing deeply and throwing back his shoulders. "Holy Frija, you need new clothes! It's too late to make anything proper now . . . Hmm. I think your shoulders are broad enough that we might be able to fit one of Alapercht's tunics on you, if we cut it down in the sides and belt it in tightly enough. As for breeches . . ." Herwodis sighed, then nodded decisively, looking down the road. "And where did you leave Ragin? Should we be waiting for him, or did he go off on his own?"

"He'll be coming, I think," Sigifrith said carelessly. "He walks so slowly, I couldn't wait for him. But he's afraid of the Burgundians, so maybe he won't be coming after all. What did you mean when you told him to dress me in my best?"

Herwodis' face seemed to sag for a moment, heavy jowls drooping from her strong cheekbones. "We'll talk about it later, when things are more . . . well, when things are settled. I never told you much about my first wedding, did I?" she added—irrelevantly, Sigifrith thought.

"No," he answered. "Can you tell me while I'm eating? I'm awfully hungry. Ragin wouldn't let me hunt much while we were traveling."

The two of them walked into the hall side by side. To Sigifrith's pride, he was the same height as his mother now. Alapercht's stone-built hold had once been a keep of the Romans, and a fine sandstone relief with Roman runes at the bottom still graced the wall by the main door: as guardian of the house, the Romans had set a stately walkurja who held a spear in one hand and a shield bossed with the furious head of a snake-haired woman in the other, to whom Herwodis never forgot to pour out ale at the Winternights feast. Daylight rippled through the glass windows over the rugs and furs that eased the coldness of the stone floor. At the end of one of the long tables stood a tall pitcher of bluish green glass adorned with curving squiggles of white, whose handle was wrought into a garland of clear flowers; like many of Alapercht's best goods, it had been made by Frankish craftsmen farther down the Rhine. Three graceful goblets stood beside the empty pitcher.

Herwodis raised her voice, its deep resonance echoing through the stone hall. "Claudia? Frithelinde? Mathilde? Somebody bring out food and drink, please. Sigifrith is home!"

A few moments later two of Herwodis' serving maids came in, Mathilde carrying a platter of bread and cold meat and Claudia taking the pitcher out to fill it. Gratefully Sigifrith plunged into the food with both hands, spraying crumbs as he chewed until he noticed the cynical twitch of his mother's lips. He gulped twice and began to eat at a more measured pace, as Ragin had taught him, cutting the meat neatly with his new knife, which he turned this way and that to display.

"I see Ragin has managed to teach you some manners," Herwodis said. "Did you make the knife yourself?"

"All by myself," Sigifrith answered, before honesty forced him to admit, "Ragin helped a bit." He wiped the blade off and handed it, hilt first, to his mother. She weighed the knife in her hand, then tested the edge with her thumb.

"The balance is a little off," she said critically. "Other than that, it's very good."

"I had to grind it in a hurry," Sigifrith said. "I'll know better when I go back."

"I don't think you should expect to go back soon," his mother told him. "Thank you," she said to Claudia as the dark-haired servant returned with the pitcher and poured a golden-green stream of the wormwood-flavored wine that Herwodis brewed in the Frankish style into two of the goblets.

Sigifrith sipped gingerly, trying not to wrinkle his nose at the faint hint of bitterness that underlay the fruity sweetness of the wine. "Why not? What's supposed to happen? Are you going to send me to the Burgundians for fostering?"

"Oh, no. No, Alapercht feels that it's time for you to start learning your duties as a ruler, now that Ragin has trained you to behave more carefully. We are hoping Ragin will stay here with us and continue to teach you, since he seems to have taken such a surprising interest in you. Of course, as a kinsman of mine, he is always welcome in our hall, and a smith of his skill would be greeted joyfully in any case." Her gray eyes met Sigifrith's glance firmly for a moment. "I expect you to mention this to Ragin, if he should fail to recognize the length of the welcome I give him."

"I will," Sigifrith promised. He took a bolder swallow of his drink, letting the warmth of the wine and the deeper glow of the wormwood soothe his road-sore body. "What about your wedding, then. Will you tell me more about my father?"

Herwodis' eyes were hooded as those of an old falcon as she studied her son. She was quiet for so long that Sigifrith began to wonder if he had accidentally said something awful.

"My father gave me a choice between two kings," Herwodis said finally. "I was lucky then—though far luckier after Sigimund's death, when Alapercht took me away from the battlefield and offered me another honorable marriage. A king's child, daughter or son, very rarely has a choice in these matters. As a man, you will be able to bring your wife to your own lands, but Alapercht and I will almost certainly choose her for you. Nor will she have a choice; remember that, if you should be less happy with the woman we pick than we would want you to be. Also, the honor of your kin and the peace and strength of your lands, which are upheld by treaties and the bonds you forge with other folks as much as by your own strength, are more important than the way you feel about your marriage bed."

"All right," Sigifrith agreed. "I understand that. But I'm not getting married for years yet, am I? Not till I've had a chance to prove myself in battle?"

"No, but you need to be aware of things like this. The treaties we hope to make with the Burgundians in the next few days are . . . very delicate. I won't say more to you now because I don't want you to be too disappointed if things don't go altogether as we expect—and I don't want difficulties to be caused if you discover that you dislike any aspect of the negotiations. Can I put my trust in you without having to say more?"

"Of course."

Herwodis patted her son on the shoulder. "Anyway, you'll spend most of the time with the Burgundian children. King Gebica and Queen Grimhild have three—"

"Gundahari, Gundrun and Hagan," Sigifrith finished for her. "Hagan's a bit younger than I am—he must be the youngest—and the other two are close to my age, right?"

Herwodis' lips curved in approval. "That's right. Gundrun was born near the beginning of the winter in which you were born, and Gundahari is a year older than she."

"And Hagan's the strange one," Sigifrith went on proudly. "Although I like him . . . I think."

If Herwodis was surprised, no hint of it showed on her dignified, heavy-jowled face. She only regarded her son calmly as she said, "And where did you learn that?"

"I met them in an inn along the way. I was pretending to be Ragin's apprentice, and no one recognized me except Hagan, and he promised not to tell anybody." Then Sigifrith clapped his hands over his mouth, remembering. "And I wasn't supposed to tell anyone either," he admitted, feeling his cheeks heat with shame. "But you won't let anybody else know, will you? I trust you," he added, staring hopefully at his mother.

"A secret more than one knows . . . "

"Is not a secret at all. I know."

"You do realize how much harm a prank like that could do if you boast about it to anyone else?" Herwodis persisted.

"Hagan said it was important for me not to," mumbled Sigifrith. "I really don't see . . . it was Ragin's idea for me not to tell anyone who I was. And then he went and hid himself somewhere when the Burgundians showed up. But what harm could it possibly do? It was just a joke. I wouldn't mind too badly if someone tricked me like that."

"If you tell anyone, you'll have cast shame on the Burgundian royal family by making them look like fools. Then, for their own honor, they'll have to start fighting with us again."

"Oh." Sigifrith turned his glance down to the smooth gray floor, staring at a long crack in the mortar between two flagstones. An ant trundled along an invisible pathway leading out of the crack, along its side in an arching loop and back down again.

"Sigifrith," his mother said, more softly. "Not everyone is as strong or as sure of themselves as you are." She rubbed her sore ribs ruefully. "Try to keep that in mind and be careful of what you say in the next few days."

"I will," Sigifrith promised. "Where's Alapercht?"

"He's gone hunting with some of the thanes." As Sigifrith started to stand up, she laid a hand on his shoulder. "You're not going after him. You need to stay here so that we can get some feast clothes ready by tomorrow—and first you need a bath."

"Urhm," Sigifrith complained, but he sat back down.

Sigifrith was sitting inside the hall with King Alapercht and his thanes, waiting for the midday meal to be brought out, when the sentries' horns—the brassy tubas taken from the Romans—blew the warning note of strangers in the land. Alapercht rose unhurriedly from his seat and gestured for his men to follow him out. Those thanes who owned swords carried them at their sides; but the peace strings were tied over the hilts and the men wore no byrnies in token of their assumed trust in the Burgundians. Sigifrith, newly dressed in an embroidered red tunic that his mother and her women had spent half the night cutting and stitching to fit him, a blue summer cloak rippling lightly down from his shoulders, took his place by King Alapercht's side as the warriors arranged themselves before the door of the hall.

The Burgundians began their show of fine riding well before they reached the foot of the hill. Like the Alamanns, some of them wore swords, but they had put away their byrnies as a sign of peace and the shields they carried were white. Alapercht's men shifted, murmuring to one another. As Sigifrith had been, they seemed evenly split between awe at the eastern folk's skill and amusement at the little steppes horses that wheeled and leaped or reared under the light touches of the Burgundians' reins, behind the proud banner of Gebica's golden boar.

"Gebica!" they shouted as they thundered to a stop below Alapercht's hall. The Sinwist, the king and his family rode to the front of the band halfway up the hill, leaving the throng of their warriors below. Courteously, as a gesture of respect to his host, Gebica dismounted before he reached the top, giving his reins and those of Grimhild's horse to his head gudhija, who sat as still and erect as a wooden post in his saddle. The Gebicung children followed their father's example, walking behind Gebica and Grimhild in the sudden silence. Sigifrith suddenly became aware that all three of the young Burgundians were watching him. Hagan stared with the same straight, unnerving gaze that had met Sigifrith's eyes at the inn; Gundahari, though his step was as wide and confident as his father's, turned his glance away when Sigifrith looked at him. The eldest Gebicung clenched his hands on his green tunic's hem, crumpling and uncrumpling; his mouth worked in a sudden tic, as though he were chewing on the inside of his cheek. Gundrun held her short, squarely built body very erect, smiling slightly, her long honey-brown braid swaying as she walked. She met Sigifrith's eyes for a moment, then glanced away with the excessively casual grace of an embarrassed cat.

"Alapercht," said Grimhild, stepping forward before her husband could speak. She favored the Alamannic king with a brittle, polite smile, patting absently at the back of the dark braids coiled around her head. "I'm so glad to be able to meet you. I gather this is your—son, Sigifrith?" There was no trace of Burgundian in her voice; she spoke with a Frankish accent as clear as Sigifrith's mother's.

Sigifrith bowed courteously. It seemed to him that he could feel a thrill of tension running through his stepfather's body, but Alapercht's voice was perfectly calm when he answered.

"Indeed he is. And your children, Gebica? Gundahari, Gundrun, and . . . ?"

"Hagan," Gebica supplied, patting the youth's arm. Sigifrith saw Hagan twitch, as if to shake off the touch. Hagan, thought Sigifrith: hedge-thorn. That's a strange thing to call a king's son. I wonder what his real name is?

Herwodis and two of the thanes' wives, Hilde and Herware, came out of the hall bearing tall glass goblets of wine, which they offered to the Burgundian couple, then to Alapercht. "Be welcome here, King Gebica and Queen Grimhild," Herwodis said, her voice very soft. "You and all who come with you are welcome guests in the hall of King Alapercht of the Alamanns."

"We thank you for your gracious hospitality, King Alapercht and Queen Herwodis," Gebica responded. Though he spoke slowly and clearly, his thick Burgundian accent made him difficult to understand. He tossed back his head, the golden torc beneath his thick chestnut beard glittering in the sunlight, and drained the goblet. Alapercht drank with him, but Grimhild only sipped at her wine. The gla ss rang softly as she tapped a pointed nail against the goblet's conical bowl, considering Sigifrith and his stepfather.

Sigifrith thought that Alapercht breathed more easily as Herwodis tilted her pitcher to pour more wine into the kings' glasses. "We have a garth readied for your horses," the Alamannic drighten said. "If you wish, my thanes will show your men to it."

"That is kind," Gebica agreed. He gestured to the Sinwist, shouting something too rapid for Sigifrith to understand as Alapercht's warriors began to file down the hill toward the Burgundians, leaving the two royal families alone together before the hall. Alapercht opened the door, gesturing Gebica and his wife and children in under the watchful eyes of the stone walkurja and her fearsome shield. Thralls were carrying in more heavy wooden benches as the serving maids and some of the thanes' wives readied the hall for the evening feast and laid out platters of bread and cheese for the warriors to eat during the day. The Alamannic king brought his guests to the end of the hall, where the high table stood on a raised dais of stone under mosaic tiles in an elaborate pattern of blue and white circles and squares. Sigifrith hung back, following Gundahari, Gundrun and Hagan in. The youngest Burgundian glanced back at him suspiciously, but said nothing.

When the two families were seated, Gebica, a piece of bread in his hand, leaned against the wall and looked at the children. Sigifrith and Gundahari had already started to eat; Gundrun and Hagan sat neatly with their hands folded in their laps, backs very straight—Gundrun proudly, her strong chin lifted, her shoulders squared to display the pin of filigreed silver and garnet just above her right breast; Hagan like a sentry keeping watch. Gebica coughed lightly, then he looked across the table into the Alamannic king's eyes. "Alapercht," he said, "why don't we let the children go off together and get to know each other on their own? After all, we won't get to . . . well, their part in anything . . . until the feast tonight anyway. What do you think?"

Grimhild looked at her husband, then at Sigifrith. Her glance felt to Sigifrith as though she was stroking him softly with a hundred nettle leaves at once. There was something about her that made him feel uncomfortable—as though he ought to know something, though he couldn't put a name or a shape to it.

"Gebica," she said warningly, "do you think that's proper? Gundrun is, after all, of an age that might be prone to . . . misunderstandings. Not that I would mistrust your Sigifrith, Alapercht," she added, "but a young girl's name is a very fragile thing, and especially at this . . . critical juncture." She shrugged expressively, favoring Alapercht with a smile as bright and brittle as clear ice in winter sunlight.

"She'll have her brothers to protect her," Gebica said heartily. Then he spoke very softly, so that even Sigifrith's keen ears could barely make it out under the sound of Herwodis raising her voice to direct two of the thralls as they moved a bench across the hall. "You know Hagan has the sense to keep her away from anything that might look even slightly questionable, and the gods know nothing can distract him from what he thinks needs doing. Don't be so worried, Grimhild, my precious."

"You insist," Grimhild said.

The Sinwist entered the hall, blinking his half-blind eyes against the shadows within; behind him followed the Burgundian warriors and Alapercht's thanes. He came up to the high table without waiting for an invitation; Alapercht graciously gestured him to sit as Herwodis poured wine for him. Grimhild's eyes flickered nervously up to his long, deep-graven face. He nodded slowly, the flow of silver hair from his topknot swaying like a willow in a slight breeze.

"Very well," the Burgundian queen murmured. "Alapercht, is your son ready to be a host to our little horde?"

"I'm sure Sigifrith would be more than glad to show your children around our land," Alapercht said, looking significantly at Sigifrith, who stood up at once, a hunk of bread in one hand and a piece of cheese in the other.

"Of course I would," Sigifrith agreed. "Come on," he said to the Burgundians. "Let's go."

The four of them walked out through the throng of warriors in the hall and down the hill, stopping at the large pen by the edge of the wood where the Burgundian horses were chewing peacefully on hay and oats. Sigifrith and the others stood considering each other for a moment before Gundahari spoke.

"I'm Gundahari, and these are Gundrun and Hagan," he said, rather unnecessarily Sigifrith thought, and stuck his arm out for Sigifrith to clasp. Silently Hagan followed his example, his face a frozen mask. "What is there to do around here?" the elder youth went on. "Any good hunting? We went on a boar hunt at the beginning of last winter and I helped to kill it, but I got this." He pulled the sleeve of his green tunic back to show a long pink scar down his forearm.

"He was very lucky," Hagan said. Something in the eerie resonance of his harsh voice was almost beginning to remind Sigifrith of something, though he couldn't think what. "If you hadn't turned when Gebica shouted at you, you would have been badly gored."

"But I did, didn't I?" Gundahari replied, smiling. "Hagan's always worried about something," he explained to Sigifrith. "Not only does he worry about what is happening and what might happen, the way other people do, he also stays up at night worrying about things that have happened."

Gundahari pushed his brother affectionately; Hagan shoved back and the two scuffled a moment, Gundahari laughing, Hagan grim.

"Is he always like that?" Sigifrith whispered to Gundrun while the Gebicungs pummeled each other. "Doesn't he ever smile?"

"You mean Hagan?" Her voice was shadowed by a soft veil of resignation. "No. He's been like that all his life."

Gundahari and Hagan stepped apart, straightening their tunics. "Can you wrestle?" the older youth asked Sigifrith.

Sigifrith grinned, feeling more at ease. "I can," he answered. "Can you?"

"Try it and find out," said Gundahari. The two of them circled each other for a moment, then Sigifrith sprang. Gundahari braced himself well against the attack; the two of them grappled a moment until Sigifrith bent his opponent over backward by brute force and threw him down, landing with a knee in the thick, knotted muscles of the Burgundian boy's stomach. "I give in," Gundahari gasped. He got up, dusting himself off with an astonished look on his open face. "Shit, you're strong. You're even stronger than most of the men in my father's warband, and he's got the best fighters north of Rome."

"The Alamanns are the best fighters north of Rome," Sigifrith contended. "But I could wrestle down half of Alapercht's warband before I left for fostering last Winternights, and I bet I could beat the rest of them now. You want to try me, Hagan?"

"I'm supposed to be watching out for Gundrun, not playing," Hagan said roughly.

"You're afraid, that's all. You think you'll get beaten like your brother was."

"We'll see. I suppose we're safe enough here." Hagan crouched down, wary as a wolf, sidestepping Sigifrith's leap with blinding speed and grabbing his arm. Sigifrith shook the smaller youth off easily, but Hagan's foot was already between his legs, tripping him up. He grabbed the other boy, throwing him down as he fell himself. To Sigifrith's surprise, he could feel the links of a byrnie beneath the red wool of Hagan's tunic. The two of them rolled over in the grass, each trying to get on top. Between Sigifrith's strength and size and the chain-mail weighing Hagan down, it was hardly an even fight;

in a few moments, Sigifrith was twisting the other's wiry arm up behind his back and kneeling on his legs. Hagan tried to buck him off, but the Burgundian was exhausted from the effort of wrestling in mail and Sigifrith had him well pinned.

"Give up?" Sigifrith asked. Hagan shook his head, trying to twist away. "Come on, you know I've got you." He pulled on the youth's arm. Hagan's breathing sounded a little harsher, but he said nothing.

"He gives up," Gundrun said quickly, a faint nasal note edging her alto voice. "Let him go, you're going to hurt him."

"Nod your head, if you don't want to say it. You don't have to be ashamed of yourself, you put up a good fight," Sigifrith coaxed, beginning to feel embarrassed by the whole thing.

With an effort, Hagan turned his head to glance at Gundahari, who nodded. "Say it, Hagan."

"I give up," Hagan admitted. Sigifrith let go of his arm and lifted him to his feet. "We'll try it again sometime," he went on.

It was impossible for Sigifrith to tell whether the other meant his words as a threat or a friendly promise. He looked closely at Hagan's face, trying to see if he could find any lingering hostility. Ragin had warned him that his strength could make enemies for him if he were too proud.

Sigifrith smiled brightly at Hagan. The Burgundian stood still for a moment, as if he were trying to remember something. Then his lips slowly pulled back to show his sharp white teeth, the corners of his mouth twitching with the strain. At first Sigifrith thought Hagan was snarling at him; then he realized that the other youth was trying to smile. He felt oddly complimented, as though Hagan's attempt at friendship was more of a tribute to his own prowess than his earlier surrender.

"Let's," he said, and Hagan's face relaxed into its normal frown. "Why are you wearing a byrnie, anyway? No one else in your band is—you're supposed to be coming in peace, aren't you?"

"I always wear it. It's good practice for fighting and besides, you never know when someone might decide to attack."

Ragin, thought Sigifrith. I knew he reminded me of someone. "You really are a thornbush, aren't you? Is that truly the name your father gave you?"

"Yes."

"Why isn't it something starting with a G?"

Sigifrith got his hand up just in time to block Gundrun's slap as she flew at him. "You leave my brother alone!" she snapped. "Don't Alamanns have any manners?"

Sigifrith grinned at her and held his hands out in surrender. "I'm sorry, Hagan. I didn't mean to make fun of your name, honestly I didn't."

"My mother chose it," Hagan said. "It's all right, Gundrun." He drew her aside, whispering something, his slanted eyes flickering warily toward Sigifrith's.

Gundrun clenched her fists. For a second, her dangerous frown matched her brother's. "Well, he shouldn't say things like that when he's just met you."

"What about flytings, then? Warriors are supposed to be able to defend themselves with their wits. It's as silly for you to get angry when someone teases me as . . . as it would be if you put on a byrnie and started to fight for me."

"Well, you and Gundahari better not get into any fights while I'm here, then, because I will," Gundrun flared at her brother.

Gundahari, standing a little way back with his fists on his hips, broke into a hearty laugh. "They're always doing that," he said to Sigifrith. "When you marry her, you'd better watch out. Our sister is a wild woman . . . a real walkurja."

Sigifrith's mouth dropped open. "Marry her? I'm not—"

Gundahari clapped his hands over his mouth. "Oops. I wasn't supposed to—"

"You weren't supposed to," Hagan said, "but now that you have, I think he'd probably better be aware of what's going on, if only so he can respond presentably at the feast tonight. Assuming, that is, that the negotiations go as expected."

"Respond presentably? You mean instead of fleeing in terror?" Gundahari chuckled. "All right, Sigifrith. You must have wondered why we came with our father's warband, and now you know. You're supposed to be betrothed to my sister as part of the peace between us. They're probably haggling over the dowry at the moment."

Sigifrith looked at Gundrun. Her fair skin went very red and she glanced downward, her pale blue eyes slipping away from his gaze. "They weren't supposed to tell you," she said. "You were supposed to . . . oh, I don't know." She turned around and ran up the slope to the hall, as nimble as a young doe. Hagan followed her with rather more dignity.

"Moon blood," Gundahari said softly, with a wicked sideways glance at Sigifrith. "What do you bet?"

He saw the confusion on Sigifrith's face and laughed, shaking his head. "You'll find out soon enough, I guess. It's something to do with the Moon—he drives them mad once a month. Hai, you're shocked about finding out you're going to be betrothed, aren't you? Our parents told us because they didn't want us messing things up. They didn't want us to say anything to you because they thought if we started talking about it to anyone here, it would make some sort of difference to what they hoped to gain. Perhaps your parents didn't want you to be disappointed if it didn't work out, or something."

"Perhaps," Sigifrith said slowly.

"Don't worry. You won't have to get married for a few more years, at least not until you have thanes and a hall of your own. They're looking for a wife for me, too, but none of the other kings around us who might be allies have daughters yet. I'll probably get stuck with some barbarian princess from so far north she's got icicles hanging out of her nose. You're lucky to be getting Gundrun—I think. She's got a pretty fierce temper on her."

"So I noticed," said Sigifrith dryly. "Why does she think she's got to protect Hagan? He seems to be able to take care of himself."

"He can. Better than the rest of us, I think sometimes. But older sisters . . . you know. No, you don't, do you? Why don't you have any brothers or sisters?"

"Grandmother Perchte—King Chilpirich's frowe—says I was too big when I was born, and something inside my mother broke so she can't have any more children. She was awfully lucky to have lived through it."

"How do you stand being all alone?"

"I've never thought about it, really. And I'm not actually alone that often. I train and go hunting with my father's thanes and their sons, and my foster-father Ragin is around a lot. Actually I was staying with him up on the Rhine when we got the message that you were coming. We passed through your lands on the way back," Sigifrith added. Then, remembering what his mother had told him, he stopped abruptly before he could say too much.

"Ragin? Ragin the Smith? The dwarf?"

"You know him?"

"He's our uncle. Sort of our uncle," Gundahari amended quickly. "Hagan could tell you all the generations if you wanted to know; he's better at remembering stories than I am. If his voice weren't so awful, he could be a skop."

"If you say so," said Sigifrith dubiously. "What's wrong with him, anyway? Why's he so . . . ?"

Gundahari glanced around. Only the little steppes horses were within earshot, watching the two youths through the wooden fence of the pen with mild interest as they flicked flies away with dark coarse tails or chewed reflectively on bits of hay. "That's one of the things we're not supposed to talk about outside the family, but you're going to be part of the family so maybe you need to know. Look, I don't want anyone hearing this who shouldn't. Are there any places nearby where we can talk?"

"Come on," said Sigifrith. He and Gundahari walked over the meadow, stepping around piles of horse dung and stopping every so often to pick the sweet red strawberries that dotted the grass, their white starlike flowers gleaming from clusters of deep green leaves. Sigifrith led his new friend to the creek that wound around the slope below the hall, following it upstream into the woods where it widened out to run shallow over a bed of pebbles. Finally they reached the bottom of a small hill where the burn sprang from beneath an overhanging ledge of yellowish sandstone streaked with the glistening white of quartz. "Down here. Now what's the deep, dark secret?"

Gundahari looked him in the eyes for a moment, his wide-cheeked face very earnest. A tic jumped at the side of his mouth, as though the muscles were fighting against each other. "All right. I want you to understand first that I'm telling you this for a reason, so you won't tell anyone else. Occasionally people say things, and I hope that once you know the truth you'll

STEPHAN GRUNDY

be able to head them off, for the sake of Hagan's reputation—and our family's. Do you understand?"

"I understand," said Sigifrith.

"All right. We don't think Hagan's actually Gebica's son."

Sigifrith could feel his jaw dropping. He closed it. "No wonder Gundrun got so angry with me," he said slowly. How could I have missed it? he thought then.

"It's more than that, actually. Our father acknowledged him, and it's often the way of our folk to share the kingship between brothers or sometimes even cousins anyway, though one is usually first over the others. It wouldn't make any difference, I don't think, except there's this other thing."

"Which other thing?" Like Ragin, he thought again. A sudden, ludicrous image of Ragin and Grimhild in bed together came to Sigifrith's mind, and his laughter pealed out across the splashing stream. "He's not Ragin's son, is he?"

A giggle broke out of Gundahari's mouth. He struggled to contain his mirth for a moment, then gave up. "That dwarf's just the right height to find Grimhild's . . . " The two of them laughed together for a moment, but Gundahari sobered quickly. "Actually, you're getting pretty close. Nobody except Grimhild knows for sure who his father is—or what. Our cousin Giselhari's father, who is a Christian, said once when he was very drunk that Hagan was the child of some sort of unholy ghost that the Christians believe in. But Gundrun says she's heard people saying that he was fathered by a mirk-alf at the Winternights feast when Grimhild went out alone to the rocks by the Rhine to make sacrifice to the alfs, and we think that's what most people think. But there's never been any proof that he's not Gebica's son, except that Mother insisted on his name. Nobody ever thought he wasn't until a couple of years after he was born. Anyway, we try to put down the rumors when we hear them, which I hope you will now, too."

Sigifrith shifted beneath the shadow of the stone, pulling off his shoes and dipping his bare toes into the cool water that bubbled up from the roots of the hill. "Why should you be worried about it?" he asked, then, suddenly, "It's true, isn't it? When I first saw him, I felt . . . " For a moment he tried to think of words to describe what he had felt at the inn when he first met Hagan, and failed.

"Frightened?" Gundahari supplied. "That's how most people feel about him." The Burgundian loosed the ties around the jagged tops of his own shoes, splashing his feet into the burn. Absently he picked up a flat rock with his toes, which were remarkably long and agile, and skipped it once downstream.

"Not frightened," Sigifrith insisted, shaking his head. "I like him, I think, but I could sort of feel that he wasn't . . . well, that there was something eerie about him."

"But you won't tell anyone."

"Not since you don't want me to. I don't think it's so bad. Maybe if Hagan weren't so worried, it wouldn't make any difference to him either."

"That's the other thing. Don't tell him I told you. If you do, he'll be furious with me and you won't be able to get three words out of him for the rest of our stay. It embarrasses him, knowing that other people know."

"I won't tell him," Sigifrith promised.

"Or Gundrun either. If she doesn't tell him straight away, she'll start shouting at you or me, and then he'll find out. The boy's got ears on him like a wolf's, and I swear he can hear through stone, especially when someone's talking about him."

"I gather that was meant to be a compliment," Hagan's harsh, eerie voice said from above them. Sigifrith and Gundahari both started, looking up guiltily. Hagan came out from between the fir trees on top of the little hill, his slender bare feet braced against the rocks. Farther back, they could hear the sound of Gundrun's alto swearing as she trod on something sharp. "I got here," he went on, just after 'Don't tell him I told you.' " He climbed down gracefully, stopping only to brush his fine black hair out of his eyes. "Which I assume means that you did tell him, to the accompaniment of the usual assurances that he won't tell anybody else. Am I right?" Hagan looked directly at Sigifrith. The eerie tingle ran through Sigifrith's spine again, and he stared at the other till Hagan dropped his eyes.

"You could be right," Sigifrith said. "So? I'm not King Alapercht's natural son. Really, in a way, I was born in captivity, which is a lot worse than being whatever you are."

"Thank you so much," Hagan said, his words carefully spaced to give the impression of a sarcastic inflection.

"Sigifrith!" Gundahari hissed. "He doesn't need that!"

"Sorry. But my mother was captured by Alapercht while she was carrying me. It doesn't bother me, and I don't think you have anything to be ashamed of, either."

"I am ashamed neither of myself nor of my father," Hagan said. "However, I have difficulty enough without that particular thing being known any more widely than it is already, and having my birth thrown in my teeth by the simple-minded really makes me very angry." He stared significantly at Gundahari, then glanced swiftly at Gundrun as she limped over the top of the hill. "Have you hurt yourself?" he asked her, seeming to dismiss the whole subject.

"It's not bad," she said. "I stepped on a sharp rock."

"Let me look at it." He climbed to her, kneeling down and turning her foot up. She balanced precariously on the other leg, an irritated expression on her strong face. Sigifrith could see to her knees beneath her white gown. If I were just a little closer, he thought.

Gundahari snickered. "Stop looking up my sister's dress, Sigifrith," he whispered. "You'll get your chance to see everything soon enough."

Sigifrith felt a warm flush coming to his cheeks. He swatted at Gundahari, who brushed his hand away and poked him in the stomach.

"You're bleeding," Hagan said to Gundrun. "I'll take you down there to wash it out."

"Hagan!" she squealed. "What in Frija's name . . . ? Hagan, don't, I hate it, you'll drop me!"

Ignoring his sister's protests, Hagan swept her up in his arms and began to carry her down the hill.

"Put me down, damnit!" she shouted, trying to wriggle out of his grip.

"Be quiet," Hagan grunted. "If you keep squirming around, you'll make us both fall." For a moment he teetered on an edge of rock, but he recovered his balance and made it down to the side of the creek without dropping his burden. Carefully he set Gundrun down on a large boulder by the side of the spring and crouched again to tend to her foot. "It needs bandaging." He reached to the edge of his tunic, about to tear a strip off.

Gundrun grabbed his wrists. "Don't you dare," she told him. "That's your best feast tunic, and Mother will be furious with you if you ruin it."

"All right," Hagan conceded. "How are you going to get back to the hall, then? I suppose Sigifrith could go and fetch your shoes and some bandages."

Sigifrith stretched himself to his full height, grinning. "You can't be too heavy, if Hagan can carry you around. Don't worry, men, I'll take good care of your sister."

"I wouldn't," Gundahari warned. "She'll hit you. She hates being picked up."

Gundrun edged back on the rock, putting up her fists in a fighting stance. "Don't you try it, you . . . you Frank. If you want to be helpful, you can go and tell Ildiche to get my shoes out of my baggage again. No, you go, Hagan. You saw where I put them, and Ildiche couldn't find her own feet without a guide."

"I'm supposed to stay with you," Hagan insisted. He looked at Gundahari and Sigifrith. "Why don't you two go?"

Gundrun tossed her head irritably. "Oh, never mind." She held her foot up to show the little tear in its dark-calloused pad. "It's stopped bleeding already. You can stop making such a fuss over it now, I'm not crippled for life."

Sigifrith shook his head in bewilderment, secretly wondering for a moment if he would be marrying into a mad clan. "Are you all right?" he said to Gundrun. She gritted her teeth together in frustration, glaring up at him.

"You're a bunch of fools," she said to them. "I stepped on a damn stone, that's all. You'd think the Muspilli had come, or something, from the way you're acting." Gundrun dipped her feet in the stream, eyeing them as though daring them to say anything.

"You Alamanns fight very well from horseback," Hagan said flatly after a few moments. "And raise horses. Will you show them to us? My brother is very good at riding."

"I'll be glad to," Sigifrith said, relieved. The four of them started back, the boys walking slowly to keep pace with Gundrun's limp.

Sigifrith took the Burgundians around the pens where Alapercht's horses were kept: the fighting stallions in their separate enclosures; the geldings and mares for riding and work; the brood mares which Alapercht kept carefully barred away from accidental contact with amorous studs; and, in a high-fenced garth of her own, his prize mare Harifaxa.

"She's never dropped a foal that wasn't one of our very best," Sigifrith said proudly, reaching through the fence to stroke Harifaxa's deep brown nose. The mare lipped gently at his hand to see if he might have brought her an apple or pear. Finding nothing, she raised great liquid eyes reproachfully to Sigifrith's face. He patted her fiery gold forelock. "All her fillies are brood mares and her colts are war stallions."

"If she's such a fine breeder, why hasn't she got a foal now?" Gundrun asked.

"It's her one fault," Sigifrith admitted. "She doesn't always catch in season—Hrodkar says she'll only foal if the stallion's seed is strong enough. She was being rested last year, and this year nothing came of the breeding. Come on, I'll bring you in so you can see her better."

He opened the gate in the tall wooden palisade and led the Burgundians through, latching it carefully behind him. The beautiful mare paced deliberately over to him; though her step was slow, there was no laziness in the crisp sound of her gleaming hooves against the earth. Sigifrith petted her glossy neck as she butted her forehead against him. "There, there, my frowe," he murmured to her, blinking back the first prickling of tears as her warm touch brought home to him how he had missed the horses—and Harifaxa especially—in his half-year with Ragin.

"Why do you have her penned up like this, when the others are in plain garths?" Gundahari asked. "Is it to keep the wrong stallions away from her?"

"She jumps over the other fences, or else kicks them down, and we can't keep her tied when the weather's bad. Hruodgar—he's our Master of Horses—says she's really a witch with runes of unbinding hidden in her mane somewhere. And she's as strong as any fighting stallion, too—you can see that just by looking at her. If she weren't a mare, and if she weren't far too valuable as a brood mare to risk, Alapercht would ride her into battle himself."

"Is it safe for us to be in here with her?" Hagan questioned, stepping forward to get between Gundrun and the large mare.

"Perfectly safe. She's also the cleverest horse we have, and the best trained. Watch." Sigifrith vaulted lightly onto Harifaxa's back, nudging her into a full gallop. They circled around the palisade a couple of times. The wind of their running whipped his hair and Harifaxa's mane and tail back, tearing the shout of joy out of his mouth. He leaned this way and that as though brandishing a sword in battle, the subtle movements of his knees and feet guiding Harifaxa through a mock fight where she dodged, spun, kicked and finally reared to her full height to batter an invisible foe with her hooves. At another touch, she dropped down and trotted lightly over to stop beside the Burgundians. Sigifrith, flushed and exhilarated, slid down from her back.

"Can I try that?" Gundahari asked.

"Please do."

Gundahari heaved himself up. Although it was clear to Sigifrith that the

Burgundian horses must be trained quite differently from their own, Gundahari managed to get Harifaxa to trot, then canter, then gallop, holding his seat with sturdy confidence. "The Huns shoot from horseback, you know," he shouted as Harifaxa tore past. He mimed shooting an arrow at a crow that was flying overhead. "How did you get her . . . to do that other stuff? The fighting?"

"You've got to be trained as well as the horse," Sigifrith shouted back. Gundahari slowed to a walk, nudging Harifaxa over to him. "There are signals with the knees and things, see."

"I guess it's the same as with ours. Holy Engus, she's fast. Do you ever race her, or ride her out or anything?"

"My mother rides her when we go to the halls of other kings or athelings, but racing and horse fighting are for stallions."

"I want to try riding her," Gundrun said. Reluctantly Gundahari got down and lifted his sister up, supporting her as she arranged her skirts. Harifaxa started off at a light, bouncy walk, as she was accustomed to do when Herwodis rode her. Gundrun smiled brilliantly at Sigifrith, urging the mare to a trot. "She's wonderful! It feels strange to be riding up so high, though." The Burgundian girl stroked Harifaxa's neck as she rode. "Yes, you're a beauty," she murmured to the horse. "Ever so much prettier than our little ponies. A bit faster, now?"

"No," said Hagan. "Not without a proper woman's saddle." He locked eyes with Gundrun, as if daring her to disagree. She flushed and looked down. "It's my turn, anyway."

Gundahari helped Gundrun off and Hagan walked to the horse, who sniffed cautiously at him. He edged away from her muzzle, as though expecting her to bite, and in one swift movement he had leapt to her back. For a moment Harifaxa stood stock-still. Then she raised her head, a ring of white showing around her black eyes, and snorted, pawing the ground with one forehoof. The horse began to run, clouds of dust thundering up from her hooves as she tore around and around the pen. Hagan clung to her back tightly, his face a lightning-pale blur. For a moment, Sigifrith stood enspelled by the storm of wildness he had accidentally unleashed within the horse's garth, the pounding of Harifaxa's hooves almost drowning out the distant sound of Gundahari and Gundrun shouting.

Sigifrith shook the dizziness from his head. The mare, he saw, was gathering speed for a final leap that might take her over the high wooden posts of her enclosure—or might not. As she neared the fence, he ran in front of her.

"Down!" he shouted, his high voice cracking like lightning splitting a tree. Harifaxa stopped short, frozen in place, and Hagan quickly slid down from her back. Sigifrith laid a reassuring hand on the Burgundian's shoulder. A shock of trembling thrummed against his palm, shaking through him with an echo of nameless, familiar wildness, so that he could only stand and stare at the other for a moment. Hagan twitched the touch off, stepping away.

"What did you do to her?" Gundahari asked his brother, at the same moment as Gundrun said to Sigifrith, "Why did she do that?"

"He must have stuck his heel into her the wrong way or something," Sigifrith said slowly. "She's very sensitive to that sort of thing. Are you all right, Hagan?"

"I'm fine."

"Why don't we go on back, then? I expect you're getting hungry. Even if we have to wait for the feast, we can probably scrounge something from the kitchen."

"I'm hungry," Gundrun agreed. "Since I didn't start grabbing food at midday like some people did." She looked accusingly at Gundahari, then at Sigifrith. Suddenly her eyes widened as she stared over Sigifrith's shoulder. The blood ebbed from her face, then flowed back in a red flush. "What are you doing here?"

Sigifrith turned his head. Behind him stood the tall figure of the Sinwist, as thin and dark as a withered tree against the pale sky. The old man's mist-whitened eyes lighted on Sigifrith for a long moment, his long fingers making a curious gesture toward the youth.

"The tent has been readied," the Sinwist said. His voice was very deep and soft; it seemed to Sigifrith that its undertones reached down further than he could hear, twining and coiling about like roots beneath the earth. "You shall come with me."

"Why?" Sigifrith asked boldly. "What do you want?"

"Before the betrothal is spoken, I must see the will of the gods and the ghosts in this matter. They who have kept and warded our holy kindred since we fared forth from the farthest Northlands may not be scorned, or else our kingly line shall come to an end and our folk go under forever."

The Sinwist laid his hand on Sigifrith's shoulder. Light as its weight seemed, Sigifrith felt that the gudhija's grip would not be easily shaken off. Still, it was not the Sinwist's strength that turned him to follow the old man, but his own wish to know more.

The Sinwist's tent, a low structure of brown hides stretched over gnarled tree branches, had been set up in the woods some way from Alapercht's hall. Half-hidden by the bushes and tree shadows, it might at first glance have been taken for the slumped body of a stag or aurochs, but a thin curl of greenish smoke rose from its flap. When Sigifrith came closer, he could see the four whitened skulls set at its corner. Two horses' heads grinned emptily at him; two boars' skulls still threatened with curling tusks.

Supple as an adder coiling into its hole, the Sinwist crouched down and disappeared between the hides. Sigifrith followed more slowly, careful not to bump into any of the branches that held the tent up. He could feel how delicately it was balanced, each stretching of hides and crossing of stakes set against another to the very least finger-brushing of pressure.

It was very hot inside the skins, stiflingly dark except for the low glow of coals in the middle of the tent. Sigifrith felt sweat prickling out over his body, thousands of burning droplets melting together to run down his face and back. The Sinwist's robes and topknot shadowed black against the darkness; the coals cast no light on his face.

"Now we shall see," the old gudhija murmured. His voice grew softer and softer as he spoke, until Sigifrith felt that he was not hearing it with his ears any more, but only as a soundless murmuring through the bones of his skull. "The eagle sits at the top of the tree; his wings blow the wind from the east. Long ago we dwelt in the North: we were one kin with the Gauts, we who dwelt in Burgundarholm. Then you led us onward, holy ones: we fared forth, south over sea, south into the steppes. Still the eagle sits in his ancient stead; his wings blow the wind from the east."

The Sinwist leaned forward, sprinkling a handful of something to flare up on the coals. The smoke that rose from it was sweet-scented, but burned roughly in Sigifrith's nose and throat. Sigifrith put his hand over his mouth, trying to stifle his cough as he strained to hear the gudhlia's words.

"Eldest Gaut, you ancient one, Ansus who fathered our folk, look upon us. Engus, remember us; your boar tusk ward us, your wisdom lead us. Halja, wise frowe, loose your thralls and let them speak: give tongue to the runes of the dead. You ghosts who dwell about us, you who dwell in the hallowed stocks and hallow skulls, come and give rede: tell me what I will know."

The Sinwist cocked his head as though listening. Sigifrith heard only the whisper of the long hair falling against his rough linen robes and the crackling of the leaves on the coals.

Then something else rustled in the darkness. Sigifrith heard a brushing as of feathers against leather, and the Sinwist brought his hands up. There was something between them, something that moved and struggled until the gudhija twitched sharply, snapping the thing he held. Now it lay limp, but his hands were still moving, tugging until something gave way and dark blood dribbled out to hiss blackly on the coals.

"Food for you old ones," the Sinwist whispered. "Come now, you ghosts, come and feed. You who have become snakes in death, you who are eagles; you who dwell in the roots of the tree, you who nest in its highest branches." He laid down the thing that bled and sprinkled more leaves on the coals. Their smoke sparkled lightlessly, rainbow colors bursting against the darkness. Sigifrith's head was swimming now, numb warmth wrapping his limbs. Small bones clicked and rattled in the Sinwist's hands, spattering onto the earth before the coals. At first the runes were black against the white bone, then Sigifrith saw the flames springing forth from them, searing their shapes onto the backs of his eyes.

"*Fehu, gebo, perthro*," the Sinwist chanted, touching each of the carved bones in turn: ᚠ ᚷ ᛈ. "Wealth causes strife among kin, but here it is wedding's lust, and here it is set in the Well. Aaaah . . ." His sigh hissed around Sigifrith's ears, rising to the rushing of wind through bare branches. "I must know more. These runes are grim runes, their riddles hiding them from me. Who will speak with me? Who?"

He pushed the small corpse onto the coals. Its feathers flared in a bright stink that set Sigifrith coughing again until the Sinwist's cold dry hand brushed over his mouth to still him. The meat caught fire more slowly, blackened skin crackling and bubbling under the twisting flames.

Like a scattered pattern of ruddy leaves on the ground leaping suddenly to a fox's shape in the eye, the sound of the fire eating the dead bird resolved into words—words spoken by a swift high hissing voice of flame. Sigifrith knew that he had heard it before, but could not think where. He leaned forward, trying to hear more clearly.

"I will speak to you, old man, for you have called me rightly; but you'll never train this boy to your ways. Where is the youth who should be by your side, to be Sinwist after you? I think you've given up hope for the Burgundian kin already, haven't you?"

The Sinwist's voice was as still and dark as an unstirred pond. "I know you well enough, Sly One. I have heard your taunts before. You never tire of scorching where you are bidden to warm, or doing harm where there is need of your help. Even so, I have called you rightly, and you have come. You know what I will as well as any of the wights. Tell me what should lie before this betrothal, if it is made now: the betrothal of Sigifrith and Gundrun, before the gods and ghosts."

The flames writhed like bright snakes, and Sigifrith could smell the bird's charring bone; but the voice in the fire was silent for so long that he began to fear he had lost the hearing of it.

"Much is yet to be shaped," the fiery words hissed at last. "Wyrd is yet to be known, for the hero may turn it again in his moment of might: that is the meaning of the *perthro* rune you cast here. I can tell you only what might be, if your work is wrought rightly. Bind Sigifrith to your kin, for only so will the hoard of the Rhine come to Gundahari in Worms, and only so can the Burgundians gain rule over the dragon's gold. I say to you that the bonds wrought now shall not lightly be broken. Go on with the wedding, and set your might to bringing it about: this is the rede I give you. Leave it be, forsake the betrothal, and the Burgundians shall dwindle and become a forgotten folk, nor shall any stead in the Middle-Garth ever bear their name: the Gebicungs shall go under unknown."

"What sign do you give me for trust, Sly One? You are not best known for your troth."

"The gray Wolf I fathered gapes at the gods' dwelling; but the fetter that binds him is yet unshaken, nor shall its edges fray while the World-Ash stands. The great Wyrm I fathered lies in the sea, ringed about the Middle-Garth; though Thonar's Hammer scathed his head and the waters run black with bale-filled blood about that wound, he lives yet and shall wind the Middle-Garth while the World-Ash stands. I swear by them that I have given you good rede, and that you cannot hope for a better. If you do not trust me, trust in the fetter that binds the Wolf; trust in the Hammer that struck the Wyrm. I swear by them that I have given you good rede, and that you cannot hope for a better. You shall not find a better husband for Gundrun, and if Sigifrith is wedded to her, he shall bring it about in time that Gundahari has the highest atheling-bride of the Northern folks."

The Sinwist was silent; the flames were burning down again, dying away from the charred corpse on the coals. At last the fire voice spoke again. "You know that Wodan blended his blood with me, in the earliest days: why should I be foe to his will?"

The words died down with the last of the flames. At the same time, Sigifrith felt his limbs easing as though he had set down a heavy burden. The smoke no longer rasped in his throat, and the sweat streaming down his face and back felt as soft as warm summer rain. Whatever had been there was gone: the old man and the youth were alone in the tent again.

Suddenly a strong gust of wind tore the flap aside, shaking the tent as it swept a great drift of smoke out. The wind was as cold as winter through Sigifrith's wet hair, sharp in his aching lungs. He arched his shoulders back in a careful stretch, yawning as though he had just awakened.

Sigifrith crawled out of the tent and got to his feet. For a moment he saw the Sinwist's hand against the brown leather; then the gudhija had pulled the tent flap closed behind him. Sigifrith waited a few moments to see if anything more would happen, but he could hear nothing from within, and his stomach was feeling more and more empty. He turned to trot toward the hall, wondering whether the Gebicungs had been able to steal or beg any food from the kitchen.

The tables were carried out after the feast and the benches pulled closer together for the beginning of the symbel. Alapercht and Gebica sat together in the center of the raised dais, Sigifrith to his stepfather's right and Gundahari and Hagan to the Burgundian king's left. On Hagan's other side sat the Sinwist; Ragin sat at Sigifrith's right hand, as silent as a squat boulder, only his eyes glittering from his craggy face to show that he lived. Of the women, only Herwodis, Grimhild and Gundrun stayed in the hall, bearing wine to the athelings gathered there. When all the cups were full, Alapercht rose to speak the first toast.

"To Ziw, who metes out battle-victory to the worthy!" the Alamannic king called. Many echoed him; others, trusting in their own might and main, drank to Donar.

As he had been taught, Sigifrith raised his glass to toast Ziw according to the Alamannic custom, but the wine caught the torchlight, gleams of orange and yellow fire melting and swirling within, and as he stared at it he heard his own voice whispering, "To Wodan, for victory's gift."

Gundrun came to refill his goblet, her trembling hands clinking the lip of her pitcher against his glass. Impulsively Sigifrith put his hand over her smaller one, squeezing it reassuringly for a moment. She bit her lip, then smiled fleetingly at him before she pulled away.

Alapercht made the next toasts as well, to Nerth and Nerthe and to Fro

Ing for peace and fruitfulness. Then Gebica rose to stand beside him, planting his thick legs well apart as he clenched his glass in both fists and spoke for all the hall to hear.

"King Alapercht of the Alamanns, our fathers were foes, as were their fathers and their fathers before them, since before the time when we warred over the springs of salt. Now the time has come for our strife to end, as we dwell together again under the roofs of the Romans. What gift do you offer us as a sign of peace that all men may see its bond?"

"I will give twelve of the best horses of the Alamanns, nine mares and three stallions, and two of the thralls who know best how to tend them. What gift do you offer, Gebica, Hending of the Burgundians? What do your folk have that might be worthy of our steeds?"

"The horses of the steppes are for those with the blood of the steppes," Gebica answered. "But the house of Gebica has a greater treasure than horse or hoard. See our open-handedness: to weave peace between us, I offer this treasure to your clan." He put a heavy arm around Gundrun's square shoulders, drawing her forward to stand before Alapercht and the assembled men. She shook her long hair back and stood very straight, the firelight staining her white dress with shifting patterns of glowing orange and yellow, glittering from her silver brooch and the gilded hilt of the eating knife at her waist and gleaming deep red from the smooth garnets of her girdle clasp. "Behold Gundrun, my daughter! As a sign of our peace, I give her to your son Sigifrith as betrothed, to be wed when he has gained a man's full years and fame. And she shall be dowered with sixty ounces of gold and twice that of silver, and with four and twenty of the best cattle that none shall say our kin lack in wealth. So shall the years of strife between our folks be at an end with this oath: hereafter we shall aid one another in war and in peace, as sworn kin should."

"Let the gods and goddesses hear us swear it!" said Alapercht.

The Sinwist rose from his place at the end of the bench, bearing a heavy arm-ring of twisted gold to the two kings. Each of them laid a hand upon the metal, lifting their goblets. "Before Tius and Fro Engus, Donars and Wodans, Frija and Fulla, and all the mighty ghosts of our folk, you have spoken. Do you swear to hold to your words, by your blood and your lives?" His deep whisper carried throughout the hall like a rustle of wind through fallen leaves.

"I swear it," said Alapercht.

"I swear it," said Gebica, his accented voice sounding like a rock-distorted echo of Alapercht's in Sigifrith's ears.

"Then the holy ones now hear!" the Sinwist said. The two kings drank together, pouring half of the draught in a pale stream over the oath ring.

Alapercht raised Sigifrith to his feet, bringing him forward to stand beside Gundrun. The two fathers joined the hands of their children as the knobbly fingers of the Sinwist traced a complex sign over their heads.

"Sigifrith and Gundrun," he said, "I bind you by your fathers' oaths. By the runes of frith wrought by the Gebicung's gift in this wedding that our folks shall ever win battle-victory together. So shall it be!"

"So shall it be!" the assembled men echoed. The fiery glimmer of the glasses around him as the host drank dazzled Sigifrith's eyes for a moment. He held tightly to Gundrun's hands, only realizing that he might be hurting her when she pressed her lips together hard and glared at him. Guiltily he loosened his grip.

Grimhild gave her daughter a full pitcher of wine, with which Gundrun refilled Sigifrith's glass again. Everyone was staring at him, waiting to see what he would do. He put an arm around Gundrun's shoulders and drew her small body closer to him. "Drink to my betrothed, Gundrun, the daughter of Gebica!" he called out, his high voice ringing clear and hard against the stone walls. "Before we are wed, I shall have done such deeds and become such a hero as to be worthy of the highest of atheling-maids!"

He drank as Burgundian and Alamann alike shouted approval of his brave words, a heady roar that rushed through him with the warmth of the wine. Exhilarated as Sigifrith was, he was aware of a faint glow of unease beneath his boasting, as unreal as the half-seen green foxfire glimmering from the depths of a horn full of dark, yeast-muddied ale. The shadowed curve of his mother's lips as she watched him was wistful; Grimhild's smile was as brittle and polite as before. Gundrun glanced up at him, her squarish face suddenly softening into a look of vulnerability. He hugged her gently before he went back to his place and she began to pour out drink again for the men who now rose by rank to hail the gods and those kinsmen who had gone before them, or else to make boasts that they would now be sworn to fulfill.

3

THE COLT

A few white flakes of snow glimmered through the blackness of the early Yule morning, hissing to nothingness in the heat of the torch Sigifrith held as he stood watching his mother mount her mare. Harifaxa tossed her head and whinnied, her hooves crunching through the thin layer of snow on the ground. She stepped lightly out of her pen, responding perfectly to each nudge of her rider's knees or touch of the reins along her proudly arched neck. Even Herwodis, heavy as she was, was no burden for the great mare, who shook her fiery mane with eagerness to be off. Alapercht's bay stallion seemed as pale as a ghost in the darkness as the king rode up to Sigifrith, who vaulted lightly up behind him, holding his torch carefully out to the side. He could see crystals of snow twinkling from the deep brown fur of Alapercht's bearskin cloak, a few of them beginning to melt under the warmth of his own breath.

"Ragin says the weather won't get worse before nightfall," Alapercht called to his wife, his voice carrying sharply through the frosty air. "We won't have any trouble getting to my father's hall."

"That's all right, then," Herwodis said. "I've never known Ragin to be wrong about the weather. Will he come with us?"

"He's in the wain."

Sigifrith looked over to the road, where the glowing torches were beginning to cluster around a large dark shadow as the thanes of Alapercht's guard came up, waiting beside the wain for their king. Herwodis and Alapercht turned their steeds, nudging them into a perfectly matched trot as they rode down to meet their band of picked warriors. When they had satisfied themselves that everything was as it should be—that the gifts they had chosen for Chilpirich and Perchte were packed away in the wain where Ragin, Herwodis' maidservants, and Hilde sat, that everyone who was coming was there and ready to go—the two of them rode to the front of the procession, the clear light of the torch in Sigifrith's hand burning like a beacon to their followers.

The Rhine was running swiftly, his churning waters broken every so often by a dead tree limb or a chunk of ice. A big, flat-bottomed barge waited by the river's shore, its shape misty in the lightening dimness of the morning. Sigifrith heard a few groans from the thanes behind him as they dismounted: it would take all of them to ferry the wain and their steeds across the Rhine to Chilpirich's lands. He took up his oar with the others, waiting till he heard Alapercht's command "Pull!" through the anxious neighing and stamping of the horses. The barge glided slowly across the river, its weight and the strength of the men who rowed it holding it steady against the rushing fury of the waters till it jarred to a stop on the other shore.

"You can sit in the wain with Ragin if you'd like," Alapercht offered as the warband began to disembark and remount. "He'd probably like someone to help with the driving."

Sigifrith raised his head, sniffing at the clean, cold morning air. Far above, the light veil of clouds was beginning to break up, showing pale sky streaked with the first yellowish pink brightness of dawn. "Maybe a little later," he said. From inside the wain, he heard Hilde's giggle above Ragin's low indistinguishable mutterings of annoyance.

After the midday meal had been eaten, Sigifrith moved to the driver's seat of the wagon, taking the reins in his hands and clucking the two chestnut geldings who pulled it into a brisk walk. The snow on the ground was getting deeper as the small band rode higher into Chilpirich's lands, along the road that wound and twisted through the high pines. Sigifrith could hear the twittering of birds calling from tree to tree in their hidden speech like the music of tiny wooden flutes. The breeze was swiftly strengthening, becoming a biting wind; Sigifrith tasted the steely scent of coming snow on it and looked up to the heavy gray clouds rising above them like crags of shifting stone.

"I thought you said the weather wasn't going to get any worse before nightfall," he said teasingly to Ragin, who huddled beside him, wrapped in the heavy fell of a wolf. The dwarf turned to glare at Sigifrith from the dark cave of his fur cloak's hood as the youth went on, "Has the cold frozen your weather-wisdom?"

Sigifrith's foster-father coughed, spitting neatly between the two horses. "The snow won't fall till after nightfall," he croaked. "We'll be able to get to Chilpirich's hall and inside before dark. Are you afraid of being out in the woods at night? Are you afraid of what might come riding between the worlds of the dead and the living? Of the hunger of the Hunt?"

One of the women behind them made a muffled noise of terror. Sigifrith laughed. "Why should I be? I'd like to see it."

"Don't say that!" Hilde said. The plump wife of the thane Heriman put her arms around herself and shivered inside her red woolen cloak. "Ragin, Sigifrith, you're frightening me."

"It's ill luck to talk about things like that at Yule time," Mathilde added. "It might . . . well, I wouldn't go outside the hall tonight for twelve ounces of gold."

Sigifrith looked back in bewilderment. "Why are you so frightened? It's not even dark yet, and you're acting like a bunch of rabbits."

Hilde, Mathilde and Frithelinde glanced nervously at each other. Only Claudia murmured, "Barbarian superstitions," but she looked down at the floor of the wagon and her voice trembled as she said it.

"Would you stay out tonight?" Frithelinde asked her sternly. For a moment Claudia was still, then she jerked her head in a quick shake.

"Men say," Ragin muttered, "that those who see the Wild Hunt must either go mad or ride forever with the host of the dead—without rest, without hope of rebirth, howling through the worlds in their endless strife until the Muspilli come to the doom of the gods. Doesn't this frighten you?"

"And why should it? Walhall isn't supposed to be a hall of peace either, and those who fight there are as mighty as any mad ghosts," Sigifrith answered.

It seemed to Sigifrith that a glint of tooth gleamed from the dwarf's mouth, but whether Ragin smiled or grimaced, the shadows of his wolfskin cloak hid his face from Sigifrith.

The gray sky was rapidly darkening by the time Alapercht's band rode up to the door of Chilpirich's hall. A comforting glow of firelight shone from within as the old king walked out in dignity to greet his kin, embracing Alapercht and Herwodis as they got down from their horses, then turning to Sigifrith. Chilpirich's hair and beard, which Sigifrith had remembered as heavily silvered black, were grayish white now, and he moved more slowly, but his grip was strong as he clasped the youth's arm, stepping back to look up into his face for a moment.

"I believe your boy is growing to fulfill all I expected of him," Chilpirich said softly to his son, then, louder, "Come in, all of you, and be welcome." The women scurried from the shelter of the wain into the warm hall as Alapercht and his thanes began unloading the gifts.

"Hai! Sigifrith," Hildkar called, crouching at one end of a long wooden box which, Sigifrith knew, held fine glasswork. "It's too heavy for one."

"No, it's not," Sigifrith answered, heaving the box onto his shoulder with a grunt.

"You drop that, you're going to die," Hildkar warned, hovering behind him as he carried it into the hall. "Your mother will carve the blood eagle on you if you break anything."

Sigifrith laughed, easing his load down onto the table. "Everyone's got to die some time, but this isn't it for me. Anyway, if I can't trust my own strength, what can I trust?" He lifted his head, sniffing hopefully at the scent of roasting meat that filled the hall.

"You can trust the fact that glass breaks if you drop it," Hildkar said darkly. "You can also trust the fact that you're going to have to help see to the horses before we eat anything. Umm, and you can pretty well trust that it's as cold as week-old shit out there, too. Come on, the sooner we get it over with, the sooner we can get back inside."

The two of them went out to help guide the horses into the crowded barn. Despite the cold outside, the bodies of the horses, cattle and pigs that filled the building made it cozy, if smelly; when Sigifrith and Hildkar came out again, the wind flayed their unprotected faces with an icy knife and cut through their woolen cloaks. Together they ran back to the hall, Hildkar shivering, Sigifrith laughing with exhilaration from the shock of the cold.

Chilpirich's hall was adorned for Yule with branches of holly, the red berries bright among the thorn-edged leaves. Thick beeswax candles burned from green wreaths of fir woven with twining ivy, their light gleaming from nutshells and deep red apples; more dark-needled wreaths hung on the walls. Herwodis, Ragin and Alapercht were already seated by Perchte and Chilpirich at the head of the central table and an empty place awaited Sigifrith between his foster-father and Alapercht. He hurried to them, scuffling through the herb-scented straw on the earthen floor. Perchte stood to hand him a polished white horn with silver binding its rim and the end of its black tip. Its smooth curve was very warm in his hands, the rich scent of ale heated with butter, honey and pieces of apple rising from within.

Perchte stretched up on tiptoes and Sigifrith bent to kiss her before she raised her own horn to him. "Hail Sigifrith, and wassail!"

"Drink hail!" Sigifrith answered, and drank. The sweet ale was good and strong, its warmth flowing out through his whole body. "And merry Yule, Grandmother."

Perchte hugged him around the waist, her touch as light as the brushing of a leaf. "Merry Yule, darling. My, you really are almost a full-grown warrior now, aren't you, with an atheling bride betrothed, and I hear she's a very pretty girl as well. I can hardly believe that it's been fourteen winters since you were born here in this hall—fourteen to the day, even!" She looked up at him proudly. Her blue eyes were as bright as he remembered, although her fine skin was veiled with a sunken net of a thousand tiny wrinkles.

As often, Sigifrith had no idea what he should say. To hide his confusion, he took another drink of the ale and hugged Perchte very carefully, amazed at the fragility of the old woman's thin bones beneath his hands. He was about to speak when the singing started at the other end of the hall.

> Battle-tusk, earth-   turning plough,
> Yule blitheness   blesses he,
> Bristles fierce   as fire's glow,
> Ingwe's keen, bright,   kingly boar.

Four of Chilpirich's thanes—two burly men with big black beards, whom Sigifrith knew were brothers, though he had forgotten their names, one tall young man with wildly curly yellow hair and a smaller, older warrior—had begun to bear a roast boar wreathed with rosemary and apples around the hall on a huge wooden platter. Sigifrith took his place and joined in the singing as the gathered folk rose, one by one, to touch the boar in his round.

> Round the hall   runs Ingwe's steed,
> (Battle-tusk, earth-   turning plough),
> Holy boar, the   hero-helm,
> (Yule blitheness   blesses he)
> In the coldest,   cruelest night,
> (Bristles fierce   as fires' glow),
> Shines his gold   to shield his folk
> (Ingwe's keen, bright   kingly boar).

> Battle-tusk, earth-   turning plough . . .

When the boar reached Sigifrith and he stood to touch him and speak his oath, he saw that hazelnuts had been put in for the swine's eyes and an apple thrust into his mouth, his yellowed tusks curling up on either side of the fruit as if to guard it. "I will remember," Sigifrith said softly, beneath the noise of the song.

> Now we bear the   slain boar round,
> (Battle-tusk, earth-   turning plough),
> Wreathed with apples   aye for life,
> (Yule-blitheness   blesses he)
> Only tried hearts   in troth brave,
> (Bristles fierce   as fires' glow)

This boar may carve   and keep his worth,
(Ingwe's keen, bright   kingly boar).

Battle-tusk, earth-   turning plough . . .

As everyone sang the last chorus, the four thanes stood before Chilpirich
and set their burden down on the table in front of him. The old king raised
his knife and traced the sign of the whirling sun-wheel over the boar in
blessing before he plunged the blade in. Chilpirich carved off the hero's
portion first and held it up, drops of sizzling fat dripping onto the table
from the rich meat.

"For my son Alapercht, who has wrought mightily in his own lands this
year!" he said. "Would anyone here challenge?" Only cheers and friendly
laughter answered him as he set the meat on a platter and gave it to his son.
Thereafter he carved off portions for each in turn, which Perchte, Herwodis
and Hilde carried around the hall. "And does your wife," he asked Alapercht
as he carved, as he had asked at every feast for as long as Sigifrith could
remember, "still take drinks of milk from the cows every morning?" His lips
curved beneath his beard, and Alapercht laughed.

"The ring her father gave still grows cold on her finger at dawn," he
answered, as he always did.

Sigifrith was about to start pestering after the story of their strange re-
marks again, but when Perchte set a platter of hot pork in front of him, its
scent rising to his nose and starting his mouth watering, he could think of
nothing more interesting than stuffing the meat into himself as enthusiasti-
cally as he could, though his awareness of the silent heaviness of Ragin at
his left side kept his bites no larger or messier than courtesy allowed.

Some of the gifts—most of those between family and friends—were given
before the symbel had begun; others waited upon the oaths of the drinking
rounds. When the toasts to Ziw or Wodan, Donar and Fro Ingwe had been
made and the toasts in memory of the dead or boasts of deeds past and
deeds to be done were raised by each man in turn, Sigifrith stood to make
his Yule oath and drink on it before the gods and the men gathered there.

"I swear to become a hero worthy of my father and my line!" he called
out. He raised the horn to his lips and drained it in a single long draught,
gasping as he lowered it. Alapercht beamed proudly at him; but Ragin
glanced up as warily as a wild beast, and the flickering of the candlelight
cast a veil of shadowy sadness over Herwodis' face.

Chilpirich drew a spiral ring of gold from his arm, holding it up to glitter
in the candlelight. "Sigifrith of the house of Chilpirich," he said, his deep,
slow words weighty as the metal in his hand, "you have come to a man's
age and a man's strength. Son of the house of the Alamanns, will you also
take your place as a thane in the warband of the Alamanns, helm of the
kings Chilpirich and Alapercht?"

"I will," Sigifrith said, taking the ring and slipping it over his wrist and
halfway up to his elbow. The smooth metal binding his arm was still warm

from Chilpirich's body when Perchte refilled his horn from her new glass pitcher and Sigifrith drank on the oath with the two kings.

It was not much longer till the wind of Alapercht's yawn put out one of the candles, and not long after that when the rest were blown out and the men began to curl up in the blankets they had brought with them, muffling themselves against the cold. Sigifrith, too, wrapped himself up and lay down near one of the low-burning fires with the other thanes. He could hear the wind rushing through the pines, moaning low and eerie over the roof of Chilpirich's hall as the men inside settled down into a deep sleep. Only Sigifrith lay awake in the dark hall, the hairs prickling on his arms with the thrumming of the hidden lightning through the air.

A sudden banging jerked Sigifrith out of his blankets and to his feet. He pulled his cloak over his shoulders and raced on tiptoe to see what it was. The biting wind tore the door open beneath his hand, whirling his cloak in a shower of snowflakes. He heard the banging again, more loudly, and knew that it was coming from the barn where the horses were kept. A shock of memory shot through him: Harifaxa would not stay tied or penned when the weather was stormy; she must be trying to kick her way out. And what would become of her if she got lost in the blizzard? He pulled the door of the hall shut against the wind and ran blindly through the driving snow and the darkness, finding his way to the barn by memory till a flash of lightning lit the driving whiteness with an eerie glow and showed him the black shadow ahead. A crack of splitting wood echoed the thunder's roar as something huge and dark tore out of the barn and past Sigifrith, knocking him flying to land on his back in the snow.

The blood was hot and sweet in his mouth as he got to his feet, gasping the breath back into his lungs, and began to run into the woods after the fleeing horse, crying, "Harifaxa, Harifaxa!" The wind swept his voice away, its cry rising to an echoing moan like a pack of dogs or wolves howling in full throat through the pines.

In only a few moments, Sigifrith had lost all sense of direction. He halted for a moment, panting, straining his eyes through the blind night for any trace of the lost mare. Then a white flash of lightning seared his sight with the stark blackness of the wind-whipped trees against the whirling torrents of snow and the sound of a hunting horn rang through the thunder and the gale, its irresistible wod trembling along Sigifrith's veins till he lifted his head and howled at the storm. Looking up, he could see the far-off glowing of the wolves' red eyes through the snow, the streaming clouds in the tree tops twisting and writhing into the shapes of the mirky riders, their dead faces shining pale through snow and night as they spurred their misty steeds on. And before them stormed the mighty figure of Wodan on Sleipnir, the ghost-gray horse's eight hooves flying wildly through the sharp pines and his rider's dark cloak streaming out behind into the wind like the long hair of the wolf-riding women around him, the mad walkurjas whose piercing song shrieked their blood-lusting wod through the storm.

The Wild Hunter raised his horn and blew it again as his one glinting eye fixed on Sigifrith. The youth rose to his toes in a burst of eagerness as though hoping for the wind to lift him up. He could no longer think as the dark ghosts rode down toward him, the black wings of ravens beating around his head in the wind and the harsh coats of the wolves brushing around his body like the needled branches of firs as he ran—or did he ride, swept up in the wod that whelmed him, mad with the brightness of the lightning burning sharp through the howling snow of the storm? A high clear voice shouted wordlessly into the wind, crying out in wild longing and joy as he rode screaming through the night sky, the deep pounding of hooves beneath him beating the dark madness of the Hunt up through his body. Now he ran as a wolf with hot blood in his mouth; now blood streamed from his open throat as he howled between the doors of life and death, lost and hungry, following the night-shape of a raven who wheeled through the flashes of lightning above. Then the black branches of a yew tree whipped around him, its hidden fire glowing deep and steady. He reached out to catch hold of it, and tumbled into the snow with a thump that knocked the breath from him.

Sigifrith was not sure how long he had lain there—not long: despite his trembling he was hardly cold—but the sky was beginning to grow light when he grasped one of the yew's branches and used it to pull himself to his feet. He gasped with disbelief as he saw the shadow of a horse through the tree's needles, and hurried around to the other side. Harifaxa stood there, one back hoof tilted in rest. Her fiery mane was twined with the yew's green needles and red berries. Wonderingly, he stared at her, putting out his hand to touch the warm solidness of her neck. She leaned her proud head toward him, nudging affectionately at his shoulder.

"I hope you remember how you got here," Sigifrith said to her, his voice a hoarse, raw croak. He warmed his numb hands against her neck for a few moments before hauling himself onto her back, clinging tightly to her against the cold that was beginning to creep into his bones. "Go on, Harifaxa, go home."

The mare began to walk surely, if slowly, through the deep snow, lifting her feet no higher than she needed to. The wind and snow had hidden any tracks they might have left, but Sigifrith trusted the mare to choose her own way, letting her strength bear him back from the woods to the hall. Now and again he rubbed gingerly at his throat; he could still feel . . . teeth biting through as he ran through the forest of Gautland in a warg's hide, the long wandering in the dark, and beside that the grief and guilt of his long watch by the death-wounded wolf's body. "Sinfjotli," Sigifrith murmured; then, although he could feel his lips splitting in the dry cold, he smiled in quiet joy. No more memories came back to him, but now, as he wrapped his arms around his thumping ribcage against the icy breeze, he could feel their deep roots waiting unshaken within, and was content for the time.

By the time they got back, the Sun was well up, her light shining whitely through the winter sky and glittering off the fields of snow. Sigifrith could hear the sound of men's voices shouting, "Hai! Sigifrith! Where are you?" as he rode nearer. He nudged the tired mare lightly, and she raised her head, lifting her feet into a high-stepping trot.

"Hai! Hildkar!" he called as he rode up behind his friend, the words rasping up from his throat. Hildkar jumped, whirled and then, to Sigifrith's shock, let out a horrible shriek, his angular face going dead white as he stumbled backward.

Sigifrith stared at him, completely taken aback. "Hildkar? Are you all right?"

The young thane, panting for breath, did not answer for a moment. Then he shook his head, rubbing furiously at his eyes with his knuckles as color flooded back into his cheeks. "I must have been looking at the snow too long," he muttered in embarrassment, then, "Shit, Sigifrith, you startled me, that's all. I'm fine. What in Ziw's name did you think you were doing, riding off before dawn without telling anyone?"

Sigifrith sat collecting his thoughts together for a moment. "Why not?" he said finally, turning Harifaxa toward the barn where a group of men stood by the broken door, shaking their heads.

"Last night was a bad one, for sure," one of Chilpirich's older thanes said. "The wind could have done it. I've been saying for weeks that door needed fixing."

"Look here," said a thin warrior whose blond hair stood up in a crest on one side where he had slept. He pointed a chapped red finger at the split boards. "That was broken out from inside. One of the horses must have wanted out pretty badly."

Sigifrith dismounted and led Harifaxa in as the men stared at him. The mare went placidly to her place and began to munch on some hay.

"You know anything about this, Sigifrith?" Alapercht's thane Adalprant said to him. One side of the warrior's brown-stubbled face smiled, as always, where the huge scar slashing across his cheek had drawn his lips up; the other corner of his mouth was turned down.

"It was broken when I came out before dawn," Sigifrith said truthfully. "I think Harifaxa did it during the storm."

"Likely enough," Adalprant grunted. "What were you doing out at that hour, anyway? Well, go on in. I think your mother's starting to worry about you."

Sigifrith hurried back to the hall, his stomach growling as he went. He was glad to help himself to some bread and cold pork and to sit on a bench by one of the fires as the warmth soaked into his body.

"Where were you this morning?" Herwodis asked him as she came to sit beside her son. She spread a red cloak over her knees and began to stitch along the border, her embroidery following the faint traces of interlacing chalk marks.

"I felt like going out for a little ride. Harifaxa broke down the barn door," he added.

Herwodis sighed. "Your hair's a mess." She stuck her needle into the cloak and drew her gold comb out of her belt pouch. Sigifrith ate while his mother pulled the comb carefully through his tangled mass of hair. Every so often she tossed a few pine needles and bits of stuff to hiss in the fire. "Are you sure you weren't doing anything else?" she asked after a while.

Sigifrith put his hand up to cover a wide yawn, wincing as his cracked lips split again. "I'm sure," he said.

For the first time since Sigifrith could remember, Harifaxa did not come into season near winter's end when the other mares did. Alapercht shook his head in disappointment, lifting the mare's tail to look closely for any signs of her readiness to breed as she stamped a front hoof impatiently on the icy ground.

"Maybe she's waiting for the thaw," he said.

In less than a moon the icicles had all dripped from the eaves of the hall and the muddy earth was green with new shoots of grass, but Harifaxa was still stubbornly unready, and stayed so, unbred that year. Though Alapercht often stood looking at her through the fence as though his reproachful gaze could bring the mare into season, his hopes came to nothing: she never showed the least sign of heat, nor did the stallion that he led into her pen take more than passing interest in her. It was a great surprise to everyone when after Winternights, Harifaxa's belly and teats began to swell. Because of her size, she had always been late to show; now Alapercht pressed knowingly along her stomach and nodded, sighing in relief that his fears of her barrenness had been unfounded.

"She'll drop a foal before Yule," he said, frowning at the strangeness of it. "One of Chilpirich's stallions must have gotten to her when she broke loose—I should have known better than to put her near the other horses there."

"What else could you have done, dear?" Herwodis asked him as she brushed the mare's dusty coat.

Alapercht shrugged his thick shoulders, straightening up. "She's never gone into season that early before. Well, we'll see. Still, I would have thought I would have noticed. And it's more than odd that she should be foaling in winter. I've never known a mare to drop at that time of the year; they need the grass of early summer for their milk. Sigifrith? You didn't see any sign of her being ready to breed last Yule, did you? Or anything strange about her?"

Sigifrith had been helping Hrodkar to mend the hinges on the gate of Harifaxa's pen. He glanced up at Alapercht, shaking his head. "I don't think so," he said slowly. "Except kicking the barn door down, but I guess that's not strange for her."

"Hmph. Anyway, a foal of hers won't be too much of a waste, whoever its father was. My father's got some fine stallions, too, but I'd like to know which it was. I'd planned . . . well, next year." He brushed back his sandy hair and patted the horse briskly on her neck. "Always had a mind of your own, haven't you, old girl?"

It was a bright clear day a little before Yule when Sigifrith heard the anxious whinnying from the stables. His boots crunching through the thick fur of frost on the hard ground, he hurried to see what was wrong.

Harifaxa lay on the stable floor with her legs spread apart, straining to force her colt out of her grossly swollen body. Her dark coat was lathered with sweat and froth dripped from her nostrils and mouth as though she had been ridden far longer and harder than even her great strength could bear; the fresh straw Hrodkar had spread was already wet and dirty beneath her. Sigifrith could see the foal moving beneath her taut hide, kicking against her in its struggle to be born. Hrodkar knelt between her legs, frowning, with two rope-ends in his hand, and Sigifrith crouched down beside him: they might soon have to tie the ropes around the colt's forelegs and pull it out together.

Harifaxa heaved, opening wider: Sigifrith saw something dark and slick pressing outward then sinking in again as the contraction ended. The other mares were beginning to stamp and shift restlessly, as though they sensed that something was wrong.

"All right, darling, all right," Sigifrith crooned to his mother's mare. "Push, go on, you can do it." He clenched his fists, trying to will some of his strength into her. She heaved again, then raised her head with an odd whickering moan. Hrodkar rocked back on his heels staring at her bloody dilation.

"Wouldn't have believed it," he grunted.

"What's wrong?"

"The foal's too big for her. Only seen this a couple of times before, with little pony-mares bred to a big stallion. Afraid we'll have to cut if it doesn't come out soon." He raised his voice, shouting at the top of his lungs. "Hariwolf! Get in here now, you useless turd!"

The door banged open and one of the stableboys hurried in. "What . . . ?"

"Run for Alapercht—go on, run! Get him in here now!"

Harifaxa shifted on the straw, nostrils flaring and breath coming more harshly as she strained over and over to get her foal out through the passage that, wide as it was, was still too narrow for it. A sudden wave of dizziness swept over Sigifrith; he leaned against Harifaxa for a moment (as the darkness in his skull suddenly brightened to the misty, dreamlike sight of a woman attended by shadows, clutching at a sword's hilt as she struggled to give birth, as he felt the hilt of a knife and the rough wood in his hands, carving runes to bring the child out). One rune, one strange name, glowed in his mind as he breathed deeply, trying to steady himself before tracing, as he half-remembered, the upright stave with its two slanting downstrokes,

, and whispering softly, "Ansuz . . . ansuz . . . ansuz . . ." It seemed to him that a soft wind was blowing through him, out through his mouth and down through his hands into Harifaxa, as he sang the galdor-song of the rune to open the way and bring the new life forth from the hidden worlds.

Harifaxa tossed her head and screamed as her womb suddenly tore open and the foal struggled forth in a great gush of hot black blood. A gust of wind rushed past Sigifrith's head, banging the stable door, and the mare sank down to the earth below, the dark pool spreading out from under her as her foal wobbled to its feet. Without thinking, Sigifrith did as he had seen his father and Hrodkar do so many times: rubbed the caul from the newborn's nose and mouth so that it could breathe, tying a knot in the slimy cord that ran from foal to mare, and biting it free. He wiped the smears of thickening blood from his face, swallowing the salt taste in his mouth. Hrodkar was kneeling by Harifaxa, but even as Sigifrith looked, the horsemaster straightened up, shaking his head grimly.

Alapercht rushed in, slowing as he saw that it was too late. Gently he took Sigifrith by the shoulder, raising him up. "You've done a fine job," the Alamannic king said to his young thane. "Look, it's a healthy colt."

Sigifrith didn't answer.

"No one could have done better," Alapercht went on softly, as though he could read the thoughts Sigifrith had not even spoken to himself yet. "It's not your fault."

But it is, Sigifrith thought. He did not know how or why it had happened, but he was sure that he had somehow been the cause of Harifaxa's death, and the guilt swelled to a hard lump beneath his breastbone as Alapercht patted him on the back.

"Strangest thing," Hrodkar muttered, shaking his head as he looked down at the mare's corpse. "We'd better get her out and shovel this up before the blood smell soaks in too deep—no, there's milk in her teats yet, and a colt seldom thrives if it doesn't get a share of the birthing milk early on. Later we can put him in with Whitenose, since she's still nursing." The horsemaster got a bucket and began to milk Harifaxa's body, muttering under his breath as he did.

When Hrodkar was done, Sigifrith silently bent down, locking his arms around Harifaxa's chest and beginning to pull her out. Hrodkar crouched to help him, but he shook his head.

"I'll . . . do it myself," Sigifrith panted.

"Sigifrith, don't try. You'll strain yourself," Alapercht warned, but Sigifrith pulled at Harifaxa until it finally became clear to him that he could not move the mare's body more than a few inches by himself. In the end, the men had to drag her from the stable and out onto the icy ground by her hind legs. Sigifrith wanted to weep, but could not; his head throbbed as though the tears were bound up hot and aching behind his eyes.

When Sigifrith went back in to help clean out the stable, Alapercht and Hrodkar were watching the new colt warily. The milk-bucket was empty, the colt moustached with a ring of white froth, and a new bruise was already swelling purple on the fair skin of Alapercht's arm.

"Can't lead him if we can't hold him," Hrodkar grunted. "Have to bring Whitenose here."

"Mmph," Alapercht agreed, still staring at the colt and rubbing his arm. "I'd like to know which stallion sired him. I've never seen a newborn kick like that before."

"We're going to have Loki's own time breaking him," Hrodkar warned. He took the manure shovel from the wall and dug it into the sodden straw and blood-soaked earth, leaning on it with all his weight. "If he lives that long."

Without speaking, Sigifrith took the shovel from him and began to dig furiously, flinging the dark mud out the door as Alapercht and Hrodkar cautiously herded Harifaxa's colt toward the mares.

When he had shoveled all the blood out of the stables, Sigifrith went into the forest and began to collect dry branches for a pyre. He broke and tore at the wood with his hands until his own blood was running freely, the pain of the scrapes fresh and hot through his cold-numbed fingers. Only then—hands muffled in his cloak so that his mother would not try to bandage them for him—did he go into the hall to get one of the big axes the men used for cutting firewood. Still he worked at building up the wall of branches around Harifaxa's body, his entrails knotted tightly within him by the knowledge that he had somehow killed her. He did not know how much wood it would take to burn her body to ash; only that it would be a great lot, more than the big heaps that the thralls cut for feast-cooking.

The Sun was down by the time Sigifrith had completely covered Harifaxa's body with wood, the light of the waxing Moon cold on the frost-slick tangle of branches. It would be a great burning, he thought, like the burning of a hero—a bale-fire fit for the mighty mare.

After a moment's thought, Sigifrith went to the stables, finding his way to the saddles by touch: Harifaxa should not fare without signs of the high worth in which they had held her. It was her fairest gear he brought out, saddle and straps adorned with little plates of wrought silver. He laid it on top of the pyre, then went back for an armful of oats so that she would not go hungry on her last faring. Finally, he went to the hall to fetch out a burning brand.

Sigifrith stood for a few moments with the flaming stick in his hand. The fire shone red off the patches of ice that smoothed the branches' rough bark here and there, glittering from the chip-carved silver on the saddle. He could see nothing of Harifaxa herself; only the dark crevasses in the heap of wood hinted that something might lie within.

Although he tried to think of some words that might ease his heart, no words came. He knew that he had brought about her death, and there was no way to make that fairer in his own sight.

"But not alone." Sigifrith's voice sounded as quiet as an echo in his own ears, ringing softly through the frosty air. A sudden fierceness seized him: he cried out, "To Wodan!" and plunged the brand into the pile of branches.

The fire spread slowly from stick to stick, droplets of melting ice hissing away from the flames. Sigifrith had to watch it carefully at first, poking it about and feeding it with small twigs until it got a good hold on some of the larger logs. It was not too long before the scent of roasting horsemeat sweetened the air. Sigifrith realized that his mouth was watering: he had not eaten since midday, and he was almost shaking with hunger. Appalled, he swallowed hard, the tears coming to his eyes. I might as well think of eating the flesh of men, he said to himself; but it seemed that he could taste the warm meat in his mouth already, the blood running freely down his jaws . . . A forest path, the dry leaves of summer's end gray against the silver sky and the howl winter-cold through the hot blood of the slain in his mouth . . . the warmth of the wolf hide on his back . . .

Sigifrith shook himself, trying to shake the half-dreaming thought from his mind as if he were shedding a heavy fur cloak from his shoulders. He crouched down closer to the fire. He could not forget how warm Harifaxa's back had been when he rode her through the snow, warm as the flames that now scorched her saddle and burned her flesh.

Although Sigifrith went into the forest twice more for wood, in time he saw that he would never be able to build the fire hot enough or keep it going long enough to eat the mare's great corpse to ashes. The Moon was down by the time the wood had burned away, and Sigifrith was glad of that, for Harifaxa's body was no more than half-burnt: but the faint starlight showed him little more than he needed to see. Although the flames had not done the work he had hoped, their heat had melted the ice beneath the pyre, softening the ground enough so Sigifrith could begin to dig a grave.

He dug steadily until he was down deeper than the warmth of the fire had sunk, to the depth where his shovel rang off the frozen earth as though it were iron, his strength no longer enough to break it. Harifaxa's charred flesh was hot, burning Sigifrith's torn hands painfully as he heaved her body into the grave. Although he pushed at her head until the last burnt flesh sloughed from her hot skull, the hole was not long enough and he had to scrape at the earthen wall with broken nails, scratching chunks of mud aside until he could get her head all the way down.

Standing at the edge of the grave, Sigifrith looked down into the darkness. It would have to do. He had done all he could. He wished he could have buried her deeper, but the earth would freeze hard again that night, and he did not think it likely that the nails of hounds or foxes could dig more strongly than his own shovel.

Sigifrith began to fill the hole in again, breaking up the harder clumps of earth with his shovel and sifting them around the edges of Harifaxa's body.

He worked until a knee-high mound of earth showed where the mare was buried, then went into the stable to put the shovel back. It was warm inside, and very dark. Sigifrith stood listening to the comforting breathing of the horses around him, at last finding his way by touch and memory to the door of Whitenose's stall. The colt was suckling. Sigifrith could hear the little noises it made as the pregnant mare shifted restlessly. For a moment he thought about going in, but suddenly felt that he could not bear to see or touch the colt that had killed Harifaxa.

Sigifrith crept out of the stables and back to the hall. He had thought everyone would be asleep, but his mother rose from her seat as he came in. A loaf of bread and a cup of wine rested on the table; she ladled a bowlful of stew from the big iron cauldron hanging over the low fire and set it beside the bread.

"You must eat something, Sigifrith," she said. Even in the dim firelight, he could see that her eyes, too, were swollen; like him, she had loved Harifaxa deeply.

Sigifrith's fierce hunger had ebbed—he only felt cold and sad now—but he sat down anyway. When he picked up the spoon to start eating, he saw that his hands were bleeding.

Herwodis moved closer, drawing in her breath as she saw his blood blackening the spoon's horn. She grasped him firmly by the wrist and turned his hand over to look at his palm, then examined his other hand in the same way. "You stay here. I'll clean and bandage those."

"They are hardly worth it," Sigifrith argued. "No one would say that I am hurt."

"I would." Herwodis hurried off and came back in a few minutes with a bowl of water and strips of clean linen. Sigifrith sat quietly while she tended to his hands, till they were washed and wrapped to her satisfaction.

Herwodis hugged her son about the shoulders. "More like your father . . ." she murmured, but did not finish her thought. "There's more stew there if you want more. Sleep well, Sigifrith."

To Sigifrith's disappointment, Alapercht's lands stayed at peace that year and so he had no chance to go into battle. He thought about asking if he could go north and fight in another drighten's warband for the summer, as kings' sons often did, but Ragin gave him sharp rede against it and so he stayed at home with Alapercht's other thanes, to hunt and break horses and fight with blunted sword and spear.

"All four of you at once!" Sigifrith challenged, flickering the weighted practice sword from side to side and spinning his shield.

Adalprant shook his head, leaning against the side of the hall to watch. "I'm an old man, Sigifrith. I think I've done my part in exercising your arm today."

"What about you three, then?" Sigifrith asked Hildkar, Perchtwine and Theodipald. "Come on, you can't be tired yet."

Perchtwine groaned, shaking back his sweat-frizzed tangle of sandy hair. His face was reddened, the thumb-sized purple birthmark on his forehead standing out brightly from the effort of fighting and the summer heat. "Can't

I?" he muttered. But he crouched into a fighting stance as Hildkar and Theodipald took up their places around Sigifrith, wearily lifting their weapons again.

As always, the battle was short and sharp. Sigifrith leaped among his opponents, flicking their blades away with his own as easily as flicking flies with a willow wand, tapping them here and there to show where a real sword would cleave neck or head, pierce chest or gut. Once Theodipald, coming in low from behind and diving as Sigifrith whirled, got in a lucky stroke to bruise the back of his thigh. Sigifrith dropped down, touching Theodipald's back lightly where he would have chopped through his foe's spine in a battle, then turned on one knee to parry the blows of the other two, mock-gutting Perchtwine with an upward stroke and coming down with a diagonal slash that knocked Hildkar's shield aside and would have taken his legs in a real fight. They tumbled to the ground with realistic moans, Hildkar rubbing his thighs ruefully.

"You're going to break my legs doing that one day," he complained.

"You need a better grip on your shield," Sigifrith countered.

"I had a better . . . well, you know what I mean!"

"I thought he was holding it pretty well," Theodipald said, picking up Hildkar's shield. "It was the way you hit it on the edge there." His brows drew together as he held up the round shield, stubby finger pointing to a long crack running through the linden wood to the rough boss. "Look, you broke it."

Theodipald handed the cracked shield back to Hildkar: the wood was good for little, but the metal grip and boss could easily be fitted on to another shield.

The five of them walked to the hut where the practice weapons were kept together with the spare shields and spear shafts. It was rare for a shield to last through more than one battle so most drightens kept a heap stockpiled against need; but when Hildkar opened the hut to get one out for himself, Sigifrith saw that there were no more spares.

Hildkar groaned as he looked in. "Shit, what happened here?"

"Woodworm got into them," Adalprand answered. "I was going to tell you earlier, but it slipped my mind. The drighten sent me to order more from Chludowich the Woodworker a few days ago, so they ought to be ready by now."

Hildkar looked at Sigifrith. "You were the one who broke it, you ought to go and get the new shields."

Sigifrith glanced up at the Sun, near her summer height. It was a long and boring way down a dusty road to Chludowich's home and, although he had nothing else to do that day, he didn't want to fetch the shields either. "I'll tell you what," he said. "I'm thirsty. Let's race to the stream, and whoever gets there last has to go."

"I'm thirsty too, and I want beer," Hildkar replied.

"So do I," agreed Theodipald. "And I'm not racing anywhere. Anyway, whoever loses we know who'd get there first, so there's not much point to choosing that way. I say we should go in and throw dice over it."

The thanes went into the hall together and Herwodis' servant girl Mathilde came out with cups and a pitcher of small beer for them.

"It's hot out there today," she said. "You look as though you've been working hard."

Perchtwine drained his beer and let out one of his tremendous belches, holding out his cup for her to refill. "Some of us have," he said. He drank again, then pulled three wooden cubes out of his belt pouch, blowing on them and rattling them briskly between his palms. "You know, we could make this more interesting by adding more things to the betting. I've had my eye on your dagger for a while, Theodipald."

The stocky thane put his hand protectively over the smooth red garnet that adorned his knife's pommel. "Ha, if you think I'll wager it while we're using your dice, you must be joking. What rules are we playing by?"

"Three throws, straight threes get a half and throw again, sixes take all, ones lose all. When someone's lost everything he's willing to wager and loses again, then he's got to go and fetch the new shields."

"Good enough."

The five of them cast dice for a little while, with Mathilde offering giggles at good throws and encouragements at bad ones. Before long, however, Sigifrith had begun to feel restless. He stood up, stretching to his full height—he was taller than any of the other thanes except Arnwald, Chelmwich and Chlodomar now, and he thought he might overtop them in the next year—and looked down at his bench companions.

"Any of you feel like going out for a ride?" he asked. "We could race horses on it instead of throwing dice; you'll have long enough to sit inside this winter."

"Maybe later," answered Perchtwine. "Come on, Hildkar, that was a bad throw and it's my turn now."

As Sigifrith went down the hill, he met Alapercht puffing upward. Splotches of sweat stained the Alamannic king's yellow tunic; his plump face was red and wet and his hair plastered down to his skull.

"That colt again," Alapercht panted before Sigifrith could ask. "He got in with the mares. Trying to mount them already, would you believe it?"

"But you're going to set him to stud anyway, aren't you?" Sigifrith asked.

"Not . . . till we find out if he can be broken. What good's a line that can't be trained or ridden? Harifaxa was trouble enough, but this beast . . ." He wiped his forehead with the sleeve of his tunic, sighing in exhausted resignation. "Well, he's still young. Is your mother around anywhere?"

"I haven't seen her."

"Well. All right, then."

Alapercht went on up to the hall, and Sigifrith ran to the large enclosure where that year's foals ran untamed. Even from a way off, Harifaxa's colt stood out among them like a leek among grasses: bigger than many yearlings, deep-chested and long-legged, he galloped as restlessly as a penned wolf around the foals' garth, rearing now and again and battering the air with his hooves. The wild colt was the deep cloud-gray that the Alamanns called "wind-color," with a silvery mane and tail; though no one could stand close to him long enough to groom him, his hide gleamed with health and strength. Sigifrith clenched his fists and turned away, glancing at the grass-covered mound in front of the winter stables before he went on into the wood.

Sigifrith ran along the twisting path through the trees, oak and ash rustling above him in the soft wind. A young roedeer dashed across the path, turning its head to give him a fleeting glance of startlement before fleeing again. As Sigifrith ran on, coming closer to the stony crag which jutted out of one of the hillsides like a jagged shelf, he could hear the rhythmic ringing of metal on stone growing louder.

Ragin thrust the spearhead he was working on back into the fire with a grunt, beginning to pump the bellows again as Sigifrith burst out of the woods and through the open door of his earth cave.

"Can I help?" he asked, not out of breath in spite of his long run.

"No."

"Why?"

"You'll pump the bellows too hard and then you'll break them or melt the metal. You have better things to do."

"Like what?"

"Atheling-things."

"I can't go to battle, because we're not at war with anyone," Sigifrith complained. "I haven't got anyone to fight or wrestle with, and I've gone hunting every day since before Midsummer. What other atheling-things are there?"

"If that's all you know . . ." Ragin muttered. He pulled the spearhead out and laid it on the stone again, tapping its edge out into the curve of a long steel leaf. As the dwarf worked, he looked critically up and down the length of Sigifrith's body. He drew his thick eyebrows together till the creases of his black-pored forehead became deep crevasses and glared up at the youth. "What do you know? You don't even dress like an atheling. You walk around without breeches or shoes like a poor carl's son or a thrall, and you don't know how much gold you have—or could have."

"What are you talking about?" Sigifrith asked.

Ragin gave the spearhead a couple of final taps and set it back into the fire, adding a few more pieces of coal. "Do you know how much wealth your father had when he died?"

"Well . . ." Sigifrith remembered that his mother had once or twice mentioned treasure that would be his when he was old enough for it; something glittered far in the back of his mind, a misty vision of gold and silver, furs and fine cloth, laid in chests and hidden behind a hedge of thorns, but he could remember no more. "No," he admitted.

"Do you know who holds it now?"

"Mother said . . . Alapercht and Chilpirich keep it for me."

"And are you happy with this? Don't you want more for yourself?"

"They give me what I want. Why should I worry about more? I'm sure they take better care of it than I would."

"Hah," Ragin muttered. "Treasure to buy ships with, to gather men to you . . . that's why an atheling needs gold. Think of how you could go harrying down the Rhine, to Gaul and Britain and to the lands of the North, if you only had the gold to gather a band together and ready yourself as an atheling ought to be readied." He held up a gnarled hand to halt Sigifrith as the youth turned to dash out. "Not now," he warned. "You're still too young. But think on it, because you're almost a man grown. Perhaps no more than a year—you'll know when you've become ready." The dwarf's beard twitched, his teeth showing in one of his rare yellowed smiles. "Or if you don't, I will. You can trust me for that."

"And where are your shoes?" Ragin asked Sigifrith, scuffling his heavy boot through a frosted tangle of dry grass to make his point. Although it was well past Winternights—almost the middle of Blotmonth—Sigifrith stood barefoot in the white light of the pale winter sun, his long curly hair tumbling over his shoulders and halfway down his back like a short brownish red cloak.

"I didn't feel like wearing them," Sigifrith said carelessly. "They're too small for me anyway, and it's not that cold out here. Your blood's just thin, that's all."

"My blood's thin, is it?" Ragin asked, setting his fists on his squat hips and tilting his head back to stare at Sigifrith's neck. "And what shall we say about your blood, if you're not proud enough of it to show yourself as might befit it?"

Sigifrith smiled, turning his elbow so the wide curve of his gold arm-ring dazzled out a blaze of light. For a moment he saw its reflection gleaming in Ragin's dark eyes like sunlight glittering off choppy water.

Then the dwarf snorted. "Your troth's bought cheaply. Can you name me any one of King Alapercht's other thanes who doesn't have a horse of his own? But you walk as a poor man must."

Sigifrith thought for a moment. It was true: each man had his steed, and each horse's face and name, gait and skills, were as well known as those of his rider. Only Sigifrith rode the unchosen geldings or walked, as he might need to, and he had never thought to ask why.

"What business is it of yours?" he asked, roughness edging his high tenor voice. "Why should you care? You never have anything to do with anybody, and you won't take a horse when it's offered to you."

Ragin looked across at the interlaced wyrms of Sigifrith's belt buckle, the twisting design carved chip by chip from the fine frost-white silver—a gift he himself had made and given Sigifrith after the last Yule feast.

"My foster-son should be worthy of his line," he said, his raspy voice muffled as if he were chewing on his beard while he spoke. "Shall be worthy of our line, to win the hoard of our estate back from the one who holds it. I want you to appear as you should—I have worked so that you shall become a hero, Sigifrith, and a hero needs a steed to bear him."

"But my father didn't . . . " Sigifrith started, and stopped. He knew that Sigimund had never ridden a horse; but he remembered the rush of wod bearing him up and along the wind-paths of the Hunt as the wolf shapes had borne Sigimund and Sinfjotli through battle. He did not understand or know how to tell what he felt to be true, but he could not argue with Ragin any longer. "What should I do, then?"

"Ask the king for a horse. You're always boasting that he'll give you whatever you want."

"Now?"

"I think it's time."

Alapercht was sitting in his hall, talking quietly to Herwodis and two of the older thanes. They all looked up as Sigifrith rushed in, flushed from his run through the forest.

"I need to talk to you," Sigifrith said, adding, "my drighten."

Alapercht smiled beneath his moustache.

"My thane," he said, patting Sigifrith on the back, "what do you want?"

Sigifrith shifted uneasily from foot to foot. "I want to ask you for a horse of my own—as Ragin gave me rede to." He gazed anxiously down into his stepfather's face. "Is that all right?"

Alapercht laughed in a kindly way. "I'd been wondering how long it would be before you decided to stop wandering around like a poor man's son. Of course you can have your choice of steeds. Did you have one in mind?"

There was a promising gold-maned bay among the three-year-olds on whom Sigifrith had been keeping an eye; but the words choked in his throat as he opened his mouth to speak. Mutely he shook his head, feeling like a fool.

"Well, you can choose when you please. You can even," he went on, glancing down at Sigifrith's bare feet, "have some new boots as well, if you'll sit still long enough to be measured for them."

Sigifrith could feel himself blushing under the friendly smiles of the others. Alapercht patted him on the back again. "There you are, then. Go on, you look like a man with things to do."

"Thank you," Sigifrith said belatedly, and made his escape from the hall, letting the cold morning air cool his burning face. He had meant to walk down to the horses, but instead found himself turning to follow the ice-edged spring up into the woods, wandering as if dazed between the bare trees and splashing through puddles of frosty mud.

A raspy, croaking cough startled him into looking up, and he found that he was face to face with a strange man in a dark blue cloak, whose wide-brimmed hat was tilted to half-cover his face. The man's sturdy boots were scuffed and covered with mud, his long gray hair and beard flowing in dirty tangles from the shadow of his hat. He was very tall, even taller than Sigifrith, though he leaned heavily on the shaft of his spear.

"Where are you going?" he asked, his deep, hemp-rough voice shivering down Sigifrith's spine. Sigifrith gathered all his will to meet the keen glare of the eye that gleamed from beneath the brim of the forest man's hat.

"To choose a horse," he answered. "Will you give me rede on it?"

"Come with me."

Sigifrith followed the wanderer back along the muddy brown bank of the stream and down to the pens where the horses had been let out for the day. Instead of going to the enclosure where the three-year-olds who were ready for riding were kept and trained, he stopped before the garth of the unbroken yearlings. The stranger opened the gate and went in, flapping his cloak to drive the horses out. Sigifrith shouted to them, guiding them from the other side. Together the two of them ran, driving the herd of young horses in full gallop along the road and down to the Rhine. Sigifrith was panting hard by the time they stopped at the river's banks, gasping in gusts of icy air and rubbing at a stitch in his side, but the old man by his side betrayed no sign of tiredness, waiting only a moment for Sigifrith to recover himself before raising his cloak again and beating at the yearlings' flanks with the flat of his hand. Sigifrith fell to helping him, shouting at the horses, pushing and waving his arm till the whole herd stood belly-deep and shivering in the rushing waters of the Rhine. The old man splashed back to shore and Sigifrith followed him, his feet too numb from the cold water to feel the sharp rocks over which he stumbled.

"What now?" Sigifrith asked when they stood dripping on the bank again. He bent to loosen the bottom cords of his breeches, spilling out the little pools of water trapped inside.

"Watch."

The horses were beginning to turn back, breasting the flood to force their way to dry land. Only one moved out toward the middle of the Rhine: Harifaxa's wind-gray colt had begun to swim through the water, tossing his long mane and snorting as the brown river churned into froth around him. A tangle of bare branches floated toward him, catching in his feet and dragging him under for a moment; Sigifrith caught his breath, clenching his fists as he moved, only half-aware, toward the water again. But the young horse kicked his way out of the branches without any help, blowing a spume of water from his nostrils and swimming as strongly as before.

"Take him and rear him carefully," the old forest man said, the keen glance of his single eye piercing through Sigifrith's head like a long steel thorn. "He is descended from Sleipnir, and shall become the greatest of horses." He put two fingers in his mouth and let out a whistle so shrill and pure that Sigifrith had to wince, closing his eyes and raising his hands to his ears. When he looked again, the old man was gone and Harifaxa's colt was swimming toward him.

Sigifrith waited until the horse had come to shore, water dripping from the tip of every strand of his mane and coat. The yearling trotted up to him, butting against Sigifrith with a wet nose and almost knocking him over. Sigifrith braced himself to stand up to the horse's affection, and for the first time, he stroked Harifaxa's colt, feeling the warmth beneath the cold dampness of his soaked hide; then, unable to help himself, he embraced the young horse around the neck, trembling with the realization of what he had hidden from himself for almost a year.

"You're mine," he murmured fiercely. The horse turned his head, lipping gently at Sigifrith's hair. "Grani," Sigifrith said. "I name you Grani."

Grani whinnied gently as though approving of the name, his breath warm on Sigifrith's head.

"Hai!" Hrodkar's voice shouted. "Who let the damn horses out?"

The yearlings were prancing about, wandering farther away as the realization that they had been loosed came to them. Hrodkar was limping down, his lumpy face heavy with thunderous anger. "Sigifrith! Did you leave the gate open?"

"I did," Sigifrith admitted lightly. Reluctantly he let go of his horse, stroking his soft nose one last time.

"You'll be cleaning the stalls till Yule, boy! Now help me get them back in before they're all lost."

Sigifrith looked at Grani, whose eyes met his with a glance of keen understanding. "Come on," he said softly. "Let's do it."

When the yearlings were back in their pen and Hrodkar's wrath had been soothed by Sigifrith's promises of good behavior and shoveling of manure to come, Sigifrith began to look around for a saddle, but could find none big enough. At last he simply put the flat of his hand on Grani's back to keep the colt still and leapt up, holding tightly to the horse with his knees as he felt Grani's muscles surging like a great wave with the movements of his own hips and thighs, bearing him onward. Sigifrith guided the gray steed around the pen three times, until he heard Alapercht's voice ringing sharp with anger.

"Sigifrith! What do you think you're doing?"

Grani whirled to face the Alamannic drighten and reared up, beating at the air with his hooves like a trained battle-steed as Sigifrith struggled to keep his seat on the horse's slippery back. Grani must have felt his rider's balance shifting, for he dropped again, standing still while Sigifrith steadied himself.

"This is the horse I've chosen," he called back. "This is my steed; what more need I say?"

"You may have him freely if you wish, but I thought you knew better than to try riding such a young horse! Have you learned nothing in all your years of life?"

Of course, Sigifrith remembered now: before three years or so, a horse was still growing, bones soft and unformed—likely to be harmed by a rider's weight. Alapercht had full right to be angry with him—or would have, had Sigifrith leapt onto any other yearling. But Grani bore him too easily for Sigifrith to fear that he could hurt the young stallion, and he knew well that the old man would not have come to make his choice before it was time.

"Does he seem bowed beneath my weight?" Sigifrith answered. "Or even unbroken—when I need no saddle or tack to ride him?"

Alapercht's mouth fell open as he stared at the two of them, and Sigifrith nudged Grani into a run again, shifting his weight back as they came to the fence. Grani leapt into the air for a dizzying moment, flying over the wooden bounds of the garth without effort. He landed smoothly, so steady that Sigifrith was never in danger of losing his seat.

"Can you doubt that Grani is ready to bear me, or I to ride him?" asked Sigifrith.

Alapercht shook his head, staring wide-eyed at his foster-son. "There has been nothing of this foal's life that could have been expected—not his breeding, nor his birth, nor his growth. If he has the strength to bear you thus at a year of age, and carries you willingly, then I can say nothing further, except that he is yours indeed."

Grani neighed as if he had understood Alapercht's words. As Sigifrith waved his thanks, the young stallion turned to gallop over stock and stone into the winter-bare woods.

"Hai, old dwarf!" Sigifrith shouted as he rode to the crags above Ragin's earth cave. "Ragin! Come out and see what your rede has done!"

Ragin stumped out of the cave, blinking his eyes blearily in the sunlight. He stared up at Sigifrith for a moment, then, slow as toppling stone, nodded his hoary head. "Yes," he rasped. "Yes . . . Well, my hero. Now that you have your steed, are you ready to know more?"

"What?"

"Come in, and I'll tell you."

Sigifrith slipped down from Grani's back, stroking the horse's drying neck. "You'll wait for me, won't you?" he whispered into the arched cup of Grani's silvery ear. "Or at least come back when I call?"

Grani fit his nose into the curve of Sigifrith's collarbone, pushing affectionately at his master in agreement.

When Sigifrith and Ragin had gone in, Ragin sat down on the smoothed top of a half-carved tree stump, from which the rough figures of wyrms and beasts, men and weapons, had just begun to emerge. Sigifrith settled himself at the dwarf's feet, his back to the warm glow of the forge's banked coals.

"You think well of yourself for having gotten this horse, don't you?" Ragin began, peering down at Sigifrith.

"Why shouldn't I?"

"Because there's far more that you need. You need wealth, and you need to prove yourself with the deeds of a hero."

"What can I do?" Sigifrith asked. "We're not at war with anyone and I don't have a reason to ask Alapercht for anything else, now he has given me my choice of a horse."

"I can tell you where there is much gold to be had, and it would be a deed of a hero to seek it out and gain it."

"Where is it?" Sigifrith asked, leaning closer to Ragin's knees and looking up into the craggy shadows of the dwarf's face. "Who guards it?"

Ragin turned away, turning the tap of the barrel that stood against the wall and filling two clay cups with his dark, bitter ale. He handed one to Sigifrith, drinking deeply himself. "You should know that already," he said. "You should remember."

"I should . . . " Sigifrith murmured. Something about the way the firelight glittered from Ragin's eyes, from the wrought gold of his belt buckle, stirred him deeply and he shifted his weight with uneasy eagerness and hitched himself a little closer to the dwarf. "I don't," he admitted, ashamed. "I know . . . I should remember, but I can't, quite. Tell me."

"You've heard of Fadhmir, who lies north along the Rhine in the Dragon's Crag by Gnita Heath. When you go there, you shall think you have never seen more gold gathered in one place, nor will you ever need more as long as you live, no matter how famed you become," Ragin murmured to him, the words gliding smoothly from his mouth.

"The dragon Fadhmir . . . I've heard songs of him. But no one dares to go against him, because he is so great and cruel." Though I might dare, Sigifrith thought to himself. In the depths of his awareness, he felt his hand moving to his side, closing only on the hilt of his knife.

"You should know by now how tales grow, Sigifrith," Ragin chided gently. "He is no greater than any other ling-worm—and would have seemed so to your kin who have gone before you. Are you really a Walsing? You can't have the courage of those who were said to be first among men, if tales of a dragon frighten you."

"You've been telling me for years that I'm too young to do this or that," Sigifrith answered angrily, bitterly stung by Ragin's taunt. "Why are you urging me to this now, if you don't think I have the strength or skill of the Walsings? Since my wisdom seems to have failed me, I will hear from your own mouth what Fadhmir is to you."

"There is a tale to it," Ragin said, refilling his cup again.

"Let me hear it!"

"This is the beginning of my story. There was a man called Hraithamar . . ." Ragin said.

It was too warm to sit by the fire. Sigifrith moved until his back was to the cool stone cave wall, staring into the patterns of red heat that writhed through the ash beneath the light breeze blowing in through the cave's mouth. He sipped at Ragin's brew as the dwarf told his tale, letting the strong drink wend him into a pleasant daze. Although Sigifrith had never heard the story, it seemed to him that he knew it already—that he had seen it in a dream, the fires leaping from the coins and bracelets and chains of purest gold.

A gust of wind stirred the coals, brightening their glow as Ragin spoke of the three wanderers who had come to Hraithamar's hall, and of Otter's weregild. It seemed to Sigifrith that there was something of laughter in the stirring of the heat within the forge; that he could almost hear the swift voice murmuring to him from the fire.

But he is not telling you the truth; he is not telling all the truth. Ask him whose sword felled Hraithamar; ask him who carried the gold away.

"My brother Fadhmir was the strongest and fiercest of us, but it was he who was maddened by the gold," Ragin said, as if he had heard the voice. Sigifrith glanced at him, but the smith was not looking into the fire, nor yet into Sigifrith's eyes. He stared at the stone over Sigifrith's head, and it seemed to Sigifrith that he could hear an ache of grief in the old dwarf's voice. "He killed our father; he fled to the Dragon's Crag with the gold. There he went into the iron-bound cave the Romans had dug years ago when they brought out stone for their working; and there, by the might of the Helm of Awe, he became a dragon. And that is the tale of how I missed a share in my brother's weregild and my father's heritage."

Now it seemed to Sigifrith that he could see a pair of eyes in the coals— hot amber eyes, with heat lightning flickering behind them—and he heard the voice murmuring from the forge again.

But he is not telling you all the truth; he tells you only half the story. Ask him why he fled into the wood; ask him how he came to dwell with the dwarves. I shall warn you now, for I am your friend: Ragin means to betray you, and keep the gold for himself.

Sigifrith's guts twisted in on themselves as Ragin went on speaking, as the hot gaze from the coals flickered over him. Summoning his strength, he stared back at it, trying to fix the half-seen amber eyes with his own. I have never had anything but good from Ragin, nor are his redes to me other than wise, he thought back silently. But the Sinwist, who knew you, did not trust you; why should I?

No answer came from the coals, though their heat rippled through the air like clear water under a light breeze. Sigifrith turned toward Ragin, who was filling his cup with ale yet again—the strong beer's wod did not shake a dwarf's earth-strength as it did a man's—and he felt a sudden warmth as he watched the old smith carry out the familiar action. The Sly One's tricks shall not shake our trust, he thought.

"Tell me of the Helm of Awe," Sigifrith said.

Ragin stared into his cup for a while before answering. "It was wrought by the craft of the dwarves in elder days, and was part of Andward's hoard; after his ring, it was the fairest treasure he held and the one the dwarves most begrudge to Fadhmir. If the dragon were only a beast, he might be slain—would have been slain for the gold long ago, although it took a full warband to do it; neither his might of body nor the poison he sprays would have stood against as many warriors as would have banded together for the sake of winning his hoard. But the dragon is Fadhmir's ghost, to which the Helm gave the might to come forth in the Middle-Garth as his body died and fell away; and from that might springs the terror that drives folk far from the Dragon's Crag. No man dares to raise eyes to the cave where Fadhmir dwells, for no man's gaze is strong enough to meet his, or to look upon the Helm of Awe where it burns between the dragon's brows—though while Sigimund the Walsing lived, there were some who thought that he might have dared to meet Fadhmir in fight."

"You have lost a lot," Sigifrith agreed slowly, "and Fadhmir was evil toward his kin." Sigifrith stood, bending his knees to keep from scraping his head on the roof of the cave, and looked down at the dwarf. Then he dropped to his knees to stare into Ragin's eyes, grasping the smith's thick shoulders and forcing him to meet his gaze. "Make me a sword," he commanded. "Since you won't teach me any more forging, you'll have to make it for me. Make me a sword better than any other, a sword with which I can do whatever deeds I have enough courage for, and I will slay Fadhmir for you."

"And do you think you have the courage to meet the dragon?" Ragin asked, turning his eyes away from Sigifrith's. "You're young and untried. What makes you think you can do what no one else has dared to?"

"I may be young and untried, but I'm the strongest man in King Alapercht's hall. Ragin—foster-father—I think you know me better than anyone else. Have I ever flinched from anything I set myself to? Have you ever had a reason to call me a coward?"

"No," the dwarf admitted. "You've broken or ruined plenty of things through clumsiness and over-eagerness, yes. I've called you a fool plenty of times, on good grounds. But if you have the strength and the will to face Fadhmir, no one will ever be able to call you a coward."

"I will do it!" Sigifrith said boldly. "Make me a sword worthy of the deed."

"I shall do that, and you shall be able to kill Fadhmir with that sword," said Ragin, leaning forward and clasping Sigifrith's hand in his own. Sigifrith gripped his hand tightly, until the dwarf hissed between his teeth with pain and burning drops of blood sprang out from beneath his cracked nails on to Sigifrith's palm. Ragin bared his teeth in a grin of angry satisfaction as Sigifrith let go and wiped his hand on the side of his drying breeches. "And so it shall be."

4

GRAM

Sigifrith rode to Ragin's cave the next day, sitting proudly on Grani's back as the young colt bore him lightly up over fallen branches and stones, leaping for the joy of it. Regretfully Sigifrith slid down when they had reached their goal, leaning his head against Grani's warm gray neck for a moment. He could already taste the metallic sharpness of steam hissing from quenched iron in the air and hear the low muttering of the dwarf's voice within the cave.

Ragin crouched before his forge, the firelight throwing his shadow huge and hulking on the rocks above. On the big stone that served as his anvil lay several slim bars of steel rods twisted together. He held another in his hand, a flat bar with a mottled pattern. Sigifrith recognized something he had seen Ragin do before, something the dwarf would have taught him in time: the twisted bars would be split, folded over and welded till they looked like the one Ragin held now. Then the smith would weld them together around a softer iron core and edge the sword blank with his best steel before forging it into shape and hardening its edges with the eating venom. So the finest swords were made, the atheling-blades with their wyrm mottling and wyrm-sharp bite.

"Is that for me?" Sigifrith asked eagerly. "When will it be done?"

Ragin turned his face away from the firelight to look at his foster-son. "Be patient, Sigifrith," he answered. "The best work always takes a long time."

"I know that. But when do you think—?"

The dwarf coughed, laying the flat steel down and moving one of the wound pieces of metal away from the others. He took up the chisel and hammer that rested on the anvil and began to split the bar down its length with delicate, precise strikes. The sharp clinking went straight through Sigifrith's head with each blow, making it difficult for him to think clearly or pay much attention to Ragin's broken words.

"I make it . . . " (clink) "the rest of the day . . . " (clink) "for this . . . " (clink) "then another five or . . . " (clink) "six, until . . . " (clink) "it's done. If I don't do anything else in all that time." Strong as pincers, the dwarf's gnarled fingers pried the two split halves of the bar a little away from each other. He moved his chisel down another inch and began to tap at it again.

"Can I help?" Sigifrith offered. "Surely you've taught me enough?"

"No."

"I'll be careful, I promise," Sigifrith said, but the piercing ring of the chisel cut through his words so he wasn't sure if Ragin had even heard him. The dwarf shook his head without meeting Sigifrith's eyes, staring down at the metal he was splitting.

"Go on," he said between blows. "Come back in . . . " (clink) "a week . . . " (clink) "and then we'll see . . . " (clink) "how your new sword fits you . . . " (clink). "Now go and ride your horse."

"Is there anything you need? Is there anything I can bring you?"

"Umph," Ragin grunted, turning the twisted bar over to examine the straightness of his cut. "Some bread wouldn't be too bad. Won't have much time for cooking, I think. Whatever your mother wants to send up to me." He put the iron back down on the anvil. "Or . . . " (clink) "see if . . . " (clink) "your hunting's . . . " (clink) "worth your boasting." (clink) "Whatever . . . " (clink) "you can catch."

"I will," Sigifrith promised. He went out of the cave, straightening up and stretching the cramp from his limbs, face turned to the cold sunlight. Grani was nibbling on the thorny leaves of a holly bush a little up the path. When he saw Sigifrith, he tossed his head back and whinnied, trotting eagerly to his master. Sigifrith leapt up on his back. The gray horse reared, pounding the wind with his hooves before he dropped back down.

"Hai, we'll catch a fine stag for the old dwarf, won't we?" Sigifrith said to Grani, nudging his steed with a knee to turn him along the path that led deeper into the wood. The stallion raised his head as if he caught a scent on the breeze, breaking into a light canter.

The stag's hide gleamed ruddy-bronze in the sunlight where he stood between two bare trees. His large dark eyes stared at Sigifrith and Grani for a moment. Then he wheeled and ran, leaping over bush and stone. Sigifrith and Grani followed, the wind-gray horse gaining swiftly on the stag.

Twist and turn as he might, doubling back and dashing away, the hart could not get away from the hunters who pounded down closer and closer upon his track. Sigifrith threw his head back in a howling laugh of excitement as they drew near enough to see the rolling whites of the stag's terrified eyes, the flecks of foam upon his mouth and the sheen of sweat darkening his bronze pelt.

Sigifrith pulled out the knife he had forged. Grani galloped in a wide circle about the stag, coming along his side to avoid the slashing of his branching antlers. With a quick sweep of his hand, Sigifrith caught the stag by the prongs, jerking his head up to drag him, stumbling, along for a couple of steps before the knife's blade slashed across his throat.

Grani halted, shaking as the deep crimson torrent of hot blood poured over Sigifrith's leg and down his side. The stag's eyes were dulling already, the knees had given way; only Sigifrith's strength held the dead atheling-beast up from the earth. Slowly the youth let his burden down, leaping to the ground beside it. The stag's blood was already beginning to clot on his own body. Its taste was strong and musky-salt in his mouth as he licked his hands clean, filling him with a sudden hunger. In a sudden burst of strength he tore through skin and muscle. The stag's ribs cracked beneath his hands as he wrested its chest open to show the heart still quivering faintly between the limp masses of lung.

The meat was tough, spurting warm blood into his mouth and over his face as he chewed. When his hunger was sated at last, he heaved the stag's body over Grani's back with a mighty grunt. The forelegs and head dangled down on one side, the hindquarters and legs on the other. Sigifrith wiped his mouth on his arm, leaving a dark smear on the white skin, and slapped Grani lightly on the flank. The colt turned his head questioningly, sniffing at Sigifrith's face.

"Go on," Sigifrith said, his voice sounding suddenly harsh and choked in his own ears. Grani tapped a forehoof on the ground, his eyes staring expectantly at Sigifrith.

"All right, then." He vaulted up behind the stag's body, and Grani began to trot back toward Ragin's cave.

Sigifrith carried the stag in slung about his shoulders, its hooves hanging down at his thighs. Carefully he squatted to lay the body down by the cave's door.

It was a few minutes before Ragin turned from the fire to plunge a new-welded bar into the clay bucket of water beside him. The steam hissed white around him, clouding his shape for a moment. When it cleared, he was staring hard at Sigifrith, tugging at his beard with one hand and hefting his tongs in the other.

"What in Dwalan's name happened to you, boy?" he grunted. "Are you wounded?"

"Of course not," Sigifrith answered, offended. "I've killed you a stag—see? The blood is his."

To Sigifrith's surprise, Ragin whirled, crouching down to look at the hart's body. He ran his hands over the opened ribcage, lifting its head to stare at the glazed eyes for a moment. At last he let his breath out in a sigh.

"Is something wrong?" Sigifrith asked, confused and faintly troubled.

"No," Ragin said, his voice no more than a soft mutter. He was looking over Sigifrith's shoulder, staring out of the door of the cave to the unfettered horse standing outside. "But you'll give me an oath."

"What?"

"Swear that if you ever see a stag with a swarthy hide in the wood, you'll leave it be."

"I swear," Sigifrith said at once. "I wouldn't kill—"

"Kill what?" Ragin said, his voice sharpening to a saw-toothed edge. He took a step closer to Sigifrith, staring at the middle of the young man's chest with eyes that gleamed oddly out of the shadow cast by Sigifrith's body.

"More than a stag," the youth murmured slowly. "A dwarf's daylight fetch—I'd know."

"So you remember!" Ragin said, his thick finger jabbing into the muscles of Sigifrith's stomach. "And what else?"

"I don't . . . I just knew."

"Nothing else?"

"No . . . nothing."

Ragin stood looking at his foster-son for a little while longer before he stepped back again. "So," he grunted quietly, as if to himself, then, "Well, you'd better wash yourself before you return to the hall. You're likely to be mistaken for a troll or a werewolf if you come in with blood over your mouth and hands like that."

Sigifrith glanced down at the broken bones gleaming from the chest of the stag, a dark ruin in the shadows of the cave. It came to him what he had done, what the other thanes—or Alapercht, or his mother—might think if they had seen him. The thought writhed coldly through the pit of his stomach; he put his hand to his mouth as if to hide the traces of his deed, feeling the rough bloodstains flaking away from his face.

"Fool," Ragin said, dipping a cloth into the warm water of the quenching pot and handing it to Sigifrith. "Of course you didn't think about it, did you? The gold . . . ach, no. Be careful of what you do in the hall—and when you go hunting with others." He paused, tugging at his beard as he considered his foster son. "And stop pretending to be sick. I can tell damn well you're not. Since you killed the stag, you can clean and cook it; I don't have time."

The dwarf pulled the new-welded bar from the water and laid it on the anvil, beginning to beat it flat with firm, even strokes. Sigifrith stood with the dripping cloth in his hand, listening to the comforting, familiar sound of ringing metal and stone for a moment before he began to wash his face. It was true: he couldn't bring himself to feel any revulsion, and the twisting of shock and shame in his guts had already eased. He cleaned his mouth and hands carefully; he knew he would have to soak and beat the stiff blood from his breeches in the stream before going back to the hall. They would still be stained, but then, his clothes often were.

Sigifrith brought Ragin fresh bread and wine every day that week, till at last he arrived to find the finished sword laying on the anvil. Its twining patterns gleamed dully in the afternoon sunlight that shone through the cave's mouth.

"There you are," Ragin croaked. "Go on, pick it up."

Sigifrith took the sword, swinging it to hiss through the air in a couple of practice strokes. The blade was balanced so finely that he felt a hair's weight might tilt it. It was very light in his hand—almost uncomfortably so, as though the weight of its steel were not enough for his arm.

"A sword that will slay a dragon?" he wondered aloud. A master smith's work, yes; a blade fit for an atheling, as well-wrought as it might be. But it seemed to him that his arm knew a different weight and a different blade, his palm knew the smoothness of another hilt resting comfortably in its grasp . . . (and the rasp of steel cutting through stone).

Sigifrith swung the sword and brought it down one-handed to crash upon the rock of Ragin's anvil. With a sound like an icicle breaking at winter's end, it shattered, splinters of steel flying everywhere. One grazed Sigifrith's forehead; another stuck in his shoulder. Ragin's short bark of pain sounded behind him.

Only a single twisted shard still jutted from the hilt in Sigifrith's hand. He stared at it in disappointment, but not surprise. The metal was hot enough to burn his fingertip when he touched it.

Sigifrith wiped the blood out of his eyes and yanked the shard of metal from his left shoulder. A deep, numbing pain twinged through his arm as the steel slid out.

"Idiot," Ragin said harshly. A dark stain was spreading through the dwarf's gray hair, already beginning to drip down his sooty-pored forehead. He pressed a hand to his head, wincing in pain as he looked about for bandages. "Did you want to kill us both? You'll be lucky if you haven't crippled yourself."

Sigifrith tossed the hilt onto the coals of the forge, then lifted his wounded arm, raising and lowering it as if he were swinging a shield. It hurt, but not too badly, and the movement was free. He pressed his other hand to the scratch on his forehead, holding it tightly to stop the flow of blood. "I'm all right," he said. "But that sword was no dragon's bane. You'll have to do better than that if I'm to kill Fadhmir for you."

Ragin stared fiercely at the floor, wrapping a rag about his skull. The wool darkened swiftly. "My head," he growled, then, "From behind. Damn you. My own . . . "

Sigifrith remembered that once he had enjoyed the old dwarf's fits, waiting for one to come to a fight so he could try his strength against the smith's. But Ragin was no challenge now, and Sigifrith had no way of knowing how deep Ragin's head wound—the wound he himself had given him—was; the old dwarf might be near to death for all he could tell.

"Ragin?" Sigifrith said softly. "It's only me. Are you all right?"

Ragin gritted his teeth as he pulled the rag away and parted his blood-sodden hair to show Sigifrith the long, shallow trench in his scalp. "I'll live," he muttered. "Much you care. If you'd said the sword wasn't good enough for you, I could have at least got a fair price from someone else for it. You think I like seeing my work smashed?"

"I didn't . . . " Sigifrith began, then, "How else was I to know? I had to—"

"Hah. Of course you had to. You haven't gone a day without breaking something since I've known you."

"That's not true," Sigifrith protested lamely. Realizing how feeble his complaint sounded, he decided to change tactics. "You can forge a better sword, I know you can. I've never heard anyone tell of a living smith who might be your equal."

"If you can't kill me with flying steel, you'll choke me to death with flattery, is that it?" Ragin asked. Nevertheless, Sigifrith thought he heard a glint of satisfaction in the old dwarf's rock-rough voice. "You're not such a fool as you act sometimes, I suppose. It's true: I made that sword with skill alone—but a skill no human could match. Think on that, before you look too scornfully on what you broke."

"What about the next one, then? Will you use magic in it?"

Ragin put his fists on his hips and made a harsh croaking noise. The wrinkles creasing his sooted skin deepened to crevasses, his bearded lips pulling back to show yellowed teeth. It took Sigifrith a second to realize that the dwarfish smith was laughing.

"What did I say?" Sigifrith wondered, a trifle aggrieved as well as bewildered by Ragin's sudden mirth.

At last the dwarf stopped laughing, tilting his blocky head to one side as he stared at Sigifrith. "I'll need you to get certain things for me. There might be a thing or two you'll have to do in the course of the forging as well, but the main thing is keeping out of my way and not coming in at the wrong moment. I'll go to the hall when I need you. Don't you dare to interrupt me! Do you understand?"

"Of course," Sigifrith answered. "What can I get for you?"

"Now? You can get those wounds cleaned up before you take sick from them, that's what. Then you can get this mess cleaned up, and after that you can get out of my way so I can start work again. You needn't expect this one to be finished soon, either. I won't do the last work on it till sunrise on Yule."

Sigifrith pulled his tunic off, looking with regret at the splotch of blood staining the cream-colored wool. He prodded gingerly at the puncture in his left shoulder. It was beginning to throb steadily, the ache pulsing down his arm, but it had bled well and seemed clean.

Ragin pushed Sigifrith down onto a stool. His rough fingertip poked gently at the wound. "Urmph," he grunted. "You'll live. Sit still." The old smith wetted a rag, twisted one corner into a point and swabbed out the hole as best as he could before tying another cloth around Sigifrith's shoulder. He washed the scratch on Sigifrith's forehead as well.

"I don't need a bandage," Sigifrith protested when Ragin was about to wrap cloth around his head.

Ragin tossed the rag at the chest he had taken it from and handed Sigifrith the little broom that leaned against the side of the cave instead. "All right. If you're not badly hurt enough for a bandage, you're not too badly hurt to clean up the mess you've made." He uncorked the clay bottle of wine that Sigifrith had brought the day before and poured himself out a mugful, sitting down on the stool as Sigifrith rose and began to sweep the floor.

Although Ragin wouldn't let Sigifrith into the cave, the youth wandered about near it every day. Short as the days were, he had plenty of time to run in the woods, working off some of the restless strength that drove him from before dawn to well past dusk. The other thanes were hardly willing to fight with him anymore; he hunted better alone, and none of their horses could hope to keep up with Grani for more than a few moments, riding or racing.

When Sigifrith stood on top of Ragin's hill, he could sense something thrumming through the rock beneath his feet and hear the faint rumbling of the dwarf's deep chanting, though he could never make out any words. Sometimes the smoke that drifted from the forge's chimney into the cold air outside had the clean smell of burning ashwood, sometimes it was tinged with black and the smell of scorching fur. Once it came out greenish; when Sigifrith sniffed the tainted steam, he had to turn away from the foul reek, leaning on Grani to hold himself up and coughing till his racked lungs ached.

Despite his earlier words, Ragin did not appear in Alapercht's hall during the forging of the second sword. Sigifrith often left loaves of bread or rabbits he had caught down by the door, then hid himself to see when Ragin would come out, but he could never sit still long enough to outwait the dwarf.

As Yule drew nearer, Sigifrith could feel a prickling sparkle in the frosty air about Ragin's hill, a tingle that filled him with a maddening excitement. He knew the old smith's enchantments—for his sword!—must be weaving in more tightly, Dwalan's runes running through the blade's hot steel, wrought in with hammer and fire, word and worts. Each night he stayed longer past dark, sitting on the hill and staring into the shifting, lightless glimmer of tiny blue sparks in the blackness or dashing around it in a circle that seemed to spiral upward with each turn till he grew dizzy enough to close his eyes.

The night before Yule, Sigifrith did not go back to the little house that he now shared with Hildkar and Hludowig. Instead he brushed the light snow away from a patch of ground and lay down, rolling himself in his cloak. Grani folded his legs and lay beside his master, the heat of his body keeping Sigifrith's back warm.

Above, the clouds were breaking up, the new Moon gleaming cold and silver between the icy stars. Sigifrith lay wrapped in the comfort of his steed beside him and the steady, deep rumbling of the rock below. Half-dozing, he could hear the names murmuring just below the edge of his mind: Northren, Suthren, Austren, Westren; Althjof, Dwalan, Nar and Nawan; Nyi, Nithi, Niping, Dawan; An and Onar, Ai, Wind-Alf . . . Where his skull touched the stone, Sigifrith could hear the voices rumbling through it, as slow and deep as the grinding of glaciers.

"Wyrm-bale for a wyrm; bale from the roots of the worlds, from the wyrm Swefnir who eats at the World-Tree's roots. Keen be the edges of wyrm-forged blades; kin to us are the snakes there, to us who creep through the old etin's earth-corpse and dwell among his rocky bones."

"Kenaz the rune, torch and rot, the eating-water to shape the sword. Thus is the craft of the dwarves: no work without bale, if it be not bought at our price."

"Young Ragin's price is high; he has wrought for this longer than most."

"The dragon shall melt in his death; the sword shall melt in his blood when Fadhmir's ghost-might is freed to run hot down the crag. Ragin, beware that molten river when Fadhmir's might runs unbound; but one hotter fire has been set outside Muspell-Home, and if we have wrought rightly, it shall never be crossed."

When Sigifrith closed his eyes, it seemed to him that he could see down through the rock, into the darkness lit only by the forge fire; he could see the wyrm pattern of the sword writhing into the black venom, green ripples of foxfire snaking out from it as the lightless fires of red eyes watched.

"Another sword must hew to Fadhmir's heart when this one's work is done. Let Ragin roast the dragon's heart and eat it; then he shall grow wise."

"Swiftly were that done, if it should not melt in the bale of Fadhmir's corpse. His fiery blood shall not be death-cooled long."

"So is it ever with wyrms: their bale turns swift on itself."

"So with the wyrm we have wrought: the eater is eaten in turn."

The sword burned green along its edges, glowing through the dark eating-water, its lines rippling and coiling as though it were melting in the poison instead of hardening. But it glittered cruelly when it came out again, glinting with bale in the low fires of the forge.

Sigifrith was awake well before dawn, pacing around the top of the hill and staring into the clear black eastern sky for the first streaks of light. In the distance, he thought he could hear the crowing of an early rooster. Only a few faint wisps of smoke still rose from the hole in the roof of the hill—the smoke of plain firewood that Ragin might burn to warm himself with.

Grani stamped his hoof eagerly and snorted white puffs of frozen steam into the icy air. Sigifrith began to stroke him, feeling the trembling excitement of his own body mirrored in his steed's as they waited for the dawn.

The sky had paled, shadowy trees and bushes gradually clearer in the growing light of Yule morning. Sigifrith went to stand before the door of the cave, shifting from one foot to the other as he stared at the mossy rocks around it, trying to will Ragin out.

"Come on," he muttered softly. "Are you asleep, old dwarf?" But he spoke only to himself, although he knew Ragin's work was done.

Sigifrith waited longer and longer, till he could see the first red rim of the Sun through the bare winter trees. Then he stepped forward and knocked boldly on the oaken door of Ragin's cave.

"Come in," the dwarf's voice rumbled, echoing through the stone as the chanting had all night. Sigifrith pushed the door open and walked in, bending his knees to keep from hitting his head on the low roof.

The sword shone darkly from the stone of the anvil. It was bigger than the first had been, longer and wider in the blade, its wyrm-marks writhing and coiling over each other like true snakes.

"Go on," the smith rasped. "Pick it up." Ragin's dark eyes were red-rimmed, his brown tunic and breeches stained, face and hair almost black with soot. He waved a shaking hand at the sword. "This one ought to please you, even hard as it is to be your smith."

Sigifrith hefted the new sword. Its smooth cold hilt moved easily in his hand, the blade turning as if by its own will. He raised a finger to test the edge.

"Don't do that!" Ragin snapped.

"Why?"

"Its edges are forged with venom, as they ought to be. No one wounded by it will live long after." The dwarf stroked his beard, smearing the grains of soot in black streaks through its mottled gray. "When it strikes flesh, it will not stop till it has gone through the body and into the earth, nor can it be sheathed except with a human's warm blood on it. The name I have given it is Swefnir."

"It is a fine blade," Sigifrith agreed cautiously, swinging it a couple of times as Ragin stepped hastily back. Swefnir hissed through the air like a cold living thing, as though it hungered for warm flesh already. Its coiling patterns drew the light in, melting and swirling darkly as it moved in Sigifrith's hand. He remembered how it had wavered beneath the venom's dark surface. Slowly he walked toward the anvil again.

"Sigifrith!" Ragin shouted, then, as his foster-son lifted the sword, scuttled out of the cave.

Sigifrith felt Swefnir turning in his hand, writhing against him. Clasping the hilt in both hands, he brought it down with a sharp flick of his wrists. Swefnir struck the anvil with a crash that almost jarred the hilt from Sigifrith's hands. Half the blade flew off, sticking into the cave's stone wall; a faint wisp of greenish steam seared Sigifrith's lungs. He coughed dryly once and spat the foul taste from his mouth, looking down at the twisted half-sword in his hands.

A sudden wave of anger and disappointment swept over him. He flung Swefnir's hilt across the cave, crying out to Ragin, "You must be as treacherous as your kinsmen!"

Ragin stood in the doorway, his sooty face cracking into a grimace of anger.

"Cursed boy," he said, the rasp of the file in his voice. "What in Hella's name does it take to satisfy you? You won't get such a sword so easily again, I promise you." The dwarf looked at the long shard sticking out of the stone wall. "Lucky," he added bitterly. "What if Swefnir had shattered as your last sword did? You'd regret destroying my work a lot more than you do now, believe me."

"It wasn't the sword I need," Sigifrith answered.

"The sword you need? It would have done for slaying Fadhmir." Ragin walked across the cave and picked up Swefnir's hilt, considering the broken metal that jutted from it. Then he went to the tall pot of dark liquid that stood near the forge and lowered the remains of the sword in carefully. "Now it will be eaten by the bale it was meant to deal—more work wasted for your pleasure." He paused, glaring at Sigifrith. "Other heroes have killed and died to hold lesser blades. Only you would break the best craft of the dwarves with your first blow."

"What shall I do for a sword, then?" Sigifrith asked. "If that was the best craft of the dwarves . . . if you can't forge one for me?"

"Get out of my smithy!" Ragin snapped. "Go back to your mother. You won't find a better smith than I am, so you'll have to do without a sword. If no weapon will suit you, you'd better stay in the hall with the women and learn to weave."

Furious, Sigifrith raised his fist and moved toward the smith, who stepped hastily back. Ragin bared his teeth in a grimace of fear like a cornered rat's as he cowered from his foster-son. Sigifrith cried out in anger and shame, slamming his fist against a stone jutting from the cave's wall. The rock broke under his blow, its pieces rattling onto the stony floor.

Sigifrith heard Ragin choking off a gasp. Meeting the dwarf's eyes again, he saw what they both knew: his blow could easily have killed Ragin, if he had followed his first thought and struck the old smith instead of the stone. Sigifrith stumbled out of the cave and heaved himself onto Grani's back.

"What should I do, then?" he asked the stallion. "If Ragin can't forge my sword for me, who can?"

Grani began to walk slowly along, every so often turning his head to munch bits of twig and dead leaf from the side of the path. Sigifrith closed his eyes, trusting the horse to find his own way.

It was not long before Grani stopped at the side of a little pool. The thin ice coating the water shone like a polished silver mirror in Frowe Sunna's new light.

"You're thirsty, hmm?" he asked. "I'll break the ice for you, then."

Sigifrith got down, raising his boot over the pool. Suddenly he stopped, surprised by the clearness with which he could see every detail reflected in the ice. The sole of his boot, mud caked into the neat sinew stitches, showed huge, leg and body tapering off above it. Curious, he knelt down in the snow at the pool's edge and looked into it.

Sigifrith had not used a mirror for months; the man he saw in the ice almost seemed a stranger to him. Masses of light brown hair, shining with soft gleams of muted reddish-gold where the light caught it, spilled around his broad shoulders and down his back in a long curly tangle. The Sun's light glittered from the sparse brown hairs along the edge of his jaw and his upper lip. He could see the heaviness of his mother's bones in the broadness of his face; his dark eyebrows were thick like hers, but grew in straight arches above his eyes. As Sigifrith stared at his reflection, he could almost see the face behind it, the shadow of a pale beard over a sharper jaw and narrower mouth, fair hair falling over the same wide forehead as his own, framing the same high-ridged cheeks. It seemed to him as though his father's ghost lurked hidden within his bones, staring out through icy-brilliant blue eyes.

"My father had a sword," Sigifrith murmured. "I think I shall not bear one till I have my own in my hand again." And who, he asked himself then, would know about his father's sword if not his mother?

He stared into the icy mirror for a while longer. Grime, he noticed, smeared his cheek on the left side where he had slept the night before. His hair hadn't been properly combed for weeks and was rucked up into tangled messes. Indeed, it had, if he remembered rightly, been a good while since he had bathed last. If he were to go to his mother to ask her about his father, he decided suddenly, he would go as befitted an atheling—and Sigimund's son.

Sigifrith shattered the ice with his fist. After Grani had drunk, slurping the clear cold water in huge gulps, the young man stripped off his clothing and braced his heavy muscles against the frosty air. He crouched, then leaped to fall in the very middle of the pool with a great splash. The cold shocked his breath from him, tingling sharp and painful through his veins. He laughed as he broke the surface again, splashing into the cold sunlight. He scrubbed at himself with his hands till he was sure he was clean, then hurried from the pool. He dried himself with his cloak, the scratchy wool harsh against his wet skin, and dressed as fast as he could.

Only Hildkar was in the house they shared, lying on his bed. He leaned on one elbow, looking up at Sigifrith with bloodshot eyes and holding his head.

"Ohh," he groaned. "Where were you last night? Why aren't you suffering from the wine's revenge like everyone else?"

"I thought the feasting didn't start till tomorrow," Sigifrith answered, suddenly worried. Had he lost count of the days? But Ragin had said . . .

"We went down to that Roman village down the way. You should've been there. There's a woman who runs a house there—plenty for everyone, if you know what I mean." He gave Sigifrith a lopsided, exhausted smirk. "Hludowig's probably still there. He passed out about halfway through. I could've tied him over his horse's back, but I don't think either of them would've liked it too much."

The young thane lay back, groaning again. "Oh, gods, my head! Sigifrith, you wouldn't mind bringing me a drink of water, would you?"

"Will you let me borrow your comb if I do?"

"I'll let you borrow my first-born son. Come on, I'm dying."

Sigifrith picked up a clay pot from the corner and went out to the stream. Hildkar reached out a skinny arm to grab it from his hand when he came back, draining it in one draught.

"Aah, better. My comb's under the bed, I think."

Sigifrith lay down on his stomach and rooted around through the dirt and crumpled clothes beneath Hildkar until he found the coarse-toothed piece of bronze. He sat up, brushing dust from the front of his tunic, and began to yank the comb ferociously through his hair.

Hildkar winced in sympathy as Sigifrith tugged at a particularly tight knot. "Damn, it hurts just watching you do that," he complained.

"Don't watch, then."

"Urf." The thane closed his eyes and rolled over to face the wall.

It took a long time before Sigifrith could run his fingers through his hair from roots to ends without finding any more tangles, but at last he was done.

He opened the chest where he kept his clothes and dug out his light blue feasting tunic, a pair of dark blue breeches and a rag to clean his boots with.

Sigifrith had not worn his good clothes since Winternights; now the breeches were short on him and the tunic was so tight across his shoulders that he knew he would have to be very careful to keep from breaking its seams. He brushed the mud off his cloak and folded it to hide the worst stains before draping it over his shoulder and pinning it with a square brooch of Roman gold. The wyrm-wrought silver of his belt buckle glittered icy at his waist, and his golden ring coiled warmly around his left forearm below his sleeve.

As Sigifrith opened the door to go out, Hildkar looked up at him, shading his eyes with his hand as if blinded by a sudden brightness.

"Have I seen you before?" he asked. "You don't look like the Sigifrith I know. Shit, you almost look like a human being." Beneath his sardonic words, Sigifrith could hear a solid ring of genuine admiration.

"Merry Yule to you too, Hildkar," he said, laughing.

Herwodis was standing as calmly as the solid trunk of a tree in the middle of the hall, directing her serving maids and the thralls as they scurried about arranging the benches and tables and draping the walls with wreaths of fir and holly. A finely embroidered dress of deep apple-red under a dark green cloak draped her considerable bulk; crimson garnets gleamed from the hilts of the golden pins holding her silver-threaded braids in their coils about her head. Sigifrith breathed deeply, if cautiously, trying to settle his excitement as he went to his mother.

"Sigifrith," Herwodis said, smiling up at her son. "How nice to see you again. We were beginning to wonder if you would be here for Yule, though it is your birthing-day."

"I am sorry I've been gone so often," Sigifrith answered, speaking almost as slowly and choosing his words as carefully as his mother did. "I hope it hasn't caused you any worry."

"A man of your age goes where he will," Herwodis said. "In any case, I know that Ragin will have been giving you wise redes. Speaking of our kinsman, shall we need to set a place for him at this feast?"

"I don't know. Mother, I can see that you have work you want to do in this hall before nightfall, but will you have any time to speak with me alone?"

"Of course I will." Herwodis clapped her hands. She hardly seemed to raise her voice, but its deep tones echoed from the stone walls, muted only by their woven hangings and the rugs on the paved floor. "Claudia, bring us wine and the best glasses. The rest of you, go out and chop some more firewood or see to the beasts. You know what you ought to do."

Herwodis led Sigifrith to the raised dais at the end of the hall, seating herself in her own chair and gesturing him to the one where Alapercht usually sat.

"So, my son," she said when Claudia had brought the wine and left. "What is in your thoughts, then?" She lifted the pitcher by its clear flower-wrought handle and poured for Sigifrith, then for herself.

Sigifrith picked his goblet up, twirling its long clear stem about in his fingers and swirling the wine inside the conical bluish green bowl before he sipped at it.

"I asked Ragin to make me a sword," he said. "He made one with craft alone and one with magic, and . . . I broke both of them. He told me to come to you. He was very angry with me," Sigifrith added. He sipped at the wine again, savoring the edge of wormwood that sharpened its sweetness.

Herwodis looked into the depths of her glass for a moment before raising it to her lips. She drank without haste, but the goblet was almost empty when she set it down.

"I expect he would be," she said. "How did you break them?"

"I struck them on his anvil to test their strength."

Sigifrith's mother considered her son for a while. It seemed to Sigifrith that something in her gray eyes rippled like light through window glass, as though she were looking past Sigifrith and out of the hall.

"One does not usually cut stone with swords, even dwarf-forged swords," she said at last. "Surely you had a reason for doing this?"

"I did it because I needed to."

"There are not many who would question the worth of Ragin's smithing. Even hard as you can hew, I think that his swords would not often be expected to break against helms or byrnies. What did you mean to do with your blade, that it needed such a test?"

"I mean to slay the dragon Fadhmir," Sigifrith answered. His words fell clear as breaking glass in the stillness of the hall.

Herwodis gripped the stem of her goblet tightly with one hand, lifting the pitcher in the other. Her hand was shaking badly enough to splash some wine over the side of her glass, the greenish gold drops spreading into splotches on the creamy linen table covering. Almost as an afterthought, she refilled Sigifrith's glass as well.

"What's wrong?" Sigifrith asked his mother. "Is there something else I need to know?"

"When your father and I sailed north on his last faring—when we would have gone to his lands to gather his people—we passed by the foot of the Dragon's Crag. I think that I am no coward, but I could not look up to the cave where Fadhmir dwells. I have heard it said that he bears the Helm of Awe, and that therefore no man may dare to stand against him. But your father raised his eyes to the dragon's hole and put his hand to the hilt of his sword, and I knew he had it in his mind that one day he would try his strength against Fadhmir's. If he had not been slain . . . " Herwodis coughed and drank hastily. Sigifrith could see the gleam of unshed tears in her eyes, and clenched his teeth against a grin of excitement. He leaned forward, trying to breathe deeply enough to calm himself without ripping the seams of his tunic.

Before he could think or weigh his words, the cry burst out of him, as sudden and terrible as a crack of thunder, "What became of the sword's two shards?"

Herwodis' glass shattered on the stone floor. She had gone white, her flesh seeming to fall away and the heavy bones of her face standing out starkly against the shadows beneath. For a moment, it seemed to Sigifrith that he saw Herwodis as she had been in her youth; then, that he looked upon the sagging face of an old woman.

"Sigimund gave the pieces of the sword to me. I kept them well and hid them in a secret place I made in King Chilpirich's hall, where no one but I would ever be able to find them and bring them out again."

Sigifrith grasped his mother by her hands, being careful not to crush them. Herwodis' skin was very cold to his touch, her flesh clammy with sweat and soft except for a thin hard line of jagged scar tissue down the palm of her right hand.

"Give them to me. I would have them!" he said. Without his willing it, his fists tightened with excitement. He heard the ripping of the seams over his shoulders as his tunic gave way at last.

Suddenly Herwodis grasped Sigifrith's hands with a strength that surprised him, as though she were holding her whole weight by that grip alone. "You are likely to win glory with that sword," she whispered, her voice rough and edged keenly with pain. "We shall go to Chilpirich's hall for the feast of Ostara, and then I shall give you your father's sword to be made whole again." The first teardrops began to swell from the corner of her closed eyelids. "Wyrd writes as she will. I knew this should come one day, but . . . it had been a long time, and I had almost stopped expecting it."

"Why are you weeping, Mother? I think there is little that you or I need fear in this."

Herwodis wiped her eyes with the gold-embroidered sleeve of her red linen dress and blinked hard several times. "Of course there's not, Sigifrith," she said briskly, patting her coiled braids straight. "You will do what you must, in any case, and I would not keep your inheritance from you if I could—that would betray your father's memory. No; there is no reason or good in weeping now."

She stood and clapped her hands together. "Claudia!" she called. "Tell the others to bring the firewood in. We have plenty of work left to do."

The thralls began to bear in their loads of wood for the fires that would be kindled around the hall. Sigifrith spread the folds of his cloak, tugging it around his back to hide his rent tunic before he stood.

"Can I help with anything?" he asked.

Herwodis looked about in distraction, then nodded her head decisively. "Go and apologize to Ragin and see if he's willing to come to the feast. I should think," she added, "that he deserves more thanks than you seem to have given him."

Sigifrith shifted uncomfortably. "Maybe so," he muttered. Then he smiled brilliantly at his mother. "Don't worry. I'll take care of everything, you'll see."

Although Herwodis' lips curved in answer to her son's grin, her drawn brows still cast low dark shadows over her eyes and Sigifrith could see the little lines pulled tight around her mouth. "Of course you will, Sigifrith," she said lightly. "Go on, now."

The clouds had come up swiftly since the dawn. By the time Sigifrith reached Ragin's cave, the sky was dusky gray and the first snowflakes were beginning to float downward. The door to the dwarf's smithy was shut. Sigifrith knocked on it without hesitation, but no answer came.

"Ragin?" he called. "Ragin, it's me."

The smith did not answer.

"Are you there? Ragin, come on, say something. I know you're angry with me. I'm sorry. I've come to apologize."

After a few moments, the dwarf's grating voice rumbled, "Go away."

"Ragin," Sigifrith coaxed. "Come on, let me in. I want to talk to you. Please?"

"Go away."

"Will you come to the Yule feast tonight?"

"No."

"My mother will be angry with me if you don't."

"Good."

"Ragin, I really am sorry. I didn't mean to—"

The door banged open. Ragin was already stumping away from it, his back turned on Sigifrith.

Sigifrith bent his knees and crept into the cave, sinking down cross-legged beside Ragin's low stool with his back to the fire. Warm from his run through the woods, he pulled his cloak over his head without bothering to unpin it and dropped it beside him. The dwarf seated himself and glared across at Sigifrith.

"What do you have to say for yourself, then?" he muttered fiercely. "No, don't bother. If you go on as you have been, there may very well come a day when you'll regret having broken that sword—it was the blade of a true hero, whether you know what that means or not."

"Will you forgive me?" Sigifrith asked softly.

"It doesn't matter whether I do or not," Ragin answered, folding his thick arms across his chest and sitting as stolid as a boulder before his foster-son. "But if I can altogether trust you to follow the redes I give, maybe things won't work out so ill in the end."

"What could go ill?"

Ragin turned his head slowly from side to side. "Foolish boy," he murmured. "We'll see, then."

"Are you willing to forge another sword for me?"

Sigifrith saw a torch of true anger kindling in the dwarf's eyes, and braced himself for a blow that never came as the fires sank back into darkness.

"Tonight I'm going to sleep, and nothing more. Perhaps if you ask me in a year or two I'll say yes."

"A year or two?" Sigifrith cried in dismay and shock. "But my mother is giving me the pieces of my father's sword at Ostara's feast."

Ragin's head sagged down into his hands, as slow as a rock tearing itself grain by grain away from a mountainside. "Go away," he said again, overtones of tiredness rasping through his voice like the sharpness of small files through the grumbling of a grindstone. "Leave me be. Let me think about it."

Sigifrith waited for Ragin to say or do something else, but the old dwarf only sat with his head in his hands. When Ragin's harsh snores began to rumble through the cave, Sigifrith lifted him from his stool and laid him down on the pallet at the side of the cave, covering him with his rough woolen blanket. Ragin's heavy muscles were tightly knotted even in his sleep, as though he still held himself wary against attack, but—limbs and mind fettered by the exhaustion of his long work—he did not wake.

It had been warm when King Alapercht's household started their journey to King Chilpirich's hall in the morning, but the air grew colder and colder as they traveled farther into the mountains. Although it was the day before Ostara's feast, which would be the first day of summer, thin patches of snow still lay under the shadows of the spreading fir branches, and the puddles on the road were rimmed with muddy rime. Sigifrith could hardly keep still on Grani's back; the two of them dashed up ahead of the troop and back over and over again, Grani prancing about from side to side of the road like the wild colt he had been and Sigifrith's shouts of exuberance ringing through the icy air. Ragin watched them dubiously from the shelter of the wain where he sat huddled into his wolf-hide cloak, muttering to himself.

When Perchte and Chilpirich came out to greet their son and his family, Sigifrith noticed that the old king dragged his left foot a little and the corner of his mouth drooped even when he smiled; that Perchte had grown thinner, except for the swollen joints of her bony fingers, and that a faint hint of blue like a light river mist tinged her lips and fingernails. But they met their guests with great cheer—more than usual, Sigifrith thought. It seemed to him that Alapercht and his queen might not fare to Chilpirich's hall many more times. The thought troubled him and he twitched his shoulders as if to shake it from them like a cloak, smiling down at Perchte as she fluttered, as always, about how large he had grown and embracing her as carefully as he would cup a butterfly in his fingers.

Hard as it was for Sigifrith to hold himself back, he waited in silence while the glass goblets had been passed about and filled with Perchte's thick ale, sitting still as the two kings and their wives spoke together over what had happened since they saw each other last.

"Really, the most news comes from the Burgundian lands," Alapercht said, settling himself down comfortably and leaning back in his chair. "Gebica died of a sickness before Winternights and his son Gundahari was chosen as king over the Burgundians. Folk expect things of him. The last we heard he was gathering his men together and beginning to press the Romans into a new treaty. They say he might even be looking to have a voice in what goes on in the Empire."

"What of your alliance, then?" Chilpirich asked. He stroked his beard thoughtfully, turning to Herwodis' son. "Will your betrothal hold, Sigifrith?"

Sigifrith sat at a total loss, only now realizing how little he had seen of Alapercht's folk that winter. He had not heard any of this news before.

"There is no sign that Gundahari won't hold to the alliance his father made through Gundrun," Herwodis answered. "It is said, too, that his mother Grimhild still sits high in his counsel, and that it was she who wished the alliance in the first place."

"Grimhild is said to be a wise woman," Chilpirich said, his voice betraying no hint of his thoughts.

"It's her other son that we've heard more of here," Perchte added. "Hagan—he was sent as a hostage to the Hunnish drighten Attila at this past Midsummer. Since then, he's been making a good name for himself as a warrior together with another young hostage, a Frank named Waldhari. We've heard that there are a lot of Goths who've gathered in Attila's warband around the exiled King Thioderik."

"What of the Huns, then?" Alapercht asked. "Do you hear more about them on this side of the Rhine?"

"They take a little here and a little there," Chilpirich answered. "For the time, they seem to be at peace with the Romans, though that could change any day."

Sigifrith sat listening to the talk of the others till he could bear it no longer. Then it seemed to him as though a wave were swelling beneath him, bearing him to his feet. The talk broke off, Chilpirich, Alapercht, Perchte and Herwodis staring up at him.

"Mother," he said softly. "I think it's time."

"Yes," murmured Herwodis. She, too, stood. "We'll be gone for a while," she told the others. "Please excuse our bad manners. Sigifrith and I have something we must do."

Perchte laughed, shaking her silver-wound head. "Herwodis, darling, you know there's nothing to excuse. Can we help you?"

"I think not," the younger woman answered. "Though I do thank you. Come, then, Sigifrith."

Sigifrith followed his mother out of the hall. She walked with slow dignity, keys jangling at the waist of her rich reddish brown dress. Her deep green cloak belled out behind her in the icy wind as they stepped outside, and she quickly pulled it tight.

Together they walked around the hall to the storehouses, going to the farthest one. Herwodis loosed the knot holding her keys to her girdle, fumbling with stiff fingers for a large key of iron as Sigifrith shifted impatiently from foot to foot. She slid the key into the rusty lock, twisting and moving it for a time that seemed far too long to Sigifrith. Just as he was ready to take it from her and see if his strength could break the seal of years, the key turned with a grating squeak of metal and the door swung open.

The first thing Sigifrith marked was the musty scent of old linen, wool and furs. As his eyes slowly adjusted to the light, he saw two great wooden chests lying beneath a thick fur of dust. The lid of one had caved in and a few gleams of silver shone from the blackened coils beneath. He moved over to it.

"Not that one," Herwodis said. She pointed to the larger of the chests, the one that rested against the back wall of the storehouse. "You will need to move that one away before I can get the shards of Gram out."

Sigifrith squatted, putting his arms around the huge wooden box and blowing away the cloud of dust that rose around him. It was heavier than he had thought it would be, but with a mighty heave from his legs he rose to his full height and carried the chest across the storeroom. "Where do you want it?" he asked, breathing only a little harder as he stood before his mother with his great burden.

"Anywhere," Herwodis answered.

As Sigifrith put the chest down, she walked forward and knelt before the shallow, sharp-cornered hole that the chest had pressed into the earthen floor. To Sigifrith's shock, she began to dig with her hands, her fingernails scratching into the hard earth like a beast's claws.

"Let me do that!" he said. "You shouldn't . . . "

Herwodis shook her head. "I buried the shards of Sigimund's sword here before Chilpirich's thralls set the chest on top of it. I guided them myself. I meant that no single man should be able to lift it away and come upon Gram by chance, even if another should come into this house where Sigimund's inheritance has lain since your birth."

She kept digging until she was elbow-deep in the earth, scraping out a long trench. The afternoon light began to fade swiftly; soon it was dusk outside the hut and almost as dark as night within.

At last Herwodis drew in her breath, sitting up and wiping some of the dirt from her hands.

"Is that it?" Sigifrith asked, crouching and leaning over her shoulder as though he could see into the dark hole she had dug.

Herwodis bent and lifted out a long wooden box. The leather cords around it had rotted, falling away at her touch. She worked the lid off carefully. Inside was a dark cloth bag that she handed silently to Sigifrith.

Sigifrith reached into the bag's mouth. His fingers closed around the well-greased hilt of a sword, the stone icy-smooth against his palm. As he touched it, it seemed to him that a bolt of cold lightning shocked up his arm and through his body, bursting within his skull in a jagged flower of blue-white fire as he sprang to his feet. He cried out, a shout that seemed to ring through his head and echo through halls upon halls of unseen stone around him, "Gram!" The linen opened before the weapon's edge as he drew the broken sword forth from the bag that had held and hidden it for the length of his life.

Gram's blade was twisted where it had shattered, the wyrm mottlings warped and darkened as if by a great fire. Sigifrith pulled out the other shard; it, too, was bent and discolored. He could feel the might within them thrumming through his arms with the painful tingling of blood flowing back into a sleeping limb. For a long time he stood breathless, staring at the pieces of his father's sword till he could see them only as shadows in the darkness of the hut.

Herwodis got to her feet, supporting herself against the wall as she did. Sigifrith could hear the rustling as she brushed dust from her dress, then the clinking of her keys. She held out the iron key that had opened the door to the storehouse.

"All of this is yours now, to do with as you will," Herwodis told her son, her muted voice trembling faintly with tiredness. "I cannot hold it for you any more, nor should it rest in the darkness: this hoard can be kept no longer. Now, my Sigifrith, you know how your father fell. It was by Lingwe's plans, and Lingwe's treachery, to gather a host and attack him when he was far from his own folk. Hunding and the sons of Hunding were ever foe to the Wolfings and the Walsings: this I have heard in the songs from the north . . . that might be oftener sung in our hall," Herwodis added in a whisper, "if Alapercht thought that I had ever ceased to mourn for Sigimund." She wiped the back of her hand across her eyes, leaving a muddy smear on her pale skin.

"Your father had meant this wealth to be used in resettling his folk in my father's country, for the North Sea was eating the lands of the Saxons and they needed a new home. That is no less so; nor are his folk less yours, though your father's foe rules them now." Suddenly Herwodis' deep voice sounded clear and loud, as Sigifrith had never heard it before; his ears rang with the echo, and he thought it must shake the old dust from the wealth chests. "You must go north, Sigifrith. You must avenge your father Sigimund: you must finish what his death left undone. I was taken as a battle captive, and you were born in captivity. Until Lingwe's blood has reddened your father's sword, you cannot count yourself free, nor shall your soul—his soul, that lives in you—ever gain its full might."

She pressed the iron key into his hand. "Your father's wealth shall buy ships for your faring. It shall not be long now before you are counted a man full-grown, and ready to lead the host. I know there are many of our young thanes who are eager to see fighting after these years of frith."

Sigifrith bent to kiss his mother gently on the cheek. "Thank you, Mother. I know no bride has been truer to her man than you have been to Sigimund through these years, nor kept her trust better than you have kept this. I shall bear this sword well, and it shall not be too long before Lingwe's blood has reddened it."

Sigifrith uncurled his fingers from the hilt of the sword, swallowing down the choking thickness in his throat. Soon you shall be whole, he thought, and always at my side. He wrapped the slit linen around the sword's pieces again.

Ragin stood shivering outside the hall, waiting for them. He grasped Sigifrith by the arm and pulled him aside as Herwodis went in. "Do you have what you went for?" he hissed.

"I have it."

"Let me see."

Only half-willingly, Sigifrith handed the shrouded shards to his foster-father. Ragin folded back the cloth overlapping the pieces of the blade, holding it carefully by the linen beneath. A glint of red foxfire glowed from his eyes in the darkness as he ran his fingertips over the warped metal, muttering under his breath.

"Go to bed," he said to Sigifrith at last. "You'll have to get up well before sunrise tomorrow if we want to start our work at dawn."

"We?" Sigifrith asked in surprise, taking the broken sword back and re-wrapping it.

"I know the metal of this sword," Ragin said shortly. "It's a sort of star iron; it's too hard for my strength alone. I think this is one piece of work you won't be able to ruin, even though you're too eager for the task."

Sigifrith awoke before dawn, opening his eyes to see Ragin's dark shape crouched beside him. He slid out of his blankets, clutching the shards of his father's sword to his chest as he had all night in his sleep. Ragin heaved a clinking sack of tools into Sigifrith's grasp, slinging another bag over his own back.

Without disturbing the sleeping thanes, the two of them crept out of the hall. No stars glittered in the black sky; only the white patches of snow gleamed pale through the darkness. It was much colder now, the chill striking through Sigifrith's cloak as he followed Ragin along the long twisting path through the fir trees and up one of the mountains to the rock-built hut that served the dwarf as a forge here in Chilpirich's lands.

Ragin was breathing hard from the climb, but he did not speak as he arranged his clinking tools upon the block of granite in the center of the hut. He propped the door open with a piece of wood; through it, Sigifrith could see the first hint of gray beginning to show through the clouds in the eastern sky. From the smaller bag he had carried himself, the smith dug out charcoal and kindling, arranging them neatly by touch in the stone-lined forge. A soft wind blew through the cracks between the rocks of the walls and the open door, its icy caress sending a shiver down Sigifrith's bones as the first crystals of snow floated in.

Ragin stood without speaking, staring at his foster-son. It seemed to Sigifrith that something in the tightness of the old dwarf's shoulder ridges and the corners of his eyes spoke of an eagerness to begin; that as Ragin looked at the linen-wrapped bundle Sigifrith held, his pupils began to glow as if the smith's keen flame were flaring within his skull.

"Why don't you light the fire?" Ragin asked gruffly.

Sigifrith looked around for flint and steel, but couldn't find them. "With what?"

"Look in the bag."

Sigifrith felt in one of the sacks with cold-numbed fingers, but brought out nothing more than two sticks and a flat-topped chunk of wood with a hole drilled into it. One of the sticks was strung with sinew like a miniature bow of yew; the other was carved to a dull point at one end. The second bag was empty.

"Did you forget something, old dwarf?" Sigifrith asked, half-teasing, half-angry. The thought of having to go back to the hall again, of having to wait any longer to begin his sword, maddened him as he considered it. He clenched his cold fists, stamping his booted feet impatiently on the living bedrock of the hut's floor.

Ragin shook his head, picking up the pieces of wood and pushing them into Sigifrith's stiff hands. "For this you must kindle the need-fire." He took his foster-son by the elbow, turning him toward the stone and guiding his steps till the young man stood on the far side, facing the open door. The snow was falling more thickly now, a soft, shifting tapestry of white ice flakes through the darkness of early dawn.

Sigifrith set the pointed tip of one stick into the hole of the flat wood and slipped the bow over it, pulling it back and forth as hard and fast as he could. Before long he could feel his breath rasping harsh and hot through his throat. The taste of the air was sharp and metallic in his mouth as he strove, shivering, to kindle the fire with wood on wood, staring into the swiftly falling snow outside.

The white-shrouded night began to lighten as Sigifrith worked the bow of the need-fire, turning and turning the drill. It seemed to him that he could feel the heat beginning to burn in the pit of his stomach, warming the wood under his hands as the bow drill whirled back and forth. The dawn kept brightening, its clear light stronger and stronger through the heavy snow till whitened earth and snow and clouds glowed with a pure silver light that pierced through Sigifrith's head like the ringing of steel on steel. It seemed to him that he could see the tiny hex-shape of each falling snowflake before him, the ice crystals' edges keen as tiny blades. Flashes of brightness glimmered at the edges of Sigifrith's sight like white-gowned ghost-women hurrying away from his glance.

The wood on the stone anvil was glowing red through the silvery-white air, a wisp of smoke writhing up from it; Sigifrith sawed harder with his bow, the fire within him flowing through his arms and out into the wood as a little yellow flame sprang from the root of the drill.

Ragin was there at once, feeding the flame with dried leaves and moss, then small sticks, till it burned strong. He gestured toward the forge. Sigifrith bore his need-fire carefully to the stony enclosure, setting it into the kindling and charcoal. The flames leapt up almost at once, the wood crackling under their bite. The sweet-scented smoke of applewood rose from the forge as the charcoal began to catch, mixed with something dry and strong that sparked and singed, setting Sigifrith's head to spinning dizzily as he breathed it in. He was sweating now, hands and feet tingling with warmth; he cast off his cloak and pulled off his boots as swiftly as he could, kicking them into a corner.

Sigifrith unwrapped the shards of his father's sword, tossing the linen bag to flare in the fire. Ragin brought a fistful of thick dark stuff out of a clay pot, smearing it over the hex-cut ice stone in the sword's hilt. The dwarf put the two pieces of the sword into the forge as Sigifrith began to pump the bellows, their stormwind-strong blast whipping the flames into a mighty blaze. The grease on the blade burned fiercely for a moment, a puff of black smoke rising from the yellow-white flame that died away as swiftly as it had sprung up.

When the sword's twisted pieces glowed red-gold, Ragin drew them from the forge with his tongs, laying them on the anvil and stepping back. Sigifrith took up the heaviest of the dwarf's hammers and struck at the fiery shards with all his might, the shock jarring his arm as steel rang hard against steel. Again and again he smote the warped metal of his father's broken blade, striving against the strength of its first maker and the might that had shattered it, fighting to pound the shards straight again. He felt his strength growing instead of lessening as he beat on the blade, springing through him in a mighty peal of laughter that rang against the piercing sharpness of his hammer striking on steel and stone.

"Hai!" he cried, taking the cooling metal up in his hands and thrusting it into the fire again. Twice more Ragin brought the glowing pieces of Sigimund's sword out of the stony forge; twice more Sigifrith pounded upon the shards till at last they lay straight upon the anvil, their wyrm mottlings blackened and warped into spreading ripples of metal where Sigifrith had struck them and their broken edges beaten to spreading flatness by the hammering so that it seemed they could never be joined again.

Ragin's craggy face was ruddy from the heat of the fire, his eyes alive as he took the hammer from Sigifrith's hands and stepped behind the anvil. Carefully the dwarf turned the hilt half of the sword, striking against the flattened break with sharp, precise blows. He grunted softly with the strain each time metal met metal as he slowly worked the shattered steel into the straight lines of a sword again. Now and then he would put it back into the forge, Sigifrith would pump the bellows, feeding the coals till the fire grew hot enough to soften the star iron and the soft gray smoke filled the little hut with its sweet apple scent, its strange dry undertone blurring Sigifrith's vision into dizzy sparks when he breathed it in. Where the metal was too hard, Sigifrith had to strike it again; but it was Ragin's craft that shaped the rippling steel till the two pieces fit together as a whole. Then Sigifrith blew the fire up to its full heat again, howling in a burst of mighty wod as he pumped the bellows faster and faster until the coals were too bright to look at and the crack in the sword glowed yellow-white, drops of burning metal flowing down the blade as hot rivulets of sweat flowed down Sigifrith's forehead and back, dripping together to weld the two shards into a single weapon again. After that it was Ragin's task to smooth and sharpen the edges, hardening them in the eating venom till they glittered in a rim around the rippling patterns of dark and light star steel.

"Once more," the dwarf husked. "Blow up the fire once more, and then we quench."

Sigifrith's glance fell on the quenching trough carved into the rock of the hut's floor beside the anvil. The stone was dry with dust. Before he could open his mouth to ask what Ragin meant, he heard Grani's whinny outside. The tall horse stood in the doorway, snow crystals tangled in his mane; he arched his neck, and Sigifrith could see the pulsing of the vein beneath his wind-gray hide. The youth did not stop to think, but let his hand rise with the knife in it, gently nicking the horse's neck.

Grani's blood steamed in the snowy air, running hot over Sigifrith's cupped palms as he ran back and forth from his steed to the quenching trough. The wide groove in the stone was almost full by the time the stallion's neck had stopped bleeding. Sigifrith wiped his clotted hands in the soft snow, leaving reddish black streaks to freeze into trails of blood crystals. The steady fall of new flakes was already whitening the dark gouges in the snow, furring over Sigifrith's stains.

Ragin stood waiting by the forge with the sword laid across his hands, watching his foster-son. Without hesitating, Sigifrith took the blade from him and nicked his own wrist, holding it over the quenching trough. The bright red blood spread in ripples through the darker, melting slowly into it as Ragin watched, stroking his soot-flecked beard.

Then the smith nodded. For the last time they put the blade into the stony forge and Sigifrith set himself to blowing the coals to a glow again.

When Ragin reached in with his tongs and drew the sword forth, the bale-hardened edges glittered with a flame of their own. Sigifrith set his hand to the black-crusted hilt and together the young atheling and the dwarf sank the burning blade into the quenching trough. The blood hissed and bubbled from the sword, the scorched coppery scent of its steam cutting through the apple-sweet smoke of the forge's coals.

Ragin and Sigifrith watched till no more steam rose from the quenching trough, till the burnt blood began to clot on the edges of the stone.

"Take it," Ragin whispered. "If this one breaks, I am no maker of swords."

Sigifrith reached into the quenching trough and drew his father's sword forth, the blood clinging to it like a sheath of red-black silk. The burnt stuff with which Ragin had warded the ice stone of the hilt from the heat of the forge flaked away in his hands as he raised it above his head.

"Gram!" he shouted, and brought the sword down upon the stone anvil with a deafening crack. In a shower of bright sparks, the great boulder split to its base beneath his blow, his sword plunging to its full length into the living rock below. With a mighty heave Sigifrith brought the weapon out again, its wyrm-mottled steel shining as clean as the feathers of a swan's wing. Gram sang keenly through the air as he whirled it, laughing for joy.

"Now you have wrought a sword fit for a hero!" Sigifrith cried.

Unable to stand still any longer, he ran barefoot out into the snow with his sword in his hand, the crystals melting away as they blew against him. Grani cantered beside him, following him along the winding path through the snow-weighted fir trees that shadowed the mountains around them with a thick fell of silver-frosted blackness, misted white by the shifting waves of wind-borne snow.

They did not stop till they came to the snow-crusted edge of a lake between the firs. The water was dark gray-black as polished iron, the wind blowing silver ripples across it. Sigifrith looked into it for a few moments, stroking Grani's neck with his left hand and raising Gram in his right.

A chunk of the horse's ragged winter coat came away under his touch, the hair surprisingly fine and soft in his hand. Sigifrith blew on it; it floated out over the water a little way before a gust of wind cast it down to the surface of the lake, blowing it back toward the shore.

Sigifrith dipped Gram into the water with its edge toward the floating clump, holding the sword still as the ripples bore it to him. As the hair met the edge of his blade, it split cleanly into two pieces.

He drew Gram out of the lake, wiping the weapon dry on his tunic. The sky was already growing darker. His empty stomach was beginning to rumble and his bladder was full. Sigifrith realized that he had not even thought of stopping work for food or a rest as much as once in the day. As he thought about it, it seemed strange to him, but at the same time he knew that things could not have gone otherwise.

Sigifrith loosened his breeches and pissed, the yellow stream melting a deep hole in the snow. When he was done, he tightened the string at his waist and climbed on his steed's back. Gently he nudged Grani into a trot and rode him back to the stone hut where Ragin was cleaning up the forge and gathering his tools.

As Sigifrith came in, the dwarf fixed him with a glittering glance.

"Are you satisfied now?" he asked.

"No sword could be better," Sigifrith answered. "Thank you, foster-father." The warm flood in his heart spilling over, he went over to Ragin and crouched down to hug the dwarf around the shoulders. Sigifrith could feel the smith's thick muscles tightening, but Ragin did not move away till his foster-son stood again.

"Watch what you're doing with that sword," the old dwarf rasped dryly.

Sigifrith laughed.

"Now you must make good on your boast and go to meet Fadhmir, since I have made the sword," Ragin said, his voice deepening and cracking like treacherous ice.

"I shall keep my word," Sigifrith said. "But not before my father is avenged." He went to the corner where he had thrown his cloak and boots, pulling the boots on and wrapping the cloak around his shoulders.

Together Ragin and Sigifrith finished collecting the smith's tools from around the broken anvil and packing them away, as Grani waited patiently outside.

"Will you make me a sheath for my sword?" Sigifrith asked his foster-father.

"When we get back to Alapercht's lands. You'll have to do without till then."

When they went outside, the snow had stopped. The two of them loaded the bags of tools onto Grani's back and Sigifrith walked beside the colt, his left hand on the sacks to steady them and Gram resting in his right.

Slowly Ragin and Sigifrith began to make their way back to Chilpirich's hall. With difficulty, Ragin broke his way through the snow that came up well past his knees; Sigifrith stepped lightly over it, holding himself back so that the dwarf could keep up with him.

KINSMEN

The snow fell harder after Ostara's feast, as often happened in the mountains, so Alapercht and his folk stayed longer in Chilpirich's hall than they had meant to. Often, when the winter was long, the thanes would become quarrelsome and begin to fight over their ale; but the wines Perchte brewed from wild cherries and pears mixed with honey seemed to soothe the mood of warriors, and most of them were content to stay in and drink and dice, or play at the hunting game called tables. Though Ragin seldom came into Alapercht's hall and shunned the company of men, even he did not complain too much about the weather that kept him in with the warriors here, but sat closest to the fire warming his rocky bones at Chilpirich's hearth and drinking Perchte's wines while he carved at wood and cast the shavings to flare in the flames.

Hildkar and Perchtwine were casting dice, a pile of beads and pieces of Roman copper on the table before each of them. Sigifrith lay on the bench beside them, stretching to his full length and propping his head on his right arm to watch. At the moment, he was content to rest there with one of the hall's fires warming his back and a cup of wine in his hand, his sword sleeping upon his left thigh in a leather sheath that glittered with the finest of gilded interlace work.

"Ow," complained Hildkar, glaring balefully down at the treacherous dice. He pushed the three wooden cubes over to Perchtwine along with two amber beads.

"Hah," Perchtwine said. He grinned smugly, then winced as the air hit the jagged stub of his newly-broken front tooth and closed his mouth. The young thane belched in disgust, flipping his long fringe of sandy hair out of his eyes before he took up the dice. Cupping them in his hands, he blew on them and rattled them briskly, casting them with a practiced flip of his wrists. "Got you!" he said triumphantly. "Two more and you pay again."

"You couldn't make two more good throws if those dice were loaded with all the tin in Britain," Hildkar told him. "You're going to lose it on this one, just you wait and see."

Perchtwine juggled the dice in an arc from hand to hand, finally tossing them up into the air and knocking them to the table with a light tap of his fingers.

"Dumb luck," Hildkar said darkly when the cubes had stopped bouncing, twisting one side of his thin mouth as his glare tallied the spots on their upward faces. "Sheer dumb luck."

"I knew I was going to have a good day today," Perchtwine said, taking up the dice again. "I dreamed about cattle last night, and you know dreams of cattle always mean wealth."

"Dreams of cattle mean you're going to be slaughtered like cattle at Winternights, your wealth cut down like a bull at the idises' blessing," Hildkar insisted.

Perchtwine laughed uneasily, rattling the dice and passing them from hand to hand behind his back. "You're no spae-man, Hildkar," he said. "You couldn't read a dream if it were written out in runes and Roman letters together. You wouldn't know what a dream about cattle meant if the Weleda came back from the dead to tell you herself."

"I know what I know," Hildkar said mysteriously. "You're afraid to toss those dice. You know you're going to have to pay, and you're stalling to get out of it. Dreams of cattle, my arse."

Perchtwine let the dice fall from his hand. They clattered on the table, spinning about. He watched them carefully till they had stopped, then turned and spat into the fire.

"I told you so," Hildkar gloated, grabbing the dice.

"The game's not over yet," Perchtwine answered. "I dreamed what I dreamed, and I've told you what it means."

"Ha," said Hildkar, casting. "See? I'm right and you know it."

"Why don't you ask Ragin if you really want to know?" Sigifrith said lazily. He let a draught of cherry wine flow down his throat, its sweetness veiling the strength that flowed out through his gullet, then belched softly.

Hildkar and Perchtwine glanced at each other. "You ask him," Hildkar said hastily as the fair-haired thane shifted his weight uncomfortably from buttock to buttock.

"All right."

The other groups of thanes who sat playing tables or talking together looked up in surprise as Sigifrith raised his voice, shouting across the hall, "Hai! Ragin!"

"What do you want?" Ragin asked, his heavy head bent over the piece of wood he was carving into an elaborately adorned bowl.

"Does dreaming of cattle mean wealth?"

Ragin grunted. "Sometimes."

Sigifrith shrugged, grinning at the other two young men. "There you are," he said. "Sometimes."

Hildkar cast the dice again. "But not this time." He smirked at Perchtwine, who shook his head and picked up the clay pitcher that stood on the table between them, pouring more wine into his cup.

Hildkar's next throw fell badly. He struck the dice lightly before handing them over to Perchtwine. "Sure you don't want to play, Sigifrith?" he asked. "The luck's always better with three."

Sigifrith swung his legs over the side of the bench, pushing it back to make room for his knees under the low table. "I might as well," he said.

The three of them passed the dice around for a while. Sigifrith won a copper cloak pin and three crystal beads from Hildkar, got a horn comb with one broken tooth and a small ring of purple stone from Perchtwine, then lost the comb to Hildkar. Although he was beginning to feel pleasantly mellow from the wine, a restlessness stirred in his mind.

"I wonder what he meant by 'sometimes'?" Sigifrith said, shoving the dice over to Hildkar. "I'd think either a dream means something or it doesn't."

"Well, that one meant just what I said," the skinny thane answered. "Didn't it?" He elbowed Perchtwine in the side, moving over on the bench quickly before Perchtwine could shove him in return.

"I've never heard that a dream of cattle meant anything but wealth," Perchtwine insisted.

"Hmph," said Hildkar, casting the dice, then, "Shit!" Three single spots faced up, dark as little holes against the light wood of the dice. He slid the dice, the horn comb and a small piece of Roman copper over to Perchtwine.

"You see?" Perchtwine said triumphantly.

"I'll be back in a minute," Sigifrith told the other two.

He got up, dropping his winnings into his belt pouch, and walked across the hall to Ragin. The dwarf's head was hanging low, gray beard splayed out across his thick chest. If not for the narrow slits that gleamed between his wrinkled eyelids and the constant movement of his knife as its tip pared away the thinnest slivers from the twining interlace of the bowl in his lap, Sigifrith would have thought that the old smith had gone to sleep. He squatted down, looking Ragin straight in the face as the dwarf's eyes opened wider.

"What do you want now?" Ragin said gruffly.

"How can a sign in a dream not mean what it's supposed to?"

Ragin flung a few tiny wood parings over his shoulder into the fire, turning the bowl in his hands.

"Many ways," he answered. "Sometimes it deals with one thing, sometimes another; sometimes it's for oneself, sometimes for one's foes. Ravens can show the way to victory or to death; cattle may be wealth or strife or a slaughtering. Often a dream's might is wrought as much by how it is read and who reads it as by what it shows the dreamer of what should be. Why are you asking? Have you dreamed something?"

"No. But . . . sometimes you've spoken to me of things that might come to pass. Do you really know something about what is going to happen? About me?"

Ragin closed his eyes for a second, a sigh rattling from his throat. "Don't you think I'd tell you what you need to know?" he asked, lowering his gray-tufted brows in a fearsome glare. "When have I ever given you an ill rede?"

"You haven't, yet," Sigifrith admitted, smiling at the grimacing smith. Then he fixed Ragin with his keenest stare, till the dwarf had to drop his own gaze downward. "You do know something, I can tell! What is it? What have you seen?"

"Hush," Ragin grumbled, moving his head from side to side as though the weight of his skull was too great for his thick neck to bear in one stance very long. "Can you never be still? Did you ever think that there might be something you might not want to know, that your brave mood might fail before?"

"Only a coward fears what has to be," Sigifrith answered. Then he laughed. "No, really, Ragin. What have you seen for me?"

"Your mother's brother would tell you sooner than I will," Ragin answered.

"My mother's brother? But my mother doesn't have a . . . is that your way of saying no?"

Ragin began to carve a ring of tiny triangular notches around the base of the bowl.

"What did you mean?" Sigifrith persisted. "You've never given me an ill rede yet."

"Then trust my rede now and don't ask any further!" Ragin hissed in a harsh whisper.

A burst of laughter came from the corner where Alapercht, Adalprant and three of the other older thanes sat talking. Ragin's eyes flickered toward them as swiftly as a snake's black tongue tasting the air, as though he thought they might be laughing at him.

"Did he do something shameful? Is that why I've never heard of him?"

"There is no shame in your mother's line!" Ragin snapped, straightening his back and chipping more fiercely at his wood-work. "It's not out of disgrace that Herwodis has never named Gripir to you."

"So he does live! You didn't dream him up."

"I didn't say that," Ragin muttered.

Sigifrith's breath was coming more quickly. It seemed to him that he could feel the blood in his veins sparkling like a rushing stream's water in the sunlight as he leaned forward. "But he has a name, and he is a king's son. What land does he rule? Where can I find him?"

"If you go to the territories of the Salian Franks, where your mother's father Aiwilimo ruled, you might find Gripir's hall," Ragin admitted grudgingly. "But it's a longer and a worse journey to his lands than you might think, and few people go willingly on that faring. Nor is he often willing to speak—though it's true that he is foresighted and able to read the orlogs that Wyrd has written. But I tell you that it is a fool's errand to try seeking out your mother's brother where he sits now and asking him for rede. I think you will have a hard time getting him to answer you, if you keep on with this recklessness."

"Tell me yourself, then!" Sigifrith said, tossing back his hair and settling down on his heels to stare up into the dwarf's face.

"No. If you won't listen to me, you'll have a long ride through the rain and most likely nothing to gain from it. But that will be no one's fault but your own."

"Ragin," Sigifrith coaxed.

The smith shook his head.

"All right, then!"

Sigifrith sprang up and hurried over to Alapercht. "I'm going away for a few days," he said hastily. "I'm going to visit my mother's brother Gripir."

King Alapercht's hazel eyes widened, his cheeks pouching out as he shut his mouth firmly. "Sigifrith . . . " he began after a moment, but Sigifrith was already out of the door and running through the snow to the stables where Grani waited for him.

The colt's head lifted as Sigifrith opened the door, his ears cocked as if he heard a far-off call. When he saw Sigifrith coming toward him, he reared back, knocking the gate of his stall from its hinges with a single blow of his hooves and hastened toward his master. Sigifrith swung himself onto Grani's warm back, guiding the horse out of the stables with a nudge from his knees and turning his head toward the road that led down to the Rhine.

The clouds were drifting low and swift over the hills before the cold wind, white curtains of snow shadowing the purple-black pines into twilight gray. The icy grains of snow scoured Sigifrith's face, but he laughed at the storm as he rode, turning his face up to the dark sky to catch the white flakes that streamed into his mouth on the keen wind. Pale lightning flickered in the north ahead of him; he counted thirteen breaths before the rumble of Donar's hammer shuddered deep through the stormy air.

"Hai, Grani!" Sigifrith shouted. "Faster, faster!"

Grani leapt ahead, galloping toward the lightning that shimmered blue-white through the snow ahead of them. Without slowing or breaking, he sailed over wooden fence and stone wall, the blows of his hooves crushing the deep snow and breaking through to the brown stubble left over from the harvest. Now and again his hooves shattered the last sheaf that had lain bound in the middle of each field since Winternights, scattering the seeds into the snow to wait for melting time.

Sigifrith slept curled against his horse's belly that night, and thought he was as warm as he would have been near the fire in the hall; but he awoke soaked through, for he was out of the mountains and the snow had turned to rain in the night. He thought little of that, though he wished he had thought to bring food with him. But he was in Chilpirich's lands, and not far from the Rhine where he would cross into Alapercht's; he had no doubt that someone would recognize him and feed him along the way.

It was growing dark by the time Sigifrith rode up to the inn marked by the sign of the wolf's head. As he dismounted, the fat little woman—Guthrid, he remembered her name was—came bustling out of the inn. The top of her head did not come nearly so high as the tip of his breastbone now.

"Fro Sigifrith!" she squeaked breathlessly. "Will you be staying here for the night? I'll have dinner ready straightaway, and send one of the boys out to see to your steed."

Sigifrith could only smile, remembering how she had greeted him two and a half years ago. He thought that he might tell her how she had tried to chase him off, but then thought it still might be too chancy to break his secrecy in the matter.

"How did you recognize me?" he asked, instead.

Guthrid stared up at him over his shoulder, not meeting his gaze—eyes and mouth wide. "Who else could you have been? Even here, men say there is no young atheling bigger and stronger—or more generous—than King Alapercht's son Sigifrith."

Sigifrith laughed at the flattery. He patted Grani on the neck as they walked round to the hut of leaky boards that did for the inn's stable. "Have someone bring out some oats, if you will. He'll care for himself otherwise."

Guthrid peered at the horse, her round face screwing up in surprise. "With no bridle, or reins . . . is it safe to leave him like that, Fro Sigifrith?"

"Safe for him," Sigifrith assured her. "And for everyone else, as long as they don't try to ride him."

He followed her into the inn. At first he perched himself on one of the wooden stools in front of the fire, but its slightly miscut legs tilted under his weight and he had to draw his knees up uncomfortably to fit on it. He got off the creaking stool and seated himself cross-legged on the earthen floor, letting the warmth of the fire soak through his wet clothes.

A young woman came out bearing a mug of steaming ale and a big wooden platter heaped high with hot stew and fresh bread. Her child-swollen belly stood out from her scrawny body as though she were carrying a cauldron beneath her coarse brown woolen skirt. The woman's blond hair was straggly with sweat, her sharp nose red from the heat of the kitchen.

When Sigifrith looked at her, she turned her face away. Her raw-knuckled hands shook as she gave him his food and drink.

Before she could run away, Sigifrith caught her bony fingers in his, pressing the crystal beads he had won that morning into her palm. "For you," he said gently.

The serving woman dipped her head and whispered thanks, still not looking at him. She scurried back to the kitchen as though Sigifrith had given her a threat instead of a gift.

He slept in a room alone that night, lulled by the steady rhythm of the raindrops beating down on the roof and the wind blowing outside. Vaguely he wondered what Hagan was doing at the Hunnish drighten's court—if he wandered out alone at night and what the Huns, those strange, troll-faced folk, made of him. Sigifrith thought back to the feast of peace and betrothal at the end of his fostering, and how odd the three Burgundian children had seemed, bound so closely to one another even as they teased and fought each other without ceasing. Long-toed Gundahari, playing barefoot in the stream—Sigifrith could not imagine the boy he had wrestled as king of the lands through which he had traveled that day. And what about Gundrun? He tried to remember what she looked like, but could call to mind no more than a long golden-brown braid and the tight grip of her strong hand in his own. It seemed to him that another woman's face, high-boned and pale, shimmered through the darkness of his mind, but when he tried to see it more clearly, it vanished like mist in the Sun's morning light.

Sigifrith was up early in the morning, riding through the dawn rain. Twice he passed Burgundian patrols on the road. They nodded their long warped skulls and muttered to each other, letting him pass without challenge as he and Grani reared and danced lightly over the wet stones of the Roman road to show the steppes folk and their little horses what fine riding was.

After Grani had leapt over the raised stocks and cairns of stone that marked the far edge of the Burgundian marches, the road became worse and worse, mud and trampled brown grass covering the Roman stones. In a while they came to the edge of a storm-swollen river, its mirky rushing laced with white froth like the foam on a mad dog's mouth.

The bridge over the flood was wide, but badly kept. Its rotten boards creaked beneath the weight of Sigifrith and Grani; three times they gave way, and only the gray colt's swiftness kept them from falling into the river.

The road on the other side of the bridge was marked only by a few scattered stones, so it was hard to tell its puddled width from the dark mold around it. Grani was lifting his hooves high out of the thick mud with each step, leaving a track of deep water-filled pits in the wet earth behind them. The stubble of the wheat fields was sparse up here, drooping as thin and wavery as the hair on an old man's skull. Only a few scraggly trees grew on the low brown hills, dead leaves hanging sodden from twisted branches. The rain was falling more heavily, shrouding the wintry land in shifting veils of dark gray and misting the gallows that stood by the side of the muddy road till Sigifrith was almost upon it.

A dead man hung from the cross-piece, swinging in the wind that blew the smell of his rot coldly into Sigifrith's face. The bone of his skull shone through the rims of his empty eyesockets, gleaming white here and there where the ravens' beaks had torn the meat away. His filthy breeches and tunic were matted into the melting flesh of his body, so that it was hard to tell where one ended and the other began. Beside him a scraggly wolf rode high on the gallows, its clotted fur sloughing off in the rain to show black streaks of meat beneath.

"Hai, old gallows bird," Sigifrith called. "Will you and your wood-hound show me the way to Gripir's hall? I've seen better guides than you, I think, or at least more cheerful. I don't think you'll be much company on the road." He waited a moment, laughing, before he nudged Grani onward.

Still, he thought, if there was a warg hanging by the road, somewhere about must be the drighten who had hanged him. The food he had brought from the inn that morning was gone, and Sigifrith was beginning to want his dinner. He urged Grani on faster, stretching his sight through the rainy dusk for the glimmer of a hall's light before him. He was sure that sooner or later he would come upon something. After a while he began to sing light-heartedly, his high tenor bright above the steady patter of the rain.

> Onward! The cold sea's   foam-necked steed is riding,
> raising her sail   swan-white to the sky.
> Wind howling darkly   over the waters,
> forth the waves bear us,   faring away.
> Let the green land there   lie in her stillness,
> behind us the hall   and home that we know.
> Where the great wyrm   writhes through the sea-deeps
> we sail onward   seeking our way.
>
> Onward! The foam-plough   digs a white furrow
> graving it deep   into grim Ran's wave-field . . .

Even Sigifrith's keen eyes could barely make out the dark figure standing by the side of the road, a shadow through the rain and dusk. The smaller shadow at his feet moved restlessly, letting out a sharp bark.

"Hai!" the young atheling called, breaking off his song and bringing Grani to a halt. "Who are you, there?"

"I am called Geithirth, the goatherd. Who are you, riding so boldly along the way to the north? You must be a proud man. Your horse's hooves sound louder than those of a whole troop."

"Don't you know me, then? You're the first one on this path who hasn't."

Sigifrith heard Geithirth hawking, the goatherd's spittle lost in the rain. "Why should I know every bedraggled warg who comes riding on this road? Go on, there's nothing for you here."

Sigifrith leaned down, staring through the darkness at where he thought Geithirth's face should be. "I'm seeking the hall of the drighten Gripir, the son of Aiwilimo. Tell me where he is, and I'll go on and leave you alone. Lie to me, and I'll leave you lying in three pieces on the road."

The goatherd cackled roughly above the growling of his hound. Sigifrith could smell his foul breath; swiftly he shot out an arm in hopes of grabbing the man, but Geithirth had already leapt back from him.

"What do you want with the drighten Gripir? He doesn't speak to such as you. Didn't you see the warg back there with his hound? But you know how a drighten should deal with his men; he gives his thane a good steed to ride to his hall." The goatherd laughed again. After a while, his chortle deepened into a racking cough, gurgling and choking as though he were bringing up chunks of his lungs.

"Are these Gripir's lands?"

"Gripir holds the land," Geithirth gasped. "Or say, if you will, that the land holds him. Ha! You'll never get into his hall, anyway."

"Is Gripir your drighten, goatherd?" Sigifrith demanded, his patience coming to an end at last. "By the gods, he'll roast you when he hears that you've tried to chase his sister's son from his lands."

"It's been a long time since Gripir sought his sister's side, and longer still since she came to meet with him," the goatherd whispered, a hollow ring of cunning in his voice. "Did it take Herwodis this long to remember where her kin have gone?"

"If my mother was greeted like this, it's no wonder she comes seldom to her brother's hall!"

Sigifrith leapt from Grani's back, his boots sinking halfway into the mud as he landed. He heard the sucking sounds of Geithirth moving back and the panting of the goatherd's hound. With a heave, he dragged his right foot from the bog and kicked high, his boot catching the hound halfway as it sprang for his throat and flinging it away to land with a splash. Another leap through the darkness, and he had Geithirth's soggy throat in his hand, his rough beard as prickly as a hempen rope against Sigifrith's palm.

Sigifrith spat the goatherd's reek from his mouth, holding him at arm's length by the neck. He could feel the cold mud at his knees creeping in around the tops of his boots.

"Ha!" he shouted, grinning with fierce joy. "Will you tell me now? You may not be much of a guide, but you're the best I've got, and I'm not letting you loose till I stand before Gripir's hall."

"You've gone off the road," the goatherd croaked. "There's no way for you now."

Sigifrith laughed, hauling his legs from the mud and slogging back along the path he thought he had come by, dragging Geithirth along behind him. It was not long before the weight of the bog and the effort of tearing each step out of it began to tire him, but he kept going, heedless of the burning in his calves, and soon he kicked one of the marker stones. He grunted as he stepped on to the firmer mud, heaving the choking goatherd with him.

"Grani!" he called. The gray horse whinnied, bumping wetly against Sigifrith. He mounted, holding fast to Geithirth's throat, then took his guide by the slimy shoulders and swung him up. Geithirth's legs dangled limply in the air until Sigifrith lifted him higher, setting him down on the horse's back.

"Forward," whispered Geithirth. "If you ride this road long enough, you'll come to Gripir's hall."

A gust of wind whipped Sigifrith's soaked hair against his face, raindrops battering at him harshly as hailstones. He tightened his knees on Grani, feeling the horse's muscles gathering and surging beneath him, bearing the young atheling and his burden onward. Grani's hooves spattered drops of wet mold from the road; the goatherd's hound splashed howling beside them, its gaunt shape hidden in the darkness. Lightning flashed, pale, showing Geithirth's head lolling to one side, showing the raven that wheeled black through the white-lit torrents of rain above them.

"Faster!" Sigifrith shouted to Grani, then to Geithirth, "Hai, goatherd, have you ever had such a ride? What atheling's steed bore you to this land?" He slapped Geithirth's back, wrinkling his nose at the musty reek. "I've had cleaner comrades than you, I think. Forward, Grani! Show this stinking carl what you can do!"

Grani galloped faster as the thunderless lightning blazed over their heads again. Leaves whirled on the wind, slapping wetly past Sigifrith's face in the flashes of blackness between the lightning that seared his eyes again and again with the vision of the dead land rising in heaps of twisted rock around him, turning and writhing like a thousand stone wyrms winding together, rearing their folded heads high above his. Sigifrith tossed his head in wild mirth; a faint hint of rot tainted the rain falling into the back of his mouth.

"On!" he called, hearing his voice echoing far ahead of him. "Gripir, can you hear me? It's I, Sigifrith, Herwodis' son!"

A high cliff of rock flashed before him in the lightning, rising vaster than anything Sigifrith had ever seen to tower far above his head. Only a narrow gap of blackness cracked down its middle, thin as a thread against the huge wall of stone. He tightened his knees on Grani, leaning forward and digging his fingers past the second knuckle into Geithirth's shoulders as the wind-gray steed sprang into the darkness. For a moment they seemed to soar, borne up by the stormwind around them; then Grani's hooves came down with a great wet crash, jolting Sigifrith forward into the stallion's flying gallop.

Ahead, Sigifrith could see a red-gold burning, a fire that cast no light but showed the black shape of a low hill beneath its leaping ghost flames.

"There!" Geithirth hissed. "There is the hall you have sought. Now let me go ahead to tell the drighten Gripir who has come to meet with him."

The goatherd sagged sideways, toppling from Grani's back. Sigifrith grabbed for him, but caught only a handful of rotting skin and cloth. He shook the slime from his fingers, letting the storm wash them clean.

Herwodis' son rode to the burning howe, the cold rain growing icy around him as he neared it. When he shook his hair back from his face, he could feel the rime cracking from it. Grani's hair was freezing into tattered points of ice under his hands, though the stallion's skin was warm beneath.

"Gripir!" Sigifrith called. "My mother's brother, come forth! You within, awake—Aiwilimo's son, if you are more than mold. Awake! Sigifrith, your sister's son, calls!"

The voice from within the earth-heaped cairn was very deep and slow, as though sleep were fast upon the speaker. "What do you wish, Sigifrith? It would have been more seemly if you had come here to your kinsman's howe before."

"If you are wise, Gripir, tell me what you know. Say to me how wyrd shall turn for Sigifrith hereafter."

"Foolish boy," Gripir's slow voice answered. "That would do me no good to speak, and you no good to hear. Go hence, Herwodis' son, and bid my sister not to forget me when she pours drink to the ghosts of our line. Bring meat and wine to my howe; then my blessings will be upon you."

"I have not ridden here to be sent away by my kinsman!" Sigifrith shouted. "Open the doors to your hall, for I would look you in the face. I have no fear of a dead man."

The ghost fire rimming the howe spread outward, the lightless flame of a red err-light glowing from a long hole in its middle. A dark shape rose in the middle of the cold howe fire, standing in the keyhole gate of the flame-ringed mound: the shadow of a tall, thin man girded with a sword and leaning upon a twisted staff.

"Now the grates of Hella are open," Gripir said, his deep voice warped by its own echoes as if he were speaking from the bottom of a well. "Now the draug stands in the doorway; do you tremble, kinsman?"

Sigifrith rode forward. As his keen gaze met the cold flames, they flickered and faded beneath his eyes till Grani stood at the edge of the howe. "Tell me of what must come to pass, Gripir. By Wodan, Wili and Wih, I say to you that you must answer before I let you sleep again, whole in your howe."

"Do you know how my words may wreak your doom?"

"I have no fear of doom. Speak as you will, I am ready to meet it."

"Then hear me, Sigifrith, Herwodis' son, and be content with these words:

Of men you will be   under sun mightiest
and highest born   of hero any
giving of gold   but grudging to flee
fairest of wights   wise in your words.

"Now let these staves suit you. You will get no better rede."

"Speak still, King!" Sigifrith said. "Ready yourself, for I will hear more. Wise one, say to Sigifrith if you see further. What will come to pass first, when I fare from your hall?"

First shall you, folk-warder   avenge your father
and drive out all   Aiwilimo's woes.
There all Hunding's   hardy sons
Sigifrith fells   in swiftest strife.

"Now let me be, Sigifrith. Go your ways; let me sleep, whole in my howe."

"Speak still, King! Say to me, your kinsman, Herwodis' son who speaks bravely with you: do you see deeds of daring before Sigifrith, that fare highest under the heavens?"

> You should alone slay   the shimmering worm
> who greedy lies   on Gnita Heath.
> You ought to both   then be the bane,
> Ragin and Fadhmir   rightly says Gripir.

"Now ask no more, Sigifrith. No higher hero could you be than when you have slain Fadhmir; you ought to ask no more, for there is a hero's tale done. So let that be an end; end your asking and let me sleep, whole in my howe."

"I shall have wealth if I do as you have said, and battle honor if you speak rightly. But let me know—speak longer! What lies before me after that?"

> You ought to find   Fadhmir's dark lair
> and with you take   the wealth most bright
> load the gold   on Grani's back,
> ride to the Gebicung   grim hero then.

"Enough, Sigifrith!" groaned Gripir. "Ask me no more! It will do me no good to tell it; it will do you less to hear it. If you have any of my sister's wisdom, if the foresight of our line has lighted upon you even once, ask me no more!"

"There must be sorrow in what you will not say," Sigifrith said. "I know you can see beyond that. What grief is written in my wyrd that it is too heavy for you to speak willingly?"

> All your life   lies here before me
> lightest before   look I onward.
> I have wrought full   your rede is tallied
> I see nothing further   though forward I gaze.

"There is no man above the mold who can see further than you, Gripir. Do not hide it from me, though my life be ugly and my end luckless. Tell me!"

The icy crimson light shining through the keyhole door of the mound began to dim, the cold loosening its grip as Gripir's dark shape moved backward.

"No!" cried Sigifrith. He leaned forward, his gaze piercing into the darkness of Gripir's shadowy face as if to spear and hold him where he stood. Two red sparks gleamed from the dead man's eyes, growing brighter and brighter till it seemed to Sigifrith that twinned rays of power rang between his kinsman and himself. He breathed deeply and slowly, feeling his will strengthen and steady as he stared into Gripir.

"Tell me," he said softly. "I will know. Tell me of my deeds and my death."

Gripir stood as still as a dead tree stump for a moment, leaning heavily on his staff. Then he began to speak again, his words echoing through Sigifrith's skull and ringing dizzyingly around him.

> No shame shall blot   Sigifrith's glory.
> Now you shall see   so shall you learn!
> Ever your name   shall noblest be held,
> atheling of heroes,   while ages last.

Gripir raised his staff, pointing upward to the twisted pillars that writhed above them. Now Sigifrith saw that the howe stood beneath the roots of a tree that was huger than his sight or his mind could grasp; now he saw that the roots were wound about by gnawing wyrms whose teeth dripped green-black bale. In the cold red fire that shone through the mound's keyhole door, Sigifrith could see the rippling of water all around him, as though he were at the bottom of a giant well. He did not know whether he was breathing air or water; only Grani's warmth beneath him told him that they still lived.

The waters rippled out from Gripir's staff, brightening around it to the fires of sunset; and those fires were darkened by the rising shadow of a high crag where two figures stood. One was white-clad beneath her byrnie, her long fair hair flowing out from under a steel helm, a shattered shield in her hand. Sigifrith caught his breath as her face grew clearer and clearer in his sight, blue eyes glimmering like ice stones with the tears that filled them but did not spill over. He felt his hand rising from Grani's withers, reaching out to her, and was hardly able to pull it back. The hoar-bearded man who stood on the crag beside her wore a deep blue cloak and a wide-brimmed hat tilted to hide one eye. The sunset's red glinted from the tip of the spear in his hand as he raised it and turned it toward her; the runes on its shaft flared as the iron thorn-tip pricked through her byrnie. The cloaked man caught her as she fell, easing her down upon the rock and laying her broken shield carefully over her. He straightened, rising to his full height and raising the spear over his head. The sunset fires flared brighter and brighter from the weapon's tip as he lifted it, flashing out into a widening ring of fire that burned around the top of the crag.

Sigifrith stared breathless at the vision before him; he was not willing to turn his gaze from it, but Gripir was speaking again and as he spoke the shimmering sight faded into the darkness of his deep voice.

> Sigimund is not   from Sigilind torn,
> but shining the fire   shields her crag.
> Byrnie-clad, sleeping,   bound is the maid.
> The hero should wake her   the Walsings should live.

> Runes he might have   and redes of might,
> leech-craft, and all   the lore fit for kings.
> If his high heart   could heed that wise gift,
> wyrd might turn to weal   though words he must break.

"What words must I break?" Sigifrith asked. "What must I do to awaken the maid?"

Gripir did not answer at once; instead, he pointed his staff toward the door of his howe. It seemed to Sigifrith that the mound was growing greater and greater, until its keyhole door had become a cave's mouth leading into the depths of a mountain. Looking through it, Sigifrith could see that the fires burned over heaped gold, burned from it, its fire lighting the darkness inside the mound. The gold coiled like a wyrm, wrapped over and under the goods of a grave—linen and chests, drinking vessels and weapons, the food set out for the dead man and the horse slain for his last faring—and now Sigifrith saw that the gold was the dragon crawling from the chest of the big warrior who lay in the middle of the howe with the rotten flesh melting away from his bones like metal melting in a crucible. Something had been laid over the dead man's face: it looked like a coif of chain-mail, but it glowed so brightly between his eyes that Sigifrith could not look straight at it. The gold-fires blazed up fiercely enough to dazzle his sight; when he blinked, he saw only Gripir's tall shadow standing before the howe's doorway.

> *What's given to have   hold must the dead,*
> *darkly aye deal   the dwarves with all thieves,*
> *yet gold must be given   as gift among men*
> *for bonds of betrothal   broken, must pay.*

> *Though warder be grim   is worse the gold ring,*
> *Rhine-fire burns   to the ruin of all.*
> *Sigifrith falls   by spear he had trusted,*
> *the horse of his drighten   but to howe rides.*

"How can I win free of this?" Sigifrith asked. "What can I do?"

It seemed to him that he could hear the sadness echoing deep in Gripir's voice as the dead man spoke again, as hollow as the sound of a stone dropping into an empty well.

> *Better for hero   if brought down by Fadhmir,*
> *his hour of death   his highest of all.*
> *Better, if Ragin   betrayed him with counsel*
> *and blood with the dragon's   bale melted sword.*

"Now let me be, Sigifrith. I have told you more than I would, and I can say no more. Let that be an end; end your asking and let me sleep, whole in my howe."

"There is more to tell," said Sigifrith. "I trust in Ragin and, more, I trust in my father's sword, whose edge is mightier than the hardness of stone. I know no bale shall melt it, and it is not shaped that Fadhmir shall be my slayer. Now, Gripir, I know that there must be more, nor shall you hide it from me. Show me how it may be when I have wakened the maid—show me how I may turn wyrd to my will."

Slowly the dead man stepped aside from the door of his howe. He spoke softly as Sigifrith leaned forward to look within again. The light in the mound had changed: though the ice still numbed Sigifrith's hands and face outside, the rainbow-shimmering flames within were bright as sunlight.

Wodan swore an oath on the ring.
Who can trust in his troth?
The sword breaks on his spear,
the god is not kind to his kin.

Sigifrith did not heed Gripir's dark words, for it seemed that he looked into a great hall whose spear-shaft pillars rose straight and smooth to a roof shingled with golden shields. The hall was bigger than any he had seen, with doors set along its length. The thanes who sat upon the benches drinking were mighty men, none of them unscarred by battle. Some Sigifrith recognized from Alapercht's warband, but most of them were strange to him. Fine and fierce-looking hounds, as keen-eyed and thick-pelted as wolves, lay chewing at their meat in the clean straw beneath the tables or followed the fair maidens who walked about with glass pitchers of clear golden mead and dark amber ale. The hunting bird perched by the empty high seat was no mere hawk or falcon, but a full-grown eagle, its keen eyes scanning over the warriors gathered there.

Suddenly one of the doors flew open. Looking through its posts, Sigifrith saw a gray horse with two riders on its back galloping through a fair green land to the hall. The foremost rider was the white-clad maiden from the crag, and she seemed sorrowful no longer, joy brightening her eyes in place of tears. She was laughing as they rode in the morning light, like a bride at her wedding. Behind her Sigifrith himself sat on Grani's back, wearing a tunic of gold-worked scarlet with the golden coif from the howe glittering on his head. The dream-Sigifrith seemed older—his shoulders heavier and his short-cropped beard thick along his jaw, the lines of wear on his face not wholly hidden by his grin—but Sigifrith knew without a moment's thought that he saw himself.

"I will have this. I will dwell in that hall with her!" Sigifrith cried out. "Let it be so!"

Grani leapt forward at the nudge of his heel; but as they were about to pass through the doorway, the vision vanished from his sight. The two of them stood as they had before, and Gripir's staff was raised to bar the door to the howe.

The draug struck the ground with his staff three times: it rang from the frozen earth beneath with the dull sound of iron striking ice, nor was his voice brighter as it tolled from his dead throat.

Though wyrd is now spoken   the wise still might turn it,
beware of masked battle   as of battle hid.
The draught that held memory   shall hide it also,
and shield-wood tree   shall be your bane.

"I understand your words ill; but if I may have what I have seen, that is enough for me," Sigifrith said. He could no longer see the immense roots stretching down from above; it seemed to him that the light from the howe was beginning to fade, the blackness behind it lightening, and he knew that he had but little time left to ask. "Now tell me, Gripir, you who are wisest of all: what shall become of Gundrun and the Gebicungs, to whom I am sworn? What part have they in the shapings of my wyrd?"

Gripir's dead voice was softer now, as if the rot-tainted wind that blew from the howe door were bearing it to Sigifrith from very far away.

Gundrun and Hagan   and Gundahari,
Wyrd doomed in the shape   wove in eldest of days.
Your line-mother saw   your slayer before her,
three women's hands   weave Sigifrith's fall.

Woe to your kin!   No king shall ever
—who keeps the dwarf's gold—in gladness long live.
Gundrun shall weep,   grim all her days,
all Grimhild's wiles   bring woe to her kin.

The sky was lightening more and more swiftly with the dawn, the cold howe fires fading into the dark hump of the mound.

"Fare well, Gripir," Sigifrith said. "No one wins over the shapings of Wyrd. Now you have done well what I asked of you. You would have told me a fairer tale, if you could have."

Gripir's shadow was almost lost against the darkness of the mound door. Sigifrith heard his voice only as a whisper.

"Let this comfort your heart: no one shall ever come upon the earth in Sunna's sight who shall be counted greater than you. Fare well, Sigifrith, Herwodis' son."

Sigifrith waited in the cold, watching the morning light rise around the high mound before him. The wind from the north seemed warm now, easing the chill that had gnawed at his bones all night. Grani put his head down, chewing at the grass that grew thickly around Gripir's howe.

After a while, Sigifrith turned his horse's head toward the south again, Grani's hooves squishing through the wet wheat stubble that grew thickly in the rich fields of the Franks. He had not gone far from the road. The light of dawn was already casting long shadows from the tree beside the way and the neat stone markers that laid out the path between the hills where the dry grape leaves rustled in row upon row of well-kept vineyards.

Sigifrith saw the two figures dangling from the ash tree's branches before he reached the road. The wind turned the corpses, man and wolf, about for Sigifrith to see. He shrugged and rode onward, thinking on the strange redes Gripir had given him.

Sunna was warming the left side of Sigifrith's face as he rode across the border of the Burgundian lands. Some way to the west, he could see her glitter shining on the distant and indistinct shape of a warband riding toward him. He turned Grani and galloped over the fields toward the host.

The challenging note of a horn shook through the cool, clear air in welcome as one man rode out ahead of the warband to meet Sigifrith. No helmet's steel, but a ring of gold sparks shone around his dark head. He sat easy and confident in the saddle as his brown horse—smaller than an Alamann's, but bigger than the steppes ponies Sigifrith remembered—reared and danced in welcome.

"Hai! Gundahari!" Sigifrith called, the strength of his voice singing high through the long gap still between them. Gundahari raised a hand to hail him, shouting back something that the breeze carried away. The Burgundian king nudged his own horse into a gallop, slowing only as he came within a hall's length of Sigifrith and Grani.

"Hai, Sigifrith!" Gundahari said. "Welcome and well met! Are you in a hurry to get somewhere, or can I offer you and your men a share in our victory feast?" He scanned the horizon behind Sigifrith, looking for a warband.

"I came alone," Sigifrith admitted softly. "I had to visit one of my kinsmen in his lands on a personal errand. I'm on my way back now. Where have you been?"

"I've been in the west. We had trouble with some of the Romans near our Gaulish borders who weren't willing to be as hospitable as they should have been toward us. They thought they could take advantage of harvest season." Gundahari shrugged heavy shoulders. "Very rude people. But that's taken care of and next harvest they'll be too busy tending their lands for us to worry about making trouble. Come on, we're not too far from the hall of my drighten Ulfas where we're holding our feast."

Harvest season? Sigifrith wondered. It was only just past Ostara when I set out to seek Gripir! But no green shoots showed through the stubble under Grani's hooves; the dried leaves still hung on the grape vines and the trees, and when he looked farther, he marked for the first time that the hills were not misted with the yellow-green of summer beginning to unfold but dry with the sere yellow leaves of its end.

Wordless, Sigifrith followed Gundahari back to the Burgundian band, which wheeled around in formation behind their king. Sigifrith noticed that many of them rode the larger horses now—crossbreeds, he thought, between the Burgundian ponies and the horses that Alapercht had given to seal the alliance. The Burgundians bore the signs of battle, all of them smeared with dirt and sweat and a few wearing black-crusted bandages. But gold and silver glinted in coils from beneath the grime, garnets gleaming richly like fresh blood drops on boar-crested helms and gems glowing in rainbows from sword hilt and sheath. If the riches of his men showed anything, the songs of Gundahari's battle-luck and open-handedness did not lie.

"Ulfila!" Gundahari called. A skinny blond youth with only a few sparse golden hairs on his chin rode out of formation and halted before his king. "Go on to your father's hall and tell him to set another place of honor beside mine—a seat big enough to hold Sigifrith of the Alamanns."

Ulfila looked at Sigifrith, his blue eyes widening. "Yes, my king," he blurted out. He spurred his horse on, galloping ahead of the troop.

Gundahari laughed heartily, scratching below his dark scruff of beard. "He's still getting used to the idea of a world outside his father's hall. It was the boy's first battle, you know. Shit, he'd never even been in a real city before."

Sigifrith shifted uncomfortably on Grani's back as they rode on, wondering how he could admit to Gundahari that he himself had never been in battle.

"Are you weary?" the Burgundian king asked. "Don't worry, it's not far. You must have been riding an awfully long time."

"I had a long way to go," Sigifrith said.

"I'm sure," Gundahari agreed, "since no one has seen or heard from you from Ostara to harvest time. You look as if you've come a long way, too. When did you sleep last?"

"Uh . . . night before last."

"Holy Engus, you're getting as bad as Hagan. You'll have to take better care of yourself than that, or Gundrun will be severely disappointed."

"What is she doing now?" Sigifrith asked, glad of a chance to turn their talk to something else.

"She's up in Worms with our mother, making sure the lands don't fall apart before I get back. You couldn't have asked for a better queen. I'd never have managed without her. I tell you, she will be glad to see you. When are you going to come and get her, anyway? She's been complaining about being left to become an old maid." The Burgundian's face showed no sign of guile as he smiled at Sigifrith, but his hazel eyes met Sigifrith's gaze firmly without flinching or turning away.

Sigifrith rubbed his grainy eyes with a knuckle, trying to gather his thoughts together for an answer that would make sense. Until Gundahari had pointed it out, he hadn't realized how tired he was; now he felt as though his brain had melted to a soggy lump inside his skull. "As soon as I've taken my full and rightful place," he answered, almost by rote.

Gundahari nodded. "Good enough."

"Is Hagan still in Thioderik's warband? I've heard the songs about him and Waldhari the Frank."

"I'm here." Hagan's monotonous voice had deepened further and cleared a little with age, but it was still unmistakable. Sigifrith turned to look at the younger Gebicung as Hagan rode up beside him. A short beard grew over the sharp edge of the Burgundian's jaw; his black hair, silver-threaded and dirty from days of riding and fighting, was tied back in a Hunnish knot and he carried a thrusting spear. "I came home at the last full moon." His dark gray eyes scanned Sigifrith, resting for a moment on the hilt of the other young man's sword. "That looks like Ragin's work. I see you've been a good apprentice."

Sigifrith stared at Hagan in disbelief, then a startled laugh burst out of him as the other's upper lip lifted in his painful half-snarl.

Gundahari looked oddly at both of them. "What are you talking about?" he asked Hagan. "What's so funny?"

"Never mind. It's not important," his brother answered. "Will Gundrun be able to see her betrothed again tomorrow when we get back to Worms?" He stared pointedly at Gundahari as he spoke.

The elder Burgundian coughed. "Ah. Sigifrith, will you accept our hospitality in Worms tomorrow night? We would consider your visit to be a great honor."

Hagan was watching Sigifrith again, his gaze unnervingly steady and unblinking. "Our sister will be glad of it. She has been waiting for news of you."

Sigifrith looked into Hagan's eyes to see if he could find any hint of sarcasm behind the Gebicung's grim mask.

"You'll greet her for me," he said.

"Always. But will you not come to greet her for yourself?"

"I must be getting back. King Alapercht and Queen Herwodis will be looking for me." And what would Alapercht think of a thane who had announced that he was going to visit a dead man, then run from the hall? Sigifrith knew he would have a lot of explaining to do when he got back.

The chair Ulfas had found for Sigifrith and set between Gundahari and Hagan was rather too small for him; he would have rested more easily on one of the long benches. Out of politeness, he stayed with the company until the tables had been carried out instead of curling up in the corner to sleep as he would have liked to do. The drighten Ulfas was a hearty man whose blond wife kept pressing food and drink on Sigifrith and gasping in amazement over his appetite. Sigifrith wondered guiltily if they might think he had fought beside their son in Gaul. I won't be unblooded much longer, he promised himself.

"You don't know anyone, do you?" Gundahari asked Sigifrith, who jerked himself awake with a start.

"What? Sorry, I missed something."

"I was saying we have a betrothal arranged for Hagan, but Grimhild insists that none of the eligible women around are worthy of my station. I think she might have some idea of marrying me off to a Roman after we've moved farther out into Gaul. There's something to be said for that, I suppose, but I think the real danger's more likely to be at my back in a few years. If Attila had an eligible daughter or I had another sister, it would make my life a lot easier. I even thought about offering him Grimhild, but Huns want fertile wives."

"Who are you marrying Hagan to?"

"A Frank named Costbera. Her father has taken the lands a little way up from our northern borders. He'll be running things for me up there and leaving me free to work on what I'm doing in the west."

Sigifrith nodded, trying to look as though he knew exactly what Gundahari was talking about as the Burgundian went on to tell about his plans for expansion into the rich lands of Gaul through treaties with a Rome that was slowly losing its grip and through the growing strength of the Burgundian warband.

"We're not tied to the land the way we were, because the Romans who give us guest-right—the hospites treaty—do all the tilling and work for us. In return we protect them from the barbarians across the Rhine, the ones who want more than we do. But that means I've got a place in my warband for just about anyone who wants to join and can use a weapon well enough." He paused, eyeing Sigifrith speculatively. "I bet I could find a place fitting for you, if Alapercht could spare you for a couple of seasons."

"Alapercht's lands have been at peace for a long time," Hagan added. He swirled the wine in his silver-bound horn, sniffing at it. It was good red Gaulish wine, brought in from Gundahari's most western lands. "If you wanted to win fame for your deeds as well as your size, you wouldn't do badly by leading a host under Gundahari." Hagan tilted his head to look into Sigifrith's face, firelight glittering from his slanted eyes. Sigifrith glanced down at him and then at Gundahari. There were no songs about Sigifrith's fame in battle; Sigifrith had won no land and signed no treaties with the Romans. He wondered how many men each of his companions had slain in fight—fewer than the songs claimed for them, surely. "I understand that Alapercht is in good health," the younger Burgundian went on. "If you mean to wait till you have succeeded him, you will have a long wait. Nor is he likely to give over power to an untried boy."

Sigifrith set his wine glass down carefully on the arm of his chair before he clenched his fists, leaning over Hagan. "Why are you insulting me?" He spoke so softly that he knew only himself and Hagan could hear.

"There's a time to hide things that other people have said, and a time to say them out loud," Hagan answered, equally quietly. "Why has Sigifrith, who rides the finest of horses and wears the best of swords, no better parents to boast of than a battle captive and an unavenged dead man? Is this a suitable inheritance to bring to Gundrun?"

Sigifrith glanced at Gundahari, who in turn was watching him. "Think about it," the Burgundian king said. "There's rich land to be won out there—half an empire to be taken, if we go about it the right way. If we fight together, there's no one who could withstand us. You could win enough land and thanes of your own to marry my sister by next Winternights, if you wanted."

The noise in the hall was getting louder as the men drank, shouting toasts to their victory and their king now and again through the noise of boasting and argument. Beneath the sounds of merriment, the gravelly rumble of Hagan's voice was almost hidden. "You need to do something."

"Will you?" Gundahari asked.

"I'm already sworn to King Alapercht," Sigifrith said. "I couldn't join your band without his leave."

"Then join our house now!" Gundahari said, reaching his hand out to Sigifrith. The old boar's scar had faded to white, stretched and puckered across the heavy muscles of the Burgundian's massive forearm. "Swear the blood oath and become our brother."

"Why do you want me to? All I have that's really mine is my sword and my horse. I haven't done anything . . . and I'm already betrothed to your sister."

"Because I know what you can do," said Gundahari, rising from his chair to stare intently up at Sigifrith. "Because we want you to be part of our family—and a betrothal isn't yet a wedding. And, mainly, because I feel that it's right and I didn't get where I am by ignoring what I feel."

Sigifrith looked down at the hand Gundahari was still holding out to him.

"I won't withdraw it till you've taken it," the Burgundian king insisted. "We shall stand side by side—shield-brothers till death."

It seemed to Sigifrith, as he looked into Gundahari's face, that he saw a shadow of something familiar behind the Burgundian's dark tangle of beard. He remembered a voice in the moonlight; remembered that Grimhild was said to be a foresighted woman; and he thought there might be more to Gundahari's hoard of victories than strength and luck alone. Still he held his hand back, remembering that Gripir had spoken dark redes for the Gebicung clan.

Sigifrith felt the rasping of Hagan's deep voice, rather than hearing it. He wasn't sure whether the words had been spoken aloud or whether, in his tiredness, he was dreaming them: "After all, we are bound by blood already."

Sigifrith reached out his arm and clasped Gundahari's so firmly that the Burgundian rocked on his feet for a moment before getting his balance again and drawing Sigifrith up from his seat.

"Come out!" Gundahari shouted to his men. "Come witness our oath!" The Burgundian king grasped a torch from the wall in his left hand, pulling Sigifrith along with the right. Sigifrith, still bewildered, allowed himself to be led out of the hall at the head of a line of torch-bearing warriors, the trail of flames flickering through the night like a serpent of fire winding around behind him. Hagan walked silently on Sigifrith's other side, bearing his spear and a horn of wine.

Gundahari led his troop out over a winter-dry sward of grass till they came to the middle of the field. Then the warriors formed a ring of torches around Gundahari and Sigifrith as Hagan turned the point of his spear downward. The younger Burgundian scored two marks through the grass, then crouched to cut through the roots beneath. He lifted the middle of the long turf with his spear, propping it up so that it formed an arch with the two ends still holding tightly to the earth.

Hagan stepped back into the ring of thanes, leaving Gundahari and Sigifrith together before the earthen arch. Sigifrith looked down at the Burgundian king. He could see that Gundahari's face was pale beneath the coarse black of his beard. Gundahari's mouth moved, but no sound came out as he pulled at his tunic to straighten it. Then his stance became firmer as he looked around at his men and drew in a deep breath.

"I, Gundahari, of the Gebicung line, call you to witness," he cried. The pitch of his voice rose as he began to chant the words of the Burgundians' rite, half-singing in a surprising light tenor:

> Brother to brother   born of one womb,
> the blood of life   is blended there.
> Kin cannot be   cleaved from that bond
> unless with the gods'   unending curse.

> Earth is the mother   of mighty ones' blood;
> earth is the mother   all pass through her womb!
> Born of one blood   when blended within her,
> holy turf-round   the ring where we swear.

> Blood-brotherhood   bind our troth for ever,
> Earth-mother bears us,   men, new from her womb.
> And if bond be broken   blood only can pay,
> the gods shall take   for geld, death alone.

"I shall swear this oath with you," Sigifrith said. "Brother to brother, bound to our troth, as if of one mother born."

Gundahari grasped his forearm again. "Then let us pass through the turf-ring and blend our blood, so we shall be sworn before gods and men."

The two of them crouched down, creeping under the earthen arch. A few crumbs of dirt fell on Sigifrith's neck, rolling cold and damp down his spine when they stood up on the other side. Gundahari drew his boar dagger and slashed lightly first down his own arm, then down Sigifrith's where they were clasped together. The warm blood welled up from the two clean slices, flowing together across their arms.

Hagan held the horn out to them. They raised their hands, letting their mingled blood stream into the dark Gaulish wine.

"So I am sworn to you, Sigifrith of the Alamanns, my brother," Gundahari said.

"So I am sworn to you, Gundahari the Gebicung, my brother," Sigifrith answered. Then he turned to Hagan. "Come through the earth-ring," he said. "I would be bound to you in this oath as well."

It seemed to Sigifrith that Hagan's eyes widened as he heard those words. "Would you have my blood in your veins?" Grimhild's son asked him.

Sigifrith smiled charmingly at him, a spark of satisfaction glowing at having unsettled the grim Burgundian.

"I have already blended mine with your brother's. Do you think it is not worthy of yours?"

"So you have chosen," Hagan said, his monotonous voice as heavy as a stone dropping. Sigifrith took the horn from his hand and he walked around to the other side of the turf arch, ducking lithely through. His bare forearm flashed white beneath his black tunic as he struck it across the spear's blade, knocking the weapon free. The raised sword fell inward, spattering cold clods of earth over the three who stood in the middle of the ring.

Hagan laid his arm over Sigifrith's and Gundahari's clasp, his cooler blood flowing slowly through theirs and into the wine.

"Now I, too, am bound to your troth and your orlog again," the younger Burgundian said.

"So we are all." Sigifrith raised the horn to drink. The rich salt taste of their blood ran beneath the full-bodied wine in a heady current. He passed the horn to Hagan, who drank silently and gave it to his brother in turn.

When Gundahari had drunk his share, he raised the horn above his head. "Now let our blood flow back to our mother again! Be the bond sealed for ever!"

He poured the last of the draught out to flow over their clasped arms and down onto the sward. As one, the Burgundians ringed around turned their torches over and plunged them to darkness in the earth.

"And I swear also," Sigifrith said in the moment of stillness, "that before next Midsummer I shall have come to wed Gundrun, adorned with the honor and fame that befits such an atheling-frowe."

"We shall await you gladly!" Gundahari said. Then the men began to cheer, hastening them back to the hall and the drinking again, and no more could be said.

Sigifrith slept late the next morning. When he awoke the Burgundian warband was already gone. Hastily he ate the breakfast that Ulfas' wife gave him, then hurried out to Grani.

Sunna had already sunk behind the mountain peaks, her light fading swiftly around their craggy edges, by the time Sigifrith rode up to Alapercht's hall. After he had stabled and fed Grani, he went to wash himself and change his grubby clothes. When, refreshed, he went into the hall, he found only Alapercht, Herwodis and Ragin sitting by the fire and talking quietly. Overcome by curiosity, Sigifrith tiptoed through the shadows behind their backs till he could hear what they were saying.

"I told him not to," Ragin grumbled. "I told him he wouldn't get any good out of it."

"But why didn't you tell him Gripir was dead?" Alapercht asked.

"I thought he had the sense to work it out."

"Where do you think he's gone, then?" said Herwodis, winding a trail of dark hair through her fingers. Her voice was calm as always, but Sigifrith could hear her grave depth of concern.

"I suppose he rode up north to the Frankish lands. Sooner or later someone will tell him what he needs to know and he'll come dripping back in, apologizing for having frightened us and swearing he'll never do it again. Hah! He won't go looking for dead kinsmen again soon, that's true enough."

Sigifrith saw Alapercht's head shaking. "He just ran out of the hall without bothering to ask anything. Maybe we should have sent him to another king while he was younger. I don't know what we're going to do with him when he gets back."

Sigifrith flattened himself into the shadows as Ragin's dark glance flashed glittering about the hall. The youth held his breath for a moment, but if Ragin noticed him he showed no sign of it. "He has a duty to do," the dwarf hissed. "He's old enough for it now, and I've . . . we've waited long enough for him to do what he's been raised for. Keep him here over the winter, but let him go when summer comes. There is a task he's sworn to fulfill."

"But I have to be finished by Midsummer!" Sigifrith protested aloud, then clapped his hand to his mouth. Three heads jerked up, turning as Sigifrith stepped into the circle of firelight.

Herwodis leapt to her feet, wrapping Sigifrith in an embrace that he knew would have cracked a weaker man's ribs. Though the tears did not spill onto her cheeks, he could see them shining in her eyes. "Sigifrith, my son," she murmured. She cleared her throat hard. "Where have you been? And what is it you must be finished with before Midsummer?"

"I have to avenge King Sigimund, and . . . " The words stuck in his throat, but Ragin nodded slowly, the corner of his beard twitching in what Sigifrith thought was a smile.

"Do you have any idea what you'd have to do?" Alapercht asked.

"Sail up north—now, before the winter seas get too fierce—and do battle with the Saxons until King Lingwe is dead." Sigifrith knelt, so his eyes were on a level with those of the seated king. "I have to do it, my drighten. I promised Gundahari that I would have proved myself in battle before Midsummer and would go to Worms to marry Gundrun then."

Herwodis sighed heavily; Ragin groaned. Alapercht closed his eyes for a moment, as if in pain.

"Whyever did you do that, Sigifrith?" Alapercht asked. "Isn't trouble with the Burgundians the last thing we need?"

"Well . . . I've never had a chance to prove myself here. We've been at peace all my life. Hagan's a full half-year younger than I am and he's been famed as a warrior for years, and even the least of Gundahari's warriors has fought more than I have. People are saying that Sigifrith is a useless lump of meat without the spirit to avenge the death of Sigimund the Walsing."

"I think you are, perhaps, exaggerating a little," Herwodis said calmly. "Where did you hear this?"

"Hagan told me so."

Ragin, Alapercht and Herwodis exchanged glances. "Where did you meet the Gebicungs?" Herwodis asked. "Tell us what happened to you."

"I rode to Gripir's howe and then I rode back. On the way I met Gundahari and his warband . . ." Sigifrith told the three of them what he and the Burgundians had said and done.

"So Grimhild had nothing to do with this?" said Ragin. "It was one of Gundahari's impulses?"

"As far as I know." Sigifrith reached out to Alapercht, gripping him by the shoulders and gazing directly into his adoptive father's eyes. "Please help me with this! I've been here a long time and I owe you a great deal for the love and honor you've given me. But now I must leave these lands and find the sons of Hunding. I wish them to know that not all the Walsings are dead—and I would like your help and blessing in this."

Alapercht looked away from Sigifrith's gaze at last, blinking as if to clear sunspots from his eyes. Absently the Alamannic king rubbed his lower back as though the aching he often complained of had become worse.

"He has Sigimund's treasure," Herwodis murmured. "And we've known for a while that we couldn't keep him much longer."

"Yes," said Alapercht. It seemed to Sigifrith that the king's eyes were faintly clouded, as though a veil of smoke had risen between them from the fire. "But now? Sigifrith, you've never sailed anywhere in your life. You can't imagine what the North Sea in winter is like. It's so rough in summer that my ships nearly foundered when I first went harrying in the north. Wait at least until winter is over and the sea is calm enough to sail in again."

"But I swore to the Burgundians . . ."

"Hella take the Burgundians!" Anger cracked in Alapercht's voice, as shocking as lightning lashing from a sheep-white cloud. "I'm not going to see you killed because they trapped you into making a stupid oath. They've waited long enough; it won't hurt if you're a month or two late. What kind of idiot do they think you are?" Even in the firelight, Sigifrith could see Alapercht's cheeks reddening as if the flames had leaped up to burn him.

Herwodis laid a hand on her husband's arm, gently turning him toward her. For a moment she sat without speaking, the steadiness of her bulk and stillness calming both Alapercht and Sigifrith as they looked at her.

"He's my only son," Alapercht said. "I don't want to see him do this. There's no need for it—not now. He can wait till summer."

"You know he has to keep his oath," she said quietly. "All we can really do is make sure he can."

"And what about the men he takes with him? Who can I tell to go through the North Sea in winter? There are not more than twenty left of the thanes who sailed north with me on my last voyage, and the rest haven't seen any more water than the Rhine. Going through the North Sea with a crew like that at this time of year—it's not bravery, it's madness. I can't order my men into something like that."

"Let Sigifrith ask them. See who's willing to go with him," Ragin croaked. "It's time for him to see what a king really has to do."

"You both think he should do this crazy thing?"

"Let us take the omens tomorrow," said Herwodis. "See what signs fall for this journey, then find out who wishes to go with Sigifrith. Then, if all is well, we must make as much haste as we can to ready his ships and train his men for the voyage."

"I suppose there's nothing else we can do," Alapercht sighed. "Very well, then. If the omens are good, and if my men will follow you in this, Sigifrith, I will give you everything you ask for. And I will offer sacrifice to Ziw and to the god that you call on that you may be blessed with victory and with battle-luck."

Sigifrith leaned forward and hugged Alapercht. "I'll always try to be worthy of the line and the name you gave me," he said. "Please don't ever think that I want to forsake you."

For a moment Alapercht didn't answer; Sigifrith could feel the tightness of the muscles beneath the king's flesh. At last he straightened. "I always knew it would come to this one day," he said. "So. Go to bed, Sigifrith. We'll take the omens at dawn."

"Thank you." He turned to Herwodis. "And thank you, Mother." He hugged her too, quickly, before going out of the hall.

Sigifrith had only gone a little way before he heard the clumping sound of Ragin's footsteps behind him. He stopped and turned, crouching to look into the dwarf's face.

"What do you want, Ragin?" he whispered.

"Kill Fadhmir, as you have promised! Do it now, and you will have more than enough gold to build a whole fleet and to call a host the like of which has never been seen to your side. Then there will be no doubt about your revenge."

"First I must avenge the kings Sigimund and Awilimo, who fell in battle with the sons of Hunding," Sigifrith insisted. "Do you doubt that I will keep my oath afterward? Gripir told me that I would not die in gaining my vengeance."

Ragin's hands closed on Sigifrith's arms, pincer-strong fingers digging into the young man's muscles. Sigifrith remembered how painful the dwarf's grip had been when he was younger; now he barely felt it.

"What else did Gripir tell you?" the dwarf demanded.

"I hardly understood any of it," Sigifrith answered. "He spoke unwillingly, but it seemed to me that he didn't promise me much happiness, though he spoke of great deeds I would do—and the first of those was my vengeance."

Ragin coughed, his hot sulfurous breath spraying over Sigifrith and stinging tears into his eyes. The young man drew back, wiping his face with his sleeve. In the darkness, he couldn't see the look on Ragin's face. Tentatively he reached out to his foster-father, but Ragin stepped away from his touch.

"What did he say to you of Fadhmir?"

"He said that I would slay him, but it also seemed to me that he said I might die of it."

"And is it because of this you fear to face the dragon?"

"I will not fall with my father unavenged. Let me do what I must. I think that you, more than any, know what it will mean."

"I fear that I do," Ragin muttered. He turned around and stumped off into the darkness without another word. Sigifrith watched till the dwarf's shadowy shape was hidden in the night.

The sky was turning pale gray when Sigifrith, freshly washed and dressed in his finest clothes, stepped into the holy grove where oak and ash grew around a circular clearing. A cold wind rustled the dry brown leaves above his head, stirring his hair; fallen acorns crunched like little bones under his boots. He stroked the ice stone in Gram's hilt, its coolness tingling through his hand. Most of the time, weapons were not to be borne in the grove; but Sigifrith knew he would keep his sword.

Herwodis and Alapercht stood in the clearing, flanking the huge flat-topped boulder in the middle. Behind them towered the great oak trunk with the bearded and spear-holding figure of Ziw carved into it—the Irmin-pillar that held up the might of the Alamanns. The round eyes of the god stared sternly down at Sigifrith as though Ziw were weighing his worth; Sigifrith hoped that he would deem well and mete out a fair fate.

A white cloth was spread out over the stone harrow; upon it was set a bag of ancient, cracked deerskin. Sigifrith had not seen those things since he was seven, when Chilpirich and Alapercht had cast the signs in the sight of all their folk to decide whether the Alamanns would join the other tribes in the crossing of the Rhine. Beside the bag was a huge blowing horn, bound at lip and mouthpiece with gem-set silver wrought in graven spirals such as Sigifrith had never seen before. A few scraps of rotting leather still hung from the strap fittings, but the metal shone fresh-polished in the new morning light.

Without speaking, Herwodis lifted the horn and handed it to Sigifrith. He understood that he was supposed to blow the call and summon the host. His mouth was dry from excitement and he had to lick his lips and cough before blowing into the horn.

The deep note, rougher and starker than that of any Roman tuba, shivered through the brightening air, tingling down the length of Sigifrith's body. When his breath finally faded, it felt to him that the sword against his thigh was ringing with its echo. Twice more he blew; by the time the last note had sunken into the gold streaks of the sunrise, sleep-tousled thanes were beginning to make their way through the trees and into the grove.

Alapercht waited until everyone was gathered; until no more footsteps crackled in the fallen leaves of the holy grove and only the rough breathing of the men and the rustling of the wind through the hallowed trees stirred the silence. Then he raised his arms, his gold-wrought red cloak blowing free from his shoulders.

"Ziw and Wodan, Donar, Fro Ingwe, Frowe Holda! High and holy ones, hear!" he called, his voice sounding light and squeaky after the deep note of Sigifrith's horn. "What do you wish, Sigifrith?"

"I would bring battle to the sons of Hunding, so they may know that not all the Walsings are dead!" Sigifrith shouted. "As soon as I may, I would sail to the north with all who will follow me through sea and storm to my fight. What signs do the gods give for this work?"

"Be still," Herwodis said. "We will let the gods speak."

At first there was only the lightening blue of the sky above and the wind in the brown leaves. One or two men shifted restlessly as Herwodis took up the ancient bag, rolling it from hand to hand as if she were silently shaking dice. Then, slowly, Sigifrith became aware of the stillness around him as if it were a sound too mighty for human ears to hear, a light too clear to brighten human eyes. He drew in a deep, careful breath of awe, waiting with the others in the hallowed place until the bond that held them seemed to loose a little and Herwodis could cast the graven slips of wood from the bag.

The signs fell on to the cloth with a muted clatter. Herwodis gestured to Sigifrith, and he stepped forward, not sure what to do.

"Close your eyes and pick three of them up," she whispered.

Sigifrith closed his eyes and stretched his hand out to the stone, feeling the three smooth pieces slip beneath his fingers. He picked them up and handed them to his mother.

Herwodis stared at the signs. She began to sway from side to side for a moment, then spoke:

"There will be no easy faring. Nevertheless, I believe you may win, if you heed the counsel that you get along the way. In any case, you may not turn away from this battle, except if you be a coward or nithling—and I think that a Walsing is neither."

She gathered the pieces of wood back into the bag and tied its mouth closed again, folding the square of white linen around it. Sigifrith shut his mouth, suddenly feeling the stares of the assembled throng pressing on him like two hundred assayers' hands testing gold for alloy. He looked at Alapercht, who stood as if carven into a stately pillar, then glanced about for Ragin, who was nowhere to be seen. What can I do? he thought. What am I supposed to do? He waited for a moment, but no visions rose out of his blood.

Hildkar stood in the front row, his dark hair rucked into a peak like a Burgundian's skull; like many of the others', his eyes were half-closed and clouded with sleep. There was Adalprant near him, his scar twisting his face into a badly carved mask. And there was Perchtwine, rubbing at the purple birthmark on his forehead; and there the rising sunlight glittered off Chlodomar's red hair; and there Kunitrut's dark eyes glared from beneath a single tangle of grizzled eyebrow as he tapped his hairy fingers on his belt pouch. Sigifrith began to speak as he would have spoken to any one of them, the men who had been his companions and his teachers for most of his life.

"We've kept our lands in frith for a long time," he said. "I've been able to grow up in peace and honor. Because of our strength, no one threatens us— but many of us are young men who have never gone into battle as men ought to do. Now I have made a vow that I will avenge Sigimund the Walsing before Midsummer. This is my own fight, and if no one will come with me, I must go alone; but if you want to follow me to the north, I can offer you battle-glory and treasures. I've heard it said that the Saxons are rich pirates, raiding up and down the coasts of Britain and Gaul. It seems to me," he added, smiling, "that it would only be fair to relieve them of some of the booty they've taken from our good friends the Romans." The men were laughing now, especially the older thanes who remembered how the Alamanns had gained the treaty giving them the lands west of the Rhine. "Will you come with me?" he asked, more soberly. "Frowe Herwodis says it will be no easy faring. I have never seen the North Sea by summer or winter; I just know that I must go, if it means that I must bear my sword against Aegir himself. And if faring and battle are hard, the treasures we win will be all the richer and the songs bearing our fame through the lands more brightly wrought."

He swept his gaze over the thanes, meeting the eyes of each for a second, then, in a single swift movement, leapt to the top of the harrow. The new sunlight filled his eyes with a dazzling flood of brightness. He spread his legs to brace himself firmly on the stone, tossed his hair over the pale blue cloak that flowed out behind him and drew Gram to burn in the morning Sun.

"See!" he cried. "I give myself to this oath, through storm and strife. If I should fail or falter in what I have sworn, my death shall be the only geld that can pay for it." He nicked his arm with Gram's point, letting the drops of blood fall onto the stone. "Who will come with me?"

Hildkar was the first one forward, the last mists of sleep burned from his eyes by the light glittering from Sigifrith's sword and his doleful face livened by excitement. He reached out to touch a drop of the blood darkening on the harrow-stone. Then Otkar shouldered his way past two other thanes; then Agilo, then Perchtwine, Theodipald, Kunitrut; in groups of two and three they hurried to the stone where Sigifrith stood with his hands uplifted to the gods, Gram in his right hand and blood dripping from his left arm. Almost half of Alapercht's warband stood about the harrow when someone began to shout, "Sigifrith!" and the rest of them took up the chant, baying, "Sigifrith! Sigifrith!" like a pack of joyful wolves.

Sigifrith looked down at them through the blur of light in his eyes, his heart straining against his ribs as he realized that they were calling his name, had chosen to trust him, unblooded and unproven as he was. It seemed to him that a weight was upon him, steadying his exhilarated dizziness and clearing his sight until each hair of beard or stubble on the faces of his thanes was sharp as a bolt of lightning against a black sky to him. He leapt down from the rock; standing among them, he still towered over the tallest of them, Chlodomar, by almost a head. They were pounding him on the shoulder and back, buffeting him lovingly with blows that they might have used to fell men of their own size and strength. Sigifrith laughed, answering their rough play as gently as he could.

The next days went by in a fury of work, Sigifrith awakening before dawn every morning and going to bed long after dark. The ships on which Alapercht had sailed north had not rotted, but needed repair badly. In any case, they were too small for Sigifrith's host and too flimsy for the winter seas. Muscles that had begun to slacken with early winter idleness tautened again as if summer's battles were about to begin; the older thanes were out on the Rhine with the younger men daily, showing them how to sail and warning them of the perils of wave and current that they would meet in the North Sea. The women of the hall and the wives of the thanes worked all day weaving the woolen sails cross-plaited to stand up to the winds that would meet their men at the mouth of the Rhine. It seemed to Sigifrith that he could not turn a corner without tripping over Ragin's squat figure as the dwarf tested the timbers of the ships for flaws, running calloused fingers as gently as feathers over the joins. When he found the least fault, he would shout at whoever was nearby for as long as it took him to pull his tools and compounds out of his pouch and smooth the wood into a seamless whole. The ships grew as the treasure in Sigimund's chests shrank. The weather was windy, but the skies stayed clean and blue, promising Sigifrith a clear way to the north.

At Winternights, Herwodis slaughtered a bull to the ghosts of their kin and the keepers of their home. Her voice did not tremble as she asked the idisi for a safe journey for her son, for his protection and victory in his battle and his return in frith; but when she spoke the name of her brother Gripir as she poured out the bread and wine, Sigifrith saw the raven-wing of fear pass behind her tear-bright eyes and remembered that he had never asked how Gripir had died.

The Blotmonth moon was new on the night that Ragin came through the darkness to Sigifrith's hut to tell him that the ships were ready for the voyage.

"They're as well made as you'll get," the old dwarf croaked grudgingly when Sigifrith opened the door. "You can call the men to them tomorrow and set sail at dawn, I think." He turned his craggy face up to the sky, the Moon's white light silvering his dirty gray beard and casting his sunken eyes into pools of darkness. "The weather will hold for a day or two, at least.

After that, don't eat anything you don't want to see again!" Ragin coughed out a short, sharp bark of a laugh.

Sigifrith only shrugged. "Come in for some wine?" he offered. "It'll help you sleep better, if you're worrying about the voyage."

"Me? Why should I worry about it? I'm not going with you."

Sigifrith looked down at his foster-father and smiled as charmingly as he could. "Of course you are," he urged. "Who'll keep me out of trouble if you're not there? Who'll sharpen our swords and spears?"

"What kind of thanes can't sharpen their own?" Ragin grunted in answer. "I'm not going. You think dwarves were made to sail on the Deep?"

"But you will come, won't you? You're just teasing me now, aren't you?" Sigifrith crouched down to Ragin's height, reaching out to steady himself on the dwarf's thick shoulder.

"You shouldn't need me by now," Ragin complained, but Sigifrith could hear the wavering in his voice. "You've offered these crazy young men gold, glory and a chance to get killed beside you. I don't want glory, I don't want to get killed and there's far more gold in Fadhmir's cave than in the whole of the Northlands. No, I'm not going."

"Why not?"

"Because you're doing it against my rede. Kill Fadhmir first; then I'll go with you wherever you ask."

"But . . ." Sigifrith started. Ragin turned around without another word and clumped off into the night. Sigifrith closed the door, sitting down on the bed that creaked alarmingly under his weight. The coals were burning low, showing him Hildkar's skinny shape and Hludowig's square one only as shadows. He could hear the low sound of the whetstone stroking along the edge of Hildkar's dagger; wine gurgled and splashed as Hludowig raised his wooden cup and drank.

"What was the dwarf on you about this time?" Hludowig asked. "Donar, you'd think he'd realize you were old enough not to need a nursemaid by now."

"Compared to him, nobody's old enough," Sigifrith said. "Anyway, now that he's sure the ships are ready, it'd take Donar's hammer to knock a leak in one of them."

"Don't tempt the gods," Hildkar warned him in sepulchral tones. "You never know when they might be listening in. I've heard the stories the Greeks tell about their gods—"

"Then that's what you get for listening to Greeks," Hludowig broke in. "What good are foreign gods, anyway?" He spat casually on the floor. "Well, we've been ready for weeks. When are we going to sail, then, O mighty drighten?"

"Tomorrow at dawn," Sigifrith answered firmly. "I'm going out to look at the ships one more time myself to be sure everything's all right."

"Isn't that what Ragin just told you?" Hludowig asked.

"Yes, but he's not going to be sailing on them. I want to be sure for myself before I trust our lives to them."

"Getting cautious in your old age?" Hildkar said, a note of grudging admiration in his voice.

"Do you want to come with me?"

"I'll trust you," Hildkar said slowly, his surprise glimmering through his words like ore through rock. The thane's dagger rustled softly into its leather sheath as Sigifrith opened the door to go out; behind him, the young drighten could hear Hludowig's whispered, "Good faring and rich return," as the other man poured out the last of his wine before his clay statue of three basket-holding idises.

The five ships at the dock tugged their ropes northward, as though eager to begin their faring down the Rhine. Sigifrith did not notice the figure at the prow of his flagship until a great wyrmlike head rose from it, turning itself this way and that as though sniffing about in search of something. Sigifrith shouted in excitement, drawing his sword and running eagerly toward the water-wight. As he leapt from the pier on to the deck of his ship, there was a loud wooden clatter.

"Damn you!" Ragin shouted. "What in Hella's name do you think you're doing?"

The dwarf stepped out of the shadows cast by the sides of the ship, his brawny arms heaving what looked like a long log until Sigifrith got close enough to see the dragon head carved at its end. Without speaking another word to his foster-son, the dwarf leaned the figurehead against the side of the boat, running his hands carefully over it. "If you're that eager to kill a dragon . . ." Ragin started, then shook his head. He spat over the side. "Ach, Sigifrith, what are you doing out here anyway?"

Sigifrith sheathed his sword. "I came to check the ships for myself. What are you doing?"

"Putting up your prow. This will guide you through the waters and bring terror to the land of your foes; it's wrought with wisdom to bring you back so you can fulfill your oath."

Sigifrith moved closer to the dragon carving, putting out his hand. A strange cold tingled through him as he touched it; for a moment he saw the patterned coils of an adder twining up around his arm like serpentine fetters. He blinked quickly, driving the strange sight away, but a faint cold unease remained.

"Do you swear it will do no harm to my men or myself?" he asked quietly.

Ragin dropped his head. Sigifrith could hear his teeth grating against one another. "All this work," he said, his voice muffled. "What haven't I done for you? What more could I have done for you? Now I've given you what help I could for this fool venture, and you ask me to swear it isn't harm. By Dwalan and Dawan, boy, do you have nothing better to do than to insult me?"

Sigifrith felt his stomach cramping with guilt as he looked down at the spot in Ragin's hair where the Moon shone from the dwarf's bald skull. "I didn't mean to insult you, but I felt strange when I touched it—and I'm not just responsible for myself anymore. Ragin, they trust me, and none of them is as strong as I am. I don't know what they can withstand and what they can't."

"You're growing into a hero," Ragin murmured. "And they're only men. . . but they're men who want to follow where a hero leads. Don't let yourself give in to their weaknesses or fears, and you'll make them closer to what they want to be. Just wait, there'll come a day when no man can make a prouder boast than, 'I sailed with Sigifrith, the Dragon's Slayer.' "

"Then why won't you come with me?"

"Because I'm no man, but a dwarf, and I have no need to boast of my deeds. Go on, now. Do what you've got to do and go to bed." Ragin turned to lift the dragon prow into place, the light tapping blows of his hammer marking sharp stops in the words he whispered under his breath. Troubled, Sigifrith watched him for a few moments more before turning away, walking over each ship in turn. The ropes were sturdy and thick, with no signs of fraying; their knots were pulled tight. The barrels of salt fish and dried bread, of small beer and light wine, were stowed where high seas would not knock them about. By them stacks of spears and arrows were made fast, greased against the greedy gnawing of rust and salt. The hulls were as strong and light as Ragin's skill and the best craftsmanship of the Alamanns could make them. Their clean straight lines and narrow keels were still a surprise to Sigifrith, used to the flat-bottomed river barges. Racehorses against draft ponies, he thought, stroking his hand along the silk-smooth oaken planking. Above the mast, the banner his mother had given him drooped dark against the moonlight, like a raven's wing folded for sleep.

6

SIGIFRITH'S INHERITANCE

Sigifrith took a deep breath of the white morning river mist, bracing his bare feet on the boards of his deck as he blew three long blasts on his father's horn. Excitement prickled down his neck as he saw the dark shadows of men gathering in the fog, coming toward him; the mist blurred friendly faces and well-known shapes so that for a moment Sigifrith could see foes blurred by battle-madness and feel its wod singing through his veins. Then he heard the replying shouts, "Hai! Sigifrith!" and felt the fire sink down into a tingle of anticipation. He leapt to the side of the ship, balancing easily beside the dragon's head Ragin had raised, then jumped down to squelch through the cold mud and river grass as he helped his thanes load their last things on to his ships. Each vessel was crewed by twenty young men and four of the old thanes who had sailed north with Alapercht.

A fresh breeze was beginning to lift, thinning the river mist in the growing light till Sigifrith could see all his ships clearly, their reflections shining from the rippling river. With a rustle of cloth, his banner flapped straight out in the wind: the apple of the Walsings, deep red against a white field. Sigifrith grunted, heaving up the anchor of his ship by himself. When the men who had been given the same task on the other vessels had finished their struggle, he went to the side of the ship and untied its moorings. "For Wodan and vengeance!" he shouted, casting off. The sail arose creakily behind him, fighting against the thanes who held it as it caught the wind. Herwodis and her women had wrought elaborate embroideries into it, red and gold writhing through the woven strips of wool; now it seemed to glitter with glory in the sunrise, finer than Sigifrith had ever imagined.

"Sigifrith!" shouted Adalprant, the captain of the next ship, as they cast off behind the flagship. Sigifrith turned, about to ask what the older man wanted, when he realized that Adalprant's call was not a hail, but a battle-cry. Almost embarrassed, he raised a hand in thanks and recognition. After Adalprant followed Kunitrut, Paltwini and Anshelm—experienced men, whom Alapercht had insisted command under Sigifrith.

"I hope you know what you're doing," Hildkar said, leaning against the dragon prow and looking up at Sigifrith. "I think these men actually trust you. Amazing, isn't it?"

"What about you, then?"

Hildkar brushed a wave of dark hair out of his eyes, staring at the embroidered sail. "I'm here, aren't I? You know, I think Perchtwine's getting sick already. Gods help him when we get out on the ocean."

"Hella take you!" Perchtwine answered, straightening and clamping his teeth together. "I am not sick." In spite of his words, the thane's freckled complexion showed a faint greenish tinge, and he swallowed violently.

"Take a little wine or strong ale to settle your stomach," Sigifrith ordered. "That's what we used to do when . . . " He stopped, bewildered. Vaguely, he seemed to remember strong ale or mead being doled out to new sailors in small doses; but he wasn't sure where or when he had seen it.

"If I play sick, can I have some wine too?" Hildkar asked. Sigifrith cuffed him gently on the side of the head.

"There's no cure for you," he said, then, noticing that one corner of the sail was beginning to work loose, he added, "Go and tie that rope down tightly before our sail flies away."

Hildkar gave him a sardonic Roman salute, but he went quickly over to fasten the sail as Sigifrith had ordered.

"You might want to lower that a bit, actually," Harthpercht said. The old thane's crooked forefinger pointed back at the other ships straggling in a row behind Sigifrith's flagship. "Give 'em a chance to catch up to you. It may be a while yet before everyone learns what they're doing, and you don't want to push 'em too fast yet."

"Urmph," Sigifrith muttered, helping Harthpercht and Hildkar to lower the sail. "Will I have to worry about losing the other ships on the ocean?"

"Worry about it? You can just about count on it, if the gods aren't holding us together with their own hands. That's why you've got experienced captains on the other ships, so everyone ends up where they're supposed to be. Old men like me, we know what we're doing." Harthpercht cackled, running a hand across his bald head. "It's all that knowledge crowded out the roots of my hair."

Sigifrith laughed with him rather uneasily. Harthpercht whacked him across the small of the back in a friendly way. "Don't worry about it too much," he advised. "You do your job and let everyone else get on with theirs. . . . Wake up, Hludowig, you fool!" the old thane shouted at the steersman. "Have you forgotten there's rocks in the Rhine? Push to the right, Ziw curse you!"

For a moment the ship swung about wildly, till Sigifrith got behind Hludowig and added his weight and strength to the rudder. The young thane looked up, pale beneath his swarthy tan. "I'm sorry," he gulped. "I didn't see . . . Do you want someone else to steer?"

"No, you stay where you are. I wouldn't have chosen you if I didn't think you could learn the job. Harthpercht, stay here and help guide him till he knows what to look for."

"I'll be here a long time, then," Harthpercht said. "Old Father Rhine gets mean at this time of year."

"Keep you on your toes, won't it?" Sigifrith said flippantly. He walked to the stern of the ship, looking back at the other vessels swinging about behind him. For the first time, he began to wonder if Alapercht was right; if an untried boy taking an inexperienced crew out into the worst seas around the Middle-Garth at the stormiest time of the year could really have any chance of reaching Saxony, let alone conquering it. We'll have learned how to handle these by the time we reach the North Sea, he told himself, and it won't be so bad then. If I trust in Wodan . . . A laugh rose from somewhere within him. Wodan's given me enough already, he thought. Better for me to trust in those gifts: my strength, my wit, and my father's soul.

"What do you think you've got to laugh about?" a familiar voice grumbled behind him. Sigifrith turned, grinning.

"I thought you weren't coming!" he said to Ragin, delighted. "What made you change your mind?"

"You need someone with a brain to look after you," the dwarf said, staring down at the square toes of his boots. "If I thought you could do it alone, I'd be safe in my cave now. Have I ever told you how much I hate going on the water?"

"I'm glad you're here. You'll be able to see me use my sword for the first time—if you've got the bravery to get close enough to the fighting, that is."

"Hrrmph. If you won't treat me with respect, I'll get off and walk home."

Sigifrith laughed, bending down to give Ragin a quick hug around the shoulders. "No, you won't. What would happen if we sprung a leak in the middle of the North Sea and you weren't there to mend it?"

"You'd drown. Which is just what you'd deserve for doing something as stupid as this in the first place."

"You don't mean that."

"I do." Without asking, Ragin went over and filled his mug from the barrel of strong ale, then sat down on one of the benches muttering to himself.

The weather was fair all the way down the Rhine, the wind blowing the ships along swiftly. By the second day, the younger men could handle their vessels as smoothly as the experienced thanes, weaving through rock and flood with the same graceful skill that they used in guiding their horses through the forest. The string of ships wound down from the high Alamannic lands, passing by the red stones of Worms and through the low mountains and hills of the Frankish territories. The lands looked different from the river, and though Sigifrith scanned the red-gold hills in search of landmarks he knew, he could not tell when they had passed by Ragin's old forge. But he marked when his men began to eye the hills nervously, hands twitching toward sword hilts. They had not sailed much farther when the air began to prickle as though a flight of unseen spears were besetting their ships.

Ragin gripped Sigifrith by the elbow, turning him to look at the mountains rising on the eastern side of the Rhine. "Up there," the dwarf grunted, though he kept his own gaze down, staring into the river. "Look up, Sigifrith. There is where the dragon comes down to drink."

Though it felt as though a heavy helm were weighting his head downward, Sigifrith forced himself to raise his eyes along the side of the mountain—along the track of scorched and scattered stone that led down from the dark cave. Gram's ice stone was cold and smooth against his palm. Sigifrith held the sword's pommel firmly as he stared at the mountain, his eyes fixed on the ghostly shimmer of gold fire within Fadhmir's lair. He did not turn his gaze away until the river had borne his ship out of sight of the Dragon's Crag.

After they had passed through the Frankish lands, the river turned westward, running through lands that grew flatter and lower as they traveled, fields of winter-brown stubble giving way to boggy plains of tall bulrushes and marsh grasses, until Sigifrith awoke to the first light of morning on the North Sea.

Dazed from sleep, Sigifrith thought at first that the huge green-gray plain stretching out in the distance beyond the mudflats was a field of some late grass till he heard the shout of "The sea!" behind him. A flock of geese, startled, rose from the long brown marsh-sedge and flew honking above the ships.

"Gods, it's so big," Perchtwine muttered quietly. "I never expected . . ."

The wind gusted about, a cold blast of salt tainted with dead fish striking them head-on; the dragon prow dipped and rose as the ship began to lurch. Perchtwine wrapped his cloak tightly around himself, blowing his nose on one edge of it.

"Yah, this is where the fun starts," Harthpercht said. He cocked an experienced eye at the wispy clouds feathering out across the blue heavens. "Looks as though we might be getting a bumpy ride. Do you want to lay low for a while, Sigifrith?"

"Why?"

"See those fox-tail clouds up there? See how fast they're moving? They're running from a big mean wolf of a storm—a real ship-eater. It's not going where we want to go, either. We could end up in Britain or Gautland—or Nibelheim, maybe."

Sigifrith looked at the wide stretch of sea ahead. They were close enough to see the little white-frothing waves leaping and sinking, as if the water were a great cauldron of wind-stirred ale. The wind had swung about behind them, pushing the ships forward. Sigifrith looked up at the sky again, at the thin tattered banners of cloud flying before the faraway storm. A flash of white caught the corner of his eye. Turning, he saw three swans flying north across the wind, their wings beating silently above him. The sight seemed to twist something in his chest; a glimmer of tears prickled through his eyes. He clenched his hand on the ice stone in the hilt of his sword.

"We can't stay here, and I won't turn back," he answered. "Through storm and strife, I said."

"Through storm and strife," Harthpercht muttered, dipping his head to avoid Sigifrith's glance.

The waves that had looked small from the river caught the dragon ship's prow so that it lurched violently, throwing the men from side to side. The older thanes, remembering the voyages of their youth, had braced themselves; the younger warriors were caught by surprise. Chlodomar hung grimly on to the rudder, the ship turning as the weight of his body pulled it to one side till Sigifrith could stumble across the tilting deck and brace him, steering to cut straight through the long waves. A *V* of white spray frothed out around the ship's sharp prow like a watery mane; Sigifrith stared at it in delight, humming to himself, "Onward! The sea's foam-necked steed is riding . . . " He was ready for the next rise and fall, swaying with it as he would move with the leaping or lunging of Grani. The other young thanes, more cautious, held to the sides of the ship, and Perchtwine was leaning over, the sound of his vomiting lost in the splashing of the waves. Sigifrith took Chlodomar's place, the red-haired thane scrambling and slipping along the deck between waves to find a more secure place, and waved Harthpercht to his side.

"How do I turn it around?" he shouted, looking over his shoulder to the other ships wallowing at the river's mouth behind him.

"You don't. Wait . . . ah, there they come." Harthpercht took the rudder from Sigifrith's hands, turning the ship this way and that. A big wave caught Paltwine's ship broadside and it rolled half-over. Sigifrith bit his lip, watching anxiously as the vessel straightened. "Good work, there," Harthpercht said. "No one overboard. These are bad waters to get lost in. If a man isn't pulled out straightaway, the cold kills him. You sure you want to go on right away?"

"I'm sure."

Ragin, holding tightly to the mast, gestured Sigifrith over to him with one hand. "You can turn back any time, you know," he grunted. "This is stupid. Are you trying to get everyone killed?" The dwarf's teeth were chattering; Sigifrith couldn't tell whether it was from fear or from cold.

He took off his cloak and wrapped it around Ragin's shoulders. "Go and hide among the barrels," Sigifrith suggested. "That way you won't have to look at the water, and you'll have a bit of shelter. All right?"

"No, it's damn well not," Ragin complained. "Can't you wait a few days till the storm's blown out? You'll get where you're going just the same."

"Maybe, but we're going now."

Sigifrith supported the dwarf over the lurching deck to where the supplies were stored. Ragin wedged himself between two barrels of beer, clutching his own cloak and Sigifrith's about him as he glared up at his foster-son. "Go on, get us all drowned," he muttered. "It's no good trying to talk sense into you, is it?"

"You didn't have to come," Sigifrith reminded him cheerfully.

All the ships were out now. Sigifrith waved to the captains of the other four, gesturing northward. "Along the coast!" he shouted. "Stay as close to me as you can."

Paltwine raised a skinny arm in answer, Adalprant nodded and Kunitrut and Anshelm waved, wrestling their ships through the waves to follow Sigifrith. The wind was blowing harder, yanking Sigifrith's long tail of hair about painfully and stinging his face with cold till the blood glowed warmly in his cheeks. He took the rudder from Harthpercht, guiding the ship out through the swells that rolled her from side to side. A gull cried above, flung about by the wind; Sigifrith thought suddenly that flying must be like this for a bird, lifted up and tossed about by the wild currents of the sky. Strange as it was to him, it also felt comfortable, as though he had fared like this for years. He grinned, looking back at the land, which was already fading into a cloud on the horizon.

It was harder to sail across the wind as they had to do, following the coastline; the ship bucked and fought, her mast creaking alarmingly. Perchtwine had vomited himself out and was huddled by the side; Chlodomar had gone a greenish pale, and even Hildkar had a hand to his mouth as he stared into the heaving sea. Hludowig, Agilo, Notkar and Hermann seemed all right, sliding and skidding across the deck and laughing at their sickly comrades. The older thanes, Ansbrand, Otho and Hathopart, stood by the sail, ready to haul it in at Sigifrith's word.

"How's your breakfast doing?" Harthpercht chuckled at Sigifrith. "Don't worry about them. The ones what don't get used to it, they'll fight twice as hard when we land 'cause they'll want to die before anyone can chase them back on to a ship again. They . . . shit!" A sudden gust of wind caught the sail wrong, swinging the vessel around before Sigifrith could right it and shoving it into the swell of a wave. Icy water swept over the side, knocking Perchtwine sprawling beneath it and weighting the boat dangerously low. Sigifrith forced the rudder straight as Notkar and Hildkar hauled their struggling friend up and the others leapt to the bailing buckets.

The wind had already blown Sigifrith's ship away from the others, which still toiled across it. He thought for a second, then made his decision. "Follow me!" he shouted. "Must stay together!" The young drighten gestured as wildly as he could to get the attention of the other captains. For a couple of seconds, he thought they hadn't seen or heard him; then, one by one, his fleet turned, the wind bearing them swiftly toward him.

The dark clouds were rising higher over the land now, roiling and seething like steam from an etin-wife's cauldron. Sigifrith's ship plunged down into a trough, a huge wave looming above it for a breathless moment, then leapt up in the spray of icy water before diving again. The wind grabbed at the sail, wild gusts shaking it this way and that before a single howling blast of flying sleet caught it from behind and drove the ship straight through the heaving waves. Sigifrith saw Hildkar's face white against his dark hair, mouth a working black hole and eyes squinted shut against the furious wind as the thane bent to bail frantically.

Sigifrith held to the rudder, facing forward with the waves breaking over his head, laughing between mouthfuls of salt water as they ran before the storm. The waters rose and leapt around him, darkening beneath the black thunderclouds sweeping down; it seemed to him that he could hear mocking laughter in their roar, the laughter of etin-women tossing their foamy heads and reaching with great watery claws to grasp his ships and drag them down to Ran's sea-cold hall. It was no dream, the streaks of deep red through the frothing green-black; the sea itself was bloodied, the wild hair of Ran's daughters stained with wound-dew. He could hear them howling to each other as they flung his ships about in the water, their voices like the screeching of gulls, screaming in the wind that tore at his banner and pounded the spray from his sail.

"Hai, wild women!" Sigifrith shouted, his voice almost lost in the noise of the storm. "I'm not here for your sport. Go and tell Ran to rob another; you'll get no game here."

The laughter of the waves rose cruelly as the bloody sea pounded down on Sigifrith's deck. Out of the corner of his salt-blurred eyes, he could see his thanes each hugging mast or spars with one arm, bailing madly with the other.

Come down, come down, he heard them crying through the wind. Come to us, little man. Are you afraid? Because you've never had a woman yet? It's what you did with the old dwarf in the cave—ha! That might make you a walkurja, but never a hero. Are you man enough to come to us?

A huge wave rushed over him, beating the breath from his lungs and almost knocking him down. Sigifrith gasped air in, laughing. "No more strength than that?" he taunted. "You women aren't fit for me, then. Seek a mate who's more your match—if you're tired of scaly nicors, there's plenty of hairy trolls in the north to warm you."

Great fingers of frothing brine curved about his ship, pulling against the wind that bore him up. The ship listed from side to side, timbers creaking and sail fraying between the two struggling mights. Harthpercht slowly made his way along the side to Sigifrith, cupping his hand and shouting something in his drighten's ear.

"What?" Sigifrith called.

"Reef the sail! It's ripping!"

Cold seaweed slapped Sigifrith in the face as the next wave broke over them, its black tendrils twining about his neck. Angrily he tore the slimy stuff off and flung it away.

"Raise it higher!" he shouted back. As Harthpercht shook his head, Sigifrith pushed the rudder into the old thane's hands and leapt across the lurching deck himself, pulling the frayed sail up to catch the full might of the wind. The ship shot ahead, skimming like a spear over the bloody waves, her sharp prow cleaving them neatly as a foam-shedding blade. It seemed that the stormwind held the ship up as much as the sea now, rolling as smooth as a galloping horse over the seething waters. Sigifrith glanced behind; whether from desperation or loyalty, the other four ships had also hoisted their sails to full height, driving through the long showers of rain and spray behind him. Lightning lashed yellow-white through the clouds as if to whip them onward. The thunder was far away, but followed more closely in their wake with each bolt.

Sigifrith's fleet ran before the storm all day without hope of changing course; nor could they see through the purple-gray thunderheads to chart their path, even if they could have fought across the wind. Now and again, Sigifrith and his men would scrabble over the deck for a few pieces of hard bread that was soaked through with rain and spray almost as soon as they drew it from the barrels or for some of the salt fish. Ragin glowered from where he sat crouched among the supplies; once or twice he tried to speak to Sigifrith, but couldn't raise his voice high enough to cut through the raging of the wind and the sea.

No land came into sight until Sunna's setting light began to glow a deep, bruised purple through the thinner clouds in the western sky. Then Sigifrith, straining his eyes through the veil of sleet and rain, could see the dark shadow of an island ahead as the ship balanced on the crest of a wave before plunging down between the waters again. He took the rudder, steering for it; his thanes, too tired to cheer, hung from the sides of the ship as he wrestled it toward the land.

Closer, Sigifrith saw that the waves were breaking on the faces of great overhanging cliffs of craggy stone, clawed and torn by years of storms like the one they rode. The current had his ship now; he spared a moment to gesture the others frantically away before using all his strength to force his vessel out of the stream bearing it toward the rocks. Around the island, he thought; if I can find a place fit to land . . .

Sigifrith rounded the foot of the island, sailing along its western side. Squinting through the huge waves and the blinding storm, he thought his eyes were tricking him at first; but ahead was a single pillar of rock like a limbless tree trunk carved from dark- and light-layered stone, standing well free of the cliff that curved around behind it. On top of the stack, just above the crashing stormwaves, stood a dark figure, hooded cloak flapping in the wind behind it. Sigifrith saw the man, if it was a man, cupping hands to mouth. Then the deep, rough-edged voice rang through the howling of the wind,

"Who rides the sea-king's steeds there over the high waves? Your sails are sweaty and splintering—the wave-mares won't stand the wind much longer!"

Crablike, Ragin crawled from his shelter, slipping and stumbling back and forth on the pitching deck. His lips were drawn back from yellowed teeth, eyes fixed on the strange man with grim fury as he struggled over to the side of the boat. Sigifrith was about to go and help him when a lurch of the ship flung the dwarf onto the planking. Still staring at the man who had hailed them, Ragin pulled himself up and growled, his voice whipped away by the wind, "Sigifrith's men are on the sea trees, and the wind would give us our bane itself. The waves fall over our prow, and the roller-horses plunge. Who is it asking?"

"I was called Hnikarr, when Huginn was gladdened," the man answered, looking Ragin straight in the face. The dwarf looked away, spitting, and the stranger turned his single sharp glance on to Sigifrith. "Young Walsing, you may call the carl of this berg Fjolnir or Feng. Now I wish to fare with you."

Sigifrith turned his ship into the current again, letting it sweep toward the high-towering crag. The waves were stronger near shore, tossing the craft up and down; only Sigifrith's might held it from being dashed and broken on the rock as he worked it nearer and nearer till a wave lifted the ship nearly to the top of the stack and Fjolnir leaped into the boat. As Sigifrith tacked away from the crag, the waves sank down and down. The rain lightened to mist, floating away on the soft breeze as the western clouds parted to let the golden-red light of Sunna's setting through. In the space of a few breaths, the ships of Sigifrith's fleet were rocking gently on a calm sea beneath a cliff and a free-standing stone column that, Sigifrith thought, must have stood at least twelve times as high as the mast of any ship ever built.

The thanes were gathered at the other end of the boat, staring at Fjolnir and Sigifrith in wonder and awe. Hildkar's mouth was gaping open; Harthpercht was rubbing at his eyes with both hands as if to wipe impossibility from them; Perchtwine sat huddled in a sickly heap. Ragin was still flattened against the side of the boat, glaring at the man of the berg with—recognition? Hatred? Beneath the wind-warped tangle of wet hair and beard that covered the dwarf's face, Sigifrith could not tell what feeling warped his foster-father's expression.

Fjolnir pointed around the island, the way they had come. "That way, and east," he commanded. "We'll reach the land of Hunding's sons by midday tomorrow. Well done, Sigifrith." A hint of a grim smile turned beneath his gray-streaked brown beard.

"Thank you, and welcome." Sigifrith untied the carved wooden mug at his belt and filled it at the barrel of strong wine. Although the wind was filling the sail again, the deck seemed as steady as dry land after that day's wild faring, and Sigifrith did not spill a drop as he carried the full cup to his guest.

Fjolnir took the cup and drank half, then gave it back to Sigifrith. "Drink with me, my host, in token of the coming night in which you shall be my guest," he murmured. Sigifrith met the old rock-man's eye steadily as he raised the cup to his lips, draining the wine to the bottom. The rush of wod through his head was more than familiar, like the rushing of blood through his veins or the tingle of Gram's hilt in his hand, and it seemed to Sigifrith that he knew the wanderer who had helped him choose Gram. To his own pride, Sigifrith saw that he and the old man were of the same height now.

"In token of that night," Sigifrith said gravely. He turned to his men. "Well done. My thanes . . . I'm proud of you. Go ahead and drink. I think we've made it through the worst."

Exhausted, stunned by what they had weathered and seen that day, it seemed to take a while for Sigifrith's words to sink in. It was Chlodomar who recovered first, lanky legs and arms flailing as he ran across the deck to the wine.

"Hail the gods!" he whooped. "We're still alive. Come on, you slugs, wake up. Hai!" he shouted to the other ships. "The drighten says we can drink!"

Sigifrith waved to the other captains in agreement. He saw a few men on the other vessels untying themselves from their posts, each crew gathering around its own store of provisions. On Sigifrith's ship, Hildkar had appointed himself to pass out fish and bread as well as wine. One of the thin thane's hollow cheeks bulged like a squirrel's as he tried to chew and talk at the same time.

"Early for a victory feast?" Fjolnir asked, his mouth quirking ironically.

"Say . . . a rest between battles," Sigifrith answered. "More wine? Fish? Bread? It's not very good, but it's what we've got."

Fjolnir unslung a great drinking horn from beneath his cloak—an aurochs' horn, bound with silver at the rim and tipped with a silver eagle's head, graven with a branching tracery of dark-stained runes. He drank deeply, a few drops falling from his beard into the bilgewater, then passed it to Sigifrith. The two of them sat down on the foremost bench, facing the eastern sky. The clouds were breaking up, a few stars shining from the cracks between them like water glimmering beneath broken rocks.

"Say to me, Hnikarr," Sigifrith said after they had been drinking for a while, "all you know of the signs that are best for gods and men going into battle."

"There are many which are good, if men only knew them when about to swing their swords. I think that the raven's flight is a fair following to the doughty warrior. The second is that, if when you are going out and prepared to leave, you see two strong thanes standing on the path. Thirdly, if you hear a wolf howling in the woods, you'll fare well among helmet-bearers if you see them faring first. Never fight your foe widdershins, or against the shining of the Moon's sister—the one who can see best will have the victory, when you are arranged into the battle-wedge I shall teach you. But if your foot should stumble when you go in the ways of battle, then you are fey; then the idises stand guileful on both sides and would see you wounded. The keen man should be combed and cleaned, and eat well in the morning: it is unknown where one may come in the evening, and it is ill to miss your own gain. Hold these signs in your mind: if you can find them and follow them, you can win both victory and frith, but if you should forget them, another may turn them against you."

"Tell me of the battle-wedge, then. In what way should I lead my men to war against the sons of Hunding?"

Fjolnir leaned closer, till Sigifrith could smell the wine on his breath like a sweet wild scent in the wind. "This is the way my sons draw up their hosts to fight against the foe. You must stand at the front, with sword but no shield. Behind you your men are arrayed in nine ranks, spreading out in a wedge with their shields locked along its two edges. Place your archers and men with throwing spears and axes in the middle behind you. This wedge will drive into the host of your foemen and split them; thereafter you will lead one side against Lingwe, the other will turn against his allies. So it will be known, who has my rede. Take with you a throwing spear, and cast it over the host of your enemies to give them to Wodan. Should you take Lingwe alive, make him a gift to the god in the way that will best revenge the greatest of athelings and the strongest of men; and if he proves his own bravery by enduring the sacrifice, then you will know that you have won a fit revenge for Sigimund the Walsing. Do you trust my rede?"

"My mother told me that I ought to follow the counsel I got along the way," Sigifrith answered. "That I shall do."

Fjolnir laughed, his one eye bright through the darkness. The clouds were shifting across the Moon, breaking up like ice in the floodings of winter's end and letting the clear light shine through. "No more trust than that? Maybe Ragin's managed to teach you some wisdom after all." The old man gestured to Ragin, who still stood watching him mistrustfully. "Sit down," he commanded. "Share our drink."

"I won't drink with you," Ragin answered. "For all you claim the wardings of guest-right, you brought my father to his death and my family to ruin when we guested you in our hall. Eagle, I remember you and your brothers. Why have you come to torment me again?"

"Sit and drink, Ragin," Fjolnir said. "I mean you no more ill. Indeed, I owe you a debt for your careful fostering of my kinsman." He raised his horn. "See, I drink to the memory of your father Hraithamar, first paid by the Rhine's gold, and your brother Fadhmir, long dead and become Fadhmir the Wyrm." He took a draught from the horn, then held it out to Ragin.

"What do you want of Sigifrith?" the dwarf grunted, staring at the glittering silver rim around the dark draught. "You've said yourself that a gift always looks for a gift. What gift are you asking of him in return for your rede? It's more than a few men slain, isn't it, old barrow-walker?"

"The one who plans to rob his brother's howe shouldn't speak so rudely of what can be taken from barrows," Fjolnir replied. "Nor is the dwarf himself so far from the land of the dead. How long ago was it that Ragin went into the same stones in which Nar and Dawan dwell?"

"Why have you come back?" Ragin asked again. "Sigifrith can do well enough without you."

"Well enough for your goals, maybe. But Sigifrith called me and I came. I have always heard the calls of the Walsing race."

"Sigifrith?" said Ragin, turning to his foster-son. The Moon was to his back, his face in shadow as he looked up at the young drighten. "Do you know who broke your father's sword? Who are you going to avenge yourself upon?"

"Lingwe the son of Hunding slew my father by treachery," Sigifrith answered. He could see the handsome face in his memory, the golden curls bleached to silver by the moonlight shining into his skull through his eyes; he could hear Lingwe's high voice calling him to battle, the echo warping it into the voice of an aging man.

"And what shattered the sword we reforged?" Ragin asked. "Do you think Lingwe's blade was stronger? Who chose victory for Hunding's son?"

"Sigimund chose for himself when he took the sword from the Barnstock," Fjolnir said. "No more, Ragin. You were never a brave man. What do you know of heroes?"

"I know what I have crafted, and I know that you and your kin are robbers—you, breaker of oaths especially, for you betray the souls of those true to you."

"I shall have showed him more faith than you by the end," Fjolnir told Ragin softly.

"You will torment him for your own ends and give him to an unworthy death," answered Ragin. Then, "At least let him forget what we have spoken. Doesn't he have enough to bear without these dark words added to it?"

Sigifrith heard the rustle of Fjolnir nodding within his cloak. "There will come a day when he must remember all. But then . . ."

Ragin took the horn from Fjolnir's hand and drank at last—deeply, as though trying to become drunk on one draught, the rivulets dripping from the corners of his mouth. He wiped his beard with his sleeve as Fjolnir's long, knobbly hand emerged from the folds of his cloak and moved toward Sigifrith's face. The youth tried to move backward, but it was too late; he was already falling into a deep sleep as Fjolnir touched him.

Sigifrith awoke to the clear brilliance of the Sun rising over the water into a sky swept clean by the sharp breeze blowing his ships toward the east.

He swung his legs down from the bench, shivering as his bare feet splashed into the icy bilgewater, and stretched to his full height. Running his tongue over his teeth, he spat the stale taste of sleep from his mouth. To his disappointment, he could see no trace of Fjolnir. Remembering the evening, Sigifrith thought that he had gone to sleep before he had finished asking the old man everything he wanted to know, though he couldn't think of what other rede he had thought he'd needed. The other thanes were stirring slowly, groggy as if they had drunken themselves dead the night before; Ragin sat like a stump with his cloaks over his head, and Sigifrith couldn't tell whether the dwarf was awake or asleep.

"Rise up!" Sigifrith called out merrily. "Are you ready for battle? We'll be landing by midday."

He filled his cup with small beer, dipping his hard bread into the drink to soften it, and munched as he watched his men pull themselves together. To Sigifrith's surprise, no one cursed at him or complained as they usually did when he woke them up in the morning; it almost seemed that his friends were avoiding his gaze as they hurried to ready themselves. He sloshed to the end of the boat where the thanes had gathered while he spoke with Fjolnir.

"Are you all right, Hildkar?" he said. "You seem awfully quiet."

"I'm all right," Hildkar muttered, looking down at the piece of bread in his hand as he turned it over and over.

"Nervous?"

"Of course not. Um, just a moment." The thane walked over to one side of the boat, tested the wind, shook his head and moved toward the bow. The breeze flung the stream of yellow droplets forward past the prow.

"Chlodomar? Ready to go and kill some Saxons?"

"That's what we're here for," the lanky redhead agreed, his eyes darting around as if he were watching something over Sigifrith's shoulder. His mouth slithered into a quick grin; he seemed about to say something, but turned it into a rough stuttering cough. Hludowig's glance flicked away when Sigifrith looked over at him.

Sigifrith walked back to his place by the prow. It was because of Fjolnir, he knew, and there was nothing he could say or do about it. The Sigifrith who had talked with the man of the rock was not the Sigifrith they had know within Alapercht's hall. For a moment, Sigifrith wished Hagan were there—Hagan, who walked out at night to speak to whatever it was he saw in the river—or else Gundahari, to whom his brother's strange doings seemed a matter of course. Then he shook his head. He was imagining things: his men had fought through the storm all day and then drunk enough to send them straight to sleep. Why should he expect them to be lively?

"Eat and rest as much as you can," he called, getting up to help himself to a second serving of breakfast. "We'll need all our strength when we go ashore. I mean to have Lingwe's lands half-conquered by the time he's called three of his thanes together."

Harthpercht nodded, grinning to reveal a mess of half-chewed fish between the gaps in his teeth. Perchtwine had recovered from his seasickness well enough to nibble on a bit of bread and beer; he was still pale, but looked better than he had. "How are you feeling?" Sigifrith asked him.

"Ready to kill someone," the sandy-haired thane said with the ghost of a grin. "My stomach wants revenge."

Sigifrith clapped him gently on the shoulder. "You'll get your chance soon enough. This is what I mean to do . . . Gather round, everyone."

With hunks of bread and salt-fish, Sigifrith showed his thanes the battle array that Fjolnir had taught him, giving each man his place by his skill. Otho drew his grizzled eyebrows together as he looked at the formation.

"Seems to me I've heard tell of something like this once or twice before," he said. "I heard there's only one man who can teach it. As long as Lingwe don't know it too, maybe we've got nothing to worry about."

"Don't praise the battle till it's won," Ansbrand chided him. The swarthy thane ran his whetstone along the edge of one of his throwing axes—a Frank by birth, he still used the weapons of his tribe, though he'd been fighting beside Alapercht for thirty years. "Sigifrith, how are we going to know where to go and what to do? None of us've been up here since before you were born."

"We'll find out where the sons of Hunding are when we land, then raid our way through and do just as we like till they get up the courage to come and try to stop us," Sigifrith said. "If they don't want to meet us, then they're cowards not worth venging ourselves on, and we'll take every snippet of gold and silver in the whole of Saxony."

As he finished speaking, he noticed that the thanes were looking over his shoulder at something. The younger men had gone pale, staring wide-eyed. Harthpercht thrust his thumb through his fist in a gesture to ward off evil and Otho stepped back, fumbling for the Ziw's spear amulet at his neck. Faintly, Sigifrith could hear the gasps from the other ships. He whirled, eager to see what had come upon them.

A great swan winged toward the group of ships, blood dripping from its pure breast. It was blindingly white against the clear sky with the morning sunlight on it, its brightness searing its shape within Sigifrith's eyes to flash black in his sight as he blinked. Wounded as it was, the swan flew strongly, each beat of its wings fanning a gust of wind into the sails. It began to circle the ships, its blood falling onto them. A drop struck Chlodomar's upturned face just below his left eye, splashing across his blotchy skin like brighter freckles; the red-haired thane began to curse and scream in horror as he rubbed and tore at the spot where it had fallen. A few men on the other boats cried out in disgust and fear when the blood spattered onto them.

The swan flew around the fleet three times, then turned northward, flying on till it could be seen no more. Chlodomar had gone to the barrels of small beer, dipping his hands into the drink and splashing it over his face again and again till Sigifrith caught his bony wrists in one hand.

"That's enough, Chlodomar," he said gently. "You've got it off."

"I can still feel it," the thane said in bewilderment. "It . . . ugh!" His cheek was red and raw from his scratching at it. "It was an evil sign," he insisted. "That was our blood splashing over the ships. We're all doomed to fall in this battle."

The other thanes hid their fear better, but Sigifrith could see the paleness beneath their sun-browned skin and he knew what it meant when Hildkar bit his lip and twisted his long fingers together like that. Harthpercht's feet shuffled nervously, as if they would betray his courage by running away with him. Otho's massive, gray-stubbled jaw grated from side to side, moving as if he were already rehearsing some counsel of prudence. Sigifrith felt no fear, only a little disgust with his men. He knew that if he didn't speak at once, Chlodomar's words would come true and his battle be lost.

"What kind of heart do you have in you?" he asked, laughing. "A sign? So it was. It's not our blood, but the blood of our foes that will cover our ships before the battle's done. Chlodomar, you've fought before—you should know what an enemy's blood in your face feels like. Maybe you've been sitting in peace too long?" He bent down, wiped a drop of blood from the deck with two fingers, and licked them clean. "See? There's nothing to be afraid of here. We'll feed the ravens well enough . . . " Sigifrith paused. It seemed to him . . . he could see the white image of the swan flashing black behind his eyes, and suddenly he knew another meaning of the sign. "And a raven is called a swan of wounds," he went on, half-amazed at himself. "It's a good sign to see a raven before a battle; it means a worthy fight and victory at the end. Do you hear?" he shouted to the other ships, turning and gesturing to them. His call rang high and clear between them, carrying over the water. "A sign of victory!"

"Hail Sigifrith!" Kunitrut's deep growl echoed back. "Victory!" Adalprant and Paltwine shouted; gold flashed from Anshelm's arm as he raised his fist in a gesture of acknowledgment, his teeth showing in an uneven smile.

Sigifrith's glance flickered over to Ragin. The dwarf heaved himself from his bench and stumbled over to Sigifrith, still unsteady even in the light swells through which the ship rolled with ease. Sigifrith caught Ragin as a tilt of the deck threatened to pitch the dwarf straight into him, holding him upright and setting him down on another of the oarsmen's benches.

"It's a risky business, interpreting signs," Ragin grumbled. "Do you think you're a wise man now?"

"Wise enough to know weal from woe," answered Sigifrith. "Does this mean more to you?"

"It might, if I chose," the dwarf muttered. "I think there's more ways than one to read—or write—every rune. But now I'll leave it as you have spoken it."

Before the Sun had reached her midday height, they could see the clouds rising from the land over a dark mass of marsh. Sigifrith turned to Otho, looking at him questioningly. The older thane shrugged.

"Looks like Saxony to me," he said. "Ever since I've heard anything about it, they've had bad flooding at this time of year. Most of 'em will be living on top of mounds and such—terpen, they call them—that they've piled up against the sea." He blinked bloodshot hazel eyes, staring at the land ahead of them. "We could be anywhere along the coast. Go on far enough, we'll find one of their settlements."

"Right." Sigifrith took the rudder, steering the ship along the coast. The sands at the edge of the marsh were white and as bare as bone, marked only by scatters of black seaweed here and there. A faint mooing floated over the water. Straining his eyes, Sigifrith saw a scrawny dun cow picking its way through the swamp. They sailed on for a while, till brown marsh-sedge gave way to bare tree trunks and branches twisting dark against the blue winter sky where the ground rose. The wind was dying down. Sigifrith helped reef the sail and then called for the oars, steering as his men rowed the ships in. They beached, the keels grinding to rest in the white sand, and tossed the anchors over the side.

"Is this high or low tide?" Sigifrith asked, looking at the four older thanes, then at Ragin.

"Probably midway, till another storm comes," Ansbrand decided. "Then it's well out to sea." He watched the low waves curling in for a few moments. "Tide's going out," he judged finally. "If we want to get away fast, we'd better think again about mooring here."

"There's nothing here we want to flee," Sigifrith said. He raised his voice to carry to the other ships. "Get your weapons and some food. We're going ashore!" To Hildkar, he said, "And get my banner down. You don't mind carrying it, do you?"

"Me?" Hildkar said, his jaw dropping to make his long face even longer.

"Yes, you."

"You sure about that?"

"Yes."

"Shit . . . I mean—er—I'm honored," Hildkar corrected himself quickly. The thane's ears were glowing bright pink. "Er, yes. Of course." He scrambled over to the banner, fumbling with the fastenings that held its pole to the mast.

When they had stumbled and splashed ashore, Sigifrith asked who would be willing to stay and guard the ships. Except for Ragin, no one was and they had to draw lots, three men from each crew. Hludowig threw his short twig to the ground, spat disgustedly at it, then ground it into the sand with the heel of his boot; the other unlucky guards mostly eased their feelings with curses and mumblings. Only Chlodomar seemed relieved by the lot that kept him on the ship; he had not spoken much since the swan's blood spattered him.

"Shall we get into the wedge now?" Perchtwine asked.

"Not till we actually come to meet Lingwe," Sigifrith answered. "I think it'll only work in a real battle, not in raiding."

Adalprant, Paltwine, Kunitrut and Anshelm looked at the two of them, and Kunitrut growled, "What are you talking about?" Sigifrith explained the formation as quickly as he could to the commanders of the other ships. They nodded their heads wisely.

"We'll want to practice that," said Adalprant. And so Sigifrith arranged his warband as Fjolnir had told him. Shields locked along the sides, the wedge of men ran up and down the beach behind Sigifrith. At first they stumbled on the solid ground, shields slipping as the men on the edges tried to match each other's pace and height, those within bumping into each other when they mimed the motions of shooting and throwing their weapons. But it felt good to be off the ships with the long day of storm behind, able to stretch cramped legs and sore muscles in the sunlight. Sigifrith could hear the thanes shouting and laughing behind him as they ran and waved their arms about, playing at the fight like a horde of boys beneath the mocking laughter of gulls and terns. The cool breeze from the sea quickly dried their sweat, and soon they were running and mock-fighting in step, shields locked into a solid frame around their wedge. Sigifrith felt that he could have led them like that all day, but after a while he could tell that some of them were wearying, so he called a halt. They ate their midday meal on the beach while Sigifrith explained his campaign plan, such as it was, to the men off the other ships.

After lunch, they walked along the beach till they found a path that led into the wood. There were fresh cow tracks in the wet leaves, the deep hoofprints just filling with water, and the pathway was well kept enough not to be too far from a settlement. Vines dangled soggily from the lower branches of the trees. Out of curiosity, Sigifrith picked one of the long, broad leaves off and found that it was seaweed.

"Flooding," Otho grunted as Sigifrith tossed the leaf away. "That keeps up, the north won't be worth living in soon. Not that it is anyway," he added cynically. He settled his helmet more comfortably on his head, using his casting spear to point ahead with a meaningful grunt.

Sigifrith could see the neatly smoothed edges of a huge low mound through the bare trees. "Is that one of the terpen?" he whispered.

Otho nodded. "Kill what we can, eat what we can, steal what we can and burn everything else?"

Sigifrith put his hand over his mouth to muffle his laugh. "Yes . . . Ready?" All along the line, his men nodded their heads, drawing swords or gripping axes.

Sigifrith drew Gram, whirling it over his head, and ran forward. The bare branches whipped past his face, but soon he was clear, running up the soggy side of the hill and shouting, "Wodan and vengeance!" Before him a skinny youth looked up from between two gaunt cows, choking for a moment in shock before he dropped their ropes and scrambled away through the slippery mud. Sigifrith let him go, charging up into the settlement. The women were fleeing into their houses, men in rough homespun running out with spears and axes. The edge of an arrow feather-flicked Sigifrith's cheek in a sprinkle of blood as he turned to meet the first group, the little men crowding around him like dogs around a stag. Gram cleaved through the iron of their weapons, a single stroke parting blades and arms in two as the screaming began. The shouting of his men behind him roared as distant as the sea in his ears as he pressed onward to the largest hut. A few men with swords and helms were coming out of the door of the tiny hall. Sigifrith ran gladly to meet them, Gram whirring and flicking between them like a willow wand that sliced steel and bone till they lay in a bloody heap before him. He leapt over their bodies into the hall, looking about in hopes of finding worthier foes, but only a plain woman in a drab brown dress huddled in the far corner, her arms around two young children.

"Is there anyone else here?" he asked. The woman glanced up, shaking her head as the children began to cry. "Who are you?"

"I am called Herborg," she said. Her speech was choppy, harsher than Sigifrith was used to hearing. "I am . . . I was the wife of Wulfric, fro of these lands. What do you want? Why have you done this?"

"I've come for revenge for Sigimund the Walsing," Sigifrith answered. "Tell me where I may find Lingwe the son of Hunding."

"Will you swear not to hurt my children?" she asked. Her voice cracked, spilling tears; she swallowed hard and wiped her eyes on her long woolen sleeve.

"I swear," Sigifrith said at once. "Tell me where he is, and you and your children may go free."

"Three days' sail to the east, if the wind is good, and one day's march overland. Then you'll come to Lingwe's hall, that once was Sigimund's," Herborg told him.

"How long will it take you to get there?"

"Five days if you let us have our horses. I don't know how long otherwise."

"Take what you can carry, get your horses and ride to Lingwe," Sigifrith told her. "Bear him this message: that not all the Walsings are dead. If any of my men tries to stop your going, tell him that Sigifrith has sent you."

Herborg spoke to her children too swiftly for Sigifrith to understand her words through her heavy accent. They hurried about the hall, gathering this and that into a cloth bag, then went out of the back door without another word just as Hildkar, Kunitrut, Theodipalt and Perchtwine came in the front. Perchtwine's axe was in his belt and he was carrying a flaming brand, black smoke coiling up to snake along the low roof of the hall. Sigifrith could hear the roar of flames in the village.

"Anything in here?" Theodipalt asked. He held up a twice-coiled arm-ring of thin gold wire. "I guess this is yours—you killed the man it belonged to." He tossed the ring to Sigifrith, who caught it one-fingered and absent-mindedly slipped it on as he looked around for something to clean Gram with. The thanes rummaged through the hall, going into the back room and coming out a few minutes later.

"Not much here worth taking," Kunitrut grumbled. "You didn't see any women, did you?"

"There was an older frowe, but I've sent her off," Sigifrith answered. "She said something about horses . . . "

Kunitrut spat, grinding the spittle into mud on the earthen floor. "I'm not that hungry, and Saxon horses aren't good for anything else." He turned and walked out.

"Can we burn it now?" Perchtwine asked. The young thane's face was flushed red from heat and excitement, the birthmark on his forehead almost black with blood.

"Might as well," Sigifrith said. They left the hall and Perchtwine set his torch to the thatch. The sodden straw hissed and sputtered for a few moments before flaring up. A gust of wind blew the smoke into Sigifrith's face, so that he coughed and rubbed at suddenly streaming eyes, waving it away.

"What shall we do with these?" Hildkar said, gesturing at the stripped bodies by the door.

"Leave them for the ones who want them," Sigifrith said. Out of the corner of his eye, he thought he saw Hildkar shaking off a shudder, but when he turned to look straight at him the thane was grinning lopsidedly. Sigifrith noticed a dark spot soaking through the shoulder of Hildkar's green tunic. "Hai, you're wounded, aren't you?"

Hildkar put his hand to his shoulder, pulling the frayed linen away. "Not bad, I think." The cut was a couple of inches long, but not deep. Sigifrith could see that the blood was beginning to clot already. "You got scratched yourself, along the cheek there. Letting your guard down, were you?"

Sigifrith wet his finger and rubbed off a thin crust of dried blood, then shrugged. "Arrow graze."

He could hear high screams over the sounds of the flames as the hamlet burned; a couple of the thanes had grabbed women already. Sigifrith stared at Otkar's thick white buttocks pumping beneath his flapping tunic, breeches about his knees, as he pressed a struggling girl deeper into the mud. Sigifrith knew what was happening—what had to happen; he had heard about it often enough, but never seen . . .

Shaken, he turned away, bumping into Harthpercht. A few dark red drops glistened on the grizzled hair around the old thane's mouth; and for a wild moment Sigifrith thought that Harthpercht had been drinking blood till he saw the clay bottle in the other warrior's hand. Harthpercht held it up, grinning. "Wouldn't have thought we'd find any of this here, hey?" he laughed. "Drink some, it'll do you good. You look a little pale. First-battle shakes? You just about won this one by yourself."

Sigifrith tilted the wine bottle and took a healthy swallow. "Thanks," he said. "Think I can call everyone back? We've got a lot more fighting to do before we're done."

Harthpercht gazed around. "There'll be one or two who won't come as fast as others, so to speak." He aimed a kick at Otkar's rear. "Might as well wait a bit. You weren't the only one first-blooded this time, you know."

It was a while before Sigifrith called his men together. He gave orders that the women and children be turned loose to go to Lingwe with news of what had happened; some food was given to the survivors and the rest carried back to Sigifrith's ships, together with such loot as Sigifrith's men had found. When they were gathered on the beach, Sigifrith stared at the smoke rising from the burning settlement, and a sudden fierceness took hold of him. His father had had neither pyre nor mound; only the flames of his own revenge would do for Sigimund's honor. The thought fired him with the need to move, to do something. He strode among his men without speaking for a few moments, looking down at them.

"Tired?" Sigifrith asked at last, his voice ringing hard as metal on metal in his ears. "I hope not. Those practice swings barely loosened my arms. Shall we see if we can find men enough to give us a fight before sundown?" He shoved Otkar's shoulder roughly, knocking the plump thane to the sand. Otkar's blue eyes stared up at him, his mouth open to speak. "You didn't wear yourself out back there, did you?" Otkar shut his mouth and shook his head, a sheepish grin spreading across his face as he hoisted himself up. "Back to the ships, then. There'll be something better to the west."

"Not till the tide comes in," Adalprant said, the unscarred corner of his mouth quirking ironically as he looked at the stranded ships in the sand, well above the edge of the sea.

Sigifrith laughed, running lightly over to his own ship. He lifted the anchor and heaved it over the side, then put his shoulder to the bow and dug his feet into the sand, pushing the boat out toward the water. "Come on!" he shouted. "If you won't help with the others, get in and I'll push you myself!" The foam was starting to curl around his ship's keel. With a glad cry of enthusiasm his thanes rushed forward, several of the younger men gathering around each of the other boats and heaving them toward the sea. Sigifrith shoved his own out till he stood thigh deep in the icy water and the ship was floating free, then hauled himself over the side, cheering his men on as they splashed out to him. One by one he lifted his crew up, swinging them onto the deck. Ragin sat cross-legged on a bench, its wood now freshly adorned with finely carved knotwork. He watched Sigifrith sourly as his laughing men congratulated him.

"Did you clean the sword properly?" the dwarf asked Sigifrith. "No matter how good you think that metal is, if you sheath it dirty you're going to regret it."

"I cleaned it," Sigifrith said. He drew Gram three-quarters from the sheath.

Ragin leaned over and peered short-sightedly at the blade, swinging his head from side to side as he scrutinized the glistening metal for the smallest mar of blood. Reluctantly satisfied, the smith snorted. "Hah! Killing thralls and farmers—it wasn't made for that. Might as well use it to cut cheese with, if you've got to exercise your arm on something."

"I'll find better when we land next," Sigifrith said. He put one finger up to test the wind. "Ready to row, men?"

Sigifrith's fleet rowed along the coast a fair way. They passed a few small hamlets, but it was mid-afternoon before they came to a large settlement by the mouth of a river. A horn sounded over the water as they rowed up; sunlight glinted from the byrnies and weapons of the men assembling at the edge of the village.

"That's more like I expected," Hildkar said to Sigifrith. He lifted the banner high, brandishing it at the warriors above. "We'll have a real fight this time."

"Maybe even loot worth taking," Harthpercht added. "Is that gold I see on their drighten's helmet?"

In answer, a shower of arrows sliced hissing through the air as Ragin scrambled for shelter among the ale barrels. A few of the shots thunked into the ships' planks, though most fell into the water. Sigifrith laughed delightedly, taking up a throwing spear.

"You all belong to Wodan," he shouted, casting it to the top of the mound with his full strength. It passed over the gathering host; he saw their heads turning to watch as it slammed through the wooden door of the great hall behind them. Sigifrith gestured his men to row in faster. "Shields up!" he said, seeing the archers bending their bows again.

The thanes put their shields over their heads, rowing one-handed toward the shore. More arrows struck the boats, quivering shafts jutting from shields. Sigifrith thought at first that no one had been hurt; then Chlodomar toppled sideways, falling into the bilge with a splashing thump. Sigifrith hurried to his side, turning him over. Chlodomar's left eye drooped out over an arrow's gull-feather fletching, bright blood oozing around it. Sigifrith tried to lay his thane's lanky body down on one of the oar benches, but Chlodomar's arms and legs kept flopping down, pulling his corpse to one side or the other. Two more arrows whirred past Sigifrith's face to stick between Chlodomar's ribs and in his right leg.

The ships grounded. Sigifrith left Chlodomar and tossed the anchor over the side, following it himself. He brandished Gram above his head as he waded through the waist-deep water while his men struggled along behind him, holding their shields against the storm of arrows and throwing spears and trying to keep their balance through the low waves breaking off their chests. When Sigifrith got closer to the land, he waited for his thanes and then, with a cry of "Wodan and vengeance!" they plunged ahead, forward to the host of the defenders waiting above on the slope of the terp.

Battle-wod laughed through Sigifrith as he fought, striking with all the strength he had feared to use against his friends in practice. Shieldless, a blow from his shield arm's fist was enough to split a spear shaft or bend a sword, shatter a skull through helmet or splinter a linden shield. His hair had come loose from the thong that bound it, whipping about him in the wind of his fighting; he could hear his voice shouting wordlessly as he struck and slashed and destroyed everything in his path. It was far too soon when his eyes cleared; when he stood, sticky with drying blood, in the middle of the settlement where nothing moved except his own men and the women they were dragging from the houses. He pushed back the thick mass of blood-clotted hair around his face and looked down at the slaughtered bodies that lay about him, a quiet disappointment beginning to settle in. Then he saw Perchtwine bringing a torch from inside one of the houses.

"Don't burn them yet!" he shouted. "Over here!"

The thane hurried over, a questioning look on his face. "Why not?"

"We'll stay here the night. It's better than sleeping in the bilge, isn't it? Did any of our men get killed?"

"Otho, Adalrat and Arnolf."

Sigifrith gazed at the heaps of dead lying around the settlement. "I suppose that's not too bad."

Perchtwine laughed. "No, these folk were so busy trying to get at you that they didn't look out for anyone else. Hai, you're all bloody. You look like a werewolf or a troll or something. Are you wounded?"

"I don't think so. We'll give our dead a proper pyre. Get someone to haul the rest of these off the terp for the ravens and wolves, then tell some of those women to roast meat for a feast."

"Right you are, my drighten. Will we burn this down tomorrow?"

"Yes."

Perchtwine went off; for a moment Sigifrith stood wondering what to do, then he remembered that he would be expected to deal out treasure that night and hurried to the great hall. His throwing spear lay just inside the broken door. Perhaps out of respect for their drighten, no one else had tried to loot the hall yet. Sigifrith went through, swiftly collecting whatever valuables he could carry easily. The drighten here had been a vain man: he had owned a shield inlaid with too much gold to make it fit for fighting with, and many of his tunics were embroidered with gold wire and set with gems. A small chest lay open; although there were fine dresses in the drighten's chamber, there were no adornments fit for a woman. Sigifrith guessed that the frowe must have taken her jewelery and fled when the fighting began. Good luck to her, he thought. He used one of the fine linen dresses to clean Gram with, polishing the sword until its snake ripplings gleamed even in the darkness of the hall.

Sigifrith laid the treasures he had found in the high seat with his spear across them. He knew that none of his men would touch what he had claimed.

They burned the bodies of their fallen that night, together with their weapons and some of the loot from the settlement. Sigifrith stood and watched till Chlodomar's limbs had stopped coiling and twitching in the fire, till Otho's face had burned away, till Adalrat and Arnolf had melted into torches of flaming meat with the sword blades across their bodies sagging and dripping white drops of iron and the gold around their burning arms flowing away in red rivulets like glowing snakes. The fire burned all night as the warband feasted; in the morning they woke to the screaming and flapping of the sea eagles fighting over the bodies of the fallen where Sigifrith's men had cast them down onto the beach. They lit the thatch of the hall and the huts around it with brands from the funeral pyre and marched away, not back to the ships but through the woods along the river. Some of the women had told them that there was another rich settlement up the river, one with which their drighten had carried on an ancestral feud over trading rights; a fat little redhead with cold black eyes had even begged Sigifrith to go and raid the other town as well.

Sigifrith and his men heard the crashing through the trees and the harsh grunting bellows long before they reached the fighting. When they rounded the bend in the path and reached the clearing where the battle was taking place, they stopped, staring in awe. They had all seen stags fighting before— the hunting was good around Alapercht's lands—but not like this. The two stags were true atheling-beasts, big as the horses of the Alamanns. Sigifrith guessed that one's rack carried fourteen points, the other's sixteen. They were not struggling for lordship, but in deathly earnest, shattering together with tree-shuddering crashes. Drops of blood spattered outward as sharp hooves struck and antlers locked, turning this way and that as each tried to force the other down. Awesome as their fight was, it was sickening to see them, torrents of white foam dripping from their mouths and red-streaked whites rolling and flashing in their madness-glazed eyes. Sigifrith and his men stood frozen, unable to turn their eyes from the unspeakable fury of the two great beasts loosing all their might against each other.

The battle of the two stags seemed to go on for a long time, till one, turning as if to gore the other's belly, slipped on the wet grass and crashed to his knees. His enemy's forehoof crunched down in his skull, but his last spasm jerked his horns up, stabbing the other deeply. The gored stag screamed, a horrible harsh guttural noise, as he tried to struggle off the other's branching antlers; he half rose, then the two fell together, the weight of the one on top forcing his foe's tines out through his back like bloody fingers outspread.

Sigifrith heard gagging coughs from behind him. "That's not natural," someone whispered. "What does it mean?"

Sigifrith saw Anshelm shaking his head. "Nothing good," the older thane muttered softly. "Whatever madness came over them, that's no good sign."

Sigifrith looked at the stags again. The one on top was still kicking weakly, its mouth opening in soft, hair-raising moans. "That's not a fit death for the atheling-beast," he murmured to himself. He walked over, careful to keep as far as he could from the deadly antlers. Gram flashed once, stabbing down.

"That was a sign," Harthpercht said, more loudly. "Sigifrith, I don't think we should pass this place."

A mutter of agreement came from the thanes behind him. "The omens . . . that swan . . . Chlodomar . . . "

"Are you afraid?" Sigifrith asked. Harthpercht flushed and scuffled one boot through fallen leaves.

"No one can fight against wyrd," he said. "If this is doomed to failure, we'd best leave it be and do something else."

"But it's not," Sigifrith said. He looked back at the dead stags. Two fallen atheling-warriors . . . two warriors in his pathway . . . "It's a sign, yes—it's a sign for victory, if we have the wit to understand it. Fjolnir told me that one of the best signs, going into battle, was to meet two warriors on the way. So we have: two mighty athelings fighting more fiercely than I have ever seen. It's only death to those who read it so and lose their brave mood." He looked fiercely, furiously, at the men. None of them would meet his gaze. But then Hildkar straightened his shoulders and raised the pole of Sigifrith's banner. "Onward!" Sigifrith said, waving his arm and striding firmly past the two stag-warriors locked in their death. He did not look back, but he heard the sound of his men trooping behind him and smiled to himself.

Sigifrith and his thanes loosed fire and slaughter, slaying men, burning settlements, and laying waste wherever they fared within Lingwe's lands. And wherever they went, Sigifrith sent the survivors to Lingwe to tell him that not all the Walsings were dead. The moon was two days from full by the time the white-shielded messenger rode to the beach before Sigifrith's ships.

"Hai!" he shouted. "Is Sigifrith the son of Sigimund on board?"

Sigifrith leapt up to stand on the side of the ship, swaying to keep his balance as it rocked with the swells. "I am he," he called back. "What do you want?"

"King Lingwe the son of Hunding sent me!" the messenger answered. His voice was hoarse, straining to shout his full message. "He says that he will meet you on the great plain north of his burg, if you have the brave mood you need to meet him in open battle. If not, he will hunt you and your wargs down with his hounds."

"We will meet Lingwe on the morning after the full moon!" Sigifrith replied. "Say to him that the geld for Sigimund and Aiwilimo is still owing, and the last of the Walsings has come to claim it."

The messenger spurred his clumsy Saxon horse, trotting in a wide circle to turn and ride away from the beach. Sigifrith turned to Hildkar, grinning; the skinny thane stepped backward. "Now for a real fight," he said cheerfully to his man. "Looking forward to it?"

"You mean someone besides you has a chance to kill somebody?" Hildkar muttered. "I suppose so. Do we have enough men left to fight a real battle?"

"Eighty-four and myself," Sigifrith said, surprised. "Why wouldn't that be enough?"

"We started out with a hundred of us, and that wasn't really a very large host, was it? And Lingwe's in his homeland."

"A half-wasted homeland. Anyway, all the signs have been in our favor. Cheer up, Hildkar. Another month or so and you'll be home drinking and

S
T
E
P
H
A
N

G
R
U
N
D
Y

⊕
3
9
0

looking for a wife again, if we haven't found you enough Saxon maidens to keep you busy."

"Are we going to take thralls home?"

"I don't see why not. I didn't want to haul them along with us while we were raiding, but afterward . . . ?" Sigifrith shrugged. "Anyway, we're going to win. Don't be so nervous."

Because Sigifrith remembered Lingwe's treachery, his host waited in their ships the night before the battle, anchored off the shore near Lingwe's burg. Toward midnight, the wind began to come up, dark clouds streaming across the full Moon in thinning and thickening banners, and the vessels began to pitch and roll in the rising waves. Sigifrith prowled ghost-quiet around the deck of his flagship, his feet splashing through the icy bilgewater as he stepped over the body-laden benches. Perchtwine muttered in his sleep, pulling his cloak over his head and turning restlessly on the narrow board. Hildkar lay quietly, one cold bare hand clinging to the pole of Sigifrith's standard.

Sigifrith heard what sounded like the creaking of the mast, then a raspy shifting of the bags of food and booty they had brought aboard. It was a moment before he heard the words, another before he looked down to see Ragin sitting among the half-empty barrels, his eyes gleaming stones in the darkness.

"Do you really think you can make those signs mean what you want them to?" he whispered to Sigifrith. "Do you really think you can win tomorrow?"

"Of course," Sigifrith answered, then, with some disgust, "Holy gods, Ragin, doesn't anyone else think so? You of all people should know—"

"You may be a hero, but what if an arrow hits you when you're not looking? What will you do when some greasy thrall gets behind you and sticks his eating knife between your ribs? You'll die just the same, even if it's not a hero's death. None of your men think they're going to live out the day."

"Why are they still here, then?"

"Pride," Ragin whispered. "Pride and troth. And maybe they don't want to leave you to face an army by yourself. But I can tell you, each of them is hoping you'll decide you've done enough for Sigimund's sake and turn around to go home tomorrow morning."

Sigifrith turned his face to the wind. A few spatters of rain flew into his eyes as the last light of the Moon sank beneath a drift of black cloud.

"I don't think the weather will let us go home so soon," he said. "We'll be lucky if we can sail back by Yule."

"You won't see Alapercht's hall for Yule," Ragin said painfully. "Sigifrith, this is a stupid thing to do."

"You raised me to be a hero," Sigifrith answered. "You did your best to teach me wisdom, but you never let me forget about my honor and my line. If I wanted to run away from danger, wouldn't you shame me into staying?"

Sigifrith could hear only the harsh rasp of his foster-father's breathing. After a while the young drighten turned away and walked to the bow of the ship, leaning against the smoothly carved scales of the dragon's head with his back to the sharpening wind. He closed his eyes and tried to put the dwarf's words out of his mind. It seemed to him as he dozed that he could see a black swarm of flies crowding around his ships, stinging and sucking blood in thousands of little droplets. Only where he stood was the air clear, as if a wind were blowing the flies away. Sigifrith half-roused himself, drowsily lifting a hand to wave against the flies on his men.

The rain was falling harder now, a few cold drops splattering through the warmth of his sleep, and he knew he had been dreaming; flies wouldn't swarm in the rain. He pulled up the hood of his cloak and closed his eyes again.

Sigifrith roused his thanes at dawn, as soon as the sky began growing light. A thin rain was whipping across the bay in sheets, the waves leaping in torrents of white froth. The men woke shivering and cursing. As soon as each had some bread and stolen meat or cheese in his hand, Sigifrith ordered them to their oars. "The rowing will warm you up," he called, seating himself on the foremost bench and taking one oar in each hand. "Come on, my heroes—one last fight, and then we'll have our victory and our frith together. We'll sleep in Lingwe's burg tonight and drink his ale." He gestured at the hall whose wide-shingled roof showed dark through the bare trees.

The five ships wallowed in to shore, fighting against the waves. Sigifrith saw after a while that most of his men wouldn't be able to wade through the wild sea, and ordered a dinghy to be lowered. He rowed it in and out himself, ferrying his troops to the shore till only two men, chosen by lot as always, stood on the deck of each ship.

"Gather into the wedge!" Sigifrith called. He waited till his men had fallen into place behind him, shields locked and weapons ready, then turned from his stead at the front to face them. "This is the battle for which I was taught it. Hold your places till we've split their host, then turn and take them. The gods have given us signs of victory, and I know you won't fail me. For Wodan and victory!"

"Sigifrith!" the thanes answered. Their voices were ragged, but Sigifrith could hear the brave mood burning in them. He raised a fist in acknowledgment and turned again to lead them up the slope of the beach. There was a wide path through the winter forest, wide enough for the host to pass easily, though the wind whipped the wet branches against the shields and faces of the men on the edges of the wedge.

They were not yet out of the wood when they heard the shouting, a dreadful howling like a host of mad dogs together with the clashing of weapon against weapon and linden wood. Sigifrith looked back; his men were exchanging uneasy glances.

"Berserkers," Anshelm murmured. "Lingwe's got berserkers in his host."

It seemed to Sigifrith that he could feel the sinking of their hearts like the timbers of a bridge giving way under his feet. Hildkar's eyes were very dark in his white face as he stared at his drighten; Perchtwine's birthmark stood out like a blotch of blood on his forehead and Kunitrut's hairy eyebrows were drawn almost low enough to hide his deepset little eyes.

Sigifrith whirled, drawing his sword. The sound of the howling seemed to fan the mad joyous wod that had run hidden and quiet through his blood like glowing coals hidden beneath ashes, fire springing up again in the wind. "The third sign!" he shouted softly. "The old man told me that if I heard a wolf howling in the woods, and then saw my foes before they could see me, that it was a sign for victory! Forward, my men, forward and on them!" His gaze leapt like lightning from one thane to the next, sparking their courage to light. He ran forward, bursting from the wood above the edge of a great plain.

The size of Lingwe's army flashed in Sigifrith's mind first: a great horde of men and horses waited ahead of him. Clearest to him was the banner that fluttered at the western side of the host—the snarling dog's head of the line of Hunding, its red dimmed a little by the sheets of rain whipping across the battlefield—and the men who stood beneath it in gold-wrought helmets and bright byrnies, the sons of Hunding and their sons. They looked up. Sigifrith could hear them shouting, though they were too far for the words to be clear.

"You all belong to Wodan!" Sigifrith shouted back, hurling his throwing spear at the banner of Hunding's sons. It seemed to him that the spear keened in its own wind as it flew over the host, piercing through the banner and hurtling onward. The arrows came in answer as Sigifrith blew his father's horn, a shower of long hail falling harmlessly around him and thumping into the trees beyond. Then his thanes were behind him, thundering down the slope of the field.

Sigifrith's momentum carried him on as they smashed into the first line of Lingwe's host. In one eyeblink he saw Gram carve a glittering line through a horse's dun belly, entrails tumbling out in the sword's trail; in the next a man's byrnie and helmet were parting before his blade, the sweetness of blood spurting over Sigifrith's face and into his mouth. A taunting horn was blowing ahead of him, the red banner pressing closer. He saw twisted faces coming at him, froth spilling from their mouths, their howling lost in the clashing and screams of the battle. Gladly he pressed forward to deal with the band of berserkers, his laughter ringing high over their growls as he found that their wod-given strength could almost meet his. Now he was fighting for his life, the berserkers around him; they fought on with gray-pink lungs pulsing through gaping wounds, struggling up on half-severed legs. The face of one dangled from his bared jawbone like a ghastly red beard; eyeless, he swung his sword around him till Sigifrith cut his hand

R
H
I
N
E
G
O
L
D

ᚻ
3
9
3

from his wrist. The blade of the last buckled as it met Gram's flat, wrapping around Sigifrith's sword. Dropping its hilt, the berserker leapt on Sigifrith, clinging to him with an unbreakable grip as his jagged teeth crunched against the young warrior's collarbone. Angry, Sigifrith lowered his head, crushing the berserker to him and fastening his own teeth on the man's bearded neck. He whipped his head back and forth, biting deeper till the berserker's throat came out in a great gush of blood. Sigifrith cast his body away, swinging his burdened sword in a half-circle to clear the way in front of him for a second till his thanes could come up around to guard him while he slid the bent blade off Gram with his boot. Then he pushed on again, hewing his way through Lingwe's host at the point of his wedge of men.

Now and again a flash of sun gleamed through the drifting clouds onto the battling hosts. Once it seemed to Sigifrith that Sunna was straight overhead; when the clouds cleared again, he saw her lowering into afternoon. He blinked her dazzle out of his eyes, turning—not widdershins; he remembered the old man's advice—fighting his way around deosil to put his back to the sun. His wedge had split into two long lines; the hound banner was ahead. Sigifrith, looking over the heads of the men around him, saw one of Hunding's sons—safe in the middle of his brothers and their sons—taking his helmet from his head. A mass of gray curls sprang from beneath the helm and Sigifrith recognized Lingwe's thin, high-arched nose and blue-green eyes at once, though his handsome face was wrinkled and worn and his thick moustache tarnished silver. Hunding's son raised the horn to his lips, blowing it to call his men to him.

"Lingwe!" Sigifrith shouted through the sound of the horn, cutting his way through the men who thronged to their drighten. "Lingwe! Come and face me! Have you learned courage since Sigimund's fall?"

"Come and fall as he did!" Lingwe called back, his nasal voice cracking with the force of his cry. He gestured to his men, a sword-edged pathway opening between the two of them. Sigifrith was down it before Lingwe could step forward, Gram turning in his hand so that the hilt struck the northern drighten on the head. Lingwe fell, a light burden to Sigifrith's arm as he whirled to strike down the other sons of Hunding. Last to fall was the banner bearer. Sigifrith stabbed Gram through the pole as it dropped from the dead man's hand, holding it high for a second so that all could see, then slung it violently away.

"Lingwe's dead!" someone shouted. Blades swirled around Sigifrith more fiercely than ever for a few minutes as the last of Lingwe's sworn thanes came to their deaths. Slowly the battle stilled, little whirlpools and eddies of fighting rising and ebbing away for a time longer. Sigifrith laid Lingwe's unconscious body down across a couple of corpses, then unslung his father's horn from across his chest and blew it thrice. The long notes faded away into the moans of the wounded, just now starting to feel pain through their shocked numbness. Those of Sigifrith's men who were left began to limp up to him, stopping now and again to make sure a fallen foe was really dead.

Hildkar's right arm hung limply by his side, but he lifted Sigifrith's standard high as he came to stand beside his drighten.

"I suppose . . . you were right," he gasped.

"I knew we were going to win," Sigifrith said. His voice was hoarse, rasping painfully through the back of his throat.

"You . . . won it. Really."

Sigifrith shook his head absently, trying to count the men who were able to walk. Thirty or forty of the eighty-five who had marched out that morning with him; more probably lay living on the field. The ravens were already circling in the sky, a couple of them beginning to drift down to the slain like huge black leaves against the afternoon sunlight.

He waited until everyone had gathered close to him, tallying up the missing. Perchtwine wasn't there, nor Harthpercht, nor Ansbrand. Theodipalt was and so was Kunitrut, though the hairy older thane was bent around a wound in his gut, supporting himself with the shaft of his spear. Sigifrith rubbed at his bitten collarbone; the ache was beginning to pulse pain through his left arm with each beat of his heart.

"You badly wounded, rest where you are," he commanded. "The rest of you go and see if any of our fallen can be saved and make sure none of their fallen can."

"What about those who can't be helped?" Anshelm croaked. "Do we . . . ?"

Sigifrith gave one short nod, pressing his lips together. He bent down again, heaving Lingwe onto his shoulder. "I have one more thing to do, and then I'll be back."

"Do it here." Sigifrith looked down, his jaw dropping in surprise. Ragin, dark streaks clotting in his gray hair and beard, was struggling along between the bodies of the fallen. The sword in his hand was stained with drying blood.

"Ragin! What are you doing here? You're not . . . " Sigifrith asked before he could stop himself. Suddenly he wanted to bite his tongue out. He turned his cringe of embarrassment to a sheepish grin. "What kind of smith's tool is that you're carrying?" he added teasingly. "Is it a hammer or a file?"

"It's the sword Ridill. Do you think I was always a smith?" Ragin challenged. He averted his eyes. "Do what you have to do here, on the earth your father used to hold." The dwarf bent and tugged bodies away to clear a place in the muddy weeds.

Sigifrith flung Lingwe down again. The Jutish drighten was beginning to move, struggling weakly in his grasp. In a few moments, Lingwe's eyes fluttered open, the blue-rimmed pools of darkness drawing in as he tried to focus on Sigifrith.

"You," he gasped. "Sigimund's son."

"You murdered my father."

"I slew him in battle. Not . . . fair, maybe, but in fight for all that." His lips curved weakly in a familiar, ironic smile. "The spae wife warned me. That . . . one day I would regret wooing Herwodis, even if I won my battle."

"You are my gift to Wodan now."

"Do what you have to do, Walsing," whispered Lingwe. He closed his eyes, as if he were too tired to hold them open any longer. Ragin crouched by the head of Hunding's last son, pinning down his wrists with hands as heavy as iron manacles; at Sigifrith's glance Theodipalt and Irmingeld took Lingwe's legs.

"To Wodan," Sigifrith said, standing over Lingwe's body, Gram's point just touching his foe's breastbone. "For vengeance . . . and victory."

He looked up for a moment. High above the ravens' dropping flight, he saw the great spread wings of an eagle riding the wind; the atheling-bird's scream sounded faint in his ears.

"Turn him over," Sigifrith said.

His first cut parted Lingwe's tunic and skin alike, blood welling up to darken the red linen down the length of the northern drighten's back. A matching stroke sliced lightly down the other side; the third opened a rent along the tops of Lingwe's shoulderblades. Sigifrith took hold of the top of the sark digging his fingers down into flesh and skin, and with a slow, firm movement, tore the flap away to reveal ribs and backbone white for a second before the blood washed over them. Lingwe raised his head, his fingers clawing up handfuls of mucky weed, but he did not scream. Suddenly dizzy, Sigifrith had to stop for a moment. He could see . . . Lingwe, younger, sitting with his blond head bent toward Herwodis as the two of them spoke together, heat lightning flaring through his own body as he watched . . . Awilimo nodding quietly, the Frank's face with the awareness of his wyrd but content with the knowledge that his daughter would escape the coming slaughter . . . He saw Herwodis bending over him as with his last strength he lifted his hand to lay it upon her quickened womb . . .

Sigifrith straightened, setting Gram's point against the edge of the top rib to the left. Carefully he began to cut through the milky band of tough cartilage, sawing lightly back and forth to free the bone from the spine. Lingwe was not struggling wilfully, but the pain racking him heaved his body back and forth. Gram broke through the first rib, then the second, and another wave of dizziness swept over Sigifrith as he looked down . . . at the body of his son Sinfjotli, a few drops of ale drizzling from the corner of his mouth into his fair beard . . . at Borghild, her hazel eyes gleaming with tears of hatred and grief . . . and unloosing the ash-blond hair of the slender maiden in the bridal hut, the maiden walled off from him, even when their bodies warmed each other, by the same hedge that held back his tears over Sigilind—which he had never shed in Borghild's unbound hair . . .

"Are you all right, Sigifrith?" Ragin asked softly. "Can you go on with this?"

Sigifrith wiped his bloody face with his blood-caked sleeve, smearing the tears across it. He nodded, moving Gram's point to the next rib. Lingwe cast his head back again as Sigifrith cut. His teeth were locked in his tongue, blood dribbling down his clean-shaven chin. Through that bone, and the next and the next . . . and smoke was blowing in his eyes, the smoke of

Sigigairar's hall. Sigilind, burning . . . his sword in his hand again, the ice stone cool and smooth against his palm . . . then he was in the forest; the taste of men's hot blood in his wolf mouth as he howled at the silvery sky through the gray leaves of autumn . . .

Hildkar was holding him up with his good hand, wincing in pain as his drighten's swaying jarred his broken arm.

"Thanks," Sigifrith whispered. He breathed deeply, slowly . . . as the Herulian had taught him, how to gather his strength from the earth beneath him and the paths of the winds above . . . and set himself to sawing through Lingwe's ribs again. His father's slayer was not screaming or begging yet; but for all his bravery, he was making a low noise through his clenched teeth. Sigifrith started on the other side . . . and saw Sigilind's face ghost-pale through Freyjadis', crying in joy beneath him; saw his sister glimmering in the dawn by the Herulian's white howe, which faded into the heaped stones of the harrow as Sigilind and Sigigairar clasped hands on the gold oath ring, the mare's blood pooling in the crannies of the rocks . . . Gram moved through the blood washing over Lingwe's back, cutting the ribs down the other side. He was here again, he knew, but where was Sigilind? He had seen her shape flashing white above him through storm and battle, shielding him till the last; now she was gone, and no matter how he tried he could not touch her as they had always touched, all of their lives and after her death.

Sigifrith knelt, the tears flooding down his face. He took hold of Lingwe's ribs on either side, hooking his fingers beneath bone and muscle and sinew. Swiftly he opened his arms, splitting Lingwe's ribcage open. The two sides of Lingwe's chest cracked away like two halves of a nutshell, white ribs arching between streaks of red like eagle's wings shaped of blood and bone. Lingwe made a horrible noise, the pink-gray masses of his lungs flattening, pulsing up, and flattening again. His dark heart clenched like a fist, then loosened.

"So I have my vengeance," Sigifrith said, standing up. Ragin, Theodipalt and Irmingeld let go of Lingwe's corpse and stood as well, rubbing sore arms and cramped legs.

Sigifrith was about to sheath Gram when Ragin's hand closed on his wrist. "Clean it first," the dwarf insisted.

Sigifrith nodded numbly. His steps wavering a little, he found a body whose clothes weren't too filthy and crouched down to wipe his sword. Afterward, he still felt dizzy and faint, too dazed to do more than wander about the battlefield for a while.

Eventually he noticed that the western sky was beginning to flush, and that no one except himself, the ravens and the first foxes and wolves sniffing at the edges of the field was moving among the slain. His hair was a clotted tangle over his face and shoulders, his tunic stiff with dried blood, and where his arms and face weren't sticky with blood it was flaking off. The smell of the battlefield was beginning to ripen, and it seemed to Sigifrith as though the same might be said for himself. He cracked his stiffened tunic and pulled it off, dropping it onto the field; it would never be clean again. He had seen a stream by the path that morning, and he wanted to wash.

Sigifrith sat in the high seat of the hall that night, dressed in a clean white tunic with his hair falling over his shoulders and down his back in long glistening coils. Although the earthen floor had been paved with flat rocks mortared edge on edge, he could see the slight mound in the middle of the hall where the Barnstock had once grown if he looked carefully. But the tapestries on the walls were new and strange, and the thanes who sat on the long benches before the fires that burned down the length of the hall were his Alamanns now. As befitted a good drighten, he had dealt out the gold and silver they had won in their fighting. The wounded wore their treasures where they could, the winding of red gold shining over the red-stained windings of their bandages; the whole arched their arms as they ate and drank, admiring the glitter of precious metals in the firelight. Kunitrut and Wigpercht had died that evening. Ragin said that the rest of the wounded looked likely to mend.

The door of the hall was open; the roasting meat of the pigs and cattle over the cooking fires within hid the scent rising from the flames that burned without, the fire where the dead of Sigifrith's host lay with their weapons and treasures around them. As always, Sigifrith had commanded that the enemy dead be left to feed Wodan's creatures, the wolves and the ravens, but he had lit the burning to bear his own to Walhall.

Sigifrith watched the downcast women, the wives and thrall-women of Lingwe and his sons, bringing meat and ale to his men. One girl with her hair in blond coils and a bruise already darkening the fair skin above her cheekbone looked familiar, as though he might have known her mother or grandmother; the thrall woman tending the meat had the square face and heavy build that he remembered from a Saxon thane. After a few minutes Sigifrith got up and walked over to her.

"Was your father named Odger?" he asked.

She nodded sharply, looking down at the pig she was turning. Her freckled face was flushed from the heat, her short-cropped hair spiky with sweat. She mumbled something, too softly for Sigifrith to hear.

"Could you say that again?"

"My mother said he fell with Sigimund," she murmured.

"He deserved a better fate for his children," Sigifrith said. He waved one of the other women over, taking Odger's daughter by the arm and leading her to the empty seat beside his own. Agilo whistled through the new gap in his teeth; a couple of the other thanes cheered, though Sigifrith heard Harthpercht muttering from the wall where he sat nursing his wounded leg, "You'd think he could choose . . . "

Later that night, Odger's daughter followed him obediently to the drighten's chamber.

"Stand still and close your eyes," Sigifrith said. She obeyed, trembling, an awkward figure in her stained and shapeless woolen dress. Before she could open her eyes, Gram had cut through her iron thrall's collar. Sigifrith prised it from her with the strength of his hands and cast it into the fire.

"Oh!" she gasped, staring up at him. Even in the shadowed room, Sigifrith could see the terror quivering at the corners of her mouth, glazing her blue eyes.

He sighed, turning away. Lingwe had had a proper bed, but it was far too short for him. He stripped the furs and blankets off the down-stuffed linen mattress, tossing it onto the floor and beginning to arrange a pallet for himself.

"Do you want me to . . . ?" the woman began hesitantly.

Sigifrith shook his head. "I just want to go to sleep," he said.

She walked to the door, stopped, turned again. "Are you going to be ruling here now? Will you go away again?"

"I'm leaving as soon as the weather lets me. Whoever wants to come, I'll take." Sigifrith took off his tunic and hung it over the chair in front of the fire. "Go on, now."

"Sleep well, my drighten . . . and thank you," Odger's daughter said. She slipped out, closing the door behind her as Sigifrith worked himself comfortably in among the bedclothes.

Sigifrith lay staring at the glowing shapes shifting through the coals beneath the sinking flames, the embers brightening into torcs and arm rings of fiery red gold and dimming again as the air shifted with his breath. As he drifted to sleep, the coals still glowing behind the darkness of his eyelids, it seemed to him that he could almost feel the pure precious weight in his hands, the high ringing of gold on gold in his ears . . . almost . . .

The storms came before the Moon had waned down to half again, the sea rising and frothing like a great cauldron of working ale-wort as flurries of snow lashed over the waves. The hall which was now Sigifrith's was almost an island; there was no way to think about faring south again, so they rested peacefully there while the wounded healed; and, as Ragin had warned Sigifrith, they held Yule there and waited for winter to break and ease Agwijar's fury.

Though everyone else was willing to sit and drink and dice for the treasures they'd won, Ragin did not rest idle for long. The Saxon smith had been slain in the battle; Ragin moved into his forge the day after the fight and heated it up, though he scorned the dead man's tools as shoddily made next to his own. Sigifrith saw little of him before Yule: he felt the need to know his new folk as his father had known them, to see who wished to come with him and whom he might trust with the leadership of those who wished to stay behind in their old lands. There would be few enough who stayed: the sea-eaten mounds were no place for farming now, and most of those who had won their wealth by piracy along the shores of Britain and Gaul were dead.

For the first time, it was Sigifrith who gave the holy Yule boar to the gods and goddesses, standing on the low mound in the middle of his hall where the Barnstock had once bloomed and holding the twist in the pig's nose firmly while each of his thanes and the Saxon folk came forward to speak their Yule vows in turn. Only Ragin held back, sitting in a shadowed corner by the bag he had hauled in from the forge; and Sigifrith remembered that he had never seen the dwarf take part in the Yule oath-swearing, nor in any of the symbols that the other folk shared during the holy nights.

"Hai, Ragin!" Sigifrith called. "Now that you're no more an outlander in my hall than I am, you need not hide in the corner there. Come, foster-father, swear your Yule oath with the rest of us. There are no strangers here!"

Ragin did not speak nor rise; his dark eyes glared warily up at Sigifrith as though he thought his foster-son might be making a mock of him.

"Come, foster-father," Sigifrith repeated more softly. "Of all the folk here, I hold you most welcome in my garth. Do not shame me by turning away from me."

Still Ragin did not speak. Only when the silence began to hum dizzily in his ears did Sigifrith realize that he was holding his breath, waiting for the dwarf's answer. It seemed as though the other folk in the hall were no more than ghosts, waiting like the shadows of all the folk who had once dwelt beneath the Walsings' roof and came unseen to keep the Yule feast with their living kin.

Sigifrith stretched his free arm toward the old smith, his hand open. "Come, Ragin, my kinsman."

At last Ragin stood, stumping slowly over to Sigifrith. His calloused palm was as rough and cold as rock, and though he could not grip Sigifrith's hand hard enough to harm him, Sigifrith felt the strength that would have broken another man's bones in Ragin's grasp. The dwarf set his other hand on the boar's back.

"By the bristles of the boar, I swear . . . I swear that I shall be true to you, Sigifrith, and work for your weal—however others may see it—so that the shape of your wyrd may be turned to one fairer than seems to be set now." Ragin let go of Sigifrith's hand, turned and clomped back to his seat.

Sigifrith laid his own palm on the boar's bristles, feeling the beast's restless shifting beneath his touch as he rolled eyes up at the man who held him. Does he know . . . ? the young drighten wondered, but he had no more time for thought: everyone was staring at him, and he had not made his own oath yet.

"By the bristles of the boar," Sigifrith called out, his voice as clear and bright as the first gleam of blue sky through breaking storm clouds, "I swear that I shall stand against Fadhmir the Wyrm in single fight, and that one of us shall not live past our battle's end. So let Fro Ing hear my holy oath on his boar; so let Wodan witness it!"

Sigifrith heard the soft gasps around him, like the wind sighing through the dry leaves of summer's end. He did not hesitate so much as a heartbeat, but drew his sword and brought it swiftly across the pig's throat. The boar's blood fountained out to splash over the bowl that Odger's daughter stretched for it. Sigifrith held the beast upright, the drighten's strength stilling his struggles until his eyes glazed over and his trotters no longer scrabbled at the earthen floor. Only then did Sigifrith lower the boar's body and dip Gram's tip into the blood. The folk crowded closer to their fro as he raised his sword and whirled it three times over his head so that the blessing droplets spattered everyone in the hall.

Once the gift to the gods had been given, and the boar's body cut up to be seethed and eaten, it was time for the human folk in the hall to give their gifts to each other. As the drighten, Sigifrith was most open-handed; but the pile of treasure by his high seat grew instead of lessening as the evening drew on. It was not only his thanes giving him choice items from their booty, but each of the Saxons seemed to have found or made something for him. They must truly love me, Sigifrith thought, a little bewildered as he gravely thanked a small Saxon girl named Ealwynn for the belt pouch she had embroidered with an eagle's head for him. True, the work was a little clumsy, but Ealwynn was no more than eight winters old, and the look of joy on her face as Sigifrith praised its beauty and promised to wear it faithfully thereafter made him feel warm and mellow as though he had just drained a hornful of hot buttered ale. I shall have children like this one day, he thought, stroking Ealwynn's flaxen braids and listening to her cheerful talk until her mother Wynswyth bid her to come back and leave the drighten be.

For Ragin, Sigifrith had kept something special: hidden in the back of one of the storehouses he had found a small cask marked with the runes _berkano_ ᛒ and _hagalaz_ ᚺ, as Borghild had always marked her finest brewing. Sigifrith had only taken the smallest sip to find out what it was and discovered that the cask was full of a mead brewed with honey and fruits, mellowed by at least eighteen years of aging and good beyond anything Sigifrith had ever tasted. He was about to get up and carry it over to Ragin when he saw that the dwarf was already coming over to him with the great sack he had brought from the forge.

Before Sigifrith could say anything, Ragin opened his bag and pulled out a jumble of riding tack, the strap-mounts glittering and flashing gold from the leather as he gave it over into Sigifrith's hands and reached in again to lift out a finely tooled saddle that he laid across Sigifrith's lap. Sigifrith could tell without a second glance that it was too big for any horse but Grani and for any man but himself; he had no doubt that Ragin had measured his steed before they left. He lifted up the bridle, admiring the gold mounts that shone from each crossing of the straps and the square chip-carved plates that Ragin had fastened along them as ornaments. Some showed eagles with curling beaks and garnet eyes; some showed straight-beaked ravens gripping emeralds; others had wolf heads with tiny slivers of ivory inlaid for their fangs or boar-heads with inlaid tusks. Many of the strap-mounts were shaped like the heads of beasts of prey, with other beasts intertwined over their surfaces and tiny face-masks glaring out from between the writhing limbs.

Awed by the gift's beauty, Sigifrith unwillingly turned his gaze back to Ragin, who stood gnawing at his gray beard. "This is as fair a piece of work as you have ever made, I think. I thank you, foster-father."

"You deserve to have joy while you live," Ragin mumbled. "And a drighten needs a saddle fit to adorn a fine horse."

Sigifrith leaned forward across the saddle to hug Ragin swiftly about the shoulders. "What would I do without your redes?"

"Very little, and none of it right. Hmph, I don't suppose you've bothered with a gift for me."

Sigifrith grinned down at him. "You're wrong, old dwarf. You see that keg there?"

Ragin hefted the keg in the crook of one arm, easing the stopper out of the bunghole. His shaggy eyebrows rose as he sniffed at the brew. "I might have misjudged you," he admitted. "Yes, I think you haven't done so ill here. And a merry Yule to you."

It was almost a month after Yule, with the feast of Donar just past, when the storms blew out for a time, leaving the seawater calm. Then Sigifrith and his thanes loaded their ships and Lingwe's with their treasures, with the thralls they had won and with those children of Sigimund's men who wished to come with them—who would have come south eighteen years ago, if Sigimund and Aiwilimo had finished their voyage. Of the remaining Saxons, there was only one—a youth just coming into manhood, whom fever had kept out of the battle—whom Sigifrith had watched through the winter and thought might take a drighten's place. So at the feast the night before they left, he hung a heavy golden chain around the neck of Hengest the son of Wihtgils, charging him to keep and lead the folk well and asking for the gods' and goddesses' blessings upon him. The youth looked up with eyes nearly as bright as Sigifrith's own, his sandy-brown hair flopping away from his face, and squeezed back with all his strength as Sigifrith clasped his wiry arm—a salute of friends and equals.

"I'll do a good job . . . you'll see," he said, his voice cracking with passionate intensity.

Sigifrith smiled down at him; there was not more than three years' difference between them, but he was a blooded warrior and a proven drighten now. Still there was something about this youth that burned in his sight. Something about Hengest's angular, horsy face and the jut of his long jaw spoke of his strength and ambition, but more than that it seemed Sigifrith could almost see a hero's red strand twining out from him, stretching as far into the distance as the eyes of Sigifrith's soul could follow.

"I know you will," Sigifrith said. "I expect your name will not soon be forgotten after your death."

Hengest drew in a breath, suddenly sobered, as though he himself sensed a hint of the uncanny in Sigifrith's words. Sigifrith led him to the high seat, taking his own place with his thanes at the head of one of the benches.

The faring back went smoothly, though more slowly, since they were rowing against the current for most of the way rather than sailing with it. So it happened that Sunna was already setting by the time they got within sight of the Dragon's Crag.

"Pull over to the west!" Sigifrith shouted. "We'll set up the night's camp on the shore there."

Anshelm tapped Sigifrith on the shoulder. The shadow of the mountain to their west lay over the thane's face, dusking his blue eyes and darkening the gray strands in his deep brown hair. "Is this wise? I think there will be few who will sleep this night if we camp there; it is too close to the Dragon's Crag for us to feel easy."

Although Sigifrith knew the older warrior to be a brave man, he could give no name other than fear to the shiver he saw rippling over Anshelm's skin. The young drighten laughed, raising his voice so that everyone could hear. "What have we to be afraid of? I've never heard that the Wyrm sought to swim the river." He turned to Ragin, who sat carving on one of the ship's benches. "Will we see Fadhmir come down to drink tonight? I think that would be a sight worth stopping for."

"Hush and listen," the dwarf grunted. "If he means to drink this evening, you will hear him soon—but no one here will thank you for that wish."

It seemed to Sigifrith that he could see the gold-fire burning brighter in Fadhmir's cave as the day swiftly darkened into night, but he heard no sounds except the tight breathing of his men as they tied up the ships and set up the tents for the night. It was a moment before he realized what was wrong: no one was speaking, not even to curse as they pounded the tent pegs into the frozen ground. The Saxon children and their mothers stood huddled together, wide eyes glancing everywhere but toward the Dragon's Crag.

"You have nothing to fear," Sigifrith said to them again. "The Wyrm is not even leaving his cave tonight. You are quite safe—and I have sworn that he shall not have much longer to brood on his gold. There is nothing to be afraid of."

The sound of his voice breaking the frightened silence seemed to ease some of their fear, but Sigifrith could still feel the tension stretching through the camp like a taut rope as the darkness rising from the East pressed Sunna's last red light farther down the sky and the stars glimmered more brightly around the Moon's thin sickle blade. Perchtwine had often kept several of the others up half the night casting dice to see who would have to stand the late watch, and there was an old Saxon named Beornstan in the company who had kept the custom alive in the last few nights. No one was throwing dice that evening, though, and the fires were few and small, yellow flames flickering uneasily against the darkness.

It was not long before the company had settled in their tents; but it was a very long time before Sigifrith heard the soft breathing around him deepening into the first snores. Though he lay in his blankets, he was not tired himself; he could feel the might that beat out from the Dragon's Crag prickling through the earth beneath him and up through his veins. Finally, he rose and crept outside, looking up toward the faint glow halfway up the mountain across the river.

Sigifrith did not think about what he was doing until he stood in his ship with the rope in his hand, ready to cast off. He stopped, standing stock-still and trying to think what had come upon him: it seemed to him that he was not moving at his own will.

A dry cough sounded behind him. Sigifrith whirled. Ragin sat on the ship's bench, tracing the lines of his carving in the starlight.

"So you're here at last," the old dwarf muttered. "Go ahead; cast off now. We're going to cross the river so you can have a better look at what lies before you."

Sigifrith's flagship had not been made for one man to row it straight across the current and doing it stretched his strength more than he was used to, but Sigifrith was not tired by the time he had made the boat fast to an alder on the other side of the Rhine. He and Ragin got off and made their way slowly up the dragon's track. Even in the faint starlight, Sigifrith could see how pale the dwarf's face was—corpse-pale, white as moonlit quartz beneath his beard—and feel his trembling as they climbed higher.

"I go no further," Ragin panted when they were halfway up to Fadhmir's cave. "Beware of coming too close: this is not yet the time for you to strike at him, for you will have no chance of slaying him in his own den."

"I understand."

Sigifrith kept climbing, creeping between the heat-shattered rocks. The closer to the cave he came, the stronger the prickling through his veins grew till he seemed to be standing in the heart of a bee swarm. There was something in the feeling that drew him nearer and nearer, until he was close enough to see the ghost-fire glimmering over the gold within the iron-bound cave.

Sigifrith drew in a long, deep breath of awe and desire, moving closer without thought. He had not dreamed of how the coins would feel rippling through his fingers, nor given heed to the sinuous writhing of thick wire about wire in the carefully wound arm-rings and torcs; the weight of gold chains had never seemed a fair binding to him before, but now he could feel their links about him as if he bathed in the hoard's pure fiery gold.

Caught up in the brightness dazzling before him, Sigifrith thought at first that the gold itself was moving, raising a huge head to glare about through glowing rubies. Then the black forked tongue flickered out, its tips sharp and cruel as iron spear points, and Sigifrith knew that the Wyrm was testing the air for thoughts of theft. He looked up at the dragon, unwilling to back down; but the sign that flared between Fadhmir's eyes was too bright for Sigifrith and he had to turn away, blinking back the brilliance in flashes of lightless color against his eyelids.

Now Sigifrith knew the truth of what Ragin had told him—he could not meet Fadhmir in his den—and more: he could not go against the dragon till he had finished with his duty to his father's folk. Though he was loath to leave the sight of the hoard, Sigifrith let the waves of Fadhmir's awe-might push him away and crept clumsily back down the mountain. His gold-dazzled eyes almost missed Ragin in the darkness; if he had not known where the dwarf waited, he never would have seen him.

"Now do you see?" Ragin hissed.

"I do."

Half of that hoard is to be mine, Sigifrith thought; and the thought filled him with a strange trembling excitement that he had never felt before. But though his knees were not steady beneath him, his strength brought him back to the river's edge unhurt, ready to cast off for the other side.

When they came nearer to the territory of the Alamanns, Sigifrith took down the dragon's head to keep it from frightening the land-wights. He stood in its place at the bow of the flagship himself, keeping watch as they rowed toward the jagged mountains. After a time, they rounded the foot of a snow-covered hill and Sigifrith could see Alapercht's dock ahead. He loosed a blast on his horn, its deep call shivering through the frosty air.

The first ships were tying up as a horseman came down from the hall, spear in his hand and byrnie jingling icily. He stopped ahead of the dock, then whirled, his steed's hind legs kicking up a fine cloud of snow as he galloped back. By the time Sigifrith had leaped from the ship to the pier, Alapercht and Herwodis, muffled in their furry winter cloaks, were already halfway down the path to greet him. Forgetting his dignity, Sigifrith ran to meet them. In his excitement, he stopped only a heartbeat before his embrace crushed his mother's ribs.

Herwodis gasped for breath as Sigifrith put her down. When she could speak again, she said, "It seems that you have done well, Sigifrith."

Alapercht was beaming at him, but the Alamannic king's eyes slid about uneasily, looking around Sigifrith's body to the diminished warband and the Saxons who had come home with Sigimund's son.

"So," Alapercht said heartily, as if trying to drown out a soft muttering, "you avenged Sigimund?"

"I did."

"And you'll be staying at home for a while, I hope?"

"As long as I can," Sigifrith answered. Half a year; likely less, he thought, sobered.

Alapercht was still looking at the Saxons, who were lifting their bundles from the ship and beginning to file up behind Sigifrith. Finally he asked, "Who are these people? Are they captives?"

"No, they're free now. They were some of Sigimund's folk, or their children. I . . . Sigimund would have brought them south to better land, away from the winter floodings, if Lingwe hadn't. I wanted to finish what had been started, as much as I could, anyway," he said in a final breathless rush.

Alapercht considered, stroking his white-streaked moustache. "How many did you bring?"

"Perhaps two hundred."

"Two hundred," Alapercht said musingly. He glanced at Herwodis. "Can we feed two hundred people over the winter? What will we do with them?"

"We can buy food," Herwodis answered. "I'm sure that Sigifrith has not returned without winning more than a victory and a troop of hungry Saxons." She stared significantly at her son, who nodded, slightly raising his gold-laden arm. "So. And the gods know there is plenty of work that needs doing, especially since Sigifrith seems to have left quite a large piece of your war-band in the north."

Alapercht's sigh sounded as though a big rock had landed on his chest, crushing the breath out of his lungs. He looked at the men who were coming to meet him, his glance flicking over each of them swiftly, tallying who had come back and who had not.

Hildkar, his arm still in a sling, was directing several Saxons as they lifted three heavy chests out of the flagship. "You drop that in the river, and I'll flay you alive with a rusty dagger," he threatened lugubriously. "We didn't do all that fighting just to brighten the Rhine's fire again, you know."

Sigifrith smiled proudly, gesturing at the chests of booty. "That will feed our Saxons over the winter, and more," he boasted. "The North Sea may be eating their land, but they're richer as pirates than they ever were as farmers."

Alapercht gazed at the chests for a moment, then at the five long, sleek Saxon ships docking behind the vessels that had sailed out with Sigifrith. Finally he turned to Herwodis again, looking her in the eyes but raising his voice so that everyone could hear. "We should hold a feast tonight or to-morrow, to celebrate Sigifrith's victory, to welcome our new folk—and to honor the warriors who fell in the northlands."

7

FADHMIR AND RAGIN

Sigifrith left his hut before dawn, his shoes crunching through the light layer of new-fallen snow. The Moon was waxing toward his Ostara's fullness—it was less than a week till the first day of summer. The young warrior went first to Ragin's hill, but no smoke rose from it and the door was firmly locked.

Sigifrith banged on the door until he could hear the echoes rolling around inside the rock. "Where are you, Ragin? You're not sleeping late this morning, are you?"

No answer came. At last Sigifrith thought to look down at the snow beneath his feet. Although his own shoe prints had broken many of the tracks before the door, he could see where Ragin's smaller feet had trodden through the fresh snow. The dwarf's tracks led around from the door of the hill and into the woods behind; there were no tracks leading back.

Sigifrith followed the path Ragin had left, walking as quietly as a wolf through the woods as though he were seeking to ambush a foe. Now and again, he came upon a place where the snow had been scratched away, the earth thrown up in dark streaks through its whiteness: Ragin had been digging for something shallowly buried, though Sigifrith could not guess what.

A soft cold wind brushed over the top of Sigifrith's head; startled, he glanced up to see the silent shadow of an owl sweeping through the branches above him. The Moon lit the trees cold and white as winter, hiding their new buds. It seemed to Sigifrith as though he could not move for a moment, fettered by the brightness of the Moon's light through the stark branches. Then he thought of how he had spoken his Yule vow, and of Ragin waiting ahead somewhere with whatever he had dug from the ground, and his limbs loosened.

Sigifrith saw the dwarf's fire well before he came to the clearing. Ragin's shadow squatted beside the flames like an old tree stump. He was muttering something, but Sigifrith could not tell what. The young warrior crept closer, careful to make no sound.

"Dwalan give me rede," Ragin was saying. Now Sigifrith could see that he had a pot of something cooking on the fire. Though a spoon jutted from the pot, the dwarf was not stirring his meal; instead, he crouched with both hands palm down on the big flat stone where he had laid the fire. A thick cloak of wolf's fur warded him against the cold, its heavy hood muffling his voice.

Ragin was still for a while, as though he were listening to something Sigifrith could not hear. Then he answered, "Dwale and poppy gum, and Tiw's Helm for the old wolf's son. I had the blossoms dried, and I've dug the roots." The names of the herbs meant nothing to Sigifrith, except that he knew poppy gum came from the south and was more costly here than amber.

Ragin waited, leaning closer to the rock. "Salve for the burns; you warned me of Fadhmir's blood. It is hardly likely that he may come through without scathe." Ragin lifted one hand from the stone, taking the dark-stained wooden spoon from the brew and sniffing at it, then stirring the pot a few times, muttering something under his breath.

Sigifrith backed away. He had little thought that he would need the medicine Ragin was cooking up for him, but it touched him that the old smith had thought to rise so early and had called on the craft of the dwarves in his brewing for Sigifrith's weal.

Once out of earshot, Sigifrith ran light-footed to the stables, his frozen breath showing in white clouds against the moonlit darkness. He let himself into the warm horse-hall, finding his way to Grani by touch and memory. His colt whinnied, leaning over the wooden gate to lip at his master's hair for a moment before Sigifrith saddled and bridled him, and then loaded him with their bags of spare clothes, food and drink for the journey.

It was not too long before Ragin came out of the woods. The dwarf stopped with hands on hips, looking mistrustfully up at Grani as Sigifrith led the wind-gray horse toward him.

"You don't really think I'm going to ride that beast, do you?" Ragin asked at last.

"I don't notice you offering to carry Fadhmir's hoard yourself," Sigifrith answered. "And he'll fret if I lead him by the reins all the way. Speaking of that: how do you mean for us to bear the gold from the cave? You can't be hiding enough bags under your cloak to hold it."

Ragin scuffed the snow with the toe of his boot, scowling. "There is no need for that. The dwarves have told me . . . to those who truly know the hoard, there is a way. Thus the Fox brought it to us; thus we shall bring it here. Trust me, Sigifrith: this is not something you need worry about."

Grani shifted his hooves uneasily, as if eager to be off. Sigifrith patted him on the neck, and he quieted. "Come on, old dwarf, we'll get there all the faster if we ride. You've ridden a horse before, haven't you?"

"I might have," Ragin mumbled. "But that's not a horse, it's an elephant from a Roman circus."

"I'll hang on to you. You don't need to worry about falling off."

"If you don't break my bones in the process," the smith complained. "Ach, go on, then . . . at least you're eager to meet Fadhmir."

Even through the wolf's-hide cloak, Sigifrith could feel Ragin shaking as he lifted him to Grani's back before vaulting on himself. He noticed that the leather tip of Ragin's sheathed sword was sticking out from the concealment of the dwarf's cloak.

"You're becoming fierce in your old age, Ragin," Sigifrith said as he nudged Grani into a trot. "Do you mean to stand beside me when I face Fadhmir?"

"No!" Ragin spat angrily. Sigifrith saw that the old smith's trembling hands were wound tightly in Grani's mane, the long skeins of silky gray pouring over and through his gnarled fingers. The horse tossed his head up and down, stamping his hooves as he trotted.

"Loosen your hands, you're hurting him," Sigifrith told Ragin. "You want a smooth ride, don't you?" He waited till Ragin had let go of Grani's mane, then put an arm around the dwarf's thick shoulders, holding him tightly as he brought the stallion into an easy canter. Ragin said nothing, but Sigifrith could hear the sound of his teeth grinding even through the pounding of Grani's hooves and the wind rushing around them.

They rode down to the Rhine, along the river beneath the snowy darkness of the mountains. The Moon was just beginning to pale as the sky brightened around him. Heedless of his double load, Grani leapt forward along the path as if he were as eager as Ragin to bring Sigifrith to Fadhmir.

"How long will it take us to get there?" Ragin asked Sigifrith after a while, as the sunrise's rose-gold glow began to fade from the bright peaks above them and the Sun rode higher in the clear heavens.

"It was two days to Gripir's howe; I'd guess another to your forge and half a day after that to the Dragon's Crag—maybe less if we can find a ferry down the river."

"Good enough. I suppose."

"Are you getting impatient?" Sigifrith teased him. "After all you've told me about waiting for the right time?"

"You've waited long enough for this," Ragin answered absently. "Maybe too long. Now that you have all the strength of your father's soul in you . . ." He stopped with a sudden grunt, as if Grani's trot had brought his teeth together on his tongue.

"What?"

"I'm getting old, Sigifrith. Pay no attention to it," the dwarf snapped. "And while we're talking about it, how do you think you're going to get through the Burgundian lands without Gundahari dragging you to his sister's marriage bed? Well? If you stay on this path, we'll ride straight through Worms."

"Swiftly, I should think," Sigifrith answered, smiling. "At Grani's best speed, we might be able to pass through Gundahari's territories in less than a day. I'd wager that none of his messengers can get back to him faster than I can get away into the Frankish lands."

"Messengers?" Ragin snorted. "Say spies. And what about Grimhild's spies? Some of them move far faster than any Gebica's son can hire."

"What are you talking about?"

"I'd be surprised if she didn't already know where we're going. What will you wager that Hagan meets us at the march between your lands?"

"But no one knows where we're going," Sigifrith said in surprise. "I haven't said a word to anyone."

Ragin turned halfway around, looking into his foster-son's face for a moment. His dark eyes burned with a shocking feverish madness. Sigifrith almost flinched before he straightened himself to meet Ragin's glance. "You fool! She told me . . . she warned me . . ."

"Warned you about what?" Sigifrith asked. The smith dropped his gaze. Sigifrith could feel the fury easing from the thick muscles beneath the wolf's hide. It seemed to him that a grayness of age or tiredness had fallen over Ragin's face like a thin mist over rocky crags. The dwarf turned and faced ahead once more.

"Ach, it's nothing. I was thinking of something else for a moment. Well if Grimhild doesn't send someone out to meet us, we'll pass in peace—at least going. Coming back may not be as easy."

"You're a worrier, Ragin," Sigifrith grinned, the twisting within him easing at his foster-father's well-known fears. "The Burgundians are our friends now, remember."

"Oaths can be broken, you know," Ragin muttered darkly. "And you and Gundahari have no more from each other than promises of oaths to be made."

"Well, we'll find out soon. It's not so far from here to the marches."

Sigifrith and Ragin rode past the Burgundian bounds without incident, but when a swallow swooped past them, twittering softly, Ragin jerked up his head and stared angrily after it.

"It's only a bird, Ragin," Sigifrith said as the swallow circled them. "Do you think it's laughing at you? Or that it's going to peck us to death? Hai!" he shouted at the bird. "Go away, you're frightening the dwarf!"

"Think what you want to think," Ragin muttered.

"Will it take news of us back to Grimhild?" Sigifrith asked teasingly. He tried to picture the Burgundian queen pulling a cloak of feathers over her head, her long-nailed fingers changing into talons and her sharp nose lengthening into a swallow's beak. The vision was an easy one, the more so as he watched the bird's swift flight, its slim body darting from side to side. "Grimhild!" he called. "Is it you?"

"Stop that, Sigifrith," Ragin rumbled, his voice deep in his chest. "Don't speak her name again."

"You think it is her, don't you?"

Sigifrith stared enviously up at the swallow, remembering how it was to run through the wood in a wolfskin. What would it be like to fly? he wondered. If she could teach me . . .

"Grimhild!" he shouted again, but before he could say anything else the swallow had darted away down the river and out of sight.

"If you were ever to come back here again . . . if you ever should have fallen into her snares it would have gone badly with you," Ragin murmured. A tone of regret tinged the old dwarf's voice, like the bitter edge of wormwood beneath wine's sweetness.

"But now I can take care of myself, hmm?" Sigifrith said, laughing.

Ragin coughed twice, then blew his nose noisily on his cloak. "Well enough."

They stayed away from the inns this time, stopping by the road whenever Ragin could bear no more riding and munching on the white cheese and tough black bread they had brought with them. Often the smith would trail off between one word and the next, staring into the river and mumbling beneath his breath. It was almost evening when they came within sight of Worms, the Roman buildings rising above the plain of budding trees.

"What are we going to do now?" Ragin asked Sigifrith, twisting his neck to look back and up at his foster-son.

Sigifrith glanced down the river, then up it again. In the gathering shadows behind them, he saw something moving—a tall figure gliding along the river like a water-ghost. It took him a moment of peering through the dimness to make out the length of a staff in the figure's hand.

"I think we may have a swift passage after all, if that raft is strong enough to take Grani as well as ourselves."

The raft floated nearer, the ferryman poling it purposefully toward the shore. As he got closer, Sigifrith saw that he was bent and aged, his body hunched around itself like an eagle wrapped in its own wings. A long fringe of gray hair fell over both eyes, straggling into his long beard.

"Are you two going down the river?" he asked. "Have you the money for a ferryman's fee?"

Ragin started, twitching away and almost falling from Grani's back. Sigifrith steadied his foster-father with one hand as he leapt from the horse, then carefully lifted the old dwarf down.

"I think no one says that Sigifrith is stingy with his wealth," Sigifrith said. "Is your raft strong enough to bear us and my horse as well, ferryman?"

"Aye, strong enough," the ancient man croaked. "I mind me of a time— though it was some age past—when it carried a heavier load."

"And so may we be in a few days," Sigifrith answered, grinning. "Wait, and you'll see what happens."

Ragin kicked him sharply in the ankle. The impact was surprising, but not painful. Sigifrith laughed, picked Ragin up by the shoulders and set him down on the raft, then led Grani on. The raft swayed beneath the stallion's weight, ripples lapping over the log planking. Sigifrith eased his steed to the middle of the raft, standing beside him to keep the weight balanced, and slowly the craft steadied. The ferryman pushed off into the grip of the current; the raft swung about a little, then straightened and floated swiftly downstream.

"He knows," Ragin muttered. "He knows . . . " The dwarf clenched his fists, loosened them and tightened them again as though he were squeezing metal into shape.

"What are you talking about?" Sigifrith asked. "I didn't know we had any reason to keep quiet. What shame could there be . . . ?" He trailed off; he had started to think about it too late.

Ragin did not speak again until they took their food and wine out for dinner. Then, grudgingly, the dwarf offered some to the ferryman, who refused the food but drank from the wine bottle with them. The gibbous Moon cast the jagged shadows of the rocks by the Rhine's bank black over the silver-rippling water; the wayfarers passed around the wine. Grani shifted, lowering his head and settling himself for the night. Sigifrith leaned against his steed's warm side, stroking Grani's silky coat and murmuring softly to him, "It's not far now, my beauty, my wind-horse. A night or two and then you'll have a test worthy of your strength."

For a moment Sigifrith saw the moonlight gleaming through the ferryman's long, dirty beard, reflected from his teeth.

"What are you muttering about?" Ragin said crossly to his foster-son. "Anyone would think . . . ach, never mind. I suppose you didn't think to pack any blankets, did you?"

"You can have my cloak," Sigifrith offered. "I'm not cold."

"You'll be stiff and sore by morning if I do," Ragin predicted gloomily. "No, you keep it. I'll be all right."

The dwarf wrapped himself in his wolfskin and lay down, careful to keep away from Grani. For a while, Sigifrith and the ferryman sat in silence. Occasionally the old man would nudge the raft to one side or the other with sweeps of his pole. After a few moments, Sigifrith went to the fore of the raft and sat beside him.

"How long have you been a ferryman on the Rhine?" Sigifrith asked.

The old man turned his head a little. Sigifrith could barely see the twin glints in his eyesockets beneath his straggly hair, but he felt that he was being watched all the same. "A long time," he said in a creaky, scratchy voice. "Long enough to have ferried many men along this river. It's not often that I've carried a warrior and a smith to the same place together, though. Tell me, how far do you mean to go?"

"To the Dragon's Crag," Sigifrith answered.

"Few go there of their own will, since the Romans left their stone quarry behind," said the ferryman. "What do you know of Fadhmir?"

"That he holds the hoard of the Rhine, lying about it in the shape of a wyrm with the Helm of Awe upon his head," Sigifrith answered. "But I have sworn to slay him."

"Beware of his blood," the ferryman croaked. "It is full of bale, heated to burning by the fire of the gold on which he lies. If that blood should flow over you, it shall scorch you to the bone; despite your strength, its fire shall be your bane and your death pyre at once. But if there is any fear in your heart, you had better flee now, for no man has yet lived who could withstand the glance of the one who wears the Helm of Awe between his brows."

Sigifrith laughed. "Old man, I have run with the Wild Hunt. I have sailed the North Sea in winter and ridden through the land of the dead to meet my kinsman Gripir in his earth hall. I think that if I have not felt fear by now, I am not likely to. This sword was shattered once, but the soul that bore it was not; while I remain, there is nothing for me to fear, and if I should be destroyed, there will be no more fear."

"You're full of your brave mood, aren't you?" The ferryman coughed, spitting a pale blob into the river. "You're wrong, too. You may have reforged your sword, but your soul still lies in two shards. Take it from an old ferryman, who has sailed on the Rhine longer than your life: till you have felt fear, you will be neither human nor whole."

"What are you talking about?"

"Have you ever loved anyone? Or do you only smile when you want something and when you get it? See the old dwarf there, who raised you with endless time and toil? What have you ever done for him? Can you wonder if he hates you in his heart?"

Even bundled in his furs, Ragin seemed a very small lump as Sigifrith looked back at him.

"You're at least half-mad, you know," the ferryman went on, his voice smoother and gentler now. "If you were sound in your mind, you'd never have done the things you've done. It's not your fault, of course. The Walsings were all more than a little mad, and the taint of Otter's weregild runs in your mother's blood. You feel it calling to you, don't you? Like a low fire thrumming through your veins? You've seen the flickering flames around the gold in your dreams, and dreamed of being able to run your fingers through the hoard—to lie down in it, bury yourself in it?"

It seemed to Sigifrith that he could see the fiery glimmering through the strands of hair tangled over the ferryman's face, as though his eyes sparked and glinted with flame. He stood up and held his gaze steady, moving closer to loom over his companion.

"Who are you, old man?" Sigifrith asked. "I don't think we've ever met before."

"I'm an old friend of your family," he answered. "If you go back far enough, we might be related indeed." A flash of heat lightning flickered through his amber eyes as he cocked his head, looking up at Sigifrith. "Think about it," the ferryman said. "You're not really planning to share the hoard with the dwarf, are you?"

He turned away from Sigifrith's gaze, pushing the raft around an outcrop of rocks. From the corner of his eye, Sigifrith thought he saw something dark slithering away from the oar, but it was gone in his next blink.

"You seem to know a lot, ferryman," Sigifrith said by way of changing the subject. "Tell me, while we're talking about strange things: what else have you seen on the Rhine? Do you know if it's true what they say about Hagan's father?"

R
H
I
N
E
G
O
L
D

4
1
3

"I've seen many things," the old man answered, his voice sinking into a low cackle. "Why do you ask? You have no reason to care for him."

"I've been curious for years. I saw him along here once, staring into the Rhine at night. He wouldn't tell me what he'd seen or what he'd been doing."

The ferryman laughed, a strangely high-pitched giggle. "I know," he said. "But why should I tell you? Go to sleep, Sigifrith. You'll need it . . . you've got a hard day's work ahead of you." He laughed, a strangely high-pitched giggle like the hissing of damp wood in the fire. The sound brought back a memory to Sigifrith . . . the choking smoke of the Sinwist's tent, the sound of blood scorching in the flames . . . and the ferryman's amber eyes staring at him out of the coals in Ragin's forge.

"I think that's the first rede you've given me that I can trust. But if you'll answer my question now, I'll leave you alone."

"Why do you want to know?"

"Because I swore blood-brotherhood with him when I came back from Gripir's howe, and I want to know if I've mixed poison into my veins," Sigifrith said sarcastically, exasperated. "I don't really know why, but I'm curious. Isn't that enough?"

The ferryman threw back his head and laughed again. "Blood-brotherhood's been sworn with less knowledge on either side than you have already," he answered. "But I'll tell you this: when your blood-brothers Hagan and Gundahari stand beside you, you'll be better warded than any man in the world. That, I can swear, is the truth."

"Thank you." Sigifrith went back to lie down beside Ragin. He was just drifting cozily off into sleep when, like a loose thread tugging at the edge of his mind, it occurred to him that the ferryman hadn't really answered his question.

The Sun was up when Sigifrith awoke, shining brightly into his eyes. "Close the door, Hildkar," he muttered, pulling his cloak up and turning over drowsily to get back to sleep.

Ragin's voice, rough as a file, rasped through his doze; he didn't hear the words clearly, but their sound reminded Sigifrith where he was. Suddenly wide awake, he leapt to his feet, staring downstream at the seven hills rising tall and brown on the eastern side of the Rhine.

Ragin nodded, his eyes also fixed downstream. "It's there," he said, a strange undertone trembling through his voice like a swift current running beneath the river's slow-rippling surface. "Do you see? That scorched trail through the trees . . . that's where Fadhmir comes to drink."

Sigifrith's hand went to the hilt of his sword. He could feel the joy beginning to run hot in his blood as it always did before a battle, laced this time with a sparkling, glimmering tingle that grew stronger as they drifted closer to the Dragon's Crag. Now Sigifrith could see the twisting black path through the crags and budding trees. It wove down from the dark cave near the hill's peak like the burnt bed of a river of fire, over cracked rocks and charred wood, and though he had seen it before, he still shuddered in disgust.

"Here we are," the ferryman said, steering the raft in to shore. "What do you have to pay me with, then?" He tossed his head back and cackled.

Sigifrith heard Ragin's low, gasping snarl. "You!" The dwarf stood in the middle of the raft with his sword half-drawn, quivering between attack and flight. Sigifrith stepped quickly between them, drawing a thin ring of wound gold from his arm to snap off a piece. It was harder to break than he had thought, as though a little strength had drained from his fingers in that moment; but at last the gold parted and he dropped the length of metal into the old man's wrinkled palm.

"Generous, for one of Hraithamar's kin," the ferryman said. "I've heard men say that his line was greedy for the least little finger-ring. Isn't it so, Ragin?"

Sigifrith reached out, putting his hand on the ferryman's bony shoulder. His skin was hot even through his tunic, as though Sigifrith had picked up a boiling iron kettle with his hand shielded by cloth. "Don't insult my line, old man," he warned, looking into the gleams within the tangle of dirty-white hair.

After a moment the ferryman turned away from Sigifrith's gaze. "Go on, then," he said gruffly. "I haven't got all day to sit here nattering with . . . people like you."

Sigifrith loaded their bags on Grani again and led his horse with one hand and Ragin with the other as he got off. The dwarf stared after the raft till it had turned a bend in the river and disappeared.

"Is there part of the story you haven't told me?" Sigifrith asked Ragin. "Who was that? Had you seen him before?"

"Of course not," the dwarf said hastily.

"Then why were you so angry? You're still shaking."

"He reminded me of things that might have been better forgotten," Ragin said, staring at the rocks beneath his feet. Then he glanced suspiciously up at Sigifrith. "What did he say to you?"

"Not much."

The two of them walked along the edge of the water till they came to the charred edge of Fadhmir's track. It was twice the height of two tall men in width, the crushed black ashes steaming from the morning dew.

Sigifrith thought about it for a moment, then spoke. "You said, Ragin, that the dragon was no greater than any other ling-worm, but his tracks look very large to me."

Ragin stood twisting his beard, looking at the black path down the side of the Dragon's Crag. In the stillness, Sigifrith could hear the clear high piping and twittering of small birds calling back and forth through the trees.

"Dig a pit and sit in it," the dwarf said. "And when the wyrm slithers to the water, stab him to his heart and so be his bane. You will get great fame from that."

"What will happen if I get in the way of the wyrm's blood?" said Sigifrith.

"None may give you rede, if you're afraid of everything—and you're unlike your most courageous kinsmen."

As he spoke, Ragin glanced at the cave's dark mouth again and again. Sigifrith could see the glassy pearls of sweat breaking out on his black-pored forehead, as if the smith were standing over the fires of his forge.

"When will he come to drink?" Sigifrith asked.

"Not during the daytime—day is for the living. Wait till Sunna is going down, for the light between day and night. That is the time when men most fear to come near the Dragon's Crag."

"Well enough," Sigifrith said, grinning. "Go on, Ragin. Since you're not going to stand beside me, you won't be much help behind me either. If the dragon is as great as his tracks, I imagine you'll be able to see what happens from a good way away."

Ragin came closer to Sigifrith, reaching out his hands even as his eyes flickered around his foster-son's body to the cave. "Fare well, Sigifrith," he whispered, clasping Sigifrith's right hand in both of his own. "May all your luck and might help you in meeting Fadhmir—and, for both our sakes, may this be the fight of a true hero's wyrd." He looked into Sigifrith's face, the deep lines of his dripping forehead wrinkling together as if he were in pain and rheum-tinged water blurring his eyes for a second. Then Ragin dropped his gaze and let go, hurrying off between the trees with a crackling of branches and leaves.

Sigifrith shrugged, then studied the path again. The face of the mountain was not so steep as some of those in the Alamannic lands, but Fadhmir's path was that of a creature moving slowly, a creature that had tested its footing with great care—as if the dragon knew that one day he would be challenged for his hoard. Sigifrith thought about it, staring at the mountain until he saw one place where the green mist of moss over the scaly layers of brownish gray rocks had been scorched away—where, when Fadhmir had slithered half-over, he would be vulnerable to a stab from beneath.

Sigifrith began to climb the path, the cinders hot under his boots. Some of the trees had fallen; others stood with charred curves in their trunks where the dragon's sides had brushed against them, the crumpled brown tendrils of scorched ivy dangling above the burnt places. Beyond Fadhmir's track, the trees were budding green with the first delicacy of spring. Here and there Sigifrith passed a white-blossoming cherry tree, the fallen petals laid softly over the dry leaves layering the forest floor. Laughing, Sigifrith dashed from the path to clasp one of the slender trunks, turning his face to the warm snow of fair petals that showered down upon him. The uneasiness of the night had melted away; he felt light and joyful.

He picked up a double handful of cherry blossoms and dry leaves, showering them down on Grani. The colt tossed his head, snorting. A few of the white petals clung to his coat like snowflakes against a winter cloud. "Go on, Grani," Sigifrith said. "Go on, there's nothing for you to do till I call you."

Reluctantly the horse left the track, glancing back at Sigifrith as he picked his way over fallen branches and through the wood. Sigifrith leapt on upward, hoisting himself easily over the rocky outcrop to the place where he meant to dig his pit. He broke a wrist-thick branch from an ash tree that stood near the side of Fadhmir's track and set to scraping through the thick layers of hot cinders. After a while he took his cloak off, then his tunic, tossing them onto the low-spreading branches of a nearby linden, one of the few trees in full green. Winter's last sunlight was pleasantly warm on his back as he worked, stopping every so often to crouch in his pit and see if it was deep enough yet.

"What are you doing here?" a man's resonant, hemp-rough voice asked from behind him. Sigifrith straightened and turned around. An old man in a deep blue cloak, his hood drawn over his face, was looking down at Sigifrith from the edge of the path. The long-bearded man leaned on the shaft of an ancient spear, its pale ashwood dark as old oak from long use.

"I'm digging a pit to sit in and wait for Fadhmir. I have an old feud with him to settle, and I was told that this was the way to slay him."

The old man replied then, "That is an ill rede. Make many pits and let the blood run into them, but you sit in one and strike to the wyrm's heart."

"How shall I know where his heart is?"

"First you must find the might to look straight at him, and not be whelmed by the Helm of Awe which he bears. That might is in your gaze, in the keen eyes of the hero. Do not let his gold dazzle you, for if you do, you shall never find the strength to strike at him. Trust in your sword: the tip of Gram's point is sharp enough to prick through any spell, even Andward's curse. Take care that you see the Wyrm before he sees you; and if you can strike him with the might of your eyes, your gaze shall guide your blade to his heart."

He turned and stalked off, his dark cloak billowing around him in the cool breeze blowing from the north. Sigifrith went back to digging through the ashes of Fadhmir's passing.

When he was done, he had four pits: the highest and shallowest for himself to lurk in, the other three, connected by a hole at their lowest point, for the dragon's blood to run into. Sweating with his work and the heat of late afternoon, he sat down in the shade of the linden tree, leaning against its trunk. Its lightly fissured bark felt comfortably rough against his bare back. A few honey bees, the sort which the Saxons called sig-wives, buzzed around the creamy buds and early-opened flowers that dangled beneath the undersides of the linden's spear-tipped leaves.

The land across the Rhine was mostly flat and forested, though farther to the south Sigifrith could see the buildings of what had been a Roman town and was now a Frankish settlement. A low, table-topped hill rose from the wooded plain, and it seemed to Sigifrith that he might be able to see a dark shape standing on it, keeping watch from across the river. The pale green budding of early summer faded into ruddy-brown as Sigifrith looked farther away, the more distant hills seeming as dry and dead as if summer were ending rather than springing forth. He turned over to lie down in the dry leaves and springing green grasses, stretching out and resting his chin on his hands. The wood-master was coming into bloom early down here, its tiny white flowers like delicate froth above its spreading stars of long dark leaves. If Alapercht had taken his household to the hall that had been Chilpirich's for Ostara's feast as he had said he would, Herwodis would be gathering the unbloomed herb to steep overnight in her fragrant Ostara wine. For a moment Sigifrith wondered if Gundrun also steeped wood-master in wine at summer's beginning; if she was waiting now, hoping that he, with his deed of vengeance done, would come to share it with her. Could she remember his face better than he remembered hers? He tried to imagine what she would look like now, but it seemed as though his memory was numb with sleep, bringing him only a darkened blur that might have been any woman.

Above him a pair of small woodbirds were twittering clearly to each other, calling back and forth from the wind-stirred leaves of the linden to the sharp-budding ash. Sigifrith turned on his side, supporting himself on his elbow in the dry winter leaves and leaning the soft-bearded edge of his jaw on his cupped palm as he looked up at the little brown birds hopping from branch to branch. "Hai, are you talking about me?" he murmured to them. "Can you understand me better than I can understand you? No? I'll try to speak in your own tongue, then."

Sigifrith pursed his mouth to whistle, blowing as gently as he could. The first sound he made was a breathy squeak, hardly a whistle at all. He laughed ruefully. "That's not very good, is it?" Wetting his lips, he tried again. This time a pure note wavered and trilled from his mouth. The birds ignored it, chirping and singing above Sigifrith's melody. "You don't really care, do you?" he asked softly, in a tone of mock insult. "All right, then. Stay in those trees for a while, if you dare, and you'll see something you may think more of."

The mists rose from the Rhine as Sunna sank lower, blurring the rocks below Sigifrith and veiling the wood on the other side of the Rhine. As the sky darkened and the river mists thickened, the wind blew harder and colder, raising the hairs along Sigifrith's spine in a prickle of anticipation. Suddenly a silence fell on the wood as the twitters stilled and the birds rose from the trees, flying swiftly away.

It seemed to Sigifrith that he felt the shivering of the stone through the soles of his feet before he heard the grating bass note of boulder against boulder, the deep stirring, slow as the roots of trees writhing through the mountain. He ran to his pit, drawing Gram and crouching down in the warm cinders. Through the earth he could feel the great Wyrm slowly uncoiling himself, movement as vast and unstoppable as the grinding of glaciers. Sigifrith saw the fiery gleam of gold at the mouth of the cave first, a gleam that set his head ringing with a high pure note and his hands shaking with need on Gram's hilt. He swallowed the water in his mouth, watching as Fadhmir's huge golden head, flatly long-jawed as a snake's but swept up into great ridges over his mad ruby eyes and back to sharp ears, swung out of the darkness. His mouth opened to a vast empty darkness ringed by cruel teeth, hissing poison spraying out of it before him. A black tongue like a forked spear flicked from his mouth, testing the air. Then the mountain shook, trembling at each tread, as the Wyrm began to crawl.

Sigifrith rose a little way out of his pit, watching Fadhmir wend from side to side. There was a terrifying beauty in his rhythmic swaying as he uncoiled more and more of his length from around the hoard, pouring from the darkness of the cave like a fiery river of gold coins; the might of awe beat against Sigifrith from the brightness that flared between the Wyrm's red eyes. Enthralled, Sigifrith felt that he wanted to run his hands along and through the precious metal, the gold scales graven along the sides of the Wyrm; felt that he needed to sink into the heaps of the hoard, to curl about the living gold and into it, letting the fires that leaped within his skull burn through his blood and around his body. His eyelids were drooping down, weighted by the sight of the coiling gold flowing down the mountain toward him and the unbearable brilliance of the Helm of Awe.

A sharp sting in Sigifrith's right palm woke him from his glimmering daze, shocking through his body like a bolt of ice. Gram had fallen from his grasp, landing point up; leaning forward toward the dragon, Sigifrith had pierced his hand on his own sword. He crouched down again, holding the ice stone in his bloody grip and striving to quiet his harsh breaths as he stared upward.

At last Sigifrith's gaze pierced the brightness between Fadhmir's eyes, staring straight upon the eight-rayed star of golden tridents graven into the Wyrm's skull. Though Fadhmir swung his ruby-eyed head from side to side, tasting the air, Sigifrith knew that the dragon had not seen him, and a fierce joy flared in the warrior's heart. He thought no more of the gold; but he knew that it was Fadhmir's day to die—he could feel it, the might of Wyrd flowing through his body with the strength of the Rhine in flood.

The sharp reek of the dragon's poison struck Sigifrith first. As he choked back a cough, the fine spatters of burning mist began to fall over his shoulders and back like a thousand hot needles. Such pain is little to a Walsing, he thought to himself. He felt no fear: the bale itself would not harm Sigimund's son, only the heat. Then Fadhmir was upon him, his great clawed feet thudding down on either side of the pit as the wide shield scales of his underside slid over Sigifrith's head.

Sigifrith cried out wordlessly as he stood, ramming Gram between Fadhmir's burning golden scales up to the hilt. His cry was echoed by a great deep howl that rang off the hills around as the dragon reared like a snake, tottering a moment as he peered about to see who had wounded him. In that second Sigifrith leapt from the pit, wrenching the sword out again. The dragon's blood sprang out in a glowing cherry-red torrent, spurting over Sigifrith's arms up to the shoulders. The heat was so great that it seemed to Sigifrith as though he had plunged his arms into ice-water, shocking them numb. He leapt back as Fadhmir began to thrash, the concussion of the dragon's fall throwing him out of range of the wyrm's sweeping head and tail as Fadhmir's immense blows shattered the trees and rocks about him.

Lying on his back, too dazed and battered to draw breath, Sigifrith saw blazing fragments of wood hurtled through the air like comets, kindled by the dragon's heat. Now I will be burned to death, he thought; but the fire consumed the shards before they ever struck the earth.

Fadhmir roared again, his awful cry shaking through Sigifrith's body like an earthquake. In a moment, Sigifrith realized that he could almost hear words in the dragon's voice—ancient words, guttural and buzzing, like the speech of Widuhundaz the Herulian.

WHO ART THOU? WHO IS THY FATHER, AND WHICH IS THY FAMILY, THAT THOU ART DARING ENOUGH TO BEAR WEAPONS AGAINST ME?

Sigifrith gasped for air, his body convulsing twice. It was hard for him to sit up and his arms would hardly help. He could see charred skin breaking apart over swelling red blisters, see his hands clenched tightly over Gram's hilt; but none of it touched him yet. Who am I? he thought dazed. Alapercht raised me, his clan named me, but I am not their son . . . The Saxon lands are eaten by the wave, their folk scattered, I have no place in the north . . . I am like none of the others in the hall, and have no living clan to claim . . . His voice rang in his ears, free from any thought of his own—almost singing, its pure high note cutting through the dragon's earth-deep moan. But there was no sound in his throat; he could hear the harsh rasp of his struggling breaths behind the words in his head.

My family is unknown to men! I am called Atheling-Beast, and have neither father nor mother, and have fared alone.

IF THOU HAST NEITHER FATHER NOR MOTHER, OF WHAT WONDER ART THOU LIVING? AND THOUGH THOU SAYST NOT THY NAME TO ME ON MY BANE-DAY, THIS THOU KNOWST: THAT THOU ART LYING NOW.

Sigifrith could feel a tree's smooth bark, painful and cool against his back. He tried to raise his sword, but his arms could only bring it halfway up, and a hiss of pain broke through his teeth even as his voice sang out untouched in his skull. But the sword thrummed in his hand; though Fadhmir cursed him with his dying breath, Sigifrith's wyrd had been bred in his blood and bone, and taken up again when he lifted the blade of his line against the ancient Wyrm.

My name is Sigifrith, but my father is Sigimund the Walsing and my mother is Herwodis, of Hraithamar's kin.

Fadhmir heaved his head above the treetops. It swayed weakly from side to side. Despite the darkening sky and the thickening mists, Sigifrith thought he could see a man's eyes in the huge golden head, though the dragon's fire was fading.

WHO EGGED THEE TO THIS WORK, AND WHY DIDST THOU LET THYSELF BE EGGED ON? HADST THOU NEVER HEARD HOW ALL FOLK WERE TERRIFIED OF MYSELF AND MY HELM OF AWE? BRIGHT-EYED YOUTH, THOU HADST A KEEN FATHER.

I had a strong heart for this, and to stand up to it I had a strong arm and a keen sword, which you now ken; and few are hard in age if they are timid in youth.

I KNOW, IF THOU HADST GROWN UP AMONG YOUR KINS-
MEN, THAT THOU WOULDST BE KNOWN AS WRATHFUL IN BAT-
TLE, BUT IT IS MUCH STRANGER THAT A BATTLE-TAKEN CAPTIVE
SHOULD HAVE DARED TO BRING BATTLE TO ME, FOR FEW PRIS-
ONERS ARE BRAVE IN BATTLE.

You reproach me for being far from my kinsmen? Sigifrith cried silently, anger
beginning to heat in him as the first fires of pain kindled through his
arms. *But though I was battle-taken I was not captive, and you have found that I was
loosed.*

WHATEVER I SAY, THOU TAKEST IT TO BE SAID IN HATE. BUT
THAT GOLD WILL BECOME THY BANE, WHICH I HAVE HELD.

Sigifrith answered, *Everyone wants to have wealth till that one day, but everyone
shall some day die.*

The bright spots rose and swirled behind his eyes; he thought he might
have slept for a moment, but the burning in his arms gnawed him with too
much pain for him to stay asleep.

THOU WILLST NOT BE GUIDED MUCH BY WHAT I SAY, BUT
THOU WILT BE DROWNED IF THOU FAREST UNWARY ACROSS
THE SEA, SO BIDE ON LAND TILL THE FURY IS LAID.

Sigifrith heard his silent voice speaking without his will again: *Say you,
Fadhmir, if you are greatly wise: which are those Norns, who choose sons from their
mothers?* He giggled through the fiery agony that seemed to have spread
through his body; he thought that if he didn't hurt so much he would feel
quite light-headed and merry.

THEY ARE MANY AND SUNDRY. SOME ARE OF THE ASES' KIN,
SOME ARE OF THE KIN OF THE ALFS, SOME ARE THE DAUGHTERS
OF DWALAN.

*What is the island called where the Muspilli and the Ases shall blend weapon-shed
blood?*

IT IS CALLED UNSHAPED.

Then Fadhmir spoke again. RAGIN, MY BROTHER, BROUGHT
ABOUT MY DEATH, AND IT GLADDENS ME THAT HE WILL BRING
ABOUT THY DEATH ALSO, AND IT WILL GO JUST AS HE WILLED.

The dragon paused, his head sinking down to the earth. When he spoke
again, his voice was hardly more than a trembling through the stone.

I BORE THE HELM OF AWE ABOVE ALL FOLK, SINCE I FIRST LAY
ON MY BROTHER'S INHERITANCE, AND SO I SPRAYED VENOM IN
ALL WAYS AROUND ME SO THAT NO ONE DARED TO COME
NEAR ME, AND I FEARED NO WEAPON, AND I FOUND NEVER
SUCH A MIGHTY MAN BEFORE ME THAT I DID NOT THINK MY-
SELF FAR THE STRONGER, AND ALL WERE TERRIFIED OF ME.

Sigifrith managed to crawl a step away from the tree, forward toward
Fadhmir. *The Helm of Awe that you spoke of gives victory to few, for he who comes
against many may find sometime that no one is the strongest.* His knees gave way
beneath him, and he slumped back again.

THIS REDE I GIVE THEE, THAT THOU TAKEST THY HORSE AND

RIDE AWAY AS SWIFTLY AS THOU CANST, FOR IT IS OFTEN SEEN THAT HE WHO GETS HIS BANE-WOUND AVENGES HIMSELF.

That is your rede, but I shall do something else. I shall ride to your lair and there take the great gold that your kinsmen owned.

THOU SHALT RIDE THERE TO FIND SO MUCH GOLD THAT IT WILL LAST THEE ALL THY DAYS, BUT THAT SAME GOLD SHALL BECOME THY BANE AND THAT OF EVERY OTHER WHO HOLDS IT.

Sigifrith clenched his teeth together and with one swift movement he lurched to his feet. Only his will turned his scream of pain into words, shouting defiantly at the dying Wyrm. "I would ride home, though I were to miss that great wealth, if I knew that I should never die! But every brave one wishes to have wealth till that day comes. And you, Fadhmir, lie in your death throes till Hella has you!" He could hear his voice laughing hysterically; hear the crashing as the convulsion ran down the length of the wyrm, smashing his body and tail into the shattered rocks. Then everything was still except for the sound of Sigifrith's feet through fallen leaves and broken tree limbs as he staggered forward.

The last light through the mist showed him the heap lying dead across the forest wrack. The dragon's thrashing had torn the trees to shreds; only the linden, broken and charred, stood near the stead of Fadhmir's death. Sigifrith collapsed onto the warm wall of the Wyrm's body. The huge scales, as smooth and strong as polished metal, were all that kept him from plunging to the ground. Firelight flickered from Fadhmir's side; a branch of the linden had kindled at last, its leaves floating around Sigifrith like smoldering moths, brushing lightly against his back.

Sigifrith did not know how he turned; but somehow he was leaning his back against Fadhmir when he heard the clumping footfalls and the sound of his horse's hooves crunching through the wood together.

"Sigifrith!" Ragin's voice called, rasping harshly against his aching eardrums. "Sigifrith, are you living?"

A moan escaped Sigifrith's lips as he raised his head. He tried to blink the swarm of glimmering sparks from his eyes, licked his blistered lips and spoke:

"I have slain Fadhmir. Now my kin are avenged and Otter's weregild lies for the one who would claim it."

He saw a burning branch break from the linden tree and float closer till he could see Ragin's short, squat shadow beneath it. He closed his eyes until something hot and wet splashed across his cheek. Opening his eyes, he saw Grani standing between himself and Ragin. The horse licked his master's cheek again. Sigifrith turned his head.

"Hail, my fro," Ragin said to Sigifrith. His voice was too hoarse for Sigifrith to hear any taint of sarcasm in it; it sounded as though the dwarf had gone sleepless for days. "You have won a great victory in slaying Fadhmir, when before no man was daring enough to sit and wait for him, and this hero's work will live as long as the worlds stand."

"Ungh," Sigifrith moaned. The light of the torch gleamed around him, flames reflecting from Fadhmir's scales and whirling into a circle of sparks. "Have you . . . salve? I think I'm hurt."

Ragin said nothing. Sigifrith's head drooped to the right, his sight turning sideways around Grani. He could see the gold-red sparks glinting out of Ragin's eyes; but the dwarf was not looking at his foster-son.

Ragin stood and stared down at the earth for a long time.

"You have slain my brother," the old smith murmured at last, "and I can hardly be free of blame for this work." After a while he lifted his head. "Move your horse and I'll see to your wounds. I thought you might be burnt."

Sigifrith moved his head weakly, gesturing Grani aside. The stallion stepped back a pace, letting Ragin bring his fire closer. The dwarf poured something dark out of a stone bottle on to a cloth and wiped it gently over Sigifrith's arms. At first he had to chew at his tongue to keep from screaming as the pain of the dwarf's touch bit into his burns, but then the blessed numbness began to spread from Ragin's salve, seeping warmly through his body. The dark stain and the flickering torch hid the worst of the charred blisters from Sigifrith's sight; when he looked away, it no longer seemed to him that he was grievously hurt. He felt drowsy, as though he had drunk a bottle of wine and then crawled into a warm featherbed, but no worse. Ragin's eyes were fixed keenly on him, the dwarf's heavy shoulders canted forward as if he were bracing to catch a heavy burden.

"Thank you," Sigifrith said weakly.

Ragin shut his eyes. "Sigimund's son," the smith murmured, as if to himself. "It is told of Sigimund . . . " He shook his head.

The dragon's blood had clotted on Gram's blade. Pushing himself off Fadhmir's body, Sigifrith walked unsteadily over the cinders to the trees and crouched down to clean his sword on the grass and dry leaves.

Ragin said something ending in " . . . won the hoard"; Sigifrith could not tell whether he had said "we" or "I".

"You went a good way off while I did that work," Sigifrith said mildly, soothed all through by the sweet warmth of the salve. "I tried out this keen sword with my own arm, and with my own strength I strove against the main of the Wyrm while you lay in a heather bush and did not know where heaven or earth were."

"The Wyrm might have lain long in his lair if you had not had that sword which I made for you with my hand, and neither you nor any other would have won that victory yet," Ragin replied, his rocky voice glinting hard with anger.

Sigifrith sheathed Gram, his burnt hand lingering on the ice-stone without feeling it. When he unclenched his grasp, the hilt was black with tatters of charred flesh. His tongue was thick in his mouth, moving slowly as he spoke. "When men come to do battle, then a good heart is better for a man than a keen sword."

Ragin chewed fiercely on a strand of his beard. One gnarled hand lifted, as though reaching toward the fire mirrored golden in Fadhmir's scales, then dropped again; his torch drooped in his grasp. He walked a few steps toward the crag over which the dragon's body drooped and paused, looking down into Fadhmir's dull, lidless eye.

"You slew my brother, and I can hardly be free of blame for this work." His voice was a murmuring of gravel, almost too soft for Sigifrith to hear over the sea-roaring in his ears.

Then Ragin drew his sword and walked back toward Sigifrith, the light of the torch in his other hand glinting cold and red from the steel. Sigifrith, his senses dimmed as by night and mist, watched him dully as Ragin turned the weapon, pressing Ridill's oaken hilt into his palm. He could not feel it, but his fingers closed about it as they had been taught from his earliest childhood.

"I shall hold your blade, while you cut out the dragon's heart," Ragin said, unbuckling the swordbelt from Sigifrith's waist. "It must be done swiftly: now Fadhmir's corpse is cool enough to touch, but soon the might that gave his ghost an earthly body shall be unbound, and the dragon shall melt in the heat of that loosing."

Sigifrith's numbed legs bore him over to Fadhmir's side; the sword in his hand slid into the great dark wound Gram had made. The dragon's mushy flesh melted away easily under the steel's edge till the sword's point speared something hard. Sigifrith braced his legs and drew it out. Spitted on the weapon was a black lump, like the heart of a man but thrice as big. Sigifrith thought vaguely that it seemed a very small heart for such a great wyrm, but Ragin smiled.

"That's it," he croaked. The dwarf came to Sigifrith's side, reaching into the wound between Fadhmir's scales. He drew his cupped hands out, dark blood and flesh dripping from them, and drank greedily. Sigifrith watched the dwarf's black-stained mouth open in a soundless cry as he clenched his wet fists, his thick body convulsing and shaking in the grip of the might he had taken into himself. It seemed a very long time before Ragin stood straight again, his fiery eyes burning into Sigifrith's dimmed gaze. It seemed to Sigifrith that the dwarf had grown taller and larger. From the corner of his eye he could see a shimmering orange-red foxfire playing around Ragin in the darkness, lightless and unreal as the winter banners of light in the northern sky.

"Now do me one boon," the smith said. His voice had taken on a new resonance and power, echoing through Sigifrith's skull. "It will be a little thing to you. Go to the fire with the heart and roast it and give it to me to eat."

Sigifrith nodded dumbly. "But there's no fire," he said after a moment of trying to think.

"Then make one!"

Sigifrith crouched down, awkwardly gathering fragments of half-burnt wood together and laying a fire with his free hand as he held up the spitted heart with the other. Ragin thrust his brand into the wood till the flames leapt up before him, shining on his bloodied lips and showing the black streaks through his beard. The dwarf stood watching a moment as Sigifrith lowered the heart over the fire, then turned and walked off into the darkness.

Sigifrith sat turning the dragon's heart without thinking, watching its skin shrivel and bubble above the flames. Now and again his head would nod down, and he would have to jerk the roast from the fire.

After a while juice began to hiss and foam out around the blade. He reached into the fire, touching it with his finger to see if it was done. A shock of coolness ran through his arm, as though he had touched a block of ice. Without thinking, he brought his finger into his mouth, sucking the heart-blood from it.

A great roaring rose up around him, glimmering through the air till he could see nothing but shimmering light. Slowly it cleared away into the darkness again. Sigifrith was lying on his back with the sword across his body. He could hear something chirping and whistling clearly through the trees; it seemed strange to him that the woodbirds should be singing at night, but he lay listening because he could think of nothing else to do. The glittering twitter rose, breaking into wordless song, then into words that Sigifrith could understand.

"There sits Sigifrith, and roasts Fadhmir's heart," the woodbird sang. "That should he eat himself. Then would he become wiser than any man."

A second bird-voice came from the broken trees, "There lies Ragin, and wants to betray the man who trusts him."

"Strike he then the head from him," a third voice sang, its high beauty rising above the other two. "Then may he rule over the gold alone."

"He would be wiser if he did that which rede was given him to do, and rode after to Fadhmir's lair, took the gold which is there and rode after on Hind's Fell where Sigrdrifa sleeps. And there he would take great wisdom. He would be wise if he had your rede and thought of his own need, for I ween that there is a wolf where I see a wolf's ears."

Another chirped, "He is not as wise as I thought, if he spares him, having killed his brother before."

"That were a keen plan," another bird sang, "if he slew him and ruled the wealth alone."

"There Sigifrith lies wounded," one of the woodbirds twittered. "He need not suffer such pain if he were wise enough to bathe in Fadhmir's blood. Then no sword or shot could scathe the dragon's slayer; the blood that burned him would be his byrnie then."

"Dwalan's son has drugged him with dwale; a weaker man would lie dead now," another bird sang. "But if Ragin eats his brother's heart, he will gain the strength to slay his slayer."

Sigifrith heaved himself up. He could not stand, and when he put his palms down the pain bit through the warmth of Ragin's dwale salve. On his knees he moved away from the fire to Fadhmir's body, leaning against the cooling scales as he worked his way over to the pits which the old man had counseled him to dig for Fadhmir's blood. As he toppled forward, the cinders seemed to open beneath him.

Coolness tingled through the warm fog wrapping Sigifrith. He tried to breathe; a draught of thick, musky liquid poured into his mouth, its salty sweetness kindling a hidden fire through him. His throat convulsed in a cough, but no sound came out. I am underwater, he thought. Did my ship sink? I was warned about sailing in bad weather . . . No! He struggled through the pool till his head broke the clotting rind and he gasped in gulps of the cool night mist.

Sigifrith laughed for joy, crouching down and springing out of the pit. He was naked except for the coat of dragon's blood clinging to him, and filled with a strength that thrilled through him like nothing he had felt in his lifetime, a might of which Sigmund's wod had only been a shadow. He remembered how Ragin's swords had shattered in his hands, thought of the death rede the dwarf had given him and tears of anger began to well from his eyes. "It is not shaped for Ragin to be my bane!" he cried. "Rather should both brothers fare on one way."

He looked about for the glimmer of Ragin's torch glowing through the night and mist. The flame burned farther up the mountain; the dwarf had toiled almost to the mouth of Fadhmir's cave. Sigifrith was not sure what he meant to do; only that he needed some deed to voice his betrayal.

Ragin whirled as Sigifrith leaped behind him, drawing Gram and stabbing toward his foster-son. Sigifrith's heart clutched in angry shock as the blade flashed toward him again.

"You're dead, gods curse you," Ragin hissed, his eyes as huge and dark as caves in his stony face. "Fadhmir, you're dead. I saw you lying . . . " Sigifrith backed away, trusting his naked feet to find a path through the rocks as the mad smith pushed toward him.

"Ragin, I'm Sigifrith!" he shouted. "Your brother's dead. I'm Sigifrith."

"Sigifrith . . . " Ragin murmured. Gram drooped for a moment, then the dwarf sprang forward again, the blade singing keenly through the air in a sweep meant to take Sigifrith's head from his shoulders. "The gold's mine! Sigifrith, you're dead. You were burnt . . . the dragon's blood killed you. I gave you dwale to make you sleep into death." And he hacked so fiercely that Sigifrith was barely able to keep a step ahead of the hissing steel, dodging and turning among the rocks as Ragin swung at him with sword and torch. "Die now! You should be dead."

"Ragin, stop," Sigifrith cried, backing up along the mountain path. "Ragin, I don't want to fight you. I'll share the gold with you. I always meant to. Don't do this to me."

Ragin's snarl hewed deep into the stone of the dwarf's craggy face, warping it to an ill-wrought monster's. One of his wild swings drove Gram deep into the rock of the mountainside; before he could wrest the sword out again, Sigifrith ran forward and grabbed him by the wrist. Ragin's bone was cold and hard, his earth-heavy strength more than Sigifrith had looked for. "Not while I live," the smith whispered. "It's mine, mine alone; you shall not have it while I live."

"Ragin, I don't want the gold. I'll leave it to you—you can have it all."

"You'd come back . . . I killed you and you came back. You'd never leave me . . . Die, Sigifrith! You've lived too long already. Die a hero's death as you ought." Red-gold sparks burned far back in his eyes, like fires in the empty blackness of a cave. Sigifrith could not bear to meet them and did not dare to look away. They strove there for a terrible moment, Ragin whispering, "I saw it. I saw you kill me . . . my sister warned me. You were the one she meant. You must die, or I can never live."

Then Sigifrith broke Ragin's fingers from Gram's hilt and ripped the weapon loose from the rock. The sword they had forged together swept through Ragin's beard, cutting off his last cry, "Sig—!"

The torch fell from their clasped hands, guttering out in its own ashes. Its last flicker of light showed the dwarf's headless body toppling as slowly as a felled tree stump.

As Sigifrith stood above his foster-father's cooling corpse with Gram in his hand, his fury ebbed and drained away.

"Now my kin are truly avenged," he murmured. Then, "Ragin, why? Wasn't there gold enough for both of us?" He swallowed against the hot choking in his throat. "If you had only asked me, I think . . . I think I could have left it all to you. Why didn't you believe me? Why did you have to . . . ?"

I could have, he thought. I could have.

He spoke again. "You gave me rede all my life. What should I do now?"

Nothing answered him but the cold rustling of the wind through the leaves and the soft dripping on the cinders of Fadhmir's track. For a time Sigifrith stood, looking down at the dark path. Then he cleaned his sword and went down to the fire where Grani stood beside the dragon's roasted heart.

The colt nuzzled his master anxiously, his warm strength comforting. Sigifrith stood with his arms around his horse's neck, leaning his wet face against Grani's soft coat. "I feel so alone," he whispered. "I didn't want to . . . I wouldn't have . . . "

After a while, he picked up Ragin's sword, sliding Fadhmir's heart from it. The heart had shrunk to a shriveled lump hardly bigger than Sigifrith's fist. He raised it and bit into it.

As he chewed the tough meat, it seemed to Sigifrith that something glimmered from the depths of his memory, like gold shining through dark water. The draught Ragin had given him on Thrimilci Eve . . . Otter's were-gild . . . As if he were looking through a rippling pane of glass in his mind, Sigifrith remembered the frenzy of the gold seizing Hraithamar's sons, burning the madness into Ragin's brain. He understood how the coals of Andward's curse had smoldered over the long years within the dwarf's skull and the dragon's mound, waiting for Sigifrith's deed to blow the flames to life again. Yet . . . mad as he was, Ragin had cared for Sigifrith and wished him well.

Sigifrith said aloud, "That would have been a hero's death, worthy of fame. But now I must write my own wyrd."

He placed what was left of the dragon's heart in one of the saddlebags. Taking a brand from the fire, he mounted Grani and guided him up the wyrm's burnt track to the mouth of Fadhmir's cave.

Sigifrith stared in wonder as he came into the dragon's lair. Great bands of rusty iron—the Romans' work from years long ago, when they had dug stone from the mountain—shored up the rocky walls; blackened where Fadhmir had touched them, they arched over his head like the ribcage of a giant beast holding up the ceiling. Below, the flame of his torch was multiplied a thousand times, a million, multitudes of little fires glimmering from golden Roman coins, from coiled arm- and finger-rings and from heavy chains, all of them shining as if new-minted.

Sigifrith had never truly believed in so much gold; before he had been too dazzled by the dragon and the Helm of Awe to see the hoard in its full richness. But here it was, heaped about him and burning with orange-red foxfire around the edges of each tiny mirror-flame.

Curious, Sigifrith bent down, running his hands through the ringing gold. Great as the hoard was, it seemed to him that he had won little from Ragin's death; the saddle that the dwarf had made for Grani was as fair to him, and more useful.

Through the sliding of the smooth metal, Sigifrith's blood-crusted fingers touched something crumbly and dry. Carefully he, remembering at last, moved the gold away to uncover the brown skeleton of a large man. Fadhmir's last remains were still decaying, the larger bones falling in on dark marrowless corruption like hollow tree trunks collapsing into their own rottenness. The Helm of Awe had sunk into his skull, cheese-soft bone coming through the links of the golden chain-mail; the splinters of Fadhmir's fingerbone pierced through Andward's dragon-ring.

Sigifrith pulled the helm loose from the disintegrating skull. The Helm of Awe chimed musically as he shook bits of rotten bone from it. For a moment he looked at the ring, then picked it up. He thought it would be too small for him, but it seemed to twist in his grasp, the little dragon's golden tail coiling about the middle finger of his right hand as he thrust it on without thought.

"I ought not to leave my kinsmen like this," Sigifrith said softly to himself. He carried the torch down the path to where Ragin's body and head lay. Setting the dwarf's head on his chest, he heaved the corpse up one-handed. The granite burden was great even for his strength; in death, Dwalan's adopted son had gone into the rock again.

Sigifrith carried Ragin to where Fadhmir's decaying bones lay on the floor of the iron-bound cave. Carefully he placed the dwarf beside his brother, putting Ragin's head against his neck again. He tried to close his foster-father's cold lids, but he might as well have been trying to shape stone with his fingers. Instead he took two Roman gold coins from one of the chests and laid them across Ragin's staring eyes.

Going out again, Sigifrith went to fetch Ragin's sword Ridill. In the darkness and mist, he did not notice how far down the path he had gone till he felt warmth rushing around his feet and smelled the scorch of hot metal. Looking down, he saw that he had stepped into a shallow, steaming river that hissed from the half-melted corpse of the wyrm. The light of his torch showed him the stream of hot venom burning through the rocks where it flowed; but when Sigifrith stepped out, his feet were clean and untouched.

Sigifrith searched till he found Ragin's sword by the embers of the burnt-out fire and brought it to lie across its maker's chest. There they would be until the end of time, he thought: Fadhmir and Ragin, with their brother's weregild spread about them as their grave-goods. Sigifrith knew that both dragon and dwarf had been dead men for many years, since Fadhmir starved in his gold and Ragin went into the rock; he did not know whether any part of them lingered past the second death he had dwelt them. Still, their howe would be filled with the riches they had longed for, as befitted Sigifrith's kinsmen.

Sigifrith lit another branch from the last of his torch and began to look for boulders by its light, bearing them to wall up the mouth of the cave till no one else could have thought to come into the cairn or disturb Fadhmir and Ragin's sleep.

When Sigifrith was done there, he took Grani by the bridle and tugged, meaning to lead him down the dark and rocky pathway; but the stallion stood as if his hooves were held fast in the stone, snapping angrily when Sigifrith pulled on his bridle again.

"Come on," Sigifrith murmured coaxingly. "So . . . so." But Grani would not move, not even when Sigifrith slapped his haunches with the flat of his hand. Then Sigifrith saw what the horse wanted. He leapt on Grani's back, touching his sides with his heels, and the stallion galloped away as if he had been loosed from all burdens.

8

THE AWAKENING

Grani galloped down the Dragon's Crag and through the mists by the Rhine. Sigifrith could hear the river's rushing, but he could not see it through the fog. It was not long before the horse took another path, his hooves ringing on the stones below. The night grew colder and brighter as they rode, the full Moon shining silver-gold through the frost-white mist. At last Sigifrith and Grani broke free of the fog, galloping out over a field of glittering hoarfrost flanked by dark woods on either side.

Sigifrith raised his heat-flushed face to the icy wind of their running, calling out, "Faster, Grani! Faster! On to Hind's Fell!"

The wind-gray stallion sprang swiftly forward, his pale mane whipping about like a row of banners in a storm as he leapt over the stone wall at the edge of the field and bore Sigifrith into the wood. Above, the budding branches lashed dark against the Moon like skeletal shadows, and owls swooped silently away from the horse and his rider as Grani's hooves crashed through the fallen leaves and rotting wood beneath.

Sigifrith rode through the forest till he saw the first light of dawn beginning to glow in the eastern sky, crowning the shadow of a great wooded peak with a rainbow-shimmering fire that seemed to light up the heavens. He laid the reins across Grani's neck, turning his steed toward the fell.

At the mountain's foot was a dark lake, its surface coldly mirroring the towering crag and the sunrise flame above. Grani plunged into it, his hooves churning the water to a wake of froth behind him. Sigifrith laughed as the icy waves splashed over his bare legs; as Grani leapt from the lake's bottom, blowing a spume of water from his nostrils, and began to swim as though no burden weighted his back. When they had reached the other shore, the horse sprang forth from the lake and galloped through the dark firs. The growing light sharpened the trees' needles to a million thorn-tipped spears, brushing harmless as fur against Grani's coat and Sigifrith's blood-smeared skin as they rode up the side of the mountain. Ostara's hidden might seemed to shimmer through the land around him; from the corners of his eyes, Sigifrith could see the shining white of the light alfs flashing through the trees and over the low hills around the mountain.

Breaking forth from the trees, Sigifrith saw a wall of white and red shields locked together before him. The golden morning flames leapt from the shield burg, glimmering with brightness; it seemed to Sigifrith that he could see a banner waving above on the point of a spear, though it shone too strongly for him to see what sign it bore.

"Up, Grani!" he shouted. "Let me bathe in the fire to win my dear bride!" Gram flashed in Sigifrith's right hand as he raised his arms, gazing upward in joy.

Grani did not stop to gather his might; he sprang higher than he ever had, leaping straight into the shining shield flames. The fire flared up around Sigifrith, burning the last of the dragon's blood from his naked body in a burst of rainbow brilliance as his steed bore him through the flame.

The rock rang like a bell beneath Grani's hooves as they landed, echoing from the brightening arch of the sky. The horse slowed from his furious rush, standing still at the mountain's peak.

Sigifrith looked down to see the rainbow flames glimmering from the polished helmet and chain-mail byrnie of one who lay beneath the shattered pieces of a white linden shield. The shield rose and fell gently with the sleeper's breath; beneath it, the mail seemed as tight as if it had grown to the flesh.

Sigifrith got off his horse and knelt beside the still body. Gently he pulled the helmet from the sleeper's head with one hand, lifting the shield away with the other.

It seemed to Sigifrith that a bolt of lightning had shot through his eyes to pierce his skull. He caught himself before he fell, staring wildly at the face beneath the helmet. Long fair hair tumbled around the high-boned, icy face of the woman who had glimmered, unknown, through his young dreams like a swan through the storm—of Sigilind, Sigimund's sister and bride, swept from him in his last struggle.

Tears streamed down Sigifrith's face as he gazed at the sleeping maiden. His hand trembled on Gram's hilt; his whole body was shivering with terrible awe. He was afraid to move; afraid to awaken her and look into her eyes, more afraid lest she should sleep forever and his soul never be seared by the lightning of her walkurja glance.

Sigifrith drew a deep, shuddering breath, turning his face up to the shining sky for a moment. Before he could turn and flee, he grasped Gram in both hands. His sword's keen edge sheared through the iron of her byrnie as if it were no more than cloth, down from the neck and along both sleeves. The hauberk fell away, leaving her slim white body naked beneath the brightening heavens. But her eyes were still closed in sleep.

"Now you have slept too long!" Sigifrith cried. "The night is ended: awake!" Carefully he lowered Gram to touch her between her breasts, the sword's tip pricking her like a thorn. A single drop of blood, crimson as a yew berry, welled up against her snowy skin.

Slowly her lids opened, the pale blue sky of the new day gleaming from her eyes. Sigifrith's heart clenched as though her glance had shot a spear of ice through it; he could not move or breathe, his joy so great that it seemed to him he was dying of it.

Her clear, high voice rang in his ears like the steel of a drawn sword, "What bit my byrnie? What broke my sleep? Who felled the leaden fetters that bound me?"

"I am Sigifrith, Sigimund's son!" he answered. "Fadhmir the Wyrm lies slain by my blade; with his bane I broke your sleep."

"Long was my slumber," she murmured. "I was long asleep; life is long to the sad. It was Wodan willed that I might no longer brandish battle staves."

Then the walkurja maiden sprang to her feet, tossing back her fair hair and raising head and hands to the light of the rising sun as she sang joyously,

Hail, day!   Hail to day's sons!
  Hail, night and her daughters!
Light thy eyes   unwrathful on us,
  Give victory to those sitting here!

Hail to the gods!   Hail the goddesses!
  holy be need-giving earth!
Speech and human wit   give to we, the well-known two,
  and healing hands, while we live!

When she brought her arms down, there was a horn in her hands, the golden mead brimming over and dripping down onto the ancient rock beneath their feet. She lifted it up to Sigifrith, who drank off the sweet draught and embraced her, holding her lithe, strong body against his own. The walkurja's brilliant blue eyes stared into his; his tears of unbearable joy glimmered like clear ice stones on her face as he bent to kiss her.

"What shall I call you now?" he asked the maiden.

"On this crag I am Sigrdrifa, your sig-wife, since you have wakened me," she answered. "Two kings did battle, an old warrior and a young. I wished to choose victory for the elder, my brother whom I loved; but Wodan had chosen otherwise. He stuck me with the sleep thorn in revenge for this, and said that I should never choose victory in battle again, but be given in marriage. But I swore an oath to meet that: that I should never be given in marriage to one who knew fear. So my walkurja soul was set to sleep here on this mountain peak, ringed around by a fiery shield wall; while I was also born again as the earthly maiden Brunichild. Now that you have wakened me, I may be one again and made whole."

"You are the bravest of women, who has borne all this," Sigifrith murmured to her. "Sigrdrifa, wise maiden, give me rede. I must learn from you, for I know that you know tidings from all the worlds."

"You are better able to do that than I," she said. "But if I know anything that will please you, I will gladly tell it to you, whether of runes or other matters. Now we shall both drink together, and the gods give us a good dawn that my wisdom may bring you weal and fame and that you may hold in your mind what we two speak of."

She took the horn from him, holding it to the sky till white froth ran over the rim to stream into her open mouth. Giving the horn to him, she began to chant, her galdor-song rushing through Sigifrith's head with the wod and magic of the draught as he drank.

Beer do I bring you   byrnie-moot's apple!
blended with might   and mainful fame
full of wisdom songs   and winful staves,
of good galder-charms   and gleeful redes.

You shall ken sig-runes   that you shall be wise . . .

Sigifrith drank, the wod mounting to his head at once as she traced the victory-runes before him: the sun-rune *sowilo*, ⚡, whirling golden, the sharp red arrow of Ziw's own rune, *tiwaz*, ↑ . . . "and scratch them on the blade's hilt. Scratch some on the sockets, some on slaying grip, and call twice upon Ziw."

Sigrdrifa laid her own hands over his on the horn. "You shall ken ale-runes, that another's wife not betray your troth, if you trust." And Sigifrith saw the hidden green bale-fire that Sinfjotli had seen in Borghild's hate-brewed ale: it would have helped the Walsing if he had known these staves against poison then. "On horn shall you scratch them, on your hand's back, and the need-rune, ᚾ , mark on your nail. You shall sign the filled cup against foe's work, and cast a leek in the cup. Then, I wot, the mead shall never be blended with bale fore you." The rune she traced was *laguz*, ᛚ , its might shining with the brightness of a fresh-springing leek, like a leaping fountain flowing through to cleanse the draught. "Though you be Sigimund's son, and Sigimund born again, these redes you shall need: do not scorn them when you see the drink brewed with betrayal!" She lifted the hallowed horn to his lips. "Now be this a memory-draught: you shall remember my rede, for you shall have need of it, my hero."

Now Sigrdrifa held an apple to her heart, the fruit shining wound-red between her white breasts. "The line of the Walsings is often born to death, our might too great for earthly flesh to bring forth. You shall take birth-runes to help birthing, and free the child from frowe. You shall scratch them on palm, on span of the hand's back, and bid the idises aid." The walkurja raised the apple, biting into it before she dropped it into Sigifrith's horn. It sank beneath the ale at once; but when Sigifrith drank again, he tasted its sweetness and felt its might tingling in his seed.

Thus Sigrdrifa gave Sigifrith rede: she taught him the brime-runes to ward ship on the sound, scratched on stem and steering rudder, burned into the oar's blade; she showed him the limb-runes to heal hurts, the mighty leech-runes to be laid on bark and leaves of a tree with east-leaning limbs.

"Wise you shall be, if you heed and use these, but there are yet more, and those more needful for you," the walkurja murmured, and as she spoke, Sigifrith saw the staves shining before him. "You shall ken speech-runes, seeking that no one pay you harm out of hate. Wind them around, weave them around, set at each other's side, at that assembly where folk shall fare to set full doom. You shall take thought-runes, if you would be recked wiser than any among warriors. These runes were spoken and scratched by Hropt, dark-cloaked Wodan: he laid upon them the drops from the head of Haith-draupnir, from the horn of Hoddrofnir. He stood upon the rock holding the sword Brim, a helm upon his head: then Mimir's skull spoke wisely the first word, and said sooth of the staves."

It seemed to Sigifrith that her words bore him on the wind like the mighty sweeping of a swan's wings; that he looked down at the dawning world from a great height, and saw the runes burning through it as they had since the first shaping of the World-Tree. They shone upon the shield that stood before Sunna, on the ears and hooves of her horses Arwaki and Alswith; on the wheels rolling beneath Wodan's wain; on Sleipnir's teeth and on the sledge straps. The strength of the bear's paw burned with the runes, and they sang from the tongue of Bragi, the scop-god of the Ases' Garth; they lay beneath the darkness of the wolf's claw, and screeched in the eagle's beak. Sigifrith saw the runes graven in the bloody wings of Lingwe's back, when he had made the gift to Wodan and won his father's memory; they

R
H
I
N
E
G
O
L
D

ᚻ
4
3
3

stood on the bridge's head, on the palms of midwives loosening bairns from their mothers, and on the tracks of healing. Glass and gold shook with the might of the holy runes roaring through them, and men's good luck flowed from the runes within; they seethed and worked in the wine and the wort. The point of Wodan's spear Gungnir shone bright with runes, and Sigifrith saw how they glimmered on Grani's breast, on the nib of the owl and on the nails of the Norns who sat by the Well of Wyrd and cast its holy water on to the World-Tree. And above all, at the Tree's crown by the great eagle, stood Wodan, the hempen noose of his hanging falling loosed about his neck as he raised the runes he had won, the bloody stave shapes risted into a piece of the great evergreen's wood. The runes burned in Wodan's hand; they flowed forth in a stream of shining red might, flowing into the silver-bound aurochs horn he held and glowing in the ruby eyes of the silver eagle's head at its tip.

Sigifrith heard his own voice blending high and golden with Sigrdrifa's as they sang together,

> All were scraped off   that were scratched on,
>   and blended with the blessed mead,
>   and sent on wide ways.

> These are with the Ases,   those with the alfs,
>   some are with the wise Wans,
>   some had by human beings.

> Those are beech-runes,   those are birth-runes,
>   and all are ale-runes
>   and mighty runes of main.

> Who knows them unconfused   and all unspoilt,
>   shall bear them to his blessing.
>   your good, if you get them,
>   until the doom of the gods!

The rainbow-fire shimmered in Sigifrith's eyes as he stood on the mountain with Sigrdrifa, drinking the last of the draught with her. She looked up at him, her day-blue eyes as clear and bright as the ice stone in Gram's hilt, and spoke again. "Now you shall choose. The choice is given to you, tree of true weapons. Speech or stillness you have in heart yourself—meted the meanings all."

"Though you know me fated to fall, I will not flee you," Sigifrith answered Sigrdrifa. "I was never born a coward. Now I will have all your loving rede as long as I may live." Andward's ring glittered upon the hand he held out to her, the six-rayed star blazing from the great ruby in its center. "See! I do not fear my orlog, whatever it may be; Wyrd writes as she will. But now we are together after our long parting, and that is geld enough to repay many sorrows."

He kissed Sigrdrifa again. Her lips were warm beneath his, sweet from the honey mead and hallowed malt they had drunk together. The walkurja's arms twined around him, holding him to her; her breasts pressed softly against him. It seemed to Sigifrith that the shimmering shield fire was burning through him again, filling him with a joy so great that it was painful. All the desire that had slept in him while other thanes sought and loved was kindled by his need now, its song roaring in his ears as he gently stroked Sigrdrifa's hair.

"I had waited so long," she murmured. "Sigifrith, come to me."

Sigrdrifa drew him down to the rock as his hands and mouth sought the sweet curves of her body. Her touch loosed the unfelt sorrows of his years alone; he felt the bands of iron falling from his limbs, fetters of loneliness cracking away like ice at winter's end, freeing the rivers that seemed to sweep through him, sweeping him away in their warm flood of shining waters. Sigifrith cried out, clasping Sigrdrifa to him as he had always, unknowingly, longed to do.

"Now take my rede with you when you ride forth again," Sigrdrifa said to Sigifrith as they sat together, watching Sunna rising toward her height in the heavens. "Though you have no fear, yet you may use your wisdom and strength to turn wyrd about again for yourself."

"Give me your rede, wisest of women," Sigifrith answered, kissing a loose strand of fine hair from her fair brow.

"I will tell you as clearly as I may: hear what I say carefully, my beloved. Act well toward your kinsmen and take little revenge against them for their offenses. Bear with their deeds, and you will get lasting praise. Beware of ill things, both against the love of a maid and of a man's wife; for ill often comes of these. Do not hold angry thoughts against unwise men at the meeting of many men. They often speak worse than they know. If you fare along a way where evil wights dwell, be wary of yourself. Do not take shelter near the path, although it is night, for ill wights often dwell there. Do not let fair women entangle you—though you see them at feasting—so that they stand before your sleep or that you get pain of soul from them. Do not lure them to you with kisses or other blithenesses. Fight against your foes, rather than be burned. And swear no crooked oath, for grim revenge follows the breach of troth. Do rightly by dead men, whether dead of sickness or dead at sea or dead of weapons; prepare carefully for their bodies. And trust no one, of whom you have felled father or brother or other near kinsman, although he be young: there is often a wolf in a young son. Be careful against the rede of your friends." She stopped for a moment and looked up at him, the warm tears glimmering ice-bright in her eyes. "Yet I can see little of your life to come, if the hate of your wife's kinsmen does not come upon you."

"I have found no one wiser than you," Sigifrith said. "Now I swear this: I shall have you in marriage, for none can be more truly matched with me."

"And I would wish to marry you, though I chose among all men," Sigrdrifa answered.

Sigifrith took Andward's ring from his finger, holding it out to her. "I swear this oath to you upon this ring, which I took from Fadhmir's hoard. Take it, if you will, as morning gift and wedding ring; let the gold bind us in place of the iron."

Sigrdrifa took the ring and slipped it on to her hand. "And I swear this oath to you upon this ring: that I will be wed to no other than you, the fearless hero who has ridden through my ring of flame."

He caught her up, lifting her onto Grani and vaulting on behind her. "Let us go forth from this rock together, my bride, as we shall always be—Wodan grant that we not be parted again."

Sigrdrifa leaned back to gaze up into his face, her hair streaming over his shoulder. "I cannot come with you now," she said sadly. "Though here I am living, I am no more than a ghost in the world below. When I leave this shield-burg, I must fare to my earthly body, and she is far from here. So you must go forth and find the maiden Brunichild, the daughter of Theoderid. She shall be waiting for you with your ring around her hand; a fire like this shall burn around her hall, so that none but the boldest of heroes shall win her. Then we shall be wed in all the worlds, as we are in truth here between them."

"Now that you live," Sigifrith answered, "I shall not be alone again. Trust in Grani's swiftness, for he will bear me back to you as soon as he may." He embraced Sigrdrifa again, kissing her mouth one last time as he touched Grani with his heels. The wind-gray steed sprang over the shield wall, through the shimmering fire.

When the rainbow brightness had faded from Sigifrith's eyes, he saw that he was alone on Grani's back again, riding down among the fir trees. The Sun had passed her height; the lengthening shadows showed his way eastward, back toward the Rhine.

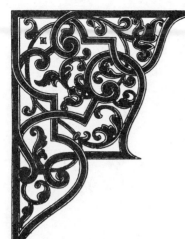

BOOK III

THE DEATH OF ATHELINGS

Unbound
through all the worlds
the Wolf Fenrir shall go
till in his destroying tracks
kings of equal worth
are found.

—EYVINDR SKÁLDASPILLR,
"HÁKONARMÁL"

Bragi: "Why did you take victory from
him, if he seemed the bravest to you?"
Óðinn: "For that which is unknown of
knowledge: the gray wolf gapes ever at the
dwelling of the gods."

—ANON., "EIRÍKSMÁL"

1

ALONG THE RHINE

rimhild did not hear the door to her hidden chamber opening; the one who came in bore no torch whose light might warn her that she was not alone. Only when he let the door close with a muffled thump did the Burgundian queen whirl from her three-legged stool, her skirts brushing dangerously close to the little fire that burned in the middle of the floor as she tilted her head to stare angrily up at the tall shadow of the intruder. Her seith-flame glimmered back at her from a single dark eye; the other was a blot of blackness.

"What are you doing here?" she demanded, unnerved.

"You have been seeking out Sigifrith," he said flatly, his eye narrowing as he looked past her into the flames.

Grimhild turned her back on him, lifting a bucket of sand and dumping it over her fire. A cloud of white smoke puffed up, filling the chamber with a charred sweetness like singed honey edged by bitter-strong herbal scents. She waited until the smoke had melted into the air, then stalked out without speaking.

He followed her till she got to the chambers that she had shared with Gebica. These rooms were larger, with windows of Roman glass overlooking the Rhine; the torches burning around the walls and the big fire at the northern end lit it well. Grimhild sat in her own chair, sinking down on to the cushion of northern fox fur and tapping her pointed nails impatiently on the falcon-headed armrest. Her guest took his seat on the bed. As always, he sat straight as if he were braced for an old Roman military inspection. Although his face was turned from the torches, in the better light Grimhild could see the shiny red track of the fresh scar running jaggedly from beneath his black eyepatch down into his silver-threaded beard. A familiar shiver went up her back as his dark glance met hers; but Grimhild was well used to dealing with the uncanny.

"Hagan," she said, "you know I don't like being spied on. Why have you decided that you need to know everything I do?"

"Because it is my duty to know everything that might concern my family," her son grated. "Tell me, what have you seen?"

Grimhild rose from her seat, darting over to one of her chests. She took out a clay wine bottle and two goblets of swirling green Roman glass, pouring a pale stream into each of them.

Hagan sniffed carefully at his glass, holding it up to the torchlight and staring into its depths for a long time before taking a drop on to the tip of his tongue. Grimhild waited patiently, sipping at her own draught. She was long used to her son's ways, as he was to hers.

"Sigifrith is coming back," she admitted at last.

"With Fadhmir's hoard?"

"Yes."

"And Ragin?"

"Dead."

"That is a great loss," Hagan said. "Sigifrith slew him?"

"Yes."

"It might have been expected." Hagan looked into his wine again, swirling it about and finally sipping a little. "Your Ostara wine is very good this year."

Grimhild smiled, her teeth white as bare stone. "Thank you."

"If Sigifrith is coming back with the hoard, why aren't you rejoicing?" Hagan asked suddenly. "Tell me what has gone amiss with your plans."

The Burgundian queen sighed, setting her goblet down on the glass-inlaid top of a birch table. "Will you leave it be if I tell you that there is nothing you need to worry about?"

"No."

Anger curled Grimhild's thin hands into talons as she stood, gripping Hagan by the shoulders. Her nails dug deeply into the thick layers of muscle armoring his light bones; she tried to shake him, but he was too strong for her to move. "Damn you, Hagan!" she hissed. "I've told you not to come into my rooms unasked, I've told you to leave my affairs to me and I've told you that you don't need to have anything to do with this one. For someone with ears as sharp as yours, you're doing a damn good imitation of a deaf man."

"You're not really angry with me," Hagan said. His rough, deep voice was unchanged, as always; but Grimhild could tell from the way her son spaced his words and the tightness of muscle under her hands that he was working very hard to stay calm. "You're angry because Sigifrith either has done or is about to do something you don't like—perhaps something that may interfere with his marriage to Gundrun. If that is so, I want to help you do whatever needs to be done so things will go as they should. Now tell me what has happened."

Grimhild dropped her hands, sighing. "Will you believe me if I say you don't want to know and everything will go much better if you don't?"

"Do you expect that I'll betray your secrets to Sigifrith?" Hagan asked. "Will my face give them away?"

"Hagan, you swore blood-brotherhood with him. I assume that you must like him."

"My truest friend was Waldhari the Frank," Hagan answered. He turned his face so the torchlight shone angry red off the scar beneath the black eyepatch. "I cut his hand off in fight for Gundahari's sake, as you know, though I made peace with him again when he had paid back the score. If

Sigifrith means to do something that would shame our family, I must do what I can to keep it from happening."

"Sigifrith means to marry Brunichild, the daughter of Theoderid of the Goths, and to pay us for this with gold."

"Enough gold will pay for many things," Hagan said. "But Gundrun will marry Sigifrith or no other man, and I believe that you had thought to forge an alliance between Theoderid's daughter and Gundahari, if it might be done. And besides . . . Ragin told me the length of our lineage when I was young. We have as great a claim on Otter's weregild as he. Where is Sigifrith now?" Hagan stood, as though he meant to leave the room.

Grimhild stepped between her son and the door, her slight figure a feather blocking his way out. "Tell me what you know first. I know that great mights are moving upon the Rhine: my seith-sight was blurred by the northward storm."

Hagan cocked his head as though listening to something. Grimhild did not know what sound came to him through the thick stone walls, for Hagan's hearing was sharper than any other's. It might have been the far-off rumble of earthly thunder he listened for; it might have been something else altogether.

"Great mights are moving upon the Rhine indeed," he said. Though no change of tone eased the weight of his voice, his words came slowly, as though they sounded from far away. "I know that Donar goes with his Hammer, chasing after Loki; for the Sly One shall come no more into the gatherings of the gods. Loki flees along the Rhine, but shall find no friend there for his rape of the swan-maiden is not forgotten, nor have the river-wights forgotten how he stole Andward's hoard. Not long past, he went as a ferryman; now he flees in fish shape, for no beast is harder to find or fasten upon—but Donar follows him swiftly, and will catch Loki in the end as he himself caught Andward in the elder days. Yet these things have little to do with us, now that the dragon is dead. Sigifrith has seen the last of Loki, and Wodan only waits for his son to live out his wyrd. The tale of what shall become of him is not whispered upon the Rhine; it is for us to see it through."

"You cannot fight Sigifrith," Grimhild warned her son. "Even if he weren't said to be the strongest man and the best warrior in Germania, he has bathed in the dragon's blood and no weapon can scathe him."

"So what do you mean to do?"

"I shall brew a draught that shall blind his memory to all that happened after he took Fadhmir's hoard, and bind him to Gundrun. I have found that Brunichild the daughter of Theoderid will not be so easy to win now as she would once have been; it may be that Sigifrith shall help with that."

"I have heard it said that no bale could scathe Sigimund, whether he drank it or were touched on the skin by it. Why do you think that your brewing can touch his son?"

"The Walsing line is proof against poison, not against enchantment," Grimhild answered. "Since no bale can slay him, the mightiest herbs may be used to snare his senses and his soul. It is true," she added, "that if he should come to doubt the draught, he could use the wisdom he has learned to overcome it easily enough. Then we should have to content ourselves with Fadhmir's hoard, Attila as marriage-kinsman through your sister, and a king unwed or married to a Roman maiden. I think there have been worse outcomes, though nothing could be better than to hold Sigifrith to us as closely as we may."

"When his deeds become widely known, no one will be more famed than he," Hagan agreed. "Tell me then: what must I do?"

"The draught must be swift in the brewing," Grimhild said musingly. Her fingernails clacked on the golden hawk's head of her girdle's clasp. "Mighty as Grani is, Sigifrith has tired him; even if they find passage up the Rhine, they will not be here for two days. So, this is what I need: Go into the woods tonight and find me Witch's Violet and Balter's Brow, keyflower and Frowe's Glove, sowthistle and mist twig. Dig out a root of Allruna—you know how to ward yourself against her howl. Bring these worts back to me before the first light of dawn." She showed him her teeth again. "If you don't think picking flowers and digging roots is too much of a shame to an atheling-warrior."

"You know my line better than any living wight," answered Hagan.

He left as silently as he had come, slipping out like a shadow, untouched by the torches' fire.

It was nearing dusk when Sigifrith rode to the Dragon's Crag, past the scars his battle with Fadhmir had left on the earth. He was little willing to come back; he had hoped to leave Ragin's grave behind him forever. But he had thought and thought on it as he rode, and it seemed to him that there was no choice but for him to claim the hoard. He would not hold it long: it would be his gift to the Gebicungs, to pay for his broken betrothal to Gundrun and keep the peace between the Burgundians and Alamanns. Though it was not unknown that a man have two wives, or that a second woman be his concubine in law with rightfully-born children, Sigifrith knew that neither Brunichild nor Gundrun would willingly hold second place and that a house with two such women in it would not long rest in frith.

If Sigifrith had not known where he was going, he would not have recognized the heap of boulders before the door of the cave. Hauling them away was a wearying job—he had blocked the cave's mouth well and thoroughly—but at last he had the opening clear enough for him to crawl inside.

Although the warm sunset light shone into the iron-bound cave, it was very cold inside. There was no warmth to the ruddy brightness that the hoard shattered into thousands of glimmering reflections, and Sigifrith felt the adder-chill coiling into the marrow of his bones. Though he did not wish to, he could not help looking toward the place where he had laid Ragin's body, but it no longer lay amid the gold: only a heap of broken rocks marked where Sigifrith had set his foster-father's corpse. Nevertheless, a strong smell of rot tainted the icy air inside the dragon's cave: Sigifrith could not get away from the knowledge that he had stepped into a stead that belonged to dead men, and come to steal from the dead.

The two chests Sigifrith remembered were clear in his mind's sight: great ancient things, held together with bronze nails from a time when iron was dearer, carved with the rayed stars and crude figures of many generations ago and bound with leather straps. There had been two makeshift bags as well, wide cloaks tied at the corners—but that had been many years past, he realized. A pile of shattered wood lay against one wall, the broken planks blackened with age and the scorch of the dragon's passing; nothing was left of the second chest, or either of the bags.

Sigifrith squirmed out of the cave and back in, carrying his empty saddlebags. They would not hold so much as a tenth part of the gold, but he remembered Ragin's words: "To those who truly know the hoard, there is a way."

Sigifrith clenched his fists tight on the saddlebags. His gaze blurred as he stared at the rocks lying upon the gold. "What did you mean by that?" Sigifrith whispered, his throat choking his words to unechoed softness. He stood very still, holding his breath as though he might hear a whisper from the stones, but no sound came.

Finally he crouched down, beginning to sweep the gold into his saddlebags. The smooth metal felt slimy beneath his hands, as though he were lifting it from rotting flesh. Although he could still feel the might tingling through the pure gold, it was no sweeter to him than the prickling of wasp stings against his hands. I shall take what I can, at least, he thought; perhaps the Gebicungs can send men for the rest later.

Though the Sun's light no longer shone straight into the cave, it seemed to Sigifrith that the gold's fires were burning brighter than ever around him. He breathed deeply, sitting back on his heels with his hands still in the gold. It seemed to him that the hoard had become a river of fire flowing around him, its might burning like the veins of melted stone that flowed through the depths of Ymir's corpse where the dwarves toiled and forged their wonders. The flowing gold, the fire—Sigrdrifa had shown him its rune, *fehu*, ᚠ: wealth, the kinsmen's strife, serpent-path and flood-tide flame.

Half-dreaming, Sigifrith chanted the rune's name as his hands traced its ringing shape through the gold. The breath of his galdor-chant blew through the cave like a mighty wind, blowing the fires to burn brighter and brighter around him till Ragin's rock and Fadhmir's bones were hidden in its pyre light. The hoard seemed to have risen to fill the whole cave with gold, straining against the bands of Roman iron that bound it into the rock. Sigifrith drew the fire into himself with every breath; it was as though he could feel all the gold touching him at once, its tingling might flowing through him—as though he himself had melted into the flame. But Gram still hung at his side, the stone in its hilt a single grain of clear ice holding him to his human shape and the task he had willed for himself; and so Sigifrith stretched out his left hand to open his saddlebags again. With his right, he guided the burning flow of the gold, still chanting the rune *fehu—fehu*, the fiery might that rushed unstilled, that could be grasped no better than a flame and burned the one who would hold it.

The seething river of howe-fire flowed into his bags until only the gold's red shadow flared within the cave. As its after-image faded from Sigifrith's blinded eyes, it seemed to him that a great many dark figures stood about him, and that before him a fiery shadow lay lashed about with writhing bonds like serpents or living entrails, black and cold as ice which its might could not melt. A serpent hung twisting above it, green-glowing drops of bale falling from its jaws. Sigifrith thought he could see the bound shadow's mouth open, and feel the rock tremble beneath him with its agonized struggles. But it was no more than shadows he saw: shades cast forward, ripples of light reflected from the waters of Wyrd's well. What he had seen might come to pass . . . or else . . . and then the flames of the bound figure burned higher and higher, burning away the shadows. In its light he saw a city of stone-built Roman halls standing proud between humbler dwellings—Worms, he knew, though he had never seen it—and then the wild horsemen screaming through, the flames rising behind them to eat the city, stone and wood together. Sparks shot from the burning like arrows of fire, landing on Alapercht's roof; the thanes were fighting before it, their foemen pressing them back to the burning hall where Alapercht lay in his blood before the doorposts, and Sigifrith heard Herwodis' scream ringing within. Then it was not Herwodis who stood in the doorway, but Brunichild, the circle of fire around her tightening on her like a noose until her white gown burst into flame and a burning river ran up her fair hair.

Sigifrith leapt to his feet, lurching forward toward the fire and drawing Gram; but the flames were gone, the cave was cold and gray inside, with no echo of the visions nor any sound but Sigifrith's hard breathing and the jingling of Grani's tack outside as the horse shifted about. A darker shadow lay over the heap of broken rocks; the gold's fire had scorched them black, but it had burned Fadhmir's ancient bones to ash.

Sigifrith quickly closed his saddlebags without looking inside to see what they held. He could feel it too easily, straining against the bounds he had set on it. He would be glad when he had given the gold away—when, free of its burden, he could ride to Brunichild as lightly as he had ridden to Hind's Fell. The memory of Gripir's vision gleamed keenly in his mind then: the shield-roofed hall with its mighty thanes and bright maids, and through the doorposts the green world outside where he and Brunichild rode Grani together.

"That I shall have soon; that shines brightly before me," Sigifrith murmured to himself, gazing at the bare place on his finger where Andward's ring had rested for a little time.

Outside once more, Sigifrith hauled the boulders back where they had been. He knew that earth would fall over them; that one day trees would grow over the scorched ground, and no one would be able to see his work nor dig through to disturb the grave again. His breath caught sobbingly in his throat as he slung the saddlebags over Grani's back. Though Sigifrith thought to lead his horse, the gray colt stood until Sigifrith mounted him. Sigifrith could not help thinking of the ride from Alapercht's land, when it had been Ragin's weight that burdened Grani as well as his own—but he did not turn his head back, nor look through the shadows to the heaped stones that hid the cave's mouth.

As they rode toward the Rhine, Grani broke into a gallop, hurtling down the path like a stone flung from a cliff. Swiftly as Grani ran, Sigifrith could feel the hidden weight of the gold dragging them even more swiftly down, the river's fire eager to flow into its old bed. Grani covered the last of the path with a great leap that ended with the colt standing hock-deep in the Rhine's mud, water lapping about his knees.

Slowly the gray horse began to walk southward through the water. Soon Sigifrith realized that Grani was trying to go more deeply into the river, and tugged on the reins to stop him. Sigifrith could feel the water's pull as though he were already swimming in it, mingling with the fire of the gold. He knew he would have to find the ferryman again: he could not ride to Worms like this, and only the Rhine's water could bear him safely to his goal.

Sigifrith cupped his hands to his mouth and shouted, "Hai! Ferryman! Can you hear me?"

His cry echoed across the steel-dark water, sinking into the shadows on the western shore. Though he shouted twice more, no answer came back to him. Then a breath of wind stirred the branches of a willow tree that drooped into the river a little way from him, the blue ripples coiling out from it like water-wyrms; and when the branches no longer rustled something beneath them continued to move, swaying back and forth in the current. Sigifrith nudged Grani with his knee, and they splashed over toward it.

Though the light was fading swiftly, Sigifrith could not think how he had missed seeing the raft lodged between two of the willow's gnarled roots. The ferryman's pole lay across its planking, but there was no other sign of him.

"So I must be ferryman for us," Sigifrith murmured to Grani, urging his horse up the bank, then dismounting and leading him on to the raft. He took the pole firmly in both hands and pushed off. Although he was poling against the current, it put no strain on his strength; he could still feel the gold's might surging forward with him, on toward Worms.

Gleams of red gold shone from the wing feathers of the hawk riding proudly on Gundrun's leather-gloved hand, the bird's rich plumage glowing in Sunna's afternoon light. The fierce bird was large as an eagle, heavy for her to bear; but she knew that she could far less bear to lose it. She was horsed, riding along a pleasant meadow by the Rhine. The river flowed slow and calm, golden light rippling across its deep green waters. Every so often she saw the flash of a pike or trout in the depths, sudden as a stone turning underfoot, but she was not hawking for fish.

A gust of wind flattened the grass ahead of her to show the rusty streak rustling through it. For a moment the fox's eyes fixed on hers, its narrow jaw opened as if to laugh.

She flung up her arm, loosing her hawk. It circled into the air, strong, beautiful and wild. The wind of its wings caught the breath from her lungs and blew her long hair back as her arm, free of its burden, fell to her side. She felt tears of joy in her eyes as she watched her hawk's mighty wings beating at the air, carrying it higher and higher till it was a dark speck against the glass-blue sky.

Suddenly, swift as two spears cast on the wind, a pair of eagles arrowed in to strike her hawk. Bloody feathers scattered; the hawk tumbled, striving against the air with broken wings as its blood spattered onto her face. She heard her own scream as she spurred her horse toward the falling bird, and the scream in her ears awoke her to a frantic struggle with the sweat-damp blanket that bound her in a twisted rope.

When she had managed to free herself, Gundrun lay breathing heavily until the pounding in her ears had slowed and dulled to the sound of her heartbeat. After a while, she stood up and went to her window, pulling the curtain aside from the glass. Only a few ripple-warped stars glinted from the night sky; the moon was down, the Rhine sunken in darkness.

Gundrun went back to bed and lay down again, pulling her blanket over stone-chilled feet. She drew in her breath and let it out as slowly as she could, trying to calm herself and go to sleep. Tomorrow would be Ostara's feast, and Sigifrith—Sigifrith might come to meet her, for now he was a man tried and proven in honor. He had sworn that he would come to her before Midsummer and that he would avenge his father. There was no reason for him to wait longer. She could remember him: the keen glance of his blue eyes, too strong for her to meet straight on and yet more painful for her to look away from; high-arched nose and wide cheekbones; light brown hair tumbling down his back in long thick waves; and the clear rich sound of his voice as he called out his vow like a challenge. She remembered how easily he had smiled, how friendly and joyful he had seemed—as though he had nothing in the world to fear. Even then, he had been coming into his great strength: her hand had been sore from his careless grip for more than a month, as though he had cracked her bones. But she had not asked her mother for a poultice, because she had prized even the lingering ache from her betrothed's touch.

And now men sang songs of Sigifrith's deeds in the north, and their eyes turned to her where she sat at the high table beside her brothers and her mother—with honor, yes; men honored her and women envied her because she was Sigifrith's betrothed, but sometimes she thought that she could hear the whispers stilling when she came within earshot. If not yet, it would not be long before folk started to ask one another whether Sigifrith truly wanted

Gebica's daughter, or whether—like Gundahari—he might be turning his eyes southward to some woman of Rome or of the Gothic folks.

Wrapping her coverlet about her shoulders, Gundrun crept back to her window. She thought she could see the three stars of Frija's Distaff glinting through a rippling line of glass. Between her breasts lay a pendant her mother had given her when she came to womanhood, a gold falcon gripping an amber disc. She clutched it with both hands, staring at the stars.

"Frowe Frija," she whispered, "I know you hold the oaths between men and women holy. Please bring Sigifrith—my betrothed—back to me."

To her horror, Gundrun found that she was about to cry. She coughed, straightening her back; surely Frija had no reason to listen to someone who lacked the strength of soul an atheling-maid ought to have. "The oaths are sworn and sealed," she went on, more briskly. "It's a fair match. Sigifrith is the strongest man on the Rhine, but my brother Gundahari is the most powerful king between the Northlands and Rome. Frowe Frija, I know your husband loves strife and slaying, but you're the mother of frith-weavers— don't let the peace our folks wove at our betrothals be broken. For I think that if Gundahari and Sigifrith ever turned against one another, the German lands would have cause to remember the slaughter for a hundred generations.

"Frowe Frija, I've always given gifts to you at the slaughtering times and feasts. Now it's only fair . . . let Sigifrith keep his oath to me."

The starlight through the wash of window glass was too faint to show Gundrun any sign of answer, if Frija gave one; but she went back to bed feeling easier in her heart and sleep came quickly.

The morning dawned clear and sparkling, a cool breeze blowing through the budding boughs of the summer wood. The sorrows of the night forgotten, Gundrun was out gathering flowers for Ostara's feast with the other young women of the household, her attendants and the daughters of her brother's thanes. Purple-flowering tendrils of sorceror's violet trailed from her basket; she and Fridlinta tossed the round blossoms of keyflower at each other like yellow coins fluttering into Gundrun's honey-brown hair and on to the dark red coils of Fridlinta's braids. Now and again the girls stooped to pluck the white flowers of Balder's Brow that starred the grass, the bruised fringes sending up a rich green scent where fingers or bare feet crushed them. The crimson-violet bells of Frowe's Glove were just beginning to open at the bottom of their long bud-hung spikes, but those blossoms they left alone: they were said to cause quickening of the heart and madness.

"Look," one tall, white-clad maiden murmured, tossing her long fair hair as she pointed. Ahead of them, between two black-budding ash trees, a huge stag stood with his wide-antlered head proudly upraised. The white flowers of wild spear leek shone around his hooves, higher and fairer than the lesser grasses beneath them. A golden sheen gleamed from the stag's light brown pelt; his sky-pale eyes were so bright that Gundrun could neither look into them nor look away. She thought that she had never seen anything so beautiful as the stag standing with the tapestry of sun and branch-shadows woven over him.

Heedless of the danger to herself, she hurried toward the stag, flowers spilling from her basket. She was not alone; the tall blond girl caught up with her easily and ran ahead, but the stag turned as her fingertips brushed his hide, slipping from her grasp and leaping high over a fallen log to come down beside Gundrun. Trembling, she embraced him as tightly as she could, awed by his warm strength against her body and the silkiness of his pelt beneath her cheek. The stag seemed to her dearer than any other thing she had ever seen or touched, and she thought that she could not be happier.

Then his legs began to crumple beneath him. Although Gundrun was strong, she could not begin to catch him. The weight of his fall and the crash as he struck the earth shook her from her feet. She fell to her knees beside his body, crushed down by an unbearable grief.

A raven-fletched arrow stood out from the stag's side; beside them, the tall blond girl held a bow in her hands. Her white dress was flecked with blood, her twisted face melting into a flood of furious tears. Gundrun scrambled to her feet, ready to leap upon her, but Grimhild already had her daughter by the wrist, her slender fingers gripping as sharply as a falcon's claw. No matter how Gundrun twisted and struggled, she could not break free of her mother's hold until Grimhild had led her far away.

"See, I have another pet for you," Grimhild said, loosing the leash of a great hound from around the branch of an ash. The hound came eagerly up to Gundrun, licking her hand and fawning about her; but when it raised its head, she saw that its jaws were bloody, and when it shook its head, it spattered her with the blood of her brothers.

Gundrun awoke again with a hoarse shout. She was sitting bolt upright in bed, her throttled bedclothes twisted in her hands. The flame of a candle haloed her mother's fragile figure against the darkness of the hall beyond.

"Gundrun," Grimhild said softly. "Gundrun, dear, what's wrong? I heard you cry out."

The Burgundian queen came closer, setting her candle down on Gundrun's table and put her arm around her daughter's shoulders, smoothing the sweaty hair from Gundrun's forehead with a quick brushing movement.

"I had a dream," Gundrun said. "That's all it was."

She tried to move away, but Grimhild's thin arm held her in a firm embrace.

"Tell it to me, darling, and don't be frightened. Most often, all dreams mean is a coming storm. When the air grows thick it often presses against the heart."

"This is no weather dream," Gundrun said. "I dreamed that I saw a fair hawk on my hand. His feathers had a golden sheen to them."

"Many have heard of your beauty, wisdom and courtliness," Grimhild told her soothingly. "A king's son will soon be coming to claim your hand."

"I thought nothing finer than this hawk, and I would rather have lost all that I had in the world rather than him. Then I dreamed of a stag, whose pelt was golden. It was far better than other deer. Everyone wished to capture the stag, but I alone could do it. The deer seemed to me more precious than anything else." She stopped, unwilling to go on.

"You have no need to worry," Grimhild said, her thin lips curving as she stroked her daughter's hair. "You shall soon be wed to the mightiest of atheling-warriors, for Sigifrith shall be coming to you and bringing the gold of Fadhmir's hoard with him."

Gundrun looked out into the darkness, at the lightless swirls of red and blue sparks that seemed to spin around the fuzzy circle of the candle's light. "The dreams seemed very dark and troubling to me," she murmured, so softly that Grimhild had to tilt her head closer to hear her.

"You have nothing to fear," her mother answered. "Now I will bring you some warm milk and honey so you may sleep and be joyful in the morning for Ostara's feast. You must be at your most beautiful to give her proper honor, for the shining goddess shall be bringing your husband to you soon. Let her see you at your fairest, and so Sigifrith shall also see you for ever."

"Have you heard news of him?" Gundrun asked, her eagerness beginning to lighten the shadow of her dreams. "Will he be here for our feast?"

"Not for the feast, I think; he has ridden a long way with a heavy burden, and his horse is tired. But it will not be long afterward that he comes to you."

Gundrun swung her feet over the edge of the bed, grasping her mother's bony fingers in her hands. "Do you know . . . does he remember me? Is he . . . ?" She could not finish, even to herself, but Grimhild's head bobbed swiftly.

"No other woman has ever delighted him within the ring of the Middle-Garth," Grimhild answered. "When you see the joy your welcome cup gives him, you will be sure that you need fear no rival for Sigifrith's love." The older woman pressed her daughter gently down into bed again, pulling the coverlets over her. "Rest now, darling," she said. "I'll bring you your posset."

"Thank you, Mother," Gundrun said, closing her eyes against the darkness as Grimhild bore her candle out.

Several days after Ostara's Feast, Gundrun sat beside Helcha and Fridlinta on one of the stone benches in the garden outside the great hall, trying to chat with the other two young women as they embroidered on the tapestry spread out over their knees. Every now and then she glanced unwillingly at the road that led from the Alamannic lands, straining her eyes for the least puff of dust against the distant blue mountain shadows.

Helcha nudged her with a plump elbow, giggling. "What are you looking for?" she asked. "Can I guess?"

"You don't have to guess," Fridlinta answered, her low voice cool and amused. She pulled the tapestry farther up on to her lap, fingers fluttering as she stitched light green around the edge of a leaf. "But really, Gundrun, don't you think he'll send a proper messenger to warn you before he gets here? Has he learned barbarian manners from the wild Saxons he brought back from the north?"

Gundrun dug her needle fiercely into a hunter's blue tunic, pulling the thread tight till it thrummed at breaking point.

"I'd be insulted if he came without a proper band of thanes around him," declared Helcha cheerfully. "Now, what color shall I do the boar's hooves in, hmm?"

"That brown there, I think," Fridlinta told her. "But who knows what Sigifrith might do? I've heard that he goes off into the wilds with Ragin the Smith for months at a time, and nobody knows where they are or what they're doing." She rested her pointed chin on the tips of her fingers, looking sideways at Gundrun. Glints of yellow seemed to shine from her brown eyes as she murmured in a lower voice, "The songs say Sigimund and his other son—the one with the outlandish name, that Sigimund got on his sister Sigilind—were werewolves in the Gautish forests together. Aren't you afraid of marrying someone with blood like that, Gundrun?"

"No, I'm not!" Gundrun snapped as her thread broke. "Shut up, damn it! You're jealous because there's no man who might be Sigifrith's equal except my brother, and he doesn't want you."

Fridlinta laughed, brushing a tendril of dark red hair from her freckled forehead. "Your brother?" she said. "Even if Hagan weren't married—that poor woman!—I couldn't bear to have him touch me. But you're right, it's not much choice between a wolf-skinned berserk and a mirk-alf's son." A quiver of real fear seemed to tremble beneath the exaggerated movement of her shudder as she brushed her fingertips across the ivory-set gold cross at her throat.

Shaking with anger, Gundrun stood, dumping part of the tapestry and her coils of threads onto the grass, and slapped Fridlinta across the face as hard as she could, knocking the other girl off the bench. Helcha shrieked, scooting away from her.

Fridlinta disentangled herself from the tangle of embroidery and got up. The mark of Gundrun's squarish hand stood out against her white cheek.

"I'm sorry, Gundrun," she mumbled. "I didn't mean to insult you, really I didn't. I was just teasing."

"It is good to know that," Hagan's deep voice grated from behind them. They whirled in surprise, staring at him. Fridlinta stepped back so hastily that her feet caught in the tapestry and she went down again, landing hard on her buttocks as she stared up at him in terror. A horrified giggle squeaked out around the edges of the hand over Helcha's mouth.

"Ready yourself quickly, Gundrun," Hagan said. "Sigifrith will be here before long."

Gundrun looked up the road, then down it. Brilliantly clear as the day was, she could see no sign of a rider.

"How do you know?" she asked.

"I saw the raft on the Rhine. He is some way downriver—almost to the Frankish march—but it will not be long before he is here."

Gundrun glanced at the river, frothing with the rising floods from the mountains. "How could you see him from that far away? How do you know it was Sigifrith?"

"Because he was poling upriver as easily as another man would row down the current, with a horse and a heavily laden raft. Who else could it be? Hurry now, since you need to race against him."

Gundrun ran to her brother, flinging her arms around his mailed chest and standing on tiptoe to kiss his scarred cheek. Hagan suffered her embrace for a moment, then gently turned her toward the hall.

"Go on. Grimhild will have the greeting horn prepared for you to give to Sigifrith when he gets here." He bent down, sweeping up the twisted mess of tapestry, threads and needles in one powerful arm and thrusting the bundle into Helcha's hands before she, too, could back away from him. "You two go and alert the other women. Have the hall readied for a feast."

Sigifrith leaned his head back as he poled easily up the flooding Rhine, letting the Sun warm his face. Ahead he could see the stones of Worms where his raft's weight would be lightened with the loosing of his betrothal to Gundrun. Then he would be free to seek out Sigrdrifa—Brunichild—and wed her within the Middle-Garth as he had already done without. The planking was warm on his bare feet; he had put no spare boots in his saddlebag with his extra clothing, nor had he wanted to break his faring along the Rhine for as long as it would have taken for more to be made. I will have this done with swiftly, anyway, he thought; no one except the Gebicungs will see me, so it hardly matters how I am clad.

"Ragin would have . . ." he murmured. Then his ribs twinged as though they had healed crooked after a break, and he could not say anything more. He reached to pat Grani on the neck.

As he drew nearer to Worms, he heard the brassy blare of Roman tubae from the ruddy sandstone walls of the city. A train of people was already standing by the stone jetty that jutted out into the Rhine. He could see the glint of sun from chain-mail over a dark tunic on one side, gold over light blue on the other—Hagan and Gundahari, flanking a small figure gowned in deep red.

Sigifrith whispered the runes that had come to him from Sigrdrifa, the runes of speech by which he could soothe Gundahari's and Gundrun's disappointment and Hagan's wounded pride. His fingers moved, tracing their stave-shapes as he summoned their might within him and readied it to flow forth with his words.

"Hail, wanderer!" Hagan called out, his deep voice reverberating across the water. "Where are you faring?"

"To Gundahari, Gebica's son!" Sigifrith answered.

"Come to his hall as guest! Hail and welcome, Sigifrith, Sigimund's son!"

Hagan walked over the stones to the end of the jetty as Sigifrith poled in, helping him to moor the raft. Sigifrith could feel his face flushing with the scrutiny of what looked like half the Burgundian athelings on him. He glanced curiously at Hagan's eyepatch and the fresh scar crawling down from it, but decided to wait until later to ask.

Before Sigifrith could stop him, Hagan took Grani's reins to lead him from the raft. The colt rolled his eyes wildly, dancing to the side. Water poured over the planking around his hooves, cold on Sigifrith's bare ankles.

"There, go on," Sigifrith said, laying his hand on Grani's flank and giving a push. While Sigifrith touched him, the horse moved docilely forward; but when he took his hand away Grani stepped backward again.

Hagan shrugged as though settling the chain-mail across his shoulders, handed the reins back to Sigifrith and waited for him to lead his horse off before stalking along the jetty behind them.

As Sigifrith set foot on the land, Gundahari strode forward and clasped his forearm. Their gold arm-rings clashed together dully as metal met metal in the embrace.

"Welcome, brother!" Gundahari said. "We've been waiting for you. Come, Gundrun is waiting in our hall." He looked past Sigifrith to Grani. "Let one of our grooms stable your horse. You'll find your bags in your room when you get there."

"I think Grani can bear his load better than any," Sigifrith answered, distracted by the thought of what he would very soon have to tell Gundahari and by the weaving and winding of the runes that would make his news bearable to the Burgundian king.

"It is true, then, that you have slain Fadhmir and have claimed his hoard?" Grimhild murmured. Her deep red cloak swished around her as she stepped from behind her elder son to stare up at Sigifrith. Although the slim woman seemed no bigger than a swallow before him, Sigifrith felt her presence as if it were a stone crag blocking his way.

"It is true," he declared boldly, leading Grani forward. "And thus I have brought Otter's weregild here to the land of Gebica's son, for—"

"Then surely no deed has been done to match yours!" Grimhild exclaimed, cutting him off before he could begin to speak the words he had readied. She took him by the forearm, though her long-nailed hands did not reach halfway around it, and guided him up the tree-lined path to the Roman burg that stood in all its renewed glory beside the Rhine. "Come, your betrothed is waiting for you."

The least flick of his arm would have freed him from her grasp, but

Sigifrith knew that it would be unspeakably rude of him to pull away from the dry touch of the Burgundian queen. Fearing that the carven stone and glazed clay would splinter beneath Grani's hooves, he guided his steed to the side of the path as he and Grimhild walked along the cracked mosaic of Roman paving.

A small, white-clad maiden, her waves of honey-brown hair crowned with pale green leaves and tendrils of purple-flowering vine, stood in the arch of the gateway. She held a horn-shaped vessel of clear glass ornamented with squiggles of opaque white and blue over the greenish wine within. He recognized the hilt of Gundrun's knife, set with its garnets and emeralds, before he remembered her square-jawed face and solid little body. The top of her head did not quite reach the tip of his breastbone.

Gundrun's blue eyes gazed up at Sigifrith as she lifted the horn toward him—not quite meeting his gaze, not quite turning away. She was breathing hard, as if from struggle or fear; the nasal twinge in her low voice was almost a squeak as she spoke the ritual words of greeting to him.

"Hail and welcome, Sigifrith, Sigimund's son, to the hall of the Gebicungs. Gebica's daughter offers you guest-drink."

Sigifrith took the horn from her hand and raised it. As Sunna's light glowed golden through the green-tinged wine, he saw the unmistakable fox-fire of bale around the edges of the horn and felt the warning thrumming through his arms. Shocked, he glanced down at Gundrun, but the sight Sigrdrifa had given him showed her soul glass-clear and unstained by guile. Grimhild then; in that sword-edged moment of sight where he rested unmoving, Sigifrith remembered Ragin's warning and knew that Grimhild, Lofanohaith's daughter, had brewed venom into the draught to gain Otter's weregild for her own.

Unfettered by fear, Sigifrith laughed joyously. He needed none of the runes Sigrdrifa had given him to deal with this draught of bale: was he not Sigimund's son, with all his father's might within him, able to bear poison both within and upon his hide? Instead he silently called up the runes of frith and soothing that he had readied against any anger at his breaking of the betrothal, and spoke as Sigrdrifa had made him able to.

"Let this drink be peace and honor between our houses, fitting to the love that offers it," he said, half-chanting, seeing the golden ghost light of his power brightening invisibly where the sound of his voice rang. Sure in the memory of his dark hall where he had drained such a draught twice before without scathe, Sigifrith tilted his head to face the Sun's light and emptied the horn of envenomed wine.

A wave of dizziness hit him as the warmth of the wine began to glow from his stomach. He could feel his heart beating as rapidly as a bird's wings inside his chest, his breath coming quickly as he looked down at Gundrun. He wanted to blink the bright spots of flashing crimson from his eyes, but could not bear to shutter his glance from her for a moment. His hands were shaking on the horn as he gave it back to her; the light touch of her fingertips on his seemed to shock through his nerves. Gundrun's wide-eyed gaze was fixed on his face as if in terror, a flush of red creeping over her strong cheekbones. Her breasts heaved with her breath, kindling a raging need-fire in Sigifrith. Only the thought that he might harm her held him back from grasping her where she stood.

Sigifrith's throat seemed to close, choking off his words; he was barely able to whisper, "Greetings, my betrothed."

"You have had a long faring, Sigifrith," Grimhild said, swiftly stepping between Sigifrith and her daughter. "Will you come in and have something to eat?"

"Y—yes," Sigifrith stuttered. He was about to follow Grimhild and Gundrun into the hall when Hagan's voice broke through his daze.

"What shall we do with your horse, Sigifrith?"

For a moment he stood irresolute, poised between Gundrun and Grani. Then Gundahari clapped him on the shoulder with a hearty laugh.

"Go on," the Burgundian king said. "My sister's waited four years for you, after all. She's not going to run away now."

Embarrassed, Sigifrith picked up Grani's reins and followed Hagan to the stables. There was one empty stall, bigger than the others and freshly swept, with clean straw on the floor and a bin filled with oats.

"This is yours," Hagan told him. "My brother had it built for your steed so that he, too, would have a fitting place when you came to us. You are pleased with Gundrun?"

Sigifrith stared down at Hagan, surprised beyond speaking by the question.

"Of course," he said at last. "I have never seen a fairer maiden, nor one I would . . . would wish more to . . . be wedded to . . . " He trailed off, overcome again by bewilderment at the aching passion awakening through his body as his heart fluttered harder and more swiftly against his ribs. He could not think of anything except Gundrun's light touch on his fingertips, could not see anything except her leaf-crowned face staring at him from a curling frame of honey-brown hair; and each breath felt like a blow in the pit of his stomach.

"Are you well?" Hagan asked, his single eye scanning Sigifrith intently.

"Yes . . . Yes, I think so. I hadn't remembered . . . hadn't realized she was so . . . "

"I hope that you may have joy in your wedding." Hagan unlatched the stall gate and stepped aside so Sigifrith could lead Grani in. The two of them reached together to lift the saddlebags from the gray colt's back. Sigifrith saw Hagan stagger under the weight, his scar flushing an angry purple-red as though the blood were about to burst from it again; and in that moment the leather bags gave way at their strained seams, gold spilling out like sunlit water bursting from a dam. Sigifrith stared with his mouth open. He did not know how he had packed it in; there was far more than his saddlebags could have held—more weight, he would have thought, than he could have lifted or Grani carried. He did not doubt that the whole of Fadhmir's hoard was there, to the last finger-ring.

"So you have learned Loki's secret," Hagan said. Closely as Sigifrith listened, no shade of mockery or accusation tinted the Burgundian's rough voice. "What tidings do you have of him?"

"What are you talking about? I don't know—"

"How did you get the gold into those bags?"

"I don't know," Sigifrith said again. He shook his head as if to shake water out of his ears, shake the blur from his memory. He must have done it . . . he had killed the dragon . . . he had . . . "Ragin gave me dwale to dull my pain."

"Dwale often makes men forget—or see strange things. Do you remember what you saw?"

Sigifrith searched his memory, but saw no more than a spark of light leaping like a flame within the cave. "I remember that Grani wanted to go into the river. And the ferryman—" He remembered the scorch of recognition from the Sinwist's flames. "He ferried us to the Dragon's Crag, and left his raft for me. After that I know nothing of him."

"So he may yet be free," Hagan mused. Sigifrith thought that he might say more, but he did not.

After a few moments of silence, Sigifrith laughed. "So long as he doesn't get in the way of my wedding, it is little to me! When will it be? Have you chosen a day?"

"You must speak to Grimhild about that. I am seldom asked about such things."

"Are you . . . I mean, Gundahari said you were betrothed. Have you been wed yet?"

"Yes."

"What is it like? I mean, can you . . . can you tell me?"

"The frowe Costbera, my wife, shall be giving birth some weeks after Midsummer," Hagan answered. "What else is there to tell?" After a few moments under Sigifrith's glance, he added, "She is a Christian. More Goths have come among us, and there are more followers of the new god than there were since my brother spread his reign into Gaul. Has this touched your folk yet?"

"Not much. A few of the thralls who were Romans or owned by Romans."

Hagan nodded, then gestured toward the gold lying heaped on the straw. "What shall we do with this?"

Sigifrith shrugged. "Leave it be, if you like. I think Grani can guard it well enough."

Hagan's tilted eye flickered up and down the horse, as if measuring the strength in Grani's muscular flanks, the weight and sharpness of his hooves and his swiftness in striking.

"I had not heard that the Alamanns trained their horses as sentries," he commented. "Are you sure? I will watch it myself, or send trusted thanes if you would rather."

"Grani knows what to do," Sigifrith insisted, stroking his horse's neck.

"You don't seem over-worried about the safety of your gold," Hagan said as they walked into the sunlight. "The songs about Otter's weregild made me think that you might be expected to care more about it."

"Ragin cared," Sigifrith admitted, looking down at his bare feet. The square Roman tiles of the path were marked with lacy blue crosses over a yellow background. Most of them were chipped, a few cracked across. "He tried to kill me. First through the dragon, then by drugging me and taking my sword."

"A smith of his like will not be seen again soon. I regret the death of my kinsman. But you did not slay him over the gold."

"No. It seems better fit for giving than for keeping, to me. Indeed . . ." Sigifrith turned, dragging Hagan back to the stables with him. "Help me choose gifts for your family from it. What does Gundrun like? What will make her happy?"

Sigifrith flung open the stall door, Grani stepping aside to let his master at the hoard. The heaped gold gleamed red even in the dim light from the open door at the end of the stables.

"As I heard the tale, the last treasure of the hoard was a dragon ring," Hagan said at last. "Have you hidden it well?"

"I suppose so," Sigifrith answered, surprised. "I remember finding something like that, but I'm not sure where I put it."

"Let it stay hidden, then." A gleam seemed to glint from Hagan's eye for a second, but his stone-pale face did not change as he crouched to run his fingers through the gold. After a few minutes he pulled out a gold-set boar's tooth dangling from a thick chain. "This would please Gundahari, I think."

"What about Gundrun?"

Sigifrith dropped to his knees beside Hagan, rummaging through the hoard with him till they found a wide-disced brooch with the figures of running does and stags raised from its glittering surface by thousands of delicate hammer-taps crafting them to the last hair. In the center of the brooch was set a smooth round garnet, red as a transparent holly berry.

"What about you, then?" Sigifrith asked Hagan when they had chosen gifts for the rest of Gundahari's family. "Do you see anything you'd like?"

Hagan shrugged. Then, remembering, Sigifrith scrabbled through the gold with both hands, strewing chains and coins into the straw as he felt about for the piece of work he remembered. Triumphantly he held up the coif of gold chain-mail—the Helm of Awe which he had taken from Fadhmir's skull.

"I think this would suit you," Sigifrith told Hagan. "Since you wear a byrnie everywhere, you ought at least to have one fit for feasting in. Now choose something for your frowe."

Hagan took the Helm of Awe from Sigifrith's hands, turning it over carefully and looking at the sign graven on the gold plate welded to the forehead—the eight crossed tridents radiating out from a single point. Then he shook his head, giving it back.

"This is not for me," he answered. "This is a thing of might, which you must ask Grimhild about. She will tell you how to use it as you need."

"Why should I need it?" Sigifrith asked.

Hagan's eye looked very large and dark in the dimness of the stables as he stared at Sigifrith for a moment. "Keep it," he said. "It is the fairest and finest of the things you have won, excepting only Andward's ring. I have heard it said that it was by the might of the Helm of Awe that Fadhmir was able to become the dragon, and that one who knew how to use it properly could have still greater power."

Sigifrith thought of the swallow swooping and dancing above him as he and Ragin crossed the Burgundian marches, and how he had longed to fly. He dropped the Helm of Awe into his belt pouch and tied it shut.

"Choose for yourself, then," he offered, gesturing sweepingly toward the glittering hoard. "Do you want the ring? I'll see if I can find it."

"I would not wear it by choice," Hagan replied.

"Why not?"

Hagan did not answer. Instead he drew out a spiral arm-ring, whose terminals were cast in the shape of eagles' heads and adorned with delicate filigree. He considered it a moment, rocking back on his heels, then slipped it over his hand and bent it more tightly so that it would fit on his fine-boned wrist. Taking it off again, he handed it to Sigifrith.

"I should like that, if you must give me something," he said.

"Of course. Now choose something for Costbera, or she'll be likely to beat you tonight."

"I think not. She is not so vigorous as Gundrun."

Despite himself, Sigifrith laughed, remembering how his betrothed had flown at him when they first met. "Am I in danger, then?" he asked teasingly. "Will you be marrying me to a wild walkurja?"

"If you can keep her temper calmed, you have nothing to fear."

Something about Hagan's monotonous grimness as he gave this warning threw Sigifrith into a hysterical fit of giggles. The Burgundian watched him calmly, as if trying to decide whether he had gone mad or not.

"I'll . . . try to protect myself . . . " Sigifrith gasped.

"See that you do. A woman's fury is a fearsome thing." Hagan's unscarred cheek twisted painfully, half his upper lip pulling back to show a gleam of teeth.

Sigifrith sat at Gundahari's right that evening, Grimhild to the Burgundian king's left, with Gundrun beside her. Hagan was seated on Sigifrith's other side. An empty chair separated him from two boys barely at the edge of manhood, who had been introduced as Gundahari's cousins. Gisalhari was sandy-haired, his limbs just beginning to lengthen into the first spurt of youthful growth. He was continually looking about himself, scratching at the razor burn down his left cheek or tugging at the long-stemmed cross of enameled silver that hung from his thin neck. Gernot was a little larger, dark-haired and heavy-set with a moustache like a smudge of coal across his upper lip. He seldom moved and had not spoken since being brought forward to greet Sigifrith.

Grimhild and Gundrun rose from their seats when the hall was about two-thirds full, taking blue pitchers ornamented with scrolls like sea foam and coming round to pour out the wine. Sigifrith could not turn his eyes away from Gundrun's graceful movements as she filled his goblet, the quivering of the smile at the tender edge of her lips and the way her eyelids flickered when she looked at him, as though she were staring into the Sun's blinding brightness and yet was not willing to let herself blink. He reached out to cover her square hand with his palm as she set his wine glass down again, his breath shaken from him by the feeling of her warm skin under his touch. Gundrun stood poised with one foot half off the floor as though his glance had frozen her in the moment of fleeing. Wisps of honey-brown hair curled out of the long braid down her back, framing her face in fragile tendrils.

Grimhild's sharp cough broke Sigifrith's passionate entrancement a moment before he could rise to embrace her daughter. The queen's eyes flicked over and away from the startled gaze he turned on her; he could just see the white edges of her teeth between her thin lips as she smiled at him. Abashed, he let go of Gundrun's hand so that she could go on to pour drink for the other men.

"When may I wed your sister?" Sigifrith asked Gundahari breathlessly as the women passed on.

The Burgundian king raised thick eyebrows in a look of bemusement. "You've certainly become eager all of a sudden, haven't you? Sigifrith, you're blushing. You look like a fourteen-year-old who's just found out what it's for."

Gundrun's white dress rippled over the curves of her back and buttocks like a waterfall of froth as she walked about the hall, her sturdy ankles as pale as birchwood beneath its gold-wrought hem. Her heavy braid, intertwined with the pink and yellow blooms of keyflower, swayed with each movement she made.

Gundahari passed his hand slowly back and forth in front of Sigifrith's eyes. "Are you still there?" the Gebicung asked teasingly. "Wake up, Sigifrith. You have seen women before in your life, haven't you? All that time up in Saxony, killing, looting and burning, and you never took a moment to rest and enjoy the fruits of victory?"

Sigifrith could feel his own blushing, as hot as a brand laid across his cheeks. "There were other things that I needed to do," he admitted in a low voice. "I never thought about it."

Gundahari opened his mouth, shut it again and grinned at Sigifrith. "Well, it's about time then." He leaned across Sigifrith to Hagan. "Where's Costbera? Is she all right?"

"She will be here soon," Hagan answered. He cocked his head slightly, as if listening to something. "You can hear the Christians ringing their bells. Their spring ritual should be over."

"You can hear the Christians ringing their bells, you mean," Gundahari answered amiably. "All I hear is stomachs grumbling." He leaned back, glancing around the hall. "I suppose we shouldn't have the food served till the rest of my thanes get here."

Gisalhari leaned forward and twisted his neck to look at his cousin, pulling at his yellow tunic to straighten it. "If you were going to wait anyway, why did you make me come early?" he asked in a high, pleasant voice. He smiled at Sigifrith, showing a missing tooth halfway along his upper jaw. "I wouldn't have wanted to be rude to you, but I would have liked to go and celebrate spring with the other Christians."

"Because life is not easy, boy," Gundahari answered flippantly. "When you're older, you can decide where you go and with whom. You can have your own personal priest to follow you around if you like—and if you can find one silly enough to do it."

The last of the thanes began to wander in, their faces flushed as if with strong wine. A young woman wrapped in a thick green cloak stumbled clumsily among them. Warmly dressed as she was, her clothing could not hide either her swollen belly or her stick-thin arms and puffy ankles. Her brown braids were coiled over her ears so that her head looked too large for her neck. Sigifrith thought her turquoise eyes seemed oddly bright against the dark sags of flesh beneath them, as though she looked through the clear dreams of a raging fever.

Hagan rose from his seat to help his wife to hers. She did not flinch from his touch, but she drew back from him when he released her to stand before Sigifrith.

"This is my frowe Costbera," Hagan told Sigifrith. "Costbera, this is Sigifrith the son of Sigimund, of whom you have heard so much told."

"It honors me to meet you," she murmured softly. She did not raise her eyes to meet his. Her head swayed from side to side; for a moment, it seemed to Sigifrith that her tired face sagged into a look of pity.

"And I, you," Sigifrith answered, unsure of what he ought to say. "I hope your spring rite went well and your gods are pleased."

To his surprise, Costbera's thin lips curved up, the faintest breath of a laugh puffing from her mouth. "I might have expected . . . " she whispered, then, "It's not quite like that. But thank you for your good wishes."

A wash of pain seemed to flow across Costbera's face. She covered her belly with both hands, her fingers whitening as she pressed. Hagan caught her, supporting her and easing her into her seat.

"My frowe has not carried easily," he said, then to Costbera, "Do you want to stay? You don't have to. Sigifrith will understand."

"I'll stay," Costbera insisted.

Hagan took Gundrun's pitcher from her hand as his sister passed, pouring his wife's goblet full of wine. "You're in pain. Do you have the powder Grimhild made for you?"

The Christian woman lifted her hands as though she wanted to take her husband by the shoulders and turn him to face her. She did not touch Hagan, but he turned so Sigifrith had to look down over the Burgundian's dark head to see Costbera.

"Not here," she said to Hagan, so softly that Sigifrith could hardly hear her. "Later. Please . . . I'm all right."

Sigifrith shifted his buttocks on the padded fur cushion beneath him, turning uncomfortably away to face Gundahari again.

"Is she well?" he asked.

Gundahari's heavy shoulders rose and fell in a ponderous shrug. "Grimhild says the first child is usually hard to bear. Other than that—who knows? And she won't take her medicines," he added under his breath, so Sigifrith had to lean down to catch his words. "She says it's heathen sorcery. I hope Brunichild is more sensible."

"Who's Brunichild?"

"The daughter of Theoderid, the king of a tribe of Goths who have settled around Tolosa as *foederates*. We knew this would be coming, and so we've been readying ourselves toward offering an alliance."

"Oh. Well . . . congratulations, then."

"Save it till the wedding feast," Gundahari advised him. "It's bad luck to praise a maiden too quickly, you know." Then he laughed. "I've heard that she's one of the fairest women north of the Vandals' Sea. It's surprising she's stayed unmarried for so long. She's seventeen, the same age as you."

Gundahari's last words were lost in the glittering stream of wine pouring from Gundrun's pitcher into the goblet before Sigifrith. His chest tightened on his breath as the Gebicung maiden returned to her own place beside her mother. When Sigifrith sat up straight, it was easy for him to look over Gundahari and Grimhild to see the soft gleam of torchlight from Gundrun's hair.

"Sigifrith," Gundahari hissed, elbowing him in the ribs, "you're being very rude. Sit down and act like a human being, for the gods' sakes. You'll see her every day for the rest of your life, after all."

Sigifrith allowed himself to slump down till he was closer to the height of Gundahari and Hagan. The serving thralls were bringing platters of sizzling meat to the high table; though summer had just begun, the smell of crisped fat rising from the roasted beef was as rich as if the cattle had been feeding in good fields for months. There was plenty of fresh honey-sweetened bread and soft cheese to go with the meat, as well as crimson strawberries heaped in bowls of Roman-wrought silver.

"Is this also your Ostara feast?" Sigifrith asked between mouthfuls. As the food calmed his raging hunger, it was also beginning to steady out the faint dizziness that had blurred the back of his mind since his arrival in Worms. He had not been able to eat his fill like this, he thought, since his victory feast in Saxony.

"This? Oh, no. We had that a few days ago, just after the full Moon. It's surprising how rich the Gaulish lands are, you know."

Sigifrith nodded absently. The full Moon . . . but surely the Moon had been full the night he slew Fadhmir, and he had not been on the river more than a day and a half on his way back to Worms? It seemed to him that he had wandered redeless after walling Ragin up with his brother in the Dragon's Crag, but not for so long.

"I'll be back in a moment," he muttered, rising from his seat.

As Sigifrith relieved himself in a corner of the garden, he looked up at the sky. The Moon had waned almost to half, floating low and golden between the gathering streaks of black cloud like a frost-brightened leaf.

The thought that he had somehow missed something scratched at the back of Sigifrith's mind, dry and light as a dead twig down the back of his tunic. He pushed it away, retying his breeches. When he thought of that night, it was too easy for him to see the golden coins over Ragin's stone eyes again, or feel the terrible wrenching in his guts as he realized that his foster-father had betrayed him to his death. Better, he thought, to leave the dead resting as still within the white howe of his skull as they were within Fadhmir's iron-bound cave above the Rhine.

When Sigifrith came back into the hall, the twanging of a harp and the sound of a man's strong baritone voice were already rising over the noises of eating and talking.

Long the Wyrm lay   in his lair coiling
on treasures uncounted,   on treachery's gold.
High upon head   the Helm of Awe burned
that none be so fierce   fighting to dare him.

Flame-sparks he spewed   and sprayed out his bale
when atheling-bold Sigifrith   stood up before him.
Grim though the dragon   Gram's blade was matchless
—each hating the other—faced hero and Wyrm.
Mighty the struggle   and mountain roots shook
as fire blazed up,   far away, men saw clear . . .

Grimhild sat with her chin in her palm, pointed nail tapping against her sharp cheekbone and a lingering smile on her face as she glanced from the warp-skulled singer to Sigifrith and back again. Gundrun's eyes were fixed on Sigifrith alone, like a ray of sunlight warming the spot on his chest where her gaze seemed to be resting. Gundahari was talking to Hagan across Sigifrith's empty seat; Costbera sat huddled inside her cloak, her luminous eyes shut.

When the eating was done, Sigifrith brought the bag of treasures that he and Hagan had chosen from Fadhmir's hoard out from beneath his chair. He stood, drawing himself up to his full height, and held the bag out at arm's length. "See, I have not come empty-handed to my kin," he said. "I have brought you these gifts from Fadhmir's hoard. I hope they will please you."

He reached into the bag, feeling around till he found the broad rim of

Gundrun's brooch. With a turn of his wrist, he displayed the golden disc upon his palm. "Gundrun, this is for you—as all I have is to be yours."

She stared at the fire-glittering gold, the running figures of doe and stag around the dark garnet, with her mouth half-open—as suddenly everyone in the hall was staring at it, as though the round brooch had become a whirlpool of light drawing their gazes into itself. Sigifrith walked around Gundahari and Grimhild to lay the piece into Gundrun's hand. He closed her fingers gently on the rim. "The gold will never be as fair or as dear as the woman who bears it," he said softly to her.

"Thank you," she whispered, looking at the brooch in disbelief. "Oh, it's beautiful."

Sigifrith drew out Gundahari's gold-set boar's tooth next. "For you, my brother. Frith in times of stillness and warding in times of war—and my troth with it."

Sigifrith could see the old scar twisting white across Gundahari's browned forearm as the Burgundian king raised his hand to take his gift.

"May you ever stay with us," Gundahari answered hoarsely, his fingers clenching around the gold chain. The beads of sweat beneath his hair and beard gleamed as red as drops of molten metal in the torchlight. A strange pang, sharp as the taste of copper, twinged through Sigifrith as he watched his sworn brother drape the pendant about his neck and uncurl his hands from the pure soft metal. Then the sparks of the gold no longer reflected in Gundahari's hazel eyes. He grinned at Sigifrith. "Thank you. I wish I had thought of a gift for you."

"What more could you give me than you have already?"

"Well . . ."

To Grimhild, Sigifrith gave a girdle clasp carved with a design of whirling interlace; to Gernot and Gisalhari, torcs twined out of gold wire, finally presenting Hagan with the eagle-headed arm-ring. At the same time, Sigifrith gave him the delicate brooch wrought with filigreed spirals that they had chosen for Costbera, letting Hagan himself offer the present to his wife.

Costbera's hand trembled as she accepted the brooch from her husband. She thanked both of them in a choking voice, moving as if to pin it to her cloak. Then her face paled to an odd greenish white color, her hands shaking so violently that the brooch flew out of her grasp. It struck the stone floor with a light, musical clang, skittering a little way along before fetching up against one of the sheepskin rugs that lay scattered about. Hands to mouth, she got to her feet and hurried clumsily from the hall.

Hagan rose to pick up the brooch. "I'm sorry, Sigifrith. My frowe is not well. I think she would not have tried to stay so long for anyone of less worth. If you don't mind, I will take my leave and see her home."

"Of course." Sigifrith gestured helplessly. "Go, go on. I hope she gets better soon."

"Thank you. It should be easier for her when our child is born."

Hagan followed his wife's path out of the hall. Gundahari shook his head, sighing. "I'm sorry about that," he said. "It was bad timing. I think she was holding it in all evening."

"Never mind."

"You're not insulted, are you?" Gundahari went on, leaning forward. This close, Sigifrith could see the spider-threads of red lacing through the whites of his eyes and the tiny creases of strain raying out from their corners. "She'll apologize as soon as she's feeling better. I hope you don't think she meant to seem ungrateful or anything?"

"Why would I think that?" Sigifrith asked.

"Some people . . . " The Burgundian king sighed, rubbing the creases from his broad forehead. "It's dealing with these messengers and political people. It's making me nervous about every word anyone says. It was easier when we were just going out to fight. Now it seems as though everyone around me is the kind of person who can find a black dog in a dark room on a moonless night, even when there's no dog there. You know what I mean?"

Sigifrith's laugh sounded like a jangle of tin in his own ears. He drained his goblet quickly, holding it up to be filled again.

"So, tell me about Fadhmir," Gundahari went on. "I saw his track once, that scorch of poison and fire . . . How did you manage to face him without being burnt to death? The old wanderer told us only that you had slain him in single combat."

"I didn't quite face him," Sigifrith admitted. He took a swallow of the sweet wine, leaning back in his chair. Big and sturdy as it was, he could hear the wood creaking beneath him. "Whatever you may have heard about me, even I'm not that unwise. Ragin told me to dig a pit . . . "

He told the story of how he had killed the dragon, and Gundahari listened, enthralled.

"And you bathed in the dragon's blood after being burnt by it," he said wonderingly when Sigifrith's tale was done. "Does it really keep you from being wounded? How?"

Sigifrith grinned, picking up his eating knife. "Test the edge."

Gundahari rasped the ball of his thumb across the blade's glittering rim. "It's sharp," he agreed. "You're not going to . . . ?"

"Watch this," Sigifrith said, taking the knife and drawing it hard across his bare wrist. It passed over his skin like the brush of a leaf; when he took it away the point was bent slightly out of line and the edge was as dull as if he had tried to scratch Gram's star iron with it. He sheathed the knife and stood, walking to one of the fires along the edge of the hall and reaching in. When he blew the ash off, the live coal in his hand flared rose-orange beneath his breath.

"That's very impressive," Grimhild said, her eyes glittering like mica. "So there is nothing that can wound you?"

"Not that I know of," Sigifrith answered. He tossed the coal back into the fire, a shower of sparks scattering from its glowing path. Taking his seat again, he raised his goblet, holding the glass carefully so as not to crush it.

"But what I have won is for Gundrun: that I might be worthy of the highest of atheling-maids. Hail to my betrothed! I drink to her, and to our wedding." The moment his goblet's base touched the smooth oak of the table again, he added, "How soon can the hall be ready for it?"

Grimhild looked over her elder son's head at Sigifrith. Her eyes narrowed as she turned them away from his keen glance. "Rather more slowly, Sigifrith, please," she said. "Famed and mighty as you are, certain things have to be seen to in their due course."

"What things? Tell me, and I swear I will do what I may to bring our wedding about more swiftly."

"You are swift to swear," Grimhild murmured, her words almost lost among the rumble of Gundahari's thanes talking. "One would hardly think you had been Ragin's foster-son."

"What must I do?" Sigifrith repeated, more urgently. He rose to his feet, staring down at the slender woman before him. Grimhild tilted her head back so far that the thin band of gold about her wound braid began to slide off.

"Please sit down, Sigifrith," she said, one delicate hand gesturing him to his chair. "Surely we shall have plenty of time to talk about matters of state. This is a feast of joy, after all, in honor of your deeds and your return to us."

"If I could, I would hold the wedding this very night," Sigifrith answered her. "At least tell me when it should be, if you will."

Grimhild turned her head, considering Gundrun. Sigifrith could see the maiden's knuckles white on the hilt of her eating knife as she looked at her mother. The two women's voices rustled as high as dry leaves above the sounds of the feast, but Sigifrith could not hear their words for a moment. Then Gundrun's sharp-edged alto cut through her mother's murmuring, "You never said anything like that before! You said . . . "

As Grimhild grasped her daughter by the shoulders, Gisalhari leaned over to Gernot. Although he was speaking straight into the other boy's ear, Sigifrith distinctly heard him say, "They're fighting again! I think it's going to be a good one this time."

Gundahari leaned behind Sigifrith to thump his cousin before he could say anything else. "We've tried to teach him not to piss in the house, but that doesn't work either," the Burgundian explained to his guest. "Ignore him if you can."

Gundrun twisted herself from her mother's grasp, standing up and bracing her fists on her hips. Her square cheekbones were flushed with the firelight that paled the blue tinge from her light eyes. "I don't want to wait any longer either," she declared. "Either you tell him now or I will, so may Frija help me!"

Sigifrith saw Grimhild's shoulders rise and fall in a sigh. "Gundahari, tell your sister to sit down so that we can talk about this in a fitting manner," the queen commanded. She muttered something else, more quietly; the only word Sigifrith caught was the sound of his own name.

Sigifrith looked into Gundrun's eyes; standing while he sat, she was only a little taller than he. "It will be soon enough," he told her. He tried to speak as firmly as he could, but he could hear his voice shaking as his ribcage arched like a drawn bow under her glance.

After a moment the flush on Gundrun's cheeks brightened and she dropped her eyes. "You swear?" she asked, the quaver of her voice aching through Sigifrith's body.

"I do," he replied. "Do you doubt that I can do whatever has to be done?"

"Oh, no!" Gundrun's glance flickered over Sigifrith's face again, and behind her gaze flowed a sparkling wave of the light-headed dizziness he had felt when he drained the first draught she had given him. "But I've waited so long," she added softly. "And I'm not sure . . ."

Grimhild laid her hand on Gundrun's arm and drew her back. This time, the maiden let her mother guide her to her seat.

"It will be better if sooner done, I suppose," Grimhild said. "Well then: we have been consulting, and found that it would be unfitting for Gundrun to be married while Gundahari has no queen to sit beside him and bear him heirs. Therefore we are afraid that you and Gundrun must wait to wed until the day of Gundahari's marriage to Brunichild the daughter of Theoderid."

"But when will that be?" Sigifrith asked, a thin-stringed note vibrating through his voice.

"We had sent messengers to her father before, but it will be needful for Gundahari to go himself for the betrothal to be made, let alone sealed. Matters can be so difficult with these newly settled *foederates* . . . We had thought he might go sometime soon, perhaps, though no day had been set; we were trying to gather a band of athelings whose births and fame might be high enough to make them a fitting escort for Gundahari and his bride."

"Let us go tomorrow!" Sigifrith cried. "You, I and Hagan, Gundahari. Surely the three of us will be enough to bring Brunichild to the Rhine, if you think my birth and fame are high enough for you."

Gundahari stood and wrapped his arms around Sigifrith in a great bear-hug. "So we shall, then!" he answered joyfully. "My brother, I would trust no one at my back more than I trust you and Hagan. It's an honor to me to have Sigifrith Fadhmir's-Bane with me."

"Are you not tired from all you have done?" Grimhild asked, her voice clear and precise as breaking glass. "Surely you will want to rest for a few days."

"I need no more rest," Sigifrith declared. "I could go tonight, if you wished to."

"I think tomorrow would probably be better," Grimhild suggested. "Gundahari must have time to ready himself at least a little. And there are all sorts of things you will need . . ." She tidied her skirts around her as she got up. "Will you excuse Gundrun and I? We must set our women to work, if you're to be able to leave tomorrow."

"Of course," Sigifrith said. Then he remembered Hagan's rede, and beckoned Grimhild closer to him. "May I talk to you later tonight?" he asked her quietly. "There is something I need to know about, and I think it would be better if we were alone."

The curve of a smile rippled across Grimhild's lips for a moment and was gone. "I am always willing to speak to you," she said. "Aren't you of our kin? It delights us that you are here, and we wish to lay all good things before you. I shall be your mother and Gundahari and Hagan are your brothers."

Sharp-featured and small-boned as Grimhild was, Sigifrith thought that he could see something of Gundrun in the firm set of her jaw and the stance of her feet—as balanced as a warrior's—beneath her deep red skirts. It seemed to him as though the warmth within him rose and spilled in a flood like a great wave breaking over the side of a ship. He did not know what to say, but Grimhild seemed too brittle for him to embrace without breaking her bones, so he sat staring at her and feeling stupid.

Grimhild's fingers brushed against Sigifrith's cheek in a light pat, as dry and fragile as twigs at winter's beginning. "Perhaps when you and Gundahari are finished, you will let Hagan know your plans. I should think that he, too, may want to get ready for your journey. After all, he has a wife with child to arrange for."

Sigifrith rose. "Shall we go, then?" he asked Gundahari. "Or if you want to stay, maybe one of the boys could show me where Hagan's house is."

"No, I'll come with you. He'll take it better if we both tell him."

Two steps brought Sigifrith before Gundrun. "Till later, then," he said.

Her fingertips had barely brushed his before Grimhild's sideways glance pinned them. "Till later," Gundrun murmured.

The pathways of Worms were laid out in neat intersecting lines, marked by pavements of cobblestones and lit by long torches at the street corners. Deep grooves had been worn into the clay between the stone walks by the wheels of carts and hooves of horses. "We've had Roman workmen in to do most of the work," Gundahari said. "It was a barracks town for a long time after real Romans didn't live here anymore, and it had been ill-kept before my father got it. I've done my best to keep up everything that Gebica started and take it further along."

"Why doesn't Hagan live in your hall?" Sigifrith asked, stepping neatly over a dark heap and wrinkling his nose at the smell that wafted up from it.

"Because he prefers being alone. I think he likes it better down by the river anyway. He can go out and creep around at night without disturbing anybody except his frowe."

Hagan's house had been a Roman villa, built of whitewashed clay smoothed over neatly fitted stones. Smooth pillars held up the roof over a tiled porch. Though the door's knocker was crusted with greenish black corrosion, Sigifrith could see that it had been the bronze mask of a man with wild, curly hair and beard. If there had been tiles on the porch floor, they had been removed to leave bare paving stones.

Gundahari and Sigifrith looked at each other, both unwilling to knock. Then Sigifrith raised the knocker, clashing the bronze beard three times against the metal plate beneath.

The door opened outward, sliding smoothly on its hinges. A candle cast its light over the thin features and fair curls of the girl who opened it, its flame leeching the blood from her face and shining white from the slender silvery thrall-ring around her neck. Seeing the two of them, she dipped her knees and head in a curious sort of bob that Sigifrith had never seen before.

"Greeting and welcome, Fro Sigifrith, King Gundahari," she said to them. The voice that rose from her thin throat was startlingly rich and warm, like Gaulish wine sweetened with honey. "What do you wish here?"

"Greetings, Ada," Gundahari replied. "Is Hagan at home?"

"I fear that the fro has gone out. Would you care to come in and wait? Or is there any message that you would like to leave for him?"

"Tell him to ready himself and his horse for a journey. We are leaving for Tolosa tomorrow morning."

"It shall be done," she answered with another of her bobs.

"Is the frowe Costbera better?" Sigifrith asked.

Ada lowered her head, glancing at Sigifrith through thick blond eyelashes. "She is sleeping, if you please. King Gundahari, I know that your brother would bid me to tell you to carry his thanks to your mother for the medicine which she gave to Costbera. He gave it to her this evening when it seemed to him that her pain had become too great for her safely to bear, and it has eased her greatly."

"Did she take it willingly?"

"She took it, King Gundahari."

"Will it be all right for Hagan to leave her alone?" questioned Sigifrith. "If she's having so much trouble, shouldn't he stay with her?"

"Of course the frowe will be saddened at parting from her husband," the thrall-girl murmured smoothly. "But she will be well attended. I think, Fro Sigifrith, that you will have no need to trouble yourself about the frowe Costbera during her husband's absence."

"Oh. Well . . . that's good."

"Now if you will excuse me? I have a great deal to do before tomorrow. Be well, Fro Sigifrith, King Gundahari."

Gundahari made a gesture of dismissal, and Ada closed the door.

"I've told Hagan that his wife needs more than one girl to take care of her, but he won't hear of it," Gundahari said as they walked away. "He seems to think . . . well, never mind what he thinks. He does it far more than is really good for him, anyway."

"Hmm."

Sigifrith and Gundahari walked down along the side of the Rhine for a while. Here, the only light was that from the torches in their hands and the paleness of the lowering Moon. The river seemed to flow and splash more loudly than it had in the daylight, the waters swollen with the melted snows of winter's end flowing down from the mountains. Here and there lacings of flood foam gleamed white through the blackness, showing for moments before the ripples drowned them in darkness. Sigifrith found the sound of the waters oddly comforting, their rhythmic rushing soothing the tremors that still twitched through him now and again.

"Are you planning to stay with us after the wedding?" Gundahari asked after a while. "You know there'll always be a place for you here."

"I doubt it. King Alapercht is getting older, and I don't really like the thought of leaving him too long. One day I'll have to lead his warband and rule the Alamannic folk, after all."

"Our lands aren't that far apart. You could rule the Alamanns as well from Worms, and Gundrun would rather stay here with the folk she's known all her life."

"How could I rule the Alamanns from Worms? Their king has always lived among them. I don't know why that should change."

"I think the day of scattered tribes is coming to its end, and the ones who will be victorious are the ones who realize it soonest. What are the Alamanns but a tribe that started as a federation—Alamanns, "all the peoples"—no more than six or seven generations ago? I've had a book read to me that was written by a Roman about the Germanii back almost as far as the days of Harimann of the Cheruscii, and he names scores of tribes in the north where the Saxons are and all through the other lands where single folks like the Alamanns and the Franks now rule. Think what we could win together, you and I, while the Huns and the other tribes who came east are busy harrying Rome! No fame would equal ours."

They turned away from the Rhine's slippery bank, walking through the muddy clay of the street. The Moon was hidden behind the rows of houses around them, and the torches in their hands were beginning to burn low.

"Perhaps we could see . . . at least while Alapercht lives," Sigifrith added thoughtfully. "After all, he is in good health and his father Chilpirich reached a great age."

"You can think about it anyway. Hai, it's not far from here to a house that has the best women in Worms. Would you like to . . . ?"

"I don't want any woman except Gundrun," Sigifrith answered.

"Then why did you take so long getting here?" Gundahari said teasingly. "Folk were starting to wonder if you still wanted her."

"Well . . . I hardly thought about her in the last few years. I don't know why. But now that I've seen her again I couldn't imagine living without her— as if she were my own shield arm. I'd do anything to keep her by me."

"Even stay in Worms after the wedding?"

"Even so," Sigifrith said finally, then, "Why not? Alapercht holds his lands in peace; he doesn't need a young man looking over his shoulder. I fear . . . I think I was more harm to him than help when I took half his warband up north and came home with less than half of that."

"We'll have plenty for you to do," Gundahari told him. "You won't need to worry about languishing away in peace."

They walked through the gates to Gundahari's hall. "This is where we part ways for a while," the Burgundian king said. "I've got some things to take care of. You go on, any of the thralls will show you where your room is. If you want anything, you only have to ask. Oh, by the way—where did you put those bags you brought with you?"

"They're in the stables. Grani can guard them better than anyone, I think."

"All right. But you don't mean to take them with us, do you?"

"No, I suppose not. Where should we put them?"

"I've got a good underground storehouse. I don't know what the Romans used it for, but it's built of solid stone beneath the earth and there's only one key. Would that be all right?"

"I don't see why not."

"Good. When you've finished talking to Grimhild, send someone to find me and we'll see about moving them. I don't know about you, but I think I'll sleep better when they're locked safely away."

Grimhild was sitting on a three-legged stool next to the fire burning by the north wall of Sigifrith's room, her frail hands fluttering over a piece of embroidery. A decanter of deep red wine and two full goblets rested on the ivory-inlaid ebony of the table before her. She looked up as he came in, her eyes narrow cauldrons of blackness in her sharp-angled face.

"Come and sit down, Sigifrith," she said, patting the carven bear's-paw arm of the great chair beside her stool. "Did you find Hagan?"

"His thrall-girl said he had gone out," Sigifrith told her, sitting down and picking up his goblet. The dark wine had a musky scent, but he didn't want to say anything; for all he knew, the best southern wines might smell strange. He drank it in a gulp, the full plummy richness of its taste only bursting over his tongue when he had swallowed it. Grimhild refilled the glass and he drank again, more carefully.

"It's from the finest of our Gaulish lands," she said. "The true dark grapes won't grow as well here by the Rhine, I'm afraid. I suppose it's the price we pay for not having to swelter eight months out of the year. Do you like it?"

"Very much. Thank you."

Grimhild settled herself more comfortably on her stool, swirling her own wine around in her goblet and sipping at it. "What can I do to aid you, then? You said there was something you needed to know about."

Sigifrith drew the Helm of Awe out of his belt pouch, laying it over the black-and-white squares of the tabletop. Like an adder about to strike, Grimhild drew back from the glitter of its golden links. Her breath hissed in between her teeth.

"So the songs spoke true," she muttered. "I thought . . . Do you know how to use this?"

"No. I tried to give it to Hagan, but he said that I ought to keep it and that I needed to ask you how to use it."

"So," she said again. She reached out her hand toward it, moving as gingerly as if her fingertips were nearing a burning coal. Her hand stopped just before the points of her nails touched the metal.

"It would take a brave man to meet you when this is on your head," Grimhild said musingly. "But you have no need to awe anyone with more than the keenness of your gaze and the strength of your body. I think what you really want to know is the way to use this as Fadhmir did, in changing your shape."

"Yes." Sigifrith picked the Helm of Awe up, dangling it gently from his hand. The links clinked together, their piercing note ringing and echoing from the glassware like high bells clashing against each other till Grimhild raised her hands to her ears and frowned at him. He laid the golden mail down and stilled the goblets and pitcher with a gentle touch.

"With a thing of might like that, magic is much simpler," Grimhild said. "But you still have to judge your degree. The easiest way of shape-shifting is to change your soul and fare forth from your body. If you wish to do that, all you must do is put the Helm of Awe on your head and think of how you are changing—feel the change in every bone and sinew. Then it is an easy thing to fly or swim or run forth from your earthly body. The danger there is that you may stay in your borrowed hide too long; then all your might will feed your soul till, like Fadhmir's, it has become a real thing within the Middle-Garth and your body, like his, has starved to death. But there may come a time when you need to change your seeming. Then you will do the same, but instead of going forth you will strengthen your soul more and more till it shows through your body—till at last your form is completely hidden. Though you will hear and see according to the shape you have chosen, you cannot do anything which is not natural to you because your body will only be hidden, not altered. You can take a bird's seeming, but not fly without leaving your earthly form; you may take a fish's seeming in the water, but your body will drown. It is very easy to change your seeming to that of another human, harder to become something else. The third is true shape-shifting: if you change your soul or your seeming, and keep it so within your body long enough, then everything will change in the course of time. But that takes longer than you would ever wish for— and I think it is a kind of madness that you need not fear. Still, you must be wary of yourself whenever you walk in the worlds outside the ring of Middle-Garth, if you wish to come back as a human again."

Grimhild stopped, drinking deeply of the wine that seemed black and fathomless as her eyes in the fire's darkening shadows.

"And that's all I have to do? Could I do it now?"

"You could. If you wish, I shall watch to be sure you come back safely."

Sigifrith was about to refuse when he thought that it might be good to have someone who could tell him if the might of the Helm had really worked to change his shape. "Please," he said.

He put the Helm of Awe on his head, the plate of gold graven with the eight-spoked wheel of tridents resting between his eyes.

"It will be better if you lie down to do this," Grimhild said, her sharp voice suddenly echoing as loudly as a bird's shriek between his ears. "Lie down and close your eyes."

Sigifrith lay down on his back, stretching to his full length. In a dim chamber of his mind, he marked that the huge bed must have been made for him; but that thought was already being washed away by the flow of might tingling through his skull from the plate of gold on his forehead. It seemed to him that he could feel his arms spreading and stretching as long feathers sprouted, his feet crooking into powerful claws, his nose and mouth jutting out into a lordly beak as his whole shape shrank to the size of a hawk. Remembering Grimhild's words, he drew more and more of the Helm's might into him till he could no longer feel his human body on the bed. Opening long-sighted eyes, he looked at her blurry shape before him and opened his beak in a screech of triumph. He could not see the body beneath him, though he knew it must be there; it seemed as though a hidden thread still bound him to it.

"Well done, my golden hawk," Grimhild said. To Sigifrith's hawk ears, her voice was startlingly loud, its glass-smoothness rimmed with roughly broken edges. Her body was ringed with a shifting glow of red-tinged gold shot through with flashes of green. "Now you may leave your body and fly, but be careful not to go too far. If you don't come back of your own will, you shall come back when I speak your name thrice."

Sigifrith spread his wings and leapt upward, the might that had cloaked his body falling away to leave it lying beneath him. He hovered for a moment, looking down at the huge long-haired warrior, pale and still as a statue, who lay with only the slightest rise and fall of his chest to show that he still lived. The Helm of Awe seemed to be a net of darkness now, the graven piece in the center black as a hole through the forehead of an empty skull.

He beat his wings, rising easily up through the roof and out into the night sky. The Rhine below was a dark green streak of shining might, glimmering with the cold silver streaks of fish and blotted black where darker things hid. He could see people wandering through the streets of Worms; looking closely, he saw a thin tabby cat scampering through the grass at the river's edge. Her eyes glowed in the night like two tiny moons seen through the bottom of a wine glass; lithe as a snake she twisted and leapt, coming up from the weeds with a bundle of small black legs kicking feebly in her mouth. A dark shadow blotted her from Sigifrith's sight for a moment; she turned and fled, a fluid streak through the grass.

Sigifrith floated higher, tilting his wings to circle on the wind that bore him up. He could see the snow on the peaks of the southern mountains. It would not be so far to fly home, he thought, to see Alapercht and Herwodis again—maybe even to bear them word that he lived and was well?

He began to wing strongly along the Rhine, the wind flowing through his feathers and around him as if he were swimming against the river's stream.

Soon he could see the staves that marked Gundahari's marches below, but then he heard the distant voice calling his name.

"Sigifrith!" Grimhild said once; and he stopped, hovering in the air, unable to go farther. "Sigifrith!" she called again, and without thought he fell into a long dive, tearing through the sky and swooping downward toward the lights of Gundahari's hall. "Sigifrith!" and he slammed into his own body, gulping in great gasps of air as he pressed at his aching chest with human hands and blinked human eyes against the sudden blindness of the firelight.

Grimhild was stroking his forehead, gently pulling the Helm of Awe away from him and laying it on the table. He sat up, catching her in his gaze. "Why did you bring me back so soon?" he asked, the winds of the height aching in his voice. "I was about to go . . ."

"Too far," Grimhild said kindly. "Strong as you are, Sigifrith, you must be careful not to strain yourself at this."

She filled his goblet again and put it into his hand. His senses still unnaturally keen, he had to sip at it carefully; the least sniff sent its rich musky fruit bursting through his mouth and nose as though a hundred bottles had been boiled down into the one mouthful. Slowly the hammering in his chest faded away and he could breathe easily.

"You should not try this again for a few days," Grimhild advised him. "It would really be best if you waited to fare forth till your return from Tolosa, so I can keep watch for you till you have become more used to it. If you are very careful and discreet, you may practice shifting your seeming in private along the way, but you must be sure to let no one else know what you are doing unless it becomes absolutely needful. Do you understand?"

Sigifrith thought of the way people looked sideways when Grimhild's name was mentioned, the coldness that had come into the voices of Alapercht and Chilpirich, Herwodis and Perchte, when they spoke of the Burgundian queen; and he thought he understood very clearly. No one openly named her seith-woman, but the words lay beneath her name like an adder in a rotting log, and there were worse names for a man who worked that sort of sorcery.

"I'll be careful," he promised.

A muffled knock sounded on the door. "Sigifrith?" Gundahari's voice called, sounding very thin through the weight of stone and wood. "Are you ready?"

"Go on," Grimhild told him. "I think you know all you need to for now."

Sigifrith followed Gundahari down to the stables where Grani stood guarding the gold. As they neared the colt's stall, the shadows seemed to thicken beneath the torchlight and solidify into Hagan's shape. A hooded dark cloak muffled the clinking of his byrnie and hid his single eye in shadow; a number of large sacks lay folded over his arm.

"What are you doing here?" Sigifrith asked.

"I was told that we were leaving tomorrow. I knew you would be coming to move your hoard, and I am the keeper of the key to the king's storeroom. I thought I would save you the trouble of trying to find me again."

"All right."

Sigifrith stepped forward into the darkness of Grani's stall, stroking his horse's flank. "There, it's all right," he whispered into the cupped ear. "We're going to move the treasure to a place where it'll be safe while we're gone. You don't really want to carry it halfway down Gaul and back, do you?"

Grani whinnied softly in answer, butting his head against Sigifrith's shoulder like a velvety battering-ram. Sigifrith laughed. "Hush, we've got work to do—yes, you as well."

Sigifrith took the sacks from Hagan as Gundahari handed his torch to his brother. Crouching in the fresh straw, the two of them loaded the bags with gold.

"Not too full," Hagan warned Sigifrith when he laid the first sack aside. "The seams will break under the weight if you fill them all the way." He stuck the torch into a socket on the wall and slipped into the shadows again; but even through the ringing of the gold, Sigifrith heard the sound of horses being saddled. By the time Sigifrith and Gundahari had finished their work, two steeds stood ready before the stall.

Though Gundahari struggled with all his strength to lift the bags, and would not own the weight too much for him, it was Sigifrith who had to do most of the loading, just as Grani bore most of the gold. The floorboards creaked threateningly under the horses' weight as Sigifrith and the Burgundians led their steeds out, and the last board splintered beneath Grani's hooves.

Once they were outside, Hagan turned the torch upside down and plunged its flame into the earth.

"Why did you do that?" Sigifrith asked him, rather annoyed. "How are we going to find our way?"

He could just glimpse Hagan raising his hand in a beckoning gesture. "Follow me closely. It will be better if we are not seen. Be as still as you can."

Sigifrith led Grani by the reins, following the Burgundian's cloaked figure and his steed through the trees of the garden. As they passed through an arch in the wall, the paving stones changed to chill earth sinking beneath Sigifrith's bare feet; instead of the neat shapes of the trees within, a wild wyrm-tangle of branches grew around and above the dirt pathway, the twisted black limbs blotting out the faint stars. The creaking and rubbing of branches in the wind wove through the rhythmic sound of Gundahari's hoarse breathing; the crackling of twigs and fallen leaves under their feet and the horses' hooves might have been no more than the nightly struggles of fox and bird, owl and mouse. Beside his steadily plodding horse, Hagan seemed to melt in and out of the night and the thin mist, leaving his steed unguided for long breaths at a time as he glided along the twisting path before Sigifrith and Gundahari.

The whisper of the wind through the trees grew louder as they walked, rushing along and flowing into the sounds of the river. When they stopped by an outcropping of black-mossed stone, the wood and the darkness hid the Rhine's banks, but Sigifrith could feel the cool river-mist around him and hear the waters close by.

"Here," Hagan said, his harsh voice muffled by his hooded cloak as he bent down, scraping a layer of dirt and old leaves away from something with his bare hands. "Here, behind these rocks."

Sigifrith heard the click of a well-oiled lock, followed by the smooth singing of metal sliding across metal and the grating of steel on stone. Iron hinges rang as Hagan heaved a wide iron plate up and over beside him.

"Set those down," the younger Burgundian commanded. "Sigifrith, you must get in there so we can lower the gold to you."

The three of them set to unloading the horses, heaving the sacks down carefully. When all the bags lay beside the hole, Sigifrith leapt in without a second thought.

The fall was longer than he had thought it would be, half again his own height. Hard stone shocked up the bones of his legs through the numb soles of his feet as he landed in a half-crouch on the storeroom floor. Against the blackness surrounding him, the circle of misty night sky above seemed very bright.

"Are you all right?" Gundahari's worried voice floated down to him.

"I'm fine," Sigifrith answered. His words boomed eerily low and hollow against the stone walls, as though he were speaking through the deep brass length of a Roman tuba. "Are you going to throw the gold down, or will I have to come up and carry it myself?"

Sigifrith heard only a muttered grunt from above. Then a shadow blotted out the dim brightness of the hole above him. He stood to his full height, reaching upward; his fingertips just brushed against cold iron.

"Are you ready?" Hagan asked.

"Let it down."

The soft cloth of the first bag settled into Sigifrith's hands, the loose gold slithering about within it like a nest of hard-muscled adders as he tried to get a firmer grip. Gundahari and Hagan lowered it carefully, easing more and more of its weight onto him till he called out, "I've got it!"

"Are you sure?" Gundahari queried.

"I'm sure."

Sigifrith heaved the bag of gold out of their hands, letting it down onto the stone floor. "I'm ready for the next one," he told them. "Are you?"

"Give us a minute," said Gundahari. "You don't want us to drop it on you, do you?"

"I'm not worried. I could catch two at a time, if you'd toss them down here."

"Shit on that," the Burgundian king replied in disgust. "I'm not going to be the one to tell Gundrun how we squished her betrothed. You think we could ever turn our backs on her again? And we would have to sleep some-

STEPHAN GRUNDY

☩ 474

time, you know. No, if you want to get us killed, you can climb out of there and do it yourself."

Sigifrith thought that Hagan said something else then, but his words were no clearer than the grating of iron on stone.

"All right, you do it," Gundahari told his brother, his voice echoing faintly around Sigifrith. Then the younger Burgundian's shadow was gone from the rim of the hole above Sigifrith's head, leaving only the black silhouette of Gundahari standing with his hands on his hips and staring into the darkness of the storeroom. "Ready?" he called.

"I'm ready."

The second bag blacked out all but a few faint cracks of dimness as Gundahari took one end from his brother and the two of them let it down into Sigifrith's hands. He took it away from them and set it beside the first.

By the time they lowered the last bag, the Burgundians seemed near the end of their strength; they very nearly did drop it on Sigifrith, but he caught it easily enough.

"Stand back, I'm coming out!" Sigifrith crouched and sprang, head and shoulders bursting out of the hole. He grabbed on to the grassy earth, trying to hoist himself out, but it gave way beneath his weight and the strength of his grasp, collapsing in toward the edge of the hole as he began to slide back.

Gundahari grabbed his right wrist in both hands, Hagan his left. The two Burgundians dug in their heels, pulling him out inch by inch. Sigifrith could feel the trembling of their muscles and wanted to help, but he knew that he could not grip their arms to pull himself up without breaking them, so he merely let himself be dragged across the rim of stone below the earth's surface and up. When he finally stood and tried to brush himself off, the skin of his chest and thighs gleamed white through the tattered shreds of his tunic and breeches.

Gundahari and Hagan were both gasping from their labors. The king's breath was loud and hissing, his brother's as silent and rapid as the panting of a cat.

When Gundahari could speak easily again, he looked at Sigifrith and shook his head. "There might have been a brighter way to do that, you know. Just what do you think you're going to wear on the journey tomorrow?"

"Well . . . if you want to start without me, I could stay here for a day or two and then catch up with you."

"Fadhmir's hoard in your hands, and not a single thing to wear," Gundahari went on. Sigifrith could see the whiteness of his grin through his beard as the shorter man dropped his gaze to Sigifrith's feet. "And no shoes, either. Who else but Sigifrith would travel in state like this?"

"Stop teasing him, Gundahari," Hagan broke in. "If you don't, you may wake to find snakes in your blanket tomorrow morning. Remember, Sigifrith has no need to be afraid of picking up adders."

A shudder wriggled down the Burgundian king's back and he glanced away as if in embarrassment while Hagan hauled the iron lid back over the opening to the storeroom, bolted it and locked it. The keeper of the store-room looped the chain bearing the key over his neck and dropped it under byrnie and tunic, then began to scratch dirt and leaves over the portal until no sign of it could be seen.

"He only does this to torment me," Gundahari complained softly to Sig-ifrith. "He knows how much I hate snakes. I was bitten by an adder when I was four winters old. My father thought he'd have to cut my hand off if Grimhild's medicines didn't work."

"Oh. What am I going to wear?"

"You don't have to worry about that. Grimhild had clothes and shoes made to your size. We expected that you would be staying with us for a while, and we wanted to have everything you might need ready for you."

Hagan stood, wiping the dirt from his hands. "If we mean to leave early, we ought to go home now. There are things I have to do."

Gundahari put his hand to his mouth, quieting a yawn. "Yes, it's late. Come on, then."

They left silently, as they had come, leading their horses single file along Hagan's path through the wood to the archway in the wall of the garden around Gundahari's hall. None of the three spoke again until they had sta-bled the horses; then Hagan took his leave and slipped into the night.

Gundahari led Sigifrith to the room that had been given him. "Is there anything else you need?"

"I don't think so," Sigifrith answered.

"All right. Sleep well, my friend, and we'll meet again in the morning."

"Sleep well."

BRUNICHILD

Heavy gray mist cloaked the yard of the Burgundian hall so thickly that Sigifrith had to trust to his memory when his eyes failed, picking his way through the fog to the stables. He felt the cold only as a tingle in his face and hands; though a cloak of red wool wrought with golden wyrms around the hem was draped around his shoul-ders, he wore it for show rather than warmth. The boots Grimhild had ordered to be made for him were rather tight, rubbing against the outer joints of his feet and the ends of his toes, but the slight misfit was easy to put from his mind.

Grani's whinny guided him surely to the stable door and in. Well built though the stables were, the straw beneath his boots drooped with morning dampness and only a dim light filtered in through the open door. Sigifrith saddled and loaded Grani half by touch then led him out into the yard.

Boots clacked on tile as someone approached, but Sigifrith didn't recognize the shape moving through the mist till Gundahari was almost upon him. The Burgundian king was dressed plainly for traveling, wearing breeches woven of gray and white wool and a brown cloak over a dark green tunic. The brooch on his shoulder was a small circle of copper with a pin through it; but the tip of the gold-set boar's tooth Sigifrith had given him gleamed out of a fold in his cloak. A full pair of saddlebags was slung over his left arm, saddle and bridle over his right.

Gundahari looked first at Grani, then Sigifrith. "I see you're ready to go. Just give me a minute or two to saddle up, and I'll meet you out here."

"Where's Hagan?"

"He was up early. He'll meet us at the city gates. Is there anything else you need to do?"

"I can't think of anything."

"Let's get going, then." Gundahari went on into the stable and came out a few minutes later leading his brown horse.

The stallion looked askance at Sigifrith's steed; Gundahari hauled his head back as his teeth snapped near Grani's flank, clouting him lightly across the nose. "Hai! None of that. It's hard keeping Goti near other stallions," he explained to Sigifrith. "Especially ones that really are bigger than he is. There's something about it he can't bear to live with." He turned Goti's head, looking deep into one of the horse's brown eyes. "But you'll keep the peace on this trip, won't you, Goti? Yes, you will or we'll be eating horsemeat from here to Tolosa and back."

The stallion made a low, rumbling noise, shifting his forehooves as if readying himself to strike, but he followed Gundahari docilely enough as the two young men led their mounts out of the yard and on to the muddy streets of Worms.

As Gundahari had promised, Hagan was waiting by the city gates. Like his brother, he was clothed plainly for traveling; his byrnie was almost hidden by the cloak that covered his sword, and he carried a throwing spear in his hand. His hair was tied back by a leather thong knotted at the nape of his neck.

He nodded when he saw Sigifrith and Gundahari coming through the dripping arch of the gate, waiting for them to mount before he climbed onto his own horse.

"Which way are we going?" Sigifrith asked.

Hagan gestured toward the south, his pointing finger outstretched like a long white bone. "Near to the march between my brother's lands and yours, then bearing straight southwest. It's a rougher ride than following the Roman roads, and there's only one inn along our path, but it will get us there more quickly and with less trouble on the way."

"Do you really think that's necessary?" Gundahari asked, nudging his horse to a walk. "What do we have to be afraid of? What can you think of that the three of us can't handle?"

Hagan's single-eyed gaze slanted over to Sigifrith. "Would you rather get there sooner or later?"

"Sooner, of course. I don't mind sleeping on the ground or in someone's barn, if I have to."

"All right, I see I'm outnumbered," Gundahari sighed. Then, "Stop that, you wretch!" as Goti snapped at Grani's neck. He yanked his horse's head around, forcing him to circle off the road and come back on the other side of Hagan's chestnut gelding. "I think we'd better ride like this, if we don't want to have horse-fighting all the way."

The mists hung heavy all morning, thickening into a slow drizzle by noontime. The earth was too wet to sit for their midday meal, so Sigifrith, Gundahari and Hagan ate standing, leaning their backs against tree trunks cushioned by damp moss. They remounted quickly and rode on.

By late afternoon, the drizzle was a soft but endless rain. Their clothes were soaked and water dripped from their hair and the ends of their noses. Hagan sneezed twice, a startlingly ordinary sound.

"Shitty weather," Gundahari complained. "Too bad the old Sinwist isn't here anymore. You remember how folk used to say he had power over the wind and the clouds, Hagan?"

"Folk said a lot of things about him. You met him once, Sigifrith. What did you think?"

"I thought he was strange . . . I liked him. Who do you have as a chief gudhija now?"

Gundahari and Hagan looked at each other, then Gundahari turned his gaze back to Sigifrith.

"I haven't chosen one." A tic twitched at the corner of the Burgundian king's mouth, fierce as a small living thing. "Times are changing. The folk need different things . . . there's less place for the old ways. And what kind of leverage would it give Rome and our other neighbors against us, knowing that we had a *gudhija* who could not be set out of office and a king who could? It was different when we were just a tribe fighting to stay alive. Now Grimhild and I do most of the rites, and the gods have still blessed us with victory and frith" —he grinned at the pun on Sigifrith's name— "so who's to complain?"

"The old Sinwist taught no successor and left no chosen name behind him," Hagan added. "It had always been the way before, that the Sinwist adopted a son for himself and readied him to do his work after his own death. It was said that the ghosts of our folk showed him the one who was chosen; and this was the way it was done from the time we left Burgundarholm till our wanderings led us to the banks of the Rhine."

Sigifrith closed his eyes for a moment, trying to think. It seemed to him . . . vaguely he thought that . . . no, Ragin had never chanted runes to charm the weather, though he had carved their angular staves into steel and stone for his own reasons. Nor had he ever taught them to Sigifrith, though he had said once that he would.

Sigifrith shook his waist-long hair back, wringing wetness from its tangled waves. He laughed, spurring Grani ahead of the other two. Cold droplets of dirt and water splattered from the colt's hooves like little muddy hailstones. Gundahari's horse shied viciously from the spattering; Hagan wiped a bit of wet clay from his eyepatch, leaving an uncomfortable smear of reddish brown across the black cloth.

"Well, let's hurry, then!" Sigifrith called back to them. "Since we can't change the weather, we may as well move along. Who's for a race?"

Goti was already champing and tugging, eager to chase Grani. Gundahari leaned forward in the saddle, his eyes narrowing as if he already felt the rain-sharp wind of full gallop blowing in his face.

Hagan shook his head. "You'll wear out the horses."

"We can't be that far from the inn, anyway," Gundahari argued. "Come on!"

The Burgundian king touched his heels to the sides of his horse, urging him to a wildly splashing gallop through the ragged puddles of Grani's tracks. The sound of Grani's hooves drowned out the sounds of the chase in Sigifrith's ears and when he looked back Gundahari was only a far-off shape, as vague as a ghost of horseman and rider in the rain.

Sigifrith let his steed run for a while, glad to be free on the road with only the woods around him and Grani's powerful muscles moving evenly beneath his thighs. The first scents of wet summer earth and springing leaves were as rich and strengthening as the taste of roast boar, as sharp and sweet as the new bubbling feather-white wine at Winternights; and Sigifrith rode with the swiftness of a loosed hawk, his laughter torn from his mouth by the wind of Grani's running.

Although Gundahari was long out of sight, Sigifrith kept going till he saw the black wolf's-head sign of Guthrid's inn through the darkening gloom. The inn was in good repair, and the boy who came out to take the reins of Sigifrith's horse was clothed well. Sigifrith twitched Grani's reins out of the youth's freckled hand, saying, "Go on, boy, he won't be tended by anyone but me."

"Y . . . yes, Fro Sigifrith," the boy said, his hazel eyes staring in wonder from a long-jawed face. "What can I do?"

"Tell Guthrid to ready rooms for myself, King Gundahari and his brother Hagan," Sigifrith said, watching the boy's mouth open like the hungry beak of a young bird. "And have some warmed wine and a good fire ready as well. I expect that when Gundahari and Hagan get here they'll need it." He paused, a thought springing and growing in his mind. "You keep out of sight for a while, understand? I'll deal with greeting them myself."

"Yes, Fro Sigifrith!" the boy said, running back into the inn. Sigifrith quickly unloaded Grani and rubbed him down. He carried his saddle and bags into the inn and set them down by the fire, then hurried back out into the rain and around behind the building before anyone could say anything to him. He looked around but saw no one nearby; no sound pierced through the dripping of the eaves except for a woodbird's high chirp.

Sigifrith drew the Helm of Awe out of his belt pouch and put it on his head, settling the graven plate between his eyes. He thought back, trying to remember: a boy of thirteen winters, as tall as many grown men, but lanky, slim muscles just beginning to swell from his long bones . . . a tangle of hair, not so long or thick as it was now, matted and dirty from days of sleeping on the ground with no one but the old dwarf to see him . . . eyes cast down as if in fear, but worried only that he might be recognized by his gaze . . .

It felt to him as though he was dwindling, the weight of strength on his limbs lightening as his beard shrank away to leave chin and upper lip bare to the wet cold of the wind that brushed against the soft boy-fuzz on his cheeks. Sigifrith raised a hand to his head; but though the Helm of Awe still tingled between his eyes, no smooth links of metal met his touch. Looking around him, the buildings of the inn and the trees seemed larger, as though they had grown by a hundred years in a few moments. He laughed, and the sound of his own laughter in his ears was the pure and piercing highness of a boy's mirth. Cold mud was caked in a thick rim around the edges of his bare feet and between his toes; his dirty tunic was bound at the middle by a length of hempen rope, and he could not touch or see Gram at his side.

Grani raised his head and whickered enquiringly as Sigifrith came around the side of the inn again, then walked over to him and rubbed his head against his chest. Sigifrith stroked his horse for a moment, gladdened that Grani could see through the magic that cloaked him, then pushed him gently away as he heard the sound of two sets of hoofbeats through the rain.

Smiling to himself, Sigifrith watched as Gundahari and Hagan, catching sight of the inn, began to urge their horses more swiftly onward. Wet and disreputable-looking as they were, Sigifrith thought that if he hadn't known them, he would think the two wanderers were traveling with no worthy purpose in mind.

He hurried forward to take the reins of their horses as the inn-boy had taken his, ducking his head beneath their glances.

"Welcome to Guthrid's inn, atheling-fros," he muttered softly. "Let me tend to these for you."

Gundahari and Hagan dismounted, handing their reins over to him and lifting off their saddlebags. Though he had always thought of the Burgundians as short, Sigifrith noticed that Gundahari was taller than he now—a little taller than most men, and much broader with muscle—while Hagan stood half a hand's width higher than his brother.

"Hai, you there," Gundahari said as Sigifrith turned to tether their horses. "Look at me . . . no, here. Who was your father, boy?"

"Don't know," Sigifrith mumbled, his gaze sliding away from Gundahari's.

"Well, who was your mother, then? What are you doing here?"

Sigifrith shrugged. "Just the inn-boy," he muttered, trying to roughen his voice. "Tend horses, fro. I'll be beaten if I take too long about it," he added, suddenly inspired. "Please, fro."

"Leave him be," Hagan grated. "You can see he's a young fool with no sense and no knowledge."

Sigifrith scurried so he could say no more. He took the Burgundians' horses down then stabled them. After he was done, he went behind the inn and, breathing in deeply, began to feel his body swell with growth at each rush of air till he stood, bearded and finely if wetly clad, with Gram at his side and new boots on his feet. He lifted the Helm of Awe from his head, stifling his giggles as he walked to the front door of the inn in a leisurely way.

Gundahari and Hagan were already seated by the fire, sipping at steaming mugs of wine by the time Sigifrith came in. Gundahari's boots were off, his feet propped at the stone edge of the firepit, and the smell of wet wool heated was beginning to rise from his socks and soak through the garlicky air of the inn. Hagan had his cloak spread out like wings to enfold the fire's warmth; now and again he tried to dry his wet face with a wet sleeve.

"Where have you been hiding?" Gundahari asked, gesturing Sigifrith to sit down.

"I went out for a piss. Why?"

"You don't have any younger brothers you don't know about, do you?"

Sigifrith tried to hide his smirk with a bewildered look, succeeded in raising his eyebrows and twisting his face around. "I wouldn't know, would I?"

Gundahari looked disgusted. "You know what I mean."

"My father died before I was born, and my mother was barren afterward. I don't think so."

"I saw that boy here when we came through for Gundrun's betrothal," Hagan said unexpectedly. Sigifrith tried to flash a warning at him in his glance, but Hagan's eye was turned away from him, staring into the eaves. "You just weren't paying attention."

Gundahari shrugged. "Maybe not. Still, it was the strangest thing . . . He looked so like you, Sigifrith. You sure you didn't steal a march on us and play stag and doe with a serving maid when you were four or five winters old?"

"I'm sure," Sigifrith answered. He put his hand to his mouth, turning his laughter into a coughing fit till he began to choke.

Hagan reached out to tap the serving maid on the shoulder. She whirled, staring at him and backing away until the planks of the wall stopped her. "Bring more hot wine for Sigifrith," he told her. She fled to the kitchen, nearly tripping over her own feet in her haste. "That's a bad cough. Perhaps you ought to go back to Worms and get some medicine from Grimhild."

"I'll be all right," Sigifrith wheezed. "Thanks."

The next day was bright and warm as Midsummer, the sky polished as clear as glass by the soft dry wind that blew steadily from the south. Clumps of drying mud clotted quickly about the horses' hooves as they rode along the southwest pathway through the woods. It seemed to Sigifrith that Gundahari was growing quieter as they rode, often staring off into the woods as if he thought he might see something half-hidden between the cool green shadows of the trees and the woven traceries of gray-brown branches springing from their long knotty bodies.

Playfully Sigifrith rode around beside Gundahari, darting in to ruffle his hair and guiding Grani skilfully away before Goti's snapping teeth could close on him. "Hai, why so sad?" he asked. "Are you worrying about something? I thought you had Hagan to do that for you."

"Just thinking," Gundahari answered. "This may surprise you, but I do think once in a while. It keeps the spiders from building webs inside my skull." His voice sounded thin and pale, like a trickle of watered beer, his usual humor soured.

"What are you thinking about, then?"

"Brunichild."

Sigifrith waited a few moments.

"I don't know what to expect, and I'm rather nervous, all right?" Gundahari finally admitted. "This wasn't what I had planned."

"What could you possibly have to be nervous about?"

"I've heard that she's a very strong-willed woman. Suppose she turns me down? We'd have to go to war over the insult."

"She won't turn you down. You're a famous king, you're young, you're not ugly . . ."

"And I don't pick my nose where people can see it. Yes, I know."

"So what are you worrying about?"

"I'm not sure dashing off like this was such a good idea. We could have made a proper visit in state with a full band of thanes around us. What are Theoderid and his folk going to think when three strange wanderers arrive on their doorstep?"

"They'll think that they are honored to be guesting the king of the Burgundians and the heir to the Alamannic lands, Sigifrith the Dragon's-Slayer," Hagan answered, riding between them before Gundahari's angry stallion could make another attack on Grani. "I'm sure we will not be difficult for them to recognize."

"Maybe not. I don't know what I'm worrying about. I just have a feeling that this may not work out as well as Grimhild planned it. Don't ask me why."

The back of Hagan's head was turned to Sigifrith as he spoke to his brother. Sigifrith felt a sudden urge to pull the tail of fine black hair dangling from beneath the Burgundian's steel cap, but held back.

"Drinking too much hot wine on an empty stomach will often sour your sleep. You should know better."

"I didn't drink that much," Gundahari argued. "Less than you; you were the one sneezing and creeping out to the kitchen all night. What else could you have been doing out there, hmm?"

"You have no need to worry about how this journey will end," Hagan said flatly.

Gundahari snorted and poked at his brother's stomach. Hagan's hand blurred across to knock the mock blow aside. "Hah! You were doing something you shouldn't have been," Gundahari chortled. "Did you enjoy yourself? Did that girl enjoy herself? What will you do for me if I promise not to tell Costbera?"

"Costbera knows that hot wine is good for sneezing fits."

"And that's the only reason you look so self-satisfied this morning. I understand."

Hagan ignored his brother's words, staring ahead at a hill that rose near the side of the path. His hand lifted halfway toward his face, as though his missing eye had twinged viciously, then fell back. For a moment it seemed to Sigifrith as though he were about to speak, but he said nothing.

"Is something wrong?" Sigifrith asked.

"Let us stop for our meal here."

They dismounted by the side of the hill, Gundahari and Hagan tethering their horses to the low-spreading branches of one of the oaks growing by the pathway. The three of them climbed to the crest of the hill where a flat-topped outcropping of cracked rock formed a natural table.

"Why are we stopping here?" Sigifrith asked as they settled themselves and began to eat. "What have I missed?"

"This is where we met Waldhari the Frank in battle—where he lost his hand and I my eye. Gundorm, the father of Gernot and Gisalhari, also fell here together with some others."

"Why were you fighting him? I thought the songs said that you and he were the closest of friends."

"And so we were. But it became needful for my kin to fight against him."

Hagan fell silent, resting his dark-bearded chin in one hand and leaning on his throwing spear, the butt of which was braced against the rock. His head was turned as if he were looking down at the horses as they grazed peacefully on the long grass by the pathway, but the slight tilt of his eye seemed to warp his gaze away from them.

"I'll be back in a moment," Sigifrith said when they had finished eating. He stood and walked down the other side of the hill, off into the woods. When he was sure that he was far enough out of sight, he took the Helm of Awe from his belt pouch, weighing the gold mail thoughtfully in his hand. His companions needed a chase, something to draw them out of their melancholy . . . Grimhild had said that unless he truly changed his body he could do nothing outside his nature, but he knew that he could outrun both Gundahari and Hagan . . .

Sigifrith settled the Helm of Awe over his head, crouching down on all fours. Hands narrowing and hardening to sharp-cloven hooves, yes; hair crawling over his body, becoming a silky pelt of gold-sheened brown; tail dropping down from lean and powerful flanks; his head raising proudly to hold the huge crown of antlers that sprouted from his skull: twelve points, fourteen, sixteen, no hunter could hold his arrows back from this atheling-beast.

He raised his stag head, sniffing at the wind as a true deer would. Like a man, he smelled only the raw odor rising from the white flowers of wild spear leeks beneath his feet; the green of the springing leaves against the shining blue of the sky was unchanged, and his stag hide gleamed as warm as a gold-rubbed hazelnut in his sight. Sigifrith trotted through the brambles and around the hill, coming up from the south.

It was Gundahari who saw him first, touching his brother on the arm and pointing silently toward Sigifrith where he stood between the trees. Slowly, raising and lowering one pointed hoof at a time as if the nearness of men was a thing of no meaning to him, Sigifrith turned his back on them and began to walk away.

He felt the first blow like the sudden nudge of a knuckle in his lower back, blunt and hard. Looking behind him, he saw Hagan's throwing spear lying on the ground, the tip of its blade bent backward. Gundahari was already at the bottom of the hill, the lower end of his great bow braced against his foot as he bent it down to his height and slipped the noosed string over its end. Sigifrith dashed down to the pathway, stopping in a slant of sunlight for a moment and glancing back as if to taunt the Gebicungs.

Gundahari's first arrow grazed the top of his head; the second thunked solidly against his leg. Hagan was running toward the stag, his sword in his hand. Twin flashes of wonder shot through Sigifrith's mind: What does he think he's going to do with that? and, I thought he was too wise to attack a stag close up. But even weighted by his byrnie, Hagan was faster than Sigifrith had expected; the edge of his blade was already lashing out toward the stag's spine before Sigifrith recovered himself and leapt forward, out of reach.

He ran before the Gebicungs for a while, leading them along twisted trails, through ankle-deep mud and through a shallow stream. Sometimes he dodged Gundahari's arrows; other times he let them hit where they would, their thumps drowned out by the odd yelp of "Got him!" and "Shit, I saw that . . ."

At last, Sigifrith noticed that Gundahari was lagging behind badly and, though Hagan was still struggling to keep up with his quarry, his face was flushed dark as a dead man's. Sigifrith leapt over a clump of thornbushes— Gundahari's last arrow dropping uselessly away from his side—and ran as swiftly as he could away and back through the woods in a circle toward the hill where they had eaten their midday meal. His companions did not follow him, as he knew they could not.

He rose to his hind legs, his borrowed shape dropping off him as he stood into manhood again. Casually he walked back up the hill, settling himself on the rock and waiting for his companions to return.

It was a good time before Gundahari and Hagan came limping back down the pathway. Hagan's right hand was pressed to his side as if to soothe a stitch, and his eyepatch was askew showing the lumpy red rim of the wounded socket. Gundahari was panting like a bellows, his face pink and hair lank with sweat.

"Where were you?" Gundahari gasped when he got close enough. "You missed it."

"Missed what?" Sigifrith asked. "I was having a shit."

Hagan walked over to pick up his throwing spear, bending its blunted tip straight again. "There was a stag worth hunting, we thought. We chased him, but he got away. If you had been with us, it might have gone differently."

"I could have sworn I hit him a few times." Gundahari held up a handful of arrows, some with broken shafts and others with bent points. "But there it is. I suppose I've been inside the hall doing administrative work for too long. It seems I was shooting rocks and trees most of the time. It was the strangest thing . . . we tried to track him after we lost him, but we couldn't find as much as one print, even in damp earth. The only tracks we could find were from a man in boots, and those were old prints. They'd swollen out the way tracks do in the wet, till they were almost the size of a giant's."

"It was a fine stag," Hagan said, and Sigifrith thought he could hear a faint wistfulness in the other's harsh voice, like a thin mist graying the blackness of a deep and rocky ravine. "When we return to Gundahari's hall, you must come hunting with us, Sigifrith."

"I'll be glad to."

"The woods around Worms are better for boar than for deer," Gundahari said. He grunted as he unstrung his bow, letting it spring free; the length of the unbowed stave nearly matched Sigifrith's height. "You'll see when we take you out there . . . Come on, then!" he added cheerfully, untying Goti and mounting. "We've wasted enough time here, and we have a long way to fare yet."

The city of Tolosa lay on the bank of a wide, sluggishly moving river turning northward from the foot of a range of mountains that reared high and jagged like a dark ridge of pine trees against the bright sky of midmorning. Sigifrith, Hagan and Gundahari were beginning to sweat in the warmth of the Gaulish Sun; the weeks of their journey had not accustomed them to the southern heat yet.

Two sentries stood by the gate of the city. They were both fair men, one of middle height and one taller; they wore matching red tunics, dark breeches and Roman helms. The larger one was leaning against the gate, his eyes half-closed; his companion was flipping a copper coin idly from hand to hand.

"Who are you and what do you want?" the shorter one called out to the three wanderers. To Sigifrith's ears, his speech sounded very like that of a Burgundian's, if thicker and more difficult to understand.

From his slouch against the wall, the taller one looked them up and down, then spat a thick gobbet into the dust. "Why are you traveling on a holy day?" he asked. His voice was very deep, as slow as a mule plodding over a muddy field. "You're late for the Mass, if you've come to church."

"I have come to speak with King Theoderid about his daughter Brunichild," Gundahari said, riding forward to face them.

The tall sentry moved his right hand—its back was crusted with a scabby red rash, Sigifrith noticed—from forehead to navel, then shoulder to shoulder, in a sign a little like that of Donar's Hammer. The other peered up at the Burgundian king suspiciously, his eyes narrowing to slits against the glare of the Sun at Gundahari's back.

"Are you here on behalf of the Burgundians?" he asked.

"We are."

"I don't suppose you could give me any proof of that, could you? I've got orders to show someone from Gundahari in, but King Theoderid and his thanes are at the Pentecostal Mass and I don't want to trouble anyone I don't have to."

Sigifrith rode in front of Gundahari, careful to give his horse a wide berth. Staring down at the guards, he waited till they turned their faces away from his glance and then said, "These are King Gundahari of the Burgundians and his brother Hagan. I am Sigifrith, Sigimund's son, Fadhmir's Bane, of whom you may have heard some tales told. If you should still doubt us, I will prove the truth of these stories to you with this sword." He pushed his cloak aside so that the ice stone in Gram's hilt caught the sun, flashing a burning dazzle of white light into the sentries' faces.

Without another word, they both snapped to attention, stepping aside and letting Sigifrith, Gundahari and Hagan ride in. The man who had done most of the speaking followed them, taking the reins of Gundahari's horse and guiding them along. The streets of Tolosa were paved with slabs of dusty stone and splotched with drying dung; a few chickens wandered along the side of the road, clucking like old women at the wash together.

"Over there are the baths, if you want to refresh yourselves after the long ride as I should think you will," the guard said, pointing at a white marble-fronted building with Roman runes graven in gold over the door. "As a matter of fact, there won't be anyone much at the king's hall till after midday today, so I wouldn't blame you if you wanted to stop there now. I'll take your horses and your things over to the hall for you and see that they're taken care of, if you like."

Sigifrith looked at Gundahari and Hagan. They both appeared as grimy and itchy as he felt, their traveling clothes caked with three weeks of dirt and sweat. Gundahari's hair clung lankly to his skull, his beard a dull and ragged tangle; Hagan's face was streaked with smears of mingled sweat and dust. Sigifrith caught the slight flare of the younger Burgundian's nostrils, as if he had suddenly become aware of a questionable smell.

Gundahari glanced at his brother, then at Sigifrith and moved his head up and down. "Baths, everyone?"

The three of them dismounted, taking the saddlebags that held their spare clothes. Gundahari and Hagan left their horses to the care of their guide, but Sigifrith waved him away when he came to take hold of Grani's reins.

"He won't follow you if you try to lead him, but he'll go where I ask him to," Sigifrith explained when the man looked questioningly at him. He stroked Grani's neck, speaking coaxingly to the horse. "Hai, Grani, there's plenty of food in the stalls and I'll come to tend to you later. You follow the others and behave yourself."

Grani looked at the sentry's crested helmet and whuffled as if disgusted, but he followed the other horses along reluctantly, turning his head with every step to look back and roll his eyes at Sigifrith.

"How did you get him to do that?" Gundahari asked admiringly as they went into the baths. "He seems to understand every word you say. You'll have to teach me how you train horses."

"He just does it. I don't think I could train another like that," Sigifrith answered, staring at the mosaic pictures on the walls and floor. Hugely muscled men wrestled with bulls and strange beasts; creatures with human torsos set on the bodies of horses or the hindquarters of goats swept up screaming women at the edge of a vine-wreathed forest hung with heavy bunches of grapes.

A little man with masses of dark curly hair hanging over his thrall's collar came padding barefoot up to Sigifrith. "Take clothes, master? Byrnies?" he said in broken Gothic. "Have cleaned, three coppers each?"

To Sigifrith's surprise, Hagan had already taken off his sword belt and was bending down to slide his chain-mail from his shoulders as Gundahari stripped off his clothes.

"We undress in here," Gundahari explained, stepping out of his breeches and handing them to the thrall together with his tunic and sword belt; the gold-set boar's tooth around his neck was the only thing he did not give over. A long pink scar ran the length of the Burgundian king's right thigh, twisting between the thick muscles like a pale snake. Here and there, a few lesser marks marred his heavy torso—the sort of nicks and grazes that branded almost every warrior by his third battle. When Hagan took off his tunic, Sigifrith saw a puckered swath sweeping from below his navel to the tip of his breastbone; only great luck and a kind wyrd, Sigifrith thought, must have kept him from dying of that wound. A thinner scar, pink and lumpy in places, slashed from Hagan's left shoulder to his nipple and down into a wide crescent, as though the tip of a blade had twisted in its path; and the fading bruises of a rocky bed showed bluish yellow against the white skin of his right shoulder and hip. The eagle-headed arm-ring Sigifrith had given him, hidden beneath the sleeve of his tunic for the past weeks, gleamed from Hagan's bare arm like a coiled noose of gold.

Sigifrith hurried to undress himself, but when the thrall tried to take Gram from him he lifted the blade out of the man's reach. "No one shall care for this but me."

"It will be quite safe," Hagan assured him, looking him in the eyes. "This thrall's life shall pay if he lets any harm come to our belongings. So it is done here. I should think that you, of all men, would not need to fear being weaponless."

Sigifrith shifted uneasily from foot to foot as the Burgundian's gaze flickered pointedly down and up the unscarred and unmarked length of his body.

"I will not entrust Gram to another," Sigifrith insisted.

"Leave him be," Gundahari finally ordered the thrall, speaking slowly and carefully. "Have these other things cleaned, they need it. If you do it well, you'll be rewarded."

"At your will, master," the thrall answered. "*Unctorium* through that door, please."

Sigifrith had to bend his knees and duck his head as they passed through the low arch of the doorway. The next room was wrought in geometric mosaics of pink, black and white marble, with smooth marble benches along the walls. A shaven-headed, swarthy thrall with the thick neck and shoulders of a wrestler and a white latticework of lash scars across his bare back gestured them to lie down. The oil with which he anointed the three had a sweet and curiously heavy scent, like nothing Sigifrith had ever smelt before. Still, it was pleasant to lie while the thrall massaged his shoulders and back, rubbing away the tightness around his spine and the faint aches left by three weeks of riding.

When Sigifrith, Gundahari and Hagan had been anointed with the gleaming oil, the thrall showed them into a room that had thick mats of woven straw and cloth on the wooden floor around a big rectangular pit filled with sand. He bowed and left them.

"What do we do now?" Sigifrith asked.

"We're supposed to exercise till we've worked up a good sweat. It helps to clean the blood as well as the skin," Gundahari told him.

"You want to wrestle, then?"

Hagan and Gundahari glanced at each other, as if speaking silently between themselves.

"I'll take on both of you at once, if you like," Sigifrith offered.

Hagan seemed to consider a moment before he stepped into the shallow sandpit.

"That's fair enough. Come, then."

Sigifrith followed him in, Gundahari coming down behind him. The two Burgundians leapt on Sigifrith like dogs on a stag, trying to drag him down. Oiled as all three were, it was easy for Sigifrith to wriggle free of their grips; harder for him to grasp and hold them in turn, or to keep his footing in the face of their double attack. Between Hagan's wiry quickness and Gundahari's strength, Sigifrith found himself more fairly challenged than he had been in any match since his beard began to grow.

It was some minutes before they finally broke off, none of them quite victorious. Gundahari and Hagan were panting hard, close to exhaustion, and even Sigifrith had worked up a good sweat, a glistening sheen of perspiration mingling with the scented oil over his body and the sand that had stuck to all of them as they wrestled.

The next room was filled with a thick, hot fog. Sigifrith could hear a hissing along the walls as if several large snakes lay hidden in the mist.

"It's only steam from vents," Gundahari said to Sigifrith. "You don't need to worry. Surprising what the Romans can do, isn't it?"

"Over here, masters," the thin voice of the thrall who had met them at the door said through the steam. "Step careful, please. Floor slippery."

Gundahari, Hagan and Sigifrith followed his blurred shape to benches by the wall, where two other thralls waited with thin, curved pieces of metal in their hands. Seeing his companions stretch out, Sigifrith did likewise, leaning his sheathed sword against the wall and letting the thrall scrape the grimy coating of dirt, sweat and oil from his skin. He could feel his muscles relaxing like loosened harpstrings beneath the soothing touch of the hot steam, his cleansed skin tingling from the thrall's ministrations.

When the three of them had been thoroughly scraped and allowed to rest a bit, the thralls showed them into a room with several marble-lined pools sunken between tiled pathways and stone sculptures of women dressed in thin flowing garments with curled ringlets dripping down from high-piled hair. Sigifrith, thinking of how his mother brewed beer, wove and dyed cloth, and often rode her husband's horses, wondered what kind of frowes could possibly go about all day in such flimsy-looking and elaborate clothes. But perhaps, he thought, this was only how Roman women dressed for high feasts; surely they couldn't work in those delicately draped veils.

Three tall cups waited beside one of the pools, water-frost already beading white on their red-glazed sides. Gundahari and Hagan each picked up a cup and lowered themselves into the pool; Sigifrith set Gram down by its side and followed them in. The water felt cool on his body; the wine was cold and refreshing, like the rain of a thunderstorm bursting through summer's muggy heat.

"One day we'll have the baths in Worms set up like this again," Gundahari murmured reflectively. "One day . . . maybe soon, if Brunichild wants to be able to go to a proper bathhouse."

"That will be nice," Sigifrith agreed. He rolled over, resting his crossed forearms and chin against the edge of the pool and kicking his feet languidly as he stared at the polished marble toes peeping in an unnaturally lifelike way from beneath the hem of one of the statues' dresses.

"That is an odd mark on your back there," said Hagan. "Were you born with it?"

"Where?"

Hagan waded through the waist-high water to Sigifrith's side, the waves of his passage shifting Sigifrith's floating body about. "Here, behind your heart."

Sigifrith felt the cool pressure of the other's finger a little to the left of his spine, just below his shoulderblade. He craned his head, trying to see the spot that Hagan was touching. "What does it look like?"

"It is like charcoal or ash, and shaped rather like a leaf. Does it hurt when it is touched?"

"No." Sigifrith shrugged. "I'd never noticed it, but then, I wouldn't have, would I?"

"I suppose not. If it gives you no pain, then there is probably no reason to worry."

Hagan went to where his wine cup sat at the pool's edge, sliding under the clear water till its ripples blurred the entire length of his white body and half-closing his eye.

"Good timing, coming when the Christians are at feast," Gundahari commented after a while. "I've heard that bathhouses like this are usually full."

"There must be a lot of them here, then," Sigifrith said.

"Well, the Romans are supposed to be, and so are the Goths, although I think they worship a different Christian god or something. They call themselves Arians. There's been some tension through the Empire because of this, I've heard. I expect Brunichild will be able to explain this to us more clearly."

Outside, a bell began to toll, its ringing vibrating through the marble floors of the bathhouse. Hagan put his hands to his ears and rubbed at his temples as if pained by the sound.

"Obnoxious, isn't it? Ready to move on?" Gundahari asked, finishing the last of his wine. The three of them climbed out of the shallow pond and went to the next room, where a pool as big as a small lake stretched almost from side to side. The mosaic on its floor, deep beneath the water, showed a bare-chested man with a wild green hair and beard. He held a three-forked spear in his upraised right hand; with the other, he drove a chariot drawn by green horses tossing frothy white manes.

Sigifrith laid Gram on one of the benches at the wall, then ran light-footed across to the edge of the pool and dived in. The cold of the water caught him like a heavy blow across the chest; he surfaced gasping and laughing, shaking a shower of glimmering drops from his hair over Gundahari and Hagan as they walked more slowly toward the water.

"Come in!" he called to them.

Gundahari narrowed his eyes, looking down at Sigifrith, then leapt up and plunged in with a great splash, sending a cold wave over his friend. As Sigifrith wiped water from his eyes, he saw that Hagan had slipped quietly into the pool in his brother's wake and was treading water toward the middle as he tightened the leather thong that held his eyepatch to his face. His black hair had frayed out of its knotted plait, hanging over his wide shoulders in silver-threaded strings. With his hair loosed from its severe bindings, Hagan hardly looked older than his sixteen winters.

"Take that patch off," Sigifrith told him. "You'll be more comfortable, and it won't make us sick."

Hagan shook his head. As Sigifrith swam toward him, he dived down, slithering through the waters and away before Sigifrith could touch him.

"You won't be able to catch me," Hagan said as he surfaced at the other end of the pool. "I'm a good swimmer."

Gundahari launched himself off the wall toward his brother. Hagan dived again and Sigifrith tried to follow him. His sight was blurred underwater, ripples of greenish light fluttering over the mosaic below and the green-tinged tiles of the pool's walls and floor. Still it was strange to be able to see through the water, to float free of a river's pull; he felt, for a moment, like a hawk circling through a clear sky. Then a cold hand tugged at his ankle, dragging him downward. He coughed in a gasp of water, sputtering and choking as he tried to twist away and fight his way toward the air. With nothing to brace against, he kicked out at his attacker. Half by luck, his foot caught Hagan's shoulder and tore him away.

Freed, Sigifrith swam upward, choking and sputtering as he broke through the surface. Hagan appeared beside him, hardly more than an arm's length away.

"Are you all right? I didn't know you were having trouble."

Sigifrith coughed out a gout of water and breathed raspily in. "Don't worry. I'm all right." He lunged over to duck Hagan, but the Burgundian had glided out of his way.

Gundahari had hauled himself out and was sitting on the edge of the pool with his legs in the water as he watched them. "Have you two finished playing?" he asked, kicking a spray of water toward them with one long-toed foot. "If you have, I think it's time to get dressed and be on our way. We can always come back later."

Sigifrith swam to the edge and vaulted out, landing on his feet. Hagan followed, easing himself out of the water without leaving so much as a ripple behind him.

The curly-haired thrall met them in the outer chamber, where their bags and washing-damp clothes lay beneath the Burgundians' sword belts. The three of them took the feasting clothes they had brought with them out of their bags. Grimhild and Gundrun had packed a sky-blue over-tunic for Sigifrith; Gundahari's was red and Hagan's deep green. All three were embroidered at the sleeves and hems with interlacing patterns of woven gold. Hagan shrugged into his byrnie, standing straighter against the burden weighting down his shoulders as he pulled his loose upper tunic on to conceal it. He pushed his arm-ring down to his wrist where it could be seen, and Gundahari took several rounds of twisted gold from his bag to adorn himself as befitted a king.

Sigifrith sat patiently while the thrall combed out his hair; waist-long as it was, matted in thick curls, it took some time. He refused to let the man cut his hair, but allowed him to clip his beard back close to the jawline.

When all three were properly trimmed and combed, Gundahari paid the thrall in Roman coin and asked him the way to Theoderid's hall.

"Down the street, left, right and left again, then along through big gardens to the villa," the man said, nodding his head so energetically that his masses of curls bobbed up and down like seaweed on choppy waves. "Easy to find, masters. You get lost, anyone tell you where."

The guard who had brought them in was standing outside the door of the bath with another man, a stocky red-haired warrior who wore the same red tunic and dark breeches, but whose crest ran from side to side of his helm instead of front to back. The two of them thumped fists to chests, then snapped their arms straight as Gundahari, Sigifrith and Hagan came out.

"King Theoderid bids you welcome!" the red-haired man said to them. The bridge of his nose, clearly once broken, had been set so badly that when the guard gazed along its twisted line, Sigifrith could not tell whether he was trying to meet his own eyes or Gundahari's. "If you will, King Gundahari, allow us to show you the way to his hall."

"We are glad for your guidance," Gundahari answered. The guards turned toward him, repeating their gesture of fists clapped to chests, then whirled on their heels and marched out before the Burgundian king and his companions.

As they passed between the white columns upholding the roof over the entryway to Theoderid's hall, a tall, thin man dressed in a draped piece of purple-bordered white wool hurried out of the door and stood before them. It seemed for a moment that the guards were about to brush him aside, but he gazed fiercely down his beaky nose at them, holding up his hand palm outward, and they halted.

"This is still my house, hospites," he said slowly. The voice rising from his thin chest was surprisingly resonant and clear, though heavily accented. "If you have brought someone to visit your drighten, it is only the behavior of civilized folk to warn your host—and his—first. If these are also to be guests of mine, you must at least tell me their names." Firmly as he stood, Sigifrith could see the little beadlets of sweat welling along his forehead and beginning to roll toward the edges of the dark wings of hair that framed his bare crown. His brown eyes were veined with red; corpse-blue flesh sagged beneath them, as though he did not sleep well often. "If you cannot follow the customs of civilized men," he added mildly, "at least have the goodness not to commit barbarisms against barbarian custom by insulting the man who has given you guest-right."

"King Gundahari of the Burgundians; his brother Hagan; the fro Sigifrith, Sigimund's son," the red-haired guard growled. "You tread on the hem of your luck, Agrippus. They have come for Brunichild."

Agrippus' mouth twisted into a puckered laugh, as though he had bitten into bad fruit and found it vastly humorous. "I will stand in your way no longer, then. Come, guests, and welcome to my house." He flung the door open wide, gesturing them in with an extravagant bow.

The guards stalked past him without another word. Gundahari and Hagan followed as if they knew what had happened, and Sigifrith, in his confusion, could only go wordlessly after.

Their guides led them through a marbled passageway and out into an open garden where a table with food had been set up in the shade of a great oak tree. Sitting about it and eating were perhaps fifteen men, all clothed in plain white tunics and breeches.

"Hail, King Theoderid!" the guard who had spoken to Agrippus barked.

The largest of the men at the table, a massively built warrior with a long blond beard and fair hair bound by a golden circlet, rose to his feet to return his thane's salute.

"Hail and welcome, King Gundahari," Theoderid said. Strong as his voice was, it seemed strangely thin, like wine from a middling bad year. "Come and eat with us. If you will not share our holy rites, at least share in the joy of our feast."

"Hail, King Theoderid," Gundahari answered. "My brothers and I will be honored to eat with you."

Theoderid's thanes moved aside to make space for Gundahari, Sigifrith and Hagan on the bench beside their king. Sigifrith glanced behind him, waiting for Brunichild to come out with cups and wine; but it was Agrippus who carried out three goblets with stems and bowls wreathed by vine leaves of green glass, and the other men were pouring their own portions from three pitchers of wine that stood on the table.

"I hope you have been refreshed well after your long journey?" Theoderid said, neatly carving a steaming leg from one of the roast geese and lifting it to the plate before him. "I had not expected you to arrive so soon."

"We were lucky in our faring," Gundahari replied. "And I was eager to meet Brunichild, of whom I have heard so many fair tales. I trust the maiden is well?"

Theoderid chewed the bite of goose in his mouth carefully, as though no question had been asked, washing it down with a leisurely sip of wine. "She is," he answered at last.

"And will we be meeting her soon? Or will she be at the rites for the rest of your holy day?"

"How soon you meet her must depend on your courage. Brunichild is the strongest-willed of my daughters, and I made a vow to her that I would not force her to marry against her will or to marry anyone she found unworthy." The hand Theoderid raised to gesture Gundahari back into his seat on the bench was heavy with rings of gold and silver, square-cut and weighted with sign-carved stones in the Roman manner. "You understand, King Gundahari, that nothing will delight me more than for a ruler as famed as you are to fulfill the test Brunichild has set and take her to wife. I myself think that nothing could be better for our two folks than this alliance, especially if you are the hero who can win a victory over Brunichild's pride."

"What test are you talking about?" Hagan's voice rasped, harsh as the call of an aurochs horn through the soft air of the Roman's garden. "What brings your daughter to question the might of Gundahari of the Burgundians—or to stand against her father's will?"

Theoderid stood up, leaning over the table with both ringed hands braced against it so that it creaked and swayed under his weight. He did not look at his three guests, but, rather, stared upward toward the sharp-edged mountain peaks cutting darkly into the clear sky.

"This has become known to all the folk in Tolosa and to the peoples of the Gothic tribes, wherever word of my kinsmen is spoken. At the Paschal feast of this year, Brunichild swore an oath that she would never be married to a man who knew fear, but only to the highest-souled and strongest hero in the world. Near the city, at the top of a mountain, is a hall which was first built as a Roman watch-post. Brunichild had it readied for herself, then went in with three of her maidens. By her own strength or by the grace of God, I know not which, she set a fire to burn around it, saying that none but her chosen warrior would be able to cross through the flames and take her as betrothed bride; and there she will stay till the man who is worthy of her comes for her. Are you that hero, Gundahari? If you fear that you may not be, go back to the Rhine and seek another bride; my daughter will not wed a lesser man, nor can anyone force her will now. But if you can win Brunichild, then you may have her with my blessing."

"I have come for Brunichild, and I shall not leave without her," the Burgundian king answered, rising to his feet again. He and Theoderid were almost of a height, facing each other with less than a hand's breadth of space between them. Gundahari spoke softly, staring closely into the Gothic king's eyes, but his words carried all through the garden, as hard and clear as hammers striking against stone. "Nor will I flinch before her flames, spaewife though she be. I would measure myself well against any man within the Middle-Garth's ring. Enough thanes have heard the words you have spoken to me that I would be shamed forever should I name myself a lesser man by turning away. Show me the way to Brunichild's mound, and I will pass through her fires or die in the doing."

"Follow the road from the city southward into the mountains, and I expect that you will find Brunichild's burg by sunset. But will you not stay with me and rest from your journey for a day or two first?"

"No. I thank you for your hospitality, King Theoderid, but I will go to seek Brunichild."

"Will your companions go also?" the Gothic drighten asked, his eyes flicking mistrustfully toward Hagan and Sigifrith. "If they are not Christians, they may feel themselves more comfortable with you."

"I will follow my brother as far as I may," Hagan said, getting up. After a moment, Sigifrith rose as well. Theoderid's forehead furrowed as he looked at Sigifrith, his heavy blond eyebrows lowering as if to shade his eyes from the young warrior's glance.

"I have heard tales of Sigifrith the son of Sigimund, whom men now name

Fadhmir's Bane," the Goth murmured, so softly that Sigifrith was not sure whether the words had indeed sounded in his ears or merely been shaped by his imagination and the wind-ruffling of the fair beard over Theoderid's lips. "I might have thought . . . " Then he spoke aloud again: "If you wish to go at once, I will not hold you. Alaric, Recceswinth, fetch these athelings' horses from the stables and bring them whatever else they may need. May Christ and your gods aid you in this, King Gundahari."

"Be ready for our return," Gundahari answered.

As Sigifrith, Gundahari and Hagan stood by the outer door of the hall, Agrippus came out carrying three bags. Though his burden was not great, the Roman was breathing hard from his labors. A faint blueness tinged his lips, like the dusty bloom on ripe grapes.

"So you still wish to seek out the furious witch-woman," Agrippus said, setting his bag down. "Fortunate for Theoderid that Brunichild is sought by a heathen who cannot turn away from her challenge for his soul's sake."

"What are you talking about?" Sigifrith asked.

Agrippus twisted his neck to look up at Sigifrith, his broken teeth showing white as eggshell through his half-smile. "Why, a Christian would not have to face Brunichild or her ring of fire; only to cry "Witchcraft!" Then he might leave Tolosa with his fame whole and Theoderid's that much more cracked. I believe the flames they call upon today at Pentecost are far cooler than Brunichild's," he added mysteriously.

"Aren't you a Christian?"

"Sigifrith," Gundahari murmured warningly. "I'm not sure . . . "

"Unwilling as my kind guests are to hear of it, I am too old to turn away from the gods of my family," Agrippus said, ignoring the words of the Burgundian king. "But I shall be dead of one thing or another soon enough anyway, and then my carcase can be what Theoderid pleases. Come, your horses are here and you have a long way to go before sunset. *Ave atque vale*, Sigifrith, Gundahari, Hagan."

The Roman turned and went in again, closing the door of his villa softly but firmly behind himself as Sigifrith, Gundahari and Hagan stepped down to the road where Grani waited behind the other horses and two of Theoderid's thanes.

They rode along without speaking until Gundahari turned to Hagan and said, "How could this have been foreseen? What should I have done?"

"The only thing you can do. Ride through the flames and win Brunichild. Such a deed will be sung of and add greatly to your fame."

"If I succeed."

"It will do you no good to doubt. Theoderid has arranged this very neatly. Even the Goths are not Romans yet. You could not have refused the challenge and still been honored as king among our folk. Word of such things travels swiftly. If we do not come back with Brunichild, it would be better for us not to come back at all."

"If you ride fast enough, it shouldn't be hard to leap through a ring of flames," Sigifrith said. "Our master of horses at home told me once that he had seen a warrior ride a horse over a burning fence around a burg that Alapercht's warband had set on fire. He said the man was going so swiftly that the flames blew back from the wind of his riding and never touched him. Of course, they got him with throwing spears as he came over, but if Brunichild isn't waiting for you with weapons on the other side, you shouldn't have anything to fear."

Gundahari nodded thoughtfully, his hand dropping to stroke his stallion's gleaming brown flank. "He's a fast horse and a good jumper. I suppose we'll find out what his fierce mood is worth."

"I wonder if Brunichild has other skills of magic," Sigifrith said. "If she can call up a wall of fire, perhaps she also knows how to cut and read runes, or the charms of healing. That is worthy lore for a queen."

"Gundrun knows a little of it," Hagan said. Only his black eyepatch met Sigifrith's glance of surprise; his sighted eye was turned upward, toward the mountains. "I myself can read runes carved by others, at least somewhat, though I was never taught in their use. Grimhild did not think it wise that I spend too much time among such things."

"Why not? I would have thought, of all people—"

"I can read Roman letters, if not runes," Gundahari broke in unexpectedly. "It's a needful skill for a king in these days. A thrall has to do my writing for me, though. I tell you, once you start using Roman writing for messages and such things, it's hard to imagine how our fathers ever managed without it. Did you ever learn to read or write, Sigifrith?"

"No. Why would I have?"

"Maybe Gundrun can teach you when we get back. We even have two Roman books in our hall. They're books of what the Romans call poetry, so they're hard to understand, but they're by the greatest poets of the Empire and the pages are bound and worked with the very finest southern crafts-manship. Would you be interested in learning to read?"

"Of course. Would I have to learn Latin as well?"

"Everything's written in Latin, or in Greek—but that's supposed to be a lot more difficult. Anyway, no one needs to know Greek anymore."

"Do the Romans do magic with their runes?"

"How could they? They use them for everything, and far too many people know how to write them."

"I suppose that's true."

"With a bit of luck, Brunichild will have good Latin. The Goths came through the Empire, after all."

"I hope she turns out to be worth your trouble," Sigifrith said.

"So do I," Gundahari said. He looked pointedly at Hagan. "You know, if Grimhild was as wise as everyone thinks she is, she would have warned me about this and saved us a long journey."

"Perhaps Grimhild, too, thinks that you should wed Brunichild. Certainly there is no maiden of more worth than she now."

"Not if worth is measured by cost," Gundahari muttered into his beard.

It seemed at first that the red-gold glow of Sunna's setting shone reflected from the southerly mountains as the sky darkened around their black crags. It was only when Sigifrith, Gundahari and Hagan rode closer that they saw the shapes of flames writhing and twisting around the shadow of a hill, burning from a wall of interlocked linden shields and upward-pointing spears of ashwood. The fire-ringed mound was crowned with a square-built burg, whose gold-mounted roof gave back the brightness in a thousand red-glittering points like the spear tips of a far-off host.

Sigifrith heard Gundahari's hiss of breath, as though the Burgundian's ribs had clutched inward at his lungs. Then the king flung his weight back in the saddle, clamping his knees on Goti's sides as he urged his horse forward in a gallop. For a moment Gundahari's shape was a shadow against the flames; then the stallion shied sideways so violently that his rider was almost flung from the saddle. As Gundahari struggled to regain his seat and wrestled with his horse's reins, Goti ran in a half-circle around the side of the road.

"Why did you shy, Gundahari?" Sigifrith called. "You were almost there."

"Horse . . ." Gundahari panted as he brought his stallion under control. "He won't leap into the fire. Thought I was going off . . . Sigifrith, will you lend me Grani? I think I can trust him not to be afraid, and I don't know a better horse."

"I'll be glad to," Sigifrith answered, sliding from the gray's back and taking Goti's reins. "You don't fear any fires, do you, Grani? Carry Gundahari well, my horse; you aren't likely to bear a burden more worthy of an atheling-steed."

Gundahari placed his palms against Grani's side, crouching as he gathered his strength. Leaping as high as he could, the Burgundian just managed to scramble on to Grani's back. The wind-gray stallion swished his tail, tossing his head and pawing at the ground with one hoof, but he stood still.

"Go on, Grani," Gundahari said, touching the horse's flanks with his heels. "Go on!"

"Go!" Sigifrith commanded, slapping Grani's hindquarters with his free hand. Grani swung his head around, showing teeth as large and bright as silver coins, then stamped his forehoof down and stood like a carving of gray stone, blood-tinged by the glare of the sinking Sun.

"He won't go for anyone but you, Sigifrith," Hagan said. "Grani will give us no help in this."

From his high seat, Gundahari stared despairingly at his brother. Then his lips pulled back in the snarl of a war-cry.

"Gebica!" he screamed, and leapt from Grani's back. He landed hard, stumbling to his knees, but was up and running again in a heartbeat, charging toward the flame-ringed hill as swiftly as if he were both horse and rider.

"Stop him!" Hagan cried to Sigifrith, sliding from his own steed's back and running after his brother. Sigifrith dropped Goti's reins and followed, overtaking Hagan and grasping Gundahari just as the Burgundian began the leap which would have taken him into the fire.

"Let me go!" Gundahari shouted.

"You can't do it!"

Gundahari struck out angrily at Sigifrith, trying to wrench free with more strength than Sigifrith had felt yet in another man. Then Hagan was there as well, helping Sigifrith to hold his brother back from the flames. This close, the heat was fearsome, and sweat, lit red as blood by the fire, streamed forth over the three of them in rivulets as they wrestled back and forth.

At last Gundahari's desperate might began to sink away, and Sigifrith and Hagan were able to drag him away from the fire.

"Why didn't you let me go?" the Burgundian king panted bitterly, staring up at Sigifrith, then at Hagan. "I could have . . ."

"You would have died," Hagan answered. "That fire would be deadly enough to a man on horseback at full gallop."

"Then you should have let me die! What kind of shame will I win from this? You said yourself that I had no choice but to try this. Let me try your horse," he added suddenly.

Hagan shook his head. "You know I am no good rider, and Holkwer is no better steed than I can manage. Even if he had the brave mood to go through the fire and the wit and training to leap when he ought, he could never go fast enough or jump high enough to get you through alive. No. But I think there is one of us who can pass through fire without hurt, who might safely bring Brunichild forth."

Gundahari's despairing glance kindled into hope again as he looked to Sigifrith. The memory of the dragon's scorched track . . . the glow of a coal in the darkness of the hall at Worms . . . Then the Burgundian's face twinged, as though he had bitten on the bitter-sharp tang of a copper coin.

"You would be Brunichild's chosen one, then, not I," he said, his voice low. "What good would that do? Would you shame me and forsake Gundrun for the fame of winning Theoderid's fire-ringed daughter?"

"Of course not," Sigifrith answered, without a moment's breath between question and reply. He looked at the flames again, shining redder and more furious against the darkening heavens in the east to pale the gibbous glow of the rising Moon as he mounted into the sky from the edge of the plain. Then he knew at once, hard and ringing as the blow of a sword's hilt against the back of his skull, why Grimhild had been willing to teach him how to use the Helm of Awe before he began the faring to Tolosa.

Sigifrith drew the golden coif from his belt pouch. In the light of the fire, a half-seen flame seemed to waver around the Helm's links. "It will be you who rides through Brunichild's fire on Grani, Gundahari! Enchantment to meet enchantment: with this we shall change our shapes until I have made your betrothal to Brunichild and brought her safely out again."

"So," Gundahari said, staring wide-eyed at the golden mail that dangled from Sigifrith's hand. "I must win my hero's fame and my bride by a trick, or else be shamed before all?"

"This is hardly a fair test for you," Sigifrith argued. "And am I not of your blood, as if I had been born your brother? What falls to one of us ought to fall to us both."

"There is more than your pride in question," Hagan said. "You must also think of your folk and your duty to them. Would you allow the destruction of everything you have built up for the sake of the honor hidden in your heart? My rede is that you follow Sigifrith's plan. No one will know but the three of us, and I would not count it shame."

Gundahari turned his broad back and walked down the road toward the horses who grazed quietly by its side. For a moment Sigifrith thought he was going to mount again; but instead the Burgundian king dug about in his saddlebag for a moment. Sunna's last light blinked a green gleam from his hand as he came back to Sigifrith and Hagan.

"Here is the ring that I brought to wed Brunichild with. Now you must wear my shape and put it on her hand in my name."

Sigifrith took the ring from Gundahari. Its smooth circle of gold clasped a great round stone as deep green as the waters of a slow-moving river. Sigifrith slipped it on the little finger of his left hand and closed his fist over it, then set the Helm of Awe upon his head.

"Now look into my eyes," he murmured to Gundahari, staring into the Burgundian's hazel depths. Squared cheekbones and jaw beneath the fresh-trimmed beard framed by thick waves of chestnut hair; low forehead already scored with the thin lines of the young king's struggle for understanding, for rule; a squint at the corners of the eyes, as if he were always straining to see the path ahead for himself and those who followed after him. A shorter body, heavy muscles knotted over bone like the hard gnarlings of oak— thick legs spread in a deep-rooted stance—shoulders bent in as though a heavy cloak weighed hard upon him and he could not shake it off . . .

In Sigifrith's narrowed sight, Gundahari's features seemed to swirl into fog around eyes that slowly, slowly lightened to a blue so bright and painful that he could hardly look into them any more or meet the faint smile of sureness curling into the other's short-trimmed light beard. He stared at Sigifrith's powerful chest, half again as wide as his own; at the glistening torrent of thick brown hair that fell across Sigifrith's shoulders and down to his sword-girt waist; and for a moment it seemed to him that he had been caught in an ill dream from which he could not awaken. Then his right hand reached beneath the web of seeming to touch the cold ice stone in Gram's hilt, and he knew that he had worked all he had chosen to work.

"Sigifrith?" his own clear tenor voice asked, soft with wonder; and for a second he could not believe that his own mouth had not moved. He nodded, surprised at the lightness when no weight of long hair pulled against the movement of his skull.

"I'm ready," Sigifrith said, then laughed as his eyes flickered around against his will, looking for Gundahari.

Only a glowing rim of fire showed on the western horizon as Sigifrith mounted Grani. The flames around Brunichild's mound rose higher from the wall of shields and spears; Sigifrith drew Gram, pricking his steed on the flank with the tip.

The fire flared up with a mighty roar as Grani galloped toward it. Sigifrith felt the earth trembling beneath him, shaking Grani's stride as if the horse were drunk on strong mead. The flames seemed to be mounting to the sky, drowning out Sunna's last light in a burning so bright that Sigifrith's eyes were dazzled and he rode through its shining as blindly as if he were riding through the mirkiest fog, with the roaring of the flames stilling all other sounds in his ears.

The fierceness of the fire slowly faded from his hearing, the brilliance dimming from his eyes till he could see that he stood before a fine burg. The flames around the hill cast their light over the carven pillars flanking the heavy door; he could see the shapes twisting through the wood, but not make them out clearly.

Sigifrith dismounted and raised his right fist, beating thrice on the door with Gram's hilt. A deep booming rang from his knocks, as if he had struck against the wall of a great hollow chamber built of iron. He waited for a few heartbeats, but no one came to answer the door, so he pushed it open and walked inside.

Fires burned the length of the hall, their flames as bright as blades. Two high seats were raised at the far end; one was dark, but white steel gleamed from the other. Sigifrith walked down till he stood in front of the dais, raising his eyes to the woman who sat there, shining as a swan on the wave.

Brunichild was clad in a glistening byrnie over a white gown with a white linden shield before her. Long fair hair flowed down from her steel helm around her high-boned, pale face; eyes as blue as the ice at a mountain's peak stared down at Sigifrith as he stood leaning on the hilt of his sword before her.

"Who are you, who has ridden through the flames to my hall?" she asked. Though her voice was clear, it shook as if she were crossing a river on a flimsy plank of wood that trembled beneath her feet.

"I am Gundahari, son of Gebica, king of the Burgundian folk. And you are to be my wife, with your father's consent, since I have ridden through your leaping flames as you willed."

"I hardly know how I must answer this," Brunichild murmured. Her gaze was as keen and bright as snow mirrored on steel. Sigifrith thought for a moment that it would shear through the weaving of the Helm of Awe, that his borrowed shape would fall away like cut cloth before the maiden's glance. Then she straightened herself, looking over his head to the firelight flickering through the open door behind him. "Gundahari, you should not speak so to me unless you are a better man than any other. You do not seem like the man for whom I set these flames around my mount, nor is your shape the one I saw in my dream. But if you would have me for your wife, you must slay whoever asks to have me, if you trust enough in yourself. I have been in battle with kings. My weapons gleamed with men's blood, and that is what I still long for, for I am a walkurja in soul and in truth."

"Then you have done many great works," Sigifrith answered. "But now you must remind yourself of your oath: that if anyone rode through this fire, you would go with the man who had done it, and so you must be betrothed to Gundahari, Gebica's son."

"I did swear that oath, and may not be loosed from it," Brunichild said reflectively, as if she spoke to herself. Then she arose briskly from her seat, stepping down and taking Sigifrith by the hand. The grip of her slender fingers was so strong that he hardly needed to hold his own might back, or to worry about crushing her bones in his grasp. "Since you must be my husband, come and sit beside me."

Brunichild led Sigifrith to the empty throne where he sat with Gram laid across his knees, then clapped her hands. Three white-clad maidens, one fair and two brown-haired, hurried into the hall. The blond girl's gray eyes were wide in her narrow face; as she saw Sigifrith, she touched two fingers from forehead to bosom, then shoulder to shoulder. The other two, whose stocky shapes and plain freckled faces were so alike that they could only be sisters, looked at him with open curiosity.

"Childeburg, bring drink and food. Matasuntha and Ragnachild, ready my bed," Brunichild commanded them. "This man is Gundahari the son of Gebica, and I must be wed to him since he has ridden through the flames that none but the strongest could pass. You may be joyful for this, since we will leave this hall for the lands of the Burgundians when the three nights of the betrothal are passed."

"God be thanked," the fair-haired girl whispered, and the other two smiled at Sigifrith before they left the hall again. The shorter of the sisters came back quickly, carrying a plate of bread and smoked ham together with a goblet big enough to hold as much golden wine as a full horn, which she laid on the table before the two thrones.

As Brunichild cupped both her hands around the wide bowl of the goblet and raised it to drink, Sigifrith saw that she wore a ring like that which he had taken from Fadhmir: a little golden dragon coiled about the smooth curve of a deep red stone, with its tail wrapped around her finger. Except for Ragin's crafting and the jewels of Fadhmir's hoard, he had not seen such fine workmanship; it seemed to him that the piece must have been dwarven-made.

"Where did you come by that ring?" he asked curiously.

"Don't you know, Gundahari? If you are the man who rode through the fire, surely you have seen it before."

"It appears to be one of the treasures Fadhmir kept. Tell me."

"It was given to me by the hero who awakened me in my dream, as his token that he would come back to wed me. I remember . . . It was so clear when I awakened, as if my dream had been fixed in a crystal. Then I knew who my true betrothed was and how he would come riding through the fire to me, and I knew how to set the flames around my hall so that none but he could pass. I thought I could never forget, but it was less than a week before the knowledge of my dream sank from my mind as suddenly as though I had drunk a draught of forgetfulness and I awoke remembering only that he would come and that I must wait for him. I thought that I would know him at once when I saw him . . . "

She was still then, looking down the length of the hall as she gave him the goblet. Sigifrith took it from her hands and raised it to her. "And now you are to be my bride, Brunichild. I drink to your joy in our wedding and the greatness which you shall bring to the house of Gebica."

When Sigifrith lowered the empty goblet, he saw that Brunichild had cast her gaze downward; the firelight glimmered a ruby tinge into the ice-stone brightness of her welling tears.

"Why are you weeping?" he asked gently. "Surely you do not find this orlog so ill-laid?"

"It does not seem to me that this is how things should have been."

Sigifrith arose, taking Brunichild's arm in his right hand and lifting her to her feet as he sheathed Gram with his left. "Don't think about that any more. You shall be the queen of a great people in a fair city by the Rhine; you shall have all the gold you wish and your fame shall be sung throughout the northlands. I shall build you a chapel if you follow your father's cult, or you may stand beside me and pour the blessings to the gods and goddesses at our holy days. If you wish to go hunting, there are rich woods about Worms; if you wish to stay in the hall to weave and embroider with the other women, my own sister Gundrun shall be your companion; and if war is still your delight, it was never said that the Burgundians languished overly long in peace. Whatever else you ask for, I shall do my best to give it to you. What more could you want?"

"I don't know," Brunichild murmured. "I suppose Wyrd has written as she must, and I can do no more. Do you wish to take me to your bed, then?"

"That is the custom of betrothal."

Outside Grani neighed. Brunichild's head sprang up, and she stared piercingly at the horse's shadow against the flames. "I know that horse," she whispered.

"I must tend to him!" said Sigifrith. "Have you a stable here? He is not my own; my horse was fearful where I was not, and so I was obliged to borrow him from one of the athelings with whom I fared here."

Grani raced to his master as the two of them walked out of the hall, first rubbing his head against Sigifrith's shoulder, then, to his great surprise, against Brunichild's. For the first time, he saw her smile, as brief and bright as a flash of lightning.

"Grani," she whispered, stroking the horse's soft nose. "That is your name. Surely only you . . . " She stopped, as if suddenly aware that Sigifrith was staring at her. "This way," she said, taking Grani's reins. The gray followed her as though he had never refused to move at another's bidding, and Sigifrith, bewildered, could only follow the two of them. The flames around the hill gave enough light for them to see their way clearly, though the last brightness of Sunna's setting had faded into night.

"Romans built this, many years ago," Brunichild said as she led Grani into the stables. "Eleven men and their horses could stay here, with a month's worth of food stored up and water for all of them from the well."

One white horse's head and three duns swung about over the gates of the stalls to watch Grani passing; he turned his head to whicker at them, but no more.

Brunichild guided the colt into a freshly cleaned stall. Sigifrith came in behind her, bending to rub some of the hay in the horse's trough between his fingers. It was dry and a little musty, but it would do, and the water smelled fresh. Grani lowered his head and drank thirstily, spraying Sigifrith and Brunichild with a spatter of droplets from his mouth when he raised his head again and blew out his lips in a noisy snuffle.

"Will he be all right here?" Sigifrith asked.

"I think that he will. My mare, Snowbright, is not in season yet, so you won't need to worry about him breaking out."

The two of them went back into Brunichild's hall. She led Sigifrith through one of the small doors at the far end and into a large chamber. Torches burned around the walls; every so often one would flare up, hissing and crackling, and the scent of pine sap would curl forth in a twist of smoke. The bed was made with a blanket of fox fur laid over fine white linen and a mattress stuffed with goose down and sweet herbs; in its middle the maidens had set a loaf of fresh-baked bread and a thorny crimson-pink rose, its petals already beginning to droop.

Brunichild stood silently before the bed, holding her back very straight under the weight of helmet and byrnie. Sigifrith reached out to take her hand in his. Though her arm hung with the heaviness of dead weight as he lifted it, she did not struggle against him.

"Now I shall take this, and you shall wear Gundahari's wedding ring," he said, tugging at the golden dragon ring on her finger.

Brunichild tore her arm from his grasp, whirling away. "How dare you try to take my ring?" she screamed, her face suddenly twisted wolflike in angry wod. "You shall not have it, no matter who you are or what you have done! It is mine . . . the only token I can trust. If you were really the one—"

Her madness was gone as quickly as it had fallen upon her, and she leaned against the frame of the door, weeping softly. "I shall wear your ring as well, if I must, but leave me this. It was given to me in my dream, and I prize it above everything else that I have." She looked at Sigifrith in beseechment, her finely wrought face glimmering with a sheen of tears beneath the bright steel of her helmet. "I must stay as true as I can to the one who gave it."

A twinge of sympathy vibrated through Sigifrith's body, as though his entrails had been plucked like a harpstring. The hot blood of guilt rushed after: this was Gundahari's bride, and he, too, had sworn an oath. Before his will could weaken, he had ripped the dragon ring from her finger and replaced it with the heavy gold and emerald of the Burgundian. He slipped the dragon on to his own finger; it seemed to him for a dizzy moment that it twisted in his hand, its tail reaching into a wider coil to pass over his knuckle and tighten on him again.

Brunichild did not move as Sigifrith lifted the helmet from her head, but she had to raise her arms for him to pull the byrnie off. Much as he tried to keep the iron links from tangling in her long hair, she still winced when he lifted the mail shirt over her shoulders and off. It slithered into a glistening heap of silvery rings on the floor beside Brunichild's helmet.

When Sigifrith lifted her up, Brunichild was as light in his arms as swandown on the wind. He set her on one side of the bed, then walked about the chamber, turning the torches down in their sockets one by one. When he had plunged the last flame into darkness, he drew Gram from its sheath and walked toward the bed, reaching out with his right hand till he touched Brunichild's cool bare shoulder. This might be—will be—Gundrun in bed beside me, Sigifrith thought, and felt a stirring of heat as he thought of how it would be when he and Gundrun were wed.

"Stay where you are," Sigifrith said to Brunichild, laying his unsheathed sword down the middle of the bed. "This blade must lie between us for these three nights."

He heard the long shudder of Brunichild's inward breath, then the soft hiss as she let it out again. As his eyes began to settle into the darkness, her slender shape seemed slowly to lighten into a pale shadow against the fox-fur blanket.

"Why?" she asked.

"Because it was shaped as part of my orlog that I should ready my bridal bed in this way, or else get my bane from it."

"Then so it shall be," Brunichild said softly.

Sigifrith turned over on his side, his back to her, and closed his eyes. Though his sleep came swiftly, it was shallow, stirred into muddy fragments of half-dreams by Brunichild's thrashing and twisting about and by his sense of Gram's keen blade always laid at his back.

The morning of the third day was so foggy that a faint mist palled the chambers within Brunichild's burg. When Sigifrith went outside, he had to feel his way around the outer wall to the stable; fire rose through the fog, but the brightness of the mist did not lighten its thickness.

Brunichild was saddling her white mare. She did not look up as he came nearer, but only said, "If you're ready, Gundahari, we'll go now. There is no need to stay longer, and we may find better cheer somewhere else."

Sigifrith made sure Grani was bridled then led him from the stall. "What shall we bring with us? Grani can carry whatever belongings you wish."

"There is nothing more here. We shall have to go back to my father's house to claim my wedding-goods. Theoderid will not be able to come to the marriage feast himself, since you insist on holding it in Worms, but he will send an honorable band of warriors with us."

"All right. Where are your maidens?"

"They will follow after us. They're busy clearing up; when we are gone, this burg will be as I first found it."

She gathered her pale green skirts, swung them briskly to one side and mounted her mare. Sigifrith hauled himself on Grani's back, careful to leap no more easily than Gundahari's borrowed shape would allow.

"Follow me," Brunichild said, nudging her mare's white flank with the heel of one boot. The horse moved into a trot; Grani began to walk, keeping a few paces behind her as they rode down the hill.

Suddenly the sunrise glow of the fog died, leaving Sigifrith alone in a blindness of dark gray. Grani stepped over a linden shield between two spears, brushing the ashen shafts to either side as he passed through.

Sigifrith rode about for a few minutes, lost in the mist and the darkness of early morning. He could not see or hear Brunichild, and he was not sure where he was. Finally he raised a shout. It did not seem so strange now to hear Gundahari's voice calling, "Brunichild! Sigifrith!"

"Sigifrith!" a higher voice answered, the golden shaft of Sigifrith's own tenor cry ringing clear through the fog.

Sigifrith urged his steed to a gallop, riding swiftly toward the sound till Grani stood face to face with the Walsing's long-haired shape who held Goti's reins. He slid down and grasped the other's larger hands tight in his. His own blue eyes flashed bright at him through the mist; one deep breath of fog, cold and damp as if he were drawing water into his lungs, and Sigifrith looked down again into Gundahari's heavy-boned face.

"Sigifrith!" Brunichild cried, riding ghost-white out of the fog before them.

Sigifrith dropped Gundahari's hands, standing straighter to face her. Goti's reins dangled from his right fist.

The Visigothic maiden stared down at him. Her shoulders were trembling, as though she were about to be sick. "Sigifrith, Sigimund's son, Fadhmir's Bane. Where have you been?"

"I . . . I waited and held Gundahari's horse, while he rode through the fire to wed you," Sigifrith answered, lifting the stallion's reins up to her as proof. Goti tugged angrily at the leather straps, stamping his forehooves very near to Sigifrith's feet.

"He has been with me all this time," Hagan said from farther off in the mist. The fog seemed to warp his voice so that it rang roughly all around them. Sigifrith could not tell where the Burgundian stood.

Brunichild glanced quickly about her, as if looking for an ambush, then turned her gaze back to Sigifrith. "It was you who rode through the fire as I lay sleeping; you had my love, and you pledged then that I would be your bride. What have you done to me?"

"What have you done, Sigifrith?" Gundahari echoed in a whisper, his brown eyes as wide and blank as those of an ox stunned for slaughter.

"That is Gundahari's ring you wear, and you pledged yourself to him on your mound!" Sigifrith shouted at her, shocked into fierceness. "I have broken no oaths. I pledged myself to Gundrun, Gebica's daughter, many years ago and shall be wed to her alone." Had the Helm of Awe betrayed him? Had this woman's keen gaze cut through the weaving of dreams after all, and seen the true shape of his soul?

"Gundahari forced me to become his bride. He is no Walsing, and he did not pass the flames that Wodan set about my soul. Why should the god have betrayed me so, to keep me from you when we had been parted so long already?"

"I have never seen you before in my life!" Sigifrith answered. He mounted Grani. As if in answer to his master's rage and confusion, the stallion reared, beating at the fog with heavy hooves. "Now I have heard enough of this madness!" Sigifrith roared as Grani's forefeet crashed against the ground. "Gundahari, take your betrothed back to her father's hall, if you will. I shall ride ahead to tell your folk of your deed, and warn them to ready the wedding feast for you and Brunichild—and for myself and Gundrun."

"Will you swear first that you are without guilt in this thing?" Hagan asked, darkening out of the mists on his horse. He held his throwing spear upright in his hand; though it offered no threat so, Sigifrith felt as though he would be able to lower and hurl it in less than a heartbeat. "That no pledge and no oath binds you to Brunichild now, that you can make no claim to her nor she to you?"

"I will swear it gladly and freely," Sigifrith said. Hagan rode closer, turning his spear straight so that the tip of the blade hovered only a hand's span from Sigifrith's chest. Cold beads of mist melted together and rolled in long shining trails down the oiled steel as Sigifrith laid his right hand on the weapon's thorn-sharp tip.

"Bright spear, holy weapon, by you be my oath sworn. Hear me, Wodan, god of my father, and judge my troth! I swear that I have never loved Brunichild nor sworn myself to her, that no bond of body or soul binds she and I. If I swear falsely, let this spear strike me down; let the line of the Walsings, Wodan's children, come to a woeful end!"

Hagan sat on his horse's back, staring one-eyed at Sigifrith for a long moment before he turned his gaze away. "Are you satisfied?" he asked Brunichild. "Sigifrith has sworn a fuller oath than I asked of him."

"He has earned his doom," she answered, so softly that Sigifrith was hardly certain he had heard her words. Then she raised her voice. "Come, Gundahari. Take me to my father's hall, as you said you would, and I will gather my marriage goods together. Let these two go where they will. I do not want them by me."

"Brunichild," Gundahari protested, riding close enough to lay his hand gently on her arm. "Beloved. Hagan is my brother by birth and Sigifrith by blood. Remember that, and behave toward them as you ought. I will have peace within the walls of my hall."

"I ride ahead," Sigifrith declared again. "Fare well, Gundahari, Hagan, Brunichild. I'll see you when you get back to Worms."

He wheeled his horse toward the north, riding swiftly into the mist. The shapes of his three companions were quickly lost in the fog, their voices fading away behind him.

THE WEDDINGS

Although Sunna, near to her Midsummer's height, shone hot on Sigifrith's back as he rode along the path toward Alapercht's hall, the mountain wind was cool as a rushing stream after the long road through Gaul. Grani trotted lightfootedly past the enclosures of the Alamannic horses, raising his head to sniff the breeze. Sigifrith had to knee the gray stallion hard, turning him away from the pen where the young mares frisked.

"Not yet," Sigifrith said, patting his steed affectionately. He smiled, his heart swelling against his ribs as he thought of Gundrun. "Hai, I know how you feel, Grani." He shifted in the saddle as the horse began to trot around to the stables.

"So you're back, are you?" Hrodkar grunted, seeing Sigifrith ride up. "Took you long enough to get here. Go on, I'll get him fed and watered. Herwodis and Alapercht will want to see you. I think they've got some news you'll want to know about."

"What kind of news?" Sigifrith asked, sliding off Grani's back. "Has there been word from Worms? Is it anything to do with Gundrun?" He unsaddled the horse and hung his tack on the empty hooks that had always been his alone.

Hrodkar grinned at Sigifrith, showing stumps of teeth like mud-streaked sandstone through his yellowing beard. His cackling laugh turned into a cough; he turned his head, spitting the thick gobbet in a high arch over the side of the path.

"Might say so in a little while," the horsemaster told him. "Not right now, I hope." Hrodkar's knowing eyes flicked over Grani, noting how the gray stallion lifted the long waterfall of his tail, how he shifted his hooves and shook his mane as he caught the restless scent on the wind. "On second thought, you'd better lead him in with the ready mares. I can't keep him out if he wants to get in, and we won't find a stronger stud anyway."

"Grani," Sigifrith said to his horse. The stallion twitched his ears forward and nuzzled at Sigifrith's shoulder. "Go on, then. It's all right."

As soon as Sigifrith had spoken, Grani sprang forward into a gallop, his coat glimmering silver in the sunlight as he ran back over the road they had taken, back to the young mares' pen. Sigifrith watched proudly as his horse leapt into the air, flying over the high fence as if he rode the wind.

Hrodkar shook his head, scratching beneath his beard as if flea-bitten. "Never seen anything like that horse, not since he was a foal," the old man muttered. "Don't know how you ever trained him like that. Damn good bloodline, though. Go on, Sigifrith, go up to the hall. They've probably guessed you're here already."

Alapercht's hall seemed very dark and cool inside, restful after Sunna's summer brightness. Herwodis and her husband rose as Sigifrith stepped over the threshold and nodded to the stone walkurja who held her shield with the frightful head as its boss to ward the hall.

"What news have you had?" Sigifrith asked excitedly, hurrying forward to embrace his mother.

Herwodis held her palm out to slow his rush toward her. "Careful, Sigifrith," she murmured. "You mustn't crush me too hard."

He hugged her with exaggerated gentleness, laying his cheek on the top of her silver-threaded crown of dark braids, then turned to embrace Alapercht as well. Looking at his adoptive father, it seemed to Sigifrith that a new flush of youth had come to the Alamannic king's face, just as Herwodis seemed as pink-cheeked as a maiden, the creases about her eyes and mouth hidden in the dim light of the hall.

"What news have you had?" he asked again. "Hrodkar said there was something I needed to know."

"Sit down, Sigifrith, and be welcome," Alapercht said cheerfully, gesturing to the end of the table where a wine pitcher and three goblets were set out by a plate of bread, cheese and strawberries. "I can see you haven't changed a bit."

Sigifrith followed him to his seat. Herwodis came afterward, pouring wine for the three of them. Then she settled herself comfortably between her husband and her son, leaning into the crook of Alapercht's arm.

"The songs about you have traveled swiftly, my son," she said. "You have certainly honored Sigimund's inheritance, as well as the clan that raised you. Now tell me, are you going to bring Gundrun home with you, or will you stay in Worms with your bride's family?"

"I . . . I don't know. Gundahari has offered me a place beside him. What do you think?"

"It is more usual for a husband to bring his bride back to his own lands," Herwodis commented. "Still, we have seldom heard anything but good about Gundahari himself. I think the choice must be yours alone."

"You know you will always be welcome here, Sigifrith," Alapercht added. He sipped at his wine, then smoothed down his moustache. "Though Gundahari is a young man, and very ambitious; you would not do badly to take a place with him, at least for the time being."

"Do you think so?"

Herwodis patted her son on the shoulder. "You would not be giving up your place here, after all. And it is, I think, past time that you learned more about the world beyond our forests and fields. Ragin was a good teacher of some things . . . " Her voice wavered for a moment, like a bird caught by a gust of wind; then she went on as strongly as before. "But he was very old, and you need to know more than your ancestors knew if you are to rule in this world."

Sigifrith sat up in his seat, looking impatiently down at Herwodis and Alapercht. "Will the news you had for me have anything to do with this?"

"Oh, no," Alapercht said at once, shaking his head in a sudden flurry. "You mustn't think that it does."

"What is it, then?"

Herwodis and Alapercht exchanged a quick look; it seemed to Sigifrith that the still calm of his mother's face softened like a lake melting into ripples as she smiled at her husband.

"We shall be having another child around Yuletime, if all goes well," she said, placing a hand over the curved mound of her belly. "After all these years, Frija has heard my call and healed my womb at last."

Sigifrith stared at his mother in surprise, unsettled and unsure of what he could say. It seemed to him for a moment as though he were looking at two strangers, the gray-moustached man and the heavy woman with silver in her wound braids, flushed as pink as newlyweds with the first child of their marriage just planted. He felt shocked into dizziness, as though the stones of the hall floor beneath his feet had suddenly failed and fallen; and yet at the same time he could not help thinking of the solid curves of Gundrun's hips and breasts that would bear and suckle his own child in the near course of time.

He raised his untouched cup of wine to Herwodis and Alapercht. "Then hail to Frija for her gift! May your child be born safely and grow up in health and joy, with the blessings of the gods."

"May it be so," Alapercht agreed, lifting his own glass. The three of them drank together.

The glass foot of Herwodis' goblet chimed through her soft laugh as she set it down again. "They say the second bearing is always easier than the first. I think we will not need to fear. But tell me, Sigifrith, when shall you be wed? We had thought it would have been before now."

"As soon as Gundahari and Hagan can get back to Worms with Brunichild. Grimhild said that it was not fitting for Gundrun to be wed before her brother, and so she had me fare with Gundahari to win his bride."

Herwodis and Alapercht exchanged glances again. Sigifrith thought he could see an edge like the first sour sharpness of wine just starting to go bad showing through their joy.

"What is it? What's wrong?"

Alapercht bit his lip, looking down at the paving stones beneath his feet. Herwodis' gray eyes met Sigifrith's, her long gaze of consideration as quiet and weighty as he remembered from his earliest childhood.

"Did Ragin ever say anything about Grimhild to you? I think he might have been able to explain things better than I," she said finally.

"He warned me about her once," Sigifrith answered, thinking of how he had shouted at the swallow when they crossed between the march lances. The sharpness of the memory felt like the shock of cold water through sleep's drowsiness; he could not close his eyes to shut out the sight of the dwarf's dark eyes glinting with anger, or the gold coins on Ragin's stone lids afterward.

"That was well done, then, if you heed it," Alapercht said in a breath of relief. "Perhaps, after all, it would be better for you to stay here."

"Why?"

"Because of . . . what Ragin told you about her. And even beyond the matters about which he should have counseled you, Grimhild may be expected to use you to her own ends and sacrifice you for the sake of her own children," Herwodis answered. "I don't doubt that Gundahari is an honorable man and that his mother's rede has served him well, but you must be careful in the kingdom of the Burgundians for your own sake."

"What do I have to fear?"

"You trust others, my son, because you yourself are true," his mother murmured.

Am I? Sigifrith wondered to himself, but Herwodis was still speaking. "I think you don't understand fear or jealousy of others' strength because you've never known either. I wouldn't worry if you were going to do battle with your sword, but in struggles within the world of men your might is the last thing that can help you. You need to rely on your wisdom instead. And if you do stay with the Burgundians, you must be aware that Grimhild will always see you as a threat to the place of her own son and she will do her best to hold you in her power."

"What threat could I possibly be to Gundahari?" Sigifrith asked, bewildered. "He is their king, and he's been a good king for years. I wouldn't want to take his place if I could."

"But now you are Sigifrith Fadhmir's-Bane, and men are starting to think you the greatest hero of the northern lands," Herwodis said gently. "Perhaps it would be better for you to bring your bride home after your wedding feast. At least you ought to think about it." She put her hand on his shoulder again as he started to rise to his feet. "No, sit down and eat. We can talk about it later if you like. But now you must tell me about your faring through Gaul. What are the lands like, and what sort of folk are living there?"

Sigifrith sat and talked to Herwodis and Alapercht till they had eaten the food set out and drunk all the wine. Then Alapercht stood, saying that he had some work with the horses to attend to, and Herwodis said that the new batch of bread must have risen by now and she needed to go and bake it as well as seeing to bedding and such for Sigifrith. He would have to sleep in their chambers that night, since Hildkar had wedded one of the Saxon girls, Olwyn, and there was no more room in his house.

Sigifrith wandered out of the hall, uncertain what to do with himself. Without thinking about it, he found himself following the stream up into the woods, turning off along the path that led to Ragin's cave. He shrugged, then walked back to the stream and sat down cross-legged on the bank.

It seemed to him that he could hear the soft voices under the high bright twittering of the birds; that if he only listened more closely they would speak to him again. He sighed, closing his eyes.

"Where is Ragin? Where is Ragin? Where is Ragin?" a wood-pigeon called.

"Gone, gone. To rock; to stone," a cuckoo answered it. "Gone, gone."

"Why did Sigifrith forget so soon?" another bird's voice glimmered above the rustling of the leaves.

"Why does he wear Andward's ring? Where is the maid he should wed?"

"She longs for him day and night. She is pale and sad since he left."

"Come back; come back; come back," another cuckoo cried, deeper in the wood, and the first sang back to it, "Untrue; untrue; untrue."

Sigifrith put his hands over his ears, shaking his head as if to dislodge a host of burrs from his tangle of hair. When he opened his eyes again, the words in the birds' voices had cleared to meaningless song. He could not stay where he was; he got up and walked toward Ragin's hill.

The outcropping of rock was the same, but the door he had waited at was no longer there, only craggy stone showing through earth like jagged bones. Sigifrith, moved by the echo of a memory he could not shape more clearly in his mind, walked up to the side of the hill and placed his palms against the cold rock, listening. He half-expected to hear Ragin's grumbling voice, or the clink of metal on stone from within, but there was nothing except the buzzing of the bees on the flowers growing through the grass above and the melodic chattering of birds through the leaves.

Sigifrith had planned to leave at dawn the next morning, but when he got up he found that the hall was full of people, his Saxons and the thanes who had sailed north with him. One of the long tables was heaped high with wedding gifts: linen sheets and embroidered quilts of goosedown; finely carved things of wood, chests and plates and bowls; and, most precious of all, twenty-four clay jugs of honey mead for Sigifrith and Gundrun to drink on the wedding night and the nights after so that their marriage would be fruitful, standing beside a clear pitcher garlanded with flowers of frosted blue glass and two matching goblets with rippling blue stems twining up from their feet to the blossoms around the bowls. Alapercht and Herwodis sat at the head of the table, smiling at Sigifrith as he stood amazed in the doorway.

A cheer went up when Sigifrith stepped into the hall, the gathered folk rushing to greet him. Afterward, he remembered Hildkar banging him on the back, a grin cracking the thane's long face in two; he remembered Otkar's daughter Otfrith smiling shyly up at him for a moment before Theodipald's wide shoulders crowded her away and Kunitrut's fat widow Donaridis cackling with friendly laughter, but the rest was as blurred as if he had been in battle, except that he had stood and smiled helplessly, muttering, "Thank you. Thank you," and wondering what he had done to earn this outpouring of joy for his wedding. But at last a path cleared through the thanes and their wives and he could get through to his mother and Alapercht.

"You didn't think you were going to steal away empty-handed and alone, did you?" Alapercht asked, getting up to embrace his adopted son. "Since Herwodis and I can't come with you, we'll at least make sure that the Burgundians know we haven't forgotten you're getting married. We've reached two of your ships, so you can take thanes and horses with you."

"Oh. I . . . Thank you! That's wonderful."

"You'll go as befits your house," Herwodis told him. "And here, this is my present for you and Gundrun."

A tiny mew pierced the air as she stood, lifting a scrap of tabby fur from her lap. The kitten gazed up at Sigifrith and mewed again, showing little white thorn-teeth in a pink mouth. He stared at it, nonplussed; he had seen tamed cats in Gaul, but they were rare among the German folks.

"Oh. Thank you," Sigifrith said, letting his mother set the small creature into his hand. "What should I do with it?"

"If you're kind to her, Frowe Holda will bless your marriage with children and love. If you're not, it will rain on your wedding day and your wife will beat you."

Sigifrith petted the kitten between her ears with the tip of one finger. She let out a purring noise, walking about on his palm and peering over the edge. He caught her before she could teeter off, bringing her to his chest where she snagged her claws in his tunic at once.

Alapercht and some of the thanes were laughing openly, and Herwodis' hand was before her face as if to hide a smile. Sigifrith could feel his ears heating with embarrassment. "Um. What do I feed her on?"

"Milk and meat and fish and bread soaked in milk. When she gets bigger, she'll catch mice for you."

Sigifrith bent down to kiss Herwodis on top of her head, holding the cat carefully to keep her from falling. Then everyone had to show Sigifrith which of the gifts they had brought and tell him how they had made it or found it or bought it. He thanked the thanes and their wives till he was dizzy with it, still wondering how he had earned so much love.

"I will come back. I promise I will," he said, over and over.

At last the throng of folk began to unload the table and carry their gifts down to the ships at the pier.

"Frija bless you," Sigifrith said to his mother, hugging her about the shoulders as gently as he could.

"And may all the gods and goddesses fare with you, Sigifrith." Herwodis looked up at him, her gray eyes glimmering. "May your drighten Wodan deal more kindly with your marriage than he did with your father's. Be careful, and come back to us soon."

"I will," Sigifrith answered. They stood there in silence till the kitten tried to crawl down Sigifrith's arm, lost her balance and dangled from a fold of his sleeve by her claws, miaowing piteously. Then he had to laugh, disentangling her and holding her out before him. "Is this . . . cat supposed to climb on me all the way to Worms?"

Herwodis pulled a lidded basket out from under the table. "Keep her in this, but be sure you let her out often enough or you'll have a little mess to clean up."

The basket was roomy, with a stuffed woolen cushion inside. The kitten wriggled and mewed when Sigifrith thrust her in, her plaintive cries creeping out for a few moments, but in a short while she seemed to settle down.

"Fare well," Herwodis said.

"Stay well," Sigifrith answered. He and Alapercht got his tack from the stable, then walked down to the pen where Grani stood tall amidst the serviced mares, silvery in the morning light, his neck arching high above theirs as if they were bowed before him. Sigifrith and his adoptive father stood leaning on the wooden fence, watching the horses.

"We'll have some good colts out of those," Alapercht said.

"I should hope so." Sigifrith smiled quietly with pride. "I don't think you'll find a sire from more of an atheling-line."

"No. Um . . . Sigifrith, about siring and such."

"Yes?"

"I've never talked to you about this before . . . I think probably I should have." Alapercht looked down at the horse-cropped grass, away from Sigifrith's gaze. One late-flowering spike of wild spear leek had sprung up by a fence post, its bloom shining white above the green blades around it. Sigifrith knew the worried look drawing Alapercht's forehead down into wide ridges, knew the way his cheeks pouched as if he were uncertain as to whether he should let his words loose or hoard them for the winter. "Um, as far as I've heard, you never went to any of the hamlets nearby to do, well, what young men do. Hildkar said you'd taken one of the Saxon girls to your bed up north, but Irmingeld wedded her after Ostara and he said she was still a maiden. Now, some young men are just shy, or late coming to it, but no one's ever said that you were unduly held back in anything you chose to do. Well . . . you see what I mean?"

"I don't want anyone but Gundrun. I never have."

"But you do—?"

"Oh, yes. More than anything. When I came back to Worms and saw her . . . " Sigifrith's heart hammered faster even as he thought about it, and the heat began to rise through his body.

Alapercht nodded, satisfied. "Yes, you do, don't you? Well then. There are some things you need to know about. It's never easy for women the first time, and I expect Gundrun will have a worse time of it than most, if you know what I mean. Remember, no matter how badly you want to leap on her and start swiving, you'll have to be careful with her, or you'll hurt her badly. And there's something else you'll have to be aware of too, especially the more you come to love her . . . "

The Alamannic king gazed into the pen again, watching Grani among the mares, and it seemed to Sigifrith that his hazel eyes were blurred, as though he were looking through a ripple of water. "Do you know why it's customary to give your wife her morning gift after the wedding night?"

"It's the price for her maidenhead. Isn't it?"

Alapercht shook his head, staring beyond Grani to the dark roof of the stables. Grass grew thickly over the low mound near the stable door, starred with the white flowers and blood-drop fruits of wild strawberries. "Young men often think so. No. You're paying her weregild in advance, because when you plant your seed in her, you're putting her in the greatest danger she'll ever face in her life. How many wives of my thanes have died in childbirth since you can remember?"

The first childbed death Sigifrith remembered was Hildkar's mother, who had died giving birth to her eighth (though only Hildkar had lived past two winters) the summer after the Alamanns had crossed the Rhine; from all the men that had fallen in the north against Lingwe's folk, only eighteen widows had been left behind; and Arnolf's widow Swanhwita, who had been with child when they sailed out, had died of childbed fever around lambing time.

"You know what injury your mother took giving birth to you; and for all she was only fifteen winters old, Herwodis was as tall as she is now and nearly as broad in the hips. Gundrun's older, so that may do some good, but though I'm told she's strong and healthy, I've also heard that she's a small woman and not likely to bear with ease. I'm telling you this because . . . well, I can tell how you feel, and I'm afraid you'll come to care for her more than might be good for you. Do you understand what I mean?"

Sigifrith nodded, his breath strangled in his throat. It was all too easy for him to see Gundrun torn from within, the blood mixed with water streaming around the red dome of a child's skull too large to pass through the narrow way . . . it almost seemed as though he had seen it before, in a dream or a flash of foresight, and none of his strength could help to shift it.

"What can I do? Is there anything . . . ?"

"Call on the gods and goddesses for their blessing, maybe. But I think . . . In the end, all you can do is hope that Wyrd has written kindly for Gundrun and that a good orlog is laid for your wedding. Maybe that's all anyone can do about anything."

Sigifrith was silent for a while longer.

Alapercht laid a hand upon his arm. "Sigifrith, you have to go on with it and you have to beget children. There is no other choice, unless you want to run away and live like a wolf in the woods. I hope I haven't distressed you too deeply; but you have to know about the dangers that might come so you can be ready if they do. Herwodis wasn't my first wife," he added in a softer voice. "No more than I was her first husband. Their children and our fighting; we each have the same risk of death, though our battles are on different fields. But now is the time for you to be joyful, because that day is a long way off and there's no good worrying can do about it."

"I understand," Sigifrith said, and the words seemed to rise from the well-spring of his heart without his willing it, because he wasn't sure that he did. But the sun was beginning to warm the meadow and Gundrun was waiting for him, so he put two fingers in his mouth and whistled shrilly for Grani. Alapercht winced away from the sound; but the wind-gray colt rose in a great leap from where he stood, clearing the wooden fence and landing beside Sigifrith.

Alapercht shook his head in wonder, staring up at the horse as Sigifrith began to saddle and bridle him, but he said only, "I suppose it is time for you to go, then. Gods and goddesses be with you, and fare well."

"Stay well," Sigifrith answered. The basket in his hand let out a sharp startled mew as he leapt on to Grani's back and nudged the horse into a canter, heading toward the Rhine where his ships were waiting for him.

Only Hagan was waiting on the dock as the current bore Sigifrith's ships down the Rhine. Sigifrith knew him from a long way off by the dull gleam of his mail-shirt. No wind was blowing; here on the plain around Worms the weather was very warm and weighted with the heavy mugginess of a building thunderstorm, though no clouds darkened the hazy blue sky or shielded the earth from Sunna's hot gaze.

"I remember him," Hildkar said balefully, looking over the ship's railing at Hagan. "He was wearing that same damn byrnie when the Burgundians came to pledge peace with us."

"Probably not the same one. He's grown since," Sigifrith pointed out.

"You know what I mean. Is it true what they say about him?"

Sigifrith remembered how earnestly Gundahari had made him swear not to tell anyone, and answered almost at once, "Of course not."

The Burgundian had turned his head; far off as they were, it seemed to Sigifrith that he could feel the spear tip of cold in the other's glance. As he watched, Hagan raised a long black horn to his lips as if about to blow a warning, and Sigifrith realized that the apple of the Walsings was hidden in the drooping folds of the windless banner. He cupped his hands over his mouth, shouting before Hagan could sound his horn.

"Hai! Hagan! It's Sigifrith!"

"Sigifrith!" Hagan shouted back, his voice carrying easily across the water. "Come on, then!"

Sigifrith took the foremost pair of oars and began to row, and his flagship skimmed down the river ahead of the other vessel. It was not long before he was tossing the rope out for Hagan to make it fast around a post of the dock and jumping out without waiting for the gangplank to be set.

"You traveled fast," he said to the Burgundian. "I would have thought it would take longer with women and a whole band of Visigoths."

Hagan shook his head. "I came alone. I was asked to ride ahead so I could help ready things for the wedding. You might have told me that you planned to bring a host of your own folk with you."

"I didn't plan to . . . " Sigifrith began, when Theodipald interrupted him.

"Hai, Sigifrith! You want to get your horse off the ship before he finally succeeds at sinking it?"

Sigifrith beckoned, and Grani came walking along the gangplank, setting one hoof neatly before the other. The wood creaked and dipped alarmingly under the great horse's weight, springing up behind him as he stepped onto the dock.

"Sigifrith, you forgot your cat," Hildkar told him, grinning maliciously as he thrust the basket into Sigifrith's arms. "Your mother would never forgive you."

"Getting jittery before the wedding, are you?" Ehwamar asked. "Forgetting things already?" Two bottles of mead bulged from under each of his thick arms. Sigifrith decided it would be too risky to shove him into the Rhine.

"Your cat?" said Hagan, his eye flicking toward the basket with what Sigifrith almost thought might have been amusement.

"Don't you start. Where's Gundrun? When is the wedding?"

"I believe that Gundrun has retired to her room with a slight headache, though the news of your return may work a cure upon her. If their faring goes smoothly, the other wedding party shall have arrived when the Moon is full again."

But he was only full a night ago, Sigifrith thought in silent protest.

"As you guessed," Hagan went on, "they ride more slowly than the three of us alone. Brunichild herself would be no hindrance, but she has brought several of her maids and a wain full of wedding goods."

"Oh."

For the next month, Sigifrith was almost too busy to worry about how the wedding would go. By custom, he was allowed to see Gundrun as little as possible; instead Hagan put Sigifrith and Grani to work hauling stones to build the marriage baths in which the separate parties of men and women would be cleansed according to the Burgundian tradition. When that was done, he went with his thanes to hunt and to fish along the Rhine, catching their own meat and bringing in enough to ready for the wedding feast as well. The weather stayed hot and muggy with no storm to clear the air, so the hunting was more work and less of a game than it might have been, and the women complained about the trouble of storing the meat.

It was almost midmorning on the day after the moon had begun to wane when at last Gundahari and Brunichild, riding at the head of the band of Visigoths and followed by the maidens' wain, came into sight on the hazy edge of the southern horizon. Sigifrith and Hagan were standing in one of the old Roman watchtowers, watching as they came nearer. Brunichild was riding close to Gundahari, as if they were talking together, and it seemed to Sigifrith that she must be easier with her betrothed than she had been.

"Come," Hagan said to Sigifrith. When the band had reached the gates of Worms, they walked down the steps of the watchtower. Instead of going to the road, as Sigifrith had thought he would, Hagan led his companion through the city and along a narrow path between the river and the edge of the wood to a great heap of sandstone that jutted out high above the river's bank.

"What are we doing here?" Sigifrith asked.

Hagan lifted the aurochs horn that hung around his neck on a leather strap, slinging it over his back so he could climb onto the high rocks without risking any damage to it. He stuck his throwing spear in his belt and began to clamber over the stone.

"This has been the holy stone of the Burgundian folk since we came into these lands by the Rhine. When I blow the horn, it will summon the folk to the beginning of the marriage rites."

Sigifrith climbed on the heap of wind-eaten stone beside him, noticing how the folds of red rock were stained darker in streaks and driblets, as if by years of blood and drink poured out to the gods and ghosts of the land. It seemed to him that he could feel a low thrumming through the palms of his hands and the soles of his feet as he pulled himself up the rough sandstone, as though the sap of the earth were rising through the rock's deep roots. Sitting beside Hagan at the top of the stones, he felt oddly at ease, as if he had come at last to a place of rest without knowing how tired he was; and at the same time he was filled with strength, wanting to draw his sword and do some deed, though he did not know what.

"When will you blow it?" he asked.

"In a while. But you must go back to the hall and tell Grimhild that they are coming, then ready yourself for the feast."

Sigifrith leapt off the rock, his boots sinking to the ankles in the earth as he landed. He pulled his feet free and began to run back to Gundahari's hall.

Grimhild sat in the garden with two gray-haired women of her own age, embroidering the last stitches upon what Sigifrith thought might be a coverlet or a tapestry.

"Gundahari's here!" he called, dashing along the path toward her. "Hagan said to tell you and then ready myself."

Grimhild rose to her feet, bundling up her work and thrusting it into the hands of the woman on her left. "Has he gone to the rock yet?"

"Yes."

"All is as it should be, then. Go to your room. You'll find your feast clothing laid out, and I'll send your men in to you. When you hear Hagan's horn, go to the rock. If you should see Gundrun, do not try to speak to her. Hurry, you don't have much time."

Sigifrith hastened to his chamber. As Grimhild had promised, his best tunic and breeches were laid out on the bed; the young cat was curled up in the middle, a tabby stain against the gold-embroidered scarlet. When he lifted her gently to move her to one side, she let out a miaow and swiped at the back of his hand with her claws.

"Why did you do that?" Sigifrith asked her, stroking her with one hand as he dusted loose cat hairs from his tunic with the other. The cat looked up at him through slitted golden eyes, putting back her ears, and miaowed again. As Hildkar, Theodipald, Ehwamar, Harthpercht and Irmingeld rushed in, she leapt off the bed and ran under it.

Before Sigifrith could say anything, the thanes were clustered around him, stripping his clothes off against his token efforts to fend them away.

"Hoo, Gundrun's going to have a night of it!" Harthpercht cackled when they pulled Sigifrith's breeches down around his ankles. "What'd the horse say, boy?"

"What horse?"

"The horse you stole that thing from!"

"He's blushing," Hildkar chortled as the men, laughing, pushed Sigifrith on to the bed. Harthpercht pulled off one boot, Theodipald the other; Irmingeld waved his hand as if to fan away a stench and made a horrible face.

"Have your feet died in there, Sigifrith?" he asked. "When did you wash them last?"

The thanes tugged Sigifrith's feasting clothes out from under him and began to argue over how they should be put on.

"Hai, you've got those back to front," Sigifrith protested when they finally began to work his breeches up over his legs. He kicked out lightly and knocked Ehwamar to the floor.

"Why not? We thought you might need more room in there," Theodipald said, but they turned the breeches around, then the thanes pulled him up to his feet.

"Put your arms up, Sigifrith," Harthpercht ordered. "No, not like that, none of us can reach that high."

"Get a ladder!" Ehwamar said. "Or Hildkar can stand on my back . . . yah, there!"

Harthpercht and Irmingeld made a cradle of their hands, lifting Hildkar to balance on the shorter man's wide shoulders. Theodipald handed the tunic to him.

"You sure this is a tunic?" Hildkar asked, flapping the big piece of scarlet cloth around. "Hai, Sigifrith, now we know why you didn't worry about our ships in the storm up north—you were wearing the extra sail." He dropped the tunic over Sigifrith's head, making Sigifrith thrash about in red darkness for a few moments before he could get his head and arms out of the right holes while Harthpercht gleefully shouted obscene advice.

"You've got it on crooked," Hildkar said, leaning down as if to straighten the tunic. He teetered, overbalancing, and fell into Sigifrith's arms to the laughter of the others.

"Can't you wait for Gundrun?" Irmingeld asked as Sigifrith threw Hildkar onto the bed.

"He's like a ram in spring—once the scent hits him, he doesn't care what he's going after!" said Ehwamar. Hildkar got up, his face red; it was only then that Sigifrith noticed that the thane had put his tunic on inside out.

He had the garment halfway over his head again when the muffled winding of Hagan's aurochs horn blew deep beneath the men's laughter. As he struggled frantically to get the tunic off without tearing it, they began to push against him, trying to hurry him along. Sigifrith stood firmly against their prodding, whipping the shirt over his head, turning it, putting it on again and belting Gram on before he let them rush him out to where the other Alamannic thanes waited in the hall with a band of Burgundians. Down at the end of the passage, he could hear Gundahari cursing and struggling as he tried to turn a tunic that had been put on him backward while his men shoved him along.

"Hurry, hurry," the thanes shouted, pushing the two bridegrooms out of the hall as Hagan sounded his horn again. "Your brides are waiting for you, don't let them be lonely. Go on, go on, there's no time to waste!"

The band of men ran down to the Rhine, going along the narrow path by one and two. Gundahari had managed to straighten his tunic and belt his sword on, but he was breathing hard as he struggled to keep up with Sigifrith. They could see Hagan standing on top of the red stones with his spear in his left hand, a dark shadow against the thickening haze of the sky. As they neared, he lifted his horn and sounded it once more.

The men gathered in a quarter-circle by the rock, pushing Sigifrith and Gundahari forward to the base of the stone stack.

"What do we do now?" Sigifrith whispered to his fellow bridegroom.

"We wait for the women's party. They won't be long."

Nor was it long before Grimhild, dressed in fine southern brocade woven of deep red and purple, led the two white-clad maidens down the path before a train of women who carried green branches and flowers. The circlet resting on Brunichild's fair head was made of pale Roman silver, wrought into a ring of tiny arrow points; but Gundrun's bride circlet was a smooth fillet of gold. Both young women's hair flowed freely, snow-blond and honey-brown. After this day, Sigifrith knew, they would not wear it loose again; that was only for maidens.

The women arranged themselves to fill out the rest of the arc around the holy stones. Grimhild took Gundrun's hand with her right and Brunichild's with her left, leading them forward to where Sigifrith and Gundahari waited.

"Why have you called us here?" she cried up to Hagan, her voice thin through the muggy air. "Does a foe threaten? Is war upon us?"

"Our foes do not threaten; it is not time for war," Hagan answered. "The horn is sounded in frith. I call the folks here to witness the weddings of Gundahari, Gebica's son, King of the Burgundians, and Brunichild, daughter of Theoderid, King of the Visigoths; of Sigifrith, Sigimund's son, Fadhmir's Bane, of the house of Alapercht of the Alamanns, and Gundrun, Gebica's daughter. But Gebica and Sigimund are fallen; Alapercht and Theoderid dwell in their own lands. Are there any kinsmen here who witnessed the pledges of betrothal, who can vouch for the dowries of these maids and say that this is rightly done?"

"I witnessed my sister's betrothal to Sigifrith, Sigimund's son, and I shall keep the oath my father Gebica swore in the matter," Gundahari answered. "Gundrun is given as peace-weaver between the folk of the Burgundians and the folk of the Alamanns. As dowry I give with her thralls, twelve maids and twelve men; I give four and twenty cattle of our best breeding; twice twelve gold arm-rings of three ounces each, and twice again that of silver, more than my father first swore. So shall it be seen how I prize my sister."

"Who speaks for Theoderid?"

One of the Visigoths, a heavy-set man in a tunic of Gaulish checkered weave whose blond beard overspread his chest, stepped forward from the men's side. "I, Totila, the son of Theoderid's mother's brother, witnessed Theoderid's betrothal of his daughter Brunichild to Gundahari. Theoderid has sent with us a dowry of twenty-four lengths of the finest silk from the South, forty-eight ounces of silver and forty-eight of gold in the coinage of the Emperor Valentinian, which all men say is the purest within memory, and a full hundred-count of bottles of the best red wine of Gaul; and with that I say that it shall be rightly done if these two are wed."

"Does any challenge this wedding, or know of shame darkening the names of bride or groom?"

Sigifrith heard the low hiss of breath between Brunichild's teeth, saw Grimhild pale with pain as the Visigothic maiden tightened her fist on the older woman's thin hand. He met Brunichild's steel-blue eyes calmly, fixing her with the might of his gaze as if he could hold her still. At last the water of tears blurred the keenness of her glance; but she did not speak. Again he wondered what he had done, what he could have done, and found no answer. When she is married, he thought to himself, this strange fancy will go from her and she will be content to be queen over the Burgundians.

"They are not cleansed according to the way of our folk!" Grimhild called. "Not till this is done can they come before our gods and ghosts to be wed."

"Then go to the place which has been readied!" Hagan commanded. "Let the fire and clean waters, the smoke of the holy herbs, cleanse their bodies and their souls so they may come whole and holy to swear their oaths to each other, as is the way of our folk."

"So shall it be," Grimhild cried. She waved her arms, gesturing to break the half-ring of gathered folk into two parties again. The women circled around Gundrun and Brunichild, guiding them back along the path.

Hagan climbed down from the rocks to join the men's band as they ringed themselves around Sigifrith and Gundahari, following at a safe distance from the women. The two groups went to the mound-shaped houses that Sigifrith had built of stones and the Burgundian women had calked with clay and twigs. At Hagan's direction, he had left the doors on opposite sides of the mounds so that no one standing before one could see anyone at the other. Now, as the men began to strip before the door of the bath, he knew why. He took his clothes off with the rest, laying them on the ground beside the wooden tub that the thralls had hauled up and filled with cold water, and crouched to pass through the narrow doorway.

The first unexpected breath of steam mixed with the sweetish smoke of burning herbs seemed to tear at Sigifrith's lungs, making him cough and choke. Then the warmth began to spread out from his chest as it soaked in from the steam already beading on his bare skin, easing his muscles. He lowered himself to sit cross-legged before the glowing coals from which curls of bluish smoke rose into the thick steam that filled the mound-hut, breathing in deeply as Gundahari came to sit next to him and the others gathered around them.

"Are you ready to hear words of wisdom?" the Visigoth—Totila—who had spoken for Brunichild asked them.

"We are," Gundahari answered. Sigifrith nodded his agreement. It seemed to him that the dark walls of the stone house were beginning to sparkle with lightless gleams of blue and crimson in his eyes, as though he had held his breath too long. He drew in another deep lungful of mingled steam and smoke, listening carefully to Totila's words.

"You shall praise the day in the evening, a woman when burned on her pyre; a blade when it is tried, a maid when given in marriage; ice when it is crossed, ale when drunk. Let no man trust the words of a maid, nor that which a woman speaks. For on a whirling wheel were their hearts shaped, and brittle in breast were laid."

"Heed now my speech," one of the Burgundian men went on when Totila fell silent. "For I know them both: brittle are the thoughts of men to women. For we speak most fairly when we think the falsest, for so work the wisest wits. Let no man mock at the love of another ever. Often the wise fall where fools would not to the lure of a lovely maid. It is unwise for one to mock at another about that which befalls many warriors. Foolish or wise are by fairness fooled, and by the might of love."

Harthpercht spoke next; "Do not let your wife visit her kinsmen often, although she asks to; only sorrow will come of it. Nor should you stay out with a mistress. And you should never foster the child of a man who is higher born than yourself."

Sigifrith's head was spinning with the strong smoke; he felt as though the dark hut had grown to the clouded dome of the night sky and he were floating above the coal-glow of the setting Sun. The sparks of stars flashed and wheeled behind his eyes; men's voices muttered and grumbled their wisdoms far below in the steam-hut, as they had since the Goths had fared in their ships from the Northlands and the forefathers of the Saxons had scratched for oysters in the sand with sticks. He could feel the middle of his forehead growing numb, as though something were pressing hard against it.

A deep voice, rough with the scarring of hemp, rang echoing through the hot clouds. "I sought the old etin, I am come back again, well did my speech serve me there. With many words I spoke my will in the hall of Suttung. Gunthjoladho gave a drink of the dearest mead to me upon her golden stool; I left her an ill reward afterward for her faithful soul, for her heavy heart. I made good use of the well-bought thing, and little lacks to the wise, for the wod-roaring mead has come up now for the oldest of earth's holy ones. Ill were it to me, I could not have come out of the garth of the etins if Gunthjoladho had not helped, the good woman in whose loving arms I lay. An oath on the ring did Wodhanaz swear: who can trust in his troth? He swindled Suttung, took his symbel-mead, and beguiled Gunthjoladho."

A second voice, higher and cracked with pain, hissed through the steam. "Are you mindful, Wodan, how in earlier days we blended our blood together? You swore you would not let ale be borne unless it were borne for us both. Now the wyrm's bale drips into my mouth; will you share this draught with me?"

Sigifrith could see the fire's glow through the white clouds of wet smoke, writhing and twisting into a fog-veiled shape like a man lying on his back; rings of black broke his brightness at wrists and ankles. Something dark loomed behind the glowing shape, the shadow of a hooded cloak stretching through the steam.

"You doomed my son to Hella's high halls; he shall not come hither again till the worlds' wyrd is dreed. I know that it was your hand which aimed the mistletoe that slew Balder the Bright, you who broke brothers' troth first. What meeter than that your son's ice-cold guts should bind you and the wyrm hang above?"

"You have many sons who yet live, and you yourself have betrayed many to their deaths. Bale-Worker, sworn brother, you have dealt no more fairly in battle than in love: often you give victory to the worse man, and death to the better."

"I have often dealt so; but now Balder has fallen and drinks Hella's mead while you drink of the wyrm's bale, bound beneath the earth. It shall be long before I come to this cave again, for Wyrd's web is not yet fully woven, and much may yet go amiss with my work. Stay, as you must, and I shall fare as I will."

The roaring in Sigifrith's ears almost drowned out the reply, but he could still make out the pain-gasped words, "But what shall you do . . . without Loki . . . to bear the blame of your bale?" Then the sea-sound broke into the muttering of men's voices again, stinging and tingling over his body, like the slapping of leaves and slender twigs. Trying to focus his eyes, he saw the glimmering shadows of white birch rods lit by the glow of the coals through the fresh cloud of steam hissing up from them, and realized that the men were switching each other with bundles of the fine twigs. Someone thrust one of the bound sprays of leaves into his hand, and he swished it about the other dark figures in the steam-hut, laughing with them as they beat at each other. The ritual wisdom now given, the men were calling out their own advice to the two bridegrooms.

"Beat your wife before the week is out, or she'll think she owns you!"

"Don't neglect your marriage duties, and don't leave her alone too long! Get her with child soon, and she'll be a better wife."

"Don't fight with her kinsmen, because she'll never let you sleep in peace afterward."

"Bring her presents, and don't get in her way when she's trying to manage the household."

"Never argue with a woman, because you can't win, and if you do she'll make you suffer the rest of your life."

"If you're not careful, your wife will lead you around by your wedding tools. Remember, there are other women in the world if you get too needy."

"Beware if your wife casts her eyes on to another man too often, especially if he's younger and stronger than you are. Men have died over women before."

After a while, the men came out of the steam-hut and jumped into the tub of cold water. The freezing shock cleared Sigifrith's mind as though a block of ice had shattered over his skull; he came up gasping and red-faced with the rest of them, laughing as the blood tingled freshly through his limbs.

"Will you remember all that, Sigifrith?" a long bony Visigoth asked him as they crowded together to let the last of the men into the tub.

"Hai, look at his eyes," one of the Burgundians said, peering into Sigifrith's face. "He's dazed from the smoke. You Alamanns don't do this, do you?"

"Which what?" Hildkar asked blearily, as the men from the steppes tribes laughed.

"That one's gone," said Gundahari. "Quick, get him out of the water before he drowns."

Two of the Burgundians lifted Hildkar by his shoulders, heaving him over the wooden edge of the tub. He started thrashing and landed on his bottom in the grass, protesting incoherently.

"It's the herbs we put on the coals," Gundahari explained to Sigifrith. "He'll be all right in a little while when it wears off."

A loud splashing, followed by shrill squeals, rose from the other side of the steam-huts. "Eee, that's cold!" a high voice shrieked in a thick Visigothic accent as the other women giggled.

The men began to get out of the tub, drying and dressing themselves. When Hagan had put on his byrnie and taken up his spear again, he went to stand between the two mounds, calling, "Ready yourselves and come to the rock! We cannot wait any longer. And have your weapons ready, for there is slaying to be done!"

The group of men waited till they saw Grimhild lead the train of women out past the mounds, then followed behind to the holy rocks by the Rhine. Sigifrith felt curiously light on his feet, and the wind shimmered with rainbow-bright sparks around him; at the same time, he thought that the call of a battle-horn sounded, too deep for him to hear yet loud enough to shake the earth beneath his boots and send a shiver through his bones. His sight blurred as he and Gundahari stepped forward to their brides, so that it almost seemed to him as though great white swan wings swept up behind Bruni-child's shoulders; that she was clad in byrnie and helm again, as he had seen her first, and her eyes were bright as dawn through his half-dreaming sight. For a strange moment, he could not remember which of the women he was supposed to wed; then Grimhild raised her arm and he turned his gaze downward to Gundrun, who looked joyously up into his eyes. He knew that she was the dearest thing to him in the world, and he would rather have lost all that he had than her.

Sigifrith started as the bleat of a goat broke through his thoughts, and looked toward the stone. Several of Gundahari's men stood at its base with nanny and buck, sow and boar and cow and bull tied before them. Totila held a hammer in his hand, swinging it in a slow half-arc. The Walsing could hear the far-off rumbling of thunder; the clouds were rising over the Rhine at last, weighting down the thick air more heavily than before.

Grimhild stepped before the stone, spreading her feet and raising her hands to the sky. In her left she held a wooden bowl; in her right a bundle of pine twigs. "Holy gods and goddesses, hear us!" the Burgundian queen called, her thin cry as sharp as a swallow's. "Fro Engus and Frowe Holda, Donars and Sibicho, Tius, Frija, we call on you and on all the gods and ghosts who have fared with our folks. Hallow the oaths these athelings swear; hold them in troth and keep them whole."

The lightning flickered like a whip, closer now; the storm was riding toward the Rhine on wheels of thunder. Sigifrith could see that the men who stood by the bound beasts smiled at the sound: it was well-done for Donar to hallow the wedding vows.

"What blade shall you swear on, Gundahari?" Grimhild asked.

"On the sword of my father Gebica."

"What blade shall you swear on, Sigifrith?"

"On Gram, the sword of the Walsings."

"Then give your brides their rings upon the hilts, and take yours by the same, for ring and sword shall bind your oaths."

Sigifrith drew Gram and pulled the ring he had taken from Brunichild—the dragon ring, so like that Fadhmir had worn—from his finger, laying it upon the cold ice stone in the hilt. Carefully he stretched it out to Gundrun, who took it and slipped it on, placing the ring she had brought on the sword. Except that it was larger, the ring she gave was made like the one Gundahari had given Sigifrith for Brunichild, smooth gold clasping a large green stone. For a moment, Sigifrith wondered how Brunichild and Gun-dahari had chosen to manage their rings; but his back was to the other couple, and Gundrun was before him.

He took her ring from the sword and her hand in his, so that the metal of their rings touched in their clasp and on the blade of the sword.

"Do you vow to hold yourselves wed before the gods and all folk; to be true to each other in love and frith; and to honor the clans to which you bind yourselves now?"

"So I swear," Sigifrith and Gundrun said together. Gundahari and Bruni-child echoed them a half-moment later, lower and higher.

"Then may Tius and Donars witness it! May Frija and Frowe Holda bless your weddings, as you hold to your oaths; may many atheling-children be born of these two marriages so that your clans may wax great in the years to come."

Grimhild moved back, gesturing to Totila. Thunder boomed as the Visigoth swung his hammer in three great arcs: first over the heads of Gundahari and Brunichild; then over Gundrun and, because he could not reach much higher, before Sigifrith's face; lastly over the heads of the three pairs of beasts who lay bound for sacrifice. "Hammer hallow, holy hold you, free be you from all ill," Totila chanted, then spoke softly to Sigifrith and Gundahari. "Now you shall give these gifts to the gods, that they may bless your weddings with joy and fruitfulness."

Grimhild crouched down beside the animals, fingers curved about her wide blood bowl, as the two bridegrooms came to do the sacrifice. A few heavy drops of rain spattered down as their swords opened the throats of boar and sow, buck and nanny, bull and cow. The dark blood flowed out in torrents of mingled life, overflowing Grimhild's bowl and soaking the hem of her rich dress, spreading around the stained foot of the rocks and streaming into the waters of the Rhine.

The Burgundian queen set the bowl down on a wide ridge of sandstone, taking Sigifrith and Gundahari's sword hands in her own and joining them to the ringed hands of Gundrun and Brunichild. She dipped her twigs into the blood; cold drops of rain mingled with the hot as she sprinkled the two couples with the blood of the sacrifice till red drops hung in Gundrun's hair like garnet beads strung on bronze wire, glowing against Brunichild's pale face as yew berries against new-fallen snow, and the gold-set tooth around Gundahari's neck dripped as red as the wild boar's goring tusk. "So the gods' and goddesses' blessings be upon you," she cried, taking her bowl in both hands and whirling to fling the blood onto the holy stones. The splash sank into the sandstone almost at once, leaving a stain very dark among the many worn and ancient spoors of spilt sacrifice that deepened the reddish pink of the rocks. "Kiss your brides; then it is done and sealed."

Sigifrith bent down to Gundrun, his eyes closing as he felt her lips soft beneath his. The clean herbal scent of her thick wavy hair, the wine-sweetness of her breath; the feeling of her arms about his neck as he held her body close to his—slender, but more solid-boned than he had thought, her strength rising from the hot stew of love and anger seething within her. He tightened his arms, careful not to crush her, and felt her pressing closer to him in turn, her breasts against his ribs and the padded cradle of her hips against his groin . . .

He was aware of nothing else till he felt Gundahari's fist pounding against his shoulder. "Hai, Sigifrith, you'll have her all to yourself later. It's custom here for the new bride to kiss all the men for luck, and the new groom to kiss all the women. So move over and do your duty!"

Reluctantly Sigifrith straightened, holding Gundrun a moment more. The maiden's eyes were closed, her shoulders rising and falling with quick breaths; her half-parted lips were very pink, a little swollen from the strength with which he had kissed her. Opening her eyes as Sigifrith passed her to her brother, Gundrun almost staggered, but recovered herself quickly and smiled up at her new husband. He kissed her once more, swiftly; then wiped Gram on the grass and sheathed it before he moved over to Brunichild.

The Visigothic woman's eyes were downcast; she turned her face aside as Sigifrith took her lightly in his arms, as if she were unwilling to give him the ritual kiss.

"Come on," Sigifrith said to her. "Gundahari says it's custom here."

Brunichild looked up at him at last, tilting her head back. Sigifrith bent to brush her mouth with his.

A white blast of lightning scarred the sky, bursting off the inside of Sigifrith's skull. I've been struck, he thought first; then, as his sight cleared again, he saw Sigrdrifa's day-blue eyes staring into his, the rain beginning to wash the spatters of blackening blood from her bone-white face. . . . *While I was also born again as the earthly maiden Brunichild. So you must go forth and find the maiden Brunichild, daughter of Theoderid. She shall be waiting for you with your ring around her hand; a fire like this shall burn around her hall. . . .* And she had been all his thought, he had been coming to buy himself free of the betrothal to the Gebicungs—until he drank of the horn Gundrun had brought him, the drink in which he thought he had seen death-bale glowing.

Too late, Sigifrith knew what draught Grimhild must have brewed for him; too late, he knew the oath he had sworn for his own doom. And so he whirled her away into Totila's arms before he could break the last of his oaths and turned to kiss, first Grimhild's adder-cold lips, then each of the women in the bridal train with the same easy lightness with which he had embraced Brunichild.

The rain was beating down harder and harder; Sigifrith felt that he could hardly breathe, that he was drowning in water as deep as the skull bowl of the sky. But he laughed as he loosed the last maiden, hoping that no one would hear the ragged edge that scarred his throat. "What now?"

"We race back to the hall," Gundahari answered. "If the women come last, they have to serve the mead; if we come last, we do!" He slashed his hand through the rain; at once everyone began to run, slipping through the muddy grass and trying to push each other toward the riverbank. Though Sigifrith knew he could easily have outraced the rest, he paced himself, running along easily beside Gundahari.

It was not long before the bridegrooms and their thanes had outdistanced all the maidens except Brunichild. In spite of her skirts, she ran ahead of the men (running with Sigilind's swift light strides, white ankles gleaming below the hem of her dress).

"Go on," Gundahari panted to Sigifrith. "You've got to get there first— keep her out of the hall."

Sigifrith knew how this was done: it was traditional among the Alamanns as well, that a husband must bar the door and lead his bride over the threshold, lest she stumble. He stretched his legs into full stride, catching up with Brunichild and then passing her; he could not turn his head to look at her, but pounded his soles against the earth as if the numbing beat could shock his legs to dull the furious-edged emptiness within him.

Sigifrith reached the door of the hall and turned, drawing Gram and standing with his sword point down against the threshold as if he were threatening a downed foeman.

Brunichild was breathing hard as she dashed toward the door, her face flushed and her eyes bright as she looked up at him. "Are you Gundahari's watchman? His servant?" she asked, her voice sharp as the acid-hardened edges of a keen blade. "Or will it be you who leads me into the hall?"

"Your husband is almost here," Sigifrith answered. His hands trembled on Gram's hilt; he wanted to reach out to her, to draw her to him again. He remembered the strength of her grip, her lightness in his arms (and Sigilind standing in the brightness of dawn, fair and grave as she spoke of revenge; and the fires flaring around her), and he felt the hot pricking of tears behind his eyes as he tightened his fist on the smoothness of the ice stone, trying not to feel the faint ringing of her presence echoing through the clear crystal against his palm.

The men were laughing as Gundahari led them through the gardens around the hall, shouting, "Hai, Sigifrith, did you win? Or will we have to serve the ale tonight?"

"Come here, Gundahari, and lead your bride in. I can't keep her out much longer," Sigifrith called. His words came high and cracked from his smiling mouth, as if with laughter.

The Burgundian king slowed to a walk. Sigifrith stepped back and turned aside, letting him cross the threshold, whirl, and stand in the doorway with drawn sword for a moment. Sigifrith did not see Gundahari take Brunichild's hand, but he heard his friend say, "Come, my beloved, into the hall where you shall be queen." At her gasp of surprise Sigifrith looked back to see Gundahari's powerful arm bearing her up in her stride over the threshold; and he heard her breath of pain as she came down on a suddenly twisting ankle. Her husband held her so she did not seem to stumble, but Sigifrith had seen it and he knew Gundahari must have felt the fall of weight on his arm.

The Burgundian picked his wife up in his arms, carrying her to their seats at the end of the hall and kissing her before he set her down. Sigifrith turned back to the door, looking resolutely out as the women began to straggle into the garden. Gundrun was first among them, her thick hair fluffed out in windblown disarray and cheeks pinkish from the run. Sigifrith longed for the enchantment that would have filled him with joy at the sight of her hurrying toward him, but he smiled down at her when she stopped before his drawn sword, reaching out to brush her hair back from her face with one finger before he enfolded her firm hand in his own grasp. He hardly guided her as she stepped boldly in.

When she had crossed the threshold, Gundrun let go of Sigifrith's hand and clasped him about the ribs in a sudden, surprisingly tight embrace. He stroked her long mane of tangled hair, smoothing it beneath the maiden's circlet again; but he could not help glancing sideways to see the uncomprehending betrayal widening Brunichild's eyes as she watched him with Gundrun. He thought it must be the thing that would hurt him more than anything else, that he could not tell her how he, too, had been betrayed—how he had betrayed himself.

Sigifrith walked Gundrun to their chairs, his step light like that of a man who was merry. When he had seated her, he excused himself and went out into the garden as if he were going for a piss; but instead he rounded the hall and came in dripping through the back door, making his way through the passages to his rooms.

The cat, recovered from her fright, was creeping out from under the bed. She glanced up at him suspiciously, flattening her ears, but she stayed and watched until Sigifrith had taken the Helm of Awe from the bottom of his clothes chest and put it on with the graven sign between his eyes, then she fled back under the bed again.

Simple as it was, this disguise was surprisingly hard for Sigifrith to bring to his mind. But no one had ever named his will weak, and he knew that to keep the seeming of his honor and hold that of his blood-brother whole, he would have to achieve this. His body did not shrink, nor sprout horns nor wings—when he left his room no one would take him for anything but Sigifrith, Fadhmir's Bane—but when he was done the polished gold of his arm-ring reflected a face that was a little flushed with merriment and drink, the shadows of sorrow in his eyes hidden by the brightness of a bridegroom's love. His voice would be the voice everyone knew, singing out his brave mood and joy high and clear—stone with a gleaming glamor of gold cast over it—and the gold of the Helm of Awe, in the last dream of the disguise, was hidden by the woven net of magic so his head was adorned only by his waist-long flow of light brown hair, its thickness and length (so his mother had always told him) showing forth the strength of his manhood and the blood of his atheling-line. If Sigifrith's shoulders were bent as if his body clutched around a gut wound; if his face was stupid as a stunned ox's with shock, or his fists clenched in fury and grief; if tears of bitter longing and shame scalded his eyes to blur Brunichild's shining shape, no one but himself would ever see or know; and the words he spoke to others, helped in secret by the runes she had taught him on the mountain's peak, would be as light and merry as a man's might be.

"Wyrd writes as she will," Sigifrith whispered. Because of the dragon's enchantment that warded him, no droplets of blood fell from his palms where his nails drove into them and the Helm of Awe hid the deep white dents in his skin.

So, laughing, he went out into the thundering rain again, and so he came back into the hall.

"What took you so long?" Theodipald asked as he came in. "The women won't start serving the ale without you."

"Hush," Hildkar said to his fellow thane with mock severity. "We always knew he was full of shit."

Sigifrith put his hand over Hildkar's skull and shook it rapidly back and forth, leaning his head down close to the other's.

"What was that for?" Hildkar asked when Sigifrith let go.

"I didn't hear any rattling . . . I suppose the last rock has fallen out and it's completely empty in there now."

Hildkar's fist bounced back from Sigifrith's ribs; Sigifrith felt his mouth stretching to grin at his thane before he went to his seat between Gundrun and Hagan. As Sigifrith sat down, his new bride rose to her feet.

Gundrun and Brunichild lifted their glass pitchers, pouring the dark ale into their husbands' goblets together. Sigifrith reached for the glass, but Gundrun had lifted it first, making the sign of Donar's Hammer over the foam and then sipping delicately from it.

"My husband, I give you holy ale," she said, her words heavy with the measured rhythm of ritual. "Luck and joy I bring with this cup, and weal for our wedding years."

Sigifrith took the goblet from her hand. For a moment he wanted to crush the glass to powder beneath his fingers, spilling the drink out to stain the flagstones at his feet, though he could see that this cup was clean of any witchcraft or ill runes. But the net of glamor about him was already pulling his hand upward, speaking words through his mouth:

"Hail to thee, my bride, mother of sons to come!" He drained half the ale in an easy gulp, holding out the cup for Gundrun to finish off and fill again before she began to tend to some of the other men. Grimhild was already walking among the athelings and thanes with her pitcher; so were Brunichild and another woman whose red hair was bound up around her head. It took Sigifrith a moment to realize that this was Costbera, freed from the burden of her child; he had not seen her nor heard her name spoken since the faring to Tolosa.

"Your frowe looks very well," Sigifrith said to Hagan. "How did the birthing go?"

"It was not easy. She had much pain, and would not accept more help than our thrall-maid and a Christian priest could give her. This is the first time she has left our house since. Still, she bore a strong and healthy son to me, to whom I have given the name Nibel."

Nibel: it meant "Mirky Darkness"; and Nibelheim, the world of mists and darkness, was the land of the dead. "Will Gundrun slap me if I say that you've chosen an odd name for your son?" Sigifrith asked teasingly.

"It seemed to me fitting," was all Hagan answered.

The women went around again and again, pouring out ale and wine as the laughter of the thanes rose to drown out the sound of the thunder battering against the roof of the hall. Three of the Visigoths were singing a song about Thinderik's exile; every so often, a line or a few words would sound clear through the waves of talk and merriment. Ehwamar and a black-haired Burgundian thane were circling each other in one corner, stripped to the waist for wrestling, as the men nearest to them called out bets and insults. Sigifrith drank steadily, emptying his cup as fast as it could be filled, till at last a merciful fuzziness began to blur the edges of his sight.

"Hai!" Gundahari shouted suddenly. "We'll have to test the luck of our marriages. You see the pillars behind us, Sigifrith?"

There were two, carved of wood blackened with age and years of smoke, placed to either side of the great hearth as if to hold up the roof, though they came short of it by a handspan's height.

"Our folk brought them with us when we came here. You've got to stand on a chair and stab your sword into the top as deeply as you can. The depth of the mark you make will show the luck of your wedding."

In spite of the Helm of Awe and his rising drunkenness, Sigifrith thought that his face must have shown something because Gundahari made a gesture of waving away protest. "No, go on, you try it first."

Harthpercht, Hildkar and a few Visigoths and Burgundians crowded in at once as Sigifrith stood up, shoving and wrestling against each other to get at his chair and carry it over to the left-hand pillar.

"Go on, Sigifrith, show us how you can stick it in," Gundahari said, laughing.

Slowly Sigifrith climbed up on the seat of the chair and drew Gram. He held the sword's hilt clasped between his hands as he positioned the point in the middle of the pillar, very near to the top. For a moment he closed his eyes, trying to silence the rustling memory of apple blossoms, then drew the sword back and stabbed in a sudden burst of anger.

"Look out!" someone shouted; but Gram's blade had already passed over the scatheless top of the pillar; and Sigifrith, overbalanced by the strength of his thrust, was diving face first toward the slab of neatly edged black marble that served as the hall's hearthstone. Gleaming and swift as a flash of lightning, Gram struck the stone with a thunderous crash, the shock breaking through Sigifrith's hands and wrists as he landed full length on the hall floor.

For a moment he lay there, getting his breath back and letting the ringing in his ears fade into the ringing of laughter from the walls around him. Shakily Sigifrith spat a mouthful of black marble dust into the fire and stood, looking down at the shattered stone. The impact had driven the pain from his body, leaving him numb and aching all over.

Gundahari stood next to him, laughing so hard that he had to bend over with his arms braced against his thighs. "Are . . . you all right?" the Burgundian king finally managed to gasp out.

Sigifrith looked carefully up and down Gram's edge, making sure that no nicks or scars showed in the wyrm-patterned weave of dark and light steel and that the ice crystal was not cracked. "I'm fine. Uh, I'm sorry I broke your hearthstone."

Gundahari's face was red with laughter; he whooped so convulsively that Sigifrith might almost have thought his friend was having a fit. "You'll have. . . a fine marriage," he finally managed to wheeze out. "No one . . . has ever . . . made a mark . . . like that before . . . Hail Sigifrith!"

"Are you all right?" Gundrun demanded furiously from behind him. He felt her hands on his arm, trying to tug him around, and turned to face her. "Why did you do that, you idiot? Are you hurt?"

"Gundrun," Sigifrith said, as lightly as he could, "you should have heard by now that I'm not easy to wound. I'm afraid the stone I landed on is hurt much worse than I am."

"Well, don't do anything silly like that again. I've just got you and I'm not ready to get rid of you yet." Her jaw was firmly set as she stared up at him; he could not tell whether she was really angry, or only playing at it. "You great lout," she said, her voice softening. "I'm rather fond of you and I'd like to keep you for a while."

Sigifrith was about to pick her up to kiss her, but remembered in time how she had raised her fists to him the last time he had tried lifting her. Instead he bent down to her, noticing, for the first time how awkward it was. If she were as much as a handspan taller, he thought (if she were Brunichild's height, he could not help thinking), this would be easy.

"Go and help my brother," Gundrun told him as he straightened. Sigifrith nodded, lifting the chair and setting it down beside the other pillar. Gundahari was still laughing so hard he had to steady himself against the wooden post in order to climb onto the chair.

"Watch out, or you'll bring the whole hall down!" a Burgundian voice shouted from the benches. Gundahari convulsed in mirth again, snorting like a wounded boar.

"All . . . your fault . . . Sigifrith . . ." he choked. Everyone except Sigifrith backed away as Gundahari drew his sword, its blade shaking in his hand with his laughter.

The Burgundian king coughed several times, quelling his laughter with a frown of furious seriousness. The exaggerated sternness of Gundahari's face as he sighted along his blade and drew it back with both hands, gathering the strength of his shoulders and arms in readiness to drive the point into the pillar, undid Sigifrith completely, and against his will he let out a whoop of hysterical laughter.

Gundahari, caught in mid-stroke, doubled over. The tip of his sword skidded off the wood of the pillar; the scratch it left behind was hidden by the depth of the ancient soot stains and the shadows near the roof. Glaring at Sigifrith through his laughter, he pulled the blade back again, stabbing it deeply into the post and jerking it out. "There! Marriage luck and many children—that's how it ought to be done." He climbed down from the chair to the cheers of the gathered folk and went back to his seat where Brunichild silently waited to hand him another cup of ale.

The door from the kitchens opened and twelve husky thralls came out, their backs bent beneath a huge wooden platter on which the sacrificial boar and sow, now roasted, rested in brown and crackling state. They circled the hall once, then brought the roast swine to lay on the table before the two wedded couples. Hagan stood, knocking the haft of his spear against the flagstones for quiet. "Who claims the hero's portion?" he called. "Who has done the greatest deed this year?"

The cold gleam of Hagan's gray eye darkened in Sigifrith's sight as he realized that everyone was looking at him in the sudden hush after Hagan's challenge, two hundred gazes glittering as taut as bronze harpstrings stretched from a single point. He had slain the dragon: who, in all the tales he had ever heard, had done a greater deed?

Sigifrith began to rise from his seat; but in that moment he saw that one alone was not staring at him. Brunichild's ice-bright eyes gazed into Gundahari's—in triumph? In hope?—and Sigifrith remembered the terms of her enchantment and what she had said to him in the hall. He sat back in his chair, waiting.

Another moment passed before the Burgundian king jerked himself to his feet, lifting the carving knife that lay by the boar. "I claim the hero's portion," he said harshly. "For I have won Brunichild as my bride, though she was ringed by a fire that only the strongest might cross. Would any challenge me for it?"

The hall was so still that Sigifrith could hear the drumming of the rain on the roof, men leaning forward with their teeth clenched on eager breath to see if Sigifrith Fadhmir's-Bane would rise to his feet. Gundrun's hand tightened on his forearm; he felt the faint trembling running through her bones like the echo of an avalanche through rock, but could not tell whether she wished to hold him back or spur him on.

"Would any challenge me for it?" Gundahari called again. His face had gone pale; he stared straight ahead, not looking at Sigifrith, but the flickering of Brunichild's glance seemed to leave an after-image in the damp air of the hall, like the scar left by lightning through the clouds. Once more, Sigifrith thought; then it will be done.

"Is anyone here counted a higher hero than I? Does anyone question my right?" Gundahari's voice went up on the last words, its shrillness a hair's breath away from breaking. This time his gaze did waver toward Sigifrith; but the Walsing sat still, hoping that if he did nothing no one would dare rise to speak for him.

The Burgundian king breathed out gustily, creases deepened his brow, but the straight brace of his back seemed to ease. "Then so it is deemed!"

The Burgundians and Visigoths cheered, though the Alamanns muttered darkly. Sigifrith was careful not to meet Ehwamar's dark glower or Harthpercht's scowl, and turned his eyes away from the crushed-hound look of disappointment on Theodipald's face. He knew that he had wronged his men in not challenging, and there would be a reckoning later; but he had done what he could.

Slowly, as the cheering and the mutterings beneath it died away, Sigifrith felt the overstrung tautness around him melting into talking and laughter again, the lightning-copper taste fading from the air as Gundahari stabbed the carving knife into the crackling skin of the boar. Sigifrith's mouth watered at the rich smell of the juices flowing from the roast, and he could feel his stomach rumbling.

After Gundahari had lifted the hero's portion on to the plate that he and Brunichild shared and served Grimhild, Sigifrith took the knife from him and carved a piece out for himself and Gundrun. Only when he had sat down again did he notice a few men looking at him and realize that though Gundahari had taken the best portion, he had cut a much larger piece for himself.

"Are you stocking up for the winter?" Gundrun asked, looking at the heavily laden plate. Hungry as he felt, Sigifrith's throat tightened like a noose as he swallowed the first bite. Trying to loosen the knot, he drank some more ale, which helped him to choke the meat down. After the first few bites it became easier, though he had lost his joy in the rich taste.

Gundrun drew her gold-handled knife and began to cut a slice of pork into bits. The thralls were bringing platters loaded with loaves of bread; Sigifrith took a whole loaf, holding it out to his wife so she could break off as much as she pleased. Gundrun ate very neatly, he noticed, wiping the grease from her fingers with her bread and sipping delicately from her wine glass between bites; Brunichild was hardly eating at all, shaking her head as Gundahari tried to give her the choicest bits on the plate.

Cauldrons of soup were brought in next. Grimhild rose, ladling out a large bowlful for each of the two wedded couples. Sigifrith knew that the meaty broth had been seethed from the other sacrifices, the cattle and the goats; he could smell leeks and spear leek in it as well, and other herbs he could not name. He marked how Hagan, as always, sniffed at the soup before dipping a sop of bread in and tasting with the tip of his tongue, and thought he could guess why now. Sigifrith knew that the Helm of Awe would hide the look on his face, but he had to put his silver spoon swiftly beneath the table so he could straighten out the metal that had crumpled in his grip before anyone noticed.

When the eating was over, the women rose again to pour out streams of dark ale and golden wine into the cups of the gathered men. Gundahari's scop, a golden-haired young man who might have been very handsome had it not been for the elongated Burgundian troll-skull rising above his clean-cut face, stepped out before the king's table and began to chant.

> Far from Burgundarholm,   faring from the north,
> wandered our folk,   wind on the plains.
> No home we had then   no holt was builded,
> the eagle's wings beat   from east blew his might.
> Far from Burgundarholm,   faring from the north,
> first of the god-kin,   Gaut he was called,
> led us on our way,   left his kin behind him,
> Goes his line thus onward   to Gebica's sons.

> Far from Burgundarholm,   faring from the north,
> We dwelt then with Huns,   witch-children dark.
> Fury drove forward,   fighting from eastward,
> Sunna's way led us   we sought for new lands . . .

Sigifrith drank again and again as the scop told the tale of the Burgundian folk: how they had come to the Rhine, the long years of war with the Alamanns, by turns skirmishing with the Romans and allying with them against the other tribes pushing into the lands they had chosen to build in. When he began to chant the deeds of Gebica, Sigifrith looked down the hall to where two men he didn't know had stripped to the waist for a wrestling match. One was tall and thin with a curly shock of blond hair; the other was of medium height and sturdily built, two long brown braids dangling from his round head. The tall man dodged his opponent's charge, grasping at one of his braids and yanking his head around. The attacker grunted, but instead of trying to break the hold, he stepped in closer. His knee struck hard against his foe's thigh a finger's width from the groin; the next two blows fell almost at once, the blond man slamming his knuckles into the other's face even as the fist in his stomach doubled him over. They broke for a moment, gasping in air, then fell upon each other, their fists hammering brutally down. When the shorter man's face showed, Sigifrith saw that it was bloody and red welts were rising on the fair wrestler's shoulders and ribs. Sigifrith strained to pick out the bets that were being shouted back and forth through the scop's chant; even so he could not help but hear some of the words telling the tale of fair peace-weaver Gundrun and Fadhmir's Bane, Sigifrith, of the flames ringing Brunichild and the bravery of Gundahari. He drank more deeply, and with relief, as the scop chanted his last lines:

> The songs shall be sung   so, for our children,
> we who fared from Burgundarholm   forget we shall not.

It did not seem so long, then, before the women left the hall; before six of Sigifrith's thanes took torches and led him down the stone passageway toward his room, laughing the whole way and making ribald jests about Sigifrith's chances of doing his wedding duties properly. He laughed with them, uncertain. It seemed to matter less, now; their laughter made it easier to come to the door of his room where Grimhild waited with Costbera and four other women who bore torches in their hands.

Grimhild opened the door and led Sigifrith in. The fire was burning in the fireplace, and the room was bright with candles; to Sigifrith's drunken eyes, it seemed that a thousand gleams of light glimmered and wavered in the rush of wind from the passageway. Gundrun lay in the bed already, the sheets pulled up over her; the little cat sat tall at the foot of the bed, glaring at Sigifrith through slitted eyes that gleamed like chinks in the wall of a firelit hut.

Somebody nudged Sigifrith in the back, pushing him forward toward the bed. "You can't escape now! We're not going to let you out until dawn comes," one of the men—Theodipalt, Sigifrith thought—shouted behind him.

Slowly Sigifrith went to Gundrun, lifting the circle of gold from her head and setting it aside. He could see the twelve pairs of bright eyes gleaming in the passageway, witnessing what he had done and ready to speak for the final sealing of the wedding. Even as the door closed, he could hear Harthpercht's raucous voice outside—"Put out the candles, Sigifrith! If she ever gets a good look at what you've got, she won't stop running till she gets to the Danes' land!"—the sound of laughter, men's and women's, and a high Burgundian voice saying, "If it's half of what I've heard, I'd walk all the way from the Danes' land for a chance at it!"

He and Brunichild had been alone, with only Gram drawn between them. But now the mad wod was rising in him till his head swam; he felt, but did not hear, the sound in his throat. Gundrun paled, bracing herself as he kicked off his breeches and pulled back the coverlet. She raised her arms so that he could rend her white gown easily from her, then let him open her legs, clenching her fists like a warrior in readiness for what would happen to her, but making no move against him. Flung onto her, driven into her by the fury of his body, Sigifrith felt sick and dizzy as he never had in his life. It seemed that he was pitching up and down on the ocean; he heard the rending of the mast beneath the stormwind in Gundrun's shrill screaming, the waves rushing up to drown out the sound in his ears. He did not feel her hands pushing against his shoulders, nor the blow of her fist on his cheekbone, but he saw her eyes widen with shock, then droop suddenly shut as her last cry faded into his first.

Gundrun slumped back as Sigifrith withdrew from her. She was still breathing, but unconscious, her legs splayed at a strange angle as if Sigifrith had torn their sinews loose. He was shaking so badly that he had to brace himself against the wall to stand, sure that he was about to throw up. The pooled blood soaking into the linen beneath her was black in the candlelight, with pearl-pale streaks like sea-foam; her blood gleamed dark red on Sigifrith's sinking phallus, smearing the white skin of his inner thighs. Carefully, as if arranging a corpse, he moved her legs back together and pulled the blanket up over her. It was not long before the blood began to soak through it.

As Sigifrith tore the Helm of Awe from his head, it became visible again, flying across the room from his hand to strike the wall and drop in a jingling heap of gold. A noose of hot guilt choked his throat shut, unshed tears chafing like sand at the back of his eyes, but he could not help thinking: what if she died now? In time he might win Brunichild . . . in time . . .

He found his belt knife by his breeches and knelt beside the bed, reaching out to take Gundrun's small palms in one of his and holding his knife with the other. Though he lacked Ragin's skill, point and edge were as sharp as his own whetstone could made them. The eastward post: this was no living tree, but sap had flowed through it once and twigs sprung out. That life was still there, leaf and branch, though hidden beneath layers of years; and now

Sigifrith could see the ghostly shapes. He breathed deeply thrice, beginning to chant the healing-runes he knew from Sigrdrifa as he carved them into the bedpost: *uruz,* ᚢ , the aurochs-rune, cut thrice for health and strength; three times *nauthiz,* ᚾ , the strength of need, the slanted cross of the need-fire's bow drill; and thrice *berkano,* ᛒ , rune of Frija, the Birch-Goddess, to make Gundrun whole and fruitful, healing her wounded womb.

The galdor-chant of the rune names flowed forth on the wind of Sigifrith's breath as he drew the coverlet back and dipped the point of his knife in the blood, dyeing each of the runes red. He could see their angular stave-shapes glowing with ghostly fire as he brought Gundrun's hands carefully up and clasped her palms around the bed-post. She did not waken; but the bleeding slowed to a trickle, then stopped. Sigifrith felt the pulse in her neck with the tip of one finger. It was slow and faint, but steady. He knew that she would heal and live, and that she could bear him children in health.

Cloths and a bowl of cooling water rested on the table by the bed, together with the glassware and one of the jugs of mead Herwodis and Alapercht had sent. Sigifrith lifted his wife away from the clotting muck beneath her and clumsily set about trying to clean her before she awakened. He saw that Gundrun had lost the contents of her bowels and bladder under his attack, and now he did weep, his tears dropping onto her white face.

Gundrun's eyes opened, focusing dizzily. Her fist snapped out fast enough to startle Sigifrith, bouncing off the bridge of his nose. The blow did not hurt him, but the look on her face as she pulled the cover over herself and sat bolt upright felt like dirt grinding into an open burn.

"Don't you dare touch me!" Angry tears welled in her eyes as she stared at him. "What did you think you were doing?"

"I thought . . . I thought . . . "

"The women told me . . . you were supposed to . . . " Her shoulders began to shake with sobs of fury. "Damn it, Sigifrith, it wasn't supposed to be like that!"

"What should I have done?"

Sigifrith sat down on the edge of the bed and reached out to put his arm around her, but she shook him off, moving away.

"Don't . . . " Sigifrith started to say, but he was too late.

Gundrun choked off a cry of disgust as she jumped back toward him, staring down at the blood-drenched mess in the linen. When she turned her face upward again, the iron of her anger was gone, leaving only white hurt scored by lines of fear around her mouth and tear-reddened eyes. "You could have . . . I think you might have killed me." She pressed both hands against her thighs, as if unsure of their wholeness. "My mother and the married women said that even if you were gentle, it would hurt the first time and there would be a little blood, just enough to show on the sheets. Even Costbera told me that it was nothing that would hurt a strong woman too badly. And they said that you were likely to kiss me first, and tell me that you loved me, and touch me and try to ease everything for me."

. . . and Sigifrith knew that Gundahari, who knew exactly what he ought to do, was kissing Brunichild and stroking her body; and he did not know whether he hoped that Brunichild was taking joy in her husband, or that beneath Gundahari's caresses, she was thinking of him. Slowed by the knowledge he could not drown, Sigifrith opened his mouth to answer, but Gundrun spoke again before he could get any sound out.

"They didn't say you were going to rape me."

"I'm sorry," Sigifrith choked. He was weeping again, his tears as scalding as the dragon's blood where they fell on his arms and thighs. And he had thought of her death . . . He felt that not only she, but he had been raped by his raging wod; his groin ached as though the blood drying between his legs were his own. "Can you forgive me?"

"We'll see."

Gundrun reached for her gown and pulled it on. Sigifrith had not torn it too badly in his haste, though when she stood he could see that one of the side seams had split halfway up the thigh. She sopped one of the cloths in the bowl of water and tossed it at him. "Go on, clean yourself."

Awkwardly Sigifrith turned his back, sponging her blood off himself. Still keeping his back turned, he walked around the bed to find his breeches and put them on. Gundrun was sitting on the edge of the bed when he looked around again, pouring mead from the clay jug into one of the goblets. He sat in a chair at a careful distance from her, close as a husband should be and not near enough to frighten her again, as she raised her glass, drank deeply and refilled it.

"May I have some?" he asked meekly after a few moments. He thought at first that Gundrun would tell him to pour his own, but she nodded and filled his goblet as well, pushing it over the table to him.

They sat uncomfortably together until a miaow broke the stillness and Sigifrith felt something furry writhing over his bare feet. He picked the kitten up, setting her on the table.

Gundrun's smile eased his heart all the more because he had not expected it. She stroked the little cat, who purred and butted a tabby head against her hand. "Aren't you a pretty thing," she crooned. "What do you call her?"

"I don't know. My mother gave her to me as a wedding gift for us. She said . . . " Sigifrith coughed out a hoarse bark of salt-bitter laughter as his eyes began to water again. "She said if I was kind to her we'd have good weather for the wedding day."

Gundrun ran her fingers along the kitten's plump sides. "Well, I don't think you've been starving her." She traced the black markings on the animal's forehead with the square tip of one finger. "She's marked with a Roman M, or an *ehwaz* rune: M. Hmm . . . *ehwaz* for Ehegabe—marriage gift. That's your name, little cat. It will bring us luck and love in our wedding."

Ehegabe jumped down into Gundrun's lap, curling up as the new bride stroked her with one hand, filling her goblet again with the other.

"Hagan said that you knew the runes," Sigifrith said musingly, sipping at his mead. It was stronger and sweeter than the wine he was used to, its warmth easing his aches.

"A bit. Well enough. He understands them better than I do, even though Grimhild wouldn't teach him and I had to show them to him myself." The mead was thickening her tongue, slurring her speech, but she kept drinking steadily.

"Are you all right?" Sigifrith asked. "Do you need anything?"

"I'll be all right. I still hurt, though."

Pain, eased by the drowsy soothing of numbness . . . suddenly Sigifrith remembered something that had lain hidden in the darkness at the back of his mind since the night he had slain the dragon (slain Ragin, echoed his thoughts). He got up, went to the saddlebags that lay in a heap in the corner and dug down to the very bottom in first one, then the other.

The remains of Fadhmir's roasted heart had dried out completely, becoming a thin black slab of tough, flattened meat. It seemed to Sigifrith that this gift would be a fair geld for what he had done to Gundrun; he hoped that she would get more joy from the birds' song than he had.

"What's that?" she asked.

"It's Fadhmir's heart. If you eat from it, it will give you wisdom and strength. It was the best treasure I won from the dragon."

Gundrun took the dry meat in her left hand, staring at it. "They say dragon's blood is poisonous," she murmured.

Sigifrith could not answer; he did not know, for the bale would not have scathed Sigimund's son, and though Ragin had been human once he had passed beyond the walls of the Middle-Garth so long ago that what could slay a man might not have touched the old dwarf (except for Gram's blade, Sigifrith thought; though his eyes were empty of tears, they clenched with a tightness like dry heaving).

Gundrun looked up at Sigifrith, then held out her hand to him. He knelt and her hand tightened on his shoulder, tugging him closer as she tilted back her head. He kissed her as best he could, gentled by guilt like a spearpoint just touching his skin, holding him at a marked distance.

A slow, nagging feeling was beginning to rise through Sigifrith's body: that he should keep Gundrun from eating the dragon's heart, that her reluctance was right, that it would only harm her. He was about to speak when she raised her other hand to her face, sinking her teeth into the tough heart and jerking her head viciously sideways to rip a bite of the black meat off. The muscles along her square jaw bulged and jerked as she chewed and swallowed.

Twice more, and it was done. Gundrun reached for her mead, drinking it down as if to wash a horrible bitterness from her mouth. Only Sigifrith's swiftness kept her from dropping the half-empty glass as the first shudder hit her.

Gundrun gasped, her body straightening convulsively and then snapping over as if her spine were a broken twig. Sigifrith caught her before she could fall to the floor, lifting her and putting her on the bed. Her breathing hissed in and out between her clenched teeth; her pupils had swollen till the blue was only a faint rim of smoke around the cauldrons of darkness in her eyes. She raised her dragon-ringed hand slowly, letting it hang in the air.

Sigifrith bit down on his tongue, sucking at the pain and the taste of blood as if he could draw the strength from himself to change what he had done. Gundrun's whole body was twitching now, as if a great knot of wyrms were writhing over her. He stood watching, helpless, waiting for the bale to run its course as her torso twisted and she cried out again.

Gundrun's moans sank down to a low muttering; her restless movement stilled. The blackness filling her eyes slowly began to draw back into their depths; her gaze was still fixed on the golden ring binding her hand.

"Where did you get this ring?" she whispered.

"In Gaul. Your brother's horse wouldn't go through Brunichild's fire and Grani wouldn't move beneath him, so we traded seemings through the might of the Helm of Awe, and I stayed the three nights of the betrothal with her in his shape and under his name. It was then that I took this ring from her and gave her Gundahari's."

"Does anyone else know about this?"

"No one but Hagan."

She sighed, easing her body to its full length and stretching before she sat up. "I feel . . . I don't want to sleep," she said suddenly. She got to her feet, prowling restlessly about the room.

"What shall we do?" Sigifrith could hear the faint sounds of talking and a burst of laughter from outside. The witnesses would, as they had promised, keep watch over the bridal chambers till dawn.

"I don't know."

She came over to the bed and stood beside him, close enough for him to feel her dragon-stoked warmth through the gown that lay over her body like a thin layer of white ash over a glowing coal. The rent linen had fallen away from her leg and her thigh was almost touching his.

"Do you still hurt?"

"No." Then, slowly, wonderingly, "No, I don't. I feel . . . so much stronger . . . and listen!" Gundrun, eyes alight, hurried over to the window. Sigifrith followed. He could hear the piping song of one nightbird, answered by another. He did not wish to know what the birds might say to him; but he stood there till Gundrun turned to embrace him about the waist.

"Did you hear?" she whispered. "They spoke, and I understood them! They said that if we were to bed together again now, we could get a son on this night who would bear all the might of the Walsing line within him. Sigifrith . . ." Gundrun's arms tightened around his waist; she did not pull away as she felt him rising against her. Her eyes glowed as brightly as the silver-blue sparks of stars in the shadows of the guttering candles.

"Are you all right? Can we—?"

"I'm not afraid any more."

Sigifrith drew Gundrun back to the bed, sitting down and taking her on his lap so he could hold and kiss her comfortably. Breathless with desire as he was, he was no longer seized by fury or sickness, but instead with a warmth answering to the new fires he could feel within her. He could feel the tightness that bound his chest loosening beneath the mead-sweet eagerness of her kisses, knowing that he had been able to mend at least one of his wrongs.

Even with his eyes closed, Sigifrith could not take Gundrun for Brunichild, but he murmured, "I love you," to her, and knew that he would be able to believe it. "And you shall have Fadhmir's hoard as your morning gift," he added. Gundrun did not answer, but kissed him again.

OSTARA

Sunna shone from the thin layer of snow furring the ground and dark pines, the glittering crystals crunching beneath Sigifrith's bare feet and Gundrun's boots. Here in the mountains, at the hall that had been Chilpirich's but was now Sigifrith's, the snow often lasted through Ostara, sometimes not melting till a week or two before Thrimilci Eve. Still, the days were longer than the nights now, and the Moon had almost reached his first summer's fullness. Soon, Sigifrith hoped, the snow would melt; then the woods would no longer be the silver-wrought wilderness of that Ostara when Ragin had forged Gram and he would walk easily in them again.

Sigifrith let go of his wife's hand, going ahead to the bench before the hall that he had fashioned from two fallen logs. He brushed the snow off, then came back to help Gundrun to her seat. Even the thick cloaks of fur that muffled her body did not hide the heavy curve of her swollen womb; she walked awkwardly, as though her thighs had bowed outward like birch branches beneath the weight that she bore within her.

Gundrun sighed as she eased herself down, turning her face up to let the Sun's light fall on her pasty skin. Sigifrith sat beside her, putting his arm around her shoulders and letting her lean against him. Plump as Gundrun had become during her pregnancy, and seldom as she had been able to leave her bed in the last few days, she seemed as tired and pale as if she had not eaten nor slept for a week. It seemed to Sigifrith that holding and keeping the babe was taking all her strength from her.

"It's good to be out again," Gundrun said. "I was beginning to think the storms were never going to end, and I couldn't go out and run around in them like some people."

"I wish you could have."

"I know, dear. It's not your fault . . . well, I suppose it is." She smiled at him, patting his cheek. "You can't help it. I'll just be glad when this is over."

Sigifrith put his hand on the curve of his wife's belly. Even through her thick woolen dress and her cloak, he could feel the thump as a tiny hand or foot struck against the wall of Gundrun's womb. "A little warrior," he said, as he had said twenty times a day since the windy night when he had felt the first stirrings within her.

"A little Walsing," Gundrun said. "It will be nice when he's got someone apart from me to pound on."

"Who will it be? The Huns?"

Gundrun caught herself before she could glance eastward. As far through Mirkwood as the Huns dwelt, and as much respect as they had for the strength of Sigifrith Fadhmir's Bane, they were uneasy neighbors. Although, Sigifrith thought, when Attila had sent his messengers to greet the young drighten of whom he had heard so much, Gundrun and her Burgundian women had been easier with the warp-skulled warriors than his own thanes had been.

"Maybe so," she said. "Or maybe he'll conquer Constantine's city. There won't be much of Rome left by the time he's grown."

A white bird with black wings was hopping from one snowy branch to the next on a pine tree nearby. It cocked its head and opened its beak, letting out a chattering like a tiny hammer beating on wood.

"The Moon was just past full when we got married," Gundrun said thoughtfully. "It shouldn't be too much longer now." She paused for a moment. "You know, I almost wish my mother were here. I never learned a half of the herb-lore and such that she knew, but she had plants to ease pain and help birthing along when it wasn't going well."

Sigifrith felt himself stiffening like a corpse in the cold as he thought of Grimhild. He had never spoken ill of her; but Gundrun did not speak of her often, either.

"There's not time to bring her from Worms, I think," he said finally. Unless she's been spying on us in her fetch-shape, Sigifrith added to himself, though he was sure that he would know Grimhild under any seeming now.

"I know. I was only wishing."

After a while, Gundrun began to wiggle her feet about, stamping them lightly in the snow.

"Are you all right?"

"They're numb. They've been getting that way whenever I'm up for too long. It's because they're so swollen, and because these boots make them swell more and that cuts off the flow of blood."

"Do you want to go and lie down?"

"I don't want to, but it looks as if I'll have to."

Gundrun got up painfully, bracing herself against the bench and wincing as her full weight shifted on to her feet. Then she cried out softly and sat down again with a heavy thump.

"What's wrong?"

"I'm . . . oh!" Her eyes closed for a moment. When she opened them to look up at Sigifrith, her lips curved into a trembling smile. "I think my waters have burst."

"What does that mean?"

"I'm going to bear our child today."

Sigifrith let out a whoop of joy. Gundrun put her arms out to ward him off, and he caught himself before he could sweep her up in his arms and swing her around. Instead he ran to a waist-high boulder that stood near the path into the woods, heaving the granite from the ground and slinging it through the pines. He heard the crash as it struck one, saw the slushy loads of snow slide from the tree's branches as it began to topple sideways.

"Are you quite finished?" Gundrun asked. "I need to go in now. In case you hadn't noticed, it's not quite over with yet."

Sigifrith managed to get, "I'm sorry," out through his grin of delight.

"You can carry me back, then."

He lifted her carefully in his arms and bore her back toward the hall. The wetness in her cloak and skirt was soaking through his tunic as well, a sign sure as the blood of a wound.

As he hastened toward the hall, Sigifrith looked for a woman he could call to aid him. He knew that most would be inside working or off in the woods gathering things for Ostara's feast. Only Hildkar's wife Olwyn sat between the wooden door posts of her home, with her young daughter at her breast. "Olwyn!" Sigifrith called. "Come quickly! My frowe's waters have broken and she's starting to give birth."

Sigifrith hurried as fast as he could toward the chamber he shared with Gundrun. One of her maidens, a tall, rawboned girl named Fredegund, was sweeping the hard-packed earthen floor of the hall. She put her broom down at once when she saw Sigifrith carrying his frowe.

"Is it starting?" she asked. Gundrun nodded. "Let me put the birthing blankets on the bed before you get in."

Sigifrith set Gundrun in her chair and crouched down before her to unlace her boots and pull them gently off. The constriction of the footgear had left deep white creases like bloodless wounds in the puffy flesh of her feet and ankles. He rubbed Gundrun's feet gently as Fredegund came in with her arms full of bedding and began the work of readying the birthing bed. Olwyn followed her, panting from her run up to the hall, and stood watching as Gundrun's maiden did her work.

Though the blankets Fredegund was putting on now were clean, Sigifrith could see that they were worn and darkened by stains that would not wash out. He wondered if this might be the same bedding on which he had been born nineteen winters ago; but only Perchte could have told him, and she was dead.

Gundrun clenched her fists, her face whitening as she bent forward.

Olwyn nodded sagely; to Sigifrith, it looked as though her frail neck were drooping beneath the heavy crown of thick ash-blond braids wound about her narrow head.

"There you go. Hold this for me," the Saxon woman said, thrusting her baby into Fredegund's arms. It twisted its face and began to howl at once as the maiden helplessly jiggled it. Olwyn gathered the goose-down pillows together and stacked them so Gundrun could recline half-upright. After helping Sigifrith's wife to the bed, she took her crying child back into her arms and pulled her dress down on one side, far enough to thrust her nipple into its mouth. "That's better for you; you won't strain as much," she told Gundrun. "Now, Fredegund, see if you can find some of the older women to help. Heat some water and bring clean cloths, as well."

Fredegund left the chamber as Olwyn fussed about, moving the pillows to help Gundrun sit more easily. "Now you take her hands, Sigifrith, and let her hold on as tightly as she needs to when her womb cramps . . . there!"

Gundrun grasped her husband's hands, closing her eyes as she strained against the child inside her. Her hands, like her ankles and feet, had swollen with water in the last weeks of her pregnancy, and her own grip left white grooves in her soft flesh when she let go of Sigifrith. Gently he stroked her palms, then, seeing how a frizz of hair had strayed from her coiled braids, he brushed it out of her face. She tossed her head irritably under his touch.

"I'm not completely helpless," she said. "If you want to be useful, you could get me my comb so I can tidy my braids."

"Oh, no," Olwyn broke in. "You mustn't have any knots about you, or your womb will knot. Let your hair down and make Sigifrith comb the tangles out of it instead."

Sigifrith fetched Gundrun's comb out of the chest where she kept her mirror and scented oils. It was a pretty thing, gracefully carved out of Roman ivory, but with teeth strong enough to pull through Gundrun's heavy tresses without breaking. By the time he sat down beside her, she had already ripped out the gold pins that held her braids up, letting them swing free. Though his fingers felt thick and clumsy at the work, Sigifrith unbraided her hair and began to comb it.

It was not long before Fredegund came in again with cloths and bowls of hot water. Behind her came Harthpercht's wife Adalflad and Gundolind, the mother of a carl from a nearby farm.

Gundolind planted her feet firmly on the earthen floor, bracing her hands on wide hips. "What are you doing here?" she asked Sigifrith. He glanced at her, and she dropped her eyes and her scratchy voice mellowed a little. "Fro Sigifrith, I think you'll be happier if you go away till the birthing's done. This isn't the place for an atheling-drighten."

"I want my husband with me," Gundrun stated. "And if you try to get rid of him, I'll get up and throw you out myself." Then she arched against the pillows with another cramp. Sigifrith put down the comb and gave her his hands to grip again as she moaned softly in pain.

"If you're lucky, it won't be too much longer," Gundolind said.

"I don't know," Adalflad said dubiously as the two of them spread Gundrun's swollen legs apart, bending her knees into a crouching position. "There, stay like that. As small as she is, and a first birth too, this isn't going to be easy." She pursed her thin lips, iron-gray braids swinging as she looked between Gundrun's legs and shook her head. "She'd be spread well enough for a middling-size babe already, but this one's going to have a big head."

"Sigifrith, where's the cat?" Gundolind asked suddenly. "She's been the luck of your wedding so far; it would be good to have her here, for Holda's help and blessing."

"I'll go and get her," Sigifrith said, walking to the door of the chamber.

Ehegabe was napping on the lingering warmth of the hearth beside one of the fires of the feasting hall, a lithe coil of dark and golden stripes like a thickly wound arm-ring. Only her tail stuck out toward the fire, untwisted into her circle; the thick layer of ash over the coals kept its tip from singeing. She purred as Sigifrith picked her up and began to stroke her, curling closer to the warmth of his chest.

He hurried back to the chamber, where the women were taking it in turns to let Gundrun grip their hands as her womb tightened against the babe. Eyes clenched shut, she was holding on to Olwyn now; the Saxon woman had gone white with pain under the strength of her agonized grasp.

Sigifrith closed the door behind him and set Ehegabe down by his wife's side. The cat stood and stretched to her full slim length, sniffing about, then settled down. She had grown used to people and fusses. Gundrun opened her eyes and smiled palely as she felt Ehegabe's warmth nestling against her. She loosened her hold on Olwyn, leaning back and breathing deeply.

"The cramps are getting much stronger, and coming more quickly," Gundrun told Sigifrith. "Maybe it won't be too much longer."

Adalflad grunted. "Frija makes some women quick bearers. As fast as you're going, you should have had it out already, but the head's too big."

Sigifrith saw Gundolind elbow her in the ribs, dragging her head down to whisper in her ear. Adalflad frowned, drawing her sparse eyebrows together to glare at Sigifrith till his eyes met hers again; but she said no more.

Sigifrith nudged Olwyn away and took his wife's hands himself as her next contraction began. Gundolind and Adalflad moved to opposite sides of the bed, pressing flat-palmed down on the mound of Gundrun's belly.

Gundrun shut her eyes and moaned through clenched teeth, her body racked with strain as she bore down to force their child out. Sigifrith felt his own innards tightening with sympathy as Gundrun's small fists ground the bones of his hands against one another; it seemed to him that he could feel the echoes of her pain spreading like river ripples through his own body. He wondered if it was time for him to call on the lore he had learned to ease her, but he knew the price of Wodan's gifts and knew, as sure as he knew the winding of his own entrails, that the weaving of Wyrd would turn more kindly for his son if Gundrun could bring him forth with her own strength. And the women were standing about, watching; if he were to work those spells, he would have to send them away. But they knew about birthing and he did not.

It seemed to Sigifrith that Gundrun had time for no more than a breath or two between each contraction. The crown of the babe's head showed between her legs, as pale and rounded as a new steel shield-boss against red-dyed linden; but it was too large to pass through. After a while she began to scream; then, exhausted, to moan again.

The torches that had been new before noon-time had burned halfway down when Gundolind sent the other women out.

"I can save your child," the old carline whispered to Sigifrith. "But you'd best leave now, because you won't want to watch."

"You leave," Sigifrith answered. "Go."

"I can save your child!" Gundolind insisted in an angry whisper. "You don't know what to do."

Sigifrith looked at her and she turned and fled in haste, almost tripping over her skirts. Sigifrith drew Gram, laying the sword's point against his palm and beginning to trace the runes he had learned on the mountain's peak, trying to still the sound of Brunichild's voice ringing in his mind like the echoes of a sword struck on stone. *Uruz, nauthiz, berkano;* Ing's rune for the seed planted, *berkano* again, for the birthing womb and the idises' aid, *jera,* rune of harvest, for the seed come to fullness. He laid his hands against Gundrun's swollen womb, chanting the galdor-song of the rune names and letting the rushing wind of his call bear his sense away to the hidden worlds. It seemed to him that he saw an apple as red as a yew-berry, fully ripened at last. A swan-winged maiden cupped the fruit in her hands; its redness shone from the links of her byrnie and from the steel cap on her fair head. Wodan had sent the walkurja Hleod to Wals' father with an apple for the birth of his son; now, as Sigifrith chanted the god-rune *ansuz,* rune of Wodan, opener of the way between the worlds, he saw the shining might flowing apple-red through his body and into the little body of his son, reddening the gold-burning strength of the dragon's blood and heart.

Gundrun cried out as the child's white-shrouded head pushed through between her legs, straining the narrow passageway open. Sigifrith bore down slowly and steadily with the might of the runes he had called. It seemed to him that he could see the dark and bright ghost shapes of women standing to either side of him, the idises guiding his hands. He thought that he knew the daughters of Hraithamar, that white-clad Lingwohaith stood at his right elbow and dark-clad Lofanohaith at his left, come at his bidding to help their daughter give birth to the child of their son; and it seemed to him that the shapes of the women glimmered back farther than he could see. Together they pushed the child out, pulling the blood-streaked hood of his milky caul back from his head and slapping him gently so that he coughed and wailed, staring about furiously at the unfocused world before his adder-bright blue eyes. One more push, and the slippery mass of the afterbirth slid out into a dark-stained wooden bowl that was somehow there beneath Sigifrith's hands.

Then Sigifrith's sight cleared to the world of the Middle-Garth where his wife was lying back amid her pillows, breathing easily at last. Gundrun's hair was dark with sweat; she could barely raise her head to look at her husband.

"Is he all right?" she whispered.

The child began to cry, a high thin penetrating wail. Sigifrith held him gently to Gundrun's milk-full breast, pushing the nipple into the corner of his mouth with one finger. He coughed, sputtered, and then began to suck greedily.

"He's fine."

Nine days later, Sigifrith stood with his boots sunk deeply into the green-sprouting mud before the harrow stone in the holy grove near his hall, where he himself had been given his name. He faced eastward, toward the blood-pink sky where the rising Sun shone between the mountains. Gundrun was standing to his left, their white-swaddled son in her arms. Herwodis and Alapercht had crossed the Rhine, coming to Sigifrith's hall in answer to his message bidding them to his son's naming feast, and stood at his right hand now. Herwodis had loosed the top of her dress and was suckling Alapercht's son Alaswinth. Alapercht held a horn full of water, still as icy as the three snowmelt-swollen streams from which Sigifrith had just drawn it. Before them the thanes and their wives stood in a half-ring about the stone, holding in their hands the painted eggs and tansy cakes for Ostara's feast.

"Hail to Sunna, sig-queen bright!" Sigifrith called.

> Hail to dawn's light,   day of the year,
> Ostara rises   in awesome morn.
> Holy ones, round   the harrow standing,
> High gods and goddesses,   hear me all!

He took his son in his arms, lifting him high over his head. The Sun brightened the babe's white wrappings, glimmering in Sigifrith's light-dazzled eyes. "So I, Sigifrith, Sigimund's son, call this child my own and of the Walsing line."

Alapercht held the horn toward him. Sigifrith dipped his fingers in the cold water and sprinkled droplets on the fair wispy hair of his son's head. The child at once began to wail, his angry cries echoing through the air as he glared into his father's eyes. Sigifrith could not keep from smiling as he went on. "I name you Sigimund the Walsing, Sigifrith's son. And this gift I give you, though I shall hold it for you till you are grown enough for its use."

Sigifrith set his son down on the harrow stone and drew Gram. He wrapped Sigimund's tiny fingers around the hilt, holding the blade upward. Gram shone as straight as the stalk of a leek in the sunlight, its pattern of dark and light steel flowing upward like a fountain. "So shall the sword of the Walsings be yours, and all the might of my father's line."

At that moment, Sigifrith saw two black flecks winging across the red-gold light of the rising Sun and heard one raven's deep call to the other: "Remember," it croaked; and the other answered, "Remember."

But now Gundrun was embracing him beneath the kindly gazes of Herwodis and Alapercht, and his folk were coming forward to lay their eggs on the harrow by his son and press honey-sweet tansy cakes on him with their good wishes for young Sigimund. Hildkar and Olwyn, Theodipald, Ehwamar, Harthpercht and Adalflad, Gundolind and her son Hludowic and all the rest of them crowded around Sigifrith and Gundrun, wishing them O-stara-blessing; and Sigifrith could only smile at them and answer with the same joy.

THE QUEENS

Grani galloped with the north wind, its flow whipping brown and golden leaves into Sigifrith's long hair as it beat against his face and his son's. Sigifrith held on to Sigimund's waist as the boy stood up on the saddle before him, reaching out to catch a flying ash leaf in his little fingers. Sigimund looked over his shoulder at his father, grinning.

"Look, Father!" he said, tossing the leaf over Grani's head for the wind to bear away. "Where is it riding to?"

"Over the mountains and far off, southward to Rome," Sigifrith answered. "And one day you'll ride there too, at the head of a band of loyal thanes, and take it for your own."

"And fight?" Sigimund said, sitting down and bouncing on Grani's withers. "With spears and swords?"

"With spears and swords," Sigifrith agreed, rustling his son's light hair with his free hand. "You have three winters now; when you can count ten more you'll be a man and have Gram in your hand. The skops will make songs about you, and you'll have a fine stone-built hall to hear them in, where you hold your feasts and give out gold rings to your men."

"And kill a dragon? You killed Dragon Fadhmir."

"Yes, I did. There aren't many dragons in the world, but there might be another one for you if you look hard enough for it."

"Kill a dragon," said Sigimund happily, slashing an imaginary sword through the air as they rode.

"Kill a dragon," Sigifrith agreed. "Not from horseback, though. You fight men from horseback, like this." He guided his son's arm through a couple of strokes, feeling the child's strength with pride. He could already see Sigimund grown to manhood, as tall and strong as Sigifrith himself, his light hair flowing over a glittering byrnie and Gram bright in his hand as he called his men to gather beneath the apple banner of the Walsings.

"Do you fight Huns from horseback?"

"Yes, we fight Huns from horseback." The Huns had been troublesome neighbors in the past three years; thrice a desperate messenger had arrived from Hrodgar calling Sigifrith and his thanes to ride to their ally's aid. "When you're old enough, you'll be fighting Huns too."

They rode out of the stand of ash and oak, back to the road that turned toward Sigifrith's hall in the mountains.

"Look!" Sigimund cried, pointing back the other way. "Someone riding!"

Farther down the road from the Rhine, Sigifrith saw a man on a dappled gray horse. At first Sigifrith thought the man must be very large; then he realized that the horse was far smaller than his own breeds. The rider was not close enough for Sigifrith to see his face clearly, but his skull sloped sharply upward, making him either a Burgundian or a Hun. Sigifrith turned Grani, riding toward him at full gallop.

"Hail Sigifrith!" the Burgundian shouted when they got closer. His voice was familiar; now Sigifrith recognized Gundahari's golden-haired skop, though he could not remember his name.

"Hail and welcome!" Sigifrith shouted back, slowing Grani to a trot, then a walk.

"Who's that?" Sigimund asked.

"A messenger from your mother's brother," Sigifrith told his son softly. "Hush now, and be a good boy. I hope all is well in the kingdom of Worms?" he said to the scop.

"All is well, indeed. And with you? Is this your son Sigimund? He has your look, but surely Sigimund can be no more than three winters old?"

"This is indeed Sigimund," Sigifrith answered proudly. "He's grown very fast."

"Ah, you'll be as mighty a man as your father then," the scop said to Sigimund.

The child nodded vigorously "Are you a Hun? You've got a funny head like Huns, but your hair's the wrong color."

"I am a Burgundian," the scop answered. "I'm from the tribe of your mother."

"Mother doesn't have funny head!" Sigimund protested indignantly.

"Indeed not." The scop smiled, his teeth very bright beneath his blond mustache. "Only warriors have heads shaped for helmets."

"I'm a warrior!" the boy declared.

"You are, truly."

Sigifrith turned his horse to ride by the Burgundian's side as they continued along the road toward his hall. "So what message brings you here?" he asked. "Has Brunichild given birth?"

"Not yet, but it is said that she may be with child. As often as the king goes in to her . . . By the laws of our folk, he might have named her barren after three years and put her by for a more fruitful bride, but he loves her and will not be parted from her. And now it is known that the queen's courses have stopped for three months; and before the queen Grimhild left to keep Winternights with her kinswoman the queen Thonara in the Danes' land, she said that she thinks Brunichild carries a son."

"And Brunichild is happy with Gundahari?"

"It seems so now. It was not easy for her to come and live among a strange folk, and she had seemed to think . . ." The scop fell silent, the clean-shaven planes of his fair cheeks flushing as if, without meaning to, he had almost spoken of some family shame. "Hagan's wife has given him another son, to whom he has given the name Adalulf."

"Three in four years," Sigifrith mused. "Who would have thought it of him?"

"The Christian faith teaches that a wife shall submit to her husband," the scop said, laughing. "But you are not lagging too far behind. I remember it was not three months since we sent you Gaulish wine for the naming feast of a second child. I trust that your daughter Swanhild is well and strong?"

"She is."

"She's not red and wrinkly and ugly-looking any more," Sigimund broke in. "She was squishy when she was born."

"And so were you," Sigifrith said, tickling his son's ribs till he squirmed.

The Burgundian messenger did not even bother to try hiding his smile.

An hour's ride for Grani was a long walk for the little Burgundian horse, and it was well past noon when Sigifrith and Gundahari's messenger stabled their steeds. Sigifrith gave his son over to the care of his nursemaid Hildidis and the two men went to the hall.

Gundrun was waiting at the door with Swanhild in her arms. "Folkhari!" she said as the scop came nearer. "It's good to see you again. Is all well with my brothers?"

"All is very well, Frowe."

Gundrun gestured her husband and their visitor inside. "Sit down and let me get you a drink of welcome. I hadn't thought that we would be having a guest from home this late in the year."

Ehegabe was sitting in Sigifrith's chair at the end of the hall, her tail curled around her. She was heavy with her third litter; after she had gone into heat twice, Gundrun had insisted that a tom be brought in for her and now there were cats throughout the settlement. As Folkhari and Sigifrith came nearer, she laid back her ears and hissed angrily at the Burgundian scop. Another step; the cat jumped down from the seat of the chair, letting out a sort of purring grunt as she landed on the new paving stones with an audible thump, and waddled away to the other side of the fire on the right.

"What's wrong with her?"

Sigifrith shrugged. "I don't know. She hasn't done that before. Maybe it's because you're a stranger."

Gundrun came out from the kitchens, bearing the Roman glasswork that they used at the high feasts and a pitcher of mead.

"Be welcome in our hall, guest," she said as she poured the golden drink out before Folkhari.

He raised the cup to her. "My thanks for your welcome, kind Frowe." The scop drank deeply, showing enjoyment, though Sigifrith thought he shuddered a little at the unfamiliar taste of the mead. Folkhari stood. "Now I shall give you both the message I bear. King Gundahari longs to see his kin again, and so bids you both to guest with him at this year's Winternights feast, for he says that you have been parted from him far longer than he would have wished, and he is eager to see the youngest members of his clan as well."

The look on Gundrun's face was like the sudden kindling of a fire in a cold hearth, and Sigifrith knew that he could not deny his wife this. It had been three winters; he loved Gundrun and his children. He thought that he did not need to fear . . . but, aching and deep as the throbbing in a long-broken bone before a storm, he knew that he wanted nothing more than simply to look on Brunichild again.

"We will be glad to come to King Gundahari's feast," Sigifrith answered.

It took two days for Sigifrith and Gundrun to ready themselves and gather the gifts they meant to bring with them for their kinfolk. After some thought, they decided that Swanhild was too young for such a journey so late in the year and should be left with Hildkar, Olwyn and the wet nurse; but Sigimund would of course come with them. They took a wain, not only to keep the wind and wet from the heads of Gundrun and her maidens, but because Fadhmir's hoard, Gundrun's morning gift, still lay in the earth at Worms and, now that they knew that they would remain in the hall at the edge of the Mirkwood, they had decided to bring it back. Sigifrith left his hall and his warband in the care of Hildkar till his return.

The weather was warm for harvest time, and it grew warmer as Sigifrith and his household traveled down toward the flatlands of Worms. If it had not been for the red and gold of the trees burning against the clear blue sky, and the dead leaves riding the unseasonably warm winds, Sigifrith would have thought that he had somehow come to a land of endless summer. But the grass beneath Grani's hooves was brown and dry, and the bare stalks rustled in the fields around them as he rode before the wain.

Sigifrith was not surprised when he saw the gates of Worms opening before they were hailed; he knew that Hagan would have seen them from a distance and warned Gundahari. Sigimund pointed at the city. "Look, it's a big stone wall!" he cried. "What's in there? Why is it so big?"

"Because there are lots and lots of people in there," Sigifrith answered, pulling his son down. "And you're going to see them in a little while, so you can sit still, can't you?"

"No!" Sigimund tried to scrabble to his feet again, pouting when his father's hand on his shoulder held him down. "I want to see!"

Sigifrith remembered how he had always needed to run about and grab at new things, and he felt a sudden twinge of sympathy for Alapercht and Herwodis. No wonder they sent me to stay with Ragin so often, he thought.

Gundahari and Brunichild were waiting at the gates for them, together with Hagan and Costbera.

"Greetings and welcome, Sigifrith and Gundrun!" Gundahari called. "Come in joy and stay in peace."

"Greetings, Gundahari," Sigifrith answered. "We are glad to be your guests."

The wain stopped at the wall, and Gundrun leapt down to embrace her brothers. Sigifrith marked that Gundahari had put on weight; that Brunichild's belly was just beginning to curve outward against her light blue dress and that a faint flush of pink brightened her pale skin. She looked proudly away from his gaze, but he saw that her glance came back to Sigimund again and again, and then he could not bear the longing so he looked at Hagan and Costbera instead. Hagan's black hair had grown more silvered and the scar running down from his eyepatch had faded to a track of hoary purple, but otherwise he had not changed since Sigifrith had seen him last. Costbera leaned heavily on her husband's arm. Though she had grown rather plump, her face seemed somehow wasted, as if her cheeks had been dusted lightly with ashes. A slim, black-haired child—Hagan's son Nibel—stood beside them. His face seemed to be set in a minature of his father's grim mask; then he looked up to smile winfully at Sigifrith and Sigimund before greeting Gundrun.

Sigifrith dismounted, and his son jumped down into his arms. He set the boy down beside him and went forward to clasp Gundahari's forearm in greeting.

"Hail and welcome, Sigifrith. What took you so long getting here?"

"So long? Your messenger only came a few days ago, and it's more than a week till the Moon is full."

"Sigifrith, it's been three years. You knew you were welcome here."

"You never invited us," Sigifrith said, shrugging. "Anyway, we're here now. This is my son, Sigimund. Sigimund, this is King Gundahari, your mother's brother."

"Hail King Gundahari," Sigimund piped up, sticking out his forearm as he had seen his father do.

Gundahari crouched to clasp his hand. "Hail Sigimund. Holy gods, you're a strong one."

Sigimund grinned with happiness, looking back and forth from Brunichild to Sigifrith. "Who's the pretty frowe? Is she my father's sister?"

The Burgundian king laughed uncomfortably. "No, Sigimund, this is my wife, the queen Brunichild."

Brunichild's gaze was already fixed on Sigimund; now she bestowed a flickering smile on the child as she bent down to kiss his fair cheek. "You look very like your father," she said distantly.

"So do you."

"Sigimund, don't be silly," Sigifrith said sharply. "You've never met Brunichild's father."

Sigimund twisted his head around to look up at his father over his shoulder. Afraid of what the boy would say, Sigifrith bent down to grasp him by the shoulders, aiming him toward Hagan's son who stood quietly while Gundrun talked with his parents. "See, that's your cousin Nibel. Go and play with him."

"That's a funny name," Sigimund said ominously, but he ran over to the other boy obediently.

Sigifrith sighed, straightening. "I never thought children would be so much trouble."

Gundahari put his arm around Brunichild's waist, drawing her closer to him. "Did Folkhari tell you that we might be having our own soon?"

"He told me. Frija's blessing on it!"

Sigifrith greeted Hagan and Costbera, then he remounted; Gundrun climbed back in the wain, and they went through the streets of Worms to the hall. When Gundahari and Hagan had helped Sigifrith and Gundrun to unload, Gundrun said that she felt dirty from the trip and wanted a bath.

"Why don't you and Brunichild go to the Rhine, then?" Gundahari suggested. "It's still warm enough to swim, and you used to enjoy bathing there far more than you liked washing indoors. And, after all, the two of you ought to have some time to get to know each other."

Taken aback, Gundrun looked at Sigifrith. "Do you think . . . ?"

"I don't see why not, if your brothers think it's safe."

"Gundrun, you remember the secluded place along the river's banks," Hagan said. "It is safe enough. You often went there with your maidens when you were younger."

Gundrun felt rather uneasy as she and Brunichild departed through the back gate, walking along the river's edge; but it was good to be back by the Rhine again. She had forgotten how the river's rushing had whispered through everything she had done when she was young, how the sound of its flowing had wound through her girlhood like a single thread weaving her life together.

"So you are to have a child soon?" she said to Brunichild, and could not help thinking: I am glad it was not till now. I am glad it could not be Sigifrith's.

The Visigothic woman smiled and laid her hands over her womb. They were beautiful hands, white, slim and long-fingered. Gundrun could not help glancing at her own stubby fingers and square palms, which were calloused from the work she did every day in her husband's hall.

"It is due after the next feast of Ostara," she answered.

Gundrun nodded. "You must be very happy about it."

"I am not unhappy. I have felt ill now and then, but the women tell me that is to be expected."

"If you ask Grimhild, she can give you something to stop that. When I was carrying Swanhild, I was sick every morning until my mother sent me a powder of herbs for it."

"No. It is not bad enough for me to need her help."

They passed the heap of red sandstone and walked to where the river bent, eddying in a shallow swirl beneath the trees. Gundrun and Brunichild took off their dresses, hung them over the low-hanging limbs of a brown-leaved willow and stood in their shifts. Gundrun felt oddly wary of undressing before the other woman. It felt as though the white linen she wore might be as strong as a byrnie woven of steel links, and for the first time she thought she understood Hagan's unwillingness to go among others unarmored.

Brunichild took the golden pins from her coiled braids and unbound the wires of gold that held them, combing her hair out with her fingers to lie in shining, braid-crimped waves over her shoulders and down her back. She did not look at Gundrun as she did this, but rather stared out over the Rhine. After a moment of thought, she pulled Gundahari's emerald from her finger and set it down on a rock with the rest of her jewelry.

Gundrun took her own hair down, fluffing it out; it seemed to her that she could still feel Sigifrith's fingers running through it, combing her hair carefully as he did every night, his immense might gentled to the lightness of his task. She put her pins down beside Brunichild's, but closed her hand over Sigifrith's dragon ring; it had not slipped off once in the years of her wedding.

Her back to Gundrun, Brunichild pulled her shift over her head. She hung it on another branch of the willow and shook her hair out again, the lithe muscles of her shoulders and back rippling beneath white skin. Against her will, Gundrun could not help seeing Sigifrith together with her, Brunichild's pale golden hair lying across his shoulders and his arms clasped around her strong, slender body. She is so much taller than I, he could kiss her without having to bend down, Gundrun thought. But Sigifrith had chosen her . . . her, not Brunichild: the Visigoth was his concubine, not his wife.

Gundrun took off her shift and hurried into the Rhine, gasping at the water's cold bite on her milk-swollen breasts. She was all too aware of how little and dumpy she must seem to Brunichild—but she will not look so perfect when she has had children! Gundrun thought, easing herself farther in to let the gentle eddying tug of the river wash the travel dirt from her body.

Brunichild stepped into the shallows slowly and with great dignity, as if she did not feel the cold. She lowered herself till only her head was out of the water, her long hair floating out around her like golden waterweed, then suddenly ducked under and came up laughing, her hair plastered down to her head.

Gundrun caught her breath and blinked in shock, deaf to the meaningless words coming out of the other woman's mouth. She had never seen Brunichild laugh before; but the eerie familiarity of the sound, of the grin on that strong, high-boned face, caught her like a blow between the ribs. It seemed to her for a dizzy moment as if she might somehow be looking at the ghost of a younger Sigifrith, seeing the more delicate features and hearing the higher voice of the boy she had first met.

" . . . don't you think?" Brunichild said.

Gundrun nodded with no idea what she was agreeing to. She ducked under the river's surface, eyes open to the rippling green light, and began to run her fingers over her itchy scalp to clean it. Brunichild's body was only a vague white shape through the Rhine, tinted with the water's green as though she were one of the river-maidens who called men to their deaths.

When Gundrun came up, shaking water from her ears and turning her face up to the warm light of the Sun, Brunichild was standing beside her with a scrubbing cloth.

"Here, I'll do your back if you'll do mine," she offered.

"Gladly." Gundrun stood up, offering her back to the pleasantly rough touch of the wet linen.

"What are these bruises on your sides?" Brunichild asked as she rubbed in circles along Gundrun's spine.

"I don't know . . ." Gundrun twisted her head to look down at the stripes of purple-blue. Only when she touched the sore places along her ribs did she remember. "Oh, that's where Sigimund holds on to me when I pick him up. He doesn't know how strong he is yet, and so he'll squeeze more tightly than he means to."

"He looks very like his father. He is a handsome child."

"He is that," Gundrun agreed, pleased. "I'm rather fond of him myself."

"Perhaps he'll keep that sly little beast of Hagan's out of trouble for the afternoon."

Gundrun laughed. "Sigimund? He's not the one to keep anyone out of trouble. Is Hagan's son a bother?"

"He is. He slinks about prying into everything . . . I would almost swear that he can open every lock in Worms, and he moves so quietly he might as well be invisible. Then he wanders off by himself and vanishes for whole nights, and Hagan keeps everyone awake looking for him."

"It's fair enough that he should have a son like that," Gundrun said as she took the washcloth from Brunichild and rinsed it out. Brunichild parted her hair and draped the two waist-length golden ropes over her shoulders. She leaned forward, resting her elbows against a rock so Gundrun could scrub her back more easily.

"Hagan did the same thing when he was a child," Gundrun went on. "I remember he hardly slept at night, and he couldn't bear to be kept indoors."

Brunichild tried to muffle her laughter. "I'm sorry," she said. "I just can't imagine Hagan as a child. It's hard enough to believe that he's half a year younger than I am. Was he any different than he is now?"

Gundrun thought about it a moment. "He was smaller."

The two of them laughed together, though Gundrun noticed that Brunichild glanced about her as if she, too, had grown used to Hagan's habit of silently appearing whenever his name was mentioned.

"But tell me, what is Sigifrith's hall like?" Brunichild asked after a while.

"Ah. Well, it's not Roman work, not so far east of the Rhine. But we've just put in a stone floor, and we were talking about looking for a glass-worker while we were here so we could have real windows."

"I would have thought Sigifrith could do better than that."

"It was the hall of Chilpirich, Alapercht's father, while he lived. It's fine enough, and we're happy there. We won't run out of treasure while there are Huns to fight eastward of us—there's no folk greedier for gold rings than they are, and Sigifrith and his men will often bring nearly as much treasure back from quashing a raid as my brother would get in a month of fighting westward. And there's Fadhmir's hoard as well, of course."

"Why did you go across the river instead of staying with Herwodis and Alapercht?"

"Sigifrith insisted. He said Alapercht's hall had too many memories for him to feel comfortable there any more, and it would be better left to Ala-percht's own son anyway."

The lithe muscles of Brunichild's back tightened under Gundrun's hands like a corpse stiffening into rigor. "What memories did he speak of?"

"He didn't say. I'm sure it had something to do with Ragin the Smith. Nothing else bothers him too much for him to talk to me about."

"I see." Brunichild straightened, taking the washcloth back from Gundrun and beginning to wade farther out into the river. She stopped and began to rub her arms and legs clean. Gundrun came nearer to her; when the other woman saw her move closer, she stepped farther and farther out. At last Brunichild was standing with only her head and shoulders out of the water, and Gundrun had to stand on tiptoes, almost treading water as she beat at the current with her arms.

"What are you doing?" Gundrun asked. Brunichild turned her gaze to the face of the smaller woman, her blue eyes searingly keen and bright; but Gundrun was used to meeting Sigifrith's glance by now, and stared fearlessly back at her. "What does this mean?"

"Why should I reckon myself equal with you in this more than anything else?" Brunichild curled her upper lip back, baring her teeth like a wolf in a trap. "I think that my father was more powerful than yours, and my husband did many great deeds and rode through the burning fire while yours was a bondsman of the king Alapercht."

Gundrun clenched her fists. A thousand words, burning like a hoard of molten gold, flooded into her mind, but she said only, "You would be wiser to silence yourself than to slander my husband."

"Why? For all Sigifrith's strength, he did no more than hold the bridle of Gundahari's horse when Gundahari came to woo me. My husband is a great king, whose might stretches out through Gaul and whose name is known as far as Rome, while yours contents himself with staying at home and breeding children. No one could ride through my fire but Gundahari, and no king of the northern folks is more famed or powerful."

"It is said by all men that never has anyone come into the world who is Sigifrith's equal in any way. He conquered the Saxon lands and avenged his father Sigimund the Walsing; he has proven himself mightier in battle than any man, as he is greater in strength; for he slew Fadhmir the Wyrm."

"But although he could freely take whatever he wishes, Sigifrith was content to live in a dirt-floored hut in the mountains. What is fighting Huns to him? He should be matching his might against Rome itself. Did Fadhmir's flames burn out his heart?"

The fire was roaring through Gundrun again, as it had when she ate of the dragon's heart; she looked at Brunichild's sharply chiseled beauty, golden hair streaming wet over strong white shoulders and dawn-blue eyes as bright as Sigifrith's own, and cried out in anger and jealousy, "It is not well for you to slander Sigifrith, for he was your lover, and he rode through the leaping flames when you thought it was King Gundahari, and he lay with you and took Andward's ring off your hand, and you may ken it here now!" She stretched out her fist toward Brunichild, the white star in the dragon's red stone as dazzling as sunlight on the river. He chose me and not you, Gundrun repeated furiously to herself. He chose me and not you!

The brightness of Andward's ring glittered from Brunichild's eyes as from ice stones. Her high cheekbones flushed, then paled so suddenly to white that Gundrun reached out to catch her in a sudden shock of fear, thinking, Have I killed her? But Brunichild pushed through the current, fighting her way through the Rhine to the shore. She dressed without looking back, her hands moving faster and faster, then began to run barefooted toward the hall.

Gundrun breathed deeply, trying to still the furious drumbeat of anger and fear that her heart pounded through her body like a summons to battle as she stared at the ring on her hand. For a moment she felt an urge to tear it off and fling it into the river, as if her angry words would sink with the gold, but she knew that nothing could unspeak the staves of fury she had spoken.

She will not make her shame known, Gundrun thought to herself. She will not. Slowly she made her way back into the shallows, forcing herself to stretch out in the cold water and deliberately rubbing her limbs clean, then working her fingers through her hair again and again. Only when she was shivering too hard for her hands to do their work did she get out of the river and put her clothes on again.

Brunichild was not there when Sigifrith and Gundrun came to sit with Gundahari, Hagan and Costbera that night. Sigifrith did not know whether the loosing in his chest at the sight of the empty chair beside Gundahari was sorrow or a relief great enough to be painful. Only the five of them were eating in the hall that night; there would not be feasting till Winternights.

Costbera had barely poured out the wine when a high shout echoed down the length of the hall as Sigimund and Nibel came in. The two of them were carrying clay pots in their little hands; their hair, fair and dark, was matted into sticky peaks. A number of swelling red lumps dotted Nibel's face and arms, though Sigimund was unscathed.

"Somebody has been poking into a beehive," Gundrun said, rather severely. "Don't you know that bees bite?"

"They didn't bite him," Nibel said. "They landed all over him, but they didn't sting."

"They did," Sigifrith's son contradicted. "They just didn't hurt me. They didn't hurt any more than thorns."

"Anyway, we got their honey from them. See the honey we got?"

The two boys held their golden booty up for their parents to admire. Sigifrith stuck a finger into Sigimund's pot and licked the drips off. "That is very fine honey," he said gravely. "And you're both very brave."

"Did you get all the stings out of you?" Costbera asked her son.

Nibel nodded. "They weren't that bad. I've trodden on bees before."

"You must be more careful," Hagan told him. "Too many bee-stings can be as baleful as an adder's bite."

Sigimund and Nibel put their pots of honey on the table.

"Have you had all you wanted?" Gundrun said.

"Yes," answered Sigimund.

"He ate a lot more of it than I did," Nibel told them. "I thought he was going to be sick."

"I'm never sick," Sigifrith's son protested.

"Well, I think it's time for you brave bee-wolves both to go off to bed, and you shall have honey cakes in the morning," Gundrun promised them. "Costbera, I know some herbs that will ease your son's stings."

"Thank you very much," Costbera said, even as Nibel objected, "I don't need any help for them."

"You shall let Gundrun treat you," Hagan said, locking eyes with his son. Nibel set his chin defiantly, staring back at his father until Gundahari's laugh broke their attention.

"It must be true that a father is born again in his son," the Burgundian king said lightly. "I seem to remember someone else who didn't much like treatment when he was hurt."

"My son will be grateful for your help," Hagan told Gundrun as she stood and took one boy by each hand. Costbera also got up, ready to follow her out.

Without warning, Sigimund broke away from his mother, running to climb on his father's lap and squeeze him about the chest with all his strength. "Goodnight, Father," he said breathlessly.

Sigifrith laughed in pride, hugging his son back with just enough force to startle a squeak out of him. "Goodnight, Sigimund. Dream well."

"You too." The boy clambered down and dashed out of the hall before Gundrun, Nibel and Costbera.

Gundahari watched them go, silent until he said, "I think Brunichild must surely be carrying a son. Grimhild says her temper shows it."

"Has she been ill-tempered?" Sigifrith asked. "Is she unhappy?"

It was Hagan who answered him. "No one should fairly call her unhappy. She says often that she has the most distinguished of husbands, and the one she most wanted. She has not behaved ill toward my brother, but she is prone to changing her mood swiftly."

"Where is she tonight?"

"Sick," Gundahari said. "She has taken to her bed. I asked her if she would be willing to have Gundrun see to her, and she said she would not."

"But she has been well and happy?"

"Of course. Why wouldn't she be?" Gundahari turned and looked over his shoulder at the door to the kitchens. "I wonder what's taking our food so long? I thought the fish had been caught this afternoon, but it seems as though the cook must have gone down to the river to get more."

Later that night, Gundrun lay curled against Sigifrith in their bed. They had put the candles out; the dying fire was only a faint glowing after-image against Sigifrith's closed eyelids. He was almost asleep when he felt the shivering through his wife's flesh.

"Are you all right?" Sigifrith's tongue felt thick and furred by a drowsiness like heavy drunkenness, speaking through the drowning warmth of the feather quilt over them.

"I think so." Then, "Did Gundahari say why his wife wasn't at the table tonight?"

"No." Muzzily Sigifrith added, "I think we shall find out soon enough." Something in his own words pricked at him like a wakening thorn; he opened his eyes, staring into the shifting of light through the embers as Gundrun spoke again.

"Why can't she be content with what she has? She has wealth and happiness, praise from everyone, and she said that she had won the husband she wanted."

Sigifrith knew he should be silent, but he spoke anyway; thus Chlodomar had torn at his blood-spattered flesh till it was raw, raw as his throat felt now. "Where was she when she said that she had won the husband that she most wanted?"

Gundrun's voice sounded very queer and choked. "I shall ask her tomorrow whom she would most like to have."

"I would advise you not to," Sigifrith said heavily. "You shall regret it if you do."

He put his arms around Gundrun, and she suddenly turned to cling tightly to him, crushing her soft body into him. Feeling her tears hot on his shoulder, he brushed them from her cheeks. "Say no more about this, if you can, unless it is to make peace with Brunichild. My name is strong enough to bear a few harsh words, and we shall cross the Rhine and fare home again soon enough."

"Soon enough," Gundrun echoed. "I'm sorry, Sigifrith. I swear I never meant to . . . but she was slandering you, and I couldn't let her keep on."

Sigifrith took her hand in his, running the tip of one finger along the smooth star stone ringed by the rough gold of the dragon's scales. So Andward's ring had clasped Brunichild's finger when he set it on her hand; so it had felt in his hand, hot from the life blood warming her body when he, blinded of memory yet driven, knowing her only as his blood-brother's chosen yet racked by unstilled and unanswerable feeling, had silenced his soul and ravaged it from her. He could think of nothing to say, so he said nothing until the need he could not still forced his words out. "What did she say about me?"

"I've forgotten."

"No. Tell me."

"She said you were meant for better things than staying at home and breeding children . . . that you were unmindful of your rank and had lost your courage."

Sigifrith smiled ruefully; he could hear Ragin's harsh voice echoing in the depths of his memory, as from the bottom of a well. "The time is past when words like that stung me. And if I were not in the east, the Huns might well be gathered at the gates of Worms."

"For your sake, I will try to make peace with her."

The next morning, Gundrun found Brunichild in her chambers, stitching on a tapestry of the hunt. The door to the garden was open and the windows unshuttered, a flood of sunlight pouring over the tapestry frame and brightening the room to summery warmth. Brunichild's head was down as she worked grimly, sewing the green tunic on to one of the hunters with swift jabs of her needle. She had not bothered to braid her hair and put it up again; it fell down her back and over her face in a long soft tangle.

Gundrun sat down beside her and took up another needle, beginning to fill in the shape of the stag with neat brown stitches. Brunichild said nothing.

"Be cheerful, Brunichild," Gundrun said after a while. "Are you upset because of what we said? What stands in the way of your happiness?"

"You are saying this out of nothing but malice, because you have a grim heart," Brunichild answered dully.

"Don't talk like that. Tell me what's wrong."

Brunichild tossed her head, flinging her hair out of her face without breaking the rhythm of her stitches. Tiny red cracks ran through the whites of her eyes, as jagged as broken glass. "Only ask about what is good for you to know. That is more seemly for powerful women. And it is good to be content with good things when all is going as you wish."

"It's early yet to boast of that, and there is something of foresight in it. What do you reproach me with? I have done nothing to cause you grief."

"You shall pay a geld for getting Sigifrith. I grudge your enjoyment of him and of Fadhmir's gold."

"Brunichild," Gundrun said, "you sound as if I had deliberately taken him away from you. He was betrothed to me not long after your king Alaric took Rome, five years before any talk was made of marrying you. Now I think my father could surely arrange my marriage without asking your consent, and if either of us has a quarrel against the other, it is I who have it against you."

"The betrothal of a child!" Brunichild scoffed. "Did Sigifrith love you then? Did he swear of his free will to marry you, and put a ring he had won with his own might on your hand?"

"What are you talking about? That was not how Sigifrith told me the story. Brunichild, I think you're half-mad, and you've made a better match than you deserve. I'm afraid your pride won't be stilled without some evil being done, and many will have to pay the geld for you then."

Brunichild stared at her tapestry. With a sudden jerk she broke the green thread, tying it off. After scrabbling in her basket of wools for a moment, she brought out a black skein and threaded the needle again.

"I would be content," she said in a low voice, "if only you hadn't got a far better man as husband."

"My brother is so famed that no one can say who is the greater, and he has wealth and power in plenty while we sit at the eastern gates by Mirkwood to beat back the Huns. You have lived in Rome, and Hispania and Tolosa; would you choose to dwell in a simple hall in the mountains rather than at the heart of the greatest realm of the Northern folks?"

"Sigifrith struck at Fadhmir, and that is worth more than all King Gundahari's power. That deed shall be told as long as there is life on earth, but your brother did not dare to ride at the fire or leap over it."

"Grani would not gallop through the fire when Gundahari mounted him, but my brother dared the ride well enough, and none may question his courage."

"I think there has been dark trickery through this matter, and I can't pretend that I think well of that seith-witch Grimhild. If you did not cut mirk-staves to blind Sigifrith into loving a lesser woman, then it must have been she."

Gundrun dropped her needle, letting it dangle from the tapestry, and stood up to look down on Brunichild. "You are telling many untruths, and that is a great lie!"

"May you enjoy Sigifrith to the degree that your clan has not deceived me. The two of you don't deserve your life together, and I hope things turn out for you both as I expect."

"I shall enjoy him more than you shall like. No one ever said that he even once had pleasure of me when it was not fitting."

"You're speaking ill, and when you're quieter you'll regret it. Everyone knows that you have a fiercer mood than any woman born, and that it has caused more trouble than anything. Now let us speak no more spiteful words."

"You first cast spiteful words at me," Gundrun replied. "Now you act as if you'd put things right, but you are grim underneath it."

"Let us lay this pointless chatter aside, then," Brunichild said heavily. "For a long time I hid the sorrow that had settled in my breast, but I love your brother alone and we shall talk of something else."

"Your thoughts see far before this." And Gundrun thought: she is plotting some ill, I must ward myself. She drew her dagger from her belt and cut another thread. Instead of sheathing it at her side, she laid it on her other knee where Brunichild could not reach it easily, silently thanking Wodan for the strengths that warded her husband from scathe of bale or blade.

The Sun's slanting light was only a pool on the threshold when Brunichild said, "I am not well. I want to lie down. Close the door and the windows and then go away."

Gundrun bit back her angry reply and went to shut out the light. Only cracks of brightness crept through the shutters on the windows—just enough for her to see where Brunichild was and keep well out of her arms' reach. "Sleep well, and dream of peace," she said. "If you like, I shall have honey cakes or wine or whatever you please sent in for you."

"I want no food. I told you, I am not well."

Gundrun left her quietly. She knew that she would not find Sigifrith; at breakfast, Sigimund and Nibel had coaxed him into promising them a ride on Grani, and they had taken some food for a midday meal with them. It seemed to her often that Sigifrith was happier when he was away on his horse than at any other time, and that now he sought to cure the sorrows that had kept him awake most of the night. Instead she went outside into the garden where Gundahari and Hagan were sitting and eating in the shade of a tree.

"Come and join us," Gundahari called to her, patting the dry grass beside him. "There's plenty for you as well."

Gundrun sat down with her brothers, cutting off a piece of bread and a hunk of cheese. Although the bread was soft and the cheese white and fresh, she found them dry and as hard to swallow as ashes.

"Where have you been all morning?" Gundahari asked.

"I was with Brunichild."

"Is she feeling better? What is she ill of?"

"She will not say. I think . . . I think you'd better talk to her before any of the things she's saying are overheard."

Gundahari felt his chest and belly clenching in on him, driving the air from his lungs as if the butt of a spear had struck him beneath the breastbone. "What is she saying?"

"I think you'd better talk to her," Gundrun repeated.

His sister had gone very pale, as though she were about to be sick; Gundahari stood up, brushing the crumbs off his blue tunic and breeches. "All right. Is this something to do with Sigifrith?"

She nodded. "Take care and watch out for her. I don't know what she might try to do."

Gundahari went around the hall to the door leading from the garden to his wife's chambers. He raised his hand and knocked thrice, but Brunichild did not answer. Hesitantly he pushed the door open and stepped inside.

Brunichild lay on the bed with her hands crossed over her breast and the covers pulled up to her waist. Her eyes were shut. She lay so still that Gundahari feared that she had died until he saw the faint rising and sinking of her breasts. He stood staring at the curve of her high cheekbones, her lips as white and cold as wind-shaped snow, and remembered how the flush of love had warmed her cheeks like red wine poured into clear ice-melt, how she had come to welcome his kisses and embraces, laying her fair head upon his shoulder as they sat together in the evenings. He thought he could see the soft beginning curve of her womb beneath the blankets—filling with his child, he was sure of it.

"Brunichild," he said. "Brunichild, what is wrong with you? Who has offended you?"

She made no reply, lying as if she were dead.

"Brunichild, speak to me. My love . . ." Gundahari's voice cracked, and he could not keep on. He knelt down beside her, reaching out to stroke her tangled hair.

Brunichild rolled over, turning her back to him. His hands shaking, Gundahari took her by the shoulders and lifted her to face him. She twitched beneath his touch, trying to shake him off; her eyes were still closed.

"Look at me," he said, his hands tightening. "Brunichild, tell me what's wrong and I will do what I can."

At last her eyes opened and she looked upon him. He could not meet the red-crazed brightness of her blue glance, so he turned his eyes downward to where his child—he was sure of it, he could not doubt it—grew.

"What did you do with the ring you took from me?" Brunichild asked.

Gundahari lifted his hand to show her the twisted circle of gold on which they had sworn their marriage vows, and which had never left his finger since.

"That is not the ring, and you should know it. I mean the dragon ring, which was once a part of Fadhmir's hoard—which, as I told you upon my mound, the hero who was meant for me gave to me in my dream. You rent it from my hand and forced yours upon me in its place; but you put Andward's ring on your own finger. Now I wish to see it or know what you have done with it."

Gundahari stared at her, stunned, thinking: Sigifrith was false to me after all, Sigifrith was false . . . what else did he do that he never told me of? Did he . . . ?

"Grani was the horse that rode through the flames," she went on mercilessly. "Will you ask Sigifrith to let you ride him again, so you may show me how willing he was to bear you?"

Gundahari took his hands from his wife's shoulders, for he was afraid that in his rising anger he might do her some harm. The shame was hot as a brand on his cheeks; furious, he was powerless, and he knew that Brunichild could not miss the meaning of his angered dishonor.

"Sigifrith was my first love and my deepest, brother and lover both; long though we were parted, Wodan brought us together again, and I thought I would never be gladder. And it was he who slew Fadhmir, and he who rode through the flames, while you were as pale as a corpse through fear. I swore it to Wodan, and again before my father Theoderid, that I would love only the highest of atheling-heroes, and that was Sigifrith. But now I am foresworn, for through your treachery and his he is not mine, and for that I hope to cause all of your deaths. And worst of all are Gundrun and Grimhild, for they are witches and I shall have to pay them back. I know of no women more cowardly and worse than they."

Gundahari glanced at the open door behind him, and answered quietly, "You have spoken many lying words, and you are an ill-thinking woman to misspeak so of those who are better than you. Neither Gundrun nor Grimhild is discontented with her lot, though they are not seated as highly as you are, and all men hold them in esteem. But in the years before your womb quickened with my child, the rede of my advisors was that I put you away and find a wife who would be no walkurja, but peaceable and fruitful. Brunichild, I have kept you as my queen because I love you, but I will not have you saying these things that you have said behind my back or making threats toward my kin. No kingdom is so strong that it can withstand these slanders."

"I've held no secret meetings and done no outrages," she answered, "but I would be ready enough to kill you."

Before Gundahari could speak to soothe her again, Brunichild sprang up from the bed with her dagger in her hand. He was hardly able to catch her wrist before the point did more than scratch his throat, trying to force her dagger hand back from his neck and the other from his eyes as he twisted sideways to ward his groin from the battering of her knees. Though he knew she was stronger of body than other women, he could hardly believe the mad might of her wod; she was slowly pushing him backward with brute, furious strength, pressing her dagger down toward his throat again.

Gundahari stepped sideways and threw up his hands before Brunichild could react, letting her own force fling her away from him. She caught herself before she could crash into the stone wall, turning to spring at him again; but it was at that moment that Hagan stepped into the room and caught her arms behind her in a painful fetter lock. All her might seemed to drain from her at once, and she sagged down against him, her breathing harsh.

"It would be better if she were put in chains," Hagan said. "She might have killed you, and she might try it again. Think if she attacked our sister like that."

Gundahari shook his head. "No. Let her go. I do not want her to be put in chains."

Reluctantly Hagan let go of Brunichild. She straightened herself, walked over to sit by her tapestry and stared grimly at both of them. "Do not heed that wish," she said to Hagan, then to Gundahari, "for you will never see me glad in your hall, neither drinking, nor playing at tables, nor speaking kindly, nor embroidering cloths in gold, nor giving you rede. My deepest sorrow is this: that I am not married to Sigifrith."

Then Brunichild raised herself up again and struck at her tapestry with her hand, rending it to shreds so that the half-embroidered stag and hunters and trees hung in tatters from the wooden frame. She opened the door leading from her chamber into the hall and began to howl so her lament could be heard through all the passages.

Hagan walked past her and shut the door firmly, facing her down. "Have you no thought for your husband's honor or your own?" he asked her. "It would be better for you to keep yourself in silence, or else to go into the woods where you may put on a wolfskin and howl as you please."

Gundahari did not see Brunichild's hand move, but he saw Hagan brace himself. Her blow rocked his head back; blood welled and began to trickle from the corner of his mouth. The tip of Hagan's tongue flickered out to lick it away as his single eye stared calmly down at her.

"Have you finished?"

"You are no man," she said to him. "Why do you taunt me with Sigimund's memory?"

"Why do you not behave as is fitting for a woman such as yourself?"

"Have I not suffered enough? Would it be better for me to sit meekly and plot behind my husband's back? Now this shall be ended as it must be, nor shall I shrink from what must be done." She turned to Gundahari. "And you, go away. You shall not see me again or share in anything that is mine."

Before Gundahari could say anything, Hagan spoke to Brunichild again. "*Haven't* you suffered enough? You could, if you chose, be content with a kingly husband and his child in your womb; you might be content to know that Sigifrith lives and is happy, and that the Walsings are not all dead."

"What are you?" Brunichild whispered. "Do the dead tell you these things when you go out to the river at night?"

"A walkurja should not scorn the dead. But you have no business reproaching my speech, for you have already said far more than you should."

Brunichild walked over to her bed, laid herself down in it, turned her face to the wall and pulled the covers over her head. Gundahari and Hagan stood looking at one another, then Gundahari knew that he would not stay in that chamber any more. He gestured his brother out to the garden, and they closed the door behind them.

No one said anything of Brunichild's deeds to Sigifrith when he brought the boys back that evening; they told him only that she was ill, and he seemed to take it for truth. But the next day Gundrun came to Gundahari again, and said that she wanted to speak to him in private.

Gundahari sighed at her words, heaving himself from his seat and coming with his sister to the chamber that she shared with Sigifrith at night. The bed that took up more than half the room had not been made yet, the blankets tossed about and tangled. He knew how it was with Gundrun and Sigifrith; he knew that Sigifrith's manhood was as mighty as the rest of his body, and he could not help seeing Brunichild opening herself to Sigifrith with more desire than she had ever shown toward him.

Gundrun sat down on the edge of the bed. Gundahari could not bear to touch it, sitting on one of the two chairs instead. "So," he said. "What now?"

"The maidens of the hall are talking about what has happened to Brunichild, and why she lies in her bed like a dead woman without taking food or drink. Gundahari, you must go and see her. Tell her that her misery is an ill thing for all of us."

"She has banned me from seeing her, or having any part in what is hers," Gundahari answered. "But I will go to see her anyway."

Brunichild did not answer his knock on the door. When he tried to open it, he found that she had bolted it.

"Brunichild!" he called. "Let me in!"

There was no answer. Gundahari went outside and tried the other door, but got no more reply there. After a while he gave up and went to find Hagan. His brother was not anywhere about his hall; he had to walk down to Hagan's house, where the blond thrall-maiden told him that her fro was sleeping.

"Well, wake him up!" Gundahari shouted at her. He felt ashamed at once when she cringed from the harshness of his voice. "I'm sorry, girl, I didn't mean to frighten you. Go and wake him up; it is important."

"I'm sorry, my king," she flustered. "It's only that this is the first time he's been able to sleep for two days, and I don't like to—"

"Did he finally get laid or something?" Hearing his own words, Gundahari flinched. "No, I didn't mean that. Just go and get him, all right? Please?"

The thrall-girl scuttled away into the dim house, and a little while later Hagan came to the door. His hair was loose and his eyepatch askew, but he had put his byrnie on and girded himself with his sword.

"What do you want?"

"I want you to go and speak to Brunichild. She won't answer when I knock on the door and call her."

"What makes you think she'll speak to me?"

"Hagan, I know you know something about this which you haven't told me. Now either you tell me what's going on or you go and talk to her, since you know what her problem is better than I do."

"I want you to know that I am not eager to do this, but since you ask it of me I suppose I have no choice. Do you promise you will not follow me or listen or try to talk to me till I am done with her?"

"I promise."

So Gundahari waited in his feasting hall, pacing about and looking up at the two great pillars behind his chair. He had had a new hearthstone made to replace the one Sigifrith had broken, and the marks his own blade had made in the left post were already sooted over and hidden in the shadows.

"I got no word from her," Hagan said behind him. "But I said what I could. Perhaps in a few more days she shall be more willing to speak."

"She'll have starved by then, if she keeps on as she has been."

"It takes longer than that to starve to death. If she keeps wine in her chamber you have no reason to fear for her health. Now, since I can do no more here, I am going home."

"I'm sorry I had to disturb you."

"I have done what I could. I wish it could have been more."

As Sigifrith came in from the stables, he heard Gundahari and Hagan speaking in the great hall, but the echoes against empty stone warped their voices too badly for him to understand them. Then Hagan pushed the door open and came out.

"I must speak to you," Hagan said.

The two of them walked out to the garden. Hagan led Sigifrith along the path to the back gate in the wall and out into the wood.

"Is something wrong?"

"I want you to speak to Brunichild. She will not talk to any of us, and it is for your sake that she is ill."

For the first time, Sigifrith found himself cursing whatever darkness of blood or magic had made Hagan too grim of look and harsh of voice for him to read the other's thoughts in his face or words. He could not tell whether Hagan was accusing him or begging, or only stating how things were.

"Why?"

"If you wish to know, you must ask her yourself."

Sigifrith thought about it for a few moments, then said, "I'll go if you lend me your byrnie."

"It won't fit you. The rings can only shift so much."

"It may be short in the sleeves and at the bottom, but I think I can wear it."

"What need do you have for a byrnie? Even if she attacks you with steel, she can hardly scathe Fadhmir's slayer."

"I don't need it because I fear anything that she may do."

"Why, then?"

"Because . . . " For the first time, Sigifrith found that he could not meet Hagan's dark eye. In a low voice, looking down at the dry grass beneath their boots, he said, "Because I could not bear it, if she were to touch me. Then I would break my troth and shame us all."

"And you have not already?"

Sigifrith said nothing.

Hagan ungirded his sword and set the belt aside. He bent over, letting the weight of his chain-mail strip it from him, and handed it to Sigifrith without a word. "Do what you can to still this slander before it spreads any further. You and Gundrun seem to have begun it, and I think no one else can end it."

"I shall," Sigifrith said.

Hagan's chain-mail was short in the sleeves and hardly reached the top of Sigifrith's thighs; but though it was tight over his shoulders and chest, it was not too small for him to move in. Seeing this, Hagan belted his sword over his ring-marked tunic and walked away down the river path.

Sigifrith returned to within the walls of Gundahari's hall and went to the door that led into Brunichild's room. When he touched the lock, it sprang open beneath his hands and he went in.

Brunichild was lying on the bed wrapped in her blankets, and Sigifrith thought she might be asleep. He flung her shutters open to let in the light, then threw off the bedclothes and spoke.

"Wake up, Brunichild! The sun is shining about the house, and you have slept enough. Cast off your sorrows and be glad!"

Brunichild sat up in her bed, clutching the blankets back around her. She was very pale and disheveled, her eyes red and swollen from weeping. Her voice was soft and choked when she asked, "How dare you come to see me? No one was worse to me in this deception."

"Why won't you speak to anyone? What distresses you?"

"I shall speak of my wrath to you."

"You are bewitched if you think that my thoughts are grim toward you. Your husband is the man you chose, as you said yourself."

"No. Gundahari did not ride through the fire, nor was it he whom I warded in battle and for whose sake I was set to sleep long years. I was confused by the man who came into my hall, and I thought that I knew your eyes, but I could not see clearly because of the veil that lay over my soul."

"You have no cause to weep. I am no more renowned a man than the sons of Gebica. Gundahari is a mighty king, and Hagan's deeds in Attila's warband were being sung long before anyone outside Alapercht's hall knew my name."

"There are many ills I have to settle with them. Don't remind me of my sorrows. You, Sigifrith, struck at the Wyrm and rode through the fire for my sake, and Gebica's sons were not there. I have never looked at Gundahari and found that my heart was joyful, but I have always felt grim toward him though I helmed my anger from others."

"It would be unnatural not to love such a king for his own sake, as well as for the sake of his child whom you bear in your womb. Brunichild, it is no fault of Gundahari's that distresses you. It seems to me that his love should be better to you than gold."

"It is bad enough that I must bear Gundahari's child, but the sorest of my sorrows to me is that I cannot get a bitter blade to be reddened in your blood."

Sigifrith stood looking down at her. From outside he heard a cuckoo's first hollow note, suddenly cut off as though a bird of prey had seized upon it in mid-call. "Do not worry about that. It shall not be long before a bitter blade stands in my heart indeed, and you need not ask worse for yourself for you shall not live after me. The days of our lives shall be few after this."

"Your words do not come from little malice, since you deceived me from all happiness and I do not heed life any longer; life is far too long to the sad."

Sigifrith knelt beside Brunichild; he feared to touch her, but he could feel the rustling of her breath on his cheek. "Live. Love King Gundahari and myself, and I will give you all I have if you do not die."

"You do not know my nature. You are the best of men, and no woman grew more hateful to you than I." Brunichild closed her eyes, her face tightening in pain. "Go away, Sigifrith. Do not mock me any longer. We all know what happened, and you have no need to make my shame worse."

"The truth is something else," he whispered. "I loved you better than myself, though I was deceived, which may not be changed now. But when my wits were unveiled it grieved me more than anything that you were not my wife, though I bore myself as best as I could since I was in a king's hall and sworn to him as a blood-brother. Brunichild, why do you think I went so far away? I could not bear to see you and be near you, and not share in your love. But even far away I knew that you were woken from your sleep and that you lived, and I was happy enough because of that—because we were not forever parted. It may be that the spae-words spoken before shall come true, but you should not worry about it."

"You have said too late that my distress sorrows you, and now there is no ease for us."

Sigifrith drew in a deep, shuddering breath, reaching out to lay his hand over hers. She stiffened, looking into his eyes, and then he could be silent no longer. "I wish that the two of us would both go into one bed, and you would be my wife," he murmured. He felt his face reddening with shame and desire; but he could not draw his hand back from her, nor she from him.

"Such things must not be said," she answered broken-voiced. "I shall not have two kings in one hall, and I would rather leave my life than deceive King Gundahari. On Ostara dawn we met on the top of the mountain and said our vows to one another. I poured out holy mead and gave you my wisdom with it, and you gave me Andward's ring as a sign of our love. But now that is broken, and I do not want to live."

"I had no memory of your name, and I did not recognize you before you were given in marriage. That is my greatest sorrow."

"I swore an oath to marry that man who rode through my leaping flames, and I wished to keep that oath or else die."

Sigifrith could hardly breathe; he felt that a great wave had swept over his head, dragging him down into a dark world of sorrow and grief, and he knew that the cold weight crushing his heart from him was Brunichild's despair added to his own, a stone set on top of stone to build a burial cairn. He clasped her to him. Even through their sorrows, the feeling of her body against his sent a thrill of joy through him. He heard Brunichild gasp as her arms tightened about him, and knew that if it were not for the rings of metal between them they would love again there and then.

"Rather than that you should die, I'll marry you and leave Gundrun," Sigifrith whispered. "It is no great matter to break a wedding. We can stay in my hall in the mountains, or go wherever you want—to Britain, to Rome itself; it will not be long before I make myself a king in whatever place." For a moment, his vision seemed to glimmer in the dark pools of Brunichild's pupils like the icy blue and crimson banners of ghost light against the black winter skies of Gautland. Sigifrith could hear himself breathing hard; then the clear sound of steel rings breaking cut into his ears, as sharp as the snapping of icicles. Hagan's byrnie fell loose down his chest and back, its fettering tightness split along his ribs.

Brunichild broke his hold as if all the strength had left his arms, pushing him away.

"I don't want you," said Brunichild, "nor any other."

Sigifrith went away.

Sigifrith did not come into the hall again until Sunna had begun to set. As he walked around from the back gate he saw Brunichild sitting beneath her window staring at the darkening eastern sky. He skirted a wide path through the trees and around to the front doorway where Gundahari stood waiting for him.

"Do you know what is wrong? Is she able to speak?" the Burgundian king asked in a rush of breath, his heart pounding with fear beneath Sigifrith's grim gaze.

"She can speak. She is by her window."

Gundahari nodded. "I'll go to her." He began to walk away, then stopped and looked back at the two flaps of chain-mail that hung free over Sigifrith's breast and back. Worried as he was, he could not help asking, "Sigifrith, why are you wearing a broken byrnie?"

"Go and talk to Brunichild."

Gundahari found his wife as Sigifrith had said, sitting by her window with her knees drawn up to her chest and her fair hair hanging loose over her face. He sat down beside her, watching the heavens deepen to ocean-blue above the walls of the garden.

"Is there anything that can ease your grief?" he asked.

"I don't want to live," said Brunichild. "Sigifrith betrayed me, and he betrayed you too, for he was my first lover. Now I will not have two husbands at once in one hall, and that shall be Sigifrith's bane or yours or mine, for he has told Gundrun everything and she taunts me with it. He boasted to her that he had taken my maidenhead, and he gave her the ring that he took from me when he wore your shape and came to play the part of a bridegroom with me upon my mound."

"Has he spoken of this to anyone else?"

"I should be surprised if everyone in your hall did not know what had come to pass by now—how he took your honor together with mine."

Gundahari laid his hand over one of Brunichild's, but she jerked angrily away from him. "Don't touch me! Everyone knows that you are a lesser man than Sigifrith, though he let you claim the hero's portion at the wedding."

"Brunichild," Gundahari murmured. "Brunichild, I love you. Why must you do this to us?"

She did not answer.

"I swear that when this feast is done, I shall send Sigifrith and Gundrun far away and they shall never come back again while you and I live in this hall. Then all shall be as it was, and we shall forget this and be content again."

"And will your mother brew a seith-drink to make sure of it?"

"Brunichild, Grimhild has always treated you like a daughter. You should not speak ill of her."

"I cannot bear the sight of her, for I think much of this is her fault."

"Tell me what I must do to make you happy again, my love."

Brunichild was silent for a long moment. Then she whispered, "You can never make me happy again. But you shall lose kingdom and wealth both, your life and me, and I shall fare home to my kinsmen alone and sit sorrowfully in that hall if you do not kill Sigifrith—and his son. You must not rear the wolf's whelp."

Gundahari got up and walked away among the dry rustling of the trees, driven by his distress. How can I betray my blood-brother? he asked himself. I am bound to Sigifrith by oath.

But Brunichild bears my child in her womb, and if she fares from me my son shall go with her. Nor have I ever known such happiness as in her rare smiles, nor is there anything I would not give to keep her with me.

. . . Yet another thought coiled like a wyrm, gleaming and baleful, in the caverns of his skull: if Sigifrith goes away, he shall take the gold with him, and it shall never come back to the place where you keep it hidden by the Rhine.

Sigifrith is my blood-brother and my friend, and my sister's greatest joy in life. And I could not slay Gundrun's child, my own sister-son; this is a monstrous thing my beloved asks of me.

Whose songs are sung more often? What have I done to match the slaying of Fadhmir? What right did I have to the hero's portion, and why did Sigifrith let me take it? Wasn't it because he felt no need to prove his might against me, because he had already proven it before Brunichild's leaping flames? And he gave the ring to Gundrun, and he boasted to her of how he had won it; does that shame not burn in my blood? Should he not die for that, whether he knew it for ill or not?

. . . And the thoughts writhed and hissed at the roots of his mind, tingling through the gold-set boar's tooth that lay over his heart: if Sigifrith fell, the Rhine's gold would be mine—how can I keep my kingdom if the folk know that he is the better man? How can I keep the Gebicungs' honor safe, if men doubt that my sons are my own?

How could I ever still the shame of a broken oath of blood?

Gundahari looked at the slumped shape beneath the window, staring at her till his eyes blurred in the darkness.

I know that Brunichild is better to me than all, and she is the most well-famed of women. I would rather die than lose her love. And no shame could match mine if she left me; would she not tell everyone why? And then all I have done would be destroyed, and all I have built would be broken for ever, and it would surely be Sigifrith's fault and Gundrun's . . .

. . . Yet might not a woman who could give me rede to slay my own sister-son be mad enough to be her own bairn's bane?

Gundahari went out from the walls and through the darkened streets of Worms till he came to the door of Hagan's house. His brother answered with a torch in his hand.

"Sigifrith's speech with Brunichild did not go well," Hagan stated. "Come in."

As far as Gundahari could tell in the torchlight, Hagan's house was as clean and well-kept as he might have expected. Hagan led him into a small, plain bedroom, setting the torch into its socket on the wall and shutting the door behind them. "Costbera has gone to your hall to relieve Gundrun of Nibel and Sigimund, and our thrall has enough to do with my other children. We shall not be disturbed. Now, sit down and tell me what your thoughts are."

"There is a great problem before me," Gundahari said as he seated himself on one of Hagan's spare wooden chairs. "Sigifrith has broken troth with us, and I mean to slay him."

"It would not be right to break our oaths with such unfrith. And he is a great help to us. No kings are a match for us while he lives; for the last three years, he had guarded our eastern gates from the Huns. Believe me, no one knows better than I what would happen if there were not such a hero as Sigifrith in the eastern marches."

"Hrodgar holds the lands east of Sigifrith."

"But it is Sigifrith's might that has kept him free of Attila's rule. We should never get a kinsman like him again, and think how good it shall be when such sister-sons of ours as he shall beget come to be fostered in our warband. But I see where this stems from. Brunichild has wakened it, and from her rede deep shame and scathe shall come to us."

"Still it must be carried out, or else our line shall lose its fame forever, and all because of Sigifrith's boasting and Gundrun's pride in her man."

"I think this is an ill rede, and although we carried it out, we should have a great geld to pay for betraying such a man."

Gundahari leaned forward, resting his elbows on his thighs and his chin in his hands. "Sigifrith must die, or else I must, for I cannot live with the shame which has been brought upon us. He took my wife's maidenhead and deceived me, and he broke his oath for a woman's golden ring."

"For Andward's ring. Others have broken troth and died for that gold before—even our own kinsman Ragin the Smith."

"Hagan, what is our family's honor to you?"

"Do you need to ask me that?"

"What is my life to you?"

Hagan only looked at him.

"If you will not help me in this," the king said slowly to his brother, "I shall fight with Sigifrith alone, and only one of us will come from it living."

"Do you think Sigifrith would kill you? Why should he even try, when you cannot scathe him either with weapons or worts?"

Gundahari had not thought of that, but his brother's words stopped him like the blow of a spear. "What can we do?"

"We shall ask Brunichild. This was her rede; none should know better than she how Sigifrith could be slain."

Brunichild was still by her window when Gundahari and Hagan came back within the walls. Her eyes were sunken cauldrons in the frightening paleness of her moonlit face; Gundahari stepped back a pace when she turned her gaze toward him.

"What have you come for?" she asked. Her voice was harsh, as raw as the green wood of a linden with its smooth gray bark rasped off.

"We've come . . . " Even now, Gundahari's heart failed him at the thought. It was one thing to speak to Hagan, who would give him rede and keep his secrets silent; but he knew that words given to Brunichild would be staves carven in stone that his hand would not have the strength to chip away again.

"How may Sigifrith be slain?" Hagan asked. Quiet as his speech was, Gundahari seemed to feel the earth grinding beneath his feet with the sound of his brother's rock-rough voice.

Black in the Moon's gibbous light, Brunichild's eyes fixed on Hagan. She opened her mouth, and her words rode out in a single rush of air like a torrent of winter leaves on the wind: "On Sigifrith's back, two fingers to the left of his spine and a little above his heart, there is an ash-hued mark shaped like a linden leaf. It is where a smoldering leaf clung when he had slain Fadhmir, and when he bathed in the dragon's blood that one spot was not warded, so if you should pierce that place with a blade the spell on him would be broken and he would die like any man, and he may be slain in no other way than by the thrust of a spear in his back. This do I know, for I was Wodan's wish-maiden and Sigifrith's first beloved."

"We thank you," Hagan said. He turned and walked away from her without looking back, and Gundahari followed him.

Hagan stopped when they were outside in the street again. "Now go home and go to sleep. Tomorrow is Winternights and we must go hunting to bring in food for the feast."

"And what shall we do about . . . ?"

"You shall do nothing. You are his blood-brother, and it would be as unseemly for a king to break such an oath as for any of the other ills we have spoken of to befall you. If this thing must happen, it would be better for the dishonor of Sigifrith's murder to befall me."

"Hagan . . . but what of Gundrun? What will happen to her?"

"If it were not for her tongue and her temper, we should not have to do this thing. We shall make another marriage for her, and in any case she shall have Sigifrith's son and daughter to comfort her."

"Must we really do this?"

"We must. If it were not for my oath and the care I had for Sigifrith, I would have seen what needed doing when the men and maids of our hall first began to talk—when Folkhari came to me and told me what they were saying."

"Is it that widely known?" Gundahari whispered.

Hagan nodded.

"Then there is no choice for us."

"For me. You need only do as you have always done."

"How can I let you do this? It is my shame; the deed should be mine. A man kills his own foes."

"Murder is not the deed of a man. But I had more of a hand in this than you know, and it is mine to pay for it."

Gundahari stepped forward and embraced his brother quickly. To his surprise, he could feel the ridges of muscle raised over Hagan's sharp bones; Hagan's tunic hid no chain-mail. "Where is your byrnie?"

"I lent it to Sigifrith."

"He broke it."

"I told him it was too small. I have another."

"Be careful."

"I am. Always."

Gundahari waited until he could no longer see his brother in the shadows before he passed through the gates again. "Will you come inside now?" he asked Brunichild. She did not answer; it seemed to him that she did not hear him, but stared instead at a world that he could not see. Heavy and sick at heart, Gundahari went into his hall to greet his kin.

WODAN'S GIFT

The morning before the day of the Winternights feast, Sigifrith arose at dawn while Gundrun was still sleeping. The rising light of morning through the shutters lay over their bedclothes in long slanting lances, brightening Gundrun's sleep-pale face and gleaming here and there from her hair's tangles as if they had been strung with little golden beads. Sigifrith stretched to his full height, taking a deep breath of the cold morning air. He did not know why, but he felt quite whole and well, as though some gift of the gods had cracked off the heavy rings of sorrow that had fettered him and they had fallen suddenly away from his limbs. He was hungry and eager to be out at the hunt.

Sigifrith bent to kiss Gundrun's cheek. He pulled the covers up to warm her back where he had been lying, then got into a plain crimson tunic and dark breeches for the hunt. He did not bother with his boots, for he thought that today he might choose to chase stag and boar on foot and he wished to be able to run freely; but he girded Gram to his side.

The men were gathering in the great hall, where loaves of steaming new bread and wheels of cheese were set out on the tables together with pitchers of milk warm from the cows. Sigifrith broke off half a loaf and a piece of cheese the size of his fist. He ate as he walked up to the high table, where Gundahari and Hagan were trying to explain to Sigimund and Nibel why the boys could not go hunting with them, to the amusement of Gisalhari and Gernot. The white cheese was very fresh and firm, squeaking under his teeth, and the bread was rich with butter.

"You are too small," Hagan said. Sigifrith could see the lines of a byrnie beneath the Burgundian's black tunic, and wondered if he should say anything to Hagan about the one he had broken.

"I am not!" Sigimund insisted. "I can shoot a bow and arrow. A small bow and arrow," he admitted when his father's eyes lighted on him. "But I could ride with someone."

"I am almost a year older than he is," Nibel added. "I could carry a throwing spear." He reached out to grasp the shaft of his father's spear, showing that his fingers were long enough to wrap around it, and smiled brilliantly up at Sigifrith. The bee-stings had almost faded from the boy's face and arms, but a network of fresh bramble-scratches criss-crossed his white skin. "I'm not afraid of the hounds, even though they bark at me and the Irish ones are taller than I am."

"I'm not afraid of hounds either. I'm not even afraid of wolfs. We have lots of wolfs in the woods where we live," Sigimund told Nibel.

"Why shouldn't they come with us?" Gisalhari asked. Though he had become taller and broader in the shoulders since Sigifrith's wedding, and now sported the first tufts of an orangeish beard, his voice had not deepened yet. He wore a large golden cross around his neck, which stood out brightly against his blue tunic. "Gernot and I went hunting from a very early age, didn't we?"

Gernot nodded. Like his brother, he had grown a great deal in the last four years; his heavy limbs were padded with fat now, and his dark beard was full.

"Not that early," Hagan said.

"Neither of you is going hunting with us today," Sigifrith told the young boys firmly. "But tomorrow I'll make you some bows and arrows and take you out to shoot birds. Will that be enough for you fierce warriors?"

Sigimund and Nibel looked at him, then at each other.

"We'll shoot lots and lots of birds, and have them in a pie for dinner," Nibel said.

"I'll shoot an eagle!"

"What good is an eagle dead?"

Sigimund thought about it a moment. "Maybe I'll wound it a little so I can catch it and take it home and heal it and teach it to hunt."

Sigifrith laughed, putting a hand on each of their shoulders and giving them a gentle push. "Run along, now. Go and find whatever poor woman is supposed to be taking care of you today and make her give you breakfast or something. Go on."

Sigimund hugged his father about the legs as Sigifrith tousled his hair, then sped off to overtake his friend on the way out of the hall.

"Oh," said Gisalhari. "Poor things. Gundahari, are you going to let them get rid of their sons that easily?"

Gundahari did not seem to notice his cousin. "Ready for the hunt, then, Sigifrith?" he asked, hollowly echoing his usual cheerfulness. The Burgundian king's face was pasty above his black beard; beneath his brown cloak he was wearing the same green tunic he had the night before, and it was creased as though he had slept in it.

"I am. Are you sure you are? You don't look so well."

"I'm just tired. I'll be all right once we get out into the air."

Sigifrith finished his food and helped himself to some more, following it with a big mug of milk. "Are things any better with Brunichild?"

"The same."

"Are we ready to go?" Folkhari asked, coming up to the high table. "Sunna's rising higher every minute, and the deer will soon be going to their dens." The golden-haired singer smiled at them. "Come on, or we'll have a thin feast tomorrow."

Gisalhari and Gernot sprang up at once, and Gundahari and Hagan followed more slowly. Gundahari's thanes were picking up the bows and spears that lined the walls of the feasting hall; the king went to get his own bow and arrows from where they rested against one of the ancestral posts.

"What weapons are you taking, Sigifrith?" Hagan asked, tapping the butt of his throwing spear against the flagstones.

"The sword Gram and my own strength. What more should I need?"

"I suppose what did for slaying a dragon will do well enough for stalking deer and wild swine."

Gundahari led the hunting band out to the stables. It was colder outside than Sigifrith had thought and the men wrapped their cloaks more tightly around themselves, muttering against the biting wind. Grani whickered and stamped restlessly when Sigifrith went to stroke and talk to him as the other men saddled up. "No, my friend, you're not going this time. You and I together would be too much for them. We want to leave some game for the rest, after all. Be patient; we shall have time enough together afterward."

Grani reared in his stall, beating at the air with his hooves. Sigifrith did not step back; he knew that his horse would not strike him, and so he did not move in time when Grani's right forehoof crashed down on his left shoulder and knocked him to the ground.

Sigifrith lay where he had fallen, looking up at the gray stallion in disbelief and testing the bones of his shoulder. It seemed that nothing was broken, though the ache ran numbingly deep through his whole arm.

The stallion snorted, bending over Sigifrith and snuffling at him. Sigifrith moved his shoulder in a circle to work some of the pain out, then looped his right arm over Grani's neck and let the horse pull him to his feet.

"You didn't mean to do that, did you?" he asked. Grani whuffled, spraying wetness from his velvety lips. "It's all right. I'm not hurt too badly." Sigifrith patted his steed reassuringly. "I'll take you for a good long ride tomorrow."

It was easy for Sigifrith to jog along by Gundahari's stirrup, hardly stretching his legs as he ran by the two Irish hounds whose heads almost reached his waist. He turned his face to the cold wind that blew the woods into their last summer fire, red and gold leaves stark-edged against the clear blue sky of winter. Acorns and dry twigs crunched beneath his bare feet, softened by the year's rotting leaf-mold below them. With a light kick to the side he knocked the white-flecked cap from a crimson toadstool, spinning the spotted wheel out ahead of the horses into a thorn bush. A startled fox streaked from the bush across the path, its ruddy pelt flashing almost golden in the slanting spears of sunlight through the trees. An arrow—Sigifrith was not sure whose—sped after the fox, just missing its tail; it glanced from the face of a half-buried stone, and Sigifrith heard a Burgundian voice muttering, "Shit."

"Nice try," Folkhari called to the luckless shooter. The singer nudged his bay into a canter, coming along the path to the leaders of the hunt. "Hai, Sigifrith, since you're so swift, why don't you run ahead and chase some game back here for us? Can you outrun our wolfhounds?"

Sigifrith glanced up at Gundahari.

"Go ahead," the Burgundian king said. "I'd like to see that." Though the wind had reddened Gundahari's face, his voice was still dull and his eyes no brighter.

"Cheer up, and I'll give you something worth seeing."

Sigifrith slapped his thigh, whistling to the Irish hounds that leaped and barked around him and breaking into a full run. The huge gray dogs followed him eagerly, their long-legged clumsiness sweeping into a grace as breathtaking as flight. They ran behind Sigifrith with all the swiftness bred in them for chasing down Irish deer and wolves; but the pair of hounds could only keep up with him so long before Sigifrith sped ahead of them, laughing as he leapt over half-rotted logs and thorn bushes. The biting air was as refreshing as ice-chilled wine in his throat against the heat of his running.

Looking down to the path before him, he saw the cloven prints of a deer cut deep and neat in the leaf-mold as if a goldsmith's sharp-edged tool had stamped them there. The depths of the tracks were just beginning to fill with water.

Sigifrith followed the deer tracks down to the Rhine, where a ruddy ten-pointed buck stood drinking. Carefully he circled till he stood downwind of the stag, then crept up as quietly as he could till he was almost upon it. With a sudden bound he broke cover, springing toward the deer as it swung its antlers about to meet him. He grabbed the stag by its rack, torquing its head about till it went down on its side in the river mud with a great thump. White-rimmed eyes, shiny and dark as chestnuts, rolled up to stare desperately at Sigifrith; the stag's breath came hot and strangled, the thick veins of its neck pulsing swiftly.

One hand holding his prey, Sigifrith took off his belt with the other hand, looping it around three of the deer's legs and pulling it tight with his sheathed sword braced around the atheling-beast's belly like an extra limb. He heaved the stag onto his shoulders and began to jog back along the path, following his track as well as he could till he heard the sounds of horses' hooves and men's voices.

"Hai!" he shouted. "What have you caught?"

"Nothing yet," Gundahari called back. "What about you?"

Sigifrith rounded a bend in the path, coming into view of the hunters. He raised the stag above his head. "I've brought you some game, as I said I would." Laughing as the Burgundians gaped at him, Sigifrith lowered the stag and whipped his belt from its legs. "Now it's your turn to hunt!"

Startled by its sudden freedom, the stag stumbled a few paces before it began to run in earnest. A few arrows whipped around Sigifrith, then the dogs leapt forward and the men stopped shooting, kicking their horses to full gallop. Sigifrith stayed a few paces ahead of them, chasing the stag as it doubled back on the track through the wood and ran in a jagged path through the trees with the hounds barking behind it.

At last they came to a hedge of thorns that the stag could not leap or break through. It halted a moment, about to turn, and then the dogs were on him and bringing him down.

"Hai!" Gundahari shouted at the hounds, shoving them away from the corpse with his boot before they could rend it to shreds. "Good dogs, there . . . that's enough. We'll be giving you your part."

Well trained, the giant hounds sat back on their hindquarters, tongues lolling out as they grinned bloodily at him. Three of the Burgundian thanes dismounted, unsheathing their knives for the butchering.

"That was well run," Folkhari said to Sigifrith, grinning. "I would hardly have believed it in one of my own songs."

Sigifrith shrugged. "There you are, then. It wasn't so much."

The hunting band waited till the hounds had gobbled the entrails of the stag, then mounted again and began to ride westward while the thanes who had done the butchering loaded the meat onto their horses to take back to the hall.

They stopped an hour or two after midday for a meal, eating bread and apples and smoked meat. Each man filled his horn or cup from a barrel of Gaulish wine that they had brought with them, but the wine ran to red-brown sludge before half the thanes had had a second drink.

"Your kegs don't hold very much," Sigifrith said to Gundahari.

"It's my fault," Hagan broke in. "I knew that one of the barrels in the storeroom was half-empty. I should have looked at it before I had it loaded."

"Don't feel bad," Gundahari told him. "There'll be that much more for the feast. Do you think you'll live without a third horn, Sigifrith?"

"I'm sure I will." Sigifrith smiled at his kinsman, only to see Gundahari go suddenly pale. "Are you all right?"

"Sat on something," Gundahari grunted. He heaved himself up off the ground, scrabbling about beneath his buttocks to bring out a small stone and fling it away. "That's what I get for not looking where I plant my arse."

"What other game are we seeking today?" Hagan asked. Gundahari started, turning toward him and half-flinging up his hand as if to ward off a blow.

"Brunichild's made you jumpy, hasn't she? And to think you were warning me about Gundrun's temper once," Sigifrith said lightly. He poured half the wine from his horn into Gundahari's, splashing some over the Burgundian's hand. "Drink, Gundahari, drink. See, your brother has brought you wine. Why are you so pale?"

Gundahari stared down into the horn. "It seems to me," he muttered in a muffled voice, "that the horn is full of blood."

"Then let yours be mixed with mine!" Sigifrith took the horn from Gundahari's hand, pouring a thin stream of the dark wine back and forth and dripping a little on to the earth from each horn before he gave Gundahari's back and raised his own to drink.

"There is a wild boar's den some ways from here," Hagan said. "He is a fine boar, bearing many scars from hunters who have not been able to slay him. Perhaps with Sigifrith's aid we might be able to do that and serve him up for our Winternights feast."

"If you think so," Gundahari answered. "Let one of the men take the hounds from their meat, then, so they'll be fiercer for the hunt."

The hunters mounted when they had finished their meal and rode along the paths Hagan pointed out to them, laughing and talking to one another. They had no fear of frightening their quarry away; it was mating season, and Sigifrith gathered from the talk that this boar, whom the Burgundians called Gold-Tooth because his long tusks had grown yellow with age, was particularly fearless and fierce. Now and again Sigifrith would dash on ahead of the other men; once he followed a wolf's spoor back to the cave where three of the gray beasts slept, shadows in the dimness, before he came back to the path.

Sunna was more than halfway down the sky when Sigifrith saw the first signs of boar. Here and there, the earth and leaves were torn up where Gold-Tooth had fought with his rivals in the wod of rut; and more than once, a trail of blood led away.

"He is likely to be at the river drinking," Hagan said to Sigifrith, who marked how the other men were readying their spears and arrows. "What part would you like in this hunt?"

"Whatever you wish."

Gundahari had borrowed Gernot's boar spear; now he rode up on Sigifrith's other side. "I want this kill, if I can do it," he said.

"All right. Shall I start him toward you?"

"Are you sure you want to do that?"

"How can he hurt me?"

Gundahari nodded slowly. "If you will, then."

They rode toward the Rhine, Sigifrith leading the Irish hounds a little ahead of the hunters till he found the boar's fresh spoor. The tracks lead to where the river's banks spread out into marsh; and there between the trees, his head lowered and snorting as he drank, was the biggest boar Sigifrith had ever seen. His back came almost to the middle of Sigifrith's thigh; his scarred shoulders were as thick as a bull's with muscle and the two yellowed tusks that jutted from his lower jaw seemed better than a handspan long. He raised his head, glaring red-eyed at the hunters and letting out a deep, grunting bellow.

Gundahari quietly got off his horse, giving the reins to Hagan. Sigifrith and the hounds circled splashing through the marsh, coming up on Gold-Tooth from either side. Wyrm-swift, the boar turned to slash at them with his tusks, leaving a bleeding graze through the grizzled coat of the wolf-hound bitch. Her mate snapped at the boar, growling, but could not bite through the hardened skin armoring his sides, and in the next moment he had to tumble back from the swine's deadly gore.

The hounds circled the boar more warily, leaving Sigifrith standing before him. Sigifrith did not draw his sword; instead, he kicked flat-footed at Gold-Tooth's snout just hard enough to enrage the beast. Gold-Tooth charged him, tossing his head as he battered into Sigifrith with an impact that bowled the man over. Sigifrith rolled with his momentum and came up laughing.

"You're not the only one with a sturdy hide," he chortled. "Come on, then."

"My kill!" Gundahari shouted to him.

Sigifrith raised his fist in acknowledgment, side-stepping the boar's next charge and leaping over his back. "Come on!" he called, running toward the horses with Gold-Tooth behind him. Gundahari stood before the others, his spear clutched firmly in both hands. "Get down!" Sigifrith said, running straight toward him. Gundahari dropped to one knee and braced the butt of his spear against the ground, its broad blade pointing straight at Sigifrith. Sigifrith brushed it to the side and leapt over Gundahari's head, turning as he landed to see his brother whip it back into place, ready to take the boar through the more vulnerable hide of his chest as he charged.

Gundahari's aim was off only by a couple of inches, but it was enough for Gold-Tooth to wrench the spear from the king's hands and fling him sideways to the ground. The boar grunted horribly, backing a step or two and shaking the shaft that stuck from his chest before he lowered his head and charged forward to gore and toss the downed man. Desperately Gundahari rolled to the other side; but he would not have got out of Gold-Tooth's path if Sigifrith had not dived forward to slam his shoulder into the boar's with all his might.

Sigifrith's blow stopped the boar long enough for Gundahari to get to his feet again. Instead of running as he ought to have, the Burgundian grasped for the spear shaft as it whipped about. He was knocked down again, but this time he held on to the shaft, grunting as fiercely as the boar as he tried to get his feet under him and brace himself. Then the Irish hounds sprang into the fray, snapping at Gold-Tooth as he vainly tried to turn away from the spear in his chest and gore one or the other of them. They did not bother with his thick-skinned sides this time, but twisted their heads under to rip at his belly with their powerful jaws.

At last the spear wound and the rending of the hounds weakened the boar enough so Gundahari could push the shaft the rest of the way in. Gold-Tooth's eyes closed and he slumped back. Gundahari straightened, grinning in exhausted triumph; and the moment his grip loosened, the boar leapt up and charged forward again, bearing him down. Sigifrith was upon them in a heartbeat, grabbing the boar around his sharp-bristled shoulders and wrestling him away from his kinsman. He could feel Gold-Tooth's last burst of strength waning beneath his grip, and then it was an easy thing to heave him away from Gundahari.

The dying boar lay on his side, blood running out of his mouth and along his tusks as the heaving of his chest grew less and less. Sigifrith helped his kinsman up. He could feel Gundahari's bone-deep trembling as the king gasped his thanks.

"You don't need to thank me," Sigifrith said. "It was your kill. I've hardly seen such bravery."

"That was not very wise," Hagan said as he dismounted, his throwing spear still in his hand. He walked over to the boar and put the point straight into his eye; Gold-Tooth kicked once and then was still. Hagan pulled his spear out and wiped the blade off, blood and brains vanishing into the black of his tunic. "You might well have been slain, Gundahari."

"But I wasn't," Gundahari said, a faint smile ghosting across his muddy face as his thanes hastened to offer their praise. He looked at his brother. "You see, we should be ill off if we did not have Sigifrith with us," the Burgundian king added, his voice strained as with exhaustion. "I think we have enough game today."

"And now I am thirsty, and I expect you are too," Sigifrith complained laughingly. "But the river's too mucky to drink from here. Hagan, why don't we have any more wine? It's all your fault, isn't it?"

"It is," Hagan said.

"And you didn't even help in the kill. Is it the weight of your byrnie that slows you down too much to be of use?"

"It is said that I am the swiftest runner among the Burgundians, but we shall see. If you are really thirsty, there is a place not far downstream where a clear stream flows into the Rhine. I shall race you there, if you like, and wear my byrnie and carry my spear while I run as well."

"And what does the winner get for a prize?"

"He gets to drink first."

"That's not much of a prize," Gisalhari objected cockily. "You ought to have something more to offer than that."

"Shut up, Gisalhari," Gundahari told him, cuffing him lightly. "No one asked you."

"And who shall be the judge of this race?" Folkhari asked merrily. "How shall we know who has won?"

"Whoever likes can run with us," Sigifrith said, sweeping his arm in a wide gesture to include all the thanes. "Then we'll find out whose boasts are worthiest." He drew a line in the marshy muck with a mud-caked toe. "Come on, then."

Hagan, Folkhari, Gisalhari, Gernot and four or five of the other Burgundians lined up beside Sigifrith, who glanced back at Gundahari. "Aren't you going to run too?"

"I'm too tired . . ." Gundahari began to protest, then looked around at his thanes. "Oh, why not?"

He took his place behind Sigifrith, and Folkhari began to count. "One . . . two . . . three!"

The men sprang over the line, splashing through the marsh till they got to firmer ground and then beginning to run before the wind in earnest. The two wolfhounds dashed ahead of them, barking cheerfully at the game. At first Sigifrith trotted only a little ahead; but soon he saw that Hagan was close on his heels, the one-eyed warrior running swiftly between the gray hounds and bidding fair to overtake him within a few heartbeats. Sigifrith widened his stride, pulling ahead again. He was outstripping the wind now; though it blew from behind him; the wind of his own running tossed his hair back.

Sigifrith almost missed the stream when he came to it; he was running too fast to stop, but had to leap over the creek and back again before he knelt down to drink.

The freezing water cooled his hands; he splashed the first draught to drip over his hot face before he cupped his palms and lowered them into the stream. As he raised his hands, he heard the croaking of ravens to the west.

"Remember," one called to the other; and the other's harsh voice replied, "Remember."

Sigifrith raised his head, looking westward through the trees. Two dark shadows winged against the burning light of the setting Sun.

"Do you hear what those ravens are saying?" Hagan's rough bass called. Sigifrith glanced back, meeting Hagan's single eye where he stood with his spear raised between the two hounds. "They give me rede for revenge!"

Sigifrith gasped as the blow struck his back, falling forward on his elbows in the water of the stream. Slowly he raised himself, looking down to see the steel tip of the spear sticking out through his tunic like a bloody thorn. He did not feel any pain; it was as though his whole chest were numbed by Ragin's salve of dwale, but when he coughed he could taste the blood hot and thick on his tongue.

Sigifrith turned and looked up at Hagan. "Why?" he whispered, his voice weak. "I did nothing to deserve this from my kin."

Hagan stood looking down at him, Sunna's light glinting from the mail of his raised arm. Slowly he let his hand fall.

"Hagan, what are you doing?" Gundahari whispered as the men came up behind the slayer. "What have you done?"

"I avenged a false oath," Hagan answered harshly, staring at Sigifrith.

Sigifrith turned his face to the burning wheel of the Sun. The ruddy and gold leaves were black against her light now, falling upward in the rising wind. It seemed to him that he was no longer looking west, but east; that Sunna was rising in a ring of flame, brightening to shimmering rainbows.

"Sigrdrifa," he murmured, reaching out with his last strength, then, as he slumped forward toward the stream, "Sigilind!" He could see her white swan-wings glimmering before him in the cold wind that blew over his face, its ice mingling with the hot wolf blood in his mouth as the brightening before him took the last of his breath away.

Hagan's breath caught on the taste of blood as the ring of unseen flames faded around Sigifrith's fallen body, leaving the hero's corpse a dark shadow half-athwart the stream. A sudden, terrible heat coursed through his veins, its wod burning within the cool white bone of his skull to shatter the clarity of his thoughts like a shattering of light reflecting from clear rushing water as the hounds fled howling from his side.

The faces of the other men paled when he turned to look at them, gray as frost-stricken grass in the ruddy light. Folkhari backed hurriedly away from him, Gisalhari, Rumold and Dankrat crossing themselves as their mouths hung open. He reached out to touch Gundahari's shoulder, and his brother stumbled back from him, shaking in horror. The croaking of the ravens sounded in his ears again, the call too far off for the others to hear it: "Ready the benches, measure the mead. A hero comes to the shield-roofed hall."

Only when he heard the echo of his own raspy voice from the rocks did Hagan realize that it was he who had spoken. Driven by the wod within him, he could not stand still, but leapt down to where Sigifrith lay with his face in the water and his long hair drifting like a drowned man's. He lifted the great body in his arms, breathless at its lightness, and bore it to where the hunters stood staring at him as if bound by battle-fetter.

"Kindle your torches!" Hagan commanded. "It grows dark. Bind this on to a horse and bear it back with our other game, for the queen will be ready to come to her feast." He laid Sigifrith's corpse on the dry grass. Bracing his foot against Sigifrith's ribs, he heaved his spear free and raised it, slamming the butt down on the earth again.

No one moved; it was several moments before Hagan realized that they did not dare to come nearer to him. He strode away between the trees, then stood to watch as Gundahari slowly walked over to Sigifrith's fallen body. The king of the Burgundians knelt beside his dead rival; Hagan saw his brother's shoulders shaking as he turned Sigifrith over and tried to wipe the earth and bits of grass from his face with the muddy sleeve of his own tunic. It seemed to Hagan that he heard his brother's voice whispering something, but Gundahari spoke too softly for even his ears to catch the words.

The king gestured; Gernot, Gisalhari and Irtwine came forward, crouching down on either side of the body. Together they heaved, lifting Sigifrith with their shoulders under his hips and shoulders on either side. His limbs rolled limply to flop down as the men rose; his right arm fell across Irtwine's slim back, and the young warrior let out a muffled sound of terror, jerking sideways so that the other corpse-bearers staggered and were barely able to right themselves again before they began to walk. To Hagan's one blurred eye, in the fading light, the four men carrying the dead body melted into the single shape of an eight-legged horse with its head hanging low. He waited between the trees till the men had gone along the path; they hurried before him as though they feared to look back and see what followed.

The mellow light of Sunna's setting glowed into the feasting hall through the open door. Gundrun sat in her chair next to Sigifrith's empty place, watching the serving maids. Some swept the benches and strewed fresh herbs and straw beneath the tables; others were measuring out wine into the tall pitchers of Roman clay that would stand among the thanes. Now and again she would get up and go to the door, looking anxiously out for signs of the hunters.

Brunichild had not come out of her room all day. Gundrun had sent maids with food and drink for her, but Gundahari's wife had taken nothing. Gundrun did not know whether the woman was alive or dead, whether she slept or was working some deathly walkurja magic within her chamber. She comforted herself with the thought that nothing could scathe Sigifrith, at least, that Sigimund was away with Costbera and her children while Swanhild was safe with Hildkar and Olwyn. If Brunichild wished to work some harm, she would have to deal with Gundrun herself . . . and Gundrun clutched the gold hilt of the knife at her belt, wishing that she might, like Hagan, be able to bear byrnie and weapons to the night's feast of frith.

Suddenly a hoarse scream shuddered through the air, its rough anguish seeming to rasp against Gundrun's very skin. She was out and running, following the sound as it howled out again over the sound of wood crashing beneath furious blows.

Gundrun was almost to the stables when the door burst outward, long splinters of wood flying around Grani as the wind-gray stallion galloped out into the yard, rearing with a high horrible neighing. His muzzle dripped white with froth as though he had drunk from the ocean's waves; his eyes rolled in furious blindness. Falling to all fours again, he began to run in wide drunken circles, staggering from side to side.

"Grani!" Gundrun cried as the stallion dropped his head down almost to the ground. "What is wrong? What is wrong with you?" She had never seen a horse go mad, but she could think of nothing else. Somebody must shoot him; we must not let Sigifrith see this, she thought. But before she could shout for help or go to fetch bow and arrows herself, Grani straightened himself and galloped toward the wall, flying up in a breathtaking leap that took him cleanly over it.

"What can have happened?" Gundrun whispered to herself. Trying to calm her shaking and walk with dignity, she hurried back to the hall and caught her maiden Harirad by the shoulder.

Harirad's brown eyes went wide as she looked at her frowe. "What's wrong?" she whispered.

Gundrun heard the thin edge of fear cutting through the maiden's voice, and knew that she must be all the stronger. "Go to Costbera's house and have her bring my son to me."

"Yes, my frowe, but Costbera will be at her evening rite with the Christians now."

"Of course . . . where is my son, then?"

"I . . . d-don't know, Frowe," Harirad stuttered, tugging anxiously at one of her thin braids. "She may have left the children at home with the thrall-maid, or some such. I really don't know! Frowe, don't hold so tight, you're hurting me."

Seeing that her fingers were sunk deep into the maid's plump shoulders, Gundrun loosened her grip. "Go and find him, then!"

Harirad scuttled out of the hall the moment Gundrun let go of her. Gundrun looked around to see the other women staring at her. "Get back to work," she said, trying to keep her voice even. "You, Frederid, go into the kitchen and see how long it will be before that roast is done, and be sure there's enough bread baked. The hunters should be back shortly, but whatever game they've caught today there won't be time to cook it before they need feeding. Anyway, we'll need most of what they've hunted today for tomorrow's feasting."

Gundrun sat herself firmly in her chair again, clenching her jaw as tightly as she could to keep from screaming or moaning as she watched the blushing gold of the sky darken to crimson beneath deep blue, then to black.

When she could endure the waiting no longer, she stood up again. "I am going to my chamber," she announced to the women. "Someone come to tell me when the hunters get back; or if Harirad returns with my son first, send them to me." She paused a moment, then pointed to the largest of the maidens, a tall, broad-shouldered carl's daughter named Hadeburg. "You stand guard outside Brunichild's door. Don't let her out until everyone is back, and don't listen if she speaks to you."

"I'm not afraid of magic, Frowe," Hadeburg said, touching the amulet at her throat—a fish made of copper wrought with runes that Gundrun could recognize as Greek, though she could not read them. "I'll be glad to."

"Good."

Shivering, Gundrun hurried to her chamber and lay down on the bed, wrapping herself in the feather-stuffed blanket. Perhaps I am with child again, she thought; this cold is like that which came over me when I was carrying before. She remembered how Sigifrith had laughed lovingly at the unreasoning fears or angers that had swept over her like sudden whirlwinds as she grew heavier with each of the babes growing in her womb, his big hands stroking her hair and soothing her into contentment again, and she curled about herself with her hands laid on her middle as if to protect a new-seeded child within.

Had she not herself seen Sigifrith stand up unhurt from blows or falls that would have killed another man? Didn't his thanes use sharp weapons when sparring with him, because no edge could scathe his hide? Gundrun knew there was no need for her to fear for Sigifrith's sake; she knew, but she could not stop her trembling.

Perhaps I am fevered, she thought, turning restlessly over on to her other side and curling up again. She laid one palm against her brow. Cool as her skin was, it was damp with a cold sweat like the dew whitening the side of a glass pitcher filled with icy water. I need to rest; it would be better if I went to sleep so that I can be well for the feast tomorrow. Yes, I must sleep; if I should be carrying a child, it will draw my might from me till it is born, as Sigimund and Swanhild did.

Gundrun breathed deeply, forcing her shuddering breaths into a regular pattern. Though she tried to loosen her limbs, the trembling in her muscles rose until her whole body tightened convulsively on itself. She seemed to be awake for a long time, then fell into a doze from which her twistings and struggles against her bedclothes and the choking air of her room could not more than half-awaken her from a dream of swords and twisted black shapes like dead trees fighting by torchlight, the hemp-scarred voices of hanged men shouting roughly,

"Hai! Torches here! Wake up, Gundrun! Wake up!"

Something cold and heavy fell across Gundrun's back, jolting her upright to scream at the looming shadows that wavered and flickered in the torchlight around her. A corpse's ash-pale face hung above her, his single eye mirroring the flames of his torch as he raised a mailed arm to point at her. Though he came no closer than the bed's edge it seemed that she could feel the ice of his touch already; she shrank back from him with a gasp of horror, then let out another cry as her hand fell on a stiff cold arm.

Behind the mirk-ghost at the foot of her bed, a shadow-hand went to a shadowed mouth; she heard Gundahari's voice clearly whispering, "No . . . no, don't."

The torch lifted higher, its ruddy light spilling over the bedclothes, and Gundrun could no longer keep herself from looking down.

Sigifrith lay beside her, his lips half-parted and his glazed eyes wide open, as if he were calling silently to someone. She could see the little dark-stained rent in the front of his tunic; she did not need to turn him over to know that there must be a much greater wound in his back. Her scream rose higher and higher, ringing from the stones until its echoes through the passages of the hall broke upward into the screaming sound of a woman's wod-wild laughter.

Brunichild's wordless howl of triumph still bitter in her ears, Gundrun fell over her husband's dead body, kissing his cold mouth as if she could warm him back to life. Then she felt the faint movement of his arms trying to draw up toward her; she caught her breath in hope, raising her head to look at him as she held more tightly to him. But Sigifrith's eyes were glazed and unmoving; her heart choking, Gundrun knew that it was the stiffening of a corpse that she had felt. Raising herself to her knees, she drew her dagger and would have flung herself at her attackers if the icy glow of Hagan's eye meeting hers had not stolen the strength from her heart.

"Which of you has done this?" Gundrun demanded of her brothers. The tears were bound in her eyes, pulsing hot within her skull; for all her grief, she could not weep.

She saw the gleam of Hagan's teeth; a fierceness that she had never heard before lit his harsh voice as he replied, "Sigifrith was slain by a wild boar, by the banks of the Rhine."

"You, and none other, are that boar, Hagan!" Gundrun cried. "Why have you given me this sorrow? The ravens should feast on your heart in a stranger's land where you know no man."

"It shall only be more sorrows for you, when the ravens feast on my heart," Hagan said. "If not for your unbridled tongue, I should not have had to do this deed. Now get up and find Sigifrith's best tunic and such adornments as you wish to send with him, for I am taking him to the great hall where his body must be made ready for the funeral pyre." He grasped Sigifrith's feet and dragged the huge corpse toward himself, crouching down and heaving Sigifrith to his shoulders with a soft grunt. No one moved to stop him as he bore his burden out into the passageway.

Only when Hagan was out of sight did Gundahari begin to speak. "Gundrun . . ."

"Don't talk to me, you traitor! You and Hagan are the most shameful of men, for you murdered Sigifrith who was my husband and your blood-brother. Henceforth you yourself will have to ride first in the army, and when you come to battle you will find that Sigifrith is not at your other hand. Then you shall see that Sigifrith was your luck and strength, and you shall deserve whatever befalls you without him."

Though Gundrun had not spilled more than a few drops of the vast hot tide of fury flooding within her, she closed her mouth when she heard the sound of a door banging open. Hadeburg's voice shouted, "Stay in there! Frowe Gundrun told me . . ." and then she heard the thud of a body striking the stone wall.

Thinking of Sigimund, Gundrun was out of the bed in a second, dodging around Hagan and out into the passage where Hadeburg lay slumped beside Brunichild's open door. She lifted her skirts and ran for the feasting hall as fast as she could, with Gundahari and his thanes pressing closely behind her.

Hagan was straightening up beside the high table on which Sigifrith lay. Brunichild, wearing only a white shift, stood beside him; though her lips trembled in a laugh of triumph, her face was as death-pale as his.

At that moment, the outer door opened and Costbera stepped in, holding Sigimund by one hand and Nibel by the other. "I'm sorry I'm so late," she began. "The boys ran off and—" She stopped as if her sight had suddenly cleared through the firelit gloom of the hall, dragging the two children closer to her body as her eyes widened to take in the scene before her.

Before anyone could say or do anything, Brunichild reached across Sigifrith's waist and snatched Gram out of the sheath, flashing across the hall toward Costbera. Hagan's wife tried to back away, but Brunichild already had her by the wrist, twisting with one hand as she stabbed with the other. The wyrm mottlings on Gram's blade glimmered bright red in the firelight as the steel went in; when Brunichild pulled the sword out again, it was dark with Sigimund's blood.

Brunichild caught the boy's body in her shield arm as he fell, lifting him off his failing legs into the air. Gundrun began to rush forward; Gundahari grabbed her dagger arm, swinging her back. In the next heartbeat, Gundrun realized that her brother had almost certainly saved her life, for Brunichild still held Gram in her right hand, the blade's bloody point toward the Gebicungs.

Brunichild carried Sigimund's body to the high table, laying him down beside his father. "Now the geld is almost paid," she cried. "For when Sigifrith denied me, he swore his death by his kinsman's spear and swore the line of the Walsings to a woeful end. Now I, too, shall fare to my kinsmen in Walhall; and so shall the wyrd of Wodan's line all be turned." She raised Gram again, bringing the sword's bloody point to touch the white linen between and just beneath her breasts.

Gundahari ran toward her as though he would grab her arms from behind, but Hagan stepped between them, facing his brother. Gundrun saw Gundahari's hands drop as his shoulders slumped; saw the shudder running down his back and knew that he, like she, could not bear to come any closer to their mother's last son.

"Let no one hinder her in dying," Hagan ordered. "She has been of no good to us or to anyone since she came here. Let her fare to Hella; may she never be born into the ring of the Middle-Garth again!"

A binding pain choked Gundrun's throat so that she could neither laugh nor weep at this; but she watched silently as the dawn-bright tears spilled from Brunichild's eyes, the sunrise fire glowing between her fingers from the ice-stone in Gram's hilt as Sigifrith's first beloved drove the Walsings' sword deep into her body. Brunichild's mouth opened in surprise, as if she had not thought of how it would hurt; she coughed, leaning against the table where

Sigimund and Sigifrith lay, and a drop of blood dribbled darkly on to her chin.

"Now let my gold and riches be given to those who want them, and to the serving maids and men of my household," she ordered in a harsh whisper, speaking as swiftly as she could. "Take the gold, whoever will, and enjoy it."

Her hands fell limp from the hilt of the sword; slowly she half-raised her right arm again, pointing at Gundrun before it dropped back. "You shall soon be reconciled with your brothers by Grimhild's craft. Your daughter Swanhild shall be the fairest of women, but you need not rejoice. After the death of your brothers, you shall be married to King Jonakr and Swanhild shall be married to the Gothic King Ermanarik. Through Sibecha's plotting, Ermanarik shall have her crushed to death by wild horses; though your sons by Jonakr avenge her, they shall be slain in the doing. And then all your line shall have fared away, and Gundrun's sorrows shall be greater."

Brunichild closed her eyes, her head drooping toward her shoulder for a moment before she opened her eyes again to stare at Gundahari. "Though burning is not the way of the Burgundians, you must have a great funeral pyre built on the flat ground for all of us—Sigimund, Sigifrith and myself. Let there be a covering as red as men's blood over us and burn me at one side of this king with my men at the other side—two at his head, two at his feet and two hawks. Then is it equally dealt. Lay there between us this drawn sword as before, when we got in one bed and were named as betrothed. And the door will not fall on his heels if I follow him, nor will our burning be little if the five bondswomen and eight thralls whom my father gave me follow Sigifrith and his son. And you must slay Grani there also, that Sigifrith may ride his horse to his drighten's hall."

Brunichild's head rolled to her shoulder; her knees gave way beneath her and she slumped down to sit on the floor, held up only by the table leg against her back. "I would say more if I were not wounded, but now the wound is frothing, the gash opening and I have told the truth."

When she next opened her mouth, only a bubble of blood came out. Brunichild's lips curved slightly; then she shut her eyes again. Slowly her body slid down, toppling toward the side as it fell. Her flesh muffled the clang of Gram's hilt striking the flagstones.

Hagan stepped aside, letting Gundahari go to Brunichild's side. The Burgundian king lifted his wife's body up, careful of the keen blade sticking out of her back. He turned to lay her upon the high table beside Sigifrith and Sigimund.

"No," Gundrun said. Her throat was very dry; she coughed, trying to gather enough spit to swallow. "Not yet. Sigifrith was my husband and Sigimund my son. I shall lay them out, and I shall do it without her there. Burn them together, if you must, but leave me this night."

Without speaking, Gundahari bore Brunichild from the hall. Gundrun felt a shiver of ice through her veins as Hagan turned his gaze on her. He took a step forward; she stepped back, holding out her dagger in a shaking hand. "Get back. Get out of here. Don't come near me."

Hagan looked down at her knife, and Gundrun realized how fragile a warding the three inches of steel blade must seem to him. He said only, "So," and walked down the hall to where Costbera and Nibel still stood by the door.

As Hagan came closer to his wife, she shrank away, and Gundrun saw her eyes widen with terror, stark black against white in the shadows.

"My wife," he said.

Her lips pressed together, Costbera shook her head, dragging her son back with her. "Please," she whispered. "Please don't touch me. I can't . . . please. Don't come any nearer."

Hagan tilted his head, looking down at Nibel. In a single swift wriggle, the boy twisted from his mother's tight clutch and ran over to his father, clinging tightly to his legs.

"I shall take him home. You stay here with Gundrun."

"Yes."

Hagan and his son left through the outer door. It closed behind them with the solid sound of loose strands cut and knotted. Gundrun saw some of the color returning to Costbera's face, felt her own breath flowing more easily as she went to the table where her husband and son lay dead together. Sigimund's mouth was open as though he were snoring in his sleep, his arms and legs splayed out; the front of his tunic was a single dark stain. His small muscular limbs were still warm under Gundrun's hands when she brought them together, but she could feel the heat fading into the cold air of the hall. She began to shiver herself, but she could not weep, though the eyes of Sigimund and Sigifrith were as lightless as night clouds after a flash of lightning. Dead, Sigifrith seemed like a great carving of stone: too large and perfectly shaped to have been human, colder and heavier than a man could become. Only the look of longing on his face seemed, as she stared at him, to change: a seeking at once terrible and painfully joyful, trembling dawnlit on the edge of fulfilment like sunrise treading over the marches of night.

They are dead, she thought; I must weep. But her tears were locked in her throat, hot and painful. Though her breath came in shuddering sobs, she could not bring her grief forth, not with her son's body lying small and still beneath her hands, gone where she could not follow. She clasped Sigimund about the waist, lifting him to hold him again. When she had held him like that before, he had grasped her around the back of the neck and heaved himself up to sit on her shoulders, his own strength lifting his weight easily—and he had laughed in delight to be so high, though he had loved even better to be swung up by Sigifrith and sit on Grani's back. Gundrun bit her lip as hard as she could, letting the blood weep in her mouth; Sigimund's arms hung limp, head rolling to the side and mouth hanging open, and the cooling blood seeped faster from her son's chest as she tightened her grip on him.

The women were gathering around, coming from the corridor or out of the shadows where they had hidden. Costbera laid a soft hand on her arm.

"Why don't you weep, Gundrun?" she asked. "I will not think it is from weakness."

Gundrun's throat knotted tighter as she shook her head, unable to speak.

"There was nothing I could do!" Costbera cried. "You saw, I tried . . ."

Gundrun nodded. She forced herself to swallow, breathing raggedly several times before she could reply, "I know. I saw."

"You must weep, Gundrun. If you don't loose your grief, it will choke your heart till it stops."

"Don't you think I want to?" she asked in a furious croak. "Sigifrith was as much better than other men as gold is better than iron, standing above them like a spear leek above the other grasses or a stag above other beasts. Now here are my husband and my son both dead: who has more cause to weep than I?"

"It is hardly easier for me, though Hagan lives," Costbera answered. "There was little joy in our wedding for me. Now I do not know what he has become, only that I am afraid of him; he seems more like a draug or other ill wight than a man. I do not know whether the Church thinks our wedding is valid or not, since he could not set foot within hallowed walls; but if I were to leave him and seek another, my priest would name me a whore and I would have no other place in the world."

"Would you wish him dead, then?"

Costbera looked down at the floor where Brunichild's blood stained the stones black. "I don't know," she admitted, very softly. "He is the father of my children . . . and I think he has been as kind to me as he can."

"There was nothing in my marriage with Sigifrith that I might have wished otherwise, but now he is dead and my son with him. If you cannot be glad in your husband, at least you have not lost as much as I have."

Gundrun brushed a loose strand of damp hair from Sigifrith's cold forehead. Gently she tugged his eyelids down, but the moment she took her hands away his eyes opened again.

"Gundrun," another woman murmured. Gundrun did not look up, but she recognized the deep voice of Gebiflag, her father's sister. "You must weep, otherwise you will die of your sorrow. Who should know better than I? I have buried five highborn husbands, three of my daughters, three of my sisters and my only brother; yet I live on."

Gundrun did not speak.

"Gundrun," said Herborg, one of her mother's serving women who had come from the Danes' land, "I have suffered yet sadder sorrows. My seven sons and my husband fell in battle in the southern lands, fighting beside your brothers. Before that, I lost my father and mother and my four brothers on the sea, when the ship on which we were faring foundered around the Orkneys. I had to bury all their bodies; I laid them out alone, and straightened their limbs. In that same half-year I was taken a captive and kept in bondage. I had to trim the hair and tie the shoes of an atheling's frowe every morning; she scolded me and beat me to my work. I never had a more friendly master than he, but never a harsher housewife to serve than she, and the best luck that befell me was when Thonara bought me free and sent me south to your mother. I wept every night of that half-year; if I had not, I should have died of my sorrows."

Then another of the women, Goldrand, spoke. "Although you are old and wise, foster-mother, you do not know how to comfort a mourner." The other women moved aside as Goldrand heaved her bulk through them to Gundrun's side. She raised a heavy arm and set her hand on Gundrun's shoulder. "Now you should lay your lips upon Sigifrith's and embrace him as you did when he was whole, for you shall never see him again when he is burnt."

Gundrun stooped; and the moment Sigifrith's cold mouth touched hers, her cheeks grew hot and a rain of tears flooded from her eyes. Sobbing, she threw herself on to the table, embracing Sigifrith and Sigimund together as she had when they lived.

"I never knew greater love beneath heaven than was given to you," Goldrand went on softly. "You were never at ease, without or within, except when you were by Sigifrith's side. You must weep all you can; but when you are done, you may comfort yourself by knowing that no woman was more joyful than you while you and Sigifrith were wed."

"I was honored higher by the king's heroes than any one of Wodan's maidens," Gundrun said through her tears. "Now that Sigifrith is dead, I am as little as the leaves hanging on dry twigs, and it is my brothers' fault that I bear this grief." Then her tears fell too thick and fast for her to speak any more; she stood shaking with sobs, standing as bent as an old woman over her husband and her son till she could weep no more.

"Bring me water and cloths so that I may clean them, and bring me the feast clothes which I laid out, which they were to have worn tomorrow," Gundrun commanded. "I, and I alone, shall ready them for their bier."

But in the end Sigifrith's strength was still too much for her; she could not move his limbs alone, it took all of the women together to get his blood-stiff tunic off him and dress him in the gold-embroidered scarlet that Gundrun had worked for him. Goldrand brought her four ancient coins of pure Roman gold, two larger and two smaller. Setting the coins on Sigimund's eyes seemed very like tucking her son's blanket up to send him to sleep, but though she could hardly bear to look into Sigifrith's darkened eyes, it was even harder for her to close them for the last time.

"You shall not sleep here," Goldrand said firmly, when Gundrun closed her own eyes and would have sagged down against the table's leg. "If you do, the dead shall drag you down into death with them. You have done what you must, and you should do no more."

Gundrun was shivering too hard with cold to protest when the big woman took her by the arm, leading her off. Only when they passed by the door of the chamber she had shared with Sigifrith did she ask, "Where are we going?"

"You shall sleep with myself and the other women tonight. It would not be good for you to be alone. And I shall mix some poppy juice in wine for you, because you must sleep."

Too worn out to complain, Gundrun followed Goldrand meekly to the room where the serving women slept. She sat on the edge of the bed where the woman put her, waiting till Goldrand returned with the dark draught.

Paying no heed to the taste, Gundrun gulped the wine then lay down in the bed and wrapped herself in the feather quilt. Slowly her shivering began to ease into drowsy warmth, letting her float easily away from her sorrows.

Hagan had searched through the woods for Grani all night, but did not find the wind-gray horse till he came back to his brother's hall at dawn and saw the steed's great shape gleaming silver through the morning light. Grani stood by the door of the hall. His head drooped downward, but his eyes were open as though he kept watch for his dead master.

"Aside, Grani," Hagan ordered. "It will not be long now; but men must use this door first."

The Roman tiles cracked beneath the stallion's hooves as he stepped aside to let Hagan in.

Hagan walked swiftly to Gundahari's room, careful not to tread too close to the serving maids who shrank away from him and signed Donar's Hammer or Christ's cross behind his back. His byrnie muffled by his tunic, he made no sound as he opened the door and stepped across the threshold.

Gundahari lay on the floor, wrapped in his cloak and snoring softly. Hagan knew his sleep was not feigned. He had heard his brother's low snuffle most of his life; he recognized it so clearly that he could find his way to Gundahari through an army of sleepers by the sound alone.

The king had laid Brunichild's corpse on his own bed. If he had set her out peacefully, with her hands crossed over the hilt of Sigifrith's sword where it stuck out of her breast, she had not stayed so. The stiffening of death had drawn her white arms upward as if she were reaching out for someone; two Roman coins gleamed against the splay of pale hair behind her head. Her eyes were wide open as if she had been suddenly awakened, and her body and legs were twisted as though she were struggling to rise against the blade that pinned her to the bed.

It seemed to Hagan as though some warmth lingered in her limbs when he went to force them straight again; that, though unmoving, Brunichild fought against him with all the strength she had had in life. When he took her hands to pull her arms down, they were not so cold as his.

"It is well that you are to be burnt, walkurja," he whispered to her. "I think you would not rest easily in the howe. If you must ride forth to the slaughter hereafter, it shall be only as a ghost; nor, for myself, do I care whether Ygg leads you in the Hunt from Walhall or from Hella's lands."

Then Hagan took the aurochs horn of the Burgundians that was mounted above Gundahari's door and left again, going out to stand in the middle of the yard and blowing three long blasts to summon the men and women of the hall.

They gathered fearfully, standing close together in little clumps like bunches of dead leaves clotting in the river. The men and maids looked sideways at him and whispered to one another, shivering in the sea-cold morning wind, but they fell silent as he began to speak.

"Gather dry wood, fit for burning, in as great a pile as you can make," he ordered. "You men who are strongest, bear out the table where the bodies of Sigifrith and Sigimund lie and set it here. Let the wood be heaped around it. You women of Brunichild's household bring out the wealth and goods that were hers; but let whoever wishes take from it what they will, as was her bidding. What has become of Gundrun?"

"Fro Hagan, she is sleeping," Goldrand answered nervously, flinching away even as she spoke. "I gave her poppy . . ."

"You did well. Let her sleep till this is over, or if she should wake of herself give her another draught. I shall see to Sigifrith's treasures myself, that he may fare to his drighten's hall as befits him."

They stood watching him. "What are you waiting for? Go on," he commanded, and they scattered as though a whirlwind had come down in their midst.

"Come with me," Hagan said softly to Grani, who still stood before the door. "I shall take you to the stables and saddle and bridle you in your best, with trappings of gold as is fitting for the steed of Sigifrith Fadhmir's-Bane. Then you shall eat and drink as well as you can, for you have a long faring before you and there are three whom you must bear on your back."

When Hagan had saddled Grani and left the horse standing by the bier, he went to see about gathering Sigifrith's belongings from the room that he had shared with Gundrun. They had brought a great many treasures with them, clearly meant as gifts to be given at Winternights. Hagan recognized the Hunnish style of goldsmithing, as well as the work of Romans and of the tribes against whose borders Attila constantly pressed—a mixture he remembered well from his years of fostering with Thioderik in Attila's warband. Then there had been much treasure to be won fighting beside the Huns; he had not doubted that Sigifrith would win a like amount from them. It would go hard with Hrodgar and the Alamanns east of the Rhine now that Sigifrith was no longer there to ward them with his strength and fame.

The Helm of Awe was placed inside one of the bags; now that Sigifrith was dead, Hagan did not choose to consider why he might have brought it. He held the golden links, the might in it tingling up his arms. Desire to put the Helm on prickled itchily in the middle of his forehead. Hagan stared at the eight-rayed sign graven upon the golden plate, thinking that he alone kept the keys to the hidden chamber: one lift of his hand, and helm and hoard could both be his. He could feel the hidden sparks stirring in the cold rivers of his blood, answering the fire of the gold.

"This must go with Sigifrith," he said aloud to himself. "Fadhmir's Bane should not fare without one prize of his deed." He opened his hand; the Helm of Awe tore away from it in a painful flare of unseen blue sparks to jingle on the bedcovers.

Under the bed, Hagan found the byrnie that he had lent to Sigifrith, broken all down the sides. He stretched it out on the bed, loading the wrought gold and silver on to the steel weave and bringing the edges up to make a weighty bag that he bore out into the yard. The women were creeping out with Brunichild's treasures, holding the precious metals and fine cloths with the tips of their fingers as though they carried the burning stubs of candles. They skirted carefully around Grani, nervously putting their burdens by the legs of the table on the other side and scurrying away.

Hagan laid the broken byrnie out over Sigifrith. Smoothing the dead man's hair back, he set the Helm of Awe upon Sigifrith's head, then arranged the rest of the treasure around the two corpses, moving them carefully to leave room for Brunichild. There; it was done, and only one thing remained before the pyre could be built.

Gundahari was still sleeping, though he had turned over and was not snoring any more. Hagan lifted Brunichild from the bed, careful of Gram's keen blade. He knew well that it was the way of the ill dead to grow heavy, bound to Hella's realm so that no man could lift them till they rose to walk again; but Brunichild was as light in his arms as swandown on the wind. He bore her over the threshold without a stumble, laying her down on her side beside Sigifrith. He placed one hand on her shoulder and wrapped the other around Gram's hilt, then drew the sword out in a single swift movement. No blood followed, nor did Brunichild's body move.

Hagan hefted Gram in his hand, its keenness rippling through him as he turned it to see the sunlight glimmering from the wrought wyrms of light and dark steel writhing down the sword's blade. "Come, Grani." He beckoned to the horse with his other hand, but Grani did not move. "Will you wait, then?"

Still holding Sigifrith's sword, he bent to pick up Brunichild's adornments and arrange them about her one-handed. The men were bearing in the loads of wood and when Hagan had finished his task he stood back so that they might arrange the pyre. It was done clumsily, for the Burgundians did not burn their dead, but when it was finished Hagan judged that it would burn hot and long enough to eat all the bodies to ashes.

"Bring out the five bondswomen and eight thralls who were sent with Brunichild," he commanded. The two sisters Childeburg and Ragnachild stepped forward nervously, glancing at one another. Hagan could see from their faces that they knew what was to come; he thought that he might speak words of comfort to them, but recognized that his care would only frighten them more. Erminrad and Liutgard were quickly seized as they made for the door of the hall, but in the end Hagan had to send Iring to find the Christian girl Matasuntha and drag her out by force with his hand over her mouth to stop her screaming. The thrall-men were brought as well, standing stolidly in a row before the bier; one or two of them stretched out their shoulders as they looked at it, and Hagan knew they thought that they would have to carry it somewhere. He signaled to the warriors, who closed in a ring. One of the thralls, a tall, balding man with keener sight than the rest, turned and tried to run; but before he had taken two steps Grani reared and came down on his shoulder with a hoof, knocking him to the ground. The thrall screamed in pain when Folkhari reached down to help him up, so they let him lie there.

"You shall go as you came, faring back with your frowe to her kinsmen who have gone before her. Be honored; you could not hope for a greater atheling-bier."

Hagan slew the fallen thrall first, picking up his body and tossing it onto the heap of branches around the funeral table. He walked to the other seven one by one; as his gaze met each of theirs they stood quite still before him, bound by fetters he could not name. Gram keened in his hand, its crystal icy against his palm beneath the runnels and spurts of hot blood as he plunged the blade neatly through the heart of each man, then of Childeburg and Ragnachild. He did not dare to stab the other women, for one of his warriors stood behind to hold each; but only the barest touch of Gram's tip opened their throats. Erminrad's windpipe bubbled as if she were trying to speak before she slumped against Dancwart. Matasuntha, held tightly and silenced by Iring's palm, rolled her light blue eyes up and down, then from side to side, crossing herself the only way she could; but Liutgard fainted before Sigifrith's sword ever touched her and died sleeping.

As Hagan had thought they would, Matasuntha's screams had awakened Gundahari. Pale and speechless, he came to stand with the others, watching as Hagan built the bier up. The bodies were arranged as Brunichild had bidden, at the heads and feet of the dead. Then two hawks were fetched from the mews. Hagan bound them, laying them fettered and living by Sigifrith and Brunichild. Three men had to hold each of the Irish hounds as the great dogs raged and struggled, howling mournfully at Hagan's approach. His hand was steady as Gram's tongue bit through their throats, then he lifted their warm bodies to lie over the thralls at Sigifrith's feet and head.

Grani raised his head at last, the high whinny of his neighing clanging oddly through Hagan's ears, as though a ghost-steed's voice sounded behind it. "Are you ready, then?" he asked softly.

Sigifrith's horse lifted his hooves, stepping carefully over the branches to stand beside the funeral bier. Hagan set Gram's point against the great artery that pulsed slowly against the stallion's wind-gray coat. "Now."

Grani leaned forward into the sword, drawing the blade through his neck as he turned his head toward his master's corpse. The blood fountained out, spreading over the bodies of Sigifrith, Brunichild and Sigimund like a coverlet of red silk as the horse fell to his knees, leaning against the table; and Hagan deemed that Brunichild's last bidding was fulfilled. He went around the other side to lay Gram down between Sigifrith and Brunichild; it measured the length of Sigimund's small corpse.

"Now bring the fire," he said.

Gundahari turned and went into his hall without a word. When the king came out again, he held a torch that had burned down almost to its haft, sending up coils of black smoke. He did not look at Hagan, but walked to the edge of the pyre and thrust the flame into the reddened leaves and dry twigs.

The flames were very small and thin at first, little needles of light flickering up through the branches. Then, as they spread, they rose higher and higher, clutching on to the dry wood and gnawing at it with a greedy crackling. It was not long before the first smoke began to rise as the fire caught hair and clothes; the screaming of the bound hawks was lost in two brilliant stinking flares of burnt feathers. Hagan knew the scent of men's flesh burning well enough, the scorch and hiss of blood in the fire over the muffled thumps of meat bursting. His eye saw through the brightness of the rising flames as he stood and watched: saw Brunichild's white skin blackening and cracking under the fire that burned around her, its ring burning from her own flesh now; saw Sigifrith, no longer warded by the spell of the dragon's blood, swelling beneath the red-hot rings of the broken byrnie as with the grief that had burst it, a river of fire running up his long hair.

The wind was rising, sweeping palm-sized flakes of black ash before it with the dead leaves that flared as the reaching flames caught them. Hagan saw the fire eating Sigifrith and Brunichild down to the bone, hiding the child who also lay there with a coverlet of flame. The ice stone in Gram's hilt glowed hotter and hotter, burning from red to golden to white till he could no longer look at it. Then the crystal burst with a searing crack as the steel around it began to melt, melting like the flesh that flowed about it and the gold that flowed into its glowing river. Hagan did not doubt what he saw as the oaken table top came crashing down, as the wind whipped the fire up; but the molten metal, the stream of gold and iron and flesh and bone, burned of itself, the flames feeding from the metal and rising higher from the very earth before all was eaten and the fire began to sink down.

Gundahari's voice was so hoarse that he had to speak twice before Hagan could understand him. "Where is Gundrun?"

"She sleeps. Goldrand gave her poppy."

"You should not have done this without her."

"There were enough dead on the pyre already. Now it is done, she is likelier to live."

"I did not see Fadhmir's gold there."

"No. It lies where it lay. There were riches enough to honor the dead without it."

"Still, I . . ."

Gundahari did not finish his thought, if thought he had had, but walked away. The other men and women were also beginning to drift off. Hagan caught Iring's eye, then Folkhari's, but they ducked their heads beneath his gaze, each muttering about something he would have to do at once. So Hagan stood and watched alone till the last flames had died down, leaving only a huge black stain upon the cracked flagstones.

The heat burned his feet even through the thick soles of his boots as he walked over the place where the fire had burned. Half from curiosity, Hagan scuffled through the ash with one toe. The glazing of the Roman tiles had melted into a brownish smear shot through with swirling colors; but there was no trace of the treasure that had been burned there, nor of anything else.

"So it is," he murmured. He would go into the woods by himself, he thought, and hunt in his own way as he often did. That night was the feast beginning Winternights: though he knew there would be no feasting in the great hall, while he lived his own household would keep—no matter what came to pass—to the honoring of his kinsmen who had fared before him; and now that Ragin and Sigifrith were dead, there were few indeed left living.

Gundrun awoke to darkness lit only by moonlight through the window. The feast, the feast! she thought; I shall be late! She had already sprung out of bed when she remembered, her crushing grief crumpling her back down as she pressed her fists into her thighs.

"Sigifrith," she mourned softly. "Sigimund."

There was no one in the feasting hall, and the high table was gone. Gundrun hastened outside into the yard, but saw nothing there. Frantically she ran to the room she had shared with Sigifrith and belted his knife around her waist, then hurried to Gundahari's chambers, knocking on the door.

"What do you want?" his dull voice called.

"Where are they? What have you done with them?"

"We've burned them. It's done, Gundrun."

Gundrun dragged the door open, stamping in with her hand on the hilt of Sigifrith's big dagger. It seemed to her that it would be no ill thing to sheathe the weapon her husband had made in Gundahari's heart; the thought was no joy, but a flash of searing fire through the gray cold shaking her limbs. "Why did you do it?" she rasped at him. "Why didn't you wake me?"

"It was Hagan's idea. He was afraid . . . well, he was afraid you'd want to join Sigifrith and Sigimund on the pyre."

"And do you think I'm better off now?" Gundrun demanded of him. "Do you think I shouldn't have? What's going to happen to me?"

"Gundrun, I have lost my beloved and a child as well . . . a child not even born." Gundahari's voice caught in his throat. He coughed painfully twice before he went on. "I shall marry again, most likely before next Winternights. You shall stay here for another year or so, till you are ready to wed again, and then you shall have a husband and more children."

"Do you think I could ever love another man after Sigifrith? Who could match him? Not you," she added, and had the bitter satisfaction of hearing her brother's breath catch as if she had indeed stabbed him.

"He is dead, and many other men are alive. And you shall stay here till you are healed and ready to wed again."

"I know what kind of healing Grimhild would give me. And I will not stay here with you. You are an oathbreaker without any thought of troth, or else a weakling who moved only to your wife's will, and I do not know which I think is worse. And you let my son be killed—you let that woman run free in our hall, though you knew she was as mad as a frothing wolf. I think there is no geld that can be paid for Sigifrith's death, except the red gold of your blood and Hagan's spilled on the earth." Gundrun was crouching, balancing lightly on the balls of her feet as she had learned to do when she was young, sparring against Hagan and Gundahari with a wooden sword in her hand.

Gundahari lifted his right hand toward her, drawing in a deep, sobbing breath. "Listen to me, Gundrun. It was not by my will Sigifrith died. I told Hagan that our day's hunting was at an end; he must have understood what I meant, but he had made his choice for himself."

"And where is Hagan now?" she asked bitterly. "Sigifrith will not speak to him from the river, nor will his son find Sigimund's ghost to play with when he creeps out into the night. It seems to me that he raised his spear for your sake, and that you are not worth it."

"And was your pride worth wrecking the realm of the Burgundians?" Gundahari cried out. "It was you, not I, who told Brunichild our secret; had you held your tongue, they would be alive today!"

Gundrun drew Sigifrith's dagger and lunged in a single movement, Gundahari's shocked face blurring before her. She shouted fiercely as she felt the point strike him, but the knife skidded on a rib, glancing away with a trail of blood spraying behind it. Before she could stab him again, Gundahari had caught her wrists in his hands, tightening his grip on her right arm and twisting until the dagger dropped from her numb fingers.

For a long time the two of them stared at each other. Gundrun could see the wound she had dealt her brother through the rent in his bloodied tunic; the scratch was long, but not deep.

"Must I have fetters put on you, or set Hagan to guard you?" Gundahari asked.

"If he comes into my sight, be sure I shall serve him the same way— though with better aim, I hope!" Yet even as she spoke, Gundrun remembered how the corpse-fire in Hagan's eye had stilled her heart and frozen her limbs, and could not keep from shivering. But no garth of the living will give him greetings henceforth; though he was little liked before, now he shall not be welcome even in this hall! she thought. Not till his clan calls his soul back in, and that I shall never do.

Gundahari let go of her, bending down to pick up the dagger and slide it back into the sheath at her side. Gundrun drew it again, stepping back, but she could see that her brother was ready for her, and she would have small chance of getting through his guard again. The thought of his hands grasping her wrists made her sick with anger.

"You shall do Hagan no harm," Gundahari told her calmly. "If you wish, I shall tell him to stay out of your sight as long as the two of you live.

Indeed, I shall find you a husband and a home far from here so you may forget your sorrows, though I must continue to sit at feasts in the hall where Brunichild died with our bairn in her womb."

"You shall find no husband nor home for me; if Wyrd will not let me take your life, there is nothing else I shall take from you."

"Gundrun," Gundahari called as she whirled and slammed the door behind her. "Gundrun . . . " But Gebica's daughter was already out in the hall, grasping a torch from one of the wall sconces and striding purposefully toward the chamber that she had shared with Sigifrith.

As she had expected, the treasures they had brought as gifts were gone—burned with Sigifrith and Sigimund, she hoped, though she was no longer sure of her brothers. But her jewelery was where she had left it. She swept the jingling gold and silver into a bag with her two plainest dresses, then pulled the gold pins from her hair and fluffed it free around her shoulders before getting into her traveling clothes and boots.

Gundrun did not know where she was going as she hurried out into the moonlit garden and through the rear gate into the forest, only that she must get away somehow before her brothers and Grimhild bound her into their plans again. Sobs shook her as she half-ran through the piles of dead leaves, wandering along the side of the moon-rippled river. When she passed into the shadow of the heap of holy stone, she could not go on any longer but sank to the ground weeping; it was too easy for her to remember Sigifrith standing above her in the lightning that had hallowed their wedding as Grimhild sprinkled them with the holy blood of the gods' gifts that had bound them for the rest of Sigifrith's life.

It was not long before she had no more tears left and had to rise and go on. Past the stones the path was overgrown with brambles; Gundrun had to kick her way through, gritting her teeth and lowering her head against the cold wind from the river.

Far away, she heard a wolf howling. Another answered nearer, then another. She did not bother to draw her blade. Her womb was starting to cramp with the pangs of emptiness; she would be weeping blood in another day, for she was carrying no child.

"If I could only die now," she whispered. To die; to be with Sigifrith in Walhall, or safe in Hella's quiet reaches; that seemed to her a better weird than wandering in the woods or turning back to her brothers. And Grimhild would be starting back from the Danes' land the next morning before the waters grew too rough for faring, and Gundrun had no wish to meet her mother again. But though she drew Sigifrith's knife out; though the Moon's light, broken by the shadows of tree branches, glittered from the edge her husband had forged in his youth, she could not bring it closer to her heart or throat, nor do more than dent the moonlight-whitened skin of her wrist with its sharp tip.

Gundrun put the blade back in her belt and kept going. In her despair, she took no care for the crunching of her boots through leaves and branches and did not worry about wild beasts or wild men coming to the sound. It might have been that her very noise frightened the wolves from her; though she heard them howling all about her, they did not come near.

She walked through the wood by the banks of the Rhine till Sunna had risen. Then, when she could walk no more, she curled into a hollow between the roots of a huge oak tree to sleep. It was a little past noon when she awoke again and, thirsty and hungry, went to the river to drink.

"Hai!" a man's voice shouted from a raft on the river. "You, woman! Are you seeking passage?"

Gundrun raised her head. The man's brown hair was mixed thickly with white. He was stooped with age and bending to his pole and oars, unarmed as far as she could see. I do not need to fear him, she thought. "Where to?" she asked.

"I'm going downriver to the Roman city Colonia. Do you know where that is?"

He sounded amused; Gundrun thought that he must take her for some bondswoman or poor carl's daughter.

"Will you go farther, if you're paid?"

"All the way to the mouth of the Rhine, if you've got the right payment." He gave her a brown-toothed grin, his eyes opening as he considered her. "You're too pretty to worry about Roman coin in hand, ay?"

Gundrun drew herself up to her full height, glaring at him as she took one of the gold hairpins out of her bag. "If you'll take me to the mouth of the Rhine, I'll give you this."

The man sucked his breath in an airy whistle. "Is that gold all through?"

"It certainly is."

"What are you doing running around in the woods with things like that?" He poled his raft in to shore, moving toward the edge. "Come aboard and let me have a look at it."

Standing her ground, Gundrun drew her knife. "My husband left me two things. This"—she held up the pin—"and this. If you'll take me north, I'll give you the one. If you give me any trouble on the way, I'll give you the other. Do you understand me?"

The ferryman gulped. "I understand you, Frowe. Why do you want to go that far? There's nothing but wild Frisians there, and the weather's getting too bad to sail on."

"I must go to the Danes' land, to the frowe Thonara daughter of King Hakon. Can you take me there?"

The ferryman bit his lip, frowning. "For a faring like that . . . Frowe, this is no seagoing boat. I might find a way to the Danes' land, I did it once before, but this is an ill time for it. I'd likely ask more gold than you'd be willing to give."

"How much?"

He stared at the gold pin she held. "That might weigh a full ounce; but once I got to the Danes' land, I'd have to keep myself through the winter and then wait for the first summer floods to sink before I came back up the Rhine. Frowe, I'd ask a mark and a half."

"For a mark and a half you could buy lands and cows and live well enough in the north the rest of your life," Gundrun answered sharply.

"You won't find passage cheaper anywhere, Frowe. There are few enough ferrymen on the Rhine, and none like to go much farther than from Worms at the one end to the Colonia at the other."

"I'll tell you what, ferryman. Take me to Thonara, and you can ask what you will of her for having brought her cousin's daughter safely to her. I've heard that Thonara is an open-handed frowe; it's likely you could get more from her than you could from me—even if you'd thought about robbing me in my sleep."

"If you think you'll be riding on my raft all the way north, you'd best not start insulting me. Give me that pin, and I'll wait to see what Thonara will give. But you must swear to make good as much of my mark and a half as you can if she proves to be less open-handed than you think."

"I swear it, by Frija and Holda," Gundrun answered, stepping onto the raft. It tilted beneath her weight so that she staggered, but the ferryman did not reach out to help her. Then she saw that she was still pointing her knife at him; and by the time she had sheathed her blade, she had regained her balance.

"Thank you, Frowe," the ferryman said as she gave him the pin. "I shan't fail you. My name's Einhard; what's yours?"

"Um . . . You should call me Wewurd." Woe-Wyrd, spoken with an Ala-mannic accent: Gundrun knew no name more fitting to herself.

"Were I an atheling, I would give my daughter a more joyful name," Einhard said, poling off from shore. He looked shrewdly at her from beneath beetling brows, turning away again when she met his glance. "But maybe I shouldn't ask any more questions of you."

"A wise choice," Gundrun said, settling herself to rest with her bag nestled against her leg.

7

ATTILA

Gundrun and Thonara sat outside the hall in the sunlight, working on the great tapestry they had been embroidering together for three and a half years. When the tapestry was unrolled, it stretched the full length of Half's feasting hall and was half again the height of a man. It showed many great deeds and mighty hunts, swords and byrnies and atheling-halls. On the tapestry were worked King Sigimund's ships as they sailed among the coast, with golden dragon prows and graven stems. They had also embroidered Sigar and Siggeir fighting on the island of Fyn; and the kings' blades were wrought in silver threads, but their byrnies were of gold and glittered finely in Sunna's light. Now Gundrun and her kinswoman were working with white threads, stitching carefully along the feathers of Danish swans such as the three who floated on the lake before them.

"You do not seem as unhappy as you did," Thonara said. "I think the Sun's light is good for you."

"The winters are so long and cold up here," Gundrun said, shivering in spite of the summery warmth. "By the time the Yule feasting is done, I always long to be somewhere else."

Thonara smiled, smoothing down her gray-salted coils of auburn braid. "And yet weren't you telling me that the snow on the edge of Mirkwood once came up to your waist at Ostara's feast? Surely you should have got used to the cold there."

Gundrun did not answer, looking at the white star glowing from the deep red stone of her ring. Her kinswoman patted her on the shoulder. "But there you were wed, and here you are still mourning. Be of better heart, darling. Remember the news of your daughter Swanhild; she lives and is growing into a beautiful and strong young maiden."

"But what will become of her when the Huns come through Mirkwood?"

"You need not fear that just yet. I have heard that Hrodgar swore his troth to Attila more than a year ago. Attila has contented himself with that for the moment, and has turned more of his might against the south."

"I am still uneasy about it."

"It will soon be time for her to be fostered elsewhere, anyway."

"But how may I have that done without betraying that I am here? You know that if my kin find out where I am, they will come and get me at once and force me to marry again—and I could not bear to live with another man after Sigifrith."

Thonara put down her wool and stuck her needle through the tapestry, turning to face Gundrun. Her lips tightened, scoring the lines around their corners deeper; the straight groove between her brows was as deep as a scar. "Gundrun, you cannot hide from your kin much longer. You are no longer a young maiden but a woman with duties, nor is it seemly for you to stay here as a spinster. If you wish, I will find you a fitting husband here in the Danes' land—there are several young atheling-men whose fathers have already broached the subject with me, and you may choose for yourself among those who are best of them."

Gundrun shook her head, not trusting her tongue to speak.

"Gundrun," Thonara murmured more gently, "you must choose soon, for it cannot be so long before Grimhild and your brothers know you are here. I have held your secret, as I swore I would, but nothing fares so swiftly as words on the wind, and there is nothing that can stay hidden from my cousin for long."

"I cannot," Gundrun said. "Am I so much trouble? I will work for my keep as a bondswoman. I'd rather that than go back to my kin or be married off."

"That is silliness, Gundrun." Thonara began to embroider again. "You know that I will keep you as long as there is no other place for you. Nor is it my wish to see you given in marriage as a pawn for your brothers' ambitions, but I see no way of keeping you from it save to marry you to another. Now Thonarbernu is a fine young man with a hall of his own, who has won himself honor and a good portion leading men on raids along the coast of Britain; if you wed him, you would be kept well all the days of your life. Or, if you would rather, there is Aiwimundur, who is not quite such a famed warrior but well known enough to be welcome in any battle-moot of kings. He is said to be the most handsome young atheling in the North, skilled at harping and skald-craft as well as at word-play, and your days with him would be a round of the finest delights. Those are the two whom I think would be the best match for you—but you can choose for yourself, you have seen them and the others in our hall often enough."

"If they are so fine, why should they wish to marry an old widow?"

"Gundrun, I think you do not know how beautiful you are. You do not look older than sixteen—indeed, you are far fairer than you were when I saw you ten years ago. Even in your sorrows, you shine more brightly than other women in their joys. Although you sit with your eyes cast down and have not marked our thanes and guests very well, I think there is not a man in our hall who has not wished to have you for his own—not even my own husband Half. If you are not wedded soon, there will be fighting over you."

"You are flattering me. That can't be true."

"Gundrun, you have told me how Sigifrith gave you meat from Fadhmir's heart to eat. Do you think you could have done that, and borne the children of Sigifrith's line unscathed, without taking some of that might into yourself? I am telling the truth when I say that there is no one living who might be like to you."

"Then if my like does not live, let me be left alone."

"Gundrun, you must marry."

The two women sat sewing for a while, listening to the buzzing of the bees on the greensward around them as the warmth and the sunlight slowly soothed them. Far off, by the sea-strand, Gundrun could hear the mewing of gulls; she closed her eyes for a moment, listening to their calls sharpen into words. "A ship! Three ships! Men in weeds of war!" "Is fighting to come? Will food lie fallen?" "A dame stands on deck! Be no battle here!" Then the gulls called again, "Wyrd is turning! We cannot unwind it!" "Let Gundrun go swiftly!" "Her kinsmen are come!"

Gundrun opened her eyes even as the deep warning cry of the bronze horn from the beach brought Thonara to her feet, looking anxiously about her.

"You need not fear, Aunt," Gundrun said sadly. "That is no warship, but Grimhild and my brothers."

She knotted her thread and cut it off with her eating dagger, putting the needle back into its case. Together the women rolled up the tapestry and called for the thralls to carry it inside.

Standing at the top of the dunes, Gundrun saw the golden boar banner of the Gebicungs gleaming from the flagship with the small dark figure of her mother below it. Her brothers and their men were fitted out as if for war, gold and steel gleaming from beneath short cloaks of sorrel-red fur. Waldemar, the thane who kept watch along the coast by day, blew another deep blast on the ancient bronze horn that coiled about his body, and Hagan's aurochs horn answered him from the ship.

"If you come in peace, be welcome!" Waldemar called, his voice thin through the echo of his horn.

"We come to claim our kinswoman Gundrun!" Hagan shouted back.

"You ask a great thing. It were better for us if you never landed here!"

"By the leave of your drighten Half, we shall land here and do what we have come for."

"If Half has given you leave, I cannot stop you. Land, and be as welcome as you may."

Some of the thanes, their byrnies crooked and swords girded askew, were already running down from the hall toward the shore. Most of them slowed as they saw the banner of the Gebicungs, but Gundrun heard them muttering angrily to one another. Some glared at the Burgundian ship; one or two glanced up at her, and she felt her cheeks redden beneath the warmth of their gazes. With as much dignity as she could, she turned her back toward her kinsmen who were tying up by the shore and walked to the hall where she shut herself in Thonara's chamber and sat on the bed, staring at the wall.

She could hear the tread of the men coming into the hall, her aunt's low voice clear above their deep mutterings as she said, "Take this drink of greeting, King Gundahari, and be welcome in our home."

Then Grimhild's words broke through Gundahari's answer like glass: "Where is my daughter? Half sent me word that she was with you."

"That was ill done," Thonara said calmly. "Cousin, your daughter is not ready to go home yet."

"We have come to be reconciled with her," Hagan said. Gundrun shuddered at the rough sound of his voice. She could see, as if she were there, the others drawing back from him, the movement hidden beneath light summer cloaks as men thrust thumb through fist to ward off his gaze. "Half has given us leave to do this."

"He did not ask nor tell me about it," Thonara said, and Gundrun could hear the hidden thunder in her aunt's words. "But Gundrun has gone to my chambers; if she will speak to you and go with you of her own will, then I shall not stand in her way."

Gundrun had only taken a few more breaths before her mother's rings rapped sharp and light against the door. "Gundrun, let me in."

Gundrun did not answer.

"Let me in now!" Grimhild commanded. Then Gundrun heard her whispering.

The lock clicked aside and the door swung open. Grimhild, gold gleaming from her black linen gown, strode in and stood looking down at her daughter. "This has gone on far too long, Gundrun. It is time for you to accept your brothers' gifts and to be reconciled with them."

"Why should I, when they killed my husband? I only wish that I might never see them again."

"Gundahari and Hagan are your own blood kin, whom you have loved best all your life. You should be together again, as you were before."

"And Sigifrith was their blood kin by troth, and they slew him by treachery!" Gundrun answered passionately. "Even if you have brought with you Fadhmir's treasure, which was Sigifrith's morning gift to me, and as much gold again to match it, none of it would be worth a drop of the blood my brothers spilled. How can you think that anyone could ever pay weregild to me for such a man, or for a love such as mine?"

"Let your brothers speak to you. Maybe the sight of them will soften your heart."

"I do not want to see them," Gundrun declared, but Gundahari and Hagan were already coming in the door. A heavy gold chain dripped from Hagan's hands, gleams of garnet-red and green glowing from the pendant in his palm; Gundahari carried a cloak cunningly wrought of green Roman silk edged with the blue-tipped white fur of Northern foxtails.

"Will you make peace with us, sister?" Gundahari asked, kneeling to look into Gundrun's face. "We have missed you for a long time."

"Why did you go away without telling us?" Hagan said, almost at the same time. "Anything might have happened to you."

"I shall not make peace with you. You broke your oaths; you killed Sigifrith. I do not want to see you or have anything more to do with you. Take those gifts away and give them to your wives or whatever unfortunate women you like."

"You cannot live wedded to a dead man forever," Gundahari told her. "Come home, and we will find you a living husband, one whose fame will live as long as Sigifrith's."

"Many men are great in battle but only one could slay the dragon Fadhmir and ride through Brunichild's flames. And even if Sigifrith had never done any of that, I should have loved him more than anyone anyway, and then perhaps you might not have killed him out of envy and fear. Go away, both of you!"

Gundrun turned her back to them. She stiffened as she heard Hagan move behind her; then it seemed that some gesture of Gundahari's had halted him, for he stepped away again.

"Leave her be," Gundahari said in a low voice. "We shall not take her against her will."

"You have not fared well with Gundrun," Thonara said as Grimhild and her sons came out of the chamber. Hagan shut the door behind them, dropping the chain and its pendant back into his belt pouch. Gundahari stood uncomfortably with the cloak draped over his forearms to show its fineness off.

"She is overwrought," Grimhild answered.

"What do you mean to do?"

"We shall stay here for a few days, by your leave, and talk to her. I expect in a little while she will be easier with the idea of going home."

"Might she be married to one of the athelings here? There are several young men with whom she could be matched. I shall have the families of the best speak to you, if you would know more."

"There is a greater king in the south who would have her," Grimhild told her cousin. "The betrothal is already made."

"Why are you doing this to your daughter?"

"Because it will be to everyone's weal, not least Gundrun's own. Now I will ask your leave to mix a drink which may calm Gundrun's sorrows and ease her mind."

"Whatever might do that would be good. You have my leave, Grimhild. Our brewing house is outside, behind the hall." Thonara took one of the keys off the ring which jangled at her belt and gave it to her cousin. "Your thanes may sleep in our hall; there is plenty of room, since Half and most of his warband are away raiding in Gautland. I expect we will even be able to feed you, though I had no reason to expect so many."

"We thank you," Gundahari said gravely. "I trust you will not take it ill if I say that we have brought some food and drink of our own—not because we doubted your hospitality, but because we thought it rude to ask you to feed a horde on such short notice. We will be honored by whatever you can spare."

"I appreciate your thoughtfulness, but surely your men will be glad of fresh food after such a long faring. If you'll bring them in . . ."

As Thonara and Gundahari spoke, Grimhild beckoned quietly to Hagan. He followed his mother out to the brewing house. The room was thick with the musty warmth of the working wort, the yeast bubbling and gurgling around them. Grimhild walked among the casks that lined the walls, tapping at them till she found one that did not quite ring empty.

"Go down to the ship and fetch the small locked chest that I brought, then ask Thonara for a plain drinking horn," she commanded her son.

Gundrun did not sleep that night; in Thonara's windowless chamber, she had no way to tell the time, except that the torches had burned three-quarters of the way down when the door opened and Grimhild glided in. Her long fingernails clacked against the drinking horn in her hand as she stood looking down at her daughter.

"You are not sleeping well."

"Why should I?" Gundrun answered bitterly. "Wherever I go, no one is willing to let me rest. Is it any wonder that I don't sleep?"

"I have brought you something to ease you and give you rest."

"Will I die of it? I cannot see much rest for me otherwise."

"I hope that you shall not die. Indeed, I expect you to live and be joyful through your life."

"There is not much likelihood of that." But Gundrun reached out and took the horn from her mother's hand. It was graven with a sharp-edged network of runes like twigs locked through each other, so bound that she could not tell where they began or ended, nor might she read the reddened staves. "What have you brewed into this? I will not drink. I think there is some bale in the beer."

"Drink, my daughter; when have I ever done ill toward you? Did I not bring you the husband you desired, and what part did I have in his slaying? Had I been there, I should have given another rede altogether. Now I want only to heal the harm that has been done by Sigifrith's death, so that nothing shall be worse than it might have been before."

Gundrun sniffed at the draught in the horn. A scent as cold as sea rime rose from it, icy, bitter and sharp; yet it was oddly enticing, so that her mouth watered as she raised the horn to her lips. Once she had caught its scent she could not help but drink, pouring the draught of ale down as swiftly as she could swallow until the last thick drop had rolled from the graven rim into her mouth.

The rime-cold of the drink slowly melted into a warmth that spread through Gundrun's limbs, easing the tightness in her chest. Slowly she lowered herself back on Thonara's bed, propping herself on the thick goose-down pillows. It seemed to her that once, far away, she had been angry and sorrowful, but now she could no longer think of it.

"What was in that draught?" she asked blurrily.

Her mother's eyes gleamed like chips of polished jet in the torchlight as she came closer, laying her hand on Gundrun's forehead. It felt to Gundrun as though the cool dry feathers of a swallow were brushing against her warm skin, as though her mother's face were sharpening to a bird's little beak. When Grimhild spoke, the dance of her words enthralled and soothed Gundrun so that she could not hear their meanings behind the swirling sounds.

Forth brought I the cup—full for your drinking
sea-cold and sharp—your sorrows mind not.
The drink is mixed   with the main of the earth,
sea ice-cold   and sacred boar's blood.
A long ling-fish   from land of Haddings,
barley uncut,   tooth bones of beasts.
Were in the beer,   many bales together,
worts all of the wood,   and acorns burnt,
dew of the hearth,   hallowed entrails,
a swine's liver seethed,   your sorrows to deafen.

"Now you shall sleep, and when you awaken you shall have forgotten your sorrows over Sigifrith and your wrath at your brothers, and you shall be glad to see them again."

Gundrun awoke to the sound of Gundahari's voice calling, "Hai, sister! Gundrun, awake! Are you still asleep? It's almost midday."

She got out of bed, shaking her hair down around her shoulders. She still felt oddly drowsy, as though she were wrapped in a goose-down quilt, but glad enough for all that. "I'll be out in a moment," she called. "Wait for me."

Gundrun remembered that her mother had brought her a draught of ale and that she had gone to sleep, but she could remember nothing more save that her brothers had come and she had been too ill to greet them properly.

Gundahari and Hagan were sitting on the bench before Half's high table when she came out. Before them were spread out a fine green silken cloak with white fox trim and many rings and ornaments wrought from gold and silver.

"Are you ready to make peace?" Gundahari asked, smiling at Gundrun.

Her anger drowned, she went forward and embraced him about the shoulders, and he hugged her gently back. She turned to Hagan then, but though she had wanted to, she could not bring herself to touch his cold flesh or look too closely at his face.

"Greetings, my sister," he said; if any note of hurt softened his harsh voice, Gundrun could not hear it. "We are glad to see you well again."

"See, we have brought these gifts for you. Will you take them?"

Gundrun lifted up the cloak, swirling it around her shoulders. Light as it was, it was wonderfully warm—too warm for summer, even in the Danes' land. She let Hagan lift the round gold pendant, whose spirals swirled and writhed around stones of deep red and green, and drop its heavy chain over her head. Gundahari waved his hand at the other jewelry. "These are yours, if you will take our peace and come home with us again."

"I will," Gundrun answered. She slipped a twisted coil of gold on to her arm, another on to her finger. "These are beautiful." She took off the cloak, setting it carefully on the table before she sat beside Gundahari. "Tell me of home. What has happened since I have been gone?"

"We've been fighting a bit; we made another treaty with the Romans in Gaul so that we have more lands—that's where the silk for your cloak came from. I have married a woman named Glamwer, and Hagan is still wedded to Costbera; though they have had no more children, those they have are hale and strong. Folkhari has also wed, and he wished to stay behind because his wife was ready to bear."

"And southward? Have you news of my daughter?"

"Hildkar holds the lands by Hrodgar's now; he and Olwyn will soon send Swanhild to Herwodis and Alapercht for fostering. Alapercht's son Alaswinth is also growing and prospering. When he is a man, he will be able to hold his father's lands well." Gundahari's hands twisted nervously at the ends of the belt he wore, twining the woven gold and green into a coiled band. Gundrun could feel Hagan's gaze on her as well, like the odd feeling of being watched that sometimes came over her when she was alone in the woods.

Grimhild and Thonara came into the hall carrying pitchers and cups of hammered silver. Grimhild was dressed in light blue linen that draped loosely around her thin body and was fastened at the shoulders with two rounded silver brooches; her taller cousin wore a tightly laced gown of creamy wool, pinned with little bosses of gold. The two older women poured drink for Grimhild's children, then for themselves, sitting across from the siblings as two of Thonara's bondsmaidens, Audur and Hallgerdar, came in with bread and meat.

After they had eaten, Grimhild rose and said to the others, "Gundrun and I must talk alone now."

Gundahari and Hagan glanced at each other, then at Grimhild. Gundahari nodded. Hagan said nothing.

Gundrun got up and the two of them walked out to the lake. The day had cooled, a grayish haze filming the Sun. The water mirrored the clouds so palely that the three swans floating at the far edge of the lake almost vanished into its whiteness.

"So you are reconciled with your brothers, and ready to come home again."

"I am."

"Would you be ready to leave again soon after?"

"Why should I wish to? What would I look for outside Worms? If I wanted to stay somewhere else, I should have asked Thonara to marry me to one of the young athelings she keeps thrusting at me."

"I shall give you gold and treasures of all kinds to have as an inheritance from your father, the dearest rings and bed hangings woven by the most skilled of Hunnish maidens: then your husband shall be paid for. Then I shall give you in marriage to the mighty King Attila, and you shall rule over his power and wealth beside him, if you do as we bid you."

"You want me to marry Attila?" Gundrun asked in dismay. "Surely it would not be seemly for us to carry on my line together."

"It was not so long ago that your father's folk dwelt with the Huns, and married among them too; don't some of our kin still bind the heads of their newborn sons and make sacrifices to the ghosts of the steppes? And Attila is no little king, but the most powerful next to your brother. Nor can he be such an ill man, since Thioderik has fought under his command for these many years; and didn't Hagan enjoy his time as a fosterling in his band?"

"He was as happy there as he might have been anywhere, I suppose," Gundrun admitted. "But that hardly means that I would enjoy it."

"I think Attila's hall is little different from what your father's was when you were young and the Sinwist lived. And it is shaped already that you shall marry this king, and you shall marry no other."

"When I lived at the edge of Mirkwood, we heard ill things of Attila. At the beginning of every winter, he sent messengers of peace to Hrodgar and to us, and when every winter had ended, he was attacking again. He is not a man who holds to his oaths, and an evil ghost dwells in his sword. Mother, we shall do badly if we bind our clan to Attila. It will not protect my brothers and the realm of the Burgundians, but rather set them in danger."

"How might you know enough to speak about that?" Grimhild asked, clenching her hands into clawed fists. Gundrun saw that her mother's thin face had paled, her fine bones standing out stark and sharp against her skin. "The Huns were born to be our bane; but I say that this wedding is our hope for Gundahari and Hagan to hold their lives and lands in safety. Do as we ask, and for it you shall have great honor and our friendship. And we shall give you the steads of Wineburg and Walburg that lie westward; the wine raised there and the fees from each year's crops shall be sent to you, that you may be rich in your own right as well as your husband's. Do you think your spae-sight is keener than mine, or how else do you see doom in the one thing I see that might fend it from us?"

"Only that I know Attila's ways," Gundrun said in a low voice. "And he is said to be a greedy man, whom no gold has sated yet. He will not share his winnings willingly, even with his kin by marriage, when he sees another way to have the whole."

"Yet I say that this must be. We can no longer trust in the strength of our men to ward the eastern marches against the Huns; that can be done only by women's strength. Do not forsake your brothers in this battle, Gundrun, for I feel that I have spent the last of my might in this faring and the work I have done. I may not be here much longer to show them the way."

"I will not. This must go forward, although against my will, but there shall be little cause for joy in it, but rather for sorrow."

"Do not say that!" Grimhild told her. "Your words are not without weight; if you fear an ill wyrd, you must try to turn it aside rather than to call it forth."

"Then let this wedding be, and I shall do my best to turn it toward weal."

Grimhild embraced her daughter; Gundrun clasped her mother carefully, frightened by the fragility of the bones beneath her hands. It seemed to her that Grimhild's wiry strength had drained from her like ale drawn from a cask, leaving a shell brittle as a dried-out spider's.

"Now let us go within, give Thonara the gifts we have brought for her and make our farewells. We cannot tarry, because it will not be long after our return that Attila and half a hundred of his men come to our hall, and we must be there when they arrive."

"So you meant to marry me off in any case?" Gundrun asked, breaking off the embrace. "With or against my will?"

"We had no more choice than you. As strong as Gundahari is in the west, he is weak in the east; the Alamanns do not have the strength to attack him themselves, but they would rather fight against us than for us if Attila gives them the chance, and we could not win such a war."

"No. If Sigifrith lived . . . "

"But that is done, and we can do nothing about it, save what we must to save ourselves and our folk."

"Let me go and gather my things, then, while you and my brothers ready farewells for Thonara. She has been kinder to me than she needed to be, and I owe her a great deal."

"We shall not forget that," Grimhild assured her daughter.

Only three nights passed between the day Gundrun went back to Worms and the morning Hagan blew the ancient horn of the Burgundians to warn of a warband approaching the gates of the city. Curious, Gundrun hurried up the steps of the old Roman watchtower to stand near his side and look down at the host of the Huns.

Attila and his men rode little steppes horses like those the Burgundians had ridden before mixing the fine blood of the Alamannic steeds into their own horse lines. Gundrun counted half a hundred—a full sixty riders— behind the man on the roan steed whose blood-red cloak flowed out over his horse's back and whose steel helm gleamed dully beneath the clouds sweeping across the plain.

"Women have borne worse husbands," Hagan said unexpectedly. "I hope you have more joy in your marriage than Costbera has had in ours."

Gundrun, taken by surprise, could hardly answer him. At last she choked out, "You might try to be kinder to her."

"How?"

Gundrun remembered how Costbera had shrunk from her husband's touch; and remembered, too, that Hagan had fathered no children on her since.

"I'm sorry."

"It is no fault of yours."

Even with her eyes closed, Gundrun could feel Hagan's nearness shuddering through her nerves like a grating note too deep for her to hear. But though the hairs prickled up and down her back and she could not stop herself from shivering, she stepped in and clasped her brother quickly about the shoulders. Hagan said nothing, but she felt better when she had done it.

"It is the way of the Huns," Hagan told her as they walked down the steps of the watchtower, "to keep their women hidden away and powerless. You must never let Attila think that he can treat you as if you were a Hunnish woman. He knows our ways are different from theirs in many things, and because there are several folks who fight in his warbands he lets all keep to their own ways whenever they are willing to defend them. Go to the feasts and pour the ale out for the men; walk freely where you will; as Attila's wife you need not fear any man in his band. If something troubles you or someone offends you, go to Thioderik or his hoary thane Hildebrand. They are the trustiest men living, and you can be sure that no one will ward and help you better than they . . . If it had not been for them and for Waldhari, I should have been most unhappy in my first months with Attila. But you must never weaken or soften yourself in dealing with the Hunnish drighten, for if he once thinks that he can bear over you in the least of things, he will allow you no choice in the greater. However, if you make him respect you, you will have as fair a life as you might anywhere."

Gundrun could not help asking her brother, "Were you truly happy there?"

Hagan did not answer for a few moments, as they walked out toward the gate. His voice was lowered when he said, "Happier than I have been since, except once."

Then they were at the city's great gate, where men on either side waited for the command to open. Hagan nodded to them. The gates swung open, and the Huns rode in.

"Hail, Attila!" Hagan said, stepping out in front of the lead horse. Gundrun could not see the Hunnish king's face beneath his helmet; but she thought from the shape of it that his skull would be lengthened like those of their own men. The muscles of his chest and shoulders pressed against his scarlet tunic, his thick belt holding in a swell of belly.

"Hail, Hagan," Attila replied. "You might have kept yourself better in my warband; an eye is a large thing to be careless of." Gundrun noticed that he spoke as clearly as a Roman, his voice lilting where Burgundian speech was guttural.

"Waldhari fared worse than I," Hagan answered grimly.

"So I have heard. Who is this woman with you? Why do you let your wife walk freely through the streets? You should keep her as we keep our women. I shall surely take more care of your sister."

"I am Gundrun, whom you have asked to marry!" Gundrun stepped forward beside her brother, glaring up at the Hun. "If you think that you can force your ways on me in place of my own, you may take them and yourself back through the Mirkwood and find yourself a Hunnish woman who will put up with them."

To her surprise, Attila laughed, the sound ringing from his helmet as from the depths of a cave. "You do not need to fear me, little one," he said. "If you are good and obey me as a wife ought to, I shall not beat you but bring you rings of gold from my wars. Now come here and walk at my stirrup."

"I certainly shan't fear you, but it is not our way for an atheling-wife to be her husband's bondmaid, and you must know that before you even think about wedding me. If you want me to come to my brother's hall or anywhere else at your side, you must lift me on to your horse or give me a horse of my own. Surely you are not too poor to afford one."

"Indeed I am not. And you shall have the finest of our horses on the way back, if you choose to ride rather than following in a wain, but none of ours are fitted with a woman's saddle. Will you ride before me?"

"I will."

Attila leapt down from his horse, grasped Gundrun around the waist and heaved her up in front of the saddle. Before she could draw a breath, he was mounted again, lifting her on to his lap where she could sit comfortably except for the hilt of his sword chafing the top of her left hipbone. Attila smelled little worse than any other man after a long journey; only a faint odor of rancid fat hung about him, and Gundrun was well used to the Burgundian thanes who greased their hair with butter when they could.

"Hai, Hagan!" a young Goth shouted from behind Attila. "Where are we going, then?"

"Follow me."

As they neared the walls of Gundahari's hall before which the Burgundian king and his thanes stood, Attila's men rode up around their king. "Hold on tight," Attila said to Gundrun, crooking his forearm around in front of her like an iron bar. She grasped it with both hands as his horse reared beneath them then dropped forward into a gallop. The Hunnish horses dashed about in the narrow space of the Roman street, missing the houses to either side by a finger's width as they rode in their tight pattern that ended with Attila at the fore again.

"Attila!" the men shouted as one, thrusting their fists into the air.

Gundahari waited, standing silently until Attila spoke to him.

"Hail, Gundahari! Do you make me welcome?"

"As my sister has greeted you and you come in peace, you are welcome in my lands and my hall."

"Where shall we stable our horses?"

"You shall stable your horses within, as shall Thioderik and Hildebrand for the love my brother bears them. Hagan shall show your men to the place where our thanes keep their steeds."

"Well enough," Attila said, riding in. Gundrun looked carefully at the two warriors who followed him. She guessed that the younger of the two, a fair man who wore a dun cloak over a cream-colored tunic, was in his early middle years—younger than she had expected Thioderik to be; she had heard songs of him as long as she could remember. The other, a silver-haired, powerfully built warrior with long drooping moustaches, was certainly Hildebrand; the old man wore a dark byrnie over his dark tunic, and his craggy face was cut deeply with cruel scores of age and hardship.

When they got to the stables, Attila was about to lift Gundrun down to Gundahari, but she pushed his hands away and climbed down herself. She could see her brother's embarrassment in the way his broad cheeks puffed up a little, as if the blood that reddened his face also made it swell.

Unfazed, Attila dismounted and led his horse into the stable, followed by Thioderik and Hildebrand. When he came out again, Gundrun looked closely at the sword at his hip, of which she had heard rumors. Its hilt was crudely made, the iron pitted as if it had been buried for a long time. The sword was not particularly long or wide; indeed, it was little larger than a Roman gladius. He had it in a plain leather sheath, adorned only with an eagle's head of carven amber such as any Burgundian warrior might be likely to brighten his weapon with.

"Let us go to your hall and set down the terms of this marriage," Attila said to Gundahari. "I am eager to wed your sister and take her home."

"We shall do it according to the ways of our folk," Gundahari replied. "I am told that you are careful of all men's customs."

"There are many gods and ghosts, and a wise man angers none of them if he can help it. Well, then, let us do whatever is needful for your gods to consider this wedding well done."

The five of them went to the hall, where the wine was set out for Gundrun to pour. Grimhild was not there: she had been in her bed since they came back from the Danes' land, eating little and hardly speaking, and Gundahari's wife Glamwer was staying close by to tend her. Attila took his helm off for the first time, putting it on the bench beside him and taking the goblet from Gundrun's hand. His black hair was rucked up over his long skull from the helmet, greasy with his long faring. The Hun's skin was swarthy and his face broad; his black eyes were tilted with tiny folds at the corners.

"Be welcome here, my betrothed," Gundrun said, as sweetly as she could. There was something cold about Attila; he seemed as untrustworthy as a brown-mottled adder lying stick-still. Now that she saw him herself, she understood her mother's words: her kin would be better off with one of their own watching him. "I look forward to pouring out wine in our own hall. Be welcome here, Thioderik," she said, moving on. "It is an honor to greet such a hero in the Gebicungs' home." Up close, she could see that the Goth was older than she had thought at first; though he moved with the restless grace and strength of a young man, the tracks of his years of exile ran deep beneath his fair moustache and across his high forehead.

Thioderik smiled at her as he took the cup from her hands, showing unbroken white teeth. His blue eyes were not so unbearably keen as Sigifrith's had been, but something in their brightness warmed Gundrun's heart. "It is an honor to be greeted by such a frowe," he replied. Even in the simple words, she could hear the fire of the Amalung kings crackling beneath his voice; she wondered why he had been content merely to lead a warband under Attila for so long. Her time with Attila would be easier, she thought, with Thioderik to trust in.

"Hail, Hildebrand, and welcome to my brother's hall," Gundrun told the old warrior as she gave him his wine.

"Hail, Gundrun. I am glad to meet you. Hagan spoke of you often." Hildebrand's voice was a deep growl, heavy with his years. He sniffed at the wine, then gulped it down with the carefully straight face of a man more used to mead or ale.

"It is better than khumiss, is it not?" Hagan asked as he came in. To Gundrun's surprise, he had taken the time to tie his hair into the Hunnish knot that he had favored when he came back from Attila's warband.

Hildebrand coughed. Thioderik laughed as he sipped at his own goblet. "The wine of these lands is well famed," he said. "To my taste, it is often better than the red wines of the south."

"I expect you will not let your sister languish without her accustomed drink," Attila told Gundahari. "As part of the wedding agreements, we shall arrange for wine to be shipped from your lands to mine each year."

"I am certain that trade in wine shall enrich both our folks," the Burgundian king answered. They spoke of prices and harvests as Gundrun rose twice to refill her pitcher and pour out more drink, and then the talk turned to the price of the wedding.

"I am willing to offer a good bride fee, in gold and in beasts. Thioderik has told me that the worth of a woman is measured by the wealth her husband has given for her; and so I will give half a hundred ounces of gold and twice twelve of our finest horses to go with it."

"That is a fine price, almost worthy of my sister," Gundahari agreed. "And she shall come with a dowry of twelve gold arm-rings of three ounces each, and twelve lengths of Roman silk and twice twelve casks of our best wine, half from Gaul and half from the banks of the Rhine."

"An atheling-maid's price indeed." Attila leaned forward, gazing hard into Gundahari's face. "I have heard, as well, that Sigifrith Fadhmir's Bane gave the hoard of the Rhine to Gundrun Gebica's daughter as her morning gift, yet it never came to their hall by Mirkwood. Shall Gundrun's own gold come with her?"

His challenge hung within the stones of the hall till Hagan's answer shattered the silence. "Where Fadhmir's hoard lay, there it shall lie."

"And where does it lie?"

"Only two know that." Hagan stared flatly at Attila until the Hunnish drighten grasped the knobbed pommel of his sword's hilt like an amulet against his fosterling's gaze. A ruddy flush washed beneath Attila's swarthy cheeks as he looked back at Gundahari.

"We shall talk of this later, then. What might you offer me for an ally's protection against the anger of the Alamanns?"

"We need no protection. Had they the strength to attack us, Sigifrith would be avenged or else his kin would all lie dead."

"Alaswinth shall not be a child forever. Do you mean to marry Swanhild to him?"

"They are too close kin," Gundrun interrupted. "But while she dwells with the Alamanns, they shall not be my foes, at least. It seems to me that it would be enough for your wedding oath to bind you and your sword to the aid of my kin in times of battle and need, and them to your help."

Attila raised his thick brows, looking down at her. "Do Burgundian women always set the terms of their men's dealings?"

"You know that we place trust in the wisdom of women," Hagan answered for her. "Gundrun should be the more precious to you, since she has inherited her mother's understanding and craft."

"And you know that such things are not seen so fairly among us," Attila replied. "I have heard a great deal of Grimhild."

"The frowe Grimhild is famed for her deep mind," said Thioderik, and no one could speak against the sparks echoing bright in his words. "It seems to me that Gundrun's rede is good, and you would all do well to heed it since the bonds of blood shall bind you soon through the children of Gundrun and Attila."

"That is well enough to be prized," Hildebrand growled sadly, and Gundrun suddenly remembered the words of a song she had heard in Thonara's hall not half a year ago:

> Hildebrand and Hadubrand   two hordes among
> son and father, kin   straightened their war gear . . .
> "Witness now, ruling god,   Woe-wyrd shapes . . .
> Now shall my own child   with the sword hew me,
> beat down with his blade,   or his bane I must be."
> Then they let first   fly the ash shafts
> sharpest warders   in shields stood . . .

For Hildebrand's son had believed his father long dead, and never known him when they stood face to face between the armies, nor trusted in Hildebrand's words when the old warrior tried to turn him from their fight.

"If the Gebicungs are willing to hold by this, I am no less so. Your fame in such matters has gone before you." Attila smiled broadly at Gundahari, who shifted in his seat.

"As long as we may trust in you, you will find nothing lacking in our troth," the Burgundian king answered him. "So it has always been."

"When shall we hold the wedding, then? Or is there anything else that must be settled first?"

"We shall be clear that I shall have rule over my own wealth and the things that are mine," Gundrun told him firmly. "So it was when I was wed to Sigifrith; so it has been in my father's house, and I do not mean to lose what is mine by this marriage."

"Then shall you bring the Rhine's gold with you? That, too, is yours, and you should not let your brothers keep you from it."

"The Rhine's gold shall lie where it lay," Gundahari said before Gundrun could speak, looking fiercely first at her then at Attila. "Now that is settled, we would do well to speak of when we shall hold the wedding. There is no need to wait longer than we must, since I can see that you are eager to gain its delight. We might as well cleanse ourselves in the hemp baths tonight and have the wedding tomorrow, if my mother is well enough to bless it."

"The Rhine's gold shall not lie where it lay!" Attila said angrily. "Do you mean to cheat your sister, after widowing her? If Gundrun is to be mine, I shall speak for her where she is too shy and weak to speak for herself, for that is the way of our men to our women. I shall defend her rights against her own kin, if I must. I say now that she shall have the gold Sigifrith gave her; her fairness deserves no less to adorn it." Attila patted Gundrun clumsily on the shoulder, his fingers lingering a moment on the golden disk brooch Sigifrith had given her when he first came to Worms. "Speak as you will, little one. You need not fear your kinsmen while I am beside you."

Gundrun looked down at the golden dragon ring coiled about her finger, its brightness a thorn of sunlight pricking through the mist that lay over her memories of Sigifrith. It would be fair to look upon the hoard, she thought— he meant for me to have it. But then she thought of Attila running his hands through the fine work, gloating over the gold till he was lost in it: she would see little of her first morning gift if it came to his hands.

"Sigifrith's wealth shall lie where it lay," Gundrun murmured.

Attila lifted her chin with a rough finger, his dark eyes staring closely into hers. "Speak louder, my betrothed: I did not hear you, and I think none of these folk did either." Gundrun heard the threatening rasp of sword on scabbard in his voice, and grasped his wrist angrily, jerking his hand away from her face.

"I said . . . " she answered loudly, but Hagan was already speaking.

"I heard my sister's words clearly, as did you. Sigifrith's wealth shall lie where it lay, and no one may say that we robbed her of it."

"She answers so only because you have taught her to fear you. That is as it should be, but soon she will be my wife, and need fear no hand but mine. I mean for her to have what is hers, whether she has the sense to take it now or not."

Thioderik's voice was cool as the clinking of river-smoothed flints, but Gundrun could hear the seeds of fire ready to spring forth. "It is often said that wealth causes strife among kin; but this wedding must be kept with the gifts of frith, not of battle. If the gold is so well kept, there is no need to hurry in claiming it. Should Gundrun wish to claim her wealth in a year, or three, I trust there is no one here who would not see her have it; there will be no need to fight for it. But think on this, Attila: we are only half a hundred in this band, and must pass through the land of the Alamanns, who might think that they have a claim to it as well—for Sigifrith's daughter, if not for his mother and stepfather. And when we get to your hall, where would you keep it? We have no storehouses of stone such as the Romans built, where one man might lock out an army; and whom would you set to guard the gold? You might trust myself, or Hildebrand, but we have more to do than sentry duty and you cannot be awake forever. Let the Rhine's gold stay here where it is safe, and Gundrun may claim it when she has a sure storehouse to keep it in." Thioderik's blue gaze locked with the eyes of the Hunnish drighten, even as Hildebrand rumbled, "Aye, we Goths will not strike where we have not been wronged."

"So be it, then," Attila grumbled. "We shall hold the wedding tomorrow, and come back for the gold when we are ready to take it."

"That shall be as it may," answered Gundahari.

Although Grimhild, drawn and wasted, had to lean on Gundahari's shoulder, her voice was strong enough as she called the gods and goddesses to the stead of the stones where a white cow and a dun bull lay bound for the wedding sacrifice. Attila drew his sword, its grainy blade gleaming under the gray-yellow haze of the sky. Gundrun put her hand unwillingly on his other palm where it lay over the Greek alpha graven on the pitted steel. She could feel the sword's might surging beneath their touch, the greasy slickness of the blade prickling with painful sparks of power.

"So I swear my troth to Gundrun on this sword, by the gods and ghosts of my kinsmen and hers," Attila called. "I shall not raise it against those of her blood; if it is drawn, let it be drawn to aid them. By this sword let us be wed; may the god of war bring me strong sons to hold it after me."

"So I swear my troth to Attila on this sword, by the gods and ghosts of my kinsmen and his," Gundrun repeated. "Thus I shall be his wife, after the ways and according to the customs of my own folk; and let this oath be woven as binding for the weal of all our kin."

Then Thioderik and Hildebrand together lifted the hammer to hallow the two bound kine. Attila slew the cattle with his sword, and Grimhild bent painfully down to dip her oak twig in the blood, straightening again to sprinkle it over her daughter and the Hunnish king.

"Now you are wed." Grimhild's words weakened as she spoke on, becoming scratchy and thin. "May the gods bless you and both our folks in this marriage, and bring you joy of it."

But as she and Attila drank the bridal ale from one cup, her husband dashing the foam from his black moustache with the back of his hand, Gundrun knew that her heart would never smile upon Attila and there would be little blitheness in their life together.

8

GRIMHILD'S DEATH

Gundrun sat on a bench beside Attila's hall, closing her eyes against the warm sunlight of summer's end as she stretched her legs and leaned back against one of the hall's doorposts with her hands over her belly. She had not felt the child within kicking yet, but she knew that it was growing; it stole more of her strength from her each day, leaving her sleepy and easily chilled.

"Attila's child," she murmured, and the words seemed to leave a bitter-edged slime in her mouth. It had been different bearing Sigifrith's children, feeling their strength wax within her like a fresh spring bubbling inside her body; this one was a swelling lump of rock that weighted her down. She tried to remember how miserable she had been during her earlier pregnancies—swollen ankles, waddling from the fifth moon onward, aching back and weighted bladder—but the memories kept fading into the leap of joy she had felt whenever Sigimund had beaten against the walls of her womb or Swanhild stirred in her sleep.

Resolutely, Gundrun opened her eyes and sat up again. She had more to do than dream of the past: there were sacks of grain to be listed and stored, cheese and ale sent to Attila as tribute from the drightens around him—the Huns did not farm, but lived off those who did—and a thousand other things that must be taken care of before the winter came. These tasks were not strange to her, but in Sigifrith's hall there had been other women to help her with her work, whereas Hunnish women had no rule over their halls or goods. Hildebrand would help her if she asked, but she thought there was no need to take him away from his work of training Thioderik's warriors or whatever the old thane might be doing now; managing the hall was a frowe's work.

As she stood and brushed off her skirts, the light breeze brought her the sound of men's voices quarreling. She hardly noticed it at first—no sound was commoner in Attila's hall—but then she heard the Burgundian accent in one of the voices and hurried to see what was happening.

The Sun's light slanted down through the red-tinged leaves, shining brightly from Folkhari's elongated cap of golden hair. He sat easily on the back of his dappled gray horse, looking down at the two Hunnish sentries who stood blocking his way.

"And I say that I shall pass, in the name of King Gundahari of the Bur-gundians," the skop said, the sharpening edge of his voice cutting through their mutterings. "If you can't understand plain Gothic, go and fetch someone who can! Attila will hardly be pleased with you for daring to stop his kins-man's messenger, nor will Gundrun be glad that you have delayed this mes-sage."

"And I say that he shall pass," Gundrun called to them. The sentries whirled about, hands dropping from their sword hilts as their eyes stared at her. As she smiled up at Folkhari, she felt the huge bitter-salt wave of home-sickness swelling and cresting within her, pooling in her eyes. Quickly she blinked the water away. "Be welcome here, Folkhari. I hope your news is glad." But even as she spoke, she saw that the skop was clad in black. No gold gleamed from his arms or fingers, and only a small plain brooch of silver closed his cloak.

"I would bring you gladder tidings if I could. Gundrun, your mother is dying and she has sent me to call you home for her end."

Gundrun felt as though a horse's padded hoof had caught her in the chest, knocking the breath from her. Even as the first shock faded, though, she knew that she had awaited this since coming back from Denmark; she had known that her mother had little longer to live.

"Come up to the hall, so that you may bear the news to Attila," she answered, her voice as calm as it might be. "How swiftly must we be there? It will be difficult for us to leave before tomorrow morning."

Folkhari drew his cloak more tightly about him; though he tried to hide it, Gundrun could not mistake the shiver that ran through his body. "Grim-hild said that there would easily be time for you to get there before her end. If she does not know the hour of her death"—his breath did catch in his throat then, and Gundrun saw the blackness at the center of his eyes wid-ening as though he looked into a dark room—"then no one is wise enough to say."

Attila was sitting inside the hall, drinking wine and talking to Thioderik and Hildebrand. The Gyula sat nearby, carving on a small piece of wood with his curved bronze knife and mumbling softly around something that he turned steadily in his toothless mouth. The three warriors looked up as Gundrun and Folkhari entered, but the old man did not turn his gaze from the tiny troll shape taking form beneath his hands as he whispered to it.

Attila's brow lowered over his brooding eagle's glare; he opened his mouth to speak, but Folkhari's words were out first.

"From King Gundahari of the Burgundians to Attila, drighten of the Huns, greetings. It is our sorrow that Grimhild, our beloved mother, has reached the end of her life. Therefore we ask that Gundrun come back to Worms for the space of two weeks, that she may aid in her mother's funeral rites as is fitting, so that Grimhild's ghost not be angered nor stirred against her kin by neglect. We give you thanks for your help in this, and ask the frowe our mother to look well on you for it."

Attila touched the amber eagle head on his sword's sheath, his black gaze flicking nervously toward the Gyula. "Two great rivers run between our lands and Worms. Have we aught to fear from the Burgundian dead?"

The old man carefully traced a circle thrice about his half-carved wood before laying it aside and looking up at Attila. "Grimhild . . . " he murmured, his dark eyes softening. He did not look straight at the drighten, nor at Folkhari, but stared into the fire for a few moments. "Hagan's mother is a mighty woman, and shall be mighty among the ghosts should her wrath be roused. Ill to keep Gundrun from her now; seek, rather, what you may gain. That is my rede to you."

"Will you come with us?"

"No." The Gyula picked up his carving again and turned his back to Attila, his muttering running under the sound of the crackling fire like the rushing of an underground stream.

"Seek what I may gain . . . " Attila mused. It seemed to Gundrun then that the swarthy fingers closed on the hilt of his sword were the thick talons of a claw that would grasp what it took and never loose it. The Hunnish drighten looked from the sunlit doorway to the fire, gazing at the glowing coals as if the gold lay nesting there, and it was as though a scaly mask shadowed his face for a moment. Then he laughed, pulling Gundrun to him by the wrist and giving her a rough pat on the rump. "Go and ready your things, my sweet. You shall not ride this time, since you are with child. I will have a wain made ready."

"I rode till the fifth month when I bore Sigifrith's children, and it did them no harm. Is your seed less strong than the Walsing's, or does it take root less firmly?"

Though Attila was still smiling as he said, "That is not so! Ride then, if you will," the second pat he gave to send Gundrun on her way stung as if he had struck her with the flat of his sword. She turned to glare at him, touching the knife at the side of her belt threateningly; on their first night together, she had sworn that if he ever tried to beat her she would knife him in the back. He grinned at her and said, "We must ready the wain anyway, for your maids; you should not go without them."

The setting Sun cast long spears of light across the plain as Gundrun, her husband and their folk rode toward the open gates of Worms. Gundrun rode between Attila and Thioderik; the Hunnish drighten had wished to leave the Goths to guard his hall, but Thioderik had prevailed in the end so that they came as a mixed band, a hundred and a half of each folk.

Gundrun did not see Hagan until they had ridden to the gate; then her brother stepped out of the shadows beside one of the stone posts. Gundrun's mare shied away as he took her reins.

"Come swiftly," he grated to her. "Our mother is dying and will not live out the night. She has called for you."

Without speaking to the others, Hagan led Gundrun ahead of them toward Gundahari's hall. He did not try to help her down from the horse, though he held the reins while she dismounted.

"Go. I must fetch Costbera."

"Why? What good will she do? She was never a friend to our mother." Gundrun's voice was sharper than she had meant for it to be; a low trembling ran through her bones, draining her strength and gnawing at the roots of her will.

"Grimhild asked me to bring her. Do not worry about your husband and his folk; Gundahari waits in the hall to greet them, for he has already made his farewell to our mother. It is the three of us she wishes to have watch by her tonight while Gundahari carries out the kingly duties for which she raised him."

Hagan turned away, leading Gundrun's horse into the stable and leaving her to make her own way into the hall. Though the Sun had not yet set, Gundrun had never seen their home so bright: the thralls were already lighting the lamps and candles, until every room and corridor burned with light. More of the serving folk wore the Christians' cross than Gundrun had remembered, and as she hurried to her mother's room she heard the soft muttering of Latin prayers before and behind her, like the frightened rustling of mice through dry leaves.

Although the shutters were closed, only a single candle burned in Grimhild's room and it was guttering low. For a moment, Gundrun thought that the bed was empty. Then a little twist of blankets stirred, and Gundrun saw the fever-hot brightness of the candlelight gleaming off her mother's eyes. Grimhild's skin had not withered, but drawn tight over the sharp bones of her skull; the arm she half-lifted to her daughter was hardly more than bones, thinner than a child's limb. Her hand fell back onto the blanket.

"Come closer, Gundrun," Grimhild whispered harshly "You did not arrive too soon."

"Attila would take the wain for my maidens, since Hunnish women do not ride, and so we fared more slowly than I wished," Gundrun answered. Though the words caught painfully in her throat, no tears came to her eyes—she did not know why. "But I am here now, and not too late. Only tell me what I need to do for you and I will do it."

"I shall die tonight, no matter what you do," Grimhild replied. Gundrun had to bend closer to understand her; pain and sickness had roughened Grimhild's voice to the rasp of rock on dry rock, and she stopped often to cough dustily. "I knew the price for my wreakings, and I chose to pay it willingly from the first to the end when I poured out the last of my might in the draught I gave you in Denmark. If you would ease my need-faring, open the chest by my bed and take out the flask of black glass. There should be a few drops left in it; mix them well into a pitcher of the good Gaulish wine. Take care that no one else drinks of it, and that you throw what is left into the river and wash the pitcher well afterward."

"Are you asking me to give you poison, Mother?"

"And if I were, would you deny it?" Grimhild asked, some of her old sharpness cutting through her ravaged voice. She coughed again. "No. I am used to the draught. It may hasten my end by a few hours, but it will strengthen me while I last and ease my pain."

Grimhild closed her eyes and turned over in bed, and Gundrun had no choice but to begin to prepare her mother's draught.

The bells were ringing for the evening Mass when Costbera wrapped her cloak around herself and began to make her way down the street to the church. She breathed deeply of the clean wind, looking up to the clouds streaming black against the sunset. As always, simply stepping outside of the house she shared with Hagan was enough to ease her soul, and Grimhild's long illness had made living with him no easier. Hard as it was to imagine, she thought that he must care for his mother. Though neither his face nor his voice showed it, it had seemed to her of late that the weight that always crushed against her when he was near was shot through with bitter streaks of sorrow now, like white veins of quartz running sharp-edged and brittle through a block of granite. Still, the sound of the church bells ahead turned Costbera's heart upward, so that she stopped for a moment and tilted her head, staring at the blue of the sky darkening back from the sunset's deepening rose, the swallows darting to and fro through the evening air.

She knew Hagan was near before she saw him, as surely as if she had heard an aurochs horn's deep note of warning. She paused—he might be passing for any reason, he had never raised his voice against her churchgoing—and then he was before her, looking down into her face, and she could not bear to meet his gaze.

"Come. Grimhild has asked that you, Gundrun and I attend her in her last hours."

Costbera clutched at the gold cross that hung about her neck, that her mother had given her before her wedding. It had not warded Hagan away from her, as she had half-thought it might, nor kept Grimhild from giving her potions while she was pregnant, but the touch of the suffering Christ had given her strength to meet the heathen terrors about her. She could feel her heart thudding hard beneath the crucifix as her sweat smeared the gold.

"Why me? Surely a priest . . ."

"Grimhild has not forsaken her ancestors yet," Hagan answered. "I do not know why she wishes you with her—but she is dying now. Come."

He took her by the wrist—the first time he had touched her for four years. Costbera could not help thinking of their wedding night; she could feel her legs trembling with the old echo of fear and pain as she followed her husband helplessly down the street. Hagan's touch had grown no easier for her to bear, and she wanted to tear herself away and flee, but she knew that the gentle grip on her arm would tighten like a noose the moment she moved away. O Christ, she prayed, give me strength for this and ward me from Grimhild's sorceries, for I know my living God is stronger than a dying witch.

Gundrun was in the chamber when they got there, holding a glass goblet for her mother to drink from. A pitcher of wine stood by the bed, but there were no other cups. Costbera swallowed twice as the wine's rich smell wafted over to her; her throat seemed suddenly very dry. Although she knew it was rude, she could not help stretching out a hand toward the pitcher.

Gundrun started, spilling a few drops on Grimhild as she rose halfway from the bed.

The old woman coughed roughly, raising a spider-thin hand to halt her daughter. "Ach, no . . . only a swallow, Costbera. More will do you harm."

Costbera took the drink, the wine's smoothness slipping easily down her throat until Hagan took the pitcher from her hand. "I shall get you more if you are still thirsty," he said.

Costbera shook her head, stepping away from him to still the shiver running through her nerves. It seemed to her that the low candle was burning brighter than it had before, its halo of light trembling against the darkness with a crown of half-seen colors sparkling around it, like the halo and jeweled crown of the Blessed Virgin in the church. It did not seem right to her that the light should shine so in Grimhild's death chamber, jeweling the witch's wide eyes in their white setting of wire-fine bone. She hardly noticed when her knees gave way beneath her, settling her into the chair that Hagan had swiftly moved under her.

"Why did you send for me?" she asked Grimhild.

"Help me sit up, Gundrun," Grimhild croaked. Her daughter lifted her by the shoulders, leaning her mother's body against her own as though Grimhild were a little shock of straw. It seemed to Costbera that she saw a bright fire burning through Gundrun's glass-clear flesh, its pure golden light flaring with angry red lightning streaks now and again, even as the candle flame guttered lower and lower in Grimhild's darkened breast.

Grimhild reached out to Costbera, her grip no tighter on the younger woman's wrist than the brush of a spider's legs. "Because you must see!" she hissed. "After I am gone, there will be no rede-giver for my sons except you; your sight may yet save their lives and lines. I chose you to come after me . . . I would have taught you . . . I saw the strength and soul sleeping in you, and hoped you would learn the bravery to bear them."

"And so you had me wed Hagan," Costbera said wonderingly. She felt as though her body were wrapped in wool, but her sight was keener than it had ever been and she could see every corner of the room as well as if the Sun's full light shone into it. The least rustle of Grimhild's bedclothes sounded as sharp as the splintering of twigs to her.

"You might have learned his heart, if you were not afraid," came Grimhild's words, final as rock settling on rock.

Costbera could not answer. She turned her head to her husband, who stood beside her without speaking. Alone of those in the room, Hagan's cloaked shape was as dark as a cloud on the night wind, lightened only by the streaks of moonlight lying silver through his hair. His single eye was as black and flat in the shadows as its hidden twin, showing nothing to her gaze. The chill still lay on Costbera's wrist where he had touched it, as it had lain all through her body in the long nights after he had fathered his children. His grim mask did not change as he watched her, nor could she hear his steady heart beating more swiftly. Grimhild must have once . . .

"What line are my children come of?" she asked, the question she knew everyone had whispered and no one had dared to face Grimhild with for Hagan's lifetime. She could hear Gundrun's gasp as the fires burning through the Gebicung flared red with fury, but Gundrun could not leave her mother to strike Costbera.

"Of the line of Lofanohaith, daughter of Hraithamar, heir to Otter's were-gild—the Nibelungs, the children of the Rhine. They are kin to Fadhmir and Ragin, to Sigifrith the Dragon-Slayer: be proud that you have borne them, for few can boast a mightier line than ours." Grimhild's teeth were very long and yellow against her sunken gums, and her face trembled with the strain of smiling before it sank into the mask of her sickness again.

"Gundrun," murmured Grimhild, "ease your anger. When I am dead, no other shall have the bravery to ask me of this. Now it seems to me that it is shaped for you to be the longest-lived of our line—the one who has eaten of Fadhmir's heart will not die easily, for I can see its fires burning in you still. Know that if your kin shall be slain, their ghosts shall not sit in Walhall nor their might pass to their kin until the last seed of their slayer is spilled in blood and his line come to an end. Seldom does it fall to a woman to avenge her brothers, and if I have wrought mightily enough, it shall not fall to you—but if I have failed, let nothing hold your hand from the greatest vengeance you may wreak: I know that you are a match for any of the Walsings in this. Swear it to me."

"I swear." Gundrun's voice caught as she spoke the words; her sorrow-fined face shone bright as a gosling's white down in the candlelight's glow.

"And one thing more: do not let the gold go from the Rhine. It were best if the ring you wear should lie with the rest of it, but I know you will not give it up. But do not let it be brought from where it lies, for Attila will try to claim it in your name. Though it is Sigifrith's winnings, and your inher-itance, let it lie as you love the honour of your kin."

Gundrun raised her hand, looking at the dragon ring. The ruby's star slept under the candle's pale light; it needed a stronger flame to bring it forth, but Costbera could not forget how she had seen it flare white beneath the Sun. "I swear," she murmured again.

"Hagan," Grimhild whispered, so softly that Costbera knew only she and he could hear. "Come here."

Costbera did not miss how Gundrun moved aside on the bed as her brother stepped closer, sitting down at his mother's other side. Gundrun held the goblet to Grimhild's lips again, wiping away the single drop that dribbled down her chin.

"You must ready my funeral rites, for now that the Sinwist is dead there is no other who can do it rightly."

"But he never taught me how," Hagan said. "No more than you did; you would not teach me the runes."

"You learned them anyway. Did you think I could miss that? No; I know that the folk you get your lore from ken the rites of the dead better than any. You shall set me in a howe beside Gebica's, with my horses and a wain to bear me to the green worlds of the gods, and you shall know better than I what ought to come then." Grimhild closed her eyes. For a moment, Costbera thought she was dead, but then the Burgundian queen gasped softly and the last glimmer of life flared with her breath.

"Take care of your brother, Hagan. Gebica lives again in him, and I . . . I loved him, and . . . owe him . . . a great geld."

Grimhild's head slumped, rolling onto Gundrun's shoulder. Hagan took her thin wrist in his fingers, and the three of them waited in silence beneath her tilted gaze.

Something struck the window, feathery wings battering the glass. Costbera choked back a shriek, half-rising from her chair.

"A night bird," Hagan said. "She is dead." He lifted his mother's body and clasped her one-armed against his chest, closing her eyes with the other hand. "The two of you wait here in this chamber until I come back. Someone must keep watch over her."

It seemed to Costbera that Hagan's voice rang oddly from the stone walls, as though it echoed back and forth between the crags of great mountains. She shrank aside as he passed, unwilling for even the hem of his cloak to brush against her as he bore the dead woman forth into the night.

Gundrun did not speak until long after the door had closed behind her brother and his burden. Costbera saw her eyes glance here and there, as if seeking a spot to stare at that bore nothing of the strangeness of her mother's last hour. Finally she looked Costbera straight in the face.

"Are your children well?" she asked.

Costbera began to laugh and could not stop, overwhelmed by the relief of Gundrun's ordinary question. The tears were raining from her eyes with it, her belly cramping and throat choking with laughter so hard it was almost soundless. She was afraid it would stop her breath, but she could not do anything but laugh harder and harder in light-headed madness.

Gundrun's hand cracked across her cheek twice. Costbera felt no pain from the blows, but they sobered her. She wiped her wet face with the corner of her cloak.

"I was afraid for you," Gundrun said. "I wouldn't have hit you otherwise. Are you all right?"

"I am now, I think," Costbera answered shakily. "Thank you. Is there clean wine in this room?"

"I wouldn't trust it. I'll go and get some."

"Hagan told us . . . "

Gundrun smiled grimly. "He's gone. I'm sure he's gone out, and my little brother isn't going to order me around in my father's hall."

Costbera saw how Gundrun's lips trembled as she spoke, and guessed that the bravery of her words was no more than a gilding, but she said nothing.

As the Gebicung opened the door, the draft blew the guttering candle out. Costbera hastily got up, supporting herself against the wall until she reached Gundrun's side. "I'll come with you."

The two of them kept carefully away from the main hall, where they could hear the sound of men's voices rising and falling. Costbera thought uneasily of Gundahari feasting with the Goths and the Huns while his mother lay dying, but she was not deaf to what the women whispered when they went to the Rhine to wash. She had never seen Gebica, but she had often heard that the father lived in the son—and that Gebica had died of a sudden illness as soon as Gundahari had grown old enough to take his place. The wonder, she thought, was that Gundahari had borne his mother's rule so long after Gebica's death; but Costbera had often felt the fear that ran through the king's veins like slow poison when Grimhild was near, the awareness of it so deep beneath the sunlit surface of his mind that she thought Gundahari himself did not know that he felt it. She knew that if she were closer to him she would hear her own sighing breaths of relief echoed in Gundahari's chest.

But what will he do without her? Costbera thought. She shuddered: she had no wish to take Grimhild's place as rede-giver, nor, she thought, would Grimhild's sons heed her words as they had their mother's.

"Here, take my cloak," Gundrun murmured, wrapping it around Costbera's shoulders before she could protest. "I think you'll feel better after you've eaten something."

The women got bread and cheese and wine from the kitchen, and as many candles as they could carry. They began lighting them at once when they got back, setting candles everywhere around the room until no corner was unlit. Gundrun began to tidy the tangled bedclothes; Costbera was stretching to put a candle on one of Grimhild's top shelves where Gundrun could not reach when she heard the other woman gasp.

"Costbera," Gundrun said in an odd, choked voice, "she's here."

The wind of Costbera's turning blew her candle out as she whirled, setting the other flames to leaping wildly among their wavering shadows. She opened her mouth to scream, but no sound came out: her throat was dead with fear, even as she saw what had happened. Grimhild had been lying there all the time, her corpse so thin that the tangle of blankets had hidden its shape until Gundrun had moved them. Her eyes were open again, as bright as if she still lived, but her head was canted limply to the side. Hagan must have brought her back, Costbera thought. There is nothing strange or wrong about this. The thought loosened her throat; though she tried to stop the sound, she was already screaming, the cry ripping up from her chest. Horrified, she put her hands over her mouth, stifling herself into silence.

Gundrun was staring at the body as well. Slowly she reached out with one hand, closing her mother's eyes and straightening her head.

"I saw Hagan . . . " she started. Then, "He must have brought her back while we were gone."

"He must have. We'd best put something on her eyes so they'll stay closed." Costbera dug into her belt pouch and brought out two silver coins—coins from Constantinople, stamped with crosses. She watched to see if Gundrun would say anything about that, but the Gebicung laid the silver circles over her mother's lids without looking at them.

"Should we cover her face?" Gundrun asked.

Costbera thought of the dead woman lying before them all night; and then she thought of Grimhild shrouded in darkness, without even the candles' light upon her. "No. We'll leave her as she is." Although Costbera still felt warm and dazed from Grimhild's draught, she knew that neither of them would sleep that night while they watched by Grimhild's corpse.

The first light of dawn was showing through the edges of the shutters when Hagan opened the door to Grimhild's chamber. Even by candlelight, Costbera could see the grayish blue tint beneath his pallor; he might have been dead longer than the corpse who lay shrouded in her blankets.

"I see that you kept your watch well. Have her dressed and laid out in her wain with her grave-goods before sunset, and set the thralls to digging the mound so she can be put in it while there is still light. I must sleep; wake me when everything is ready."

Costbera and Gundrun stared at each other as Hagan left soundlessly. They both knew how keen his hearing was; neither of them spoke for some time.

It was Gundrun who broke the silence at last. "Then he didn't come back while we were—?"

"He will have gone home to sleep," Costbera said dully. "May I rest here? If there's a room . . . "

"Of course. Give me a moment." Gundrun stepped out into the hall, and Costbera heard her shouting for a thrall.

When Costbera had been led away to sleep, Gundrun called in the other women of the household to ready Grimhild's body. She herself put the drugged wine into the chest of Grimhild's potions and heaved it onto her shoulder. Her mother had taught her something of gathering and preparing herbs, but the brews Grimhild had made for her own use were not something with which Gundrun was willing to meddle.

Attila was standing in the hall's doorway. Little streaks of blood reddened the whites of his eyes, but Gundrun could not smell the stink of stale wine or ale on him.

"Where are you going? What do you have in there?"

"It's likeliest to be poison," Gundrun answered roughly. "I'm going to throw it into the Rhine. It's heavy—you could carry it for me."

Attila took the chest from her, glancing into it before he tucked it under his arm. "Heavy only for a woman's strength," he said straightforwardly. "No weight for a man. Is she dead?"

"Yes." Gundrun glared at him; to her surprise, he turned his eyes aside and did not speak again until they had reached the river's bank. The two of them stood for a moment, looking at the ripples brightening beneath the rising Sun.

"Shame to foul the river with brews like these," Attila grunted. He lifted the chest high above his head and flung it out over the Rhine. It fell open at the top of its arch, glass bottles of many colors tumbling out like huge drops of glittering water. One or two bobbed up at once, turning slowly with the current as they floated downstream; it took longer for the wooden chest to surface. "And too bad about that glass. Still, there's no using a thing once it's been witched, unless a stronger witch can take the curse from it. I wish the Gyula had come with us."

Gundrun kept her thoughts to herself; her husband seldom spoke so openly to her when he was sober. Then Attila turned, taking her chin gently in one hand and tilting her face up to him. "They say the Rhine holds something fairer. I wonder what you would know about it. Did Sigifrith ever tell you where the gold lies?"

"He had meant to bring it back when we came to Worms for the last time," Gundrun answered slowly. "He said that he, Gundahari and Hagan had hidden it in the earth, but he never told me where."

"It would be fair to have the dragon's hoard for our own," Attila went on, his voice soft and smooth as Gundrun had seldom heard it. "I should like to see you adorned in such goldwork. I have seen the pieces Gundahari and Hagan wear, and your brooch and ring. Of all the gold my men win in fighting, none is so fairly wrought nor so warm to the touch." He stroked the disc-shaped brooch that closed Gundrun's cloak—the brooch wrought with leaping stags and does that Sigifrith had given her. She leaned away from his touch, but he did not seem to notice. "Your brother pays no heed to my wishes in this; but if you speak to claim it at your mother's grave, no one will doubt your right and Thioderik will be as eager as I to fight for you if Gundahari and Hagan should deny your own possessions to you. I had thought . . . "

To leave the Goths behind so you could try to take the gold by force of arms, Gundrun finished silently for him; you had thought that without Grimhild's rede Gundahari would waver like a willow in the wind, because the Huns believe that men who trust in women's wisdom are weak.

"I will tell you something else, so you may feel sure in your wealth's safety; no other living person knows this. I have had a place built for the gold, far from our hall, hidden beneath the earth and lined with slabs of stone so no one can dig into it. Once our gold is locked away there, none but I—and you—will know how to reach it and be able to touch it. Now nothing need hold you from asking for the dragon's hoard, and it will be a joy to us both when we have it."

"I will ask Gundahari for the gift I desire at my mother's grave," Gundrun said, knowing that she was doing no more than slowing what must happen, but too tired to do more or to resist Attila when he pulled her close to him with one arm and kissed her, his free hand fumbling at the string of his breeches. He will be done with this soon and I can rest then, Gundrun thought.

Although she had slept most of the day, Gundrun felt little better as she and Hagan led the two horses pulling Grimhild's finely carved wain along the road that led to the place where Gebica's howe had been raised from the plain to overlook the Rhine. The long dry summer had dusted the grass over his mound with a tinge of brown, but the earth heaped about where the second would rise above Grimhild's corpse was a deep reddish black, as though a draught of blood were blended into the soil. Twelve strong thralls, bare backs running with sweat and arms dirty to the elbow from their digging, stood beside an oxcart piled with the stones and timber that would roof the mound before they heaped the earth up again.

The horses, sorrel and roan, jingled with their fine trappings of silver and gold, but behind their hoofbeats and the creaking of the wain's wooden wheels, there were no sounds except muffled footfalls and hushed breath. Gundrun knew that it was fear rather than love that stilled the folk coming to Grimhild's burial; but her mother had never looked for their love for herself, only for Gundahari. This show of honor would be enough for Grimhild—enough to send her off gladly on her last faring, sure in the knowledge of the well-built kingdom she had left her son.

Hagan and Gundrun stopped before the timber-shored pit where Grimhild would lie. Hagan handed the reins of the horse he led to Gundrun, standing before the wain and waiting in silence as those who followed them came closer to ring the pit about. It took some time: although most had taken their place by rank, the kingly family and the athelings nearest to the grave and the rest farther away, Thioderik and his Goths, most of whom were Christians, stood separately at a distance, as did those Burgundians who had turned to the faith of Rome—except Costbera, who waited in the front rank with her children standing silently about her. Now and again she touched her crucifix uneasily, looking everywhere but at the wain where Grimhild lay. Attila also stood at the front, within a step and sword's stroke of Gundahari. The Hunnish drighten twisted the gold ring on his arm back and forth, up and down, as he stared down his beaky nose at his wife. Gundahari did not seem to mark Attila's closeness; his face was pale and puffy, as though he had also slept ill, but less sorrow furrowed it than Gundrun would have thought. Still, he had seen Grimhild failing over the last months; he had had time enough to grieve already.

At last Hagan began to speak, his harsh voice carrying easily over the plain. "Far is the faring, along wet wilderness ways. Wodan, Wanderer, well do you know them: guide Grimhild along her path. Donar, I call you: ward her wain from wyrm and wolf and all ill wights. High are the halls that Hella keeps, beyond the ringing bridge that spans the waters running between the worlds. You bridge's warder, let Grimhild by: you have no right to hinder her riding, for she fares with the blessing of her folk and kin beside her from a life made mighty by deeds. Let the thurse-maid sink before her! Hella's benches are readied for a bride decked with brightest linen, and a shining shield is laid over her mead, where Gebica waits for his frowe's true step."

Hagan moved to the wain where Grimhild lay among her treasures. First he lifted out a rune-carved slab of stone; though Gundrun craned her neck to see it, Hagan had set it in the wagon's shadow and she could not make out the runes clearly enough to read it. Next he brought forth a silver-bound horn, which he filled with wine from the keg beside Grimhild's body and lifted above his head.

"Let the queen's kin drink to her good faring, her joyful dwelling hereafter. No frowe has worked more tirelessly for the good of her children and their realm than she: may she be reborn into the Middle-Garth's ring, within the line for which she ever wrought!"

Hagan drank and passed the big horn to Gundrun. The draught he had poured was the Gaulish wine that Grimhild had ever favored: rich and plummy on the tongue, its heavy berry flavor lingering in the back of the mouth long after it had been drunk. Gundrun drank as deeply as her brother had—another such toast, and she would be drunk—and passed the half-empty horn to Gundahari. He stared into its depths for a few moments, as though thinking on something; then she saw him raise his eyes to look upon Gebica's mound before he drank. He might be our father born again, Gundrun thought, and it struck her at that moment that Gundahari was only a few years younger than Gebica had been at his death. A cold shiver clutched at her bowels as she thought of Grimhild's words to her: would she live to see Gundahari laid in a mound beside his father and mother, and drink his funeral wine like this? And would Hagan die before her, leaving her to carry out the death rites for him as well as she might, in hopes that he would sleep more easily in the grave than ever in his bed at night?

Hagan was lifting the horn again. "Drink with us, you gods and goddesses; our words be set in Wyrd." He poured the last draught on to the earth, the red wine stain darkening the dry grass, then lifted a silver bowl full of wild apples. "Seed sprout ever from fruit; we share the apples of life with you, our kin who have fared before us." He took one apple from the bowl for himself and gave one each to Gundrun and Gundahari. They ate as he did, chewing the fruit down to the seeds. The apples were barely ripe, tasting sharp and clean through the wine's heavy echo. Grimhild's three children strewed the seeds about them. Hagan laid the bowl of apples in his mother's lap.

Climbing down from the wain, he picked up the rune-carved stone and went to the edge of the grave, considering a moment before he slid it carefully down the pit's earthen side. "Bring the horses closer," Hagan said to his sister. She led them over without question, the wain creaking behind them. "Unloose them."

Hagan's sword moved so swiftly that Gundrun hardly saw its flicker before the blood of the two horses was spilling into the pit, reddening runes and stone and earth together in a single warm sheet of shining red. Gundrun barely gathered her wits in time to let go of the reins and move aside as the horses dropped.

Hagan gestured Gundahari forward, and together Grimhild's sons heaved the sorrel, then the roan into the grave. The thralls came around after that, lashing their ropes around and under the wain so that they could lower it gently in on top of the dead horses.

"Fare well, Mother," Hagan said, as softly as he was able. Gundrun murmured the words after him.

For a moment it seemed that Gundahari would say nothing, but when both his brother and sister fixed him with their gazes, he spoke clearly. "Fare well, Mother."

The three of them turned away from the grave as the thralls began to heave the roofing materials from their oxcart. Attila raised his arm, gesturing to Gundrun, but she did not speak. Although the Hunnish drighten coughed impatiently, she kept silent, hoping that Attila would not break the stillness of the burial.

"Gundahari!" Attila called, and Gundrun's breath hissed from her in an angry sigh. "While Grimhild witnesses, my wife has a boon to ask of you!"

Gundahari swung around to face Gundrun. This close, she could see her brother's lips tightening beneath his beard, his brown eyes narrowing. His feet were planted wide apart in a way she knew well, her brother rooting himself in the earth like an oak.

"What boon do you wish?" Gundahari asked. As he dragged his next words from his throat, his fist came up to clutch tight on the gold-set boar's tooth Sigifrith had given him. "My honor binds me to give it." He spoke so softly that Gundrun could hardly hear him; she was sure that no one else, except perhaps Hagan, would be able to witness his words.

Gundrun shut her eyes tightly for a moment, but she could not close out the sound of the thralls heaving wood and stone to build Grimhild's mound. "It was part of my first wedding portion, and will bring great joy to my life. I wish for a breeding pair of our horses from the Alamann stock. I cannot grow used to the Hunnish ponies. And let them be sorrel and roan, like the two that drew our mother's wain. Her memory and her wishes shall ever stay clear in my mind."

If Gundrun had not been watching Hagan closely at that moment, she would not have seen his slight nod; she was sure Attila did not mark the faint smile that glimmered on Costbera's face for a moment, but he could not have missed how the set of Gundahari's shoulders eased as she spoke. The blood darkened the Hunnish drighten's cheeks, but he could not raise his voice again.

"I will gladly give them to you in our mother's memory," Gundahari said, his voice raised so everyone could hear. "Come with me to choose them now: let them be the first gifts of her funeral arvel." He swept his arm about as though to take in all the gathered folk. "Follow us back to my hall, where we shall feast and drink this night to the honor and hallowing of my mother Grimhild's memory!"

As Gundahari took her arm and led her forth, it seemed to Gundrun that she could feel Attila's glare pressing hot on the back of her head. It would be a long faring back through the Mirkwood, and a longer winter with this strife between them; but she had awaited nothing better from this wedding, and she knew her mother's last redes had been true.

9

THE FALL

The ninth shipment of new harvest wines arrived from Worms on a clear winter's day, not long after Gundrun and those Goths of Thioderik's band who still kept to the old faith of their folk had kept the feast of Winternights. Gundrun was busy counting the casks according to the list in the letter Gundahari's steward Rumold had sent with them and directing the men who had brought them as to unloading and storage. It had been a good year along the Rhine; huge as Attila's army was and much as his men drank, she thought they would have more than enough wine to fill them through the winter. This was much to her liking; she shuddered at the thought of running out of wine and beer and having to drink the fermented mares' milk of the Huns again, as she had four winters ago. It was bad enough when the snows were at their worst and the warriors came into the great hall from their skin tents without having the threat of their thirst to deal with too.

"Frowe, Frowe," a young man's high voice called from behind her. She turned around impatiently, raising her list and the charcoal stick that she had been marking casks off with as though she would hit him with them.

"What do you want, Wolfhart? Can't you see I'm busy?"

Hildebrand's nephew smiled amiably down at her, smoothing his thin brown moustache. "I'm sorry, Gundrun. Can you stop them for a minute? There's a Roman here who says he has a message for Attila from Valentinian's warleader Aetius."

"If he's come that far, he can wait a while longer. Attila's out with the horsemen. For all I know, he's making one last quick raid before the snows set in. Have him in, sit him down and I'll be there in a while." She turned around, catching the stares of the men who had put down their casks to stand looking at her and Wolfhart. "Get back to work, you fools! You won't be fed until you're done."

When all the casks had been unloaded and stored in the locked huts behind the great hall and Gundrun had sent for thralls to bring out food and drink for the workmen, she smoothed her braids and went into the hall where she had told Wolfhart to bring the Roman.

Aetius' messenger stood stiffly braced before Attila's high seat, the end of his courier's staff planted on the earthen floor as firmly as a hall pillar. He was taller and slimmer than most Romans, olive skin planed tightly over the chiseled features of the highborn. He did not so much as glance down his thin arch of nose at Gundrun till she stepped in front of him and spoke in her best Latin, "What brings you to our hall, Roman?"

The messenger's nostrils flared, as if her speech carried the stink of old butter and garlic. "I have a message which I must give to King Attila alone," he replied sharply in Gothic. "Will you bring him to me, or direct me to him?"

"You must wait here until he returns. I do not know where he is."

"I have little time. Aetius told me that this message must be delivered and I must return at once."

"You have enough time to sit down and behave as a guest ought to! Now if you will settle yourself, I shall bring you some wine and food and then I shall send someone to search for Attila."

The Roman thumped his courier's staff on the ground. "I am not your guest, nor do I need to be." He held out a piece of folded parchment, sealed with purple wax. Gundrun recognized the emblem of Valentinian's ring; she had seen it a dozen times before on messages that Aetius had sent to her brother in the Emperor's name and on one or two of the treaties that the Burgundians had made with the Empire. "This is Valentinian's seal; you may argue with me, but not with it."

Gundrun breathed in and out slowly to keep herself from shouting at the man. After a moment's thought, she chose to speak Latin again; the time it took her to gather her words in the stranger's tongue was long enough to damp down her flare of anger. "Valentinian is a great distance from here. Comport yourself like the civilized man you claim to be and respect the practices of the one who is suggesting hospitality while I summon Attila to you."

"Are you the sister of the Burgundian chieftain Gundahari?"

"I am."

"This message is not for you. I am to give it to Attila in private. Go and find him, tell him that Aetius has a message for him and do not come back here till your husband tells you that you may."

"Hella take it if I will! Do you think I'm a slave? Get yourself and your message out of this hall. If you want Attila badly enough to insult his wife over it, you can find him yourself!" She was standing on tiptoes, shouting into the Roman's face. He pressed his lips together into a thin white line; his brown knuckles whitened against his courier's staff, and she could see him forcing his other hand out of a fist to lie flat against his thigh. "You strike me and you're a dead man," Gundrun warned him in a low voice, shaking with anger. Nine years in Attila's hall had taught her that it was best not to still her temper; the Huns might honor self-control in men, but they took any quietness in a woman as a sign of fear. "Get out of my hall, you dog, or I'll kill you myself and throw your cursed letter into the swine's wallow."

Gundrun did not know what would have happened then if Attila's two sons had not come running into the hall, shouting, "Gundrun, Mama! Atta's here!"

The Roman lifted his staff and turned on his heel, quick-marching out past the boys without looking at them.

"Who was that man?" Bleyda, the eldest, asked.

"I don't like him," his younger brother Humla added. "He looks like a Roman."

"That's because he is a Roman, stupid," Bleyda said, cuffing his brother hard on the shoulder and knocking him to the ground. "Didn't you see the stick he was carrying? I bet he came from the Emperor. I bet the Emperor wants Atta to go fight someone for him."

Humla picked himself up, glaring at Bleyda for a moment before he dived in and tackled his elder brother about the knees. The two of them went down in a heap, rolling over and over as they bit and kicked each other.

Gundrun walked over to them and shoved them apart with her foot. "That's enough of that, boys. If you want to fight, go and get your practice swords and do it outside."

"It's no fun with swords," Humla complained. "He always beats me."

"That's the way you get better. You learn by being beaten in practice, and then you don't make the same mistakes in battle."

"You don't get beaten when you practice on us. Why do you do it?"

"To teach you. Women don't have to go to battle."

"If getting hit's so good, why don't you practice with Wolfhart?" Bleyda asked. "I'd like to see that."

Gundrun looked grimly down at her eldest son, who smiled up at her. Both children had inherited her wavy hair, though it was as dark as their father's. Bleyda's eyes were blue, Humla's brown; both of them were fairer than Attila, though their skin had an odd yellowish cast to it.

"All right, you wretched brats. Go and find Wolfhart, get the cursed practice swords and I'll show you."

"Mama's going to fight! Mama's going to fight!" the boys yelped, running off.

Why am I doing this? Gundrun asked herself as she brushed a few sweaty wisps of hair from her forehead with the back of her shield hand and squared up to Wolfhart again. Attila's sons, standing at the edge of the long practice rectangle marked in the dirt, clapped their hands in anticipation. The big youth grinned down at her, looking obnoxiously untired, though she knew she had left a few bruises on him. Her own shoulder hurt so badly from the one solid blow he had managed to land that she could hardly move her shield; and she was sure that he was holding back.

"Go, Gundrun, go!" Bleyda chanted. She glared at the boy, stepping forward to close with Wolfhart. It was surprising, she thought as she swung her shield up again to crash against his wooden sword and flicked her own weapon around, how little her body had forgotten since the days when she had practiced fighting with Gundahari and Hagan. She was not thinking about blows and counter-blows, but the anger seething in her burned like dragon's blood in her veins as she began to move faster and faster. She saw Wolfhart's green eyes widening as he countered and struck, half-stumbling backward under her attack; his blows beat harder and harder against her shield, as if he had forgotten that he was sparring against Attila's wife.

"You're out!" Humla cried, pointing gleefully at Wolfhart. The young warrior glanced down at the line he had stepped over. Gundrun's wooden sword, moving too fast for her to stop it, struck his side beneath the ribs with enough force to cut him half-through if she had been using a real weapon.

Wolfhart gasped in surprise and pain, then grabbed his side and spun around into the dirt. "Oh, I'm dead, don't hit me again," he moaned, to the vast amusement of Bleyda and Humla.

Gundrun went over and clasped his arm, helping him up.

"Where did you learn to fight?" he asked her. "If you were the size of a man, you'd be the strongest warrior I ever faced."

Gundrun was still trying to decide whether she had been complimented or insulted when Wolfhart clapped her on the shoulder. "Really, I'd like to practice with you more often. A lot of the warriors don't fight as hard when they're not using steel, so it's not like real fighting."

"You were holding back, I know you were."

"At first I was. I thought you were joking when you said you wanted to spar with me, but at the end you would have pounded me into raw meat if I hadn't given you my best."

Gundrun could not help smiling. "All right, then. Frija knows, I needed to hit someone after a day like this."

"I could have done without that Roman myself. The way he came in here, you'd think they still owned the world."

A movement near the edge of the wood caught Gundrun's eye; looking intently at the bushes, she did not answer him. If she had not been watching very carefully, she would not have marked it as the Gyula rose from the underbrush; she would only have seen a mass of dry leaves and twigs, and a moment later been surprised by the small wizened figure in brown furs standing there holding a bulging fur bag in his hand. Wingi, the fair young man who followed him everywhere, appeared from the bushes less skillfully. Maybe it was because his height and large bones made him clumsier; maybe, being only half-Hun, he had only a half-portion of the uncanny blood that the dark ghost-fathers of the race had bequeathed to the Huns long ago, and therefore could not master the Gyula's craft so easily.

The practice sword in Gundrun's hand rose without her thinking about it as the Gyula and Wingi came nearer; she heard Wolfhart mumbling, "Donars, holy Warder . . . " under his breath as he touched the amber axe that hung from his throat on a leather thong.

The Gyula smiled toothlessly, spreading out his hands and letting the mouth of his sack fall open as if to show that he held nothing harmful, nothing worse than a bagfull of mushrooms whose white flecked crimson caps gleamed from the dimness. Wingi flushed as he looked away from Gundrun's gaze, his bare brown foot scuffling through the dry grass.

"Be happy, Gundrun," the old man said. "You will see your brothers before long."

"Why do you say that?" Gundrun asked, shocked by the reasonless rush of angry wod that rose in her at his words. Wingi stepped forward as if to ward her off from the Gyula, but the Hun waved him back.

"Don't you trust what I know? You shall know soon enough."

"What are you talking about? Has this something to do with the Roman?"

Laughing, as at a silent joke, the Gyula swung his bag of mushrooms up and caught it by the leather drawstring, letting the bag's weight jerk the noose at its neck tightly shut. "See what Attila has to say to you at evening-time. And if you have room in your letter, bid Hagan remember what I told him when we left each other last: that he would always come back to his father's folk."

Although it seemed to Gundrun that her eyes blurred as she watched the Gyula turn and glide toward his tent, she was still able to keep him in sight till he had raised the skin flap and vanished inside. Not speaking to her, Wingi walked after his master.

"What was he talking about?" Wolfhart said. "I thought Hagan's father—"

Gundrun grabbed him by the front of the tunic, dragging his face down to her level and glaring into his eyes. "Hagan is the son of Gebica and Grimhild. If I ever hear you say anything else, I shall cut every finger's-width of skin from your body myself and throw you into a salt stream. Do you understand me?"

S
T
E
P
H
A
N

G
R
U
N
D
Y

⊞
6
3
8

"Well, yes." He straightened up as she let him go. "I didn't mean any harm by it."

"I'm sure you didn't," Gundrun said between her teeth.

Wingi crouched down beside the Gyula, sitting on his heels and staring into the pit where the adders slithered over one another as his master spread the mushrooms out upon a drying rack of woven twigs above the coals that kept the wyrms warm. The Gyula had told him that the ghosts of their folk sometimes dwelt within the wyrms, telling him things in words only the wise could hear, and Wingi too should come to understand their speech one day if he dwelt with his master long enough.

"Attila has work for you," the Gyula said to him, speaking in the high singsong speech of the Huns as he always did when they were alone. Though Wingi's father had been a Goth, and he had been baptized in Arian fashion, Wingi spoke the tongue of his mother with an ease that none of Thioderik's other Goths could gain. It was the speech of wisdom to him: the speech of the true tribe, whose ways were dark to all the foolish folks about them, Goths and Romans alike.

"What work has he, my eldest grandfather?" Wingi asked. The title was one of honor; he was no blood-kin to the Gyula, but the aged loremaster had no one else to teach his arts to.

The Gyula leaned down to the slithering adders, as though listening to their hissing. "You must bear a message to Worms, to Gundrun's kin. Beware what you say; there is great danger for you in this faring, if you are not careful."

"The Burgundians have forgotten even the ways of the Gothic folk," Wingi answered in disgust. "They remember nothing of the wisdom we shared once, that their Sinwist brought from the steppes when they fled before our might. What is there to fear from them?"

"Hagan is wiser than you think; he might have become a mighty master of lore among us in his time, if he were not bound so tightly to his own kin. Beware of him, and of your own words." The Gyula gestured toward the tent flap. "Go now, and listen to what Attila and this Roman have to say."

Wingi bowed from his squat, brushing his forehead against the dry earth. "Thank you, my eldest grandfather."

The hall door was locked, but the Gyula had taught Wingi to open it long ago—half a skill of the ghost, half a cleverness of twisted wire. He slipped in almost as silently as his master could, creeping up behind Attila who sat by the fire with his back to the door, and the Roman who stood leaning on his staff as though he feared to soil his uniform on Attila's benches.

"I have no wish to anger the gods and ghosts of my folk," Attila was saying. "Rome is far, and they are near. I have seen no sign that your Christ's power might stretch toward me from them."

"We think it more fitting to deal with Christian folk, with whom we share a single faith and a single way. Let our priests and bishops come among your men, with churches to house them and Latin writing to keep tallies of lands and goods and folk, and you will see how much more smoothly your realm runs. Many kings have found that a well-ruled Christian soul leads to a well-ruled Christian land, where men understand that God has set their ruler over them, and Church and king work to a single goal."

"A fair thought, if it succeeds," Attila grunted. "But I have not seen that Christianity has done my Goths any good. Thioderik is still an exile, and his men follow him because he is of the Amalung line, not because a priest tells them to."

"Thioderik is an Arian," Aetius' messenger corrected. "But let us talk of a matter closer to hand. You might say that the Burgundian ruler Gundahari is still a heathen, yet he rules a great realm."

"That is so. Holding to the ways of his folk has done him no ill."

"But the Empire looks another way on it. We have no common cause with Gundahari, who is no kinsman of ours in Christ. Indeed, we see the Burgundians as a danger looming at the edge of our lands, a threat to the lives and souls of all the Christians under our rule and those with whom we are allied. In the last years, the Burgundian realm under Gundahari has grown far too great for Rome's comfort. Now, if something were to befall this proud king—if he were to visit his kinswoman in this hall for the heathen Midwinter's feast, and some mischance came to happen along the way—Rome would consider it a judgment of God and be greatly pleased with its earthly instruments. Should this come to pass in full safety, you might indeed take it as a sign of the might of our Christ, in whose sign we conquer."

The Roman sketched a sign over his breast. Wingi spat silently on the floor.

"I might," Attila said grudgingly. "Now tell me of what favor Aetius would show me if I do this. It is a long way to Rome; what help can he send me before the deed is done? I cannot tell how many men the Burgundians will bring, for the trust between us is not endless."

"Half a hundred trained soldiers are already drawn up but a few days' march away," the messenger answered smoothly.

Wingi had heard enough; he slipped away and out of the hall as silently as he had come. He would bring Gundahari and Hagan to the Huns' hall, in truth. It would not do for them to come with too many folk—the Huns would have to win the day, in the end—but he had already made up his mind to warn the Burgundians as they arrived at Attila's hall, so they would not be caught unawares and could offer enough fight that Attila would not dare to think of forsaking the gods and ghosts of their folk again, no matter what favor Rome might offer him.

It was not yet evening when Attila came to Gundrun, grinning as he waved a scrap of parchment, a quill and an ink stick at her. "Will you be glad to see your kin again?"

"Do you mean that we are going to Worms? It is a long ride through the Mirkwood," Gundrun said cautiously. Her anger had sunk into a quivering at the pit of her stomach; she did not know what it might have meant. She pulled her cloak more tightly about her shoulders, its wolfskin edging brushing roughly against her neck.

"I am bidding Gundahari and Hagan here for our Yule feast, where I shall offer them much honor. Aetius, too, is not unimpressed with the way the might of the Burgundians has grown in the past years, and this sign of friendship shall be much to his liking."

"Was this the idea of your Roman? What sort of feast do you mean to set?"

"One which befits their great deeds," Attila answered. "Now I should like for you to write them some word of bidding at the bottom of the message, and sign it according to whatever the custom of your folk is so they shall know it is you who has sent it."

Gundrun took the parchment from his hand, spelling the smoothly rounded Latin letters out slowly to herself. It was as he had said: greetings, and the bidding of Gundahari and Hagan to a feast at Midwinters'.

A bird's sharp wordless cry seemed to pierce through her skull; Gundrun started, looking around.

"What's wrong?" Attila asked her, reaching out to lay his hand on her shoulder as if to steady her by his touch as though she were a skittish horse.

"Nothing. Why do you need me to sign this? It is clearly written enough, and there is hardly room left for me to write more than a letter or two."

"If you don't want to . . . " Attila moved as if to take the parchment back. Gundrun stepped away from him.

"I didn't say I wouldn't."

Gundrun squatted down, laying the message across her knee. She spat on the ink stick, rubbing the quill back and forth on it. Hagan knew the runes at least as well as she had taught them to him: a simple message, easily unraveled and read, would put an end to whatever her husband was planning.

The first rune she scratched was *raidho*, the rune of journeying: ᚱ . Behind it, larger, she scratched the stave called *thurisaz*, or sometimes thorn, ᚦ , its sharp point piercing through the *raidho*'s stem to form its upper angle: ᚱ . Together, they shaped a bind-rune of warning: the journey would be threatened by thorns and ill wights, the faring would be a faring of doom. But then, as she blew on the ink to dry it, she thought that Hagan might well take the warning stave as a bidding to himself: Hagan, the Hedge-Thorn, thus given rede to make the journey.

RH
I
N
E
G
O
L
D

ᚼ
6
4
1

Sigifrith's dragon ring came off her finger as easily as if it had not clung to her hand for seventeen years. Hagan will send it back to me, she thought, and then knew that if she thought any more she would never be able to let it go. Gundrun pulled a long wolf's hair out of the trim on her cloak and knotted it about the ring, wrapping both in the parchment.

Attila's slanted eyes narrowed to black slits as he watched her. "What do you mean by that?"

"There wasn't enough space for me to get a clear message in. But this will tell my brothers that if they do not bring my ring back to me themselves, they shall bear the shame of being as wargs," Gundrun lied boldly. "It is a common custom among our folk."

Her husband nodded in satisfaction as she laid the message into his open palm. "Very good."

"Where is the Roman?"

"I have sent him away. He told me that your mood seemed unfriendly toward him." Attila laughed, drawing her close in to him with an arm about her shoulders. The hard leather byrnie he wore creaked against her cheek; Gundrun closed her eyes, letting him stroke her coiled braids. It seemed to her that she could feel the shadow lying in his very bones, winding deep into the soul of the sword at his side; she did not fear, but her senses pricked her on to a wakeful wariness.

"Will you try the new wine?" she asked. "While you were off riding, I had it unloaded and stored."

"So you were fighting with Wolfhart today," Attila said later, as he and Gundrun sat before the fire at the end of his hall. He had drunk six large cups of wine, and the flush on his broad cheeks glowed through his swarthy skin. "That must have been what my dream foreboded."

"What did you dream?" Gundrun had drunk but little; every now and again she would glance at the bare finger beside Attila's circle of garnets, and a deep ache would spear up the bone of her arm from where Sigifrith's ring had rested.

"I dreamed that you laid about me with a sword!" He chuckled and emptied his cup again, holding it out for her to refill. "Ah, my little mare, fierce as you are, I think you are not so strong of temper as that."

"You're drunk," she told him flatly. "You ought to go to bed. You only talk like that when you're drunk."

He unpinned one of her braids and grasped it firmly near the root, tugging her head toward him. "Of course I'm not drunk. I was raised on a wine brewed from mare's milk. Do you think this Gaulish grape can touch me?"

"I think you're drunk."

"I had other dreams, too," he said, letting her go suddenly. "Hagan told me that the women of your folk are able to read dreams."

"Some are. Tell me."

"I dreamed, and it was as if two reeds were growing here, and I wished never to harm them. Then they were ripped up by the roots and reddened in blood and born to the bench and given to me to eat. Then I dreamed that two hawks flew from my hands, but they were without prey and fared thus to the ghost-lands. It seemed to me that their hearts were blended with honey, and I thought that I ate them. After that it was as if two fair whelps lay before me and barked aloud, and I ate of their flesh against my will."

Gundrun was about to speak as Attila heaved himself to his feet, flinging the rest of his wine to hiss and sputter in the fire. As the steam scorched up, he whirled to bang his cup down on the table behind him, then drew his sword and slashed it through the regathering flames. "Now may my god fend the ill omen from me! You do not need to say anything about this, and if you do I shall cut your head from your shoulders."

"I'll say what I like!" Gundrun answered. "Put that sword away and go to bed. You've had far too much to drink, and that often brings bad dreams. But I think these have more meaning to them than wine, and whatever you had thought of doing you should think of doing something else. And that is all of my rede: you may take it, or Hella may take you."

"Don't try to frighten me, woman. I can get a wife to take your place whenever I choose. Didn't my concubine Hedlo just bear me a son, and a son of pure Hunnish blood at that?"

"You can't put another wife in my place if you want to keep peace between you and the Burgundian folk."

Attila stood unsteadily, glaring down at her for a few moments before he sheathed his sword. He turned and walked off toward their chamber, stopping at the door to look back. "Follow me," he ordered. "I shall get a son tonight."

"Not on me. The Moon is just past dark and my blood is flowing."

The Hunnish drighten spat into the fire and touched the amber eagle's head on his sword's sheath to turn the threatened curse aside, then closed the door behind him. Gundrun took her cloak off and wrapped it about herself like a blanket, lying down on the bench in hopes that she would be able to get to sleep that night.

The weather in Worms stayed bright for almost a month after the Winternights Feast; then, a little before the full moon of Blotmonth, the biting winds from the north whirled a bitter snowstorm down upon the city. Even Hagan stayed inside more often, going from his house to Gundahari's hall and coming back from one to the other whenever it seemed to him that others were not bearing his nearness easily. Of his own children, only Nibel—now grown almost to a man's full height and strength—was willing to bundle himself in his warmest cloak and follow his father through the frozen streets to sit near the other warriors by the king's fire.

So it happened that the two of them were there when the faint knock sounded against the door of Gundahari's hall, beating softly beneath the talk and laughter of the men gathered on the full benches.

No one else looked up at the noise; if Hagan and Nibel had not marked it, it would have sounded unheard. No louder, it fell again, unsure as if the knocker's hand trembled from cold on the door. Nibel rose to his feet.

"I will go," Hagan said, forestalling him. He walked quietly to the outer door and opened it.

Outside stood a shape so thickly bundled in furs that Hagan could hardly tell it was human, let alone know who it was at first. But the furry cap pulled down over its ears was cut in the Hunnish style, although the head beneath had not been lengthened. The man's hands were muffled in mittens with the fur turned inward, but Hagan recognized the gesture of warding he made. This man was not the Gyula: he was too tall, and light eyes gleamed from under snow-whitened brows as he muttered the word of protection that went with the gesture.

"Greetings, Wingi," Hagan said. "What brings you to us so late in the year?"

"How did you know my name?" The slight folds at the corners of Wingi's blue eyes deepened as he squinted up at Hagan. "I was scarcely two when you left Attila's band."

"It is too cold for you to stand outside. Come in and warm yourself, and tell us what news you have of our sister." Hagan stepped back from the door to let the shaman's youth in.

"What have you found out there in the snow?" Gundahari shouted from his seat at the other end of the hall. "It looks like a lost wood-wight to me!"

Hagan led the shivering man through the hall to stand before his brother. "This is Wingi, whom Attila has sent to us with a message of some considerable meaning. When he has had a chance to warm himself, shall we hear it out here or in your chambers?"

Gundahari seemed to consider a moment, leaning heavily on the arms of his chair as he looked down at Attila's messenger. "What manner of message is it?"

"A message of joy and honor," Wingi answered, as smoothly as he could through chattering teeth. "If you will give me leave to stand by your fire for a while, I shall tell you everything—though it were better done in private, since what Attila has to say is something that should not be known to everyone."

"But Gundrun is well?"

"She is very well, and sends her greetings and thanks for the fine wine which you sent at the beginning of this winter."

Gundahari nodded, stroking at his short-cropped beard. Although this was his thirty-seventh winter, no gray hairs had yet invaded its darkness. "Hai!" he called. "Build up the fires!"

Thralls and serving men hurried with more logs to feed the flames till they roared up on either side of the hall. Feeling oddly uncomfortable in the new warmth, Hagan moved back past Gundahari's seat; but Wingi spread his cloak out and crouched so closely to the fire on the left side that Hagan began to look about for water to quench the half-Hun's clothes with before the blaze he seemed to be courting could spread through the hall.

Glamwer was coming out of the kitchen, a pitcher of wine in each of her large, bony hands.

"There is a guest here you will need to greet," Hagan told her.

Glamwer started, slopping wine on to the flagstones. "You startled me," she accused him. "Why can't you stand where people can see you instead of sneaking up on them?" Gundahari's Ostrogothic wife glared short-sightedly up at Hagan, her fair eyebrows drawing together in disapproval.

"Attila has sent a messenger to us. I think he shall wish food and hot wine."

"You know where the kitchen is," she said. "Tell them to see to it. Oh, never mind, I'll do it myself."

They had all drunk several cups of hot spiced wine by the time Wingi was ready to go to the king's chambers with Hagan and Gundahari. Gundahari could feel the drink's heat flushing his face, but his thoughts were as clear as if the winter's icy wind blew through his head. There was something he misliked about this fair young man, whose blue eyes were slanted like a Hun's in his wind-scorched face. Gundahari could not put a name or a shape to his misgivings, but could not deny them either. The Gebicung rubbed absently at the twinned scars of the old adder's bite below his left thumb, trying to think if he had heard Wingi's name before.

Glamwer followed them, setting down another pitcher of warmed wine on the table with the slow care of the short-sighted. The sharp angles of her body jutted against her cloak as she moved; though they had been wedded ten years now, childbearing had not rounded her long shape to softness, and none of her bairns had lived past infancy. Gundahari sometimes thought to take a second wife in hopes of getting stronger children, but he had not had much time to consider the matter. There was always something else that needed to be done first. I should, he thought as Glamwer walked from the room. I should have heirs by now . . .

Wingi took the Hunnish skin cap from his head, letting his braided hair fall free, and pulled a piece of rolled parchment out from an inner pocket in his clothing. "Attila the king sends me here," he began to recite, "and wishes that you visit him in great honor, and receive from him great honor, helmets and shields, swords and byrnies, gold and fine clothing, hosts and heroes and great lands, for he says that he is best pleased to bestow his power upon you." The half-Hun unwrapped the parchment, catching the small object that fell from it and hiding it in his fist before he gave the message to Gundahari.

Gundahari traced slowly over the letters with the tip of one finger. His lips moved as he read, whispering each sound to himself. He had struggled with Latin for most of his life, since a king could not be without it in these times, but it had never come easily to him; he often wished that Hagan had learned to read the Roman tongue, for he was sure his brother would be better at it than he. It took him some time to unravel the message, but at last he said, "Attila gives us greetings and bids us to visit him at Midwinter time."

"He says that," Wingi broke in, "and Gundrun sent you this also, to show you that it is needful for you to come."

He opened his fist, letting the thing he held roll out onto the table. The firelight spattered into glittering sparks over the tiny golden scales of Andward's dragon ring, pooling dark red in the stone around which the wyrm wound. Something marred the smooth twist of the dragon's tail halfway along the band: a long wolf hair was wound thrice around it and knotted thrice.

Gundahari sat pondering the ring for a moment. It stirred something that had lain in the depths of his soul for the past years, quieted by the swift growth of his realm's might and the awe in men's voices when they spoke his name. But once the hero's portion had not been his by right, and his claim had been a glittering ring wrapped around empty bone.

As a king must, Gundahari had long since learned to show his feelings when he needed to and hide them when they were best hidden. Now he spoke calmly to Hagan, giving no sign that he recognized the ring which Gundrun would never let go from her—the ring which had been Sigifrith's. "How shall we take this offer? Attila bids us to take power from him; but in the nine years since Gundrun wedded him, we have grown so that there is no need to fear him. I think that there are no kings who have as much gold as we. As it is said, 'I know my horse is the best, my sword the keenest, my gold the most awesome.'"

Hagan's eye did not turn away from the ring; it seemed to Gundahari that he could see its red glitter reflected deep in his brother's icy gaze. At last Hagan said, "I did not expect such an offer, for he has seldom done such things and we would be ill-advised to fare to his home. I was surprised to see the warg's hair knotted around the gold ring with Attila's message. It may be that Gundrun thinks that Attila's soul is wolfish toward us, and that she does not want us to go."

"The other message she sent will make it clearer," Wingi insisted. "Look closely . . . there, at the bottom of the parchment, beneath her signature. Can you read the runes she risted?"

Gundahari handed the parchment over to Hagan, who brought it close to his eye.

"The runes are a little smeared," he said, "and there is a smudge above them, as if she rubbed out something miswritten, but they are not hard for me to understand. First she must have written a *raidho*-rune"—he traced the stave, ᚱ , on the parchment—"that stave should speak of the faring. Behind it, here, is a larger *wunjo*, the rune of joy: ᚹ. See how its upper angle pierces through the *raidho* to bind the staves, thus: ᚱ. She seems to urge us to come." Hagan paused; his next words came more slowly. "Still, this ring is an uncanny thing for her to have sent to bid us to a faring of joy."

"I remember what I was told of it," Wingi interrupted hurriedly. "Attila said that she said it was to mean that if you did not bring her ring back to her, you would bear a warg's curse."

The fire seemed to glitter round and round the ring, as though the little dragon shifted in its endless watch. Gundahari saw Hagan move his hand toward it then pull back, as though he could not turn away from it but did not wish to take it up.

"She wouldn't have let it go if she didn't mean for us to bring it back," Gundahari could not help muttering, and thought: if she is still alive, there is something dire in this sign. "I think it was the dearest thing she had, after . . . " After Sigifrith. But he would not say that aloud, not to this half-Hun and still less to Hagan.

"She must trust you greatly," Wingi said. "All Attila's bidding would not take it from her hand, though it was hardly fitting for her to keep the sign of such an ill-fated wedding by her."

It seemed to Gundahari that the tight corners of Wingi's lips reined back a smile, but the Gebicung spoke civilly enough, though he had no hope of a truthful reply. "How does Gundrun fare with Attila? Is she happy with the match our mother made for her, and content to be queen over the Hunnish folk?"

"She lives well enough. Attila is more patient with her than he would be with another woman, for he loves her well. He has turned from the ways of the Huns in this, that he lets her have rule over herself and such things of the household as she chooses, just as if she were one of his thanes. The king's sons are growing into large and fine youths in whom the ancient and holy blood of their father's kin runs strong; they are like him in all ways, so that no one can say Attila did ill to take a foreign woman as his wife."

They spoke of such things for a while, passing over the matter of Attila's invitation like water spiders skittering over the surface of a pond. To Gundahari's surprise, it was not Glamwer who came to pour more wine when they had been talking for a while, but Costbera, wrapped in a thick fur cloak with the melting snow still dripping from its folds.

"What are you doing out in this weather?" Hagan asked his wife. "I should have thought you would have stayed at home with the children. Has Alfarik's fever broken yet?"

"It has," Costbera answered. "He is much better than he was." She looked down at the floor, where the firelight glimmered in the puddles about her feet. "I became frightened," she went on, her voice so soft that Gundahari could hardly hear it, "and came to see where you and Nibel had been staying so long."

"We shall be here longer yet, I think. You need not be afraid."

RHINEGOLD ᚻ 6 4 7

Gundahari patted Costbera awkwardly on the shoulder as she filled his cup. He remembered that she was a learned woman—and more than that, she was a Christian who often dealt with Latin writings: he could not deny that the ways of Christianity matched well with the Empire.

"Will you read something for me?" he asked her.

"Yes. What?"

"Have a look at this letter, if you will, and tell me what you make of it."

Costbera put her pitcher down and took up the message. Her gaze scanned swiftly over the parchment, down to linger on the signatures, then up to the writing again. Gundahari saw the worried crease graven in her brow growing deeper as she thought over what was written there.

"Attila gives you greeting and wishes you to come to his feast in the middle of winter—he must mean Yule—there. This is likely to have been written by a real Roman at his asking; the grammar and the hand are as fine as I have ever seen, and his signature is very different from the writing." She put the parchment down carefully, well away from where the ring rested, as though its mirrored fire might scorch the fine sheepskin.

"Hah!" Gundahari said, feeling the solid coal of triumph that kindled in him whenever he succeeded in understanding a piece of Latin writing. He laughed as he drank. "You see, I unraveled it well!"

Hagan picked up the parchment, but his gaze never left the darkness bound within the gold ring. "Why should a Roman have come to Attila? Why should a Roman care whether we go to his feasting or not? They are still a proud folk, not a race of tame scribes."

"There are many people who pass through Attila's lands, and he is—as you are, Gundahari—bound to Rome by treaty. Truly, it should be no surprise that a Roman traveler should guest overnight in his hall, and was willing to do a small favor at our drighten's bidding."

"Shall I bring more wine?" Costbera asked, topping up their cups with the last of her pitcher.

The green-blue glass lent an odd cast to the deep red wine, as though some subtle rot had crept into the grapes. Gundahari's cellars held better than this, but its color reminded him of the rich Gaulish wine Grimhild had drunk—the wine they had drunk at her funeral.

"Bring out the best we have," he answered her. "I think now is the time to drink it."

The three of them had been drinking and talking for some time when Wingi leaned unsteadily forward and said, "There's something else . . . the most secret message, about Attila. You know there's no drighten to compare to him—except, of course, yourself and Valentinian's warleader Aetius," Wingi added hastily, and Gundahari realized that the half-Hun was not so drunk as he seemed. "But he's getting old—just past fifty winters, very old for leading his warband. Far too old for a Hunnish leader," Wingi added, his pale eyes glittering adder-cold for a moment. "It's work for a young man who can ride all day and sleep in the saddle. But Bleyda's only nine and his brother Humla is seven. They're too young to rule the host."

"Go on," Gundahari told him, gripping the bottom of his wine glass more tightly as his heart beat faster. "What are you trying to say?" If Brunichild had borne the child that lay in her womb, that bairn would have been old enough to take up weapons in the host by now, Gundahari thought—not so much younger than I at my father's death. But old as he is, and young as they are, even Attila has living heirs—and I have none.

"I shouldn't be telling you this," the young messenger said, leaning so close that Gundahari could almost feel the heat of the wine flush in his reddened cheeks. "He wanted to surprise you with it, you see. But your brother over there doesn't trust Attila. It's too bad when a man's own brother-in-law doesn't trust him."

"Tell us what you have to say," Hagan ordered, fixing Wingi with his cold gaze. The messenger swallowed his mouthful of wine the wrong way; he was just able to turn his head in time to keep from showering a spray of the drink over Gundahari.

"Don't frighten him, Hagan. Let him speak."

"You're mother's brother to Attila's sons, Gundahari," Wingi said when he got his breath back. "No one's closer kin to them. That's why he wants you to rule over his lands till they've come of age. He can trust you to watch out for Gundrun's children, and he'd rather have you profit from his realm while they're growing up than another."

"And has he ceased to desire the Rhine's gold?" Gundahari asked. "I have not forgotten what he said when we last spoke of gifts and kin."

"Attila says that he holds by far the fairest part of Sigifrith's marriage portion." Wingi smirked. "He says it is easy to tell why Sigifrith chose your sister above Brunichild, the daughter of Theoderid."

It seemed to Gundahari that the wine had not fogged his memory, but cleared it to the keenness of glass shards. This wyrd had been long in turning: since Brunichild's death, he had not heard her name spoken in any voice save that of his own thought, but now the flame-glittering ring blurred in his vision until it seemed to him that he stood before the wall of Brunichild's fire again, ready to plunge in on his own feet after his horse had failed him, with the cry of despair surging up in his chest like a wave rising and rising before it broke.

It was Hagan's stone-cold voice that brought Gundahari's mind back to the matter before them: "This seems hardly likely to me. I remember that Attila would no more loosen his grasp on any might or wealth that he thought ought to be his than he would loosen his right arm from his shoulder."

Although Wingi's words answered Hagan, the messenger stared at Gundahari. "Attila was young when you knew him, Hagan; you've been away a long time." He raised both fists together, then opened them slowly. "Will you let this slip from your grasp, Gundahari? Sigifrith was not so frightened of the Hunnish folk, though he dwelt near to our borders."

The cry surged up in Gundahari's throat as he grasped the table edge and heaved himself to his feet. "Before the gods, I am not afraid of Attila or his folk! Do not speak of Sigifrith to me again, if you wish to keep breath in your body! This faring seems better and better to me; you have no need to shame me into it. Even though my brother should be fearful, I am not— even if Attila had sent you with a call to face death in battle rather than feasting with kin I should go, and go gladly!"

Hagan stood as well, facing his brother. "Say what you will; but if you listen to my rede, you will think longer on it before going. Even Sigifrith's strength could not ward him well enough to keep him alive; will you walk into the hall of a man who is so greedy for your gold, and may think to have good reason to betray you?"

"Don't speak of Sigifrith to me again!" Gundahari shouted. His breath was coming in harsh pants, like the breath of a wild boar at bay; like the boar, he could only strike with his tusks at the spear that gored him, his fury the sole answer he could make to the death whose long tooth bit him already. "It was you who counseled me to his death; and you slew him even when I said that there would be no more hunting that day, though the brightest hope of our folk lived in him. In such things, your rede to me has been no better than the rede your father gave my mother!"

The glass cup in Hagan's hand shattered, spraying green-blue shards and crimson drops over the table. Gundahari felt himself paling at the sharp crack, the blood falling all at once from his face like the wine from Hagan's broken glass. Then he set his jaw firmly, rucking up his shoulders as though bracing himself to charge.

"Are you afraid?" Gundahari asked his brother softly. "Has it always been fear that held you back? You never came before me in battle or when we were hunting boar, nor have you ever taken the hero's portion at feast."

"If you doubt my bravery, you may judge it by this: I say that your choice in this matter must stand, and I must follow you, although I am not eager for this faring. You should not have said what you did; you shall not say it again. When shall we leave?"

"Tomorrow, as soon as everything can be made ready." Gundahari leaned against the heavy oak of the table's edge for a moment. His head was spinning; he had drunk too much wine, and its flow tide was beginning to whelm him now. "With the weather as bad as it is, we shall need all the time we have if we are to reach Attila's hall in time for Yule."

"Then you may stay here and drink, or go to bed as you choose. I shall see to what needs to be done."

And this one last time, Gundahari thought, I shall try to get an heir with my wife; but he knew already that his struggle would be of no use.

"Let us drink on it first!" said Wingi heartily. "Don't leave in anger; that would be a bad start to a faring of joy."

Attila's messenger lifted his cup and drank, passing it to Gundahari afterward. A hint of musky saltiness strengthened the Gaulish wine's heavy fruit; he drank slowly, thinking of how Brunichild had kissed him when she first knew that a child lay in her womb.

Only a few drops were left clinging to the blue-green glass when Gundahari passed the cup to his brother; but Hagan spilled them over his tongue, tasting the cold earth that lay beneath the wine's richness. Then he put the cup down and took the dragon ring, slipping it on to the middle finger of his right hand. Its gold burned hot and pure on him, as though it had just come from the smith's fire; its weight seemed to drag his arm down to the earth, but at the same time its scaly curves felt so smooth and comfortable against his hand that he might have borne it forever.

Hagan strode out of his brother's chamber, closing the door beside him. Nibel was only a few steps down the corridor; but the torches were out and, dark as it was, no one else might have noticed him.

"How long were you there?" Hagan asked his son as the young man fell into step beside him.

"Since you went in."

Costbera was waiting by the fire when Hagan and Nibel came in, stamping snow from their boots and shaking crystals of melting ice from their cloaks before hanging the wet garments by the fire. "I must talk to you alone," she said to Hagan at once.

"In your bedchamber? Or here?"

"Out here."

Hagan looked at his son, who smiled at him before walking over to kiss Costbera on the cheek. "Good night, Mother," Nibel said. "Good night, Father. Wake me when it's time to go." He glided quietly out, as if going to the room that he shared with Alfarik and Adalulf.

Hagan sat down near his wife, waiting for her to speak again. But Costbera only sat staring into the fire. The low flames showed her paler than usual, the scars of worry wrinkled deep between her eyes and around the corners of her mouth.

"What is wrong?" he asked. "Why are you so distressed?"

"Do you really mean to go to Attila's hall?"

"Gundahari has decided to, and I must go with him."

"If you mean to go, that is ill-reded. It would be better if you went at another time. And you're not so good at reading runes if you think your sister had bidden you to come."

"What do you mean? Why are you speaking to me like this? I never knew you had learned to read the runes."

Costbera turned her face to Hagan, and in the soft light he could see through the flesh that sagged along her cheeks and jawbones—see the frightened girl he had married, who had flinched from her first sight of him and whose bravery had just been enough to hold her still beneath his touch.

"When I was young, before I became a Christian, I was taught some lore. I read the runes tonight, and I was surprised that a woman as wise as Gundrun could have written them in such a confused way. But underneath I could feel that she had meant to show your death, and I know that someone must have tampered with them after she had finished writing."

Hagan looked down at the dull gleam of the fire shining from the ruby on his hand; it seemed that he, too, could see the sharp line at the top of the bind-rune where it had been scratched into a smear, warping the warning thorn into the stave of joy.

Costbera's voice trembled when she said, "And now you shall hear my dreams. I dreamed that a raging river seemed to sweep into the hall and broke up the great stocks that stand to either side of the end hearth."

"There is no need to expect evil without cause," Hagan answered her, speaking as Thioderik had often spoken to him. "It may be that Attila will welcome us."

"If you test it, you'll find that there is nothing friendly about his bidding. And I dreamed that your bed-clothes were burning, and fire shot up from the hall."

"Our cloaks are hanging too near the fire. We must move them away before we go to bed."

The corners of Costbera's mouth were trembling as she looked up into his face. She had not come so close to him since Sigifrith's death, but now she whispered so that he had to bend closer to hear her, "I thought an eagle came into the hall and sprinkled me and all of us with blood, and that must show something ill, for it seemed to me that it was the fetch of King Attila."

Hagan remembered the eagle's head of carven amber sewn to the sheath of the war-god's sword; he had always seen the brooding beak and the hooded eyes in Attila's swarthy face, and now he knew how true Costbera's sight might be. Still he said, "We do a lot of slaughtering and strike down great beasts for our enjoyment. Dreaming about eagles has to do with oxen. Attila will be of a good spirit toward us. I expect no more treachery from these dreams than I had before."

"Hagan, you would be better if you did not go. Stay here, at least till spring; if you must see Gundrun, invite her here to you."

"Why should you say this? I have thought more than once that you would be happier in another place than the one you have now."

"I think you have never wished ill toward me, and I cannot wish it to you. But if you must go, at least do not take our sons with you. Will you swear that to me?"

"That I shall swear. I had not meant to take them, although they are all of age to go to war now; but there is something for which Nibel must stay behind."

"What?"

"That is between myself and him."

"As you wish." Hagan could see the water filling her dark eyes, the golden-orange flickers of the fire mirrored in it as Costbera rose from her seat. For a moment Hagan thought that she might take a step forward to embrace him, but she only said, "Please wake me before you leave."

"I shall."

Nibel came into the room so swiftly after his mother had left that Hagan knew he had been listening at the door.

"What is it?" the youth asked his father. "Why must I stay? Do you expect me to take care of the women while you go off to battle?"

"There is something else that must be taken care of, and I trust no one else."

"What?"

"Come with me."

Hagan and his son crept through the streets to the edge of the Rhine, following the snowy bank along its rushing ice-edged road. Hagan had never asked Nibel if he could hear the voices murmuring from the river; it seemed to him that it was something of which the living should not speak. Although he kept his ringed hand hidden beneath his thick mantle, he knew that the ones who dwelt below could feel that Andward's ring had come back to the banks of the Rhine. He could hear their restless murmuring in the voices of the water; and so he trod cautiously along the snowy path, careful of hidden slicks of ice and traps woven of rotten sticks beneath the soft white blanket. For he knew that if he should slip he would never come breathing out of the river again.

The outcropping of black-mossed stone was almost hidden beneath the snow, only a few dark patches of rock showing through its white shroud. But Hagan had come to this place often enough before; in only a few paces his foot scraped against the trapdoor. The might of the gold thrummed up through the soles of his boots, warm even through the layers of ice crystals that hid the stone.

"Can you find this place again?" he whispered to his son.

"I know I can," Nibel answered, just as softly. He glanced back over his shoulder toward the Rhine as though he expected to be overheard. "I've been here a hundred times before. Is it a holy stead? I've always felt—"

"Not holy. Beneath us is the stronghold where Fadhmir's hoard has lain since Sigifrith brought it here." Hagan drew the key to the stone chamber, which had hung around his neck for sixteen years, out from beneath his tunic and byrnie and pulled the chain over his head. "See, here is the door and here is the key. I am giving it into your keeping; but you must be careful to tell no one, for it could well be the end of your life if you did."

"Is the treasure as great as the songs say?"

"It was, as is told, the dragon's broad bed; and that wrought by the craft of the ancient dwarves." Hagan pushed back the sleeve of his byrnie to show his son the eagle-headed arm-ring that still coiled above his wrist. "You have seen this often enough before; it was part of the hoard, as was this ring."

"It must be fine to look upon," Nibel mused.

"You must not think about it. Fadhmir's gold has bred nothing good since it was taken out of the Rhine. What you must do is hold this key and keep the secret silent, and you must do nothing more. Do you swear?"

Nibel straightened himself to his full height, slim as an upright spear. He set his left hand on the hilt of his sword and raised his right. "I swear, unless there is a time of such need that I have no other choice."

"Well enough." Hagan draped the key's chain over the right hand by which his son had sworn. "Now you shall be the keeper of the gold, for as long as I do not come back."

Nibel put the chain over his own neck, letting the key fall beneath his tunic where it could not be seen.

"Now go home and sleep. I shall wake you well before we leave. I think Gundahari will not be rising too early tomorrow."

"But where shall you be? Aren't you coming home?"

"Not yet. I want to stay here for a while."

"All right."

Hagan watched Nibel till he could see him no longer. It was hard for him to believe the easy grace with which his son moved through the woods, rustling no more twigs than a slight breeze might stir. We shall travel well armed with as many of our thanes as we can gather tomorrow and be ready for treachery, he reminded himself. Though his warband has grown greatly since I fought in it, he is still not likely to attack us unless he thinks he has a clear victory. If we are watchful enough . . .

As he thought, he walked farther along the riverbank. The snowflakes glimmering through the darkness fell smaller and fewer, finally stopping altogether; now that the wind had stopped, the snowy wood seemed oddly warm. After a while he took off his cloak, folding the heavy garment over his arm. Then the ice struck through the iron of his byrnie, chilling deep into his bones. He knew that he could not ease the bitter cold by putting the cloak back on; there was not enough heat in his body to warm the metal again. Loath though he was to do it, he bent over and shook the byrnie off his shoulders, wrapping it in his cloak to protect his arm from the ice.

The first light of morning was showing through the clouds when Hagan heard the harsh calling of wild swans above him. He looked up through the white-laden branches of the trees to see the three great white birds circling slowly down from the silvery sky, as if they meant to land on the jetty of heaped rocks that jutted out into the river. The wind of their wings seemed to stir his hair; the women's voices echoed high and pure beneath the hissing and calling of the swans, and Hagan drew back into the wood so that they might not see him.

"There are no men about."

"No men on the shore, no men in the wood, no boats on the rushing river."

"Only the river-ghosts, water-wights hidden, wait in the dark of the stones."

"The dawn is brightening; here may we bathe?"

"Here on this march between river and shore?"

"Here we are safe? May lay feathers aside?"

"Unthreatened, unseen by Middle-Garth's wights?"

"We may wash us in peace, sisters all."

Hagan bit his breath into silence as the three swans landed on the rocks of the jetty with a great fanning and rustling of wings. Then he was stilled by awe as they cast off their cloaks of white feathers, rising from the three snowy pools on the rocks. The swans were maidens as tall and fair as birches, their pale skin and hair gleaming in the light of dawn as they slipped silently into the dark icy waters of the Rhine. They sank and rose again, staring raptly toward the east where Sunna's brightness turned the clouds to blood-tinged silver.

Hagan made no noise as he laid his cloak-muffled byrnie down and slipped his boots from his feet. He gathered his strength in stillness.

A single rush took him out onto the jetty. The swan-maidens' fingers just grazed the feathers of their garments as Hagan swept the three white cloaks up in his arm. Their dark eyes opened wide as they sank back down into the water; they threw their heads back in a single piercing keen of loss, white throats and breasts gleaming against the blackness of the river.

Hagan stood waiting till the echoes of their cry had faded into the rocks beneath his feet.

"I shall not harm you or your cloaks," he told them. "Only answer my questions, and then I shall give them back to you."

"What do you want to know?" one maiden asked, swimming closer. She crossed her arms over a rock at the jetty's edge, looking up at him. "It will hurt us little to tell."

"There are some things we must not say," another warned her, but her voice trembled as she spoke. The third said nothing; she only stared angrily up at Hagan, her black eyes hard as polished jet.

"But I know what you want to know," the one who leaned on the rock murmured. "If you will give me back my cloak, I shall tell you how your faring to the land of the Huns shall be."

"I would gladly know that." Hagan took one of the feather garments from his arm; although it was too light for him to feel the loss of its weight, he missed its warmth at once.

"You may ride safely to Attila's country," the swan-maiden said when she had taken the cloak from him. "And I swear that you shall win great honor and glory there. You need have no fear that anything else shall befall you or the men with whom you fare."

With her last words, she wrapped her cloak around her. The swan's wings beat a shower of icy droplets over Hagan as she rose from the river, circling below the clouds to watch him with her sisters.

"Is there anything else I need to know?" he asked the other two who floated in the water below him. The maidens shared a dark glance, then the silent one pressed her lips tighter, shaking her head at her sister. "It seems by your look that there is. Now tell me, or swear that there is not anything in this faring threatening Gundahari and myself, and I shall give your cloaks back at once."

The two pale heads disappeared beneath the water without a ripple. The day was brightening; when Hagan glanced up at the swan flying above him, he could see streaks of blue showing through the breaking clouds.

Silently as they had sunk, the maidens' heads and white shoulders rose from the river again. "Let me warn you, Hagan, son of Grimhild," one of them cried. "Our sister lied to you for the sake of her cloak. If you ever get to the Huns' land, you will meet with bitter sorrow. Do not go—there is still time. For you brave warriors have been bidden to Attila's country so that you may die there. All who ride to that land have linked their hands with death."

"It would be ill for me to tell my king that we were fated to die in the Huns' land. But now, I think, there is no more that you can say."

He gave the second feather cloak to the one who had spoken; she donned it and flew at once to circle above his head with her sister. Then he held up the third, speaking to the last of the maidens. "If you have no more to tell me, I will not torment you any more. Take it and fare well."

The swan-maiden climbed out over the rocks, standing naked and fair in the morning light before him. The dripping ends of her hair were already beginning to freeze to points of ice, but the cold that numbed his feet and ankles did not seem to touch her. Standing so close to her, Hagan saw faint pink scars like the blisters of old burns marring the clean whiteness of her breasts and shoulders. She met his eye without blinking or flinching as she reached out for her swan's hide; she was, he marked, almost of a height with himself.

The swan-maiden stood with her feather garment dripping white from her hand, looking at him. At last she said, "Why didn't you seek to gain anything from me while you had my cloak?"

"Because I know all I need to, unless you can tell me how to turn away this wyrd."

"Do not go."

"Gundahari has already made up his mind. Whatever I say to him, he will cast away and say that I have spoken words of fear. If you cannot give me some rede by which we may ward ourselves, there is nothing else I need to hear."

"Whoever crosses the Danube to Attila's land is doomed to die. Neither I nor you can change that; that orlog was laid long ago, and you turned the wyrd upon yourself when you took up Andward's ring."

"Then so it must be." He turned to leave the jetty.

"Hagan, wait!" the swan-maiden called. "Do not go yet. There is something else I have to say to you."

Hagan's legs were trembling as he walked back toward her. "What more can you tell me than you have?"

"Hagan, it is already written that Gundahari's house need fall, but you do not need to fall with it." She raised her swan-draped arm, pointing at his heart. "You are no more bound to the world within the Middle-Garth's ring than I, except as you choose to be. You have always known it: your place is not truly with them, and you yourself broke the last wall keeping you within their stead. Since you slew Sigifrith, have you known a woman's love or the friendship of a man?"

Hagan could not help thinking bitterly of Gundahari's words to him; unwillingly he shook his head.

"The ravens should not feed on your heart in a stranger's land; the Rhine is your own, and you must stay here. This is my rede: cast Andward's ring into the river. Then you shall be loosed from the threads of its wyrd, and you may come away with me."

Her brightness before his eyes and her words pierced him with a spear of pain as keen as joy; his whole body was shaking now, battered between the icy cold of the rising wind and the longing that sang through his blood in every limb. It seemed to him that her dark eyes held everything haunting that he had half-heard in the river at night; that the gleaming whiteness of her breasts was the brilliance of byrnies in the joy of battle, and the swan-maiden's voice sang the promise of everything that his own being had barred him from among the dwellers in the Middle-Garth. But once Gundrun had embraced him, and Gundahari had trusted him not only with his life, but with his honor.

While he still might, Hagan shook his head. "My place is beside my brother. If he must die of this faring, he shall not die without me."

"You are foolish," the swan-maiden said sadly. "Now I must go, for my sisters are waiting for me; I cannot wait any longer for you. You shall not see me again while you live."

"That shall be a sorrow to me."

He stood on the jetty and watched as she flung her feathered hide over her shoulders. The swan flew up, the wind of her rising cold against him. She circled once over his head, letting out a shrill mournful cry, then winged off behind her sisters in their eastward flight.

It was well past noon by the time the Burgundian thanes began to gather themselves and their horses at the southern gate of Worms, ready to be ferried across the Rhine. Hagan had been in Gundahari's hall most of the day, seeing to the packing of weapons and armor and such things as they might need on the way to Attila's lands. His brother spoke little, perhaps from the after-effects of the wine.

It was not until Hagan and Gundahari went out to the stable for their horses that Gundahari said, "Where are your sons? Surely Nibel and Alfarik, at least, are old enough to ride with us."

"Alfarik has not recovered from his fever completely yet, and would only slow us down. I am leaving Nibel here."

"Why?"

"Because I trust him." Hagan shifted his byrnie forward, tugging the neck of his tunic down to show that no key-laden chain hung around his throat.

"Hagan . . . you don't think we're coming back, do you?"

Hagan did not answer.

"Glamwer had ill dreams last night. There were some that might have showed weather, and another that seemed to me to mean the snapping of small hounds and the snarling of dogs, but the last dream she told me of was one where women came in, looking downcast, and they chose me as their husband. She thought that these were my idises, and I could not give that dream a fair meaning." Gundahari looked down at the straw-strewn earth of the stable's floor. "Hagan, you don't have to come with me. I forced you into it, and now I think it might be better if you stayed to look after things here at home. At best we shall be gone for a long time, and the land cannot be left wholly unattended."

"I have already chosen to come with you. Who will keep watch for you at night, if I do not? Who will see that we are warded properly against the ways of the Huns to their foes, if I am not there to warn you what to expect? You are the king; you have spoken your words, and we all drank on them. And I must bring Gundrun's ring to her." He raised his hand so that Gundahari could see the golden dragon coiled about his finger.

"I hardly believed that she had sent it. Do you think she is still alive?"

"She was when she signed the letter. We shall find out further when we are there, I suppose."

Glamwer, Costbera, Hagan's three sons and some of the Burgundian thanes were waiting together in the courtyard when Gundahari and Hagan led their horses out. The members of the little group looked at one another nervously before the oldest of the warriors, a gray-headed man named Rumold who had been in Gebica's warband and now oversaw the administration of Worms, spoke, as if for all of them.

"We cannot help being sad that you are going on this faring," he said. "Is there any way to turn you from this purpose? You know as well as we that Attila is not worthy of very much trust."

"I trusted my sister to him, and he has not betrayed her yet, nor has he broken any of the oaths he swore to us or the agreements he made when he married her. There's no reason for this weeping; why shouldn't we think well of Gundrun's husband?"

"To whom will you trust your land and your folk while you are gone?"

Hagan saw Glamwer's long face crumple a little in pain; the sharp winter sunlight underscored the deep lines marking mourning on her face—three stillbirths and two sons dead in infancy—with cruel clarity. If Gundahari did not come back, no child of her blood would rule over the Burgundians; and there was no place for a queen alone.

"To you, Rumold. I trust my land and my folk to you until my return, for I know that you will keep them well, as you were always true to my father Gebica and to me afterward."

"I shall pray to the Christ and the gods of our folk for your safe home-coming," Rumold replied. "May we all be blessed by it!"

"Now, Glamwer," Gundahari said to his wife, "bring us all great goblets of the best wine, if you will, for this may be our last occasion to feast. The old wolf shall come to our gold if we die, and so the bear shall not spare biting with his fangs."

It seemed to Hagan that the blackness in the middle of his brother's eyes had swollen to swallow their hazel rings as he spoke, as though Gundahari were looking through very dim light. But that, he thought, might have been a trick of his own eye; his sight often showed him things that were not there to see.

Then Gundahari laughed. "Stop looking so grim, all of you," he said. "The Muspilli haven't come to burn the world yet. Anyone would think there was nothing worse in the world than visiting one's brother-in-law."

One or two of the thanes strained to laugh with him, but even their best smiles were crooked and white about the edges. Glamwer came out with large silver goblets on a tray, and each of them took one.

"I drink to a good faring!" Gundahari said, raising his high. A few crimson drops sloshed over the shining side, dribbling down into the snow over the flagstones.

"To a good faring," Hagan and the others echoed him, drinking deeply. The Gaulish wine was very smooth, with a rich taste like smoky plums, and chilled from the frosty air.

When they had finished their wine, Gundahari and Hagan took their horses by the reins and, walking, led the group to the south gate of Worms where Gisalhari and Gernot had gathered the other thanes by the ferryboat.

Wingi was also waiting there, standing near Gisalhari's priest Augustinius, who watched him suspiciously. He greeted Gundahari with a wide smile. "Are you ready to go?"

Glamwer turned upon him before Gundahari could speak. "Wingi, it is likely that much ill-luck rested upon your coming, and there will be many things following upon your faring." She rested her fists upon her hips, staring him fiercely in the face.

"I swear that I'm not lying," Wingi said quickly. "May a high gallows and furious wights take me if I've lied in one word that I've said."

His plump face paling in the icy sunlight, Augustinius crossed himself, and so did Gisalhari and several of the other thanes who stood nearby.

"What are you waiting for?" Hagan asked. "Who will be the first on the ferry?"

Folkhari rode forward toward the raft. "I shall," he answered. The singer was brightly dressed, in a blue tunic under a thick yellow cloak wrought with silver embroidery, as if the feast were that night. But though many of the others were clad in plain traveling clothes, gold and silver shone from their arms, nor were Gundahari and Hagan any less richly jeweled; the Burgundians would ride as befitted the strongest folk-king in Germania and his thanes. "Surely there's no need to stand here any longer."

The skop rode his horse onto the king's ferry-raft, which swayed and tilted a little under his hooves but stayed fast. It could take twenty men and horses; five men were needed to pole it across the Rhine, but there were half a hundred thanes gathered to go on that journey.

Hagan and Gundahari waited on the bank until the last boatload was ready to push off.

"Fare well and have good luck," Nibel said to them, embracing his father quickly about the shoulders. Not knowing how to reply, Hagan patted his son on the back.

"Stay well," he said at last. "I know you shall keep my trust."

"I shall."

"Fare well and have good luck," Costbera repeated softly. Hagan gazed at his wife for a moment, trying to remember what she looked like. Sags of deep purple underscored Costbera's brown eyes; white-threaded strands of hair fell free of her auburn braids and the drooping flesh of her jawline trembled with the quivering of her mouth. He was not sure what it would mean to her if he did not come back.

Costbera half-raised her hand as if to reach out to him, then drew it back.

"Stay well, my wife," Hagan said. "Be cheerful, however things fare with us."

Gundahari and Glamwer embraced, and then Hagan and Gundahari led their horses onto the ferry.

The Burgundians were not eager to ride through the lands of the Alamanns; instead they rode due eastward from Worms, skirting the wooded edges of the mountains for twelve nights. The thirteenth day was warmer than most, though cloudy; they moved slowly, their horses slogging with lowered heads through melting slush and mud. It was not until afternoon was deepening into evening that they heard a rushing that Gundahari first took for the wind through the leafless branches of the trees.

"That is the river," Hagan said. "We shall have reached the ford by nightfall." He reined in his horse—an old piebald gelding, it was obedient if not swift or spirited—and listened to the water for a moment. "The Danube is in full flood. It shall not be an easy crossing."

"Why should we worry about the flood?" Gundahari asked. "There are enough of us to make each other fast through the waters if this ford is worse than it has been. I think you're looking for trouble."

Gisalhari rode up beside them. "Why have you stopped, Hagan? Getting saddle-sore? Even if the river's too high to cross, there'll be a ferryman. There always is in places like this."

"Go and play with your priest," Gundahari told him gruffly.

"He's not just my priest, you know."

"If there weren't so many other Christians who wanted him along, I wouldn't have let him come to slow us down, and you know that as well as I do."

"I bet there's a ferryman," said Gisalhari, retreating.

Gundahari sighed. "How old is he? Thirty winters? Something like that. Why hasn't he grown up yet?"

"He has the gift of endless youth," Folkhari said pompously, coming up on the other side. The singer puffed out his cheeks, dropping his jaw to lengthen his face into that of a self-important old man, then laughed with Gundahari.

"His only gift is that someone hasn't knocked him on the head yet. I may do it myself one day."

The Burgundians followed the road through a stand of slush-dripping trees and out on to the top of a small hill overlooking the river. The Danube roared in their ears, hurling dead trees along on its frothing brown waters; black branches reached up from the side of the river where it had overflowed its banks. Even with a stout ferry it would be no easy crossing.

"It seems to me that there will be hardly any way to do this without the loss of good men," Hagan mused.

"Don't say that!" his brother said. "You don't need to dishearten us any further. You raided through these lands with Thioderik and Attila often enough; can't you find us another way over, so we can get our horses and ourselves across?"

"My life is not so miserable that I wish to be drowned in this broad river. There shall be many men slain by my hand in Attila's realm first, I am well certain of that." He looked around at the thanes who were riding up alongside their king. The farther faces were already fading into dimness as the day was darkening more swiftly. "It is time to make camp, in any case. Gundahari, you stay beside the water tonight with the thanes. I myself will seek the ferry over this river, which will bring us, if I remember rightly, to the lands of the drighten Gelprat." With that Hagan heaved his shield over his shoulder and rode down the hill toward the east.

Hagan had no luck in finding the ferryman that night. Now and again he fell asleep in the saddle, waking with a start whenever his chin drooped far enough for the cold of his byrnie to bite through his short beard or when drops of freezing slush dripped from the branches above on to the back of his neck.

He did not come fully awake until a little before dawn, when the small birds began to twitter and chirp about him in a sparsely scattered chorus. He was not sure how far he had come; but behind the flittering birdsong he could hear the tinkling splash of a stream, which he expected would flow toward the river.

Hagan slid down from the back of his horse, taking the reins in his shield hand and leading it along the overgrown path toward the stream. He was almost within sight of the water when he heard soft high laughter.

Getting a good grip on the hilt of his sword, Hagan stepped boldly forward through the muddy leaves and muck, readying himself to either fight a foe or ask where a ferry across the Danube might be found.

The two who bathed in the pool from which the stream flowed seemed to be young women, one fair-haired and one darker; but as the fair maiden dived gracefully under the water, Hagan saw the silvery flash of what he took to be a forked tail behind her. She surfaced in a spray of droplets with her arms above her head, laughing as she looked up and saw him. "Childohaith, there stands a fool. Does he know he is going to his slaughter?"

"None of them know well enough," the darker mere-wife answered. "Only the Christian priest shall escape that doom; only his wyrd is not turned toward death there." She, too, laughed merrily. "If the rest cross the Danube whole, they shall be drowned in a river of blood."

"What do you know about crossing the Danube?" Hagan asked.

"There is a ferryman," the fair mere-wife chanted. "He is a fierce man; you must treat him carefully, or he will not let you live. But follow this path till you come to the river's edge; if the ferryman is not there, call over the flood and say that your name is Amelrich. He was a good hero who left this land because of a feud. The ferry will come as soon as the name is named."

"I thank you for that."

Both mere-wives threw their hands up and sank beneath the pool's surface, their laughter bursting into a trail of bubbles; as they leapt from the depths again, the thrashing of their forked tails splashed a spray of icy water over Hagan.

"You had the best counsel of all on the Rhine, and you did not heed it," the fair maiden giggled.

"You have been living among men too long; you may as well cast your life from you," laughed her sister.

"Such a fool, such a fool; your trust is sure to betray you, and you mistrusted the only man who might have saved you."

The fair-haired mere-wife stretched herself backward, floating langorously on the surface. Water ran from the pale tips of her breasts, pooling in the hollow below the arch of her breastbone; beneath the ripples, her tail seemed to shimmer and shiver into bright legs. The darker maiden lay forward in the pool, thrashing her tail a little to keep herself afloat; the white curves of her shoulders and silver-sheeened buttocks rose from the water like sea-smoothed stones. She slanted her gaze at Hagan through her tangle of wet hair; her sister stared at him with eyes slitted like a sleepy cat's.

Suddenly Hagan could bear their taunting no longer; the nameless wod that lay sleeping in his blood-paths rose in wakened anger. He dropped his horse's reins and stepped forward, knee-deep in the pool, with his naked sword in his hand. One slash each, where maidens' skin glimmered into scales; then they thrashed and writhed like wyrms, shifting into silvery coils around the pool. The waters rose up in a great froth from their thrashing, foaming so fiercely that Hagan had to fight his way out through waters that had risen as high as his breastbone with great sweeps of his arms.

The day was well begun by the time Hagan caught his horse again; he was wet, cold and aching, and in no mood to deal more kindly with anyone than he had to. When he finally reached the river again, he saw no mena-

bout; only a large raft moored across the water, riding high on the flood near a house built of mixed wicker and wood.

Hagan tied his horse to a tree, then breathed deeply, gathering all his strength into his broad chest for the shout. "Now fetch Amelrich, who fled from this land through a great feud!"

He pulled a plain ring of gold from his arm, holding it high on his sword point to gleam dully beneath the clouded sky.

A man came slowly out of the house, carrying an oar; even from across the river, Hagan could mark his great height and broadness of body. The ferryman's head was overgrown with a thick tangle of dark hair, beard and hair merging into a common fierce mat. He looked across at the gold on the end of the sword and seemed to consider a moment. Then he stepped onto his raft and poled off across the flood one-handed, using the oar in the other hand to fend off floating branches and, once, the bloated corpse of a deer.

As the ferry came into shore, the ferryman lowered his head and glared at Hagan through thick, beetling brows, and Hagan saw his great shoulders swelling with rage. His voice hard and flat with anger, the ferryman said grimly: "You may well be named Amelrich, but you are unlike the one I awaited. He was my own brother, of one father and mother with me. Now you have betrayed me, you shall have to stay here."

"No, let these riches make it good. I am a stranger in a foreign land and have thanes in my care. Take this pledge in friendship, and ship us across; I shall be truly grateful to you."

"This shall not be, for my drighten has many foes and I was ordered to ferry no strangers into his land. If you love your life, One-Eye, you should leave this place swiftly."

"Do not refuse, for my mood is not kindly. Take this good gold in friendship and ferry us and our steeds across."

"I shall never do that," the angry ferryman said, and with that he heaved up his thick oar and hewed at Hagan's skull. Hagan was able to step aside quickly enough for the wooden blade to crash down on his shoulder instead of his head; but the might of the blow knocked him to his knees. He was just standing up when the swinging pole in the ferryman's other hand caught him across the side of his head with a shattering crack. Then he tasted blood in his mouth; and then the wod rushed out from the bright pain in his skull and did not still until blood ran through every crack in the raft's logs and the ferryman's severed head dangled from his shield hand by the hair. Angrily he flung the bearded sphere into the mud beside the river; the raft, unfettered, had already drifted past his reach and was beginning to float downstream.

By the time the raft had drifted close enough in to snag itself on the branches of a drowned tree, Hagan was tired, muddy and bruised from chasing it. Wearily he climbed on, and picked up the oar. It was cracked from where the ferryman had struck him, splitting in his hand after a few strokes;

whirling downstream on the flood, he had to lash it swiftly together with the cords of his shield sling and then paddle back over the distance he had lost to the place where his horse was tied before he could let the river take him to the Burgundians' camp again.

As Hagan pushed the ferry in toward shore, he heard Folkhari shouting, "Hai, here he is! I knew he wouldn't fail us!" Gundahari and his thanes hurried toward the river's edge to meet Hagan; but their laughter and grins dimmed as they came close enough to see the blood blackening the ferry's planking.

"What happened to the ferryman?" Gundahari asked. "I think your strength must have proved the death of him."

"I found the ship beside a wild willow; my hand loosed it. There was no one else there."

Gundahari cocked his head to one side, looking dubiously at his brother for a moment before he said, "What cause did the ferryman give you to kill him?"

"I do not wish for any word of our faring to go before us to our enemies. Now he can tell nothing of it."

"Who's going to take us across?" Gernot grumbled. He crossed his arms over his paunch, looking at the raft and the water. "This is worse than the Rhine. We need a ferryman."

"I myself will ferry us," Hagan said. "Get on."

Again, the king and his kin waited until the last ferrying. By this time Hagan had become tired, so Gundahari took his place while the others carried the last of their baggage on.

"Don't set that down there," Augustinius ordered Gisalhari, lowering his fair head and pulling with both hands at the bulging sack the king's cousin held. "I will not have the sacred utensils profaned by the blood of a murdered man."

Gisalhari swung the sack up higher. "Where shall I put it?" he asked meekly. "There's blood all over the raft."

The priest tugged at his blond beard, teetering as he picked his way over the stained logs to the far corner. "Over here. You, Gernot, move aside."

Gernot stepped away so that Augustinius and Gisalhari could bring the sacred baggage onto unsoiled wood. Augustinius took the bag by the neck and stood holding it upright as Gundahari pushed off.

Only the Christian priest shall escape that doom; only his wyrd is not turned toward death there. . . . Hagan remembered the mere-wife's words as he watched the plump priest scowling over the side of the ferry. Without speaking he walked over to Augustinius, took him about the waist and heaved his body into the water. Hagan felt a sudden wash of relief as the priest went under, but a few moments later his head bobbed back up.

Choking and sputtering too badly to speak, Augustinius tried to claw his way toward the raft. Hagan grabbed the lashed oar, watching him.

"Get him out!" Gundahari shouted, turning the raft and trying to pole closer to the struggling priest. As Augustinius reached out for the ferry's edge, Hagan pushed against him with the pole, shoving him back under and away from the raft.

"Why are you doing this?" Gisalhari yelled furiously in Hagan's ear. "Stop it, you hear me? Get him out!"

When the priest's head came up once more, Gundahari tried again to turn the ferry toward Augustinius, but the water bucked too fiercely and sent the raft into a spin from which he was hardly able to straighten it.

"I can't swim!" Augustinius coughed as the river whirled him downstream. "Help, someone! In Christ's name, help!" But they were already too far away for anyone to reach him. Now the brown water sucked him under; now he rose again. When he went under for the fourth time, Hagan thought that he surely must drown. But the Burgundians were not yet to the other side when a scrabbling movement among the bare branches sticking up from the river's edge caught Hagan's eye. The water had washed Augustinius to shore where the river bent a little and he was pulling himself out, soaked and shivering but alive. Crouched over with cramp, he still lifted one hand to make the sign of the cross toward the boat. Hagan thought he heard the priest's voice, but they were too far away to make out his words.

"Why did you do that?" Gundahari asked. "Hagan, if someone else had thrown the priest in to die, you would have been angry. What did he do to you?"

Hagan, staring at the humped brown shape of the Christian priest, did not answer.

When they came to shore at last, Hagan waited till the others had left the ferry. "Lend me your axe, Folkhari," he said.

The singer took his weapon from his belt and gave it to Hagan at once. Hagan bent down and began to chop at a crack between two of the split logs, widening it till the raft began to sink. Then he leapt to shore and cut the mooring rope in two, giving the ferry a last push with his foot to carry it out toward the middle of the river. It whirled downstream in a swift spray of water, tilting as it sank.

"If there is some coward who wishes to flee from us after this, he must die a shameful death in these waves," Hagan said.

He gave Folkhari his axe back; the fair singer lifted it high in the air. "Well done and well said: we shall fare and fight together. Hail Hagan!" he cried; and many of the thanes answered with a shout of "Hail!"

The other side of the Danube was thickly wooded; the road led into a hoar-whitened forest of dark pines. "We should not be far from the eastern border of Hrodgar's lands," Hagan said when they stopped to make camp in a clearing. "We must be careful, for he is sworn to Attila, and I do not know how he shall receive us."

"Hrodgar is said to be a generous and honorable man," Gundahari said as he and Gernot drove in the stakes around the king's tent. "Hagan, will you give me your word that you won't attack any of his men unless they strike at you first?"

Hagan began to clear away a ring in the middle of the encampment where a fire might be lighted. Black clouds were massing against the darkening eastern sky and his byrnie was already growing colder; he thought there might well be snow that night.

"Will you?"

"I give you my word."

"All right. It will be good if we get Hrodgar's friendship; if he gives us guest-right he cannot harm us, and the more so if he offers to come through Attila's lands with us." Gundahari dusted his hands off and stood up. "There, that's got it. Just think, Hagan, you can sleep under cover tonight. You look as though you might need rest."

"Yes; slaughtering is hard work," Gisalhari said from behind the king. One of Gundahari's elbows swung back and he grunted as the tip caught him beneath the ribs. "Hey! What was that for?"

"Just because."

Folkhari came out of the trees carrying an armload of wood. He squatted down where Hagan had cleared the ground and began to lay the sticks over each other so that they would catch fire easily. As he worked, he began to chant.

> *Wroth was Donars   when he, wakening,*
> *for his hammer's   haft sought around,*
> *shook he his beard,   and shaggy head,*
> *Earth's bairn fumbled   and found it not.*

The other thanes, hearing his voice, came to gather around the first leaping sparks when they had finished their tent-setting. Folkhari blew up the fire between lines, chanting the tale of how Loki had borrowed Frowe Holda's falcon hide and flown to the world of the etins to find that the giant Thrum had stolen Donars' hammer. The singer made his voice deep and raspy, affecting a coarse speech as he chanted Thrum's words.

> *I have Donars'   hammer hidden,*
> *eight rosts deep   the earth below.*
> *None the hammer   home shall carry,*
> *unless Frowe Holda   fare as my wife.*

A cask of wine was opened at Gundahari's gesture, and the men filled their cups while Folkhari sang of how Frowe Holda's wrath had rocked the roots of the gods' garth, bursting the fiery necklace of gold that the dwarves had made for her: she would in no wise go to be an etin's bride. Folkhari walked about as he sang, untying his harp from his saddlebags and plucking it to tune till he could strum it along with his chanting. The warriors gathered more closely around the fire, drinking and eating and laughing as Folkhari told them of how Donars was then dressed as a bride for the etin, his beard hidden by a veil and Brisingamen draped around his neck; and how Loki, dressed as a bondmaid, took him to Thrum's hall and said that he had brought Frowe Holda to her wedding. They cheered as Folkhari told of how the etin gave Donars' Hammer to his bride to hallow the wedding, and of how the god arose with the skirts still about his knees to strike down the giants gathered there.

So Wodans' son won his hammer back.

Gundahari, leaning against a rock, took a gold ring from his arm and tossed it to Folkhari. Hagan saw his brother's teeth bright in the firelight; it seemed to him that the king was easier in his mind than he had been since the faring began.

"Sing something else—sing another song of merriment, skop," Hagan said.

"If I might coax you to laugh, I would sing all night and count it easily done," Folkhari replied. "What do you wish to hear?"

Hagan thought of the songs he had heard—the songs he could not sing, but knew the words and the tune to in his head as well as he knew the care of his sword and the counting of the fees collected from Gundahari's lands. Some were the songs that men beat time to with spear on shield; others were the songs at which a few might brush tears from their eyes in the darkness of the hall.

He was saved by Gundahari, who said, "I'd like to hear the tale of how Loki and Donar went to the hall of Loki-of-the-Outgarth, and how they were tricked by his seemings."

Folkhari wrinkled his nose, squeezing his face into a squint till the chiseled lines of his cheeks bulged out in wrinkly pouches, then sticking out his tongue at Gundahari. "Shall I tell the tale or shall you?" the singer asked in a tone of mock offense.

Gundahari held up his hands, palms outward. "It's all yours."

Hagan crept away from the fire into the king's tent early that night, hoping to be able to sleep. He was tired enough that when he had rolled in his blankets his thoughts faded into a warm dozing buzz; it was, he thought, much later when he came fully awake to the sound of Gundahari's snuffling snore and knew that he could sleep no longer. He crept out of the tent, moving as slowly as he could so that the muffled noise of his byrnie would not disturb his brother.

There was no light except for the fire's red glow through the ashes; the Moon and stars were thickly blanketed in clouds. Hagan picked his way between the tents to the path and followed it along, half-seeing, half-hearing where he was going.

The sky had just begun to lighten when he came out of the forest on to a broad plain. If Hagan had not heard the soft breathing of the man sleeping before him, he would have trodden on the dark hump. Instead he crouched down, searching about till he found the hilt of the sword sticking out from beneath the sleeper.

Hagan took the sword and drew it. He stood and nudged the man with his right foot. "Wake up," he said. "I think you have slept too long."

The sleeper let out a cry, leaping to his feet at once and stumbling back from Hagan as he felt for his sword. He was a short man, but heavily built. Hagan judged from the swiftness with which he balanced into a fighting crouch that he would be a good warrior. For a moment he thought of offering battle, but then he remembered his word to Gundahari.

"Woe, I am disgraced!" the man cried. "I have lost my sword; I have failed my drighten. Warrior, slay me now, for I slept while Hrodgar's land was threatened and I have lost my sword. But I was awake for three days and nights, and I could stay awake no longer."

Hagan took the gold ring he had offered the ferryman, sliding it over the hilt of the sword and holding them both out to the land's warder. "You are a man true to your drighten, I think. I shall give you this ring for your bravery, and it shall fare better with you than with the last man it was given to; and you shall also have your sword back. Nor do we mean to threaten Hrodgar or his lands, if he offers no threat to us. Tell me, how will he receive Gundrun's kin?"

"He will joyfully bid you to feast with him," the short warrior answered at once. "Songs of King Gundahari and of you, Hagan, are often sung in his hall, and he would be glad to host the kin of Attila's wife in any case. I must warn you that there are some who would be your foes for Sigifrith's sake, for he was well-loved when his arm helped to ward Hrodgar's lands. But that was long ago and my drighten has done well as Attila's man, so the king's kin shall be particularly welcome in his hall."

"What is your name?"

"I am called Ekeward."

"Well then, Ekeward, will you show us the way to Hrodgar's hall at daybreak?"

"I shall do that gladly."

A few light flakes of snow were beginning to lighten the leaden sky when the Burgundians came within sight of Hrodgar's hall, which stood in the middle of a brown meadow ringed by dark forest. Hagan was used to the smaller buildings of wood that served for even the greatest of drightens this far from Roman lands; but he heard Iring muttering to Gisalhari, "Is that supposed to be a hall? It looks more like a swineherd's hut." Hagan turned around to glare at Iring, who closed his mouth and looked down at the ground.

"If you will, wait here," Ekeward said to Gundahari. "I'll go and tell Hrodgar so he can come out and greet you properly."

Hagan loosened his sword in his sheath as the warder rode away. "If he is a man who holds by guest-right, he may have reason for wishing to meet us outside," he murmured to his brother. "Be ready."

"You're looking for trouble," Gundahari whispered back. "I don't think you'll find it here." Still Hagan kept a careful watch, eyeing the wood for any trembling of branches and listening for a rustle that might betray waiting warriors.

Only a few moments after Ekeward had entered Hrodgar's hall, a tall, thin man dressed in a rich cloak of gray Northern fox fur came out. He was alone; he spread his arms wide in greeting, and Hagan noted that he was not armed beneath the cloak, unless he carried a dagger hidden in his boot or sleeve. His brown hair had thinned and long wrinkles drew his narrow face down, but Hagan still knew Hrodgar on sight; the faint look of worry through his smile did not seem strange for a man who had shared a march with Attila for twenty-five years and finally sworn troth to him. His mouth twitched into a brief frown when his gaze lit on Wingi, and Hagan remembered that Hrodgar was a Christian, though he wondered how much deeper the drighten's mistrust might run.

"Welcome, Gundahari and Hagan and the thanes of the Burgundian folk!" Hrodgar called. His voice was deep and hollow, with a faint nasal rasp like that of a roughly cut reed pipe. "Be guests in my hall and my lands."

"Greetings, Hrodgar," Gundahari responded. "We will gladly guest here."

"Shall I have my men see to stabling your horses?"

"We will do it ourselves," Hagan told him. Gundahari looked sharply at his brother, then shrugged as if to say, "Do what you like."

The Burgundians dismounted and followed Hrodgar around to the stables, which were larger than their own in Worms but mostly empty; there were more than enough stalls for their steeds.

"Why are your stables so big?" Gisalhari asked.

Hrodgar gave him another half-worried smile, stroking his moustache. "The extra places are for Attila's band; they often come here, especially at the beginning of summer and the beginning of winter when they mean to make longer journeys away from his hall."

When the Burgundians came in from the stables, they found the long wooden tables in Hrodgar's dark little hall laden with bread. Clay cups were set out along the tables and two women, an older and a younger, were walking the length of the hall with their pitchers. The older woman was short and dumpy, with gray hair crowned by a silver circlet. The younger was tall and slender: she was clearly Hrodgar's daughter, for her long fall of golden brown hair framed a face as narrow as his, though the sharp angles of her cheekbones and chin were delicate rather than knobby and her fair skin was not eroded by any of the care that had worn her father down. A cross of silver set with five red garnets lay upon the white linen over her bosom.

"Come, dears, and greet these warriors," Hrodgar said to them. "These are Gundahari, Hagan, Gisalhari and Gernot—Gundrun's kin."

"Greetings, Frowe Gotelind," Hagan said to Hrodgar's wife before the drighten could introduce them.

Gotelind smiled without opening her mouth, as many women did after their teeth went bad. "We are honored to have such guests," she said, and began to pour ale into a cup for each of them.

Hrodgar's daughter came shyly forward. She kissed Gundahari on the cheek, then Gernot, then Gisalhari; but she flushed pink and then paled when she looked at Hagan.

"Hagan is a well-famed warrior; you have often heard songs of him, Garlind," Hrodgar told his daughter. Hagan stood quite still as she came to him and stood on tiptoes, suffering her to brush her lips against his cheek. He could feel the heat of her flushed face for a second before she backed away. Garlind's gaze was already sliding toward Gisalhari, who likewise blushed and looked down at the earthen floor as if he were considering how flagstones might be laid upon it. Hagan took the cup Gotelind offered him, raising it as Gundahari, Gernot and—after a moment—Gisalhari raised theirs toward their host and his women.

"Hail and thanks, Hrodgar," Gundahari said, and they drank.

Hrodgar insisted on holding a feast for them that night; though Hagan wanted to press on, disliking the idea that Attila might have more time to ready for the moment of their coming, Gundahari would not hear of leaving until the next day. The king and his near kin, together with Folkhari, sat at the high table with Hrodgar, his wife and his daughter. Hagan marked that a large and well-wrought shield, adorned with a raven worked in silver on dark blue, hung on the wall behind the drighten's head. It bore a few gashes, the depth of which showed its sturdiness; the light linden wood most often splintered beneath such blows.

During the meal Gisalhari and Garlind hardly looked away from each other once, and it seemed as though their feet might be pressing together beneath the table. Hagan thought that he had not seen a pair so enraptured with one another since Sigifrith and Gundrun, and the melancholy droop of Hrodgar's face seemed to lighten as he watched the two of them gazing into each others' eyes.

When the eating was finished and the tables taken away, Gotelind and Garlind rose to walk among the men with their ale pitchers.

"So, Fro Gisalhari," Hrodgar said, leaning forward to rest his elbows on the table, "you are not yet married?"

Gisalhari turned to face his host. "No, nor betrothed. I was to have been married a year ago, but the maiden died of a fever before we met."

"Why?" Hagan asked. "Do you mean to offer your daughter to him?"

"I do. It seems to me she could not make a better marriage, and I would count it a great honor to give her to the kin of the Burgundians' king. Gotelind and I spoke of it before you came, for we knew that Attila and

Gundrun had invited you to their Yule feast and were sure of meeting you there."

For the first time, Hagan began to wonder about the redes he had been given. If Attila meant to betray them, at least Hrodgar knew nothing of it—if this were a true offer and not merely an attempt to lull their wariness. Gisalhari, after all, might make many better matches; perhaps Hrodgar knew this, and did not think the Burgundians would accept the offer.

"This seems to me a good match," he said aloud, watching Hrodgar carefully. "I think, Gundahari, that it would be a fine thing if Gisalhari were to wed Hrodgar's daughter."

The tightness at the corners of the march-drighten's eyes and mouth loosened at Hagan's words; the ridges of muscle along his bony shoulders sank as if in relief. If no treachery were set in Attila's hall, Hrodgar had won a finer husband for his daughter than he might have expected.

Gundahari seemed to be chewing over a stubborn morsel as his hazel eyes flickered about the low-roofed hall. Finally he said, "Gisalhari, would this be to your liking?"

"Very much so," Gisalhari answered. "If my priest Augustinius were here, we could be married now. Or . . . have you a priest, Hrodgar?"

"Sadly not. But we are Christians here all the same, and you shall have a rightful Christian wedding. Shall we drink on it?"

Gundahari looked over to Garlind, who was pouring out ale as if she didn't know what the men were discussing. "Is your daughter agreeable to this, Hrodgar?"

The march-drighten raised his voice. "Garlind!" he called "Come here!"

Her gaze on Gisalhari, Garlind hurried so swiftly that Hagan was certain she had been told earlier what her father wished.

"Do you want to marry this man?" Hrodgar asked his daughter.

Garlind glanced down at the dirt floor, then up through her eyelashes at Gisalhari. Blushing, she made an odd little noise, as if she could neither bear to speak or not to speak. Then she nodded her head strongly thrice.

Hrodgar smiled at her, then at Gundahari. "Well?"

"I can't think of any reason why not," the Burgundian king replied at last.

Gisalhari's grin stretched the edges of his short brown beard as he stood, clearly meaning to throw his arms around Garlind. Gundahari grabbed him and pulled him down again. "Wait, at least till we've settled the terms of betrothal. You'll have the rest of your life for that."

The men drank and talked over the marriage arrangements for some time, till at last they had agreed that Hrodgar, Gotelind and Garlind should go back with them to hold the wedding in Worms. They drank several cups of ale on it, and when they had become well-mellowed Hrodgar went into his own chamber and came out with two bulging bags.

"I should like to give you these as a sign of our friendship and the new kin-bond between us."

The first thing he pulled out was a helmet, inlaid with golden boars whose eyes were red garnets. "This is for you, King Gundahari. I hope it shall always ward you well."

Gundahari turned the helm over in his hands, admiring it. "I'm honored, my friend. This is a great treasure."

To Gernot the march-drighten gave a well-wrought red shield, bound with iron and ornamented with woven bronzework bright as gold; he gave Gisalhari a sword whose blade and hilt were inlaid with silver knotwork.

"I did not know what you might like, Hagan," Hrodgar said at last. "So you shall choose for yourself: is there anything in my hall or my lands that you would like to have for your own?"

Hagan looked up to the shield hanging above his host. "I think I could bear no truer shield than the one on the wall there, if you wish to give it to me."

Gotelind followed his glance to the shield; she snuffled back a tear.

"Naudung was your brother, dear," Hrodgar said gently to her. "It's your choice."

"I will gladly give it to you, Hagan," she said. "I weep only for my brother, who bore it in battle and fell beneath it; but it will comfort me to know that it is borne again by a famed and brave warrior." The plump little woman went to the wall and heaved the shield down herself, bearing it over to Hagan. "Take it and use it well. May you—" She choked deep in her throat, coughed, then spoke very quickly before the tears came. "May you have better luck with it than Naudung did."

"I shall honor your brother's memory," Hagan said, lifting the shield to his shoulder. For all its sturdiness, it felt very light on his arm; he thought he had not borne a better one.

Folkhari stood, lifting his harp from the bench beside him. "A true atheling's gift, Frowe, and you could not have given it to a truer hero! Now would it please you to hear a song that we are fond of in our land, that tells of the Visigothic King Alaric and how he took the city of Rome itself?"

Gotelind wiped her face with the back of her hand, smiling through her snuffles. "It would please me greatly, singer." She filled Folkhari's cup again before he started, moving among the men with her pitcher as he sang.

The winter was harsh   and hoary the earth,
and cruel those nights   of need had grown.
No longer the Goths   in land of their home
might dwell, but Rome   rings bitter gave . . .

Although Hrodgar wished for them to stay longer, Hagan and Gundahari decided the next morning that they would go on to Attila's hall that day. Hrodgar said he would call his thanes together and join the Burgundians in two days' time, when Attila had meant to hold the Yule feast itself; and so they parted.

It was beginning to grow dark when the Burgundians reached the edge of the Hunnish encampment around Attila's hall, and snow was falling again.

A high fence of pointed wooden stakes surrounded a ring of tents, which was set around a large wooden building. The gate was barred, and there was no watchman there. Hagan could hear the sounds of men laughing and shouting within Attila's hall.

Gundahari rode up to the gate and knocked on it. "Open!" he cried. "Your guests are here."

"I think they cannot hear you," Hagan told him. "Folkhari, will you lend me your axe again?"

The singer tugged his pointed fur hat down to warm his neck and ears. "Gladly," he answered, shivering.

Hagan dismounted, took the axe from him and chopped a long slit in the gate, then stuck the blade through and levered the bar up so he could push the door open.

"You would have been well advised not to do that," Wingi said, smirking at him from beneath his Hunnish cap of hardened skins as he rode in before the Burgundians. "Now bide here while I seek out a gallows tree for you. I bade you come here blithely, but it won't be long till you're strung up."

"It shall turn out worse for you," Hagan warned, hastily remounting his horse.

Wingi spurred his horse, but Gundahari's steed had dashed before him already, cutting him off and forcing him back toward the Burgundians who rode around him. Hagan's first blow to the back of his head with the butt of his spear unhorsed him. Hagan thought that he had knocked Wingi unconscious, because the man made no sound as the other Burgundians leapt from their mounts and struck at him with their swords.

When they were done, Iring and Dankwart heaved Wingi's body onto the hindquarters of Dankwart's horse. Dankwart mounted again and rode toward the forest. The rest were hardly in past the gate when the door of the hall opened and two men walked out, black against the light.

Gundahari's hand was on the hilt of his sword, but Hagan stayed him with a gesture. "Those are Thioderik and Hildebrand. We need not look for treachery from them."

"Greetings!" called Thioderik as the two Goths came nearer. "Greetings and welcome. I think Attila had not looked for your arrival so soon."

"What manner of welcome has he prepared for us?" Hagan asked.

"There are no signs of war yet." The exile's blue eyes flickered pointedly over Hagan's byrnie. "I see you are as watchful as always. I might not be surprised if that served you well. Where is Wingi?"

"He met with an accident along the way."

"Then the world is a little cleaner," Hildebrand growled.

Gundahari dismounted and as the rest of the Burgundians followed his example, he asked, "Is Gundrun well?"

"She is both well and alive," Thioderik assured him. "Did you have reason to think otherwise?"

"Only that the winters are harsher here than in Worms, and when she was younger she often caught chills."

"Ah. King Gundahari, if you and Hagan will let Hildebrand take your horses, you may come into the hall and see your sister at once."

"We thank you, but we will all stay together," Hagan answered for his brother.

Thioderik smiled. Dark as the snowy dusk was growing, Hagan could see that his teeth were as sound and white as they had been when Hagan left Attila's band. "You haven't changed at all, have you? Come then, let's get this done with so you can come in by the fire. It's too cold for standing out here." To Hagan's great surprise, Thioderik wrapped an arm about his shoulders as he had sometimes done before their first parting, as if no time had passed between them; and so they walked to the stables together.

Although Attila's hall was little bigger than Hrodgar's, the rough oaken walls were hung with tapestries and booty. It seemed to Hagan that he recognized some of Gundrun's embroidery; the fine work of other pieces showed that they had been brought from Rome. The stink inside was thick and hot after the clean icy air outside. Goths and a few Huns sat and drank together on benches that could easily have held three times their number, but they were shouting and laughing so loudly that no words could be heard.

Thioderik took them to the end of the hall where Attila and Gundrun sat. Hagan marked that his sister had grown thinner and her eyes did not light in one place long. He thought her flickering glance was not that of fear, but rather like a wolf's or wildcat's: half-wary of a hunter, half-searching for prey. Her back was not bent; she sat with the straight tautness of a bowstring, as proud as she had ever been. Beside her Attila seemed very large and coarse, his lengthened head like a misshapen shadow under his thinning mane of gray hair. Hagan remembered the Hunnish drighten's adder-smile; but his heart leapt like a salmon within him when he saw the sudden flare of joy on Gundrun's face.

It was more what he awaited when her grin tightened into a gasp of silent shock, thought following hard on the heels of thought. As surely as if he touched her, he could feel the blood draining from her head and limbs in the cold paths of realization. She stopped rising halfway out of her seat, twisted awkwardly for a second as though she could neither stand nor sit.

Hagan did not know now what might come to pass, or who might know what Attila had planned. He only knew that he could do no more than wait and watch carefully till some sign betrayed more to him. So he lifted the hand on which Andward's dragon coiled and listened for the sudden hiss of Attila's breath as the firelight glittered from the gold.

"See, I have brought your ring back as you bade me," he said; he had to shout his words twice more before Gundrun could hear them clearly. Hagan could not bring himself to take it from his own hand, but stretched his arm out toward Gundrun so she had to push herself to her feet. It seemed to him that his hand became no lighter when the weight of gold left it, as though the ring were merely cloaked by a subtle seeming like the Helm of Awe's on his newly bare finger.

"Be welcome among us. And have you brought the other gold belonging to your sister, the treasure which was Sigifrith's and is now Gundrun's?" Attila asked, his voice booming hollow through the noise of the hall.

"You have your answer to that already," Gundahari replied.

As Hagan remembered, though there were few Huns eating in the hall, most of them were at Attila's own board. A brown man dressed in skins and dangling tassels stood up, clearing the warriors away from the benches by the high table with a few short gestures. Wizened as the old Gyula had become, Hagan hardly recognized him at first; indeed, it was hard for him to believe that the Hunnish shaman still lived. The Gyula made a swift jerky bow toward Hagan, smiling toothlessly, then faded into the shadows cast by the fire.

"Sit, then. My men will take your byrnies and shields for you. This is a feast of peace; you ought to sit in comfort. You can see that none of us are armored for battle."

Gundahari glanced over at Hagan, who shook his head. "It is not the way of our folk to sit unarmed in another man's hall, although we be there in peace," the Burgundian king said. "You may have marked that yourself when my brother lived among you."

"Is this true?" Attila asked Gundrun.

"Certainly," she answered at once.

"Well, sit, then."

Gundahari, Hagan, Gisalhari, Gernot and Folkhari sat at the high table beside Thioderik and Hildebrand; the rest of the Burgundians jostled for places between the Goths on the farther benches.

"Did you pass through Hrodgar's lands on your way?" asked Thioderik as Gundrun picked up her pitcher of wine and began to pour the dark drink into the horns and thick wayfarers' mugs of clay that the Burgundians had brought with them.

"I'm to be married to his daughter," Gisalhari answered. "We would be married already, if Hagan hadn't thrown our priest into the river."

Thioderik looked at Hagan, shaking his head. Hagan could see the curve of amusement beneath the Goth's dusty-blond moustaches. "But you swore the oaths of betrothal and drank on troth together?"

"Oh, yes. She and Hrodgar and Gotelind will come back to Worms with us and hold the wedding feast there."

"That is a worthy honor," Thioderik said gravely. "Tell me, why did Hrodgar not come with you?"

Pricked by the sudden sparks of the Amalung's last words, Hagan answered the question himself. "He said that he and his men would be here in two days' time, when the Yule feast itself is held. Did you wish to see him sooner?"

"If he is so late, then he will miss the feast!" Attila boomed. "Since you are here, we shall have feasting tonight and the great celebration tomorrow as I have planned it, when I shall give you the honors that both I and Aetius mean for you to have."

"Now that is an unkindly way for you to treat a man who has been true to you so long," Thioderik said, and he laughed as if to show Attila that his words had no sting in them. "Rather than that Hrodgar be left hungry and late, I shall ride to his hall myself so that he and his band can share in this feasting—since there is a betrothal to celebrate, he has more right to be here than anyone. I know Hildebrand can keep watch over my men and your hall well enough while I am gone."

He rose again and strode away before Attila could say anything. The Hunnish drighten's wolf-gray brows lowered in a glare as he watched Thioderik's back.

Gundahari also stood, raising his cup toward Gundrun, then Attila, before he drank. "Hail to our kind host, who has bidden us here as guests," he called in a voice loud enough for everyone at that end of the hall to hear. He sprinkled a few drops of wine onto the earthen floor and drained the cup at a draught, dashing the last drops from his beard with the back of his hand. "I trust you have no quarrel with Hrodgar," he went on when he had sat down again. "It would be a great pity to have strife between two of the drightens bound to our clan."

"Since he swore his troth to me, Hrodgar has been as loyal as a man may be. But why should I delay our delights for the sake of one man's tardiness? Come, drink and be merry." Attila's slitted eyes skewed over to Folkhari. "I remember you, singer. Will you give us a song of Sigifrith, in honor of the fròwe of this hall?"

"I would not remind Gundrun of her sorrows," said Folkhari, his voice so low that even Hagan had to lean close to catch his words. Then the singer smiled at Attila and spoke clearly. "It seems that you must have heard all of them time and again. Let me sing to you a song that came down from Gautland, about Sigifrith's kin and the revenge which Sigimund and Sigilind took on Sigilind's husband for Wals and his sons."

Folkhari bent his long blond head close to his harp, plinking it into tune, then stood to sing. The sound of the strings was lost in the noise of the hall, but the words came through clearly enough as he chanted the tale of Sigigairar's children slain, of the begetting of Sinfjotli and the burning of the Gautish hall.

"I have heard that Sigifrith reforged that same stone-cutting sword," Attila said when the song was over. "What became of it after his death? Was it laid in a howe with his ashes, as I have heard is often the custom?"

It was Hagan who replied. "The sword was burned with him, and melted with the brave man's flesh. There was nothing left to lay in a howe."

Hagan thought he heard Attila muttering, "A waste," beneath his breath, but could not be sure.

The Hunnish drighten turned to his wife. "Bring out my sons, so they may see the heroes of whom they have heard in the songs of the Gothic folk."

"You insisted that Bleyda and Humla should go out with the hunters," Gundrun replied. "The only child of your getting in the hall is your concubine's new son Artleb."

"Then bring him. I wish your brothers to see him."

Gundrun snorted. "Why should I?"

"Because wrangling with your husband in front of guests is not even fit for a Gothic queen."

Gundrun stood up with a toss of her head, as though her hair still fell free about her face instead of being pinned up in a wife's crown of braids. Angrily she stalked off toward the door at the back of the hall.

When Gundrun came back, she was followed by a small dark woman so heavily wrapped in swathes of linen that even her face was barely visible beneath the white hood. She bore in her arms a swaddled child, whose face was clearly marked by Attila's eagle nose; the boy's head was bound on to a slanted board, the little skull already lengthening into the Hunnish helmet shape. He let out a furious wail, struggling against the bindings of his swaddling cloths and glaring red-faced at the Burgundians.

"See what a warrior he is already?" Attila said proudly. "He carries my blood truly. There shall come a day when many warriors ride to his hall for the sake of fighting in his band."

Hagan looked at the child; and it seemed to him that a stain of shadows spread over the white swaddling linen in the firelight. "The child has a look of unluck to him. I think that men will seldom see warriors such as myself coming to his hall."

Attila's lips drew back from his jagged yellow teeth as he leaned forward with a hiss of fury; but Hagan never knew what he meant to say, for at that moment the door burst open to the shrieking of Hunnish war shouts and Dankwart staggered in with his bloody sword in his hand and blood running down from the shoulder of his limp shield arm.

"Treachery. . . . !" he gasped into the sudden silence. "Ambush . . . "

In a blinding moment, Hagan saw the shape of his doom as clear as the stark shape of a winter tree black against a lightning flash. He was the first to move; his sword flicked from his sheath and through the neck of the child in the Hunnish woman's hand, stopping halfway into her body. He wrenched it out and turned to face Attila as the horde of armed Huns began to pour into the crowded hall.

The Hunnish king was already fighting with Gundahari, who was slowly pressing him backward. Hildebrand had climbed onto one of the tables and was shouting, "Get back! Outside! Find Thioderik!" to the Goths. Some of them seemed to be pushing their way out; others, caught up in the fury of the bloody press, were stabbing with their eating daggers or bashing about them with whatever came to hand. Hagan stood to guard Gundahari's back, with Folkhari at his left side; together they fended off the Huns trying to reach their king, but Attila's thanes were pushing them back.

As two more Huns came in on his right, Hagan heard a high-pitched shout, and there was a small warrior with a sword between himself and the attackers. He could not spare more than a fleeting glance, but the shock of seeing Gundrun by his side with a weapon in her hand was almost his death: he barely got his blade up in time to fend off another attacker. He knew there was not time or space for her to get out unscathed; well as she was fighting, she was safer than she would have been in the close thick of battle without a weapon, and he hoped that Attila's men would hold their hands rather than strike at her. Indeed, out of the corner of his eye, he saw a burly Hun check his swing so that his sword did no more than graze Gundrun's arm; and he saw the blade she had caught up take the man through the belly.

Hildebrand's shouting had finally got through to Thioderik's Goths: they were falling back toward the door of the hall, and without their Gothic allies beside them the Huns could not keep the Burgundians from fighting their way through to rally together.

"Attila's fled!" Gundahari shouted, and the Burgundians took up the cry as they pushed the Huns back. Hagan gestured to Gernot; the two of them heaved up one of the heavy oaken tables, quickly barring the door to Attila's chambers so that no attack could take them from behind without warning.

Seeing that their drighten was there no longer, the Huns retreated from the hall, leaving the Burgundians alone there with the dead and those wounded too badly to move. A few of the worst injured were beginning to moan softly; other than that there was no sound except for the harsh breathing of the warriors.

"Are you all right, Gundrun?" Hagan asked his sister. Gundrun looked up at him, smiling fiercely. Sweat sheened her forehead redly in the firelight; her braids had come loose from their crown, flopping down over her shoulders. Her flickering shadow, tall on the wall behind her, showed Hagan the trembling of the sword in her hands. He could see a stain on his sister's shoulder, and another on her hip. "Let me see your wounds."

Gundrun looked down as if noticing for the first time that she had been hurt. She lifted the torn linen up, letting Hagan search through the holes.

"Neither is deep. The gods must have favored you."

"I couldn't let you fight alone. Why did you come? I sent you all the warning I could."

"The runes were muddled. Wingi might have done it, but he is dead now, in any case."

Gundahari embraced Gundrun, careful of the shallow cut above her arm. "My brave sister . . ." Then the words seemed to choke in his throat.

A Hun who lay gripping the stump of his wrist tightly with his other hand suddenly raised his head and screamed, a cracked keening ululation that seemed to go on endlessly.

"What shall we do with these?" the thane Nantwin asked, waving his hands at the wounded Huns.

"Get them out. Let their own take care of them."

Nantwin and Gernot lifted the screaming warrior first, heaving him up by shoulders and feet and flinging him out of the door. When he struck the ground, he lost his grip on his maimed arm; the blood sprayed black into the new snow and he slumped into silence. Other thanes were tending to the wounded Burgundians, slashing their tunics and tearing off strips to use as bandages.

"I can see that what I have heard is true," Folkhari called from the door when Nantwin and Arnulf had finished their task. "The Huns are cowards; they wail like women when they should be coming to tend their wounded."

The singer drew back a pace or two, picking up a Hunnish throwing spear and waiting beside the door with the weapon poised in his hand. It was only a moment before he stepped forward and hurled it: a gasp of pain, quickly chopped off, and the sound of cursing outside told Hagan that Folkhari's aim had been true.

Hagan went to the door himself to see what was taking place outside. The Goths had withdrawn into a band near the palisade; the Huns were ringed outside, and more and more armed warriors were coming in through the gate. "If we had been a day later," he said to Folkhari, "I think we should have been ambushed on the road." He could see that some of the men outside, though they were bundled in fur cloaks like the Goths and Huns, marched in straight lines with the even steps of men trained in the Roman army. "And now I think I know what honor Aetius wished to give us."

"They arrived less than half a moon ago," Gundrun told him.

Hagan nodded. "Indeed. Get back to the back of the hall, Gundrun. There will be fighting here in a moment, and the space is narrow: we need trained warriors at the door."

Gundrun looked up as if she were about to argue with him. Hagan shook his head. "If they break through into the main hall, then we shall truly need you to fight beside us. Here, you'd be as likely to hit one of us as one of them."

Gundrun went back as Gundahari, Gisalhari and Gernot came to the fore. The Huns outside were beginning to shout and clash weapons against shields, while Aetius' men gathered into a narrow wedge.

"Why isn't Attila in front?" Hagan called roughly to the Huns. "It would be more fitting if the folk-warder fought before his thanes, as King Gundahari and his kin do."

"Take care, Attila!" Gundrun shouted from the rear of the hall. "Be sure to offer your warriors gold by the heaped-up shieldfull, for if my brothers reach you there you must surely die."

Although Attila's face and hair were fearsomely masked in dried blood from a scalp wound, Hagan could not mistake the Hunnish king's roar as he leapt forward, and Folkhari laughed merrily as Attila's warriors dragged him back by the shield strap.

"Forward!" Attila shouted, waving his sword in his free hand. "Take them there! Kill them all!"

Hagan, Gundahari and Folkhari stood firm at the door as the formation of Aetius' men thundered down upon them. The first shock of the meeting knocked them back, so that perhaps twenty or thirty men poured into the hall before they could recover their place. Gundahari and Folkhari stood in the doorway battling against those trying to get in while Hagan defended their backs.

Hagan felt the shock of a blade against his byrnie on his blind side, but no pain; the steel rings had not been broken, so he thought nothing of it, whirling quickly to ring his sword off the helmet of the man who had struck him. Steel and skull broken, the warrior fell forward into the bloody mud; Hagan leaped over him to meet another attacker.

The fight was fierce and sharp, but quickly over. Hagan guessed that there were still forty of the half-hundred Burgundians whole enough to stand and fight when all the foes who had broken into the hall were slain. Even as he turned to look, the last Huns were retreating from the door.

Gundahari spat after them. "That's evened the odds a little, I think."

Gisalhari was leaning on his sword, gasping with the exertion. "I hope . . . Hrodgar comes soon. Need all the help . . . we can get."

Hagan looked at his younger cousin, feeling an irritating prickle of pity. "If Hrodgar chooses to help us. He owes some troth to each side."

Suddenly one of the fallen sprang from the floor, slashing at Hagan so viciously that he hardly had time to step back. The Burgundian could not see the man's face through his helm; a big man, a yellow braid hanging down his back, Hagan thought he might be a Goth or Frank by birth, but his short sword and style of fighting showed that he had been trained in Rome. Hagan defended himself with all his strength; sparks flew as his blade clashed on his foe's helmet, but the sword's edge was blunted and the metal thicker than most. The big man answered with a cut that flicked down on Hagan's blind side, cracking through the battered raven shield and slicing along his thigh; but at the same moment the man's shield shattered under Hagan's blow and the Burgundian's sword stabbed through his byrnie and into his body. Aetius' warrior pulled away and fled from the hall; and as he ran Hagan picked up a spear and hurled it. The point stuck in his helm, knocking him to his knees. When he rose again, he staggered in circles till his comrades came and led him away.

"Well done!" Folkhari said as Gundrun hurried forward. Hagan sat down on one of the bodies; he had barely enough strength to make sure the man beneath him was dead before he leaned back and stretched his leg out for Gundrun to see to.

The wound was not so deep that he could not stand and perhaps even fight at need—Naudung's shield had saved his leg—but a wide shallow piece of flesh had been sliced off and the pain was beginning to wash up through his body in waves.

"Bind it tightly," Hagan said to Gundrun. "I shall not have rest enough for it to heal."

She wrapped jagged strips of linen from the hem of her dress around and around his thigh, pulling it as tight as she could. "It will feel worse than it is. You could be whole again within a moon."

Gundahari peered out of the door, pulling his head back before Hagan could tell him to. "They've backed off. I don't think they'll come at us like that again, at least not for a while. Is there any food or drink left?"

Most of what was on the tables had been knocked off or trampled underfoot. They moved the table barring the back door aside and twelve of the unwounded went with Gundahari and Gernot to make sure that no Huns had come in through the rear chambers. Hagan heard the sound of heavy wood scraping across the earthen floor, and guessed that they were securing the other door into the building.

There was some food in the kitchen and half a barrel of wine left—a slice of bread with a sliver of cheese and a full cup for each man, with a little left over for the morning. Gundrun's hands were shaking as she poured, but she walked among the thanes as gracefully as she had when, as a maiden, she had dealt out the drink in Gundahari's hall in Worms. She went first to the badly wounded, who sat propped against the wall or lay on the benches and tables. The sinews of Arnulf's right knee had been severed so that he would never walk again, but he held the cup to the lips of the man beside him. For Bernward's arms, one broken and one cut half-through, were bandaged against his body with strips of red and blue cloth; and so the wounded helped one another to eat and drink.

"I wish we could have had a better meeting," she said when she came to fill the king's cup and Hagan's horn. "I have missed you both." The tears stood unspilt in her eyes, as red as watered wine in the low firelight.

"What about me?" Gisalhari demanded. "Haven't you missed me?"

Gundrun looked at him, smiling wryly. "Let me think about it."

Gisalhari's even features drooped and he let out a whine like a hurt puppy. Gundrun laughed and went to hug him about the shoulders with one arm before she poured his wine. "I suppose I've even missed you. Frija's blessing on your wedding, by the way."

"Thank you. Will you come to it? We're holding it in Worms."

"When we get out of here . . . Yes. I'll come if I can."

"Hrodgar," Gundahari murmured to Hagan. "Thioderik."

"Maybe." If Hrodgar chose to defend them—if Thioderik chose—they might be able to force Attila to let the Burgundians go free. If . . .

When everyone had finished his small meal, Gundahari rose to his feet and knocked against a table top until the thanes looked up. "We've fought like heroes today, and our battle isn't lost yet. If you think about it, we're in a better place: they have to sleep outside in the snow, while we're in here with the fires, and we've seen that they can't get in here very easily. Now I think we should sleep while we can, and see what tomorrow brings. Does anyone want to keep watch to make sure they don't try any treachery?"

Hagan pulled the bloody fur cloak off the dead man beneath him and wrapped it around himself before he rose and limped over to sit by the door. "I shall. I don't think I can sleep."

"I'll stay with you," Folkhari said at once. "What's a little sleep? Those dogs scratched my harp and broke a string. I'll be happy enough if I can kill a few more of them." He squinted his eyes, glancing around at the other thanes. "Any of you know what Huns really are?" he asked, raising his voice so that it could be heard outside.

"What?" asked Gisalhari.

"They're living proof that lonely Gothic women really will sleep with swine!"

Hagan twisted his lips back in the grimace that was as close as he could come to a smile, while a roar of laughter went up from the Burgundian thanes and some of the men outside muttered viciously.

Folkhari took a string out of his belt pouch and bent to repairing his harp. It was not long before the clear notes rang from the bronze wires, soothing the talk of the men into quietness as they rolled themselves in their cloaks and lay down on the benches or on the floor. Hagan got up to take a helmet from one of the dead men and set it on his head. His leg was beginning to stiffen, but he had had worse wounds; he thought he would not need to worry too much about this one.

When most of the thanes seemed to have gone to sleep, Folkhari laid his harp aside. He began to talk softly to Hagan about new rumors and songs he had heard of late. They talked about Gisalhari's wedding and about what they meant to do when they got back to Worms, speaking together as they had not since Sigifrith's death. Hagan remembered that it was the night before a battle when he and Waldhari the Frank—rather drunk—had sworn brotherhood together. Had it been Waldhari's idea, or his own? He could not remember: that had been seventeen years ago, but he remembered the startling blueness of Waldhari's eyes in his tanned face, Roman-cut brown hair streaked with fairness from years of riding bare-headed, and the blood-slick grip of his square hand as they had sworn. Nor could he forget the browned hand lying in the grass and dust beneath the little hill, and the blinding pain in his face as Waldhari threw the jagged stump of his shattered sword up.

"What are you thinking?" Folkhari murmured. "Do you hear something?"

Hagan shook his head.

Folkhari pointed out of the door, toward the right. "Look."

Hagan thought he saw the dull gleam of helmets in the darkness; now he heard the whisper of boots through the snow. As one, he and Folkhari stood, drawing their swords.

A voice muttered a Hunnish curse; the stealthy movement faded away, and Hagan heard a tent flap opening.

Folkhari laughed softly. "Shall I go out and join them? I have a tune I should like to play them." He moved his fingers as if plucking strings along the hilt of his sword.

"No; if you get into bad straits, I shall have to come to your aid, and then there should be no one guarding our sleeping friends. If we were both busy fighting, two or three of them could run in and do such harm among the sleepers that we should never stop mourning."

"Then let us at least let them know that we saw them." Folkhari raised his voice, calling out through cupped hands, "Hai, why do you go armed like that, you atheling-warriors? Are you off on a raid? You should ask us to go with you, then."

No answer came other than a rustle of angry whispering in Hunnish within one of the tents.

"Foul cowards! Would you have murdered us in our sleep?" Folkhari called softly. "That would not have been a man's deed."

"Enough," Hagan whispered to him. "You'll wake the others."

In the dim glow of the coals, the sleeping Burgundians were only shadows against the darkness; but Hagan could make out Gundahari's snuffle and the soft breathing of Gundrun where she lay with her head against her brother's shoulder. He did not know whether the enchantment of Grimhild's brewing still worked on her, stilling her sorrow and rage over Sigifrith's death, or whether the wearing of years and the loneliness of her loveless exile among the Huns had worked more deeply in her, so she had forgotten her fury and remembered only the closeness of her childhood. Whichever it might be, he knew that he was glad of it.

Hagan pushed himself to his feet. At Folkhari's questioning glance, he murmured, "If I don't move, my leg will stiffen and I won't be able to stand." He limped back to Gundahari and Gundrun, staring down for a long moment at his two siblings as they slept before he made his way back to his watchpost by the door.

The ice chilling through Hagan's byrnie warned him of the nearing dawn before any light glimmered in the snowy sky. He was tired and his leg ached, but no sleep weighed on his eyelid yet.

"Should I feed the fires up?" Folkhari asked, his voice as raspy as Hagan's own. "It's getting awfully cold."

"I think that would be good."

At first Hagan thought that the orange-gold glow outside was the light of dawn; then his eyes focused and he saw the flames leaping one by one from the torches, reflected from helms and shield bosses and glittering from the tiny crystals of fresh snow underfoot.

"Awake!" he shouted. "Awake and arm yourselves!"

Those who were strong enough rolled out of their cloaks and leapt to their feet at once, hurrying toward the door with their weapons in their hands.

"Kindle the hall!" Attila shouted from outside. "You cowards, go closer— what can they do? They have no bows."

Hagan felt around in the icy mud of the hall's floor for a throwing spear, as he saw other men doing, but there seemed to be none left. An arrow hissed past him, thunking into a table; in the torchlight outside he could see a ring of Huns with drawn bows standing about the door. He could only watch as the torch-bearers came to the corners of the hall, tossing their brands up onto the thatched roof.

Hagan heard three torches hiss out in the snow before the first flames began to crackle along the left side of the hall, the wind whipping them with a whispering *sssh* of snowflakes scorching into steam. The icicles dangling from the edges of the roof ran to still the flames, but the Huns kindled the fire again and again till it began to burn through patches in the roof.

The hall grew warmer, hot water and wet ashes dripping down together with flaming sticks.

"Stand near the walls! Tread the fire into the mud," Hagan called.

Then the flames began to burn along the doorframe. Biting his lip against the pain in his leg, he caught up the stiff body of a young warrior and began to beat out the fire with it till the sweet scent of roasting pork rose from the smouldering flesh. He saw the others doing the same wherever the flames flared through the straw chinking the thick wood of the walls.

Though the Huns tried again and again to kindle the fire on the thatch, there was too much snow for it to burn very long. Still, the hall had grown terribly hot. Hagan's mouth was so dry that he could hardly speak.

"I'm ready to . . . die of thirst," Folkhari panted. "Hagan, you're said to be wise: what shall we do about this?"

Hagan knew there was little wine left, and wine would only make them thirstier; except for the sooty droplets from the roof, there was nothing of anything other than the dead in the hall.

Struck by a sudden thought, he bent down and prodded at one of the corpses with his sword. It did not bleed, but when he pushed at the wound he found that there was blood in the body.

"You atheling-warriors, if thirst torments you—drink of the blood of the slain! In this heat, it will be better for you than wine; and at this time there is nothing better to be had." He crouched himself, raising the body he had cut to his lips and sucking the thick salty blood from it till his thirst was quenched. Looking up, he saw that Gundrun had not waited to do the same.

Dankwart also raised his head, wiping darkness from his mouth to stain his sleeve. "Now the gods reward you, Hagan, since I have drunk so well through your rede." Though he smiled, Hagan saw his ruddied lips trembling. "Seldom has better wine been given to me. If I live for any time, I shall always think well of you for it."

Though a few of the men looked faint and ill, more crouched down at Dankwart's words and began to drink from the dead.

Gisalhari stood, irresolute, over the body of Bernward who had died in the night. Hagan caught his eye and would not let him look away. "Don't you Christians drink the blood of your god? And wouldn't Bernward want you to have his strength? Drink; we'll need you to fight at your strongest before this is over."

The light sprinkling of freckles on Gisalhari's nose and cheeks stood out like a splatter of wine against his paleness as he bent, choking; but he swallowed when the liquid filled his mouth, and he kept the drink down.

Folkhari grinned at Hagan when he had finished his draught. "I feel that this drink has given me great strength, and many a Hunnish wife shall pay for it with her dearest friend."

The Huns seemed to have given up trying to set the hall alight. Hagan heard them drawing back, and then the sound of shouting.

"Hrodgar, Hrodgar!"

"Now," Gundahari breathed, hurrying to the door. "Now we'll see."

Hagan closed his eye and bit back his breath, listening to the sound of hooves nearing. Not a large band; he deemed that it was not more than thrice twelve.

"Hai!" Attila's raw voice shouted. "You're here early in the day, Hrodgar. Where is Thioderik?"

"I haven't seen him. Because I know you are sometimes impatient we left at midday yesterday and last night we stayed in the tavern on the march between my lands and yours, the one with the sign of the Red Eagle. Why are you out here? What has happened?"

"The Burgundians slew my son Artleb and attacked my men for no sake at all. They are in there and we are out here, and I charge you to earn the rings and swords I have given you, according to the way of your folk."

"Woe to me, then, that I was ever born! Is there no way to halt this? I gave the Burgundians guest-right in my house, I hardly believe that they acted with no reason."

Hagan heard a man's voice saying in a speech lilting with the rhythms of the Hunnish tongue, his whisper nearly as loud as a shout, "See how he stands there, who has his rulership from Attila's hand—who was to earn the life and the folk and the hall that Attila gave him! In all of his storming, he has struck no praiseworthy blow. I think he does not care what goes on here, since he has everything he wanted to keep. I have heard that he was courageous, but these conflicts prove that false."

"You think I am a coward?" Hrodgar cried. "You have spoken too loudly." The thunk of bone on bone was as sharp as an axe striking into wood. Hagan heard the unmistakable steel jingling and deep thump of a man's armored body dropping to the ground. In the murmurs that followed, he recognized the Hunnish word for "dead," then a Goth's awed whisper, "And with only one blow of his fist!"

"Away, nithling!" Hrodgar said. "Don't I have enough sorrows? Why should you curse me for not fighting here, since I had no reason to be here? And I gave the Burgundians guest-right, and the troth of my kin in betrothal besides. I may not fight them."

The words were clear enough for everyone to hear. Hagan saw the hope flowering on Gisalhari's face as he stared at the dawn light coming in through the doorway and heard Gundrun's soft inward breath.

"What kind of help is slaying my men?" Attila asked angrily. "We have so many dead in the land that we don't need any more. You've told me for twelve years that you would fight for me as my thane, and serve me as if I were a drighten of your own folk; and I have never needed your troth more than I do now."

"I will lose life and lands for you gladly, because I swore my oath, but I never swore to lose my soul. It was I who welcomed them into the farthest marches of your rule, and they must still be my guests."

"I have heard that you are honorable; you owe me a great geld of troth and oath, and so you ought to make good this harm to me."

"God pity me that I have lived until this! I must give up my honor, my troth and the honor of my line that God gave me. God in Heaven, that death should not have taken me from this! Whichever path I forsake for the other I shall have acted evilly, but all folks shall blame me if I leave them both. May He give me rede, who called me to life!"

"Think of your oaths and your honor. Your daughter may yet marry Gisalhari, if he lives; but your sword is sworn first to me. And remember: it is only by my grace that you hold your land and your hall, which I could have taken from you at any minute. I could have slain you and given your wife and daughter to my warriors, as I still might if I choose."

"My drighten, take my land and hall. Let my family and myself go into exile and become wretched wanderers; let me go on my own feet."

"Who would help me then? I shall give you freely your land and your followers if you will revenge me on my foes, and you shall be a king beside Attila."

"I bade the Burgundians to my own home, and gave them meat and drink and my best gifts—how should I plan to kill them now? It would make me seem a coward. I gave my daughter to Fro Gisalhari, nor could I have found a better man for her."

Hagan heard the whisper of a sword being unsheathed; the prickling along the end of his nerves, gathering to the pain in his leg, made him think it was Attila's.

The Hunnish king spoke again. "I swear on my sword that if you lead your men against the band in the hall there, I shall treat your wife and daughter as if they were of my own blood. Gotelind shall hold your hall if you are slain. Garlind shall have the best husband I can find between here and Rome." His speech halted for a moment. Then he went on so softly that Hagan could hardly hear him, as if he had put his arm around Hrodgar's shoulders and was whispering into the march-drighten's ear. "I know I don't need to threaten you, Hrodgar. You know men say you are honorable. I expect you to live up to the songs."

The deep sigh pressed out of Hrodgar's lungs as if Attila had punched him beneath the breastbone.

Hagan opened his eyes to see Hrodgar and three times twelve thanes approaching the door. As Hrodgar led his men nearer, he put his helmet on. Except for the eyeslits, the steel was a faceless gray mask; the helm the march-drighten had given Gundahari was far finer than his own.

"Now my wife will be a great boon to us," Gisalhari cried cheerfully, peering over Hagan's shoulder. "See, Hrodgar is coming to give us aid."

Folkhari turned to give him a sour look. "I don't know why you're so cheerful. When did you ever see so many armed men putting their helmets on for the sake of peace? Hrodgar means to earn the lands and hall which Attila has allowed him until now."

"Ward yourself, Burgundians!" Hrodgar shouted, the metal of his helm ringing with his words till his voice sounded like a stranger's. "You were my friends before, but now I must break our bonds."

"Our gods and yours forbid it!" Gundahari called as he turned the helmet Hrodgar had given him over in his hands. "I cannot believe you would ever do this to us."

"I cannot hold back. I must fight you, since I am bound by oath. Now ward yourself, as you love your life. Attila has held me to my word."

"It is too late for you to forswear yourself," said the Burgundian king. "May your god reward you if you can bring this to a peaceful end. Hrodgar, high atheling, think of the gifts you gave us when we came into your land and the troth that binds us."

"I would be happy if I could thus bid you to my hall again. I wish you were back on the Rhine and I were dead with honor."

Gisalhari pushed his way past Gundahari and stood in the door. "Look, Hrodgar!" he shouted. "I am wearing the sword you gave me. I doubt whether atheling will give such a fine weapon again—but if you slay any of my friends or kin here, I must take your life with your own sword, and then I shall mourn for you and your frowe."

"I wish that what you are waiting for had already come to pass. Gisalhari, I place my wife and daughter in your trust."

Hrodgar raised his shield as though he were about to lead the charge into the hall. Then Hagan said. "Halt a moment, Hrodgar. What good can our deaths do your drighten, if peace could be made?"

"There is no hope of peace," Hrodgar replied, his words muffled.

Hagan lifted up the broken raven shield. "See, the shield which Gotelind gave me to carry has been hacked to pieces by the Huns. If the gods would give me one as good as the one which you bear, I would need nothing else to ward me in battle."

"I would gladly help you with my shield if I dared give it to you before Attila . . . Take it, Hagan, and wield it! I should be joyful enough if I knew you were to bear it back to the Rhine."

Hagan came out of the hall, blinking against the sunrise, and took the shield from Hrodgar's arm. "The gods reward you, and may your atheling-virtues ever be reborn into the ring of the Middle-Garth. However this fight goes, I myself shall not raise my sword against your body, though I shall deal harshly with your thanes if I must."

"Since Hagan has set peace between you and him, I shall keep it also," called Folkhari. "You well deserve it for the welcome you gave us when we came here."

Then Hagan went back into the hall, walking as straight as he could so that the Huns might make less of his wound. He and Folkhari stood next to Gundrun on the bench which had stood before the high table before it was moved. She, too, had found a dead man's helmet and put it on her head, waiting with a sword clasped in both hands.

Hrodgar and his band of thanes rushed into the hall, meeting the Burgundians with a shattering crash. In only a few moments, Hagan and Folkhari had seen five of their comrades fall before the better-rested warband. Hrodgar was at the front; silver glimmered from the sword he had given Gisalhari as the two of them hewed at each other. So Folkhari and Hagan ran forward, Gundrun following closely behind them as they attacked Hrodgar's band.

The hall was very quiet when the clashing of steel stilled. Hagan felt faint; he leaned the point of his sword on the helm of a corpse, breathing deeply and pressing one hand against the reopened wound on his leg as he looked about him.

Gundahari and Gundrun were standing, seemingly unhurt, as were Folkhari, Gernot and perhaps fifteen of the other thanes, but Gisalhari lay dead on the earth. A great bloody dent had caved in his acquired helmet; he still clutched to the silver-wound hilt of his sword, whose blade was embedded deeply between Hrodgar's neck and shoulder.

"His troth deserved a better geld than this," said Hagan. He sat down to tighten the bloody bandages on his leg.

Gundahari bent to disentangle weapon from man, and Folkhari aided him to carry the bodies of Hrodgar and the king's cousin over beside the wall, laying them next to the wounded and dying Burgundians.

Outside the Goths were muttering, "What has happened? Who is yet alive?" Then a young man's voice said clearly, "Uncle, we must go see what's happened—shit, we owe it to Hrodgar. Remember how he spoke for our drighten when Attila's first sons were killed in battle under him? I'll go ask what they've done, and then come back to tell you. If they slew Hrodgar they shall all give up their lives for it, or else we shall be shamed."

Hildebrand's deep growl answered him, "I do not want you to go and ask, Wolfhart. I don't think you will be a peace-weaver."

"Take up your shield and sword, then, and put on your helmet. If you go there unarmed, they're like to insult you, and then you'll have to come back ashamed. But if you go weaponed, they'll behave better."

Hagan heard the sound of byrnies jingling and weapons clinking, then Hildebrand spoke again. "Where in Hella's name do you think you're going?"

"We're coming to the hall with you," another Gothic voice answered. "You're more likely to get an honorable answer if you come with the full warband behind you."

Hagan rose to look out of the door as Hildebrand and the Gothic thanes drew themselves up outside it, holding their shields before them.

"Is Hrodgar dead?" Hildebrand demanded.

Gundahari stepped before his brother, standing in the doorway. "We wish that he were not."

The Goths muttered and sighed into their helmets. Hildebrand said, "Now give us Hrodgar, dead as he is, from the hall so that we may mourn him and honor his body as is fitting. Remember, we too are wretched exiles. Why do you keep us waiting? Let us come in and carry him away so we may give him our thanks in his death." The old warrior paused, then murmured softly, "It would have been better if we had done so while he lived."

"No honor is so true as that which a friend gives to a friend after death," answered Gundahari. "It is fitting that you should honor Hrodgar thus." But he did not step aside from the door.

"How long do we have to beg?" Wolfhart cried. "Since you have slain our best-trusted ally and we must do without him, let us come in and carry him away to bury him. Are you afraid to let us in?"

"They're afraid!" Attila's voice shouted from outside. "Give up the body, if you dare!"

Folkhari jostled through the gathered thanes to stand at the door beside Gundahari. "No one is going to give him to you. Come and get him in this hall where he fell into the blood with his death wound. Then the honor you pay him will be true honor!"

"You're trying to provoke us, singer," Wolfhart said. "If we were supposed to fight here before our drighten Thioderik says we can, you'd be in real trouble now."

Folkhari spoke with the strong clarity that he used for chanting over the shouting of men in a crowded hall so everyone outside could hear him well. "There's too much fear when a man is ready to hold back from everything that's forbidden him. I can't call that a true hero's mood."

"Now I'll jingle your harp for you!" shouted the young Goth. "I can't let that pass without shame."

"Come on! I'll take the shine out of your new helmet."

Hagan saw Wolfhart try to leap for the door of the hall, and Hildebrand grab him about the shoulders. "Anyone would think you'd gone mad!" the old warrior scolded his nephew. "You would have lost our drighten's favor forever. We are not to fight till he comes back."

"Let him loose!" called Folkhari. "If he once gets near me, no matter if he had slain all the thanes in the world, he would have no chance to tell the tale."

At that Wolfhart wrested himself free of Hildebrand's grip and, drawing his sword, ran for the doorway. Hildebrand followed him; at first Hagan thought that the aged Goth meant to try to hold his nephew back, but Hildebrand was inside the hall before Wolfhart.

Hildebrand sprang at Hagan, and the two of them traded blows for a few moments before the rest of Thioderik's thanes pushed in and got in their way. In flashes through the tumult of fighting, Hagan saw the crippled Arnulf sitting on a bench and striking out at every Goth who came within his reach; he saw Gundrun's small shape between Wolfhart and Folkhari, hewing two-handed at Wolfhart with her blade as the Goth tried unsuccessfully to fend her off and get around her without being gutted. Even in armor from the rear, he could not mistake Hildebrand's wide shoulders and squat body as Thioderik's thane came on Folkhari's other side; the steel dust sparked from the singer's byrnie before the spraying gush of blood drenched the air and Folkhari fell.

Hagan shifted his shield up higher and slashed like a boar, trying to reach Hildebrand.

"Turn toward me!" Gernot shouted at Wolfhart. "This cannot last much longer."

Hildebrand was exchanging blows with Gundahari. Hagan could see no one else to fight. He stood resting on his sword for a moment as Gernot's blade broke through Wolfhart's byrnie. It is done, he thought. But Wolfhart dropped his shield when he felt his death wound, lifting his sword with both hands while Gernot tried to wrest his blade out and bringing it down on Gernot's head through helmet and chain-mail, so that the two of them fell together.

Hildebrand backed off from Gundahari, glancing about him. He and the three Gebicungs were the only ones still standing, though a few wounded were beginning to moan from the blood-mixed mud of the floor.

The old warrior held up his hand to stay Gundahari, who nodded, stepping back so Hildebrand could go to his nephew's side. Wolfhart was not quite dead yet. Hildebrand crouched down and took him in his arms as if he would have carried him away, but the young man was too heavy for him to raise.

Wolfhart lifted his head, then let it fall again. "Uncle, you can't do anything for me now. If my kin want to weep for me when I am dead, tell them not to. I've died well enough, slain by the kin of a king. I paid my own weregeld, too, in a red gold that the wives of strong thanes've got good reason to cry over." Then he said nothing more.

Hagan turned Folkhari's body over. Bloody mud masked the singer's face, brown-red streaks bedraggling his long fair hair. Hagan looked at Hildebrand, faceless beneath his helm, and a sudden angry wod swept over him. "You shall pay for this life!" He pushed himself up against a bench and limped toward Hildebrand, who rose swiftly to defend himself.

Hagan's shield held against the old Goth's blow; but Hildebrand's byrnie gave way, steel links scattering into the mud, and Hagan saw the blood flowing from Hildebrand's shoulder.

"Thioderik!" someone shouted outside.

As if in answer, Thioderik's call burned through the icy air: "Hildebrand!"

Hildebrand backed away, then slung his shield over his back and left the hall.

Hagan made his way to one of the benches and sat down. Now there were only the three Gebicungs living, except for Dankwart who lay in the mud trying to hold his guts in and a Goth whose lungs pulsed through a great hole in his chest. Gundrun took off her helmet and went to the Goth first.

Dankwart made the sign of the cross over himself as Gundahari knelt down beside him. "Do it quickly," he gasped. "No . . . better way out of here for me."

"May your Christ guest your soul well."

Then there were only the three of them. Gundahari had lost his helmet; a fresh trickle of blood was running down the side of his head and his left forearm had been laid open almost to the bone. A few more scrapes had bloodied Gundrun's ragged gown, but she was otherwise unharmed. She bound Gundahari's arm, then eased the caked linen from Hagan's leg and rewrapped it.

"Will you come out?" Thioderik called. "Or must we come in to fetch you?"

The Gebicungs went to the door together. Thioderik and Hildebrand stood outside; the Huns and such of Aetius' men as had survived had gone away or hidden in the tents.

"You have slain my truest thanes," the Amalung said. "I am as alone and wretched as I was when Hildebrand and I fled Odoacer's hate, before we came to Attila's hall. One way or the other, you shall make it good to me. Gundahari, give yourself and Hagan up to me, and I shall see that no one here does you any harm—for the sake of my honor, Attila will have to kill me before he kills you if you become my prisoners." Thioderik's eyes were very bright, the dusty gold of his hair gleaming in the winter sunlight that shone through the breaking clouds. Hagan found it hard to breathe under his gaze. The stink of the hall seemed to choke in his throat, and he longed to be outside.

"Isn't it rather late for that?" Gundahari asked. "There are three of us and two of you. Why should we give ourselves up?"

"You know we may not fight with Gundrun, and thus in fair honor she may not strike at us either."

Thioderik's words seemed to hang in the air for a moment, glittering as hard as ice stones.

Slowly Gundrun laid down her sword. She turned to kiss each of her brothers. The tears on her face shone bright as fine steel as she stepped out into the shifting sunlight.

"Go to your husband, Gundrun," Thioderik said. "He has already sworn to take you back and keep you in safety, and your sons are waiting for you. You shall not suffer more from this."

Gundrun walked unsteadily through the snow to the largest of the tents, fumbling at the flaps as if her fingers had gone numb. At last she got it open and disappeared inside.

Thioderik turned to look at the Burgundians again. "Now we are two and two, and you are wounded and weary from battle. Give yourselves up, and I shall see that you get safely home to the Rhine again."

"It would be shameful for us to do so when we still stand on our feet and our thanes and kin lie dead around us," Hagan replied.

R
H
I
N
E
G
O
L
D

⊞
6
9
1

"God knows the time has come when you should be glad to accept peace!" cried Hildebrand. "You ought to agree with my drighten's terms, for no better shall ever be offered to you."

"I would agree with them before I would run from a hall as shamefully as you did here. I thought you could stand up to your foes better, Hildebrand."

"I left to do my duty to my drighten. Nor should you reproach me with that, Who sat on his shield by the Waskenstein while Waldhari the Frank slew his kinsmen and friends?"

"Enough of that!" Thioderik snapped. "Are you two warriors or old women? Listen Hagan and Gundahari, for the honor of my oath and of my thanes whom you have slain, I shall take either of you on in single combat, or each after the other if you choose. Which of you will fight first?"

Hagan put his helmet on and limped out into the clean icy wind which chilled through his helm and byrnie at once. He heaved his shield to his shoulder as Thioderik also put his helm on, and the two of them began to fight.

The clashing of swords seemed to go on without end. Hagan's sight blurred in and out as they fought, his arm warding him without the guidance of his mind. When Thioderik began hewing with both hands grasping his blade, Hagan noticed that he, too, held only the hand grip of his shield; the rest had been hacked away. He tossed it into Thioderik's face, hoping to distract him; but it bounced harmlessly from the Amalung's helmet and Thioderik ignored it.

It seemed to Hagan, after a time, that he could see a glimmering of sparks around Thioderik's head; that the pale fire of the Amal kings burned from his foe's mouth as the Goth cried, "Yield, if you wish to live." Hagan staggered back; he could hardly stand or raise his sword, but he shook his head all the same.

Thioderik dropped his weapon and leapt forward, wrapping his arms around Hagan. Hagan's helm slewed around, darkening his eye; he tried to fight, but Thioderik's strength and weight bore him to the ground. Then he felt rough hands wrapping ropes around his wrists and ankles, and then, at last, he slumped into sleep.

A splash of water in his face awakened Hagan. Half-delirious with thirst, he opened his mouth as the next drenching hit him, swallowing gratefully. He could feel that his byrnie had been taken from him and a stinking cloak of ill-tanned fur thrown over him to keep him from freezing while he slept.

When he opened his eye, he saw that he and Gundahari were both in Attila's hall, propped on a bench with their hands bound behind them. The dead had been carried out, and he thought he could smell their flesh burning outside—or did his mouth water from the scent of the boar turning on a spit over the fire in the middle of the hall? He could not see Gundrun, but Thioderik and Hildebrand stood nearby with Attila and the Gyula and the rest of Attila's men.

"Now I have you," Attila said, snarling a triumphant smile at them. "Now, Gundahari, will you buy your life with Sigifrith's gold? It has done you no good all these years when it lay in the ground, and it will do you no good when you and your brother are dead."

Gundahari's hazel eyes met Hagan's, and Hagan thought that he could read what was to come in his brother's look. He nodded.

"There is no way out of this with honor," the Burgundian king answered steadily. "I may tell you where the Rhine's gold is, but first I must see the bloody heart of my brother Hagan before me."

Attila threw back his head and laughed, slapping his hand against the hilt of his sword. "Hagan, do you hear how dearly your brother loves you? If you'll tell me where the hoard is, you may go free and have his life to do with as you will."

"Gundahari may tell you what he pleases. I cannot stop him, and still less if I am dead. But for myself, I shall never tell you where the gold lies."

"Take him out!" Attila commanded. "Cut out his heart, as his brother has asked."

Thioderik stepped before the two captives. "This is a shameful way to treat warriors and kings, and I shall have no part of it. Slay them if you must, but slay them honorably and swiftly, or I shall do it myself."

Attila walked up to him, almost treading on the Goth's toes as he glared into his face. "Your men are all dead except one. What makes you think you can force me?" He stepped back a pace, drawing his sword and setting the tip just below Thioderik's breastbone.

"Go ahead if you like. You will never have the aid of the Goths again, and all the folks will turn against you if you slay me for no good sake."

After a moment Attila resheathed his blade. "If you will not aid me in this, get out of my hall, you and Hildebrand both. You know that if you ever strike at me, you shall have broken the oaths that you swore in your blood and on your honor and hope of regaining your kingship, and the Amalung line will be dishonored."

"There is no fair end to this. Now I say that you are no longer my drighten, nor I your thane; and may we meet again where my sword can take your life."

Thioderik turned and walked out of the hall, Hildebrand following behind him. Attila waited for a while, staring down at Gundahari and Hagan. "This is your last chance to save your brother's life together with your own, Gundahari. Will you tell me where the Rhine's gold is?"

"Not while Hagan lives."

"So be it."

Two Huns dragged Hagan to his feet, but his leg gave way beneath him when he tried to walk, so they picked him up and carried him outside. His wounded leg had gone quite numb and so had his hands; he could hardly struggle as they untied his arms from behind his back and laid him in the snow, binding his hands to two stakes of one tent and his feet to the stake of another.

"Aren't you afraid?" Attila asked. "I remember that you were always cautious where you might come to any harm."

Hagan shook his head weakly. Attila drew his sword and stood over him, scratching the ragged tunic from Hagan's chest with its point.

"That's a waste of a good warrior," one of the Huns said. "Let's cut out the heart of Hialli the swineherd instead. No matter how long that coward lives, he won't be good for anything."

Hagan heard feet running through the snow, a short struggle and then a whining squeal, "Let me go, master. It's an evil day when a wretched swineherd has to pay for athelings fighting, and leave his fat pigs and good scraps and his warm place by the fire to be slain."

The Huns laughed, dragging the struggling thrall over beside Hagan. "Let this fool die in your place; he's not worthy of life."

Hialli let out a searing scream, and the Huns roared with laughter. "The point hasn't even touched you yet!"

Hagan turned his head to the side, sucking in enough snow to wet his throat. "Let him go. I don't want to hear his shrieking any more. It will be easier and more pleasant for me to play out this game myself."

"There are not many men who would say that in your place," Attila commented. "But we must have a heart to show your brother, though for your sake I shall still his screams first."

With that the Hunnish king slit the swineherd's throat, then chopped through his ribs to cut out the heart, lifting the quivering fistful of dark muscle and shaking a few spurts of blood out of it.

Hagan lay in the snow as the Huns trooped inside. Faintly he heard Attila say, "See, we have brought you Hagan's bloody heart, so you must tell us where Fadhmir's hoard is hidden."

"That is not Hagan's heart," Gundahari said. "It quivers greatly now, and I think it quivered more in the breast of the coward from whom you cut it; it was not my brother who screamed outside."

Attila led his men out again, and this time they did not speak. The sight in Hagan's eye was darkening even as the tip of the war god's sword grated against his breastbone. Then, as the searing pain sliced jaggedly through the numbness of his body, Hagan saw a white glimmering through the blackened sky above him: the wide wings of a swan circling down toward him. He tried to reach up to her; his arms were tied, but he felt the tightness that bound his chest loosing under Attila's sword at last. Freely and joyfully, Hagan laughed as he saw the dark eyes of the swan-maiden bright in her pale face beneath the white shadow of her wings, and he reached out to clasp her hands as the last strings of his breast fell free beneath the blade's edge.

Gundrun came out of the rear chambers of the hall in time to see Attila coming in. His hands dripped with dark blood; she had cleaned deer and boar and cattle often enough to know that it was a heart he carried.

Attila held the bloody heart before Gundahari. The Hunnish drighten's hands were shaking. "You cannot doubt that Hagan is dead. No other man might have laughed as the living heart was cut out of him."

"That is indeed the heart of my brother," the Burgundian king said sadly. "It hardly quivers now, and it quivered less when it lay in his breast." Then Gundahari grinned fiercely through his tears. "Now, Attila, you shall never find out where the Rhine's gold lies, and you shall lose your life as we are now losing ours. If you had tortured me, Hagan might have told you for my sake; but now I alone know where the gold is, and Hagan won't tell you. May the Rhine swallow the hoard before the Huns wear it on their arms!"

"Do you say so? Take him to the Gyula's tent," Attila ordered his men. "I think we know how to make him speak."

Gundrun could not help but follow, clutching the empty knife sheath at her belt with white-knuckled hands. Attila flung Hagan's heart away into the bushes at the edge of the wood as he walked.

Gundrun did not look at the white bone and frozen blood of her brother's gaping chest, but at his face. Hagan's eyepatch had slipped sideways, showing the pale scars beneath. His other eye was wide open, brighter than she had last seen it. She could hardly believe that it was her brother lying there, for his mouth was open as if he laughed yet, the grim mask of his face broken into a look of joy. She did not like to leave him lying there, but there was nothing she could do for him and Gundahari was still living.

The Gyula's tent was large, but stuffily warm, smelling of badly cured hide and drying mushrooms. Coals glowed in a ring around a deep pit. Gundrun heard the sound of scales slithering over scales, and saw Gundahari's face whiten. Dear gods, she thought, why this, of all things? She could not forget that once she had told Attila how Gundahari had been bitten by an adder as a child, and of fear he had had of snakes ever after. The wyrms were quite lively in the warmth of the tent, raising their mottled brown heads and hissing.

"I shall not tell you," Gundahari said again, though Attila had not spoken. "This shall be over soon enough."

Gundrun turned and dashed for the hall with two Huns behind her. She snatched up Folkhari's harp, which lay overturned beside the door, holding it to show the warriors that she meant no violence. "I shall take this to my brother. Let me do that, at least."

She took advantage of their moment of indecision to hasten back to the tent where Attila and two of his men were lowering Gundahari slowly into the pit as the frightened adders slithered to the sides.

Before anyone could stop her, Gundrun bent and dropped the harp in after her brother. Too late she realized that his hands were bound; he had no way of striking the strings.

Gundahari looked up at her and tried to smile through chattering teeth as he kicked off his boots. She had forgotten how long his toes were, how easy it had been for him to throw rocks or pick up fallen rings with them when he was a child and went bare-footed.

Before the adders could come back from the sides of the pit, Gundahari bent his legs and began to pluck rhythmically at the strings with his toes. Slowly, soothed by either the measured sounds or his even movements, the snakes stopped slithering, their dark jewellike eyes fixed on the Burgundian king as he played. Gundrun was afraid to breathe or move. For a moment she felt a painful twisting of hope beneath her breasts.

Then a shudder went through Gundahari's body. He shook his shoulders convulsively and the strings snapped beneath his toes. As he flung himself backward, Gundrun saw an adder dangling from his neck, his flesh already darkening with poison.

Gundahari twitched and moaned as the snakes struck at him. For a second he thrashed and tried to shake them off him; then he gave a long groan and was still.

"Gundrun," said Attila, "you've lost your brothers and it is your own doing, because you wouldn't tell me or get them to tell me where Sigifrith's gold is hidden."

"You say that, but you may be sorry when you find out what shall come afterward. While I'm alive, you shall regret this."

"We must be reconciled, and you shall serve in my hall as my wife, as you always have."

"You can never pay a geld for my brothers that will satisfy me," Gundrun said. Then she thought that open enmity would not bring her any chance to take revenge. "But we women are often subdued by your strength. My kinsmen are dead; you alone have rule over me. I must accept what has happened, if you will only let me give a great feast to honor the memories of my brothers and clan, and of your fallen as well."

"So you may."

Gundrun worked numbly in the kitchen, cleaning out the entrails of the two pigs she had ordered slaughtered for the funeral feast. Several barrels of wine, three full and one half-empty, had been brought in from the storehouse and stood by the door to the hall; the bread was rising on the hearth.

Her hands shook so badly that she could hardly wield the knife. She pulled out the boar's lights, then its heart, and wept again at the sight of the dark-bloodied organ.

What can I do? What must I do? she thought. It will not be enough to stab Attila in his sleep. He must suffer for this. I want him to know exactly what I feel.

It was worse for you when Sigifrith was slain, a voice in her mind seemed to say. It was a harder grief for you to bear when your husband lay dead on the feasting table, with his son slain beside him. Then you might have been glad to know the end to which your brothers should come from it.

But that was long ago: though she had never quite stopped mourning Sigifrith, he was more than twelve years dead. And now she remembered what Hagan had said to her then: *It shall only be more sorrow for you, when the ravens feast on my heart.*

Gundrun did not know why, but somehow she was furious with him for it—perhaps because he was gone and could not hear her anymore.

"You were right, Hagan, curse you!" she wept angrily. "You were always right, and you always warned us about everything. Why in Hella's name did you have to be stupid just this once?"

Gundrun sat over the pigs and cried till she had wrung out her last tears. Then she wiped her face with the back of her sleeve and began to work again, slicing through sinew and breaking through bone with the sharp heavy knife.

The door swung open and shut as Bleyda ran through it. "What are you doing, Gundrun?" It banged open again behind him as Humla chased him in.

"Can we help?" the younger boy asked. "Can we cut something? Let us cut the swine, Mama! Cutting is men's work."

The stamp of Attila's blood seemed clearer and clearer in the faces of her sons as Bleyda looked eagerly up at her and Humla stared at the entrails of the boar. Gundrun's answer choked in her throat, but she moved her head silently.

At most Yule feasts, Attila's hall was so tightly packed with men that it was hard to move along the tables; this year it was less than half full. Since the Goths were either slain or gone with Thioderik, there was no one who cared to put wreaths of pine and holly up along the walls. Only Attila, Gundrun and the Gyula sat at the high table.

"Go and pour the wine, my wife," Attila said to Gundrun.

"Only for you; these others may serve themselves."

She went to the kitchen and filled her pitcher with the drink she had blended for her husband, then picked up the platter of food she had prepared for him.

"I have made this for you alone, as a sign of the new peace between us," she said, pouring Attila's wine and setting his food before him. He dipped his fingers in and ate eagerly. Gundrun had taken great care in the making of it, blending honey and nuts and apples in with the chopped meat.

"You must have opened a new barrel of wine," he said when he had drained his cup and she had refilled it.

Gundrun could not speak; she only nodded.

Attila looked keenly about him. "This is a good feast you have made. I don't remember when you've taken such care of your duties as a wife."

"I wished to honor the dead rightly."

"Indeed. But where are my sons? They should be sitting beside me, to show that the holy blood of our clan still lives and we have yet cause for rejoicing."

Then Gundrun could not help but laugh, shrieking hysterically. She saw Attila's mouth twist like a wounded adder as he half-rose from his seat, his hand cracking across the side of her face. "Where are my sons?"

"I'll tell you, and make your heart glad in the holy blood of your clan. Now you shall hear my words: your sons are here. You have lost your sons, and you yourself drank their blood mixed with wine. Then I roasted their hearts on a spit and chopped them up with honey and other good things, and you've eaten them." And she spat in his face.

Attila drew his sword. Gundrun thought he would have cut her head off then, but the Gyula grabbed his elbow.

"Stop!" the ancient little man shouted, his twiglike fingers holding Attila's muscular arm back. "You may not touch her. Her deeds have made her . . ." and though Gundrun had learned some Hunnish in her years in Attila's hall, she knew that she had never heard the word the Gyula used.

Attila's swarthy face was red with fever and sickness; she saw him choking beneath his beard, forcing himself not to spew before his men. He stared angrily down at the Gyula, who gazed back unmoved. "What may I do? She must be punished for this; she ought to be torn apart by four horses and burnt."

"You may not. No human woman might have done what she has done: she belongs to the gods and ghosts. It is for them to deal with her."

"What may I do? She cannot be let free."

"If you will not turn her loose, build a cage and keep her in it. If you keep her and she is treated well, the gods and ghosts may favor you, for she belongs to them." The Gyula's voice rose to a shriek above the shouting of the men as he turned to face the warriors who were pressing in with drawn eating knives. "Do not touch her! Death and rot to the man who touches her! Do not ask what the gods have done!"

Unwillingly the Huns backed off, muttering; Gundrun saw several of them clutch at amulets or make signs of warding as her gaze swept over them.

"Fetch stout branches, then, and build a cage," Attila ordered. "She shall never walk free again."

The Gyula looked at Gundrun, his lips curving into a smile. "Stay where you are, and do not move till your cage is done. We must burn this bench with the dead, for your touch has made it . . ." and he used the strange Hunnish word again.

Gundrun settled herself more comfortably on the bench. "Do you feel the curse on you yet, Attila?" she asked. "Can you still taste your sons' blood?"

Attila gulped twice, convulsively. Gundrun laughed as he hastened back through the kitchen, laughed harder when she heard the sound of his spewing. "Drink for the dead!" she shouted. "This begins to make good the geld for my brothers!"

Between retches, Attila called to her: "Wait till summer, if you still wish to laugh. My kin shall come from the east then, and we shall sweep down upon Worms and burn it to the ground."

"Brave words!" Gundrun taunted. "But I didn't see you fighting very well here, when even I had taken up a sword." And when Gundahari doesn't come back, they will ready themselves for war at home, she told herself; but she was not as sure as she would have liked to be.

THE RHINE'S GOLD

Gundrun counted the passing of days by making marks on the branches of her cage with her thumbnail; she knew when the Moon was past his darkness by her monthly bleeding. A bitter dry cold settled in after that; despite the fires in the hall it was so cold that Gundrun had to wrap her fur blankets thrice about and sit on her pot to warm it for a while before she dared lift her skirts and let the frozen clay touch her skin. Even the Gyula did not sleep in his tent any more, but came into the hall with the other Huns at night. Gundrun wondered if his adders had frozen to death, or if he had buried them so that they could come out alive again in the spring. But in spite of the cold, there was no snow: the light through the hall door was clear enough to burn Gundrun's eyes when she looked out, and little sparks of dry lightning often flashed between the Huns when they brushed against one anothers' furs.

It was the coldest night that year; the men did not even have the mood to toss dice or argue, but sat huddled together by the fires. Now and again someone would get up to stuff more straw into a chink against the harsh dry wind whispering into the hall through every crack, or else to fill his cup with *khumiss*—Attila had ordered all the wine poured away.

Suddenly a sharp knock sounded on the door. Attila raised his head at once, sniffing about him like a fox catching the scent of wolf on the wind as he touched the amber eagle's head on his scabbard. "Are all our men within?"

"They are," the Gyula answered. "If you doubt this guest, I shall open the door myself."

"Do you think I'm afraid?" demanded Attila. He stalked angrily down the length of the hall and flung the door open, wincing from the blast that burnt his face with cold.

The knocker was tall and cloaked in black. A hood covered his head and shadowed his face; he carried a long throwing spear in his hand. He forced the door shut behind him.

"I thank you for your hospitality, King Attila," he said, his deep voice carrying easily through the hall. For an eerie moment, Gundrun thought that she was hearing Hagan's ghost. Her heart clutched within her, but then she realized that the tone was too clear, its rhythms too expressive, to be that of her brother: for all she had ever loved Hagan, his voice had never sounded other than harsh against her ears.

"Who are you? What are you doing out on a night like this?"

"I am a singer, traveling from the Rhine to a drighten's dwelling where I have kin and business. I became lost, and a goatherd showed me the way to your hall."

"Come and share our drink, then, if you're thirsty. But your lodging won't be free: you must sing for us tonight."

"I will gladly do that."

The singer unslung a horn from beneath his cloak, going to the fire where Attila had been sitting. The Hunnish drighten handed him a full skin of *khumiss*. "If you can drink this, you're a true man."

The wanderer squirted the fermented mare's milk into the horn. Gundrun felt her tongue curling in sympathy as he raised it and drank. But if the taste sickened him, the shadow of his hood hid any sign that might have marred his face.

"Now I shall sing a song for you which is seldom heard on the Rhine these days, but which I think shall gladden your heart anyway. And this is the lay of the Rhine's gold: how it was drawn forth from the river, and how the children of Hraithamar fought over it till at last it was won by Sigifrith the son of Sigimund and Herwodis.

> *Wodan and Hoenir   wandered with Loki*
> *to Middle-Garth   as men by the Rhine.*
> *There an otter   eating saw they*
> *a goodly fish   the flood beside . . .*

As the singer recounted the story of Sigifrith, Gundrun could not help weeping; she had to muffle her face in the furs to keep her tears from freezing to her chapped skin.

> *No hero, say men,   higher has lived,*
> *Than Sigifrith Fadhmir's Bane   slaying the wyrm*
> *to get for himself   the gold's red-bright fire,*
> *glittering by   the banks of the Rhine.*

Wyrd loves no fosterling   more long than a moment,
and no man may breathe   for more than his days,
Nor trust long in Wodan   Walhall's high drighten,
for raven and wolf   wait for his thanes aye.

Now lies the weregild   all lost by the Rhine,
and no man may say   nor see where it's hid.
For only two living   owned Fadhmir's secret,
now that secret's kept   in cairn with the dead.

"Well sung!" Attila said, and filled the wanderer's horn himself before he drained off the rest of the skin at a single draught. "Bring more *khumiss*, and build up the fires! We'll need both of them on a night like this. Singer, you will have to lose the last verse from your song, for when summer comes my kin and I shall fare to the Rhine and find the gold, if we must dig up every piece of earth from Worms to the Dragon's Crag. Then you shall have something else worth singing about."

"That would be a deed deserving of song indeed."

Gundrun marked that Attila drank a great deal in a very short time, and it was not long until he stumbled off to his chambers, leaving his warriors to wrap themselves in furs and lie down together as close to the fires as they dared.

The Gyula sat on the bench beside the stranger, speaking to him softly. Gundrun could not hear what they were saying, but at last the Gyula nodded. The old man gathered together all the blankets he could find to wrap himself in, then made his way out of the door, muttering to himself, as the singer sat down beside the fire again.

It was not until all the flames had died down to coals that the dark-cloaked man stood and glided between the heaps of sleeping Huns to Gundrun's cage. "Make no noise," he whispered.

She did not see the knife in his hand, but she heard the sounds of the sinews parting. The wanderer caught each branch in turn, lowering them carefully and setting them on the floor. He held out his hand to Gundrun; she took it, and he bore her up as she stumbled out.

The singer waited a few minutes while Gundrun got her balance, then gestured to the door Attila had left through, beckoning her to follow him.

Attila was snoring beside the coals in his chamber. He lay on his back with fur rugs heaped over him; his gray hair was spread out around his head, his eagle nose hooked over his moustache. Beneath his beard, Gundrun could see the gold chain of the boar's-tooth pendant he had taken from Gundahari's corpse.

The wanderer drew a sword from beneath his cloak. He held it one-handed above the sleeping king. With his other hand, he took Gundrun by the wrist and brought her palm to the hilt. She closed her fingers around his and together they drove the sword into Attila's chest.

Attila let out a strangled gasp, his eyes opening. "Who are you? Who has given me this hurt?"

"I am Hagan's son Nibel. Gundrun and I have done this together, and so are my father and King Gundahari avenged."

"You'll . . . pay this summer. My kin . . . " Then Attila spoke no more; the slanted black eyes glaring up at them were the eyes of a dead man.

"Where is the oil kept?" Nibel whispered to Gundrun. He pulled the sword out and wiped it on his cloak. She crouched to lift Gundahari's chain and Hagan's eagle-headed arm-ring from Attila's corpse, then stripped his neck of the torcs he had robbed from the bodies of Gisalhari and Gernot; she would not have him adorned with their treasures.

"The storerooms. Through here."

The two of them braced themselves, stepping out into the cruel wind that cut through all their wrappings. They hurried to the storage huts and back with two great jugs of oil, which they poured over Attila and his chamber.

"You do it. You have suffered more at his hands than I," murmured Hagan's son.

Gundrun took a glowing coal out with the hearth tongs. They went out of the door again, and she tossed it back into the oil. The flames flared at once with a crackle of mocking laughter, running up the walls in a brush of fire like a burning foxtail and leaping through the thatch of the roof where the wind tossed it the length of the hall in a few heartbeats.

"We can do nothing more. Hurry, quickly. Where are Attila's horses?"

Gundrun and Nibel ran to the stables, swiftly saddling the first two horses that would hold still for them and mounting up. It seemed to Gundrun that her buttocks were bruised after the first few lengths, but she clung desperately to the horse as it galloped behind Nibel's, grateful for its warmth against her body.

They could still hear the sounds of burning behind them when they had to slow down in the thick underbrush of the forest. Gundrun thought longingly of the inn on the march between the lands that had been Attila's and those that had been Hrodgar's, but there was no way of knowing whether the Huns had escaped or died in the fire.

Nibel and Gundrun rode till the Sun was well up, her winter-weak light easing the grip of the cold a little. Then they dismounted and built a fire, huddling by its warmth to sleep for most of the day. They fared like this for several days, riding at night when the cold was worst and sleeping beneath the Sun's light, until they had got far away from the lands of any drighten who might have owed troth to Attila.

Gundrun had begun to think that she would never be warm again when, near Sunna's thirteenth setting since they had left the Huns' land, they saw a sign painted with a wreath of golden apples hanging above the door of a small inn.

"I think we may safely stay here tonight," Nibel said. "If the Huns are so close behind us as to make it dangerous, then we have no hope of escaping them."

"I think you're right."

There was only one other guest in the inn, an old man who sat half-asleep by the fire. His tangled gray hair fell over his face; he clutched tightly to the shaft of a long staff that leaned against the wall beside him, as if he were afraid someone would steal it from him.

"Food and hot ale for two," Nibel said to the fat man who came to greet them. "And feed for our horses—we've stabled them already." The two of them argued over the price while Gundrun unlaced her boots and stretched her numb feet and hands out to the fire. She could not believe how good it felt to be sitting down, to be inside, not to be glancing over her shoulder and listening for the swift light hoofbeats of the Huns. When Nibel carried her ale over to her, she wrapped both hands around the warm mug and drank as quickly as she could without burning her throat. She thought that she had never tasted such good drink, neither the mead at her wedding nor the Gaulish wine in her brother's hall.

By the time the innkeeper brought them their plates of bread and stew, Gundrun felt as though she had been wrapped in a great sheep's fleece. The painful prickling had faded from her feet and hands again; she could move her toes easily and even feel them. She ate ravenously, asking for another platter when she was done.

"It's good to see you eating so heartily," Nibel said. "I was beginning to worry for you."

"I'm all right."

After the meal, the innkeeper brought them some more hot ale. They leaned back against the wall, drinking more slowly.

"Tell me," Gundrun said after a while, "why did you come? How did you know?"

"My father expected treachery. He told me to stay at home, but when he didn't come back I knew that he was dead and it was my duty to avenge him, so I left. If I had known you were kept like that, I should have come faster."

"I didn't suffer too greatly from it. I killed Attila's sons and the Gyula said that I could not be touched, but Attila wouldn't let me go free." Gundrun stared at the fire, into the shifting glow within the cavern of the flame-eaten log. "What did you say to the Gyula? Why did he leave the hall?"

"I told him that Hagan had called me to avenge him, and that the Gyula might live or die as he chose."

"And he believed it?"

"Why shouldn't he? The Gyula thought a lot of things about my father." Nibel stared into the darkness of his cup for a while. "He would have chosen him to take his place in time, if Hagan had stayed with Attila's band when his fostering was over."

"I never knew that."

"The Gyula told my father just before he left. He wanted him to stay."

"Oh." Gundrun swirled the dregs of her ale around in her mug. "Had a new king been chosen when you left?"

"No. I expect they're still waiting for Gundahari to come back."

"You're the only full-grown man of the Gebicung line now, you know. And it was you who avenged Gundahari. I think you will have to be the folk's warder from now on."

"It may be." Nibel stood up lithely, stretching himself to his full height. Again, Gundrun thought how much like Hagan he looked—but younger than Hagan had ever seemed, with no silver in his black hair and his angular face unscarred by the harshness that had always marked his father. "I'm ready to go to sleep. Wake me at dawn, if I don't waken by myself."

He lay down and rolled himself up. Gundrun sat staring into the fire, a gentle sadness stealing over her like fog. She felt that she might begin to weep, or that she might quiet her heart by thoughts of rest.

"You are not ready to sleep yet, Gundrun," a deep voice said from the darkness. Though the old man spoke softly, the might of his words seemed to thrum around her and through her and she felt more awake than she had ever been.

The aged wanderer who had seemed to sleep in the corner sat up straight, his shadow looming dimly on the wall behind him, and Gundrun saw that he must be taller than any man she had ever known except for Sigifrith. His hair fell over one side of his face. When the glance of his single eye shocked an icy lightning of fear through her, Gundrun knew who she had met and the warmth of anger flooded her fright away.

"Why?" she asked. "Why did you let this happen? Sigifrith was true to you, and my brothers had no quarrel with you."

"Why do you think you can question the ways of the gods, Gundrun? Are you so wise?"

"I shall question you, because I think that you have dealt badly with my husband, my son and my kin. What reason did you have to allow their deaths? Is it only because you joy in strife?"

"It is often said that I joy in strife; and it was never said that I offered my thanes hope of long life. Sigifrith had his victories, as did his father Sigimund before him, and your brothers and yourself as well."

"You were there at the first of things," Gundrun accused. "It was at your will that the gold was brought out of the Rhine, and why did you father Sigimund's line if not to breed Fadhmir's slayer? You have caused a great deal of pain and sorrow, and no good whatsoever has been done by it."

Wodan's eye met Gundrun's gaze again, and this time the bright glance did not frighten her, but seemed to still her soul, as soothing as warm wine. "Come with me."

He rose to his feet, and Gundrun followed him from the inn. The horse that stood grazing outside was as silver-gray as a cloud in the moonlight, shadows shifting beneath it so that it seemed eight-legged in Gundrun's sight. It felt to her as though a sudden rush of air lifted her, so she was sitting on the horse's broad back. The cool darkness of Wodan's cloak swirled about her, deep blue as the rushing night wind that swept the breath from her body. It seemed to her that she could hear the sound of Sleipnir's hooves ringing on the echoing span of the bridge, but when she looked down she saw only the moon-glimmering ripples of the river rushing below them, the cliffs that towered on either side of it no more than ridges at the bottom of the abyss of air.

"Where are we going?" Gundrun asked.

Wodan made no answer; but beyond the river, behind the cliff walls, she could see the fire-bright shapes riding closer and closer on a vast empty waste. She clutched tightly to the gray steed's silky mane; she knew now that she looked on the Muspilli, the fire-wights of the worlds' doom, circling outside the walls that hedged the Middle-Garth round. Sleipnir turned, following the river's ring downward to the north where the moonlit ripples broke into white lashes of foam over cruel crags, rushing between the cliff jaws with a low howling moan that rose and rose. As Gundrun watched, the crags stirred, a huge wolf head lifting against the little thread that bound it to gape upward toward the glimmering dwellings of the gods: the Wolf Fenrir would break free when the Muspilli came, when all fetters were loosed at last, and all men knew that it was doomed to be Wodan's bane on that day.

"Now you see," Wodan murmured. "And for these sakes I have raised my warriors, and called them to Walhall in their time. No higher heroes sit at my benches than the Walsings and the Gebicungs; no greater athelings drink my mead by night or battle on Walhall's fields by day, and so our might is gathering against the doom of the gods."

They rode down and to the north, the long shadow of Wodan's spear pointing at a dark path before them till they came to the howe that stood high and shadowed on the river's other bank. Wodan dismounted then, striding toward the mound as Gundrun watched from Sleipnir's back. Three times he traced a ring of cold blue fire around himself with his spear's point; three times he struck its butt against the ground.

"Waken, Weleda! From your long sleep, from your death-wise dreams, I call you: awake!"

The keyhole-shaped door of the mound swung slowly open. The woman who came forth was aged, her long gray hair was hanging free and her white robe was stained with streaks of mold like old blood; the sickle knife that hung at her side was blackened and half-eaten by age. Her voice was slow and deep, very soft but clear, as though her words sang from a long way off.

"Who is that man who calls me from my sleep, from my fair bed in Hella's hall? I was decked by snows, beaten on by rain; I was sprinkled with dew, I was long dead."

"I, Way-Worn, call you: show me what shall be!" Wodan raised his spear, pointing it at her, and Gundrun saw the runes shining red on its shaft.

The mound seemed to shimmer in the light, its door rippling outward into a new shape. It seemed to Gundrun that they stood beneath a huge twisted tree root, looking down into a great ring of stone laid about a white spring frothing from beneath the earth. She could see the fair lands laid out within, clear as a map: Germania, Gaul, Rome, Britannia, and far Gautland and Thule. Snow whitened the forests and fells of the northlands; the south was green as summer beneath the gray chasings of clouds. Above them, she seemed to see the ghostly shapes of faces she knew, one overlaying another so that the old Sinwist's dark eyes burned faintly through the plump features of Gisalhari's priest Augustinius, Costbera's golden crucifix glimmering over the shadow of the falcon-headed dagger at Brunichild's waist. She thought she could see the churches of Rome rising over the hallowed groves, built from the slain wood of the holy oaks, and the tears blurred her eyes. Who would remember Wodan's son Sigifrith; how would Hagan and Gundahari live again in their line, if their clan turned to the ways of Rome?

The deep murmuring of Wodan's voice did not whisper in Gundrun's ears, but rang through her skull: "Though the new ways may seem to bode the death of our kin, I have wrought so that our foes' works shall not last forever, nor our voices be forever stilled. Do not weep, but watch and learn."

Gundrun dashed the tears from her eyes, staring into the waters of the well as they grew darker and stiller. She thought then that she saw the gold glimmering far down in the depths, like a scattering of golden grains—the scattering of Wodan's seed. She could feel the rushing of her blood in the riverways of her body, the might running unseen through her, flowing unbroken from him who had named himself Mannaz to father the first of humankind. The same might whispered in every breath she drew, as she knew it always had, though she had never marked nor thought of it till now; and she knew that no Christian dew-sprinkling nor Latin prayers could still Wodan's gifts in her children, or the children who would come of her folk, though the god's own kin forsook his memory.

Stubbornly Gundrun rubbed her tears away. When she opened her eyes again, she saw that the howe was closed, the woman gone; but the frothing stream now ran around the foot of the mound. The waters seemed to sink away as she watched, falling deeper and deeper into the earth until only a dry crevasse marked where they had run. But it seemed to her that she could see a seed of brightness lying within the howe's dark shadow and feel the rushing of the waters beneath the earth gathering their might to burst forth and flow along their ancient bed again, as they must in the turning of time.

The sky-bright fires of Wodan's circle died down as he stepped forth from it and mounted behind Gundrun. "Though our folk change faiths," Wodan said as his gray steed leapt forward, galloping smoothly along the wind-path, "they shall not forget the stories of Sigimund and Sigifrith, Gundahari and Hagan and Gundrun—these tales shall grow by the Rhine and live through the long Northern nights, even to the very doors of the White Christ's church. Does this content you?"

"I suppose I could not be better contented now," Gundrun answered, though her heart ached like an old wound in changing weather.

"For the sake of what you have borne, I shall give you this warning as well. At summer's beginning, the Huns shall sweep down on the Rhine, ready to avenge their kinsman Attila. If you and Nibel wish to save your folk, you must lead them southward. If you try to fight, you shall all be slain—for so Wyrd has already written it."

"I thank you for your warning."

Wodan unslung the rune-graven horn from beneath his cloak, tracing a stave above it—*ansuz*, ᚨ , rune of wind and wod, that Gundrun knew would bear his might forth through all the generations to come. "Come share this drink with me. You have earned it as well as any warrior in my hall." He drank and passed the horn to her.

The honey-wod of the mead whirled to Gundrun's head at once. After the first three swallows she felt dizzy, as if she had been drugged, but she finished the draught. Wodan took the horn back and laid his hand upon her head, like a father blessing his favorite daughter. "Be well, Gundrun, till we meet again." He swept his other arm forward to embrace her, the folds of his cloak darkening her sight.

When Gundrun opened her eyes, she was sitting alone on the bench in the inn. The fire had almost burned down and her feet had gone to sleep, so that the blood prickled painfully in them as she staggered over to the wall by Nibel, wrapping her cloak more tightly around herself and easing herself down on a heap of straw. She meant to think on what she had seen, to fix it more tightly in her mind, but Wodan's draught had already whelmed her into sleep.

The cold had broken, melting the Rhine to full flood by the time Gundrun and Nibel had crossed the river upstream of Worms. Though it would be another moon till Ostara's feast, the weather was as warm as early summer, with a light cool wind ruffling through the bare trees. Sunna was halfway down the horizon by the time they came to the walls of the city, but instead of making for the main gate Nibel followed the path around through the wood.

"Where are we going?"

"There's something I need to show you."

They rode along past the holy stones, some way up the river. The clearing where Nibel dismounted and tied his horse looked just like any other to Gundrun, but she got off and secured her mount as well.

"What is it?"

As Nibel pulled the chain from beneath his tunic, his grave look was so like Hagan's that Gundrun had to close her eyes for a second to keep from weeping. When she opened them again, an iron key dangled from the young man's hand. "This is the key to the chamber where Sigifrith and your brothers hid Fadhmir's hoard. It must be yours now, and you must decide what to do with it."

May the Rhine swallow the hoard before the Huns wear it on their arms! It seemed to Gundrun that she could hear the ghost of Gundahari's voice echoing from the rushing water. The Burgundians could not take it with them: they had to move swiftly, and it would draw every foe from Worms to Rome on to their backs.

"We shall give the gold back to the Rhine. It has done no one good since it was brought forth, and it will do us no good to keep it. Let the Huns find our land empty when they come."

Nibel scraped the earth away from a wide iron plate held down by two bars embedded in the stone around. He stuck the key into a lock Gundrun had not been able to see, then turned it till she heard a click and slid the bars aside. With a grunt of effort he heaved the iron trapdoor off. "It's down in there."

He took two ropes out of his saddlebag and tied them fast around the trunk of a black-barked tree, lowering them carefully till the ends reached bottom. "Deeper than I expected. It might be best if I lowered you down. Then you could fill the bags with the gold and I could haul them out."

A shudder crawled up Gundrun's spine as she looked into the black pit. If he left her there . . . but if Nibel had wanted gold and rulership together, he could simply have stayed in Worms, or left her in Attila's hall. "All right."

Nibel made the ropes fast around her waist. Gundrun closed her eyes, clinging to the edge of the hole as the young man braced himself against his tree. "Ready?" he asked. She nodded and let go of the stone.

Gundrun was so relieved when her feet hit the bottom that she stumbled, going to her knees on a slimy pile of cloth. The loose gold slithered away beneath the rotten stuff as though she had landed in a bag of adders. A sudden thrill ran through her as the cloth parted beneath her touch, shaking her body and leaving her breathless as she plunged her hands in and felt the scatheless fire of the pure metal beneath her fingers, warm as Sigifrith's body. *He meant it for me; it was my morning gift, all that is left of him . . .* She did not know whether she had spoken aloud or not, or what she had said, but Nibel's deep voice bit through her enthralment.

"No, Gundrun! Think of your brothers: will you forsake their memory to keep the gold, when they died true?"

"True?" Gundrun cried. It seemed to her that the gold's brightness was burning through her head, burning away the night mists of the draught Grimhild had given her in the Danes' land. She could hear the bitter sobs racking her body, but her flesh itself felt nothing but the touch of the gold thrilling through it. "They broke their oaths to slay Sigifrith, and to get the gold for themselves . . ."

Nibel said nothing, but the shadow of his arm passed over the light streaming down into the cave as he lifted the key from his neck and held it out. Hagan had held that key, Gundrun remembered; but he would have given the hoard's secret to save Gundahari's life. . . . She thought again of the look of joy on his dead face—she had seen that look before, Sigifrith staring—at the bright shields roofing Walhall, in the green world of the gods, as his corpse lay cold before her with their son's body by his side. Her little Sigimund, whose tight hugs had often bruised her ribs, dearer to her than anything except his father and newborn sister . . .

Gundrun stared down at the gold, picking up a handful of chains and letting them run through her hands like sunlit water, golden wyrms coiling on to the hoard. If my brothers were true, she said bitterly to herself, why were they not true to Sigifrith? I would not have fought so in Attila's hall, if I had remembered. . . . I might have called Gundahari and Hagan to their deaths instead, and even gladdened in them, if Grimhild had not drowned my memory.

But then another thought rose in her mind: why should Sigifrith have lived his life scatheless in battle, to die in bed like a thrall? What fit end were that for the mightiest of the Walsings, Fadhmir's Bane?

. . . And it was Hagan's troth to Gundahari that brought Sigifrith to his death, and that same troth was Hagan's own doom, nor could he have gone more bravely. It seemed to Gundrun that she could see the strands twisting back like the wires wrapped and woven into the arm-rings and torcs that lay wound through gold coins and brooches, back to the eldest ones of her mother's kin who lived only in the line-chants now—Lofanohaith and her brothers Otter, Ragin the Smith and Fadhmir the Wyrm; her sister Ling-wohaith; and their father Hraithamar, with whose name all the songs ended.

Only I am left, Gundrun thought, and there is no more revenge to take. But there is still troth for me to keep, to the living and the dead. Fadhmir's heart burned in her blood; Sigifrith's daughter still breathed; Hagan's son waited quietly above her, and the folk Gundahari had loved needed Gebica's daughter to stand beside Nibel and lead them away from their doom, as Wodan had told her.

"Fehu, 'gold,' the kinsmen's strife," Gundrun whispered: the first line of the rune-song Grimhild had taught her when she was young. The strife would be ended: Sigifrith and her brothers had worked the tangled strands of And-ward's curse clear, and she, twice given as a peace-weaver between clans, must knot its threads tight and cut it free.

Gundrun caught a deep, ragged gulp of air. She untied the ropes around her waist. "Send down the bag. I'm ready to start loading it."

When at last they had all the gold heaped on the bank of the Rhine, Sunna was burning down swiftly through the trees behind them. Gundrun and Nibel did not look at each other or speak as they began to pick great armfuls up, throwing the pieces of gold into the river like children tossing the leaves of summer's end. They worked faster and faster, afraid to let the gold linger in their hands, till the pieces Gundrun had brought with her— the torcs Sigifrith had given Gisalhari and Gernot, the girdle clasp she had inherited from her mother and the brooch Costbera had refused to wear— had splashed into the froth-laced flood after the gold from the storeroom.

"Is there anything else?"

Unwillingly Gundrun took Gundahari's boar's tooth from around her neck, swinging the chain and letting it fly in an arc toward the middle of the Rhine. Hagan's arm-ring was warm from her wrist; she cast it as far as she could, the glittering drops splashing up. Last she unpinned the brooch Sigifrith had given her, the golden disc wrought with the figures of a stag and doe, and spun it out over the water like a flat stone. Twice it skipped, then sank into the ripples.

She was ready to walk away when Nibel pointed silently to the dragon ring still coiled on her finger. "That is Andward's ring."

But Sigifrith gave it to me, Gundrun was about to say. It is my last token of him; how can I give it up? Yet Brunichild had had it before, and before her Fadhmir, and before him Hraithamar, Loki . . .

The ring had brought her brothers to their deaths through her—and Gundrun could no longer hide the thought from herself: it had been the sign she showed the walkurja at the Rhine's edge, the sign that had sealed Sigifrith's doom. Of all who had worn it, only she still lived . . .

She tugged the ring from her finger, weighing the heavy gold in her palm. The shadow of the trees reached halfway across the Rhine now; beyond their jagged darkness, the river seemed to burn with Sunna's red-gold light. The red stone in the dragon's golden embrace was very dark, its star hidden beneath the shadows of sunset.

Gundrun flung the ring over the river with all her might. It seemed to her that she saw the silver flash of a fish's back on the border between river-shadows and river-fire, just where Andward's ring splashed into the Rhine. Then it was gone, sunken into the darkness.

HISTORICAL AND BACKGROUND NOTES

*R*hinegold is based on the most widely known and most beloved story-cycle of early Northern Europe, the story of Siegfried the Dragon-Slayer and the fall of the Burgundian royal house. The oldest written reference to this legend appears in the English national epic *Beowulf,* in which the deeds of the Waelsings Sigemund and Fitela (Sin-fjotli) and the slaying of the dragon are retold as part of the feast celebrating Beowulf's victory over Grendel. The Norse preserved the story in their oral tradition as a cycle of poems, eventually writing the legend down in prose form as the saga of the Völsungs (thirteenth-fourteenth century); a somewhat different version was recorded in the German *Nibelungenlied* (early twelfth century). The popularity of the tale in Scandinavia is borne out by the unparalleled frequency with which scenes from it appear in Viking Age and mediaeval art; folk ballads recounting the story have survived in the Faroes until the present day.

Attempts have been made to locate the historical prototypes of the Wals-ings; it has been suggested that Sigimund was originally the Burgundian king Sigismund and Brunichild based on the Merovingian Brunichildis, but the parallels between the historical and legendary figures are too slight to make any identification certain. However, Gundahari (Gunther, Gunnarr) the son of Gebica, ruler of the Burgundian kingdom on the Rhine, was a very influential figure in the first part of the fifth century C.E. (Common Era—see Glossary), expanding the Burgundian power significantly. In 436/7 the Huns, encouraged by the Roman military leader Aetius, demolished the kingdom on the Rhine, killing Gundahari and most of the Burgundian royal family; the Burgundians were forced to migrate again, eventually settling in the region which bears their name today. This story developed in Germanic heroic legend, eventually attributing the slaying of Gundahari to Attila and later also setting Theoderic the Great (born in 453, the year of Attila's death) in Attila's warband.

The two best-known versions of the legend are those preserved in *Völsunga Saga* and *Nibelungenlied. Völsunga Saga,* in which Gunnarr's sister Gudhrún tries to warn her brothers about Attila's ambush and avenges their deaths after-ward (*Nibelungenlied* has Gunther's sister Kriemhild arranging the ambush as revenge for the killing of her husband Sigfrit), is generally thought to be closer to the original form of the legend. Due to the early Christianization of Germany, the mythic elements in *Nibelungenlied* were also driven underground: though the death of Sigfrit at Hagen's hands has often been compared to the slaying of the Norse god Baldr by Loki, no reference to any of the Germanic gods has survived in the German work, whereas the greatest of the Northern gods, Wodan/Odin, is one of the major characters in *Völsunga Saga.* For these reasons, *Rhinegold* follows the plot of the Norse saga rather than that of the German poem, though I have also made much use of the latter in the description of the Burgundians' journey to Attila's hall and the battle there. The Norse *Thidhreks Saga,* a Scandinavian collection/translation of German legend, also supplements the *Nibelungenlied* materials and was particularly valuable to me for the insights it provided into the character of Hagen.

In general, I have attempted to wed the historical with the legendary as closely as possible, so that, for instance, the Walsings in *Rhinegold* are pre-migration Saxons whose warlike activities are motivated in some part by the rising of the North Sea along their home coasts (and Sigifrith is succeeded as leader of his tribe by the same Hengest who later led the Saxons to Britain); and the Roman presence on the borders of Germania exerts a constant influence on Gundahari and his fellow leaders. However, where irresolvable conflicts existed, as with the chronological problem of Attila and Theoderic, *Rhinegold* has staunchly kept faith with the legendary/literary tradition.

The calendar used by the ancient Germanic peoples varied considerably but seems in some areas and at some times to have been divided into twelve months that roughly corresponded to those of the Roman calendar. Feasts, except for the solstices, were probably reckoned by either the full moons or visible changes in the seasons (the beginning of harvest and so forth). The Germanic year is broken into two seasons, summer and winter, the points of change coming at the feasts of Winternights and Ostara.

The names I have used for the months are derived from the Anglo-Saxon and Icelandic calendars. Where they disagree, I have chosen the name that seems to me likelier to be the oldest. For the sake of clarity, I have presented a degree of standardization between the different branches of the Germanic tradition, which almost certainly never existed. The year known to my characters begins with the Yule feast, held at the end of the month called Yule (Roman December). The order thereafter is: Thonri, Solmonth, Hrethmonth, Eostre (Ostara in the more southerly parts of Germany), Thrimilci, Fore-Lithe, Aft-Lithe, Weodmonth, Heilagmonth, Winternights, Blotmonth, Yule. The major religious festivals are Yule (the twelve days from the winter solstice through to New Year), Eostre, Midsummer (Anglo-Saxon Lithe), and Winternights; local festivals include, but are not limited to, the feast of

Thonar (Thórr), the early spring procession of the wagon of Freyr or Ner-thus, and various harvest celebrations too numerous to count. May (Thrim-ilci) Eve is a traditional festival throughout Northern Europe. Better known by its christian name Walpurgisnacht (after Saint Walpurga), it is a night associated with "witchcraft" and love.

In order to create a sense of historical Germanic realism, I have used a number of words, particularly titles and names of gods and goddesses, which may not be immediately familiar to the reader. Many of the names, partic-ularly those of deities, appear in various dialectal forms (Thonar in the north versus Donar in the south, or Donars among the Gothic tribes for instance).

GLOSSARY

For the sake of clarification, I offer this list of words and personal names. It should be emphasized here that this is not meant to serve as a definitive guide to Germanic religion, which, like the calendar, was probably far less consistent than I have presented it as being; also, I have committed considerable oversimplification for the sake of offering a general guide. Old Norse forms of the names, which will probably be the most familiar to students of Germanic mythology, are given in parentheses.

AGWIJAR (ÆGIR): Giant associated with the sea, perhaps a personification of it. Husband of the goddess Ran.

AIWILIMO: Herwodis' father, slain by Lingwe, avenged by Sigifrith.

ALAPERCHT: king of the Alamanns, son of Chilpirich, second husband of Herwodis and adoptive father to Sigifrith.

ALASWINTH: son of Alapercht and Herwodis.

ALF: an "elf", but not in the usual modern sense of the word. Little is known about the alfar, but they seem to have been a sort of spirit intermediate between gods and humankind, and sometimes actually powerful dead people to whose burial mounds offerings could be made. Dwarves were also called "swart alfs."

ANDWARD (ANDVARI): a river-dwarf, first owner of the hoard.

ASES (ÆSIR): "gods". The godly kin is divided into two tribes, the Ases and the Wans (Vanir). The Ases (Wodan, Thonar, Tiw, Frija, and others) are particularly associated with air, weather, war, and runic magic; the Wans (Nerthus, Fro Ing, Frowe Holda) with water, earth, protection, and visionary/shamanic magic, although their functions overlap considerably. Both tribes were called on for fruitfulness and help in battle; kingly lines were often descended from either Wodan or Ing.

ASES' GARTH (ÁSGARDHR): the home of the gods.

ATHELING: nobly born.

ATTILA: leader of the Huns. The name, "Little Father," may be taken as a title, as this particular Attila, who dies in 437, clearly could not have marched on Rome a decade and a half later.

BALDER (BALDR): son of Wodan and Frija, the "shining god" who is slain by a sprig of mistletoe. His death, at least in the Norse Eddas, marks the beginning of the end for the gods of Asgardhr, but after the final battle between gods and giants, he returns from Hel's realm to take Wodan's place as ruler of the reborn world.

BERSERKER: a warrior who fights in a state of altered consciousness in which he cannot be harmed by fire or iron, but is often incapable of distinguishing between friends and enemies. Coats of bear or wolf skin were often used to bring on the berserk state. Many berserkers were also thought to be were-beasts.

BORGHILD: Sigimund's first wife, who poisoned Sinfjotli.

BRUNICHILD: the earthly name of Sigifrith's walkurja Sigrdrifa.

C.E.: Common Era, a non-religious system of dating based on the peak of Rome's power and the rise of the Western world as we know it. C.E. dates correspond exactly to A.D. dates, B.C.E. (Before Common Era) to B.C.

CARL: a free farmer, who was also a warrior at need or went raiding between planting and harvest (typical for many Vikings in later centuries).

CHILPIRICH: king of the Alamanns east of the Rhine and into the Black Forest.

DELLING: "The Shining"; "Delling's door" is dawn.

DONARS: see Thonar.

DRAUG: a living corpse.

DRIGHTEN: "lord" in the specific sense of the leader of a warband, except in Scandinavia where it became a general term for "king" due to the development of the lord term "freyr" into a taboo name for a god (and "freyja" for a goddess). A feminine form of "drighten" only exists in the Scandinavian languages, as the Continent retained the distinction between "drighten = warleader" and "fro = ruler", and also kept "frowe" as a secular term (see Fro/Frowe below). I have generally used the word "lady" for the feminine of "drighten" to maintain both sets of distinctions.

DWARVES: the dwarves have great skills of smithcraft, wisdom and magic. Most of the names recorded in the Old Norse "Dvergatal" (Catalogue of Dwarves) have to do either with these things or else with darkness, cold and death. The list includes such names as Dáinn ("Dead One"); Nár ("Corpse"); Gandálfr (Magic Elf); and Dvalinn ("Deluder"), among many others of a similar character.

ETIN: a type of giant, usually with magical power and much lore.

FADHMIR (FÁFNIR): brother of Ragin, Otter, Lingwohaith and Lofanohaith, great-great-great-great-granduncle of Sigifrith on his mother's side, dragon. The Germanic dragon is never a natural animal, but usually a dead man guarding the treasure in his burial mound in that form.

FLYTING: a ritual exchange of insults that often became downright obscene.

FRIJA: wife of Wodan, goddess of marriage and family.

FRO/FROWE: "Fro" translates as "lord" in the sense of one who demonstrates leadership during peacetime, including the duties of arbitration, protection of the lesser people who look to him and keeping the land fruitful by proper dealings with the god/esses and his own personal power. Historically, the term became a general religious term for the gods among the continental Upper Germans, survived as an earthly title among the Anglo-Saxons (though it was also used in a godly context), and in Scandinavia was only used in the Norse form Freyr as a taboo name for the god Ingwaz (called Fro Ing here). "Frowe" was a more general title for a woman, surviving on the Continent to become the modern German "Frau." In the Scandinavian form "Freyja," this title, like "Freyr," also became a holy taboo name. The first name of this goddess is not known, but I have called her "Frowe Holda" here, as much of the German folklore about Holda seems reasonably consistent with the myths of Freyja.

GALDOR (GALDR): a magical song or incantation.

GARTH: "enclosure". Also used in a larger sense for the boundary separating human/social space from wild/magical space—see "Middle-Garth."

GAUTS: a tribe in southern Sweden.

GEBICA: Burgundian king or "Hending"; father of Gundahari, Gundrun and (perhaps) Hagan.

GINN-REGINN: "gods of might (?)," a term referring to the gods at the beginning of the world.

GODHI/GYDHJA: a full-time priest/priestess, often, though not always, to the service of one particular god/ess. In this period, the term does not carry the connotation of secular authority which it does in the later Iceland of the Viking Age. Gothic gudhija.

GOTHS: the Eastern Germanic people in general, divided into Visigoths, Ostrogoths and other tribes such as the Burgundians. Migrated southeastward from Scandinavia in the last centuries before the rise of Rome, driven from their Eastern European home by the Huns in the latter part of the fourth century C.E.

GRAM: the name given by Sigifrith to his father's reforged sword.

GRANI: Sigifrith's horse, sired on the mare Harifaxa by Wodan's steed Sleipnir.

GRIMHILD: "Masked Battle"; Burgundian queen, mother of Gundahari, Gundrun and Hagan.

GRIPIR: the late brother of Herwodis.

GUNDAHARI: Burgundian king of great historical renown, appearing as the heroic Gunnarr of Völsunga Saga and in a greatly diminished form as the Gunther of Nibe-lungenlied and Wagner's Götterdämmerung.

GUNDRUN: "Battle-Secret"; Burgundian princess, married to Sigifrith and then to Attila.

GYULA: the Hunnish shaman.

HAGAN: "Hedge-Thorn"; brother (or perhaps half-brother) of Gundahari and Gundrun.

HAITH (HEIƆR): Frowe Holda in her aspect of the witch who practices seith-magic (see witch).

HARROW: an altar of stone, often made of heaped stones.

HELLA (HEL): the goddess who keeps the kingdom of death.

HELM OF AWE (ÆGISHJÁLMAR): in Völsunga Saga, *this seems to be a literal helmet; in Icelandic tradition, the term was used even through the Christian era for a symbol which appears in Germanic holy/magical art from a very early stage and continued to be drawn between the eyes of Icelandic wrestlers to strengthen them and terrify their opponents.*

HERULIAN: member of the Herulian tribe. The presentation of this tribe as a band of Wodanic berserks/runemasters is based on the use of the Primitive Norse form of the name as an apparent runemaster's title in a number of inscriptions and the description of their fighting style in Tacitus' Germania.

HERWODIS: "Sword-Goddess", Sigifrith's mother.

HRAITHAMAR: father of Fadhmir, Ragin, Otter, Lingwohaith and Lofanohaith, Sigifrith's maternal great-great-great-great-great-grandfather.

HOF: a full-scale temple, an actual building rather than the more usual holy grove.

HOENIR: Wodan's brother, about whom little is known.

IDISES: "goddesses." The dead women of a clan who continue to interact with their living descendants, particularly at birth when the child is blessed and death when they come to claim their kin. During one's life, the idises protect, help and give fruitfulness.

ING, FRO ING, Engusi FREYJAR (FREYR): the god of holy kingship and fruitfulness, whose sign is the boar of battle. Later best known as the patron deity of the Swedes, but worshiped by everyone else as well. Twin brother of Frowe Holda (Freyja).

LINGWE: unsuccessful suitor of Herwodis, who brought about the death of Sigimund and Aiwilimo.

LINGWOHAITH: elder daughter of Hraithamar, mother of Sigifrith's maternal line.

LOFANOHAITH: younger daughter of Hraithamar, mother of the maternal line of Gundahari, Gundrun and Hagan.

LOKI: an etin, Wodan's blood-brother, often interpreted as a fire spirit. The Trickster of Norse mythology who, perhaps at Wodan's far-sighted contriving, brings about Balder's death.

MIDDLE-GARTH (MIDHGARDHR): "the Middle Enclosure", the world of humankind, which is also called "Middle-Earth" in Anglo-Saxon writings. Beyond the Middle-Garth's walls is the Outer Garth (Útgarƌr), the realm of etins and trolls.

MOON: the Moon is always masculine in Germanic language and myths (as in the "Man in the Moon" of English folklore), just as the Sun is always feminine.

MUSPILLI: "destroyers of the world (?)," beings characterized by fire, who will come to burn the worlds in the final battle, Ragnarok.

NEED-FIRE: a fire kindled through the bow-drill method with no use of flint or steel, considered to have magical powers.

NERTHUZ: a deity whom Tacitus called "Mother Earth"; appears as the Old Norse god Njördhr, father of Freyr and Freyja by an unnamed sister. It has variously been suggested that this deity was hermaphroditic, a pair of male-female twins, or masculine in some regions and feminine in others.

NIBEL: Hagan's son, who, together with Gundrun, avenges Hagan and Gundahari and ultimately leads the Burgundian folk away from the destruction of Worms to their final home in present-day Burgundy.

NINE WORLDS: the Ases' Garth (Ásgardhr), Light-Alfheim, Etinheim, Wanheim, Niflheim, Muspellheim, Swart-Alfheim, Hella's realm and the Middle-Garth.

NITHING, NITH: hate, a magical curse and insult. A "nithling" is someone with no honor, a coward.

NORNS: the three personifications of time/causality in the Norse mythos. Urdhr or Wyrd is the Norn of all that has come to pass, which shapes that which should become; Verdhandi, "Becoming," represents the present moment of change; and Skuld, "Should," is the embodiment of what ought to develop. These three are sometimes translated as "past," "present" and "future," but this is not really true to the Germanic time sense, in which the "past" is still the living and powerful reality that continuously shapes all that comes to pass.

ORLOG: fate in the sense of that which has been laid down by previous heroic/ritually significant actions (of both oneself and others) and must come to pass.

OTTER: Hraithamar's youngest son, shape-shifter, killed by Loki.

RAGIN: Hraithamar's second son, became a dwarf after the killing of Hraithamar; Sigifrith's foster-father and maternal great-great-great-great-uncle.

RUNES: literally "secrets," but normally used to refer to the staves of the Germanic alphabet (called the "futhark" after its first six letters, F, U, Th, A, R and K). Many of the runic inscriptions that have survived seemed to have been intended for memorial and/or magical purposes, although many are practical (of the "Ingrid owns this comb" type) and ordinary graffiti in runes is not uncommon. The runes used in this book are those of the oldest type, the 24-letter Elder Futhark.

fehu   uruz   thurisaz   ansuz   raidho   kenaz   gebo   wunjo

hagalaz   nauthiz   isa   jera   eihwaz   perthro   elhaz   sowilo

↑ ᛒ ᛗ ᛗ ᛚ ◇ ᛟ ᛉ

tiwaz   berkano   ehwaz   mannaz   laguz   ingwaz   dagaz   othala

The first letter or sound of each rune name shows the letter or sound it represents, with the exceptions of *elhaz* (Z or the final R of Norse words) and *ingwaz* (ng). The H of *hagalaz* should be pronounced as a guttural CH, the J of *jera* as a Y.

Those interested in further material on the magical aspects of the runes as described in this book should read Kveldulf Gundarsson's *Teutonic Magic* (Llewellyn, 1990), Freya Aswynn's *Leaves of Yggdrasil* (Llewellyn, 1990), and Edred Thorsson's *FUTHARK* (Samuel Weiser). A more historically informative, skeptical discussion can be found in Erik Moltke's *Runes and their Origins: Denmark and Elsewhere* (National Museum of Denmark, 1985). Unfortunately, the most popular and readily available book on this subject, Ralph Blum's *A Book of Runes*, is grossly misinformative and useless for either intellectual or spiritual purposes.

SEITH-MAGIC: magic that worked largely on the mind; also seems to have been related to shamanic practices of trance and working with spirits. Seething things in cauldrons and sitting on a high platform were two methods used by seith-witches. Often malicious, and sometimes considered unmanly or dishonorable for a man to practice. The difference between seith-magic and spae-magic is sometimes hard to determine, and the use of one term or the other may simply have depended on the respect in which the practitioner was held.

SIGIFRITH (SIGURDHR, SIEGFRIED): "Victory-Peace," slayer of the dragon Fadhmir.

SIGIGAIRAR: Gautish ruler of the Ingling line, Sigilind's husband, slayer of Wals and his nine youngest sons.
SIGILIND (SIGNY): "Victory-Linden," twin sister of Sigimund, mother of Sinfjotli.

SIGIMUND: "Victory-Gift," twin brother of Sigilind, father of Sinfjotli and Sigifrith.

SINFJOTLI: son of Sigimund and Sigilind, poisoned by Sigimund's first wife Borghild.

SKALD: a Scandinavian poet. Skaldic poetry in the Viking Age was highly complex, based on the use of kennings (elaborate riddle images designed to show off the poet's knowledge of his or her own religion and traditions) with a very strict alliterative form and syllable count. End-rhyme poetry was not used by any of the Germanic people.

SIGRDRIFA: Sigifrith's walkurja and destined bride, the reborn Sigilind.

SINWIST: the Burgundian high priest or "gudhija."

SLEIPNIR: Wodan's eight-legged horse.

SPAE-MAGIC: like seith-magic, it involved trances, looking into the future and "shamanic" faring between the worlds, but was more respectable and not used for malicious purposes. Spae-men were honored as well as spae-women.

SUNNA: the Sun is always feminine in Germanic languages and myth, just as the Moon is always masculine.

THANE: a warrior bound to a drighten by oaths of troth.

THIODERIK: historically Theodoric the Great, a sixth-century Germanic leader who held the Western part of the Roman empire for many years. Protagonist of the mediaeval German "Dietrich von Bern" legendary cycle. Although the historical characters never met, Theodoric being born in the same year Attila died, Germanic heroic legend presents Theodoric as an exile fighting in the Hunnish warband for many years.

THONAR, DONARS (THÓRR): god of thunder, giver of might, courage and fruitfulness; warder of humankind against trolls, giants and fruitfulness. His hammer was used as an amulet and a sign of hallowing by the Norse.

THRALL: slave.

THURSE: an elemental giant.

TIW, ZIW, Tius (TÝR): one-handed god of battle and justice, who lost his hand binding Loki's terrible son, the wolf Fenrir. Somewhat diminished during the Viking Age, but one of the highest gods of the Germanic people during the Migration Age. A goddess Tisa or Zisa, who may have been Tiw's twin sister or bride, was also known to the continental Germans, but no tales of her have survived.

WALDHARI THE FRANK: Walter of Aquitaine, from the tenth-century epic of the same name. Hostage fostered in Attila's warband together with Hagan; Hagan's best friend and blood-brother.

WALHALL (VALHOLL): "Hall of the Slain," where Wodan's heroes go after death to prepare for the final battle. They fight each other all day, are healed in the evening and drink together all night.

WALKNOT: "Knot of the Slain", a symbol found particularly on the Gotlandic picture stones of the Viking Age and thought to be connected with the cult of Wodan as the god of death in battle:

WALKURJA (VALKYRJA, VALKYRIE): "Chooser of the Slain". Wodan's daughters or adopted daughters who determine which heroes shall fall in battle and bear them to Walhall.

WALS: father of Sigimund and Sigilind, after whom the Walsing line is named.

WANS: see Ases.

WARG (VARGR): "criminal, outlaw," also used to mean "wolf" in Old Norse, a meaning that survives in modern Swedish. A breaker of the bonds of society.

WILI AND WIH (VÍLI AND VÉ): Wodan's two brothers (or alternate aspects), with whom he created the world.

WINTERNIGHTS: the feast of the first full moon after the autumnal equinox. The end of harvest and the turning point between summer and winter.

WOD: fury, madness, inspiration (particularly poetic inspiration), ecstatic state of altered consciousness, divine possession. The name Wodan/Odhinn is derived from this root and probably means the "Furious (or Inspired) One."

WODAN (ÓDHINN): god of death, particularly death in battle; giver of poetry, magical lore and inspiration; ancestor of many lines of kings (including the current royal house of Britain); leader of the Wild Hunt; and, at least in the later Icelandic materials, chief of the Norse gods.

WYRD: the eldest Norn, the personification of fate; the word wyrd or weird is also used as a general term for fate.

YGG: "the Terrible", a name of Wodan.

For those who are interested in finding out more about the religion and folklore of the Germanic peoples, there are several good books available. H.R. Ellis-Davidson's *Gods and Myths of Northern Europe* and E.O.G. Turville-Petre's *Myth and Religion of the North* discuss Germano-Scandinavian religion; the most complete collection of Germanic folklore in English is Jacob Grimm's four-volume *Teutonic Mythology*. Kevin Crossley-Holland's *The Norse Myths* retells the tales of the Viking gods in an interesting and accessible manner. The works on reconstruction of the northern European religions that have most strongly influenced the portrayal of the god/esses and rites in this book are Kveldulf Gundarsson's *Teutonic Religion* and Edred Thorsson's *A Book of Troth* (both published by Llewellyn) and *Our Troth* (edited by Kveldulf Gundarsson, privately published by the Ring of Troth).